LONDON

D0500535

CRIPLE STREET

FINSBURY

Moor Fields

Bedlam

Gresham's College

South Sea Co.

BISHOPSGATE

THREAD NEEDLE STR

Bank of England

POULTRY

St Stephen

LOMBARD

WALLBROOK

FISH STREET

The Royal Exchange

CORNHILL

CHANGE ALLEY

BIRCHIN LANE

MINCING LN

St. George's

St. Mary at Hill

All Hallows Church

Fire Monument

THAMES

St. Dunstan STREET

Trinity House

TOWER STR

TOWER HILL

Billingsgate

Customs House

The Clink

London Bridge

Tower Wharf

Tatler-Lock

The Pool

Tower of London

WHITE CHAPEL

RATCLIFF HIGH WAY

SOUTHWARK

THE BOROUGH

River Thames

To Rotherhithe

SHOREDJ

THE RULES OF FLEET PRISON

FLEET LANE

Fleet Prison

Fleet Ditch

GREAT OLD BAILEY

FLEET STREET

LUDGATE HILL

LUDGATE STREET

Fleet Prison

THE

System

OF THE

WORLD

WM

WILLIAM MORROW

An Imprint of HarperCollins*Publishers*

THE
System
OF THE
WORLD

VOL. III of
THE BAROQUE CYCLE

Neal Stephenson

THE SYSTEM OF THE WORLD. Copyright © 2004 by Neal Stephenson. All rights reserved. Printed in the United States of America. No part of this book may be used or reproduced in any manner whatsoever without written permission except in the case of brief quotations embodied in critical articles and reviews. For information address Harper-Collins Publishers Inc., 10 East 53rd Street, New York, NY 10022.

HarperCollins books may be purchased for educational, business, or sales promotional use. For information please write: Special Markets Department, HarperCollins Publishers Inc., 10 East 53rd Street, New York, NY 10022.

FIRST EDITION

Book design by Shubhani Sarkar
Endpaper maps by Nick Springer
Illustration of globe by Laura Hartman Maestro

Printed on acid-free paper

Library of Congress Cataloging-in-Publication Data

Stephenson, Neal.
    The system of the world / Neal Stephenson.—1st ed.
      p. cm.—(The Baroque cycle ; v. 3)
    ISBN 0-06-052387-5
    1. Great Britain—History—Anne, 1702–1714—Fiction.
2. Newton, Isaac, Sir, 1642–1727—Fiction. 3. Kings and
rulers—Succession—Fiction. 4. Scientists—Crimes against—
Fiction. 5. Counterfeiters—Fiction. 6. Criminals—Fiction.
I. Title.

  PS3569.T3868S97 2004
  813'.54—dc22

                        2004049943

04 05 06 07 08 WBC/RRD 10 9 8 7 6 5 4 3 2 1

To Mildred

Contents

But first whom shall we send

In search of this new world, whom shall we find

Sufficient? Who shall tempt with wandring feet

The dark unbottom'd infinite Abyss

And through the palpable obscure find out

His uncouth way, or spread his aerie flight

Upborn with indefatigable wings

Over the vast abrupt, ere he arrive

The happy Ile ...

MILTON, *Paradise Lost*

The story thus far . . .

In Boston in October 1713, Daniel Waterhouse, sixty-seven years of age, the Founder and sole Fellow of a failing college, the Massachusetts Bay Colony of Technologickal Arts, has received a startling visit from the Alchemist Enoch Root, who has appeared on his doorstep brandishing a summons addressed to Daniel from Princess Caroline of Brandenburg-Ansbach, thirty.

Two decades earlier, Daniel, along with his friend and colleague Gottfried Wilhelm von Leibniz, knew Princess Caroline when she was a destitute orphan. Since then she has grown up as a ward of the King and Queen of Prussia in the Charlottenburg Palace in Berlin, surrounded by books, artists, and Natural Philosophers, including Leibniz. She has married the Electoral Prince of Hanover, George Augustus, known popularly as "Young Hanover Brave" for his exploits in the recently concluded War of the Spanish Succession. He is reputed to be as handsome and dashing as Caroline is beautiful and brilliant.

The grandmother of George Augustus is Sophie of Hanover, still shrewd and vigorous at eighty-three. According to the Whigs—one of the two great factions in English politics—Sophie should be next in line to the English throne after the death of Queen Anne, who is forty-eight and in poor health. This would place Princess Caroline in direct line to become Princess of Wales and later Queen of England. The Whigs' bitter rivals, the Tories, while paying lip service to the Hanoverian succession, harbor many powerful dissidents, called Jacobites, who are determined that the next monarch should instead be James Stuart: a Catholic who has lived most of his life in France as a guest and puppet of the immensely powerful Sun King, Louis XIV.

England and an alliance of mostly Protestant countries have just finished fighting a quarter-century-long world war against France. The second half of it, known as the War of the Spanish Succession, has seen many battlefield victories for the Allies under the generalship of two brothers in arms: the Duke of Marlborough and Prince Eugene of Savoy. Nevertheless France has won the war, in large part by outmaneuvering her opponents politically. Consequently, a grandson of Louis XIV now sits on the throne of the Spanish Empire, which among other things is the source of most of the world's gold and silver. If the English Jacobites succeed in placing James Stuart on the English throne, France's victory will be total.

In anticipation of the death of Queen Anne, Whiggish courtiers and politicians have been establishing contacts and forging alliances between London and Hanover. This has had the side-effect of throwing into high relief a long-simmering dispute between Sir Isaac Newton—the preëminent English scientist, the President of the Royal Society, and Master of the Royal Mint at the Tower of London—and Leibniz, a privy councilor and old friend of Sophie, and tutor to Princess Caroline. Ostensibly this conflict is about which of the two men first invented the calculus, but in truth it has deeper roots. Newton and Leibniz are both Christians, troubled that many of their fellow Natural Philosophers perceive a conflict between the mechanistic world-view of science and the tenets of their faith. Both men have developed theories to harmonize science and religion. Newton's is based on the ancient proto-science of Alchemy and Leibniz's is based on a theory of time, space, and matter called Monadology. They are radically different and probably irreconcilable.

Princess Caroline wishes to head off any possible conflict between the world's two greatest savants, and the political and religious complications that would ensue from it. She has asked Daniel, who is an old friend of both Newton and Leibniz, to journey back to England, leaving his young wife and their little boy in Boston, and mediate the dispute. Daniel, knowing Newton's vindictiveness, sees this as foreordained to fail, but agrees to give it a try, largely because he is impoverished and the Princess has held out the incentive of a large life insurance policy.

Daniel departs from Boston on Minerva, *a Dutch East Indiaman (a heavily armed merchant ship). Detained along the New England coast by contrary winds, she falls under attack in Cape Cod Bay from the formidable pirate-fleet of Captain Edward Teach, a.k.a. Blackbeard, who somehow knows that Dr. Waterhouse is on board* Minerva, *and demands that her Captain, Otto Van Hoek, hand him over. Captain Van Hoek, who loathes pirates even more than the typical merchant-captain, elects to fight it out, and bests Teach's pirate fleet in a day-long engagement.*

Minerva *crosses the Atlantic safely but is caught in a storm off the southwest corner of England and nearly cast away on the Isles of Scilly. Late in December she puts in at Plymouth for repairs. Dr. Waterhouse goes ashore intending to travel to London by land. In Plymouth he encounters a family friend named Will Comstock.*

Will is the grandson of John Comstock, a Tory nobleman who fought against Cromwell in the middle of the previous century and, after the Restoration, came back to England and helped found the Royal Society. Subsequently, John was disgraced and forced to retire from public life, partly through the machinations of his (much younger) distant cousin and bitter rival, Roger Comstock. Daniel served as a tutor in Natural Philosophy to one of the sons of John. *This son later moved to Connecticut and established an estate there. Will was born and grew up on that estate but has lately moved back to England, where he has found a home in the West Country. He is a moderate Tory who has recently been created Earl of Lostwithiel. Queen Anne has recently been forced to create a large number of such titles in order to pack the House of Lords with Tories, the party that she currently favors.*

Daniel has spent the twelve days of Christmas with Will's family at his seat near Lostwithiel, and Will has talked him into making a small detour en route to London.

BOOK 6

Solomon's gold

mouth blacksmith would ever come to a formal bow. Having thus taken his leave, he turned his broad back upon them and trudged quickly downwind. Soon he became hard to distinguish from the numerous upright boulders—which might be read as a comment on his physique, or on the gloominess of the day, or on the badness of Daniel's eyesight.

"The Druids loved to set great stones on end," commented the Earl. "For what purpose, I cannot imagine."

"You have answered the question by asking it."

"I beg your pardon?"

"Dwelling as they did in this God-forsaken place, they did it so that men would come upon these standing stones two thousand years after they were dead, and know they had been here. The Duke of Marlborough, throwing up that famous Pile of Blenheim Palace, is no different."

The Earl of Lostwithiel felt it wise to let this pass without comment. He turned and kicked a path through some stiff withered grass to a strange up-cropping of lichen-covered stone. Following him, Daniel understood it as one corner of a ruined building. The ground yielded under their feet. It was spread thin over a shambles of tumbledown rafters and disintegrating peat-turves. Anyway the angle gave them shelter from the wind.

"Speaking now in my capacity as Lord Warden of the Stannaries, I welcome you to Dartmoor, Daniel Waterhouse, on behalf of the Lord of the Manor."

Daniel sighed. "If I'd been in London the last twenty years, keeping up with my Heraldic Arcana, and going to tea with the Bluemantle Pursuivant, I would know who the hell that was. But as matters stand—"

"Dartmoor was created part of the Duchy of Cornwall in 1338, and as such became part of the possessions of the Prince of Wales—a title created by King Edward I in—"

"So in a roundabout way, you are welcoming me on behalf of the Prince of Wales," Daniel said abruptly, in a bid to yank the Earl back before he rambled any deeper into the labyrinth of feudal hierarchy.

"And the Princess. Who, if the Hanovers come, shall be—"

"Princess Caroline of Ansbach. Yes. Her name keeps coming up. Did she send you to track me down in the streets of Plymouth?"

The Earl looked a little wounded. "I am the son of your old friend. I encountered you by luck. My surprise was genuine. The welcome given you by my wife and children was unaffected. If you doubt it, come to our house *next* Christmas."

"Then why do you go out of your way to bring up the Princess?"

"Only because I wish to be plain-spoken. Where you are going next it is all intrigue. There is a sickness of the mind that comes over those who bide too long in London, which causes otherwise rational men to put forced and absurd meanings on events that are accidental."

"I have observed that sickness in full flower," Daniel allowed, thinking of one man in particular.

"I do not wish you to think, six months from now, when you become aware of all this, 'Aha, the Earl of Lostwithiel was nothing more than a cat's paw for Caroline—who knows what other lies he may have told me!'"

"Very well. For you to disclose it now exhibits wisdom beyond your years."

"Some would call it *timidity* originating in the disasters that befell my father, and his father."

"I do not take that view of it," Daniel said curtly.

He was startled by bulk and motion to one side, and feared it was a standing-stone toppled by the wind; but it was only Thomas Newcomen, looking a good deal pinker. "God willing, that carriage-ride is the closest I shall ever come to a sea-voyage!" he declared.

"May the Lord so bless you," Daniel returned. "In the storms of the month past, we were pitched and tossed about so much that all hands were too sick to eat for days. I went from praying we would *not* run aground, to praying that we *would*." Daniel paused to draw breath as the other two laughed. Newcomen had brought out a clay-pipe and tobacco-pouch, and Lostwithiel now did the same. The Earl clapped his hands to draw his coachman's eye, and signalled that fire should be brought out.

Daniel declined the tobacco with a wave of his hand. "One day that Indian weed will kill more white men, than white men have killed Indians."

"But not today," Newcomen said.

If this fifty-year-old blacksmith seemed strangely blunt and direct in the presence of an Earl, it was because he and that Earl had been working together for a year, building something. "The balance of the voyage was easier, I trust, Dr. Waterhouse?"

"When the weather lifted, those horrid rocks were in sight. As we sailed past them, we said a prayer for Sir Cloudesley Shovell and the two thousand soldiers who died there coming home from the Spanish front. And seeing men at work on the shore, we took turns peering through a perspective-glass, and saw them combing the strand with *rakes*."

The Earl nodded knowingly at this and so Daniel turned towards Newcomen, who looked curious—though, come to think of it, he *al-*

ways looked curious when he was not in the middle of throwing up. "You see," Daniel continued, "many a ship has gone down near the Isles of Scilly laden with Pieces of Eight, and sometimes a great tempest will cause the sea to vomit up silver onto dry land."

The unfortunate choice of verb caused the blacksmith to flinch. The Earl stepped in with a little jest: "That's the only silver that will find its way onto English soil as long as the Mint over-pays for gold."

"I wish I had understood as much when I reached Plymouth!" Daniel said. "All I had in my purse was Pieces of Eight. Porters, drivers, innkeepers leapt after them like starving dogs—I fear I paid double or treble for *everything* at first."

"What embarrassed you in Plymouth inns, may enrich you here, a few miles north," said the Earl.

"It does not seem a propitious location," Daniel said. "The poor folk who lived here could not even keep their roof off the floor."

"No one lived *here*—this was what the Old Men call a jews-house. It means that there was a lode nearby," said the Earl.

Newcomen added, "Over yonder by that little brook I saw the ruins of a trip-hammer, for crushing the shode." Having got his pipe lit, he thrust his free hand into a pocket and pulled out a black stone about the size of a bun. He let it roll into Daniel's hand. It was heavy, and felt colder than the air. "Feel its weight, Dr. Waterhouse. That is black tin. Such was brought here, where we are standing, and melted in a peat-fire. White tin ran out the bottom into a box hewn from granite, and when it cooled, what came out was a block of the pure metal."

The Earl had his pipe blazing now too, which gave him a jovial, donnish affect, in spite of the fact that (1) he was all of twenty-three years old, and (2) he was wearing clothes that had gone out of fashion three hundred years ago, and furthermore was bedizened with diverse strange ancient artifacts, viz. some heraldic badges, a tin peat-saw, and a tiny bavin of scrub-oak twigs. "This is where I enter into it, or rather my predecessors do," he remarked. "The block tin would be packed down the same sort of appalling road we just came up, to one of the four Stannary towns." The Earl paused to grope among the clanking array of fetishes dangling from chains round his neck, and finally came up with a crusty old chisel-pointed hammer which he waved menacingly in the air—and unlike most Earls, he looked as if he might have actually used a hammer for some genuine purpose during his life. "The assayer would remove a corner from each block, and test its purity. An archaic word for 'corner' is 'coign,' whence we get, for example, 'quoin'—"

Daniel nodded. "The wedge that gunners use, aboard ship, to elevate a cannon, is so called."

"This came to be known as *quoinage*. And thence, our queer English word 'coin,' which bears no relation to any French or Latin words, or German. Our Continental friends say, loosely translated, 'a piece of money,' but we English—"

"Stop."

"Is my discourse annoying to you, Dr. Waterhouse?"

"Only insofar as I *like* you, Will, and have liked you since I met you as a lad. You have always seemed of a level head. But I fear you are going the way of Alchemists and Autodidacts now. You were about to declare that English money is *different,* and that its difference inheres in the purity of the metal, and is signified in the very word 'coin.' But I assure you that Frenchmen and Germans know what money is. And to think otherwise is to let Toryism overcome sound judgment."

"When you put it that way, it does sound a bit silly," the Earl said, cheerfully enough. Then he mused, "Perhaps that is why I have felt it necessary to make this journey with a blacksmith on one hand, and a sixty-seven-year-old Doctor on the other—to lend some gravity to the proposal."

By gestures so subtle and tasteful that they were almost subliminal, the Earl led them to understand that it was time they were underway. They returned to the coach, though the Earl lingered for a few moments on the running board to exchange civil words with a small posse of gentleman riders who had just come up out of the Gorge and recognized the arms painted on the carriage door.

For a quarter of an hour they trundled along in silence, the Earl gazing out an open window. The horizon was far away, smooth and gently varying except where it was shattered by peculiar hard shapes: protruding rocks, called Tors, shaped variously like schooners or Alchemists' furnaces or fortress-ramparts or mandibles of dead beasts.

"You put a stop to my discourse and quite rightly, Dr. Waterhouse. I was being glib," said the young Earl. "But there is nothing glib about this Dartmoor landscape, or would you disagree?"

"Plainly not."

"Then let the landscape say eloquently what I could not."

"What is it saying?"

By way of an answer, Will reached into a breast-pocket and pulled out a leaf of paper covered with writing. Angling this toward the window, he read from it. "The ancient tumuli, pagan barrows, Pendragon-battlegrounds, Druid-altars, Roman watch-towers, and the gouges in the earth wrought by the Old Men progressing west-to-east across the land, retracing the path of the Great Flood in their search for tin; all of it silently mocks London. It says that before there were Whigs and Tories, before Roundheads and Cavaliers, Catholics and Protestants—

nay, before Normans, Angles, and Saxons, long before Julius Cæsar came to this island, there existed this commerce, a deep subterranean flow, a chthonic pulse of metal through primeval veins that grew like roots in the earth before Adam. We are only fleas gorging our petty appetites on what courses through the narrowest and most superficial capillaries." He looked up.

"Who wrote that?" Daniel asked.

"I did," said Will Comstock.

Crockern Tor

LATER THAT DAY

So many boulders protruded through the moth-eaten tarp of dirt stretched over this land, that they had to stop and alight from the carriage, which had become more trouble than it was worth. They must either walk, or ride on arguably domesticated Dartmoor ponies. Newcomen walked. Daniel elected to ride. He was ready to change his mind if the pony turned out to be as ill-tempered as it looked. The ground underfoot was a wildly treacherous composite of boulders, and grass-tufts as soft as goose-down pillows. The pony's attention was so consumed by deciding, from moment to moment, where it should place all four of its hooves, that it seemed to forget there was an old man on its back. The track ran north parallel to a small water-course below and to their left. It was only visible about a third of the time, but helpfully marked out by a breadcrumb-trail of steaming horse-patties left by those who had gone before them.

The stone walls that rambled over this land were so old that they were shot through with holes where stones had fallen out, and their tops, far from running straight and level, leaped and faltered. He would phant'sy he was in an abandoned country if it weren't for the little pellets of sheep dung rolling away under Newcomen's footsteps and crunching beneath the soles of his boots. On certain hilltops grew spruce forests, as fine and dense and soft-looking as the pelts of Arctic mammals. When the wind gusted through these, a sound issued from them that was like icy water hurrying over sharp stones. But most of the land was covered with heather, gone scab-colored for the winter. There the wind was silent, except for the raucous buller that it made as it banged around in the porches of Daniel's ears like a drunk burglar.

Of a sparse line of Tors stretching north over the horizon, Crockern was the smallest, humblest, and most convenient to the main road—which was probably why it had been chosen. It looked not so much like a Tor as like the stump and the crumbs left behind after a proper Tor had been chopped down and hauled away. They broke out onto the top of the moor and saw it above them. The men and horses huddling in its lee enabled them to judge its size and distance: farther away and higher up-hill than they had hoped, as was the case with all hard-to-reach destinations. It felt as though they had toiled for hours, and got nowhere, but when Daniel turned around and looked back at the way they had come, its many long meanders, which he had hardly noticed at the time, were all compressed so that they looked like the fingers of two interlaced fists.

The Tors were out-croppings of layered rocks of the kind that Leibniz thought were built up in riverbeds. Wind had eaten out soft layers to make them flattened lozenges piled atop each other in teetering stacks that leaned together for support—like piles of time-rounded books made in a library by a scholar who was trying to find something. Remnants of fallen ones were scattered down-hill for some distance, half-sunk into the ground at crazy angles, like three-volume treatises hurled into the ground in disgust. The wind only became stronger as they went up; small brown birds flapped their wings as hard as they could and yet fell behind this invisible currency in the air, so that they moved slowly backwards past Daniel.

Daniel estimated that two hundred and fifty gentlemen had answered the Earl's summons, and gathered in the lee of the Tor. But in this place, that many men seemed like ten thousand. Few of them had bothered to dismount. For whatever sort of folk their forebears might have been, these truly were modern gentlemen, and they were as out of their rightful place, here, as Daniel was. The only man who seemed at home was the blacksmith, Thomas Newcomen, who looked like a chip off the old Tor as he stood to the side, broad shoulders an umbrella against the wind, scabby hands in pockets. Daniel saw him now for what he was, a Dwarf out of some Saxon ring-saga.

Between Stones and Wind this Tor ought by right to be dominated by elements of Earth and Air, if he were disposed to think like an Alchemist; but to him it seemed more a watery place. The wind sucked heat from his body as swiftly as snow-melt. The air (compared

9

to the miasmas of cities) had a clarity and cleanliness, and the land-scape a washed, lapidary quality, that made him feel as if he were standing on the bottom of a clear New England river at the moment when the ice broke up in the spring. So Water it was; but the presence of Thomas Newcomen spoke of Fire as well, for a Dwarf was never far from his Forge.

"Do not mistake me, I would fain be of service to the Proprietors of the Engine for Raising Water by Fire," Daniel had insisted, on the twelfth day of Christmas, after Newcomen had stoked the boiler, and the Engine he had wrought, sucking and hissing like a dragon, had begun to pump water up out of Lostwithiel's mill-pond, and into a cistern on the roof of his house. "But I do not have money."

"Consider that stop-cock by which Mr. Newcomen brings the machine to life," the Earl had said, pointing to a hand-forged valve-wheel mounted on a pipe. "Does that stop-cock make steam?"

"Of course not. Steam is generated in the boiler."

"The trade of this country is a boiler that raises all the steam—which is to say, all the capital—we require. What is wanted is a valve," the Earl had said, "a means of conducting some of that capital into an engine where it may do something useful."

THE JUMBLE OF SHRUGGED-OFF slabs afforded natural benches, podia, lecterns, and balconies that served the tin-men as well as the same furnishings in a proper meeting-house. The Court of Stannary was convened there, as it had been for half a millennium, by reading certain decrees of King Edward I. Immediately the most senior of the gentleman of this Tin Parliament stepped forward and proposed that they adjourn, without delay, to a certain nearby Inn, the Saracen's Head, where (Daniel inferred) refreshments were to be had. This was proposed without the least suspicion that it would be refused. 'Twas like the moment at a wedding when the Priest polls the congregation for objections to the union. But the Earl of Lostwithiel astonished them all by refusing.

He had been seated on a mossy bench of stone. Now he clambered up onto it and delivered the following remarks.

"His Majesty King Edward I decreed that this Court meet in this place, and it has been phant'sied ever since that he did simply thrust the royal finger at a Map, indicating a place equidistant from the four Stannary Towns that surround the Moor, and never suspecting that by so doing he was choosing one of the most remote and horrible places in Britain. And so it is customary to adjourn to the comforts of Tavistock, on the supposition that the King of yore would never have intended for his gentlemen to hold their deliberations in a place like this. But I give King Edward I more credit. I daresay that he had a suspicion of Courts and Parliaments and that he wanted his Tin-men to spend their days in producing metal and not in carrying on tedious disputes, and perhaps forming Cabals. So he chose this place by design, to shorten our deliberations. I say that we ought to remain here, and profit from the King's wisdom. For the tin and copper trades have fallen on hard times, the mines are flooded, and we have no real business to transact, other than what we gin up. I mean to gin some up now, and to go about it directly.

"My grandfather was John Comstock, the Earl of Epsom, and the scion of that branch of our ancient line, known vulgarly as the Silver Comstocks. As you know he came to ruin, and my father, Charles, fared little better, and even had to leave over the Earldom and immigrate to America when James I was overthrown. I make no bones about my ancestors.

"But even those of you who suppose that we are Jacobites (which we are not) and call us inveterate Tories (which we are) and who say that Queen Anne made me an Earl, only to pack the House of Lords with Tories when she needed to break Marlborough's power (which may be true)—I say, even those among you who think nothing of me and my line, except what is deprecating and false, must know of the Royal Society. And if you think well of that Society and its works—as every sapient gentleman must—you may not take it amiss, if I remind you of the old connexions between that Society and my grandfather. John Comstock, though wedded to many of the old ways, was also a forward-thinking Natural Philosopher, who introduced the manufacture of gunpowder to England, and whose great distinction it was to serve as the first President of the Royal Society. During the Plague Year he succoured them as well, by offering them refuge on his estate at Epsom, where discoveries too many to list were made by John Wilkins, by the late Robert Hooke, and by him who stands at my right hand: Dr. Daniel Waterhouse, Fellow of Trinity College, Cambridge, Fellow of the Royal Society, and Chancellor of the Massachusetts Bay Colony Institute of Technologickal Arts. Dr. Waterhouse has very recently re-crossed the Atlantic and is even now on his way to London to confer with Sir Isaac Newton . . ."

The mention of Daniel's name caused a sparse ripple of curiosity to propagate through the company of cold, irritable Gentlemen. The mention of Isaac's created a sensation. Daniel suspected this had less to do with Isaac's invention of the calculus than with the fact that he was running the Mint. The suspicion was confirmed by the next words of William Comstock, Earl of Lostwithiel: "It has been years since silver coins were to be seen in the market-places of this land. As many as are minted are taken to the furnaces of the money-goldsmiths and made over into bullion and sent into the East. Golden guineas are the currency of England now; but that is too great a denomination for common folk to use in their dealings. Smaller coins are wanted. Will they be minted of copper? Or of tin?"

"Copper," shouted a few voices, but they were immediately drowned out by hundreds shouting, "Tin!"

"Never mind, never mind, 'tis no concern of ours, for our mines will not produce!" proclaimed the Earl. "Else, we would have never so much to talk about. To the Saracen's Head we should adjourn, so as not to starve or freeze during our deliberations. But as all of our mines are flooded with water, the copper, or the tin, for the next English coinage shall perforce be imported from abroad. 'Twill be of no concern and no profit to us. The doings of this ancient Parliament shall remain a mere antiquarian curiosity; and so why *not* convene for a few ticks of the clock on a freezing moor, and have done with it?

"Unless—gentlemen—we can pump the water out of our mines. I know how you will object, saying, 'Nay, we have tried man-engines, horse-engines, mill-wheels and windmills, none of them profit us!' Even though I am not a miner, gentlemen, I understand these facts. One who understands them better is this fellow standing at my left hand, Mr. Thomas Newcomen, of Dartmouth, who being an humble man styles himself blacksmith and ironmonger. Those of you who have bought mining-tools from him know him thus. But I have seen him work on mechanical prodigies that are, to a mining-pick, as the Concertos of Herr Handel are to the squeaking of a rusty wheel, and I recognize him by the title of Engineer.

"Now, those of you who have seen the apparatus of Mr. Savery may hold a low opinion of engines for raising water by fire; but that of Mr. Newcomen, though it comes under the same *patent* as Mr. Savery's, works on altogether different *principles*—as is evidenced by the fact that it *works*. Dr. Waterhouse is plucking at my sleeve, I can keep him quiet no longer."

This came as a surprise to Daniel, but he did in fact find something to say. "During the Plague Year I tutored this man's father, the young Charles Comstock, in Natural Philosophy, and we spent many hours studying the compression and rarefaction of gases in the engines conceived by Mr. Boyle, and perfected by Mr. Hooke; the lesson was not lost on young Charles; two score years later he passed it on to young Will at their farm in Connecticut, and it was my very great pleasure to visit them there, from time to time, and to witness those lessons being taught so perfectly that no Fellow of the Royal Society could have added what was wanting, nor subtracted what was false. Will took up those lessons well. Fate returned him to England. Providence supplied him with a lovely Devonshire wife. The Queen gave him an Earldom. But it was Fortune, I believe, that brought him together with the Engineer, Mr. Newcomen. For in the Engine that Newcomen has fabricated at Lostwithiel, the seed that was planted at Epsom during the Plague, England's darkest hour, has flourished into a tree, whose branches are now bending 'neath the burgeoning weight of green Fruit; and if you would care to eat of it, why, all you need do is water that Tree a little, and presently the apples shall fall into your hands."

From this, most of the gentlemen understood that they were about to be dunned for Contributions, or, as they were styled in those days, Investments. Between that, and hypothermia, and saddle sores, the response was more tepid than it might have been. But Will Comstock had their attention. "Now one may see why I did not adjourn this Court to the Saracen's Head. Our purpose is to set prices, and transact other business relating to tin-quoinage. And as the Old Men were exempt in several ways from Common Law, and common taxation, this Court has long met to supersede and overrule the ones that held sway over the rest of England. Without capital, Mr. Newcomen's engine will remain nothing more than a curiosity that fills my cistern. The mines shall remain inundated. Neither copper nor tin shall come out of them, and this Court shall lose standing, and have no business to transact. On the other hand, if there is some interest among you Gentlemen of Devon—to speak plainly, if a few of you would care to purchase shares in the joint stock company known as the Proprietors of the Engine for Raising Water by Fire—why, then, the bleak situation I have just described is overturned, you shall have purchased a Revolution, and this Court will be a busy one indeed, with little choice but to adjourn to that merry Inn down the road— where, by the way, the first two rounds of drinks will be paid for by your humble and obedient servant."

The Saracen's Head
THAT EVENING

"Now you will be a Tory, in the eyes of certain Whigs," Will warned him, "and a butt for all the envenomed Darts of Party Malice."

"It is merely a repetition of when I departed my father's house on Holborn during the Plague, and went to seek refuge at Epsom," Daniel said wearily. "Or when I became part of King James's court—in part, at the urging of your father. It is ever thus, when I have dealings with a Comstock . . ."

"With a Silver Comstock," Will corrected him. "Or a Tin one, as they have taken to calling me in Parliament."

"Being a Tory has its perquisites, though," Daniel allowed. "Mr. Threader has very courteously offered to convey me to London, departing tomorrow. He is going thither on business."

The Earl looked a bit queasy. "And you have gratefully accepted?"

"I saw no reason not to."

"Then know that Tories have their factions too, and parties within the party—"

"And Party Malice?"

"And party malice. Though within a party—as within a family—the malice is more strange, and frequently worse. Dr. Waterhouse, as you know, I am my father's third son. I spent a good deal of time getting beaten up by my elders, and quite lost my savour for it. I was reluctant to be made a Tory lord, because I knew it would lead to more of the same—" Here his gaze broke free of Daniel's, and wandered round the Inn until it had sought out Mr. Threader, who was holding court with several gentlemen in a corner, saying nothing, but listening, and writing in a book with a quill.

Will continued, "But I said yes to the Queen, because she was—is—my Queen. Many blows have landed on me since, from Whigs and from Jacobite Tories alike, but the two hundred miles of bad road between here and London act as a sort of padding to lessen their severity. You enjoy the same benefit here; but the moment you

climb into Mr. Threader's coach, and begin to put miles behind
you—"

"I understand," Daniel said. "But those blows do not hurt me, because I am followed around—some would say, haunted—by a long
train of angels and miracles that account for my having survived to
such a great age. I think that this explains why I was chosen for this
work: either I am living a charmed life, or else I have overstayed my
welcome on this Planet; either way, my destiny's in London."

Southern England
LATE JANUARY 1714

TRUE TO HIS WORD, Mr. Threader—or, to be precise, Mr. Threader's
train of carts, coaches, spare horses, and blokes on horseback—collected Daniel from the Saracen's Head on the morning of 16 January
1714, hours before even the most optimistic rooster would be moved
to crow. Daniel was proffered with a courtly bow, and accepted with
sincere reluctance, the distinction of riding with Mr. Threader himself in his personal coach.

As Daniel's *person* had been deemed so worthy, his *baggage* (three
sea-trunks, two of which sported bullet-holes) merited placement
on the cart that followed right behind the coach. Getting it there
was not to be achieved without a few minutes' unpacking and
rearranging.

Daniel stayed outside to observe this, not because he was worried
(the luggage had survived worse) but because it gave him a last opportunity to stretch his legs, which was something he had to do frequently, to prevent his knees from congealing. He doddered round
the Inn's stable-yard trying to dodge manure-piles by moon-light.
The porters had unpacked from the wagon a matched set of three
wooden boxes whose deeply polished wood harvested that light and
raked it together into a pattern of gleams. They were expertly dove-
tailed together at the corners, and furnished with pretty hardware:
hinges, locks, and handles made to look like natural swirlings of
acanthus-leaves and other flora beloved of ancient Roman interior

decorators. Behind them on the cart was a row of peculiarly tiny strong-boxes, some no larger than tobacco-chests.

The three wooden cases put Daniel in mind of the ones commissioned by the more well-heeled Fellows of the Royal Society for storage and transportation of scientific prodigies. When Hooke had made the Rarefying Engine for Boyle, Boyle caused such a box to be made to carry it round in, to emphasize its great significance.

In his laboratory in the cupola of Bedlam, Hooke had used Comstock gunpowder to drive the piston of such an engine, and had shown it could do work—or in Hooke-language, that it could give service as an artificial muscle. That was because Hooke the cripple had wanted to fly, and knew that neither his muscles nor anyone else's were strong enough. Hooke knew that there were certain vapors, issuing e.g. from mines, that would burn with great violence, and hoped to learn the art of generating them and of conducting them into a cylinder to drive a piston—which would be an improvement on the gunpowder. But Hooke had other concerns to distract him, and Daniel had distractions of his own that led him apart from Hooke, and if Hooke's artificial muscles had ever been perfected, Daniel had never seen them, nor heard about them. Now Newcomen was finally doing it; but his machines were great brutish contraptions, reflecting the fact that Newcomen was a blacksmith to miners where Hooke had been a watchmaker to Kings.

That merely glimpsing three good wooden boxes on a baggage-wain could lead to such broodings made Daniel wonder that he could get out of bed in the morning. Once, he had feared that old age would bring senility; now, he was certain it would slowly paralyze him by encumbering each tiny thing with all sorts of significations. And to become involved, at this late date, with the Engine for Raising Water by Fire, hardly simplified matters! Perhaps he was being too hard on himself, though. He was of an age where it was never possible to pursue one errand at a time. He must do many at once. He guessed that people who had lived right and arranged things properly must have it all rigged so that all of their quests ran in parallel, and reinforced and supported one another just so. They gained reputations as conjurors. Others found their errands running at cross purposes and were never able to do anything; they ended up seeming mad, or else perceived the futility of what they were doing and gave up, or turned to drink. Daniel was not yet certain which category he was in, but he suspected he'd find out soon enough. So he tried to forget about Hooke—which was difficult, since Daniel was still carrying his bladder-stone around in one pocket, and Hooke's watch in the other—and got into the coach with Mr. Threader.

Mr. Threader bid him good morning and then slid down the coach's window and made some remarks to his entourage, the general import of which was that they ought all to begin moving in the direction of London. This command was received much too cheerfully, as if going to London were a sudden brilliant improvisation of Mr. Threader's. Movement commenced; and so it came to pass that on the evening of the 16th they found themselves slightly less far away from London than they had been at the start, and on the evening of the 17th, slightly less distant still. They lost ground on the 18th. Progress on the 19th was debatable. Certain days (as when they wandered north to the suburbs of Bristol) they might have been vulnerable to the accusation that they were not making any progress whatsoever.

Daniel's father, Drake Waterhouse, had once moved his person, two horses, a pistol, some bags of oats, a Geneva Bible, and a sack containing eleven hundred pounds sterling from York to London—a distance comparable to the one Daniel was attempting to cover with Mr. Threader—in a single day. And this at the height of the Civil War, when roads were so muddy, and canals so murky, as to erase the distinction. That ride, and others like it, had become proverbial among Puritan traders: examplars of Industry. Mr. Threader, by contrast, played the slothful tortoise to Drake's enterprising hare. On the first day of the journey, they stopped no fewer than five times so that Mr. Threader could engage in lengthy conversations with gentlemen who surprised them along the way—in all cases, gentlemen who happened to have been in attendance at the Court of Stannary the day before.

Daniel had just begun to form the idea that Mr. Threader was not of sound mind, when, during the last of these conversations, his ears picked up the sounds of coins in collision.

Daniel had come well stocked with books, borrowed from Lostwithicl's small but colorful library. He began reading his way through them, and gave little further thought to Mr. Threader's activities for the next several days. But he saw and heard things, which was a grievous distraction for one who was suffering from the particular form of anti-senility troubling Daniel.

Just as the end of a Parishioner's life was announced by the tolling of the church-bell, so the demise of a Threader-conversation was invariably signalled by the music of coins: never the shrill clashing of farthings and Spanish bits, but the thick, liquid clacking of English golden guineas hefted in Mr. Threader's hand. This was a nervous habit of Mr. Threader's. Or so Daniel guessed, since he obviously was not doing it to be tasteful. Once, Daniel actually caught him juggling a pair of guineas one-handed, with his eyes closed; when he opened his eyes, and realized Daniel was watching, he stuffed one coin into the left, and the other into the right, pocket of his coat.

By the time they had got past Salisbury Plain en route to the suburbs of Southampton, and thereby put all strange Druidic monuments behind them, Daniel had learned what to expect from a day on the road with Mr. Threader. They traveled generally on good roads through prosperous country—nothing remarkable in itself, save that Daniel had never in his life seen roads so excellent and country so thriving. England was now as different from the England of Drake, as Île-de-France was from Muscovy. They never went into the cities. Sometimes they would graze a suburb, but only to call upon some stately manor-house that had formerly stood all by itself in the country (or had been made, in recent times, to look like such a house). In general, though, Mr. Threader hewed to the open country, and sniffed out the seats of gentle and noble families, where he was never *expected* but invariably *welcome*. He carried no goods and performed no obvious services. He dealt, rather, in conversation. Several hours of each day were devoted to talking. After each conversation he would retire, clinking pleasantly, to his carriage, and open up a great Book—not a ledger (which would be tasteless) but a simple Waste-Book of blank pages—and joggle down a few cryptical notations with a quill pen. He peered at his diary through tiny lenses, looking somewhat like a preacher who made up the scripture as he went along—an Evangelist of some gospel that was none the less pagan for being extremely genteel. This illusion, however, diminished as they drew (at length) closer to London, and he began to dress more brilliantly, and to bother with periwigs. These, which would have been ornaments on most humans, were impenetrable disguises on Mr. Threader. Daniel put this down to the man's utter lack of features. On careful inspection one could discover a nose in the center of the fleshy oval that topped Mr. Threader's neck, and working outwards from there, find the other bits that made up a face. But without such diligent observations, Mr. Threader was a meat *tabula rasa*, like the exposed cliff of a roast beef left by the carver's knife. Daniel at first took Mr. Threader for a man of about three score years, though as the days went on, he began to suspect that Mr. Threader was older than that, and that age, like a monkey trying to scale a mirror, simply had not been able to find any toe-hold on that face.

Southampton was a great sea-port, and since Mr. Threader obviously had something to do with money, Daniel assumed they would go to it—just as he had assumed, a few days before, that they would go into Bristol. But instead of Bristol, they had traced a hyperbola around Bath, and instead of Southampton, they grazed Winchester. Mr. Threader, it seemed, felt more comfortable with cities that had actually been laid down by the Romans, and viewed the newfangled port-towns as little better than hovels thrown up by Pictish hunter-gatherers. Recoiling from salt water, they now set a course, not precisely for Oxford, but for a lot of tiny places between Winchester and Oxford that Daniel had never heard of.

Now, Daniel was not being held captive; Mr. Threader even tendered apologies to him more than once, and offered to put him on a hired coach to London. But this only made Daniel want to see it through with present company. (1) Partly it was class. To leap out of Mr. Threader's excellent carriage and dash off to London in a grubby hack-coach would be to admit that he was in a hurry—which, in Mr. Threader's crowd, was not done. (2) He had been worried, anyway, about his knees locking up if he were forced to sit for a long time; which would be true, axiomatically, in an efficient coach. The leisurely itinerary of Mr. Threader was just the one Daniel would have chosen, had he been afforded the power to choose. (3) He was not in a hurry anyway. According to what Enoch Root had confided to him in Boston, his summons from the Princess had been a single mote in a storm of activity that had broken in the Court of Hanover in the late spring and early summer of the year just concluded, after the signing of the Peace of Utrecht had brought the War of the Spanish Succession to an end, and got all the Princes and Parliaments of Europe thinking about what they were going to do with the rest of the Eighteenth Century. Caroline could be made the Princess of Wales, and Daniel's errand could suddenly be imbued with all sorts of import and urgency, by two deaths—Queen Anne's and Sophie's. Perhaps Caroline had, at that time, had reasons to expect the former, and to fear the latter. Accordingly, she had begun to set her pieces out on the board, and dispatched her summons to Daniel. But both Anne and Sophie were still alive, as far as Daniel knew. So he was not even a pawn yet. 'Twere pointless, as well as self-important, to rush to London, so long as he was on the island, and able to reach the city on short notice. Better to take his time and to see that island, so that he would better understand how things were, and be a more competent pawn when the time came. Through the windows of Mr. Threader's carriage he was viewing a country almost as strange to him as Japan. It was not only England's unwonted peace and prosperity that made it strange to him. Too, it was that he was viewing places that Puritans and Professors did not get invited to. Since Daniel had never seen those places, he tended to forget they existed, and to discount the importance of the people who lived in them. But this was a mistake, which would make him a very poor and useless pawn indeed if he did not mend it; and weak pawns were liable to be sacrificed early in the game.

They had a surprising bit of warm weather then, for a day or two. Daniel took advantage of it by getting out of that coach whenever it stopped moving. When he tired of walking, he had his great raccoon-lined cape brought out—it filled a trunk by itself—and spread upon the wet grass. There was always grass, for they always stopped in places with lawns, and it was always short, for there were always sheep. On his square of American raccoon fur he would sit and read a book or eat an apple, or lie on his back in the sun and doze. These little picnics enabled him to make further observations of Mr. Threader's business practices, if that is what they were. From time to time, through a manor-house window, across a Great Lawn, or between sparkling fountain-streams, he would catch sight of Mr. Threader passing a scrap of paper to a gentleman, or vice versa. They looked like perfectly ordinary scraps—not engraved, like Bank of England notes, and not encumbered with pendulous wax seals like legal documents. But their passing from hand to hand was always attended with much courtesy and *gravitas*.

If children were present, they would follow Mr. Threader about, and, whenever he stopped moving, form up around him and look expectant. He would pretend not to notice them at first. Then, suddenly, he would reach out and snatch a penny out of some child's ear. "Were you looking for this? Do take it—it is yours!" he'd say, holding it out, but before the little hand could grasp it, the penny would vanish as mysteriously as it had appeared, and be discovered a moment later in a dog's mouth or under a stone, only to disappear again, &c., &c. He would drive the little ones into a frenzy of delight before finally bestowing a silver penny on each of them. Daniel hated himself for being so fascinated by what he knew to be the cheap jugglery of a carnival mountebank, but he could not help watching. How, he wondered, could the wealthy parents of these children entrust money—as they apparently did—to a *prestidigitator*?

On one Lawn, while he dozed, sheep came up all around him, and the sound of them grazing became a sort of continuo-line to his dreams. He opened his eyes to see a set of blunt yellow sheep-teeth tearing at the grass, inches from his face. Those teeth, and the mass of winter wool that had turned the animal into a waddling, greasy bale, struck him as most remarkable. That solely by gnawing at the turf and lapping up water, an animal could generate matter like teeth and wool!

How many sheep in England? And not just in January 1714 but in all the millennia before? Why had the island not sunk into the sea under the weight of sheep-bones and sheep-teeth? Possibly because their wool was exported—mostly to Holland— *which was in fact sinking into the sea!* Q.E.D.

On the 27th of January they entered a forest. Daniel was astonished by its size. He thought they were somewhere near Oxford—it went without saying that they were avoiding the city itself. He saw a fragment of Royal heraldry, but old and ivy-grown. They must be on the estate that, in his day, had been known as the Royal Manor and Park of Woodstock. But Queen Anne had given it to the Duke of Marlborough in gratitude for his winning the Battle of Blenheim, and Saving the World, ten years ago. The Queen's intention was that a magnificent Palace was to be thrown up there for Marlborough and his descendants to dwell in. If this had been France, and the Queen had been Louis XIV, it would have been done by now—but it was England, Parliament had its knobby fingers around the Monarch's throat, and Whigs and Tories were joined in an eternal shin-kicking contest to determine which faction should have the honor of throttling her Majesty, and how hard. In the course of which, Marlborough, a quintessential Tory, and son of a Cavalier, had somehow been painted as a Whig. Queen Anne, who had decided, very late in life, that she much preferred Tories, had stripped him of military command, and in general made life so unrewarding for him in England that he and Sarah had gone away to Northern Europe (where he was considered the greatest thing since beer) to bask in the gratitude of Protestants until such time as the Queen stopped fogging mirrors at Kensington Palace.

Knowing all of this, and knowing what he knew of construction sites and of the English climate, Daniel expected to see a lifeless morass surrounded by a slum of underemployed workers huddling under tarpaulins and drinking gin. For the most part he was not disappointed. But Mr. Threader with his genius for skirting, and his abhorrence of the center, teased Daniel by taking unmarked tracks through the woods and across meadows, opening gates and even taking down fence-rails as if he owned the place, and sniffing out the cottages and lodges where the Duke's tame gentlemen kept records and counted coins. In glimpses between the trunks of trees (where trees still stood) or piles of timbers (where they didn't) Daniel collected vague impressions of the Palace's foundations, and some half-completed walls.

This divagation to Woodstock finally broke the ice—which had been very thick—between Dr. Waterhouse and Mr. Threader. It was clear that Daniel was as mysterious to Mr. Threader as the other way round. Since Threader had not been present at Crockern Tor—he had lain in wait for the Stannary Court at the Saracen's Head—he'd not had the benefit of hearing Will Comstock's account of the Plague Year. All Mr. Threader knew was that Daniel was a Royal Society chap. He could infer that Daniel had got in solely on account of his brains, as he was manifestly lacking in the other tickets: wealth and class.

In the early going, out in Devon where distances between fine houses were greater, Mr. Threader had not been able to restrain himself from circling round Daniel and jabbing at his outer defenses. He had somehow got it in his head that Daniel was connected to the family of Will Comstock's *bride*. And to him this would make sense. Will had married the daughter of a Plymouth merchant who had grown wealthy importing wine from Portugal. But her great-grandfather had been a cooper. Will, by contrast, had noble blood, but no money. Such complementary marriages were all the rage now. Daniel was no gentleman; *ergo,* he must be some friend of the cooper's folk. And so Mr. Threader had made certain dry, deadpan utterances about Will Comstock, hoping that Daniel would put his book down and unburden himself of some lacerating comments about the folly of using steam to do work. In the first few days' travel he had bobbled such bait before Daniel, but his angling had been in vain. Since then, Daniel had kept busy reading in his books and Mr. Threader writing in his. Both men were of an age when they were in no great hurry to make friends and share confidences. Starting friendships, like opening up new overseas trade routes, was a mad venture best left to the young.

Still, from time to time, Mr. Threader would lob dry conversation-starters in Daniel's direction. Just to be a good sport, Daniel would do the same. But neither man could accept the loss of face that attended curiosity. Daniel could not bring himself to come out and ask what Mr. Threader did for a living, as he could see that among the set who kept big houses in the country, it was perfectly obvious, and that only an idiot, or a grubby Whig, would not know. Mr. Threader, for his part, wanted to know how Daniel was connected to the Earl of Lostwithiel. To him, it was monstrously strange that an aged Natural Philosopher should materialize all of a sudden in the middle of Dartmoor, in a coonskin wrapper, and croak out a few words that would cause every gentleman in a twenty-mile radius to liquidate other holdings, and buy stock in that commercial Lunatick Asylum, the Proprietors of the Engine for Raising Water by Fire.

Daniel had developed two alternative hypotheses: Mr. Threader was a betting agent who roamed about taking and settling wagers. Or, Mr. Threader was a Jesuit in disguise, visiting the homes of crypto-

Catholic Jacobite Tories to hear confessions and to collect tithes. The polished wooden chests, according to this hypothesis, contained communion wafers, chalices, and other Popish gear.

All of these speculations collapsed in a few minutes when Daniel saw Blenheim Palace a-building; realized whose estate they were on; and, in his astonishment, forgot himself, and blurted, "Is he here?"

"Is *who* here, precisely? Dr. Waterhouse?" Mr. Threader asked delicately.

"Churchill."

"*Which* Churchill?" Mr. Threader asked shrewdly. For new ones were being produced all the time.

"The Duke of Marlborough." Then Daniel came to his senses. "No. I'm sorry. Stupid question. He's in Antwerp."

"Frankfort."

"He has just moved to Antwerp," Daniel insisted.

This occurred moments before Mr. Threader went into one of Marlborough's out-houses to do whatever it was that he did. Meanwhile Daniel meditated on the foolishness of his little outburst. Obviously the Lord of the Manor was not in residence now. Men who owned such estates did not *live* upon them, at least, not in *January*. At this time of the year they were all in London. The most important occupants of the country estates were not men, but sheep, and the most important activity was conversion of grass into wool; for wool, exported, brought revenue, and revenue, farmed, enabled gentlefolk to pay rent, buy wine, and gamble in London, all winter long.

All clear enough in its general outlines. But as Daniel had got older he had developed a greater respect for details. Mr. Threader, he suspected, was a detail.

To a merchant, England was a necklace of sea-ports surrounding a howling impoverished waste. As with a burning log on a hearth, all the warmth, color and heat lay in the outer encrustation of ruby-red coals. The interior was cold, damp, dark, and dead. The sea served the same purpose for the commerce of England as the atmosphere did for combustion of a log. Any place that the sea could not reach was of no account, save in the vastly inferior sense that it sort of held everything together structurally.

And yet England *did* have an interior. Daniel had quite forgotten this until he had been awakened by the sheep-teeth right in front of his face. Unlike, say, the interior of New Spain, which produced its wealth in a few highly concentrated mines, England's countryside made its treasure in the most diffuse way imaginable. There were no wool-mines. A given swath of grass produced infinitesimal revenue. In order to arrange it so that a Lord could wager a hundred guineas on a horse-race, some kind of frightfully tedious and complicated money-gathering process would have to take place, and it would have to take place all over England, all the time, without letup. Daniel's eyes watered, to think of the number of separate transactions that must go on, all over a given hundred-mile-square patch of English turf, in order to yield a single pound sterling of free-and-clear income, deliverable to a Fop in London.

But at any rate it happened somehow. The recipients of those pounds sterling gathered in London, all winter long, and engaged in Intercourse. That is, money changed hands among them. In the end, a great deal of that money must make its way back out into the countryside to pay for the building and upkeep of stately houses, &c., &c.

The stupidest imaginable way of handling it would have been to gather together all of the pennies in the countryside, from millions of tributary farmsteads, and physically transport them into London; let the wagon-trains feed and water while the gentlefolk carried out their Intercourse; and then load the coins back onto the wagons and haul them back out to the country again. And perhaps that was how they did it in some countries. But England had obstinately refused to mint coins of large denominations—which was to say, gold coins—in large enough quantities to be actually useful. Anyway, such coins were too enormous for small transactions on farms. Those that were minted, tended to be snapped up by London merchants, and used for overseas trade. The true coin of England, the one ordinary folk used, had always been the silver penny. But its low value—which was precisely what made it useful in market-town and countryside—made it miserably inconvenient for gentry who wanted to live in the city. The annual systole and diastole of wealth in and out of London would require movement of vast wagon-trains laden with coins.

One never saw such traffic on English roads, though. The very idea had a Robin Hood–esque, days-of-yore ring to it. And because what was out of sight was out of mind, Daniel had never thought about what was implied by the disappearance of money-chests from the highways of modern England.

Suppose one had gained the trust of many gentlefolk in London. One could then act as an intermediary, settling their transactions in the city with a word and a handshake, without the need for bags of silver to be lugged around and heaved into the doorways of posh town-houses.

Suppose one also had many contacts in the countryside—a network, as it were, of trusted associates on all of the estates and in all of the market-towns. Then one could almost dispense with the need for hauling stamped disks of silver to and from London on the highways—but only by replacing it with a torrential, two-way flow of *information.*

Winged-footed Mercury, messenger of the Gods, must have very little to do nowadays, as everyone in Europe seemed to be worshipping Jesus. If he could somehow be tracked down and put on retainer and put to work flitting back and forth from city to country and back, carrying information about who owed what to whom, and if one, furthermore, had rooms full of toiling Computers, or (engaging in a bit of Speculative Fiction here) a giant Arithmetickal Engine for balancing the accounts, then most transactions could be settled by moving a quill across a page, and movement of silver across England could be cut back to the minimum needed to settle the balance between city and country.

And forget silver. Convert it to gold, and the number of wagons required would be divided by thirteen.

And if one possessed a reservoir, a money-cistern somewhere, even *those* movements could be reduced—one could then do calculus on the curves, and integrate them over time—

"You were right," Mr. Threader exclaimed, climbing back into the carriage. "His Grace has indeed moved to Antwerp."

"When Queen Anne suffered her latest Onset of Symptoms," Daniel said absent-mindedly, "George Louis in Hanover finally got it clear in his mind that he and his mum would be responsible for the United Kingdom any day now, and that they would need an apparatus—a Council of State, and a Commander in Chief."

"Of course *he* would want *Marlborough* for that," said Mr. Threader, sounding just a bit scandalized. As if there was something clearly improper about the next King of England choosing the most glorious and brilliant general of English history to take the reins of the Army.

"Therefore the Duke has gone to Antwerp to renew ties with our regiments in the Low Countries, and to be ready—"

"To pounce," Mr. Threader said.

"Some would say, to be of service, when the new reign begins, and his exile comes to an end."

"Self-imposed exile, let us not forget."

"He is not a fool, nor a coward—he must have felt some strong compulsion to leave his country."

"Oh, yes, he was to be prosecuted for duelling!"

"For issuing a *challenge,* I was informed, to Swallow Poulett, after Mr. Poulett said, to the Duke's face, in Parliament, that the Duke had sent his officers off to be slaughtered in hopeless Engagements, so that the Duke could then profit from re-selling their commissions."

"Scandalous!" said Mr. Threader ambiguously. "But that is in the past. The Duke's pretensions as to his exile, however sturdy they may have *appeared* to *some* in the *past,* are now wholly undermined; for I have a bit of news concerning Marlborough that I'll wager not even *you* have heard, Dr. Waterhouse!"

"I am *cataleptic* with anticipation, Mr. Threader."

"My lord Oxford," said Mr. Threader (referring to Robert Harley, Lord Treasurer of the Realm, the Queen's chief minister, and leader of the Tory Juntilla which had thrown down the Whig Juncto four years earlier), "has granted the Duke of Marlborough a warrant of ten thousand pounds to resume construction of this Palace!"

Daniel picked up a London newspaper and rattled it. "What a very odd thing for him to do, when Harley's own Spleen, the *Examiner,* is jetting bile at Marlborough." This was Daniel's delicate way of suggesting that Harley was only throwing money at Marlborough to create a distraction while he and his henchman Bolingbroke were up to something really reprehensible. Mr. Threader, however, took it at face value. "Mr. Jonathan Swift of the *Examiner* is a bull-terrier," he proclaimed, and favored the newspaper with what, by Mr. Threader's standards, was a warm look. "Once he got his canines sunk in my lord Marlborough's leg it was several years' labor for my lord Oxford to pry those foaming jaws apart; never mind; Harley's *deeds* speak louder than Swift's *words;* those Whigs who would claim Marlborough's virtues for their own, must now explain the matter of those ten thousand pounds."

Daniel was about to air the observation that ten thousand pounds was a very reasonable price for the Tories to pay to get Marlborough in their camp—especially since it was not actually their money—but he curbed his tongue, sensing that there was no point. He and Mr. Threader would never agree on a thing. There was no profit to be gained by further discussion anyway, for Mr. Threader's fascination with those ten thousand pounds was the datum that enabled Daniel to solve the equation at last.

"I wonder if we might have met before, you and I," Daniel mused. "Long ago."

"It must have been very long ago indeed, sir. I never forget—"

"I have perceived that about you, Mr. Threader—that you allow certain things to slip decently into the past—which is *practical*—but you never forget, which is *prudent.* In this instance you have not forgot a thing; we were not formally introduced. In the summer of 1665, I left London and went out to find refuge at Epsom. As very little traffic was moving on the roads, for fear of the plague, I had to walk from Epsom town out to John Comstock's estate. It was rather a long walk, but in no way unpleasant. I recall being overtaken by a carriage that was on its way to the manor-house. Painted upon its door was a coat of arms not familiar to me. I saw it several more times during my stay there. For even though the rest of England was immobilized—embalmed—the man who went about in that carriage would not stop moving on any account. His comings and goings were evidence, to me, that the world had not come to an end, the Apocalypse had not occurred—the hoofbeats of his team on Comstock's carriageway were like the faint pulse in a patient's neck, which tells the Physician that the Patient still lives . . ."

"Who is that madman, coming and going in the midst of the Plague," Daniel asked, *"and why does John Comstock let him into his house? The poxy bastard'll infect us all."*

"John Comstock could not exclude that fellow any more than he could ban air from his lungs," Wilkins said. "That is his money-scrivener."

Mr. Threader was getting teary-eyed now, though it was a toss-up whether this was because of Daniel's mawkish Narration, or because at long last he understood the nature of Daniel's feeble connection to the Silver Comstocks. Daniel brought the anecdote to a swift merciful conclusion: "Unless my memory is having me off, the same arms are painted on the door of the vehicle in which we are now sitting."

"Dr. Waterhouse, I'll not sit still while you disparage your faculty of recollection any more, for truly, you have the memory of an elephant, sir, and it is no wonder to me that you were gathered in by the Royal Society at a tender age! Your account is without flaw; my late father, may God have mercy on his soul, had the honor of being of service to the Earl of Epsom, just as you said, and my brothers and I, during our apprenticeships, as it were, did accompany him on several of his excursions to Epsom."

HE HAD PROMISED that they would go into London the next day, but the matter of the ten thousand changed everything. Mr. Threader was now in the same predicament as a spider who has unexpectedly caught something huge in his web, which is to say, the news was good, but much frantic scurrying around was now demanded of him. So they were detained round Oxford on the 28th and 29th of January. Again, Daniel could have got to London easily but again he resolved to see the journey through with Mr. Threader. So he nipped into Oxford and renewed friendships or, as warranted, hostilities with scholars at the University, while Mr. Threader mended the strands of his local Web, so unused to such exertions.

On the 30th, which was a Saturday, they got a late start. Daniel first had to find a hackney-carriage to take him from Oxford back out to Woodstock. There was a lot of blundering about in the woods there trying to rendezvous with Mr. Threader's train. When he spied it, drawn up before a cottage on the edge of the wood, he saw that he was too early after all, as the horses were all in their feed-bags. He had the hackney-driver unload his trunks on the spot, so that Mr. Threader's men could get them packed on the right cart. But Daniel himself remained in the hackney-coach, and asked the driver to continue a mile down the road and drop him off, so that he could enjoy a stroll back through the woods. If they were going to attempt to make it all the way to London today, this would be his last opportunity to stretch his legs.

The woods were pleasant enough. Spring was trying to come early. Even though branches were bare, holly and ivy provided some greenery. But the road was a slough, with puddles that would have challenged an albatross. It seemed to be cutting round the base of a rise situate between him and the cottage, and so Daniel angled away from it first chance he got, taking what looked like a game trail up onto higher and firmer ground. Reaching the top of the rise he was faintly disappointed to discover the cottage just where he had expected to find it. Decades had passed since he had enjoyed the thrill of getting lost. So down he went, and approached the little compound from its back side, and thereby saw something through a window.

The three wooden chests from Mr. Threader's baggage cart had been brought in and unlocked. They contained scales—exquisite scales made out of gold, so that cycles of tarnishing and polishing would not, over the years, throw off their balance. In front of each scale sat one of Mr. Threader's assistants, weighing golden coins, one at a time. Another assistant was counting the coins out of a chest and distributing them, as needed, to the weighers, who stacked the weighed coins one at a time on embroidered green felt cloths that they had unrolled on the tabletop. Each weigher was maintaining three stacks of coins; the stack in the middle tended to be higher than the other two. When a stack grew precarious it would be carried off, counted, and deposited in one of Mr. Threader's strong-boxes. Or that was the general impression Daniel collected peering through bubbly ancient window-panes with sixty-seven-year-old eyes.

Then he remembered the warning that Will had spoken to him at the Saracen's Head. He knew instantly that, even though he had come this way with intentions wholly innocent, and stumbled upon this scene by chance, it would never be *viewed* that way. He began to feel actual guilt-pangs even though he was blameless. This was a miraculous prodigy of self-shaming that was taught to young Puritans by their elders, as Gypsies taught their children to swallow fire. He skulked back into the forest like a poacher who has stumbled upon the gamekeeper's camp, and worked his way round to the road, and approached the carts from that side, just as the scales and strong-boxes were being loaded onto the carts for transport.

They began to work their way down the gantlet of thriving river ports that crowded the brinks of the Thames. It was market-day in several of the towns they passed through, which impeded their progress, and at the end of the day they had got no farther than Windsor. This suited Mr. Threader, who perceived opportunities for conversation and profit in that district, so lousy with Viscounts, Earls, &c. Daniel was of a mind to stroll up the road to the nearby town of Slough, which was full of inns, including one or two newish-looking ones where he thought he could find decent lodgings. Mr. Threader deemed the plan insane, and watched Daniel set out on the journey with extreme trepidation, and not before Daniel had, in the presence of several witnesses, released Mr. Threader from liability. But Daniel had scarcely got himself into a good walking-rhythm before he was recognized and hailed by a local petty noble who was a Fellow of the Royal Society, and who insisted that Daniel accompany him to his house near Eton and stay the night in his guest bedchamber. Daniel accepted gladly—to the fascination of Mr. Threader, who saw it play out in the carriageway, and found it extremely singular, verging on suspicious, that a chap such as Daniel should be thus recognized and plucked out of the crowd simply because of what went on in his brain.

The next day, Sunday, January 31st, 1714, Daniel did not get breakfast, because none was served. His host had given his kitchen staff the day off. Instead he was hustled off to a splendid church between Windsor and London. It was exactly the sort of church that Drake would have set fire to with extreme prejudice during the Civil War. As a matter of fact, the longer Daniel looked at it, the more certain he became that Drake *had* torched it, and that Daniel had watched. No matter; as Mr. Threader would say, that was in the past. The church was vaulted with a fair new roof now. Daniel's bum, and the bums of the noble and gentle congregants, were kept up off the stony floor by most excellent carven pews, which were rented out to the occupants at annual rates that Daniel did not dare to even think about.

This seemed like the sort of High-Flyer church where the minister would wear glorious raiments. And maybe it was. But not today. He trudged up the aisle in burlap, his head hung low, pallid knuckles locked together below his chin, dolorous musick wheezing out of the organ, played upon reed stops that mocked the rumblings of the parishioners' empty stomachs.

'Twas a scene of pre-Norman gloom. Daniel half expected to see Vikings crash through the stained glass windows and begin raping the ladies. He was quite certain that Queen Anne must have suffered another Setback, or the French unloaded a hundred regiments of Irishmen in the Thames Estuary. But when they had got through the obligatory stuff in the beginning of the service, and the Minister finally had an opportunity to stand up and share what was on his mind, it turned out that all of this fasting, humiliation, and wearing of rough garments was to bewail an event that Daniel had personally witnessed, from a convenient perch on his father's shoulders, sixty-five years earlier.

"THOSE PEOPLE MIGHT AS WELL have been Hindoos to me!" he shouted as he was diving into Mr. Threader's carriage three hours later—scant moments after the Recessional dirge had expired.

Then he looked at Mr. Threader, expecting to see the man's periwig turned into a nimbus of crackling flames, and his spectacle-frames dripping, molten, from his ears, for Daniel's humours got sorely out of balance when he was not fed, and he was quite certain that fire must be vomiting from his mouth, and sparks flying from his eyes. But Mr. Threader merely blinked in wonderment. Then his white eyebrows, which were not on fire at all, went up, which was what Mr. Threader did when overtaken by the urge to smile.

Daniel knew that Mr. Threader was feeling that urge for the following reason: that now, in the final hours of their two-week trek, starvation and a High Church sermon had succeeded where Mr. Threader had failed: the real Daniel Waterhouse had been unmasked.

"I see no Hindoos, Dr. Waterhouse, only a flock of good English parishioners, emerging not from a heathen temple but from a church—the Established Church of this Realm, in case you were misinformed."

"Do you know what they were doing?"

"That I do, sir, for I was in the church too, though I must admit, in a less expensive pew . . ."

" 'Expiating the horrid Sin committed in the execrable Murder of the Royal Martyr! Remembrancing his rank Butchery at the Hands of the Mobb!' "

"This confirms that we did attend the same service."

"I was there," Daniel said—referring to the rank Butchery—"and to me it looked like a perfectly regular and well-ordered proceeding." He had, by this time, had a few moments to compose himself, and did not feel that he was spewing flames any more. He uttered this last in a very mild conversational tone. Yet it affected Mr. Threader far more strongly than anything Daniel could have screamed or shouted at him. The conversation stopped as dramatically as it had begun. Little was said for an hour, and then another, as the carriage, and the train of wagons bringing up the rear, found its way along town streets to the Oxford Road, and turned towards the City, and made its way eastwards across a green, pond-scattered landscape. Mr. Threader, who was facing forward, stared out a side window and looked alarmed, then pensive, then sad. Daniel recognized this train of emotions all too well; it was a treatment meted out by evangelicals to Damnable Sinners. The sadness would soon give way to determination. Then Daniel could expect a fiery last-ditch conversion attempt.

Daniel was facing backwards, watching the road pass under the wheels of the baggage-cart. On that cart, he knew, was Mr. Threader's strangely over-organized collection of strong-boxes. This put him in mind of a much-needed change of subject.

"Mr. Threader. How shall I compensate you?"

"Mm—Dr. Waterhouse? What?"

"You have not only transported me but boarded me, entertained me, and edified me, for two weeks, and I owe you money."

"No. Not at all, actually. I am a very particular man, Mr. Waterhouse, in my dealings. Had I desired compensation, I'd have said as much before we set out from Tavistock, and I'd have held you to it. As I did not do so *then* I cannot accept a penny from you *now*."

"I had in mind more than a *penny*—"

"Dr. Waterhouse, you have made a lengthy journey—an unimaginable journey, to me—and are far from home, it would be a sin to accept so much as a farthing from your purse."

"My purse need not enter into it, Mr. Threader. I have not undertaken this journey without backing. My banker in the City will not hesitate to advance you an equitable sum, on the credit of the Person who has underwritten my travels."

Now Mr. Threader was, at least, interested; he stopped looking out the window, and turned his attention to Daniel. "I'll not take *anyone's* money—yours, your banker's, or your backer's, sir. And I'll not ask who your backer *is*, for it has gradually become obvious to me that your errand is—like a bat—dark, furtive, and delicate. But if you would be so good as to indulge my professional curiosity on one small matter, I should consider your account paid in full."

"Name it."

"*Who* is your banker?"

"Living as I do in Boston, I have no need of a bank in London—but I am fortunate enough to have a family connexion in that business, whom I can call upon as the occasion demands: my nephew, Mr. William Ham."

"Mr. William Ham! Of Ham Brothers! The money-goldsmiths who went bankrupt!"

"You are thinking of his *father*. William was only a boy then." Daniel began to explain young William's career at the Bank of England but he bated, seeing a glassy look on Mr. Threader's face.

"The money-goldsmiths!" Mr. Threader reiterated, "The money-goldsmiths." Something in his tone put Daniel in mind of Hooke identifying a parasite under a microscope. "Well, you see then, it's of no account anyway, Dr. Waterhouse, as I do not think that Mr. Ham's money would have any *utility* for me."

Daniel understood now that Mr. Threader had set a trap by asking for the name of his banker. Saying to Mr. Threader, a money-scrivener, *My banker is a money-goldsmith,* was like mentioning to an Archbishop *I attend church in a barn*: proof that he belonged to the Enemy. The trap had sprung on him now; and, whether by design or no, it happened at the moment they trundled through Tyburn Cross, where limbs of freshly quartered criminals were spiked to the scaffold, festooned with unraveled bowels. Mr. Threader proclaimed, "Coiners!" with the finality of a Norn.

"They're drawing and quartering people for *that* now?"

"Sir Isaac is determined to root them out. He has brought the judicial Powers round to his view, which is that counterfeiting is not just a petty crime—*it is high treason!* High treason, Dr. Waterhouse. And every coiner that Sir Isaac catches, ends up *thusly,* torn by flies and ravens at Tyburn Cross."

Then, as if it were the most natural Transition imaginable, Mr. Threader—who had leaned far forward and screwed his head around to contemplate, at greater length, the festering shreds of Sir Isaac's latest kills—fell back into his repose with a contented sigh, and fastened the same sort of look on the tip of Daniel's nose. "You were there when Charles the First was decapitated?"

"That is what I told you, Mr. Threader. And I was *startled,* to say the least, to enter a church three score and five years later, and be confronted with evidence that these High Church folk have not yet recovered from the event. Do you have any idea, Mr. Threader, how many Englishmen perished in the Civil War? In accordance with our norms, I shall not even mention Irishmen."

"No, I've no idea . . ."

"Precisely! And so to make such a bother about one chap seems as bizarre, idolatrous, fetishistic, and beside the point to me, as Hindoos venerating Cows."

"He lived in the neighborhood," said Mr. Threader, meaning Windsor.

"A local connexion that was not even mentioned in the homily—

not, I say, in the first, the second, or the third hour of it. Rather, I heard much talk that sounded to me like *politics*."

"*To you.* Yes. But *to me*, Dr. Waterhouse, it sounded like *church*. Whereas, if we were to go there—" and Mr. Threader pointed at a barn in a field to the north side of Tyburn Road, surrounded by carriages, and emanating four-part harmony; i.e., a Meeting-House of some Gathered Church "—we would hear much that would sound like church to *you*, and politics to *me*."

"To *me* it would sound like common sense," Daniel demurred, "and I hope that in time you would come round to the same opinion—which would be an impossibility for *me*, in *there*—" Fortuitously, they had just crossed over some important new street that had not existed, or had been just a cow-path, in Daniel's day; but never mind, as looking north he saw Oxford Chapel just where it had always been, and so he was able to thrust his finger at an Anglican church-steeple, which was all he wanted to illustrate his point. "—in that there is no sense to it whatever, only mindless ritual!"

"It is naturally the case that Mysteries of Faith do not lend themselves to commonsensical explanation."

"You, sir, might as well be a Catholic, if that is what you believe."

"And you, sir, might as well be an Atheist—unless, like so many of the Royal Society, you have, on your way to Atheism, chosen to pause for refreshment at the Spring of Arianism."

Daniel was fascinated. "Is it widely known—or *supposed*, I should say—that the Royal Society is a nest of Arianism?"

"Only among those capable of recognizing the *obvious*, sir."

"Those capable of recognizing the *obvious* might conclude from the service you and I have just been subjected to, that this country is ruled by Jacobites—and ruled, I say, thusly from the very *top*."

"Your powers of perception put mine to shame, Dr. Waterhouse, if you know the Queen's mind on this question. The Pretender may be a staunch Catholic, and he may be in France, but he *is* her brother! And at the end of a poor old lonely woman's life, to expect that she'll not be swayed by such considerations is inhumane."

"Not nearly as inhumane as the welcome her brother would receive if he came to these shores styling himself King. Consider the example just cited, so tediously, in church."

"Your candor is bracing. Among my circle, one does not allude so freely to Decapitation of Kings by a Mobb."

"I am glad that you are braced, Mr. Threader. I am merely hungry."

"To me you seem *thirsty*—"

"For blood?"

"For *royal* blood."

"The blood of the Pretender is not royal, for he is no King, and never will be. I saw his father's blood, streaming out of his nostrils in a gin-house at Sheerness, and I saw his uncle's blood being let from his jugulars at Whitehall, and his grandfather's plashing all round the scaffold at the Banqueting House, sixty-five years ago today, and none of it looked different from the blood of convicts that we put up in jars at the Royal Society. If spilling the Pretender's blood prevents another Civil War, why spill it."

"You really should moderate your language, sir. If the Pretender did come to the throne, the words you just spoke would be high treason, and you would be dragged on a sledge to the place we have just put behind us, where you would be half-hanged, drawn, and quartered."

"I simply find it inconceivable that that man would ever be suffered to reign over England."

"We call it the United Kingdom now. If you were fresh from New England, Dr. Waterhouse, which is a hot-bed of Dissidents, or if you had been dwelling too long in London, where Whigs and Parliament lord it over ordinary sensible Englishmen, then I should understand why you feel as you do. But during our journey I have showed you England *as it is,* not as Whigs phant'sy it to be. How can a man of your intelligence not perceive the wealth of this country—the wealth *temporal* of our commerce and the wealth *spiritual* of our Church? For I say to you that if you did comprehend that wealth you would *certainly* be a Tory, *possibly* even a Jacobite."

"The *spiritual* side of the account is balanced, and perhaps o'er-balanced, by the congregations who gather together in Meeting-Houses, where one does not need to sign a lease, to sit on a pew. So we may leave Church-disputes out of the reckoning. Where *money* is concerned, I shall confess, that the prosperity of the countryside quite overtopped my expectations. But it comes to little when set against the wealth of the City."

Timing once again favored Daniel, for they were now on Oxford Street. To the carriage's left side, the Green Lane stretched northwards across open country, threading its way between parks, gardens and farms, darting into little vales and bounding over rises. To the right side it was all built-up: a development that had been only a gleam in Sterling's* eye twenty years ago: Soho Square. Gesturing

---

*Sterling Waterhouse (1630–1703), Daniel's older half-brother, a real estate developer ennobled later in life as the Earl of Willesden.

first this way, then that, Daniel continued: "For the country draws its revenue from a fixed stock: sheep eating grass. Whereas, the City draws its wealth from foreign trade, which is ever-increasing and, I say, inexhaustible."

"Oh, Dr. Waterhouse, I am so pleased that Providence has given me the opportunity to set you right on that score, before you got to London and embarrassed yourself by holding views that stopped being true while you were gone. For look, we are come to Tottenham Court Road, the city begins in earnest." Mr. Threader pounded on the roof and called out the window to the driver, "High Street is impassable for re-paving, jog left and take Great Russell round to High Holborn!"

"On the contrary, Mr. Threader. I know that the Tories have established their own Bank, as a rival and a counterpoise to the Bank of England. But the Bank of England is capitalized with East India shares. The equity of the Tories' Land Bank is, simply, land. And East India trade grows from year to year. But of land there is a fixed quantity, unless you mean to emulate the Dutch, and manufacture your own."

"This is where you need to be set to rights, Dr. Waterhouse. The Land Bank is an antiquarian folly, for just the reasons you have set forth. But this in no way signifies that the Bank of England holds a monopoly. On the contrary. With all due respect to the busy, but misguided men of the Juncto, their Bank's health is as precarious as the Queen's. The war we have just brought to an end was a Whig war, pressed upon a reluctant Queen by the importunities of a warlike Parliament, led by a Juncto intoxicated by dreams of adventures on foreign soil. They got the money by taxing the people of the country—and I know whereof I speak, for they are my friends!—and they got that money into the coffers of the Duke of Marlborough's army by means of loans, brokered in the City, at great personal profit, by Whig bankers and money-goldsmiths. Oh, it was very lucrative for a time, Mr. Waterhouse, and if you were to believe the representations made by my lord Ravenscar, why, you might be forgiven for thinking it was all profitable to the Bank of England. There is his house, by the way," Mr. Threader remarked, as he peered at a spreading Barock pile on the north side of Great Russell Street. "Unspeakably vulgar, quintessentially *nouveau . . .*"

"I was the architect," Daniel said mildly.

"Of the *first* bit," said Mr. Threader after only a moment's break, "which was admirable, a jewel-box. Pity what has been inflicted on it since you left. You know both the Golden, and the Silver, Comstocks. Fascinating! Ravenscar is no longer in a position to afford the best, and so, as you can plainly see, he makes up in ostentation and volume what he cannot have in taste and quality. His mistress seems to find it pleasing."

"Oh."

"You do know who my lord Ravenscar's mistress is?"

"I've no idea, Mr. Threader; when I knew him, he had a different whore every week, and sometimes three at once. Who is his whore presently?"

"The niece of Sir Isaac Newton."

Daniel could not bear this and so he said the first thing that came into his head: "That is where we used to live."

He nodded southwards across Waterhouse Square, and slipped far down in his seat so that he could get a look at the house that brother Raleigh had built on the rubble of the one where Drake had been blown up. This change of position brought him knee-to-knee with Mr. Threader, who seemed to know the story of Drake's demise, and observed a respectful silence as they circumvented the square. Gazing, from his low-down position, over the skyline of the city, Daniel was shocked by a glimpse of an enormous dome: the new St. Paul's. Then the carriage rounded a turn onto Holborn and he lost it.

"You were making some comment about banks, earlier?" Daniel inquired, in a desperate bid to purge his mind of the image of Roger Comstock putting his poxy yard into Isaac's niece.

"It went poorly for the Whigs, very poorly indeed, in the last years of the war!" Mr. Threader answered, grateful to've been given the opportunity to recount the misfortunes of the Juncto. "Bankruptcy forced England to do what France could not: sue for peace, without having accomplished the chief goals of the war. No wonder Marlborough fled the country in disgrace, no wonder at all!"

"I cannot believe East India trade will be depressed for very long, though."

Mr. Threader leaned forward, ready with an answer, but was tripped up by an interruption, of a professional nature, from the driver.

"Dr. Waterhouse, if you would be so good as to specify any destination in greater London, it would be my honor and privilege to convey you to it; but we are approaching Holborn Bridge, the gates and wall of the ancient City are within view, and you must decide now, unless you really want to accompany me all the way to Change Alley."

"That is very kind of you, Mr. Threader. I shall lodge at the Royal Society to-night."

"Right, guv'nor!" said the driver, who could overhear conversations when he needed to. He turned his attention to his horses, then, and addressed them in altogether different language.

"Bad luck that that the Royal Society has moved out of Gresham's College," Mr. Threader asserted.

"The delicacy of your discourse is a continual wonder to me, sir." Daniel sighed, for in truth, the Royal Society had been thrown out of that mouldering pile after Hooke—who, for many years, had defended their lease with his usual vicious tenacity—had died in 1703. Without Hooke, they had only been able to delay the eviction. And they had delayed it superbly, but as of four years ago they were in new quarters off Fleet Street. "Those of us who sank our money into the bonds that paid for the new building, might employ stronger language than 'bad luck.'"

"It is apropos, sir, that you should bring up the topic of investments. I had been about to mention that, should we have taken you to Gresham's College, we should have passed by the front of a new edifice, at Threadneedle and Bishopsgate, that might fairly be called a new Wonder of the World."

"What—your offices, Mr. Threader?"

Mr. Threader chuckled politely. Then he got a distracted look, for the carriage had slowed down, and tilted slightly, depressing him and elevating Daniel. They were climbing a gentle grade. Mr. Threader's gaze bounced from the left window to the right, and stuck there, fixed on the sight of St. Andrew's church-yard, a huddled mob of gray headstones fading into the twilight of the absurdly truncated mid-winter day. Daniel, who even in daylight would have been at some difficulty to keep track of where they were in this new London, realized that they were still rattling eastwards down High Holborn; they had missed several turns, viz. Chancery Lane and Fetter Lane, that would have taken them down toward Fleet Street. As St. Andrew's fell away aft, they missed yet another: Shoe Lane. They were climbing the approaches to the bridge where Holborn, like a country gentleman stepping over a turd-pile, crossed the Fleet Ditch.

Mr. Threader rapped on the roof. "The Royal Society is no longer at Gresham's College!" he explained to the driver. "They have moved to a court off of Fleet Street—"

"Crane Court," Daniel said. "Near Fetter Lane, or so I am informed."

The driver now murmured something, as if he were ashamed to speak it aloud.

"Would you be offended, affrighted, sickened, or in any wise put out, if we were to go down the Fleet?"

"As long as we do not attempt it in a *boat*, Mr. Threader."

Mr. Threader put the tips of his fingers to his mouth, lest the mere suggestion should cause him to throw up. Meanwhile with his other hand he made a coded rap on the ceiling. The driver immediately guided his team toward the right edge of the street. "The brink of our Cloaca Maxima has been shored up since you last, er—"

"Made a Deposit into a Vault?"

"As it were, Dr. Waterhouse. And it is still early enough that the nocturnal traffic shall not have built to the pitch of activity one would so desperately wish to avoid, later."

Daniel could not see where they were going, but he could smell it now, and he could feel the carriage swerving away from the foot of the Holborn Bridge, and slowing to negotiate the turn southwards. He leaned forward and looked out the window down the length of the Fleet Ditch, a black and apparently bottomless slot in a long slab of unspeakably stained pavement, running due south to the Thames. The sky above the river shed a flinty twilight on this gap, from which the buildings of the city seemed to draw back in dismay. In defiance of Mr. Threader's optimistic prediction, an ox-cart, consisting of a giant barrel on wheels, had backed up to the edge of the ditch and opened a large orifice in its rear to spew a chunky brown cataract into this, the least favored tributary of the Thames. The sounds coming up from the depths below, indicated that it was striking something other than clear running water. Making a quick scan of the length of the Ditch between them and the Fleet Bridge, about a quarter of a mile downstream—if "downstream" had any meaning here—Daniel saw two other such carts doing the same thing, or getting ready to. Other than the usual crew of idlers, vagrants, thieves, shake-rags, and disgraced preachers selling instant weddings, there was no traffic, other than a single sedan-chair, which was just emerging from an alley on the opposite bank of the ditch, and in the act of turning north towards Holborn. As Daniel caught sight of it, it faltered and stopped. The faces of the two men carrying it waxed like a pair of moons as they turned to look at Mr. Threader's train. Then the carriage in which Daniel was riding executed its turn. The Ditch swung out of Daniel's view, and was replaced by the first in a various row of cookeries and market-stalls, not all that bad here, close to Holborn, but bound to degenerate rapidly as they moved on. Daniel turned his head the other way to look out at the Ditch. A slablike wall rose from the opposite bank, ventilated by a few windows barred with heavy grids: the front of the Fleet Prison. His view was then blocked by the nostrils of an ox towing a vault-wagon. A whiff came in the window that paralyzed him for a few moments.

"Deposits must be down to-day, and vaults empty, as so many are fasting in remembrance of the Royal Martyr," Daniel observed sourly, for he could tell that Mr. Threader wanted to continue talking about Financial Institutions.

"If I were coming to London a-fresh, Dr. Waterhouse, and wished to align my personal interests with a bank, I should pass the Bank of England by—pass it right by, I say! For your own sake! And keep right on going."

"To the Royal Exchange, you mean . . . one or two doors down, on the opposite side . . ."

"No, no, no."

"Ah, you are speaking of Change Alley, where the stock-jobbers swarm."

"That is off Cornhill. Therefore, in a strictly cartographic sense, you are getting colder. But in another, you are getting warmer."

"You are trying to interest me in some security that is traded in Change Alley. But it issues from an Eighth Wonder of the World that is on Threadneedle, near Gresham's College. It is a most imposing riddle, Mr. Threader, and I am ill-equipped to answer it, as I've not frequented that busy, busy neighborhood for twenty years."

Daniel now leaned to one side, planting his elbow on an arm-rest and supporting his chin on his hand. He did so, not because he was tired and weak from hunger (though he was), but so that he could see round Mr. Threader's head out the rear window of the carriage. For he had glimpsed a peculiar apparition overtaking them. A rustic person would have guessed it to be a coffin levitating through the air. And considering the number of corpses that had been disposed of in Fleet Ditch over the centuries, there was no better place in London for a haunting. But Daniel knew it was a sedan chair, probably the same one that had emerged, a few moments ago, from the alley across the way. Looking across the Ditch Daniel could see directly into that alley, or one like it, and it seemed to him like the vertical equivalent of the Fleet Ditch itself, a black slot filled with who knew what sort of vileness. What had a sedan chair been doing in such a place? Perhaps taking a gentleman to an unspeakably perverse tryst. At any rate it was now gaining ground on them, coming up along one side. It got close enough that Daniel could sit up straight and view it directly out the carriage's side window. The windows of the sedan chair—assuming it had windows—were screened with black stuff, like a confession-booth in a Papist church, and so Daniel could not see into it. He could not even be certain that anyone was inside, though the ponderous jouncing of the box on its poles, and the obvious strain on the two massive blokes who were carrying it, suggested that something was in there.

But after several moments these porters seemed to hear some command from inside the box, and then they gratefully slackened their pace and allowed Mr. Threader's carriage to pull away from them.

Mr. Threader, meanwhile, had resorted to complicated hand-gestures, and was staring at a distant point above Daniel's head.

"Proceed to the fork in the road, there, where Pig Street leads away from Threadneedle. Whether you go right, toward Bishopsgate, or left up Pig toward Gresham's College, you will in a few moments come to the offices of the South Sea Company, which, though it is only three years old, already spans the interval between those two ways."

"And what do you propose I should do there?"

"Invest! Open an account! Align your interests!"

"Is it just another Tory land bank?"

"Oh, on the contrary! You are not the only one to perceive the wisdom of investing in the future increase of foreign trade!"

"The South Sea Company, then, has such interests . . . where? South America?"

"In its original conception, yes. But, as of a few months ago, its true wealth lies in Africa."

"Africa! That is very strange. It puts me in mind of the Duke of York's Africa Company, fifty years ago, before London burned."

"Think of it as the Royal Africa Company, risen from the ashes. Just as the capital stock of the Bank of England is the East India Company, that of the South Sea Company is the Asiento."

"Even I know that this word Asiento is linked somehow to the Peace, but I've been terribly distracted—"

"We could not win the war—could not dislodge the grandson of Louis XIV from the Throne of Spain—but we did extract certain concessions from him. One of which was the entire right of shipping slaves from Africa to the New World. Mr. Harley, our Lord Treasurer, made arrangements for this Asiento to become an asset, as it were, of the South Sea Company."

"How splendid."

"As the commerce of America grows, so the demand for slaves from Africa will grow apace with it, and so there can be no sounder investment than the Asiento, no surer foundation for a bank, for a fortune—"

"Or for a political party," Daniel said.

Mr. Threader raised his eyebrows. Then they passed by another vault-wagon, forcing them to keep their mouths, and even their eyes, closed for a few moments.

Mr. Threader recovered quicker, and said: "*Steam*, on the other hand, sir, I would hold in very low *esteem*, if you'll indulge me in a spot of word-play."

"It is lamentably late in this journey, and this conversation, sir, for you to be divulging this to me."

"Divulging what, Dr. Waterhouse?"

"That you think the Earl of Lostwithiel is launching a mad enterprise, and that you believe your clients should put their money, rather, into the Asiento."

"I shall put their money where they have directed me to put it. But I cannot help observing, that the nearly limitless coast of Africa is crowded with slaves, driven out from the interior by their more ferocious cousins, and virtually free for the picking. If I wish to pump water from a Cornish tin-mine, Dr. Waterhouse, I need not pay Mr. Newcomen to erect a frightful Engine; now that we have the Asiento, I need only send a ship southwards, and in a few weeks' time I shall have all the slaves I need, to pump the water out by stepping on tread-mills, or, if I prefer, to suck it out through hollow straws and spit it into the sea."

"Englishmen are not used to seeing their mines and pastures crowded with Blackamoors toiling under the lash," Daniel remarked.

"Whereas, *steam-engines* are a *familiar sight*!?" asked Mr. Threader triumphantly.

Daniel was overcome with tiredness and hunger, and leaned his head back with a sough, feeling that only a miracle could get him out of this conversation whole. At the same moment, they arrived at the Fleet Bridge. They turned right and began back-tracking westwards, since the driver had over-shot their destination. Daniel, who, as always, had a view out the rear window of the vehicle, was confronted suddenly by the astonishing sight of a colossal stone egg rising up out of the street less than half a mile away, reigning over the low buildings of London like a Khan over a million serfs. This was by a wide margin the largest building Daniel had ever seen, and something about it replenished his energies.

"Nothing about the English landscape is forever fixed. Just as you have probably grown used to the presence of that Dome," Daniel said, nodding down Fleet to St. Paul's, and obliging Mr. Threader to turn around and rediscover it, "we might grow accustomed to multitudes of black slaves, or steam-engines, or both. I speculate that the *character* of England is more constant. And I flatter us by asserting, furthermore, that *ingenuity* is a more essential element of that character than *cruelty*. Steam-engines, being a product of the former virtue, are easier to reconcile with the English scene than slavery, which is a product of the latter vice. Accordingly, if I had money to bet, I'd bet it on steam-engines."

"But slaves *work* and steam-engines *don't!*"

"But slaves can *stop* working. Steam-engines, once Mr. Newcomen has got them going, can never stop, because unlike slaves, they do not have free will."

"But how is an ordinary investor to match your level of confidence, Dr. Waterhouse?"

"By looking at *that,*" Daniel answered, nodding at St. Paul's, "and noting that it does not fall down. Go and examine its arches, Mr. Threader, and you will see that they are in the shape of parabolas. Sir Christopher Wren made them thus, on the advice of Hooke; for Hooke shewed that it should be so."

"You have quite wandered away from me. It is an excellent church. I see no connection to steam-engines."

"Both church-domes and engines are subject to physical laws, which are, in turn, amenable to mathematickal calculations; and we know the laws," Daniel announced. "It is at least as well-founded as what you do for a living."

They had come to a halt before the mouse-hole in the north side of Fleet Street that led to Crane Court. The driver maneuvered his team into it, giving directions to the other drivers that the baggage-cart alone should follow; the remainder of the train, consisting by this point of two large carriages and a second baggage-wain, were to remain in Fleet Street, and to get themselves turned around and aimed in the direction of Ludgate.

Getting the horses, their tack, and the carriage to pass through that archway was a bit like funneling a model ship, rigging a-luff, through the neck of a jug. At one point they drew to a full stop and Daniel, glancing out a side-window, found himself within kissing range of a pedestrian—gawky, post-smallpox, perhaps thirty years of age—whose advance down Fleet Street had been barred by all of Mr. Threader's maneuvers. This fellow, who affected a ratty horse-hair wig, and who carried a smoky lanthorn in one hand and a staff in the other, peered in on them with frank curiosity that Mr. Threader found unseemly. "Go to, go to, sirrah, we are no concern of the Watch!"

The carriage moved forward into the narrow cul-de-sac of Crane Court.

"One of the Royal Society's new neighbors?" Daniel asked.

"That watchman? No, I should think not!"

"Each inhabitant is supposed to take his turn on the Watch," Daniel said pedantically, "and so I assumed . . ."

"That was twenty years ago when the Act was passed," Mr. Threader returned, sorrowful over Daniel's naïveté. "It has become the practice for householders to pool a bit of money and pay some fellow—usually some caitiff from Southwark—to do the chore in their stead. As you encountered him this evening, so shall you *every* evening, unless you have the good fortune to pass by while he is in Pub."

Still they were making their way, tentatively, down Crane Court. Once they had squeezed through the entrance, it had broadened slightly, to the point where two oncoming carriages might scrape past each other.

"I rather thought we should be leaving you off at the home of some distinguished Fellow," said the bemused Mr. Threader. "I say, you're not on the outs with them, are you?" he jested, trying to terminate their journey on a jolly note.

I shall be soon enough. "I have several invitations in my pocket, and mean to spend them methodically—"

"Like a miser with his coins!" said Mr. Threader, still trying to haul Daniel up to the level of joviality that he considered suitable upon parting; perhaps this meant he wanted to see Daniel again.

"Or a soldier with his pouch of balls," Daniel returned.

"You may add one more!"

"I beg your pardon?"

"Invitation! You must come and lodge with me for a few days, Dr. Waterhouse; I shall take it as an affront if you do not."

Before Daniel could think of a polite way to beg off, the carriage came to a stop, and at the same moment the door was pulled open by a fellow Daniel assumed was a porter, albeit over-dressed for the job in his Sunday church-going togs. He was not a porter of the gorilla type, but rather tall, of reasonably normal proportions, perhaps forty-five years old, clean-shaven, almost gentlemanly.

"It is I," Daniel volunteered, as this man could not seem to decide which of the two passengers was the honored guest.

"Welcome to Crane Court, Dr. Waterhouse," said the porter, sincerely but coolly, speaking in a French accent. "I am Henry Arlanc, at your service."

"A Huguenot," muttered Mr. Threader as Henry Arlanc helped Daniel down onto the pavement.

Daniel glanced at the front of the house that formed the end of the court, but it looked just like the engravings, which was to say, very plain and simple. He turned to look back towards Fleet Street. His view was blocked by the baggage-cart, which had taken longer to negotiate the entrance, and was still fifty feet away, lumbering towards them. *"Merci,"* said Mr. Threader as Arlanc helped him out.

Daniel moved over to one side so that he could peer between the baggage-cart and the line of house-fronts running down to Fleet. His night vision was not what it had once been, but he thought he could see the glimmer of the inquisitive watchman's lanthorn limning the arch, perhaps three hundred feet away. He was bothering someone else now, someone in a sedan chair.

The luggage wagon suddenly got much larger, as if a giant bladder had been inflated to fill the entire width of the court. Daniel had scarcely registered that impression, when it became a source of light. Then it seemed a radiant yellow fist was punching at Daniel through a curtain of iron-colored smoke. The punch was pulled long before it reached him, and collapsed and paled into an ashy cloud. But he had felt its heat on his face, and things had flown out of it and struck him. Crane Court was now enlivened by the music of færy-bells as golden coins sought out resting-places on the paving-stones, and fell in twirling parabolas onto the roof-tiles. Some of them must have been flung straight up in the air for great distances because they continued to land hard and to bounce high for several seconds after Daniel had found his own resting-place: on his arse in the street. The court had been blocked off by a wall of smoke which now advanced to surround him; he could not see his own feet. But he could smell the smoke; it was sulfurous, unmistakenly the product of the combustion of gunpowder. Mixed in with that was a sharper chymical scent that Daniel probably could have identified if he had sniffed it in a laboratory; as it was, he had distractions.

People were calling names, including his. "I am all right," Daniel announced, but it sounded as if his fingers were in his ears. He got to his feet, spry as a twenty-year-old, and began working his way down the court in the direction of Fleet Street. The air was clearer nearer the ground, and he ended up walking bent nearly double, tracking his progress by the passage of sprayed coins and other detritus under his feet. There was a kind of snow fluttering through the smoke as well: raccoon fur.

"Watchman!" Daniel shouted, "can you hear me?"

"Yes, sir! The Marching Watch has been sent for!"

"I do not care about the Marching Watch, they are too late! I want that you should follow that sedan chair, and tell me where it goes!"

No answer came back.

Mr. Threader's voice came out of the smoke, just a few yards away. "Watchman, follow that sedan chair and I shall give you a guinea!"

"Right you are, sir!" returned the watchman.

". . . or a guinea's equivalent value in other goods or services, at my discretion, provided that timely and useful information, which would not have been obtainable through other means, is brought to me, and me alone; and note that nothing in this offer shall be construed to create a condition of employment between you and me, particularly where assumption of liabilities, criminal or civil, is concerned. Did you hear all of that, Dr. Waterhouse?"

"Yes, Mr. Threader."

"It is so witnessed this thirty-first day of January, Year of our Lord 1714." Mr. Threader muttered very rapidly.

In the next breath, he began finally to answer the hails of his assistants, who had come running up from Fleet Street and were now tramping blindly through the smoke all round, hardly less dangerous than the terrified horses. Having found Mr. Threader and Daniel by nearly running them down, they began asking, repeatedly and redundantly, whether they were all right; which soon became annoying to Daniel, who suspected that they were only doing it to be noticed. He told them to instead go and find the driver of the baggage-cart, who had been airborne when Daniel had lost sight of him.

The smoke was finally beginning to clear; it seemed to be draining, rather than rising, from the court. Mr. Threader approached. "Did anything strike you, Dr. Waterhouse?"

"Not very hard." For the first time it occurred to him to brush himself off. Wood-shards and raccoon-tufts showered from the folds of his clothing. His finger caught the edge of a coin, which had been made rough as a saw-blade by the violence of its recent career, and this fluttered to the ground and hit with a tinny slap. Daniel bent to examine it. It was not a coin at all. It was a miniature gear. He picked it up. All round him, Mr. Threader's assistants were in similar postures, snatching guineas off the ashlars like a crew of gleaners. The driver of the baggage-cart was face down, moaning like a drunk as he was tended to by Henry Arlanc and a woman, possibly Arlanc's wife. Someone had had the presence of mind to draw the other baggage-cart across the entrance of Crane Court so that the Marching Watch—when and if they arrived—would not simply march in watching for stray coins.

"At the risk of being one of those *bores* who will only venture to state facts after they have become perfectly obvious to all," said Mr. Threader, "I guess that my baggage-cart has just been Blown Up."

Daniel flipped the gear over in his palm several times, then put it in his pocket. "Without a doubt, your hypothesis passes the test that we call, Ockham's Razor."

Mr. Threader was strangely merry. For that matter, even Daniel, who had been in a sour mood all day from fasting, was feeling a bit giddy. He saw Henry Arlanc approaching, wiping traces of blood from his hands, his face blackened. "Mr. Arlanc, if you are all right, would you be so good as to fetch a broom, and sweep my things in-doors?"

This actually produced a guffaw from Mr. Threader. "Dr. Waterhouse! If I may speak frankly, I had been concerned that your coonskins would leave you open to ridicule from London's *à la mode.* But in the end, the Garment in Question was not even suffered to pass the city gates."

"It must have been done by someone very young," Daniel guessed.

"Why do you suppose so, sir?"

"I have never seen you happier, Mr. Threader! Only a fellow who had lived through very little would imagine that a gentleman of your age and experience would find this sort of thing impressive."

This hammered a bung into Mr. Threader's barrel of chuckles, and straightened him right up for several moments. In time he worked his way back to merry, but only after perilous detours through confused, astonished, and outraged. "I was about to make a similar remark directed at *you!*" He was less shocked by the explosion than by Daniel's imputation that it had anything to do with *him.* Another cycle of bewilderment and stifled anger swirled round his face. Daniel observed with some fascination; Mr. Threader had facial features after all, plenty of them.

In the end, all Mr. Threader could do was laugh. "I was going to express my *outrage,* Dr. Waterhouse, that you imagined this had anything to do with *me;* but I bated. I cannot throw stones, since I have been guilty, *mutatis mutandis,* of the identical sin."

"You thought it was for *me*!? But no one knew I was coming," Daniel said. But he said it weakly, for he had just remembered the pirates in Cape Cod Bay, and how Edward Teach, literally smouldering on the poop deck of *Queen Anne's Revenge,* had asked for him by name.

"No one, save the entire crew of the ship that put you ashore at Plymouth—for she must have reached London by now."

"But no one knew *how* I was coming to London."

"No one, save the Court of Directors, and most of the Investors, of the Proprietors of the Engine for Raising Water by Fire! Not to mention your Backer." Mr. Threader then got a bright look on his face and said, "Perhaps they were not trying to *affright* you, but simply to *kill* you!"

"Or *you,*" Daniel returned.

"Are you a wagering man, Dr. Waterhouse?"

"I was brought up to loathe it. But my return to London is proof that I am a fallen man."

"Ten guineas."

"On the identity of the intended victim?"

"Just so. What say you, Dr. Waterhouse?"

"As my life is already staked, 'twere false œconomy to quibble over ten guineas. Done."

Crane Court

EARLY FEBRUARY 1714

But what should be the reason that such a good man
should be all his days so much in the dark?
—JOHN BUNYAN, *The Pilgrim's Progress*

DANIEL'S FIRST FORTNIGHT at the Royal Society was not equal, in excitement or glamour, to that fiery Spectacle that had heralded his arrival. In the minutes after the blast, excitement born of fear had made him feel half a century younger. But the next morning, he woke in his little guest-garret to discover that the thrill had vanished as quickly as the smoke of the blast; while the fear persisted as stubbornly as the carbon-black scorches it had sprayed on the pavement. Aches and pains had appeared in every part of him, as if all the shocks and insults he had suffered since Enoch Root had walked into his Institute some four months ago, had not been registered at once by his body, but had been marked down in a credit-ledger which had now come due, all at once, and with usurous interest.

Much more debilitating was a melancholy that settled over his spirit, and took away his desire to eat, to get out of bed, or even to read. He only stirred at odd intervals when the melancholy condensed into a raw, beastly fear that set his heart thumping and caused all the blood to drop out of his head. One morning before dawn he found himself crouching before his tiny window, twitching a linen curtain, peering out at a wagon that had trundled into Crane Court to deliver some sea-coal to a neighboring house, wondering whether the collier and his boys might be disguised murderers.

His own clear awareness that he had gone half mad did nothing to lessen the physical power of his fear, which moved his body with irresistible power, as a sea heaves a swimmer. He got no rest during the two weeks he spent in that garret, despite staying in bed most of the while, and realized only one gain: namely, he arrived at a better understanding of the mentality of Sir Isaac Newton. But that hardly seemed like a reward. It was almost as if he had suffered a stroke, or a blow to the head, that had stolen away his faculty of thinking about the future. He was quite certain that his story had come to an end, that his sudden journey across the Atlantic was a flash in the pan, which had quite failed to ignite the powder in the barrel, and that Princess Caroline would purse her lips, shake her head, and write it all off as a failed investment and a Bad Idea. Really he was no better off during that time than he had been tied to Hooke's chair at Bedlam being cut for the stone. The pain was not as intense, but the mental state was much the same: trapped in the here and now like a dog, and not part of any coherent Story.

He got better on Saint Valentine's Day. The agent that brought about this miraculous cure was as obscure as the cause of the disease itself. It certainly did not originate from the College of Physicians, for Daniel had used what energies he had to keep the doctors and their lancets at bay. It seemed to issue, rather, from a part of town that had not existed when Daniel had been a young man: a place, just up the road from Bedlam, called Grub Street.

Daniel's medicine, in other words, was Newspapers. Mrs. Arlanc (the wife of Henry, an English Dissenter, and the housekeeper of Crane Court) had been faithfully bringing up food, drink, and newspapers. She had told *visitors* that Dr. Waterhouse was deathly ill, and *physicians* that he was doing much better now, and thereby stopped *all* of them from crossing his threshold. At Daniel's request, she refrained from bringing him his mail.

Now, most places did not have newspapers, and so, if Mrs. Arlanc had not brought him any, he would never have known that they were wanting. But London had eighteen of them. 'Twas as if the combination in one city of too many printing presses; a bloody and perpetual atmosphere of Party Malice; and an infinite supply of coffee; had combined, in some alchemical sense, to engender a monstrous prodigy, an unstanchable wound that bled Ink and would never heal. Daniel, who had grown to maturity in a London where printing presses had to be hidden in hay-wagons to preserve them from the sledgehammers of the Censor, could not quite believe this at first; but they kept coming, every day. Mrs. Arlanc brought these to him as if it were perfectly normal for a man to read about all London's scandals, duels, catastrophes, and outrages every morning as he spooned up his porridge.

At first Daniel found them intolerable. It was as if the Fleet Ditch were being diverted into his lap for half an hour every day. But once he grew accustomed to them, he began to draw a kind of solace from their very vileness. How self-absorbed for him to cower in bed, for fear of mysterious enemies, here in the center of a metropolis that was to Hostility what Paris was to Taste? To be so unnerved, simply because someone had tried to blow him up in London, was like a sailor in a naval engagement pouting and sulking because one of his fellows had stepped on his toe.

So, inasmuch as it made him feel better, Daniel began to look forward to his daily ink-toilette. Immersion in Bile, a splash of Calumny on the face, and a dab of Slander behind each ear, and he was a new man.

The 14th of February was a Sunday, meaning that before the sun had risen, Mr. and Mrs. Arlanc had embarked on their weekly pilgrimage to a Huguenot meeting-house that lay somewhere out beyond Ratcliff. Daniel awoke to find, next to his door, a bowl of cold porridge resting on an otherwise empty tray. No newspapers! Down he ventured into the lower storeys of the house, scavenging for old ones. Most of the rooms had no reading material whatever, except for damned Natural Philosophy books. But on the ground floor, back in Mrs. Arlanc's kitchen, he found a sheaf of old newspapers preserved as fire-starters. He re-ascended in triumph to his garret and read a few of the more recent numbers while excavating a pit in his congealed porridge.

Of the past week's editions, several actually agreed on something factual. This happened about as often as a Total Eclipse of the Sun, and was just as likely to cause panic in the streets. They agreed that Queen Anne was going to open Parliament tomorrow.

Daniel had been conceiving of this Queen as a caricature of elderliness and frailty. News that this half-embalmed figment was going to clamber out of bed and do something of consequence made Daniel feel ashamed of himself. When the Arlancs returned from church in the late afternoon, and the Mrs. trudged up to the garret to collect the tray and porridge-bowl, Daniel announced that tomorrow he would read his mail, and perhaps even put on clothes and get out of bed.

Mrs. Arlanc, who hid competence beneath a jiggly, henlike façade, smiled at this news; though she had the good manners to keep her lips pressed together so that Daniel would not be exposed to the sight of her teeth. Like most Londoners', these had been well blackened by sugar.

"You chose aptly, sir," she allowed the next morning, backing through the narrow door with a basket of books and papers balanced on her tummy. "Sir Isaac inquired after you for a third time."

"He was here this morning?"

"Is here now," Mrs. Arlanc answered, then paused. The entire house had drawn a tiny, sharp breath as the front door was closed. "Unless that was him departing."

Daniel, who had been sitting up on the edge of his bed, rose to his feet and ventured to a window. He could not see down to the front door from here. But in a few moments he spied a burly fellow plodding away, holding a pole in each hand, followed closely by a black sedan chair, and then a second pole-holding bloke. They patiently built up to a trot, weaving round a few stentorian vendors, knife-grinders, &c. who were making their way up and down Crane Court, pretending to be shocked that the residents were not flocking out of their houses to transact business with them.

Daniel tracked Isaac's sedan chair until it reached Fleet, which was a howling flume of Monday morning traffic. The bearers paused long enough to draw deep breaths and then executed a mad sally into a gap between carriages. From a hundred yards away, through a window, Daniel could hear drivers reminding them about their mothers. But the whole advantage of the sedan chair was that it could out-pace other vehicles by insinuating itself into any narrow leads that might present themselves in traffic, and so very soon they had vanished in the tide of men and animals flowing to Westminster. "Sir Isaac is on his way to the opening of Parliament," Daniel hazarded.

"Yes, sir. As is Sir Christopher Wren, who also nipped in and asked about you," said Mrs. Arlanc, who had not failed to seize on this rare opportunity to strip off the bed-clothes. "But that is not all, oh, no sir. Why, this morning you've had mail from a Duchess. A messenger brought it round not half an hour ago. 'Tis on the top of the basket."

Hanover 21 January 1714
Dr. Waterhouse,

As you are expected (God willing) to arrive in London soon, Baron von Leibniz is eager to correspond with you. I have made private arrangements for letters to be conveyed between Hanover and London by couriers who may be trusted. At the risk of being presumptuous, I have offered the Doctor (as I affectionately call him, even though he has been ennobled) the use of this service. My seal on this envelope is my affirmation that the enclosed letter came from the Doctor's hand to yours, untouched and unseen by any other person.

If you would forgive a short personal memorial, I beg leave to inform you that I have taken possession of Leicester House, which, as you may know, was once the home of Elizabeth Stuart, before she came to be known as the Winter Queen;

when I return to it, which may occur soon, I trust you will be so generous with your Time, as to call upon me there.

Your humble and obedient servant,
Eliza de la Zeur
Duchess of Arcachon-Qwghlm

This had been wrapped around a letter written in Leibniz's hand:

Daniel,

That God hears the prayers of Lutherans, is a proposition hotly disputed by many, including many Lutherans. Indeed the late fortunes of the King of Sweden in his wars against the Tsar might lend support to those who say, that the surest way to bring something about, is for Lutherans to get down on their knees and pray that God forbid it. Notwithstanding which, I have prayed for your safe passage every day since I was allowed to know you had left Boston, and I write these lines in the hope and expectation that you have arrived safe in London.

It would be unseemly for me to beg for your succour so early in this letter, and so I shall divert you (or so I flatter myself) by relating my last conversation with my employer, Peter Romanov, or Peter the Great, as he is now styled—not without perfectly sound reasons—by many (I say "employer" because he owes—I do not say "pays"—me a stipend to act as his advisor on certain matters; my Mistress and liege-lady remains, as always, Sophie).

As you probably know, the Tsar's chief occupation these last several years has been making war on the Swedes and on the Turks. What little time remains, he spends on the building of his city, St. Petersburg, which by all accounts is growing up into a fair place, though it is built on a slough. Which amounts to saying, that he has little time to listen to the prating of savants.

But he does have *some* time. Since he flushed the Swedes out of Poland, it has become his habit to travel down through that country and into Bohemia to take the waters at Carlsbad for a few weeks out of every year. This happens in the winter when the land is too barren and the seas too frozen for him to prosecute his wars. Carlsbad, which lies in a mountain valley thick with noble trees, is easily reached from Hanover, and so that is where I go to earn—I do not say "collect"—my pay as consultant to the Tsar of All the Russias.

But if you are imagining a peaceful winter idyll, it is because I have not rendered the scene faithfully. (1) The entire point of "taking the waters" is to induce violent diarrhœa for days or weeks on end. (2) Peter brings with him a vast entourage of lusty Steppenwolves who do not take well to the genteel boredom of Carlsbad. Such words as "languid," "leisurely," and "placid," common as they may be among the Quality of Europe, who are exhausted by a quarter-century of wars, do not appear to be translatable into any of the languages spoken by Peter's crowd. They stay on an estate that is loaned to them by the Polish duke who owns it. But I am certain that this fellow does so out of some baser emotion than hospitality, for every year the Russians find it in good repair, and leave it a ruin. I would not even have been able to reach the place if I had not come in my own personal carriage; the local coachmen will not venture near it for any amount of money, for fear that they or their horses will be struck by musket-balls, or—what is more dangerous—be invited to join in the revels.

I was not afforded a choice. When I stepped out of my coach in the carriageway of this estate, I was spied by a dwarf, who saw me thanking God for my safe arrival, and beseeching Him for an expeditious departure, in the Lutheran manner. "Swede! Swede!" he began to cry, and the chant was rapidly taken up by others. I told my driver to make himself scarce and he rattled away promptly. Meanwhile I had been picked up by a pair of Cossacks and thrown into a different sort of vehicle: an ordinary gardener's wheelbarrow. But it took me several moments to understand this, for it had been decked out with silver candelabras, silk curtains, and embroidered tapestries. To make room for me, they had to expel a marble bust of the King of Prussia, which was already spalled by impacts of musket-balls, and now broke in half on the icy cobblestones. Then the living Leibniz took the place of the carved King. Unlike my predecessor I did not break in two, though I was put in my chariot roughly enough that I was lucky not to have fractured my tailbone. A fragment of a lady's tiara was stabbed into my periwig to serve as a crown, and without further ceremony I was wheeled into the grand ballroom of this stately house, which was as smoky as any battle-field. By this time I had been engulfed in a motley phalanx of dwarves, Cossacks, Tatars, and diverse ill-looking Europeans who had been milling about in the stable-yard until my arrival. I did not see a single Russian until the smoke, driven by a frigid gust from the open doors, cleared from the far end of the ballroom to reveal a sort of makeshift fortress that had been erected by flipping several dining-tables up on edge, and then lashing those walls of polished wood together with bell-ropes and curtain-pulls. This fortification was supplemented by demilunes and ravelins, fashioned from chairs and cabinets; and it was manned entirely by Russians.

I collected now that Peter's entourage had been divided into two groups, viz. Muscovites, and Miscellaneous, and that a battle was being enacted. Or *re*-enacted; for the general arrangement of the redoubt, and the deployment of the Miscellaneous forces, brought to mind the Battle of Poltava. Peter's antagonist in that great clash was King Charles XII of Sweden, which role had been played by the marble bust until moments ago; but said statue had performed so miserably that his forces had been repulsed, and driven back into the bitter cold of the stable-yard. Little wonder that they had seized on me, a flesh-and-blood Lutheran, as a replacement. But if they were expecting me to display any more martial qualities than the bust, they were sorely let down, for even after I had been wheeled into the van of the Miscellaneous battalions, I comported myself in all ways as a sixty-seven-year-old philosopher. If I pissed myself it was of no account, since the Moravian prostitute who came running toward me with a two-foot-high tankard of beer, tripped on her dirndl and flung the contents into my lap.

After this pause for refreshment, the Miscellaneous forces mounted a charge towards the redoubt. We had got about halfway across the ballroom when some Russian galloped out from behind an overturned armoire and cut the chandelier-rope with a backhand swing of his saber. I looked up to see half a ton of crystal, and a gross of lit tapers, descending toward me like a glittering meteor. The men who were pushing my wheelbarrow flung themselves forward and with a mighty acceleration we shot beneath the chandelier so close that I felt the warmth of the candle-flames moments before being struck by a hail of shattered crystal. We had dodged it; but those behind us were brought up short by this spectacle, and then hindered by its sharp wreckage. So our advance *faltered;* but my heart *stopped,* when I saw barrels of muskets reach up over the wooden redoubt, and then shorten as they were leveled at us. Pan-powder flashed up and down the line, and then bolts of white fire sprang towards us. But nothing else came our way save a few chunks of wadding-material. I was struck on the arm by a smoking wine-cork and still bear the bruise on my bicep. The amount of smoke hardly bears description. Most of it came forth in an amorphous cloud, however I saw one or two smoke-rings, about the size of a man's hat, propagating across the room, and retaining their shape and *vis viva* for extraordinary distances. These rings are unlike water-waves, which consist of different water at different times, for smoke rings propagate through clear air, proving that they indeed carry their own substance with them, neither diluting it with, nor dispersing it into, the surrounding atmosphere. And yet there is nothing special about the smoke as such—it is the same smoke that hangs over battlefields in shapeless clouds. The identity of a smoke ring would appear to consist, not in the stuff of which it is made, for that is commonplace and indifferent, but rather in a particular set of relationships that is brought into being among its parts. It is this pattern of relationships that coheres in space and persists in time and endows the smoke-ring with an identity. Perhaps some similar observation might be made about other entities that we observe, and credit with uniqueness and identity, including even human beings. For the stuff of which we are made is just the common stuff of the world, viz. ordinary gross matter, so that a materialist might say, we are no different from rocks; and yet our matter is imbued with some organizing principle that endows us with identities, so that I may send a letter to Daniel Waterhouse in London in the full confidence that, like a smoke-ring traversing a battle-field, he has traveled a great distance, and persisted for a long time, and yet is still the same man. The question, as always, is whether the organizing principle is *added to* the gross matter to animate it, as yeast is thrown into beer, or *inheres in* the relationships among the parts themselves. As a Natural Philosopher I feel compelled to support the latter view, for if Natural Philosophy is to explain the world, it must do so in terms of the things that make up the world, without recourse to occult intrusions from some external, unknowable Realm Beyond. That is the view I have set forth in my book *Monadology*, a copy of which is enclosed—you are most welcome—and, right or wrong, I interpreted the smoke-rings flying past me in the ballroom in Carlsbad as a Roman would interpret owls, ravens, &c. before a battle.

The Russians had not fired live musket-balls at us; or if they had, none had struck me. I flattered myself for a moment that we were safe. But then, on the other side of the smoke-bank into which I was being thrust headlong, I heard the scrape and ring of steel blades being whisked from scabbards, and the rumbling roar of deep-chested Russians bellowing war-cries as they vaulted over wrecked furniture. They were mounting a sally from the redoubt! They came out of the haze like apparitions, as if the smoke itself were condensing to solid form, and fell upon the attackers swinging their blades. By this point I had fully convinced myself that I really was caught up in a violent insurrection, and that I would go to my death in a wheelbarrow. Then my attention was commanded by a vast disturbance propagating through the smoke towards me: not so much a single whorl or eddy, as a whole meteorological event unto itself, like the towering whirlwinds of America, and seeming all the higher for my position: as low down in the wheelbarrow as I could slouch.

Glints and gleams, not only of steel, but of diamonds, and cloth-of-gold, shone through the dark turbulence of it; and finally the smoke cleared away, like a bow-wave parting round the gilded figurehead of a ship, to reveal Peter the Great.

When he recognized me, he laughed, and given my circumstance I could do nothing but accept this humiliation. "Let us go out," he said in Dutch.

"I am afraid I will be killed!" I returned, quite honestly. He laughed again, then sheathed his saber and stepped forward until he was straddling the wheelbarrow, almost as if he meant to piss on me. Then he bent down, planted his shoulder in my gut, wrapped one arm around my waist, and lifted me up as if I were a sack of coffee-beans being taken from a ship's hold. In a moment I was upside down over his shoulder, watching his spurs glide above the marble floor as he bore me across the room with immense strides. I expected to see pools of blood and severed limbs, too, but the worst was the occasional burst of beer-vomit. The battle still raged all around, but the shouting was mixed with a good deal of hilarity. Blade still rang against blade, but where sword-blows struck home, they did so with slapping noises; the Russians were beating their foes with the flats of their sabers.

In a few moments Peter had carried me out into a formal garden that had been hewn at great expense from the surrounding forest. He bent over and tossed me onto what I first supposed was a very high bench; but it pivoted beneath me. Looking around, and shaking away my dizziness, and blinking off the brightness of the sun on the snow, I perceived that I was perched on the wheel of a wagon, which had flipped over on its side at the end of a long set of skid-marks. It had plowed to a stop in a topiary hedge shaped like a man-of-war, which was now listing to port as a result of having been rammed by this cart. The hedge served to block the wind; and the cart-wheel, which was as high off the ground as an average man's shoulder, elevated me to the point where by sitting up straight I could very nearly look the Tsar in the eye.

Now, it was not usual to see him so quickly. In previous years I have been summoned to Carlsbad most urgently, only to languish in the town for days or weeks as I beg his Court officials for the favor of an audience. My first impulse was to be pleased that I had found myself in the Presence so soon; then I had the wit to realize that he would only act in such haste if he were angry with me, or wanted me to do something. As it turned out, I was right about both.

The conversation was direct. Some would say brutal. It is not that Peter is a brute. Extremely violent and dangerous to be sure, but more in the style of a highly effective Roman Emperor than of a cave-bear. It is simply that he likes to accomplish things, preferably with his own hands, and tends to view conversations as impediments. He would rather *do* something of an essentially stupid and pointless nature, than *talk* of something beautiful or momentous. He wants his servants to be like his hands, which carry out his will immediately and without the tedium of verbal instructions—so much so that if a conversation extends beyond a few sentences, he will grow intolerably restless, his face will become disfigured by uncontrollable tics, and he will shoulder his interlocutor out of his way and take action himself. Since he and I do not share fluency in any language, he might have summoned an interpreter—but he was content to get along with a few crude sentences in a mixture of Dutch, German, and Russian.

"At St. Petersburg there is a place staked out to build the Academy of Sciences as you have suggested," he began.

"Most Clement Lord," I said, "as I have had the honor and privilege of founding such an Academy in Berlin; and as I have made some head-way in persuading the Emperor to found one in Vienna; my *joy* upon hearing this news, cannot but be commingled with *apprehension* that that of Russia will one day outshine those of the Germans, and perhaps even put the Royal Society in the shade."

You can well imagine his impatience as I croaked this out. Before I was half-way through it, he was stomping back and forth in the frozen garden like a frost-bitten sentry. I looked down to the opposite end of the clearing and noticed several portraits in ornate gilded frames, which had been taken down from the walls of the château, leaned against the hedge, and used for musketry practice. The faces of most of those paintings now consisted of fist-sized holes, and stray balls had punched out novel constellations in the dark backgrounds. I decided I had better get to the point. "How can I make this happen?"

This startled him and he spun round to glare at me. "What?"

"You want the Russian Academy to over-awe those of Berlin, Vienna, and London?"

"Yes."

"How may I be of service to your Tsarish Majesty? Do you want me to recruit savants?"

"Russia is big. I can *make* savants. Just as I can make soldiers. But a soldier without a gun is only a fire that burns food. I think the same is true of a savant without his tools."

I shrugged. "Mathematicians do not require tools. But all the other types of savant need something or other to help them do their work."

"Get those things," he commanded.

"Yes, Most Clement Lord."

"We will make that thing you spoke of," he announced. "The library-that-thinks."

"The great machine that manipulates knowledge according to a set of logical rules?"

"Yes. That would be a good thing for my Academy of Science to have. No one else has one."

"On both counts I am in full agreement, your Imperial Majesty."

"What do you need, to build it?"

"Just as St. Petersburg cannot be built without architects' drawings, or a ship without plans—"

"Yes, yes, yes, you need the tables of knowledge, written down as binary numbers, and you need the rules of symbolic logic. I have supported this work for many years!"

"With generosity worthy of a Cæsar, sire. And I have developed a logical calculus well adapted to regulate the workings of the machine."

"What of the tables of knowledge!? You told me a man was working on this in Boston!"

By this point the Tsar had stormed up and put his face quite close to mine and gone into one of his twitching fits, which had spread to involve his arm. To steady himself he had gripped the rim of the wheel upon which I was seated, and was twisting it back and forth, rotating me first this way, then that.

For what I said next, it may help to exonerate me slightly in your eyes, Daniel, if I mention that this Tsar still breaks men on the wheel, and does even worse things to those who have incurred his displeasure; which was impossible for me to put out of my mind in my current circumstance, viz. mounted on a large wheel. Before I could think better of it, I blurted, "Oh, Dr. Waterhouse is on his way across the Atlantic at this very moment, and should, God willing, reach London soon!"

"He is turning over the work *I* paid for, to the Royal Society!? I knew I should have throttled that Newton when I had the opportunity!" (For when Peter visited London some years ago he met Sir Isaac at the Mint.)

"Not at all, Clement Lord, for indeed, your humble servant and all his works are reviled by the Royal Society, which would never accept anything linked to my name, even if Dr. Waterhouse were to behave so dishonestly, which is inconceivable!"

"I am building up my Navy," Peter announced.

This, I confess, made little impression on me, for he is never *not* building up his Navy.

"I have ordered three men-of-war to be constructed in London," he continued, "and to sail into the Baltic when weather permits in the spring, to join my fleet for a further assault upon the Swedes; for I have not yet fully purged Finland of those vermin. It is my wish that when those ships sail from London, they are to be laden with tools for my savants to use at the Academy of Science, and they are to carry the fruits of the labors of Dr. Waterhouse."

"It shall be as you say, your Imperial Majesty," I answered, as it seemed unwise to give any *different* response.

Then he could not shoo me away fast enough. I was dragged, breakneck, back into the center of Carlsbad on a *troika* and re-united with my driver. Thence we proceeded to Hanover with only a brief detour to Leipzig, where all of my affairs are in a state of upheaval. Publication of *Monadology* has gone forward with only the normal amount of bickering with printers. Now that the war is over, Prince Eugene, the Duke of Marlborough's valiant brother-in-arms, has taken an interest in Philosophy—which may or may not be an affectation. At any rate, he asked me to write down some of my ideas in a form that would be readable by people like him, who are literate, and intelligent, but do not make a professional study of

Philosophy (and he is not the first. It would be interesting to ask one of these people why they assume it is possible to do this in the case of *philosophy* when they would never dream of asking Sir Isaac to write a version of *Principia Mathematica* with all of the mathematicks taken out). I have done the best I can to satisfy Prince Eugene. The tract is called *Principles of Nature and of Grace,* and *its* printing moves forward too, attended by a completely different set of distractions and controversies. But most of my time in Leipzig was spent, not on the publication of *new* work, but on the most tedious re-hashing of what I was doing forty years ago. Since you are in the bosom of the Royal Society, Daniel, you know what I refer to: the dispute with Sir Isaac as to who first invented the calculus. Letters have been flying back and forth like kites over a knacker's yard ever since this became *warm* about six years ago, but it has been *hot* during the last two years, or ever since Sir Isaac began to convene "committees" and, God help us, "tribunals" at the Royal Society to render an *impartial* verdict. In short, by the time you read this, anything I might say concerning the Priority Dispute will be out of date, and you can get better intelligence by stopping anyone in the hallway and asking him for the latest.

By this point, Daniel, you are no doubt frantic with anxiety that I'm about to ask for your help in my war with Sir Isaac. Indeed, I confess I might have stooped so low, if Peter had not laid more pressing burdens upon me. As it happened, during the ride from Leipzig to Hanover I scarcely thought of Newton at all, save in one, purely practical sense: I could not imagine how I was going to get a letter to you at Crane Court without someone—possibly even Newton himself—recognizing my handwriting, and tearing it open.

Upon my arrival, however, I learned that Providence had shed some favor on me. My old friend (and yours, I believe) Eliza, the Duchess of Arcachon-Qwghlm, had come to town *incognito.*

Several members of the English nobility have gravitated to Hanover in the last year or two, as the war ground to a halt like an unwound clock, and it became evident that England would not suffer the Pretender to succeed Queen Anne. These English courtiers—all Whigs, of course—have probably earned the scorn of London society for turning their backs on a reigning Queen and leaving their country to curry favor with Sophie and her son. And perhaps some of them deserve it. But they have performed invaluable services, not only to the

Hanoverians but to England, by forging contacts, teaching their future rulers a few words of English, and coaxing them to think concretely about preparations. If the change of reign goes smoothly, you may thank them for it. They will be sure to compensate themselves handsomely!

This is not the place to tell the nature of Eliza's work in Hanover. Suffice it to say that her *incognito* is not just a histrionic fashion statement. She is not seen in Court. Almost no one knows she is here. She corresponds frequently with a certain distinguished Englishman who lived in Frankfort until recently, when he moved to Antwerp. And if she receives letters from the Pretender's court in St.-Germain, it is not because she is in league with the Jacobites, but because she makes it her business to know every detail of the plots that are being laid there, to bring a Catholic king back to the Court of St. James. At any rate, the Duchess's network of couriers is peerless and more than equal to the task of getting a letter from my hands to yours without it falling into the grasping claws, and passing beneath the bulging eyeballs, of Sir Isaac.

So, to the matter at hand: Peter's three new warships are supposedly being completed at Orney's ship-yard in a place called Rotherhithe, across the river from Limehouse, adjacent to the Shepherd and Dog Stairs, off Lavender Street. I hope that these names mean something to you!

If you are feeling up to a minor adventure, and if it would in no way interfere with whatever it is you are supposed to be doing for Princess Caroline, I should be indebted if you were to (1) learn from Mr. Orney when those ships are expected to sail for St. Petersburg, and (2) before they do so, freight them, as much as you can, with goods that might be of use, or at least of interest, to aspiring Russian Natural Philosophers, viz. thermometers, scales, lenses, toad's-eyes, unicorn's-gallbladders, Philosopher's Stone, and the like; and (3) for God's sake give the Tsar something to show for our work of the last fifteen years. If you can arrange for your note-cards to be shipped over from Boston in time, that is ideal. Short of that, *any tangible* evidence that you have been doing *something* at the Massachusetts Bay Institute of Technologickal Arts, may help to keep your humble and obedient servant from being broken on a wheel before the Russian Academy of Sciences, as an example to Scientists who draw stipends without yielding Science.

Yours, & c.,
Leibniz

Daniel got dressed. Much of his clothing had been blown up. In the two weeks since, however, Mrs. Arlanc had brokered the procurement of new garments. Daniel had been too debilitated to meddle. Consequently he was now closer to being *à la mode* than at any time in his life.

The last fifty years had not witnessed anything like the thoroughgoing revolution in gentlemen's attire that had come about after the Plague and the Fire, when doublets, and other medieval vestiges, had finally vanished from the world by decree of Charles II. The garments stacked on the table next to Daniel's bed bore the same names, and covered more or less the same bits of the humane anatomy, as the ones that had become fashionable at that time: hose up to the knee, breeches, a linen shirt, a long, skirted, many-buttoned vest, and over that a long-sleeved coat with even more buttons. They had even managed to scare up a periwig for him. The old Louis XIV lion-mane wig was no longer in use; the new ones were narrower and more compact. A bizarre affectation seemed to have taken hold, of dusting them with white powder. The one Mrs. Arlanc had put on the block-head here was as plain as could be, and simply made it look as if Daniel had a luxuriant head of snow-white hair, tied back in a queue. Daniel put it on, if only to keep his bald head warm. He had avoided freezing to death in this room only by wearing a woolen night-cap twenty-four hours a day.

While he was putting on these clothes, which took a long time—his fingers were stiff with age and chill, and the buttons never ended—he glanced through the basket Mrs. Arlanc thought of as a repository, and Daniel thought of as a dustbin, for his mail. There were five separate communications from Mr. Threader, two from Roger Comstock, one from the Earl of Lostwithiel, and diverse cards and notes from Fellows who had stopped by to look in on him, and been turned away by the adamant Mrs. Arlanc. His London relations, some of whom he had never even heard of (these were children of the late Sterling and of Raleigh, and of William Ham) had written, somewhat perfunctorily. As promised, *Monadology* was in there from Leibniz, and there was a 2nd edition of Isaac's *Principia Mathematica,* its leather cover still reeking of the tannery. This had been dropped off, not by Isaac—indeed, there was nothing in the basket from him—but by one of his young acolytes, who had thoughtfully piled on top of it a recent issue of *Journal Literaire,* a Royal Society document from last year called *Commercium Epistolicum,* and a litter of broadsheets and pamphlets in diverse languages, all tied together with narrow black ribbon. Daniel recognized these as several years' worth of attacks and counter-attacks in the calculus dispute. Apparently he was expected to familiarize himself with them—which could only mean that they intended to call him before their tribunal to render testimony.

So much for mail from persons he actually knew. He worked his way deeper into the basket. Metallic clanking and scraping noises issued from its depths as he stirred through it. There were a few letters from Londoners who, starting as of a month ago, had become his fellows on the Court of Directors of the Proprietors of the Engine for Raising Water by Fire. There were two from chaps whose names he did not recognize at all, but who had orderly minds—or so he guessed from their handwriting. These two were the only letters he actually bothered to open and read, simply because they were the only ones whose contents were not wholly predictable. As it turned out, both were from men who had come up with inventions for determining longitude, and sought Daniel's help in bringing their ideas before the Royal Society. Daniel threw them away.

There were no letters from his wife, or from little Godfrey, which was in no way surprising, given the season of the year and the rough weather. Groping to the very bottom of the basket, he scraped his hand on something jagged, and jerked back. He was not too old to die of tetanus. His fingers emerged sooty, rather than bloody. Pulling all the mail out of the basket and then tilting it towards the window he observed several twisted and blackened shreds of wood and of metal in the bottom. The largest bit was a miniature cask, no more than gallon-sized, such as might be used to transport distilled spirits. One end of it was intact—badly damaged to be sure, but still recognizable as having once been a keg. The staves were bound together by an iron band at the end, and spread out, like lines of longitude from the pole, until they reached the equator. But none of them continued very far into the opposite hemisphere. Some were snapped off clean, some bent outwards, some smashed into splintery brooms. That end of the keg, and its metal band, were gone entirely, though they might be accounted for by some of the loose fragments in the bottom of the basket. Other things were in there, too: gears, springs, levers of wrought brass.

Part of Daniel wanted to overturn this basket on a well-illuminated table and piece the device back together. But instead he buried it again under his unread mail. He had spent a fortnight immobilized by melancholy, and tormented by unreasonable fears. Today his humours had gone back into balance. The Daniel Waterhouse who had cowered in that bed for two weeks was a different chap from the one who was standing by the door, dressed and periwigged. But they could easily change places if he dwelled too long on the dark relics in that basket. They had grown cold, waiting for his attention; let them grow colder still.

THE ROYAL SOCIETY'S HEADQUARTERS comprised two separate houses and a tiny courtyard separating them. During the fund-raising effort, some had gone so far as to style it a "compound." One of the houses was the northern terminus of Crane Court. Above its ground floor it had two addtional full storeys, plus a garret in the roof space. This garret, which was where Daniel had been lodged, had two small dormer windows facing the Crane Court side, which would have afforded a clear view all the way down to Fleet Street, and even to the Thames, had they not been partially blocked by a low parapet-wall that had been added to the front of the house to make it seem a few feet higher than it really was. So from his bed, Daniel's view had been of a sort of lead-lined ditch formed where the steeply sloping roof plunged down to die in the base of the parapet: a bathing-place for birds when it rained, and a raceway for rodents in all weathers. For a few hours in the afternoon the sun would traverse the rectangle of sky that showed above the parapet, if the weather happened to be clear. If Daniel stood up and approached the window he could see over the lip of the parapet, where moss, soot, and birdshit vied for hegemony, down into Crane Court, and scan the jumble of rooftops all around. A view of the dome of St. Paul's was denied him unless he opened the window, thrust his head out, and craned it to the left. Then it was startlingly close. Yet it seemed inapproachable because of the wide crevasse of Fleet Ditch, which broke the city in twain half-way between. If he turned one hundred eighty degrees and looked west, he was confronted by a church that was much closer, and infinitely older: the Rolls Chapel, which appeared to be sinking or collapsing into a spacious church-yard just across Fetter Lane. This medieval pile, which had been used by Chancery as a records dump for many centuries, had turned black with coal-smoke during Daniel's lifetime. A bow-shot to the south of it, fronting on Fleet Street, was the Church of St. Dunstan-in-the-West, a Wren production, duly turning black.

Much less strenuous for an old stiff-necked man was simply to gaze southward down the length of Crane Court and hope to glimpse a bit of open water between the buildings that filled most of the space between Fleet Street and the river. This view, every time he spied it, made Daniel feel as if he had, by some error in navigation, been taken to some city as strange as Manila or Isfahan. For the London in which he had grown up had been a congeries of estates, parks, and compounds, thrown up over centuries by builders who shared a common dream of what a bit of English landscape ought to look like: it should be a generous expanse of open ground with a house planted in it. Or, in a pinch, a house and wall built around the perimeter of a not-so-generous patch of ground. At any rate, there had been, in Daniel's London, views of sky and of water, and little parks and farmlets scattered everywhere, not by royal decree but by some sort of mute, subliminal consensus. In particular, the stretch of riverbank Daniel could see from this garret had been a chain of estates, great houses, palaces, courts, temples, and churches put up by whatever powerful knights or monks had got there first and defended them longest. During Daniel's lifetime, every one of these, with the exceptions of the Temple (directly across from the outlet of Crane Court) and Somerset House (far off to his right, towards where Whitehall Palace had stood, before it had burned down), had been demolished. Some had been fuel for the Fire and others had fallen victim to the hardly less destructive energies of Real Estate Developers. Which was to say that with the exception of the large open green of the Temple, every inch of that ground now seemed to be covered by Street or Building.

Turning his back on the window and opening his bedchamber door brought him back to London straightaway—not the London of average Londoners, but the circa-1660, Natural-Philosophic London of John Wilkins and Robert Hooke. For the remainder of the attic was packed to the rafters with material that Daniel recognized and identified under the broad heading of, *Science Crapp*. All had been brought over from the Royal Society's crèche at Gresham's College.

Gresham's College had been precisely the sort of structure that had no place in modern-day London: a compound, rather than a house, built around a court that was spacious enough to house hundreds of Londoners if razed and jammed with town-houses. Gresham's had been Tudor wattle-and-daub, a style that encouraged builders to make it up as they went along, and generally suffered them to get away with it. Whatever it might have looked like in Sir Thomas Gresham's mind's eye, when he had come back from Antwerp, famous from mending Gloriana's coinage, and rich from speculating in it, by the time Daniel had got there it seemed to have been made not by human architects but by wasps.

At any rate it had been huge: ten times the size of the two Crane Court houses combined. They had not had the whole thing to themselves, but they'd had a lot of it.

Also they'd had Hooke and Wren, who'd built London up from cinders. If there was a cellar, closet, attic, or shed anywhere in London that was sitting vacant, Wren would know of it, and Hooke would have the temerity to use it for something.

What it all amounted to was this: up to about the turn of the century, the Royal Society had been able to store things by the acre. There had been no need to cull out, to throw away, or even to organize. But during the first decade of the century they'd lost Gresham's and they'd lost Hooke. Their storage space had shrunk by a factor of ten, at the least. Which might have been a very favorable turn if the sorting out and throwing away had been done by someone who was qualified—who had been around from the beginning—and who had had the time to do a good job of it. To put it plainly, Newton, Wren, or Waterhouse. But Sir Isaac had been busy with the Mint, with prosecuting a war against Flamsteed, and with making the second edition of *Principia* Leibniz-proof. Sir Christopher Wren, during the same days, had been finishing St. Paul's and building the Duke of Marlborough's London house, just next door to St. James's Palace: two significant jobs for an architect. Daniel had been in Massachusetts trying to build a Logic Mill.

Who then had performed the sorting-out? One of Newton's acolytes. And he had probably done it in a hurry. If Daniel had been fully aware of this four years ago, when it had been happening, he'd have been in a panic. Now he could only look on the contents of this attic in the same spirit in which he had looked at the remains of Drake's house on the morning after the Fire.

Most of the Science Crapp was still packed in the crates, barrels, bundles, and bales in which it had been carted hither. Each of these containers was an impediment to the casual investigator. Daniel spied a crate, not far below the rafters, with its lid slightly askew. The only thing atop it was a glass bell jar covering a dessicated owl. Daniel set the bird to one side, drew out the crate, and pulled off the lid. It was the old Archbishop of York's beetle collection, lovingly packed in straw.

This, and the owl, told all. It was as he had feared. Birds and bugs, top to bottom, front to back. All salvaged, not because they had innate value, but because they'd been given to the Royal Society by important people. They'd been kept here just as a young couple keeps the ugly wedding present from the rich aunt.

He heard someone stifling a sneeze. Straightening up carefully, so as not to burst any of the juicy bits in his spinal column, he looked down the stairs and caught the eye of Henry Arlanc. Henry looked nervous, and studiously mournful, like a vicar at a wake, who did not know the deceased, but who is aware that the living have suffered a grievous loss and are likely to be in a foul mood. "I have endeavoured, Dr. Waterhouse, to preserve all that was brought here, in the condition it was brought."

"No solicitor could have worded it more carefully," Daniel muttered under his breath.

"I beg your pardon, sir?"

Daniel stepped over to the top of the staircase, and steadied himself with a hand on the wall, for this was halfway between a ladder and a stair, and it made him dizzy.

"You have done well . . . you are absolved," Daniel said. "The owl was free of dust."

"Thank you, Dr. Waterhouse."

Daniel sat down at the top of the stairs, resting his feet on the first step down. Between his knees he now enjoyed a clear and direct view of Henry's face. Up here in the attic it was gloomy, but the walls and doors of the storey below were all painted white or close to it. The doors had been left open to release the light coming in the windows, and so Henry was bathed in pitiless and revealing illumination, like a specimen on a microscope stage. He was regarding Daniel uneasily.

"How long have you served here, Henry?"

"Since you moved in, sir."

Daniel was a bit confused until he realized *you* meant *The Royal Society*.

"I like to say, that I came with the property," Henry continued.

"When *we* moved here from Gresham's College, there must have been a good deal of . . . rubbish. At Gresham's, I mean."

Henry looked inexpressibly relieved. "Oh yes, sir, more than you could ever imagine."

"Cart-loads, then, was it?"

"Yes, sir, dozens of cart-loads hauled away," Henry affirmed, in the pride of a job well done.

"Hauled away where, precisely?"

Henry faltered. "I—I would not know that, Dr. Waterhouse, there are salvage-men who pick through rubbish looking for objects of value, and sell them to tinkers . . ."

"I understand, Henry. What is more, I agree that neither you, nor any other man, can be asked to know whither rubbish has gone, after the rubbish-cart has disappeared from view. But I have a different question for you along the same lines, on which you must concentrate as intently as you can."

"I shall strain to do so, Dr. Waterhouse."

"At the time that Gresham's was being cleared out, and the *rubbish* being carted away, and the *treasures* brought safely here—I say, at that time, was any rubbish taken away, or treasures produced, from *other locations?*"

"Other locations, Dr. Waterhouse?"

"Hooke. Mr. Robert Hooke. He might have squirrelled things away at Bedlam, or in the additions to the Marquis of Ravenscar's house, or the College of Physicians—"

"Why those places, sir?"

"He built them. Or St. Paul's, or the Fire Monument—he had a hand in those as well. He might have left things in those buildings; and just as the nuts, hidden in out-of-the-way places by a squirrel, are oft forgotten, and discovered later by others—"

"I do not recollect anything coming from Bedlam, or any other place besides Gresham's College," Henry said flatly.

Henry looked curiously red in the face. He had been simple enough to fall into the trap that Daniel had set by speaking of rubbish. But he was sharp enough to see it in hindsight. His response was to become angry rather than fearful. Daniel sensed immediately that to have this man angry at him was undesirable. He explained, in softer tones, "It is only that the Royal Society is so pre-eminent among the scientific academies of the world, that what is rubbish to us, would be esteemed treasure to some who are accounted savants in backward places; and as a gesture of friendship towards such countries, we could send them odds and ends for which we have no further use."

"I take your meaning now, sir," said Henry, the flush fading from his cheeks.

"Better for one of Mr. Hooke's old clocks to be studied by a student in Muscovy, than for some Shadwell tinker to make the gears into jewelry."

"Indeed, sir."

"I have been asked by a colleague on the Continent to keep an eye out for any such items. It is probably too late for the dozens of cart-loads. Perhaps not for what might have been stowed by Hooke in other buildings to which he had keys."

"Sir Christopher Wren was an old friend of Mr. Hooke's."

"That he was," said Daniel, "though I wonder how you know it, since Hooke died seven years before you had any connection to the Royal Society."

Again Henry's face flushed. "'Tis common knowledge. Sir Christopher is here all the time—why, he stopped in just this morning—and often speaks of Hooke with a kind of affection."

Henry got a wry distracted look which proved he was speaking truth. God and the angels might speak of Hooke with outright and unalloyed affection; but *a kind of* affection was the best that could be achieved by Wren, or any other mortal.

"I should simply refer my inquiries to Sir Christopher, then."

"He has stated more than once that he would enjoy renewing your acquaintance, sir, whenever . . ."

Henry trailed off and made a furtive glance at the doorway to the garret, near the top of the stairs.

"Whenever I came to my senses. Consider me healed, Henry. And if you are seized by an urge to throw anything away, do make me aware of it, so that I can pluck out any items that would pass for wonders in Muscovy."

Daniel went out for a walk: a most imprudent act.

Henry Arlanc had let it be known that if Daniel ever summoned the will to leave, for an hour or a day, he, Henry Arlanc, could arrange a sedan chair or a carriage. This was nothing more than simple common sense. The streets of London were a good bit more dangerous now than when Daniel had last walked them, and Daniel much more vulnerable. But on a morning like this, with the streets so crowded with well-to-do persons on the move, murderers and footpads were less likely to be encountered than pickpockets. And these would reap only the meagrest of harvests from Daniel.

An odd notion had come in to Daniel's mind: perhaps the intended victim of the Infernal Device had been, not Daniel or Mr. Threader, but Henry Arlanc.

Now in his years of toil for the Royal Society, Daniel had become a stern judge of odd notions. There were abundant reasons to discard this one straightaway. Its most obvious defect was simply that Daniel had not the faintest idea why anyone would want to blow up the Royal Society's porter. Moreover, the fog that had descended over Daniel's mind since the explosion had made him susceptible to hypotheses of an extremely dark and frightening cast, and this seemed like one of those.

But the Natural Philosopher in him had to admit that it was at least *theoretically* possible. And until it had been ruled out, Daniel liked to preserve, from Arlanc, some independence—he did not wish to get in the habit of relying on the Huguenot every time he stirred from Crane Court—and some privacy. 'Twas neither necessary nor desirable for Arlanc to know everything about his movements around London.

His knees were still recovering from too long spent in bed, but they had become unlimbered by the time he reached the end of Crane Court and flung himself on the mercy of Fleet Street. He turned to the right, therefore moving in the general direction of Charing Cross, and worked his way cautiously upstream, prudently facing on-coming traffic, and with his right hand dabbing at the fronts of houses and shops in case he should be forced to save himself by diving into a door-way. Soon he had left St. Dunstan-in-the-

West behind. The Inner and Middle Temple would be to his left, on the opposite side of Fleet, lurking behind a screen of newer buildings. These were largely occupied by pubs and coffee-houses that were continual targets of arch but confusing references, and cruel but murky satire, in newspapers.

Soon he had passed through Temple Bar. The way—now called the Strand—forked into a main channel on the left and an inferior one to the right, creating a long central island with a couple of churches in it. Daniel took the narrower way—really a series of disjoint street-fragments crudely plumbed together—and grew convinced that he was lost. The buildings were held apart by splints of air, too narrow to deserve the name "alley," that jogged crazily to the right and left, and did not run in straight lines even when they could have. The fire had stopped short of this part of the city, probably because the Rolls and the Temple, with their generous lawns, had acted as fire-breaks. Hooke, in his capacity as City Surveyor, had not been empowered to bring it out of the Dark Ages. These ancient rights-of-way were as sacred, or at least as unassailable, as the precepts of the Common Law. Somewhere among them was an old, therefore low-ceilinged room that had been acquired by a printer, Mr. Christopher Cat, and made into a thing called the Kit-Cat Clubb.

I have spoken to Mr. Cat about you, Roger had let Daniel know, in a note slipped under his door. *When you venture out, stop by our Clubb for refreshment.* There had been a sketchy map, which Daniel now withdrew from his pocket, and tried to interpret. It was useless. But presently he was able to find his way to the Kit-Cat Clubb simply by following the carriages of Whig M.P.s.

The building had clearly been thrown up in an epoch of English history short on food and building materials, because Daniel, who was of average height, could barely stand up without being bludgeoned by a joist. Accordingly, the paintings that Mr. Cat had commissioned to adorn the walls were all bizarrely wide and short. This ruled out portraits, unless they were portraits of very large groups as seen from tremendous distances. Of these, the largest and most prominently displayed was of the distinguished membership of the Kit-Cat Clubb. Roger was front and center in his best wig, which was captured as a horseshoe-shaped swipe of an overloaded paint-brush.

"Let's do something about Longitude!"

He was the same Roger in a much older body. Only his teeth looked young, because they were; they could not have been carved more than a few months ago. He had deteriorated in every way save the Mental and the Dental. He made up for it with clothing.

Daniel blew on his chocolate for a few moments, trying to get it to cool without forming a wrinkled hide on the top. He could not hear himself think for all the Whigs in wigs shouting at each other. "The Queen opened Parliament only two hours ago," he reminded Roger, "or so I've been told, and she forgot, *entirely,* to mention the trifling detail of who would succeed her, after her demise. And you wish to have a chat about Longitude."

The Marquis of Ravenscar rolled his eyes. " 'Twas settled æons ago. Sophie or Caroline will succeed her—"

"You mean, Sophie or George Louis."

"Don't be a fool. Ladies run Europe. The War of the Spanish Succession was all women. In Versailles, Madame de Maintenon. In Madrid, her best friend, the Princesse des Ursins, *Camarera Mayor* of the Bourbon Court of Spain. She runs the place. Those two on the one side, fought it out against Queen Anne and Sophie on the other."

"I thought Queen Anne and Sophie hated each other."

"What's that got to do with anything?"

"Touché, Roger."

"Now if you insist on being pedantic, yes, George Louis is next in the queue after Sophie. Do you know what he did with his wife?"

"Something horrible, I heard."

"Locked her up in a Schloß for the rest of her life, for bed-swerving."

"So clearly *he* has the upper hand, at least—"

" 'Tis the exception that proves the rule, Daniel. By taking such a measure, he confesses his helplessness to the world. She made him a cuckold. Cuckolds cannot be unmade."

"Still, *she's* locked in a Schloß, and he *isn't.*"

"He is locked up in the Schloß of his own mind, which, by all accounts, has walls so thick, as to leave very little room within. The leading lady of England will be the Princess of Wales—raised personally by Sophie and by the late lamented, by all accounts dazzling, Queen of Prussia; and tutored by *your friend.*" This Roger stressed ominously.

"Er, getting back to the actual topic of conversation, don't you think your time were better spent making sure the Hanoverians actually do succeed to the throne? Longitude can wait."

Roger waved his hand as if trying for the eleventh time to knock a particular horse-fly out of the air. "God damn it, Daniel do you really think we are so feckless, as not to have thought of that?"

"I beg your pardon."

"We're not letting the Pretender in! You were there at his so-called birth—you saw the sleight-of-hand involving the warming-pan—surely a man of your discrimination was not so easily deceived!"

"To me it looked like a babe's head coming out of the Queen's vagina."

"And you call yourself a man of science!"

"Roger, if you would set aside this quaint notion that countries must be ruled by kings who are the sons of *other* kings, then it would not matter whether the Pretender entered St. James's Palace through a vagina, or a warming-pan; either way, to hell with him."

"Are you suggesting I become a Republican?"

"I'm suggesting you already are one."

"Hmmph . . . from there, 'tis only a short step to Puritanism."

"Puritanism has its advantages . . . we are not so much under the thumb of ladies."

"Only because you *hang* all of the interesting ones!"

"I am told you have a mistress of a distinguished family . . ."

"As do you—the chief difference being, I get to sleep with mine."

"They say she is extraordinarily clever."

"Yours, or mine?"

"Both of them, Roger, but I was referring to yours."

Roger did an odd thing then, namely, raised up his glass and turned it this way and that, until it had caught the light from the window the right way. It had been scratched up with a diamond. Several lines of script ran across it, which he now read, in a ghastly chaunt that was either bad reading or bad singing.

> *At Barton's feet the God of Love*
> *His Arrows and his Quiver lays,*
> *Forgets he has a Throne above,*
> *And with this lovely Creature stays.*
> *Not Venus's Beauties are more bright,*
> *But each appear so like the other,*
> *The Cupid has mistook the Right,*
> *And takes the Nymph to be his Mother.*

By the time he had lurched and wheezed to the end, several nearby clubbers had picked up the melody—if it could be so called— and begun to sing along. At the end, they all rewarded themselves by Consumption of Alcohol.

"Roger! I never would have dreamed any woman could move you to write even bad poetry."

"Its badness is proof of my sincerity," Roger said modestly. "If I wrote her an *excellent* love-poem, it might be said of me, that I had done it only to flaunt my wit."

"As matters stand, you are indeed safe from any such accusations."

Roger now allowed a few silent moments to pass, and adjusted his posture and his wig, as if about to be recognized in Parliament. He proclaimed: "Now, when the attention of all Good and Forthright Men is fixed upon the controversies attending the Hanoverian Succession, now, I say, is the time to pass Expensive and Recondite Legislation!"

"Viz. Longitude?"

"We can offer a prize to the chap who devises a way of measuring it. A large prize. I have mentioned the idea to Sir Isaac, to Sir Christopher, and to Mr. Halley. They are all for it. The prize is to be quite large."

"If you have *their* support, Roger, what can you possibly want of *me*?"

"It is high time the Massachusetts Bay Institute of Technologickal Arts—which I have supported so generously—did something useful!"

"Such as—?"

"Daniel, I want to win the Longitude Prize!"

London

DANIEL WAS LURKING LIKE A bat in the attic, supervising Henry Arlanc, who was packing Science Crapp into crates and casks. Sir Isaac Newton emerged from a room on the floor just below, talking to a pair of younger men as they strode down the corridor. Daniel craned his neck and peered down the stairway just in time to catch a glimpse of Isaac's feet and ankles as they flicked out of view. One of the men was Scottish, and sanguine, and fully agreeable to whatever it was that Isaac thought he should do. "I shall *remark* on the Baron's *remarks,* sir!"

Leibniz had published his latest salvo in *Journal Literaire* under the title "Remarks."

"I'll use him smartly, I will!"

"I shall supply you with my notes on his *Tentamen*. I found in it a clearly erroneous use of second-order differentials," Isaac said, preceding the others down the stairs.

"I perceive your strategy sir!" boomed the Scotsman. "Before the Baron presumes to pick the lint from oot o' yoor eye he ought to extricate the log from oot o' his oon!" It was John Keill: Queen Anne's cryptographer.

The three men stormed down the stairs and out into the streets, or so it sounded to Daniel, in whose failing ears their footsteps and their conversation melted together into a fusillade of hoots and booms.

Daniel waited until their carriages had cleared the end of Crane Court, then went to the Kit-Cat Clubb.

ONE OF THE REGULARS THERE was John Vanbrugh, an architect who made a specialty of country houses. For example, he was building Blenheim Palace for the Duke of Marlborough. He couldn't help but be busy on that front just now, since Harley had just flung ten thousand pounds at the Duke. Most of his tasks, just now, had nothing to do with the drawing up of plans or the supervision of workers. He was rather shunting money from place to place and attempting to hire people. Daniel knew this because Vanbrugh was using the Kit-Cat Clubb as his office, and Daniel couldn't go there and read the paper and drink chocolate without hearing half of Vanbrugh's business. Occasionally Daniel would glance up to discover Vanbrugh staring at him. Perhaps the architect knew he had corresponded with Marlborough. Perhaps it was something else.

At any rate, Vanbrugh was there when Daniel walked down from Crane Court, and within a few moments he had a great deal more reason to stare. For Daniel had scarcely sat down before a really excellent carriage pulled up in front of the club, and the head of Sir Christopher Wren appeared in its window, asking for Dr. Daniel Waterhouse. Daniel obliged by coming out and climbing right in. The magnificence of this vehicle, and the beauty of the four matched horses that drew it, were sufficient to stop traffic on the Strand, which greatly simplified the task of getting it turned around and aimed back the way Daniel had come, eastwards into the city.

"I sent a carter round to Crane Court, as you requested, to collect whatever it was you wanted collected. He shall meet us at St. Stephen Walbrook and then he is yours for the day."

"I am in your debt."

"Not at all. May I ask what it is?"

"Rubbish from the attic. A gift to our scientific brethren in St. Petersburg."

"Then I am in *your* debt. Given the nature of my work, what a scandal it would raise, if Crane Court collapsed under the weight of beetles."

"Let us consider all accounts settled between us, then."

"Did you really go through *all* of it!?"

"What I am really after is the residue of Hooke."

"Oh—er! You shan't find it *there*. Sir Isaac."

"Hooke and Newton are the two most difficult persons I have ever known—"

"Flamsteed belongs too in that Pantheon."

"Hooke thought Newton stole his ideas."

"Yes. He made me aware of it."

"Newton considered himself aggrieved by any such accusations. Hooke's legacy could only support Hooke, and never exonerate Newton—so away with all such rubbish! But Hooke, being no less obstreperous than Newton, must have anticipated this—he would therefore have placed his most valuable stuff out of Newton's reach."

Wren bore his eighty-one years as an arch supports tons of stone. He had been a sort of mathematical and mechanical prodigy. The quicksilver that had seemingly welled up out of the ground, round the time of Cromwell, had been especially concentrated in him. Later that tide had seemed to ebb, as many of the early Royal Society men had succumbed to a heaviness of the limbs, or of the spirit. Not so with Wren, who seemed to be changing from an elfin youth into an angel, with only a brief sojourn in Manhood. He wore a tall fluffy silver wig, and clothing of light color, with airy lace at the throat and wrists, and his face was in excellent condition. His age showed mostly in the dimples of his cheeks, which had lengthened to crevices, and in the fragile skin of his eyelids, which had become quite loose, pink, and swollen. But even this only seemed to lend him a placid and mildly amused look. Daniel saw now that Wisdom had been among the gifts that God had bestowed on the young Wren, and that it had led him into architecture: a field where the results spoke for themselves, and in which it was necessary to remain on speaking terms with large numbers of one's fellow humans for years at a time. The other early Royal Society men had not recognized Wren's wisdom, and so there had been whispers, fifty years ago, that the wonder boy was squandering his gifts by going into the building trade. Daniel had been as guilty of saying so as anyone else. But Wren's decision had long since been vindicated, and Daniel—who'd made his own decisions, some wiser than others—felt no trace of envy, and no regret. Only a sort of awed bemusement, as their carriage emerged from Ludgate and circumnavigated St. Paul's church-yard, and Wren parted a curtain with one finger to cast an eye over St. Paul's, like a shepherd scanning his flock.

What would it be like, to have built *that?* Daniel could only guess at it, by considering what *he* had built, and trying to appraise it in a similar spirit. But Daniel's work was not finished yet. He was not that old—or so he felt, in present company. When Wren's son had laid the last stone into its place in the lantern atop the dome of St. Paul's, Sir Christopher had been ten years older than Daniel was *today.*

St. Paul's had passed from view; they had turned onto Watling Street and come to a dead stop in the congestion; the tables had turned, and now Wren was looking at Daniel bemusedly. "I do not intend to make your business mine," he said, "but it would help me to help you, if you would allow me to know what sort of Hooke-stuff you are looking for. Some of his artwork, to adorn your walls? Navigational instruments, for finding your way back to Boston? Architectural drawings? Astronomical observations? Schemes for flying machines? Samples of exotic plants and animals? Clock-work? Optical devices? Chymical Receipts? Cartographical innovations?"

"Forgive me, Sir Christopher, my affairs divide and multiply from one day to the next, I am compelled to pursue several errands at once, and so my answer is not as plain as it might be. Almost anything will serve the end I have already mentioned, viz. giving the Russian savants-in-training food for thought. As for my own purposes, I require anything to do with machines."

"I have heard it mentioned that you are a member of the Court of Directors of the Proprietors—"

"No. It is not that. Mr. Newcomen's Engine is a huge and beastly piece of ironmongery, and he needs no assistance from me to make it. I am thinking of small, precise, clever machines."

"I suppose you mean, small, precise machines, *made cleverly.*"

"I meant what I said, Sir Christopher."

"So it's the Logic Mill again? I thought Leibniz gave up on it, what, forty years ago."

"Leibniz only *set it aside* forty years ago, so that he could—" Here Daniel was struck dumb for a few moments out of sheer awe at the *faux pas* he had been about to commit; he was going to say, *invent the calculus.*

Sir Christopher's face, as he regarded this narrowly averted conversational disaster, looked like the death-mask of a man who had died in his sleep while having a pleasant dream.

Finally Wren said, brightly, "I recall Oldenburg was furious. Never forgave him for not finishing it."

A short pause. Daniel was thinking something unforgivable: perhaps Oldenburg had been right, Leibniz should have built the damned machine and never trespassed upon the holy ground that Isaac had discovered and walled round. He sighed.

Sir Christopher was regarding him with infinite patience. 'Twas like sharing a coach with a Corinthian column.

"I am serving two masters and one mistress," Daniel began. "Just now, I don't know what the mistress expects of me, and so let us leave her out of the discussion, and consider my masters. Both men of power. One, a prince of a faraway land, of an old style, but with new ideas. The other, a new sort of prince: a Parliamentary potentate. I can satisfy both, by achieving the same object: construction of a Logic Mill. I know how to build it, for I have been thinking about it, and making test-pieces, for twenty years. I shall soon have a place to build it *in*. There is even money. I want tools, and clever men who can work miracles with them."

"Hooke devised machines for cutting tiny gears, and the like."

"And he knew all of the watch-makers. Among his papers there might be names."

Wren was amused. "Oh, you'll have no difficulty getting watch-makers to talk to you, after my lord Ravenscar passes the Longitude Act."

"That depends on whether they perceive me as a competitor."

"*Are* you?"

"I believe that the way to find longitude is not to make better clocks, but to make certain astronomical observations—"

"The Method of Lunar Distances."

"Indeed."

"But there is so much *arithmetick* to be done, with that method."

"And so let us equip every ship with an Arithmetickal Engine."

Sir Christopher Wren pinkened—not because he was angry, or embarrassed, but because he was interested. His mind worked for a while. Daniel let it. Finally Wren said, "The most ingenious mechanics I have ever seen, have not been those who make clocks—though they are admittedly very clever—but the ones who make *organs*."

"Pipe-organs, you mean?"

"Yes. For churches."

Daniel felt something very strange happening to his face: he was smiling. "Sir Christopher, you must have employed more organ-makers than any man in history."

Wren held up a steadying hand. "The furnishings are put in by the parish vestries—it is they who employ the organ-makers. But this much is true: I see them all the time."

"London must be infested with them!"

"That was more true ten and twenty years ago than now. London's churches are finished. Many of the organ-makers have gone back to the Continent, to rebuild instruments destroyed in the wars. But many are still here. I shall make inquiries, Daniel."

They arrived at the church of St. Stephen on Walbrook. Walbrook had been a stream in Roman times, and was now assumed to be a sewer flowing somewhere beneath the street of the same name, though no one was volunteering to go down and verify this. It was a good omen for the day, because this was Daniel's favorite church. (1) Wren had put it up early in his career—come to think of it, during the same years Leibniz had been toiling on the calculus. It was all domes and arches, as white and pure as an egg; and whatever uplifting thoughts its parishioners might think as they filed into it, Daniel knew it was Wren's secret anthem to Mathematicks. (2) Thomas Ham, his goldsmith uncle, had lived and worked close enough to hear the hymns being sung in this church. His widow Mayflower—who late in life had converted to Anglicanism—had attended services there with her surviving son William. (3) When King Charles II had ennobled Thomas Ham by way of apology for absconding with all of his customers' deposits, he had named him Viscount Walbrook, and so to Daniel the Church of St. Stephen Walbrook felt almost like a family chapel.

Wren had put up so many churches so quickly that he'd not had time to plant steeples on them. They all looked splendid on the inside. But steeples were essential to his vision of how London ought to look from the outside, and so now, in semi-retirement, he was going round to his old projects and banging out majestic yet tasteful steeples one after the other. From here Daniel could see another being finished at St. James Garlickhythe, a quarter-mile away, and yet another freshly completed one across the street from there at St. Michael Paternoster Royal. Apparently Sir Christopher's steeple project was rolling through London a neighborhood at a time. Eminently practical, that. This one, at St. Stephen Walbrook, was just getting underway, using men and matériel being moved over from the other two.

They were taking over the near end of an anomalous open ground north of the church, which spanned a distance of a hundred yards or so between it and the riotous Poultry/Threadneedle/Cornhill/Lombard intersection. Formerly this had been the Stocks Market. It was impossible for so much uncovered dirt to exist in a city like London without becoming a breeding-ground for Crime or Commerce, and Daniel spied instances of both as soon as he got out of Wren's carriage. At the nearer end, Wren's workmen had set up, and were guarding, supply-dumps for the masons and carpenters who would spend the next year or two working here, and were erecting a tiny encampment of shacks and tents. Their dogs were parading around, solemn as doctors, urinating on anything that did not move fast enough. Amid this mess, Daniel spied one cart laden with parcels he'd packed with his own hands in the attic of the Royal Society.

A lot of fellows were doffing their hats—not to Daniel, of course, but to his traveling-companion. Wren was clearly getting ready to part ways with him. "I have in my possession drawings of many of Hooke's buildings."

"That is just the sort of thing I need."

"I shall send them to you. As well as the names of some men, now retired, who built them, and who may have recollections of peculiarities in their construction."

"That is really splendid of you."

"It is the least I can do on behalf of the estate of the fellow who taught me how to design arches. Lastly, I shall nominate you as Overseer of Demonstrations to the Royal Society."

"I beg your pardon?"

"It will become clear to you with a little reflection. I bid you good day, Dr. Waterhouse."

"You are a perfect gentle knight, Sir Christopher."

HE HAD PHANT'SIED that London would be less congested in its eastern reaches, beyond Bishopsgate, but if anything that part of the city was worse yet. For on that front it lay open to the inroads of, on the left hand, Industry, and on the right, Shipping. Neither Daniel nor his carter cared to spend the balance of the day disputing the right-of-way against heavy wagons laden with bricks, coal, and lime, and being drawn down the street by cavalry-charges of draught-horses. They might cross the Bridge, but Southwark would be the same scene with narrower, fewer, and worse roads. So Daniel decreed a change in plans, and had the carter drive him and his parcels down Fish Street Hill to the approaches of London Bridge, and then east along Thames Street as if going to the Tower. To their right, diverse narrow ancient lanes ran down to the wharves, about a bow-shot away, each street giving him a moment's glimpse of a different controversy, mob action, or commercial transaction; but the river Thames was not present in any of these tableaux, because all he could see at the open street-ends was masts and rigging.

They passed the Billingsgate market, which was arrayed around the three sides of a large rectangular dock, or cut-out in the riverbank, where small vessels could come in from the Pool. The dock reached most of the way to Thames Street, which broadened into a plaza there, so as to shake hands with the market. Black rocks skittered out, or lodged and shattered, under the iron rims of the cart's wheels. The horses faltered. They were pushing through a crowd of children in grimy clothes who were buzzing around gleaning those black rocks out of crevices between paving-stones.

"Crimps!" said the carter, "Crimps and Meters come to meet the Hags." He was referring, not to the boys scavenging coal, but to classes of people doing business on the northern shore of Billingsgate Dock. Crimps were coal-merchants, and to judge from snatches of accent drifting on the breeze, they were Yorkshiremen. Meters were the City of London officials who weighed the chalders of seacoal on immense blackened steel-yards, and Hags were the stout tubby boats that ferried it in from the big hulks out in the Pool. All of which was new to Daniel, who thought of Billingsgate as a fishmarket; but he was reassured to see that the fishwives had not been driven out of the place, indeed still controlled most of the dock, and drove back encroaching Crimps with well-aimed barrages of fish-guts and vivid, faithful descriptions of their persons and their families.

Past Billingsgate the going was easier, but only slightly, as the Customs House was shortly ahead of them on the right. This was so crowded with men doing transactions that it was said by some to rival Change Alley. Their discourse commingled into a surfing roar, and even from here Daniel could hear the occasional crash and foam of some mighty wave of Intercourse.

"This will do," he said, and the carter took the next right turn and drove down a lane, lined with small and dingy, but very active, business concerns, to the Thames wharf. Several wee docks had been chopped out of this stretch of the riverbank and it did not take them long to find one where watermen were gathered, smoking pipes and exchanging learned commentary. Simply by standing still and dispensing coins to the right people at the right times, Daniel was able to cause his parcels to be loaded on a boat; passage to be booked across and down the river; and the carter to be sent home.

Seen from Thames Street the river had seemed less Conduit than Barrier—a palisade of honed wood thrown up to prevent an invasion, or an escape. But with a few strokes of the waterman's oar they penetrated the screen along the wharves and surged out into the main channel. This was as crowded as any water in the world, but miraculously open and accommodating compared to the streets of London. Daniel felt as though burdens had been lifted, though nothing could be further from the truth. London very quickly became a smouldering membrane, a reeking tarpaulin flung over the hill and not smoothed out. The only features of consequence were the Fire Monument, the Bridge, the Tower, and St. Paul's. The Bridge, as always, seemed like a Bad Idea, a city on stilts, and a very old, slumping, inflammable Tudor city at that. Not far from its northern end was the Fire Monument, of which Daniel was now getting his first clear view. It was an immense solitary column put up by Hooke but universally attributed to Wren. During Daniel's recent movements about London he had been startled, from time to time, to spy the lantern at its top peering down at him from over the top of a building—just as he had often felt, when he was a younger man, that the living Hooke was watching him through a microscope.

The tide was flowing, and it wafted them downstream at a fair clip. They were abreast of the Tower before he knew it. With some effort of will, Daniel swerved his gaze from Traitor's Gate, and wrenched his thoughts from recollection of old events, and paid heed to present concerns. Though he could not see through the Tower's walls and bastions, he could see smoke rising from the general vicinity of the Mint buildings; and beneath the general clamor radiating from the city he phant'sied he could detect the slow heavy pulse of the trip-hammers beating out guineas. On the battlements were soldiers, wearing black trim on their red coats: therefore, the Queen's Own Black Torrent Guards, who had been garrisoned at the Tower, yanked away from it, re-garrisoned there, yanked back again so many times that Daniel had given up trying to keep track. The whereabouts of the Black Torrent Guard were an infallible weather-cock that told which way the wind was blowing, where Marlborough—who had founded the regiment—was concerned. If the United Kingdom was at war, the Black Torrent Guards were at the front. If at peace, and Marlborough in favor with the Sovereign, they would be at Whitehall. If Marlborough lay under suspicion of being another Cromwell-in-the-making, then his favored Regiment would be exiled to the Tower, and numbed with the toils of minding Mint and Arsenal.

As they drifted down the river, the buildings gradually became meaner, and the ships more magnificent. Not that the buildings were so very mean at first. Carriageways had always coursed along both banks, but now one could not see them because warehouses, mostly of burnt brick, had been cast up between them and the river, their walls plunging sheer into the water so that boats could bump against them to be loaded or unloaded with the help of cranes that projected out above the water like the feelers of microscopic animalcules. The only relief in these warehouse-walls was at small flat wharves specializing in this or that type of cargo, and connected to the world by rays of pounded dirt. On the left or Wapping bank, those streets led into a city that had, dumbfoundingly, been summoned into being during Daniel's absence. On the right or Southwark bank, the buildings soon dwindled to a mere screen along the water-front, with open country beyond. But Daniel was only allowed to see into it when the boat swam into transitory alignment with a south-going road. Such roads were lined with new buildings for a quarter-mile or so inland, making them look like sword-cuts hacked into the city. And the country beyond was not your English farm-steads (though there were pastures and dairies) but your quasi-industrial landscape of tenter-grounds and tanner yards, the inherently land-hungry manufactures of large flat goods.

Coming round the elbow before Wapping put them in view of a mile of river, running straight up to the great horseshoe-bend between Limehouse and Rotherhithe, Daniel was surprised, and yet not, to see that the new city on the left bank extended almost that entire distance, so that the formerly free-standing towns of Shadwell and Limehouse were all but swallowed by London now. The very idea made his skin crawl just a bit, for the downriver slum-towns had always been the breeding-grounds of mudlarks, river-pirates, rabid dogs, wharf-rats, highwaymen, and Vagabonds, and the intervening belt of countryside—pocked though it might have been with clay-pits, brick-yards, and gin-houses—had been a sort of *cordon sanitaire* between them and London. He wondered if London might get more than it bargained for, by replacing that barrier with through streets.

The Southwark side was much more open, and parts of it were unobstructed, so that Daniel, and grazing dairy-cows, could inspect each other across a few yards of water, mud, and turf. But just as the sloops and schooners were giving way to proper three-masted ships as they progressed down this stretch of the Pool, so the small wharves and warehouses of city merchants were being supplanted by vast flat yards that owned long swaths of the bank, big as battle-fields, and almost as noisy: the ship-yards. Some bloke at the Kit-Cat Clubb had tried to convince Daniel that there were now no fewer than two dozen ship-yards active along the edges of the Pool, and almost as many dry-docks. Daniel had only pretended to credit this, out of politeness. Now he believed. For what seemed like miles, the banks of the Thames were lined with enterprises that ate trees by the thousands and shit boats by the score. They spat out enough saw-dust and wood-shavings to safely pack St. Paul's in a shipping-crate, supposing a crate that large could be built. Which it probably could, here. Certain things Daniel had been noticing suddenly became connected in his mind. The rafts of hardwood logs floating down the Charles, day after day, in Boston, and the fact that coal, its smoke, and its soot were everywhere in London now, both spoke of a desperate hunger for wood. The forests of Old and New England alike were being turned into fleets, and only a fool would burn the stuff.

At the last minute the waterman showed uncertainty as to which ship-yard was Mr. Orney's—there being so many to choose from, here—but Daniel knew. It was the one with three men-of-war, all being built to the same plan, resting side-by-side on the ways. The workers sitting on the ribs of those ships, eating their midday meals, were English- and Irishmen, wearing wool caps if they bothered to protect their heads from the raw breeze at all. But as they rowed closer Daniel saw two men in giant fur hats, inspecting the work.

The waterman made them drift beneath the jutting sterncastles of the three hulls. The one in the middle was nearly complete, except for the all-important carving, painting, and gilding of gaudy decorations. The other two were still receiving their hull planks.

They came in view of a pier that thrust out into the river at the downstream end of the yard, well clear of the ships. A man in plain black clothing was sitting on a keg near the end, nibbling on a pasty and reading a Bible. When he saw them coming, he put both down carefully, stood up, and held out his hands to catch the painter thrown his way by the waterman. His hands blurred and conjured up a perfect knot, making them fast to a heavy iron bitt on the pier. The knot, and the style in which it had been performed, demonstrated to all who witnessed them that this fellow was one of God's elect. His clothing was severe, and it was none of your fine Sunday stuff, but heavy woolen work-clothes, flecked all over with stray fibers and saw-dust. From the man's callused hands, and his way with cordage, Daniel took him for a rigger.

On the shore above them, wheel-ruts and plank-roads formed a miniature London of avenues and squares, except that the place of buildings was taken by stacks and heaps of logs, timbers, rope-coils, oakum-bales, and pitch-kegs. Running along one side of this supply-dump, and defining the eastern boundary of Orney's yard, was a public right-of-way that traversed the flats for a short distance and then bounded up a stairway to Lavender Lane, which was the bankside street in this part of Rotherhithe.

"God save you, brother," Daniel said to the rigger.

"And thee—sir," returned the rigger, giving him the once-over.

"I am Dr. Waterhouse of the Royal Society," Daniel confessed, "a high and mighty title for a sinner, which brings me never so much respect and honor among those who have been seduced by the pleasures and illusions of Vanity Fair." He threw a glance over his shoulder at London. "You may so address me, if you wish; but to be called 'Brother Daniel' would be a higher honor."

"Then Brother Daniel it is, if thou wouldst return the favor, by knowing me as Brother Norman."

"Brother Norman, I perceive that thou dost set a continual example of Industry to the men around you who are tempted by the false promises of Slothfulness. All of this I understand—"

"Oh, there are hard workers among us, Brother Daniel, otherwise how could we perform such works as these?"

"Thy point is well taken, Brother Norman, and yet my confusion only worsens; for I have never seen a ship-yard so prodigious, with workers so few; where is everyone?"

"Why, Brother Daniel, I am grieved to inform thee that they are in Hell. Or as close a thing to Hell as there is on this earth."

Daniel's first guesses at this riddle were *prison* or *a battlefield* but these did not seem likely. He had almost settled on *whorehouse* when he heard the sound of men erupting into cheers on the far side of Lavender Lane.

"A theatre? No! Bear-baiting," he guessed.

Brother Norman closed his eyes prayerfully, and nodded.

This outburst of cheering was the signal for several of the men who had been eating to rise up and quit the ship-yard. They ascended the stairs in a bunch, followed at a cautious distance by the two Russians Daniel had noticed earlier. Other than Brother Norman, perhaps half a dozen workers now remained in the entire yard.

"I say," Daniel exclaimed, "is it Mr. Orney's custom to suspend all work, in the middle of the day, so that his workers can run off to attend a bloody and disgraceful spectacle? It is a miracle anything gets done in this place."

"I am Mr. Orney," Brother Norman said pleasantly.

Forty years ago, Daniel might now have flung himself into the river from sheer mortification. In light of recent months' events, he knew he would survive this, like it or not. The best he could do was to soldier on. He was more concerned about the waterman who'd brought him here. That man had been listening shrewdly to the exchange, and now looked as if he might topple backward off the pier.

"I do beg your pardon, Brother Norman," said Daniel.

"Oh, not at all, Brother Daniel, for how are we to come closer to God, if our ears be not open to the criticism of godly brethren?"

"Very true, Brother Norman."

"Thou mightst never wot, O Son of Drake, what a ridiculous figure thou makest, in thy foppish periwig and whorish clothing, unless I were to lovingly put thee in mind of it."

Another cheer from beyond Lavender Lane reminded Daniel that, as usual, the unrepentant sinners were having more fun.

"I have acquainted the workers with my views on such entertainments," Brother Norman continued. "Several of our Brethren are there now, handing out tracts. Only God can save them."

"I thought you were a rigger," Daniel said idiotically.

"To be an examplar, in a ship-yard, is to show excellence in all of its tributary trades."

"I see."

"The baiting-ring is yonder. Tuppence a head. Enjoy!"

"Oh, no, Brother Norman, I have not come for that."

"Why *hast* thou come then, Brother Daniel? *Solely* to offer me thy opinions as to how I might better look after my affairs? Wouldst thou care to audit my books? The day is young."

"Splendid of you to offer, but—"

"I am afraid my fingernails are dirty, and might not meet with thine approval, but if thou wouldst come back tomorrow—"

"That is really quite all right, Brother Norman. My father, the *smuggler,* who employed diverse *pirates and Vagabonds,* was frequently observed to have a bit of dirt under his nails after we had been up all night loading contraband."

"Very well, then, how may I be of help to thee, Brother Daniel?"

"By loading these parcels aboard the first of yonder ships that, if God wills it, does set sail for St. Petersburg."

"This is not a warehouse. I cannot accept responsibility for aught that happens to them while they are stored in my yard."

"Agreed. The thief who makes off with them is in for bitter disappointment."

"You must secure the permission of Mr. Kikin."

"And he is—"

"The short one. Approach Mr. Kikin from directly in front, with thine hands in plain view, or the tall one shall kill thee."

"Thank you for that advice, Brother Norman."

"Not at all. Mr. Kikin is quite certain that London is alive with Raskolniks."

"What's a Raskolnik?"

"From the nature of Mr. Kikin's precautions, I infer that it is a sort of Russian Huguenot, bearded, ten feet tall, and good at throwing things."

"Well, I don't think I quite match that description—"

"One can never be too careful. Thou couldst be a Raskolnik disguised as a superannuated *dandy.*"

"Brother Norman, 'tis such a pleasure to be free of the stuffy courtesies of London."

"The pleasure is entirely mine, Brother Daniel."

"Tell me, please, have you heard any news of an East Indiaman called *Minerva?*"

"The ship *Minerva* of Rumor and Legend? Or the real one?"

"I have heard no rumors, know no legends . . . I assure you my interest is practical."

"I saw a *Minerva* in dry-dock, round the bend, a fortnight ago, and so I can promise thee she was not the one of legend."

"How does that follow, Brother Norman? I am wanting some knowledge, concerning *Minerva*, that would transform your *riddle* into a *story.*"

"Forgive me, Brother Daniel, I assumed you were as knowledgeable about maritime legends, as you are in *ship-yard management.* Some of the French sailors impose on the credulous, by insisting that there was once a ship, of that name, whose hull, below the waterline, was clad in gold."

"Gold!?"

"Which could only be seen when she was heeled over, as when a stiff breeze was coming in abeam."

"What a preposterous notion!"

"Not entirely, Brother Daniel. For the enemy of speed is the barnacle, which makes the hull rub the water. The notion of covering a hull with smooth metal is excellent. That is why I, and half the other shipwrights along the Pool, went to the trouble of having a look at this *Minerva* when she was in dry-dock."

"But you did not see gold."

"Copper is what I saw, Brother Daniel. Which might have been shiny and red when it was new. And if the light were to glance off it in just the right way, why, a Frenchman—a Papist, susceptible to gaudy and false visions—might phant'sy it were gold."

"So that's how the legend got started, you suppose."

"I am certain of it. Oh, but the ship is quite real, Brother Daniel, I spied her riding at anchor a day or two ago, not half a mile out—I believe that is her, there, in front of Lime-Kiln Dock." Brother Norman helpfully extended a hand across and downriver, indicating a short stretch that contained a hundred vessels, of which a third were full-sized, ocean-going three-masters. Daniel did not even bother to look. "She is a rakish teak-built sort of Dutch East Indiaman of the later Jan Vroom school, marvelous well-armed, generous tumble-home, a temptation and a terror to pirates."

"I lived aboard her for two months and yet would never be able to pick her out from that crowd, at this range. Brother Norman, when do you expect that these ships shall set sail for St. Petersburg?"

"July, if God wills it and the cannons are delivered on time."

"Sir," Daniel said to his waterman, "I am going to go have a word with Mr. Kikin. While I do, I should be obliged if you would deliver a message to Captain van Hoek of *Minerva*."

Daniel got out a pencil and a scrap of paper and wrote out the following on a barrel-head:

> *Captain van Hoek,*
>   If your intention is to make a return voyage to Boston, then mine is to hire you to collect certain goods there, and bring them back to me here in London, preferably no later than July. I may be reached at the Royal Society, Crane Court, Fleet Street, London.
>
> —*Daniel Waterhouse*

Mr. White's Baiting-Ring
HALF AN HOUR LATER

ABOUT THREE-QUARTERS OF THE RING was subtended by standing-room, the remainder by a stand of benches. Daniel shrugged off the pamphleteers and missionaries trying to block the entrance and paid a whole shilling to get a sack of straw to cushion his bony old arse, and admission to the bleachers. He chose a place at the end of a bench so he'd have some hope of jumping clear if the structure collapsed—clearly it had not been engineered by Wren. From there he was able to look directly across the ring into the faces of the two Russians, who had elbowed their way to the front. This was no mean feat, considering that the other groundlings were Southwark ship-yard workers. However, the tall one really was enormous, and he was armed. Mr. Kikin simply stood in front of him; his head came up to the other's breastbone. Behind them, fellow spectators were reduced to taking turns sitting on each other's shoulders.

Behind the stands a four-horse carriage was drawn up, defended from the Rotherhithe crowd by its staff of white-wigged footmen and coachmen. Daniel found it a bit odd that someone rich enough to own and populate such a rig would come so far to see a bear-baiting. The theatres and baiting-rings of *Southwark* were in easy striking distance of London; *that* was a simple matter of ten minutes on a boat. But to get *here* was a long trip in a coach, through a nasty sprawl of tanneries.

On the other hand, if these people were squeamish, they would never have formed the intention of coming hither. Daniel did not recognize the arms on the door of their carriage—he suspected that they were newly minted—and he could divine little by staring at the backs of the wigs worn by the owner and his two lady companions.

Aside from those three, the stands contained half a dozen other well-heeled persons who had evidently come out by water. These had all come alone. Daniel had to admit that he blended in.

The entertainment hewed strictly to the ancient Classical forms, which was to say it consisted of five minutes of actual excitement preceded by nearly an hour of showmanship. A series of pompous introductions, enlivened by cock-fights, led to some big dogs being trotted out on chains and paraded round the ring, so that wagers could be laid as to which would survive. Members of the audience who were too poor or too prudent to bet amused themselves by surging to the front and trying to make the dogs even angrier than they already were by throwing rocks at them, poking at them with sticks, or bellowing their names. One was King Looie, one was King Philip, another Marshall Villars, and yet another, King James the Third.

A fellow came in late and chose a seat at the end of a bench three rows below Daniel. It was another Nonconformist, dressed all in black, with a broad-brimmed hat. He was carrying a basket, which he set down on the bench in front of him, between his feet.

The gentleman who'd come out in the coach stood up, resting a scarred hand on the pommel of his small-sword, and stared at the newcomer. Daniel found the gentleman's profile annoyingly familiar but could not quite place him. Whoever he was, he was clearly of a mind to go and eject this Nonconformist, who was as out of place *here,* as he would have been at the Vatican. The only thing that held him back—literally—was his companions. The ladies seated to either side of him exchanged a meaningful glance behind the skirts of his coat, then reached up in perfect unison, as if they were mirror images of each other, to lay gloved hands on the gentleman's forearms. The gentleman did not take kindly to this at all, and shook his arms free with such violence that Daniel flinched, afraid that the fellow was going to elbow the ladies in the faces.

This imbroglio-in-the-making was interrupted by an announcement that "The Duke of Marlborough" was in the house. Everyone save the gentleman, Daniel, and the Nonconformist cheered. A score of groundlings were shooed out of the path of a gaudy-painted cart, a booth on wheels, which was being backed into the ring with a ponderous slowness meant to build excitement and enhance wagering.

The gentleman, preparatory to sitting down, put his hands on his arse to smooth the skirts of his coat. He glanced back behind the stands and looked moderately surprised. Daniel followed his gaze and noticed that the coach-and-four was no longer there. For this, the most plausible explanation was that the coachman had decided to move to some place quieter and not so crowded with Bankside rabble; it was certainly the case that many horses would be spooked by the entertainment that was about to begin.

Daniel turned back to look at the gentleman, who patted his belly, blindly groping up the length of a fat golden watch-chain that traversed his brocade vest, and pulled a time-piece out of a wee pocket. The watch-chain had several shriveled brown charms dangling from it—rabbits' feet? The gent flipped open the lid of the watch, checked the time, and finally sat down.

They had missed nothing: only a mock-pompous ceremony of dragging a length of chain out from under the door of the wheeled booth, and fixing it to a massive stake driven into the ground. Now, finally, the door could be opened to reveal the Duke of Marlborough. And here was where Mr. Kikin and his companion suffered a great let-down. For the Duke might be large, by the standards of European black bears, but he was a runt compared to the brown Siberian monsters that chased people around Muscovy. Worse yet, when the Duke's muzzle was pulled off by an intrepid trainer, and he opened his mouth to roar, it was obvious that his fangs had been filed down to harmless nubs.

"The Duke's most fearsome foes: Harley and Bolingbroke!" shouted the master of ceremonies.

A pause for effect. Then the door of an enormous kennel was winched up, like the portcullis of a donjon. Nothing happened. A squib exploded inside the kennel. That did the trick: out came Harley and Bolingbroke, a matched set of poodles with white periwigs strapped to their heads. They rushed out half-blind and deaf, and went separate ways; Harley headed for the edge of the ring, Bolingbroke for the center, where the bear knocked him down with one blow of his paw, then rolled him over on his back and brought the other paw down with a sort of scooping motion.

A big spongy piece of poodle viscera was silhouetted against the white sky. It was throwing off a helix of blood-spray as it spun end-for-end. It seemed to be hanging motionless in the air, which gave Daniel the idea it was headed straight for him; but then it plunged and struck, with palpable momentum, into the bodice of the powder-blue silk gown currently being worn by one of the gentleman's two lady companions. From there it tumbled into her lap and lodged in her skirt, between her thighs. Daniel pegged it as a lung. She had the good sense to stand up *first*, and scream *second*.

This performance, from the detonation of the squib to the almost as explosive ovation given by the groundlings in acclaim for the lady's role, covered an elapsed time of perhaps five seconds.

The one lady now had to be taken aside and comforted by the other. As their coach had gone missing, this had to be done there in the stands, in full view of all present. It made a sort of side-show to the long-awaited main event: the big dogs were unleashed into the ring. First King Looie and King Philip. They made straight for the bear, until the bear noticed them and stood up on its hind legs; then they had second thoughts, and decided to see what might be achieved with a hell of a lot of barking. Marshall Villars and King James the Third were then let go, and pretty soon it had begun to look like a fight.

The crowd of groundlings were now in a frenzy equal to that of the animals. So much so that they did not notice, for several seconds, when the dogs and the bear stopped fighting, and began to ignore each other. Their muzzles were down in the dirt.

The dogs' tails were wagging.

The crowd stopped shouting, almost in unison.

Bits of red stuff were hurtling into the ring from somewhere near Daniel, and plumping into the ground like damp rags.

All eyes noticed this and back-traced the trajectories to the Nonconformist. He had stood up and set his basket on the bench next to him. Daniel noticed now that the basket was blood-soaked. The man was pulling great hunks of raw meat from it and hurling them into the ring.

"You men, like these poor beasts, do fight for the amusement, and toil for the enrichment, of men such as this wretch—Mr. Charles White—only because, like these beasts, you are hungry! Hungry for succour, of the physic, and of the spirit! But prosperity temporal and spiritual is yours to be had! It falls from heaven like manna! If you would only accept it!"

To this point the meat-flinger's performance had been entertaining, after a fashion, and they'd particularly liked it when he'd called a gentleman a Wretch to his face. But in the last few moments it had taken on the aspect of a *sermon*, which the groundlings did not care for at all. They all began to murmur at once, like Parliament. Daniel for the first time questioned whether he would get out of Rother-hithe today in one piece.

Mr. Charles White—perhaps asking himself the same question—was sauntering diagonally across the stands, casting meaningful looks at several of the blokes who were running the place. From this, and from what the meat-flinger had said, Daniel collected that White was the owner, or at least the backer.

"Splendid proposal, old boy! I do believe I'll take a bit of *this*, thank you very *mumph*." White's final word was muffled by the Non-conformist's left ear.

Now, the removal of said ear was a close re-enactment of a similar undertaking Daniel had witnessed twenty-odd years earlier, in a coffee-house. The hand that gripped the victim's head, twisting him this way and that to worry the ear off, still bore an ugly stigma from Roger Comstock's dagger. Daniel had no desire to see such a thing again. But the groundlings were fascinated. This was in other words a shrewd bit of crowd control on White's part, in that it gave his audi-ence some value for their money; the only value they were likely to get, today.

He got the ear off a lot quicker this time—practice having made perfect—and held it up. The crowd applauded; and as they did, White swiveled the ear back and forth, making it "listen" to whichever side was applauding the loudest. Once they understood this witticism, they went for it with gusto, the left and right flanks try-ing to out-do each other in noise-making. White meanwhile took this opportunity to dab blood off of his lips with a lace hanky.

"This ear is rather dry and gamy," he shouted, when the crowd had grown tired of the jest. "I am afraid it has been *tanned* by listen-ing to too many hellfire-sermons! It does not merit pride of place 'pon my watch-chain. 'Twill serve for dog-meat though."

White vaulted over the barrier into the ring: a display of physical vigor striking to all. He fed the ear to the surviving poodle, Harley.

This spectacle—a dog eating a piece of a human being—seemed to give the crowd whatever satisfaction they had come for. Though none was pleased by the outcome, none complained. They began to mutter and joke amongst themselves. A few departed straightaway, to beat the crowds. Most milled out in a great herd, occasionally turn-ing their heads back to watch the poodle, its periwig askew, its black lips peeled back from its fangs, grinding up the ear in its back teeth.

It occurred to Daniel to look for the one-eared, meat-hurling Puri-tan, who, when last seen, had been exiting stage right, making a dread-ful noise: half sobbing with pain, half singing a hymn. His basket had been upset during the struggle with Mr. Charles White. Several bits of offal had tumbled out of it, and now lay on the bench in steaming lagoons of dark blood. Daniel recognized an enormous thyroid gland and decided that this had all been removed from a horse, or something equally large, that had been alive a quarter of an hour ago.

The meat-thrower had staggered down out of the stands and into the open space behind, where he was being assisted by a dozen or more of his brethren, who were all showing off forced smiles. Mr. White's carriage still had not returned; in its place was a conveyance far ruder, and much better suited to this district: a knacker's wagon, dark and crusty with old gore and bright and runny with new. Daniel from his elevated vantage point was able to see things in the back of that wagon that were hidden from the view of Mr. White, who remained down by the ring's edge: a newly cut-up horse was in there. Not a worn-out nag but a glossy and well-looked-after steed.

It was one of Mr. White's carriage-horses.

Mr. White's footmen and driver were standing very close together a quarter of a mile away, next to a motionless carriage, to which only three horses were harnessed.

Daniel took another look at the Nonconformists and noticed that every single one of them had at least one pistol in his belt.

'Twas an excellent time to be leaving. Daniel descended the benches, trying not to look like a man in a panic, and did not slow or look back until he had put the whole baiting-ring between himself and the scene that had happened, or was about to, behind the stands.

"Mr. Kikin," he said, having approached from in front, with his hands in plain sight, and offered a formal bow. "I come to you on an errand from Baron von Leibniz, counselor to his Imperial Majesty, Tsar Peter."

This was an abrupt beginning; but Charles White, on the far side of the ring, was only just now piecing together the picture of how he had been used today by those Dissidents, and was working himself up into a rage limited only by the fact that he was outnumbered by chaps who looked forward to dying, and were carrying loaded pistols. Amid such distractions, the only way Daniel could think of to seize Mr. Kikin's attention was to invoke the name of Peter the Great.

It worked. Kikin showed not the slightest doubt that Daniel was telling the truth. From this, Daniel knew that Leibniz's account of the Tsar was on the mark; he did things his own way, be they never so irregular, and his servants, such as Kikin, did not long endure if they wanted the nimbleness to keep pace with his evolutions. Thus Daniel was able to draw Mr. Kikin and his companion aside, and get them clear of the growingly monstrous spectacle in the stands. Mr. White was bellowing threats and execrations at the Dissidents, who were drowning him out with hymn-singing, while a few unusually stupid spectators were darting in to throw stones at them.

HE HAD BEEN TOLD, by people who knew Russians, to expect cheek-bones. Lev Stefanovich Kikin (as he introduced himself, once they had edged clear of the brawl, and withdrawn to a quiet corner of Or-ney's ship-yard) did have quite a pair. But the slablike elements of Kikin's face, and his overall fleshiness, hid his bone structure well enough that no one who lived north of, say, the River Seine would have picked him out as having come from a far country that was by all accounts very different from the rest of Christendom. Daniel would have felt more at ease if Kikin had had green skin and three eyes, so as to remind anyone who looked at him that he thought about things differently. As it was, Daniel tried to concentrate on the outlandish hat, and Kikin's giant companion, who never left off scanning the horizon for Raskolniks.

For his part, Kikin—who was, after all, a diplomat—listened with an air of amused tolerance that Daniel found a bit grating after a while. But never mind; his mission here was not to befriend Kikin (or Orney, for that matter) but to arrange for the Science Crapp to be off-loaded and warehoused here, that it might be shipped to St. Petersburg later. Before an hour had passed, he had accomplished it, and was on his way back across the river. He asked the waterman to convey him to Tower Wharf.

The waterman rowed hard, not to please Daniel, but out of a self-ish desire to put a large expanse of water, or *anything*, between him and Rotherhithe. They cut diagonally through the Pool, crossing from the south bank to the north whilst working upstream about a mile. This brought them to Wapping. From there another mile's jour-ney took them past the Red Cow, where Daniel and Bob Shaftoe had run Jeffreys to ground, then St. Catherine's, and then the long wharf of the Tower. This was pierced in one place by the arch that led to Traitor's Gate. Daniel had talked his way in there once, but saw no merit in attempting it now. So he had the waterman keep rowing.

Just beyond the Tower's upstream corner, the river seemed to bend around sharply to the right—a trick played on landlubberly eyes by Tower Dock which was a vestige of the outer moat-system. Looming above this stagnant channel was a bewildering complex of land-gates, water-gates, docks, causeways, and drawbridges, all more or less answering to the appellation Lion Tower, and serving as the front door of the entire Tower of London complex. This was where Daniel paid the waterman for the day, and disembarked.

The outer reaches of the complex were open to the public. Daniel got all the way through Byward Gate, and into the beginning of Mint Street, before anyone bothered to ask him what he was doing. He claimed that he was here to pay a call on Sir Isaac Newton. This got him an escort: an Anglo-Irish private soldier of the Queen's Own Black Torrent Guards, who accompanied him a short distance up Mint Street. This was narrow, noisy, and long. For the first several yards it was lined with the dwellings of some of the Mint workers. Past that, it was pinched between a porter's lodge on the right side of the way, and on the left, a building that served as the formal entrance to the Mint, with stairs leading to an office on the storey above.

Daniel's escort ushered him into the building on the left, which Daniel immediately recognized as one of those miserable places where visitors cooled their heels waiting to be admitted.

For all that, it wasn't so bad. He could use a respite. On the off chance that Daniel really was a friend of Sir Isaac's, the porter ventured in from across the street and brought him a cup of tea. Daniel sat for a while, sipping it and watching coal-carts rumble in, and manure-carts out, and feeling the throb of the trip-hammers. Presently he was given the news that Sir Isaac was not on the premises, and the opportunity to leave him a note, which he did.

On his way out, as he passed under Byward Tower, he encountered the private who had escorted him to the office.

"Did you serve in the War, private?" Daniel asked. For this fellow did not look like an utterly raw recruit.

"I marched with Corporal John in '11, sir," came the answer. Corporal John was what the Duke of Marlborough was called by his soldiers.

"Ah, the outflanking of the *ne plus ultra*," Daniel exclaimed. "Thirty miles in a day, wasn't it?"

"Thirty-six miles in sixteen hours, sir."

"Magnificent."

Daniel did *not* inquire about the campaign of '12, which had been a disgrace—the Queen had fired Marlborough on the first day of that year. "I once knew a fellow, a sergeant in this regiment—he did me a favor, and I did him one in turn. Since then, there have been twenty-five years of war. He couldn't possibly still be here—"

"Only one man saw those twenty-five years through, sir," the private returned.

"That is a dreadful figure. What is that man's name?"

"It'd be Sergeant Bob, sir."

"Bob Shaftoe?"

The private rationed himself a grin. "The same, sir."

"Where is he now?"

"On a Mint detail, sir."

"Mint detail?"

"Doing a job that needs doing for the Mint, sir."

"So he is—?" Daniel pointed back up Mint Street.

"No sir, you'll find him on London Bridge, sir. 'Tis a task of an unusual nature, sir."

DANIEL SAW NO SOLDIERS doing anything, usual or unusual, as he walked most of the length of the bridge. Here, at least, was a part of London that had changed very little during his lifetime. The clothing worn by the people, and sold in the shops lining the carriageway, was of course different. But it was late in the afternoon and the sun was shining horizontally downriver, throwing the built-up segments of the bridge into a gloom too profound for his old eyes to penetrate, and so in these stretches he could phant'sy himself a ten-year-old boy again, out running an errand in the Puritan republic of Oliver Cromwell. But these day-dreams were interrupted when he came to the open fire-breaks, where the buildings ceased and the bridge hurried on for a stone's throw as a naked causeway. As he ventured into these gaps, the sun blasted him on the right side of his face, and when he turned his head away from it and looked down the Thames, he saw two thousand ships—which annihilated the dream that he was back in the simple days of old. He scuttled across these open stretches like a rat across an unwelcome stripe of lanthorn-light, and found refuge in the cool dark canyons between the old buildings.

The last and shortest of these open stretches was practically in Southwark, seven-eighths of the way across. On the far end of this gap the carriageway was over-arched by a stone castle, of ancient-looking design, but only about three hundred years old. It was the highest structure on the Bridge, for it served both as watch-tower and as choke-point. It dated to an æra when military operations were of a more straightforward character, so that a bloke on the top of the tower, looking south to discover Frenchmen or Saracens coming up in force, could sound the alarm and slam the doors to the Bridge. It was called the Great Stone Gate.

The last of the old wattle-and-daub houses was supported by one starling, and the Great Stone Gate by the next one to the south, and the fire-break between them, above the carriageway, coincided with the broad stone arch that spanned the interval between the starlings below. The flume of Thames-water that raced through that arch was called Rock Lock, and was the broadest of all London Bridge's twenty locks. Passengers who were willing to brave the rapids of the Bridge were sometimes offered the option of detouring all the way down here to take Rock Lock, which was the least dangerous, being the widest; but to do so was generally scorned, by your inveterate Bridge-shooters, as unmanly.

The Bridge's several fire-breaks exerted a mysterious attraction upon contemplative or insane Londoners. Daniel passed one—he was not sure which—standing with his back to the carriageway, looking upstream. He was wearing a pinkish or flesh-colored coat. He was not enjoying the distant view of west London. Rather, his grizzled, scarred, close-cropped head was bent down to look at the starling beneath. He was gesticulating with an ebony walking-stick, and jabbering: "Have a care, have a care, remember the object of the exercise—there's no point in doing it, is there, if the result is crackpated, and cannot hold milk." The words sounded insane, but he spoke them with the weary patience of a man who has been ordering people around for a long time.

A soldier in a red coat was planted to one side of the carriageway, craning his neck to look almost vertically upwards. Daniel stepped to the side, so that he would not be run over, and followed that soldier's gaze to the top of the Great Stone Gate, where a pair of young men in filthy old shirts were at work.

In company with Ludgate, Temple Bar, Aldgate, &c., this was one of the old gates of the City of London. And in accordance with an ancient and noble tradition, common to most all well-regulated Christian nations, the remains of executed criminals were put on display at such gates, as a way of saying, to illiterate visitors, that they were now entering into a city that had laws, which were enforced with gusto. To expedite which, the top of the tower above Great Stone Gate had been fitted with numerous long iron pikes that sprayed out from its battlements like black radiance from a fallen angel's crown. At any given time, one or two dozen heads could be seen spitted on the ends of these, in varying stages of decomposition. When a fresh one was brought in from Tower Hill, or from one of the City's hanging-grounds, the wardens of the gate would make room for it by chucking one of the older heads into the river. Though here as in every other aspect of English life, a strict rule of precedence applied. Certain heads, as of lordly traitors who'd been put to death at the Tower, were allowed to remain long past their Dates of Expiration. Pickpockets and chicken-stealers, by contrast, were swapped through so rapidly that the ravens scarcely had time to peel a good snack off of them.

Some such operation was seemingly underway now, for Daniel could hear some authoritative chap atop the tower, chiding those men in the ragged shirts: "Don't—even—think—of touching *that* one, it is Baron Harland of Harland—peculation, 1707, hanging by a thread as you can see . . . yes, you may inspect that one."

"Thank you, sir." One of the wretches gripped an iron pikestaff and lifted it carefully out of its socket, then brought it round so that the head mounted to its end was face to face with the other wretch— who proceeded to feel the skull all over, like a phrenologist.

"I phant'sy this'n's sound, sir. It don't give when I mash it."

"Bring it down," shouted the red-coated soldier on the carriage-way.

A few moments later the wretch emerged from an internal stair-way, which he had descended with conspicuous gallantry and athleti-cism. He passed the head under the gaze of the soldier, who responded with a perfunctory nod, and then tucked it back under his arm and sauntered over to the western edge of the carriageway, within arm's length of the grizzled man in the pink coat. Taking it up in both hands, he hollered, "Oy! Heads up, mate!" and gave it a good toss. Daniel could not see its trajectory, but could read it in the pos-tures of the head-thrower and the pink-coat, both of whom were tracking it carefully: quiet anticipation as the head traced a parabola downwards, then shock and dismay as someone down below bobbled it, ending with explosive relaxation as it was caught. The man who'd thrown it wheeled about smartly, like a soldier in a drill. His face looked very much as if he had dodged a cannonball. He marched back to the Great Stone Gate.

Daniel strolled over to take his place. Looking over the bridge's parapet he could now see down to the flat top of the starling below: a puddle of rubble circumscribed by a line of pilings, just an arm's length above the level of the river. Down there were two more red-coats, supervising the labors, but standing well clear, of another pair of unfortunates, who were surrounded by partially decomposed and dismantled heads. These two chaps were working shirtless in the cold, probably because their backs were covered with whip-marks that were still bleeding. But they, too, were vigorous young men. Daniel reckoned they were private soldiers guilty of some infraction, being made to undertake this work as part of their punishment. The work consisted of catching the heads thrown down to them, and cut-ting off the tops of the skulls with handsaws.

As Daniel was taking in this scene, one of them finished a cut, and the top of a skull fell to the ground. He picked it up, gave it a quick inspection, and then underhanded it straight up in the air. The man next to Daniel snatched it at the peak of its flight, and gave it a care-ful look. To Daniel the Natural Philosopher, the specimen appeared in excellent condition: the sutures well knitted, the bone thick and sturdy.

"If you are talking to me, Daniel Waterhouse, I cannot hear you," said the man. "Unlike other men whose ears have gone bad, I have schooled myself not to shout, nor to ramble on and on. But *you* may have to do both."

Daniel perceived now that Bob Shaftoe's coat was an army uniform that had once been red, but lost much of its color from washing. From this, and from the careful mending of it, he deduced that Bob had a wife.

"Abigail is well, thank you," Bob announced. "Forgive my presumption, but men with bad ears must learn to read minds, as well as lips; and if you were not about to ask about her, why, the fault is yours."

Daniel smiled, and nodded. "What the hell are you doing?" he shouted, and pointed to the skull.

Bob sighed. "The Mint men have been melting down a lot of silver, which was taken from a treasure-galleon on the Spanish Main. When it melts, certain fumes rise out of it—surely you know more on this than I—and the men who breathe in those vapors grow ill. There is only one remedy. Sir Isaac learnt of it from some German coiners he hired during the Great Recoinage. It is to drink milk from a human skull. Several of the Mint-men have lately gone down ill; so the call has been put out for skulls and milch-cows. What are you doing here, guv'nor?"

"In London? I—"

"No, *here*," said Bob, pointing to the pavement between Daniel's feet. "Observing me like a beetle."

"I was at the Tower on other business, and took it into my mind to pay a call on you."

Bob did not seem entirely certain that Daniel was telling the truth. He removed his eyes from Daniel's face and gazed out over the river, towards Whitehall. His thumb had discovered a loose flap of scalp projecting above the rim of the skull-cup, and now he was absent-mindedly peeling the scalp away. The deceased was a red-headed man with close-cropped hair and a freckly bald spot. "I am not available," Bob said.

"Not available, for what?"

"For the Marquis of Ravenscar's bloody secret army," Bob answered. "I serve the Queen, long may she reign, and if the Pretender comes to this island, why, then, we shall have a bit of sorting-out to do, and I shall look to John Churchill for his leadership in the matter. But the Whig Army shall have to get 'long without Bob Shaftoe, thank you very much."

HOOKE, TWISTED AND BENT as he was, had been in the habit of going everywhere on his own two feet, even though his work as City Surveyor, and as a sort of partner to Wren, had made him rich enough to afford a coach and four. Daniel had not understood it fully until today. For a man who wanted to get things done in London, there simply was not time to go in a vehicle, because of the congestion. The sedan chair was a workable compromise, but still a compromise. The only reason not simply to walk was the dirtiness of the streets, and the loss of dignity. After all he'd seen today, Daniel could not, with a straight face, abhor the streets of London for their squalor. As for dignity, he had very little of that to look after, and the sight of the heads and the skulls had set loose in his mind the usual train of ruminations considering mortality, vanity, and all that. Long sour passages from Ecclesiastes were running through his mind as he tromped back up the bridge and up-hill to Eastcheap where he turned left. The sky was crimson in the west. The dome of St. Paul's, directly ahead of him, looked bluish against it. The Watch were emerging and beginning to range up and down the streets, giving Daniel reason to believe that it was not utterly suicidal to walk home alone. He happened to reach St. Paul's as Vespers was beginning, so he went in there to rest his feet for a while.

A new organ was under construction, and Daniel spent more time brooding over it than he did contemplating the meaning of the service. Wren had disparaged it as "a box of whistles." Daniel understood the complaint. For Daniel, too, had once designed a building, and savored the thrill of seeing it built, only to endure the long indignity of watching the owner clutter it up with knick-knacks and furniture. This box of whistles project was only one of several spats that Wren had conducted with Queen Anne in recent years as to how St. Paul's ought to be decorated. And so as Daniel looked about at the interior of the place, he understood that certain of the details that met his eye might not be as Wren would have wanted them. And yet, he had to admit that it wasn't in bad taste at all, at least compared to some other Barock architecture he'd seen. Or perhaps the style was merely growing on him.

Daniel thought that the fantastically complex ornamentation of Barock churches was a replacement for the complicated things made by God, that had used to surround people when they lived out of doors (or that Hooke had seen in drops of water). Entering into a place such as this, they were surrounded by complicated things made by men in emulation of God—but frozen and idealized, in much the same way as the mathematical laws of Natural Philosophy were compared to the reality they tried to describe.

When the service was over, the sun had gone down, and it were dangerous to be out alone. Daniel shared a hackney down Fleet Street to Crane Court.

A note had arrived from Captain van Hoek of *Minerva*. But it had been written out, and probably composed, by Dappa.

> *Dr. Waterhouse,*
>
> We guess that to carry your freight, though less of an honour ought too to be less of a hazard, than to carry your person, and therefore consent. We aspire to leave the Pool in the latter half of April and to return in July. If this will not be too late, kindly inform us as to the approximate tonnage and volume you wish to reserve on our return voyage.
>
> Dappa will venture ashore some day before we embark, to consult with his publisher in Leicester Square, quite near your current lodgings. With your permission he will meet with you on the same day, to write a contract; for his pen is as versatile and inconstant as his tongue.
>
> *van Hoek*

Orney's Ship-yard, Rotherhithe
12 MARCH 1714

DANIEL SUPPOSED THAT THE MATTER of Orney and Kikin and the Science Crapp was finished and settled for good. But one morning, close to a fortnight later, a note was handed to him by Mrs. Arlanc. This document was not merely *dated* but *timed*, for it had been written out in haste half an hour ago.

> *Monsieur Waterhouse,*
>
> A hellish glow on the eastern horizon early this morning gave notice to any Londoner who chanced to look that way of

Trouble in Rotherhithe. You may yet observe a column rising from that district, consisting more of steam than of smoak, as the Fire has been put out; but not before it had consumed one of His Imperial Majesty's ships. I am, naturally, bound thither in haste. This message (for whose rudeness I apologize) comes to you in a hackney-carriage. Kindly inform its driver whether you will join me at Rotherhithe (in which case he shall convey you at my expense) or not (in which case prithee send him away).

Kikin

It was by no means obvious to Daniel why he ought to heed this oblique summons from Mr. Kikin. That there had been a fire at Orney's ship-yard was unfortunate. But Daniel's connection to the matter was tenuous. Kikin, who was an intelligent man, must know this. Yet he had gone to some trouble and expense, and had unlimbered his most diplomatic English, to ask Daniel out to Rotherhithe.

In the end he decided to go there, not because he could see any clear reason why, but because he could see no reason why not, and because it was likely to be more interesting than staying at Crane Court. The endless carriage-ride gave him plenty of time to make up his mind that he had decided wrong. But by then it was too late. He reached Orney's ship-yard around midday. From the point on Lavender Lane where he disembarked from the hackney-carriage, he enjoyed an Olympian prospect over the entire ship-yard.

There was no wind at all today. A silent tide of translucent white smoke had seeped into the maze of stock-piles down on the bank, turning them into blocky islands. These had been little affected by the fire. Daniel's eyes sought out the pallet where had been piled the Natural Philosophy stuff from Crane Court. Other than a few scorch-marks where cinders had showered down upon the tarpaulin, there appeared to be no damage.

Having satisfied himself as to that, he raised his eyes to the parallel ways where the Tsar's three ships had been a-building.

The fire had started in the middle of the three hulls. As far as Daniel could make out, no attempt had been made to save this one. But expanses of sail-cloth had been drenched in the river and flung over the unfinished hulls to either side. The cloth looked very much the worse for wear—no one would ever make sails of it—but for the most part it had steamed, not smoked, in the heat of the flames. From footprints in the bankside mud and other such evidence, Daniel could infer that bucket-brigades had been formed to wet down the sail-cloth and perhaps to attack the central fire. A hue and cry must have gone up; Orney and many of his workers must have rushed to the yard. But not soon enough to save the middle ship. The fire must have worked in the belly of that hull for some time before it had been noticed. The hull-planks on both sides were charred through, and it was obvious that the keel had been damaged. It would be rated a total loss by Mr. Orney's insurer.

This much Daniel could see from a high vantage point at the top of the stairs. Swirling heat-waves still roiled out of the destroyed hull. Through them he could see a weirdly distorted image of men on small boats rowing to and fro, peering at the disaster in something of the same spirit as other men had watched the bear-baiting.

Daniel found a stairway and descended from the lane to the yard. The smoke that lingered in the lanes among the stock-piles smelled like the aftermath of any house-fire, which was to be expected. But mixed with it, Daniel was surprised to nose out a sharp nostril-stinging fragrance that did not belong there: a chymical fume. Daniel had most recently smelled it in Crane Court, the night of his arrival, just after the Infernal Device had gone off. Before that, he had smelled it many other times in his life; but the *first* time had been forty years ago at a Royal Society meeting. The guest of honor: Enoch Root. The topic: a new Element called Phosphorus. Light-bearer. A substance with two remarkable properties: it glowed in the dark, and it liked to burn. He suffered a pang of incipient guilt, thinking that perhaps this was all a terrible mishap, laid to him; perhaps there had been a sample of phosphorus in among the goods from Crane Court, which had somehow caught fire, and caused the conflagration, and Kikin had called him out here only to prosecute him. This was extremely unlikely—a fair sample of the stupid terrors that continued to bedevil him from time to time. He went and inspected his pallet, and found that nothing of the sort had happened.

Daniel found Orney and Kikin in one of the surviving hulls. This was still draped in sopping sail-cloth, presumably in case the fire in the middle hull should flare up again. Orney and Kikin roamed up and down the length of the hull on a strip of temporary decking—a sort of scaffold. Daniel reckoned it had been put there so that the workers could gain access to the upper parts of the ribs, but in present circumstances it made a suitable command and observation post for the proprietor and his customer.

They took in the curious spectacle of Daniel ascending a ladder, then—since he had survived it—greeted him. Orney was smiling in the way that bereaved persons oft did at funerals. Kikin—whatever emotions he might have felt earlier in the day—was sober, avid, acute, interested in everything. "You have come," he said more than once, as if this were a significant finding.

Norman Orney mopped his cindery visage with a corner of wet canvas. Seeing this, a boy stepped in with a bucket of beer and offered Orney a ladle-full. "God bless you, lad," said Orney, accepting it. He quaffed half a pint in a few impressive swallows.

"It started in the wee hours, then?" Daniel hazarded.

"Two of the clock, Brother Daniel."

"It burned for a long while, then, before anyone noticed."

"Oh, no, Brother Daniel. In that, you are quite off the mark. I employ a night-watchman, for these banks are infested with mudlarks."

"Sometimes they fall asleep."

"Thank you for supplying me with that intelligence, Brother Daniel; as ever, you are keen to point out any mismanagement or incompetence. Know then that my watchman has two dogs. Both began to bark shortly after two of the clock. The watchman smelled a pungent fume, and observed smoke from yonder hull. He raised the alarm. I was here a quarter of an hour later. The fire had spread with inconceivable rapidity."

"Do you suspect arson?" Daniel asked. The thought had only just come to him; even as he was giving voice to it he was feeling the first flush of shame at his own stupidness. Orney and Kikin made polite efforts to mask their incredulity. In particular, Kikin would presume arson even if there were evidence to the contrary; for these were, after all, warships, and Russia was at war.

What must Kikin make of Daniel?

"Had you, or your watchmen, seen any strangers about the ship-yard recently?"

"Other than you, Brother Daniel? Only a pair of prowlers who stole in, night before last, on a longboat. The dogs barked, the prowlers departed in haste. But they can have had nothing to do with the fire; for the ship was not on fire *yesterday*."

"But is there any possibility that these prowlers might have secreted a small object in the hull—down in the bilge, say, where it might have gone unnoticed for twenty-four hours?"

Orney and Kikin were gazing at him most intently.

"The ship is—or *was*—large, Brother Daniel, with many places of concealment."

"If you find clock-work in the bilge of the burnt ship, please be so good as to inform me," Daniel said.

"Did you say *clock-work*, Brother Daniel?"

"It may have been damaged beyond recognition by the combustion of the phosphorus."

"Phosphorus!?"

"Your men must inspect the bilges and any other hidden cavities in the surviving hulls every morning."

"It shall be done, Brother Daniel!"

"You have a fire agent in the City?"

"The Hand-in-Hand Fire-Office on Snow-Hill!"

"Pray consider me at your disposal if the Hand-in-Hand Fire-Office tries to blame this on you, Brother Norman."

"You may have hidden virtues, Brother Daniel. Pray overlook my stubborn unwillingness to see them."

"Pray forgive my hiding my light under a bushel, Brother Norman."

"Indeed," said Kikin, "there is much that is hidden in you, Dr. Waterhouse. I would see it uncovered. Would you please explain yourself?"

"The pungent reek that your watchman complained of, and that still lingers over yonder, is that of burning phosphorus, and I last smelled it on the evening of the thirty-first of January in Crane Court," said Daniel. He went on to relate a brief account of what had happened that night.

"Most remarkable," said Kikin, "but this ship was not *exploded*. It was *set afire*."

"But one who knew how to make an Infernal Device, triggered by clock-work, might rig it in more than one way," Daniel said. "I hypothesize that the machine uses phosphorus to create fire at a certain time. In one case, that fire might be conveyed to a powder-keg, which would explode. In another, it might simply ignite a larger quantity of phosphorus, or of some other inflammable substance, such as whale-oil."

"But in any case, you are saying, the machines—and their makers—are the same!" said Orney.

"Then it is a matter for your Constables!" Kikin proclaimed.

"As the evildoers are nowhere to be seen, there is nothing for a Constable to do," Daniel pointed out. "It is ultimately a matter for a Magistrate."

Kikin snorted. "What can such a person do?"

"Nothing," Daniel admitted, "until a defendant is presented before him."

"And who should do that, in your system?"

"A prosecutor."

"Let us find a prosecutor, then!"

"One does not *find* a prosecutor in England, in the way one finds a constable or a cobbler. One *becomes* a prosecutor. *We* who are the victims of these Infernal Machines must be the Prosecutors of those who made them."

Kikin was still in difficulties. "Do you mean to say that each of us pursues a separate Prosecution, or—"

"We *might*," Daniel said, "but I suppose it would be more *efficient*"— this word chosen to delight the ears of Mr. Orney, who indeed looked keen on it—"for you and you, and I, and the Hand-in-Hand Fire-Office if they are so inclined, and Mr. Threader and Mr. Arlanc, to pursue it jointly."

"Who are Threader and Arlanc?" Kikin asked. For Daniel had left them out of his Crane Court narration.

"Why," said Daniel, "you might say that they are the other members of our Clubb."

A Subterranean Vault in Clerkenwell
EARLY APRIL 1714

"THE RIVER FLEET is a parable—I would venture to say, a very *mockery*—of humane degradation!" announced Mr. Orney, by way of a greeting, as he stomped down stairs into the crypt.

Here, if he had evinced dismay, turned on his heel, and run back up the steps, no man would have thought less of him.

Mr. Threader—who'd arrived a quarter of an hour previously— had been quite aghast. "It is consecrated ground, sir," Daniel had told Mr. Threader, "not some pagan Barrow. These souls are Members in Good Standing of the Community of the Dead." And he had shoved his hand into a tangle of pallid roots and ripped them out of the way to reveal an ancient brass plate, bejeweled with condensed moisture, and gouged with a dog's breakfast of rude letters, no two the same size, evidently copied out by some medieval artisan who knew not what they signified.

Re-forming them into Latin words and sentences was a job for patient clerks, or clerics. But this was Clerkenwell, where such had been coming to draw water for at least five hundred years. De-cyphered, the letters said that behind this plate lay the earthly remains of one Theobald, a Knight Templar who had gone to Jerusalem whole, and come back in pieces. Next to it was another plate telling a similar tale about a different bloke.

Unlike Mr. Threader, Mr. Orney seemed not in the least put out by the surroundings. Daniel had been at pains to set up candles and lanthorns wherever he could, which generally meant the lids of the half-dozen blocky sarcophagi that claimed most of the floor. By the light of these, it was possible to make out a vaulted roof. This was not a soaring, lost-in-dimness type of vaulted roof. It was barely high enough for a bishop to walk up the middle without getting slime on his mitre. But the stones had been well joined, and the room had survived, a pocket of air in the dirt, oblivious to what might be happening above.

Mr. Orney paused for a moment at the foot of the stairs to let his eyes adjust, which was very prudent, then advanced on Daniel and Mr. Threader, dodging round nearly invisible puddles with sailorly grace as he made his way between the sarcophagi. He was showing a lack of curiosity, and a refusal to be awed, that in another man would have been infallible proof of stupidity. Since Daniel knew him not to be stupid, he reckoned that it was a sort of religious assertion; to a Quaker, these Papist crusader-knights were as primitive, and as beside the point, as a clan of Pictish barrow-diggers.

"Why, Brother Norman? Because the Fleet, like life, is brief and stinky?" inquired Daniel politely.

"The stench at its *end* is only remarkable because the Fleet runs so pure and fresh at the *beginning;* issuing as it does from diverse wells, holes, rills, and spaws hereabouts. Thus does a babe, fresh from the womb, soon fall prey to all manner of gross worldly—"

"We get the point," Mr. Threader said.

"And yet the interval between the two is so brief," Mr. Orney continued, "that a *robust* man" (meaning himself) "may walk it in half an hour." He pretended to check his watch, as proof that this was no exaggeration. But it was too gloomy in here to make out the dial.

"Do not let our host see your time-piece, sir, he'll have it apart before you can say, 'avast, that is expensive!'" said Mr. Threader, sounding as if he knew whereof he spoke.

"Never mind," said Daniel, "I recognize it as the work of Mr. Kirby, probably undertaken when he was journeyman to Mr. Tompion, nine years ago."

This produced a brief but profound—one might say, sepulchral—silence. "Well discerned, Brother Daniel," Mr. Orney finally said.

"After the mysterious explosion," remarked Mr. Threader, "Dr. Waterhouse secreted himself in an attic no less gloomy than this tomb, and would not return my letters for many weeks. I feared he had no stomach for Prosecution. But when he returned to polite society, behold! He knew more of clocks, and the men who make 'em, than any man alive—"

"*That* is rank flattery, sir," Daniel protested. "But I will grant you this much, that if our Clubb is to achieve its Goal, we must learn all we can of the Infernal Devices in question. They were driven by clock-work, you may be sure on't. Now, thirty years ago, I knew Huygens and Hooke, the most illustrious horologists of the æra. But when I returned to London I found that I was no longer privy to the secrets, nor acquainted with the practitioners, of that Technology. In my eagerness to redress this, I did from time to time forget my manners, prising open clocks and watches to examine their workings and decypher their makers' marks, as Mr. Threader has waspishly reminded me. The result: we are met here in Clerkenwell!"

"Vy the khell are ve meetink *khere*?" demanded a new voice.

"God save you, Mr. Kikin!" answered Mr. Orney, not very informatively.

"If you had arrived on time," said the irritable Mr. Threader, "you'd have had an answer just now from Dr. Waterhouse."

"My carriage is axle-deep in a bog," was the answer of Mr. Kikin.

"That bog is a valuable discovery," said Mr. Orney, who waxed jovial when Mr. Threader was in a bad mood. "Put a fence round it, call it a Spaw, charge a shilling for admission, and you'll soon be able to buy a phaethon."

The Russian was ill-advisedly descending a slimy twelfth-century staircase into his own shadow. A flickering orange trapezoid was projected onto the floor from above, skating back and forth like a leaf coming down from a tree. It could be inferred that Mr. Kikin's associate, who was too tall to enter the crypt, was standing in the antechamber at the top of the stairs waving a torch around, trying to get the light around his master's shoulders.

"This damp will kill us," Mr. Kikin predicted in a stolid way, as if he got killed every morning before breakfast.

"As long as the candles don't go out, we have nothing to fear from this atmosphere," said Daniel, who was deeply sick and tired of hearing semi-learned people ascribe all their problems to damps. "Yes, water seeps in here from the moist earth. But Mr. Orney was only just now remarking upon the marvellous purity of these waters. Why do you think the Knights Templar built their Temple here? It is because the nuns of St. Mary and the Knights Hospitallers both drew their water from the same well here, and didn't die of it. Why, just up the road, wealthy gentle-folk pay money to soak in these same moistures."

"Why not meet *there*?" Mr. Kikin suggested.

"I second the motion!" exclaimed Mr. Threader.

"Because—" Daniel began. But then he heard a snatch of conversation from the top of the stairs. The torch-light trapezoid grew wider and moved sideways. A new shadow appeared in its center. The fifth and last member of the Clubb was making his way down stairs. Daniel gave him a few moments to get within earshot, then continued, loudly: "because we do not wish to draw attention to ourselves! If our Nemesis has employed a clock-maker, or indeed a maker of any sort of fine instrument, why, the knave's workshop is likely within a musket shot of this Temple."

"Some would call it a temple, some a mound of rubble in the middle of a swine-yard," said Mr. Kikin, catching the eye of Mr. Threader and getting a warm look in return.

"Mound is too grand a word, sir. In English we say 'bulge.' "

"Those who did, would thereby show a grievous want of Real Estate Acumen!" Daniel returned, "for of the Three Desiderata: location, location, and location, this ruin has all! The tide of London's expansion is lapping at its foundations!"

"*Are* you the land-lord, Dr. Waterhouse?" inquired Mr. Threader, suddenly interested.

"I am looking after the property on behalf of a High Net Worth Individual," returned Daniel, "who is keen to make this vale into a world-renowned center of Technologickal Arts."

"How did this individual become aware of the ruin's *existence?*"

"I told him, sir," Daniel said, "and to anticipate your next question, I learnt of it from a fellow of my acquaintance, a very, very old chap, who had knowledge from a Knight Templar."

"Then he must indeed be very old, as the Templars were wiped out four hundred years ago," said Mr. Threader, sounding a bit irritated.

"A new building is contemplated?" asked Mr. Orney, as one man of commerce to another.

"Is already underway," Daniel confided, "to include an arcade of shops and ateliers for makers of watches, and of instruments—not only musickal, but *philosophickal.*"

He was getting expectant stares, as if he had broken off in midsentence.

"Planispheres, heliostats, theodolites, and circumferentors, e.g.," he tried. Nothing.

"If Longitude is found, I daresay, 'twill be found on this property!" he concluded.

All of this had been taken in by Henry Arlanc, the last to arrive. He was standing silently, and somewhat apart from the others.

"Right!" said Mr. Threader. "The second meeting of the Clubb for the Taking and Prosecution of the Party or Parties responsible for the Manufacture and Placement of the Infernal Engines lately Exploded at Crane Court, Orney's Ship-yard, &c., is called to order."

TO DANIEL, IN HIS YOUTH, a club had always been a stick for hitting things with.

In 1664, a Mr. Power, discoursing of barometers, had written, "The Difference of the Mercurial Cylinder may arise from the club and combination of all these causes joined together."

This extended meaning of "club" had been taken clearly by Daniel and everyone else at the Royal Society, because many of them had lately been at universities where starvelings pooled pennies to buy food or, more often, drink. The slang for this was "to make a club." Around this time, one often heard Mr. Pepys proposing to John Wilkins and others that they make a club for dinner, meaning exactly the same procedure, save with more money and better results.

During Daniel's absence from London, Pepys's merry improvisations had spread out across Time to become perpetual, while losing their freedom in Space by confining themselves to fixed quarters. The notion had struck Daniel as questionable, until Roger had finally lured him to the Kit-Cat Clubb. On entering that place Daniel had said, "Oh, why didn't you say so!" for he had understood it immediately as a Routine Upgrade of the coffee-houses where everyone had used to pass the time of day twenty years ago—the chief difference being that only certain people were let in. This all but ruled out ear-biting, stab-wounds, and duels.

This Clubb was nothing at all like the Kit-Cat. Its purpose was altogether different, its members (except for Daniel) very unlike Roger's crowd, its meeting-place even darker and more low-ceilinged.

But certain things about Clubbs were universal. "First order of business: the collection of Dues!" Mr. Threader proclaimed. He had a coin pre-positioned in a tiny pocket of his waistcoat, and now flipped it casually onto the stone lid of a twenty-ton coffin. Everyone did a double-take: it was a pound sterling, which was to say a *silver* coin, and very crisp-looking, too. Using it to pay Clubb dues was a bit like nonchalantly riding around Hyde Park on the back of a Unicorn.

Daniel threw in a Piece of Eight. Mr. Kikin paid with Dutch silver money. Mr. Orney tossed out a golden guinea. Henry Arlanc upended a purse and poured out half a pint of copper tokens. Nearly all of these had been given him beforehand by Daniel. The other members of the Clubb probably suspected as much.

Daniel had insisted that the Huguenot porter be admitted, because it was theoretically possible that he was an intended victim of the first Infernal Device. Mr. Threader had proposed that the dues be set high, as a way of keeping rabble such as Arlanc out. Orney had agreed for reasons strictly practical: it was expensive to hunt down and prosecute criminals. Kikin had gone along with any and all expenditures because it might help keep his head attached to his neck if he could show the Tsar he was sparing no expense to catch the men who'd burned his ship. So Daniel had ended up paying high dues, not only for himself but for Arlanc.

Mr. Threader opened a small wooden case lined with red velvet, took out a hand-scale, and began to weigh the Spanish and Dutch money against a calibrated brass weight, which, according to tiny but furious assertions graved on its face, was the Platonic ideal of what a pound sterling ought to weigh, as laid down some 150 years ago by Gresham. Mr. Orney took this as a signal to begin reading the minutes of the previous meeting, which had been held at Mr. Kikin's town-house in Black Boy Alley a fortnight ago.

"With the Membership's indulgence, I shall *elide* all that was to no purpose, and summarize all that was merely pedantic . . ." Orney began.

"Hear, hear!" said Daniel before Mr. Threader could object. He needn't have worried. Mr. Threader had stuck his tongue out, and his eyes were nearly projecting from his head on stalks as he gauged the weight of Daniel's Spanish silver.

"This leaves only two items worth mentioning: the interview with the unfortunate Watchman, and Dr. Waterhouse's discourse on the mechanism. Taking these in order, we interrogated Mr. Pinewood, a Watchman who witnessed the explosion in Crane Court, and was hired, or in some way induced, by verbal representations from Mr. Threader, of a highly ambiguous and still hotly disputed nature . . ."

"Is all of *that* really in the *minutes*!?" said Mr. Threader, glancing up from his scale with a look of mock amazement.

"Believing that he would be compensated, Mr. Pinewood lit out after a sedan chair that had been seen following Mr. Threader and Dr. Waterhouse immediately prior to the explosion," said Mr. Orney, looking satisfied that he had been able to get a rise out of Mr. Threader. "Mr. Pinewood informed us that he followed the chair eastwards on Fleet Street as far as the Fleet Bridge, where the two men bearing it stopped, set it down, turned on Mr. Pinewood, picked him up . . ."

"Avast, we know the story," muttered Mr. Threader.

". . . and flung him bodily into Fleet Ditch."

Everyone swallowed.

"A collection was taken up for Mr. Pinewood's boils, and prayers said for his other symptoms, some of which medical science has not even devised names for yet. Some contributed more, and prayed more reverently, than others.

"The subsequent movements of the sedan chair may only be guessed at. Dr. Waterhouse lost no time *guessing* that it had returned to the side-alley whence he himself had seen it issue only a few minutes earlier. 'I am convinced,' Dr. Waterhouse informed us, 'that they had some foreknowledge of our arrival in London, and were positioned to follow Mr. Threader's carriage through Newgate to the City, and that we foxed them by diverting down the bank of Fleet Ditch to Crane Court.' There followed some discussion as to whether the occupant of the sedan chair had any connection whatever to the Infernal Device; I opined that 'twere imprudent to follow so closely a vehicle known to be moments away from exploding, and that the sedan chair probably contained nothing more than a venturesome Courtesan. Mr. Threader was quick to take offense at any suggestion that a Whore (to use his term) would look on the arrival of his entourage in London as an Opportunity; the faces of the other members of the Clubb recorded amusement at his pious . . ."

"I move we choose a new secretary to take the Minutes," Mr. Threader said. "Monsieur Arlanc, never mind what I've said about him in the past, is quiet, dutiful, and literate; I'll pay his dues if he takes the job."

The end of Mr. Threader's sentence was garbled, because while talking he had reached up and inserted a large gold coin between his own molars.

"Mr. Threader," said Mr. Orney, "if you are feeling peckish, there are Inns up the road at Black Mary's Hole, and taverns down at Hockley-in-the-Hole, to which we might adjourn; but you'll get no satisfaction by eating my guinea."

"It is not *yours* any longer, but the Clubb's," said Mr. Threader, now examining the coin for bite-marks, "and it is not a guinea until I say it is."

"You've already *weighed* it, so what's the use of *biting* it?" asked Mr. Orney, sounding at least as curious as he was peeved.

" 'Tis a proper guinea," Mr. Threader admitted. "Pray continue your whimsical Narration, Mr. Orney."

"In short, I put forth the hypothesis that the sedan chair was a red herring," said Mr. Orney. "This led to a murky disquisition on clockwork, or so it appears in my notes . . ."

"For once your notes are accurate," said Mr. Threader.

"Not in the least!" said Daniel. "All I meant was this. Mr. Orney avers that to place an Infernal Device in a carriage, made to explode at a certain time, *and then to follow the same carriage closely down the street,* only moments in advance of the explosion, were madness. To which I answer, this depends on how knowledgeable, and how confident, one is of the correct running of the clock-work. A competent horologist would set the Device up properly, and moreover would have some idea how fast or slow 'twould run in a rocking and jouncing carriage on a cold day."

"So the person in the sedan chair was no horologist!" said Mr. Kikin.

Mr. Threader chuckled, believing that it was a witticism, but Daniel could see that the Russian had taken Daniel's point, and was wholly serious.

"Indeed, sir. I submit that the Infernal Devices might have been planted by people who had but a very imperfect understanding of how they worked. If that is true, the Device might have been expected to explode hours or even days later than it did—the person in the sedan chair might have been nearly as astonished as were Mr. Threader and I, when it went off in Crane Court."

"No one doubts that it exploded at the wrong moment," said Mr. Threader, "so your hypothesis has at least a patina of credibility."

"It is all neither here nor there," Mr. Orney said flatly, "as Mr. Pinewood ended up thrashing about in shite, and we know nothing more concerning the sedan chair."

"I disagree. It suggests a line of attack, by thinking about clock-work. The device that burned your ship went off at the right time: the dead of night. The one in Mr. Threader's carriage went off too early. I conclude that the device that was used ran too quickly in a moving carriage on a cold day, but ran at the correct rate sitting still in the belly of a ship's hull. From that I can guess as to what sort of clock-work was used, which might help lead us to him who made the Infernal Devices."

"Hence . . . Clerkenwell," Mr. Kikin said.

"What *results* can you report to us, from this line of inquiry?" demanded Mr. Orney.

"That is like asking a farmer in April what he has harvested from the seeds he planted a week ago," Daniel protested. "I had hoped to find some of Mr. Robert Hooke's notes and test-pieces at Crane Court. He was one of the first to have a go at finding the Longitude with clocks, and knew better than anyone how their rate was influenced by rocking and by changes in temperature. Alas, Hooke's residue was all rubbished. I have made inquiries with the Royal College of Physicians, and with my lord Ravenscar."

"Why *them,* pray tell?" Mr. Threader asked.

"Hooke built the Physicians in Warwick Lane, as well as certain additions to my lord Ravenscar's house. It is possible that he stored some of his things in those places. My queries have gone unanswered. I shall redouble my efforts."

"Since we appear to have moved on to New Business," said Mr. Threader, "pray tell us, Mr. Orney, of all that you have learnt on the piss-boiling front."

"Dr. Waterhouse assures us that piss-boiling on a very large scale is needed to make *phosphorus* for these Infernal Devices," Mr. Orney reminded them.

"His account left little to the imagination," Mr. Threader said.

"To do it in London would be difficult—"

"Why? London could not smell any more like piss than it does to begin with," Mr. Kikin observed shrewdly.

"It would draw attention, not because it smelt bad, but because it was a queer practice. So the piss-boiling probably happens in the countryside. But this would require transportation of piss, in large amounts, from a place where there was a lot to be had—viz. a city, e.g., London—to said countryside; a thing not to be accomplished in perfect secrecy."

"You should make inquiries among the Vault men!"

"An excellent idea, Mr. Kikin, and one I had a long time ago," Mr. Orney said. "But my habitation is remote from the banks of the lower Fleet where the Vault men cluster, thick as flies, every night to discharge their loads. As Monsieur Arlanc dwells at Crane Court, five minutes' walk from the said Ditch, I charged him with it. Monsieur Arlanc?"

"I have been very, very busy . . ." began Henry Arlanc, and was then drowned out by indignant vocalizations from the rest of the Clubb. The Huguenot made a brave show of Gallic dignity until this Parliamentary baying had died down. "But the Justice of the Peace for Southwark has succeeded where I failed. *Voilà!*"

Arlanc whipped out a pamphlet, and tossed it onto a slate coffin-lid; it skidded to a stop in the pool of light cast by a candle. The cover was printed in great rude lurid type, big enough for Daniel to read without fishing out his spectacles: "THE PROCEEDINGS of the *Assizes of the Peace,* Oyer and Terminer and General Gaol-Delivery for the *COUNTY OF SURREY.*"

Below that the letters got small; but Mr. Kikin bent over and read the subtitle aloud: "Being a FULL and TRUE accompt of ye most surprizing, execrable and Horrid CRIMES committed by the Enemies, and just, swift and severe PUNISHMENTS meted out by the Defenders, of the Peace of that County from Friday January 1, to Saturday February 27, *Anno Domini* 1713/14. . . ."

Mr. Kikin shared an amused look over the candle with Henry Arlanc. It was possible to buy these pamphlets everywhere, which implied that some people—a *lot* of people, actually—were buying them. But no man who was literate enough to read them would admit to it. This sort of literature was supposed to be ignored. For Mr. Arlanc to notice it was uncouth, and for Mr. Kikin to derive amusement from it was rude. *Foreigners and their ways!*

"Forgive me, Monsieur Arlanc, but I have not had the . . . er . . . pleasure of reading that *document*," said Mr. Threader. "What does it say?"

"It relates the case of a Mr. Marsh, who was driving his wagon down Lambeth Road one night in December, when he met three young gentlemen who had just emerged from a house of ill repute in St. George's Fields. As they passed each other in the lane, these three young men became so incensed by the odour emanating from Mr. Marsh's wagon that they drew out their swords and plunged them into the body of Mr. Marsh's horse, which died instantly, collapsing in its traces. Mr. Marsh set up a hue and cry, which drew the attention of the occupants of a nearby tavern, who rushed out and seized the perpetrators."

"Courageous, that, for a Mobb of Drunks."

"The roads down there are *infested* with highwaymen," Mr. Threader said keenly. "They probably reckoned 'twas safer to go out and face them as a company, be it ne'er so ragged, than be picked off one by one as they straggled home."

"Imagine their surprise when they found they'd apprehended not highwaymen, but gentlemen!" Mr. Kikin remarked, very amused.

"They had apprehended *both*," said Henry Arlanc.

"What!?"

"Many highwaymen *are* gentlemen," said Mr. Threader learnedly. "As 'tis beneath the dignity of a Person of Quality to work for a living, why, when he's gambled and whored away all his money, he must resort to a life of armed robbery. To do otherwise were dishonorable."

"How come you to know so much of it? I daresay you are a regular subscriber of these pamphlets, sir!" said the delighted Mr. Orney.

"I am on the road several months out of the year, sir, and know more of highwaymen than do you of the very latest advances in *Caulking*."

"What came of it, Monsieur Arlanc?" Daniel inquired.

"On the persons of these three, valuables were found that had been stolen, earlier in the evening, from a coach bound for Dover. The occupants of that coach prosecuted them. As all three were of course literate, they got benefit of clergy. Mr. Marsh does not appear again in the Narration, save as a witness."

"So all that we know of Mr. Marsh is that in the middle of the night he was transporting something down Lambeth Road so foul-smelling that three highwaymen risked the gallows to revenge themselves on his horse!" said Mr. Orney.

"I know a bit more than that, sir," Arlanc said. "I've made inquiries along the banks of the Fleet, after dark. Mr. Marsh was indeed a London Vault-man. 'Tis considered most strange, by his brethren, that he crossed the River with a full load in the middle of the night."

"You say he *was* a Vault-man," Daniel remarked. "What is he now? Dead?"

"Out of business, owing to the loss of his horse. Moved back to Plymouth to live with his sister."

"Perhaps we should send one of our number to Plymouth to interview him," suggested Daniel, half in jest.

"Inconceivable! The state of the Clubb's finances is *desperate*!" Mr. Threader proclaimed.

Silence then, save for the sound of tongues being bitten. A face or two turned towards Daniel. *He* had known Mr. Threader longer than the others; so a decent respect for precedence dictated that he be given the first chance to bite Mr. Threader's head off.

"We have just doubled the size of our accompt, sir. How can you make such a claim?"

"Not quite doubled, sir, your Piece of Eight came up a ha'p'ny light of a pound."

"And my guinea is several pence heavy, as all the world knows," said Mr. Orney, "so you may supply Brother Daniel's deficit from my surplus, and keep the change while you are at it."

"Your generosity sets an example to us unredeemed Anglican sinners," said Mr. Threader with a weak smile. "But it does not materially change the Clubb's finances. Yes, we have twice the assets today as we had yesterday; but we must consider *liabilities* as well."

"I did not know we had any," said the perpetually amused Mr. Kikin, "unless you have been taking our dues to Change Alley, and investing them in some eldritch Derivatives."

"I look to the future, Mr. Kikin. One *gets* what one *pays for*! That is the infallible rule in fish-markets, whorehouses, and Parliament. And it applies with as much force in the world of the thief-taker."

Mr. Threader reveled in the silence that followed. Finally Mr. Or-

ney, who could not stand to see anyone—especially Mr. Threader—
enjoy anything, said, "If you mean to hire a thief-taker, sir, with our
money, you would do well to *propose* it first, that we may *dispute* it."

"Even before *disputing* thief-takers, if someone would be so kind as
to *define the term* for me?" said Mr. Kikin.

"Apprehending criminals is oft strenuous, and sometimes mortally dangerous," said Mr. Threader. "So, instead of doing it oneself,
one hires a thief-taker to go and do it for one."

"To go out and . . . hunt down, and physically abduct, someone?"

"Yes," said Mr. Threader mildly. "How else do you suppose justice
can ever be served?"

"Police . . . constables . . . militia . . . or *something*!" sputtered Mr.
Kikin. "But . . . in an orderly country . . . you can't simply have people running around arresting each other!"

"Thank you, sirrah, for your advice upon how to run an orderly
country!" Mr. Threader brayed. "Ah, yes, if only England could be
more like Muscovy!"

"Gentlemen, gentlemen . . ." Daniel began. But Mr. Kikin's fascination prevailed, and he let the argument drop, asking, "How does it
work?"

"Generally one posts a reward, and leaves the rest to the natural
workings of the market," said Mr. Threader.

"How large a reward?"

"You have penetrated to the heart of the matter, sir," said Mr.
Threader. "Since the days of William and Mary, the reward for a common robber or burglar has been ten pounds."

"By convention, or . . ."

"By royal proclamation, sir!"

Mr. Kikin's face clouded over. "Hmm, so we are in competition
with Her Majesty's government, then . . ."

"It gets worse. Forty pounds for highway robbers, twenty to twenty-
five for horse thieves, even more for murderers. The Clubb, I remind
you, has ten pounds, plus or minus a few bits and farthings."

"Stiff competition indeed," said Mr. Orney, "and a sign, to those
wise enough to heed it, that 'tis a waste of time to rely 'pon thief-
takers."

Before Mr. Threader could say what he thought of Mr. Orney's
brand of wisdom, Mr. Kikin said: "You should have told me before. If
the Clubb's dues are to be pissed away on inane things, I must be
thrifty. But if it is a matter of posting a reward . . . to catch an enemy
of the Tsar . . . we could have every thief-taker in London working for
us by tomorrow evening!"

Mr. Threader looked perfectly satisfied.

"Do we really want that?" Daniel asked. "Thief-takers have a more vile reputation even than thieves."

"That is of no account. We are not proposing to hire one as a *nanny*. The viler the better, I say!"

Daniel could see one or two flaws in that line of reasoning. But a glance at the faces of Mr. Orney and Monsieur Arlanc told him he was out-voted. They appeared to think it was splendid if Mr. Kikin wanted to spend the Tsar's money in this way.

"If there is no further business here," Daniel said, "I thought a tour of the watch-makers' shops of Clerkenwell might be in order."

"To find *criminals*, Dr. Waterhouse, let us search among *criminals*, not *horologists*; and let us not do it *ourselves*, but have thief-takers— paid for by the Tsar of Muscovy!—do it *for* us," said Mr. Threader; and for once, he seemed to speak for the whole Clubb, except for Daniel. "The meeting is adjourned."

AS A WAVE PASSES THROUGH a rug that is being shaken, driving before it a front of grit, fleas, apple seeds, tobacco-ashes, pubic hairs, scab-heads, &c., so the expansion of London across the defenseless green countryside pushed before it all who had been jarred loose by Change, or who simply hadn't been firmly tied down to begin with. A farmer living out in the green pastures north of the city might notice the buildings creeping his way, year by year, but not know that his pasture was soon to become part of London until drunks, footpads, whores, and molly-boys began to congregate under his windows.

As a boy Daniel had been able to open an upper-storey window in back of Drake's house on Holborn, and gaze across one mile of downs and swales to an irregular patch of turf called Clerkenwell Green: a bit of common ground separating St. James's and St. John's. Each of these was an ancient religious order, therefore, a jumbled compound of graveyards, houses, ancient Popish cloisters, and out-buildings. Like all other Roman churches in the realm, these had be-come Anglican, and perhaps been sacked a little bit, during Henry VIII's time. And when Cromwell had come along to replace Angli-canism with a more radical creed, they had been sacked more thor-oughly. Now what remained of them had been engulfed by London.

Yet it was better to be engulfed than to be on the edge, for the city had a kind of order that the frontier wanted. Whatever crimes, dis-ruptions, and atrocities had occurred around Clerkenwell Green while it was being ringed with new buildings, had now migrated slightly northwards, to be replaced by outrages of a more settled and organized nature.

Half a mile northwest of Clerkenwell Green was a place where the fledgling Fleet ran, for a short distance, parallel to the road to Hampstead. Between road and river the ground was low, and shiny with shifting sheets of water. But on the opposite bank, nearer to Clerkenwell, the ground was firm enough that shrubs and vegetables could be planted in it without drowning, and buildings set on it without sinking into the muck. A hamlet had gradually formed there, called Black Mary's Hole.

A bloke wanting to leave the urban confines of Clerkenwell Green and venture out across the fields toward Black Mary's Hole would have to contend with a few obstacles. For directly in his path stood the ancient compound of St. James's, and on the far side of that was a new-built prison, and just beyond that, a bridewell run by Quakers. And the sort of bloke who passed the time of day going up to Black Mary's Hole would instinctively avoid such establishments. So he would begin his journey by dodging westwards and exiting Clerkenwell Green through a sort of sphincter that led into Turnmill Street. To the left, or London-wards, Turnmill led into the livestock markets of Smithfield, and was lined with shambles, tallow-chandleries, and knackers' yards: hardly a tempting place for a stroll. To the right, or leading out to open country, it forked into two ways: on the right, Rag Street, and on the left, Hockley-in-the-Hole, which presumably got its name from the fact that it had come into being along a bend of the Fleet, which there had been bridged in so many places that it was vanishing from human ken.

Hockley-in-the-Hole was a sort of recreational annex to the meat markets. If animals were done to death for profit in the butcher-stalls of Smithfield, they were baited, fought, and torn asunder for pleasure in the cock-pits and bear-rings of Hockley-in-the-Hole.

Rag Street was not a great deal more pleasant, but it did get one directly out of the city. A hundred paces along, the buildings fell away, and were replaced by gardens, on the right. On the left the buildings went on for a bit, but they were not so unsavoury: several bakeries, and then a bath where the Quality came to take the waters. In a few hundred paces the buildings ceased on that side as well. From that point it was possible to see across a quarter-mile of open ground to Black Mary's Hole. This was, in other words, the first place where a Londoner, crazed by crowding and choked from coal-smoke, could break out into the open. The impulse was common enough. And so the entire stretch of territory from the Islington Road on the east to Tottenham Court Road on the west had become a sort of deranged park, with Black Mary's Hole in the center of it. It was where people resorted to have every form of sexual congress not sanctioned by the Book of Common Prayer, and where footpads went to prey upon them, and thief-takers to spy on the doings of the footpads and set one against another for the reward money.

Baths and tea-gardens provided another reason to go there—or, barring that, a convenient pretext for gentlefolk whose real motives had nothing to do with bathing or tea. And—complicating matters terribly—any number of people went there for childishly simple and innocent purposes. Picknickers were as likely to come here as murderers. On his first visit to this district, Daniel had heard someone creeping along behind him, and been certain it was a footpad, raising his cudgel to dash Daniel's brain's out; turning around, he had discovered a Fellow of the Royal Society brandishing a long-handled butterfly net.

Just at this place where London stopped, on the road to Black Mary's Hole, was a bit of land accurately described, by members of Daniel's Clubb, as a swine-yard with a mound of rubble in it. As a boy looking out the window of Drake's house, Daniel had probably flicked his gaze over it a hundred times and made naught of it. But recently he had got a bundle of letters from Massachusetts. One of them had been from Enoch Root, who'd got wind of Daniel's plan to build a sort of annex to the Institute of Technologickal Arts somewhere around London.

> For a long time I have phant'sied that one day I should find the landlord of the ruined Temple in Clerkenwell, and make something of that property.

Daniel had rolled his eyes upon reading these words. If Enoch Root was a real estate developer, then Daniel was a Turkish harem-girl! It was typical Enochian meddling: he knew there was a Templar crypt under this swine-lot that was about to be gobbled by London, and didn't want it to be filled in, or used as a keg-room for a gin-house, and he hoped Daniel or someone would do something about it. Daniel bridled at this trans-Atlantic nagging. But Root had a knack for finding, or creating, alignments between his interests and those of the people whose lives he meddled with. Daniel needed a place to build things. Clerkenwell, though it was obviously unstable, muddy, smelling of the knacker, and loud with the screams and roars of fighting beasts, Regarded as Unsafe by Persons of Quality, was a suitable place for Daniel. He could get to Town or Country—or escape from either—with but a few steps, and none of the neighbors were apt to complain of queer doings, or pay any note to nocturnal visitors.

The parcel was an irregular pentagon about a hundred paces wide. Within it, the sunken ruin was situated off-center, away from the road to Black Mary's Hole, near a vertex that pointed back towards Clerkenwell. The gardens of a neighboring Spaw came up close to it on one side, making the parcel seem larger than it was. It was one of countless crumbs of territory that had been worried off the edges of the Church's stupendous holdings in Tudor days. Tracing the changes in its ownership since then had been a good job for an unemployed boffin who knew a lot of Latin—Daniel had made two trips to Oxford to research it. He had discovered that ownership of the land had passed into the hands of a Cavalier family that had gone to France during Cromwell days and, owing to an ensuing pattern of marriages, bastardy, suspicious deaths, and opportunistic religious conversions, essentially become French people and were unlikely ever to come back. Twenty-five years of almost continual war between Britain and France had left them profoundly ignorant of suburban London real estate trends. Daniel had passed all of this on to Roger at the Kit-Cat Clubb. Letters had been despatched to France, and a few weeks later Roger had informed him that he could build anything he wanted there, provided it might later be resold at a profit. Daniel had found a mediocre architect and told him to design houses with shops in the ground floor, wrapping around three sides of the property, embracing a court with the ruin in the middle of it.

As he emerged from the half-collapsed anteroom of the crypt—the last member of the Clubb to depart—white blindness came over him because of the brilliance of the cloudy sky. He shaded his eyes and looked down at the luminous grass. A small round wrinkled thing was next to his shoe, looking like a færy's coin-purse. He kicked it over and realized it was a knotted sheep-gut condom.

His eyes had adjusted sufficiently now that he could look at the nearby hog-wallow without suffering too much. It was all dried up, as the tenant had been encouraged to take his swine elsewhere. Finally he could remove his hand from his brow and trace the lines of surveyors' stakes marking the foundations of the new buildings. When walls began to rise up upon those foundations, they'd screen this yard from the road, and then the only people who'd be able to see into it would be a few of those Spaw-goers, and perhaps—if they had sharp eyes, or owned perspective glasses—inmates of the new prison on Clerkenwell Close, a quarter-mile distant. But for what it was worth, they'd be the better class of prisoners who could afford to pay the gaolers for upper-storey rooms.

Accustomed to the tempo of Trinity College and of the Royal Society, he'd thought that the Clubb's meeting would go much longer. But Threader, Orney, and Kikin had nothing in common but decisiveness, and a will to get on with it. His watch told him he was very early for his appointment with Sir Isaac Newton. This would have been a blessing to most, for who'd want to be the insolent wretch who kept Sir Isaac waiting? To Daniel, who was looking forward to the meeting about as much as another bladder operation, it was a damned nuisance. He desired some pointless distraction; and so he decided to go call on the Marquis of Ravenscar.

There was no way to get from here to Roger's house that was not dangerous, offensive, or both. Daniel opted for offensive, i.e., he attempted to walk through the middle of Hockley-in-the-Hole. It lay within earshot, just on the other side of some buildings. What made it offensive was the sort of people gathered there on this Saturday morning: Cockneys come up to watch fights between beasts, and to participate in others. But they also made it safe, after a fashion. Pickpockets were all over the place, but footpads—whose *modus operandi* was to beat victims senseless—couldn't work in a crowd.

At the place where Saffron Hill Road disgorged its push of Londoners into the Hole, two men, stripped to the waist, were circling around each other with their fists up. One of them already had a red knuckle-print on his cheek, and a huge smear of dirt on one shoulder where he'd tumbled into the street. They were bulky coves, probably meat-cutters from Smithfield, and at least a hundred men had already formed a ring around them, and begun to lay wagers. All foot-traffic had to squeeze through a strait no more than a fathom wide between this storm of elbows and the building-fronts along the north side of the Hole: a line-up of taverns and of smudgy enterprises that looked as if they didn't want to be noticed.

A man was lying full-length on the ground at the foot of one building, dead or asleep, creating further eddies and surges in the crowd as people dodged around him. He looked like an apparition, a prophecy of what would become of Daniel if he were to lose his footing there. So Daniel made no pretense of dignity. He sidestepped as far as he could to the right, so that he was almost cowering against the sheer brown-brick face of a building, and shifted his walking-stick to his right hand so it wouldn't get kicked out from under him, and put his hand through the wrist-loop in case it did. He let the traffic carry him into the flume.

He had got about halfway through, and begun to sense daylight ahead, when he sensed unease propagating like a wave through the crowd ahead of him, and looked up to see a great brute of a horse, in black leather tack with silver ornament, drawing a small carriage. Its design was outlandish: all stretched out and bent around, recalling the shape of a pouncing cheetah. In the moment before he realized that he was in trouble, his mind identified it as one of the new rigs called phaethons. It was going to squeeze through this bottleneck. Or rather, it would trot through without breaking stride, and let the pedestrians do all the squeezing.

The crowd couldn't believe it—'twas an impossibility! Yet the vehicle, twenty feet long and eight high, drawn by a ton of prancing, iron-shod flesh, was not slowing down. The ends of the carriage-poles protruded like jousting-lances. One of those could go through your head like a pike through a pumpkin, and if you dodged that, you might still have your foot crushed under a wheel and face the always-tricky dilemma of amputation vs. gangrene. A hundred men did the rational thing. The sum of those rational choices was called panic. Daniel's contribution to the panic was as follows: perhaps eight feet ahead of him he saw a recessed shop-doorway, and made up his mind that while everyone else was gaping at the phaethon, he could squirt forward between the crowd on his left, and the shop-window on his right, and dodge into it. He ducked under the shoulder of a bigger man and scurried forward.

Halfway there, his left peripheral vision went dark as a large number of onrushing bodies blotted out the white sky.

Daniel saw very clearly that he was going to die now, in the following manner: smashed against the front of this shop by tons of meat and bone. The shop-window would not give way; it was made of small square panes in a grid of wooden mullions as thick as his wrist. Eventually it might buckle under the pressure of the crowd, but all of his ribs would give way sooner. He tried to lunge forward another step, but it only got worse; and his foot came down too soon, on unsteady ground. He had stepped on the torso of the unconscious man he'd noticed moments earlier. He lost his balance, but gained six inches' altitude, and this triggered some sort of climbing instinct. If the mullions of the window were stout enough to crush his ribcage, then they could at least support his weight while they were doing it. He flung both arms in the air like a Baptist in ecstasy, clutched at a horizontal bar, and pulled himself up while pushing with both feet against that sleeping or dead man, all at the same moment as he was being picked up by the mob, like a reed that has fallen into the surf, and slammed against the building. His feet were no longer touching anything. The force of gravity was countered by several different blokes' knees, shoulders, hips, and heads, which had all struck him over the course of a brief, bony barrage. If they'd driven him under he'd be a sorry case, but they'd pushed him up. One of his cheeks had slammed up against a windowpane so hard that the glass had popped half out of its frame and was making ominous ticking noises very close to his eyeball.

He no longer needed to support his own weight, so he allowed his left hand to release its grip on the mullion above, brought it down right past his nose, insinuated his fingers between jawbone and window, and crooked his fingers over the edge of the frame, taking advantage of the loose pane by getting a bit of a handhold on its mullion, so that when the crowd collapsed he would not simply fall backwards and crack his head on the ground.

The air inside the shop felt cooler on his fingertips and smelt of pipe-smoke. He had no choice but to stare through the glass for about five seconds. In the architect's mind's eye, this had probably been a lovely shop-window where ladies would coo over pretty displays. And maybe it would be that some day, if Hockley-in-the-Hole ever became fashionable. But for now a board had been put up inside of it, a bit more than arm's length inside the glass. Daniel couldn't tell whether it was a backdrop for display, or a barrier against intruders. It had been covered with green fabric a long time ago, and the fabric had been bleached by the sun, as this was a south-facing window. It had gone nearly white everywhere except where the sun's light had been blocked by wares, hung on that board for display. No wares remained on it now. But their caught shadows were clearly visible. Daniel's first thought was pendulums, because the shapes were circular, depending from slim cords. But no one bought pendulums save Natural Philosophers and mesmerists. It had to have been watches, hanging on chains.

The phaethon clattered past and the crowd relaxed, presenting a whole new universe of hazards to Daniel. A lot of chaps who had been leaning against other chaps who had, in the end, been leaning against Daniel, now decided to right themselves by pushing off hard. So waves of pressure thrust Daniel against the grid, again and again, so hard that he felt it popping underneath him. One of the brass buttons on his coat shattered a pane, spraying the watch-shadows with skewed triangles of glass. Then his support went out from under him and he fell, braking himself—as planned—with the one hand he'd crooked over the windowframe. His hip swung into the store-front and cracked another pane.

Now that the loosened pane was no longer being forced inwards by his cheek, it had sprung back and trapped his knuckles under its sharp edge. He was caught on tiptoe, like a prisoner strung up in a dungeon. But his right hand was free, the walking-stick still dangling by its wrist-thong, so with some ridiculous tossing and squirming motions he got a grip on its middle, raised its knotty head, and bashed out the loose pane to get himself free. The man who'd been lying on the ground rolled over onto his back, sat up convulsively, and blew a cloud of blood from his nostrils. Daniel hurried on; and just as he walked past the front door of the building he felt it opening. Three paces farther along he heard an "Oy, you!" but Hockley-in-the-Hole had become more riotous than ever and he could plausibly ignore this. He simply could not begin a conversation with the sort of person who would lurk in the back of such a building.

He walked faster, following the leftward curve of Hockley-in-the-Hole. A miasma of watery smells, issuing from gutters and crevices in the pavement, told him he'd crossed over the entombed Fleet. He dodged right into Windmill Hill, though it was a long time since there'd been a discernible hill, or a windmill, there. He then forced himself to walk straight west, without looking back, for a hundred paces. That brought him clear of Hockley, and into the center of the largest open place in this part of town, where Leather Lane, Liquorpond Street, and several other ways came together in a crazed, nameless interchange half the size of Charing Cross. There, finally, he turned around.

"Your watch, sir," said a bloke, "or so I surmise."

All the air drained out of Daniel's lungs. For ten minutes he had felt clever and spry. Now he looked down at himself and saw wreckage. To inventory all that had gone wrong with his clothes and his toilette would take more time than he could spare; but his watch was unquestionably missing. He took a step toward the bloke, then a smaller step. But the other fellow seemed to've made up his mind that he'd not pursue Daniel any farther today. He stood and waited, and the longer he waited, the more he seemed to glower. He was a great big cove, built to chop wood all day long. He had the most profound whiskerage Daniel had seen in many a year, and looked as if he could grow a jet-black beaver-pelt out of his face in about a week's time. He might have shaved forty-eight hours ago. But he'd had little incentive to do it any more frequently than that, since his cheeks and chin had suffered badly from smallpox, leaving scars atop other scars. In sum, the man's head looked like a Dutch oven forged over a dying fire with a ball-peen hammer. His hair hung round his face in a way that reminded Daniel of the young Robert Hooke; but where Hooke had been sickly and bent, this man was made like a meat-wagon. Yet he was holding Daniel's watch in the most curious delicate way, the time-piece resting on a half-acre of pink palm, the chain drawn back and draped over the black-creviced fingers of the other hand. He was *displaying* it.

Daniel took another step forward. He had the ridiculous phant'sy that the man would dart away if Daniel reached out: a reflex Daniel had learned in childhood games of keep-away, and never quite got rid of.

Something did not make sense. He looked up into the man's gray eyes and noticed crows' feet. He was older than he looked, probably in his forties. The beginnings of an explanation there.

"You have judged me aright," the man said, in an encouraging tone. "I am a horologist gone bad."

"You deal in stolen time—"

"Don't we all, sir? Each striking his own bargain, as 'twere."

"I was going to say, 'time-pieces,' but you interrupted me."

" 'Tis a common error of those who buy time dear, and sell it cheap, Dr. Waterhouse."

"You know my name? What is yours?"

"My surname is Hoxton. My father christened me Peter. Hereabouts, I am called Saturn."

"The Roman god of time."

"And of surly dispositions, Doctor."

"I have inspected your shop, Mr. Hoxton, quite a bit more closely than I should have liked."

"Yes, I was just inside the window, smoking my pipe, and observing you in return."

"You have told me in your own words that you have gone bad. You operate under an alias that is a byword for foul temper. I think I know the nature of your business. Yet you ask me to believe that you are returning me my watch, without any . . . complications . . . and you expect me to approach within your reach . . ." Daniel here trailed off, keeping an eye on the watch, trying not to seem as interested in getting it back as he really was.

"You're one of those coves f'r whom everything has to make *sense*? Then you and I are fellow-sufferers."

"You say that because you are a horologist?"

"Mechanic since I was a lad, clock-maker since I came to my senses," said Saturn. "The piece of information you are wanting, Doctor, is this: this here is an old Hooke balance-spring watch, this is. When the Master made it, why, it might've been the best time-piece ever fashioned by human hands. But now there's a score of proper horologists round Clerkenwell who can make ones that'll keep better time. Technology ages, dunnit?"

Daniel pursed his lips to keep from laughing at the spectacle of this new, five-guinea word, *Technology*, emerging from that head.

"It ages faster'n we do. It can be difficult for a bloke to keep up."

"Is that your story, Saturn? You could not keep up, and so you went bad?"

"I *grew weary* of keeping up, Doctor. *That* is my story, if you must know. I grew weary of *transitory* knowledge, and decided to seek knowledge of a more *æternal* nature."

"Do you claim to have found it?"

"No."

"Good. I was afraid this was going to turn into a homily."

Daniel now felt safe in advancing two more steps. Then a question occurred to him, and he stopped. "How did you know my name?"

"It's inscribed on the back of the watch."

"No, it's not."

"Very clever," said Saturn. Daniel could not tell which of them was the target of the sarcasm. Saturn continued, "Very well, sir. A certain flash cull of my acquaintance, a file-cly with a specialization in tatlers, who had run afoul of a Harmon in Fleet Street, and been condemned to shove the tumbler from Newgate to Leadenhall, came by my ken of an afternoon, desiring employment of a sedentary nature while his stripes healed. And after taking sensible precautions, which is to say, making sure that he was not running a type of service-lay to slum my ken, I said to this buz, my business here has fallen on hard times because I cannot run it without transitory knowledge. And yet my brain has had its fill of the same, and all I wish to do is to sit in my shop reading books, to acquire knowledge æternal, which benefits me in ways intangible, but in no way helps me to receive and sell stolen property of a horologickal nature, which is the *raison d'être* of the shop. Therefore, go ye out into the Rumbo, the Spinning-Ken, to Old Nass, go to the Boozing-kens of Hockley-in-the-Hole and the Cases at the low end of the Mount, go to the Goat in Long-lane, the Dogg in Fleet Street, and the Black-boy in Newtenhouse-Lane, and drink—but not too much— and buy drinks—but never too many—for any flash culls you spy there, and acquire transitory knowledge, and return to my ken and relate to me what you have learnt. And back he comes, a week later, and informs me that a certain old Gager has lately been making the rounds, trying to recover some lost property. 'What has he lost?' I inquired. 'Not a thing,' came the answer, 'he is after another cull's lost property—some gager who was Phinneyed ten years since.' 'Go and learn that dead cove's name,' says I, 'and the quick one's, too.' Come the answers: Robert Hooke, and Daniel Waterhouse, respectively. Why, he even pointed you out to me once, when you walked past my shop on your way to visit your swine-yard. That's how I knew you."

Peter Hoxton now extended his arms. His left hand held the chain of the Hooke-watch, swinging it like a pendulum, and his right offered a handshake. Daniel accepted the watch greedily, and the handshake with reluctance.

"I have a question for you, Doctor," said Saturn, as he was shaking Daniel's hand.

"Yes?"

"I've made a study of you, and know you are a bit of a Natural Philosopher. Been meaning to invite you into my ken."

"Did you—sir, did you cause my watch to be stolen!?" Daniel demanded, trying to draw back; but Saturn's hand had engulfed his, like a python swallowing a gerbil.

"Did you—Doctor, did you fling yourself against my shop-window on purpose!?" Saturn answered, perfectly mocking Daniel's tone.

Daniel was too indignant to speak, which the other took as permission to go on: "Now philosophy is the study of wisdom—truths æternal. Yet, long ago you went over the sea, didn't you, to set up an Institute of Technologickal Arts. And here you are back in London, aren't you, on some similar errand. Why, Doctor? You had the life I dream of: to sit on your arse and read of truths æternal. And yet I cannot make my way through a chapter of Plato without glancing up to see you sprawled against my shop-window like an enormous spate of bird-shite. Why turn away from the study of truths æternal, to traffick in transitory knowledge?"

Somewhat to his own surprise, Daniel had a ready answer, which came out of his mouth before he had had time to consider it. "Why does the minister tell mundane stories during his homily? Why not simply quote direct from sublime works of theology?"

"Anecdotes serve to illustrate the ideas he's getting at," Saturn surmised, "and anyway, if those ideas have no relation to mundane things, why, they're probably rubbish."

"Then if Newton and Leibniz are sublime theologians, sir, I am an humble vicar. Technology is a sort of religious practice to me, a way of getting at the æternal by way of the mundane. Does that answer your question, and may I have my hand back?"

"Yes," said Saturn. "You have your watch, sir; you have your hand; and you have a parishioner."

"But I do not want a parishioner," said Daniel, turning on his heel and walking west into Liquorpond Street.

"Then you ought to give up preaching, and those religious observances you just spoke of," said Peter Hoxton, falling into step beside Daniel. "You are a Cambridge man?"

"I am."

"And is not the ancient purpose of Cambridge to turn out clerics, and send them out into England to minister to the unwashed?"

"You know that perfectly well! But I'll not minister to you or any other man, Peter Hoxton, for if ever I was a vicar, I am a fallen one now, and not fit to minister to a dog. I went astray early, and have strayed far. The only way I can think of to find my way closer to God is through the strange ministry I spoke of earlier, whereof Hooke and Spinoza were prophets. It is not a way I recommend to any man, for I am as 'stranged from the main line of religion as a stylite monk, sitting on a pillar in a waste."

"I have strayed further and grown more 'stranged than you, Doc. I have been wandering in that same waste without any pillar to sit upon—therefore, you, perched on your post, are like a Pharos to me."

"I say to you one more time—"

"There's that word again! Time. Let me speak of time, Doc, and say to you this: if you continue to walk through Hockley-in-the-Hole unaccompanied, and to wander about the city as you've been doing, your time may be measured in days, or hours. You are not leery enough. This fact has been made note of by certain coves who make unleery gagers their prey. Every foot-scamperer and bridle-cull on the upper Fleet pricks up his ears when you trudge out to your swine-yard and disappear into your hole in the ground. Your time will be up very soon, and you will wind up as a scragg'd, naked corpse, floating down Fleet Ditch to Bridewell, if you do not make some large friends soon."

"Are you nominating yourself my bodyguard, Saturn?"

"I am nominating myself your parishioner, Doc. As you lack a church, we shall have to worship peripatetically, ambling about the streets, as now, and making Hockley-in-the-Hole our Agora. As I am half as old, and twice as big, as you, why, many an idle cove, who does not wot the true nature of our relationship, may ignorantly *assume* that I am your bodyguard, and, on account of that foolish misapprehension, refrain from stabbing you or bludgeoning you to death."

They had reached Gray's Inn Lane. The lawyer-infested gardens and walks behind Gray's Inn lay to either side of the road here, and beyond them were the settled confines of various Squares: Red Lyon, Waterhouse, Bloomsbury. Roger's estate was on the far corner of Bloomsbury, where London gave way again to open countryside. Daniel did not want to lead Saturn directly to it. He stopped.

"I am dafter e'en than you guess, Saturn."

"Why, impossible!"

"Have you heard of a pirate in America, called Edward Teach?"

"Blackbeard? Of course, sir, he is legendary."

"I say that not so long ago, I heard Blackbeard standing on the poop of *Queen Anne's Revenge,* calling for me by name."

For the first time, Peter Hoxton was taken a-back.

"As you see, I am insane—best leave me alone," Daniel said, and turned his back on Saturn yet again, looking for an opening in traffic on Gray's Inn Lane.

"Concerning Mr. Teach, I shall make inquiries among the Blackguard," said Peter Hoxton.

The next time Daniel dared to look over his shoulder, Saturn had vanished.

Bloomsbury
HALF AN HOUR LATER

"A Roman temple, on the edge of the city. Modest. Nothing gaudy," had been Roger's instructions to him, some twenty-five years earlier.

"I suppose that rules out having it be a Temple of Jupiter or Apollo," Daniel had returned.

Roger had looked out the window of the coffee-house, feigning deafness, which was what he always did when he guessed Daniel was making fun of him.

Daniel had sipped his coffee and considered it. "Among your modest and humble Roman Gods would be . . . let me think . . . Vesta. Whose temples, like your house, stood outside the old boundaries of the city."

"Well enough. Splendid god, Vesta," Roger had said, a bit distantly.

"Goddess, actually."

"All right, who the hell was she!?"

"Goddess of the hearth, chaste above all others . . ."

"Oh, Jesus!"

"Worshipped around the clock—or the sundial, I should say—by the Vestal virgins . . ."

"Wouldn't mind having a few of those around, provided they were not pedantic about the virginity."

"Not at all. Vesta herself was *almost* seduced by Priapus, the *ithyphallic* God . . ."

Roger shivered. "I can't wait to find out what that means. Perhaps we should make my house a Temple of Priapus."

"Every shack you walk into becomes a Temple of Priapus. No need to spend money on an architect."

"Who said I was going to pay you?"

"*I* did, Roger."

"Oh, all right."

"I will not make you a Temple of Priapus. I do not think that the Queen of England would ever come to call on you, Roger, if you lived in such a place."

"Give me another humble, unassuming God then!" Roger had demanded, snapping his fingers. "Come on, I'm not paying you to drink coffee!"

"There's always Vulcan."

"Lame!"

"Indeed, he was a bit gouty, like many a gentleman," Daniel had said patiently, "but he got all the most beautiful goddesses—including Venus herself!"

"Haw! The rogue!"

"He was master of metals—though humble, and scorned, he fettered Titans and Gods with his ingenuity—"

"Metals—including—?"

"Gold and silver."

"Capital!"

"And of course he was God of Fire, and Lord of Volcanoes."

"Volcanoes! An ancient symbol of fertility—sending their gouts of molten stone spurting high into the air," Roger had said meditatively, prompting Daniel to shove his chair away several inches. "Right! That's it, then—make me a Temple of Vulcan—tasteful and inexpensive, mind you—just off Bloomsbury there. And put a volcano in it!"

This—*put a volcano in it*—had been Roger's first and last instructions to Daniel concerning interior decoration. Daniel had fobbed that part of it off on a silversmith—not a *money* one, but an old-school silversmith who still literally smote silver for a living. This had left Daniel free to design the Temple of Vulcan itself, which had presented no difficulties at all. A lot of Greeks had figured out how to make buildings of that general type two thousand years ago, and then Romans had worked out tricks for banging them out in a hurry, tricks that were now second nature to every tradesman in London.

Not really believing that Roger would ever actually *build* it, Daniel had sat down in front of a large clean sheet of paper and proceeded to pile element on element: and quite a few Plinths, Pilasters, Architraves, Urns, Archivolts, and Finials later, he had ended up with something that probably would have caused Julius Cæsar to clap his hands over his laureled and anointed head in dismay, and order the designer crucified. But after a brief sell job from Daniel in the back room of a coffee-house ("Note the Lesbian leaf pattern at the tops of the columns. . . . Ancient symbols of fertility are worked into the groins. . . . I have taken the liberty of depicting this Amazon with two breasts, rather than the historically attested one"), Roger was convinced that it looked exactly like a Temple of Vulcan ought to. And when he actually went and built the thing—telling everyone it was an exact reproduction of a real one on Mount Vesuvius—nine out of ten Londoners were content to believe it. Daniel's only consolation was that because of the bald lie about Vesuvius, hardly anyone knew he— or indeed *any* living person—had been responsible for it. Only the Gods knew. As long as he avoided parts of the world with a lot of volcanoes, he would go unscathed.

During his most melancholy times, he was kept awake at night by the phant'sy that, of everything he'd ever done, this house would last the longest, and be seen by the most people. But with the one exception of being cut for the stone, every fear that had ever tormented Daniel in his bed had turned out, in the light of day, to be not all that bad really. As he plodded westwards on Great Russell Street toward its cross with Tottenham Court Road, passing by Bloomsbury Square, he sensed a massy white Presence in the corner of his eye, and forced himself not to look at it. But at some point this became absurd, and he had to square his shoulders, perform a soldierly right-face, and look his shame in the eye. And, *mirabile dictu*, it was not so very bad! When it had first gone up, twenty years ago, in the middle of a hoglot, cater-corner from a timber depot, it had been screamingly bizarre. But now it was in the middle of a city, which helped a little, and Hooke had added on to it, which helped a great deal. It was no longer an alienated Temple but the buckle in a belt of Corinthian-columned arcades that surrounded Roger's parcel. The wings gave it proportion and made it seem much less likely to topple over sideways. The friezes had been added to the pediment and to the tablatures while Daniel had been in Boston, a tangle of togas and tridents that diverted the viewer's eye from the underlying dreadfulness (or so Daniel thought) of the architecture. Here Hooke had done him more favors by extending the horizontal features of the Temple into the wings, giving Daniel's phant'sies and improvisations more authority than they probably deserved. All in all, Daniel was able to stare at the place for a solid five or ten minutes without dissolving in embarrassment; London's boundaries enclosed much worse.

For the thirtieth time since crossing Gray's Inn Road, he looked to see if Saturn was following him. The answer was again no. He crossed Great Russell and walked up the steps, feeling like a wee fig-

ure sketched into a rendering to show the scale. Passing between two
fluted columns he swept across the Portico and raised his walking-
stick to beat upon one of the massive front doors (gold leaf, with details in silver and copper, all part of the metallurgical theme). But the
doors were drawn open so swiftly that they seemed to leap away from
him. It gave him a turn—his eye was foxed into thinking that the
doors were stationary, and he falling backwards away from them. He
took a step forward to compensate; and, entering the cleavage between the doors, nearly fell into the one between a pair of breasts. It
required some effort to stop himself, straighten his carriage, and
look the owner in the eye. She was giving him a knowing look, but
the dimples in her cheeks said, *All in good fun, go on, have a good long
stare then!*

"*Doctor* Waterhouse! You have kept me waiting *far* too long! How
can I ever forgive you?"

This sounded like an opportunity for Daniel to say something
witty, but it whooshed past him like grapeshot.

"Er . . . I have?"

Ah, but the lady was accustomed to dealing with numb-tongued
Natural Philosophers. "I should have heeded Uncle Isaac, who has
spoken so highly of your strength of character."

"I . . . beg your pardon?" He was beginning to feel as if he should
perhaps hit *himself* with his stick. Perhaps it would restore circulation
to his brain.

"A weaker man would have planted himself right there, where you
were just now standing, on his first day in London, and said to all who
passed by, 'Look! D'you see that House? I built it! It's mine!' But, *you!*"
and here she actually planted her hands on her hips in mock exasperation. But it seemed funny, not in the least affected. "You, Doctor
Waterhouse, with your Puritan ways—*just like* Uncle Isaac—withstood
that temptation for, what, a little more than two months! It is a mystery to me, how you and Uncle Isaac can delay your pleasures with
such stony patience, when someone such as I would become *frantic.*"
Then, because this perhaps sounded a bit risqué, she added, "Thank
you *so* kindly for answering my letters, by the way."

"You are most welcome, it was my privilege," Daniel answered
without thinking. But it took a moment to remember what she was
even talking about.

Catherine Barton had come to London round the turn of the century. She'd have been about twenty. Her father—Isaac's brother-in-
law—had died a few years earlier, and Isaac had shouldered the load
of keeping the poor survivors fed, clothed, and housed. After a short
time staying in the city with Isaac, she'd come down with smallpox

and fled to the countryside to recover or die. It was during that time that she'd sent a letter to Daniel in Boston, a letter no less sweet and charming for being cleverly written.

Which reminded Daniel that he ought to say something. "It is fortunate for me that, through your letters, I was able to meet your *mind* before I was put in any danger of being swept off my feet by . . . er . . . the rest of you."

She'd been trying to figure out why her uncle was the way he was. And not in a conniving way, but, it seemed, out of a sincere desire to be a good and understanding help-meet to this weird old man who had become, in effect, her new father. Daniel had written eight drafts of his letter back to her, for he knew perfectly well that one day Isaac would find it among her effects, and read it. He would read it every bit as shrewdly as a challenge from Leibniz.

Everyone knows Isaac as a brilliant man, and treats him as such, which is a mistake; for he is as pious as he is brilliant, and his piety taketh precedence. Mind you, I speak not of outward, conspicuous piety but of an inner fire, a light under the bushel as 'twere, a yearning to draw nearer to God through exercise of God-given faculties.

"Your advice was of inestimable value to me, after I recovered— thanks be to God—and returned to London. And insofar as I have been of any help *whatever* to Uncle Isaac, I daresay what you wrote was a boon to him as well."

"I shall not hold my breath waiting for an expression of gratitude from *him*," Daniel said, hoping it sounded like a wry thing to say. She had the good grace to laugh out loud. Daniel got the impression she was accustomed to having men blurt indiscreet things to her, and regarded it as excellent sport.

"Oh, nonsense! You understand him better than any man alive, Dr. Waterhouse, and he is keenly aware of it."

This—though she said it with dimples engaged—was really more of a threat than a compliment. What was more, Daniel knew that Catherine Barton had said it quite carefully and deliberately.

He decided to stop waiting for the formal introduction of Miss Catherine Barton to Dr. Daniel Waterhouse. It would never happen. She had vaulted over that hurdle with ribbons and skirts a-flying, and obliged him to follow. "You might enjoy a look round," she suggested, arching her eyebrows spectacularly. She did not need to speak aloud the second half of the sentence: *if you could only manage to pry your eyes off me.* In truth, she was more presentable than beautiful. But she had some beautiful features. And she was very well-dressed. Not in the sense of showing off how much money she could spend, or how *à la mode* she could be, but rather in the sense that her attire presented to the world a full, frank, and exhaustive account of all that was admirable about her body. When she spun around to lead him across the vestibule, her skirts swirled around her buttocks and thighs in a way that made their contours fully known to Daniel. Or he phant'sied as much, which amounted to the same thing. He'd been wondering, for as long as he'd been in London, what it was about this woman that caused great and powerful men to recite appalling poetry about her in the Kit-Cat Clubb, and to go all glassy-eyed when her name came up in conversation. He should have known. Faces could beguile, enchant, and flirt. But clearly this woman was inflicting major spinal injuries on men wherever she went, and only a body had the power to do that. Hence the need for a lot of Classical allusions in Catherine Barton love-poetry. Her idolaters were reaching back to something pre-Christian, trying to express a bit of what they felt when they gazed upon Greek statues of nude goddesses.

There were plenty around. The vestibule was an oval room lined with niches that had stood vacant the last time Daniel had seen the place. The decades since had afforded Roger all the time he'd needed to bankroll raiding-parties on Classical ruins, or to commission original works. As he followed Miss Catherine Barton out of the room, Daniel spun round a full three hundred sixty degrees to scan the vestibule. The two servants who had pulled the doors open on Catherine's command—both young men—were caught staring at their mistress's backside. Both of them snapped their heads away and blushed. Daniel gave them a wink, turned, and followed her out.

"I have shown this house to visitors an hundred times," she was saying, "and so all sorts of prattle is on the tip of my tongue—all of it perfectly boring to you, Dr. Waterhouse, to whom this house needs no introduction! You know we are crossing the central hall, and that the important rooms are to the left . . ." She meant the dining hall and the library. "And the odds and ends to the right . . ." (servant's quarters, kitchen, back stairs, House of Office) "and the Withdrawing Room straight ahead. What is your pleasure? Do you need to retire that way?" she asked, glancing to the right. She was asking him if he needed to urinate or defecate. "Or is there anything you would like there?" glancing left—meaning, did he need to take any refreshment. She kept her hands clasped together in front of her bodice and pointed to the left or right with tiny movements of her eyes, obliging Daniel to gaze into them attentively. "To be proper, I should conduct you into the Withdrawing Room where we might have a great argument as to who should sit in which chair. But after the war, French manners are quite out of favor with us—especially us Whigs—and I cannot bring myself to be so formal with you, who are like another uncle to me."

"I should only make an ass of myself—I who have spent twenty years in a wooden house!" Daniel returned. "Only tell me this, I pray you: if we go into the Withdrawing Room, can I see—"

"The volcano has been moved," she said, quite solemn, as if afraid Daniel would be furious.

"Out of the house, or—"

"Oh, heaven forbid! No, 'tis the centerpiece of the house as ever, Doctor! It is only that this part of the house, which is to say, the part you designed, began to seem, in some of its rooms, rather more small than suited Roger's tastes."

"That is when Mr. Hooke was brought in to add the wings."

"You know the story, Dr. Waterhouse, and so I shall not bore you, other than to say that the addition contains a ballroom that is at last large enough to exhibit the volcano in the style it deserves." And with that she wheeled around and pushed open a pair of doors across the hall from the vestibule, allowing light to flood in from the windows of the Withdrawing Room. Daniel stepped in, and then stopped, a-mazed.

When this room had been laid out, those windows had commanded a view to the north across a pasture, soon to become a formal garden: a view near to Daniel's heart, as it was practically the same as the one from the back of Drake's old house. But now the garden had been truncated to a court-yard with a fountain in the center, and directly on the other side, a stone's throw away, rose a Barock palace. This room, which Daniel had conceived as a quiet retreat from which to enjoy a vast prospect of flowers and greenery, had been reduced to a sort of viewing-gallery for contemplating the magnificence of the *real* house.

"Vanbrugh," Catherine explained. The same one who was doing Blenheim Palace for the Duke of Marlborough.

"Hooke—"

"Mr. Hooke did the wings, which as you can see, embrace the courtyard, and connect your Temple to Mr. Vanbrugh's, er . . ."

Fuck-house of the Gods was on the tip of Daniel's tongue, but he could hardly throw stones at Vanbrugh since he had started it. All he could summon up was, "What an undeserved honour 'tis for me, that Vanbrugh should finish so grandly, what I started so plainly."

The chairs in the Withdrawing Room were arranged in an arc facing toward the window. Catherine passed between two of them and opened a pair of French doors that in the original scheme had led out onto the long central promenade of the garden. Instead of which he followed her onto marble paving-slabs and pursued her around the kerb of an octagonal pool. It had a bronze fountain in the center of it, a great Classical action-scene: muscular Vulcan thrusting himself forth on massive but bent legs, having a go at Minerva, the cool helmet-head, who was pushing him back with one arm. Swords, daggers, helmets, and cuirasses were strewn all round, interspersed with the odd half-forged thunderbolt. Vulcan's knobby fingers were ripping Minerva's breastplate away to expose a body obviously modeled after Catherine Barton's. Daniel recognized the tale: Minerva went to Vulcan's forge to acquire weapons and armor; Vulcan became inflamed with lust and assaulted her; she, being one tough deity, held him at bay, and he had to settle for ejaculating on her leg. She wiped it off with a rag and flung it on the ground, fertilizing Mother Earth, who later bore Erichthonius, an early king of Athens, who introduced the use of silver money.

The sculpture was heavy-laden with clews and portents: with her free hand Minerva was already reaching for a rag, and Vulcan was ominously close to making contact with her creamy thigh. Smaller sculpture groups decorated the ends of the fountain-pool; at the end nearer to Daniel's building, a babe on the lap of a fertility sort of goddess (lots of cornucopiae) being fed grapes from a bunch. Opposite, near Vanbrugh's building, a crowned King seated on a pile of bullion. As they skirted the pool, Daniel felt a perverse urge to swivel his head and find out just how the sculptor had handled certain particulars. He was especially keen to know from where the water was spurting. At the same time, he couldn't bear to see it. Catherine was ignoring the fountain altogether; she did not want to talk about it, had turned her face away, her posture rhyming with Minerva's. Daniel contented himself with pursuing her across the court-yard, albeit with even less success than Vulcan.

What with so many distractions, they were inside the new house before Daniel had really had the time to examine its interior. Probably just as well; he'd gotten a vague impression of lots and lots of statues, prancing along rooftops and balustrades.

"Rokoko, it is called," Catherine explained, leading him into what must have been the grand ballroom. " 'Tis all the rage."

Daniel could only recollect Drake's house, with its bare walls and floors, and one or two plain boxy pieces of furniture to a room. "It makes me feel old," he said, baldly.

Catherine favored him with a brilliant smile. "*Some* say, 'tis the result of a surplus of *decorators,* combined with a deficit of *houses.*"

And a want of taste, Daniel wished he could say. "As you are the mistress of the household, mademoiselle, I shall make no comment on what some say." She rewarded him with dimples. Without meaning to, he had made a sly comment on her Arrangement with Roger.

Daniel found these moments slightly unnerving. For the most part she did not look like Isaac—not even the young, frail, girlish Isaac Daniel had met at Trinity half a century ago. He would never have guessed she had a drop of Newton-blood in her veins if he hadn't known as much already. But during the moments when she forgot to hide her cleverness, a family resemblance flashed forth, and he saw Isaac's face for an instant, as if the author of *Principia Mathematica* were stalking him through a darkened room when lightning struck outside.

"Here is a curious invention you may find worthy of your attention, Doctor. This way, please!"

The volcano stood at one end of the ballroom. It was a great improvement on the volcanoes made by Nature, which were so rude, irregular, and unadorned. This one was perfectly conical, with forty-five-degree-angle slopes converging on a polished brass nozzle or teat at the summit. A semi-ruined Classical temple, complete with half-collapsed golden dome, had been erected there, enclosing the vent, which could be viewed between Doric columns of red marble. The mountain itself was black marble, veined with red, and adorned with the usual tiresome menagerie of nymphs, satyrs, centaurs, &c., all sculpted in gold. It probably stood no more than four feet from base to summit, but was made to seem much larger by the base that supported it: a hollow plinth rising from the floor to waist level, supported all round with caryatids in the shape of Typhon and other gross earthy monsters.

"If you come round back with me, Doctor, I shall a-maze you with the most marvelous Screw."

"I beg your pardon?"

She had opened a hatch concealed in the back, and was beckoning. He came round, squatted carefully, and peered inside. Now he could see a fat cylinder that began in a copper basin on the floor, and ran up at an angle to the summit of the volcano.

"Roger wanted so badly to have a volcano that would spew rivers of molten silver. It would have been spectacular! But Mr. MacDougall was afraid it would set fire to the guests."

"Which would have been spectacular too, in a different way," Daniel mused.

"Mr. MacDougall persuaded Roger to settle for oil of phosphorus. It is prepared elsewhere, and brought here in casks, and poured into the tub. The Screw of Archimedes conducts it upwards, it gushes from the summit, and runs down the slopes as the centaurs and what-not flee in terror."

"They—flee?"

"Oh, yes, for it is meant to represent glowing streams of liquid fire."

"That I understand. But how do they flee—?"

"They are clock-work creatures."

"Also the work of Mr. MacDougall?"

"Indeed."

"I remember hiring a silversmith named Millhouse but not an *in-génieur* named MacDougall."

"Mr. Millhouse hired Mr. MacDougall to do the clever bits. When Mr. Millhouse died of smallpox—"

"Mr. MacDougall took over," Daniel guessed, "and could not stop adding one clever bit after another."

"Until Roger cut him off—somewhat emphatically, I'm afraid," said Catherine, and winced in a manner that made Daniel want to stroke her hair.

"Is he still alive?"

"Oh, yes, he works in theatres, making apparitions, explosions, and storms."

"Of course he does."

"He staged the naval battle that burned down the Curtain."

"I believe you. How frequently does the volcano erupt?"

"Once or twice a year, for important parties."

"And Mr. MacDougall is called back from exile on those occasions?"

"Roger has him on retainer."

"Where does he get his phosphorus?"

"He has it delivered," she said, as if this were an answer.

"Where may Mr. MacDougall be found, I wonder?"

"The Theater Royal, in Covent Garden, is getting ready to stage a new production entitled *The Sack of Persepolis*," Catherine said, tentatively.

"Say no more, Miss Barton."

Sir Isaac Newton's House, St. Martin's Street, London
LATER THAT DAY

"I'VE A SORT OF RIDDLE for you, to do with guineas," was how Daniel ended the twenty-year silence between himself and Sir Isaac Newton.

He had been fretting, ever since Enoch Root had turned up in his doorway in Massachusetts, over how to begin this conversation: what ponderous greeting would best suit the gravity of the occasion, how much time to spend reminiscing about student days in Cambridge, and whether to say anything about their last encounter, which had gone as badly as any social encounter, short of homicide, could go. Like a play-wright penning and burning draughts of a troublesome scene, he had scripted this reunion in his head an hundred times, and each time the script had careered off into a bloody debacle like the last act of *Hamlet*. As it seemed perfectly hopeless, and as he'd been assured by Saturn that he had only hours or days to live in any case, he reckoned, why waste time on formalities?

When the door was opened, and he first looked Isaac in the face from across the room, he did not see any trace of fury or (what would have been more dangerous) fear. Isaac looked resigned. He was feigning patience. He looked like a Duke receiving a long-lost idiot half-brother. And on the spur of the moment, Daniel said this thing about guineas as he was stepping over the threshold. The servant who'd opened the door for him gave him the same sort of look he might bestow on a gibbeted corpse suspended above a crossroads on a warm day, and closed the door behind him.

Daniel and Isaac were alone together in the study. Or Daniel assumed it was called a study. He could not imagine Isaac having a bedchamber or a dining-room. Any room he was in, was a study by default. The walls were paneled in dark wood, surprisingly uneven, almost rustic, compared to Roger's house. The door was made of the same stuff, so that it vanished when it was closed, making it seem as if Daniel and Isaac were a pair of old desiccated specimens closed up in a shipping crate. The room had windows looking out onto the street. Their massive, elaborate wooden shutters were open to admit some of the light off Leicester Fields, but much of this was blocked by half-drawn scarlet curtains. Isaac was seated behind a great table, the sort of table Drake would've owned, and he was dressed in a long scarlet dressing-gown over a good linen shirt. His face had not changed all that much, though it had got heavier, and he still had the long white hair. But his hairline had jumped back, making it seem as if his brain were trying to force its way up out the top of his head. His skin had been white when Daniel had walked in, but by the time he had made it to the end of the room to proffer his hand, Isaac had gone red in the face, as if stealing the color from his robe.

"There is nothing in my life quite so irritating as to be riddled and teased with inane conundrums, meant to prove my wit, and to try my senility," he answered. "Bernoulli—Leibniz's pawn—sent me—"

"The brachistochrone problem, I recall it," Daniel said, "and you solved it in hours. It took me rather longer."

"But you did solve it," Isaac commanded. "Because it was a problem of the calculus, meant to try whether I *understood* the calculus or not! Can you fathom the impertinence of it!? I was the first man who could *ever* have solved it, Daniel, and you the *second*, because you had the calculus from me first-hand. To be hectored thus, by the Baron's lackeys, three decades after I had invented it—"

"In truth *my* riddle is another sort of thing altogether," Daniel said. "I really am quite sorry to have wrong-footed you."

Isaac blinked and heaved a sigh. He seemed inordinately relieved. Perhaps he had feared that Daniel would dispute what he had just said: *You had the calculus from me first-hand.* That was the key. In Daniel, Isaac saw a witness who could testify to Isaac's priority in the discovery of the calculus. Whatever other annoying and inconvenient qualities Daniel might have, vanished when placed beside that. Daniel felt the muscles of his scalp and neck easing, felt his lungs filling with air. He was going to be all right. He'd make it out of the room whole, even if he said things that made Isaac a little angry. To Isaac, Daniel was more than a pawn; he was a rook, kept sequestered in the corner of the board until the end-game, then brought out at last to sweep inexorably down the board, driving the foe back to the last rank and forcing surrender. Isaac would put up with a lot, from a rook.

He wondered whether Isaac had, through some machinations, *caused* Daniel to be brought back to London. Perhaps he had exerted some action at a distance upon Princess Caroline in Hanover.

"What is your riddle, Daniel?"

"Earlier today, I was with a man who knows a good deal more than I do about money. This fellow was trying to judge the value of a guinea."

"Of a coin that purported to be a guinea," Isaac corrected him.

"Indeed—I say 'guinea' because that is what, in the end, it turned out to be."

"He should have weighed it."

"That is just what he did. And he could say nothing against the weight of the coin. Which would seem to settle the matter. But then he did something that to me was very odd. He put the coin in his mouth and he bit down on it."

Isaac made no answer, but Daniel thought he pinkened again, slightly. Certainly he was interested in the story. He clasped his hands together on the table in front of him, composing himself, rather like a cat.

"Now," Daniel said. "Even I know that coiners frequently make their counterfeits by joining two faces stamped from gold foil, and filling the void between them with solder. The solder is both lighter and softer than gold. This provides two means of detection: one may weigh the coin, or bite it. Either should suffice. In particular, if a coin has passed the test of weighing, its value should be confirmed beyond doubt! For nothing is heavier than gold. Any adulteration should be betrayed by a want of gravity. The weighing test ought to be infallible. And yet this chap—who really is extremely knowledgeable concerning coins—felt it necessary to make the additional test of biting. Is there any reason for it? Or was he being foolish?"

"*He* was not being foolish," Isaac said, and stared at Daniel expectantly. His eyes were great luminous ice-balls hanging in space, like comets.

"Do you mean to say that *I* was, Isaac?"

"To associate with such a man? Foolish, or naïve," Isaac returned. "As you have wandered in the wilderness for two decades, I shall grant you the benefit of the doubt."

"Then cure me of naïveté, and tell me, what sort of man is he?"

"A weigher."

"Well, he is obviously that, inasmuch as he weighs things, but you seem to invest the word with connotations that are lost on a backwoodsman such as I."

"In spite of all my efforts to reform the practices of the Mint, and to make each newly coined guinea identical to the last, some variation in weights persists. Some guineas are slightly heavier than others. Such errors are reducible but not eradicable. I have reduced them to the degree that, where honest persons are concerned, no

variation exists. That is, most men in London—and I include sophisticated men of commerce—would trade one guinea for another
without hesitation, and certainly without bothering to take out a
scale and weigh them."

"I well remember when that was *not* the case," Daniel remarked.

"You refer to our visits to Stourbridge Fair, before the Plague,"
Isaac said immediately.

"Yes," Daniel answered, after a moment of awkwardness.

He and Isaac had walked from Trinity to the Fair once, to buy
prisms, and along the way, Isaac had made some remarks about flux-
ions—the beginnings of the calculus. During his recent sea-voyage
from Massachusetts, Daniel had summoned that ancient memory to
mind, and brought it back to life in his head, remembering certain
queer details, like the shapes of the aquatic plants in the river Cam,
bent downstream by the sluggish fluxion of the water. It was now obvious that Isaac had been thinking hard, and recently, about the
same memory.

To go on prating of coins, when the *true* topic of the conversation
was so close to breaking the surface, were faintly ridiculous. But Englishmen, given a choice, would always prefer the faintly ridiculous
over the painfully direct. So, on with numismatics.

"It got even worse—the coinage did—later," Isaac said.

"I remind you that I did not depart until the middle of the 1690s,
when there were hardly any coins left in the country, and our œconomy was a confetti of I.O.U.s."

"Now England is awash in gold. The currency is as hard as
adamant. Our commerce is the wonder of all the earth, and even
Amsterdam is in our shade. It were vanity for me to take too much
credit for this. But it is simple honesty to say, that it could not happen
in the absence of this plain understanding, shared by all Englishmen,
that a guinea may be exchanged for a guinea without a second
thought. That all guineas are the same."

Suddenly all that Daniel had observed of Mr. Threader rearranged, in his mind, into a novel, strange, but perfectly coherent
picture; it was like watching a pile of rubble spontaneously assemble
itself into a marble statue. "Allow me to hazard," Daniel said, "that a
weigher" (he almost said, "Mr. Threader") "is a chap who to outward
appearances believes what every honest, plain-dealing Englishman
believes about the value of a guinea. But in secret, he takes every
guinea that comes his way, and weighs it 'pon scales of the most exacting precision. Such as are light, or of the mean weight, he returns
into circulation. But such as are heavy, he hoards. And when he has
hoarded an hundred such—I am only making up numbers for the

sake of argument—perhaps he has enough gold, in sum, to mint an hundred and one guineas. He has created a new guinea out of thin air."

Isaac said *yes* by slowly blinking his pink eyelids. "Of course, what you have described is only the most elementary of their practices. Those who master it, move on quickly to more nefarious schemes."

But Daniel was still new to all of this, and stuck on the elementary. "It would only be feasible," he guessed, "if one were already in a line of work that involved handling large numbers of coins."

"Naturally! And that is why the practice is so rife among the money-scriveners. *I* make guineas, and send them out into the country; *they* scurry about unraveling the tapestry I've so laboriously woven, and return the heaviest coins to London, where they invariably make their way to the coffers of the most vile and execrable traitors in the realm!"

Daniel recalled driving past shredded corpses at Tyburn. "You mean that weighers are connected with coiners."

"As *spinners* are with *weavers*, Daniel."

Daniel was silent for a moment, rehearsing every memory he had of Mr. Threader.

"That is why I was so shocked—shocked half to death, if you must know—to see you traveling in the company of one such!" Isaac said, actually shaking a bit with emotion.

Daniel was so used to Isaac mysteriously knowing things, that he was not as surprised by this very odd revelation as he ought to have been, and did not pay any particular mind to it. "For that," he remarked, "there is an explanation that you would find miserably boring if you knew it."

"I have made it my business to know it, and I accept that there was nothing untoward in your *temporary* association with that man," Isaac returned. "If I were inclined to be suspicious, like Flamsteed, I should interpret your *continued* association with him in the worst possible light! As it is, I see plainly enough that you were ignorant of his true nature, and beguiled by his charm, and I trust you to heed my warning."

Daniel was now very close to laughing out loud. He could not choose which was funnier: the phant'sy that Isaac Newton was not suspicious-minded, or that Mr. Threader possessed charm. Better change the subject! "But my question is not answered yet. Why did he *bite* the coin, if he had already *weighed* it?"

"There is a way to fool the weighing-test," Isaac said.

"Impossible! Nothing is heavier than gold!"

"I have discovered the existence of gold of greater than twenty-four-carat weight."

"That is an absurdity," Daniel said, after a moment's pause to consider it.

"Your mind, being a logical organ, rejects it," Isaac said, "because, by definition, pure gold weighs twenty-four carats. Pure gold cannot become purer, hence, cannot be heavier. Of course, I am aware of this. But I say to you that I have with my own hands weighed gold that was heavier than gold that I knew to be pure."

From any other man on earth—Natural Philosophers included— this would amount to saying, "I was sloppy in the laboratory and got it wrong." From Sir Isaac Newton, it was truth of Euclidean certainty.

"I am put in mind of the discovery of phosphorus," Daniel remarked, after considering it for a few moments. "A new element of nature, with properties never before seen. Perhaps there exist other elements of which we are unaware, having properties hitherto unknown. Perhaps there is such an element, similar in many respects to gold, but having a higher specific gravity, and perhaps the gold you spoke of was alloyed with it to make a metal, indistinguishable from gold in its gross properties, but slightly more dense."

"I give you credit for ingenuity," Isaac said, slightly amused, "but there is a simpler explanation. Yes, the gold I speak of is alloyed with something: a fluidic essence that fills the interstices among its atoms and gives the metal greater weight. But I believe that this essence is nothing less than—"

"The Philosophick Mercury!" Daniel exclaimed. The words came out of his mouth in a spirit of genuine excitement; bounced off the hard walls of dark wood; and, when they entered his ears, made him cringe at his own idiocy. "You think it is the Philosophick Mercury," he corrected himself.

"The Subtile Spirit," Isaac said, not excited, but solemn as Rhadamanthus. "And the goal of Alchemists for thousands of years, ever since the Art was taken into the Orient, and removed from human ken, by its past master, King Solomon."

"You have been searching for traces of the Philosophick Mercury since we were boys," Daniel reminded him. "As recently as twenty years ago, your efforts to find even the smallest trace of it had met with abject failure. What has changed?"

"I took your advice, Daniel. I accepted the charge of the Mint from my lord Ravenscar. I initiated the Great Recoinage, which brought vast tonnage of gold plate and bullion out from where it had been hoarded."

"And you adjusted the ratio in valuation of silver to gold, so that the latter was over-valued," Daniel said, "which as everyone knows, has practically driven all silver off the island, and attracted gold from every corner of the globe where commerce has spread its ten-drils."

Isaac declined comment.

"Prior to your—" here Daniel was about to say something like *ter-rifying spasm of dementia* but corrected himself: "change of career, twenty years ago, you were only able to work with such modest sam-ples of gold as you could buy from local sources. Your appointment to the Mint—combined with the policies you have adopted there— have made the Tower of London the bottle-neck through which all the world's gold flows, and put you in a position to dip your finger into that flow at will, sampling and testing the gold of many different lands—am I getting it right?"

Isaac nodded, and it seemed he looked almost mischievous, in a naughty-old-man sort of way. "The practice of all Alchemists since the time of Hermes Trismegistus has been to presume that the Gold of Solomon had been forever lost, and to attempt to re-discover his lost Art through patient trials and arcane study. This was the course that defeated me, before what you coyly describe as my *change of career*. But during my recuperation, as I went to inspect the Mint, and con-versed with my predecessors there, I came to realize that the ancient presumption of the Esoteric Brotherhood was no longer true. If Solomon went away into the remotest isles of the Orient, why, Com-merce has now gone that far, or farther, and in particular the Spaniards and the Portuguese have left no stone unturned, the world over, in their assiduous search for gold and silver. No matter how far Solomon may have journeyed, he would have left behind traces of his passage, in the form of Solomonic Gold, which is to say, gold made through an Alchemical process, bearing traces of the Philosophick Mercury. In the millennia since his kingdom vanished from the earth, this gold might have passed from one ignorant set of hands to another a thousand times. It might have been taken across wastes by caravans, forged into pagan funeral-masks, plundered from fallen citadels, buried in secret hoards, dug up by thieves, seized by pirates, made into jewels, and coined into specie of diverse realms. But through all of these evolutions it would preserve the traces of the Philosophick Mercury that would provide an infallible proof of its origins. To find it, I need not pore over ancient manuscripts for frag-ments of Alchemical lore, and I need not venture into far reaches to search for ancient gold with my own hands. I need only position my-self like a spider at the center of the global web of commerce, and then so arrange matters that all the world's gold would flow inwards toward me, as every point of matter in the solar system naturally falls inwards toward the Sun. If I then remained vigilant, and sampled all the gold that came into the Mint to be made into guineas, in time I should be nearly certain of finding some traces of the Solomonic Gold."

"And now you would appear to have found it," said Daniel, unwilling to weigh in, yet, on Isaac's side. "How recently has this occurred?"

"For the first several years there was nothing. Not a trace. I despaired of finding it ever," Isaac admitted. "Then, during the respite in the War, round 1701, I found a bit of gold heavier than twenty-four carat. I cannot summon words, here and now, to convey my emotions then! It was just a flake of gold leaf, found in a coiner's shop after it was raided, on my orders, by the King's Messengers. The coiner himself had been slain during the raid—most frustrating! Several years later, I found a counterfeit guinea that was heavier than it ought to be. In time, I hunted down the coiner who had made it, and interrogated him as to where he had obtained his bullion. He had gotten most of it from conventional sources. But he said that he had recently purchased, through a middleman, a quantity of gold in the form of sheet metal, hand-hammered, about an eighth of an inch thick. Six months later I talked to another coiner who recollected having seen a larger piece of such gold. He said it had been marked on one side with a linear pattern of scrapes, and stained on the other face with tar."

"Tar!"

"Yes. But I have never seen such a sample with my own eyes. I only find *evidence* of its existence in coins—counterfeit guineas of a level of quality such that I myself am sometimes deceived by them!"

"So, 'twould appear that whoever has this gold, has hoarded it, and used to spend it, in the form of plates stained with tar. But from time to time he will deliver some of it up to a coiner—"

"Not *a* coiner but *the* coiner. Jack. Jack the Coiner. My Nemesis, and my prey, these last twelve years."

"Jack sounds like an interesting chap," Daniel allowed, "and I ween I shall learn more of him from you anon—but is it your hypothesis that he has a hoard of these gold sheets somewhere, and coins them from time to time?"

"No. They're of no use to him hoarded. If he had a hoard, he would coin every last ounce of it, as fast as his coiners could do the work. No, it is my hypothesis that Jack knows the owner of the hoard, and that from time to time that person, wanting some money to spend, takes some plates out, and brings them to Jack."

"Do you have any notion as to who the hoarder might be?"

"The answer is suggested by the tar, and the scrapes. It is coming from a ship."

"There is a vague association between tar and ships, but beyond that, I don't follow you," Daniel said.

"The information you are wanting is that, among sailors and officers of the French Navy, there is a legend—"

"Ah, in truth I *have* heard it!" Daniel exclaimed. "But I failed to draw the connexion. You refer to a legendary ship whose hull was plated with gold."

"Indeed."

"But 'twould seem that in your view this is no legend."

"I have studied it," Isaac announced. "I can now trace the descent of King Solomon's Gold from the pages of the Bible, down through the ages, to the hull of that ship, and thence to the samples that I have assayed in my laboratory in the Tower of London."

"Pray tell me the tale then!"

"Most of it is no tale at all. The Islands of King Solomon lie in the Pacific. There his gold rested, undisturbed by men, until round the time that you and I were young, and Huygens's clock began to tick. A Spanish fleet, driven by a typhoon far off the charted sea-lanes that join Acapulco to Manila, dropped anchor in the Solomons, and took on board certain provisions, including earth to pack round the galley-stoves to protect the planks of the ship from fire. During the voyage home to New Spain, the heat of the fire melted gold—or something that looked like it—out of the sand, and it pooled to form nuggets of astonishing fineness, which were discovered when the ships broke bulk in Acapulco. The Viceroy of New Spain, then just beginning a twenty-five-year reign, was not slow to send out ships to the Solomons to extract more of this gold, and bring it back to Mexico to be piled up in his personal hoard. At the end of his reign, he caused the Solomonic Gold to be loaded aboard his private brig, which sailed back to Spain in convoy with the Spanish treasure-fleet. They made it safe as far as Cadiz. But then the little brig foolishly sailed alone up to Bonanza, where the Viceroy had caused a villa to be built, in which he phant'sied he would enjoy a wealthy retirement. Before she could be unloaded, she was set upon in the night by pirates, dressed as Turks, and led by the infamous criminal known to us as Half-Cocked Jack, the King of the Vagabonds, and to the French as *L'Emmerdeur*. The gold was stolen and spirited away in long stages to Hindoostan, where most of it fell into the possession of a heathen potentate, an Amazon pirate-queen, black as char-coal, who had not the faintest understanding of what she had netted. But on those shores, Jack and his confederates used their ill-gotten gains to build a pirate-ship. And from some Dutch ship-wrights they had the notion—which was in no way a faulty one, as e'en a stopped Clock is correct twice daily—that if the hull of this ship were cladded, below the waterline, with sheets of smooth metal, she would afford no purchase for barnacles, and repel the attacks of the teredo."

" 'Tis a wholly reasonable idea," Daniel said.

" 'Twas a good idea, most strangely executed! For, vain and extravagant man that he was, this Jack decreed that the metal be wrought out of solid gold!"

"So the tale told by those French mariners was in no way fanciful," Daniel concluded.

"I should rather say, 'twas none the less true, for being fanciful!" Isaac returned.

"Do you know where that ship is now?" Daniel asked, trying not to sound nervous; for *he* knew.

"It is thought that she was christened *Minerva*. But this is not known with certainty, and is of little use, even if true, as hundreds of ships answer to that name. But I suspect that she still roams the seas, and calls at London from time to time, and that some commerce plays out between Jack the Coiner, and those who sail her. Plates of gold are taken out of her bilge—for make no mistake, they were stripped from her hull and replaced with copper, probably in some unfrequented Caribbean cove, many years ago—and delivered to Jack, who coins them into excellent guineas, with which he poisons Her Majesty's stock of money. That is the tale of Solomon's Gold, Daniel. I hoped you would find it a diverting yarn. Why do you look so distracted?"

"I find it very odd that the prize you have sought your entire life, should happen to rest in the hands of the man you describe as your Nemesis."

"My Nemesis, where Mint work is concerned. In other fields, I have other foes," Isaac reminded him shortly.

"That is beside my point. Why shouldn't the hoard of Solomonic Gold lie in a vault in Seville, or at the Vatican, or the Forbidden City of Peking? Of all the places in the world where this gold might have ended up, why should it be in the possession of Jack the Coiner—the one man you'd most like to see being dragged on a sledge to Tyburn?"

"Because its density exceeds that of gold, it is valuable to a counterfeiter."

"It is *more* valuable to an Alchemist. Do you suppose Jack *knows* as much, and do you suppose he is aware that you, Isaac, are an Alchemist?"

"He is a mere *criminal*."

"Yes, and a very cosmopolitan one, from the sounds of it."

"I assure you he has not the faintest comprehension of matters Al-chemical."

"Neither do I. *And yet I understand that you desire this gold!*"

"What does it matter? He knows that I wish to hunt him down and bring him to justice—that is enough."

"Isaac, you have a habit of under-estimating the intelligence of anyone who is *not you.* Perhaps this Jack is using the Solomonic Gold to bait you."

"What matters it if a *mouse* baits a *lion?*"

"Depends on whether the lion is being baited into single combat with that mouse, or into a pit-fall with sharpened stakes at the bot-tom."

"I do not think your analogy is applicable. But I am grateful for your expression of concern. Now let us end all tedious disputes about Jack, by ending Jack!"

"Did you say 'us'?"

"Yes! Yes, I did. As there are only two men in this room, I can only have meant, *you and I.* As we shared a room, and worked together, at the beginning of our lives, so shall we do now, as we near their ends."

"What possible use could I be in helping to apprehend Jack the Coiner?"

"You have come from America on a mysterious errand. You have traveled in the company of a notorious weigher, and I am told that you are up to some occult doings in a hole in the ground in Clerken-well."

"Not true, unless you count real estate development as one of the black arts."

"If you were now to announce yourself, to the criminal underworld of London, as a weigher, in possession of gold from America—"

"I beg your pardon, but I really do not wish to announce myself to the criminal underworld as *anything!*"

"But supposing you did, why, you might be able to establish con-tacts with Jack's subtile net-work of informants and Black-guards."

"That is the second time today I have heard 'Black-guard' spoken in those portentous tones. I thought a Black-guard was a boy who polished boots."

"Some of those boys have got rather big, and found employment even lower, and even blacker," Isaac remarked.

"Then I'll have nothing to do with any Black-guard."

"If you have heard some other man speaking the word to-day, 'twould seem that you already *do* have something to do with them," said Isaac, amused, "which would hardly surprise me considering the company you have been keeping."

Daniel was silent. But only because he could not divulge to Isaac that his only motive in speaking to the sort of man who spoke of the Black-guard—men such as Peter Hoxton—was to track down whatever remnants Hooke had left behind.

Isaac read his silence as submission. Given more time, Daniel might have disabused Isaac of any such ideas, and extricated himself. But a servant was knocking at the door. A minute earlier Daniel had heard someone calling briefly at the front door of the house, presumably to deliver a message, and now it had penetrated to the study, and interrupted their discourse at the worst possible moment for Daniel. He wondered whether the servant had been lurking outside the door, waiting to knock at some subtle signal from Isaac: *I have sprung the trap, now interrupt us lest he wriggle free!*

"Enter!" Isaac commanded, and in came the servant who'd admitted Daniel earlier, holding a rectangle of good paper with a few lines scrawled over it in a lazy, important hand. As Isaac deciphered the penmanship, and considered the import, and discussed it in a hushed, elliptical manner with his servant, Daniel had his first opportunity to review all that had passed since he had breezed into this room with a riddle concerning guineas.

What had he expected? He had expected that, at best, Isaac would be cool and distant. At worst, he'd know that Daniel was striving to preserve some memory of Hooke, and corresponding with and running errands for Leibniz, and would tear Daniel's beating heart out of his chest then and there, like an Aztec priest. Those had seemed the most likely outcomes. If some oracle had let him know in advance that he was to have a long, cordial, even friendly conversation with Isaac, he'd have accounted it a triumph. And maybe it was—but it was Isaac's triumph and not Daniel's. Whether or not Isaac knew of Daniel's concealed loyalty to Hooke and Leibniz, he had clearly got it into his mind that Daniel needed to be kept close, and kept busy.

"We've not even had time to broach the subject of Baron von Leibniz's pretensions concerning the calculus," Isaac announced in a chummy voice that was very odd coming from him, "and here it is time for me to be on my way."

"I consider myself fortunate indeed to have taken up as much of your time as I have done," Daniel said, trying not to sound ironic about it.

"The good fortune is all mine, and I assure you that the meeting I go to now shall never be half so enjoyable as this!" Isaac returned. "If the Mint were strictly a temple of Natural Philosophy—as it ought to be—supervising it would be pure pleasure. As it is, I waste many hours in meetings of a *political* nature." He was getting to his feet.

"Is it Whigs or Tories today, then?" Daniel asked, rising. From here on out it would be all banter: pleasant noises that might as well have been spoken in Iroquois.

"Germans," Isaac returned, offering him priority out the door. Catherine Barton, or someone, must have taught him manners.

"Really! They'll be running the country soon enough, why are they pestering you now?"

They paused in a hall so that Isaac could shrug off his scarlet robe and have a vest and coat thrown across his shoulders by a valet. "They don't pester *me*, but *other* men, of higher station—ramifications ensue," Isaac said. "I would offer to convey you somewhere, but my conveyance only has room for one. May I have a hackney summoned for you?"

"I'll walk, thank you," Daniel said. Isaac followed him into the vestibule, which was crowded. Two large men were in here, smelling of the street. Between them stood a vertical black box, open on one side to reveal a crimson leather seat. Isaac sidled into it, smoothing the skirts of his coat under him. A servant stood at the ready to slam the door to.

"I shall hear from you concerning the proposal that I made," Isaac predicted. "And do let's not forget to have a conversation, some day soon, about the calculus."

"Not a day passes without my thinking of it," Daniel answered. With that the door was latched shut. Isaac had vanished inside the black box. His voice came out of it clearly, "God save the Queen, Daniel," reminding Daniel that the only thing between them was a sheer black screen through which Isaac could see and hear everything, though he was quite invisible to anyone outside.

"God save the Queen," Daniel returned, and then he followed the sedan chair out the door and onto St. Martin's. Isaac was carried rapidly southwards, toward St. James's and Westminster and all things great and important. Daniel, not wanting the awkwardness of walking along abreast of Isaac's chair, went the other way.

Passing immediately through a gate at the head of the lane, he came out into an open plaza, squarish, about a bow-shot on a side. This was called Leicester Fields, and on three sides—including the one where Daniel had entered—it was now hemmed in by the sort of new town-houses that had started going up all round here after the Fire. But on the north edge—which Daniel was facing directly across a few hundred feet of open turf—it was walled off by one of the few remaining old-fashioned Tudor compounds: a congeries of red brick and half-timbered buildings called Leicester House. It had formerly been one of the few houses around London deemed suitable for royalty to dwell in, and had been used by diverse Tudor and Stuart princes as a palace. Elizabeth Stuart had dwelt there before she'd gone off to Europe to become the Winter Queen and to spawn Sophie and many others. Changes in the royal line had weakened the sentimental ties to this house, and the re-building of London in a new style had quite over-shadowed it and made it seem a mere English farm-house.

As Daniel came into Leicester Fields, he gazed in that direction curiously, trying to get his bearings, like a mariner looking for the old familiar stars. He saw a lot of horses and vehicles in front of the place, and felt a pang, supposing that the wreckers had arrived to tear it down. But as he strolled across the Fields, creating localized panics among sheep and chickens, he perceived that these were not rubbish-wagons but baggage-carts, and rather well-maintained ones at that. Among them was a carriage, a coach-and-four drawn by a matched set of black horses. A woman was alighting from that carriage, walking away from Daniel toward the house, and servants were drawn up in two lines to greet her. Daniel could not see anything of the woman, other than that she was petite, and trim. Her head was shrouded in a voluminous silk scarf covering a big hat or wig. And he was too far away, and his eyes were too far gone, to resolve lips, eyes, and noses on the faces of those servants. But something in their posture, and in the way they turned their faces and bodies toward the woman as she progressed across the court, told Daniel that they were smiling. They loved her.

At the apex of this formation, where the two lines of servants came together in front of the house's main entrance, stood a man who was not a servant: he was dressed in the clothes of a gentleman. But there was something odd about him, which Daniel could not make sense of until he went into movement, extending a leg to make a low bow, and accepting the woman's hand to kiss it. The man's skin was entirely black. The woman took his arm and the black man escorted her into Leicester House; the lines of servants broke up and everyone made him- or herself busy unloading the baggage carts, &c.

As there was nothing more to see, Daniel turned on his heel and ambled toward the edge of Leicester Fields; and as he did, he became aware that he was only one part of a general slow evacuation. Diverse tinkers, vagabonds, strolling gentlemen, and boot-blacks were also making their way towards the exits, and in the fronts of the new town-houses around the square, curtains were being drawn.

Leicester House
TEN SECONDS LATER

HE WAS OBLIGED TO PURSUE her to the upper storey, for she talked as she went. She stormed a long dangerous wooden staircase and then faltered, only for an instant, as a great splintery-looking wooden door had presented itself in her way. By the time Dappa could get the words "Allow me—" past his lips, she'd clobbered it with her shoulder, got it open, and vanished into a big-sounding space yonder. The door remained ajar, shuddering from end to end.

He took the last few steps with some care. *His* legs, anyway, were unused to pushing off against things that did not pitch and roll. After all he'd been through, he didn't want to die falling down a nasty old stairway in a strange English house.

They were now in an isosceles triangle made by the converging planes of the roof and a somewhat dodgy floor of loose deals. In any house made to normal scale it would have been pigeon-nesting space, but here it was large enough to throw a country dance.

Dappa wished he had some sailors with him, so that they could all share a good laugh at this room. Persons who fell into the habit of dwelling on dry land soon acquired queer and comical ways. They forgot that everything in God's creation moved, and they fell into the phant'sy that an object, such as a wardrobe, could be dragged to a certain position in a room such as this one, covered with a sail, and let go of, without in any way being lashed down, and that twenty years later one might come back and find it just where it had been left.

Certain of these people then let themselves go altogether. Rooms such as this one were the monuments that they built to themselves. The draped furniture, crated paintings, and heaps of books were as chock-a-block as ice-floes driven into a blind cove by a boreal breeze. Spiders had been at work: a Navy of diligent riggers working day and night to tie it all down and lash it smartly together. Eliza was undoing their work, moving down the length of the room in carefully considered lunges and clever sideways darts. Her gown was growing a diaphanous train of cobwebs, and her wake in the air was visible as a serrated line of dust-explosions and plunging vortices. She was thinking hard about which way to go next, and had forgotten to talk.

Wee dormers were cut into the pitch of the roof every few yards, shedding plentiful light, and giving Dappa an excellent prospect of the many ways he could soil his dark suit if he attempted to follow her. Forgetting that this house could be trusted not to move under his feet, he reached up with one hand and braced it absent-mindedly on a tie-beam running between rafters above his head. A small avalanche of pale gray bat-shit tumbled down his sleeve and made itself one with the expensive black wool. " 'Tis well my head's grizzled *to begin with,*" he muttered, and then was struck by how well his voice carried down the utterly silent room.

"Beg pardon?"

"Never mind, only grumbling and muttering."

"It is all right," she called back in her alert way. "Do keep in mind, though, that when we are in the presence of others—especially, Persons of Quality—"

"Then you are my noble patroness," Dappa said, "and I the ink-stained wretch. So very ink-stained, as to've become black from head to toe, save the soles of my feet, where I walk about collecting slave-narratives—"

"And the palm of your hand, where you grip your quill. I recognize these phrases from the Apology of your new manuscript," she said, favoring him with a trace of a smile.

"Ah, you've read it!"

"Of course I have," she answered, affronted. "Why ever not?"

"I was afraid you might have grown weary of slave-tales. I fear they are repetitious. 'I was seized by raiders from the next village . . . traded to the tribe across the river . . . marched to the edge of the great water, marked with a hot iron, put aboard ship, dragged off of it half dead, now I chop sugar cane.' "

"All human stories are in some sense repetitious, if you boil them down so far. Yet people fall in love."

"What?"

"They fall in love, Dappa. With a *particular* man or woman, and no one else. Or a woman will have a baby, and love that baby forever . . . no matter how similar its tale might seem to those of other babies."

"You are saying," Dappa said, "that we make connections with other souls, despite the sameness—"

"There is no *sameness*. If you looked down upon the world from above, like an albatross, you might phant'sy there was some sameness among the people crowding the land below you. But we are not albatrosses, we see the world from ground level, from within our own bodies, through our own eyes, each with our own frame of reference, which changes as we move about, and as others move about us. This *sameness* is a conceit of yours, an author's hobgoblin, something you fret about in your hammock late at night."

"In truth, I have my own cabin, and do my fretting in a *bed* nowadays."

Eliza did not answer. Quite some time ago she had reached the far end of the room, which Dappa guessed was the front of the house, and during this exchange she had been peering out across Leicester Fields through a tiny round window. If this were a ship, she'd be keeping her eye on the weather. But it wasn't; so what could she be looking at?

"All that is wanted," she continued distractedly, "is for a reader to recognize a kindred soul in *a single one* of your narratives, and that will suffice to prove, for that reader, that Slavery is an abomination."

"Perhaps we should be printing them up separately, as pamphlets."

"Broadsheets are cheaper, and may be posted on walls, *et cetera.*"

"Ah, you are far ahead of me."

"Distribution is my concern—Collection is yours."

"What are you looking out the window for? Afraid you were followed?"

"When a Duchess comes off a foreign ship in the Pool and travels through London in a train of a dozen coaches and waggons, she *is* followed," Eliza said levelly. "I am taking a census of my followers."

"See anyone you know?"

"There is an aged Puritan I think I recognize . . . and some nasty Tories . . . and too many curtain-twitching neighbors to count." She turned away from the window and demanded, in a wholly new tone of voice, "Anything good from Boston?"

"They are mostly Angolans there, and my command of that language is not what it used to be. The Barkers have become so aggressive in Massachusetts—handing out pamphlets on street-corners . . ."

This, which he'd thought she'd find interesting intelligence, bored her right back to gazing out the window. Of course she would know precisely what the Barkers were up to in Massachusetts. "The result," he continued, "is that the slave-owners there are more watchful than the ones in, say, Brazil, and when they see their slave having a lengthy conversation with a strange well-dressed Blackamoor—"

"You did not collect anything useful in Boston," she said shortly.

"Am I too discursive in my responses, your grace?"

"Am I too much the Editor?" She was done peering, and was returning to him.

"This room is the reverse of a Bilge," Dappa realized. "That is, if you took *Minerva* and capsized her, so that her masts were pointed straight down towards the center of the earth, then her keel would be high and dry, like this ridge-beam above our heads, and the hull-planks would form a pitched roof."

"And it would still be crowded with stored objects, like this garret."

"Is that what you call it?"

"Starving writers live in them."

"Is that an offer of lodgings, or a threat of starvation?"

"It depends on whether you bring back some apt Narrations from your next sea-voyage," she said with a smile. She'd come abreast of him now, and took his arm. "Where to next?"

"Boston again."

They could see down those stairs now. Servants were standing anxiously below, coming in earshot. "And your grace?" Dappa added, distinctly.

"Oh—do you mean, where am I off to next?"

"Yes, my lady. You've just returned from Hanover, I gad?"

"Antwerp," she whispered. "I am here now, Dappa, for—what do you call it—the long haul."

They descended the stairs—a simple procedure made longer and more complicated than it ought to have been by the helpful strivings of the servants, and of some members of the Duchess's household. Dappa's ear, ever tuned to languages, picked out an exchange in German between two young women. They were dressed as if they were merely Gentle. But Dappa thought they carried themselves Nobly.

DAPPA HAD FIRST SEEN ELIZA some twenty years earlier. He'd been eager to hate her. He, Jack, van Hoek, and Vrej Esphahnian had sailed from Vera Cruz on a ship full of gold, bound for London or Amsterdam, and had diverted to Qwghlm only because of Jack's infatuation with this woman. The letter that had lured them there had turned out to be a trick, a forgery from the hand of the Jesuit father Édouard de Gex, and *Minerva* had fallen into a trap laid for them there by the French. A kind of justice had been served on Jack. Dappa, van Hoek, and the crew of *Minerva* had been allowed to sail away, but only after the gold in *Minerva*'s hold had been seized by the French. They'd been left with nothing more than the thin plates of gold that had been put *on* the hull, below the water-line, when the ship had been built on a Hindoostan beach. That, and the ship itself. *Minerva* was a home and an income, but only as long as they continued sailing her to and fro. They had, in other words, been condemned to spend the rest of their lives in dangerous toils and wanderings. This suited van Hoek perfectly. Not so much Dappa.

They did not own *Minerva*. The owners were, in order of precedence, Queen Kottakkal of Malabar, Electress Sophie of Hanover, van Hoek, Dappa, Jack Shaftoe, and some old comrades of theirs who at last report were dwelling on the isle of Queenah-Kootah, off Borneo. For the most part these investors were far away and had not the faintest idea of how to reach them, which were good investors to have. Even Sophie reigned over a land-locked Electorate. But in time they received a message written in her hand and bearing her seal, letting them know that she was naming Eliza, Duchess of Arcachon and of Qwghlm, as her proxy, and that they should report to her whenever they dropped anchor in the Pool of London, to hand over Sophie's share of the profits, and to be managed.

Dappa had gone to the first such meeting with dim expectations. He and the others had heard so much of this Duchess's beauty from Jack, and, at the same time, had learned to harbor such grave reservations as to Jack's powers of discernment, that he could only expect to be confronted with some one-toothed, poxy hag.

The event was rather different. To begin with, the woman had been all of about thirty-five years old. She had all of her teeth and had come through smallpox with only moderate scarring. So she was, for a start, not loathsome. She had keen blue eyes and yellow hair, which of course looked bizarre to Dappa. But he'd grown used to van Hoek, a red-head, which proved he could adjust to anything. Her small nose and mouth would have been considered beautiful among the Chinese, and in due time he understood that many European men's tastes ran along similar lines. If her nose and cheeks had not been disfigured by freckles, Dappa might have been able to bring himself round to thinking she was attractive. But she was small-waisted and bony. In every way, Eliza was the opposite of voluptuous. Voluptuous was what Dappa liked, and from the looks of the sculptures and frescoes he observed round London and Amsterdam, his tastes seemed to be shared by many a European man.

The topic of their first meeting had been Accounting. And so even if Dappa had felt the slightest attraction for the woman at the beginning of the day, it would long since have vanished when he stumbled out the door of her town-house twelve hours later. Eliza, it turned out, had a vicious head for numbers, and wanted to know where every farthing had gone since *Minerva*'s keel had been laid. Considering all they'd been through, her questions had been impertinent. Many a man would have back-handed her across the face, most would have stormed out. But Eliza was representing one of the most powerful persons in Christendom, a woman who could destroy *Minerva* in so many different ways, that her only difficulty would lay in choice of weapon. Dappa had checked his temper partly because of that, but also partly because he knew in his heart that *Minerva* ought to keep her books more carefully. They had lost their two members who knew how to keep accounts: Moseh de la Cruz, who had gone to colonize the country north of the Rio Grande, and Vrej Esphahnian, who had given his life revenging himself on the ones who had ensnared them. Since then, the books had become a mess. He'd known for a long time that a settling of accounts would have to come some day and that it would be ugly and painful. It could have come about in worse ways than over a table with this funny-looking young Duchess.

In the years since, they'd met from time to time to settle accounts. She'd learned of his strange habit of collecting and writing down slave-stories ("Why do you spend so much of our money on paper and ink!? What are you doing, throwing it overboard?") and she had become his publisher ("We can at least endeavour to make your hobby pay its own way."). Years had gone by. He had wondered how she would age. Unable to think of her as a woman (for to him Queen Kottakkal, six feet tall and three hundred pounds, was a woman), he had made up his mind, after seeing a performance of *A Midsummer Night's Dream* in London, that she was a færy. What did an old, or even a middle-aged, færy-queen look like?

THEY SAT DOWN now in a little upstairs chamber of Leicester House, less formal than a Withdrawing Room, and she fearlessly took a seat facing a window. Moreover, a west-facing window that was admitting red sunset-light. Dappa studied her.

"What do you see?" she asked, studying him back.

"I can no longer see you as anything other than my friend, patroness, and Lady, Eliza," he answered. "Marks of age, health, experience, and character, which a stranger might phant'sy he perceived in your face, are invisible to me."

"But what do you really see?"

"I have not looked at enough skinny white women to be an apt judge. But I see that bone structure is a good thing to have, and that you have it; lo, the Creator hung you on an excellent frame."

She found this curiously amusing. "Have you ever seen an Arcachon, or an honest rendering of one?"

"Only you, my lady."

"I mean, an hereditary Arcachon. Suffice it to say that they are *not* hung on good frames, and they well know it. And I owe my position in the world today, not to wit or courage or goodness, but to my being hung on a good frame, and being able to propagate it. And what think you of that, Dappa?"

"If it provides you with a sort of purchase on the sheer cliff that the world is, from which to make use of your abundant wit, courage, and goodness, why, here's to bone structure!" Dappa returned, raising a teacup high.

She lost a struggle with a smile. Creases flourished around her eyes and mouth, but they did not look bad on her; they looked well earned and fairly won. She raised her own teacup and clinked it against Dappa's. "Now you really do sound like the Apology of a book," she said, and sipped.

"Are we back to talking of that, my lady?"

"We are."

"I'd hoped I could ask you about those Hanoverian Countesses who seem to've joined your household in Antwerp."

"What makes you think they are only Countesses?"

Dappa gave her a sharp look, but she had a glimmer in her eye to suggest that she was only baiting him. " 'Twas only a guess," he said.

"Then go on guessing, for I'll tell you no more than you've already discerned."

"Why Antwerp? Meeting with the Duke of Marlborough?"

"The less I tell you, the less likely you are to be interrogated by the sort of men who loiter in my front lawn with spyglasses."

"Very well . . . if you put it that way . . . perhaps we should speak of my book!" Dappa said nervously.

She got a contented look, as if to say that this was a much more satisfactory topic of conversation, and settled herself for a moment—which gave Dappa a warning that she was about to unburden herself of a little address she'd composed ahead of time. "What you must never forget, Dappa, is that I myself might not be opposed to Slavery, had I not myself been a slave in Barbary! To most English people, it seems perfectly reasonable. The slavers put out the story that it is not so very cruel, and that the slaves are happy. Most in Christendom are willing to believe these lies, absurd as they are to you and me. People believe Slavery is not so bad, because they have no personal experience of it—it takes place in Africa and America, out of sight and out of mind to the English, who love sugar in their tea and care not how 'twas made."

"I notice you do not sweeten yours," Dappa mentioned, raising his cup.

"And from the fact that I still have teeth attached to my excellent bone structure, you may infer that I have *never* used sugar," she returned. "Our only weapon against this willful ignorance is stories. The stories that you alone are writing down. I have in one of my boxes down stairs a little packet of letters from English men and women that all go something like this: 'I have never had the least objection to Slavery, however your book recently fell under my eye, and, though most of the slave-narratives contained in it were mawkish and dull, one in particular struck a chord in my heart, and I have since read it over and over, and come to understand the despicable, nay execrable crime that Slavery is . . .' "

"Which one? Which of the stories do these letters refer to?" Dappa asked, fascinated.

"That is the problem, Dappa: each of them refers to a different one. It seems that if you put enough stories out before the public, many a reader will find *one* that speaks to him. But there is no telling *which*."

"What we've been doing, then, is a bit like firing grapeshot," Dappa mused. "Chances are that a ball will strike home—but there's no telling which—so, best fire a lot of 'em."

"And grapeshot is a useful tactic sometimes," Eliza said, "but it never sank a ship, did it?"

"No, my lady, grapeshot can never do that."

"I say we have now fired enough grapeshot. It has had all the effect it is ever going to have. What we need now, Dappa, is a cannon-ball."

"One slave-tale, that everyone will take note of?"

"Just so. And that is why it does not trouble me that you failed to sweep up any more grapeshot in Boston. Oh, write down what you have. Send it to me. I'll publish it. But after that, no more scatter-shot tactics. You must begin to use your critical faculties, Dappa, and look for the slave-story that has something to it beyond the bathos that they all have in common. Look for the one that will be our cannon-ball. It is time for us to sink some slave-ships."

The Kit-Cat Clubb

THAT EVENING

"I AM QUITE CERTAIN THAT we are being watched," Daniel said.

Dappa laughed. "Is that why you were at such pains to sit facing the window? I venture that no one in the history of this Clubb has ever desired a view of yonder alley."

"You might do well to come round the table, and sit beside me."

"I know what I'd see: a lot of Whigs gaping at the tame Neeger. Why don't *you* come and sit beside *me*, so that we may enjoy a view of that naked lady reclining in that strangely long and narrow painting above your head?"

"She's not *naked*," Daniel retorted crossly.

"On the contrary, Dr. Waterhouse, I see incontrovertible signs of nakedness in her."

"But to call her *naked* sounds prurient," Daniel objected. "She is professionally attired, for an *odalisque*."

"Perhaps all the eyeballs you phant'sy are watching *us,* are, truth be told, fixed on *her.* She is a new painting, I can still smell the varnish. Perhaps we should instead go sit 'neath yonder dusty sea-scape," Dappa suggested, waving in the direction of another long narrow canvas that was crowded with stooped and shivering Dutch clam-diggers.

"I happened to see you greeting the Duchess of Arcachon-Qwghlm earlier," Daniel confessed.

"She goes by de la Zeur—'tis less formal that way," Dappa broke in.

Daniel was brought up short for a moment, then finally got a wry look on his face, and shook his head. "You are strangely giddy. I should never have ordered you usquebaugh."

"Too long on land."

"When do you sail for Boston?"

"Ah, to business! We'd hoped to depart in the second half of April. Now, we think early May. What do you wish us to fetch from there?"

"Twenty years' work. I do hope you shall have a care with it."

"In what form is the work? Manuscripts?"

"Yes, and machinery."

"That is an odd word. What does it mean?"

"I beg your pardon. It is theatre-jargon. When an angel descends, or a soul lights up to heaven, or a volcano erupts, or any other impossible thing seems to happen on the stage, the people behind the scenes, who've made it happen, give the name *machinery* to the diverse springs, levers, rigging, *et cetera* used to create the illusion."

"I did not know you ran a theatre in Boston."

"You jest, sir, the Bostonians would never have allowed it—they'd have sent me packing to Providence."

"Then how comes it you have machinery in Boston?"

"I used the term ironically. I built a machine there—across the river actually, in a shack about halfway 'tween Charlestown and Harvard—a machine that has nothing to do with theatrical illusions. I need you to bring it to me."

"Then I must know, in order: Is it dangerous? Is it bulky? Is it delicate?"

"In order: yes, no, yes."

"In what wise is it dangerous?"

"I've no idea. But I'll tell you this, 'tis only dangerous if you turn the crank, and give it something to think on."

"Then I'll take the crank off and keep it in my cabin, and use it only to bash pirates on the head," announced Dappa. "And I shall forbid the crew to hold conversations with your machinery, unless they are devoid of intellectual stimulation: nothing beyond a polite 'Good day, machinery, how goes it with thee, does the stump of thy crank ache of a damp morning?'"

"I suggest you pack the parts in barrels, stuffed with straw. You shall also find many thousands of small rectangular cards with words and numbers printed on them. These are likewise to be sealed in watertight casks. Enoch Root may already have seen to it by the time you reach Charlestown."

At the mention of Enoch's name, Dappa glanced away from Daniel's face, as if the older man had committed an indiscretion, and picked up his dram to take a sip. And that was all the opening needed for the Marquis of Ravenscar to irrupt upon their conversation. He appeared so suddenly, so adroitly, it was as if some *machinery* had injected him into the Kit-Cat Clubb through a trap-door.

"From one *odalisque* to another, Mr. Dappa! Haw! Is it not so! For I take it that you are the writer."

"I am *a* writer, my lord," Dappa answered politely.

"I hope I do not offend by confessing I've not read your books."

"On the contrary, my lord," Dappa said, "there is nothing quite so civilized as to be recognized in public places as the author of books no one has read."

"If my good friend Dr. Waterhouse were polite enough to make introductions, I should not have to rely 'pon guess-work; but he was raised by Phanatiques."

"It is too late for formalities now," Daniel answered. "When another begins a conversation with a cryptickal outburst on *odalisques*, what is there for a polite gentleman to do?"

"Not cryptickal at all! Not in the slightest!" protested the Marquis of Ravenscar. "Why, 'tis known to all London now, at" (checking his watch) "nine o'clock, that at" (checking his watch a second time) "four o'clock, Mr. Dappa was on hand to greet the Duchess of Arcachon and of Qwghlm!"

"I told you!" Daniel said, in an aside to Dappa, and put his two fingers to his eyes, then pointed them across the room toward the phant'sied spies and observers.

"You told him what!?" Roger demanded.

"That people were watching us."

"They're not watching *you*," Roger said, highly amused. Which told Daniel, infallibly, that they *were*. "Why should anyone watch *you*? They're watching Dappa, making the rounds of the *odalisques*!"

"There you go again—what on earth—?" Daniel demanded.

Dappa explained, "He alludes to a sort of legend, only whispered by *discreet well-bred* Londoners, but openly bandied about by *drunken merry lords*, that the Duchess was once an *odalisque*."

"Figuratively—?"

"Literally a harem-slave of the Great Turk in Constantinople."

"What a bizarre notion—Roger, how could you?"

Roger, slightly nettled by Dappa, raised his eyebrows and shrugged.

Dappa proclaimed, "England being a nation of clam-diggers and sheep-shearers, must forever be a net importer of fantastickal tales. Silk, oranges, perfume, and strange yarns must all be supplied from across the seas."

"If only you knew," Daniel returned.

"I agree with Mr. Dappa!" Roger said forcefully. "The story of his *tête-à-tête* with the Duchess is racing up and down Grub Street like cholera, and will be in newspapers tomorrow at cock-crow!"

And then he was gone, as if by trap-door.

"You see? If you were more discreet—"

"Then Grub Street would be unawares. Nothing would be written, nothing printed, concerning me, or the Duchess. No one would hear of us—no one would buy my next book."

"Ah."

"Light dawns 'pon your phizz, Doctor."

" 'Tis a novel, strange form of commerce, of which I was unawares until just now."

"Only in London," Dappa said agreeably.

"But it is not the strangest form of commerce that goes on in this city," Daniel pressed on.

Dappa visibly put on an innocent face. "Do you have some strange yarn to set beside my lord Ravenscar's?"

"Much stranger. And, note, 'tis a *domestic* yarn, not imported. Dappa, do you recollect when we were being harried in Cape Cod Bay by the flotilla of Mr. Ed Teach, and you put me to work, down in the bilge?"

"You were in the *hold*. We do not put *elderly doctors* in the *bilge*."

"All right, all right."

"I remember that you obliged us by smashing up some old crockery to make ammunition for the blunderbusses," Dappa said.

"Yes, and *I* remember that the location of that old crockery was pricked down, with admirable clarity, on a sort of bill posted on a beam next the staircase. A diagram, shewing how the hold, and the bilge, were packed with diverse goods."

"There you go again with your confusion of 'hold' and 'bilge.' We do not pack goods in the bilge, as it is generally full of what I will euphemistically call *water*, which rapidly turns *goods* into *bads*. If you doubt it, I'll pack some of your machinery in the bilge on our return voyage this summer, and you may see its condition 'pon arrival. If you had any idea of the foulness—"

Daniel was showing Dappa his palms. "Not necessary, my good man. Yet your lading-diagram *does* include the bilge, and all that lies in that foulness, does it not?"

"Are you referring to the *ballast*?"

"I suppose I am."

"The *ballast* is carefully diagrammed, because it affects the balance and the trim of the ship," Dappa said. "From time to time we must shift a few tons this way or that, to compensate for an uneven load, and then it is of course useful to have a diagram of where it is."

"As I recollect that diagram, the bottom-most hull-planks of the ship are covered with flat rectangular iron pigs, laid down side by side, like floor-tiles."

"Kentledge, 'tis called. We also have some cracked cannons and old faulty cannonballs down there."

"Atop that, you have piled many tons of rounded stones."

"Shingle from a Malabar beach. Some use sand, but we use shingle, because it does not foul the pumps."

"It is atop the shingle that you pile up casks of shot, salt, water, and other heavy goods."

"As is the common—nay, universal—practice on non-capsizing ships."

"But I recall that another layer of ballast was shewn on this diagram. It was below any casks, below the shingle, below the scrap metal, below even the kentledge. It was the thinnest possible layer, a mere membrane, and on the diagram it looked like onion-skin. It was pressed against the tarry inner surface of the hull-planks themselves, and it went by some name such as anti-fouling plates."

"What of it?"

"Why put anti-fouling plates on the *inside*?"

"They are spares. You must have noticed that we carry extra stores of *everything*, Dr. Waterhouse. *Minerva*'s hull is clad in copper sheets—she's famous for it—and the last time we had a coppersmith make up an order of such material, we had him make more than we needed, so as to get a better price, and to have some in reserve."

"Are you certain you are not confusing them with the spares that are stowed in crates near the foremast step? I seem to recall sitting on them."

"Some are stored there. Others are stored against the inside of the hull-planks, under the kentledge, as you described."

"What an odd place to store anything. To get at them, one would have to unload the ship entirely, pump out the unspeakable contents of the bilge, shovel out tons of shingle, and winch up the massive pigs of kentledge, one by one."

Dappa did not respond, but had taken to drumming his fingers on the table irritably.

"It seems more like buried treasure than ballast."

"If you'd care to test your hypothesis, Doctor, you may do so the next time we are dry-docked, provided you show up with your own shovel."

"Is that what you say to inquisitive Customs inspectors?"

"We are more polite to them—as *they* generally are to *us*."

"But politeness aside, the underlying meaning is the same. The hold may be emptied, if some official demands it. *Minerva* shall then bob like a cork, but she shall not capsize, thanks to the ballast. But those anti-fouling plates may not be inspected unless the ballast is removed, which would render the vessel unstable—it could only be done if she were beached, or in dry-dock—as she was just a few weeks ago. No Customs inspector ever demands *that*, does he?"

"This is a very odd conversation," Dappa observed.

"On an arbitrary numerical scale of conversational oddness, rang-ing from one to ten, with ten being the oddest conversation I've ever had, and seven being the oddest conversation I have in a typical day, this rates no better than five," Daniel returned. "But to make it less odd for you, I shall now speak directly. I know what those plates are made of. I know that you take some out from time to time, when you are in London, and I know that they find their way into the coinage. It does not matter to me how this is done, or why. But I say to you that you are putting yourselves in danger every time you spend the treasure from that bilge. You imagine that it may be fused, in a coiner's crucible, with like metal from other sources, and that, once it has been thus con-fused, it has gone out into the world, and can never be traced back to you. But I say that there is one man, at least, who is not con-fused in the slightest, and who has drawn to within a hair's breadth of divining your secret. You may find him at the Tower of London most days."

Dappa had been greatly disquieted early in this little speech, but then had got a distracted, calculating look, as if reckoning how quickly *Minerva* could weigh anchor and get out of the Pool. "And you tell me this—why? To be good?"

"As you were good to me, Dappa, when Blackbeard called for me by name, and you refused to give me up."

"Oh. We did not do that out of *goodness*, but *stubbornness*."

"Then my warning to you is strictly an act of Christian charity," Daniel said.

"God bless you, Doctor!" Dappa replied, but he was still wary.

"Until such time as we arrive at an understanding concerning the disposition of the gold," Daniel added.

"There is something in this word *disposition* that makes me leery. How do you imagine we'll *dispose* of it?"

"You have to get rid of it before it is found by the gentleman I spoke of," Daniel pointed out. "But if you coin it, 'twill be as if you sailed *Minerva* under the guns of the Tower at noon, and ran those sheets of gold up the yard-arms."

"But what good is it, if not coined?"

"Gold has other uses," Daniel said. "Of which I shall tell you more some day. But not today. For we are approached by Peer, and must bring the oddness of our discourse down to a value of one or two on the scale I mentioned earlier."

"Peer? Who or what is Peer?"

"For a man who, moments ago, was lecturing me 'pon the workings of Grub Street, you've not been attending to your newspapers at all, have you?"

"I know it exists, how it works, and that it's important, but—"

"I read the papers every day. Let me tell you quickly then: there is a newspaper called *Ye Lens* which was started by Whigs, when their Juncto held power; several clever men write for it; Peer is not one of them."

"You mean, he doesn't write for the *Ye Lens?*"

"No, I mean he is not very clever."

"How'd he get the job, then?"

"By being in the House of Lords, and always taking the Whig side."

"Ah, so he *is* a peer!"

"A Peer of the Realm, with writerly ambitions. And as he writes for the *Lens*, and a lens is something you peer through, he has given himself the pen-name of Peer."

"This is the longest prolog to an introduction I've ever heard," Dappa remarked. "When is he actually going to show up?"

"I believe he—they—are waiting for you to notice them," Daniel said, pointing with his eyeballs. "Brace yourself."

Dappa narrowed his eyes, flared his nostrils, and then torqued himself round in his chair until he had—heeding Daniel's sage advice—braced one elbow on the table.

Facing him from roughly twelve feet away were the Marquis of Ravenscar, planted stolidly on the booze-slickened Kit-Cat floorboards, and an even better-dressed chap, who was dangling by both arms from one of the Clubb's low-hanging beams, his impeccably shod feet swinging back and forth just a few inches above the floor.

When this man saw that Dappa was looking his direction, he let go and dropped to the floor with a loud, chesty "Hoo!" His knees bent deeply, creating alarming strains in the crotch of his breeches, and allowing his knuckles to dangle near the floor. After making certain he'd caught Dappa's eye, he moved in a waddling gait to the Marquis of Ravenscar, who was standing still as a star, his face pinched up in a pickled smile.

Peer now pursed his lips, thrust them out as far as they would go, and, glancing back frequently to make sure he still had Dappa's attention, began to make little "Hoo! Hoo!" noises while circling cautiously around Roger. After completing a full orbit of Roger, he shuffled in closer, leaned in so that he was almost nuzzling Roger's shoulder, and began to make snuffling noises whilst cocking his head this way and that. Noting something apparently caught in the tresses of Roger's splendid wig, he raised one hand off the floor, reached into the luxuriant mass of curls, pinched something tiny, pulled it out, examined it, gave it a good thorough sniffing, then popped it into his mouth and began to make exaggerated chewing noises.

Then, in case Dappa had glanced away during this, he sidled around Roger and repeated the performance some half-dozen times, until even Roger became sick of it, raised one hand in the mildest of threats, and muttered, "Oh, will you stop it!"

Peer's response was extreme: he jumped back out of cuffing-range, came to rest on his knuckles and the balls of his feet, made excited screeching noises (or as near as a member of the House of Lords could come to it), then sprang into the air while flinging his arms above his head. He grabbed the beam again, knocking loose a shower of dust that sifted down, stained his white wig gray, and caused him to sneeze—which was most unfortunate, as he'd been taking snuff. A bolo of reddish-brown mucus hurtled out of his nose and made itself fast to his chin.

The Kit-Cat Clubb had become quiet as a monastery. Perhaps three dozen men were in the place. By and large, they were of a mind to find nearly *anything* funny. Rarely did a minute tick away without all conversation in the Clubb being drowned out by a storm-burst of booming laughter from one table or another. But there was something in Peer's performance so queer that it had shut them all up. Daniel, who had phant'sied that the crowding and the hubbub gave him and Dappa some sort of privacy, now felt even more exposed, and acutely spied upon, than ever.

The Marquis of Ravenscar swaggered toward Dappa. Behind him, Peer dropped from the rafters and got busy with a Belgian gros-point lace handkerchief. After Roger had moved along for a few paces, Peer followed him, cringing along in Roger's wake.

"Dr. Waterhouse. Mr. Dappa," said Roger with tremendous aplomb. "It is good to see you both again."

"And you likewise, *et cetera,*" answered Daniel shortly, as Dappa had been temporarily robbed of the power of speech.

Conversations resumed, tentatively, around the Clubb.

"I pray you will not take it amiss if I refrain from picking lice out of your hair, as my lord Wragby has been so considerate as to do for me."

"It's not even my hair, Roger."

"May I introduce to you, Dappa, and re-introduce to you, Daniel, my lord Walter Raleigh Waterhouse Weem, Viscount Wragby and Rector of Scanque, Member of Parliament, and Fellow of the Royal Society."

"Hullo, Uncle Daniel!" said Peer, suddenly straightening up. "Very clever of someone to dress him up in a suit of clothing! Was that your conceit?"

Dappa was staring sidelong at Daniel. "I forgot to mention that

Peer is my half-great-nephew once removed, or something like that," Daniel explained to him, behind his hand.

"Who are you talking to, uncle?" Peer inquired, looking past Dappa's head into a void. Then, with a shrug, he continued, "Do you phant'sy my demonstration worked? I did ever so much *research*, to get it right."

"I've no idea, Wally," Daniel returned, and then looked over at Dappa, who was still frozen in the sidelong-glare attitude. "Dappa, did you understand, from what you just observed, that my lord Wragby, here, is a member of my lord Ravenscar's ape-tribe, and that he plays a submissive role, fully acknowledging my lord Ravenscar's dominance?"

"Who are you talking to?" said Peer for the second time.

"To whom are you talking!" Dappa corrected him.

A few moments' silence from Peer, greatly savoured by Roger and Daniel. Peer raised one hand, pointed his index finger at Dappa as if holding him at bay with a pistol, and turned to Daniel with his mouth a-jar.

"What you didn't know, my nephew," Daniel said, "is that Dappa was, at a very young age, taken aboard ship by pirates as a sort of pet. And these pirates, being a polyglot group, amused themselves by training Dappa to speak twenty-five different languages fluently."

"Twenty-five different languages!" Peer exclaimed.

"Yes. Including better English than you, as you just saw."

"But . . . but he doesn't actually *understand* any of them," Peer said.

"No more than a parrot does, when it squawks out a demand for a cracker," Daniel affirmed, then let out a squawk of his own as Dappa kicked him in the shin under the table.

"What a remarkable feat! You should exhibit him!"

"What do you think I'm doing right now?"

"How was the weather yesterday?" Peer inquired of Dappa, in French.

"In the morning it was miserable and rainy," Dappa returned. *"After noon I thought it would clear but, alas, it was still overcast until nightfall. Only as I was getting ready for bed did I begin to see stars shining through gaps between clouds. Could I trouble you for a cracker?"*

"I say, the French pirate who taught him that trick must have been an educated man!" Peer exclaimed. Then he got a look on his face as if he were thinking. Daniel had learned, in his almost seventy years, not to expect much of people who got such looks, because thinking really was something one ought to do all the time. "One would suppose there would be no point in holding a conversation with a man who does not understand what he is saying. And yet he described yes-

terday's weather better than I could! In fact, I think I'll use his wording in tomorrow's edition!" Again, now, the thoughtful look. "If he
could relate other experiences—such as his *tête-à-tête* with the
Duchess—as faithfully as he recalls the weather, it would make my interview with him ever so much easier. I had come prepared to do it
all in grunts and sign language!" And Peer gave a note-book in his
hip-pocket an ominous pat.

"I suppose that whenever one speaks in the abstract—which is to
say, most of the time—what one is really doing is interacting with
some sort of image that is held in the mind," Dappa said. "For example, yesterday's weather is not here in the Kit-Cat Clubb with us. I
cannot feel yesterday's rain on my skin, nor can I see yester-eve's stars
with my eyes. When I describe these things to you (in French or any
other language) I am really engaging in some sort of internal colloquy with a stored image inside of my brain. It is an image I may call
up on demand, as a Duke might demand that a certain painting of
his be brought down out of the garret. Once it is before my mind's
eye, I may see it as if it were there, and describe it."

"That is all well and good for recollecting what you have gathered
in through your senses, and stored in the garret, as it were," Peer
said. "So I could ask you to relate your observations of the Duchess of
Qwghlm today, and rely on your account. But as you do not understand the conversation you had with her, or indeed the one you are
having with me now, I fear your *interpretation* of what went on at
Leicester House might be wide of the mark." He spoke haltingly, un-
sure of how to converse with someone who didn't understand what
he was saying.

Preying on this, Daniel inquired, "But how could he interpret *anything* if he didn't understand it?"

This stopped Peer's gob for a few awkward moments.

"I would refer you to the work of Spinoza," Dappa said, "whose
words are of course perfect gibberish to me, but who wrote in his
Ethics, 'The order and connexion of ideas is the same as the order and
connexion of things.' Meaning that if there are two things, call them A
and B, that have a particular relationship to each other, for example,
my lord Wragby's wig, and my lord Wragby's head, and if I have in my
mind an idea of my lord Wragby's wig, call it alpha, and an idea of his
head, call it beta, then the relationship between alpha and beta is the
same as that between A and B. And owing to this property of minds, it
is possible for me to construct in my head an whole universe of ideas,
yet each idea will relate to all of the other ideas in precisely the same
way that the things represented by those ideas relate to one another;
lo, 'tis as if I have created a microcosm 'tween my ears, without under-

standing a bit of it. And some of the ideas may be records of sensory impressions, for example, yesterday's weather. But others may be abstract concepts out of religion, philosophy, mathematics, or what have you—not that I'd know, since to me they are all a meaningless parade of hallucinations. But insofar as they are all ideas, they are all fungible. Whatever their origins may have been, they are now all con-fused into the same currency, and so I may speak of the Pythagorean Theorem or the Treaty of Utrecht as well as I may speak of yesterday's weather. To me, they are all just crackers—as are you, my lord Wragby."

"That is quite clear," Peer said vaguely, for he had gone a bit glassy-eyed round the point where Dappa had begun to use Greek letters. "Tell me, Dappa, were there any German pirates aboard your ship?"

"You mean, native speakers of High-Dutch, or *Hochdeutsch*? Alas, they are a rare breed 'mong pirates, for the Germans fear water, and love order. Most of them were Dutchmen. However, there was a prisoner, kept in fetters down in the bilge, a Bavarian diplomat who taught me his language."

"Right then!" And Peer flipped opened his note-book, and began to scan pages filled with laboriously botched cartoons. "Well, Dappa, you may not be aware that we Englishmen dwell on something very much like the sandbars you used to see in your rivers, save that ours is much larger, and free of crocodiles—" He held up a sketch.

"We call it an island," said the Marquis of Ravenscar helpfully.

"There is a great river of cold, salty water," Peer said, holding his arms far apart, "ever so much broader than the distance between my book and my pencil, separating us from a place called Europe which is full of nasty nasty apes. In your system of mental ideas, you might liken it to a lot of monkey-bands who are forever screeching and throwing rocks at each other."

"But sometimes we cross the salty river on things like hollow logs, except much larger," said the Marquis of Ravenscar, now getting into the spirit of things, "and throw a few rocks of our own, just to stay in practice!" He winked at Dappa, who gave back a brooding stare.

"There is a frightfully enormous and strong old gorilla, a silver-back, of whom we are terrified, just over the river."

Dappa sighed, sensing that there was no way out. "I think I've seen his image on French coins, he is called Leroy."

"Yes! He owns more bananas than anyone else, has more apes in his tribe, and has thrown a lot of rocks at us."

"That must be very painful indeed," Dappa said, not very sympathetically.

"Yes, quite," said Peer. "But we have a mighty silver-back of our own, a really stupendous and deadly accurate stone-thrower, who, some moons ago, chased Leroy right up a tree! Because of this, our little band, here on our sandbar in the salty river, cannot make out whether to worship and revere our big silver-back as a god, or fear and revile him as a devil. Now, we have an enormous clearing in the jungle, actually not far from where we are right now, where we convene to make obeisance to a certain female silver-back, rather frail—and where we beat our chests, and throw fæces at each other."

"Ugh! Until you told me that, I was about to say, I should like to see this clearing."

"Yes, it is rather frightful," Roger put in, dismayed by Peer's similitude, "but we have found throwing fæces preferable to throwing rocks."

"Do you throw your fæces, my lord Wragby?" Dappa asked.

"It is what I do for a living!" answered Peer, shaking his note-book, "and what you see here is the Instrument I use to scrape my Ammunition off the jungle floor."

"May I ask, what is special about this female silver-back, that you should brave flying fæcal material to pay homage to her?"

"She holds our Stick of Power," Peer answered, as if that settled it. "Now, to the matter at hand. There are two tribes vying for the favor of the ancient female silver-back. The leader of one of those tribes stands before you." He indicated Roger, who made a courtly bow. "Alas, we have been driven to the periphery of the clearing by the most incredible and sustained fæces-barrage this jungle has ever witnessed; and the terribly, terribly mighty and enormous English silver-back I spoke of was nearly buried alive in it, and withdrew across the cold, salty river to a place named Antwerp, where it is possible for him to sit and enjoy the occasional banana without being struck in the face by a flying turd. And we who follow Roger, here, are frightfully curious to know if, and when, our big silver-back is coming back over the river, and whether he might be in a mood to throw any actual stones at any of us if, and when, he does, and whether he has any designs on the Stick of Power."

"And what of Leroy? Is he still up his tree?"

"Leroy is halfway to the ground! And from his distance, with his failing eye-sight, he cannot easily distinguish between apes throwing stones, and apes throwing mere fæces; at any rate, if he thinks we are distracted, why, he'll scamper right back down to *terra firma* like the cheeky monkey he is, and we don't want that."

"If I may ask a direct question, why are you telling me these things, my lord?"

"That nice female you paid a call on earlier today," said Peer, "that most admirable yellow-haired chimp, why, she has just crossed over the cold salty river and returned to our sandbar after sojourning, for many moons, in the jungle that lies off where the sun rises every morning, where a thousand different German-speaking ape-tribes vie for the control of individual trees, or, indeed, individual branches of trees. She came over on a giant hollow log that seemed to have a larger-than-normal number of these German-speaking apes on board. She came from the general direction of the place where our formidable silver-back has been biding his time, and enjoying his bananas. Which band does she belong to? For in the country where she was sojourning dwells another female silver-back, who has the run of several biggish trees, and who has her eye on our Stick. Does your friend belong to her tribe? Or is she in the camp of him who bides his time in Antwerp? Or both, or neither?"

Now it was Dappa's turn to look glazed. After working this through for a moment, he guessed: "You're trying to work out whether it would enure to your benefit to hurl some fæces at Eliza."

"I say, you are spot on!" Peer exclaimed. "That Spinozzel chap really was on to something!"

Roger Comstock had a particular way of holding himself, when he wanted to say something, that caused everyone within a pike-length to shut up and turn towards him worshipfully. This everyone now did, because he was holding himself in that way. After collecting himself for a few moments, he held up one hand, thumb tucked into palm, and gave Dappa another wink. "Four silver-backs." The other hand came up, two fingers extended. "Two Sticks of Power. One of them rather firmly in the grip of Leroy and his heirs and assigns. The other, widely seen as being Up for Grabs. So, let us consider the four silver-backs." Now he was holding up both hands, two fingers extended from each. "Two female, two male, all very very old, though, 'tmust be allowed, the one in Antwerp is as vigorous as a battle-weary sixty-four-year-old *could ever* be. The German female has a son, a great oafish gorilla who is going to have our Power-Stick lodged in his fat fist quite soon, if I've anything to say about it. Now his mum is hated by the female who presides over our sandbar today; why, she begins to screech and wave the Stick about the moment she detects a whiff of this German on the breeze. So quite naturally the son is *persona non grata* here. But *he* has a son of his own, and we'd very much like to see him swinging through English trees and eating English bananas as soon as we can get him over here. So—"

"Then don't throw shit at Eliza," Dappa said.

"Thank you."

"Perhaps we should throw a *bit* so it doesn't look as if we are colluding," Peer suggested, clearly disappointed.

"Perhaps you should go pick some nits out of her hair, my lord," Dappa returned.

"Thank you, Dappa, that will be all," said Roger sternly, and led Peer away by the elbow.

"Before you ask," Daniel said, "that was a ten."

DAPPA BROODED THROUGH most of the trip to Crane Court.

Daniel ventured: "I hope I did not offend *you,* in the way I dealt with Peer. I could not think of any other way to respond."

"To you, he is just a singular imbecile," Dappa returned. "To me, he is a typical sample of the sort of bloke I need to reach with my books. And so, if I seem distracted, it is not because I am annoyed with you— though I am a little. It is because I am asking myself, what is the point of trying to reach such persons at all? Am I wasting my time?"

"My nephew simply believes whatever the people around him believe," Daniel said. "If every man in the Kit-Cat Clubb proclaimed you King of England, why, he would fall on his knees and kiss your ring."

"This may be true, but it does not help me, or my publisher."

"Your publisher," Daniel said. "The Duchess. She and you were simply talking about selling books, weren't you?"

"Of course."

"She doesn't speak to you of those matters that so concern the Whigs."

"Of course she doesn't. Don't tell me you were going to ask about it as well?"

"I admit to some curiosity about the Duchess, and what she is up to in London," Daniel said. "I knew her once, Dappa, many years ago. Recently, she has let me know that she means to renew the acquaintance. I do not phant'sy this is owed to my looks, or my charm."

Dappa offered nothing. They rattled on wordlessly for a bit. Daniel sensed that this bit of news had only made Dappa more anxious. "Will it create a tremendous hardship for *Minerva* if you follow my advice, and do not unload the anti-fouling plates?"

"It will create the need for a loan," Dappa replied, "which will have to be repaid, in gold, upon our return."

"I can arrange something," Daniel said.

In the dim light scattering into the carriage he could see Dappa's eyes flick towards the window, a gesture of annoyance. Daniel could guess what he was thinking: what sort of pass have we come to when we must look to an aged scientist as our banker?

HE INSISTED THAT THE DRIVER let him off at the entrance to Crane Court, rather than squeezing through that narrow arch and driving all the way to the Royal Society's front door. The short walk would do him some good. He bid Dappa good-bye and tottered on creaky legs through the entrance. The hackney remained where it was for a few moments, keeping an eye on him. But Crane Court was an unlikely place for footpads, as they'd have no way to escape from it if a hue and cry were raised. So presently the horses were given orders to move, and the hackney clattered away, taking Dappa down to White Friars Stairs where he could find a waterman to row him down the Thames to *Minerva*.

Daniel was alone in the familiar confines of Crane Court; and at that moment he was struck by a monstrous thought.

Now, it had been a very long day indeed, beginning with a journey up to the Templar-tomb in Clerkenwell and continuing through Hockley-in-the-Hole, an odd conversation with Peter (Saturn) Hoxton, a refreshing visit to Catherine Barton at Roger's house, the long-dreaded reunion with Miss Barton's uncle, and later the Kit-Cat Clubb. Too many threads, and too much information for his stiff old brain to cope with. Any part of the day would have given him plenty to think about during his short stroll from Fleet Street to the door of the R.S. But what his mind seized upon was Isaac's sedan chair.

Just before and after the explosion, a sedan chair had been poised at the very place where Daniel had just alighted from the hackney, there in the arched tunnel where Crane Court debouched into Fleet Street.

Tonight his way up the Court was nearly barred by a vault-wagon drawn up to exhaust the sewage from one of the town-houses. He diverted round it, desiring to give it the widest berth possible, lest he get splashed. But just before he did, he turned round and looked back toward Fleet, peering through the arch. Golden light was gleaming through from whale-oil street-lanthorns on Fleet, just as on the night of the explosion.

On that Sunday evening, the mysterious sedan chair had been framed in the entry, dead center, a black doorway suspended in the arch of light. It had followed them to that point; paused; waited (or so it seemed) for the explosion; and then it had fled, pursued, briefly, by the hapless Watchman.

Isaac had said something, earlier today, to the effect he'd been shocked to see Daniel traveling in the company of Mr. Threader. This could be interpreted more than one way; but the most straightforward was that he literally had observed the two of them together in Mr. Threader's carriage.

Which could only have occurred along Fleet Ditch in the minutes before the explosion. Perhaps Isaac had been in that sedan chair. Perhaps it had been nothing more than a coincidence that he had fallen in alongside Mr. Threader's carriage when he had. Perhaps he had been on his way from some errand—and it would have had to've been a very dark and strange one indeed—in the dangerous alleys on the eastern brink of the Ditch, en route to his dwelling off Leicester Fields. But then why had he stopped in the entrance to Crane Court?

Daniel turned about and gazed at the arch again, trying to resummon the fading memory.

But instead of seeing the remembered image of the black box, he saw a limbed shadow detach itself from one side of the arch and flit across the opening. It was a man who had been lurking there, and who had just made his departure onto Fleet Street. A moment later Daniel heard iron horseshoes splashing sparks on the brittle ashlars of the street. It was a rider, who had dismounted, and led his horse quietly to the entrance, so that he could spy on Daniel more discreetly. He had probably lost Daniel in the shadows of the vault-wagon and decided to call it a night.

Daniel had lost his train of thought concerning the sedan chair. He turned and walked quickly until his nostrils and his eyes no longer burned from the ammonia-cloud surrounding the vault-wagon. He was hardly surprised to hear footsteps behind him.

"Are you the gager Saturn names Doc?" said a pre-adolescent boy. "Don't loap off, I ain't a scamperer."

Daniel considered stopping, but reckoned the boy could keep up with him. "Are you of the Black-guard?" he asked wearily.

"No, Doc, but I've my Aspirations."

"Very well."

"This is for you, then," said the boy, and held out a folded stick of paper, very white compared to his filthy hand. Daniel accepted it. The boy darted back down the court and climbed aboard the vault-wagon he'd rode in on. "Lovely watch you've there—best keep an eye on it!" he called out, as a sort of pleasantry.

Henry Arlanc let him in, and helped stow away his coat and walking-stick. "It is a great honour to have been named Secretary of your Clubb, sir," he observed. "I've just been copying out today's Minutes."

"You will do very well," Daniel assured him. "I only wish our Clubb was one that met in a nice house and offered food and drink."

"For that, I've the Royal Society, Doctor."

"Yes, but you are not the Secretary."

"I could be. If a Secretary's job is to prick down all comings and goings, doings and discussions, why 'tis all here," said Arlanc—strangely talkative this evening—and pointed to his head. "Why're you peering at me so, Doctor?"

"I just had a thought."

Henry Arlanc shrugged. "Would you like me to fetch a quill and—"

"No, thank you. This one will rest secure up here," said Daniel, and imitated Henry's head-pointing gesture. "Henry, does it ever happen that Sir Isaac will come here in his sedan chair, on a Sunday evening?"

"Frequently!" Henry answered. "There is always business here, pressing in on him. In the week, he has responsibilities at the Mint. Then, when he comes here, there are so many visitors, distractions. But he has learnt the trick of coming late on Sundays, when no one is in the building except for me and Madame, who understand that he is not to be disturbed. Then he can work late into the night, sometimes even until sunrise on Monday."

"No one calls for him then, eh?"

"*Pourquoi non,* for no one knows he is here."

"Except for you, and Madame Arlanc, and his own servants."

"All I meant, sir, was that no one *who would dare to disturb him* knows he is here."

"Of course."

"Why do you ask, Doctor?" Arlanc said; an odd and rude thing for a porter to say to a Doctor.

"I phant'sied I had seen signs of his presence round the house on some Sunday evenings, and wondered if I were imagining things."

"You have imagined nothing, Doctor. May I assist you up stairs?"

Doc,

If you are reading this it means that the boy found you in Crane Court. You may wish to check your pockets, &c.

Know that a representative of mine is scheduled to partake of high tea with a friend of a friend of Mr. Teach on Thursday next. Inquiries will be made.

I went to your hole in the ground and chased out two culls who had gone down there, and not for the usual purpose, viz. buggery. I believe they mistook me for the Ghost of a Knight Templar, from which I conclude, they were cultivated men.

Saturn

Saturn,

Thank you for your diligence. It is what I would expect of an Horologist.

Suppose I had come into possession of some odds and ends of yellow metal; then do you know any of the sort of men who would buy them from me? Any you particularly dislike? I ask purely as an academic exercise, on behalf of a noted Natural Philosopher.

Dr. Waterhouse

Isaac,

I can think of no better way to repay the hospitality you showed me at your house today, than to respectfully inform you that someone may be trying to Blow you Up. Whoever it is, would appear to be well acquainted with your habits. Consider varying them.

Your humble and obedient servant,
Daniel

P.S. Concerning the other topic of our discussion, I am making inquiries.

Crane Court, London
22 APRIL 1714

. . . whereas here; all, as well Brandy as Wine, and all our strong compounded Drinks, such as stout Ale, Punch, Double-Beer, Fine-Ale, &c. are all drank to Excess, and that to such a Degree, as to become the Poison, as well of our Health as of our Morals; fatal to the Body, to Principles, and even to the Understanding; and we see daily Examples of Men of strong Bodies drinking themselves into the Grave; and which is still worse, Men of strong Heads, and good Judgment, drinking themselves into Idiotism and Stupidity. . . .

—DANIEL DEFOE,
A Plan of the English Commerce

A GUTTER RAN DOWN the centerline of Crane Court, in a weak bid to make Gravity do something useful. The slope was so feeble that when Daniel walked down to Fleet Street, he overtook a floating apple-core he'd tossed into it a quarter of an hour earlier, while standing in front of the Royal Society waiting for Saturn to appear.

Peter Hoxton nearly filled the archway. His hands were thrust in his waistcoat-pockets, his arms akimbo, giving his upper half the same general shape as the planet Saturn viewed through a telescope. He was smoking a clay-pipe whose stem was broken down to a mere knuckle-bone. As Daniel drew nearer, he took this out of his mouth and pitched it into the gutter; then froze, head bowed, as if a need to pray had suddenly come over him.

"Behold!" was the first thing he said to Daniel. "Behold what runs in your gutter here!"

Daniel drew up beside him and followed his gaze down. Where Crane Court's gutter ran between Saturn's feet, a sump had been formed by settling of the earth under the stones. In the deepest parts of it, the net-work of crevices between stones was plotted in brilliant lines of liquid argent.

"Quicksilver," Daniel said. "Probably discarded from the Royal Society's laboratories."

"Point to it!" Saturn suggested, still staring fixedly at the quicksilver net-work.

"I beg your pardon?"

"Point to the Royal Society, and make as if you're offering up some remark about it."

Daniel uncertainly turned round and pointed up the center of Crane Court, though he omitted any feigned remarks. Saturn turned his head to look that way; peered blankly for a few moments; then turned his back on Daniel and shuffled off into Fleet Street.

Daniel took a few moments to catch up in traffic. The church-bells had struck six P.M. a few minutes ago. Fleet was deadly crowded.

"I phant'sied you'd have a hackney," Daniel said, hoping to rein Saturn in by starting a conversation with him. "I did mention that all expenses would be reimbursed . . ."

"No need," Saturn returned, sowing the words back over his shoulder, "the place is all of two hundred paces from here." He was walking east on Fleet, glancing over his shoulder for openings between riders and coaches and wagons, sometimes trespassing in front of them to claim right-of-way. The general plan seemed to be that they would cross over to the south side.

"You had intimated it might be near by," Daniel said, "but I find it startling that a house of that type should lie so near to—to—"

"To a house of the Royal Society's type? Not at all, Doc. The streets of London are like bookshelves, you can as leave find unlike houses next to each other as find a picaroon-romance shelved alongside a Bible."

"Why did you need for me to point at the Royal Society, just now?"

"So I might look at it."

"I did not know one needed *leave* to look at it."

"That is because you are used to the ways of Natural Philosophers, who are forever peering at whatever pleases them. There is a kind of arrogance in that, you are unawares of. In other walks of life, one *does* need leave. And 'tis well we are having this talk en route to Hanging-Sword-Alley. For the ken we are going to is most certainly the sort where, Doc, you do need leave."

"Why, then, I'll have eyes only for you, Mr. Hoxton."

They had come already to where Water Lane broke away to the right, and ran straight down to the river. Saturn made that turn, as if he meant to ramble down to White Friars Dock. The Lane was a straight and broad cleft separating two jumbled, mazy neighborhoods. On the right, the periphery of the Temple. Typical resident: a practitioner at law. On the left, the parish of St. Bride's. Typical resident: a woman who'd been arrested for prostitution, thievery, or vagrancy and put to work pounding hemp at Bridewell. In his more peevish moments Daniel phant'sied that the only thing preventing those on the right and those on the left from coming together lewdly in the middle of the Lane, was the continual stream of redolent carts booming down it to eliminate their steaming loads upon Dung Wharf, which could be nosed a short distance ahead.

Water Lane was lined on both sides by post-Fire buildings, kept up in such a way as to give the casual stroller a frank and fair synopsis of the neighborhoods that spread behind them; which was to say that whenever Daniel walked down this way to the river, he hewed strictly to the right, or Temple, side, trailing a hand along shop-fronts as he went. When he was feeling bold, and was surrounded by well-dressed law-clerks and brawny, honest tradesmen, he would gaze across the way and disapprovingly regard the buildings on the left side.

There, between a certain pawn-shop and a certain tavern, stretched a narrow gap that reminded him of a missing tooth in a rotten jaw. He had always supposed that it was the result of an error by Robert Hooke, the late City Surveyor, who'd done his work sans flaw in the better neighborhoods, but who, when he got to this district, might possibly have been distracted by the charms of a Bridewell girl. Noting the sorts of people who came and went through that gap, Daniel had sometimes speculated as to what would befall him if he ever went in there, somewhat in the spirit of a seven-year-old boy wondering what would happen if he fell through the hole in an outhouse.

When Saturn had entered Water Lane, he had gravitated to (inevitably) the left side, which caused Daniel to lose his bearings, as he'd never seen it from this perspective. The strolling, snuff-taking lawyers across the way looked doltish.

After just a few paces Saturn veered round a corner into a narrow, gloomy pass, and Daniel, wanting nothing more than to stay close, hurried after him. Not until they had penetrated ten paces into it did he turn round to look at the bright façades on the other side of Water Lane, far far away, and realize that they had gone into that same Gap he had oft wondered about.

It were just to describe his movements now as *scurrying*. He drew abreast of Saturn and tried to emulate his manner of not gazing directly at anything. If this maze of alleys were as horrible as he'd always supposed, why, he did not see its horrors; and considering how briskly they were moving, it hardly seemed as if there would be time for any of them to catch up. He foresaw a long train of stranglers and footpads stretched out in their wake, huffing and puffing and bent over from side-aches.

"I presume this is some sort of a lay?" said Peter Hoxton.

"Meaning . . . a plan . . . scheme . . . or trap," Daniel gasped. "I am as mystified as you are."

"Does anyone else know where we are going, and when?" Saturn tried.

"I let the name of the place, and the time of the meeting, be known."

"Then it's a lay." Saturn darted sideways and punched his way through a door without knocking. Daniel, after a clutching, febrile moment of being by himself in the center of Hanging-Sword-Alley, scrambled after him, and did not leave off from scrambling until he was seated next to Peter Hoxton before the hearth of a house.

Saturn spooned coal onto the evidence of a late fire. The room was already stuffy; these were the last chairs anyone wanted.

"This is really not so very dreadful after all," Daniel ventured.

Saturn rummaged up a bellows, got its two handles in his hands, and held it up for a mechanical inspection. A brisk squeeze slapped lanky black locks away from his face. He aimed it at the pile of coal and began crushing the handles back and forth as if the bellows were a flying-machine, and he trying to raise himself off the floor.

Following Saturn's warnings, Daniel had religiously avoided looking at anything. But the close, and now smoky, air of this parlour was leavened by female voices. He could not stop himself turning to look at an outburst of feminine laughter from the far end of the room. He got an impression of rather a lot of mismatched and broken-down furniture arranged in no particular way, but swept back and forth across the room by ebbing and flowing tides of visitors. There might have been a score of persons in the room, about evenly divided between the sexes, and clumped together in twos, threes, and fours. At the far end was a large window looking out onto a bright outdoor space, perhaps Salisbury Square in the heart of St. Bride's. Daniel could not tell, because the windows were screened with curtains, made of rather good lace, but too large for these windows, and tarred brown as naval hemp by pipe-smoke. They were, he realized with a mild thrill, curtains that had been stolen—probably snatched right from someone's open window in broad daylight. Silhouetted against that ochre scrim were three women, two gaunt and young, the other plump and a bit older, and smoking a clay-pipe.

He forced himself to turn his attention back to Saturn. But as he did so he scanned the room and got an impression of many different kinds of people: a gentleman who would not have looked out of place promenading round St. James's Square, as well as several who belonged more to Hockley-in-the-Hole.

By his exertions Saturn had evoked light, but no perceptible heat, from the rubble of coals and ashes on the hearth. That was enough— no heat was wanted. It seemed he'd only wanted something to occupy his nervous hands.

"A lot of females!" Daniel remarked.

"We call them *women*," Saturn snapped. "I hope you haven't been peering about like some damned Natural Philosopher at a bug collection."

"We call them *insects*," Daniel shot back. This elicited a gentlemanly nod from Saturn.

"Without *peering*," Daniel continued, "I can see well enough that, though it's untidy, it's far from loathsome."

"To a point, criminals love order even more than Judges," Saturn said.

At that moment, a boy entered the room, breathing hard, and scanned the faces. He picked out Saturn instantly, and moved toward him with a joyous expression, reaching significantly into his pocket; but Peter Hoxton must have given him a glare or a gesture, because suddenly his face fell and he spun away on his heel.

"A boy who snatches your watch in the street, and runs off with it, does not do so out of a perverse longing to cause you grief. He is moved by a reasonable expectation of profit. Where you see sheep being sheared, you may assume there are spinning-wheels nearby; where you have your pocket picked, you know that there is a house such as this one within sprinting-distance."

"In its ambience 'tis rather like a coffee-house."

"Aye. But mind, the sort who're disposed to abhor such kens as this would say its hellishness inheres in its very congeniality."

"I must admit, it smells less of coffee than of the cheap perfume of geneber."

"Gin, we call it in places like this. My downfall," Saturn explained laconically, peering over his shoulder at the boy, who was now in negotiations with a fat, solitary man at a corner table. Saturn went on to give the room a thorough scan.

"You dishonor your own rules! What are you looking at?"

"I am reminding myself of the exits. If this turns out to be a lay, I shall not bother excusing myself."

"Did you perchance see our buyer?" Daniel inquired.

"Save my fellow horologist in the corner there, and this gager next to us, who is trying to wash away his pox with gin and mercury, everyone here has come in groups," Saturn said, "and I told the buyer that he must come alone."

"Gager is what you call an elderly man."

"Yes."

Daniel hazarded a look at said gager, who was curled up on the floor in the corner by the hearth, no more than a sword-length from them—for the room was small, the tables close, and the separation between groups was preserved only through a kind of etiquette. The gager looked like a whorl of blankets and worn-out clothes, with pale hands and a face projecting from one end. Resting on the hearth-stones directly before him were a clay bottle of Dutch geneber and a thumb-sized flask of mercury. This was the first clue that he was syphilitic, for mercury was the only known remedy for that disease. But confirmation could be had by looking at his face, which was disfigured by lumpy tumors, called gummas, rimming his mouth and his eyes.

"Every snatch of conversation you overhear in this room shall be riddled with such flash cant as 'gager,' 'lay,' *et cetera,* for here, as in the legal and medical professions, the more impenetrable a man's speech, the higher the esteem in which he is held. Nothing would be more injurious to our reputation in this house, than for us to speak intelligibly. Yet we may have to wait for a long time. And I fear I may fall into drinking gin, and end up like yon gager. So, let us have an unintelligible conversation about our religion."

"I beg your pardon?"

"Remember, Doc, you are my Father Confessor, I your disciple, and your portion of our bargain is that you shall help me draw nigher to Truths Æternal through the sacrament of Technology. This—" and he scanned the room lightly, without letting his eye catch on anything, "is not what I signed on for. We were to be in Clerkenwell, building things."

"And we shall be," Daniel assured him, "once the masons, carpenters, and plasterers have finished their work round the old Temple there."

"That should not be long. I've never seen stones piled up in such haste," Saturn said. "What is it you mean to make there, then?"

"Read the newspapers," Daniel returned.

"What's that s'posed to mean?"

"What's the matter, you're the one who wanted to speak in cyphers."

"I *do* read the newspapers," said Saturn, wounded.

"Have you attended to what goes on in Parliament?"

"A lot of screeching and howling as to whether our next King's son[*] ought to be given a hero's welcome in the House of Lords, or barred from the Realm."

Daniel chuckled. "You must be a Whig, to refer so confidently to George Louis as our next King."

"What do I look like to you?" said Saturn, suddenly lowering his voice, and looking about uneasily.

"A Jacobite Tory, dyed in the wool!"

Daniel's chuckling at his own jest was, for a few moments, the only sound in the room. Then:

"There'll be no such talk in this house!"

The speaker was a short, stout Welshman with a large jaw. He was wrapped in a bulky and bulging black cloak, as if he'd just come in from outside, and was making a sweep through the parlour on his way back to the kitchen. A brace of empty gin-bottles dangled by their necks between the fingers of his right hand, and a full one was gripped in his left. Daniel assumed the fellow was being wry, and chuckled some more; but the Welshman very deliberately swiveled his head around and gave Daniel a glare that shut him up. Most of the people in the room were now looking their way.

"Your usual, Saturn?" the Welshman said, though he continued to stare fixedly at Daniel.

"Have her bring us coffee, Angus. Gin disagrees with me these days, and as you have perceived, my friend has already drunk one bottle too many."

Angus turned around and stalked out of the room.

"I am sorry!" Daniel exclaimed. Until moments ago he had felt

---

[*]George Augustus of Hanover, later George II.

strangely at home here. Now, he felt more agitated than he had out in the alley.

The wretch on the floor went into a little fit of shuddering, and tried to jerk his unresponsive limbs into a more comfortable lie.

"I assumed—" Daniel began.

"That the words you were using were as alien to this place as the Calculus."

"Why should the proprietor—I assume that's what he was—care if I make such a jest—?"

"Because if word gets round that Angus's ken is a haunt of such persons—"

"Meaning—?"

"Meaning, persons who have secretly vowed that the Hanover shall *not* be our next King," Saturn croaked, so quietly that Daniel was forced to read his lips, "and that the Changeling* *shall* be, why, it shall become self-fulfilling, shall it not? Then such persons—who are always in want of a place to convene, and conspire—will begin to come here."

"What does it matter!?" Daniel whispered furiously. "The place is filled with criminals *to begin with!*"

"And that is how Angus likes it, for he is a past master among thief-takers," Saturn said, his patience visibly dwindling. "He knows how it all works with the Watch, the Constables, and the Magistrates. But if the supporters of the Changeling begin to convene here, why, everything's topsy-turvy, isn't it, now the house is a heaven for Treason as well as Larceny, and he's got the Queen's Messengers to contend with."

"I hardly phant'sy the Queen's Messengers would ever venture into a place like this!" Even Daniel had the wit to mouth the name, rather than speaking it aloud.

"Be assured they would, if treason were afoot here! And Angus would be half-hanged, drawn, and quartered at the Treble Tree, 'long with some gaggle of poxy Jacobite viscounts. No decent end for a simple thief-taker, that."

"You called him that before."

"Called him what?"

"A thief-taker."

"Naturally."

"But I thought a thief-taker was one who brought thieves to justice, to collect a reward from the Queen. Not a—" But Daniel

---

*A.k.a. James Stuart, "The Pretender," son of the late former King James II, and would-be James III.

stopped there, as Peter Hoxton had got a look on his phizz that verged on nausea, and was shaking his head convulsively.

"I see you've been sending my coal right up the fucking Chimney!" Angus proclaimed, stalking toward them. He had divested himself of the cloak and the gin-bottles and was now being followed, at a prudent distance, by a Bridewellish-looking girl with a mug of coffee in each hand.

"Rather, providing you with the service of keeping the fire going," Saturn answered calmly, "at no charge, by the way."

"I didn't want it going to begin with!" Angus returned. " 'Twas that lappy-cull who mewled and pleaded for a bit of warmth! Now you've gone and got it going again! There'll be a charge for that!"

"Of course there will be," Saturn said.

The coffee was served, and money changed hands, in the form of copper tokens, minutely examined by Angus.

"Now why do you say I should attend to the doings of Parliament?" Saturn asked, as they were beginning to sip their coffee. "What connexion could I possibly draw between the situation of the Duke of Cambridge* and your hole in the ground in Clerkenwell?"

"None whatever. Save that Parliament's more loud and obvious doings may be used as a sort of screen or blind to cover arcane, subtile machinations that might reward your attention."

"This is worse than being given no information at all," Saturn grumbled.

A man entered solus, and began to look round the place. Daniel knew immediately it was their buyer. But rather than jumping to make their presence known, he settled deeper into his chair so that he could spend a few moments inspecting the newcomer. In silhouette against the glowing screen of curtains, he could easily be confused with an actual gentleman, for he wore a wig, clamped down by a hat with a vast brim folded upwards in the style then mandatory. A sword dangled from one hip. But when he stood, he crouched, and when he walked, he scuttled, and when he noticed things, he flinched. And when this man came over to the hearth, and accepted a chair pulled up by the uncharacteristically hospitable Peter Hoxton, Daniel perceived that his wig was stinking horsehair, his hat was too small, and his sword was more danger to himself, in its sheath, than it would've been to others, out of it. He nearly tripped over it twice, because every time he whacked it off a chair- or table-leg it jumped back between his ankles. He put Daniel in mind of a clown at St. Bartholomew's Fair, got up to mock a gentleman. Yet the mere fact that he was trying so

---

*One of the English titles of that same George Augustus of Hanover.

hard earned him a sort of dignity, and probably counted for something in a house of this type.

"Mr. Baynes, Dr. Gatemouth," said Saturn. "Doc, say hallow to him we are calling Mr. Baynes."

"Dr. Gatemouth, 'tis a pleasure as well as an honour," said the newcomer.

"Mr. Baynes," Daniel said.

"Would you be one of the Gatemouths of Castle Gatemouth?"

Daniel had no idea what to do with this question.

"Doc is of a very old family of armigerous yeomen in the Gatemouth district," prated Saturn, sounding bored.

"Ah, perhaps they knew some of my forebears," exclaimed Mr. Baynes, patting his sword-hilt, "for I am nearly certain that Gatemouth Abbey lies adjacent to a certain vicarage where—"

"It is not his real name," Saturn snapped.

"Of course, that is obvious, do you think I am a child? I was merely trying to make him feel at ease."

"Then you failed. Let us speak of the Ridge, so that we may ease him out of this ken."

Said to a real gentleman, these words would have provoked a duel. So Daniel at this point was one uneasy gager. But Mr. Baynes was unfazed. He took a moment to re-compose himself and said, "Very well."

"Do you understand that the amount in play is large?"

"A large *weight* was bandied about, but this tells me little of the actual *amount* of Ridge, until the purity of the metal has been quoined."

"How large a quoin do you propose to hack off?" said Saturn, amused.

"Large enough to balance my toils and sufferings."

"Howsoever much you assay—assuming you truly *do*—you'll find Doc, here, is no Beaker. The *amount* and the *weight* are as identical as the refiner's fire can make 'em. And then what?"

"A transaction," said Mr. Baynes, guardedly.

"But last time I had dealings with you, Mr. Baynes, you were in no position to move such a quantity of Ridge as Dr. Gatemouth has on his hands. A glance at your periwig tells me your fortunes have in no wise improved."

"Peter Hoxton. I know more of your story than you of mine! Who are you to cast aspersions!?"

Now Daniel had scarcely followed a word of this, so dumbfounded was he by Mr. Baynes's appearance. But around this time, he was able to formulate an explanation that fit the observed phenomena, viz.:

Mr. Baynes had wooden teeth that had been carved to fit a larger mouth. They were forever trying to burst free of the confines of his head, which gave him a somewhat alarming, horselike appearance when it was happening. For him, speech was a continual struggle to expel words whilst keeping a grip on his dentition. Therefore he spoke in a slow, deliberate, and literally biting cadence, terminating each phrase with an incredible feat of flapping his prehensile lips around his runaway choppers and hauling them back into captivity.

The sheer effort expended—so say nothing of the risk incurred—in casting this rebuke at Saturn, gave it telling weight. Peter Hoxton recoiled, fell back in his chair, and raised a hand to run it back through his hair.

Having thus cleared the floor, Mr. Baynes continued, "Supposing a cull did have the resources" (a very difficult word for him to . . . pronounce . . . requiring a lip-wrap fore and aft) "to engage in a Transaction of the magnitude contemplated by Dr. Gatemouth—would he come *here* to meet with a *stranger*? I think not! He would delegate the matter to an underling, who would in turn choose a trusted intermediary, to make the initial contact."

Saturn grinned, which only made his unshaven face seem darker, and shook his head. "We all know there is only one coiner in the realm who can act on this scale. There is no need to flinch, I'll not utter his name aloud in this place. You'd have us believe, I take it, that you are speaking on behalf of some lieutenant of his?"

"A great big one-armed cove, a foreigner," Mr. Baynes allowed.

And now, a bit of a Moment. To this point, Mr. Baynes had been putting on a passable show. But it was bad form to have volunteered such information, and he knew it.

"You see, I do not bate at divulging such *data*, such is my confidence that he will deal only through me."

Doc and Saturn nodded sagely, but the damage had been done, and Mr. Baynes knew, though he might not admit, it.

The syphilitic gager on the floor, who had appeared dead for a while, had been stirring ever since Mr. Baynes had made his entrance. Daniel supposed this was an effect of the way they'd rearranged the chairs, for Daniel had moved to a new spot between the wretch and his precious coal-fire, and was blocking what little warmth spread out of it. The gager now made noises that indicated he was sitting up. Daniel did not turn around to look—he did not have to, as Saturn was watching all with green disgust. Something told Daniel to rise and get out of the way.

He and most other Fellows of the Royal Society recognized syphilis and leprosy as distinct diseases, spread in different ways. But most other persons had conflated the two diseases in their minds, and so recoiled from syphilitics in much the same way as they would from lepers. This explained everything about how Saturn was reacting now. Daniel, F.R.S. though he was, reverted to superstition in the clutch, and allowed the gager the widest possible berth as he half-crawled and half-staggered toward the hearth. Some of his limbs dragged senseless on the floor, while others moved in spasms, as if he were being stung by invisible hornets. Trailing his nest of filthy blankets behind him, he slouched on the hearth, completely eclipsing the light of the fire, and hunched even closer to it, rubbing his paralyzed hand with his twitchy one. His gray hair would be dangling and burning in the coals now if he, or someone, hadn't wrapped it all up in a sort of bandage-turban atop his head.

"The questions that this foreign gentleman will ask of me, may be easily anticipated," observed Mr. Baynes.

"Indeed," Saturn returned. "The Ridge is from America."

"As Dr. Gatemouth is known to have recently come over from Boston, no one phant'sied it came from *Guinea,*" Mr. Baynes said, with elaborate meanness. "The foreign gentleman will be curious: have rich new gold mines been discovered on the banks of the River Charles? Because if so—"

"If the foreign gentleman truly does represent the coiner you and I are thinking of, why, he must be a busy man, and disinclined to hear long tedious Narrations of pirate-exploits on the Spanish Main, *et cetera,*" Saturn said. "Does it not suffice for him to know that it is in fact Ridge? For the entire point of Ridge is that it may be confused with other Ridge, and it matters not where 'twas dug out of the ground."

"The foreign gentleman thinks it *does* matter, and further, is ever *alert* for inconsistencies in Narrations. Indeed, in his world, where commerce is, of necessity, informal and *ad hoc* in the extreme, to tell a coherent Story is the sole way of establishing one's credit."

"Mr. Baynes is correct as far as that goes," Saturn told Daniel in an aside. "Men of this sort are literary critics of surpassing shrewdness."

"No convincing Tale means no Credit, and no Transaction. I am here, not to quoin your Ridge, but to assay your Story; and if I do not bring him a ripping pirate-yarn to-night, why, you are finished."

An odd snuffing noise issued from the hearth, as if a handful of dust had been tossed on the coals. Daniel glanced over to see that the gager was rubbing feverishly at his eyes and his mouth. Perhaps the smoke had irritated his mucous membranes, and had made him sneeze and paw at the encrusted sores that so disfigured his face.

Daniel then noticed that the fire was blazing up, but producing a good deal more smoke than light. The smoke was drawing swiftly up the chimney, which was fortunate, because it had an evil, thick, reddish look.

He turned his attention away from the strange actions of the gager, and back to matters at hand: Mr. Baynes, who was still prating about the foreign gentleman, and an empty chair.

The empty chair demanded a second glance, and then a third.

Mr. Baynes himself was only just becoming aware that Saturn was gone. Both of them now turned to survey the parlour, supposing that their companion might have stood up to stretch, or to rid himself of his empty mug.

Twilight had come over Salisbury Square, but enough of it sifted in through the windows to show that Peter Hoxton was no longer in the room.

Most of that light was now blocked. The women who had been perched before the lace curtain were scattering away from it. One seized a fistful of skirt and hauled it clear of her ankles, and used the other hand as a flail to clear impediments out of her course: a straight line to the nearest exit. She looked as if she were of a mind to scream, but had more important things to do just now, and so all that came from her mouth was a sort of hooting noise.

For an instant it was almost completely dark in the room, and then Daniel felt in his soul the impact of something huge upon the window. Stakes of broken wood strode end-over-end across the floor, bounding through a skittering wash of sharded glass.

He stood up. A lot of people seemed to be headed his way, as half the space in the room had been claimed by a black bulk thrust in through the obliterated window. Daniel stepped back toward the chimney-corner, knowing that, in a human stampede, he'd be the first to end up with boot-prints on his face; but suddenly there was a fizzing noise nearby, and the room was plastered with hellish light. The faces of the onrushing guests burst out of the gloom, a choir of white ovals, mouths opened, not to sing, but to scream; then they all raised hands or arms to protect their eyes. They parted to the sides of the room, faltered as they bashed into one another and stumbled over furniture, and finally came to a stand.

The center was now clear, except for a treacherous rubble of up-ended chairs, and Daniel had a clear view of the thing that had come in. It was a large and heavy-built wagon, like the ones used to transport bullion, but reinforced for ramming, and painted a black so profound that, even in the dissolving radiance that now filled the room, it was nothing more than a brooding blur. One part of it stood out brightly. Fixed to the prow of this terrestrial Ram was a badge of silver metal: a flat plate of polished steel cut into the flashing silhouette of a greyhound in full chase.

Doors flew open on both sides of the wagon, and good boots began to hit the floor; Daniel could see little, but he could hear the jingling of spurs, and the ring of steel blades being whisked from scabbards: Evidence that Angus's new guests were Persons of Quality.

Daniel half-turned toward the source of the light, shielding his eyes from it with one hand, and looked at Mr. Baynes, who had lost his teeth, and seemed very old and helpless. Of all the strange things that had obtruded on Mr. Baynes's senses in the last ten heartbeats, the one that owned his attention was the emblem of the silver greyhound. Following Mr. Baynes's gaze, Daniel began to see it in more than one place: the men piling out of the wagon, and herding Angus's clients into the corners at sword-point, all wore similar badges on their breasts.

The unoccupied wagon was now withdrawn from the window and dragged off to one side. Suddenly the parlour had become an annex of Salisbury Square. A large cloaked man was cantering toward them on a black stallion, with saber drawn.

He rode right into the center of the room, reined in his charger, and stood up in his stirrups, revealing a silver greyhound pinned to his coat. "High Treason!" he proclaimed, in a voice loud enough to pelt off the opposite side of the square. "I say, on your knees, all of you!"

It was true of beasts and humans alike that when they were terrified—literally scared out of their wits, beyond the pale of reason—they either froze, or ran away. To this point Mr. Baynes had been frozen. Now his instincts told him to flee. He jumped up and turned away from all those silver greyhounds that seemed to be chasing him. In so doing, he turned full into the light. But the light was now coming over him like a burning cloud, seeming to exert a palpable force that pressed him down onto his knees, and then to all fours.

Daniel's eyes had finally adjusted to the brightness, or perhaps the light was slowly burning out. He could see now that the old gager was gone, his blankets collapsed on the hearth like a snake's shed skin.

From them had emerged what ninety-nine percent of Christendom would identify as an angel, with flowing white hair and a sword of fire. Even Daniel was tempted to think so; but on a moment's reflection he decided it was Sir Isaac Newton, brandishing a rod of burning phosphorus.

DURING THE HOUR that followed the descent of the Queen's Messengers on Angus's boozing-ken, many vivid and novel scenes presented themselves to Daniel's organs of sense. But the next time he had a moment to sit and think—which occurred on the head of a sloop anchored in the river off Black Friars, as he was taking a splendid crap into the Thames—these were the salient facts:

Isaac had tossed a handful of some chymical powder on the fire, causing thick smoke to spew out the chimney; this had been the signal for the Queen's Messengers to mount their assault on Angus's boozing-ken.

Peter Hoxton and Angus had dived through a sort of bolt-hole that led from the kitchen into the cellar of a neighboring house, gone out the back door into a little poultry-yard, vaulted a wall, streaked through a whorehouse, dodged into another boozing-ken, and taken another bolt-hole into an alley called The Wilderness (this the Queen's Messengers learned by following their trail and interrogating bystanders).

At its eastern end, The Wilderness dead-ended in the burying-ground behind Bridewell. There, Angus and Saturn had parted ways among unmarked whores' graves, and got away clean.

The sores on Isaac's mouth and eyes were fakes, made from the congealed latex, or sap, of a Brazilian tree.

The Captain of the Queen's Messengers—the big man who had ridden into the ken on horseback—was none other than Mr. Charles White, he of the bear-baiting and ear-biting.

After most of Angus's clients had been duly scared out of their wits and sent running, the Queen's Messengers, with Daniel, Isaac, and Mr. Baynes in tow, had barrelled down the length of The Wilderness with no less speed than Saturn and Angus. Before them, Bridewell rose up above its crowded burying-ground. It was a surplus Royal palace, turned over to the poor a long time ago, half burned down in the Fire, and half rebuilt. Daniel had never really taken a good look at it before, as why would anyone want to? But this was probably the right way to see it: catching the last glimmer of blue twilight, and protected from the denizens of St. Bride's Parish by its muddy necropolis. As they gathered speed down The Wilderness, Daniel phant'sied that they were about to make a frontal assault on Bridewell Palace, galloping across the pocked lumpy glacis of the burying ground to ram down the doors and round up the whores. But at the last moment they veered right on Dorset and charged straight into the timber yard that spread along the riverbank there.

Two lighters had been tucked up against the timber-wharf, screened, by stacks of logs, from the view of any underworld sentries who might have been peering down from high windows of Bridewell.

They had been well-manned with oarsmen, and ready to cast off and pull away.

A brief twilight row had taken the Messengers (half a dozen in all), Daniel, Sir Isaac, and their prisoner to this sloop, *Atalanta.* For tonight's purposes, she was all bare spars, and *incognito;* but the coat of arms on one of her furled flags was that of Charles White. *Atalanta* was his own *jacht.* No doubt, when the Queen was made aware, she would be most grateful.

Charles White had spent the brief row sitting knee-to-knee with Mr. Baynes, absent-mindedly fondling the collection of dried human ears strung on his watch-chain, and wondering aloud how long it would take them to sail downriver to the Tower of London, where all of the really first-rate implements of torture were to be found. He had held a speculative colloquy with his fellow Messengers, wondering whether it would suffice merely to keel-haul Mr. Baynes en route; whether the effectiveness of said keel-hauling might be enhanced by doing it at the place (a hundred yards away) where Fleet Ditch emptied into the Thames; whether, in other words, Mr. Baynes's ability to talk would be impaired or enhanced by being made to inhale sewage; or whether they'd have to keel-haul him *and then* use the facilities in the Tower. The problem being that traitors, who were destined to be publicly half-hanged, castrated, drawn, and quartered *anyway*, frequently saw no incentive to talk.

One of White's lieutenants—a younger gentleman, probably picked for the role because he was sweet-faced and blond—then raised the following objection: namely, that Mr. Baynes might not be destined for the man-rated butcher-block at Tyburn *at all*, as it was not really demonstrated, yet, that he was, in fact, a traitor. He was roundly hooted down. But a minute later he raised the same objection again, and finally was given leave to explain himself.

A wily barrister, he said, might argue that Mr. Baynes was in truth a loyal subject of Her Majesty.

Stay, stay, 'twas not so preposterous! For clearly *Dr. Waterhouse* was a loyal subject, merely *pretending* to deal with coiners as a trick to gather intelligence. Could Mr. Baynes's barrister not advance the same claim?

No, it was ludicrous on its face, retorted Charles White—much to the dismay of Mr. Baynes, who had begun to show stirrings of hope.

For (White went on) Mr. Baynes had not, in fact, proffered any such intelligence, indeed probably did not have any. So drawing and quartering was certainly to be the fate of him, and the only question was: how hideous would his tortures have to be, between now and then, to make him do as he ought?

Daniel had the misfortune, during all of this, to be seated in the prow of the lighter, facing aft. This gave him a clear view of Charles White's broad back, and Mr. Baynes's hairless and toothless head, which frequently strained up or sideways to scan the boat for a sympathetic face.

To Daniel it might be perfectly evident that it was a childish masque, scripted to play on Mr. Baynes's terrors, and to break him without thumbscrews. But Mr. Baynes—an audience of one—was captivated by the show. His disbelief had not merely been suspended; it had been fired out of a cannon into a stone wall. There was little question his resistance was broken. The only open question was: were his wits ruined, too, to the point where he'd be useless?

Would Daniel, put in the same predicament, have been able to see through the ruse so easily? He doubted it.

Though perhaps he *was* in the same predicament, and the show was being staged for *him* as much as for Mr. Baynes.

The shit that he took off *Atalanta*'s head was a masterpiece, exactly two well-formed packages plunging into the river like sounding-leads, and vanishing without a splash—evidence that his gut would keep functioning well after other parts of him had given way to age. He was inclined to sit there for a few minutes with his buttocks cupped in the luxuriously polished wooden annulus of the shite-hole, and to savor this triumph, just as the late Samuel Pepys had taught him to do in the case of urination. But the noises coming from belowdecks told him that he had responsibilities down there, not only to his Queen, but to Mr. Baynes.

For his fears concerning the latter had been realized. The Queen's Messengers might be very skilled at hounding traitors, but as a theatrical troupe they were rank amateurs, utterly lacking in the all-important Sense of Audience. They had let the show go on too long, and reduced Mr. Baynes to a blubbering imbecile.

Daniel pulled his breeches back on, went aft, and, at the top of the narrow staircase that led belowdecks, nearly collided with a man coming up for some fresh air. The only thing that prevented it was the other chap's white hair, which shone in the light of the half-moon, and gave Daniel a moment's warning.

He backed up and allowed Isaac to join him on deck.

"Mr. Hoxton has shown his colours, I should say," Isaac remarked.

"What—by running off?"

"Indeed."

"If he had stayed to be keel-hauled, thumbscrewed, drawn, and quartered, we'd know him to be a trustworthy chap, is that it?"

Isaac was mildly affronted. "No such fate would have befallen him, had he shown a willingness to serve the Queen."

"The only way in which Peter Hoxton *can be* of service to the Queen—or to *you*—is to bring me intelligence from the flash world. If he had *not* run away, he would have thereby declared himself an enemy of all things flash, and become perfectly useless. By escaping, along with Angus, he has enhanced his reputation beyond measure!"

"It is of no account. Your rôle is now played out. And well played. I thank you."

"Why did you send the smoke-signal? Why not wait to see what else Baynes would divulge?"

"He had already over-stepped, and divulged too much," Isaac retorted, "and he knew it. He grew reticent, and, to try you, asked you for your story. I knew you had none, or at least, none fit to withstand the scrutiny of this one-armed foreigner, or even of Mr. Baynes. My decision was: Let us advance!"

"What is it you need from Mr. Baynes now, in order to advance?"

AT DANIEL'S INSISTENCE, Charles White and his merry men left Mr. Baynes alone for a few minutes in a cabin, though they made sure to put him in irons first, so that he'd not devise some way to evade justice by committing suicide.

Daniel lurked outside the cabin door until Mr. Baynes stopped sobbing and whimpering, then counted slowly to a hundred (for he himself needed to calm down a bit), then opened the hatch and went through, carrying a lit candle.

Mr. Baynes was on a bench with his hands fettered behind his back. Before him was a plank table. He had slumped forward so his head lay on it. Daniel was certain he had expired from a stroke, until he perceived the prisoner's pinioned arms slowly rising and falling, as his lungs filled and emptied like the bellows of an Irish bagpipe.

Daniel wished he could fall asleep, too. For a few minutes he sat there nodding drowsily in the light of the candle-flame. But he could hear booted and spurred feet pacing round the deck overhead, and he knew perfectly well that he was not anchored in some placid cove, but only a few yards off Black Friars, London.

"Wake up."

"Eh—?" Baynes pulled against his irons, then regretted it and sat up, his spine creaking and popping like an old mast taking a gust. His mouth was a dry hole, pushed in like a wound. He refused to meet Daniel's eye.

"Will you talk to me?" Daniel asked.

Mr. Baynes considered it, but said nothing. Daniel rose to his feet. Mr. Baynes watched him sidelong. Daniel reached into his pocket.

Baynes tensed, getting ready to suffer. Daniel drew his fist out, flipped it over, and opened it to display, on the palm of his hand, Mr. Baynes's set of false teeth.

Baynes's eyes got wide and he lunged like a cobra, yawning. Daniel fed the teeth to him and he sucked and gummed them in. Daniel stepped back, wiping his hand on his breeches, and Mr. Baynes sat up straight, having seemingly swapped a new and better skull for the faulty one he'd woken up with.

"You are a gentleman, sir, a gentleman. I marked you as such the moment I saw you—"

"In truth I am no gentleman, though I can be a gentle man. Mr. Charles White is a gentleman. He has already explained what he means to do to you. He means what he says; why, I'm surprised you still have both of your ears. Save thine ears, and the rest of thyself, by telling me where and when you are supposed to meet the one-armed foreigner."

"You know that I shall be killed, of course."

"Not if you serve your Queen as you ought."

"Oh, but then I shall be killed by Jack the Coiner."

"And if not by Jack, then by old age," Daniel returned, "unless apoplexy or typhus take you first. If I knew of a way to avoid dying, I'd share it with you, and the whole world."

"Sir Isaac knows of a way, or so 'tis rumored."

"Spouting Alchemical rubbish is not a way to get in my good graces. Telling me the whereabouts of the one-armed foreigner is."

"Your point is well taken, concerning mortality. In truth, 'tis not fear of mine *own* fate that stopped my tongue."

"Whose then?"

"My daughter's."

"And where is your daughter?"

"Bridewell."

"You fear that some revenge will be taken on her if you assist the Queen's Messengers?"

"I do. For she is known to the Black-guard."

"Surely Charles White has the power to get one girl sprung from Old Nass," Daniel reflected. Then he stopped short, astounded to hear himself speaking like a criminal.

"Aye. Straight from there, to his bedchamber, to be his whore until he has worn her out, at which point he'll no doubt give her a decent interment in Fleet Ditch!" Mr. Baynes was as upset to *imagine* this horror, as he would have been to *witness* it, and had gone all twitchy now; his wooden teeth were chattering together, and clear snot was streaming out of one nostril.

"And you phant'sy I am a decent sort?"

"I said it before, sir, you are a gentle man."

"If I give you my word that I'll go to the Spinning-Ken and look after your daughter—"

"Not so loud, I pray you! For I do not want Mr. White to so much as know that she exists!"

"I am no less wary of him than are you, Mr. Baynes."

"Then—you give your word, Dr. Gatemouth?"

"I do."

"Her name is Hannah Spates, and she pounds hemp in Mr. Wilson's shop, for she's a strong girl."

"Done."

"Prithee, send in the Queen's Messengers."

DANIEL'S REWARD FOR THIS makeshift act of grace was a free moonlight river-cruise to the Tower of London. This was strangely idyllic. The best part of it was that Charles White and his platoon of feral gentlemen were not present; for after a short conversation with Mr. Baynes, they had flocked on the deck like a murder of crows, clambered back into the row-boats, and set off for Black Friars Stairs.

Even the passage of London Bridge, which, on a smaller boat, was always a Near Death Experience—the sort of event gentlemen would go home and write down, in the expectation that people would want to read about it—was uneventful. They fired a swivel-gun to wake up the drawbridge-keeper in Nonsuch House, and raised a silver-greyhound banner. He stopped traffic on London Bridge, and raised the span for them, and the sloop's master suffered the current to flush them through into the Pool.

Half an hour later they clambered by torch-light into the dank kerf of a Tower Wharf staircase. As Daniel ascended the stair, and his head rose through the plane of the Wharf, the whole Tower complex unfolded before and above him like a vast black book, writ on pages of jet in fire and smoke.

Almost directly ahead on the wharf stood a jumble of small buildings fenced about with a palisade. The wicket had been opened by one of the Wharf Guard standing the night watch. Daniel moved through it in a crowd, and entered one of the small buildings, troubled by the sense that he was invading someone's dwelling. Indeed he was, as this Wharf-apartment seemed to be home for (at least) a porter, a sutler, a tavern-keeper, and diverse members of their families. But a few steps on, he felt timbers under his feet and sensed that they'd passed through into a different space: they were outdoors again, crossing over a wooden causeway that spanned a straight lead of quiet water. It must be the Tower moat, and this must be a drawbridge.

The planking led to a small opening in the sheer face of the Tower's outer wall. On the right hand, a wedge-shaped bastion was thrust out from the same wall, but it offered no doorways: only embrasures and murder-holes from which defenders could shower fatal attentions upon people trying to get across this bridge. But tonight the drawbridge was down, the portcullis was up, no projectiles were spitting out of the orifices of the Tower. The group slowed down to file through a sort of postern gate into the base of Byward Tower.

To their left was a larger gate leading to the causeway that served as the Tower's main land entrance, but it had been closed and locked for the night. And indeed, as soon as the last of their group had made it across the drawbridge, the postern gate was closed behind them, and locked by a middle-aged bloke in a night-cap and slippers. Daniel had enough Tower lore stored up in his brain to suspect that this would be the Gentleman Porter, and that he must live in one of the flats that abounded in this corner of the complex. So they were locked in for the night.

With the gates closed, the ground floor of Byward Tower was a tomb. Isaac and Daniel instinctively moved out from under it and into the open cross where Mint Street came together with Water Lane. There they tarried for a minute to watch Mr. Baynes being frog-marched off to a dungeon somewhere.

Anyone who entered the Tower of London as they just had, expecting to pass through a portal and find himself in an open bailey, would be disappointed. Byward Tower, through which they'd just passed, was the corner-stone of the *outer* defenses. All it afforded was entry to a narrow belt of land surrounding the *inner* defenses, which were much higher and more ancient.

But even an expert on medieval fortifications would be perplexed by what Daniel and Isaac could see from here, which in no way resembled a defensive system. They appeared, rather, to be standing in the intersection of two crowded streets in pre-Fire London. Somewhere behind the half-timbered fronts of the houses and taverns that lined those streets lay defensive works of stone and mortar that would make the Inner Ward impregnable to a pre-gunpowder army. But in order to see those medieval bastions, embrasures, *et cetera*, one would have to raze and scrape off everything that had been built atop and in front of them, a project akin to sacking a small English town.

Byward Tower was a Gordian knot in and of itself, in that it connected the complex's two most important gates to its most congested corner. But that was only its ground floor. The building consisted of two circular towers bridged together, and was a favorite place to keep important prisoners. It now stood to one side of Daniel and Isaac. To their other side was the enormous, out-thrust bulk of Bell Tower, the southwestern bastion of the inner wall. But Daniel only knew this because he was a scholar who'd looked at old pictures of the place. Much more obvious were the ground-level structures built facing the street: a couple of taverns right at the base of Bell Tower, more sutlers' shacks, and small houses and apartments heaped and jumbled against and on top of every ledge of stone that afforded purchase.

Anyone coming into such a crowded place would instinctively scan for a way out. The first one that met the eye, as one came in through Byward Gate, was Water Lane—the strip of pavement between inner and outer defenses, along the river side. This view was half-blocked by Bell Tower and its latter-day excrescences, but none the less seemed like the obvious path to choose, for Water Lane was broad. And because it was open to the public during the daytime, it was generally free of clutter.

The other choice was to make a hard left, turning one's back on the river, and wander off into what looked like a medieval slum, thrown up against the exterior of a Crusader castle by a lot of bustling rabble who were not allowed to come in and mingle with the knights and squires. The spine of it was a single narrow lane. On the left side of that lane ran a series of old casemates, which in soldier-parlance meant fortified galleries, specifically meant to be overrun by invaders, so that defenders, purposely stranded inside of them, could shoot through the windows into the attackers' backs and turn the ditch into a killing-ground. In new forts, the casemates were burrowed into the ramparts, and protected by earth. In obsolete ones like this, they were built against the inner faces of curtain-walls. The ones on the left side of Mint Street were of that sort. They rose nearly to the height of the outer wall, obscuring it, and making it easy to forget that all of this was built *intra muros.* Gunpowder had long since made them militarily useless, and they had been remodeled into workshops and barracks for the Mint.

On the right side, packed in tight as they could be, but never rising above a certain level—like mussels along the tide-line—another line of buildings clung to the higher walls of the inner defenses.

From the corner there at Byward, it all looked like the wreckage of a burnt city that had been raked into a stone sluice where it wanted a good rainstorm to quench the flames, beat down the smoke, and wash it away. The rhythmic crashing noises echoing down the length of this dung-choked ghetto provided the only clue that something of an organized nature was going on in there; but this hardly made Mint Street seem more inviting, even when one knew (as Daniel did) that the incessant bashing was the sound of coins being minted by trip-hammers.

In a funny way, he thought, this burning gutter was a sort of counterpart to Fleet Ditch.

Since the Fleet was full of earth and water, and Mint Street full of fire and air, this was not an insight that ever would have come to Daniel's mind, if not for the fact that, just a few scant minutes before, he had been staring up the one, and now here he was, staring up the other.

On further reflection, he decided that the two had nothing in common, save that both ran in the same direction to the Thames, and both were cluttered and stagnant and had a lot of shit in them.

He had known Isaac for fifty years, and so he knew, with perfect certainty, that Isaac would turn away from the clear, cool, pleasant prospect of Water Lane, and march into the metallic seething of Mint Street. This he now did, and Daniel was content to follow in his wake. He'd never penetrated more than a few yards into the Mint; the farthest he'd ever gotten was the office that was just inside the entrance, on the left side of the Lane, and up some stairs. Of course Isaac swept past it and kept on going.

The Tower of London was essentially square, though, to be pedantic, an elbow in its northern side made it into a pentagon. The strip between inner and outer walls ran the full circuit. The southern side, along the river, was accounted for by Water Lane; but everything else was Mint Street, which was to say that the Mint embraced the Tower of London on three sides (technically four, taking the northern elbow into account).

Strange as it might seem, in a town with but a single street, it was easy to get lost. The view down the street was obstructed by ten different bastions thrust out from the inner wall, and so one could never see very far. Daniel was of course aware that he was in a horseshoe-shaped continuum, but once he lost count of the towers, this did him little practical good. By walking faithfully in one direction or the other, he would eventually come to an extremity of the horseshoe, and exit onto one end or the other of Water Lane. But the length of the Mint was a quarter of a mile, which for a Londoner might as well have been the distance between Oslo and Rome. Such an interval sufficed to distinguish between the Fleet Ditch and the Royal Society, or the Houses of Parliament at Westminster and the knackers' yards of Southwark. So by the time he'd followed Isaac past a couple of those bastions, and gone round a turn or two, Daniel felt as if he'd ventured deep into a city as outlandish as Algiers or Nagasaki.

Two hundred feet in, the way was bottlenecked by the handsome semicircular curve of Beauchamp Tower. Directly across from it, crammed against the outer wall, were the long casemates where silver and gold were melted down in great furnaces. Continuing north, they immediately passed more casemates containing the coin-bashers. Then they rounded their first corner, another bottleneck between the bastion of Devereux Tower and a low bulky fort in the vertex of the outer wall, called Legge's Mount. Both were made very strong, and both were still manned by the Black Torrent Guard, to withstand bombardment from that æternal Menace, London, which pressed in close on the Tower here.

Isaac slowed, and looked at Daniel as if he wanted to say something.

Daniel glanced curiously down the segment of Mint Street that had just come into view. He was strangely let down to see that it was quiet and almost peaceful. He'd been hoping that the Mint would only become more Hellish the deeper he went into it, like the Inferno according to Dante, and that in its deepest penetralia would be a forge of surpassing hotness where Isaac turned lead into gold. But from this corner 'twas plain that the climax had come already—that all the big, hot, and loud bits were close to the entrance (which made sense logistically, he had to admit) and that this northern limb was what passed for a sedate residential neighborhood. It was about as hellish as Bloomsbury Square. Which only went to show that Englishmen could live anywhere. Condemn an Englishman to hell, and he'd plant a bed of petunias and roll out a nice bowling-green on the brimstone.

Isaac now said something the precise wording of which scarcely mattered. The import was that Daniel was an impediment to his arcane nocturnal researches, and would he please go away. Daniel answered with some pleasantry and Isaac hurried away, leaving Daniel alone to rove up and down a quarter-mile of Mint.

He gave it a once-over, just to stop feeling lost. The northern limb sported a couple of houses at first, obviously for high Mint officials. Then it was workmen's barracks on the left side, and, on the right, milling machines of some sort, perhaps the ones that stamped inscriptions on the edges of coins to foil clippers.

As he approached the northern elbow he found himself among soldiers, and thought he'd somehow wandered astray; but after getting round the turn he began to see, again, Mint dwellings on the left and milling shops on the right. So 'twould seem the conversion of military casemates to monetary workhouses was a work still in progress.

There was another sharp right turn, pinched between the bastion where they kept the Crown Jewels and another defensive mount, like Legge's, in the outer wall. This brought him round to the eastern limb of the Mint, which ran straight south to Water Lane. A few strangely pleasant houses with gardens soon gave way to more of a smoky, glowing, banging character: probably the Irish Mint, which appeared to run all the way to the end.

By all rights he ought to've been tired. But the noise and vigor of the Mint infected his blood, and he ended up walking the entire length of it several times before he began to feel the effects of his long day.

The chapel bell tolled midnight from the Inner Ward as Daniel was rounding the northwest corner, near Legge's Mount, for the third time. Daniel took it as a signal to duck into a little court along the outer wall, a gap between casemates, which had been beckoning to him. It appeared to belong to one of the Mint officials, who kept a wee casemate-house just next to it, as cozy as a dwelling made from a last-ditch fortress defense could ever be. At any rate, the court had a bench in it. Daniel sat down on that bench and fell asleep suddenly.

His watch claimed it was two o'clock in the morning when he, and all the workers who dwelt along Mint Street, were awakened by a sort of Roman Triumph making its way up from Byward Tower. Or at least it sounded as loud and proud as that. But when Daniel finally got up from his bench, dry and stiff as a cadaver, and tottered out to look, he thought it bore the aspect of a funeral-procession.

Charles White was riding atop the black wagon, which was surrounded by cloaked out-riders—mounted Messengers—and followed by a troop of soldiers on foot: two platoons of the Queen's Own Black Torrent Guards, who garrisoned the Tower, and who (or so Daniel gathered) were in the unenviable position of being at the beck and call of Charles White, whenever he wanted reinforcements. The black wagon itself was now padlocked *from the outside.*

A strange parade it was. Yet much better suited to this horseshoe-town than any of your sunlit, gay, flower-strewing, music-playing parades. Daniel could not help but fall in step with it as the wagon came abreast of him.

"So!" Daniel exclaimed, "'twould appear that the information provided by our guest was correct."

He could feel White's glare on his face like sunburn. "All I'll allow is that our hen squawked, and laid an egg, whose savour is not yet proved. More eggs had better follow, and they had best be full of excellent meat, or else that hen shall furnish Jack Ketch with a dish of wings and drumsticks."

White's hen/egg gambit drew light applause. "How'll you try this egg we have just gathered, sir?" asked one of the foot-soldiers.

"Why, crack its shell first," he returned, "and then 'tis a choice, whether to fry it on the griddle, boil it 'til hard, scramble it—or eat it raw!"

Another round of laughter for this witticism. Daniel regretted having exposed himself in Mint Street. But they were now making the turn at the elbow, bringing new buildings and bastions in view, and White had lost interest.

"We have him!" White proclaimed, seemingly talking to the moon. But following White's gaze, Daniel was able to make out Isaac's silhouette against a narrow archway on the right side, backlit by several torches; or was that the false dawn of furnace-light?

They'd worked their way round to the best district of the whole Mint: the northeast, where the Master and Warden had their private houses and courts on the left. But Isaac was on the right. The arch in which he stood was some kind of sally-port of the Inner Keep.

"He fought like Hercules," White continued, "despite being one-armed. And we could not clap him in manacles for the same reason!" Everyone laughed. "This holds him very well, though!" He rapped on the roof of the wagon.

The procession drew to a halt there, under the embrasures of the bastion called Brick Tower. Daniel now perceived that Brick Tower had been conceived as a mustering-place where the very bravest, drunkest, or stupidest knights in the Tower of London would gather in preparation for a sally. When they were ready, they would charge down a stone stair that ran along the front of the inner wall, make a sharp left, and continue down a second flight, erupting from the door where Isaac was standing, into the ditch, where God knows what would transpire between them and any foe-men who'd penetrated that far, and survived the fire from the casemates.

All of which was of primarily historical interest tonight. Save that this sally-stair held, in the crook of its arm as it were, a large store-house, and next to it a stable, belonging to the Mint. These buildings obscured the lower half of Brick Tower, and for all Daniel knew, might be connected with it through passageways—squinting at old sooty out-buildings in the dark at two in the morning left plenty of lee-way for the imagination.

At any rate, the horses drawing the black wagon were obviously of the view that they were home, and the night's work finished. It was into those dark buildings that the wagon was now conducted. The Messengers remained within, the Guards emerged and dispersed to their barracks, some of which were all of fifty paces away.

This left Daniel alone in the street. Or so he phant'sied, for a few moments, until he noticed a red coal bobbing up and down in a moon-shadow across the way, and realized that someone was lurking there, smoking a pipe, and observing him.

"Did you participate, Sergeant Shaftoe?"

He was only making an educated guess. But the pipe-coal emerged from the shadows, and the form of Bob coalesced in moon-light.

"I dodged that detail, I do confess, Guv."

"Such errands are not to your liking?"

"Let some youngster take the glory. Opportunities for action are scarce of late, now that the war is in recess."

"At the other end of town," said Daniel, "they do not say 'tis in *recess,* but *finished.*"

"What other end of town would that be, then?" demanded Bob, feigning elderly daftness. "Would you be speaking of Westminster?" He said that in a very good accent. But then he reverted to mudlark Cockney. "You can't mean the Kit-Cat Clubb."

"Nay, e'en at the Kit-Cat Clubb they say the same."

"To Doctors they say it, I think. To soldiers they say different things. The discourse of the Whigs is cloven like a devil's hoof."

An ugly commotion now arose within the stable at the foot of Brick Tower, which, while Doctor Waterhouse and Sergeant Shaftoe had been conversing, had been lit up with torches. The doors of the wagon had been unlocked, and men were shouting in a way Daniel hadn't heard since he'd gone to the bear-baiting in Rotherhithe. From where they were standing, it was not loud. But something in the tenor of it made it out of the question for Daniel and Bob to continue their talk. Suddenly it rose to such a pitch that Daniel shrank away, thinking that the prisoner might be about to escape altogether. There was a tattoo of thumps, and a scream or two; then momentary silence, broken by a man calling out in a language of bent vowels and outlandish syllables.

"I have heard curses in many tongues, but this one is new to me," Bob remarked. "Where's the prisoner from?"

"He is from Muscovy," Daniel decided, after listening for a few more moments, "and he is not cursing, but praying."

"If that is how Muscovites sound when they talk to God, I'd hate to hear their blaspheming."

After that, all movements inside the stable were accompanied by the clanking of irons. "They put a collar on him," Bob said learnedly. The sounds receded, then vanished all of a sudden. "He's in the Tower now," Bob announced. "God have mercy on him." He sighed, and gazed down the length of the street in the direction of the full moon, which was swinging low over London. "I had better rest," he said, "and so had you—if you intend to come."

"Come where?" Daniel asked.

"Wherever we are directed by the Russian."

It took a moment for Daniel to work through all that was implied by this. "You think that they will torture him—and he will break—and lead us to—?"

"It is only a matter of time, once Charles White has him in the Tower. Come, I'll get you a proper billet, away from the noise."

"What noise?" Daniel asked, because the Mint had been extraordinarily quiet these last few minutes. But as he followed Bob Shaftoe back up the street, he began to hear, through one of the open embrasures in Brick Tower, the sound of a man screaming.

River Thames

THE NEXT MORNING (23 APRIL 1714)

"IN THE END THE MUSCOVITE spoke willingly," Isaac announced.

He and Daniel were on the poop deck of Charles White's sloop *Atalanta*. Twelve hours had passed since the Muscovite had been brought into the Tower.

Daniel had spent one of those hours attempting to sleep in the officers' quarters of the Queen's Own Black Torrent Guards. Then the whole Tower had been roused by a call to arms. Or so it had seemed, from the perspective of one savagely irritable old man who desperately wanted to sleep. In truth, only the First Company of the Guards was rousted. To the other denizens of the Tower it was the most delicious sort of nocturnal alarm: one that gave occasion only to roll over and go back to sleep.

After some few minutes of fuss and bother, which he scarcely remembered since he'd been asleep on his feet, Daniel had been sent out of the Tower of London the way he'd come in, and ushered aboard *Atalanta*. He had repaired to a small cabin and seized the first thing that looked like a bunk. Some time later he had been awakened by sunlight, and peered out a window to discover that they had moved all of a quarter of a mile from Tower Wharf. Situation Normal: some foul-up had brought the proceeding (whatever it was) to a stand; they had Hurried Up only to Wait. He had pulled a blanket over his face and gone back to sleep.

When he'd finally woken up, not long ago, and dragged himself, stiff and foul and squinty-eyed, abovedecks to piss over the rail, he'd been startled to find open country around them, and the river's width swollen to a mile. He guessed they were nearing the end of Long Reach, between Erith and Greenhithe, which would put them about halfway from London to the sea.

To get to the rail, he had to "beg your pardon" through many dragoons. The entire First Company—more than a hundred men—had been crammed aboard. Even when half of them were packed in belowdecks, this made the upperdeck so crowded that men could not sit down. Rather than trying to walk upon the deck, the sloop's able seamen scampered like spiders through rigging overhead. Fortunately, as was the practice on all well-run ships, the aft or poop was reserved for officers; and Fellows of the Royal Society were given honorary status as such. Once he'd dragged himself up the stairs to the poop, Daniel found elbow room to spare, and plenty of space along the rail to get fresh air, to urinate, and to spit out the cottony stuff that had grown in his mouth while he'd been sleeping. A cabin-boy, perhaps alarmed by the volume of fluid this already-shriveled gager was discharging into the Thames, even brought him a ladle of water.

And at some point Sir Isaac appeared at his elbow, making his day complete.

"He spoke willingly," Daniel repeated, trying not to sound aghast.

"Indeed, for a choice was laid before him: endure confinement and interrogation in the Tower to the end of his days, or tell what he knew, and be returned to Russia. He chose Russia."

"Well if you put it *that* way, *anyone* who speaks under torture does so willingly," Daniel pointed out. Normally he would have been slower to jab at Isaac, but he was in a wretched state, and moreover, had performed a great boon for Isaac during the previous day.

Isaac retorted, "I saw the Muscovite returning to his cell on his own two feet when it was over. Whatever was done to him was less violent—though it may have been more excruciating—than the beatings that are given to yon soldiers, every day, for trifling offenses. Mr. White knows ways of securing the cooperation of prisoners without inflicting permanent injury."

"He'll go back to Muscovy with both of his ears, then?"

"His ears, his eyes, his beard, and all the limbs he came in with."

Daniel had not yet turned to look Isaac in the face. Instead he was facing abaft, looking at a pair of flat-bottomed river boats that followed in their wake. These were laden mostly with horses, and all the clutter that went with them, viz. saddles, tack, and grooms. No wonder they'd been slow to get underway.

While he'd been conversing with Isaac, the sloop had been negotiating a zigzag in the river, and widening its lead over the horse-barges; now they were swinging wide round a large, marshy lobe in the south bank, and coming in view of a place, a couple of miles downstream, where bright green downs and white chalk-hills crowded the right bank, and gave purchase for a river-side settlement. There, he knew, would be Gravesend. The seamen who were manning the sloop—scattered very thin over the crowd of Guards—became more alert. The laconic, incomprehensible commands of the sloop's captain came more frequently. They were going to put in there. Indeed, they had few other choices, as once they got below Gravesend there'd be nothing but ooze all the way to the North Sea; and what was the point of barging a lot of horses down the river to drown 'em?

"What do you imagine a Russian was doing here, in business with Jack the Coiner?" Daniel asked.

"Jack enjoys the lavish support of some foreign potentate, most likely the King of France," Isaac answered. "For make no mistake, the commerce of England is envied by all the world. Those Kings who cannot raise their own realms to our level, phant'sy that they can bring us down to theirs, by polluting our coinage. If the King of France may harbor such ambitions, why, so may the Tsar of all the Russias."

"You think the Muscovite is a Tsarish agent?"

"That is the most creditable explanation."

"You said he had a beard?"

"Indeed, a long luxuriant one."

"How many years' growth, would you say?"

"Soaked and stretched, it would extend below his navel."

"He sounds like a Raskolnik to me," Daniel said.

"What's a Raskolnik?"

"I haven't the faintest idea. But they hate the Tsar. And one of the reasons they hate him is that he has decreed that they must shave off their long luxuriant beards."

This silenced Isaac for a while, by forcing him to carry out immense recalculations. Daniel took unfair advantage of it to add: "Not long ago a new warship being built for the Tsar in Rotherhithe was burned by an Infernal Device, secreted in the recesses of the hull during the night-time. It used clock-work to shatter a phial containing white phosphorus, which, when the air touched it, burst into flame. Or so I have inferred from smelling its smoke, and sifting through the residue."

Isaac was too fascinated by the news to wonder how Daniel had come by it. "That is the same mechanism as was used to set off the explosion in Crane Court!"

"Been looking into it, have you?"

"I did not ignore the warning you sent me."

"The one-armed Muscovite is no foreign agent," Daniel prophesied, "but a sort of Phanatique who absconded from Russia for the same reason that my great-grandfather, John Waterhouse, fled to Geneva during the reign of Bloody Mary. At loose ends in London, he somehow became a part of Jack's criminal net-work. I am quite certain he has not the slightest intention of going back to Russia."

"Your hypothesis is belied by your own evidence," Isaac said. He had reverted to a high, magnificent tone that he used for philosophical discourse. "You have convinced me that the same organization that set off the Crane Court explosion, burned the Tsar's ship in Rotherhithe. But a mere band of criminals does not pursue foreign policy!"

"It may be that the Swedes paid them to destroy the ship a-building," Daniel said, "which is easier than sinking it after it is launched and armed. Or it may be that the Muscovite, being, as I gad, a sort of Phanatique, did it by himself, as Puritans used to strike whatever blows they might against the King."

Isaac reflected for a moment, then said, "To carry on discourse, of a speculative nature, about Jack's organization and its designs, is idle."

"Why is it idle?"

"Because in a few hours they will be in our power, and then we may simply ask them."

"Ah," Daniel said, "I could not tell if we were going to arrest Jack the Coiner, or invade France."

Isaac briefly made a noise that sounded like laughing. "We are going to lay siege to a castle."

"You can't be serious."

" 'Tis a Jacobite stronghold," Isaac said. He was being just a bit facetious.

"So in a sense we *are* going to invade France," Daniel muttered.

"One might think of it as a chip of France on the banks of the Thames," Isaac said, showing a taste for whimsy that was, to say the least, out of character. But (as shown by the laugh and the sarcasm) he'd learned a conversational gambit or two during his decades in London.

For example, prating about the genealogy of noble families: "You remember the Angleseys, I am certain."

"How could I not?" Daniel answered.

Indeed, the very mention of the name forced him to come awake, as if he had had just been told that the sails of Blackbeard had been sighted on the horizon. He looked Isaac full in the face for the first time since the conversation had begun.

As a young man Daniel had known the Angleseys as a clan of dangerous crypto-Catholic court fops. The patriarch, Thomas More Anglesey, Duke of Gunfleet, had been a contemporary, and a mortal rival, of John Comstock, who was the Earl of Epsom and the first great noble backer of the Royal Society. Comstock had been the C, and Anglesey the first A, in the CABAL, the group of five who had run the Restoration government of Charles II.

In those days Daniel had been too naïve to comprehend just how close the connections were between the Angleseys and the royal family. Later, he'd learned that the two sons of Thomas More Anglesey, Louis (the Earl of Upnor) and Phillip (Count Sheerness), were both bastards of Charles II, fathered on a French Countess during the Interregnum, when Charles had been exiled in France. Thomas More Anglesey had then been induced, somehow, to marry the embarrassed Countess and raise the two boys. He'd done a wretched job of it—perhaps he'd been distracted by ceaseless plot-making against John Comstock.

The younger of the two "Anglesey" bastards, Louis, had been a great swordsman, and had used Puritans as practice targets during his years at Trinity College, Cambridge. He'd been there at the same time as Daniel, Isaac, and various other fascinating human specimens, including Roger Comstock and the late Duke of Monmouth. Later, Louis had become interested in Alchemy. Daniel even now blamed him for seducing Isaac into the Esoteric Brotherhood. But there was no point in laying blame today—for the Earl of Upnor had perished a quarter-century ago at the Battle of Aughrim, fending off a hundred Puritans, Germans, Danes, &c. with his rapier, until shot in the back.

By that time his supposed father, the Duke of Gunfleet, had long since died. The Duke's final years had not been good ones. Having ruined the Silver Comstocks—driven John into rustic retirement, and the rest of them all the way to Connecticut—and having taken over their house in St. James's, he had seen his own fortunes destroyed, by bad investments, by his sons' gambling debts (which must have hurt him all the more, as they weren't really his sons), and above all by the Popish Plot, which was a sort of politico-religious rabies that had taken over London round 1678. He had packed the entire family off to France and sold the London palace to Roger Comstock, who had promptly leveled it with the ground and turned it into a real estate development. In France the Duke had died—Daniel had no idea when, but it would have been a long time ago—leaving only Phillip, Count Sheerness: the older of the two bastards.

Count Sheerness. All of these names—Gunfleet, Upnor, and Sheerness—referred to places round the mouth of the Thames, and had been handed out to the Angleseys by Charles II in reward for services performed at time of the Restoration. Daniel could only recollect a few of the details. Thomas More Anglesey had been in a wee naval scrap off Gunfleet Sands, and sunk a boat-load of die-hard Puritan sailors, or something like that, and had proceeded to the Buoy of the Nore, where he'd rallied a lot of Royalist ships around him.

The Nore was a sandbar—really the extremity of a vast region of shifting sands deposited round the place where the Thames and the Medway joined together and emptied into the sea. A Buoy had always been anchored there, a few miles off Sheerness Fort, to warn incoming ships, and to force them to choose between going to port—which would, God and tides willing, take them up the Medway, under the guns of Sheerness Fort and then of Castle Upnor, and eventually to Rochester and Chatham—or to starboard, which set them on the way up the Thames to London. Anglesey's makeshift fleet had been neither the first nor the last invasion force to use that buoy as a rallying-point. The Dutch had done it a few years later. In fact, one of the peculiar duties assigned to the naval ships in this part of the river was to sail up to the Buoy and blow it out of the water whenever serious trouble loomed, so that foreign invaders could not find it.

At the time Charles II had come back, the ignominious Dutch invasion lay in the future, and Sheerness and Upnor seemed glorious names. But to any Englishman who'd been alive and awake during the Anglo-Dutch War, most certainly including Daniel and Isaac, such words as "Buoy of the Nore" and "Sheerness" connoted dark doings by foreigners, farcical bungling by Englishmen, grievous humiliation, proof of England's vulnerability to seaborne intruders.

So if Isaac's reference to Count Sheerness was the ink, then all of this history was the page the ink was printed on.

If they kept going as they were, they'd be in view of the Buoy of the Nore in a few hours.

"You can't be serious," Daniel blurted.

"If I observed faces, instead of stars, and philosophized about thinking, instead of Gravity, I could write a treatise about what I have seen passing over your visage in these past thirty seconds," Isaac said.

"I wonder if I am arrogant to think that Waterhouses are no less deeply enmeshed in the affairs of the world, than Angleseys or Comstocks. For just when I think that all have passed on, and my connections to them severed—"

"You find yourself on a boat for Sheerness," Isaac concluded.

"Tell me the tale, then," Daniel said, "for I've not kept up with the Angleseys."

"They've a French name now, and French titles, inherited from the mother of Louis and Phillip, and they dwell at Versailles, save when they are at the exile court in St.-Germain, paying homage to the Pretender. Only Phillip survived long enough to propagate the line—he had two sons before he was poisoned by his wife in 1700. The sons are in their twenties; neither has been to England or speaks a word of English. But the older of the two remains Lord of the Manor in certain pockets of land around Sheerness, on either bank of the Medway."

"And 'tis unthinkable he'd be anything but a Jacobite."

"The situation of his properties is most convenient for smugglers—or for agents of France. In particular he is lord of a certain lonely castle that stands off the Isle of Grain, in view of the open sea, and that may be reached directly from the Continent without interference by Her Majesty's Customs agents."

"Was all of this information provided by the Russian? For I am not inclined to trust him."

"The tale of the absorption of the Angleseys into France is well known. The particulars concerning Shive Tor come from the Muscovite."

"You stated a minute ago that Jack the Coiner was an agent of Louis XIV," Daniel said, "and that he was generously supported. You are telling me that this thing you call Shive Tor—"

"Has been made available to Jack," Isaac concluded. "It is the head-quarters of his criminal empire, his treasure-keep, his bolt-hole, his conduit to France."

It is a convenient explanation, Daniel said to himself, *for the fact that a varlet has been able to evade you for so many years.* But he knew if he said it aloud, Isaac would heave him overboard.

"You phant'sy that's where it is, don't you?"

Isaac stared at him, and did not so much as blink for a long time. After a bit this made Daniel nervous, and as if he needed to fill in the silence with some words. "It would make sense," he continued, "if the gold—the Solomonic Gold—came off a ship, as you suppose—what better place to unload it, and to store it, than a remote and obscure watch-tower, without most of Her Majesty's defenses and customs houses?"

"I shall thank you not to divulge this to the others. We must take utmost care until the gold is safe in the Tower of London."

"What then?"

"I beg your pardon?"

"Suppose you find King Solomon's Gold in Shive Tor and bring it home to your laboratory, and extract the Philosophic Mercury from it—that's it, then, isn't it?"

"That's *what*, then?"

"It's the End of the World or something, it is the Apocalypse, you've solved the riddle, found God's presence on Earth, the secret of eternal life—really, this entire *conversation* is idle, in a sense—none of it *matters*, does it?"

"There is no telling," Isaac said, in the soothing tones of one who is trying to calm a madman. "My calculations from the Book of Revelation suggest that the End of the World will not occur until 1876."

"Really!?" Daniel said, fascinated. "That's a hell of a long time. A hundred sixty-two years! Perhaps this Solomonic Gold is over-rated."

"Solomon had it," Isaac pointed out, "and the world did not come to an end *then*, did it? Christ Jesus Himself—the Word made flesh—trod the earth for thirty-three years, and even now, seventeen centuries later, the world is a heathenish and foul place. Never did I suppose that the Solomonic Gold was to be the world's Panacea."

"What *is* it, then? What is the bleeding point?"

"If nothing else," Isaac said, "it will furnish me with the means to give the German a *warm welcome* when he comes over the sea."

And he turned away from Daniel and went belowdecks.

Lieutenant's Lodging, the Tower of London
AFTERNOON

SAID LIEUTENANT-GENERAL EWELL THROWLEY, the Lieutenant of the Tower: "I do most humbly beg your pardon, my lord, but I simply *did not understand*."

His prisoner and guest, Rufus MacIan, Lord Gy, peered with his one extant eye across the dining-room table into the flushing face of his captor and host. Lord Gy was only thirty years old, but he was big and whiskery and banged-up and haggard. Very clearly and distinctly, he repeated his last statement: "Yeir buird is a fere bit o wrichtwork. A jiner today can never fetch such mastie straiks as these, he must send strags upaland to scaff amang the rammel, an plaister all together oot o skifting his grandfaither would hae tossed inti the chaffer."

Ewell Throwley was forced to abort, and circle back around. "My lord, we are military men, the both of us, and saw hard service in the late War. This remains true in spite of the revolutions in Fortune that have made you a condemned prisoner, and me the officer in charge of the Liberty of the Tower. I learned in *my* service, as I daresay *you* did in *yours*, that there is a time to set courtly manners aside, and speak *plainly*, one gentleman to another. There is no shame, no dishonor in so doing. May I speak to you in that wise now?"

Lord Gy shrugged. "Aye, let's hae it."

Gy was the name of a river near Arras. Back in the days when he had been named simply Rufus MacIan, this man had, on an impulse, splashed across it and cut a French gentleman in two with one swing of a five-foot-long Claymore. The Frenchman had turned out to be a Count, and a Colonel, with a poor sense of direction. The tide of a battle had been turned as a consequence of that Claymore-stroke. MacIan had been ennobled as Lord Gy.

"I knew that I could rely upon you, my lord, as a fellow-soldier," Lieutenant-General Ewell Throwley went on. " 'Tis well. For there is a certain matter never spoken of in polite society, and yet known to all, which will, if we ignore it—pretending that it does not exist—turn what should be a pleasant social occasion into an insufferable ordeal. You do know—or as you would say, 'ken'—what I speak of, my lord?"

"Crivvens!" exclaimed Lord Gy. "Wha hae foostit ben the heid-hoose!?" Then he added, with unmistakable sarcasm: "Serr's, a coud gae through the fluir."

"Brilliant, that is a paradigmatic specimen," said Throwley. "It is this, my lord: you do not speak English."

An awkward moment across the table there. Rufus MacIan drew breath to answer, but Throwley headed him off: "Oh, you understand it perfectly. But it is not what you *speak*. The polite euphemisms are many. We say, my lord Gy has a Highland lilt, a brogue, a burr. But this is to gloss over the true nature of the problem, which is that you simply and in fact are not speaking English. You could if you wanted, but you don't. Please, I beg of you, my lord Gy, speak English, and consider yourself welcome in my house, and at my table."

" 'Twas o the table—the buird—a was discoursing, when ye set in with such an uncanny rant concerning ma accent."

"It is *not* an accent. This is my *point*. My Lord."

"Sixteen month hae a lodged in the Tower o London," said Lord Gy very slowly, "and never seen th'inside o this hoose till now. A meant only to offer a compliment on the furnishings." The Scotsman gripped the edge of the tabletop with both hands and lifted it half an inch off the floor, testing its weight. "These baulks wuid serve to stop bools. Which is to say, cannonballs."

"Your compliments are accepted with gratitude," said Throwley. "As to the delay in extending my hospitality—most regrettable. As you know, it is a long-standing tradition for the Lieutenant of the Tower to take tea with Persons of Quality who have been committed to this place. As a fellow-veteran, I have impatiently awaited the day when I could share this table with you. As no one knows better than you, my lord, during the first year of your incarceration, it was felt best to keep you in heavy irons stapled to the floor of Beauchamp Tower. This I do most sincerely deplore. But since then, we have not heard from you the threats, the promises of death, dismemberment, and mayhem; or if we have, we have not understood them. It has been deemed suitable to move you to a Yeoman Warder's house, like the other guests. You and Mr. Downs have been getting along famously, I presume?"

Both Rufus MacIan and Ewell Throwley now turned their attention to the portly, bearded Beefeater who had escorted the prisoner across the Parade and into the Lieutenant's Lodgings. Yeoman Downs looked tremendously satisfied. Indeed, had looked that way, without letup, since he had opened the door of his wee house on the green a quarter of an hour ago, and led his guest across the grass in a flying wedge of armed Sentinels.

"We hae gaen alang," said Lord Gy gravely, "like a hoose afire."

The Lieutenant of the Tower and the Yeoman Warder alike seemed just a bit uncomfortable with this simile; and so there was now an awkward silence. Lord Gy filled it by humming some sort of weird aimless Gaelic chaunt.

The Lieutenant's Lodging, which was situated in the southwestern corner of the Inner Ward, was a Tudor sort of house, typical of pre-Fire London; now it was remarkable chiefly in that it had never burned down. Downs, Throwley, and MacIan were in a dining-room that had seen a lot of hard service. Throwley's maid and steward hovered in a corridor. Another maid—a servant of Lord Gy, who had followed Downs and Gy across the green—tarried in the entrance-hall with a covered basket. Several armed guards stood outside the front door, looking out over the Parade, which was quiet. Drumbeats, and the bellowing of sergeants, could be heard drifting over the fortifications from the direction of Tower Hill, where the garrison was drilling. Too one could hear the sporadic *pock, pock, pock* of carpenters building the platform where, in seven days, Rufus MacIan's head would be detached from his body.

"Splendid," said Throwley weakly, "that is what Mr. Downs has reported, and most fortunate it is that I have been able to share this table with you before your, er, departure."

"Ye spake a minute or of lang-standin traditions," said Lord Gy, and looked significantly at the Yeoman Warder. Downs relayed the signal to the young woman in the entry hall, who now ventured into the dining-room. Ewell Throwley raised his eyebrows and blinked, for she was a tall and muscular lass with enough red hair to cover three average heads. As she burst across the threshold of the room she executed a sort of running curtsey and tossed a grin at Throwley.

"On the Muir of Rannoch, they grow braw, or they grow na at all," MacIan offered by way of explanation.

"Ah, you have imported a . . . clanswoman from the . . . country to look after you."

"*A* look oot for *her*, sir . . . an orphant she is . . . a trigidy, if ye must know." MacIan cleared his throat. The red-headed lass withdrew a bottle from the market-basket perched on her arm. She gave it to Downs, then curtseyed and backed out of the room. Gy purred some phlegmy endearment to her. Downs handed him the bottle. Gy clasped it tenderly in both hands. "I have prepared an Oration!" he announced in something quite a bit closer to the English spoken by Throwley. This silenced the house. "Sir, ye treat us well here, for condemned traitors. The Tower isna a bread-and-water sort of nick, if a man will only comport himself civilly. Nay, all manner of victuals are allowed iz, and many a laird dines better in the Tower, after he's doomed, than he did a free man in London town. 'Tis a tradition, or so a am told, to share with the Warders, the Major, the Deputy Lieutenant, and—sir—the Lieutenant hissell, some moiety o the comforts ye so generously allow iz to partake of. And this hae a done with the other officers. But—sir—not yet with ye, for a hae na the privilege, till this moment, of making your acquaintance." He raised up the bottle. "Ye alluded afore to my carnaptious first twelvemonth on these premises. A do confess a was frawart and bool-horned. A did misca ye. A wes less than a Highland gentleman should be. But a Highland gentleman is never wantin the comfort of a refreshment that we know as usquebaugh. Some call it the water of life. When a wes allowed to hae it, ma mood an ma manners improved. But today a hae a guid deal more o the *water* than o *life;* for ma social calendar says a hae an Engagement on Tower Hill wi one Jack Ketch, a week frae today. And so a wanted ye to hae this, Lieutenant-General Throwley. It came to me frae a blude-friend only yesterday, and as ye can see, the bottle's never been opened."

Throwley bowed, but did not reach out to accept the bottle, since Rufus MacIan had not yet formally presented it. He contented himself, for now, with a glance at the label. "Glen Coe, twenty-two years old," he read. "Why, 'tis as old as the lassie who brought it in!"

Downs laughed in the manner of all subordinates subjected to the boss's wit. Lord Gy took it gravely. "You're rare gleg in the uptak, sir, why, the twae ir precisely alike in age."

"My lord, I know some London gentlemen who make a study of this usquebaugh, in all its varieties, even as Frenchmen do of Burgundy wine. I confess I know little of Glen this or Glen that—but I have at least the wit to recognize that any bottle aged two and a score years must be of rare excellence."

"Oh, 'tis rare—very few hae survived. Very few. Ye maun learn usquebaugh, sir. For many Jacobites wul be dwellin in this Tower in years to come, an a moiety of 'em wul be Highlanders. Nae man is better poised than ye to make o hissell a collector and a connoisseur."

"Then do let my collection, and my education, begin to-day! David, bring some dram-glasses," Throwley called to the steward who had been waiting outside the servants' entrance to the dining-room. "What can you tell me, my lord, concerning this bottle? What distinguishes it from the common dram?"

"Och, sir, ye maun no consider only its age, but its provenance, or what the French call its *terroir*. For Scotland's a big varyand countra, as crazed, riven, and pitted as ma own visage, gowstie here, cosie thare. Nae brae, nae glen, nae ben like the next. Each wi its own clime, its own sile, its own water. Adam's wine, we call water. A hae known Highlandmen who, when they were lost in smochy weather, could ken just where they were by scoopin up a handful o water frae a burn or a loch, an havin a wee gust."

"Or, I daresay, a wee dram from the nearest still!" put in Lieutenant-General Throwley, to the great entertainment of Yeoman Warder Downs. But Rufus MacIan accepted the jest with equanimity, and settled the chuckling of the two Englishmen with the calm stare of his clear blue eye.

"Dinna you make fun! 'Tis true. For the usquebaugh is the daughter of the cold clear waters tha dance in those Highland burns."

"My lord, modest chap that you are, you do not do justice to the men who dwell in those glens. For surely there is skill, there is technique—it is not a mere matter of stirring together a few natural constituents."

Rufus MacIan raised his eyebrows and held up an index finger. "Point well taken, sir, an a thank ye for gien me a fair opportunity to blaw mynes ain horn!"

Downs and Throwley laughed. A silver tray, a-rattle with small cups, had been brought in and set down. "Please, my lord, sit with us."

"A wul stand, thank ye, as befits a professor afore his scholars."

The two Englishmen were left slightly ill at ease, but Lord Gy made it plain by gestures that they were to sit, and even pulled out Downs's chair for him. He explained: "In that wee tissle at Malplaquet, which ye may hae heard of, ma company were ruggin an rivin wi some Frenchmen. A took a muckle cloot frae a musket butt, fell frae ma horse, an bemang'd my rig." He put his hands on his kidneys and shoved his pelvis forward. His sporran flew at the Englishmen and a barrage of pops and creaks came out of his lower spine.

" 'Tis true, he never sits, but drives me mad with his pacing," Downs put in.

MacIan was at such obvious pains to make them at ease that Downs and Throwley acquiesced, and leaned back comfortably in their chairs to hear the continuation of the lecture.

"As the landscape o ma countra is fractured into diverse muirs, glens, gullions, snibs, howes, scaurs, linns, lirks, *et cetera,* so ma nation, as is well known, is divided into many clans, and the clans into septs. And it is among the auld men, the lang in the horn as we say, that the wit and the airt of usquebaugh-making is concentrated—I maun wax poetic an say, *distilled.* As the septs and clans differ, so do the stills and the airt of their use, and so, accordingly, does the produce."

"Prithee, then, tell us of the sept and clan of this place whose name is on the bottle," Throwley said. "For some reason the name of Glen Coe is familiar to me; but during the War my head got so overflowed with outlandish place-names, I can no longer sort them out."

"Why, 'tis remarkable ye should inquire, sir, for it is *ma* clan and *ma* sept!"

Downs and Throwley laughed heartily at this, as it seemed to have been ingeniously laid, like a conjuror's trick. The Englishmen were looking a bit wide-eyed at Lord Gy now, seeing him anew, as a regular bloke, a merry companion.

The Scotsman made the faintest suggestion of a bow to acknowledge the glow of appreciation on their faces, and continued: "That is why a am givin ye this praisent now, Lieutenant-General Throwley. For a Highlander, the water of life that comes frae his oon glen is as much a part of him as his oon livin blude. A gie ye this so it wul aye be livin on after the deid-strake hae fallen on ma neck on yonder Hill." And now, finally, he extended the bottle across the table to Throwley.

Throwley, with an Englishman's eye for the ceremonial gesture, stood up smartly and accepted the gift with a bow. When he sat, so, finally, did MacIan.

"But my lord, again modesty obstructs your duty as our professor. We should learn something of the people of Glen Coe before we drink their, er . . ."

"The water o their life, sir."

"Indeed."

"There isna much to relate of MacIan of MacDonald," said Lord Gy. "We ir a wee sept, much more so of late. Glen Coe is an uncommon high, weather-glim scaup o land in the north of Argyll, no far frae Fort William. It runs from a lofty gowl in the Grampians down to the slate-mines at Ballachulish, at the heid of the loch called Linnhe, which runs down to plash the shores of Mull and spaw into the Atlantic. A wilsome, out o the way place is Glen Coe. When we do receive outdwellars, 'tis ever a surpreese, and more oft than na, they turn out to be lost on the way to Crianlarich. We try to show them hospitality none the less. Hospitality, we have learnt, is an uncannie thing. One may never tell how 'twill be repaid."

"Is very much usquebaugh produced in Glen Coe?"

" 'Tis odd that ye should ask, for I believe *none* is produced there *now*, or for many years. Aye, the only bottles o Glen Coe ye ir like to hae in yeir collection, shall be very auld ones."

"What—?"

"The still was shivered. No one hae made it guid."

"Then the MacIan MacDonalds must have fallen upon hard times indeed," Throwley said gravely.

" 'Tis more right to say, hard times fell on thaim. Whan all of us in this room were laddies, an order went oot frae King William that the chiefs o the Highland clans maun all sign a muckle oath o loyalty, spurnin all allegiance to the Stewart—that ye call the Pretender. Alastair MacIan MacDonald, ma chief, did sign that pledge. But dwellin as he was in the back of beyond, and it bein the deid of a vicious winter, he did miss a certain deidline. Now, no long efter, a great dooncome of snow fell ding on in oor glen. The bothies an barns were smoored under it. An then wha should appear but a company o soldiers frae Fort William, that had gang agley in the spindrift. Vagand like a band o runagates they war, fagged half to deeth, sterving, blae—a company o kirkyaird deserters! They dinna hae to beg us. A sakeless hill-run lot we wes, dacent and soothfast, goodwillie toward fellow-men. Shelter we gied them, no in oor barns, mind ye, but in oor own homes, humble as they war. For these war na outdwellars to us, though they war o a different clan. They war fellow-Scotsmen. We turned it into a ceilidh. That's whaur all o our usquebaugh went! Down the throttles o those ramscallions! But we dinna mind."

Now an extraordinary thing happened, which was that the sound of bagpipes became audible.

The Lieutenant's Lodging was packed into the corner of the Inner Ward. Indeed, though the front wall was half-timbered, the back was simply the ancient curtain-wall of the Tower of London, looking down over Water Lane. Windows had been made in the upper reaches of that wall so that the Lieutenant could see out over the Lane, and the outer fortifications, wharf, and river beyond. Both Water Lane and the Wharf were open to the public during the day-time. It seemed likely that Throwley's housekeeper had opened those rear windows to let April breezes air out the bedchambers, and haply a strolling bagpiper had wandered by, playing a Highland melody in hopes that strollers or soldiers would toss coins at him. It was the same tune that Lord Gy had been humming a few minutes previously.

Strong emotion had begun to tell on MacIan's face as he related the tale of the lost soldiers and the impromptu ceilidh that his kin had thrown for them in the snowdrifts of Glen Coe. When the bagpipe's snarl drifted through the room, his eye became watery, and he began to paw at the patch that covered the other. "Och, a need a dram," he confessed. "Ir ye havin difficulty, sir, gettin that open?"

"I must confess with all these layers of wax, lead, and wire, the contents of this bottle are as closely guarded as this Tower!"

"Haud yeir tung, much more so!" said Lord Gy dismissively. "Gie it me, there is a trick to getting it open, a'l hae oor drams poured out smairtly." He accepted the bottle back from Throwley.

Downs had been looking queasy these last few minutes. "I do confess, my lord, your tale has struck a chord, a melancholy one, in my memory. The details escape me. But I doubt its ending."

"Then a'l make it quick, and make an end o it. Efter twae weeks o dwelling amang us as blude-friends, gutting our winter victuals, burning up oor peat-bings, an dancin the reel o Bogie wi our lasses, those mangrels waukened one day at five in the morning and put the MacIan MacDonalds to the fire and the sword. Our glen they made into a knacker's midden. Some of us fled to the crags, yawin an yammerin, heart-scalded. We lived on snow an wrake-lust until the murthering wichts had gaen away. Only then durst we gae doon amang the bones an cinders to hack common graves into the frozen erd o Glen Coe."

Yeoman Downs and Lieutenant-General Throwley were sitting gobsmacked. They were petrified for now, though a harsh word or sudden movement from Rufus MacIan might have scattered them from the house.

Noting this, he closed his eye for a moment, then opened it, and managed a wry smile.

That, to the Englishman, seemed the moral to the story. It said that in spite of the horror he had witnessed as a boy, Rufus MacIan had grown up into a gentleman, and found a kind of solace in the self-control and civility that was expected of such.

"Now," he said, "wuid ye care for a dram?"

"My lord," said Throwley huskily, " 'twere disrespectful to refuse."

"Then let me get the damned thing open," said Rufus MacIan of MacDonald. He rubbed moisture from his eye on the shoulder of his coat, and drew in a big snuffle before it could escape from his nostrils. "Mr. Downs, as a mentioned, there's a trick to it. Shards o glass may fly. A entreat ye to look the other way—unless ye want me to leave ye this eye-patch in ma last will and testament!"

Mr. Downs permitted himself a controlled smile at this faint jest, and averted his gaze.

Lord Gy gripped the bottle by its neck and swung it sideways until it exploded against Downs's temple.

He was left holding only the neck of the bottle. But projecting from it was a steel dirk nine inches long, dripping usquebaugh. He was up on the table before Lieutenant-General Throwley could rise from his chair.

From the next room could be heard the sound of the red-headed maidservant throwing the door bolts to.

Rufus MacIan of MacDonald was squatting in the middle of the dining table now, giving Throwley a clear and close view of whatever it was he kept underneath his kilt. It seemed to have paralyzed the Lieutenant of the Tower. Which made his visitor's next move a simple matter. "Can ye understand *this*?" MacIan asked, and rammed the dirk into Throwley's eyeball until it stopped hard against the back of his skull.

Sloop Atalanta, *Gravesend*

THEY DREW ALONGSIDE A WHARF at Gravesend. It was near where the tilt-boat ran up the river to London, and so a sizable and curious crowd was there watching them, and calling out questions. Perhaps Isaac thought his outburst about "the German" really was an intelligible end to the conversation, or perhaps he did not care to stand in the open on the poop and be peered at.

Daniel sensed *he* was being peered at from *another* quarter. A certain gentleman had been haunting the corner of Daniel's eye for above a quarter of an hour. From his dress, he was an officer of the Queen's Own Black Torrent Guards.

"Colonel Barnes," the man said, in response to what must have been a lapse in Daniel's mean, flinty outlook.

"I am Dr. Daniel Waterhouse," Daniel returned, "and I have heard *criminals* introduce themselves to me with greater formality and courtesy than what you have just shown."

"I know," said Colonel Barnes, "one of them came up to me and did just that, a few hours ago, on Tower Wharf."

"Colonel Barnes, 'twould seem you have duties ashore, I'll not delay you—"

Barnes glanced out over the sloop's upperdeck, which had now been joined to the wharf by gangplanks in two places. Dragoons were streaming across, driven by cursing sergeants on the deck and exhorted by lieutenants on the wharf; as they came ashore they clustered by platoon.

"On the contrary, Dr. Waterhouse, I'm to stay 'board ship. Suits me better." He made a loud rapping noise on the deck, and Daniel looked down to discover that one of the colonel's legs was a rod of carven ebony with a steel tip.

"You are a Black Torrent man to the bone," Daniel remarked. Every regiment had its own type of wood, used to make swagger sticks and the like, and ebony was the trade-mark of the Black Torrent Guards.

"Indeed, been with them since the Revolution."

"Surely you need to supervise the disembarkation—"

"Dr. Waterhouse, you do not understand Delegation of Authority," Barnes returned. "Here's how it works: I tell my subordinates to get all but two platoons off the boat, and they do it."

"Who has delegated you to harry me round the poop deck?"

"Why, the aforementioned very polite criminal."

"A colonel commands a regiment, is it not so?"

"That is correct."

"Do you mean to tell me that a colonel, in turn, is commanded by a Black-guard?"

"That is the custom in most armies," Barnes returned dead-pan. "True, 'twas sometime different under my lord Marlborough, but since he was stripped of command, why, it has been Black-guards all the way to the top."

Daniel had a natural impulse here to laugh; but some other part of him was recommending that he proceed cautiously with this Barnes. What the colonel had just said was witty, but it was also reckless.

Most of the Guards were off the ship now, leaving only two platoons of some fourteen men each, each under its own sergeant. One of them had congregated at the forward end of the deck, the other aft, directly below where Colonel Barnes and Daniel were standing. This left a large clear space amidships, claimed by Sergeant Bob Shaftoe. He was facing toward the wharf, so Daniel was viewing him in profile; but now he adjusted his posture slightly toward them and glanced, for a quarter of a second, in Barnes's direction.

"Your sloop, Cap'n," Barnes sang out.

The skipper retaliated with a series of histrionic commands that caused the gangplanks to be drawn back onto the wharf, and the sloop's lines to be cast off.

"You and Sergeant Bob make war together," Daniel said. "It is what you do."

"If that's true, our life's work has been a failure!" Barnes answered, mock-offended. "I should prefer to say, we make peace, and have achieved success."

"Say it however you like. Either way, you've spent a quarter-century marching around with him, and have heard every joke and anecdote he knows how to tell, a thousand times over."

" 'Tis a common outcome in our line of work," Barnes allowed.

"Now you phant'sy you know everything about me, because ten or twenty years ago, in a tent along the Rhine or a bothy in Ireland, Sergeant Bob told you a tale about me. You suppose you may approach me in a companionable way, and divulge things to me, and thereby make me your bound accomplice, as when two boys cut their thumbs on purpose and bleed on each other and then say that they are brothers. Please do not be offended if I recoil from your tender. There is a reason why old men are aloof, and it has nothing to do with being pompous."

"You should renew your acquaintance with Marlborough," Barnes said, putting on a little show of being impressed. "The two of you would get along famously."

"An unfortunate choice of adverb, that."

Barnes was silent for a while now. The two horse-barges were coming up to the wharf at Gravesend to discharge the loads. The Queen's Own Black Torrent Guard were dragoons, meaning that they fought on foot, using the tactics and the arms of infantry. But they maneuvered round the field of battle on horseback. To put it crudely, they were shock troops. Clearly the companies that had disembarked had orders to mount, get on the turnpike that paralleled the river, and ride east, pacing the sloop.

"Everyone is scared to death just now," Barnes said. He sidled up to Daniel along the rail and offered him half a small loaf of bread, which Daniel practically lunged at. "Why, to listen to certain Whigs, a Jacobite invasion is just over the horizon, driven on a Popish wind. And yet Sir Isaac fears the arrival of the German! 'Tis an impossibility for both the Hanovers and the Jacobites to occupy the same space. Yet the Whigs' fears, and Sir Isaac's, are equally real."

When he alluded to the impossibility of two objects occupying the same space, Barnes was resorting to a verbal tic that had its origins in Descartes. He had, in other words, been to Oxford or Cambridge. He ought to be a vicar, or even a Dean, in some church. What was he doing here?

"When Sir Isaac refers, with such trepidation, to the German, he does not mean George Louis."

Barnes looked startled, then fascinated. "Leibniz—?"

"Yes." And this time Daniel could not prevent himself smiling a bit.

"So it's not that Sir Isaac is a Jacobite . . ."

"Far from it! He fears the arrival of the Hanovers, only in that Leibniz is the advisor to Sophie, and to Princess Caroline." Daniel wasn't entirely certain he ought to be telling Barnes so much, but it was better for Barnes to understand the truth than to harbor the suspicion that Isaac was a covert supporter of the Changeling.

"You skipped a generation," Barnes said puckishly. Or as puckish as a maimed colonel of dragoons could be.

"If George Louis has any interest whatever in philosophy—for that matter, in *anything at all*—'tis a secret close kept," Daniel returned.

"So am I to understand that the present expedition has its origins in a *philosophical dispute*?" Barnes asked, looking about himself as if seeing the sloop in a new light.

Atalanta had reached the middle of the channel now and, freed from the slow horse-barges, spread more canvas to the wind than she had done before. They were sailing due east on Gravesend Reach. On their right, the chalky hills would draw back from the river, widening the marshes that spread at their feet. The town of Tilbury was on the left. It was the last port on that bank of the river, for beyond it the Thames sloshed between mud-flats instead of streaming between proper banks. Even at their improved pace, they had a few hours' sail ahead of them; and Isaac was nowhere to be seen. There was no harm, Daniel concluded, in conversing with a philosophy-hobbyist.

He glanced around the sky, looking for a convenient Cœlestial Body, but the day had slowly become overcast. Instead he fastened upon the river-water rippling along the hull-planks, and glanced too at the mud-flats below Tilbury. "I cannot see the sun—can you, Colonel Barnes?"

"We are in England. I have heard rumors of it. In France I saw it once. But not today."

"And the moon?"

"She is full, and she set over Westminster as we were loading on Tower Wharf."

"The moon's behind the world, the sun's behind clouds. Yet the water that buoys us is obeying the dictates of both, is it not?"

"I have it on good authority that the tides are operational today," Barnes allowed, and checked his watch. "Sheerness expects a low tide at seven o'clock."

"A spring tide?"

"Uncommon low. Why, feel how the river's current bears us along, hastening to the sea."

"Why does the tide rush out to sea?"

"The influence of the sun and the moon."

"Yet you and I cannot see the sun *or* the moon. The water does not have senses to see, or a will to follow them. How then do the sun and moon, so far away, affect the water?"

"Gravity," responded Colonel Barnes, lowering his voice like a priest intoning the name of God, and glancing about to see whether Sir Isaac Newton were in earshot.

"That's what everyone says now. 'Twas not so when I was a lad. We used to parrot Aristotle and say it was in the nature of water to be drawn up by the moon. Now, thanks to our fellow-passenger, we say 'gravity.' It seems a great improvement. But is it really? Do you *under-*

stand the tides, Colonel Barnes, simply because you know to say 'gravity'?"

"I've never claimed to *understand* them."

"Ah, that is very wise practice."

"All that matters is, *he* does," Barnes continued, glancing down, as if he could see through the deck-planks.

"Does he then?"

"That's what you lot have been telling everyone."

"Meaning the Royal Society?"

Barnes nodded. He was eyeing Daniel with some alarm. Daniel, cruelly, said nothing, and let Barnes simmer until he could stand it no more, and continued, "Sir Isaac's working on Volume the Third, isn't he, and that's going to settle the lunar problem. Wrap it all up."

"He is working out *equations* that ought to agree with Mr. Flamsteed's *observations*."

"From which it would follow that Gravity's a solved problem; and if Gravity predicts what the moon does, why, it should apply as well to the sloshing back and forth of the water in the oceans."

"But is to *describe* something to *understand* it?"

"I should think it were a good first step."

"Yes. And it is a step that Sir Isaac has taken. The question now becomes, who shall take the second step?"

"You mean, is it to be he or Leibniz?"

"Yes."

"Leibniz has not done any work with Gravity, has he?"

"You mean, it seems obvious that Sir Isaac, having taken the first step, should be better positioned to take the second."

"Yes."

"One would certainly think so," Daniel said sympathetically. "On the other hand, sometimes he who goes first wanders into a cul-de-sac, and is passed by."

"How can his theory be a cul-de-sac if it describes everything perfectly?"

"You heard him, a short time ago, expressing concern about Leibniz," Daniel pointed out.

"Because Leibniz has Sophie's ear! Not because Leibniz is the better philosopher."

"I beg your pardon, Colonel Barnes, but I have known Sir Isaac since we were students, and I say to you, he does not strain at gnats. When he is at such pains to gird for battle, you may be sure that his foe is a Titan."

"What weapon could Leibniz possibly have that would do injury to Sir Isaac?"

"To begin with, a refusal to be over-awed, and a willingness, not shared at this time by any Englishman, to ask awkward questions."

"What sort of awkward questions?"

"Such as I've already asked: how does the water know where the moon is? How can it perceive the Moon through the entire thickness of the Earth?"

"Gravity goes through the earth, like light through a pane of glass."

"And what form does Gravity take, that gives it this astonishing power of streaming through the solid earth?"

"I've no idea."

"Neither does Sir Isaac."

Barnes was stopped in his tracks for a few moments. "Does Leibniz?"

"Leibniz has a completely different way of thinking about it, so different as to seem perverse to some. It has the great advantage that it avoids having to talk rubbish about Gravity streaming through Earth like light through glass."

"Then it must have as great disadvantages, or else he, and not Sir Isaac, would be the world's foremost Natural Philosopher."

"Perhaps he *is*, and no one knows it," Daniel said. "But you are right. Leibniz's philosophy has the disadvantage that no one knows, yet, how to express it mathematically. And so he cannot predict tides and eclipses, as Sir Isaac can."

"Then what good is Leibniz's philosophy?"

"It might be the truth," Daniel answered.

Cold Harbour

THE SAME AFTERNOON

THE TOWER MIGHT HAVE ENDURED forever with very little upkeep, had it not been for a nasty infestation of humans. From a janitorial standpoint, the problem with this particular race was not that they were *de-*, but avidly *con-*structive, and would on no account leave off bringing new building-stuff in through the all-too-numerous gates, and fashioning them into shelters. Left to the elements, such improvisations would break down naturally in decades or centuries, leaving the Tower as God and the Normans had intended it to be. But the difficulty with a human was that where he found a shelter he would occupy it, and when it broke, fix it, and if not prevented, build annexes onto it. To the management of the Tower, it was less an infestation of termites than a plague of mud-daubing wasps.

Every time the Constable brought in a surveyor, and compared his work to the plan his predecessor had drawn up some decades before, he would discover new nests that had insensibly grown in the corners, as dust-balls under a bed. If he went to eject the people who lived in them, so that he could tear them down, he would be confronted with documents and precedents, showing that those people were not squatters but tenants, and that they'd been paying rent for decades to some *other* squatter-cum-tenant, who in turn paid rent or performed necessary services for some Corporation or Office or other *sui generis* queer ancient Entity that claimed long standing or warrant Royal.

Short of a concerted arson campaign, the only brake on this infestation was a lack of space within the walls that circumscribed the hive. It came down, then, to a question of how much crowding human beings could endure. The answer: not as much as wasps, but still rather a lot. In fact, there was a certain type of human who thrived on it, and those types gravitated naturally to London.

Dart the Barber lived in a garret above a storehouse in Cold Harbour. Most of the year, Cold Harbour was cold without a doubt. To Dart and his roommates—Pete the Sutler and Tom the Boot-black—it was also a sort of metaphorical harbour. But beyond that the name made no sense at all. It was nowhere near the water, and performed no harbour-like functions. Cold Harbour was a patch of turf and a few storehouses in the middle of Tower Green, just off the southwest corner of the ancient Conqueror's keep called the White Tower.

A wee hole had been worried through the wattle near the vertex of the gable, just large enough to admit a pigeon, vent smoke from a rush-light, or frame a man's face. At the moment it was giving Dart a sort of dove's-eye-view of the Parade. Accounting for about half of the Inner Ward, the Parade was the largest open space in the Tower. A well-tended patch of English turf it was. But it was scarred, below Dart, with ridges of rain-worn stone: the exposed foundations of walls that had been thrown down, æons ago, by long-dead Constables. For perhaps the only thing that could stir a Constable to use force against the gnawing accretion of sheds, annexes, pop-outs, &c., was the combined awareness of (a) his own mortality and (b) the fact that there was no place left in the Tower complex to dig his grave. At any rate, there was evidence here that Cold Harbour had once been a bigger thing than it was now. From ground level, these ruins were a meaningless maze of tripping-hazards. From Dart's privileged viewpoint they could be made out as a page of rectilinear glyphs stroked in gray and yellow paint on green baize.

If Dart had been as keenly interested in the several centuries just past as he was in the several hours just beginning, he could have decyphered that grassy palimpsest to tell a tale about the fortifications of the Inmost Ward, and how they had changed over time, from a picket to keep out die-hard Angles, to the innermost of half a dozen lines of circumvallation, to a security checkpoint for a royal palace, to an outmoded slum, to a tripping-hazard. The part where Dart dwelt had only been suffered to remain standing because it was easily made over into storehouses.

And if Dart were one for profound introspection he might ponder the queerness of his circumstance: he (an illiterate barber), a sutler, and a Black-guard (as boys who polished boots were called) sharing an apartment twenty paces distant from William the Conqueror's chief Fort.

However none of these thoughts came to him, or even came *near* him, as he peered out through the gable-vent on the afternoon in question, heaving ruby-colored blood up from his lungs onto a crusty brown rag. Dart was living for the moment.

The Parade stretched an hundred paces from east (the line of barracks huddled along the footing of the White Tower) to west (a wee street of warders' houses backed against the west wall). A hundred and fifty paces separated its north (the Chapel) from its south (the Lieutenant's Lodging). The Cold Harbour dwelling of Dart the Barber, Tom the Black-guard, and Pete the Sutler was about half-way 'long the eastern edge of it. So to his left Dart had a good view over the northern half of the Parade, but to his right all was obliterated by the high White Tower, which squatted in the heart of the complex like a solid cube of stone. Its formidable lines had been cluttered, on its western and southern sides, by low skirts of identical barrack-houses, jammed in wall-to-wall so that their peaked roofs merged to form a sawtooth fringe. Two companies of the Guard regiment lived in these and similar ones near by. The other dozen companies were packed into various spaces around the periphery of the Inner Ward, along Mint Street, or wherever space could be found for them. All told, they numbered near a thousand.

A thousand men could not live without victuals, which was why sutlers' houses had been allowed, nay, encouraged to occupy various crannies around the Tower and the Wharf. Pete's was one such; he was the tenant of this garret, and he sublet hammock-space to Dart and, more recently, to Tom.

The Queen's Own Black Torrent Guards often drew duty of a ceremonial nature, such as greeting foreign ambassadors on Tower Wharf, and so they were more than normally concerned with the upkeep of their kit. This meant no lack of work for Tom and the other boot-blacks. And any congregation of humans required barbers to dress wounds and see to the removal of redundant hairs, whiskers, bodily humours, and necrotizing limbs. So Dart had been permitted to wind some bloody gauze round a pike and plant it outside a certain door in Cold Harbour as the customary hall-mark of his trade.

He was not plying that trade now but nervously honing a razor, again and again, on a leather strop, and peering down the line of barracks doors, watching Tom the Black-guard make his rounds. Most of the garrison was *extra muros* on Tower Hill; in their absence Tom was going to each door in turn to polish the boots that had been left out by the soldiers. To look at him, Tom was a boy of about twelve. But he spoke with the voice, and answered to the urges, of a grown man, which made Dart suspect he was really a bloke who'd not grown properly.

Tom had been doing this for the best part of two hours and had settled into a fixed routine, which was that he would squat down to polish a pair of boots, then stand up when he was finished, as though feeling a need to stretch, and look idly around the Parade, then glance up into the sky to see if any change in the weather was coming. Then he would turn his attention to the next pair of boots.

The only thing more tedious than to perform this duty was to watch it. Even though Dart had been told that he must on no account take his eyes off Tom, he found it hard going to keep his eyes open. The sun was beating against a white haze that steeped the garret in drowsy warmth. Cool gusts found their way to Dart's face from time to time and reminded him to open his eyes. True to form, he, being the barber, had the worst shave in the whole Tower. His stubbly chin pricked him awake when he nodded off and let it rest on the dove-shit-covered sill of the tiny window. The only thing he could do while he bided his time was to whet the tools of his trade. But if he did so any more, they would become transparent.

Tom the Black-guard had a yellow cloth slung over his shoulder.

It had not been there a minute before. Dart was seized by guilt and fear, and already justifying himself: I did not take my eyes off him for more than a heart-beat!

He looked again. Tom bent down to start in on another pair of boots. The yellow cloth stood out like a lightning-bolt against the usual black-stained rags.

He closed his eyes, counted to five, opened them, and looked a third time to be sure. It was still there.

Dart the Barber stepped away from the window for the first time in two hours, raked his strops, shears, and razors together into a bag, and made for the stairs.

The garret had been turned into a maze by stacked sacks of flour and kegs of salted meat, as well as by hams and gutted rabbits dangling from the rafters, and the hammocks where Dart and Tom and Pete slept. But Dart moved through adroitly, and minced down a fatally precipitous stair to the ground floor, where after a brief scamper down a stunningly foul-smelling passage no wider than his shoulders he was discharged into a somewhat wider L-shaped alley that ran from the Bloody Tower gate to the Inner Ward. Scuttling round the bend of that L, he emerged onto grass before the southwestern angle of the White Tower. Then, reversing his direction round to the left, he entered the Parade.

He'd been warned not to look about, but could not help glancing at Tom, hard at work over a boot. Tom was turned his way. Though his head was bent down over his work, his eyes were rolled up in their sockets so far that they had turned white, enabling him to mark Dart's progress over the grass.

Dart made bold to glance this way and that, trying to guess what Tom had seen. For it had seemed, during those two hours, as if Tom had been scanning the sky for something. Over the western wall of the Tower, nothing was visible except for the columnar Monument, some half a mile distant, and beyond that, the dome of St. Paul's. He turned his head to the right and looked north over the storehouses and barracks that lined that edge of the Inner Ward. Here was something: shreds of smoke were climbing up to vanish against the white sky. The source seemed near to hand. But not as near as the Mint, which lay just on the far side of those barracks. He guessed it was coming from Tower Hill. It was probably not from gunpowder, for Dart had not heard the Guard discharging any weapons. Possibly someone had lit a rubbish-fire in one of the courts tucked away in the maze of the Tower hamlets. Or possibly 'twas something more than a rubbish-blaze.

He faltered. He had made it most of the way across the Parade. But suddenly the door of No. 6, one of the warders' houses, had opened. Three Sentinels were there, in place of the usual one. It seemed that the Scotsman was due to be aired out. A Yeoman Warder emerged. It was Downs. He lived in No. 6 with the Scotsman, and he had been very particular about getting a good shave this morning.

Now he'd gone it one better by donning his best coat. He was followed by Lord Gy, a bulky man in a kilt. Then out came his maidservant, the big red-head, with a basket over her arm. Lord Gy and Yeoman Downs began to walk due south towards the Lieutenant's Lodging, beneath the parapet of Bell Tower. The three Sentinels formed a triangle around them and the red-head brought up the rear. Dart stopped to let them pass in front of him, and doffed his hat. The Laird ignored him; Yeoman Downs made an answering wink. All of this passed from Dart's mind as soon as it moved out of view. Few events were more routine than a social call by a noble prisoner on the Lieutenant of the Tower.

A lone Sentinel—a private soldier of the Black Torrent Guard—was stationed before the door of No. 4. Like No. 6, No. 4 was a Tudor sort of house that wouldn't rate a second glance if it were dropped along a village green in Essex and its peculiar occupants replaced with a petty tradesman and his family.

When Dart drew close enough to make it obvious he was headed for No. 4, the Sentinel reached round behind himself and rapped on the front door. A moment later Yeoman Clooney thrust his head out an open window nearby and inquired, "Visitor for my lord?"

"Barber," answered the Sentinel.

"Is he expected?"

Clooney always asked this. It was the most feeble of challenges. Even so, Dart had to stifle a momentary impulse to run away—or, worse, to break down and confess. But he could sense the Blackguard's eyes prodding him in the back like a pistol-barrel. "Sir," he gargled. He had to cough up some bloody phlegm and swallow it before he could continue: "I told my lord I would come this week, he is due."

Clooney's head drew back into the house. A brief exchange of murmurs could be heard through the open window. Then floorboards cracked and door-locks snapped. Yeoman Clooney opened his front door and nodded in a confidence-inspiring way to the Sentinel. "His lordship will see you," he proclaimed, in a trumpety heraldic tone that reminded Dart what an honor it was to mow an Earl's scalp, and how unworthy Dart was of it. Dart hunched over, picked up his bag, and hustled into the house, tipping his hat at the Sentinel, then making a nod at Yeoman Clooney.

The house had a front parlour looking out on the Parade through the very window Clooney had been using to exchange words with the Sentinel. The light was good there, and so that was where Dart spread out his drop-cloth. He set a chair in the middle of it.

The Earl of Hollesley was spending the twilight of his life in this house because he had been entrusted with some of H. M. Government's money during the War of the Spanish Succession, and had used it to put a new roof on his country house, instead of buying salt-peter in Amsterdam. He was near sixty, and as far as Dart knew, his entire life consisted of sitting in a chair and having his hair cut. Other prisoners strolled round the Liberty, killed themselves, or staged spectacular, improbable escapes; the Earl of Hollesley spent all his time in No. 4. Except for Dart, once a fortnight, he rarely entertained visitors. When he did they tended to be Catholic priests, for the Earl had gone Popish in his dotage. When he entered the room on Yeoman Clooney's arm, Dart said to him, "M'lord," which was all he was encouraged to say.

Yeoman Clooney had the easy, but unfathomably tedious job of keeping an eye on the Earl twenty-four hours a day. He took a chair in the corner while Dart got the Earl seated and tarped. "Sir," said Dart in a kind of stage-whisper to the yeoman, "I'll take the liberty of shutting the window, as the day's a bit gusty, and I don't want hair blowing round your tidy abode."

Clooney feigned interest in the window for a few moments, then drifted off. Dart went to it, looked out across the Parade, and found Tom the Black-guard gazing back at him. Before pulling down the sash Dart drew his rag from his pocket, loudly and distinctly hacked into it, then spat on the ground.

It went without saying that the Earl of Hollesley wore a periwig. But he still had to be shorn every so often. He preferred to have his head shaved. It ruled out lice.

By the time Dart had got his brushes and razors organized, and taken up his tonsorial post beside the Earl, Tom the Black-guard was half-way across the Parade, and staring at him curiously through the window. Which was well. For otherwise Dart could never have done, nay, even contemplated it. An Earl, or even a Yeoman Warder, was so great, so potent, so terrible to an insect like Dart. But there was a cold power behind Tom the Black-guard that overbalanced even an Earl. Dart might evade a Justice of the Peace, but blokes like Tom could nose him out even if he ran all the way to Barbados. If Dart did not do as he'd been instructed, he'd forever be a rabbit, trapped in a warren, pursued by an army of ferrets. Which is what gave him the courage—if courage was the right word for it—to announce: "Yeoman Clooney, I say that I have a blade to my lord Hollesley's throat."

"Er—what?" Clooney had been very close to drowsing off.

"A blade to his throat."

The Earl was reading *The Examiner*. He was hard of hearing.

"So, you are giving him a shave as well as a haircut?"

This was unexpected. Clooney was supposed to understand a blade to the throat of a Lord.

"I am giving him neither, sir. I am making a threat to kill my lord."

The Earl stiffened, and rattled his *Examiner*. "The Whigs will be the death of this country!" he announced.

"What possible reason could you have for doing such a mad thing?" Clooney wanted to know from the corner.

"The Juncto!" the Earl went on. "Why don't they come out and call it by its real name, a Cabal, a Conspiracy! They are trying to drive Her Majesty into her grave! It is assassination by another name."

"I know naught of reasons. Reasons are for Tom. Tom is at the door," Dart said.

"It's all right here!" the Earl continued, and leaned forward suddenly, so that he'd have cut his own throat if Dart hadn't reacted in time. "*The Duke of Cambridge*. What, his German title isn't good enough for him? You'd think he was a proper Englishman, wouldn't you?"

There came a knock at the door from the Sentinel. "Boot-black," came the call.

"Admit him, sir," Dart said, "and make no sign of distress to the Sentinel, for Tom shall be watching you avidly. Tom shall explain all."

"No wonder Her Majesty is wroth! 'Tis a calculated insult—calculated by Ravenscar. Where Age and Ague have failed to bring down our Queen, he shall do it with Aggravation, may God forbid!"

Clooney left the parlour. Dart stood for a few moments with his blade-hand a-tremble, expecting that the Sentinel would appear in a moment to blow his head off with a pistol-shot. But the door opened and closed without any commotion, and Dart could now hear the slithering voice of Tom the Black-guard, speaking to Clooney in the entrance-hall.

"That Sophie is a circling vulture," Lord Hollesley proclaimed. "Not content to wait for a dignified succession—she sends her grandson before her, like a kite to peck at our Sovereign's withered cheeks!"

Dart was straining to hear the conversation between the Black-guard and the Yeoman, but the Earl's fulminations and paper-rattling drowned out all but a few words: "Muscovite . . . Wakefield Tower . . . vertebrae . . . Jacobites . . ."

Then all of a sudden Tom thrust his head into the parlour and gave him a flat inspection, like a coroner viewing a corpse. "Stay here," he said, "until it happens."

"Until what happens?" Dart asked. But Tom was already on his way out the door, and Yeoman Clooney beside him.

Dart stood there, resting his tired blade-hand on the Earl's collar-bone, and watched the two of them angling across the green toward

Wakefield Tower—where, according to scuttle-butt, a one-armed Russian had been chained up the night before.

There was nothing else to do. So he began to soap the Earl's head. Presently he began to hear the ardent tolling of several bells on the north side of Tower Hill. This was a fire-alarm. Somewhere beyond the moat, a building was burning. Normally Dart would've been one of the first on the scene, for he loved a good fire. But he had solemn obligations here.

Sloop Atalanta, *the Hope*
LATE AFTERNOON

HAVING TAKEN DELIVERY of some Enlightenment, for which he'd have had to pay handsomely at Oxford or Cambridge, Colonel Barnes could hardly deny Daniel a look at the map. They descended to the upperdeck and spread it out on a barrel-head so that Sergeant Bob Shaftoe could brood over it in company with them. 'Twas not one of your noble maps hand-penned on gilded parchment, but a common thing, a woodcut stamped out on foolscap.

He could see a cartographer making a strong case that this part of the world did not rate mapping, for nothing was there but muck, and what features it had changed from hour to hour. The map was pocked with such place-names as Foulness, Hoo, the Warp, and Slede Ooze. 'Twas as if England, when she had worn out certain words, threw them into the gutter—like a man discarding his clay-pipe when its stem was broke down to a nub—and the Thames carried those words down-country along with litter, turds, and dead cats, and strewed them up and down the estuarial flats and bars.

The ever-widening flow swept round to the left just ahead of them. The map told Daniel that a mile or two later it would right its course again and shortly lose itself in the sea. This stretch of river was named the Hope, and an apt name it might be for Sir Isaac.

The Hope limned a hammerhead-shaped protrusion of Kent with no particular boundary between marsh and water, but instead a mile-wide zone between high and low tide—the river halved its width at ebb. Because Daniel knew where they were going, he traced the flat top of the hammerhead eastwards until he reached the semicircular peen at its seaward end. This was labeled the Isle of Grain. The Thames flowed along its northern cheek, the Medway along its southern. The two rivers met just off the Isle's eastern tip. And like a couple of porters who drop their loads in the middle of the street to engage in a fist-fight over which had right-of-way, these two rivers, at the place where they came together, let go of all the muck they'd been carrying out to the sea. In this way was built up a vast bank, a bulge growing eastwards from the Isle of Grain's indefinite shore, and as that bulge reached out into the sea, mile after mile, it narrowed, converged, refined itself into a slim prod sticking far out into brackish water between Foulness Sand on the north and the Cant on the south. At the extremity of that bar was the Buoy of the Nore. The estuary yawned east like a viper's mouth, the Nore spit thrust out in its middle like a barbed tongue. It was in that cursed in-between depth, too shallow for most vessels and too deep for any beast.

But far short of the Buoy, just off the Isle of Grain's coast, was a place that might be reached by boat *or* beast, depending upon the tide. It was a tiny thing, like a gnat crawling on the page. Daniel did not have to bend down and squint at those crabbed letters to know it was Shive Tor.

Raising his eyes from the map to scan this indistinct coastline he saw a few places where the old bones of the earth almost poked out, knuckle-like, through the flesh spread over them by the rivers. The Shive, which lay a mile off the high-tide line of the Isle of Grain, was one of those. It even had its own system of pools and bars, echoing the greater system of which it was a part. Daniel guessed that some daft person had long ago seen fit to convey stones out to this stony Hazard and pile them up, making a cairn from which to watch for Vikings or light signal-fires, and later generations of the daft had used it as the foundations of a permanent tower.

He glanced up to find Colonel Barnes gone—called away to lay plans on the quarterdeck—and Bob Shaftoe favoring him with what was very nearly an evil look.

"Do you blame me for something, Sergeant?"

"When last you slept in Tower, guv," Bob returned—referring to something that had happened on the eve of the Glorious Revolution— "you told me the following tale: namely that you had with your own eyes seen a certain babe emerging from the Queen of England's vagina in Whitehall Palace. You, and a roomful of other notables."

"Yes?"

"Well, now that babe is all growed up and living at St.-Germain and phant'sies he's to be our next King, is it not so?"

"That is what they keep saying."

"And yet the Whigs call this same bloke the Changeling, and say he's a common bastard orphan smuggled into Whitehall in a warming-pan, and never passed through the vagina of a Queen at all—at least not until he got old enough to do it t'other way."

"Indeed, they never leave off saying it."

"Where's that put you, guv?"

"Where I ever was. For my father was running about London a hundred years ago proclaiming that *all* Kings and Queens were common bastards, and worse, and that the very best of 'em was not fit to reign over a haystack. I was raised in such a household."

"It matters not to you."

"Their bloodlines matter not. Their habits and policies—that is different."

"And that is why you consort with Whigs," said Bob, finally gaining a measure of ease, "for the policies of Sophie are more to your liking."

"You did not suppose I was a Jacobite!?"

"I had to ask, guv." Bob Shaftoe finally broke off staring at Daniel's face, and looked about. They had been traveling northwards down the Hope, but were reaching the point where they could see to the east around the river's final bend and discover the startling prospect of water stretching unbroken to the horizon.

"My lord Bolingbroke, now, *he* is a Jacobite," Bob remarked. Which was like opining that Fleet Ditch was unwholesome.

"Been seeing a lot of him?" Daniel inquired.

"Been seeing a lot of *him*," Bob said, turning his head slightly toward the quarterdeck and glancing up at the banner that flew at the mizzen, carrying the arms of Charles White. "And you must know *he* is the whip that Bolingbroke cracks."

"I did not know it," Daniel confessed, "but it rings very true."

"Bolingbroke is the Queen's pet," Bob continued, "and has been ever since he drove Marlborough out of the country."

"Even a Bostonian knows as much."

"Now the Whigs—your friend in particular—they have been raising a private army, they have."

"When we met some weeks ago on London Bridge, you alluded to that, very darkly," Daniel said. He was now beginning to experience fear, for the first time since he had awoken. Not the bracing, invigorating fear of shooting under London Bridge in a small boat, but the vague smothering dread that had kept him bedridden the first few weeks he'd been back in London. It was familiar, and in that, oddly comforting.

"Whigs've been whispering in a lot of ears," Bob continued, glancing at the place where Colonel Barnes had stood a moment earlier. "Are you with us or against us? Will you stand up and be counted? When the Hanovers reign, shall they know you as one who was loyal, who can be trusted with command?"

"I see. Hard to resist that sort of talk."

"Not so hard, when there is Marlborough, just over there," nodding at the eastern horizon, "but contrary pressure, even greater, comes now from Bolingbroke."

"What has my lord Bolingbroke done?"

"He's not come out and *done* anything just yet. But he is *making ready* to do something that will make some of us uneasy."

"What is he making ready to do?"

"He's drawing up a list of all the captains, the colonels, and the generals. And according to White—who lets things slip, for effect, when he is pretending to be drunker than he really is—Bolingbroke will soon order those officers to sell their companies and their regiments, unless they sign a pledge that they will serve their Queen unconditionally."

"Sell them to Jacobite captains and colonels, one presumes."

"One presumes," Bob returned, a bit mockingly.

"So that if the Queen were to decide, on her deathbed, that the crown should go to her half-brother (I'll dispense with the pretense of calling him the Changeling), the army would stand ready to enforce that decree and welcome the Pretender to England."

"That is how it looks. And it puts a bloke like Colonel Barnes in a bit of a spot. The Marquis of Ravenscar's entreaties may be shrugged off, provided it is done civilly. But Bolingbroke offers a choice, like the Buoy of the Nore—we must go one way or t'other, and there's no going back once the decision's made."

"Yes," Daniel said. And he held back from saying what was obvious: that Barnes, with his loyalty to Marlborough, would never go Bolingbroke's way. But as Bob had pointed out, he had to choose one path or the other. He could not say no to Bolingbroke without saying yes to Ravenscar.

Daniel stood for a time brooding and fuming over the stupidity of Bolingbroke, who would force men like Barnes into the arms of the opposing camp. It was an act of panic. Panic was notoriously catchy; and the questions Barnes and Shaftoe had been directing his way suggested it was beginning to spread.

Which raised the question of why on earth they would think of *him*. Barnes owned a regiment of *dragoons*, for Christ's sake, and if a tenth of the hints dropped by him and Sergeant Bob held true, they were in communication with Marlborough.

What was it Barnes had said just a few minutes ago? *Everyone is scared to death just now.* On its face this was about Isaac and his fears concerning Leibniz. But perhaps Barnes was really speaking of himself.

Or of *anyone.* Obviously Bolingbroke was scared. Roger Comstock, the Marquis of Ravenscar, was too outward merry to let on that he was scared; but then he was apparently deep into mustering a Whiggish army, which was not the act of a man who had been sleeping soundly.

Who *wasn't* scared? The only person Daniel could think of who wasn't, was Sir Christopher Wren.

If the Duchess of Arcachon-Qwghlm was scared, she was not letting on.

Perhaps Marlborough wasn't scared. There was no telling as long as he remained in Antwerp.

Those were the only ones he could think of.

Then he had one of those moments where he suddenly stood outside of his own body and beheld himself, as from a seagull's perspective, standing on the deck of Mr. Charles White's sloop running down the tide in the Hope. And he came to ask, why was he, who had little time left on earth, devoting these minutes to drawing up a tedious inventory of who was, and was not, scared? Was there nothing better for a Doctor and Fellow of the Royal Society to do with his time?

The answer was all around him, buoying him up and keeping him and the others from drowning: Hope. According to myth, the last thing to emerge from Pandora's Box. Feeling Fear's clammy arms reaching around him, Daniel had an almost physical longing for Hope. And perhaps Hope was no less contagious than Fear. He wanted to be infected with Hope and so he was trying to think of someone, like Wren or Marlborough, who would give it him.

It was an hypothesis, anyway. And it described the actions of others as well as it did his own. Why had Princess Caroline summoned him from Boston? Why had Mr. Threader wanted to make a Clubb with him? Why did Roger want him to find the Longitude and Leibniz want him to make a thinking machine? Why did the likes of Saturn trail him through Hockley-in-the-Hole, asking for spiritual direction? Why did Isaac solicit his aid? Why did Mr. Baynes expect Daniel to look after his wayward daughter in Bridewell? Why were Colonel Barnes and Sergeant Shaftoe asking him these pointed questions today?

Because they were all scared, and, just like Daniel, they longed for

Hope, and sought anyone who might give it to them; and when they drew up their mental inventories of who was and wasn't scared, why, somehow—through what was either a grotesque error or a miracle—they put Daniel in the "wasn't scared" column.

Daniel laughed when he understood this. Bob Shaftoe might've been unnerved by that. But because Bob had got in the habit of thinking Daniel wasn't scared, he read it as further evidence of Daniel's supreme and uncanny self-confidence.

What to make of it? Daniel briefly considered hiring one of the printers in St. Paul's Churchyard to make up a broadsheet in which he, Daniel Waterhouse, declared to the whole world that he was scared shitless nearly all the time. And in other times this might have been a fair course—humiliating to be sure, but honest, and a sure way to be rid of all these needy people who wanted to feed from his supposed rich store of Hope.

But that was to take a child's view of the Pandora's Box story, and to conceive of Hope as an angel. Perhaps what Pandora had was really just a jack-in-the-box, and Hope had never been anything more than a clock-work clown, a *deus ex machina.*

God from the machine. Daniel had spent enough time with theatrical machinery to watch its workings, and its effect upon audiences, with a cynical eye. Indeed, had passed through a long phase of despising the theatre, and the groundlings who paid money to be fooled.

But coming back to London (which had theatres) from Boston (which didn't), he had seen that his cynicism had been ill-founded. London was a better city, England a more advanced place, for its theatres. It was not wrong for people to be fooled by actors, or even by machinery.

And so even if Hope was a contrived thing—a mechanism that popped up out of Pandora's Box by dint of levers and springs—it was by no means bad. Which signified that if a crowd of people had somehow deluded themselves into phant'sying that Daniel was unafraid, and, from that, were now generating Hope and courage of their own, why, that was an excellent practice. Daniel was obliged to remain upon the stage and to play his role, be it never so false. Because by doing so he might defeat the contagion of panic that was leading men like Bolingbroke to pursue such abysmally stupid gambits. False, machine-made Hope could make real Hope—that was the true Alchemy, the turning of lead into gold.

"Charles White is very like my lord Jeffreys, would you not say?"

"In many respects, yes, guv."

"Do you recall the night we hunted Jeffreys down like a rabid dog, and arrested him, and sent him to justice?"

"Indeed, guv, I have dined out on the tale for a quarter-century."

Which explained much, for the tale had probably grown in the re-telling, and made Daniel seem more heroic than he'd been in the event.

"When you and I were leaving the Tower that evening, we en-countered John Churchill—I use his name thus since he was not yet Marlborough in those days."

"That I do remember. And the two of you drew aside for a private conversation, in the middle of the causeway where you'd not be over-heard."

"Indeed. And the subject of that conversation must remain as pri-vate as ever. But do you recall how it ended?"

"The two of you shook hands, very pompously, as if closing a Transaction."

"You are almost too keen for your own good, Sergeant. Now, from what you know of Marlborough, and of me, do you phant'sy either of us is the sort to renege on a Transaction, solemnly entered into in such a pass: before the very gates of the Tower of London, on the eve of the Glorious Revolution, when both of our lives hung in the bal-ance?"

"Of course not, sir. I never—"

"I know. Stay. Only let me say to you now, Sergeant, that our Trans-action is still alive, even today; that the present voyage and mission are part of it; that all is well, and the Revolution only grows more Glo-rious with each passing day."

"That's all I wanted to hear, guv," said Bob with a little bow.

Daniel resisted the urge to say *I know it is.*

The Monument, London
LATE AFTERNOON

HALF-WAY UP THEY STOPPED to pant. The two younger pilgrims shared a stone ledge lit by a wee air-hole; some stone-masons had gone to a lot of trouble, here, to frame a toenail of gassy white sky in thunderous vault-work.

"Pity 'tis such an indifferent day," said one, but not until after he'd lunged at the window and worked his lungs, for a minute, like blacksmith's bellows.

"We'll have to gin up our own *meteor*ology," answered the other. He jammed a shoulder into a crevice of light that had opened up between the frame of the window and his fellow-pilgrim's ribs, pried him out of the way, and availed himself of some air. Being London-air it could not be called *fresh*, but it was an improvement on the congealed miasma that filled these confines: a sort of well-shaft two hundred feet high.

An older pilgrim, several turns of the helix below them, stumbled. He was too short of breath to curse. He had to be content with inhaling and exhaling in a very cross way. "Out . . . of . . . my . . . *light!*" he then managed, one syllable per stair-tread.

The younger two—who were not really all that young, being in their middle thirties—moved up. Then they came aware of an impending need to make way for three young gentlemen who were descending. These had all prudently removed their small-swords from their hangers, so as not to trip on them, and were carrying the weapons before them like saints with crucifixes.

The two ascenders by the window were garbed all in black, except for their white collars, and even had black capes reaching below their knees. They were evidently Nonconformists: Quakers, or even Barkers. The three descenders were gaudy Piccadilly boys reeking of snuff and gin.

"Beg pardon, we have been up to view Heaven," sang one of the latter, "and found it ever so boring, and now we are in a great hurry to reach Hell." His companions laughed.

The pilgrims had their backs to the light and their faces to the dark. Otherwise, un-pilgrim-like amusement might have been seen.

"Make way for them, brother," said the uppermost of the two young Dissidents, "Heaven can wait for *us;* Hell's hungry for *these.*" He flattened himself against the wall, back to the chilly stone. But his brother was disfigured by an enormous hump on the back, and had to retreat to the window, and lean backwards into the cavity.

"You're in my *fucking* light!" re-iterated the old one, now barely visible as a disembodied white collar spiraling up the dusky shaft.

"Making way for some unrepentant sinners, father," explained the humpback. "Do thou comport thyself as a good Christian pilgrim."

"Why don't you take 'em hostage!? We need hostages!"

This extraordinary suggestion welled up out of the gloom just as the foremost of the three young fops was squeezing past the pilgrim who'd backed against the wall. They were so close that the latter could hear the former's stomach growling, and the former smelt oysters on the latter's breath. They shared a Moment there, each in his own mind weighing the threats. One had a sword, but his back was to a hundred-foot abyss. The other was pinned to a stone wall, but carrying a long pilgrim's staff.

The Heaven-bound one averted his gaze politely—not a thing to be done with ease, as he had the look of one who had never lost a staredown—and called to the one below, "O Father, I have spoke with them, and found that they are all Englishmen. Not French dragoons as we had first supposed." He then winked at Sword Boy— who, getting it, said, "Ah," then, "'tis well—no fit place for an Engagement, this!" and then went on to maneuver past the humpback. A few moments later, the three Hell-bound could be heard bidding good day to the old pilgrim with the offensive politeness reserved for the mad.

"Time for a swop," said the humpback. He moved up from the window, shedding some gray glare on the staggering old man, and threw off his cape to reveal a great long helmet-shaped object strapped to his back. Getting it off, and transferring it to the other, was several minutes' feverish work. By the end of it they had made themselves near as irritable as the elder.

He had caught up with them and leaned towards the window to catch his breath. The light shone on a face imprinted with more odd and unwholesome tales than a warehouse full of Bibles. "An indifferent day," he repeated mockingly. "I know not what you mean. The weather does not make the day. We make the day, as suits us. This day it suits me to destroy the currency of the Realm. The weather is fine."

"This bloody stair has holiday-makers tramping up and down, can't you keep a secret, Dad?" said the foremost, who was now trapped in a web of lashings that bound the helmet-shaped thing to his spine.

"As long as *that* is in plain view, 'tis farcical to make a great show of discretion, Jimmy," returned Dad.

Taking the point, Jimmy's brother—who now stood straight-backed, and carried the pilgrim's staff—threw the cape over Jimmy's shoulders, turning him into a bent hunchback. "Is there really no better way to gain entry to the Tower, Dad?"

"What do you mean!?"

"There's public taverns crowded right against the foot of the wall. From there, a grapnel tossed up to the battlements—"

"The prisoners have maid-servants who go to and from market every day. You could disguise yourself as one of them," suggested Jimmy.

"Or hide in one of the Mint's hay-wains."

"Or in one of those great bloody wagons they use to bring in the Cornish tin . . ."

"Or pretend to be the barber to some noble traitor . . ."

"I myself have sneaked in with night-time burial processions, just to have a look around the place . . ."

"You could bribe the Wharf-guard to overlook you when they lock the place up for the night . . ."

The old man said, "Danny boy, if you hadn't spent the last month at Shive Tor making all ready; and Jimmy, if you hadn't been toiling over the coin-presses; you'd know that half of our number *did.* But for *me* to enter by some such subtle way would not serve the *purpose* now, would it? Don't stand there a-gawping at your Dad, move along, let's get it done before the whole venture misfires! And if you get ahead of me, and you meet with any decent London folk who'd make good witnesses, why, don't be foolish, take 'em hostage! You know how it's done!"

A few minutes later they burst out into the light, and found themselves sharing a square stone platform with four Jews, two Filipinos, and a Negro.

" 'Tis like the set-up for one of those tedious jests that are proffered in Taverns by Imbeciles," muttered the old pilgrim, but no one heard him.

Jimmy and Danny were flabbergasted by the view: the new dome of St. Paul's in one direction, about a mile away. Opposite, and only half as far, the Tower of London. Just below them, and so close that they could hear the grinding of the Dutch water-engines being impelled by the out-going tide, was London Bridge.

"Tomba! What are these bloody Sons of Israel doing here!?" he demanded of the Negro.

Tomba was sitting crosslegged at the southeast corner of the platform. In his lap was a pulley, or in nautical jargon a block, as big as a bull's head. He removed a whalebone fid from his mouth and said, "They came up to look at the view, mon. They've caused us no troubles." He had a spray of dreadlocks that would fill a bushel basket.

"Really I meant, in a larger sense, why do I encounter them everywhere I go," said the old pilgrim—though he was now stripping off the collar and cape to reveal conventional breeches, a long-skirted coat, and a breathtaking waistcoat made of cloth of gold with silver buttons. He made sure that the Jews saw it. "Amsterdam, Algiers, Cairo, Manila—now here."

Tomba shrugged. "They got here first. You can't pretend astonishment, when you see 'em." He was working on a splice. This platform on which they all stood was impaled, as it were, on the shaft of the

Monument: an immense fluted column that stood alone on Fish Street Hill. Supposedly its foundation covered the place where the Fire had started in 1666. Or so 'twas asserted by the Latin inscription on its base, which blamed the conflagration on Popish incendiaries, despatched from the Vatican. At any rate the middle of the high viewing-platform was occupied by a stone cylinder, which was the upper terminus of the stairway, as well as the support for diverse Barock decorations, knobs, lanthorns, &c. piled on top to make the Monument that much taller. Several turns of rope had been laid round this by the two Filipinos, who'd set out their street-shoes in a tidy row so that they could work barefoot, sailor-style. The same ropes passed through the eye of the huge block on Tomba's lap. To look at it, a landlubber would phant'sy that the pulley had already been made fast to the top of the Monument; but the Filipinos were riggers, and would not let it rest until a good deal more splicing, seizing, stropping, and serving had been effected. They'd been busy enough, until now; but the arrival of the man in the golden waistcoat threw them into a lather, and even the Jews backed away from them, lest they get jabbed by a marlinspike or bludgeoned by a heaver, and find their forelocks unfathomably convolved with a turk's-head.

The father of Jimmy and Danny went the long way round to the east side of the platform. A spyglass emerged from his pocket and snicked out to length. He scanned some third of a mile of London, stretching from the square at the base of the Monument to the vast killing-ground of Tower Hill. Fifty years before, this had all been smoking cinders and puddles of liquefied roofing-lead. It followed that all the buildings standing there today were Stuart, and all of 'em were brick, except for a few Wren-churches, which had a lot of stone to them. Closest was St. George's, so near by that he could jump from here and splatter on its roof. But he had no use for St. George's today, save as a landmark to establish a heading. Raising his glass then brought him straight to a view of St. Mary-at-Hill, five hundred and some feet from the Monument's gaudy plinth. A bloke with a spyglass was perched in its cupola; he took the instrument from his eye and waved. It seemed a cheerful gesture, not a warning, so he did not let his gaze linger there, other than to verify that there was a crossbowman on the roof of that church, standing next to a copper tun and facing across the street (St. Mary Hill) toward a block of buildings on the eastern side. Beyond those, a few degrees to starboard, was a great hulk of a church, St.-Dunstan-in-the-East. Unauthorized personnel had likewise gained access to roof of same. It lay all of a hundred yards from St. Mary-at-Hill; and another hundred yards to the east of *it* was another bulky fabrique whose roof too was infested with crossbowmen and other unlikely trespassers. This would be Trinity House, the Guild or Clubb of Thames river-pilots. The lower floors would be sparsely occupied with retired tillermen drunk on sherry and wondering what all the confounded fuss was about.

Diverting now a bit to port, and some five hundred feet down-range, he found All Hallows Church, easily picked out by Barking Churchyard, which wrapped around it north, east, and south. Other than a sole sentry in the steeple, the place looked innocuous; the only activity was a funeral-procession making its way into the church-yard from Tower Street.

Beyond that was Tower Hill, an open glacis between the buildings of London and the moat of the Tower. It was put to diverse uses, viz. site of public decapitations, place for drilling of troops, and picnic-ground. Some ventured to name it a green. Today it was wholly brown, but enlivened by stripes of red. The garrison of the Tower used it as a place to rehearse their tedious drills and maneuvers. This explained why it was brown, for the grass had not been able to main-tain a grip on the pounded mud. The troops were drilling at this very moment, which explained the red stripes; for the Queen's Own Black Torrent Guard, despite their name, wore red coats. They were grouped by company, which made it easy to number them even with-out aid of a spyglass. Indeed their orderly battle-lines looked like nothing so much as tally-marks scratched in red chalk on a clay tile.

"I make them a dozen! There are fourteen companies in all; the First is downriver; twelve are there on Tower Hill; one, as is custom-ary, standeth watch over the Tower. Of those, how many are out on the Wharf? Have you tallied them yet? No, never mind, ye'll be as-sembling a certain Device . . . where is my damned bagpiper? Ah, now I see him, strolling on Water Lane . . . why, I phant'sy I can even hear his Heathenish Strains. Too bad for the Lieutenant! Now, where's my Fire?" He twitched the glass hard to port, sweeping it across the whole expanse of the Tower. The northern wall and the moat flashed by, and then the stretch of Tower Hill that lay due north of the complex. This was but a narrow patch of open ground, for the city stretched out a lobe toward the Tower here, nearly pinching the Tower Hill green in half. At its closest approach, some of the build-ings along Postern Row came within a stone's throw of the Moat. These belonged not to the city of London but to the Tower of Lon-don itself; they were called the Tower hamlets, they had their own militia, their own Justices of the Peace, and their own Fire Brigade. Which was not merely a pedantic observation. For one of the build-ings in the Tower Hamlets was on fire. The trail of smoke above it told that it had been smouldering for a long time; but just now, orange flames began to billow from its windows. The Fire Brigade had been called out from the taverns where they patiently waited, day in and day out, for an excuse to do their duty, and they were hastening out of the hamlets' diverse courts and culs-de-sac, out of Distiller's Yard and Savage Gardens into Woodruff Lane. But they were out-numbered, and generally out-run, by persons who merely wanted to see a building burn down. This was the ever-present Mobility; or, for short, the Mobb.

"My people!" exclaimed the man mawkishly. Satisfied, he took the glass down from his eye, blinked a few times, and attended to the near-at-hand for the first time in several minutes. A huge Indian, blinded by sweat, was emerging from the stair carrying a bucket of silk thread. One of the Filipinos had scaled the stone knob at the top of the Monument, a good twenty feet above, and lashed himself to the base of the lanthorn. He caught a coil of rope underhanded to him by his partner. Tomba spliced away, wielding that fib like a scribe with a pen, and glancing up alertly from time to time. The four Jews had made a cabal in the southwest corner and were avidly speculating as to what the hell was going on. The only ones completely useless were Jimmy and Danny, still gazing, gobsmacked, down into the Tower.

"Wake up, ye bloody prats!" said the old man in the golden waist-coat. "Lest I come over and knock the dust out o' yer skulls." Then, before he could summon up any more such endearments, he was distracted by items of interest in the river Thames.

On the downstream side of the Bridge, a derelict-looking barge was tied up to the fourth starling from the near end. A short distance downstream, a sloop could be seen anchored in the Pool. She was in the act of weighing anchor. This was not remarkable. But she was running out her guns, which *was*; and to boot, some hands were busy on her aft end, preparing to hoist a blue flag covered with gold fleurs-de-lis.

But even more than these, what truly commanded his attention was a huge wagon coming across the Bridge from Southwark, drawn by a team of eight horses. It looked like the sort of wagon that might be used to convey great building-stones from rural quarries into the precincts of the city. But its burden was covered by worn-out sails, and it was preceded and followed by a swarm of jubilant Black-guards who, if they were keeping to form, were probably picking pockets, purses, and shop-windows clean as they went, like grasshoppers pro-gressing through a field of ripe grain. As they crossed the Square—the open fire-break in mid-span—a man jumped off the wagon, darted to the downstream side, leaned over the parapet, and waved a swath of yellow cloth over his head a few times. His eyes were directed toward the fourth starling. There, a cutlass severed a painter. The barge began to drift down with the tide.

"My boys. My doves," said the man in the golden waistcoat. "Every varlet in a mile radius is doing me a favor of some description, save you twain. Do you not wot how long it took me to hoard all of the favors I am spending in this hour? Favors are harder to get than money. Faith, what I am doing here now is like shoveling guineas into the sea. Why am I doing it? Simple, boys: 'tis all for you. All I want is to provide you lads with a proper Mum to look after you." His voice had gone thick; his face had collapsed and now bore no trace of anger. "Starin' at yon Tower as if you'd never seen the *minars* of Shahjahanabad. Remindin' me of my own self, a wee mudlark boy, first time Bob and I sallied up the river. Fascinating it might be to you, who've been 'tending to other matters, and 'tending well, I might add. But I am so bloody sick of the place, e'en though I've ne'er set foot in it. A thorough study of the Tower of London your father has made. Where the Tower is concerned, I am, as our friend Lord Gy would say, a dungeon o' learnin'. No small toil for one as unused to study as I. Spent many hours plying with drink your Irish outlaws who have garrisoned it, and know its odd corners and passages. Sent artists in to sketch me this or that tower. Stood up here on howling bitter days peering at it through a perspective-glass. Wooed the Tower's maid-servants, bribed and blackmailed the Warders. To me 'tis now as familiar as a parish church to its aged vicar. I have traced through fœtid streets the invisible boundary of the Liberty of the Tower. I know which prisoners are close kept, and which have been granted that Liberty. I know the amount of the stipend that the Constable of the Tower is paid for looking after a Commoner-of-means and a Commoner-without-means. Of the guns that look out o'er the river, I know which are in good order, and may not be fired because of dry rot in their carriages. I know the number of dogs, how many of them are pets, how many are strays, and how many of the latter are mad. I know which prisoner dwells with which Warder in which house. I know the amount of the customary tip one must give to a Warder to gain entry to the Inner Ward. When the Gentleman Porter goes into the country to take the waters, and cannot 'tend to his customary duty of locking the Tower's gates at half-past-ten in the evening, who takes over that duty for him? I know. Did you know that the Steward of the Court of the Liberty of the Tower does double duty as its Coroner? Or that the Apothecary serves by warrant of the Constable, whereas the Barber is a wholly informal and unsworn position? I do, and indeed the Barber is one of our number. All these and numberless other things I know concerning the Tower. And at the end of my studies I have concluded that the place is naught more than just another queer English town, with a rickety wooden gaol and a parish church, and the only thing of note about it is that money is made there, and its leading citizens are all Lords committed for High Treason. I inform you of this *now* so you'll not be let down *anon* when it's amply shown 'tis true; and also, so that you'll stop gawping at it, and count the redcoats in the Wharf Guard, and assemble the fucking Rocket!"

Jimmy and Danny had begun to rouse from their stupor round the point in the soliloquy when their father had brought up the subject of rabid dogs—even for those who lived a life of danger, this was a certain attention-getter. The terminal word "rocket" jolted them like the noose at a rope's end. Jimmy shrugged off his cape and let it crumple to the stone deck. For a few moments Danny looked to be committing fratricide as he worked with a dirk under his brother's arms, but he was only cutting away the web of ropes that bound the helmet-shaped burden to his back.

"Damn me, I should watch more and discourse less," remarked their father, surveying the rooftops below through his glass. "They've strung the lines while I was prating."

A thread of gossamer now connected the steeples of St. Mary-at-Hill and St. Dunstan-in-the-East, and thence ran almost in a straight line to the roof of Trinity House. But haply he focused on the streaming gutter of Tower Street just in time to see a crossbow-bolt flying above it. This pierced the copper roof-skin of All Hallows Church. It had only lodged there for a few moments when a dark-skinned, barefoot man scrambled to it, and commenced a curious hand-over-hand pantomime. He was pulling in yards of silken thread, too fine to be resolved by the glass. It was originating from a smooth-rubbed copper vat on the roof of Trinity House, and it got thicker as he pulled it in, so that if one had the patience to stand there and watch, it might in the end become visible.

He diverted his glass a few arc-seconds down into the adjoining churchyard, where the funeral had taken a macabre turn: the lid of the coffin had been tossed aside to reveal a helmet-shaped object with a long stick projecting from its base. Stored in the foot of the sarcophagus was another vat of coiled thread.

From there it was a flick of the glass to Tower Hill. The red lines were gone! The companies of soldiers had marched away. He scanned the Hill until he'd found them again: they had done just as he'd hoped. They had marched toward the smoke and the fire. As how could they not, for the fire had broken out in a building not far from Black Horse Stables, where these dragoons kept many of their horses. The protocol of London fires was as fixed and changeless as that of a coronation: first the fire brigades came, then the Mobb arrived, and finally soldiers marched out to drive away the Mobb. All was proceeding according to tradition.

He took the glass from his eye to make sure that his sons were doing their bit for the Plan. Indeed, they had lashed the pilgrim-staff to the rocket-head, and leaned it against the railing, aimed in the general direction of St. Mary-at-Hill. Several yards of iron chain trailed from the end of the stick and were now being spliced to a loose end of cord that trailed over the brim of the kettle that the Indian had lugged up here. So that was as it should be. He glanced straight down to verify that the large wagon was booming into position at the foot of the column. Then he moved in the direction of the river, to check on his naval maneuvers; but as he came near the stair exit, his progress was all of a sudden blocked by a tall slender fellow in a long robe, who emerged not even breathing hard.

"Bloody Hell—our Supervisor's here, boys."

In response, spitting noises from Jimmy and Danny.

The robed one cast back his hood to reveal black hair with gray streaks and an unfashionable, but admittedly handsome, goatee. "Good day, Jack."

"Say instead *Bonjour, Jacques,* so that our hostages shall make a note of your Frenchitude. And while you are at it, Father Ed, make the sign of the cross a few times to show off your Catholicity."

Father Édouard de Gex switched happily to French and raised his voice. *"I shall have more than one occasion to cross myself before we are finished. Mon Dieu, are these the only hostages you could arrange? They are Jews."*

"I am aware of it. They'll make better witnesses, as being impartial to the quarrel."

Father Édouard de Gex's nose was a magnificent piece of bone architecture surmounting nostrils big enough to swallow wine-corks. He put them to good use now, literally sniffing at the Jews. He threw back and cast off his long robe to reveal the black cassock of a Jesuit, complete with swingeing crucifix, rosary, and other regalia. The Jews—who had supposed, until now, that the business with the pulley was part of routine Monument maintenance—now could not choose between astonishment and fear; *We came up to take in the view,* they seemed to say, *and never expected the Spanish Inquisition.*

"Where are the coins?" de Gex demanded.

"On your climb, did you nearly get tumbled off the stair by a great Indian who was on his way down?"

"Oui."

"When next we see him, he'll have the coins. Now, if you do not mind, I'd gladly have a look at the river." Jack skirted de Gex and raised his glass, then faltered, as he did not really need it. The barge was drifting downriver with the tide-surge, and had covered perhaps a quarter of the distance to Tower Wharf. Men had emerged onto its deck and busied themselves with now-familiar preparations involving ropes and rockets. As for the sloop, she had now run out her French flag for everyone in the Pool to see, and seemed to be making a course for the Tower. Men were suddenly crowding her decks: men dressed all alike in powder-blue coats. If Jack had bothered with the spyglass, he could have seen ropes, grapnels, blunderbusses, and other Marine hard-ware in their hands.

The question was: was anyone *in the Tower* bothering to look? What if Jack threw a Boarding Party, and nobody came?

Behind him de Gex, in the universal manner of Supervisory Personages, was asking useless questions. "Jimmy, what think you?"

"I think too much pivots on outcomes within the Tower," was Jimmy's bleak answer.

De Gex seemed pleased to've been served up this opportunity to discharge the priestly office of succouring those who despaired. "Ah, I know the Tower is of an aspect very *formidable*. But unlettered man that you are, you want historical perspective. Do you know, Jimmy, who was the first prisoner ever held in the Tower of London?"

"No," answered Jimmy, after deciding not to exercise his other option, viz. flinging de Gex off the Monument.

"It was his holiness Ranulf Flambard, Bishop of Durham. And do you know, Jimmy, who was the first prisoner to *escape* from the Tower?"

"No idea."

"Ranulf Flambard. This was in the year of our Lord eleven hundred and one. Since then very little has changed. The Tower's inmates refrain from escaping, not because the place is so competently looked after, but because they are mostly English gentlemen, who would look on it as bad form to leave. If the place were managed by Frenchmen our plan would be certain to fail, but as matters stand—"

"Come, they're not *so* bad," Jack put in, "see how the redcoats swarm to the Wharf. The alarm has gone up."

"Excellent," de Gex purred. "Then a Russian and a Scotsman may achieve what no Englishman would dream of."

Sloop Atalanta, *off the Isle of Grain*
LATE AFTERNOON

WHEN NEXT THEY SAW COLONEL Barnes, they were well down the last
reach of the Hope. The tide was rushing away from them so ardently
that it threatened to ground *Atalanta* on the floor of an empty
Thames. The river drew narrower every minute as its contents fled to
the sea, exposing vast gray-brown slatherings to the air. Southend
could be seen a few miles off the port bow, stranded in a mud desert.
But what dominated the prospect was the sweep of the open ocean,
which now subtended a full quarter of the horizon.

To starboard a fat sinuous river could be seen meandering out
through the Kent marshes and nearly exhausting itself as it struggled
across the ever-widening flat, trying to connect with the Thames.

"It is Yantlet Creek," announced Colonel Barnes. "All that lies beyond it is not the mainland, but the Isle of Grain."

"How can a creek form an island?" Daniel inquired.

"Questions such as that are the penalty we suffer for inviting Natural Philosophers," Barnes sighed.

"Sir Isaac asked, too?"

"Yes, and I'll give you the same answer." Barnes unrolled his map,
and traced the *S* of Yantlet Creek inland to a place where it joined up
with a ganglion of other creeks, some of which flowed the other direction, into the Medway on the opposite side of the isle.

"Gravity seems to be mocking us here—who can explain the flow
of these streams?" Daniel mused.

"Perhaps Leibniz can," Barnes returned, *sotto voce.*

"So it is truly an island," Daniel admitted, "which raises the question: how will your mounted companies be able to cross over to it? I
assume that is what they are doing."

Barnes used one dirty fingernail to trace the line of a road from
the ferry wharf at Gravesend eastwards along the foot of the chalk
hills. Where the Thames had jogged north to swing round the hammerhead, the road angled south to cut across its narrow handle, and

then to follow the higher and drier ground a few miles inland of the Thames. "Here's where they should have got ahead of us," Barnes said. "And here is the bridge—the only bridge—over Yantlet Creek to the Isle of Grain."

"Military man that you are, you lay great stress upon the onliness of that bridge," Daniel remarked.

"Military man that I am, I have made it mine, for today," Barnes stated. "My men have crossed over it, and hold the Isle end." Then he checked his watch, to reassure himself. "Jack and his men are pent up now on that Isle, they cannot escape by land. And if they should attempt it by sea—why, we shall be waiting for them, shan't we?"

He could learn nothing further from the map, so Daniel looked up. He could now see a rectangular keep sticking up out the top of a cairn-like foundation, perhaps a mile ahead of them.

At high tide, Shive Tor might make, if not a pretty picture, then at least a striking Gothick spectacle, jutting out of sparkling water off the shore of the Isle of Grain, brooding over the traffic of ships through England's front gate. But at this moment it stood alone in the middle of an expanse of drained muck the size of London.

"If Jack lives up to his reputation, he'll have a vessel at his disposal—perhaps a bigger and better one than this," Daniel said—less to raise a serious objection than to egg Barnes on.

"But look beyond—behold what lies in the distance!" Barnes exclaimed.

Daniel now gazed past Shive Tor and perceived that there was water again, a mile or two beyond it. It required a moment or two to persuade himself that this must be the channel of the Medway. On the far bank of that lay a system of fortifications with a fishing-village cowering behind it: Sheerness.

"If Jack breaks for France, we need only signal Sheerness Fort. The Admiralty shall see to the rest," Barnes said. He said it distractedly, as he'd telescoped a brass perspective-glass to full length and was using it to squint at Shive Tor. "Not to worry, though—as we expected, he's high and dry. There's a ship-channel, you see, so that the Tor can be serviced by water, and Jack's been dredging it deeper and deeper, so he can sail right up to the Tor with larger and larger vessels—but it's no use during a spring tide. A *longboat* would scrape the bottom of that ditch this evening."

Round the time Shive Tor had emerged from behind the Isle of Grain, a new wind had flooded over the starboard bow. For the last few minutes the sailors had been attending to it, trimming the canvas. Their business masked the more subtle operations of signalmen, who were at work with flags trying to communicate (or so Daniel assumed) with the dragoons who had disembarked at Gravesend. There was, in other words, a bit of a lull. Quite obviously, it would not last, and then there was no telling when Daniel would have another opportunity to speak to Barnes.

"Don't mind Roger," he said.

"Beg your pardon, sir?"

"The Marquis of Ravenscar. Don't be troubled. I shall send him a note."

"What sort of note, precisely?"

"Oh, I don't know. 'Dear Roger, fascinated to hear you are raising an army, oddly enough, so am I, and have already invited Colonel Barnes to be my Commander-in-Chief. Do let's be allies. Your comrade-in-arms, Daniel.'"

Barnes wanted to laugh but could not quite trust his ears, and so held it in, and went apoplectic red. "I should be indebted," he said.

"Not at all."

"If my men were to suffer, because of some political—"

"It is quite out of the question. Bolingbroke shall live out his declining years in France. The Hanovers shall come, and when they do, I shall extol you and your men to Princess Caroline."

Barnes bowed to him. Then he said, "Or perhaps not, depending upon what happens in the next hour."

"It shall go splendidly, Colonel Barnes. One more thing, before we are embroiled—?"

"Yes, Doctor?"

"Your superior wanted to convey some message to me?"

"I beg your pardon?"

"The Black-guard who accosted you on Tower Wharf this morning."

"Ah yes," Barnes said, and grinned. "Great big chap, dark and a bit gloomy, would've made a fine dragoon. Spoke in words I did not fully understand. Which was probably his intent. Wanted me to tell you that it was a lay."

Daniel was frozen for a count of ten.

"You all right, Doctor?"

"This breeze off the sea is quite bracing."

"I'll get you a blanket."

"No, stay. . . . Those . . . those were his words? 'It's a lay'?"

"That was the entire message. What's it signify? If you don't mind my asking."

"It means we should all turn around and go back to London."

Barnes laughed. "Why'd we want to do such a thing, Doctor?"

"Because this is a trap. No, don't you see? They somehow—Jack somehow—knew."

"Knew what, Doctor?"

"Everything. He led us on."

Barnes took a moment to think it through. "What, you're saying the Russian was planted?"

"Just so! Why else would he have divulged so much, so soon?"

"Because Charles White had his testicles in a vise?"

"No, no, no. I'm telling you, Colonel—"

"Too fanciful," was the verdict of Barnes. "More likely, the Black-guard's in the pay of Jack, and, in a last-ditch gambit to stop us from coming out here, tried to scare us off with words."

There was no changing Barnes's mind. Daniel had committed a grave error by instilling Barnes with Hope first, *then* trying to make him afraid. If a want of hope made men desperate, a surfeit of it made them stupid in a wholly other way. Hope was tricky business, it seemed, and ought to be managed by someone with more experience of it than Daniel.

They were accosted by a lone musket-shot from shore. The captain ordered his seamen to slacken the canvas until they were only just making head-way. A skiff had pushed off from the indistinct shore of the Isle of Grain. News of it rapidly penetrated the quarterdeck and brought Charles White and Sir Isaac Newton up to the poop.

In a few minutes the skiff came alongside them, carrying a lieutenant of the King's Own Black Torrent Guards. It had been commandeered from a local fisherman and his boy, who did all the work. They were not so much put out by this turn of events, as incredulous.

The lieutenant brought a cargo of words, and unloaded it with no small pride on the poop deck. These words were accepted as valuable military intelligence by all present save Daniel, who construed them only as additional tricks put in their way by Jack the Coiner.

The gist of it was that a brilliant success had been achieved. The dragoons had galloped over the Yantlet Creek bridge half an hour ahead of schedule, and posted a platoon there to hold it. The rest of the company had made for that stretch of shore-line nearest Shive Tor, and posted a lookout on St. James's Church. This was built on the nearest thing the Isle of Grain had to a hill, and looked straight out across the tide flats. There the command post had been established. Most of the company was now deployed below it, at the high tide line, ready either to intercept any counterfeiters fleeing from the Tor on foot, or to mount a charge across the flats and storm the building. All of which had been noted by the inmates of the Tor, who had burned a few documents (or so it could be guessed from interpreting smoke) and then tried to escape by water.

Moored on the seaward side of the Tor, in the dredged channel, had been a boat of perhaps sixty feet in length, built on the lines of a Dutch ocean-going fishing vessel called a hooker. As Daniel, son of a smuggler, knew, this would be an ideal sort of craft for illicit traffic across the North Sea. Drake had used boats with flatter bottoms, because he tended to unload in shallow coastal creeks, but since Jack had his own ship-channel, he could carry out a thriving trade with a deeper-draught vessel such as this hooker. The occupants of Shive Tor had hastily loaded some items onto the hooker, raised sail, and tried to take her down the channel to open water. But she had run aground almost immediately, no more than a bowshot from the Tor. They had flung out enough stuff to refloat her, then let the wind—which was abeam—push her to the side of the wee channel, where she had run aground for good. This had opened the channel again and enabled at least some of them to make their escape in a sort of whaling boat: not much bigger than a longboat, but equipped with a mast and a sail, which had been raised once it had been rowed free of the channel. The whaler's flight was being watched from St. James's Church. But not much longer; in another hour, darkness would fall.

Having concluded this narration, the lieutenant awaited orders. Now, Mr. Charles White, who was quite obviously the master of this expedition, had the good form to look expectantly at Barnes, giving him leave to utter the command.

Barnes considered it for a long time—to the shock, then irritation, of Charles White and Isaac Newton both. Finally he shrugged and gave orders. This lieutenant was to be rowed back to shore, where he was to order an advance across the tidal flats to Shive Tor. *Atalanta* was to raise sail and pursue the fleeing whaler, pausing only to drop its longboat at the mouth of the Tor's dredged channel so that an advance party could reach the Tor, arrest anyone who hadn't made it onto the whaler's passenger list, and salvage the grounded hooker before the resurgent tide floated it off.

These orders produced intense activity from all except Charles White, who responded with a sigh of mock relief and a roll of the eyes: what had taken Colonel Barnes so long? Precious seconds had been wasted as he pondered what was obvious!

Barnes had turned his back on White immediately after giving the command. He thumped over to Daniel.

"You're correct," Barnes said. "It's—what did your friend call it? A lay."

"What brings this change of mind, Colonel Barnes?"

"The fact that I had no decision to make. An imbecile could have given those orders." He glanced over at White. "And one almost *did.*"

"Is it your intention to remain aboard, or to go to the Tor in the longboat?"

"A peg-leg's no use in muck," Barnes said.

"Daniel, I should benefit from your assistance at the Tor," announced Sir Isaac Newton, breaking in on their conversation from behind Barnes. He was shrugging on a coat, and had brought up a wooden case that, from the way that he glared at anyone who came near it, Daniel assumed must contain Natural-Philosophick or Alchemical instruments.

Barnes pondered for a moment.

"On the other hand," he said, "I could always hop about on one foot."

Lieutenant's Lodging, the Tower of London
LATE AFTERNOON

BY THE TIME HE GOT up to the late lieutenant's bedchamber, no fewer than four grappling-irons were already lodged in the sills of its open windows. As he approached, a fifth erupted through a sash, and flying glass nearly accounted for his remaining eye. He spun away, backed to the window, thrust his hand out into the breeze, and skated it back and forth until he heard an answering cheer from below.

Sixteen months ago, MacIan had been arrested for a violation of the Stabbing Act. The stabbee had been an Englishman: a Whig who had mocked him in a coffee-house, pretending that he could not understand a word the Scotsman was saying. The Prosecutor had been the Whig's widow: a more formidable opponent. By dint of various connivings and intrigues, she managed to trump up a few moments' impulsive dirk-work into an act of High Treason. Exploiting the fact that her late husband had been a Member of Parliament, she had convinced a magistrate that the imbroglio had, in truth, been an act of international espionage carried out by a Scottish Jacobite Tory against an important member of Her Majesty's Government. So MacIan had been committed to the Tower instead of Newgate Prison. He had not set foot beyond the Inner Wall since then. Now, though, he staged half of an escape by thrusting his head and shoulders out the window.

It was a different world out here. The only thing he had an eye for at first was doings on the river: not the easiest page for a one-eyed man to read, given the number and variety of ships strewn over the Pool. As a boy he had thought ships wonders. As a veteran he saw them differently, each vessel a coagulated Motive, a frozen Deed.

His eye soon picked out the triangular sails of a sloop, and a blue French naval banner, and, below them on the deck, an assembly of blue-coated soldiers. In case this were not a clear enough message, the sloop now fired a spotty barrage from its collection of swivel-guns. That, MacIan knew, served two ends: it let the Wharf Guard know that these invaders were not a mirage. But it was also a cue to the other actors in the play, letting them know that MacIan had hit his mark, and appeared in a certain window.

Within the Moat and on the Wharf, at this moment, should be seventy-two private soldiers, four corporals, four sergeants, two drums and a single lieutenant, that being a single Company, and the minimum complement deemed necessary to guard the place.

Of that number, a quarter of them—one platoon—would normally be concentrated along the Wharf, which was by far the most vulnerable face of the complex in that anyone in the world could come up to it on a boat. The other three platoons would be scattered round the complex at a plethora of sentry-posts and guard-houses: at the gates, causeways, and drawbridges, of course, but also before the doors of the Yeoman Warders' houses, in front of the Jewell Tower, and at diverse other check-points.

There were also about two score Yeoman Warders. These were, in a somewhat technical sense, soldiers—The Yeomen of the Guard of Our Lady the Queen, "the Queen's Spears," the vestiges of a sort of Praetorian Guard that Henry VII had organized after Bosworth Field. But MacIan was rather less concerned with them, for they were scattered amongst their cottages looking after prisoners, they were not well armed, and they were not really run after the fashion of a military unit.

Normally Charles White and a few of the Queen's Messengers—who actually were rather dangerous lads—would be hanging around the place. But they were off on a river cruise today.

At least in theory there was a Militia of the Tower Hamlets. But to muster these would take days, and to get their firelocks in working order would take longer. Most of them dwelt on the wrong side of the Moat anyway.

There was a Master Gunner, and under him four Gunners. By this time of day the Master Gunner could be counted on to be dead drunk. Only two of the Gunners would be on duty. And this meant sitting in a dungeon taking inventory of cannonballs—not manning the battlements ready to put fire to a loaded Piece. To actually load and fire the cannons and mortars on the Wharf and along the parapets of the walls required quite a few more bodies than that, and so it was a duty for the Guard. When the guns were fired on the Queen's Birthday or for the arrival of an ambassador, much of the regiment was kept busy looking after them.

So the task at hand was to account for the some fifty-four guards who were not presently on the Wharf, and put them out of action.

What Rufus MacIan wanted to hear, he heard now: the drummer on the Wharf hammering out a tattoo that meant *Alarm, Alarm!* He could hear it clearly through this window, indeed could've thrown a stone over the low outer wall and hit the drummer-boy on the head. But it booted nothing for him to hear it. The question was, could it be heard by the Guards sprinkled round the Mint and the Inner Ward over the alarms of the fire that was burning in the hamlets, north of the Moat?

There was no better vantage-point from which to answer such questions than the building he was in now: the Lieutenant's Lodging. MacIan turned his back on the window and strode north, exiting the room and stepping across a corridor. This brought him, for a moment, in view of a staircase. Angusina, the big red-headed lass, was coming up with a fistful of skirt in one hand and a loaded pistol in the other. Her face was flushed beneath the freckles as if someone had been flirting with her. "The Centinells ir flichtered!" she proclaimed, "weengin away like a flocht o muir-cocks at the buller o' the guns."

"The *guns*, aye, but can they hear the tuck o the *drum*?" MacIan wondered, and ducked into a small room under the gables. A long stride brought him to a mullioned window that framed a view of the Parade. What he saw was to his satisfaction: "A see reid," he announced. " 'Tis a beginning."

As MacIan knew from having watched their interminable drills through the window of his prison, when an alarm sounded, the company on guard was supposed to form up at their barracks and march as quickly as possible to the Parade. This was more or less what he was seeing now, albeit from a different window. One platoon was there, wanting a few men, and enough privates had strayed in from other platoons to assemble a couple of additional squads.

The fact that Rufus MacIan had just stabbed the Lieutenant of the Tower to death in his own dining-room had no effect at all, and would not have made a difference even if these men had been aware of it. They were carrying out standing orders, which was exactly what was wanted at this stage of the Plan. If the Lieutenant (Throwley) had been alive, or if the Colonel of the regiment (Barnes) or even its Master Sergeant (Shaftoe) had been present, any of them might have countermanded those standing orders, and dashed the whole enterprise. As matters stood, none of them was in a position to put his superior intelligence to use here. Besides them, only three other personages stood in the chain of command: the Constable of the Tower (the late Ewell Throwley's superior) and the Deputy Lieutenant and the Major (Throwley's subordinates). The Constable was presently taking the waters in the country, trying to rid his system of three dozen faulty oysters he'd tucked into yesterday afternoon. The other two had been drawn away for the afternoon on some pretext. And so the Tower guard, like a killed chicken dashing around the farm-yard, was aping the remembered commands of a head that had already been thrown to the dogs.

The ranking sergeant was in the middle of the Parade, screaming a bit of tender abuse at each solitary lobsterback who came running in. Squads were schooling like fish on the green. It put Rufus MacIan in mind of the War: of the glorious carnage of Blenheim, piercing the French lines at Brabant, crossing the morass on the right end of the line at Ramillies, breaking the French cavalry before Oudenaarde. A thousand tales of gallantry that had become mere stuff between veterans' deaf ears. Part of him wanted to stride across that green Parade, rally those troops—for excellent troops they were—and lead them to the Wharf. But his status as condemned traitor and sworn enemy would be an impediment there. To settle his mind on the task at hand was easy enough—he need only turn around and look at that red-headed girl, and remember the day when he had picked her up from the cold blue breast of her dead mother and wrapped her in bloody bed-clothes and borne her up screaming into the crags above Glen Coe.

The ranking sergeant had turned his purple face to the south. For a moment MacIan was wary of being spied in the lieutenant's window. But the sergeant was not looking his way; his gaze was directed, rather, towards Cold Harbour—no, towards Bloody Tower, the chief portal to Water Lane from where he stood. MacIan could not see what the sergeant was looking at, but he could discern from the man's silence, and his posture, that he was soaking up commands. It must be the officer in command of this company. That would fit. The lieutenant, on hearing the guns on the river, and the alarm from the Wharf, would run to investigate. Seeing the improbable, the unthinkable, but not-to-be-denied sight of a party of French Marines bearing down on the Wharf and blazing away with swivel-guns, he would dash back across Water Lane and get in view of the Parade the quickest possible way, which was through the stalwart arch in the base of Bloody Tower, and order all available units to "follow me!"

The sergeant on the green answered the only way he knew how: methodically. With a deliberation that was as agonizing to Rufus Mac-Ian as it must have been to the wild-eyed lieutenant on the threshold of Bloody Tower, he drew and raised his sword, bellowed a catechism of marching orders that caused the one company and the three squads to stiffen, shoulder arms, wheel to the south, and—finally, bringing the sword down—forward march. And once some momentum had been established he even went to the extreme of telling them to double-time it.

MacIan went back to the bedchamber on the south side and found that Angusina had already applied herself to the task of pulling in the grapnels and making rope-ends fast to the frame of the lieutenant's massive bed. Her imposing pelvis was framed in a window like an egg in a snuff-box as she hand-over-handed some burden up on a rope. Rufus MacIan thrust his head out another window and looked off to the left down Water Lane just in time to see the head of the column of redcoats sally from the base of Bloody Tower. A jog to the left then took them across the lane and into the base of St. Thomas's tower, which they could use as a bridge to the Wharf.

He was distracted by a clanging noise nearby, and glanced down to see a Claymore bashing against the stone wall as Angusina hauled it up on a rope. The blade was almost naked, clad only in a sort of thong used for hanging it on the back. Scabbards for Claymores did not exist; such weapons were to be used, not worn. This particular blade had suffered worse, and MacIan was not troubled by its sparking collisions with the wall.

The lot below numbered a round dozen. They were ordinary London tavern rabble by their looks. Or to be precise, ordinary *post-war* London tavern rabble. For the Mobility had suddenly become a lot younger and rougher in the last twelvemonth, when much of Her Majesty's army had been disbanded. Some of the veterans had gone off to be pirates or soldiers of fortune. But these happy few had been making themselves common, unremarkable features of a couple of drinking establishments spackled to the plinth of Bell Tower and the adjoining stretch of wall—directly beneath the very windows that Angusina and Rufus were presently looking out of.

"A praisent for thee, uncle, an weel to be seen!" called Angusina, and heaved the Claymore up into the room. After it several rods of iron clattered in series over the windowsill. For the great sword had been affixed to the top of a collapsible ladder, made of forged rungs separating a pair of knotted ropes. Angusina held the weapon out so that Rufus MacIan, wielding his bloody dirk, could slash the twine that bound it to the uppermost rung. This accomplished, he tossed the Claymore onto the bed—there was not room in this low-ceilinged chamber even for a practice swing—and helped the wench fix the head of the ladder to a Tudor armoire the size of a naval shot locker. Then it was back to the windows, as now came perhaps the chanciest bit of the entire Plan.

These windows were desperately exposed to view, and to more dangerous attentions, from the Wharf. What they had done until now—rope and ladder work—was *visible* but not, all things considered, *conspicuous*. Soldiers on the Wharf, distracted by the apparition on the Thames, could see it if they turned around and looked—but it was just as likely they'd not. What was going to happen *next*, on the other hand, could not be missed by *anyone*.

He hauled up a faggot of muskets on the end of a rope, slashed them apart, and began to charge one with powder and balls that Angusina had pulled up in an earlier load. A bit of covering fire couldn't hurt. But what was really wanted here was cavalry.

"They're so doughty," cooed Angusina. "Yon blae-coatit Jocks oot on the River. And whaur were such stout-hertit Marines enlisted, uncle?"

"A bankrupt theatre," he answered. "Yon French Marines ir no French, nor Marines, nor doughty, nor stout-hertit, nor aye soldiers. They ir actors, lass, an they hae been told they ir playin in a wee *masque* for the amusement o the Dutch Ambassador."

"Never!"

"Aye."

"Losh! They ir in for a stamagast then!" Angusina exclaimed.

"Fire!" came a distant scream from the Wharf. The cry was instantly buried under a barrage of mighty, hissing thuds as perhaps two score soldiers discharged their muskets. Then silence, except for a howl of dismay from the company of actors aboard the sloop.

"And that's it for thaim," said Rufus MacIan. "They'll fleg off now. Tach! Whaur is ma bludie cavalry?" He had the musket loaded by now and he approached the window, wanting in the worst way to look to the right, towards Byward Tower and the causeway over the Moat. But prudence demanded that he scan the Wharf first. The soldiers were still in line with their red backs to him, the sergeant in profile watching them reload. But the drummer—blast, the dummer was looking right at him! His grip tightened on the stock of the musket.

But blasting the drummer into the river, though it would have been easy at this range, was not a good way to be inconspicuous.

At least no one was pointing a gun at him. He turned his head to the right. Only a yard or two below the adjacent window, one of the Water Lane tavern crowd was scaling the ladder with a blunderbuss on his back. Several rungs below, another followed. Just beyond them was the sheer face of Bell Tower, which unfortunately blocked much of his view to the west. Bell was a bastion, meaning it bulged out through the planes of the walls to either side of it. This was done for a practical military purpose, viz. so that defenders, safe inside, could shoot out through its embrasures at attackers trying to scale the walls. MacIan noticed movement inside a small window cut into the near face of Bell Tower. It was really no more than twenty feet away. But a long twenty feet, in that Bell Tower was a completely different building, not reachable from here by any internal passageways that Rufus MacIan knew of. The window in question admitted a stripe of light to a prison cell, one reserved for important blokes. He could not recall who was in there just now. But where there was an important prisoner, there would be a Yeoman Warder. And how could a Yeoman *not* look out the window when he heard pitched combat on Tower Wharf? The Yeoman's hand was moving up and down rapidly, and that was what really caught the old soldier's eye of Rufus MacIan. Other eyes, reconciled to other professions and circumstances, might have read it as butter-churning, masturbation, or shaking a pair of dice. But to him it could be only one thing: use of a ramrod to shove a ball down the barrel of a weapon.

The musket could not be wielded fast enough through the small window. "Ye there," he said to the lower ladder-climber, "throw me your pistol and hold fast."

It was an exceptional sort of request. But MacIan had learned how to utter such requests in a way, and with a look, that ensured they would be heard and heeded. Shortly the pistol flew at him butt-first. MacIan caught it just as the Yeoman was swinging the window open, and cocked it as the Yeoman was thrusting his own pistol out, and pulled the trigger an instant before the Yeoman did. This had not left time for taking aim, and so the ball spalled a chunk out of the window-frame and went zooming away with a weird noise, like a drunken wasp. But it had the desirable effect of spoiling the Yeoman's aim. His shot grazed the wall short of the ladder. The man who'd thrown the pistol took advantage of the reloading-interval to scamper up the last half-dozen rungs and dive through the window; and as soon as he was out of the way, a white line flicked up from Water Lane and vanished into the sniper's window. "God damn it!" shouted the Yeoman.

Rufus MacIan looked down to discover an archer standing in the lane in front of the tavern, calmly fitting a second shaft to his bowstring. This man looked up at MacIan as if expecting a commendation; but what he got was, "Can ye see down the fookin' causeway? If ma bludie cavalry dinna come soon—" cut off by a crash and crack as a musket-ball from the Wharf smashed into the wall near MacIan's head. MacIan dropped to the floor of the bedchamber and buried his face in his sleeve for a few moments, as it felt to have been shredded on one side by numerous skirps of rock.

But he got an answer to his question. For in the sudden quiet he could hear many iron horseshoes, and a few iron wheel-rims, assaulting the paving-stones of the causeway. They could be any group of riders, followed by a wagon. But the piper down the lane, who'd been silent these last few minutes, now let pent-up breath sing in his drone, and began to play a battle-song of the MacDonalds: a tune Rufus MacIan hadn't heard since the eve of the Massacre of Glen Coe, when the soldiers had danced to it. The tune came in not through his ears but his skin, which erupted in goose-pimples all over; 'twas as if his blood were oil, and fire had been laid to it, and serrated flames were racing from his heart to his extremities, and probing through the uncanny mazes and dark recesses of his brain. And this was how he knew that they were not just any riders but his kinsmen, his bludefriends, riding at last to slake the wrake-lust that had burned in them for twenty-two years.

There was answering musket-fire now from Angusina and the few men who'd scaled the ladder. When his ears cleared he heard shod hooves biting into wood—MacIan's cavalry, drawn to the sound of the pipes, had reached the wooden drawbridge that spanned the last few yards of moat before the Byward Tower gate. They were moving at a canter—meaning that they'd seen no reason to rein in their mounts— meaning that the tavern-contingent had accomplished its paramount charge of making sure that the portcullis was not dropped.

There was an epidemic of hammering noises, and the room became very dusty. A barrage had been fired from the Wharf into the windows. Taking advantage of the reload-interval, he raised his head above the windowsill. Two more men were clambering up the ladder as sprightly as they could go. A platoon of lobsterbacks, now with their backs to the river, were lined up on the Wharf reloading; one had been shot and was curled up on his side. The other soldiers who'd been on the Wharf were no longer in sight. Indeed, since the menacing sloop had suspended its attack, there was no reason for them to remain out there. The lieutenant must have perceived this and ordered them to march back through St. Thomas's Tower. They would be flooding into the Lane at any moment—

Horseshoes below. He looked plumb down to see a line of a dozen riders in kilts trotting into the Lane from the gate; and sweetest of all, heard the Byward Tower portcullis hurtling down behind them, sealing the Tower off from London. "Fuck-all ahint ye," he informed them, "Englishmen afore, comin athort the Lane—get the bastarts!" And without bothering to wait and watch his orders being put into effect, he whirled to the bed, grabbed up the Claymore in its rude back-holster, and bore it in front of him out of the room and down the stairs.

As a lad he had plotted his wrake, his revenge, in day-dreams a thousand times. He had always seen it as a straightforward matter of wading through the intestines of Campbells and Englishmen swinging his Claymore. Fortunately, a dozen years of professional war-making had intervened between those laddish phant'sies and the opportunity of this day, and taught him that he must go about it systematically.

So he did not fly out onto the Parade and go looking for Englishmen to slay, but bided his time by the door for a moment and made a study of the place as he hung the great sword on his back.

The Parade was empty except for a single redcoat running from the barracks toward the Bloody Tower gate.

No, never mind, someone had just shot him, probably from Cold Harbour. The Plan called for ten men, give or take a few, to have slipped into the Inner Ward and taken up positions from which they could shoot over the Parade or throttle this or that choke-point. Which appeared to have been done. The Yeoman Warders looking out the windows of their houses would have seen the redcoat fall, and would understand that to step from their front doors was death. But this did not mean that the Parade was available to Rufus MacIan. For a Yeoman, or a stray soldier of the Guard, could just as easily shoot through a window or over a parapet. It had to be considered a no-man's-land for the time being.

"I need to ken if the Bloody Tower portcullis is dropped," he remarked, just thinking aloud. But hearing a man clear his throat behind him, he turned around to discover half a dozen lads, flushed in the face and breathing hard from the scramble up the ladder and the dash down the staircase, but all in the pink of health and ready to go with loaded muskets.

"Beg pardon, my lord, but we worked out a signal for that."

"And ye ir—?"

"Gunnery Sergeant, retired, Dick Milton, my lord."

"Ti the windie then, Milton, an look for thy signal."

"There it is," Milton replied after a glance across the Parade. "See there, the Chapel has a clear view of Bloody Tower, as *we've* a clear view of *it*. We've a lass in there. Came in last night for a funeral, stayed all night to pray, and stayed all day to keep an eye on Bloody Tower for us. Do you mark the yellow cloth in the middle window there? She put it up to let us know that the portcullis is dropped."

"Then the Black-guard maun hae sprung the Russian," said Rufus MacIan, "an the Russian maun hae duin his job. Crivvens! It's a clinker."

"A clinker, my lord?"

"A wadna hae believed it, tha a one-airmed man could fell so many. But he hae *surpreese* on his left flank, an mad *panic* on his right, an either o the twae, by itself, is more mauchty than Hercules. Ir ye all guidwillie, now, to practice your auld profession?"

"Aye!" and "Yes, my lord," came the answers.

"Then count to five, and follow." MacIan flung the front door open and stepped out onto the Parade, as casually as if he were the Lieutenant of the Tower on his way to church.

"One," chanted the men crouched in the building he'd just left behind.

Smoke jerked from the window of a Yeoman's house.

"Two."

A musket-ball buzzed in like a massive bumblebee, ruffled the whiskers of MacIan's beard, and destroyed the window he had lately been peering out of.

"Three!" chanted the gunners, except for one who was screaming.

Musket-smoke spurted from half a dozen odd places around the Inner Ward: from dovecotes and barrel-stacks in Cold Harbour, doors of barracks, and corners and crannies of ancient walls.

"Four!" Another musket-ball, much too high, dug a crater from the front of the Lieutenant's Lodging. "Paltry," was the verdict of Rufus MacIan. "A dowless effort." But his comments were drowned out by the echoes of the recent fire rolling around the Parade, as several other shots had just been fired to suppress the efforts of those Yeomen who were taking pot-shots at him.

"Five!"

Three men piled out the door, dropped to a kneeling position on the gravel track that ran along the front of the house, and raised muskets to their shoulders, taking aim at windows where they thought Yeomen were holed up. Their fire heaved up a cloud of smoke that covered the emergence of a second three.

Rufus MacIan was running east down the gravel track, along the fronts of the houses that looked out over the Parade. Halfway to Bloody Tower, he stopped, and cold-bloodedly turned his back to the Parade so that he could scan the windows of a house for snipers. All he could make out was the head of a maidservant peering out an upper window. No worries there; but he readied his firearm just in case a musketeer should present himself elsewhere. The second group of three men ran to a spot a couple of yards behind him, threw themselves down, and got ready to fire across the Parade. In the meantime Angusina and a few of the Water Lane tavern crew had fired a covering fusillade from the upper storeys of the Lieutenant's Lodging. The first group of three left their empty and smoking muskets on the ground, and sprinted down the track towards Bloody Tower, passing between MacIan and the other three just as the latter discharged their muskets in no particular direction.

A red garment flashed in the window of one of the houses off to MacIan's left. He wrenched the barrel of his musket that way, but the soldier saw him and dove to the floor before MacIan could pull the trigger.

The second group of three, likewise leaving their muskets on the ground, got up now and ran after their fellows towards Bloody Tower. MacIan took up the rear, following after them. But he moved only at a stroll. Partly this was because he expected a few more gunners to emerge from the Lieutenant's Lodging. And he was not disappointed, for two and then another two came out helter-skelter and ran towards him, taking their chances against sporadic musketry from the windows of a few die-hard Yeomen. But partly it was to keep an eye on this house where one or more lobsterbacks were prowling.

Of the motley line of half-timbered houses that stretched along the southern verge of the Parade, the Lieutenant's Lodging lay farthest to the west. The one Rufus MacIan was concerned with was at the opposite, easternmost end, therefore closest to Bloody Tower. It was thrust out into the green in a manner that, to the military eye, recalled a bastion. Between its eastern face and Bloody Tower was an open ground perhaps fifteen yards across—a narrow enough interval to allow for targeted musket-fire. In other words, Guards barricaded in that house could spoil their plans vis-à-vis Bloody Tower.

Another flash of red—a soldier had passed by a window in a hurry, seemingly on a downward trajectory. As if descending a staircase.

The door-handle was moving! MacIan watched in fascination

from no more than ten feet away. The front door moved outwards half an inch. Oblivious, the last two of MacIan's gunners ran by, headed for sanctuary in Bloody Tower. The soldier inside could see them, but he could not see MacIan. What would happen next was suddenly as clear to MacIan as if he'd witnessed it. He set his musket down and strode at the door of the house, reaching back behind his head with both hands and groping for the Claymore. He found it, and pulled it up out of the back-holster just as the door was swinging open. A musket emerged first, held in white hands.

MacIan drew the handle down through the air as fast as he could get his arms to move. But this was nothing compared to the swiftness achieved by the tip of the four-foot blade, which moved so rapidly that it spoke out with a wicked noise like the uncoiling of a bullwhip. Something messy happened and the musket fell to the ground outside the door. MacIan's blade had passed through the man's forearm and struck the edge of the door at an angle, skiving off an acute angle of wood and stopping when it struck a nail. The soldier had vanished inside without MacIan's ever seeing his face. Suddenly the grip of the Claymore was jerked nearly out of his hands as the door was pulled shut. The tip of the blade struck the door-frame and was knocked free so briskly that the weapon, shuddering from end to end, sprang back into the air. MacIan caught it by the cross-guards. He heard door-bolts being thrown inside—from which he guessed that there was another soldier within.

MacIan flattened himself against the wall of the house and spent a few moments getting the Claymore hung on his back, and judging the number of steps to the musket he had left on the ground. Yeomen were taking pot-shots at him from the opposite corner of the Parade. But at such a distance a musket-ball would merely accept suggestions—not obey orders. The balls were smashing out windows above him and probably creating as much of a problem for the soldiers inside as they were for their intended target.

MacIan ran, snatched his musket off the ground, wheeled, and charged round the corner of the house to the open space between it and Bloody Tower. If they had been hoping to shoot down at him, they'd now have to present themselves at different windows, and perhaps move to different rooms.

The tactic worked, as cheap simple tactics commonly did: through a ground-floor window he could see a door flying open, and a man in a red coat running through it and wheeling toward the light—then freezing up in horror as he realized he had just blundered into the enemy's sights. This gave MacIan the moment that he required to center the musket on the red breast of his foe. But as he did so he noticed a sash being flung open on the upper storey, and another flash of red appearing there.

And now a very rapid calculation: the ground-floor soldier was his. All that was required was a small movement of the trigger finger. As for the one above, if this Jock had a weapon in condition for use, then Rufus MacIan was about to be shot, no matter what he did; and if he tried to raise his musket-barrel and draw a bead on the new lad, he would probably miss. So he pulled the trigger.

What happened after that was anyone's guess, since all he could see was powder-smoke. But a moment later an answering blast came from the window above, and he felt the ground jolt beneath his feet. This, he reckoned, must be the impact of a musket-ball on his body, being transmitted down his legs into *terra firma;* and if he stood still for a few more moments he would feel the first hot shards of pain traveling away from the entry-wound, would feel an unaccountable need to clear his throat as his lungs filled up with blood.

But none of these things happened. The smoke was drifting away. MacIan looked up at the window, out of a sort of professional curiosity, wanting to lay eyes on the soldier so incompetent that he could miss that shot, wanting to relish the humiliation in the Englishman's eyes when he kenned he'd fired into the ground.

But when the smoke finally cleared, he saw no such thing, but rather an unbeast, a nightmare vision, like one of the horrors from Malplaquet that cluttered his brain, like so many stuffed monsters in an old hunter's attic, and came alive each night to torment him just as he was about to drop off to sleep. This unbeast moved, and slid limp from the window, landing on its head in the grass before him. It did not come to a decent position of repose. Rather the corpse was propped up on something: a half-pike or javelin that had transfixed its ribcage, like an enormous alien bone that had grafted itself onto the man's skeleton.

MacIan looked up into the vacant window but saw no one there— so it must have come *in to* the window from *outside*. But he was the only man in the yard, and he had no memory of chucking any spears lately. It had to have come from above, then. He turned around to face Bloody Tower and ran his gaze up forty feet of sheer stone to its parapet.

There, framed in a slot between two crenels, and silhouetted against the sky, was a very large man with a beard flowing down his front. Smaller men were active around him, hustling among the gun-carriages that were situated on the roof of this Tower, wheeling them about to aim toward the River, chocking them up with thick quoins so that they were aimed, not at the shipping in the Pool, but down upon the soldiers on the Wharf.

The big man with the beard was gripping in one hand another half-pike. He raised the other to make a gesture. It was not a hand but a barbed hook with a skein of moist detritus swinging from it, possibly hair or shreds of clothing. With this he pointed up, away from the river, drawing MacIan's eye away from the toils of the gunners and towards the penetralia of the Tower of London. Over the roofs of the Cold Harbour storehouses he pointed, and over the soldiers' barracks and the gate of the Inmost Ward, to the lofty prize that stood in the center of all, commanding the complex, the River, and the City from its four turrets: the White Tower. He thrust his hook at it thrice.

The Hero of the Gy needed no more urging. Dropping his empty musket, he unslung his Claymore for what he guessed would be the last time, and hurried between droning musket-balls towards Cold Harbour Gate.

LIKE ANY SELF-RESPECTING CONDEMNED traitor, MacIan had spent plenty of time plotting dramatic escapes from the Tower of London. He knew where the exits were. Today, though, he must think of them as entrances.

There were five gates to the Inner Ward. One of them was an old sally-port in the northeast corner, near Brick Tower, leading into the Mint. It was of no concern today. The remaining four gates were spaced unevenly along Water Lane. Bloody Tower and Wakefield Tower each contained a gate. These two structures were so close together as to constitute virtually a single, misshapen building. A stroller moving east on Water Lane would spy the Bloody Tower gate first and then, after rounding the bastion of Wakefield, see its gate. But though close together, these two portals were as divergent as they could be. The first was a broad, massive, handsome Gothick arch that led directly onto the Parade via the court where Rufus MacIan was now standing. Thanks to the Russian, the light shining through that arch was reticulated by a massive grid of iron bars. Beyond it MacIan could see several redcoats lying still in the middle of Water Lane. They'd marched back from the Wharf expecting to re-enter the Inner Ward through that arch, but had been stopped by the ancient portcullis. And at that moment a dozen Scots horsemen had charged down on them swinging sabers. When horse attacked foot the outcome was never in doubt, unless the foot had pikes, and were well drilled. The Wharf Guard of the Tower of London did not carry or use pikes.

The second gate was a little postern giving entry to the circular ground floor of Wakefield Tower. Thence one could cross into a long L-shaped gallery that ran up through Cold Harbour and broke into the open just short of the White Tower. This was not a fit way for cavalry to come in. If things were proceeding according to plan, Tom the Black-guard was ensconced beneath a window near the vertex of the L, commanding both legs of the passage, with a large number of loaded firearms in his lap. Few if any of the Tower's would-be defenders would pass in or out through the Wakefield Tower gate. But some of its attackers should have come running in that way on the heels of the cavalry charge.

MacIan ran north along the verge of the Parade, passing by the Cold Harbour storehouses on his right. There was still a damnable lot of musket-fire coming from Yeomen's windows, but none of it was directed his way any longer. When he reached the corner of the last storehouse and ducked around it, he at last had a safe vantage-point from which to appreciate why. The appearance of a few gunners atop Bloody Tower and the adjoining stretch of wall, aiming Her Majesty's cannons down across Water Lane toward the Wharf, had compelled the Wharf Guard to pitch their muskets into the river and stand helpless. They were no longer able to shoot at men climbing the rope ladder into the Lieutenant's Lodging. And so a continual parade of invaders was now emerging from the front door of that house and sprinting down to Bloody Tower where they could take stairs up to the battlements and man yet more cannons. As they did, they drew what little fire the Yeomen could muster. But even this was being suppressed by occasional fusillades from firing-points that the invaders had set up along the southern edge of the Parade.

He heard a gate groaning behind him and so turned his back to the Parade, which had become a sort of closed chapter anyway.

He had been engaged, these last few moments, on a project of looping north round the end of Cold Harbour to get from the Inner Ward (a parade for Guards and a village green for Yeomen) into the Inmost Ward (the court of a Royal Palace). He was facing now into an interval some ten or fifteen paces wide separating the Cold Harbour buildings from the corner of the White Tower. That opening was walled off; but there was a gate in the wall, which was being very considerately opened for him by a man in a kilt.

"*At last, someone I can talk to,*" MacIan said. "*Welcome to the Tower, lad.*"

"*And welcome to the Inmost Ward, uncle,*" returned this young man, and stepped back to let him enter.

This was a mere bowling-green compared to the Parade. It seemed even smaller than it was because it was mashed between the immense White Tower on the north and, on the south, Wakefield Tower (a palace unto itself) and a congeries of bulky office buildings and storehouses belonging to the Ordnance. Somewhere in the midst of that would be another tiny postern—the third of Water Lane's four portals—communicating with the Constable's Lodgings, and of no interest today. Far more important was the last gate, a proper arch, large enough for Highlanders to ride through without dismounting. That gave access to a sort of barracks-street along the eastern perimeter of the Inmost Ward, and thence to another gate, a partner of the one MacIan had just walked through . . . where was it, though? His eye, no judge of distances, had trouble making sense of the place. But the piper had taken up a position at the head of the barracks-street to lead the cavalry onwards. The sound of the music crashing from the stony environs gave MacIan the information he wanted to decypher the place. He found the gate in question. It was open. Men were beginning to ride through it. Some were slumped over in their saddles, clutching at battle-wounds earned in Water Lane, or perhaps earlier, when they had galloped out of the streets of London town to astonish the sentries posted at Lion Gate. But most were riding straight-backed and proud, and one—bless him—carrying the unfurled colors of MacIan of MacDonald.

"So that is the famous White Tower," said the lad who had opened the gate for him, "*Feich!* It's not even white!"

"The Englishmen have no self-pride. If you read their history you will see that they are nothing more than a lot of doxy and mistemious bog-stalkers. Think: what would a few gallons of white paint cost the Queen of England?"

"For the love of God, I'd come down and paint it myself just so I wouldn't have to look at it. Everywhere you go in this cursed city, there it stands, a blot on the horizon."

"I've a more expeditious solution," MacIan answered. "I know of one place, not far from here, where you can look in any direction you please without having to suffer the sight of this rubble-heap."

"Where's that, uncle?"

"The inside of it!" And MacIan beckoned to the banner-carrier.

"What—how do you get in?" inquired the lad.

"Through the bloody front door. They built it high off the ground, you see, there—to make it easy to defend—but the English, lazy as they are, have built a lovely timber staircase so they need not strain themselves."

"I cannot see it."

"The barracks are in the way. Follow me!" MacIan entered the front door of a sort of gatehouse pent between two barracks.

"I'll go before you, uncle!" cried the lad; and behind him, like exclamations could be heard from other warriors who were hastily dismounting in the Inmost Ward and running to catch up with them, encumbered by diverse cutlasses, Claymores, blunderbusses, and granadoes.

But Rufus MacIan strode out the back of the gatehouse and began climbing a rude wooden staircase towards a simple round-headed archway cut into the White Tower's south wall. "You do not understand," he called over his shoulder. "You are looking forward, now, to a pitched battle for the White Tower. As if this were a picaroon-romance. But the battle is over. You have fought it and won it."

A Yeoman Warder suddenly stood framed in the arch. He drew an old rapier from a scabbard at his hip, held it up above his head, and began to charge down the timber stairs, screaming. Rufus MacIan did not bother reaching for his Claymore. The Yeoman was butchered on the hoof by musket-balls flying in from half a dozen different angles. He sprayed and faltered at each impact, disintegrating before their eyes, and then collapsed and rolled down the stairs leaving much of himself behind.

"He's been reading picaroon-romances, too," observed Rufus MacIan. "Watch your step, lads, it's a wee bit slippery."

He took the last steps two at a time and strode across the threshold of the White Tower, saying, "I claim thee for Glen Coe."

The City of London
LATE AFTERNOON

HE WAS PRESENTABLE. He was amiable. He'd been taught to sign his name—assuming Jones really *was* his name—on command. Beyond that he was, and always would be, perfectly illiterate. This rendered it out of the question that Seaman Jones of the good ship *Minerva* would ever be an officer, or a man of commerce.

Jones did not chafe under his limitations—if he was even aware he had any. They had picked him up in Jamaica. His story at the time was that he was a wholesome North Devon lad who had been abducted from the shore round Lynmouth by a boat-load of sailors from a Bristol slave-ship anchored in the Channel—in other words, that he'd been press-ganged—and that, after a run to Guinea to pick up slaves, he had jumped ship in Jamaica. They had always assumed that Jones would jump ship again one day, and avail himself of his first chance to get back to his family farm on the edge of Exmoor. But that had been years ago. Jones had proved immune to the temptations of Exmoor on several occasions, as *Minerva* frequently called at Plymouth, Dartmouth, and other ports convenient to his supposed homeland. Indeed, he gave every indication of being perfectly content with his lot aboard *Minerva*. There had been some trouble with rowdiness at first, providing a hint as to what Jones was running away from, but as years and voyages had gone by he had ripened into a steady, reliable, if somewhat limited crewman.

So on the liability side of Jones's account, to illiteracy could be added a mysterious, probably criminal past, and a want of ambition. He had, however, one asset that was not possessed by the officer who was walking next to him up Lombard Street: he was a white-skinned Englishman. From time to time Jones was called upon to make the most of this asset by dressing up in a pair of breeches, leather shoes, a waistcoat, a long watch coat of a somewhat nautical cut, and a very plain horsehair periwig. This was the sort of get-up that a ship's officer might keep stuffed in a footlocker while crossing an ocean, and pull out after dropping anchor in some harbor, so that he could go ashore and look minimally decent in the eyes of money-scriveners, victuallers, ship-chandlers, and insurance underwriters.

If these two were to hail a hackney coach and travel a couple of miles west to the new streets round Piccadilly and St. James, where *shopping* rather than *shipping* was the order of the day, their roles, in the eyes of most casual strollers, might be reversed. For people with an eye for clothes would notice that Dappa's actually fit him, that they were of recent make, well cared for, and cleverly picked out. The lace around his shirt-cuffs had never been dragged through beer-foam, goose-grease and damp ink; his shoes shone like wax fruit. The sophisticated toffs of the West End would then take in the fact that Dappa was older, that he was alert to everything going on around them, and that when they came to street-corners Dappa went where he would, and Jones followed. Jones looked about himself curiously, but he was not really paying attention in the way that Dappa was. A West Ender, watching this procession of two stride past, might conclude that Dappa was a Moorish diplomat from Algiers or Rabat, and Jones his local guide.

But this was not the West End. This was the City of London. They were only a stone's throw from Change Alley. No one paid much heed to clothing here, unless it was as a truly vulgar and shocking exhibit of wealth. By that standard both Dappa and Jones were invisible. Dappa, darting ahead through the crowd of money-men, was assumed to be the servant—a meat souvenir picked up on a trading-voyage—beating a path through the jungle, as it were, and keeping a shrewd eye for hazards. Jones, strolling in Dappa's wake, was obviously the master, and what might in other settings have been seen as a stupid or vacuous expression could be taken, here, as the meditative phizz of a financial savant who was trying to plumb the meaning of the latest trend in Sword Blade Company share prices, and couldn't be bothered to dress himself elegantly or indeed to find his own way down the street. His absent-minded way of taking in everything around him was proof that his was a mind tuned to follow the divagating strains, and quiver in sympathy with the startling chords, of the Market.

Or so Dappa told himself, to check his own impatience, when Seaman Jones paused to chat up a pretty orange-girl on a street-corner, or reached out to accept a handbill from a dirty, bawling pamphleteer. When they came at last to the doorway of Worth's Coffee-House on Birchin Lane, just across the way from the Heraclitean riot of Change Alley, Dappa fell to the rear. Jones strode forward and entered the coffee-house first. A few moments later Dappa was pulling Jones's chair out for him as he seated himself at a vacant table, and scurrying after a maid to make Mr. Jones's desires known.

"We are early," Dappa told Jones after he had got back to the table with the coffee, "and Mr. Sawyer is ever late, and so make yourself comfortable, as I cannot. After this, there's no more leisure until we reach Massachusetts." And Dappa took up the pose of a servant, standing behind Jones, ready to dart forward and tend to emergent needs.

Everyone else in the place was either involved in a conversation or, if alone, reading something. Worth's Coffee-House was the haunt of a sub-species of petty financier who provided bridge loans, and other, less easily explained financial instruments, to the shipping trade. Of the singletons scattered about the place, some were salts consulting tide-tables or almanacks. Others looked like money-scriveners or money-goldsmiths. Their choices in reading material leaned towards London newspapers. Jones, here, was the odd man out in that he could not read at all. But at the corner of Gracechurch and Lombard, he had accepted a libel from a nasty tub-faced tout who looked and smelled as if he'd washed his face with rancid tallow, and who had bestowed an evil look on Dappa as he'd walked by. Jones had rolled it up and carried it here in one hand, looking for all the world like a man of affairs toting a Bill of Exchange to be redeemed. But now, in an effort to blend in with this literate crowd, Jones unrolled the handbill and smoothed it out on the table, and bent over it, aping the poses of the readers around him.

He had it upside down! Dappa bent his face toward the floor, and stepped forward so that he could discreetly knee Jones in the arse. But Jones was quicker than Dappa gave him credit for. Though he knew nothing of letters, he had figured out on his own that the document needed to be spun around. For this bill was *illustrated*: at the top of the page was a fist-sized blot of ink, a butcherous woodcut of a savage black-skinned man with spraying dreadlocks. His throat was clasped in a white lace cravat, his shoulders dignified by good English tailoring. Printed beneath this portrait in crusty letters an inch high was the word

DAPPA

followed by

A SLAVE, property of MR. CHARLES WHITE, ESQ., is missing and presumed stolen or astray. A REWARD in the amount of TEN GUINEAS shall be given to the first party who brings this Neeger to the dwelling of Mr. White on St. James's Square.

And then finer print, which Dappa would need glasses to read. But he could not get his glasses out of his breast pocket, because not a muscle in his body would move.

Sloop Atalanta, *off the* Shive
SUNSET

HE WISHED HOOKE WERE HERE. A Natural Philosopher could not but be enthralled by all that was laid out for view by such a rare low tide. The sun had sunk low in the west and, behind London's dome of smoke, shone the color of a horseshoe when the farrier beats it out on the anvil. That light was skidding across the tidal flats all round, making them seem not so flat at all. The surface of the muck was rippled, as if it were a pond that had been disturbed by a chill wind, then frozen. But more remarkable to Daniel was the shape of Foul-ness Sand, a few miles to the north, across the mouth of the Thames.

This country of muck, larger than some German principalities, lay concealed beneath the water most of the time. It was devoid of any features such as rocks or vegetation. Yet when the tide drew off, the great quantity of water that had been stranded in the dells of all those frozen ripples drained away, not as a streaming sheet, and not by quiet seepage into the earth, but by finding its way to the low places. One hand-sized puddle would erupt in upon its neighbor, and those two would join forces and go looking for a nearby place that lay a hair's breadth lower, even as every other dollop of water for miles around was pursuing a like strategy. The result, integrated (to use Leibniz's terminology) over the whole of Foulness Sand, was that entire systems of rivers and tributaries sprang into being. Some of those rivers looked as old as the Thames, and big enough to build cities on; yet in a few hours they'd disappear. Existing in a state of pure alienation, unsoftened by reeds or willows, and not encrusted by the buildings of men, they were pure geometry. Albeit geometry of an irregular and organic cast, repugnant to Euclid or, Daniel suspected, to the silver-haired knight who was standing next to him. But Hooke would have seen beauty and found fascination there, and wrought pictures of it, as he had done with flies and fleas.

"Do the same rivers always spring up? Or is it new ones, in different places, at every tide?" Daniel mused.

"One will recur, again and again, for years, perhaps undergoing slow alterations from tide to tide," Isaac answered.

"It was a rhetorical question," Daniel muttered.

"Then some day, perhaps after a storm or an exceptional high tide, the water draws back, and it is gone, never to be seen again. There is much in the subterranean realm that is as opaque to the mind, as it is to the eye."

Isaac now moved across the poop deck to view Shive Tor. Daniel felt compelled to stay at his elbow.

To their left, gray spread to infinity. Ahead, it extended only to the shore of the Isle of Grain, a couple of miles distant. Most of the isle barely rose above the horizon, but there was one hill, perhaps fifty to a hundred feet above sea level, grassy, with a few weather-shocked trees flinging their arms back aghast. Atop that stood a small, blocky, ancient stone church. It stood broadside to the sea, as if the masons had begun by erecting a wind-wall so that they would have something to stand in the lee of, then topped it with a steep roof to deflect the gales heavenwards. On its western front was a square tower with a flat roof and a crenellated top, which the Black Torrent Guard had pressed into service as a watch-tower.

Between *Atalanta* and the foot of that hill, the gray expanse was divided into an upper and a lower part by an irregular line of heaving froth. Below, this was tinged with blue and aqua. Above—nearer the land—it was washed with brownish and yellowish and greenish hues and mottled by scattered swellings in the mud. Sea-birds skimmed along just above it, moving in twos and threes as if hanging together for safety. From time to time they would alight and skitter about on twiglike legs, pecking at the mud. Some of them were doing so around the very foundations of Shive Tor, which stood high, but not dry, halfway between *Atalanta* and the foot of the hill.

The Tor's dredged ship-channel was aimed obliquely downriver, so to find its entrance *Atalanta* would have to glide a short distance past the Shive and come about. The sailors were making ready to accomplish that and to launch the longboat, and they were going about it smartly, for it now seemed quite possible that they might lose the fleeing whaler in the dark. A silver-greyhound flag had been produced from somewhere and was being lashed to a stunted flagpole on the longboat's transom, so that, for what it was worth, everyone who saw them would know that they were the Queen's Messengers. Two dragoons had been pressed into service throwing sounding-leads over the rail and calling out depths, one on the port and one on the starboard side of the bow.

Barnes was arguing with the sloop's captain as to which of them would need more dragoons. The latter wanted it understood that this was Mr. Charles White's pleasure-*jacht*, not an Admiralty ship, and that, in consequence, he did not have any Marines aboard; and as the fleeing whaler probably contained the leaders of Jack's organization—possibly even Jack himself—at any rate, the most notorious and dangerous criminal traitors in the Realm—most of the dragoons really ought to remain aboard the sloop.

"But you are overhauling a single boat," Barnes was saying. "We are assaulting a stone fortress. There's no telling what we shall find—"

But it was useless. Charles White—who would be staying on the sloop, that he might have the glory of catching Jack the Coiner—came down on his captain's side, and pointed out that Barnes's party would in a few minutes be reinforced by nearly a full company of dragoons charging across from the Isle of Grain. The number of dragoons put off in the longboat, not including Colonel Barnes and Sergeant Shaftoe, would be eight. If that was not enough, they could always draw back and await the onslaught from shore.

"It is like playing a part in a masque," Daniel heard Barnes muttering, "a farce entitled 'How bad plans are made.'"

"If Jack understood the true nature of the Solomonic Gold, he would not use it to coin false guineas," Isaac said to Daniel, apparently feeling some need to justify his tactics aloud. "To him it is only gold. Slightly above common gold in value, but still gold. Finding himself under attack, he would get it out of the Tor and aboard the hooker. But when the hooker ran aground, he would resolve to abandon it. For he would have other hoards elsewhere."

"You think he threw it overboard?"

"The band of criminals on the hooker, in their panic, might have thrown *anything* heavy overboard. So we might find it strewn along the bank of the dredged channel. Or it might still be aboard the hooker. I don't think it is in the Tor, or on the whaler—come! It's now!" And Isaac moved with short quick steps to the head of the stair that ran down to the upperdeck. His box of gear was slung over his shoulder on a leather strap, and it banged on his hip as he went, and threatened to pull him off balance. Daniel scurried up behind him and put a steadying hand on the box, and in this way the two old philosophers moved down the steps and across to where the longboat was a-dangle from a pair of out-thrust yards. Soon enough they, Barnes, Shaftoe, eight dragoons, and an able seaman from the sloop's crew were aboard; though Daniel nearly toppled into the water, and in the scramble, lost his periwig. Lines were worked, and the boat jostled and slanted beneath them. They fell into the looming shadow of the sloop's hull. Between the darkness and the loss of his wig, Daniel felt chilly, and called for someone to throw a blanket down to him. Soon a wadded-up lump of gray wool thudded down, followed by a knit watchman's cap, which Daniel gratefully pulled down over his naked skull. As the sloop pulled away from them he saw his wig spinning in a vortex, its long white ponytail pointing this way and that, like a compass needle that has lost its fix on true north.

The sloop—which seemed to move so slowly when one was aboard—sprang away from them. Or perhaps it only felt that way to one who was being marooned. Within a minute they were beyond shouting-range, and might signal the larger vessel only by having a dragoon fire a musket into the air.

The platoons on the Isle of Grain were not moving nearly so quickly. When this plan had first been conceived, Daniel had phant'sied that *Atalanta,* and those mounted platoons, would converge on the Tor at the same instant. But here they were in this longboat at the mouth of the dredged channel, perhaps a musket-shot from the Tor, and the companies on the isle had not stirred yet. Supposedly they were at the foot of the hill, below the steeple of the church. But they were hidden in the dusky shadows, and obscured by grass. That they existed at all was merely a comforting assumption, like that there was a God and that He meant well.

And so for a moment Daniel, and everyone else on the boat with the probable exception of Isaac, were overcome with the sense that it was all a terrible mistake.

Then they could hear the faint sound of a horse blowing air through its lips, out somewhere along the shore. Then faint crackling sounds that came and went in pulses. For the isle was belted with a strand of cockleshells rejected by the surf, and some men must be treading on them as they came down on to the tide flats.

"Let's go for a bit of a row then," Barnes said. "I'll wager Jack has some claret inside." He addressed these words to Bob Shaftoe, who bellowed something to his dragoons who were manning the oars. And rowing boats might not have been their *métier;* but they applied themselves to it cheerfully enough and began bashing their oars against each other. "Move some bloody water!" Bob told them. "This ain't duelling with quarter-staves. Do I look like Robin bloody Hood to you? Stop banging 'em together and get 'em in the water!" And much more in that vein as the longboat began to spin and dodge forward across the pale water that lay thin on the mud-bank. They had crossed over the surf-line now, and the foam of the breakers looked as if it were above their altitude. This illusion was mildly unnerving even to Daniel, who had the advantage of being in a boat; it could not have been comforting to the approaching dragoons.

Finally a horn sounded from the marshes, a cheer went up from the dragoons, and the edge of the island turned red as the First Company of the Queen's Own Black Torrent Guards emerged from the grass, all in a wide line, and began to advance over the flats at a trot.

Daniel looked at the Tor. It was square-floored, each face of the building something less than ten yards wide. Perhaps twenty yards' altitude separated its gaptoothed parapet from its foundation—a pile of boulders atop a lens of greasy black stone that poked up through the bank. "Shive" was a primeval English word for knee-cap, and Daniel, who had sliced a patella or two from cadavers, could see how the rock had come by its name. Slime and barnacles coated the lower reaches and made it difficult to tell where the natural plinth left off and the man-made work began. The Tor had been built up out of bulky brown boulders probably prised from a quarry upriver, barged down at high tide, and rolled overboard. White mortar held it together. There was but a single door, which looked out onto a silted pool at the terminus of this long gouge that they were fitfully navigating. The threshold was an arm's length above where the fur of wee crusty creatures and rank weeds gave way to bare, wave-washed stone. So that was where they had built a floor. From the situation of windows (if that was not too grand a term for them) higher up, Daniel estimated there was a wooden platform above, forming an upper storey, and above that a roof, on which lookouts and gunners might stand to look out over, or through, the woebegone parapet.

"Is there room here for so many horses, when the tide comes in?" Daniel asked.

"First you were worried they would not come at all—I could see it in your phizz—now you're worried because they're coming!" Barnes returned. "It is nonetheless a question that deserves an answer. We are dragoons, Doctor. The horses are mere vehicles. When the men are here, the beasts will be sent back straightaway—they'll be back on the Isle of Grain half an hour from now."

"I do beg your pardon, Colonel. As a wise man once told me, we are all scared."

Barnes nodded gracefully. But he could sense a Newtonian glare boring into the other side of his head, so without delay he said to the sergeant, "Let us advance, and see if we draw fire from the Tor."

"I did not understand that Sir Isaac Newton's rôle was to *draw fire*," Daniel shot back peevishly, then bit his tongue as even Isaac was smiling at Barnes's jest. Annoyed now with everyone on the boat, including himself, Daniel snatched the blanket—ten pounds of greasy Qwghlmian wool—and settled it over his shoulders. It prickled him through his clothes like a heap of thistles, but it would eventually be warmer.

The longboat balked mulishly as it scraped its keel on the sandy bottom every few yards. Sergeant Bob became exasperated, then profane, to the point where Sir Isaac became visibly offended. Half of the dragoons divested themselves of their powder-horns and granadoes, and vaulted over the gunwales to land waist-deep in the channel. This lightened the boat's load enough to get its keel out of the muck, and it enabled them to move it along by pushing on it with their shoulders, as if it were a gun-carriage mired in Flanders. "Take advantage of the shallow water," Barnes said approvingly, "we'll not have it much longer." The colonel had mostly been keeping an eye on the parapet, clearly worried about snipers. Isaac's gaze was fixed on the hooker, which was now rolling freely on the bank of the channel—the direction of the tide had reversed! The sergeant was attending to his men.

Daniel was the only one aware that the charge of the First Company from the Isle of Grain had come to a halt as soon as it had got started. Only a few yards beyond the cockle-belt, a few of the horses had gone down. The rest had halted, and the line of redcoats had split and spread into two wings, trying to probe around some obstacle. A pistol-shot tolled for a broken-legged horse. This got everyone's attention. They heard, too, a distant thudding noise: an axe striking wood.

"Jack's men drove pilings into the mud," was Bob's guess, "and stretched chains between 'em, to stop the horses. This they would've done in the highest and driest parts, where the best footing was to be had; which tells us that the flanks are now in a mire. Someone is trying to chop through a piling with an axe."

"There are nails embedded in that piling, then, and his axe is already ruined," announced Isaac absent-mindedly, without taking his eyes off the hooker.

"Sir Isaac has good ears," Daniel explained to the incredulous Bob.

"Then he'd best plug them," answered Bob and picked up a musket. A moment later the boat flinched from its recoil as he fired it into the air. He handed it to one of the dragoons, who set about furiously reloading.

"As long as you are wasting balls and powder, waste them on the parapet," said the Colonel.

Within a few moments, several other muskets had been fired at the top of the tower, and a large glutinous mass of smoke had been set adrift on the calm evening air. No answering fire came back from Shive Tor. But the little fusillade had the effect Bob wanted: the dragoons off the Isle of Grain were dismounting, sending their horses back to dry land, and advancing on foot. Daniel was noticing that they now looked like dark motes against the gray sand. A few minutes ago their coats had been a proud red. The difference was not that they were all covered in greasy mud now (though they probably were), but that it was getting dark, and the colors were draining from everything. The evening star had come out, very bright, near the Tor.

A colossal thud came out of the far west. It was impressive enough to divert Isaac's concentration from the hooker. "What was that?" he demanded—the first voice to violate the stillness that had descended upon all.

"A lot of powder was touched off at once," said Colonel Barnes. "On a field of battle, it would signify a dreadful accident. Here, I guess it was the bridge over Yantlet Creek being demolished by a mine."

"Why did you mine the bridge, Colonel?"

"I didn't."

Isaac was gobsmacked. "Then—who *did*!?"

"Now you ask me to speculate, Sir Isaac," Barnes said coldly.

"But you have men posted at that bridge," Isaac said.

"Or *had*, sir."

"How could it have been mined, when it was under guard?"

"Again, speculation: it was mined in advance, the mine concealed from view," Barnes said.

"Then, pray tell, who put fire to the fuse?"

"I've no idea."

"No man was needed to put fire to it," Daniel said.

"Then how was it lit?" Barnes demanded.

"The same way as *that* was," Daniel answered, and shrugged an arm free of the blanket to point at the Tor.

Moments earlier he had seen a blue spark in his peripheral vision, and mistaken it for the evening star coming out near Shive Tor. But by now it had become brighter than any heavenly body save the Sun, brighter by far than any Comet. And it was not in the sky, but in one of those small irregular windows in the wall of the Tor.

Everyone was now looking at it, though it was growing brilliant enough to burn the eyes. Only Daniel and Isaac knew what it was.

"Phosphorus is burning inside the Tor," Isaac remarked, more fascinated than alarmed.

"Then someone must be in there," said Bob reaching for a musket.

"No," Daniel said. "It was lit by an Infernal Device."

The door of the Tor swung inward, shouldered out of the way by a waxing draught. The archway was a gem of yellow light. A small mountain of split and dried cord-wood had been piled on the floor, and had now been set a-blaze. Sparks had begun to fountain up into the sky, jetting through orifices that had been hacked through the upper floor and the roof.

"It is an admirable piece of work," said Sir Isaac Newton, flatly and with no trace of rancor. "The rising tide obliges all to run inward to the Tor. But packed as it is with excellent fuel, this will soon become a furnace, and anyone near it will be roasted like a suckling pig. It truly is a choice between the devil and the deep blue sea."

Barnes stood up in the boat, putting all his weight on his one leg and bracing his peg against a bench. He cupped his hands round his mouth and bellowed towards the darkling isle: "Turn back! Retreat! There is not room for you here!" And then he fell back on his arse as the boat was lifted and shoved by a tidal swell. "I do not wish to hear my First Company being drowned," he said.

"Colonel, let us row toward the Isle of Grain—you can warn them all, and rescue most," Daniel suggested.

"Leave me on yonder vessel," Isaac demanded, gesturing toward the hooker, which was now upright and adrift.

"I cannot abandon Sir Isaac Newton on a derelict fishing-boat!" shouted Barnes, exasperated.

"Then do you stay with him, Colonel," suggested Sergeant Bob, "and take a few men. I'll row toward the land, advancing with the tide—warning the men off as I go, rescuing the mired."

A thud and crackle from the Tor as a floor-beam gave way. A billion orange sparks spewed from the openings and schooled in the dark.

"I too shall remain with Sir Isaac," Daniel heard himself saying, like a man lying in state, listening to his own eulogy. "We'll get the hooker clear of the fire, and navigate by the stars. Sir Isaac and I have some knowledge of the stars."

The Monument

SUNSET

"FIRE," SAID JACK, down on a knee, perspective glass steady on the railing.

This command—given in a mild conversational tone—was not answered with the expected hellish noises and exhalations. He peeled his eye from the lens and was abruptly reminded that he was two hundred feet above London. A bad time for a dizzy spell. He spanked the railing, clenched his eyes shut, and announced: "The Scotsman is inside the White Tower; I say, Fire!" Then he opened his eyes, got up, and backed round the stony bole of the Monument, for these things were as likely to explode as to fly. He heard Jimmy and Danny murmuring to each other, then a sputter as the fuse caught, then running feet. The lads came into view. Immediately a basilisk-sound, half hiss and half scream, erupted on the other side and rapidly dwindled.

Jack ran around to see a ray of black fog cantilevered out over the city. On the near side its billows were weirdly lit up, like a squall-line at sunset. But this paled and dissolved in a few moments. The only evidence that remained of this grievous and execrable crime against all known precepts of safe rocketry was a house with a hole in its roof, just short of Mincing Lane, and a gossamer thread connecting said hole with the large pulley lashed to the lantern of the Monument above their heads. From there it ran almost straight down into a polished copper kettle about three paces away from Jack, between the feet of a large Red Indian. The Indian grabbed the thread in one hand lest all of what remained be sucked from the kettle by its own weight.

Jack looked over the railing and saw the filament plunge down and away toward the east. He lost track of it in the Monument's shadow. But he could see a lot of boyish ferment on the roof of the Church of St. Mary-at-Hill, five hundred feet away: some leaping, some hopping into the air, some hurling of stones with strings tied to 'em. To any observer who did not know, as Jack did, that a thread of silk was floating in the air a few yards above these people's heads, it would have looked like the cavorting of men and boys made mad by witchcraft or syphilis, a kind of Bedlam al fresco.

A distant rocket-scream sounded from near the Tower of London. Such was the speed of this second rocket's flight that by the time its sound carried to the top of the Monument, and drew Jack's gaze that way, it was gone, and there was nothing to be seen but a black rainbow bent over Tower Hill and the Moat, connecting the Barking Churchyard behind All Hallows Church to the battlements of the White Tower. "Not a pot of gold, but close to one," Jack remarked. He was fortunate enough, now, to be looking in the right direction to see yet another dart of white flame jump up from the River Thames, pulling a shroud of black powder-smoke behind it. It reached apogee above Tower Wharf and then winked out. Momentum carried it north over the Outer Wall to crash in Tower Lane. "Damn, too short!" Jack cried, as the sound of the launch reached them.

"They've spares on the barge, Dad," Danny said.

He glanced down onto the Church of St. Mary-at-Hill. The men and boys on the roof had settled down noticeably—in fact, most of them were running away, which was, of course, the normal practice, from the scene of their crimes. Only two remained. One was working on his lap. The other was acting as a sort of lookout. He needn't have bothered; the rocket that had screamed over his head a few moments ago had ignited a fire in the attic of that house on Mincing Lane, and there, rather than the church's roof, was where the attentions of the (paltry number of mostly self-appointed) authorities and the (vastly more energetic and numerous) Mobb were now directed.

The one who had been working on his lap suddenly sprang back, jumping to his feet, and elevated his chin, as if he had released a carrier pigeon and were watching it take flight. The Indian beside Jack began to pull in string, hand-over-hand, as rapidly as he could. "Look out below!" called Jimmy, as he picked up the copper string-vat and simply dropped it over the rail.

A curse from Danny: "Hit the Lanthorn Tower this time." Then another whooshing scream from the river. Jack glimpsed another smoke-prong in the distance.

The kettle made a funny noise, a cross between a splat and a bong, as it hit the pavement below them. Tomba was grinning beneath a perspective glass. "Men in kilts on the battlements of the White Tower," he announced.

"And just what are those men doing?" inquired Jack, whose attention was fixed on the roof of the church of St. Dunstan-in-the-East, where a scene had just played out remarkably like that moments earlier on the roof of St. Mary-at-Hill.

"It appears that they are drinking usquebaugh and line dancing," returned Tomba.

"One day your wit shall be the death of you, and my hands around your throat shall be the instrument," Jack remarked calmly.

"Some of them are pulling in the string from Barking Churchyard," Tomba returned, "others raising a banner."

"*Raising a banner!?* I gave no instructions touching a banner," Jack hollered.

"A Cross of St. Andrews, and—"

"Oh, Jesus Christ. Is any of those Highlanders concerning himself with a pulley?"

"The pulley is being worked on—hold—oh, my God!" Tomba exclaimed, and drew back from the perspective glass laughing.

"What is it?"

"The rocket. It nearly knocked one of them down," Tomba explained, as yet another basilisk-shriek reached them from the river.

"So the last one flew true?"

"Skipped across the roof of the White Tower itself like a flat stone on a pond," confirmed Danny, who had watched with his naked eyes. "Passed between a Scotsman's legs and smacked into the north parapet."

"I hope that the Scotsman has had the presence of mind to stomp on the string."

"They appear to be pulling it in—there's a chap working by the pulley now—good! The pulley is threaded—"

"The roof of Trinity House is cleared!" Tomba mentioned, having trained his spyglass on a building halfway between them and the White Tower.

"Take up the slack smartly now!" Jack called down over the railing. He was awash in fiery light up here. The men at the base of the column were toiling in blue dusk, pulling in loose thread from above as fast as their hands could move. They were working in a clear space, a sort of defensive perimeter that had been set up round the base of the column. Around it the black lint of the Mobb was rapidly gathering, kept at bay by very large hoodlums with whips, and archers who had scaled the plinth of the great column to take up sniping-positions under the wings of its dragons.

"What rumor did you put out?" Jack asked of Jimmy. Directly below he could see the flattened kettle gleaming like a newly minted coin.

"That Jack the Coiner would appear atop the Monument at sundown and throw guineas," Jimmy answered.

"Barking Churchyard is clear!" announced Danny, which meant that although none of them could see it, the silken filament now stretched in a single uninterrupted catenary from the great pulley, above their heads, across a distance of a bit less than half a mile to a similar device that the Scotsmen had strung from the southeastern turret of the White Tower. From there it ran over the inner and outer walls, above the Wharf, to a barge that had drifted down the river during the last hour or so and then tossed out an anchor. Though this would not have been obvious to anyone viewing it from the level of the water, it was plain from this elevated viewpoint that a great wheel, several yards across, was mounted in that barge. Its axis was vertical, so its rim was parallel to the deck. It was not a mighty sort of wheel, not like an anchor cable's windlass, but more like a spinning-wheel laid on its side. A dozen or more crewmen stood around it, and now, evidently on some signal from the White Tower, they began to turn that wheel—reeling in the same string that they had sent rocketing over the battlements a minute ago. Within a few moments the result of their exertions could be detected up atop the Monument. For a change in the string's angle was plainly visible as the tension increased.

"Supply!" screamed Jack to the men below, who were gathered round an exceptionally large wagon chocked at the foot of the Monument. A patchwork of work-out sails had covered its contents until now. These were flung off to expose a huge cylindrical vat in which miles of cordage had been expertly coiled. But this was not ordinary line, of uniform thickness. That up here at the top of the Monument, running through the pulley at an accelerating clip, was fine silken cord. But what was emerging from the vat was noticeably coarser. And what was coiled in the bottom-most part of the vat was as thick as a man's wrist.

"Righto," Jack said, and caught the eye of the Indian. "And so 'twould seem that very soon I shall require the Chariot of Phaethon. And another for His Reverence."

His Reverence let it be known that he was amused. The Indian heaved a sigh and shambled through the door to begin the long journey down stairs.

"What are you snickering at?" Jack demanded, making a semicircular excursion round the column to discover Father Édouard de Gex. The Jesuit had, for lack of a better word, cornered the four Jewish tourists at the southwestern vertex of the platform. At his feet rested a black strong-box. The lid was open. Diverse gnarled keys and hand-hammered padlocks littered the deck all round. He had mostly emptied the casket by this point, but some of its contents could still be seen: it had been full of small leathern bags, each bag filled with something of High Specific Gravity that clinked as de Gex transferred them one by one into a stout ox-hide satchel. A second satchel, already full, sat next to the one he was packing.

"You lay a curse on yourself without knowing it," de Gex answered. "You should call it the Chariot of Apollo."

"Apollo is the sobriquet of Leroy—I was trying to show deference."

"All right, Helios then. Never Phaethon."

"Half the young blades in town are rattling about in Phaethons," Jack returned, "why can't I fly above London in one?"

"Phaethon was a sort of bastard son of Helios. He borrowed his papa's gleaming Vehicle and went for a heavenly Drive. But seeing the great height to which he had ascended, and terrified by the Heroes, Legends, and Titans hung in the sky by the Gods as Constellations, he lost his wits; the chariot ran out of control, scorching the earth; Zeus struck him down with a thunderbolt and he crashed into a river. So when you refer to your conveyance as the Chariot of Phaethon—"

"The import of your Tale is not lost on me," Jack let it be known, watching de Gex transfer the last of the clinking bags into the satchel. Then, in a different tone, he reflected: "It is curious. I always phant'sied that the rites of the ancient Pagans, prosecuted as they were in airy temples by naked maidens and prancing butt-boys, and enlivened by feasts and orgies, must have been infinitely more diverting than the insufferable ceremonies of Christians; yet the dramatick yarn of this Phaethon, intoned by Your Reverence, is as dry, tedious, and didactic as the litanies of the Baptists."

"I am speaking to you, Jack, of your pride, of your ignorance, and of your doom. I am sorry that I can not make it any more festive."

"When night fell, who rode the moon-chariot?"

"Selene. But that was of silver."

"If those layabouts on the barge do not spin that wheel any faster, we shall be compared to *her*."

"The twilight will linger for a while yet," de Gex predicted.

Jack went to inspect the rope coming up from below, and passing over the pulley and out into the air above London en route to the said barge. He was surprised to find that it had already waxed to the thickness of his finger. Surprised, and a bit dismayed, for he'd been hoping that it would snag on a weathercock somewhere and snap while it was still slender and fragile. But now that it had achieved such a thickness it was unlikely to break. He would actually have to do this thing.

Some minutes passed. London as always continued in roiling feverish busy-ness: the Mobb around the base of the Monument, swollen to a thousand, chanting for their promised guineas, here parting to make room for a mad dog, there clumping to assault a pick-pocket. The fire brigades at their pumping-engines in the Tower hamlets and now in Mincing Lane, surrounded by more of the Mobility, protected by cordons of lobsterbacks. The Highlanders atop the White Tower, victorious but somehow forlorn, as no one seemed to have noticed what they'd accomplished. The men on the barge spinning the giant wheel, like the main gear of an immense clock. The ships on the Pool as ever, going about their toils and quotidian adventures perfectly oblivious to all of these things.

Phaethon himself was just in the act of crash-landing on the upper Thames, some leagues to the west of town. With any luck he'd set fire to Windsor Castle on his way down. The radiance of his final approach sprayed flat across London and made the whole city jagged and golden. Jack looked at it all, most carefully, as he had once looked out over Cairo, and indeed the place suddenly looked as queer and as outlandish to him as Cairo once had. Which was to say that he saw all through a traveler's dewy eye, and perceived all that was overlooked by the Cockney's brass-tacks stare. He owed it to Jimmy and Danny and all his posterity to look at it thus. For de Gex was right, Jack was a bastard who had ascended to a great height and hob-nobbed with Heroes and Titans and seen things he was never meant to see. This might be the last time in many a generation that a Shaftoe might gaze down from such a vantage-point and see so much so clearly. But what was he seeing?

"Dad," Jimmy was saying, "it's time, Dad."

He looked over. The rope was as thick as his wrist now, and it no longer moved; it had been tied off down below, the plinth of the Monument pressed into service as a bitt. Half a mile distant, out in the river, the barge had chopped its anchor-cable, and flung great bags of heavy fabric—sea-anchors—into the river. The flow of the Thames had inflated them. They pulled the barge downstream with immense force, exerting tension on the full length of the rope that could be sensed from here—for the rigging that bound the great pulley to the top of the Monument had now begun to groan and tick like that of a ship that has been struck by a blast of wind. Riding on that taut hawser, now, above their heads, was a traveling block: that is to say a grooved pulley spinning on a well-greased axle in a casing of forged iron. Dangling from it were two chains that diverged slightly and fastened to opposite ends of a short length of plank. Jimmy was gripping one of those chains, Danny the other. The Chariot of Phaethon was available for boarding. Everyone up here—even the Jews, who'd left off being scared and were now fascinated—was looking at it significantly, and then looking at Jack.

"All right, all right," said Jack. He strode to it. De Gex handed him one of the two satchels and Jack slung it over his shoulder. "Padre, I'll see you anon," Jack said dismissively. Even de Gex sensed that he should draw away now. Jack climbed up to the plank, which hung about at the level of the railing. Seating himself upon it, and situating the heavy satchel in his lap, he braced his feet on the rail as if afraid the boys might pitch him off before he was ready. Which was a quite reasonable fear, as he was set to give them Advice.

"Now, lads," he said, "either this'll work or it won't. If it goes awry, never forget there's other places to be besides England; you've seen more of 'em than most, I don't need to tell you twice. The Great Mogul is always hiring good mercenaries. Queen Kottakkal would be delighted to have you back in her court, to say nothing of her bedchamber. Our partners in Queena-Kootah would give you a hero's welcome at the foot of Eliza Peak. Manila's not such a bad place, either. I do not recommend that you go to Japan. And remember, if you go the other way, to the shores of America, and travel west long enough, you ought to cross the path of good old Moseh, assuming the Comanches haven't made him into moccasins. So there's no purpose to be served in tarrying here, lads, if I end up at Tyburn. Just do me a favor before you leave."

"All right," said Jimmy grudgingly.

Jack had avoided looking into his sons' faces during this Oration, because he reckoned they'd not wish to be seen with tears streaming down their faces. But looking up at Jimmy now he saw dry eyes and a quizzical if impatient phizz. Turning the other way, he saw Danny gazing distractedly at the White Tower.

"Did you hear a single fucking word I said?"

"You want us to do you a favor," Danny returned.

"Before you embark on a new life overseas, assuming that is your fate," Jack said, "find Eliza and tell her she is my true love." And then he jerked the chains loose from the restraining grip of first Jimmy, then Danny. He leaned forward, pushed off against the rail with both feet, and launched himself into space above London. His cloak spread in the wind of his flight like the wings of an eagle, revealing, to anyone who might be gazing up into the sky, a lining made from cloth-of-gold that glistered in the rays of the setting sun like the chariot of Apollo. He was on his way down.

Worth's Coffee-house, Birchin Lane, London
SUNSET

DAPPA STOOD FROZEN for a count of ten. As if standing still would make him white.

"Sir," said Jones, chuckling, "why, this looks like you! What's it say?"

Thank God for Jones, and for his being such a perfect imbecile. Many a ship's officer, caught in storm or battle, and seized by a natural tendency to freeze up in terror, was moved to action by the vivid helplessness of his crew.

Dappa's body was not answering well to commands from the quarterdeck, so in stepping forward he bashed the table with the brawn of his thigh, nearly toppling it. But he got the libel in his hand and snatched it away. He looked round the coffee-house and met a few eyes, but they showed nothing beyond momentary curiosity at the unbalanced movements of the Blackamoor. None of them had seen this handbill.

"What's it say?" Jones repeated.

Dappa shoved it into the hip pocket of his coat, where it was about as welcome as a turd. But at least it was hidden. "It says something that is not true, about me," he said, "a perfect and abominable lie." And he wished that he could have said it in a low and quiet voice. But passion made him squawk like a strangled hen. He closed his eyes for a moment, trying to think. "An attack," he said, "'tis an attack on me by Charles White—a Tory. Why on me? No reason. Thus 'tis not an attack on *me* but on what I am a part of, namely, *Minerva*." He opened his eyes. "Your ship is under attack, Jones."

"I am well enough accustomed to that, sir."

"But not with cannonballs. This is a paper attack. Shore artillery is firing on you—what must you do?"

"Firing on *us,* you mean, sir," Jones returned, "and since shore batteries are difficult to silence, we must move out of their range."

"Correct. But the indenture that we came here to sign—*it must be signed* or our obligations to the ship-chandler shall not be met. We must meet those obligations, Jones, or our credit and our good name will be spoilt, do you understand? Mr. Sawyer is honest, as such men go—when he comes here, pretend to read whatever he places in front of you, and sign it. Then run down to the river and hie to *Minerva* and tell the Captain to begin raising anchor *now.*"

"Are you going to leave me alone here, sir?" Jones inquired.

"Yes. I shall try to get back to the ship. If I'm not aboard at the next high tide, though, then you and *Minerva* must leave *me.*" Dappa glanced up toward the window and saw the worst thing he *could* have seen: the tout who had been handing out the libels had hunted them through the crowd, and was now pressing his shiny face against the window. He met Dappa's eye. Dappa felt the way he had once in Africa, a little boy playing near the river, when he had looked up and seen the striped eye of a crocodile looking back at him. It was as if a thousand ancestors were standing round him in a great invisible chorus, screaming, "Run! Run!" And run he would have, but for the knowledge that he was the only black man in a mile, and could never run far or fast enough.

A shadow fell over the coffee-house now, like that of a cloud passing before the sun. But it was not a cloud, but a great black coach, drawn by four black horses, pulling up in front of the coffee-house, coming to a stop.

The tout paid no mind to the coach-and-four. He had got a wild triumphal look on his face—the only thing that could have made him any less pleasant to look at. Keeping his eye fixed through the window, he began sidestepping toward the entrance.

"Repeat the instructions I gave to you," Dappa said.

"Wait for Mr. Sawyer. Look at the indenture like I'm reading it. Sign it. Run to the ship. Get underway at high tide with or without you."

"And when you return from Boston, God willing, we shall sort it out then," Dappa said, and stepped out from behind the table. He began moving toward the door.

Before he could reach it, the door was pulled open from outside. The view into the street was blocked by the glossy black flank of the coach. Dappa drew his right hand up his hip, twitched the skirt of his coat behind him, and reached around to the small of his back. There, in the waistband of his breeches, was a dagger. He found its handle with his fingers but did not draw it yet. The tout appeared in the doorway, blocking his way out, ecstatic, hopping from toe to toe like a little boy who needed to piss. He looked to one side, desperately wanting to catch someone's eye—to get a witness, or recruit an accomplice. Dappa supposed he was looking at whomever had pulled the door open. The tout's head swivelled round to bear on Dappa again, and he raised one hand and pointed his index finger at Dappa's face, like aiming a pistol. He had dropped his stack of handbills and they were blowing round his ankles, tumbling into the coffee-house.

A larger man came into view just behind the tout, and over his shoulder. He was blond and blue-eyed, a young bloke, better dressed, and he had something in his hand: a walking-stick, which he was tossing straight up into the air. The brass handle at its stop leaped above his head. He caught the stick about halfway along its length and in the same motion snapped it down. The brass ball at the top stopped hard against the back of the tout's head. The tout's face and then his whole body lost tone, as if all 206 of his bones had been jellied. Before the tout could fall to the ground and block the door, the blond man stepped in beside him and checked him out of the way. The tout disappeared from view, except for his feet, which lay twitching on the threshold. The big blond man allowed his walking-stick to slide down through his fist until the brass grip was back in his hand. He bowed to Dappa in the most genteel way imaginable and extended his free hand toward the carriage, offering Dappa a lift. And it was not until that moment that Dappa recognized this man as one Johann von Hacklheber, a Hanoverian, and a member of the household of the Duchess of Arcachon-Qwghlm.

DAPPA WAS IN THE WOODEN womb of the carriage. It smelled like Eliza's toilet-water. Johann did not climb inside with him but closed the door, slapped the side, and began distributing commands in High-Dutch to the driver and a pair of footmen. The footmen sprang from their perch on the back of the vehicle and began wading through the litter on the street, snatching up every copy of the libel that they could find. Dappa watched this through the coach's window, then, when it began to lurch forward, drew the shutters, leaned forward, and buried his face in his hands.

He wanted to weep tears of rage, but for some reason they would not come. Perhaps if this had unfolded into a speedy and clean getaway he might have relaxed, and then released the tears. But they were on one of the most congested streets in all of London. Yet he felt no urgency to give the coachman instructions, for it would be a quarter of an hour before they came to any sort of turning-point.

That would be at the intersection with Cornhill, a hundred feet away.

After some moments he reached into his pocket and took out the handbill. He smoothed it out on his thigh and cracked the window-shutters to spill light on it. All of which required conscious effort and a certain fortitude, as in all ways he wanted to lean back and enjoy the gentlemanly comfort of this coach and pretend that this wretched, abominable, vile, vicious thing had never been done to him.

He did not know exactly how old he was—probably about three score. His dreadlocks were black at the tips but gray at the roots. He had circumnavigated the terraqueous globe and knew more languages than most Englishmen knew drinking-songs. He was an officer of a merchant ship, and better dressed than any member of the Kit-Cat Clubb. And yet this! This piece of paper on his thigh. Charles White had printed it up, but any Englishman could have done the same. This particular configuration of ink upon the page had made him into a hounded fugitive, laid him at the mercy of a loathsome street-corner tout, forced him to flee from a coffee-house. And it had put a cannonball in his stomach. Was this how Daniel Waterhouse had felt when a stone the size of a tennis ball had dwelt in his bladder? Perhaps; but a few minutes' knife-work and such a stone was gone. The cannonball in Dappa's stomach was not so easy to remove. Indeed he knew that it would return, every time he recalled the last few minutes' events, for the remainder of his days. He might be able to reach *Minerva* and sail out of range, but even if he were in the Sea of Japan, Charles White's cannonball would hit him in the belly whenever his mind was idle and his thoughts returned to this day. And return he would, like a dog to his vomit.

This, he now perceived, was why gentlemen fought duels. Nothing else would purge such dishonor. Dappa had killed several men, mostly pirates, and mostly with pistol-shots. The chances were better than even that, in a fair duel, he could put a pistol-ball into Charles White's body. But duels were for gentlemen; a slave could not challenge his master.

Stupid idea anyway; he needed to get to *Minerva*, to escape. The coach was negotiating a right turn onto Cornhill, therefore working its way back round toward the Pool. If it had turned left it would mean they were taking him toward Leicester House, where Eliza lived with a nest of Hanoverians. Yes, better to get out of town.

And yet the notion of challenging Charles White to a duel, putting a bullet in him, had seemed so delicious. Really the only thing that had given him any satisfaction since the shock of seeing his own name on this document.

He opened the shutters a bit more and looked round through the side and rear windows. Johann was looking right back at him from no more than twelve feet away. He was following in the wake that the coach had made through the crowd. He told Dappa, with a sharp movement of the head, to close the shutters. Then he turned round to look behind him. Dappa saw now that they were being tailed, at a leisurely walking pace, by a pair of men, each of whom was clutching a copy of the handbill. Scanning the width of Cornhill he saw more copies of the libel being handed out. He supposed that the only thing that prevented a hue and cry from going up was the reward, and the fact that those who seized him would not wish to divide it by the whole number of the Mobb. So for the nonce his pursuers were only two, and they were being held at bay by Johann, who had a sword; but Charles White could stamp out new pursuers as fast as printing presses could be operated.

How strange a thing that was! How could he have explained it to the villagers he'd grown up with in Africa? These bits of metal, put in a frame, smeared with black stuff, and pressed upon these white leaves, had the magical property that they would make one man out of a whole metropolis into a terrified fugitive, while every other man whose eyes were exposed to the incantation would become his implacable pursuer. Yet the same bits of metal put in the same frame, but in a different arrangement, would have no effect. Indeed, Dappa wondered whether he might print up some handbills naming Charles White *his* escaped slave, and putting some price on *his* head.

The notion was appealing—even more so than that of putting a lead ball through White's body. But it was idle to think of such things. Escape Dappa might hope for. Revenge was not to be thought of.

They had come to the broad intersection of Cornhill and a large north-south-running street that changed its name from corner to corner. If they turned left here they'd be north-bound on Bishopsgate, headed for the South Sea Company, Gresham's College, and Bedlam. More likely, though, they would go right, placing them south-bound on Gracechurch Street. This soon became Fish Street Hill and ran past the Monument straight down to London Bridge.

The coach halted in the middle of this intersection, for an uncommon number of persons were gathered here. When Dappa looked out the right side he tended to see the backs of their heads, and when he looked to the left he tended to see their faces; for most of them were gazing at some spectacle to the south. Dappa could not tell what. He looked to the left, trying to read the answer in their faces. He found no useful information there, save that what they were looking at was rather high up in the air. But he did catch sight again of South Sea House, a very large compound one of whose gates was situated a couple of hundred yards away, on the left side of Bishopsgate. It was bigger, and newer, than the Bank of England. It was, in a way, the Anti-Bank; its collateral, the Thing of Value against which it lent money, was the Asiento: the trans-Atlantic slave trade, wrested from Spain last year in the war.

A sudden exclamation came up from the crowd. Dappa glanced to the right, and thought he perceived a trail of black smoke drawn through the air from near the top of the Monument. And then he made a second glance, for the lantern at the top of that colossal spire was disfigured by some sort of jury-rigged block-and-tackle device. A vulgar entertainment for the Mobb, was his guess.

But back to South Sea House. The sight of this evil place, looming like a pirate-ship off his larboard beam, had caused certain notions to fall together within Dappa's mind. A plan—not a sketchy one but a Plan whole and entire—had suddenly presented itself in his mind, and it was so obviously the right thing to do that he put it into effect with no deliberations whatsoever. For this Plan had the miraculous effect of removing the enormous ball of lead from his stomach.

He dropped to his knees on the floor of the coach and flipped the libel over on the facing bench. Out of his pocket came a pencil, and touching it to his tongue, as if this would put eloquence into it, he wrote

Your grace, my lady—
Johann did his duty bravely and well. Pray do not rebuke him when this carriage is found empty.

When last you and I conversed, we spoke of my career as author of books, and teller of slave-stories. A similitude was formed, in which my works to date were likened to so many balls of grapeshot, which when fired at our Enemy pose a nuisance but can never send any slave-ships to David Jones's Locker where they ought to be all. You exhorted me to leave off gathering more grapeshot and to turn my efforts to finding a single cannonball.

Until today, I assumed that the cannonball—by which is meant, the story that will convince Englishmen, once and for all, of the absurdity and the enormity of slavery—would be found in some slave-auction in São Paulo, Kingstown, or Carolina. But to my surprise I, this afternoon, found that cannonball in the pit of mine own stomach. *Minerva* sails on the morning tide but you may find me in a gaol somewhere in London. I shall require paper, ink, and your prayers.

Your humble and obedient servant,

Dappa

Leaving this on the bench he flung open the door on the carriage's left side. A small open space welcomed him, since no spectators would stand where the view to the south was blocked by the coach. Johann did not mark him; he was as fascinated as anyone else by the spectacle at the Monument. Dappa strode, but never ran, north through the crowd onto Bishopsgate. He phant'sied he might hear reward-seekers pursuing him through the crowd; never mind, if those did not, others would soon enough.

In a few moments' time he was seated in a coffee-house literally in the shadow of South Sea House, sipping chocolate and pretending to read the *Examiner*. As if he'd a right to be there.

Busy men were all around him, unrolling documents on tables: charts of the Bights of Benin and Biafra, loading-diagrams of slave-ships, ledgers heavy with human assets. Familiar names flew around the place: Accra, Elmina, Ijebu, and Bonny. He felt, strangely, at home. Even more strangely, he felt at peace. Flipping the newspaper over, he licked his pencil again, and began to write.

Shive Tor

DUSK

IN A FEW MINUTES SIR Isaac was on the deck of the hooker, his hair gleaming like a comet's tail in the fierce light of the burning Tor. Daniel stood near him, flat-footed under the weight of his Blanket, peering from beneath his rumpled Cap. A team of four dragoons were bent over the hooker's rail, straining to heave-ho Colonel Barnes aboard without snapping off his other leg.

Very quickly the longboat rowed away from them, for the water was now deep enough that it could move free of the dredged channel. The hooker drew a bit more water than that, and was confined to the channel for the time being. Pulling his cap off so that he could feel the flow of air over his scalp, Daniel verified his suspicion that the burning Tor was drawing in a powerful flood of air, some of which was catching on the hull and the bare spars of the hooker. She was being sucked directly into the pillar of fire, like a moth into Vulcan's forge.

Barnes was aware of it. The dragoons had begun exploring the ship, looking for an anchor, or anything that would serve the same end. There were none, as the anchor-cables had been chopped through in the coiners' haste to escape.

"Is there anything that seems heavy down there?" Barnes demanded of a dragoon who had been groping around belowdecks.

Isaac pricked up his ears, as he too was very keen on finding something heavy.

"Only a great bloody chest," the dragoon answered, "too heavy to move."

"Did you look inside of it?" Isaac inquired, tense as a starving cat.

"No, sir. 'Tis locked. But I know what's in it."

"How do you know what is in it, if you did not look inside?"

"Why, I can hear it, sir. Ticking away just as steady as you please. It is a great big clock."

As if the tips of their noses were joined by a hawser that had just snapped taut, Daniel and Isaac swiveled their heads toward each other.

Daniel spoke to the dragoon, though he was looking Isaac in the eye. "Is it *so* heavy that it could not be carried abovedecks and hurled over the side?" he asked.

"I heaved with all my might and could not budge it a hair's breadth, sir."

Daniel was asking himself whether he ought to let the dragoons know what was obvious to him and Isaac: that they were trapped on a derelict vessel with a ticking Infernal Device. But Isaac made up his mind quicker, and said: "Pray forgive Dr. Waterhouse's curiosity on so trivial a matter. He and I are *amateurs* of clock-work. As we have little else to do just now, perhaps he and I shall retire belowdecks and amuse ourselves with Horologickal chit-chat."

"And I'll join you," said Barnes, who had caught on, "if you'll have me, that is."

"Please be our guest, Colonel," said Daniel. He then led Isaac and Barnes toward an open hatch, which, against the fire-lit deck planks, stood out as a crisp black rectangle.

The White Tower
DUSK

FATHER ÉDOUARD DE GEX of the Society of Jesus stood up on one leg, for he'd damaged an ankle, and turned around to survey the debris trail he had left across the roof of the White Tower. Chiefly he desired to know where the contents of his satchel were. It seemed a good deal lighter now than when he'd jumped off the Monument a few moments earlier.

Under the groaning rope, and interspersed with flattened Scotsmen and their far-flung dirks, sporrans, and tam-o-shanters, was a Milky Way of coins and the small leather bags they'd just sprayed out of. De Gex hobbled back along his track snatching them up and stuffing them into his bag. Ashamed to see a man of the cloth performing stoop-and-pick labor in their midst, the stunned and bruised Highlanders drew themselves up, shook the dust from their kilts, and went to work gleaning coins and wee bags from the roof.

But de Gex did not leave off collecting and counting them until he had worked his way back to the west parapet. There he encountered the first man he had knocked down: a bulky fellow with a patch over one eye, who spoke to him in tolerable French. "In the name of the Auld Alliance," said he (referring to an extremely spotty but æon-spanning series of diplomatic trysts between Scotland and France) "I bid you welcome to the Tower of London. Please consider it the property of France—"

"*Pourquoi non?* Since it was built by us."

"—and yours to command!"

"Very well, my first command is that you take down the banner of MacIan of MacDonald!" answered de Gex.

Lord Gy was not pleased to hear this. That much was on his face, as plain as a laceration. But he bore it with the insolent calm of one who has heard worse and would like you to notice that he is still alive. "I apologize," he said, "the lads were a trifle high-spirited. The sobriety and discretion of Paris are foreign to young blades who have just galloped down from the heather." And making a small bow, he turned in the direction of the banner. So did de Gex.

But both of them were astonished to find no banner at all: only a flag-pole that had been severed at waist level by one stroke of a very good blade. Next to it, the banner-carrier—a being made entirely of freckles, perhaps fourteen years old—was sitting in a gun-slit pinching a bloody nose.

Rufus MacIan hurried over to make inquiries. Édouard de Gex, after the obligatory rolling of the eyes, looked about and noted, for the first time, that Jack was nowhere to be seen. In the commotion of de Gex's descent upon the White Tower, Jack must have taken the matter of the banner into his own hands. He must then have gone down stairs; and the nearest way down would have been through a door, now standing open, in the round turret that held together the northeastern vertex of the building. That turret loomed above the place where MacIan was interrogating the bloody-nosed freckle-boy, and it was obvious that MacIan would be headed that way in a moment.

De Gex commanded the Highlanders around him to remain at their posts, and strode toward the round turret. Several of the Scotsmen affected not to have grasped his order, and followed him; but MacIan, who was now aimed for the same door, turned round, his face very choleric, and bit off a few words in Scots that sent them all glancing away. He entered the round turret only two strides ahead of de Gex.

"Pity," said the latter, looking around the perfectly barren room, "all the astronomical devices are gone."

Lord Gy was already in the stair, on his way down. "Eh?"

"Didn't you know? This was where Flamsteed worked, in the days before the Royal Observatory was moved to Greenwich. The Prime Meridian of the English once passed through this room—"

Which was perfectly trivial and beside the point, as de Gex well knew. But he did not like the look on the face of Lord Gy, and wanted to break his concentration. The gambit might have worked on a French nobleman whose social reflexes had been trained to quivering perfection in the salons of Versailles. It failed on Lord Gy, who had ascended to the nobility by cutting such a Frenchman in twain, and who at this moment looked as if he were ready to do it again.

The purpose of the round tower was to support a spiral stair. Finding Jack was a matter of winding down and gazing into each doorway that presented itself. They shortly tracked him down on the middle of the building's three floors. This space, formerly the royal court of a King, had been given over in recent centuries to the storage of official documents. Jack was squatting with his back to them in the middle of a cavernous fireplace shaking powder from a horn onto the Scottish banner, which he had folded a couple of times and stuffed beneath an andiron. On his career through the former throne-room he had swiped an armload of rolled-up papers from a dusty shelf and piled them under and around the banner to serve as kindling.

"Jacques—" de Gex began.

"Pardon me while I destroy the evidence, your virginity."

"Ye baistart!" exclaimed Lord Gy.

"Did I say, destroy the evidence?" Jack said, looking over his shoulder to see MacIan. "I meant that this sacred banner became torn and dirtied in the fray, and the only respectful way to dispose of it now is by a cleansing flame." And he held a pistol—an unloaded one, as it turned out—next to the banner and pulled the trigger. Sparks from the flint sprayed across powder-smeared fabric and became something more than sparks. A fizzy conflagration spread across the banner, like flames across a field of harvested stalks, only faster. Jack recoiled, staggering out of the fireplace to get clear of the smoke. Since a draught had not yet been established in the chimney, a good deal of the smoke followed him—indeed, was sucked into his wake so that he seemed to be trailing it behind him like a rocket. "Right, let's go somewhere we can breathe," Jack suggested, and strode past de Gex and MacIan, headed for the stair.

Now de Gex had seen a few duels in his day. These were at least as formal, and as premeditated, as weddings. But he'd also seen a sufficient number of sudden murderous stabbing-brawls to have understood that even they were not as spontaneous as they looked.

If you were strolling in the gardens of Versailles, you might one day hear sudden noises, and turn around to see, some distance away, one fellow—let's call him Arnauld—going after another—call him Blaise—with a drawn blade. From which, if you were a careless observer, you might think that Arnauld had just snapped without warning, like an ice-covered bough falling from a tree. But in truth the Arnaulds of the world were rarely so reckless. A careful observer, watching Arnauld for two or three minutes prior to the onset of violence, would see some sort of exchange between him and Blaise—a calculated insult from Blaise, let us say, such as a refusal to let Arnauld through a door ahead of him, or a witticism about Arnauld's wig, which had been so very fashionable three months ago. If Blaise were a polished wit, he would then move on, blithe, humming an air, and giving every appearance of having forgotten the event.

But Arnauld would become a living Exhibit. Symptoms would set in that were so obvious and dramatic as to furnish a topic of study for the Royal Society. Why, a whole jury of English savants could stand around poor Arnauld with their magnifying lenses and their notebooks, observing the changes in his physiognomy, noting them down in Latin and rendering them in labored woodcuts. Most of these symptoms had to do with the Humour of Passion. For a few moments, Arnauld would stand fast as the insult sank in. His face would turn red as the vessels in his skin went flaccid, and consequently ballooned with blood from a heart that had begun to pound like a Turkish kettle-drum signalling the onset of battle. But this was not when the attack came, because Arnauld, during this stage, was physically unable to move. All of his activity was mental. Once he got over the first shock, Arnauld's first thought would be to convince himself that he had reined in his emotions now, got himself under control, was ready to consider matters judiciously. The next few minutes, then, would be devoted to a rehearsal of the recent encounter with Blaise. Affecting a rational, methodical approach, Arnauld would marshal whatever evidence he might need to convict Blaise of being a scoundrel, and sentence him to death. After that, the attack would not be long in following. But to one who had not been there with those Fellows of the Royal Society to observe all that had led up to it, it would seem like the spontaneous explosion of an Infernal Device.

De Gex was standing behind MacIan and had watched the banner-burning over the other's epaulets. The backs of MacIan's ears had gone cherry red. He'd not so much as twitched an eyelid when Jack had strode past him to the stair. De Gex knew what would be coming soon. There was nothing he could say now to interrupt the proceedings going on in MacIan's brain: the marshalling of the arguments, the sure and inevitable judgment. But there was something he could *do.* He let his satchel down to the floor, and reached silently into the pocket of his cassock. It was not a lined pocket, but a slit that went all the way through the garment, and gave him access to what was beneath.

Father Edouard was a *member* of the Society of Jesus, but he was a *participant* in the society of *men*—to be specific, the men of London, the most beastly city he had ever seen, though he'd circumnavigated the globe. In his waistband, his fingers found the hilt of a splendid watered-steel dagger he'd picked up from a Banyan in Batavia. He drew it silently from its leather sheath. MacIan still hadn't moved. The room was silent except for the crackle of the flames spreading to the pile of ancient documents Jack had strewn around the flag. De Gex broke the silence, a little, by stepping forward.

But this triggered a greater sound from behind him. Before de Gex could turn to see what it was, his dagger-hand had been seized from behind and twisted up behind his back. The fingers opened and the weapon dropped, but did not fall to the floor; it was intercepted by another hand. An instant later that hand appeared in front of him and brought the dagger to his throat. He had been embraced from behind by a man who smelled of sweat-sodden wool, of horses, and of gunpowder. One of the Highlanders had tailed him silently down stairs.

"Ye ir a man of kirk, so a sal gie ye benefit of clergy," said the Highlander into his ear, "binna ye speik sae much as a word, an then it'll be atwein ye and St. Peter as ti whaur ye sal be expoondin yeir next sermon."

Rufus MacIan turned around. His ears were no longer red. With barely a glance towards de Gex he strode to the spiral stair and followed Jack down to the first storey.

IT WAS PACKED TO the ceiling with gunpowder. Not wanting to blow what remained of his clan to kingdom come, MacIan removed a pistol from his waistband, made sure it wasn't cocked, and laid it on a sill before turning his attention into the great room that accounted for most of the first floor.

"What were you thinking?" asked Jack.

Jack the Coiner was standing at the head of an aisle between stacked powder-kegs. He had not drawn his blade, but he had pulled it a few inches out of its scabbard to loosen it, and he was standing in a sideways attitude that, in a society where men routinely ran each other through with swords, was implicitly menacing.

MacIan kept his distance. "I dinna expect to live this lang," he said, "I hae nae thoughts concerning what we should dae after."

"Let me supply you with some thoughts, then," said Jack. "We are finished here."

"Finished!?"

"We have done all that we needed to do," said Jack, "excepting some trifles in the Mint which Father Édouard and I shall attend to after you and the others are . . . gone."

"Gone!? An how dae ye expect to hold the Tower of London agin a Regiment, with nae one to man the defenses?"

"It was never my intention to *hold* it," Jack returned. "So fly. Now. Escape to the heather. Savor your revenge. Unless . . ."

"Unless *what?*"

"Unless you prefer to go out as a hero of the United Kingdom, defending this house of your Stuart queen."

"Now that is insufferable," said Rufus MacIan. "That isna to be endured." Both hands came up in front as if he were going to clasp them in prayer. But they did not bate before his face, but kept rising and reaching back until they had found the handle of the Claymore projecting up above one shoulder. With one jerk it was out and in front of him. Suddenly Jack's weapon was likewise exposed, a handsome watered-steel blade, curved like a saber, and, in the Turkish way, slightly broader at the tip than at the guard. He held it in one hand. It would be an odd, ragged, improvised sort of duel: a medieval longsword against something that was not a cutlass and not a rapier.

"Very well," Jack said, "hero of Britain it is, then."

Jack had the lighter and swifter blade. It would be suicide for Mac-Ian to stand and await an attack, because it was unlikely he could move the Claymore fast enough to parry it. So he came on like a bull from a chute, feinting this way and that to make Jack commit himself, then winding up and swinging the weapon down at Jack's head with all his might. It was a blow that could not be fended off with any lighter weapon, and so Jack was obliged to spin back and away. Mac-Ian pursued him into an aisle between stacked powder-kegs. In these narrower confines he would have less room to swing his long blade. But Jack had done nothing to break the momentum of the great sword and so MacIan was able to swing it around and ring down another terrible blow at Jack's head. Jack barely had time to get his sword-hand up. If he had held his lighter weapon horizontally, trying to bar altogether the descent of the Claymore, it wouldn't have gone well for him. But he had the luck, or the presence of mind, to make the pommel the highest part of the weapon, and leave the point angled downwards toward the floor. The Claymore came down with little loss of speed, but it was deflected laterally, missing Jack and crashing into the stone floor, where it sent a shower of sparks against the base of a keg of gunpowder.

There was, in Rufus MacIan, a responsible and level-headed military officer. For the last few moments this person had been muscled out of the way by another that shared the same skull: the raving Celtic berserker. The sight of those sparks striking that keg caused the latter to vanish like a will o' the wisp and the former to be reinstated. There was a momentary pause as Rufus MacIan waited to see if they and the White Tower were to remain in existence. But the sparks winked out, and nothing happened.

"Lucky that," MacIan remarked, and cleared his throat, for suddenly his lungs were congested. He noticed that Jack was standing rather close—too close to be struck with the long Claymore. Indeed, he had his foot on the tip of MacIan's sword. Rufus MacIan coughed, and felt something hot and wet soaking his beard. Glancing down, he noticed the hilt of Jack's sword, all encrusted with heathenish designs, pressed up against his chest.

"Oh, it's because I am a lucky lucky fellow, my lord," said Jack—though MacIan was feeling oddly distracted, and the words did not really register. "In every respect, save the one that most matters."

"To the Pyx, then," Jack said, stepping back and snapping his sword horizontally through the air. Blood rushed down the blade, jetted from the tip, and struck a nearby wall with a sizzling noise, making a long dripping slash across the dry stones.

De Gex was frozen for a three-count. He rolled his eyeballs down in their sockets to verify that his dagger was now lying on the floor, i.e., no longer anywhere near his throat. The weight, and pressure, and the fragrance of the Scotsman were all gone. He bent down and snatched up the dagger, then spun around to face Jack—and nearly lost his footing on a spreading hot puddle. The Highlander who'd been holding him at bay was curled up on the floor, eyes half open, face gray.

"That was very risky," remarked de Gex.

"Oh, I'm sorry, we're going to begin accounting for *risk* now?" Jack returned, astonished. "Do you have any idea what just nearly—"

"That will do," said de Gex crisply, for he knew that once Jack had got into a mocking mood it was as difficult to cure as the hiccups.

They descended to the first floor of the round turret. Though the most ancient door of the White Tower was situated in the opposite corner, along the Inmost Ward, a more recent one was available at the base of the turret stair. It deposited them upon a strip of green on the north side, between the White Tower and a row of storehouses that lined the inner surface of the curtain wall. Here Jack broke his stride for a moment, because the storehouses were as regular as shocks of grain in a field-row, and offered no points of reference by which he could establish his bearings. But raising his sights above their saw-toothed roof-line he saw the slotted parapets of three bastions behind them. Here, the fire that still burned in the Tower hamlets north of the moat came in useful, as very little light was now left in the sky. But the red fire-glow shone crisply through the crenellations on those bastions. Being now a dungeon o' learning where the Tower was concerned, he knew that these three were, from left to right, Bowyer, Brick, and Jewel Towers.

Someone was hollering to him from high above. Jack couldn't make out a word. He spun on his heel, leaned back, cupped his hands round his face, and bellowed: "Run away!" to the Scotsmen on the roof of the White Tower. Then he continued striding north across the green with de Gex. He was looking for a portal that would take him through the line of storehouses and get him to the base of Brick Tower—that being the middle of the three bastions. Now that his eyes had adjusted to the twilight, he thought he could see it: a break in the half-timbered house-fronts, right in the center. It was a wide gate where wagon-loads of stuff could be trundled in or out. Standing in it were two men, one a giant and the other the size of a boy: Yevgeny and Tom the Black-guard.

"I have found the way through to the sally-port," Yevgeny announced.

"You have a Yeoman?"

Yevgeny pointed to a Beefeater who was standing inside the store-house with his arms pinioned behind his back.

"I'm glad you're finally here, mate," said Tom to Jack, "I been try-ing to explain to the Muscovite, here, this ain't the right way in!" He hooked a thumb back over his shoulder. "This here is Brick Tower! Jewel Tower's the next one down!" Tom stepped forward onto the green and pointed down the line to the bastion that stood in the northeast corner of the Inner Ward. A dozen or so men, who from their looks could have stepped off Blackbeard's flagship a quarter of an hour ago, were Loitering with Intent in that vicinity, and looking shrewdly at Jack.

"And of what significance is that?" Jack demanded.

An awkward silence.

Tom could be seen looking a bit pale.

De Gex sidled up and whispered something into Jack's ear.

"Oh, yes, of course, the *Jewel Tower*," Jack said. "That's where they keep the, what do you call them—"

"The Crown Jewels, sir," whispered Tom, now quite rattled.

"Yes, now I see where you are going—yes—of course! The Crown Jewels. Right." He considered it for a good long time. "Would you like to have a go at stealing the Crown Jewels, then, as long as we are here?"

"I thought that was the entire point of the Lay, sir," Tom an-swered, seeming very boylike indeed now.

"Oh, yes! To be sure!" Jack hastened to say, "by all means, yes, that's all I've ever wanted, really, to have some great bloody lump of gold with jewels stuck in it to put on my head. Diamonds, rubies—I'm mad for them really—go! Run along!"

"Don't you wish to—?"

"You've done splendidly to this point, Tom, and that lot in the cor-ner seem trustworthy. Go and see what you can find in Jewel Tower and I'll meet you back here—"

Yevgeny cleared his throat.

"Strike that, I'll meet you at, oh, Black Jack's Boozing-Ken at Hockley-in-the-Hole tomorrow evening, after the bear-baiting."

Jack had accompanied these improvised remarks with any amount of nods, gesticulations, nudgings, and shovings, all directed toward the a-mazed Tom and all meant to impel him toward the fabulous Jewel-trove in question. Finally Tom began to move that direction, but he walked backwards, keeping a sharp eye on Jack. "D'you really think Black Jack's Boozing-Ken is a good place to be cutting up the Sovereign's Orb?"

"Cut it up where you will, bring me some bits in a sack. Whatever you think is fair. Off you go, then!"

Tom—who was about halfway to the claque of piratish-looking blokes—scanned the roofs of the storehouses while Jack spoke these words, expecting that this was all a sort of test of Tom's loyalty, and that if he made the wrong move he'd get a crossbow-bolt through the heart. But there was nothing to be noted save a few furious Highlanders starting to boil from the door of the White Tower. Which anyway forced him to make up his mind. "Right!" he exclaimed, then turned, and sprinted for the Jewels. Jack did not even see this, for he'd already bolted, along with de Gex, into the portal where Yevgeny had been awaiting them. Yevgeny barred the heavy storehouse door behind them.

"Your name?" Jack said to the Yeoman Warder.

"Clooney! And whatever it is you want—"

"Why, Yeoman Clooney, you make it sound as if I am some sort of nefarious villain. All I want is for you to be my boon companion these next several minutes, and to survive the night in good health."

"I should not love to be your companion for any length of time."

"Then I shall remind you that I am, in truth, a nefarious villain. You may follow me on your own two feet, or I shall have the Rus put a leash around your neck and drag you up and down stairs on your beef-stuffed belly."

"I shall walk," announced Clooney, eyeing Yevgeny. By this time he had probably watched the Muscovite do any number of appalling things and was more afraid of him than of Jack.

A brief, dark, tortuous walk through the bowels of the Tower followed. After the third change of direction Jack became utterly lost. He guessed that they'd broken the plane of the curtain-wall and entered the bastion of Brick Tower.

Then a stone stair was before them, descending into a gloom that was beyond the power of their lanthorns. A man more superstitious than Jack might have recoiled, seeing it as a prefigurement of prison, death, and descent into the world below. But in the catalog of gloomy and hair-raising locations into which Jack had ventured during his lifetime, this scarcely rated notice. Down the stairs he traipsed, turning left at a landing, and then jogging left again at the foot of another flight. They must now be down in some oubliette of the Normans. But passing through a door, he found himself under the sky on, of all things, a street: Mint Street. Directly across that street was a house, a wreck of a thing, nearly black with soot. The door of this house stood open, and a single light burned within. Door and street were guarded by three men—men well known to Jack—each of whom carried the *ne plus ultra* of Mobb control weapons, a blunderbuss. And not without effect, for what crowd there was—a few grubby Mint workers—remained far away down the street, ready to duck for cover behind the elbow of Bowyer Tower if there was need.

There was no need. Jack checked his stride in the middle of the street, set his black satchel down as if to rest a weary hand, and turned around to see what was keeping the others. This movement caused his gold-lined cloak to swirl around him in a flourish that could not be missed by the cowed Mint-men. As it turned out, the black-robe was right on his heels. So Jack turned again, snatched up his satchel, and carried it into the house of the Warden of the Mint.

It was abandoned. Warden of the Mint was a profitable sinecure, usually granted to some man who knew little and cared less about coining but who had places in high friends. Such a man would not dream of living in this house, even though it was provided by the government for his use. He would as like live by a knacker's yard on the outskirts of Dublin than dwell on this smoky street in the midst of soldiers. And so most of the place went unused. But not all. Following the glimmer of lamp-light, Jack descended a stair to a vault-door, which hung open.

The vault itself was barely an arm-span in width, and the apex of the arched ceiling was scarcely high enough for Jack to stand upright. It was dank and dripping, for it was down close to the level of the moat. But it was soundly made. At the far end stood a table. On the table was a black chest with three hasps. Two of these were going unused at the moment, and opened padlocks dangled from their loops like freshly killed game from the butcher's hook. The third hasp was still closed by a padlock the size of a man's fist. Sitting before it on an overturned basket was a bulky man whose face was obscured by black hair hanging down. He was peering at the lock from a few inches away, gripping it in one great hand while the other manipulated its inner works with a steel toothpick. None of which was in the least remarkable to Jack, for he had expected all of these things, except for one.

"That's *it*?" he exclaimed.

"This is the Pyx," answered the man who was sitting on the basket. He spoke as if he had entered the serene trance of a Hindoostani mystic.

he had ever committed, and begun a ledger of sins committed since then. Did that ledger still exist somewhere? Was it still blank?

"And you, Daniel?" Isaac inquired.

"I made myself ready twenty-five years ago, when I was dying of the Stone," Daniel said, "and have oft wondered when Death would bother to come for me."

"Then neither of us has anything to fear," said Isaac. Which Daniel agreed with on a purely intellectual level; but still he flinched when a hefty mechanical *clunk* sounded from the chest, and its lid sprang open, driven by a pair of massive springs. Daniel missed what happened next because (as he was ashamed to realize) he had jumped behind Isaac. But now he stepped clear. He let the lanthorn drop to his side. It was no longer of any use. The chest was emitting its own light. Fountains of colored sparks gushed from several metal tubes that splayed from its rim, a bit like the iron pikes that adorned London Bridge's Great Stone Gate. Their light blinded him for a few moments. But when his eyes adjusted he saw a little carved and painted figure—a poppet—jutting from the top of the box, bobbling up and down atop a coil spring that had thrust it into the air. The poppet was adorned with a motley fool's cap with wee bells on the ends of its tentacles, and its face had been carven into a foolish grin. Illuminated from beneath by the fizzing sparklers, it wore a ghoulish and sinister aspect.

"Jack in the Box!" Daniel exclaimed.

Isaac approached the chest. The poppet had sprung up out of a mound of hundreds of coins. These had avalanched over the rim of the chest when the lid had sprung open, and were still tumbling to the deck in ones and twos. One of them rolled to within inches of Isaac's toe. He stooped and picked it up. Daniel, ever the lab-assistant, held the light near to hand. Isaac stared at it for a quarter of a minute. Daniel's lanthorn-arm began to ache, but he dared not move.

Finally it occurrred to Isaac to resume breathing. A tiny smacking noise came from his mouth as he re-animated his parts of speech.

"We must get back to the Tower of London straightaway."

"I am all for it," Daniel said, "but I'm afraid that the currents of the Thames and the Medway disagree with us."

BOOK 7

Currency

There was the usual amount of corruption, intimidation, and rioting.

—Sir Charles Petrie, describing a Parliamentary election of the era

Hanover

Do not pity me. I am at last going to satisfy my curiosity about the origin of things, which even Leibniz
could never explain to me, to understand space, infinity, being and nothingness . . .
—SOPHIE CHARLOTTE, QUEEN OF PRUSSIA,
ON HER DEATHBED AT AGE THIRTY-SIX

"ONCE UPON A TIME there was a penniless orphan girl named Wilhelmina Caroline, or Caroline for short. Father was a brilliant if odd
man, who died young of the smallpox, leaving Mother at the mercy
of his son by an earlier marriage. But this son had inherited neither
his father's wisdom nor his love for the beautiful mother of Caroline;
and, conceiving of her as a wicked stepmother, and of the infant as a
future rival, he cast them out. Mother took little Caroline up in her
arms and fled to a house deep in the woods. The two lived almost as
Vagabonds for some years, making occasional sojourns in the houses
of more fortunate relations. But when the compassion of her family
was spent, Mother was left with no choice but to marry the first suitor
who came along: a brute who had been hit on the head when he was
a child. This fellow cared little for Caroline's mother and less for
Caroline. He relegated them to a miserable life on the fringe of his
household while he openly made love to his vile, ignorant, and
wicked mistress.

"In time both stepfather and mistress died of smallpox. Not long
after, Caroline's mother also perished, leaving the little girl alone,
penniless, and destitute.

"Only one heirloom passed to Caroline upon her mother's death,
for it was the only thing that could not be separated from her by
pestilence or theft: the title of Princess. Without this inheritance, she
would soon have ended up in a poorhouse, a nunnery, or worse; but
because, like her mother before her, she was a Princess, two wise men

came and bore her away in a carriage to a palace in a distant city, where a clever and beautiful young Queen named Sophie Charlotte took her under her wing, and gave her all she needed.

"Of all that was offered to Princess Caroline in the years that followed, two mattered above all others: first Love. For Sophie Charlotte was both an elder sister and a foster mother to her. And second Knowledge. For in the palace was a great library, to which Caroline was given a key by one of the wise men: a Doctor who was the Queen's mentor and advisor. She spent every minute that she could in that library, doing what she loved most, which was reading books.

"Years later, after she had grown to a woman and begun to have children of her own, Caroline was to ask the Doctor how he had been so clever as to know that she would want a key to the library. The Doctor explained: 'As a little boy, I lost my own father, who, like your royal highness's, was a well-read man; but later I came to know him, and to feel his presence in my life, by reading the books he left behind.'"

Henrietta Braithwaite trailed off hereabouts, and shaped her brow into a tasteful and courtly little frown. Her finger plowed a crooked trail back up the terrain of the last paragraph, like a pig's snout rooting for a truffle. "Rather fine to this point, your royal highness, but the story becomes confused when this Doctor enters into it, and you begin to jump back and forth between tenses, and tell things in his voice—pray, how does a Doctor enter into a færy-tale anyhow? Up to *here*, it's all palaces, stepmothers, and houses in the woods, which fit. But a Doctor—?"

"Es ist ja ein Märchen—"

"In English if you please, your royal highness."

"It is indeed a færy-tale, but it is also *my* story," said Princess Wilhelmina Caroline of Brandenburg-Ansbach, "and *my* story has a Doctor in it."

She glanced out a window. Today's English lesson was in a salon of the Leine Schloß, on the side that faced away from the river. The view was across a small paved courtyard that spilled onto a busy Hanover street. Leibniz's house was only two or three doors down—near enough that she could shout a philosophical inquiry out the window and half expect to get an answer back.

"The next chapter will treat of persons, and happenings, not found in færy-tales," Caroline continued, after a pause to get the English words queued up in the right order. "For what I have written on the leaves you hold in your hands only goes up to when Sophie Charlotte died—or, as some say, was poisoned by the Prussian court."

Mrs. Braithwaite now turned in a workmanlike effort to conceal her horror and loathing of the fact that Princess Caroline had given voice to this thought. It was not that this Englishwoman had any particular love for the courtiers who infested the Charlottenburg. Mrs. Braithwaite, wife of an English Whig, would have taken Sophie Charlotte's side in just about any imaginable debate—supposing she had the kidney to choose sides. What troubled her was Caroline's forthrightness. But the ability to say things directly, and get away with it, was a birthright that came along with the title of Princess.

"It has indeed been an eventful nine years since that dolorous day," Mrs. Braithwaite allowed, "but it would still read much like a færy-tale to the common reader, if you but changed a few words. The Doctor could become a wizard, the aged Electress a wise Queen—no one in England would object to *that* change!"

"Except for all those Jacobites who want Sophie dead," Caroline returned.

This was a bit like sticking her leg out in front of Mrs. Braithwaite when she was trying to tiptoe, skirts hiked up, down a turd-strewn alley. The Englishwoman faltered and pinkened but did not come to a full stop. As everyone in Hanover, including Caroline's husband, had noted, she was the very soul of poise and grace. "The other characters and events of your last nine years—the handsome and brave young Prince, the long war against an evil King, a lost kingdom across the sea, rightfully yours, which sends emissaries—"

"Emissaries," Caroline said, "but *other* busy persons too, not fit for færy-tales at all."

Mrs. Henrietta Braithwaite, Caroline's *dame du palais* and English tutor, was also the official mistress of Caroline's husband. Caroline did not really object to her "brave young Prince" having sex all the time with the wife of an Englishman—and a rather dodgy Englishman at that. On the contrary. Sex with the Electoral Prince George Augustus had been mildly pleasant more often than it had been downright painful. But most of the time, like trimming one's fingernails, it had been a body-chore that no longer seemed gross after it had been done a few hundred times. Four children—one Prince, three Princesses—had ensued so far, and there would probably be more, provided George Augustus did not spill *all* of his seed into Henrietta Braithwaite. The arrival of this Englishwoman at the Court of Hanover two years ago, and her speedy promotion to *maîtresse en titre* of Young Hanover Brave (as Caroline's husband was styled by Whiggish Brits), had relieved Caroline of one of the less fascinating tasks that she had to put up with as a wife and a Princess, and given her more time to sleep at night and to read during the day. So there was not anything like rancor between her and Henrietta.

But relations between one who was a Princess and one who was not were governed, not by what the Princess was really feeling and thinking, but rather by certain forms that were supposed to ensure the steady functioning of the Court, and, by extension, the sæcular world. By those lights, Caroline—who was married in the sight of God to George Augustus, and who had been endowed by her mother with the incredible and priceless faculty of generating new Princes and Princesses—stood in the same wise, to the likes of Henrietta Braithwaite, as Hera to some dung-flecked shepherdess who had lately been rolling in the clover with Zeus. Caroline was expected to remind Mrs. Braithwaite of her inferiority from time to time, and Mrs. Braithwaite was expected to receive it meekly and submissively. As how could she not, for the grandchildren of Caroline would reign over the British Empire while the Braithwaites would spend their lives losing at cards and killing themselves with gin in mildewy London salons.

"It is with the greatest pleasure that I shall read the next chapter of your royal highness's færy-tale," Mrs. Braithwaite predicted. "In this Household it is an oft-told tale that when your royal highness was stricken with the smallpox, two years after your wedding, his royal highness George Augustus spurned the counsel of the physicians, and placed his own life at risk to sit by his young bride's bedside and hold her hand."

"It is true. George did not leave my bedside until I was well."

"To me—as to every other woman who can never hope to be the object of such pure adoration—that is a færy-tale we would fain read over and over, until the pages crumbled," said Mrs. Braithwaite.

"I may write it then," answered Princess Caroline, "or I may keep it to myself, as a thing rightfully mine, and not to be shared with any who does not merit it."

Some two years earlier, at a courtly *soirée* that had brought many noble persons together, Princess Caroline had overheard another Princess saying something rude about Sophie. The words that had passed between them were long since forgotten. What was remembered was that Caroline had thrown a punch at the other Princess. It happened to land on the jaw. The other Princess was carried out of the room, feigning unconsciousness.

It was not really in Caroline's nature to do some of the cruel things that a Princess was required to do. But as her færy-tale had mentioned, she well knew that being a Princess was the only thing that had kept her from ending up as a child whore in a Saxon mining-camp. So to pretend otherwise—to play with the ancient laws of Princesshood—was idle.

Suddenly weights were falling and springs unwinding in the belfry of the big old church across the square from Leibniz's house. A large piece of metal was mercilessly pounding on a bell, which stood still for it, quivering and moaning. Here in the Leine Schloß it was time for Caroline to leave off of the ritual drubbing of Mrs. Braithwaite, and to go out on her daily excursion to Herrenhausen. A skirmish of curtseys got the Englishwoman out of the Presence without violating any etiquette-laws.

Minutes later—having nipped into several nurseries and school-rooms along the way to kiss her little Prince and Princesses good-bye—Caroline was in the courtyard of the Leine Schloß telling the stable-hands that they had got it all wrong. Herr Schwartz, the retainer who was in charge of the stables, had reached an age when he phant'sied he could foretell the weather by the pains in his joints. To-day, his hip and his elbow were united in prophesying rain. Accordingly, he had given orders for the coach-and-four to be made ready. But Caroline's senses assured her that it was a perfect sunny day, and too sultry to be pent up in a wooden box. So she chided Herr Schwartz, in a playful way, and ordered that her favorite mare be saddled. The mount was led out, ready to go, before she had finished uttering the command—Herr Schwartz knew her well enough. She hitched up her skirts, ascended a little Barock stair, and perched on the saddle. A few moments later she was riding out onto the street without so much as a look back. She knew that a small escort would be not far behind; or if it weren't, the persons responsible for deploying her escort would be sent down in disgrace and replaced with others.

Anyway, the Leine Schloß was not the sort of thing any cultivated person would take the trouble to look back at. The hundred or so paces that separated it from Leibniz's house vaulted an architectural chasm. Leibniz's house was much bigger than a bachelor really needed, because he cohabited with a library. It was one of those Hapsburg wedding-cakes, thickly frosted in high-relief friezes of queer and heinous goings-on from the Bible. Next to it, the Leine Schloß need never worry about accusations of gaudiness. In a continent that was now freckled with more or less embarrassing knock-offs of Versailles, the Leine Schloß was Proud to be Dowdy. It was trapped between the sluggish Leine on one side and an ordinary Hanover street on the other, and so it would never have gardens or even a decent forecourt. To be sure, embedded in the heart of the Schloß was a single, stupefyingly gaudy room called the Rittersaal, built by Sophie's husband thirty years ago after Leibniz had come back from Italy bearing evidence that he was at least as Royal as his Sophie. But no common person riding along the street or floating down the river past the Schloß would dream that anything colorful, ornate, decorative, or lively was contained in those walls. It was a mashing-together of several blocky, four-storey wings ventilated by many rectangular windows, all of a common size, and arrayed in rows and columns. The first thing Princess Caroline saw every day, when she opened her eyes, parted her bed-curtains, and glanced toward her window to check the weather, was two intersecting stone walls of window-grid, marching off in an infinite logarithmic progression.

Merely seeing it would put Leibniz into a funk. What was only boring to Caroline was troubling to him, because he felt partly responsible. The Doctor had grown up in the aftermath of the Thirty Years' War when many towns did not have buildings at all—only ruins and shanties! The structures that survived were round-shouldered half-timbered things, as same and yet as various as a basket of apples. But the buildings of today were informed by geometry; which meant that each one betrayed the particular Idea of geometry that its architect had drilled on in school. A hundred years ago this might have meant parabolas, ellipses, surfaces of revolution, involutes and evolutes, and parallel curves. Now it meant Cartesian rectilinear coordinates—the cruel gridiron to which all of those soaring arcs had been lashed fast by the toiling algebraists. A plaything for hares had fallen among the tortoises. The non-helpless minority of Christendom—those who could read, who could travel, who were not starving—had (Leibniz brooded) got only the most superficial notion of what had been happening in Natural Philosophy and, rather than going to the trouble of actually understanding it, had fastened on to the Cartesian grid as a relic or fetish of enlightenment. A result was grid-buildings. Leibniz could not bear to look at them because more than anyone else he was responsible for Cartesian coordinates. He who had launched his career with an epiphany in a rose-garden! So he and Caroline tended to meet, not in the waffle iron of the Leine Schloß but out beyond the ramparts along the gently curving banks of the Leine, or at Sophie's garden.

Leibniz was out of town. Caroline did not know why. Court-rumors from the East had it that the Tsar's new fleet was massing in St. Petersburg, making ready to sally into the Baltic and ream it clear of troublous Scandinavians. Caroline and most of the other people who mattered in Hanover knew that Leibniz had something going on the side with Peter Romanov. Perhaps this accounted for the savant's absence. Or perhaps he'd merely nipped down to Wolfenbüttel to sort his books, or journeyed to Berlin to settle some tussle at his Academy.

Hanover was a city, and a city was, above all else, an organism for repelling armed assaults. The Leine, which flanked Hanover on the south and east, had always had some part to play in keeping the place from being sacked and burned. This explained why the Schloß rose straight from the river's bank. But the precise nature of the Leine's military duties had changed from century to century as artillery had gotten better, and gunners had learnt math.

Just past Leibniz's house, Princess Caroline turned left towards the river, and so began a sort of voyage through time. This began on a quaint, curving Hanover street, which looked essentially medieval, and concluded, a quarter of an hour later, on the outskirts of the city's fortification complex: a sculpture in rammed and carved earth as *à la mode*, and as carefully tended, as any lady's hairstyle in the Grand Salon of Versailles. The Leine threaded its way through this in whatever way was most advantageous to the engineers. In some places it had been compressed into a chute, like meat funneled into a wurst-casing, and in others it was given leave to spread out and inundate ground that was considered vulnerable.

Fort-makers and fort-breakers alike were playing a sort of chess-game with geometry. Light, which conveyed intelligence, moved in straight lines, and musket-balls, which killed over short distances, nearly did. Cannonballs, which broke down forts, moved in flattish parabolas, and mortars, which destroyed cities, in high ones. Fortifications were now made of dirt, which was cheap, abundant, and stopped projectiles. The dirt was mounded up and shaved into prisms—volumes bounded by intersecting planes. Each plane was an intention to control its edges. Lines of sight and flights of musket-balls were supposed to skim along these, seeing and killing whatever presented itself at the creases. It was hoped that cannonballs would come in perpendicularly and dig their own graves, as opposed to glancing off and bounding to and fro like murderous three-year-olds. Cavalry-stables, infantry-barracks, powder-houses, and gangways were etched into the dirt-piles in the places where cannonballs were least likely to reach. The human parts were utterly subordinated to the demands of geometry. It was a desert of ramps and planes.

All of which was actually somewhat interesting to a Princess who had learnt geometry sitting on the knee of Baron Gottfried Wilhelm von Leibniz. But artillery got better very gradually, and gunners now knew all the math they would ever know, and so none of this had changed much during the decade or so that Caroline had been passing through it almost every day. Riding among the fortifications was a time to brood or to day-dream. Her senses did not engage the world until she was crossing over the second of two causeways, strung across an inundated waste, put there to keep Louis XIV's guns at a decent remove. The extremity of the fortifications was a timber gatehouse at the place where the planking of the causeway turned into gravel.

From here Caroline could look down a straight riding-path to Sophie's orangerie, at the corner of the gardens of Herrenhausen, a mile and a half away. The Allee was striped with four parallel queues of lime trees washed with pale jackets of green moss. These lines of trees staked out three ways that ran side-by-side to the royal house. The road in the center was broad, suitable for carriages, and open to the sky. The entire length of it was visible; there were no secrets here. But it was flanked on either hand by narrower paths, just right for two friends to stroll arm-in-arm. The branches of the trees met above these paths to cover each with a canopy. Gazing down the length of the Allee, Caroline saw the entire mile and a half foreshortened into a single compact view, interrupted here and there by a little straggling line of courtiers or gardeners cutting across.

Sophie was as much an imperialist with her gardens as Louis XIV was with his fortresses. If nothing were done to stop them, her hedges and floral borders would someday collide with his *barrière de fer* somewhere around Osnabrück and conclude a stalemate.

Caroline's first stroll in the gardens of Herrenhausen had been ten years ago, when Sophie Charlotte had brought the orphan princess out from Berlin to be flirted with by George Augustus. Young Caroline had known Electress Sophie for a few years, but had never before been granted the honor of being Summoned to Go for a Walk.

Leibniz had walked with them on that occasion, for he and Sophie Charlotte shared a kind of Platonic infatuation with each other. As for Sophie, she did not mind having the Doctor tag along, as it was often useful to have an ambulatory library in which to look up obscure facts.

The plan had been of admirable simplicity and, as one would have thought, fool-proof. The garden, which measured five hundred by a thousand yards, was edged by a rectangular riding-path, which in turn was framed in a waterway. Sophie, Sophie Charlotte, and Caroline were to set out from Herrenhausen Palace, which rose up above the northern end, and execute a brisk lap around the path. Leibniz would do his best to keep up with them. The exercise would bring color to Caroline's cheeks, which normally looked as if they had been sculpted out of library paste. Just before they completed the circuit, they would dodge in to the maze, where they would bump into young George Augustus. He and Caroline would "wander off" and "get lost" in the maze together—though of course Sophie and Sophie Charlotte would never be more than two yards from them, hovering like wasps on the other side of a thin screen of hedge, jabbing away whenever they perceived an opening. At any rate, through some winsome union of George's level-headedness and Caroline's cleverness, they would escape from the maze together and part company on blushing terms.

The Electress, the Queen, the Princess, and the Savant had set out from the palace of Herrenhausen precisely on schedule, and Sophie had put the plan into execution with all the bloody-minded forcefulness of the Duke of Marlborough staving in the French lines at Tirlemont. Or so it had seemed until they got some two-thirds of the way round the garden, and entered into a stretch of the riding-path that was overhung with branches of large trees, seeming wild and isolated. There, they were ambushed by a sort of raiding-party led by Sophie's son and heir, George Louis.

It happened near the wreck of the gondola.

As a fond memento of his young whoring days in Venice, Sophie's late husband, Ernst August, had imported a gondola, and a gondolier to shove it round the perimeter of the garden, along the waterway that Sophie called a canal and that George Louis insisted on calling a moat. Maintaining a gondola in North German weather had proved difficult, maintaining gondoliers even more so.

At the time of this, Caroline's first garden-walk, Ernst August had been dead for seven years. Sophie, who did not share her late husband's infatuation with the fleshy pleasures of Venice, and who felt no affinity with his phant'sied Guelph relations, had suffered the gondola to run hard aground on a mud-bank. There, ice-storms and earwigs had had their way with it. By chance, or perhaps by some ponderous scheming of George Louis, the mother and her entourage encountered the son and his at a place on the riding-path very near the wrack of the gondola, which rested askew, occasionally shedding a dandruff of gold leaf into the canal, almost as if it had been planted there as a *memento mori* to make young princes reflect on the fleeting and fickle nature of their youthful passions. If so, George Louis had misread it. "Hullo, Mummy, and to you, Sissy," he had said to the Electress of Hanover and the Queen of Prussia respectively. And then after a few pleasantries, "Is it not sad to come upon the dingy old ruin of Papa's gondola here among all of these flowers?"

"Flowers are beauty that lives and dies," Sophie had answered. "Does this mean that when the petals begin to fall, I should order my garden plowed under?"

There followed a complicated silence.

If this had been Versailles, and if George Louis had been the sort who cared, Sophie's remark would have fallen into the category of "warning shot fired into the shoulder": nonfatal, but enough to render the victim *hors de combat*. But in fact this was George Louis's back yard, and he was not one who cared—supposing he even noticed. Sophie's remark had taken the form of a similitude between wilted blossoms and the decaying gondola. George Louis had difficulty with such constructions, as some men could not see the color green. And further he had, for better or worse, the *vis inertiae* of an ammunition cart. It took more than warning shots to stop him, on those exceptional occasions when he got moving. Sophie, of all persons in the world, knew this. Why, then, did she bother? For by making the analogy to flowers she was in effect speaking in a secret language that her son could not decypher. Perhaps the Electress was thinking out loud; or perhaps the message was intended for others.

Years later Caroline was to understand that it had been intended for *her*. Sophie was trying to teach the little Princess how to be a Queen, or at least, how to be a Mother.

One of George Louis's companions had worked at least some of this out, and now stepped forward. His motives could only be guessed at. Perhaps he wanted to receive Sophie's next shot in the breastbone, to show his loyalty. Perhaps he hoped to deflect George Louis. Perhaps he wanted to be noticed by Caroline, who was not, as yet, betrothed. At any rate, he made a courtly bow, letting everyone get a load of his plumage. "If it please your royal highness," he said in strangely distorted French, "a gardener might be instructed to pinch off the dead blossoms, to give the garden a more pleasing aspect."

This was Harold Braithwaite, who had begun coming over from England round about then to escape prosecution in London and to curry favor in Hanover. He had done something reckless, and got lucky, at the Battle of Blenheim. Now he was an earl or something.

"My English is not good enough for me to understand your French," Sophie had returned, "but I collect that you were setting in front of me some advice as to how I should manage my garden. Please know that I love my garden as it is: not only the living but also the dying parts of it. It is not meant to be some phantasm of eternal and perfect life. Such a garden did exist once, or so the Bible instructs us; but it was brought to an ill end by a *snake* who fell out of a *tree*." This with a very dubious head-to-toe look at Braithwaite, who turned magenta and backed off.

George Louis had been a bit unnerved, not by the content of Sophie's remarks (which seemed to have quite flown past him) but by their tone, which was that of a Queen at war rejecting a proffered treaty. Another man would have sensed danger, recoiled, and made amends. But inertia was all for George Louis. "I don't care about flowers," he said. "But if we cleared the gondola out of the moat, there would be room for galleys at Carnival."

It was an old family tradition to stage a Venetian-style Carnival in the spring.

"Galleys," Sophie had repeated in a distant tone, "aren't those the Ships of Force that are paddled around the Mediterranean by stinking, wretched slaves?"

"Such are too large to fit in our little moat, Mummy," George Louis had returned helpfully, "I had in mind little ones."

"Little ones? Does that mean, only a few oar-slaves?"

"No, no, Mummy. Just as Louis XIV at Versailles stages floating processions and mock sea-battles upon the Canal, for the entertainment of all the persons of consequence who dwell there, so might we enliven our next Carnival with—"

"If the next is any more lively than the last, it is likely to kill me!"

"Lively, yes, Mummy, our Carnivals have always been so. And fittingly for a sort of—"

"A sort of what?"

"Queer, peculiar family tradition. Delightful to *us*. Perhaps a bit impenetrable to outsiders." A tiny glance towards Braithwaite.

"Perhaps I do not *wish* to be penetrated by outsiders."

The War of the Spanish Succession was at its zenith. Marlborough, at the head of mighty Protestant legions, was storming round Europe at will. The Whig Juncto in England was trying to get Sophie to move to London to be a sort of Queen-in-waiting until Anne sputtered out. And so perhaps George Louis could be forgiven for seeming a bit preoccupied with his place in the world. If so, no forgiveness seemed to be coming from Sophie's direction. George Louis kept at it nonetheless, a breakaway ammo cart plunging down a bank. "This house, these gardens, are soon to become, to Britain, what Versailles is to France. Our home, Mummy, is to be a place of great consequence. What was a place for the *femmes* to dally in the garden, is to become a site of important conversations."

"Oh, but it already *is*, my little prince," Sophie had returned, "or I should say it *was*, until *ours* was interrupted, and replaced by *this* one."

This had seemed merely funny to Caroline, as in truth they had been discoursing of the tendency of a cousin of theirs to gain weight when her husband was away at the front. But she did not smile for long. It had become apparent to all that Sophie was very angry, and so her words lanced out into a febrile silence. "The blood of the house of Plantagenet flows in these veins," she said, exposing a milky wrist, "and in yours. The little Princes in the Tower died, the Houses of York and of Lancaster were united, and six perfectly delightful ladies sacrificed themselves on the bed of our ancestor, Henry VIII, to make it possible for us to exist. The Church of Rome was cast out of Britain because it was an impediment to the propagation of our line. For us, the Winter Queen roved across Christendom as a Vagabond through the Thirty Years' War. All so that I could be born, and so that you could. Now my daughter rules Prussia and Branden-burg. Britain shall be yours. How did it all come about? Why do *my* children rule over the richest swath of Christendom, not his?" She pointed to a gardener shoving a wheelbarrow of manure, who rolled his eyes and shook his head.

"B-because of that divine ichor that runs in your veins, Mummy?" answered the Prince, with a nervous glance at the wrist.

"A shrewd guess, but wrong. Contrary to what your sycophants may have been telling you, there is nothing ichor-like and certainly nothing divine about the contents of our veins. Our line does not en-dure because of eldritch contaminants in our blood, or anything else hereditary. It endures because I go for walks in my garden every day and talk to your sister and your future daughter-in-law, just as my mother, the Winter Queen, did with me. It endures because even in the fifteenth year of war I exchange letters almost every day with my niece Liselotte at Versailles. You may—if it pleases you—flatter your vanity by phant'sying that riding across the countryside in hot pursuit of vermin is a kingly pastime, and makes you fit to one day rule a do-minion that stretches to Shahjahanabad and to Boston. I shall allow you that much folly. But never shall I suffer you to trespass upon what keeps our line alive down through plagues, wars, and revolutions. I say that you are guilty of such a trespass now. Get out of my garden. Never again interrupt us at our work."

This, which would have reduced any other man in Europe, except Louis XIV, to a lump of smouldering coal, only elicited a blink from George Louis. "Good day, Mummy, good day, Sissy," he announced, and trotted away, followed by Braithwaite and the other courtiers, who rode stiff and red-necked, pretending they had not heard it. Caroline and Sophie Charlotte exchanged warm looks behind So-phie's back, trying not to get the giggles.

Leibniz had dropped onto a bench like a sack of turnips kicked off a cart, and put his head in his hands. He pulled the wig back to expose his bald skull, glistering with sweat, so that the breeze could stream over it. This had only made Caroline more disposed to giggle, as it seemed that her teacher was being comically faint of heart.

Later she had come to understand matters more clearly. Sophie would die one day, and George Louis would be Elector of Hanover, King of England, and Leibniz's boss. On that day Sophie Charlotte would still be the Queen of Prussia, and Caroline might be the Princess of Wales; but Leibniz would be the strange, incomprehensible man who had too much influence with those ladies who had ruled and humilated George Louis all his life.

Leibniz's anxiety on that score had increased tenfold a short time later when Sophie Charlotte had suddenly taken sick and died. If he'd been spending a lot of time talking to Russians since then, it might be so that he would have at least one safe harbor in which to live out a future exile.

But Caroline had no intention of allowing that to happen.

THE HERRENHÄUSER ALLEE was bedded in a swath of pleasant countryside that had been allowed to grow a bit wild. No one would devote time or money to keeping it up, partly because it was in the flood-plain of the Leine, and partly because it was in obvious jeopardy of being gobbled by any future expansions of Sophie's garden. So by default it had become a sort of park, shaped liked a folded fan, narrow near the city but broadening toward the Palace of Herrenhausen. The result—intended or not—was that at the outset of the journey Caroline felt pent between a high road on one side, and the Leine on the other. These were equally laden with traffic, fæces, and flies. But as she rode up the Allee, the road and the river insensibly spread away from her. By the time she got to the place where she could see archipelagos of green fruit hanging in the windows of Sophie's orangerie, she was riding up the center of a cone of silence, smelling nothing but the freshness of growing things.

A foreign princess paying a call would here swing round the fronts of the Orangerie and other outlying pavilions and enter into a street lined, for some distance, with the summer palaces of diverse noble families. Herrenhausen Palace had started as one of these, and grown. It looked across the road to an older and smaller garden that cushioned the family sepulchre. The visitor would allow some hours to be announced, greeted, introduced, and otherwise processed by the Court before being let into the Presence. Caroline instead nipped in through a side-gate and approached the Palace from the garden side. Her mare knew where to take her, and where to stop, and which of the stable-hands was most likely to have a green apple in his pocket. Caroline was afoot in the northeast corner of Sophie's garden without suffering her train of thought to be interrupted by anyone. Not for a Princess were idle pleasantries. Caroline could not say hello to some random Countess in a Herrenhausen salon without giving the encounter as much forethought, and as keen attention, as George Augustus would devote to mounting a cavalry charge. If she were to say it in the wrong tone of voice, or give the Countess more or less attention than she deserved, the news would be all over Hanover by sundown, and a fortnight later she could expect a letter from Liselotte in Versailles inquiring whether it was true she was having an affair with Count so-and-so, and another from Eliza in London wanting to know if she had quite recovered from her miscarriage. Better to slip into the place *incognito.*

This end of the garden, closest to the Palace, was divided into a grid of squarish parterres, perhaps tennis-court-sized. What drew the eye here was not the plantings but the statuary: the inevitable Hercules, Atlas, &c. The Gods and Heroes of Rome rose out of a sort of fanatically maintained tundra: boxwood cut down into micro-hedges no more than a hand's span high and wide, and flowered figures crowded with bees maintaining a continual low hum of golden commerce. It was a fine place for high-strung nobles—to use Sophie's phrase, the sort who took every fart for a thunderclap—to promenade about for a few moments before darting back into the Palace to regale the court with tales of their wilderness adventure. Really it was nothing more than a roofless annex of the Palace. Herrenhausen rose above these parterres in a moderately impressive way, while its wings, only a single storey high, reached out to embrace them. The central structure of the Palace couldn't have housed Louis XIV's gardening implements. A mere dozen windows were distributed among its three floors. But Sophie liked it that way. Versailles was a penitentiary for every person of consequence in France, and needed to be large. Herrenhausen was a place for getting things done, and needed to be small and tidy.

Caroline knew that she had likely been sighted from certain of those windows, and so she turned her back on the Palace and began to march away, following a gravel division between parterres. Shortly she arrived at a high hedge trimmed into a slab-wall, and penetrated it through a square opening. If the garden was a palace built of living things, then the parterres were its formal parlour, whence passageways led off to more private and peculiar spaces beyond. To one side was an outdoor theatre, walled by hedges and guarded by marble cherubs. To the other was the Maze where she had begun her courtship with George Augustus. Caroline, however, went out the back. A row of small reflecting ponds formed a quiet buffer between the front and the back half of the garden. Each was surrounded by a garden plot a little less austere than the parterres. Passing between two of these, she twirled round for a glance back at the Palace. On the parterres she had been exposed to view from any window. Now she was about to lose herself in the garden, and wanted to be certain, first, that she had been noticed. Indeed, a contingent of stable-hands had rushed together with a squadron of porters and footmen at the very head of the garden, where a pair of stairways curved down from the main floor of the Palace to the level of the ground. They were setting the stage for the ritual masque that was played every time Sophie emerged from her dwelling. Caroline only watched it until she noticed herself smiling.

She turned round again and plunged through a higher and darker barrier: a row of trees trimmed to form a wall as high as a house. In the back half of the garden, plenty of mature trees and dense hedges made it possible for her to phant'sy that she was a day's ride from the nearest building. This part was loved not only by her and Sophie but even by George Louis, who at fifty-four still went riding along the surrounding path, imagining that he was out patrolling the wild marches of some frontier duchy. Here one's lines of sight, and vectors of movement, were funneled into narrow clefts between stands of trees. Sounds carried oddly, or not at all. It seemed ten times the size of the front half.

A teeming buller had started up back in the woods. At first it might have been mistaken for a gust of wind becoming snared in the branches of the trees. But it grew relentlessly, and began to take on spattering and searing overtones. Somewhere far outside the boundaries of the garden, a man was hauling on a great wheel, flooding buried pipes that conducted Leine-water here. Caroline picked up her skirts and rushed to a nearby intersection of diagonal ways where she turned inwards toward the great round pool that stood in the center of the garden's darker and wilder half. It had already been brought to a rolling boil. A vertical jet had emerged from a stone orifice in the center and shaped itself into a blunt probe, fighting its way upwards like a sailmaker's needle pushing through a stack of heavy canvas. As it grew, it began to cast off a mantle of writhing vapor. From here, this looked almost like smoke generated by its rubbing against the air. The jet grew higher and higher until it seemed finally to reflect off the white sky (for the day had become overcast). There it shattered into an incoherent cloud of white spray. The whole garden now was suffused with the roar of the artificial tempest, perfecting the illusion that it was some wild and remote place. The clouds of mist hurled forth by this fountain spread outwards from the pool and infiltrated the corridors among the trees, blurring details of what was near and erasing what was more than a bow-shot away, so soon did things in this gleaming cloud lose their distinctness and fade into the darkness of the trees.

The land about the garden was flat, and provided no heights from which to spy down into it. There was a church-steeple nearby, with a black pyramidal roof that loomed like a hooded Inquisitor glowering down on the pagan spectacle below. Supposing anyone was watching from that belfry, by walking round the pool Caroline could vanish behind the upside-down cataract of the great fountain. By the same trick the gloomy spire was eliminated from her prospects and she was left perfectly alone.

The breeze was out of the south. It stretched the fountain-mist out into shimmering, rippling curtains that raced across the pool and rushed up the broad path that led directly to Sophie's house. The Palace was visible indistinctly, as if seen in a befogged mirror. Caroline thought she could resolve a white frock on one of the stairways, and a white head of hair above it, and a white arm waving off the carriage that had been trotted out, and shooing away the offered sedan chair.

Sophie always told Caroline to stand in the mist because it was good for her complexion. Caroline had managed to get married and have four children notwithstanding all grievances that might be leveled at her skin. But she always tried to stand in the mist anyway because she knew it would please Sophie. It was cold on her cheeks, and smelled fishy. The sheets and vortices of mist looked like pages of ghostly books tumbling towards her. Over the pool they were so white and substantial she could almost read them. But once they hurtled past her they quickly paled and vanished, diluted by vacant air.

A man was standing near her at the rim of the pool. He was already too close. A stranger should never have been in the garden anyway! But she did not cry out, for he was very old. He was not looking at Caroline, but at the fountain. He was habited something like a gentleman, but no wig covered his bald pate and no sword dangled at his side. He was encompassed in a long traveling-cloak. This was no mere affectation of style, for the garment was rumpled and spattered, and the man's boots had not been touched by a servant in weeks.

When he sensed that Caroline was looking his way, he reached into a cloak-pocket, drew out a gravid purse of crimson leather, and worried it open with parsimonious movements of his worn-out fingers. Out of it he plucked a large golden coin. This he flipped into the air above the pool. It shone, a yellow mote, for an instant before the silver torrent smashed it down into the pool.

"A penny for your royal highness's thoughts," the man said, in English.

"To me it looked like a guinea," she returned. She was annoyed beyond words that this interloper was here; but she was well-brought-up, and would no sooner let her annoyance be known than George Augustus would fall off his horse while inspecting the royal guard.

The old man shrugged, then pulled the purse all the way open and turned it inside out with a thrust of his thumbs, disbursing a shower of golden guineas into the pool.

"A village could live on that for a year," Caroline observed. "When you have excused yourself I shall have those coins taken up and put in the poor-box."

"Then do you be prepared for your Lutheran vicar to send them back to you with a curt note," the old man returned.

"To what effect?"

"He might write, 'Your Royal Highness should save these artifacts and give them to paupers in England, where they have some worth, because the Sovereign says they do.'"

"This is a very odd conversation—" Caroline began.

"Forgive me. I come from people who are no respecters of royals. Our byword is the equality of all men before God. And so when a Princess inflicts upon me an odd, unlooked-for conversation, I cannot rest until I have sought her out and repaid her."

"When and where did I do you this injury?"

"Injury? Nay, 'twas a sort of curious favor. When? Last October, though you must have set it in motion long before. Where? Boston."

"You are Daniel Waterhouse!"

"Your humble and obedient servant. Oh, how it would goad my father to hear his son saying that to a Princess."

"You deserve honors, Doctor, and all the comforts I can afford you. Why are you come to me in the style of a Vagabond? And why do you open with these queer remarks about guineas?"

Daniel Waterhouse was shaking his head. "Queen Anne has writ another of her letters to Sophie . . ."

"Oh, dear."

"Or rather Bolingbroke has, and set it before the poor woman to paw her signature at the end. The letter has been sped hence by a delegation of Englishmen: a few Tories, to inflict the humiliation, and some Whigs, to suffer it. The former are grand and consequential—many who would be in Bolingbroke's graces vied for few positions. But for the whipping-boy slots, there was very little enthusiasm shown, among Whigs. Rather, a few dried-up third-raters had to be herded aboard the ship at Tower Wharf, like so many Blackamoors on the Guinea coast. I construed this as an opportunity to come and repay my debt to your royal highness."

"What, with guineas?"

"Nay, not a *monetary* debt. I refer, again, to when you surprized me in Boston with a queer and unlooked-for conversation, which led presently to sea-voyage and adventure."

"It pleases me to be having the conversation," Caroline said, "and to be sure, I should like nothing better than to be repaid with a sea-voyage and an adventure. But such things are for picaroon-romances. Not for Princesses."

"You shall have the voyage soon enough, though it be nothing more than a Channel crossing. Once you set foot on English soil at Greenwich, an adventure—of what sort I daren't guess—will be inevitable."

"That much was true whether or not you came here," Caroline said, "so why did you come? To see Leibniz?"

"He is not in town, alas."

"It bears on the guineas, does it not?"

"It does."

"Then by the same token it must have something to do with the man who makes them: Sir Isaac Newton."

"Leibniz told me that you required little instruction—that you worked things out for yourself. I see that this was more than avuncular pride."

"Then I am sorry to let you know I have come to the end of my deductions. I asked you to go to London. It pleased me very much that you did. You have sought out Sir Isaac there, and renewed your old acquaintance with him—this is praiseworthy."

"Only in the sense that a geek at a fair is to be praised for swallowing a sword."

"*Pfui!* To cross the Atlantic in winter and enter into the Lion's Den is a Herculean labor. I could not be more pleased with what you have accomplished to this point."

"You forget that I do not care whether you are pleased. I do nothing to earn your praise. I have undertaken this work simply because I phant'sy that my ends are akin to yours; and to those ends, you have provided me with some of the means."

Caroline had to turn her face full into the mist to cool it now—like a red-hot iron that must be tempered in water lest it shatter in proof.

"I have heard that there were still men like you about England," she said finally, "and it is good that I have now met you privily and in advance, lest I should spoil my first weeks there crying 'Off with his head!' several times each day before breakfast."

"What is at issue today, is whether you, or George Louis, or Sophie, shall ever reign in England at all," Daniel Waterhouse said. "Or will a Jacobite Mobb, or a Stuart King, cry off with *your* heads?"

This thought was less frightening than it was interesting. Princess Caroline quite forgot her anger, and entertained it. "Of course I am aware that England contains many Jacobites," she said. "But the Act of Settlement has been the law of the land since 1701. Our right to the throne cannot really be in question, can it?"

"We decapitated Sophie's uncle. I was there. There were sound reasons for it. But it brought unforeseen perils. It put the heads of Princes and Princesses into play, as it were, like kick-balls on a field, to be booted back and forth by whichever gang of players was most numerous, or most adroit. Do you believe what some say, that Sophie Charlotte was assassinated in Berlin?"

"We will not speak of it!" Caroline announced; and here she really *would* have ordered his head to be struck off if any guards had been in earshot. Or done the deed with her own hand, given a sharp object. Her rage must have showed, for Daniel Waterhouse now raised his white eyebrows, elevated his chin, and spoke in a voice that was so soothing and gentle that it dissolved like sugar in the murmur of waves along the pool's edge.

"You forget that I know Leibniz, and that through him I shared his sweet love for that Queen, and his grief. Grief and anger."

"He thinks she was poisoned?" This was one of the few topics Leibniz refused to discuss with Caroline.

"The manner of her death is not as important as the consequence. If half of what people say about her is true, she had made Berlin into a Protestant Parnassus. Writers, musicians, and scientists converged on the Charlottenburg from every quarter. But she died. Quite recently her husband went to join her. Where the former King of Prussia amused himself by attending the opera, the new one plays with toy soldiers . . . I see amusement on your face, your royal highness. Familial affection, I think this must be, for this cousin of yours who adores parades and goose-stepping soldiers. But to those of us who do not share in the family joke, it is dreadfully serious. For the war is over; most of the great conflicts have been sorted out; Natural Philosophy has conquered the realm of the mind; and now—today—as we stand here—the new System of the World is being writ down in a great Book somewhere."

"The System of the World—that is the title of the book we have anticipated for so many years from Sir Isaac Newton. A new volume of *Principia Mathematica* . . . or am I mistaken?"

"Indeed. But I refer to a different unfinished work: mine and yours. We have lost Sophie Charlotte, and with her we have lost Prussia. I do not wish to lose you, and lose Britain. Those are precisely the stakes."

"But this is why I have sought you out in Massachusetts!" Caroline protested. "I cannot manage a house divided between partisans of Leibniz on the one hand, and of Newton on the other. As German and British dominions are united under one crown, so German and British philosophy must be brought together under a grand unification. And you, Doctor Waterhouse, are the one—"

But she was speaking into a cloud. Daniel Waterhouse had vanished. Caroline looked far up the path to see a crone storming towards her with a letter whipping back and forth in one hand.

Sophie as usual moved at the pace of a dragoon. But the garden was large. Caroline would have a few moments, yet, to collect herself. She turned toward the fountain, for if shock were still written on her face it were better that Sophie not read it. But all told, she was not as rattled by the conversation just finished as the average Continental princess might have been. For as long as she had been in Hanover, strange people had been coming over from England, bearing cryptic messages and making odd requests. None of it made much sense to her, since she'd never visited the place. She and George Augustus had been invited to come over by some people called Whigs—a challenging term for Germans to pronounce—but some other English called Tories were dead set against their coming. It was all academic anyhow, since George Louis had forbidden his son and daugher-in-law to leave.

High above her head, where the towering water-jet surrendered to gravity, Caroline could see clumps of water that somehow held together even as the rest of the flow shattered. These could be seen as dark streaks against the incoherent spray. But those water-clumps came down with much greater speed and force than the dissipating clouds, and as they fell, each broke apart into a shower of smaller lumps that left spreading comet-trails behind. Swarms and squadrons of these comets raced down to the pool, messengers carrying strange information from above.

She strolled round until she was very close to where most of the plume struck the pond. The spray made a solid white hiss and roar, and her dress grew heavy as it stole water from the air. She tried to follow the comets. When they smashed into the foaming surface of the pond they made indistinct noises, like individual voices trying to shout messages in the midst of the Mobb. But whatever intelligence the comets were carrying down from on high was swallowed up by the pool. When the bubbles burst and the froth died away, nothing was left but the clear water of the pond, a bit choppy from the breeze. Caroline supposed that the information was still there to be decyphered, if she'd only stand and stare into the pool long enough. But all she could make out was a constellation of yellow speckles on the stone floor of the pool.

"This cannot be a coincidence."

"Good morning, Grandmama."

Sophie was staring at the coins. At eighty-three she had no difficulty seeing them without glasses. She could even tell heads from tails, and recognize the portrait of Queen Anne stamped into the former.

"I see that bitch going and coming," she remarked.

Princess Caroline said nothing.

"It is a symbol, a sign," the Electress of Hanover announced, "planted here by one of those horrid visiting Englishmen."

"What do you think it signifies?"

"That depends on what you think of the English money," Sophie replied. "Which is the same thing as to ask, is it worth anything?"

This, being oddly similar to some remarks made moments ago by the horrid visiting Englishman in question, caused Caroline to look away from the coins, and gaze into Sophie's face. In order to do this Caroline had to look slightly down, for Sophie had lost a few inches of height. She had the loose skin that one would expect in a woman of that age, but this had lent to her eyes a marvelous clarity. The walls of Herrenhausen and of the Leine Schloß were adorned with old family portraits, not only of Sophie and her sisters but of their mother. These women stared out from the canvases with arched brows, enormous eyes, and tiny mouths, seeing much and saying little. They were certainly not the first girls in a *salon* that an insecure young man would approach, and engage in conversation. Now Caroline knew as well as anyone that portraits of royals must be taken with a grain of salt. But the visage she was regarding now did not look all that far removed from the ones in those paintings. The eyes, the mouth were the same. More so the feeling of self-possession, of completeness, the sense that this woman was by no means standing around waiting to be joined, or wishing that someone would talk to her. The only changes were in clothing. Sophie, though never responsive to fashion, had adopted the *fontange*, a tall vertical screen of white lace that rose from the hairline, added some inches to her height, and kept her thinning white hair out of view, and out of the way of those wonderful eyes.

Caroline had a funny thought then, which was that Sophie and

Daniel Waterhouse might be a match for each other. For he had great staring eyes too, and a disposition to match Sophie's. They could threaten to chop each other's heads off well into the Eighteenth Century.

"Have you spoken to any of the English? I mean the ones who have just arrived, not of the Braithwaite type."

"Briefly."

"Come, I wish to be away from those coins, and that woman," Sophie said, turning her back on the pool and leaning towards Caroline, knowing that she'd find a strong arm there. The two women clasped together like halves of a locket and began to walk away from the pool's rim. Sophie steered Caroline firmly in the direction she wanted. But she had nothing further to say for a little while.

This half of the garden was partitioned into quadrants, each of which was laid out around a fountain much smaller than the great one in the center. Small paths radiated from each of those fountains, sectioning each quadrant into several pie-wedges. Each of those wedges—thirty-two all told—had been made into a little garden-plot, and each was a bit different: some as clean and tidy as parlours, others as dark and overgrown as the Thüringer Wald. Sophie steered Caroline to one that was screened by a high wall of trimmed trees. Passing through a gap they found themselves in a pleasant green atrium with a little pool in the center, and stone benches around it. Sophie let it be known that she wished to sit on one of these—unusual since for her, a walk in the garden was precisely that.

"One of the English was using a funny word yester evening—'currency.' Do you know it?"

"It is the quality that a current has. They speak of the currency of the River Thames, which is sluggish in most places, but violent when it passes under London Bridge. It is just the same as our word *Umlauf*—running around."

"That is what I supposed. This Englishman kept discoursing of currency in a way that was most fraught with meaning, and I thought he was speaking of some river or drainage-ditch. Finally I collected that he was using it as a synonym for *money*."

"Money?"

"I've never felt so dense! Fortunately, Baron von Hacklheber is visiting from Leipzig. He was familiar with the term—or quicker to decypher it. Later I spoke with him in private and he explained all."

"What an odd coinage."

"You are too witty for your own good, girl."

"The Englishmen cannot get away from this topic. Their relationship to money is most peculiar."

"It is because they have nothing but sheep," Sophie explained. "You must understand this if you are to be their Queen. They had to fight Spain, which has all of the gold and silver in the world. Then they had to fight France, which has every other source of material wealth that can be imagined. How does a poor country defeat rich ones?"

"I think I am supposed to say 'the grace of God' or some such—"

"If you please. But in what form is the grace of God manifested? Did piles of gold materialize on the banks of the Thames, as in a miracle?"

"Of course not."

"Does Sir Isaac turn Cornish tin into gold in an alchemical laboratory in the Tower of London?"

"Opinions differ. Leibniz thinks not."

"I agree with Baron von Leibniz. And yet all the gold is in England! It is dug up from Portuguese and Spanish mines, but it flows, by some occult power of attraction, to the Tower of London."

"Flows," Caroline repeated, "flows like a current."

Sophie nodded. "And the English have grown so used to this that they use 'currency' as a synonym for 'money' as if no distinction need be observed between them."

Caroline said, "Is this the answer to your question—how does a poor country defeat rich ones?"

"Indeed. The answer is, not by acquiring wealth, in the sense that France has it—"

"Meaning vineyards, farms, peasants, cows—"

"But rather to play a sort of trick, and redefine wealth to mean something novel."

"Currency!"

"Indeed. Baron von Hacklheber says that the idea is not wholly new, having been well understood by the Genoese, the Florentines, the Augsburgers, the Lyonnaise for many generations. The Dutch built a modest empire on it. But the English—having no other choices—perfected it."

"You have given me new food for thought."

"Oh? And what think you? What think you now of our prospects, Caroline?"

To Sophie's generation of royals, this question was shocking, absurd. One who was heir to a throne did not have to think about his prospects. Royal succession just happened, like the tide coming in. But it was different now; and Sophie deserved credit for having adjusted to this new state of affairs, where many of her contemporaries had passed from ignorance to indignation to senility.

Caroline answered: "I am pleased by the cleverness of this trick that the English have played, to win wars against their betters by tinkering with what wealth is. Because of it, I do not have to marry some inbred Bourbon, as poor Eliza did, and live out my days at Versailles, or in the Escorial. But I am troubled by the uncertainty that all of this brings. To paraphrase a wise man I know, it is as though a new System of the World has been drawn up. And not by us but by some strange Natural Philosophers in a smoky room in London. Now we must live by the rules of that System. But it is not perfectly understood; and I fear that where the English have played a trick with money, to gain a temporary advantage, some other trick might be played upon them to reverse the field."

"Just so! And now you have come round to the meaning of Anne's letter!" Sophie proclaimed, and flogged the parchment several times with her ivory fan. At the same time, the tree-wall behind them let out a gasp as it was struck by a fist of cold air. The wind had changed from south to west; new weather was coming; Herr Schwartz's joints had not misled him. The tree-wall flexed toward them as if trying to spread shelter above their heads, and a dry sleet of brown leaves and twigs made the air and the ground restless with tiny itchings and fidgetings. Sophie—who of all persons was least disposed to take a fart for a thunderclap—paid this no heed whatever. Perhaps she was too absorbed in conversation to care. Or perhaps she was so comfortable in this place that she could not muster any sense of concern.

If Sophie did not wish to speak of the weather, 'twere hopeless, as well as rude, to force the topic, and so Caroline contented herself with gestures: she arched her back against the cool breeze, clasped her hands together on her knee, and glanced skyward. Then she responded, "The Queen's letter has to do with money?"

"Don't be ridiculous, she doesn't know what money *is*. And would never write of anything so vulgar even if she did. The letter concerns family matters. Several paragraphs are devoted to your husband."

"That is even more chilling to me than this recent change in the wind."

"She refers to him by his English titles: Duke of Cambridge, Earl of Milford Haven, Viscount Northallerton, Baron Tewkesbury," said Sophie, reading the outlandish names from the letter with parched amusement.

"Now you are teasing me, by not reading what the letter says."

"I am not teasing you but doing you a favor, dear heart."

"Is it that bad?"

"It is the worst yet."

"Has my father-in-law seen it yet?"

"George Louis has not read it."

"My husband and I would be in England now," Caroline complained, "and he would be sitting in the House of Lords, if George Louis merely had the backbone to let us go. Another such letter from Queen Anne only cows him all the more, and delays our departure another month."

Sophie smiled, showing sympathy. "George Louis cannot read this letter if you and I get caught in a rain-shower, and the ink is dissolved."

A cold drop came through the sleeve of Caroline's dress and sent a thrill up her arm. She laughed. Sophie did not move. A raindrop pocked into the letter. "However," Sophie continued, "you must not deceive yourself. My son won't let you go to England, it is true. But this is not simply because Queen Anne hates the idea. George Louis has his shortcomings. No one knows this better than his mama. But spinelessness is not among them! He keeps you and George Augustus pent up in Hanover, because he is envious of his son—his poise, his battle-glory—and distrustful of his son's women."

"You mean Mrs. Braithwaite?"

Sophie flinched. "She is a dust-mote. Everyone knows that except you. You, Eliza, the late Sophie Charlotte, and I—the women who walk in the garden—are to George Louis like some witch-coven. He is appalled that his son and heir is comfortable among us, and shares intelligence with us. For this reason he will never give George Augustus, and you, leave to move to England. He may use this as an excuse—" and she held up the letter so that many collected raindrops, black with dissolved abuse, tumbled down over the Queen of England's signature "—but you must never be deceived."

A strong wind-burst came through now, and cracked a branch somewhere. All the rainwater that had gathered on the leaves above was knocked loose and rushed down around them. Sophie looked around herself for the first time, becoming aware that this might develop into something more than a June shower. Her starched *fontange* was beginning to wilt.

But now it was Caroline's turn to be oblivious to weather. "When we sat down here you said that the letter had some import, having to do with currency—?"

"Not the *substance* but the *tone* of it," Sophie returned, raising her voice to match the volume of the wind. "Her previous letters, you know, written after the Whigs invited your husband to England, were petulant. Bitter. But this one is—or was—written in a haughty tone. Triumphant."

"Something has changed in the last month or two—?"

339

"That is what she believes, I fear."

"She phant'sies we are never coming at all. She's going to give the throne to the Pretender."

Sophie said nothing.

"But the throne is not all hers to give away. Parliament has some say in the matter. What could have occurred in the last few weeks to give the Jacobites such confidence?"

"A blow has been struck against the currency. An interruption in the flow."

"That is just the sort of thing I was talking about a moment ago."

"Perhaps you *are* a witch, dear, with powers of divination."

"Perhaps I receive unscheduled visits from 'horrid Englishmen.' "

"Aha!" Sophie glanced in the direction of the great fountain.

"Something must have gone awry at the English Mint."

"But Sir Isaac Newton has charge of the Mint! I have been studying it," Sophie said proudly. "When I'm Queen of England we shall all go to the Tower of London and see it." Then she slapped her knee, meaning it was time to get up. For it was absolutely raining now, and search parties had probably been sent out from the Palace. Caroline got to her feet and gave Sophie an arm, helping her up off the bench. Meanwhile Sophie went on, "Sir Isaac has reformed the English coinage, which was the world's worst, and now it is the best."

"But this proves my point! All you are saying is that English coins have an excellent reputation . . . Let's get out of here." Caroline led the way this time, ushering Sophie out the nearest gate and onto one of the radiating paths. But then she pulled up short. The way back to the Palace was not obvious, even to one who knew the garden well. Sophie sensed her hesitation. "Let us wait it out in the pavilion," she decreed, inclining her ruined *fontange* toward a diagonal path that would conduct them to the edge of the garden, where a stone dome overlooked the canal.

Caroline did not favor this idea because it would take them to a distant and unfrequented corner, and the way was hemmed in by dense wooded plots that were black and opaque and loud in the rain.

"Don't you think we should return to the great fountain? Someone should be looking for us there."

"If someone finds us, we shall have to stop talking!" Sophie answered, very provoked.

That was that. They turned their backs on the fountain and entered into a cleft between stands of trees. "It's only water," Caroline said philosophically. But Sophie seemed to have had quite enough of it, for she yanked on Caroline's arm and began pulling her onwards, trying to quicken their pace. Caroline let herself be pulled.

"I take your point," Sophie said. "A coinage based upon silver and gold has a sort of absolute value."

"Like Sir Isaac's absolute space and time," Caroline mused. "You can assay it."

"But if value is based upon reputations—like stocks in Amsterdam—or upon this even more nebulous concept of *flow*—"

"Like the dynamics of Leibniz in which space and time inhere in relationships among objects—"

"Why, then, it becomes unknowable, plastic, vulnerable. For *flow* may have some value in a market-place—and that value might even be real—"

"Of course it is real! People make money from it all the time!"

"—but that sort of value cannot survive the refiner's fire at a Trial of the Pyx."

"What on earth is a Pyx?" Caroline asked. But no answer was coming. Sophie pulled sharply on her arm and at the same moment fell into her. Caroline had to bend her knees and whip her free arm round Sophie's shoulders to avoid falling down. "Grandmama? You wish to go in this way?" She glanced at the dark stand of trees to the left side of the path. "You wish to visit the Teufelsbaum?" Perhaps Sophie had changed her mind, and wished to take shelter under the trees instead of going all the way to the pavilion.

Some sound came out of Sophie's mouth that could not really be understood. The clatter of raindrops on leaves made it difficult to hear even well-spoken words. But this utterance of Sophie's had not been well spoken. Caroline doubted that it was even words. Relying on Caroline for support, Sophie shuffled and hopped on one leg until she had brought them face to face with an iron gate. For the plot of the Teufelsbaum, the Devil's Tree, was surrounded by a wrought-iron fence as if it needed to be kept in a cage.

Sophie nodded at the gate, then looked up at Caroline with a kind of lopsided sneer: half of her face pleading, the other half sagging and vacant. Caroline reached out for the handle of the gate. At the same moment that the cold wet iron touched her skin she knew that Sophie had suffered a stroke. For this was not the first half-paralyzed face Caroline had ever seen. The symptoms were more difficult to recognize in a face she knew so well and loved so much. For a moment she froze with a hand on the gate-latch, as if some spell had turned her own flesh to cold iron. She ought to go for help, to find the doctors.

But then Sophie did something telling, which was that she looked up and down the garden path, and she did it furtively. This from someone who had never been furtive in her life.

Sophie could not speak and could hardly stand up, but she knew what was happening. She was afraid of being seen. Afraid of being rushed to the Palace, bled by the surgeons, pitied to her face and mocked behind her back. Her instinct was to hie to the deepest and darkest part of the garden and to die there.

Caroline shoved the gate open and they stepped into the dark.

The Teufelsbaum was a curiosity that Sophie had brought back from the family holdings in the Harz Mountains: a worthless tree that crawled along the ground and climbed up things, with all the mass and might of a great tree, but the writhing habit of a vine, enclosing other things and growing round them. Its boughs twisted round and divided and forked and kinked bizarrely. The bends looked something like elbows and knees, and the smooth bark and sinewy shape of the wood made the whole thing look like unidentifiable limbs of strange animals, melted into one another. The woodcutters of the Harz hated it, and cut it back wherever they could, but here Sophie had given it leave to spread. Now the Teufelsbaum returned the favor by embracing Sophie and Caroline in its sinuous arms. Caroline settled Sophie down in a crook of the tree, up off the cold ground, and then sat on a flat place and cradled Sophie's head in her lap. The rain-shower had now abated somewhat, or perhaps the leaves gentled it. Time became stretched and immeasurable as they listened to the rain, Caroline stroking Sophie's white hair, and holding the one hand that had not lost its power to grip back. But the garden was a place of quiet and of relaxation. Presently Sophie relaxed her grip on Caroline's hand, and on the world.

Caroline had a long list of questions she had been meaning to ask Sophie, concerning how to be a Queen. She could have asked them there under the Teufelsbaum, but it would have been tactless, and Sophie would not have been able to answer.

Or rather she couldn't have answered with words. Her true answer, the one that mattered, had been arranged long in advance: it was this moment and this place. Sophie's dying here was the last thing she said to Caroline.

"I am the Princess of Wales," Caroline said. She said it to herself.

Westminster Palace
11 JUNE 1714

Resolved, Nemine contradicente, that the House doth
agree with the Committee in the said Resolution,
That a Reward be settled by Parliament upon such
Person or Persons as shall discover a more certain
and practicable Method of ascertaining the Longitude, than any yet in Practice; and the said Reward
be proportioned to the Degree of Exactness to
which the said Method shall Reach.

—*Journals of the House of Commons,* VENERIS, 11°
DIE JUNII; ANNO 13° ANNÆ REGINÆ, 1714

IN WESTMINSTER, A HALL darkened Thames-bank, like a load of
gloaming spilt by a sloppy sky-god during the primordial rush to raise
the vault of the stars. Efforts had been made to pretty it up, or at least
screen it behind new work. The marshes from which it had up-
heaved had been filled and flattened to support the Hall's conta-
gions and encrustations. Some of these were styled as minsters, some
as forts, others as houses—all mere words, since none was ever put to
its builders' purpose. A man debarking on that Bank and tunneling
into the Pile, if he had a compass, and became not a-mazed in the
gaudy labyrinth of out-buildings, might penetrate to the Hall.

It was empty. Oh, law-courts, screened behind plank barricades,
had colonized the southern corners, and shop-stalls ran like base-
boards along the sides, so that the persons who came and went
through the emptiness could buy books, gloves, snuff, and hats. But
these only pointed to the problematic immensity of the Hall; for
what was the point of putting up a building so large that it could not
be used until smaller buildings were erected within it? The carven
angels at the ends of the out-thrust hammer-beams looked out on a
tub of gray space. The bareness of the place, the splintery time-
stained reach of its roof-timbers, betrayed it as a somewhat oversized

Dark Ages Viking-Hall. Beowulf could have strode in to the place at any moment and called for a horn of mead. He would have felt and looked more at home there than any of the periwigged Persons of Quality who darted across its stone floor, nervously, like stoats trying to make it across a darkling sandbar before owls could stoop on them. The smaller buildings huddled against Westminster Hall, stealing integrity from its flying buttresses, were better suited for plots, machinations, skullduggery, and arcane rites: the timeless occupations of men. So into the peripheral warrens they scurried, abandoning the hall to those bleak angels.

If this grave void at the heart of Westminster had any purpose, it was like the empty chamber that made up most of a violincello. The strings, bridge, bow, and the player itself were all to the outside. Nothing moved, nothing happened in the dark cavity; yet none of it would work unless it were built around a central emptiness that held the parts in their proper relation to one another, and withstood the relentless pulling of the strings while sympathizing with their tiniest stirrings.

There was only one man on this day who did not quicken his steps to cross that floor. It was an elderly knight who had arrived at the north end of the place in a black sedan chair, and bid his porters let him off there. He alit near the pillory, where a fat man was being whipped, writhing and hopping as each new stripe decorated his back, but refusing to cry out. The old man from the sedan chair swung wide of the post so he wouldn't be flecked by hurtling blood, and stepped into a gap between a pair of coffee-houses that had been troweled onto the ancient façade of the hall, nearly hiding its main entrance. He needed no wig, for his hair, though thin, still grew long and straight, and smallpox had left little mark on him. And he needed no powder, for his hair had been white as salt for half a century. He strolled the length of the Hall slowly, raising his protruberant eyes to meet the gaze of certain of those omniscient angels, paying others no mind. He glanced about from time to time, as if his ears could detect echoes and discern resonances to which all others were deaf. In time he reached the south end of the vault where traffic was funneled between the two makeshift law-courts. With a visible hardening of his face he forced himself into a dissolving noise beyond. He was gone from the Hall. Perhaps he had changed it in his passage, added some faint strain that echoed after he was gone, and echoes there still.

Tribes, clans, factions, sects, classes, houses, and dynasties had raised their standards, and seen them thrown down, in the Hall's outbuildings for six hundred years. It was to Power what Covent Garden was to vegetables. No point in trying to follow the ins and outs, until you stepped over the threshold. At the moment, as for the past centuries, there was here a thing called Parliament, consisting of two parallel or alternate renderings named Commons and Lords, each the ground of an on-going war between Tories and Whigs, the sons and heirs of Cavaliers and Roundheads, the sons and heirs of Anglicans and Puritans, &c., &c. Each styled itself The Party and the other The Faction. Milling about in the gloom behind them, brandishing money and weapons, were descendants of ancient warlords, currently going by the names of Jacobites and Hanoverians. The battle itself was carried forward daily with words as many as granules of gunpowder on a battle-field.

The silver-haired knight had been summoned into a high-walled Gothick chapel that for quite some few years had been claimed, occupied, and defended against all comers by the body calling itself Commons. It was dominated by the Tories just now. His summoners were a committee or subset of Commons that happened to consist largely of Whigs. Why had a body of Tories suffered a band of Whigs to form a committee that could arrogate to itself the power to summon Knights into this hallowed Chapel that they used as their Clubb-house? Why, only because the subject of that committee's deliberations was so abstruse, so recondite, and, in a word, so boring that they were only too pleased to let Whigs expend their powder on it.

"I HAVE BEEN made aware of four diverse Projects for discovering the Longitude," said Sir Isaac Newton.

"Only *four?*" asked Roger Comstock, the Marquis of Ravenscar: a Whig, and the bloke who had invited Newton here. He belonged to Lords, not Commons, and was therefore a guest in this chamber. "At the Royal Society, it seems we are exposed to four *a week.*"

That Roger did not belong to this body at all, would seem to call in question the propriety of his having invited a stranger to come and address them. But he had many friends in the room willing to overlook this and other enormities.

"I know of only four, my lord, that are true *in theory.* Of the others I make no account."

"Is that of Messieurs Ditton and Wiston among the fortunate four, or the phantastickal multitude?" asked Ravenscar.

Everyone in the chapel began barking like a dog except for him, Newton, and Messrs. Ditton (who had turned the color of a pomegranate seed, and begun moving his lips) and Whiston (whose eyelids thrummed like hummingbirds' wings as sweat coursed in gleaming rills from under his wig and pincered in on the corners of his eyes).

"Their *theory* is as *correct* as their *ambitions* are *feeble,*" answered Newton.

The House of Commons became silent, not out of shock at Newton's cruelty, but out of professional admiration. "Supposing their scheme could be executed—a supposition that might be debated, at the Royal Society, as long and as fiercely as the late War was in this House—I say, disregarding all of the practical difficulties entailed in their Project, and supposing it were effected by some latter-day Dædalus—it would not suffice to navigate across an ocean, but only to enable the most diligent mariners to avoid running aground, when they wandered close to a Shore."

General amusement in the Chapel now, occasioned by the facial expressions of Messrs. Ditton and Whiston, who were no longer even putting forth the effort to be angry or agitated. They now looked as if they were resting on slabs at the College of Physicians, about halfway through their own autopsies.

Not partaking of the entertainment was the Marquis of Ravenscar, who had just been handed a slip of paper by a page. He opened and read it, and for only a moment looked as dismayed as Ditton and Whiston. Then he got the better of himself. Like the deaf dinner-guest pretending that he heard the *bon mot,* he adopted a knowing grin, and allowed the mood of the House to infiltrate his phizz. He glanced down to review the documents spread out on the table before him, as if he had forgotten the subject of this hearing and needed to jog his memory. Then he spoke: "Merely to avoid ramming the odd continent is a low bar. What of the other three Projects that are true *in theory?* For it seems to me that if such Herculean efforts are to be made to practice a scheme, they were better directed to schemes that should enable our sea-captains to discover the Longitude *anywhere.*"

Sir Isaac Newton's answer comprised many many words, but contained no more than the following information: that one could do it by telling the time with an excellent sea-going chronometer, which no one knew how to make yet; or by watching the satellites of Jupiter through an excellent sea-going telescope, which no one knew how to make yet; or by looking at the position of the moon and comparing it against calculations derived from his, i.e., Sir Isaac Newton's, lunar theory, which was not quite finished yet but would be coming out any minute now in a book. In the timeless and universal manner of authors conversing in public places, he did not fail to mention its title: Volume III of *Principia Mathematica,* entitled *The System of the World,* available shortly where books are sold.

The Marquis of Ravenscar only heard this peroration in its general outlines because he spent the whole time jetting notes onto scraps of paper and stuffing them into minions' hands. But when his ears detected a lengthy silence, he said: "These, er, calculations—would they be similar to what are already used for finding latitude? Or—"

"Infinitely more complex."

"Oh, bother," said Ravenscar distractedly, still scribbling notes, like the naughtiest schoolboy in the entire history of the world. "I suppose every ship would then require an extra deck crowded with *computers*, and a flock of geese to keep 'em in quills."

"Or else we should need every ship to carry an *Arithmetickal Engine*," Newton returned. Then, not trusting the House to detect his sarcasm, he went on: "—a chimærical phant'sy of the Hanoverian dilettante and plagiarist, Baron von Leibniz, which he has abjectly failed to complete lo these many years." And it seemed as if Newton were prepared to enumerate the Baron's defects at much greater length, but he was interrupted, and distracted, by the hot arrival in his palm of a note still damp from Ravenscar's quill.

"So the lunar method *too* requires an apparatus we do not know how to make yet," Ravenscar said, moving to sum up with an abruptness, a dispatch, that had not been seen in this House since the last time a Papist had tried to blow it up. The benches rustled with the stirrings of many expensively clad arses. A positive start was running through the Chapel.

"Yes, my lord—"

"And so it is your testimony that our ships shall persist in running aground and slaughtering our brave mariners until we shall learn how to make certain things we do not know how to make yet."

"Yes, my—"

"Who shall invent these remarkable devices?"

"Projectors, entrepeneurs, adventurers, my—"

"What incentive could lead such a man to wager years of his life on attempting to devise a new Technology—if I may borrow a word from Dr. Waterhouse—that may turn out to be infeasible?" Ravenscar asked, standing up, and holding out his hand to let it be known that it was now permissible for someone to hand him his walking-stick. Someone did.

"My lord, some monetary—" testified Sir Isaac Newton, standing up as well—for he had read the note.

"A monetary prize—a Reward! To be awarded to such Person or Persons as shall discover a more certain and practical Method of ascertaining the Longitude? Is that your testimony? Yes? Sir Isaac, once again the Heavens resound with your brilliance and all Britannia gapes in awe at your lapidary ingenuity." Ravenscar was crossing the floor while he thus orated, a novelty that roused to full wakefulness many a senior back-bencher who had lost, or never found, the faculty of walking and talking at the same time. " 'Twere a crime to waste any more of the time of the world's foremost savant on details," Ravenscar proclaimed, arriving at Newton's side and snatching his arm. "I have unbounded confidence that Mr. Halley, Dr. Clarke, and Mr. Cotes can bat down any further questions from Commons—as for myself, I have business with certain troublous Lords—I may as well see you out, Sir Isaac, as we go the same way!" By that time he and Sir Isaac were out the door, leaving a House of more or less dumbfounded Commons; Ditton and Whiston, half-murdered but still breathing; and the three lesser savants mentioned, who had been summoned as mere acolytes to the High Priest, and been left in charge of the Rite.

NEWTON NEARLY LOST AN ARM in the lobby of Commons, for he moved left—towards Lords—as Roger Comstock, the Marquis of Ravenscar, who had possession of the arm, moved right—towards Westminster Hall. "We are summoned *by* Lords," Ravenscar explained, re-socketing Newton's shoulder-joint, and trying it with a wiggle, "but not *to* Lords." Dodging round a few bends and negotiating diverse stair-flights they came into the cleft between the two plank law-courts, and entered the great Hall again—just as devoid of Vikings, and strewn with inappropriate modern-day Englishmen, as ever. A man in quasi-genteel clothes browsed a bookshop, to let all the world know he was literate; a straw projected from his shoe, as a signal to barristers that he would give false testimony in exchange for money. A stirring in the air created a serial heaving down rows of sun-faded, smoke-stained, bullet-holed banners: the colors of French regiments that had been taken by Marlborough at Blenheim and other places. These had been hung on the walls to add a bit of color, and been promptly forgotten. A fair bit of noise was coming into the north end of the Hall from the New Palace Yard. The man who'd received the whipping there earlier had been left in the pillory, and a few score common Londoners had gathered in his sight, to fling handfuls of mud and horse-manure at his face in hopes that they might induce suffocation. This sort of thing was common enough in London that most persons could will themselves not to see it. Ravenscar, uncharacteristically, was gazing directly at the scene. His eyes were too old, and too far away, to resolve the details; but he knew what it was. "Ah, fortunate man!" he said wistfully, "if only I could trade places with him for the next hour!"

Newton straightened up and, prudently, slowed down. He glanced up and around as if wondering whether any of the over-looming angels had heard. "Where are we going, my lord?"

"Star Chamber," Ravenscar announced, simultaneously tightening his grip on Newton's arm lest these fell words cause the eminent Natural Philosopher to spin away and make a break for it. Sir Isaac did no such thing; but he was startled. He had expected that Roger Comstock would name one of the buildings of the Exchequer, which in recent decades had advanced far, and on a broad front, from the Hall's northeast corner, so that they nearly filled the space between it and the River. Star Chamber, on the other hand, was small, and ancient; Kings of England had used to meet there with their Privy Councils. "Who has summoned us?" Newton asked.

As if the answer were self-evident, Roger said, "The Eel." Saying out loud this mysterious epithet seemed to bring his concentration back. "We are only seconds away from the place. We could get more time by walking slowly; but I wish to stride into the place *enthusiastically*. The importance of this cannot be overstated. You must therefore listen carefully, Sir Isaac, as I'll only have time to say this once.

"It seems," Roger continued, "that I have only been given leave to distract myself with Longitude so that my honorable lord, Henry St. John, Viscount Bolingbroke, could prepare some sort of poppet-show. The invitation was sprung upon me while you were testifying. I am sure Bolingbroke would fainer have tied it round an arrow and shot it into my stomach, but such proceedings, though frequently seen in Lords, are still frowned upon in Commons. You, Sir Isaac, have been given a Backstage Pass to the poppet-show, which makes me suspect that you shall be called upon to play the lead role."

Sir Isaac Newton now became quiet and still, which was his customary way of showing rage. "It is an affront. I came here to discourse of the Longitude. Now you say I am caught up in an *ambuscade*."

"I beg of you, Sir Isaac, be anything but affronted. For it is when men become old and important, and peevish over the odd ambuscade, that they become most vulnerable to just such tactics. Be baffled, unconcerned, gay—what'd be best of all, *sporting* about it!"

Newton did not look very sporting just now. The portal to Star Chamber was now as large in Ravenscar's sight, as the whale's maw to Jonah. "Never mind," he said, "be as affronted as you please—just don't volunteer anything. If you see what appears to be an opening in debate, remember that it was ingeniously laid down in front of you by Bolingbroke, as coquettes drop handkerchiefs at the feet of men they would ensnare."

"Has anyone ever actually *done* that to you, Roger?" They had been joined by Walter Raleigh Waterhouse Weem, a.k.a. Peer, who was, like Roger, a Whig Lord. "I've heard of the practice, but—"

"Nay, 'twas just a figure," Roger admitted.

But this Weem/Comstock insouciance—in truth a sort of Yogic exercise to relax nerves—misfired in Newton's case. "What's the point of participating in a debate if I'm to disregard every opening?" he demanded.

"This is no more a *debate* than is Hanging Day at Tyburn Cross. Viscount Bolingbroke would be our Jack Ketch. Anything *we* are allowed to say shall be strictly in the nature of Last Words. Our reply, supposing we can muster any, shall consist of deeds not words, and it shall be delivered . . . outside . . . of . . . this . . . Chamber!" Roger timed it so that he stepped over the threshold at the moment he uttered the last word. Newton dared not respond, for the Chamber was crowded with Lords Spiritual and Temporal, Knights, Courtiers, and Clerks. And it was as silent as a parish-church when the vicar has lost his place in the middle of the sermon.

"SOMETHING MONSTROUS WAS MADE to happen in the Tower of London a month and a half ago."

It was terribly unkind for Roger to have dubbed one of his fellow-men "The Eel." And yet a visitor from another place and time, blundering into Star Chamber, not knowing any of the men in the place, would have been able to pick out the one Roger meant. Henry St. John, Viscount Bolingbroke, and Secretary of State to Her Britannic Majesty, was strolling about the open center of the chamber as he talked. All others were backed up against the walls, like so many small fry sharing a tank with something toothy and sinuous.

"London's Persons of Quality—members of the Party and of the Faction alike—have done what they could to draw a curtain over the late events in the Tower, and to promulgate the sham that it was a momentary up-welling of the Mobb, quickly suppressed by the Queen's Own Black Torrent Guard. A stable-fire on Tower Hill distracted the locals, and laid a smoke-pall over all—fortunate, that. It shall be writ down in history-books as a civil disturbance, if it is noted at all. But it would be a moral as well as an intellectual sin to mistake the events of April 23rd for anything other than a whited sepulchre. The matter must be investigated. Those responsible must be held to accompt. My lord Oxford, in his capacity as Lord Treasurer, has disappointed me by failing to do anything about it."

This frank and frontal assault on his fellow Tory Lord was new. It created a buzz in the room. Bolingbroke held his tongue for a few moments, and let his gaze stray over the heads of some of the wallflowers. These reacted as if they'd been switched across the face by a horse-tail. Bolingbroke was not looking at them, however, but simply gazing in the general direction of the various offices, courts, and receipts of the Exchequer.

After that, Bolingbroke's words poured out into a carefully maintained silence. Even men who were under attack (several of Oxford's lieutenants had been shouldered to the front rank) said nothing. This was, in other words, no kind of Parliamentary proceeding. Depending on the diurnal velleities of Queen Anne, Bolingbroke was either the first man in England, or the second, after Oxford. Today he certainly believed he was first; he might have come here direct from the right hand of the Sovereign herself. Though Star Chamber was, like Commons and like Lords, an appendage of Westminster Hall, it had nothing to do with Parliament—which was a place to discuss things—and everything to do with Monarchy of the ancient, off-with-their-heads school. The murderous Court of Star Chamber had been abolished during Cromwell days, but this room still did service as a venue for the Privy Council to effect their plans and resolves—some dictated by primordial ceremonies and others improvised moment-by-moment. This seemed to be one of the latter. In any case, no one spoke unless Bolingbroke asked him to; and he hadn't asked.

"In the Tower of London is a place called the Mint," Bolingbroke continued, allowing his gaze to slide over Newton's face. Newton did not glance away—a detail, but a noteworthy one. Roger Comstock, or any other worldly man, would have advised Sir Isaac to lower his gaze, as this was thought to have a calming effect on mad dogs and Lords of the Council alike. But Newton spent most of his time in other worlds. Those aspects of *this* world considered most important by men like Ravenscar and Bolingbroke, Sir Isaac was most apt to find trivial and annoying.

Bolingbroke did not know Isaac Newton. Newton was a Puritan and a Whig, Bolingbroke a man of no fixed principles, but with the brainstem reflexes of a Jacobite Tory. Bolingbroke was one of those *hommes d'affaires* who had sought and obtained entry to the Royal Society because it was the done thing. Out of its recondite deliberations, certain Whigs such as Pepys and Ravenscar had summoned forth magic: Banks, Annuities, Lotteries, National Debt, and other eldritch practices that had conjured latent money and power from out of nowhere. One couldn't blame a man like Bolingbroke for thinking that the Royal Society was, therefore, all about power and money. Newton's abandonment of Cambridge for the Mint only confirmed as much. If Bolingbroke had known of Newton's true reason for being at the Mint—if full understanding of Newton could have been inserted, whole, into the mind of Bolingbroke—it would have been necessary to carry Her Majesty's Secretary of State out of the room on a door, and give him tincture of opium for days. As it happened, he assumed that Newton had taken the job because the highest thing a man could aspire to was to be a time-serving hack with a sinecure, a pompous title, and as few responsibilities as possible.

And now Newton was staring him directly in the eye. Only a few men in all of Christendom had the kidney for a staredown with Bolingbroke, and until this moment, Bolingbroke had thought he knew who all of them were. For this was his first encounter of any significance with Newton, and his first hint that Newton was at the Mint for reasons that were not obvious.

"How stand matters in the Realm of the Coin, Sir Isaac?" Bolingbroke inquired, manipulating his snuff-box—which gave him a pretext to break contact with Newton's blood-freezing glare.

"Her Majesty's coinage has never been more sound, my lord—" Newton began, then stopped as Ravenscar put a hand on the small of his back. Bolingbroke had spun away as if to hide from Sir Isaac, while exhibiting to a rank of his supporters an expression of surprise and mirth that had come over his face. For as any well-brought-up person ought to discern, *Realm of the Coin* was a play on words, a mere witticism, tossed out as a sort of ice-breaker, to establish a feeling of welcome and camaraderie, while giving Newton an opening to respond with a *bon mot* of his own. Newton had missed this, which showed lack of breeding, and taken it as a literal request for information, which showed he was oddly nervous, keyed-up, trigger-happy. Odd, that! Why so defensive? Bolingbroke took snuff and composed himself, then turned back around to face Newton—but not before all of these things had been communicated to the men standing behind him, and registered on their faces, visible to everyone else in Star Chamber. All were mortified on Sir Isaac's behalf, except for Sir Isaac, who clearly just wanted to be asked questions so that he could answer them and get away from these people.

"Of course, Sir Isaac—more on that anon. I welcome you, and only wish that more Lords of the Council had not seen fit to attend you." This as an aside between two players on a stage. Then, a straightening and clearing of the windpipe, and a soliloquy: "Her Majesty's coins come out of the Mint. Her Majesty's name and her noble visage are impressed upon every one of those coins. Coinage, therefore, has ever been a State, as well as a Treasury matter. Much as Charing Cross, over yonder, is neither the Strand nor Whitehall, but rather the crux and joint of the two, so coinage is a sort of con-fusion of State and Treasury. The Secretary of State has some interest in it," Bolingbroke continued, meaning himself. "This marks the beginning, though 'tis far from being the end, of the *public* phase of the Secretary of State's investigation. I have been pursuing it *quietly* for some weeks now, and had not intended to make it known so prematurely; but when I learned that Sir Isaac Newton, who has the honor to be Master of the Mint, was coming to Westminster to testify on some trifling matter ginned up by the fevered minds of the Faction, I resolved to invite him to this Chamber that his visit would not be a perfect waste of his time."

Bolingbroke's coiling movements about the room had now led him into a position whence he could gaze directly into Newton's face across some yards of rather good wool carpet. "Sir Isaac," he said, "my investigation has already established that you were absent from the Tower on the day of the assault. But no doubt your famous curiosity got the better of you when you returned and found that a small war had been conducted there while you were out. You must have looked into those events, asked questions of those who were there. What conclusions have you reached as to the *true* nature and purpose of the outrage?"

"My lord, it was an attempt—mostly successful, I am sorry to say— by a gang of Black-guards, very likely led by no less than Jack the Coiner himself, to steal the Crown Jewels," said Sir Isaac Newton. Behind him, Ravenscar was wondering if he would get away with elbowing Newton in the throat to disable his voice-box.

"Perhaps it would help to clarify your mind as to that, if I told you that my investigators have already captured some of the Black-guards in question. Oh, they attempted to flee to Dunkirk in a boat that was overhauled and searched by a brig of the Royal Navy," Bolingbroke explained, amused by Newton's naïveté, but tolerant for now. "The missing jewels were recovered. The men were kept apart and questioned separately. They have testified, to a man, that even when Jack the Coiner had gained the Inmost Ward, and held the Tower in the hollow of his hand, as it were, standing within bow-shot of the open and unguarded Jewel Tower, he did ignore the lure of those baubles, and held them of no value. Instead he made straightaway for the Mint, and went to the vault where the Pyx is kept."

"That is absurd," Newton said. "The Pyx holds but a few samples of pennies and guineas. The Crown Jewels are infinitely more valuable."

"The theft of the Crown Jewels was an improvisation, carried out by ignorant pawns who never knew the true purpose of the assault. This much is proved by the ease with which those men were captured. I say that Jack the Coiner went to the Pyx."

"And I hear you saying it, my lord; but *I* say nothing was stolen from that Vault."

"Note the careful selection of words," Bolingbroke mused aloud to a squadron of smirking Tory admirers. "Is this a sentence, or a mathematickal riddle?" Then he whirled to face a closed door, which led not to the exit but to an inner chamber. "Bring it in!" he commanded.

The door was heaved open by a page, revealing several men who had been loitering within. The biggest led them out. He was booted and spurred, and dressed very well, complete with a cape. Dangling on his breast was a silver medallion in the shape of a greyhound. Four other men, similarly got up, followed him, each holding an end of a pole. They looked almost like porters carrying a sedan chair, and this caused a *frisson* to charge through Star Chamber as everyone phant'sied that the Queen herself was being hauled out. But the burden of those poles was smaller, yet heavier, than the Queen. It was a boxy thing hidden under a velvet cape.

"You'll all know Mr. Charles White," said Bolingbroke, "Captain of the Queen's Messengers. And, as of some weeks ago, provisional commander of the Queen's Own Black Torrent Guard, in relief of the disgraced Colonel Barnes."

A murmur of diffident greeting welled up about the place and collapsed to silence as the four Queen's Messengers set their mysterious fardel down in the center of the floor, directly between Newton and Bolingbroke. Charles White, who as the proprietor of a bear-baiting ring in Rotherhithe knew a few things about how to play on the anticipation of an audience, allowed a five-count to elapse, then stepped up smartly and whipped off the cape to reveal a black chest with three padlocks suspended from its hasps.

"As my lord commanded," White said, "direct from the Mint in the Tower of London, I give you the Pyx."

"Oh, pray don't be so absurd, this is not a Trial of the Pyx!" Bolingbroke exclaimed some time later, when everyone had calmed down a bit, and stopped murmuring in one another's ears. "As every man in this Chamber ought to know, a Trial would require the presence of the Queen's Remembrancer, as well as the Lord Treasurer, who has not seen fit to be with us this day. Oh no no no. Quite absurd. This is not a Trial, but a cursory *Inspection*, of the Pyx."

"Pray, what is the, er, procedure for such an inspection, my lord? It is a thing I have never heard of," said Ravenscar. He was acting as a second for Newton, who was still unable to speak; or so Ravenscar guessed from the fact that beneath Newton's thinning white hair his scalp was red, and covered with goosebumps.

"Of course you have never heard of it, for it is extraordinary. It has never been done before. It has never been *necessary*. For until recent times, the Pyx was always looked after by guards who could be trusted. To guard it has been a duty of the Tower garrison. Several regiments have had the honor. Of late it has been entrusted to the Queen's Own Black Torrent Guards: a regiment that enjoyed flashes of distinction until my lord Marlborough quite lost his way, and quit the country. Under a Colonel Barnes it fell into degeneracy. He has been relieved of his commission. There is an old master sergeant of that Regiment, a Robert Shaftoe. This Chamber will no doubt be astonished to learn that Sergeant Shaftoe is none other than the brother or half-brother of one Jack Shaftoe, thought to be the same person as Jack the Coiner. In spite of which, this Robert Shaftoe was allowed—through a systematic dereliction of responsibility by Marlborough, extending over many years—to remain in the regiment, under the pretext that he had become estranged from Mr. Jack Shaftoe and had not seen him in many years. It is he, and others like him, who have been given charge of the Mint in general, and the Pyx in particular, since the war ended and their Regiment was brought home. After the events of April 23rd, as I have said, Colonel Barnes was relieved, and more recently Robert Shaftoe has been moved to new quarters. Oh, he still resides within the Tower, no longer in his accustomed billet. He has been given lodgings of a rather different character. There, he has had conversations with Mr. White. Thus far, these conversations have not been terribly illuminating—but I trust this will change, as Mr. White has shown himself to be a skilled and forceful seeker after the truth. Since these changes were put into effect, the Pyx has been safe from any tampering—I dare say, as safe as the Crown Jewels. But it is impossible to know what might have been done to it during the year that it lay bare to the irresponsibility, if not the outright depredations, of Colonel Barnes and Sergeant Shaftoe. And that is why we are gathered in this Chamber today for an event without precedent: an Inspection of the Pyx."

"AND SO, TO SUM UP, I must confess that I too was absent during the onslaught of these Black-guards—a shame that I shall never out-live," said Charles White, who had just related, to an astonished Chamber, an improbable yarn about a wild goose chase down the River Thames: a venture that had been undertaken on the strength of assurances from Colonel Barnes and Sir Isaac Newton that it would culminate in the capture of Jack the Coiner, but that in fact had ended with a fire in a broken-down, abandoned coastal watch-tower, and a lot of confused and misled dragoons storming around in benighted mud-flats.

A boat or two had been sighted, and pursued, until darkness had fallen. Sir Isaac had been rescued from a drifting wreck where he and another aged Whig Natural Philosopher had been found down in the bilge playing with a jack-in-the-box.

"Your sense of duty is an example to us all, Mr. White," Bolingbroke protested, in a voice soaked with amusement over the concluding detail of the jack-in-the-box. "If you were misled, 'twas only because the Byzantine intrigues that were afoot on that day, are so alien to the mentality of an honest Englishman. Tell me, when you returned to the Tower, and found that indescribable scene, were you concerned as to the Crown Jewels?"

"Naturally, my lord, and hied thither straightaway."

"Does anyone really *hie* nowadays?" asked Roger.

Perfect was the silence at his levity.

Charles White cleared his throat and continued. "Finding several of the jewels missing, I supposed, at first, that this explained all."

"In what way, Mr White?" Bolingbroke inquired, now in a sort of friendly cross-examination mode.

"Good my lord, I reasoned that the Black-guards had been after the Crown Jewels, and that all of the day's happenings in the Tower had been parts of their plan to steal them."

"But you are using the past tense, Mr. White. Your opinions on the matter have undergone some change?"

"It was not until some weeks after, when some of the Black-guards were caught, and made to tell what they knew, that I began to perceive faults in that hypothesis." He pronounced it wrong.

"But it seemed a perfectly reasonable *hypothesis*, didn't it? No one would have found fault with it, had the prisoners not given us the information that Jack the Coiner evinced no desire to see the Crown Jewels."

"It did indeed seem reasonable, my lord, or so I tried to tell myself for quite some little while; but viewed with a more critical eye, it does not hold up."

"Why does it not, Mr. White?"

"The journey downriver, which I have just related, was, as my lord will have plainly seen, a diversion, meant to remove me and the first company of Guards from the Tower."

"So it would seem."

"It must therefore have been arranged, with some cunning and forethought, by some who were secretly confederated with Jack, and who would profit by the success of Jack's undertaking."

"A reasonable enough supposition," Bolingroke allowed. Then he reminded White, "We look forward to a confession to that effect from Sergeant Shaftoe."

"Consider it done my lord—but Robert Shaftoe is just a sergeant. A very senior one, true, but—"

"I do take your point, Mr. White. Perhaps Colonel Barnes ought to be questioned. He would have the authority—"

"*Would* have, my lord, but—and I have turned this over in my mind a thousand times—Colonel Barnes did never *exercise* any such authority on that day. *I* requested that he send a company on the expedition to Shive Tor, because, to hear Sir Isaac tell it, we would *need* a whole company, or more, to subdue the small army of Black-guards we would find there."

"Mr. White. Certainly you are not accusing *yourself* of complicity!"

"Even if I did, my lord, 'twould never stand; for the record now shows that the true butt at which Jack the Coiner aimed his shaft was not the Jewels but the Mint—to be specific, the Pyx. And how would *I* benefit from some compromise of the Pyx?"

"How could *anyone* conceivably benefit from it?" Bolingbroke wanted to know.

"It is of no account," Isaac Newton broke in, "*as the Pyx was never compromised!*"

"Sir Isaac Newton! We've not heard from you yet. For the benefit of those here who have never seen the Pyx, would you be so good as to explain its workings?"

"It would be my pleasure, my lord," said Newton, stepping forward, eluding the hand of the Marquis of Ravenscar who had groped forward, out of some instinct, trying to yank him back from the abyss. "It is closed by three locks—all three must be removed for the lid to be opened. The top, as you can see, is fashioned with a hatch, devised in such a way that a small object may be deposited into the Pyx without opening the locks. But it is impossible for a hand to reach in and remove any object." Newton operated the mechanism, letting everyone get a look at a pair of swinging doors rigged just as he had claimed.

"How is the Pyx employed at the Mint?" Bolingbroke inquired, accurately feigning the sort of elevated curiosity that was good form at Royal Society meetings.

Newton responded in kind. "Of every lot of coins that is minted, some are plucked out, and deposited. I shall demonstrate, behold!" Newton opened his own coin-purse and spilled a guinea and some pennies—freshly minted, of course—onto his hand. He borrowed a sheet of foolscap from a clerk, laid it on the Pyx, arranged the coins in the center of the page, and then rolled and folded the paper around the money to make a neat little packet. "Here I have done it with paper—at the Mint we use leather. The Sinthia, as we call this little packet, is sewn shut. The worker writes on its outside a notation as to when the sample was taken, and stamps it with a seal, kept for that purpose alone. Then—" Sir Isaac slipped the Sinthia into the Pyx's hatch, and tripped the mechanism. It vanished and dropped within.

"And from time to time, as is well known to that scholar of all matters monetary, my lord Ravenscar, the Pyx is brought hither to the Star Chamber by order of the Privy Council," Bolingbroke said, "and opened, and its contents assayed by a jury of goldsmiths drawn from the most respectable citizens of the City of London."

"Indeed, my lord. Anciently it was done four times a year. Of late, less frequently."

"When was the last Trial of the Pyx, Sir Isaac?"

"Last year, my lord."

"You say, 'twas around the time that the hostilities on the Continent ceased, and the Queen's Own Black Torrent Guard returned to garrison the Tower."

"Yes, my lord."

"And so the Pyx, as of April 22nd, contained samples of all lots of coins minted during the months that the Black Torrent Guard controlled the Tower."

"Er, indeed, my lord," said Newton, wondering what that had to do with anything.

Bolingbroke was only too happy to lead him out of his confusion. "Mr. Charles White is of the view that those who were responsible for the assault on the Tower, phant'sied that they could somehow benefit *more* from compromising the Pyx, than from stealing the Crown Jewels! How could such a thing possibly be, Sir Isaac?"

"I do not know, my lord, and I hold it to be idle, for *the Pyx was never compromised.*"

"How do you know that, Sir Isaac? Jack the Coiner might have spent as much as an hour with it."

"As you can see, it is sealed with three padlocks, my lord. I cannot attest to the other two, for one is the property of the Warden of the Mint and the other belongs to the Lord Treasurer; but the third is mine. There is only one key to that lock, and I am never without it."

"I have heard that there are men who can open a lock, without a key—there is a word for it, they say."

"Lock-picking, my lord," someone said helpfully.

"Trust a Whig to know such a thing! Could Jack have 'picked' the locks?"

"Locks such as these, perhaps," answered Newton, passing his hand over two of them. Then he turned his attention to a third, much larger and heavier. He hefted it like Roger Comstock cupping one of his mistress's breasts. "To pick this one is almost certainly impossible. To pick it and two others in an hour is absolutely impossible."

"So a clever fellow could get the Pyx open in an hour, if he had your key, by 'picking' the other two locks. But without your key—impossible."

"Just so, my lord," said Newton. He was distracted by violent stirrings in his peripheral vision, and glanced over to see Roger Comstock now frantically waving his hands about and drawing his finger convulsively across his throat. But Newton seemed to take these gestures as an inexplicable roadside mum-show.

Bolingbroke noticed, too. "My lord Ravenscar has imbibed too much coffee again and come down with the spasms," he guessed. Then he turned his attention back to Newton. "Pray take your impregnable lock away, Sir Isaac." He turned around and gestured at a pair of fellows who were standing together in a corner, each nervously fingering an elaborate key. "The Warden of the Mint has joined us," Bolingbroke said, "and even the Lord Treasurer has deigned to send a representative bearing *his* key. We would view the contents of the Pyx."

It was three-quarters filled with a jumble of leathern packets. Newton's paper-packet had tumbled down into a corner. He bent down to retrieve it; and though Newton was oblivious to this, others in the room noted that the eyes of White and Bolingbroke tracked every movement of Newton's, as if they were expecting to catch him out in some sleight-of-hand.

"Is this what you expected to see when the lid was opened, Sir Isaac?" asked Bolingbroke.

"It appears to be in order, my lord." Newton reached into the Pyx a second time, plucked out a Sinthia, glanced at it, and dropped it back in. He plucked out another. This time, he hesitated.

"Is everything quite all right, Sir Isaac?" Bolingbroke inquired, the soul of gentlemanly concern.

Sir Isaac raised the Sinthia higher, closer to window-light, and turned it this way and that.

"Sir Isaac?" Bolingbroke repeated. The Chamber was very still. Bolingbroke flicked his eyes at the Warden of the Mint, who stepped forward and stood on tiptoe to peer over Sir Isaac's shoulder. Newton had frozen.

The Warden of the Mint's eyes widened.

Newton dropped the packet into the Pyx as if it had caught fire.

He staggered back, towards the Marquis of Ravenscar, like a blinded duellist seeking refuge among his friends.

"My lord," explained the Warden, "something's a bit queer about that last packet. The handwriting—it looked forged, somehow."

Charles White raised a knee and kicked the lid of the Pyx. It closed with a boom like a cannon-shot.

"I say that the Pyx is evidence in a criminal matter," Bolingbroke proclaimed. "Put the locks on it again, and bring out my seal. I shall set my seal on this evidence to show any further tampering. Mr. White shall return the Pyx to its customary station and use in the Tower but he shall keep it under heavy guard, twenty-four hours a day. I shall bear these tidings to the other Lords of the Council. We may safely presume that the Council will order a Trial of the Pyx forthwith."

"Good my lord," said Peer, stepping forward, "what evidence suggests that such tampering occurred? The Warden has asserted that one of the packets looked a bit queer, but this hardly constitutes proof. Sir Isaac himself has said nothing at all."

"Sir Isaac," said Bolingbroke, "what is perfectly clear to most of us, is impenetrable to this Whig. He requires evidence. No man is more eligible to testify in such a matter than you. Is it your testimony, before this assembly, that all of the coins in this Pyx were minted in the Tower, under your direction, and placed therein by your hand? I remind you that every coin in the Pyx is subject to assay during a Trial, and that you are under an indenture to Her Majesty; the consequences of a failed Trial are severe."

"By ancient tradition," said Roger Comstock behind his hand, "false coiners are punished by amputation of the hand that did the deed, and castration." From anxiety he had moved on briefly to horror; but now from horror to fascination.

Newton tried to answer, but his voice did not work for a moment, and only a bleat came out. Then he swallowed, grimacing at the pain of swallowing, and got out the words: "I cannot so testify, my lord. But without a more thorough examination—"

"There shall be one anon, at a Trial of the Pyx."

"I beg my lord's pardon," said Peer, who had out of some blind herd instinct blundered out to act as scape-goat for his entire Party, "but why bother to have a Trial of the Pyx, if the Pyx has been tampered with?"

"Why, to get all false coins out of it, so that we shall know that all coins put in thereafter shall be genuine samples of the Mint's produce—*and not frauds put in as a desperate gambit to hide long-standing flaws in the coinage!*"

"The poetry of it!" Roger exclaimed, though these reflections were concealed under a hubbub, the sound of Parties and Factions mobilizing and arming. "Sir Isaac dares not assert that the Pyx is clean, for fear that Jack may have salted it with debased coins—which would be found out at the Trial, and laid to Sir Isaac. To save his hand and his balls, he must admit that it has been compromised; but in doing so, he calls his own coins into question, and names himself as a suspect in the assault on the Tower!"

"My lord," said a Tory, "it is suggested that a year's coin-samples are now simply *gone*—stolen by Jack the Coiner! If that is so, how can we gauge the present soundness of Her Majesty's coinage? Our enemies in the world shall say that the Mint has spewed out false and debased guineas for a year or more."

"It is a question of extraordinary gravity," Bolingbroke allowed, "and I say that it is a State affair, since the security of our State is founded on Trade, which is founded upon our *currency*. If it is true that the conspiracy has deprived us of our Pyx, why then we can only prove the soundness of our money by collecting samples of coins that are in circulation, and bringing them in for assay."

Ravenscar had told Newton not to pick up any handkerchiefs dropped in his way by Bolingbroke: advice that Newton, with the serene confidence of a man who had nothing to hide, had steadfastly ignored. Now was not the time for him to mend his ways. "But my lord, I protest!" he said, "there is a reason why the method you have just described is never used, and it is that a sampling of coins in circulation shall perforce include a number—an unknowable number—of counterfeits, slipped into circulation by the likes of Jack Shaftoe. 'Twere unfair and unreasonable to lay at my feet an assay of counterfeits!"

Bolingbroke seemed impressed by Newton's sheer consistency. "Sir Isaac, as a part of my investigations, I have read an Indenture with your name on it, kept under lock and key in the Cloisters of Westminster Abbey, just across the way. We can stroll over and have a look at it, if you should like to review its contents. But I can tell you that, in this solemn contract, you are sworn to pursue and prosecute coiners. Until now I have assumed that you were *tending to your duties*. Now you astonish this Chamber by *testifying to the contrary*! Tell me, Sir Isaac, if we make an assay of circulating coins, and discover that they are rife with base metal, is it because you have failed in your duty to prosecute coiners? Or is it because you have debased the coinage produced by the Mint, to enrich yourself and your Whig backers? Or did you debase the coinage *first* and *then* allow coiners to flourish in the Realm, so as to cover your traces? Sir Isaac? Sir Isaac? Oh well, he has quite lost interest."

In fact, Sir Isaac had lost consciousness, or was well on his way to it. During the last speech of Bolingbroke he had gradually softened and crumpled to the floor of Star Chamber, like a candle placed in an oven. He was breathing fast, and his extremities had gone into violent trembling, as if he were having fever-chills; but the hands pressed to his forehead felt a dry and cool brow and thumbs touched to the base of his heaving neck were drawn back in alarm at the furious drum-beat of his pulse. He was not so much sick as seized in an unstoppable paroxysm of mad, animal terror. "Get him into my coach," commanded Roger Comstock, "and take him to my house. Miss Barton is there. She knows her uncle well, and she shall tend to him better than—God forbid—any physician."

"You see?" Bolingbroke was remarking to Charles White, who was standing at his side, in the role of wide-eyed 'prentice a-gawp at the Master's skill. "It is not necessary to bite their ears off. Oh, this is nothing. I have seen others drop dead in their shoes. One needs an apoplectic for that." He seemed ready to offer up more advice in this vein, but his attention was drawn by the Marquis of Ravenscar, standing serenely on the opposite side of the Chamber as other Whigs bent their backs to the very odd job of dragging out Isaac Newton. Ravenscar held out a hand. Someone slapped a walking-stick into his palm. He hefted it. Charles White, anticipating physical violence, took half a step forward, then realized he was being absurd, and brought his hands together in front of his silver greyhound medallion, absent-mindedly rubbing at an ancient dagger-scar that went all the way through one palm. Bolingbroke merely elevated an eyebrow.

Roger Comstock raised his walking-stick until it was pointed up at the starry ceiling, and brought the butt of it to his face, then snapped it down briskly. It was a swordsman's salute: a gesture of respect, and a signal that the next thing to come would be homicidal violence. "Let's to the Kit-Cat Clubb," he said to Peer and a few other Whigs who had not yet been able to get their feet to move. "Sir Isaac has the use of my coach; but I am in a mood for a walk. God save the Queen, my lord."

"God save the Queen," said Henry St. John, Viscount Bolingbroke. "And do enjoy your walk, Roger."

Garden of Herrenhausen Palace, Hanover

JUNE 23 (CONTINENTAL)/12 (ENGLISH) 1714

"I LOVE YOU."

"I loaf you."

"I *love* you."

"I *lubb* you."

"That's not quite it."

"How can you *tell*? This 'I love you' strikes my ear like the sound of a tin sheet being wobbled. How can I say *'ich liebe dich'* with such noises?"

"To me you can say it any way you please. But you need to work on certain vowels." Johann von Hacklheber raised his head out of Caroline's lap, faltered—his ponytail had snagged in a pearl button—worked it free, sat up, and spun around on the bench so that he could get face to face with her. "Watch my lips, my tongue," he said. "I *love* you."

There the English lesson ended. Not that the pupil had failed to observe the master's lips and tongue. She had done so most attentively—but not with a mind towards improving her vowels. *"Noch einmal, bitte,"* she requested, and when he arched his sandy eyebrows and opened his mouth to pronounce the "I," she was up and on him. His lips and tongue went through the movements for "love," but Caroline felt them with her own lips and tongue, and heard not a thing.

"That was much more informative," she said, after a few more repetitions of the étude.

His ponytail was coming undone, which was largely her doing, for she had her hands to either side of his head and was tugging blond locks free from the black ribbon that bound them in back, bringing him into a state of beautiful *déshabillement*. "They say that your mother was the loveliest woman in all of Versailles."

"I thought that honor was reserved for the King's brother."

"Stop it!" She gave him the tiniest tap on the cheek-bone. "I was going to say, she gave her looks to you."

changed his mind was evanescent, for the first crunch was not followed by a second. After a rather long time she *did* hear another, but it was faint and prolonged, as if a foot were being placed very cautiously. This was followed by a "Ssh!" so distinct that she turned her head around to look.

Everyone who mattered knew that Caroline's husband had a mistress named Henrietta Braithwaite, and anyone who bothered to ask around could find out that Caroline had her Jean-Jacques (which was the pet name that she used for Johann). As a setting for trysts, intrigues, and tiptoeing about, the *Grosse Garten* almost aspired to the level of Versailles. So it was not as if Caroline had any great secret to keep here. She was not worried about eavesdroppers. Of course there were eavesdroppers. This was, rather, a point of etiquette. For such persons to be audibly shushing each other, a few yards away, was like farting at dinner. Caroline inhaled deeply and fired off a sharp sigh. *That* should fix them!

But she'd never know whether the message had struck home, for now iron wheel-rims, and the shoes of a four-horse team, could be heard above all else. This team was coming her way, and the horses were blowing as if very tired. Had they been driven all night? If so, they weren't the only exhausted horses hereabouts. The nobility of Europe were converging on Herrenhausen, using Sophie's funeral as an excuse to stage a reunion of the largest, most bizarre, violent, and incestuously cross-linked family in the world. Caroline had scarcely been able to sleep last night for all the nocturnal arrivals.

She rose from the bench. Through the tree-limbs she glimpsed a couple of tawny blurs loping down the path. "Scylla! Charybdis!" called a gruff voice, and they stopped.

Stepping away from the bench and ducking under a low-hanging bough, Caroline saw a pair of large dogs, panting and drooling. She was protected from them by the iron fence, and saw no danger in moving closer, picking her way over Teufelsbaum-limbs that undulated along the ground, unable to decide whether they were roots, branches, or vines. Along the path came the team—four matched sorrels—and behind them a black carriage, once shiny, now dusty all over. Mud-comets radiated from the wheels and lashed the polished wood. Nevertheless she could make out the arms on the door: the Negro-heads and fleurs-de-lis of the House of Arcachon quartered with the gray pinnacle of the Duchy of Qwghlm. Above that, an open window. Framed in it, a face strikingly similar to the one she'd been kissing a few minutes earlier—but without the bristles.

"Eliza!"

"Stop here, Martin."

Eliza's face was now blocked from view by a spray of leaves, but Caroline could hear the smile in her voice. Martin—evidently the driver—reined in his team. Their gait collapsed and they pocked gradually to a stop, taking the momentum of the carriage in the breeching straps slung round their backsides.

Caroline had by now advanced to the iron fence. The Teufelsbaum had been pruned back from it, leaving a clear space for the gardeners to walk the perimeter. Caroline hurried along for some yards, letting her hand count the iron verticals, in case her gown-hem should snag on a shrub and trip her.

A pair of footmen had clambered down from their perch on the back of the carriage, moving as if splints had been bound to their arms and legs. No telling how long they had been standing there, hands stiffening round the railings as they held on for dear life. Eliza lost patience with them and kicked the carriage door open. The edge of it nearly sheared off a footman's nose. He recovered in time to set down a wee portable stair and assist the Duchess of Arcachon-Qwghlm down to the path—though to be honest it was not so obvious who was assisting whom. The mastiffs Scylla and Charybdis had circled back. They had planted their eyes on Eliza, and their butts on the path, where they were sweeping out neat gravel-free quadrants with their tails.

Eliza was dressed for mourning, hard travel, or both, in a dark grim frock, with a black silk scarf over her head. She was in her mid-forties, and if she were starting to gray, it was not easy to tell, as she had been light blond to begin with. An attentive observer—and this Duchess had many—might phant'sy that the gold was now alloyed with a small proportion of silver. The skin around her eyes and the corners of her mouth gave a fair account of her age.

The number of her male admirers had not diminished over the years, but their nature had changed. When she'd been an eligible mademoiselle at Versailles she had caught the eye of the King and been pursued round the place by a horde of lust-blind fops. Now, having passed through marriage, maternity, smallpox, and widowhood, she was the kind of woman that important forty-, fifty-, and sixty-year-old men were always talking about in hushed corners of Clubbs and Salons. From time to time one of these would screw up his courage, sally forth from his redoubt, and buy her a château or something, always to retreat, defeated but not humiliated, honorably scarred, and ennobled in reputation, clustered around by other gentlemen who desperately wanted to know what had happened. To be spurned by a lady who was rumored to have bedded the Duke of Monmouth, William of Orange, and Louis XIV was to enter into a sort of communion with those figures of legend.

None of which mattered to Caroline, of course, for Eliza never spoke of it, and when the two of them were together, it was of no account to either one of them. But when they were in the company of others—as they would be for most of the day—she had to forcibly remind herself of it. To Caroline the reputation of Eliza was nothing, but to others it was all.

"I'll walk in the garden with her royal highness, Martin," Eliza called. "Drive to the stables, tend to the animals, and tend to yourself."

It was not entirely usual for ladies of Eliza's rank to be so concerned with such minutiae; but she had much concern for details, and little for class. If Martin was surprised he didn't show it. "My lady," he answered placidly.

"Our grooms and stable-hands will see to the animals—you may tell them I have said so," said Caroline. "You look after yourself, Martin."

"Your royal highness honors me," said Martin. He sounded weary—not of the long night drive, but of noble and royal ladies who phant'sied he was incapable of looking after his own horses. He allowed the team to move forward, taking up the slack in the harness. The two footmen, finally unlimbered, sprang back to their perches, and the dogs began to whine, not knowing which group to follow. Eliza silenced them with a glare and Martin summoned them with a grunt.

"Let's to the gate, and not converse through bars of iron," Caroline said, and began to walk in the same direction as the carriage was moving. Eliza walked abreast of her on the gravel side of the fence. They were separated by an arm's length, but the Princess was on a march through the forest while the Duchess strolled on a groomed path. "You couldn't possibly have come all the way from London—?"

"Antwerp."

"Oh. How is the Duke?"

"He sends his respects, and his condolences. He was a great admirer of Sophie, as you know, and much desired to attend her funeral. But the late reports from London are most troubling to him and he did not wish to put himself so far out of his countrymen's reach."

They had come to the gate. Caroline reached for the latch but Eliza was quicker; she got it open and stepped through it decisively, closing with Caroline and flinging her arms round the taller woman's neck with a kind of passion, even abandon. A very different thing from the restrained and courtly greetings that would fill the rest of this day. When she let go, which was a good long time later, her cheeks, which were devoid of any powder or rouge, were shiny with tears.

"When I was a girl of some sixteen years, I was sorry for myself, and angry at the world, because I had been separated from my mother, first by Slavery and then by common Mortality. Now, as I reckon the sum of your losses, I am ashamed that I ever so indulged myself."

There passed a moment when Caroline said nothing. This was partly because she was touched, and almost embarrassed, by this bold statement from a woman so renowned for wit and discretion. It was also partly because of a noise behind her. Martin had gotten his team to negotiate the sharp turn at the plot's acute vertex, which had not been easy, and was now rumbling along another side, not far away.

"Sometimes I think that I *am* the sum of my losses," Caroline finally said. "And if so, then every loss that I suffer enlarges me. I hope my discourse does not strike you as too grim," she added, for a little sob-shudder had run through the Duchess's body. "But this is how I make sense of my world. And if you must know, in some moments I phant'sy that I am a sort of heir to the Winter Queen—though I am not linked to her by blood—and that it is my destiny to go back to England and reclaim it for her. That is why I asked you to buy Leicester House, for she was born there."

"I did not *buy* it but *invested* in it," Eliza returned.

"Then I hope your investment will turn out to have been a prudent one."

"Why shouldn't it?"

"Your tidings from Antwerp—and other news that has reached me of late—make me doubt whether I shall ever *see* Britain, much less *rule* it."

"You shall, my dear. What concerns Marlborough is not the fate of the Realm but of a single Regiment, near to his heart, lately fallen under the sway of Jacobites. He is fretting about certain of his officers and sergeants, trying to make out what has become of them."

"What has happened to one Regiment might happen later to the whole Realm," Caroline said. Then she looked away, distracted by an eruption of barking on the far side of the vast Gordian knot of the Teufelsbaum. Martin was chastising the dogs in Dutch. They had probably lit out after one of the garden's regiment of squirrels.

When she turned back, she found that Eliza had been appraising her. The Duchess seemed to approve of what she had seen. "I am most pleased that my son has found you," she said.

"So am I," Caroline confessed. "Tell me truly, now—did you enter the garden in search of *me*, or of *him*?"

"I knew that the two of you would be together. It would appear that I just missed him," Eliza said, and reached out to pluck a long blond hair from a pearl button at Caroline's midsection.

"He hoped you'd come—and knew you'd do so without warning. He has gone for a walk with an Englishman."

Eliza got a wary look and stepped forward, pressing Caroline aside with a firm hand. Her other hand strayed to the waistband of her frock. A man came crashing through the Teufelsbaum, headed directly for them. Meanwhile Scylla and Charybdis were pelting hell-for-leather around the fence, trying to find a way in.

The man emerged into plain view and stopped. The first thing they noticed about him was that he was brandishing a dagger; the second, that he was one of Eliza's footmen. His wig had been stripped off as he'd charged through the reaching arms of the Teufelsbaum, but he was recognizable by his livery. Less so by his face, which was red, and distorted by fear and rage—battle-lust, Caroline thought.

"Jan? What is it?" Eliza demanded.

Jan ignored the question. He scanned the path until he was certain that Scylla and Charybdis had found it, and were circling around to guard the rear. Then he spun round, turning his back on Eliza and Caroline, searching the woods.

Something slammed into Caroline's shoulder. It was Eliza's body. Caroline tried to plant the opposing foot wide, to absorb the blow, but Eliza had expected this, and had already swung a leg around and hooked Caroline's ankle. Both of them fell down. Caroline hit the ground first. Eliza, rather than smashing full-length into Caroline's body, took most of the impact on her hands and knees, and wound up straddling the fallen princess, looking about herself alertly.

The second footman had circled around the other way, and now joined Scylla and Charybdis at the gate. He too had a dagger out. But Eliza stayed over Caroline, refusing to let her up. Presently the carriage roared and rattled back up the path, drawn by four insanely irritated horses who were controlled only with difficulty by poor Martin.

"What happened?" demanded Eliza, as Martin was reining them in.

Martin was in no great hurry to respond either. He stood up and scanned the woods on all sides. He had a pistol out, and was careful to keep its barrel perfectly aligned with his gaze, so that shooting could follow seeing in an instant.

"Opposite, on the far side of this weird tree, the dogs scented men who had bad intentions," he finally said, in a mild voice.

Ever the Natural Philosopher, even when pinned to the ground under a Duchess, Caroline inquired, "How do you know it wasn't a well-intentioned squirrel?"

"The dogs told me as much by their emotions," Martin returned, plainly irritated to have been questioned on such a matter. "They followed the scent from the iron fence—which these men must have vaulted—to a neighboring part of the garden, yonder, before I called them back, and told them to go and find my lady. Then, as I was rounding the corner, over there, trying to get back to you, I glanced over and saw two men running as fast as they could down the path."

"Towards us?"

"Away from you, my lady."

"Bows? Muskets?"

"They had neither, my lady."

This was the signal for Eliza to get up at last. She extended a hand and did the work of hauling Caroline to her feet, as the footmen were still prowling about with daggers drawn.

"That was an unusual procedure," Caroline remarked.

"It is not so unusual in Constantinople."

"Where did you hire your staff?" Caroline wondered.

"The deck of a privateer in Dunquerque. I once had a friend in the business, one Jean Bart, who doted on me, and wanted to see that I was well looked after." Eliza turned her attentions back to Martin. "Could you recognize those two men if you saw them again?"

"My lady, they had covered themselves in long dark hooded robes, such as friars wear, and the hoods were drawn up over their heads. I wager we might find those robes discarded on the ground within a musket-shot of where we now stand—"

"And the assassins will have blended in among the funeral-guests before we get back to the Palace," Eliza concluded.

"More than likely," Caroline agreed; then: "I beg your pardon, did you say *assassins*!?"

"THE LETTER BY which Princess Caroline summoned me was sealed in the presence of Enoch Root, and put into his hand before the wax had cooled. He traversed the west road from here to Amsterdam in no particular haste—but without let or delay. A day after, he was in Scheveningen, and three days after that, in London. A wait of one week sufficed to get him aboard a New York–bound ship. The voyage was not particularly lengthy. After no more than a night's rest on the island of Manhattan he proceeded on horseback to Boston. He delivered the message into my hand on the day he arrived. It had never left his person since the moment it was sealed in the Leine Schloß." The strange old Englishman nodded down the leafy prospect of the Herrenhäuser Allee toward the smoky bulk of Hanover's fortifications.

The young baron, noting that he had fallen a pace behind, hurried along to draw abreast. "Did you and Enoch—I call him Enoch, for he is an old friend of my family—"

"I thought he was supposed to be a *member* of your family, long ago, when he affected a different name."

"That is another conversation for another day," said the Baron, in good English. "I say, did you and Enoch discuss the matter aloud, in the presence of others, in Boston?"

"In a tavern. But we were discreet. I did not mention the author of the letter even to my own *wife*. I told her only that someone of great importance had asked for me."

"What of the letter itself?"

"That's a different matter. Mr. Root did allow some persons to see the Seal. So it could be inferred that I had been summoned from Hanover."

"Pray continue."

"Well, 'tis very simple. I was aboard *Minerva* that very night. We were held back by contrary winds for a month. Then one day a whole bloody pirate-fleet descended upon us. My god, what a thing it was. In all my days I have never lived through such a—"

Johann von Hacklheber, sensing that his Narrator was about to wax discursive, interrupted: "Pirates are said to be as common along the New England coast as fleas on a dog."

"Yes, we had some of that type, too," said Daniel Waterhouse, strangely enthusiastic. "Caitiffs in row-boats. But we shook those off easily. I am referring to a literal fleet of formidable pirate-ships, under a disaffected British sea-captain named Edward Teach—"

"Blackbeard!" said Johann, before he could stop himself.

"You have heard of him."

"He has already been the subject of picaroon-romances, which are sold by the barrel-load at the book-fair in Leipzig. Not that I would ever read such a thing," Johann said, and then waited tensely, fearing that this Daniel Waterhouse was the sort who would miss the jest, and assume he was being a snotty little baron. But the old man caught it, and batted it back: "In your *researches*, have you learnt that this Blackbeard is aligned with Jacobite interests?"

"I know that his flagship is christened *Queen Anne's Revenge*, and I collected, from this, that he had some axe to grind."

"He assaulted the ship I was on—*Minerva*—and sacrificed one and possibly two ships of his fleet to get at me."

"To get at *Minerva,* you mean, or—"

"To get at *me,* I say. He asked for me *by name.* And any other sea-captain would have given me up; but Otto van Hoek would not give a pirate a wormy biscuit, much less a passenger."

"Now, if I may play devil's advocate," Johann said, "for Enoch to come into this *Bostown,* which you describe as a sort of backwoods encampment, waving a document with a Hanoverian seal, must have drawn attention. Your departure must have been the talk of the town."

"No doubt they are talking about it *still.*"

"In every port are men of low character who pass along such intelligence to criminals, pirates, and the like. You said that a whole month elapsed while you were becalmed—"

"I should rather call it, 'bestormed,' but yes."

"That is more than enough time for word to have spread to every pirate-cove in New England. This Teach must have heard the news, and surmised that you were a man of importance, who might be held for ransom."

"This is what I was telling myself all the way across the Atlantic, to calm my nerves," Daniel said. "I even trained myself to overlook the chief fault in that hypothesis, which is that, outside of Barbary, pirates do not, as a rule, hold hostages for ransom, and especially not old men who are likely to drop dead at a moment's notice. But when I reached London, efforts were made to blast me, or someone close to me, to pieces. And during the months since, I have had intelligence from two distinct sources, one high, one low, that there is, here in Hanover, a spy who passes information to the Jacobites in London."

"I should like to know more concerning that," said Johann, who had been trying a moment ago to soothe the old Englishman's ridiculous fears, and now found himself in need of some soothing.

"An old acquaintance of mine—"

"Acquaintance, but not friend?"

"We are such old friends that we refuse to speak to each other for decades at a time. An Infernal Device, packed with gunpowder, exploded. It might have been meant for me, for him, or for both of us. He has begun to investigate the matter using his own resources—and you may be assured that his resources vastly exceed mine in almost every respect. He has heard that highly placed Jacobites—"

"Bolingbroke?"

"—highly placed Jacobites are receiving information from a source close to the Electoral Crown—someone who, to judge from the timeliness and accuracy of his despatches, comes and goes freely in the Leine Schloß and in Herrenhausen Palace."

"You said that you had a *low* as well as a high source?"

"I know a man with many connections among London's Flash: coiners, Black-guards, *et cetera*—the same element from which Black-beard recruits his seamen and what I shall politely call his 'long-shoremen.'"

"You trust such a man?"

"Unaccountably, irrationally, inadvisably, I do. I am his father confessor. He is my disciple and bodyguard. It is another conversation for another day—"

"Touché."

"This fellow has made inquiries. He has found evidence that the order to hunt me down was despatched to Ed Teach *from London.*"

"I did not think pirates took orders from London."

"Oh, on the contrary, it is an ancient, celebrated practice."

"So by combining these *data* you have settled upon a hypothesis that some spy *here* became aware of the letter that her royal highness sent to you via Enoch Root; that this spy sent word to an important Jacobite in London; who then sent a despatch to Ed Teach off the coast of Massachusetts, using some London Black-guard as his Mercury."

"That is my hypothesis, admirably stated."

"It is a good one. I have one question only."

"Yes?"

"Why are we walking down the Herrenhäuser Allee in the wee hours of the morning?"

"What, the sun's been up for hours!"

"My question still stands."

"Do you know why I came to Hanover?"

"Certainly not for the funeral, as Sophie was alive when you got here. If memory serves, you were a part of the delegation that brought Sophie the letter that is said to have killed her."

"I haven't heard anyone say that!"

"Its contents are said to have been so vexatious as to have struck the Electress dead on the spot."

"The Viscount Bolingbroke is known to have a genius for such word-play," Daniel mused, "and he probably penned it. But it is neither here nor there. Yes, I was included in the delegation, as a token Whig. No doubt you have already met my Tory counterparts."

"I have endured that honor. Again, why are we walking down the Herrenhäuser Allee at this time?"

"It occurred to me, on the journey hither from London, that if the Jacobites *did* have a spy in Hanover, why then my Tory companions would make every effort to arrange a tryst with him, or her. So I have been alert since we arrived—while spreading the rumor, and fostering the illusion, that I was senile, and deaf to boot. Yester evening, at dinner, I heard two of the Tories asking questions of a minor Hanoverian noble: what is that park that extends from the Herrenhäuser Allee north and west to the banks of the Leine? Is it solid ground, or marsh? Are there any notable landmarks, such as great trees or—"

"There is a noble oak-tree just ahead and to the right," Johann remarked.

"I know there is, for that's just what this Hanoverian said."

"So you guessed that they were arranging a spy-tryst, and needed to choose a place. But how did you settle upon such a horrid time of day?"

"The entire delegation shall attend the funeral. Immediately after, we depart for London. This was the only possible time."

"I hope you are right."

"I know I am."

"*How* do you know it?"

"I left word with the servants that I wanted to be awakened at the same time as the other Englishmen. A servant woke me up at dawn."

With that Daniel Waterhouse cut sharply in front of Johann von Hacklheber, forcing the younger man to shorten his stride. Daniel stepped off the central road of the Allee and passed between two of the lime trees that screened it from the narrower paths to either side. Johann followed him; and as he did, he glanced down the length of the road and saw a lone man on horseback approaching from the direction of Hanover.

Daniel had already hiked off into the adjoining park and found a winding lead between shrubs and trees. Johann followed him for a minute or so, until his peripheral vision was darkened by the crown of an enormous oak. In the distance he could hear voices conversing, not in German. It struck his ear rather like a sheet of tin being wobbled.

He nearly tripped over Daniel, who had squatted down behind a bush. Johann followed his example, and then his gaze. Gathered a stone's throw away beneath the spreading limbs of the oak, and looking for all the world like artists' models posing for a pastoral scene, were three of the English Tories who had come with Daniel from London.

"Sir, my admiration for your work is mingled with wonder that a man of your age and dignity is out doing things like this."

Daniel turned to look him in the eye; and his creased face was grave and calm in the morning light. He looked nothing like the daft codger who had come to dinner yesterday evening and embarrassed the other English by dribbling wine down his shirt-front.

"Listen to me. I did not wish to be summoned by your Princess. Summoned, I did not wish to come. But having been summoned, and having come, I mean to give a good account of myself. That's how I was taught by my father, and the men of his age who slew Kings and swept away not merely Governments but whole Systems of Thought, like Khans of the Mind. I would have my son in Boston know of my doings, and be proud of them, and carry my ways forward to another generation on another continent. Any opponent who does not know this about me, stands at a grave disadvantage; a disadvantage I am not above profiting from."

It was then that the hoof-beats out on the road turned into soft thuds as the lone rider from Hanover drove his mount off the beaten track and into the park. He was headed directly for the oak. At a glance they could see he was richly attired, hence, probably had begun his ride in the Leine Schloß. On a second look Johann recognized him. He crouched down lower and spoke into Daniel's ear: "That is the Englishman—supposedly a staunch Whig—Harold Braithwaite."

"It seems so obvious in retrospect," Johann lamented, a quarter of an hour later, after they had stolen back through the park to the Allee, and begun walking back toward Herrenhausen Palace.

"Great discoveries always do," Daniel said, and shrugged. "Ask me some day how I feel about the Inverse Square Law."

"He and his wife came here, what, five years ago, just as things began to go awry for the Whig Juncto. Oxford and Bolingbroke were plotting the Tory resurgence, getting the Queen's ear—as I recall, there had been a run on the Bank of England, occasioned by rumors of a Jacobite uprising in Scotland."

"Is that what Braithwaite said when he showed up here penniless? That he'd been ruined in the bank run?"

"He mentioned that the Mobb had rioted against the Bank."

"That it did. But this has little to do with Braithwaite. He is the sort of Englishman who is exported with great enthusiasm by his countrymen."

"There *were* rumors—"

"Just enough, I am certain, to make him out as a saucy picaroon, and get him invited to dinner."

"Indeed."

"The true story is depressingly familiar. He spent his inheritance gambling. Then he became a highwayman—not a very good one, for on his first outing he scuffled with one of his victims, and gashed him with a cutlass. The wound suppurated, the victim died, the victim's family—Tories, who had money—posted a reward so high that every thief-taker in London cleared his calendar. Braithwaite fled the Isle, perhaps the only prudent thing he has ever done."

"He painted himself as an arch-Whig."

"In that there was some truth, for his oppressors were Tories. But he has no principles whatever."

"That much is now proved. But why would such a man act as a spy for the Tory Lords?"

"His legal situation is awkward. This means he might benefit enormously from some adroit manipulation of certain affairs in London. He must make his peace with whatever Faction has the power to assist him; behold, the Whigs are out, and the Tories are in."

"What did you think of the letter?" Johann asked; a *non sequitur* that prompted Daniel to twitch his head around. They had come so close to the end of the path that they could smell the green fruit in the orangerie, and hear the stables and kitchens awakening: sharp crisp sounds hushed and muffled by the distant teeming of the great fountain.

"What do you mean, *mein Herr*?" Daniel asked, slipping unconsciously into etiquette now that they were in earshot of a palace. For they had moved off the Allee and were passing between stables toward the parterres at the garden's northern end, where a few early-rising nobles were already out stretching their legs.

Johann continued, "I mean, how was it written—the letter you received from Caroline? Was it in French?"

"No, English."

"Good English?"

"Oh yes, very proper. I see where you are going now."

"If it was in proper English, then her English tutor must have helped her write it. And that is Mrs. Braithwaite."

"It shall be most awkward," Daniel pointed out, "if the mistress of the Prince of Wales proves to be a spy for men who are dead set against his family acquiring the Crown."

"I know the woman. She is *immoral* but not *malicious*, if you know what I mean. After she helped Caroline write that letter, she probably mentioned it, innocently, to her husband, who, as we have seen, is the true spy."

"Difficult to dispose of him, without a scandal in the household—" Daniel observed.

"Oh, not really," Johann murmured.

Now that they had entered the garden, his notice had been drawn by a coach and four emerging from the hill of mist that shrouded the environs of the great fountain. As its outlines became more distinct, he remarked, "That looks like my mother's carriage," and then, "but the lady looking out the window, there, is not my mother but Princess Caroline. Odd for them to ride, when they could walk. I shall go and bid them good morning."

"And I shall excuse myself," said Daniel Waterhouse, "as there is no plausible excuse for me to be seen in such company."

Princess Caroline's Bedchamber, Herrenhausen Palace
LATER THAT MORNING

"MRS. BRAITHWAITE, I SHALL depend on you to have the ivory thing near to hand at all times," said Princess Caroline.

"I know just where it is, my lady." Henrietta Braithwaite rose from the stool where she had been fussing with the Princess's wig, twirled herself about in beautiful and attention-getting style, and crossed the room to where a selection of implements was arranged on a tabletop. These could have been mistaken for the trade-tools of a cook, physician, or torturer, save for the fact that the surface on which they rested was a slab of polished pink marble, topping a white-and-gilt dressing-table-cum-sculpture done up in the new, hyper-Barock style named Rokoko. It was adorned, for example, with several cherubs, bows drawn, eyes a-squint as they drew beads on unseen targets, butt-cheeks polished to a luster with jeweler's rouge. It had, in other words, all the earmarks of a gift that had been sent to the Princess by someone with a lot of money who did not know her very well. On it were diverse mortars and pestles for compounding makeups; trowels, spatulas, and brushes for inflicting it; and certain objects whose purposes were not so obvious. Henrietta picked up a long-handled implement whose business end consisted of a gently curved tongue of polished ivory, stained pink around the edges from use. "See to it that it has not become stiff, as sometimes happens when these things get old," Caroline commanded, "and inspect it for any rough edges—last time, I got an ugly welt."

"Yes, my lady," said Mrs. Braithwaite. With a curtsey, she turned her back on the Princess. Three other ladies-in-waiting were engineering her clothes, hair, and jewelry, some of which were already mounted on Caroline, others on wooden effigies. The Duchess of Arcachon-Qwghlm sat across from her, keeping her company. She was already dressed, albeit more simply. For anyone below the rank of Princess, dressing for mourning could be a simple undertaking. Eliza's yellow hair was screened behind a *fontange* of stiff black lace and the rest of her was in black silk. It was expensive and well executed as such costumes went, but still deserved the name traditionally given to such garments: *weeds.*

"My son has reprimanded me," announced the Duchess.

Caroline gasped and put a hand to the base of her throat in a gesture of mock outrage, as she understood that Eliza was being facetious. Henrietta Braithwaite, who knew the Duchess only by gossip, had to turn around and look to discern as much. Then, realizing she had been obvious, Henrietta turned back to the work at hand: running her fingertips over the ivory tool, inspecting for rough places.

"And why would such a well-brought-up young man speak to his mother so?" Caroline demanded.

The Duchess leaned closer, and spoke a bit more softly. All of the ladies in the room suddenly found ways to do whatever they were doing in nearly perfect silence. On the pretext of needing better light, Henrietta Braithwaite turned towards a window, bringing one ear to bear upon the target.

"I am sorry!" the Duchess said. "Until he told me, I had no idea that I had stupidly interrupted something! I thought I had found you alone in the garden."

"You did find me alone—but only because, when he heard a carriage approaching, he took flight, not knowing it was only you."

"Isn't that just like a mother! Interrupting her son at such a moment! You should have shooed me away!"

"Oh, no, it is perfectly all right!" the Princess assured her. "We were never truly alone anyway, for I thought I could hear one or two people skulking about."

"Spies!?"

"Oh, no, Eliza, this is not some Byzantine, spy-infested court such as Versailles. Doubtless they were some guests, here for the funeral, who simply forgot their manners."

"Those must be the ones my dogs barked at. Naughty dogs!"

"It is nothing. This evening, at dusk, Sophie shall be at rest across the way. The English delegation, and most of the noble and royal visitors, will have departed. Then he and I shall meet where we met this morning, and resume where we left off."

"I thought my son seemed . . . *frustrated.*"

"It is good for men to be frustrated," Caroline announced, "that is when they behave in the manner that is most pleasing to us, with beautiful displays of daring and gallantry."

The Duchess considered this for a long time before answering, "There is truth in that, your royal highness. But some day when we have more time I might tell you a tale of one whose frustration became perhaps too enormous."

"What did he do then?"

"Behaved in a manner that was perhaps a bit *over*-daring, and *too* gallant, and kept it up for rather too long."

"All for *you,* Eliza?"

Again this had to be considered. Eliza, who had shown no reluctance to discuss Caroline's affairs of the heart in front of an audience, was suddenly reticent. "At the beginning, perhaps it *was* all for me. As it went on and on—it is difficult to say. He became rich, and powerful after a fashion. Perhaps he then began to act out of a desire for worldly increase."

"So out of love for you, he did deeds of phantastickal gallantry and daring over many years—*then* went on to become rich and powerful? Why haven't you married him yet?"

"It is complicated. Some day you will understand."

"I see that my words have struck deeply into your heart, Eliza, for all of a sudden you are patronizing me." Caroline said this cheerfully enough.

"Please forgive me, your royal highness."

They were into it now.

"I do know *something* of complications—not a *hundredth* of what *you* do—and I know that there is always a way to surmount them. Do you love him?"

"The man I spoke of?"

"Is there any other man under discussion?"

"I believe that I *did* love him once, when he had *nothing.*"

"Nothing except you?"

"Me, a sword, and a horse. It was later, when he began to conceive absurd schemes for getting things, that we fell out."

"Why should he concern himself with *getting* when he had *you?*"

"That is what I tried to tell him. It hurt my feelings, in a way!"

"If half the stories are true, you could have made more than enough to support yourself and him as well—ah, there's the rub—it was masculine pride, wasn't it?"

"That, and a perverse desire to better himself—to prove he was worthy of me, by becoming more like me. What he did not understand—and what I could not tell him—was that I loved him precisely because he was *unlike* me."

"Why don't you tell him now? Is he coming to the funeral?"

"Oh, no no no! You don't understand, highness, I do not speak of *recent* events. This happened thirty years ago. I've not seen him since. And be assured he is *not* attending the funeral!"

"*Thirty years.*"

"Yes."

"*Thirty years.*"

" . . . . "

"THIRTY YEARS! Longer than I have been alive. The whole time I have known you, this has been going on!"

"I should not say anything was 'going on.' It is an episode of my girlhood, forgotten."

"Yes, I can see how well you have forgotten it."

" . . . . "

"Where is this man? England?"

"Two people can be a world apart, even when both are in the same city—"

"He's in *London*!? And you have done *nothing*!?"

"Your royal highness—"

"Well, this is another good reason I must go there and become Princess of Wales, or Queen as the case may be, so that I can wield my monarchical powers to patch up your love life."

"I *beg* you not to—" said the Duchess, looking thoroughly rattled for the first time. Then she stopped, for there had been an interruption.

"The rite is about to begin, your royal highness," announced Henrietta Braithwaite, gazing out a window over a crowd in black wool and black silk, funneling itself toward the entrance of the family chapel. She turned to face the Princess, then cast her eyes down in submission, and held up the ivory tool. "This is smooth," she added. "Be assured that no matter how many times we are forced to use it, your royal highness may go out this evening perfectly unmarked."

"Henrietta," said the Princess, "my life would not be the same without you." An ambiguous statement—but Mrs. Braithwaite chose the most flattering interpretation, and responded with a curtsey and even a blush.

"I HAVE A PROBLEM, MADAME," said the dark lean figure who had marred Eliza's peripheral vision for the last quarter-hour, "and you have an opportunity."

"Ugh, not *another* one!" Eliza said, and turned finally to confront this fellow, who had been following her around like a doppelgänger despite her efforts to shake him off in the crowd of mourners.

They were outside the Palace of Herrenhausen, among the parterres of the northern end of the garden. Inside the palace was a private chapel, not nearly large enough to contain all of the mourners. Sophie's funeral service had begun an hour ago. Caroline and other members of the family were within; the others were scattered like a flock of black doves across the white gravel of the paths.

In the corner of her eye Eliza had noticed that this troublesome man was dressed in black, and that his wig was white; but the same was true of every man here. Now, looking him squarely in the face for the first time, she saw that the white mane, though it was certainly fake, was no affectation. He was quite old.

"Even on the brightest days I have no desire to be pestered by men with *opportunities*. On a day like *this*—"

"It has to do with our absent friend."

Eliza was almost certain this meant Leibniz. He had not arrived yet. The remarks that several courtiers had made concerning his absence were like wisps of smoke concealing an underlying fire of gossip. Who could *this* fellow be, then? An old Englishman who knew her, and was a friend of the Doctor—

"Dr. Waterhouse."

He lowered his eyelids and bowed.

"It has been—?"

"To judge from appearances, a hundred years for me, and half an hour for you. If you prefer to go by calendars, the answer is twenty-five years or so."

"Why have you not come to call on me at Leicester House?"

"Before I *received* your summons, I *accepted* one from another Lady," Daniel said, glancing toward the Chapel entrance, "and it has kept me busy. I do hope you will forgive my rudeness."

"*Which* rudeness? Not calling on me? Or pursuing me with an opportunity?"

"If you are discomposed by it, consider that I am acting as a proxy for the Doctor himself."

"When I first met the Doctor he was at work on a scheme: a wind-mill to pump water from the mines of the Harz," Eliza recalled fondly. "He hoped they would then produce enough silver to finance his world-library-cum-logic-mill."

"Odd that you should say so. When *I* first met him, which was at least ten years before *you* did, he was working on the mill itself. Then he got distracted by the calculus."

"What I am trying to say to you, in a gentle way, sir, is that—"

"The Doctor's schemes are mad? Yes, I had already taken your meaning."

"As much as I love the Doctor and his philosophy, and as much as *you* do—"

"Stipulated," said the old man, and smiled warmly, pressing his lips together to hide whatever dental wreckage might be underneath.

"If he cannot make his project succeed with the resources of the Tsar at his back, what use am I?"

"It is of this that I wish to speak to you," Daniel began. But the doors to the family chapel now swung open. Sophie's coffin was borne out by a lot of Kings and Electors and Dukes.

They set it on a gun carriage, drawn by a single black horse. The rest of the family came out of the chapel. The coffin and carriage set out, followed by all of the mourners who were fit enough to accompany Sophie on her last walk. A procession took shape, moving southwards down the central axis of the garden towards the great fountain. Daniel strolled along at the rear of the column. Presently Eliza found him.

Daniel said, "You have probably guessed that Leibniz's absence has to do with the work that he is doing for the Tsar. I believe that the Doctor is in St. Petersburg now."

"Then no further explanation for his absence is wanted," Eliza said. "For news to reach him there, and for him to make the journey back, when there's a war on between the Russians and the Swedes—"

"Impossible," Daniel agreed. "And you have not even addressed the question of whether he would be *allowed* to leave."

A pause, a few steps down the gravel path, before Eliza answered, in a different voice altogether: "Why shouldn't he be allowed to leave?"

"The Tsar is not renowned for his patience. He wants to see something that actually works."

"Then our friend may be in grave difficulties indeed."

"Not so very grave. I have been attending to it."

"In London?"

"Yes. The Marquis of Ravenscar has supplied funding to erect a Court of Technologickal Arts in Clerkenwell."

"Why?" Eliza asked sharply, thus proving that she knew something of the Marquis.

"Longitude. He hopes that some invention for discovering the Longitude shall be devised by the men who toil in this Court."

"And they are—?"

"The most ingenious horologists, organ-makers, goldsmiths, mechanicks, and makers of theatrickal Machinery in all of Christendom."

The procession had reached the plaza surrounding the great fountain, which would probably be described in any number of diaries this evening as howling with grief, and filling the heavens with its tears. They made a slow orbit around it, reversing their direction, and then began to trudge back toward the Palace. Eliza's black *fontange* trapped some fountain-mist and began to wilt.

"If Leibniz is trapped between Peter the Great at one end, and Roger Comstock at the other, I fear he is beyond your help, or mine," Eliza said.

"It is not so dire. What is wanted is not *capital* but *financing*."

"Something in the nature of a bridge loan?"

"Possibly. Or, perhaps, an independent investment in an allied enterprise."

"I am waiting," said Eliza with the diction of one who is biting on a musket-ball waiting for the barber to saw her leg off.

"Your expertise with commodities is celebrated."

"I beg your pardon?"

"You know of Bridewell—where whores are sent to pound hemp and pick oakum."

"Yes?"

"To build the Logic Mill we shall need a large, inexpensive force of workers to carry out certain operations of a repetitive nature. We have made discreet inquiries among the wardens of Bridewell. We are optimistic that an arrangement can be made to put those women to work at a new task. No longer will they produce hemp."

"And so the price of hemp will rise," Eliza concluded. "This is not an investment opportunity but more in the nature of a Hot Tip, sir. And a reminder, as if I wanted one, of why Natural Philosophers are not often seen haunting the 'Change—except when one has been put in the pillory by his creditors."

"If the 'hot tip' makes you money, why, then, you might be able to invest in—"

"Stop—don't say it—I already know: The Proprietors of the Engine for Raising Water by Fire."

"Indeed, madame."

"It is beyond astonishing. After all these years, we have come full circle: the Doctor wants me to invest in an amazing new device for pumping water out of mines!"

"In truth, the Doctor knows very little of the Engine for Raising Water by Fire."

Now there was another interruption in their discourse as the procession met and absorbed the mourners who had stayed behind at the Palace. Several of these had boarded sedan chairs or carriages, which enlarged and enlivened the procession. A diversion round one wing of the Palace got them out of Sophie's great garden. The main road from Hanover westwards ran across the other front of the Palace. They crossed over it directly, but slowly, for a crowd of common people of Hanover had come out to stand here and pay their respects to their Sovereign. Once again, Eliza found Daniel in the crowd.

"Then this is not a silver-mining scheme? For I have had enough—"

"As have I, madame," Daniel returned.

"Tin-mining I might consider, for Cornwall is famed for it."

"And lead, and others as well. But this is not about silver, tin, lead, or any other metals, noble or base."

"Coal?"

"Nay, 'tis not a question of *any* sort of mining! I speak to you rather of Power."

"It is a frequent topic of conversation in many settings high and low," Eliza observed, glancing in the direction of the King of Prussia. He was walking arm in arm with Caroline. They were interrupted by a pair of Prussian ladies, probably Countesses or something, who threw themselves at Caroline and took turns pressing their soggy cheeks against hers several times each. Caroline exchanged politenesses with them, and then made her escape, as the gun-carriage had finally plunged across the road and entered the older and smaller garden that spread away from the Palace on that side. The crowd of mourners, pursuing the coffin, thinned out suddenly. Caroline turned around and found Henrietta Braithwaite in formation behind her. The Princess thrust her face forward, adopting the pose of a ship's figurehead, and closed her eyes. Mrs. Braithwaite stepped in close, raised up the implement with the curved ivory blade, and scraped it quickly down Caroline's left cheek, then her right, shaving off the cloud of tear-caked face-powder, and the slick of rouge, that had been deposited by the mourners. Caroline opened her eyes, mouthed *"Danke schön,"* and spun away. Mrs. Braithwaite wiped the ivory clean with a rag that had already seen a lot of use today.

"I am using the word Power in a novel sense," Daniel explained, when the milling and jostling of the crowd had brought him and Eliza together once more. By this time they were halfway along the path that ran from the main door of Herrenhausen Palace straight up the middle of the Berggarten (as this park was called) to an extremely squat and heavy Doric temple that sat in the middle, guarded and shaded by fine old trees.

Daniel continued, "I use it in a *mechanickal* sense—to mean a sort of general ability to effect change, in a measurable way. Pumping water out of mines is one thing to spend Power on, but if you had a fund of such Power you might put it to other uses as well."

"Such as pounding hemp?"

"Or moving the parts of a Logic Mill. Or other purposes we have as yet failed to imagine. Once this Idea or conception of Power has entered your mind, madame, you shall find it difficult to shake off. Everywhere you look you shall see opportunities to put Power to use; and you shall see so many enterprises that suffer from a want of Power that you shall wonder how we have gotten along without it."

"There is much to consider in your discourse, Doctor, and little leisure, here and now, to consider it. I would be alone now with my grief for Sophie."

"And I would too, madame, and I thank you."

"When we are back in London I should like to see this Court in Clerkenwell, and hear more of your plans for the women of Bridewell."

They had reached the stone temple, and pooled round it. The building was windowless. A pair of doors in the front gave entry to private crypts within; but those were storage for dead cousins and stillborns. The doors were not used today. In the front portico two immense slabs had been set into the floor, cut with the names of Johann Friedrich—the one who had brought Leibniz to Hanover—and Ernst August, Sophie's late husband. A fresh rectangular hole, of equal size, had recently been let into the floor, and a grave dug in the earth beneath it. A slab bearing Sophie's name lay to one side, ready.

The rest of the proceedings, then, were of an obvious nature. All grieved, some more sincerely than others, none more so than Caroline. But when the grave had been filled in, with handfuls of dirt from the family, and shovel-loads from almost as sad laborers, Caroline could be seen dusting the dirt from her hands, and uttering some witticism that caused several around her to erupt in shocked and shocking laughter. The procession made its way back to Herrenhausen in a gradually improving mood. None was gayer than Princess Caroline. But only Henrietta and a few others knew that she had something to look forward to.

THE SOLSTICIAL DAY HAD STRETCHED into its eighteenth hour. The English delegation had stayed long past its scheduled date of return so that they could represent Her Britannic Majesty at the funeral, and in doing so they had emptied their purses and worn out what little welcome they had enjoyed to begin with. With a celerity that was conspicuous, verging on rude, they got out of town, banging away along the west-road in a train of carriages and baggage-carts, hoping there'd be enough daylight to reach the inn at Stadthagen.

They had left behind one of their number, a frail codger, who was rumored to have been an indifferently clever chap in his prime, but who now was sadly far gone, and probably never should have attempted such a journey in the first place. He had become debilitated by the long journey to Hanover and was in no condition to make a forced march back to the Dutch coast. Some kind-hearted member of the Hanoverian court had stepped in and offered to arrange a slow and easy return journey for this man, one Dr. Waterhouse, and even to send him in a coach full of nurses and physicians if need be. The other English had accepted this proffer hastily, and with more than a few winks and smirks—seeing it as a calculated attempt by some nobody to get himself Noticed in London.

More than half of the other noble and royal funeral-guests had already gone, many headed eastwards toward Braunschweig, Brandenburg, and Prussia, others going back to wherever Sophie had family, friends, or admirers, which meant radiating to all points of the compass.

Most of those who had stayed behind at Herrenhausen had done so for a reason. That reason was George Louis, Elector of Hanover, out from under his mother's thumb at last, and next in line to the British throne. And so in spite of the long hours of afternoon sun, the mood of the place had gone just a bit chilly.

Or so it seemed to Baron Johann von Hacklheber as he strolled through the garden, on another sort of mission entirely. Like a black bumblebee he was zigzagging from one flower-bed to the next. He was gathering a bouquet to award to his lady love whenever she showed up. The fundamental laws of the universe governing young men waiting for young ladies applied here as everywhere else, and consequently it was becoming a very large arrangement. Some while ago it had grown too large for one person to hold. In fact it had now become a sort of flower-dump atop the pedestal of a conveniently located statue. Every time Johann added to the pile, he would say a little prayer to Venus—for she was the pedestal's tenant—and look up at the Palace of Herrenhausen, and lock his gaze on a window in the west wing where Caroline was being fussed over by her attendants. As long as the lace curtains remained drawn, she was a work in progress. So Johann would step back, examine the flower-pile, and ponder the balance of its colors and the variety of its shapes. He would hold an imaginary colloquy with the mute and unhelpful Venus. Then he would launch out in search of the one blossom that would make it perfect. The garden was parted into polygons—triangles and quadrilaterals mostly—and as the wait stretched out he measured with his strides many of their perimeters. A gardener of a suspicious temperament, observing his movements from a distance, might think he was some sort of spy performing horticultural espionage.

Anyone observing him more closely, though, would note that he spent more time gazing outwards toward the perimeter than in on the flower-beds. On the road that surrounded the whole garden, along the bank of the enclosing canal, a sparse but relentless traffic of riders went pointlessly to and fro on expensive horses. Mostly they traveled in groups of two and three. Spurs were jingling all round. Their sound infiltrated the garden's humid fragrant air like midsummer færy-bells. When groups met, murmuring picked up where jingling left off. Someone unaccustomed to Courts in general, and Herrenhausen in particular, would have found it as annoying as it was mysterious. Johann von Hacklheber was used to it, understanding that courtiers literally had no other way to spend their lives. Once more he was put in mind of the wisdom Sophie had shown in situating the riding-path on the extreme frontier of the garden—shouldering all equestrian conspirators out away from the part she loved.

Spotting a likely rosebud, he drew his left hand up the outside of his thigh, black wool purring under his fingertips, and over the line of tiny silver buckles that fastened his rapier's black leather scabbard to the end of a broad black leather strap—a baldric, it was called—slung diagonally over his body. Continuing up and back, his hand passed under the skirt of his black wool coat, peeling the hem up to expose its black satin lining. He bent his elbow and supinated his wrist. The back of his hand glided up his buttock and over the black leather belt that kept his breeches from falling down, and stopped above his left kidney. He closed his hand on something hard: the handle of his dagger, which lived in an angled scabbard fastened to his belt at the base of his spine. An outward movement of his elbow drew it from its sheath. He got it out in front of him smartly before his coat-skirts could settle back upon the blade and be damaged by it. This precaution would not have been necessary with many daggers of recent make, which were designed for poking, parrying, and nail-paring, and had little to nothing in the way of a cutting edge. Johann owned several such. But all of them were gloriously decorative, and so did not go well with the funeral-weeds he wore today. The same was true of his collection of swords, which was neither especially large nor small compared to those of other gentlemen. But in the back of his wardrobe he did have this old set, which he'd inherited from a great-uncle. It had been made in Italy at least a hundred years ago when styles of sword-fighting, and hence of weapon-making, had been rather different. The rapier was huge. Its blade was a good eight inches longer than his arm, and somewhat broader than was common today, bringing its weight near the practical limit of a one-handed weapon. The edge had been notched in practice or combat, and re-ground, so many times that the blade no longer looked straight, but instead, as one sighted down it, rambled from side to side.

But in this it had nothing on the dagger, which was a serpentine blade of watered steel, astonishingly sharp on both edges. This style had become necessary when some Italian fighters, more sophisticated than Johann would ever be, had learnt the trick of reaching out with one hand to grab the blade of the foe's dagger. The tactic actually worked, if the grip was firm and the dagger's blade was straight; but it was most inadvisable to try it with a dagger such as this one. At any rate, the hilts of this dagger and this rapier were comparatively simple: Renaissance rather than Barock, and a world away from Rokoko. The scabbards were as plain as they could be, being simple undecorated black leather. Johann had belted them on this morning. Round midday he had finally stopped whacking the huge scabbard against tables' legs and funeral-guests' ankles. Now he was using the dagger to harvest flowers.

The light now came predominantly from the orange western sky, not the direct rays of the sun. The bouquet had to be re-examined in this new light. Johann returned to Venus, sheathing the serpentine dagger with extreme caution, and devoted a few moments to sifting through the pile of blossoms he'd made. Then he looked back at the palace, more out of habit than hope. But he noticed that clear orange sky-light was now shining in one side of Caroline's apartment and out the other. The sheers had been drawn back from the windows; she was on her way. In a panic—convinced, suddenly, that all his flower-hunting efforts had been misspent—Johann rummaged through his harvest and drew out a generous arm-load of flowers that caught his fancy. He left the remainder as a sacrifice to the love-goddess and began moving toward the compound of the Teufels-baum in the comical gait of one who is trying to put distance behind him as quickly as possible without breaking into a run. For there was only one portal in the triangular fence that imprisoned the serpent-like tree, and it was a good distance from here; meanwhile a carriage had set out from the palace stables and was moving down the garden path at a healthy clip. God help him if *he* were late.

Johann reached the iron gate with some moments to spare and slipped through it into the realm of the Teufelsbaum, which was an hour deeper into twilight than the rest of the garden. Having passed through, he about-faced, thrust his head back out over the path, and turned it to look both ways, making sure that no evening stroller had seen him entering the place where the Princess would soon arrive for two hours' *silent and solitary meditation.*

Satisfied that no one was there, he drew back and closed the gate, carefully, so as not to make a clang. And there he stood, at attention, in the pose of a musketeer at port arms, save that he cradled a bou-quet instead of a weapon. Presently a single great draught-horse boomed around the corner, constrained between a pair of long stout carriage-poles, which led back to a little coach. The driver had a terse exchange of noises with the horse. The horse slowed, passed the gate, stopped, and then (for he'd gone a bit too far, and the driver was remonstrating) backed up until the carriage's side door was aligned with the iron gate. Quelled, the driver now set the brake, per-haps showing an excess of prudence. Johann stepped forward and opened the iron gate. Then he reached up to unlatch the carriage's side door.

He swung it open to reveal a pair of mastiffs.

Their eyes were rolling and bulging. Their nostrils were seething, as each was being straddled by a strong man with both hands clasped around its muzzle to keep it from barking. Johann stepped out of the way. The dogs were launched.

Neither Scylla nor Charybdis appeared to touch the ground until they were twenty feet inside the gate. They bounded into the Teufels-baum, bashing branches out of the way like runaway gun-carriages. Only after they had disappeared did they think to bark, and then as an afterthought. These were not hunters, bred to bay. They were workers.

On the path that ran along the back of the plot, hooves were can-tering—then they changed over to a gallop. Johann looked up to the intersection just in time to see the rider flash across drawing a cutlass. It was one of his Leipziger cousins. From the back of the Teufels-baum came a welter of furious barking and a yelp of pain. The two dog-wranglers—Eliza's footmen—dove out the open door and ran after the dogs. Johann dropped his bouquet, for it had served its purpose, and followed them. He thought of drawing his rapier, but it would get hung up in the unfathomable windings of those branches. So he drew his dagger instead, and transferred it to his right hand.

He need not have bothered. By the time he stumbled to the back fence, the matter had been concluded. One of the dogs—Johann could not tell them apart in this light—was back in the corner, attending to a long dark robe that had fallen to the ground. On the off chance that the garment was a foe, he was doing battle with it. And on the assumption that it was a vertebrate, he was shaking it back and forth in a bid to crack its spinal column like a bullwhip.

The other dog was being soothed and attended to by one of the footmen—this had suffered a diagonal gash across the muzzle, which was bleeding a lot, though it was not an especially serious wound.

The second footman was kneeling beside a man in a dark robe who lay sprawled on his stomach near the fence. This footman must have been a student of anatomy, for with both hands he was methodically driving a dagger with a foot-long blade into diverse carefully selected locations in the fallen man's back.

The injured dog—which had reluctantly been squatting on its haunches—got up. But its legs were twitching and it could not remain standing. It fell onto its side and gagged convulsively.

Johann went over to the dead man—for he had to be called dead now, even if his heart were still beating—and picked up with great care a small dagger that lay on the ground near his right hand. He raised it up into a shaft of light that still pierced the branches. One edge was red, and glistening wet, with the dog's blood; but the entire blade gleamed with a shiny brown coating glazed with an oily rainbow sheen.

"Don't touch it," said a familiar woman's voice. "Some are absorbed through the skin."

"Yes, Mother."

"I cannot imagine a state of affairs more awkward than this," Eliza thought out loud. They were walking back toward the palace, she picking up her skirts and breaking into a run from time to time to keep up with his strides. Normally Johann was more considerate. This evening, his mind was elsewhere. She wanted it back.

"Two dead assassins in the Electress's—I mean, the Elector's garden? Yes, I should say so."

It was only a few moments since they had witnessed the terminal moments of some unpleasantness in the canal. They were walking along one of the garden's transverse paths, glancing to the right at every intersection, looking for a straight route back to the palace. Now suddenly they saw it sprawling against a purple and orange sky at a distance of some five hundred Johann-paces, or seven hundred of Eliza's. Johann snapped the right turn like a soldier at drill, and stormed on.

"No, the *hashishin* are easily managed," Eliza said. "One died in the woods, the other in the canal—we'll say that the latter got drunk, fell in, and drowned. The former has already vanished."

"Then what is so damned awkward about it? By your leave."

Eliza let it be seen that she was exasperated. "Think, son. Spies are ubiquitous, obviously. But *this* spy works for the Jacobites, and he—or to be precise, his wife—is Caroline's lady-in-waiting—"

"She can be replaced."

"—and the declared mistress of George Augustus!"

"Again, Mother, almost the whole point of mistresses is that they may be hot-swapped."

"Caroline says that her husband is quite infatuated with this Henrietta. Short of actually dragging the corpses of the *hashishin* into his Presence, it is difficult for me to see how we can get him to comprehend—"

"Pardon me for interrupting, Mother, but Caroline also says that Henrietta is unlikely to be the spy. So perhaps it is Harold Braithwaite we ought to be speaking of."

Eliza *did* pardon the interruption, if only because she had to stop talking anyway to catch her breath.

"They are married to each other, the Braithwaites are," Eliza reminded her son, "joined together in God's sight." They had plunged out into the northern half of the garden, nearer the palace. This meant they'd emerged from a realm of higher trees, and deeper shadows, onto an open flat plain of clear light. A row of four rectangular pools stretched across their way. The water was perfectly smooth, and reflected the fiery colors of the heavens, creating an illusion that these were but Hell's sky-lights, lit from below.

Johann had a ready answer to this, but he bit it off. Fifty more strides along, he said: "If spoken to in the right way he might elect to remove himself."

"In a minor provincial court, who would mind such an arrangement? But when George Augustus is King of England, it will not be acceptable for his mistress's husband to be permanently absent."

"Very well, Mother, I agree with you! It *is* most awkward." Johann spoke the last sentence *sotto voce* as they were drawing near to a couple of strolling courtiers—like Braithwaite, English Whigs who'd moved here recently to curry favor with the man they were gambling would be their next Sovereign. They had names and even titles; but for all that it really mattered, they could be called Smith and Jones.

"I beg your pardon, sirs, but have you any notions as to where I—we, rather—might find Mr. Braithwaite?"

"Yes, *mein Herr*, we spied him not a quarter of an hour ago, showing some French guests round the garden. They went to see the Maze," said Smith.

"The Maze, now that is an excellent place for such an a-mazing fellow."

"No," said Jones, "I do believe that that is Mr. Braithwaite and his party, just yonder, bound for the other side of the garden." He pointed to several men in black struggling across in front of the palace.

"Finished with the Maze so soon!" exclaimed Smith.

"I'm sure it is but a miserable imitation of the French labyrinths, and quite disappointing to his companions," Johann said.

"They are going to the theatre, I'll wager," said Jones. "Oh, there is no play to-night. But they might be going to have a look round."

"And who better to escort them than Mr. Braithwaite, who is an actor of note," reflected Johann. "Mother, would you please go to the palace and relate all of the very latest gossip to our friend? She will be on tenterhooks."

Eliza suddenly looked young, because uncertain. She glanced after Braithwaite.

"I shall be in with you momentarily, after I have spoken to Mr. Braithwaite concerning his travel plans."

"Is Mr. Braithwaite to go on a journey?" asked Smith.

"A lengthy one, 'tis rumored," Johann confirmed. "Mother? If you please?"

"If these two gentlemen would be so good as to accompany you—" Eliza suggested.

Smith and Jones exchanged a look. "Braithwaite is a merry sort of chap, he shan't be offended if we cross paths with him—?" said Smith.

"I see no reason to suppose otherwise," said Jones.

"Very well. I will see you in a quarter of an hour," said Eliza, in adamant maternal style.

"Oh, Mama, it shall not even be that long."

Eliza departed. Johann stood for a few moments, watching her go, then announced, distractedly: "Let's to it. We are losing the light!"

"Er, why do you need light, my lord?" Smith inquired, after he had caught up, which took some exertion. Jones was already miles behind.

"Why, so that Mr. Braithwaite can see the going-away present that I will give him!"

THE GARDEN-THEATRE WAS A SLOPING rectangle of ground, walled in by hedges, and guarded by a picket line of white marble cherubs. These were charming in daylight but now took on the spectral, glabrous appearance of stillborns. A raised stage was at one end. Several of the French guests had climbed atop it and were amusing themselves with the trap-door. Braithwaite stood below the stage, in the orchestra, conversing with a man who like everyone else was dressed in black. But his clothing did not consist of the usual breeches, waistcoat, &c. but rather a ground-seeping cassock with a hundred silver buttons. As Johann drew nearer he recognized the man as Father Édouard de Gex, a Jesuit of noble birth, who'd figured into some of mother's more disturbing Versailles anecdotes.

Johann stopped about ten paces short of this pair—close enough to interrupt their conversation. Bringing both hands together at his left flank, he gripped the junction of scabbard and baldric with his left, and the hilt of the rapier with his right. He drew the blade out a foot or so—enough to loosen it. But knowing the weapon was too long to pull free in a single movement, he then raised the whole rig—rapier, baldric, and scabbard—up in front of his face and lifted it clear of his shoulders. A sideways gesture sent the leather goods hurtling away into the cheap seats, leaving him free of all encumbrances, with exposed rapier in hand. His left hand was now free to draw the serpentine dagger as before. He stood squarely facing Braithwaite, dagger and rapier in front of him, both tips aimed at the hollow at the base of Braithwaite's throat, knuckles down and backs of hands facing outwards, for Johann had been trained by Hungarians.

By this time Braithwaite, and all of the Frenchmen save one, had got their own swords half drawn—a cultivated reflex. De Gex had slipped his right hand into a slit-pocket in the breast of his cassock.

"Father de Gex," Johann announced, "you shall not be needing whatever that is."

De Gex's hand dropped to his side. Johann made sure it was empty. "This is not a melee but a duel. Your presence is requested, padre; first, to act as Mr. Braithwaite's second; after, to give him last rites. My second is one of these two gentlemen behind me; I care not which, and leave them to sort it out. If I should be struck by a meteorite during this combat, and killed, they will convey my apologies and my love to my mother."

Johann guessed that he might have derived some low entertainment from observing the faces of Smith and of Jones at hearing this unexpected news; but having gone this far, he could not now remove his gaze from Braithwaite's eyes until Braithwaite's heart had stopped beating. De Gex uttered something that caused all of the Frenchmen to re-sheathe their swords. Then he said something rather different to Braithwaite; but Braithwaite remained frozen with his blade half out.

"Braithwaite! It is my prerogative as a gentleman to make you defend yourself with that weapon you are forever carrying around; will you please act like a gentleman, and draw it?"

"I propose tomorrow at dawn—"

"By which time you shall be where? Prague?"

"A proper duel is never conducted in haste—"

"This looks like dawn to me," Johann answered. He could not even tell what language he was speaking now. He advanced a step, quickly, which finally prompted Braithwaite to draw his small-sword. Johann continued, "Dusk and dawn come so close to kissing at this time of year I never know which is which."

Braithwaite had finally extracted his small-sword, and, with some assistance from de Gex, got himself disentangled from the scabbard and its strap-work. He got into a stance resembling Johann's, but with the hand oddly curled under, in the English style. De Gex withdrew. Braithwaite had already cornered himself by standing with his back to the stage. Johann advanced. Braithwaite raised his weapon. Johann stung it out of the way with his dagger, put the tip of his rapier against Braithwaite's solar plexus, shoved it in six inches, and then punched the hilt downward. Then he jerked it out, turned around, and walked back towards the palace where his mother and his sweetheart were waiting for him. "So much for awkward," he said.

DANIEL WATERHOUSE REMOVED a handkerchief from his breast pocket, draped it over his hand, and used it to grip the handle of the assassin's dagger. The weapon had been borne into the room—a servants' pantry near Princess Caroline's apartment—on a silver tray, like an hors d'oeuvre. Daniel held it several inches above a candle, so that the blade split the current of warm air rising from the flame. Then he leaned forward and got his beak into a position some distance above that. He gave the air the tiniest sniff, then recoiled and turned away from it. The dagger he set back on the tray, and the handkerchief he wadded up and threw into a cold fireplace in the corner of the pantry.

Johann could smell it now, too: an acrid, smoky reek that reminded him of something.

"Nicotine," said Daniel.

"Never heard of it."

"That may be, but you have some in you right now, if you have smoked a pipe in the last few hours."

"That's what the smell reminds me of, a bit—an old pipe-bowl that has never been cleaned out."

"It is an extract of the tobacco plant. When I was your age, it was in vogue, among certain Fellows of the Royal Society, to prepare this poison and inflict it on small animals. It is soluble in oil. It is bitter—"

"You've tasted it?!"

"No, but persons who have, invariably remark on its bitterness before they stop breathing."

"How does it kill?"

"I have just told you—the victim stops breathing. But not before becoming twitchy and spasmodic for a brief time."

"That was true of the dog, when I saw it. Then I lit out in pursuit of the other assassin. He had been pursued to the edge of the canal, and jumped in rather than perish at sword's edge. He was sloshing about—for the water was but chest-deep—looking for some apt place to scale the opposite wall of the channel. Then he stopped moving, and sank below the surface. When we pulled him out he was dead."

"Did water drain from his lungs?"

"Now that you mention it, no."

"He did not drown then," Daniel said. "If you examine the corpse carefully you shall find some place where he nicked himself with his dagger, or let it brush against his skin." Daniel planted a hand to either side of the silver platter and gazed at the weapon. "This is an expert preparation, solved in some fine light oil, such as whale-oil. Smeared on the skin it would convey the nicotine into the capillaries and thence to the lungs in a few minutes' time." He looked up at Johann. "When you smoke your pipe, you feel an initial rush of stimulation, followed by a calmness, a steadying of the nerves. This is but a trace, a shadow, of nicotine poisoning. If you were cut with this dagger, that relaxation of the nerves would advance to the point where you would simply forget to breathe, and drown in air . . . every time you smoke tobacco, you are prefiguring your own death."

"Horrid . . . it makes me want to smoke something just to calm down."

"Mr. Hooke experimented with an herb called *bhang* that would cure what ails you—alas, it is harder to get."

"I shall make inquiries. It is strange. During the events, I had a clarity of mind, a sharpness of perceptions, I'd never known before. Now, sitting here, I am terrified."

"As I should be, if I had just received such a tongue-lashing from the Duchess of Arcachon-Qwghlm."

"You could hear it this far away?"

"I do believe that the King of France sat up in his bed at Versailles wondering what new war had broken out in Germany."

"It's true, I have never seen her so angry. She *did* tell me never to duel. And I *did* promise. But this—"

"You chose the moment well," Daniel assured him. "Physical violence is a means that I have never employed for any purpose. The risks are enormous, and a man of my mentality, who sees dangers where they are and are not, can always find a reason to take some other course. You are young and—"

"Stupid?"

"No, but less perceptive of risk. When, God willing, you have reached the age of forty, you'll sit up in bed in the middle of the night, covered in sweat, with the memory of this night fresh in your mind, and say, 'My God, I cannot believe I once fought a duel!' Or so I hope."

"Why do you hope for me to sleep poorly?"

"Because though I have not *done* violence I have *seen* rather a lot of it. Not all of the men who employ it are stupid, or evil. Only most of them. The rest use it reluctantly, as a way, when all else has failed, of seizing the main chance. Thus you tonight. Your mother will understand this and get her equilibrium back. But like a man who imbibes tobacco-smoke, you have died a little death tonight. I do not recommend that you become addicted to it."

"It is very good advice. I thank you for it. As I thank you, again, for giving us information that saved Caroline's life. You may expect that she will reward you—"

"I would glady forgo all thanks and rewards if I could simply take a nap."

"You can nap in the carriage, Dr. Waterhouse," said a woman's voice. Hoarse, as if she'd been screaming a lot recently.

Daniel and Johann both looked over to see Eliza in the pantry's doorway. She looked a good deal calmer.

"My lady," Daniel said, and sighed, "from any other woman I should interpret this as a jest or *non sequitur,* but from you I fear—"

"It is well known that you stayed behind in Hanover, being too ill for arduous travel—"

"Thank you for reminding me, my lady, my infirmity had quite slipped my mind."

"It is expected that you will take the slow way back, attended by a nurse. I give you your nurse." Eliza came all the way into the room now. She was followed by a young woman dressed in a severe habit, her head swaddled in a length of white linen that had been wrapped around so as to conceal all of her hair, and a good bit of her face—hardly *à la mode*, but not particularly unusual in a time and place when nearly everyone sooner or later got smallpox, and some emerged in good health but almost impossible to look at. "This is Gertrude von Klötze, a petty noblewoman of Braunschweig, who after suffering and surviving a grave illness, has dedicated the remainder of her life to succouring others in need."

"A noble woman indeed. It is my very great pleasure to meet you, mademoiselle," said Daniel, adroitly looking past the fact that this woman was, in fact, Princess Caroline.

"Fraülein von Klötze shall accompany you all the way to London."

"And how shall sweet Gertrude get *back*?" Johann demanded—having taken a few moments to recover from the abrupt transfiguration of his lover into a masked nurse. He made a step toward Caroline, but she sent him back with a dart of the eyes. "Surely her family will miss her!"

"Perhaps she won't *have* to come back, as her family may be moving to London soon *anyway*," Eliza said. "Gertrude shall lodge at Leicester House until we make rendezvous with her later."

"I did not know that I was—we were—going to London!" Johann answered.

"We are," Eliza said calmly, "but not before a detour to the chateau at Schloß Ubersetzenseehafenstadtbergwald."

"Eeyuh, *that* place? Are you joking? What'll we do there, hunt bats?"

"Some minutes ago, you may have heard a woman screaming in this wing of the palace."

"Indeed, my ears are still ringing."

"That was Princess Caroline."

"Are you certain? For during the time this screaming reached my ears I observed movements of your lips, Mother, curiously synchronized—"

"Your wit is tedious. 'Twas the Princess. Her grief over the death of Sophie is even deeper than was realized. Her braveness earlier today a mere affectation, masking a profound derangement of the nerves. Not long ago, she simply dissolved. She has been given tincture of opium and is under strict seclusion in her bedchamber. Before the sun is up, she shall be taken out in a sedan chair and loaded into my carriage. You, son, and I shall convey her to the Schloß I have mentioned—one of the most remote and desolate out-croppings in Christendom. There, her royal highness shall spend several weeks in seclusion, tended only by a few *trusted* servants, turning away all visitors."

"Especially ones carrying poisoned daggers—?"

"Rumors of assassins in the garden are absurd," Eliza said, "They are chimæras, figments of her royal highness's fevered brain. Even if they did exist, they would face grave difficulties gaining entrance to the place to which we are taking her, which, as you know if you have been studying your family history, was built on a rock in a lake by a rich Baron so concerned for his personal security that he believed that even the birds of the air were wind-up toys invented by *hashishin* to fly in his windows and put anthrax into his beer."

"Oh, was he the chap who invented beer-mugs with lids on them?" Daniel wondered aloud.

But Eliza was in no mood. "I should like it very much, Dr. Water-house, if you were to fall down and suffer a medical crisis."

"I am here to serve, my lady," Daniel returned gallantly, and began looking round the pantry for a comfortable place to hit the floor.

"Might I spend a moment with 'Gertrude' first?" Johann inquired. "There is much, er, advice I would give her concerning London and—"

"There is no time," Eliza said, "and your advice is of little value, as 'Gertrude' does not expect to participate in any *sword-fights*." And Eliza drew breath as if to expound upon this theme at greater length. But Daniel's withered hand suddenly lay gentle on her arm. She faltered. "Gertrude" and Johann had locked their eyes together across the room. Eliza could have detonated a barrel of gunpowder and they would not have heard it.

"Let's to London, then," Daniel said.

Between Black Mary's Hole and
Sir John Oldcastle's, North of London

DAWN, 18 JUNE 1714

Enlisting Soldiers without Authority. An ingrossed Bill
from the Lords, intituled, An Act, to prevent the listing of her Majesty's Subjects to serve as Soldiers, without her Majesty's License, was read a Second time.

Resolved, That the Bill be committed.

Resolved, That the Bill be committed to a Committee of the whole House.

Resolved, That this House will, To-morrow Morning, resolve itself into a Committee of the whole
House, upon the said Bill.

—Journals of the House of Commons,
JOVIS, 1° DIE JULII; ANNO 13°
ANNÆ REGINÆ, 1714

IT WAS SAID THAT Mahomet had banned bells in the *masjid,* not because they were, in and of themselves, repugnant to Allah, but simply
because the Franks were so fond of them, and used them so much,
that merely to hear one tolling was to be put forcibly in mind of the
profanities of the infidels. If that were true, why a devout Mussulman
with the misfortune to be encamped on the fields north of Clerkenwell would have suffered the rudest of all possible awakenings on this
Friday: the damp, dark, chill, sewage-scented fog that served, hereabouts, in stead of an atmosphere, was alive with the sounds of
church-bells. And none of your merry pealing carillons ringing diverse changes, but the slow stomach-walloping bongs of great solitary
bells, gravid with doom.

The tolling conveyed several meanings. First that the day had begun—a fact that most Londoners could only have determined with
careful use of ephemeris and chronometer, as it was still dark. Sec-

ond, that London was still there. The buildings, despite appearances, had not drifted away from one another in the night-time, like ships of a fog-bound fleet. Though invisible, they were still where they had been the evening previous, and a cockney with a good ear might even find his way round town by them, triangulating from the distinct voices of St. Mary-le-Bow, St. Thomas Apostle, St. Mildred, and Bennet Fink as mariners plotted courses by the lights of Ras Alhague, Caput Medusae, and Cynosura.

Heard from these fields, the sounds of the bells came not only from the south, but from east and west as well, simply because London was that big and Clerkenwell that close to it. Once he had scrambled out of his tent, stuffed Egyptian cotton into his ears, and struck his camp, the offended sojourner would therefore head north to get away from the infernal bonging. But in this he would be balked at every bridge and crossroads. For all of the traffic—mostly pedestrians—was south-bound.

Many had slept rough on these fields and greens the night before, and when the bells had begun to ring, they had arisen and begun to shuffle through the fog, like a whole battle-field of dead soldiers resurrected and ordered to march upon their respective parish-churches. All of them moved southwards, toward High Holbourn. For the tolling of so many melancholic bells had a third meaning: this was Hanging-Day. It happened eight times a year.

The people tromping southwards through the fog were common at best. Honest folk among them tended to move in packs, keeping purses stuffed deep inside their cloaks, and supporting themselves on walking-sticks that were strangely oversized. For there was a stiff proportion of Vagabonds and worse in this throng. They all hoped to make it to Holbourn before broad daylight, so that they could claim places in the front of the crowd, affording them clear views of the condemned journeying to Tyburn Cross. Failing that they might withdraw to side-streets, and execute great westward flanking maneuvers, converging finally on the vast open parks and fields surrounding the Treble Tree.

To a foreign visitor—or even to a good many Englishmen—there would be so much in these sights that was odd, and so much about the atmosphere that was gloomy, eldritch, and macabre, that he might easily over-look one or two peculiar phænomena. But the sort of person who attended Hanging-Marches eight times a year would note an anomalous gathering near an elbow in the road between Sir John Oldcastle's (a compound of stately buildings and trees, about to be enveloped by Clerkenwell) and Black Mary's Hole (a tiny alienated settlement on the banks of the upper Fleet).

Stopped by the roadside, harnessed to a team of four horses who were all in their feedbags, was a coach. The driver, with his whip, and two footmen, with cudgels, prowled around it, discouraging Vagabond-boys from coming up to ingratiate themselves with the beasts. A stone's throw away, in a field strewn with human turds and other evidence of last night's hanging-jamboree, an old man bestrode a horse. Too much horse. It was feeding selectively on whatever grew in the field, and wandering wherever it pleased to find the choicest herbs. The rider, who was wrapped in a cloak, arms crossed over his torso for warmth, occasionally unfolded himself, grasped the reins, and compelled his mount to repent of its latest wanderings. It was a big gray gelding, obviously military, with simple tack.

The old man on the gray gelding was accompanied by four other horsemen. Of these, two rode mounts similar to the first, but they kept theirs under better control. These men were big and young, dressed in very plain common garments such as yeomen might wear to venture forth on a long cross-country errand.

Even through dimness and fog, everything about the other two riders—save one detail that shall be attended to in a moment—marked them as youths of a privileged class. They had small-swords (actually not all that useful on horseback). Their horses were to the gray geldings as færies were to fishwives. In short, either one could have ridden direct to St. James's Park and gone for a genteel trot up and down Rotten Row and not drawn a second glance from the toffs and fops who frequented that place.

But first they'd have had to don wigs. Bewigged, they'd have blended in perfectly. Dis-covered, they looked more at home in the wilds of North America. For each of these young swells had carefully shaved all of his hair—all, that is, save in a longitudinal stripe, three fingers wide, running from the hairline to the nape. This had been allowed to grow to a length of several inches and then stiffened with some mysterious tonsorial compound so that it stood straight out from the head. Washed, flattened, and tucked under a periwig it would disappear, but thus deployed it looked (to the Classically educated) like the crest on an ancient helmet, or (to readers of Romances) like the battle-coif of the Mohawks.

Now, a wagon had been working its way across the torrent of Hanging-watchers. It was laden with barrels of the type used to transport ale. It seemed to be coming from the general direction of east London, and executing a movement around the northern frontier of the city to strike at Tyburn Cross around mid-morning: an excellent plan. Progress was impeded by a throng of would-be revelers who followed the wagon like sea-gulls swarming a herring-boat. But the

Shaftoe looked to the two dragoons who had pulled him out of the barrel. They confirmed it with nods.

"Am I to gather that Colonel Barnes is not alone there?" Shaftoe asked.

"I daresay the best part of your regiment is drinking up my wine-cellar."

One of the dragoons could be heard supplementing Comstock's account, muttering about "three companies." Sergeant Shaftoe was not the sort who would admit to being startled or impressed by *anything;* but at least he did not look bored or contemptuous—a signal achievement for Roger Comstock.

"I know all about your Whig Association," Shaftoe said. He had advanced now to walking, and tottered a few steps in Comstock's direction. "I have heard the rumors about all the money you have raised from the merchants of the City. And as to your efforts to recruit soldiers away from Her Majesty's regiments, and sign them up in your private army: I recruited them *first,* and trained them, so do not think that a single one has escaped my attention."

"I shouldn't dare to, Sergeant Shaftoe."

"I am too young to've witnessed the Civil War with these eyes, but as a lad I heard tales of it from ones who managed to survive. And I have seen all of the *improvements* that War made in Ireland and Belgium and other places. I could not be less inclined to take part in such an action on English soil."

"Then don't."

"Pardon?"

"Don't take part, Sergeant Shaftoe. Oh, by all means go to Ravenscar—" and here Comstock launched into the procedure of dismounting from his horse—so evidently fraught with perils for man and beast alike that the sergeant stepped forward to intervene. "Take this steed—yes—there—oh, no! I beg your pardon—thank you—that was most painful—I am in your debt—may I please have my teeth back—there! Whew! I say, take this steed, Sergeant Shaftoe, which is as glad to be *rid of* me, as *ridden by* you—ha—these two fine dragoons who, as I believe, are known to you, shall accompany you all the way to Ravenscar. Go there, drink Colonel Barnes's health, recuperate, trout-fish, as you like. There is not going to be another Civil War, Sergeant Shaftoe, if I have aught to say about it—which, as it happens, I do."

"What if you are wrong?"

"Then you are welcome, nay, encouraged to retire from military service."

"And in what way does this benefit you?"

brewer had a formidable van-guard of cudgel-men and a rear-guard of dogs, so he kept firm control of his inventory and made respectable speed. His route happened to bring him past the elbow in the road where the coach, and the five riders, were unaccountably loitering. There he stopped the wagon. Several Vagabonds rushed it. They were driven back, not only by the brewer's dogs and club-men, but also by the four younger riders, who had wordlessly joined forces with them.

The brewer and an assistant—by looks, his son—deployed a plank from the back of the wagon, making of it a ramp extending to the ground. Down this they rolled a large barrel. It seemed unusually light-loaded, for they did not much exert themselves. But the contents must have been delicate, for they took their time. While his boy stowed the plank, the brewer set the barrel upright on the ground and gave it an affectionate triple thump. When he returned to his bench at the head of the wagon, he was startled to discover a single golden guinea resting in the place where he was about to sit.

"Thank you, guv'nor," the brewer said to the old man on the gray horse. "But I couldn't possibly." And he tossed the coin back. The target was too blind to see it coming through the fog, but stopped it with his chest. It tumbled down into his lap. He trapped it under his hand.

"If it was some other bloke in there," the brewer explained, "I'd take your money, guv. But this one's on the house."

"You are a credit to your profession, sir," returned the old man, "as if it *needed* any. When next I visit the Liberty of the Tower, I shall buy a round for the house—nay, for the whole garrison."

Even large objects vanished soon in this miasma, and that was true of the beer-wagon. The four riders now devoted a minute or two to cantering back and forth driving away inquisitive Vagabonds. Then all converged on the barrel. The two Mohawks stood guard while the two common blokes dismounted and went to work on the barrel—carefully—with hatchets. Presently they tipped it over on the grass. One held the barrel. The other bent down, reached into the open end, got a grip on the payload, and dragged it out. It was a human form. From his general looks, no one would have been surprised to learn that he was dead. If so, he had expired recently, for he was still floppy. After a minute, though, he began to stir. In three minutes he was sitting on the barrel, drinking brandy, glaring at the two Mohawks, and conversing with his two rescuers. He called these by their Christian names and they called him Sergeant.

"Sergeant Shaftoe," said the old man, "I do pity the Grim Reaper on the day that he shall finally come for you in earnest. I fear you'll use him so roughly that he shall have to go on holiday for a fortnight."

"And what would be the harm in that?" croaked Sergeant Shaftoe. His voice was very raw, as if he had been shouting or screaming quite a bit in recent days. His wrists were adorned with bracelets of festering scabs.

"Oh, think of the havoc it would play with Her Majesty's annuities! Think of the carnage at Lloyd's Coffee-house!"

Sergeant Shaftoe let it be seen that he did not think much of the other's wit. "You'd be Comstock," he said, after a suitably uncomfortable silence had passed.

"I would draw nigh and shake your hand—"

" 'Tis all right, my hand does not work just now."

"—but I do not trust myself on this animal."

Shaftoe shook off a brief urge to smile. "Not to your liking, is he?"

"Oh, as an arse-warmer, he has done splendid service. But God help us all if I should essay to *ride* him."

"I s'pose it's you I have to thank for my liberty, then," Shaftoe remarked.

"From the fact that you are here, and alive, I collect that all went off as planned?"

"En route from the *dungeon* to the *cooperage* were some misadventures. Without those, it would have been as routine as removal of horse-dung. The Regiment is under new, not very competent direction."

"What of the Queen's Messengers?"

"All they do is stand in a Mobb around the Pyx day and night."

Comstock permitted himself a dry chuckle. "You are a man of many words but few specifics. You'd do well in Parliament."

Shaftoe shrugged. "I'm old. Your hirelings, who broke me out of the Tower, they are young lads, and were moved greatly by each little happening. Ask them to relate the story to you, and you shall hear a yarn far longer and more diverting than any I would tell."

"And less strictly *true*, I suspect," said Comstock.

"What's it to be now, guv'nor?" Shaftoe asked, and decided to try standing up. This he accomplished with a rolling tocsin of cracks and pops.

"Sergeant Shaftoe, 'twere absurd for me to go to the trouble of making you a free man, only to take away your liberty in the next instant by telling you what to do."

"My mistake, guv'nor. I am accustomed by long habit to being in a chain of command."

"Then, if it would be of any comfort to you, know that your longtime superior, Colonel Barnes, is now my guest. Oh, not here in London! He is at my seat, Ravenscar, on the North York Moors, above the sea."

"Always an important question to ask. I am presently engaged in a sort of duel with the Viscount Bolingbroke—the same chap you have to thank for your recent travails in Tower-dungeons. In a duel, it is customary for each participant to have a second: a friend to stand behind him to back him up. The second rarely has to *do* anything. You may think of the Whig Association's battalions as *my* second. As for Bolingbroke, he has always had the Queen's Messengers, and now, too, he has much of your old Regiment in his pocket. Most of the other regiments are too cowed to stand against him. It is important that *I* not be cowed, Sergeant Shaftoe. Having an army in Ravenscar gives me a warm feeling."

"But what's the end of it? Mr. Charles White was asking of me a lot of odd questions concerning the Pyx, and the Mint, and my ex-brother. He is planning something—"

"Oh, he *planned* it ages ago. Presently he is *doing* it. It is *I* who am *planning* something."

"A war?"

"Much nastier: a Parliamentary inquiry. Today I have punched Bolingbroke in the nose by causing his favorite witness—you—to vanish from the Tower. Tomorrow at Westminster I shall hit him over the head with a sledgehammer. He'll be frightfully angry with me. I shall fear his anger the less if I know, and if he knows, that you and others like you are drilling on the North York Moors." Ravenscar now forcibly put the horse's reins into Shaftoe's stiff and swollen hand.

"What in God's name are you going to do to him?" asked Shaftoe.

"Let us say I have told all of my friends to sell South Sea Company stock short."

"What the hell does that mean?"

"It means that grim days lie ahead for that Company. We shall be here all day if I try to explain all—go! Be off! The Hanging-March shall cover your movements, but only for so long! Mount up!"

Shaftoe did. Then he sat grimacing for a few moments as various parts of his body registered their protests. The two dragoons converged on either side of his horse and set to work lengthening the stirrups.

A dozen Barkers emerged from the fog, singing a hymn—bound for Tyburn to protest something. The two Mohawks rode out to herd them off in another direction. One of the Barkers was pushing a wheelbarrow that, because it was heavy-laden with libels, kept getting stuck in the muck.

"I wish I could be there to see it—whatever you're doing to Bolingbroke, that is, guv'nor," said Sergeant Shaftoe, sounding as close to wistful as a man of his character could.

"No," Ravenscar assured him, "no, you don't. Believe you me, the great happenings of Parliament are better to hear about than to suffer through. But make no mistake, it *shall* be a great event. After I have let the World know what *I* know concerning Bolingbroke, and what he has been doing with the Asiento money, we'll hear no more about a Trial of the Pyx, at least for a little while." Roger took a step back and slapped the horse's croup. It began to trudge forward. The two dragoons, who had mounted up, fell in behind. Roger shouted after them: "And I daresay I'll get my Longitude Act passed as a soupçon!"

Clerkenwell Court
19 JUNE 1714

Ordered, That the Directors of the *South Sea* Company do lay before this House an Account of all Proceedings in the said Company relating to the *Assiento* trade; together with all Orders, Directions, Letters or Informations which the Directors, or any Committee of Directors, have received concerning the same.

—*Journals of the House of Commons,*
VENERIS, 18° DIE JUNII; ANNO 13°
ANNÆ REGINÆ, 1714

A QUARTER OF A MILE south of the dogleg in the road where Roger Comstock had met Bob Shaftoe, the frontier of London could be discerned by the Wise in the Ways of Real Estate. The most infallible sign of which was that, here, the track leading to Black Mary's Hole had been improved with a name, *Coppice Row,* devised to conjure forth, from the fevered brains of would-be buyers, phant'sies of a cozy and bucolic character, be they never so removed from Truth. Along Coppice Row, buildings were going up, or had gone up so recently that they were still redolent of the horse-hair mixed into their damp plaster. On the left side of the road, as one departed from London, the sprawl had been baffled for the time being by the stand of trees, and root-ball of ancient property-rights, surrounding Sir John Oldcastle's. On the right were a few indifferent buildings, all made of red brick still warm from the kilns. These had shop-arcades facing the street, and flats above. The largest of these buildings commanded a frontage of some hundred feet, sliced into a dozen shop-fronts of various widths. Most were quite narrow, and most still wanted tenants.

One of them had been rented by a clock-maker. Or so it might be guessed from the new-made sign that had been hung out over the street on a clever wrought-iron cantilever. This sign had been constructed around the carcass of an ancient clock that looked to have been salvaged from a bell-tower in some Continental town—perhaps a Belgian *hôtel de ville* laid low by a mortar-bomb during the late war. At any rate it had been very old even before whatever sequence of fiery disasters, salvagings, soakings in brine, and rough transshipments had brought it to Clerkenwell. With its bent, gap-toothed gears and its scabrous corrosions it served better as an Emblem, than as a Keeper, of Time. All by itself it might have served as a conversation-piece, like a Roman ruin. But to it had been added a muscular figure, put together of wood and plaster, and styled after a God, who was with one hand supporting the clock and with the other reaching up to adjust its hour-hand. All this to advertise a shop so small that its proprietor could stand in the middle of it and touch both side-walls with his fingertips.

Clerkenwell Court—as this edifice was styled—was not *badly* situated, for it was along a way that holiday-makers might traverse en route to the tea-gardens and Spaws of Lambs Conduit Fields. And it was not too distant from Gray's Inn and diverse Squares round which wealthy persons had built their town-houses. But it was not especially *well* situated, either, for the place was difficult to reach without passing through one or more infamous Dens of Iniquity, Nests of Vipers, Pits of Degradation, &c., viz. Hockley-in-the-Hole and Smithfield.

None of which had prevented one noble Lady from making the trip out in her carriage early of a Saturday morn. She was well escorted, with a driver, two footmen, and a dog on the outside of the coach, and, on the inside, a young armigerous gentleman and a female attendant. Accompanied by the latter two, she passed through the door below the outlandish clock-sign and pulled on a bell-rope. A distant jingling was audible off beyond the back wall of the shop. She pulled again, and again. Presently a door in the back was opened. Through it the visitors glimpsed, not the expected storeroom, but an expansive, crowded, noisy, complicated Yard. Then the whole aperture of the doorway was blocked by the form of a great hulking dark bloke, coming towards them. He entered the shop, stopped, and looked straight over their heads and out the shop's front window to the carriage waiting there along Coppice Row. A moment sufficed to read the coat of arms on the door. Then he pivoted out of the way and extended an arm toward the back door. "Enter," he rumbled. Then, in case this had not been a sufficiently florid, courtly greeting, he added, "Welcome."

Johann von Hacklheber—that being the sole visitor who was male and visibly armed—had stepped in front of the two women when the big dark man had appeared. His left or dagger hand was looking a bit twitchy. This detail did not escape the perception of their host, who flung his great hands up in the air as proof that he was not armed, or as a gesture of exasperation, or both. Then he turned his back on them and vanished the way he had come.

A minute later, his place was taken by Daniel Waterhouse.

"Saturn says that he has all but scared you away," he began. "He forwards his apologies. He has gone off to brood over his unfitness as a retailer. Please come back. There is nothing *here*, save a pretense of a horologist's shop, which does not pay its rent."

Greetings and salutations of a more formal nature also passed among them, but these were so rote that they made little impression on anyone. Save one detail: Eliza, indicating her young woman attendant, made the following claim: "I present to you Fraülein Hildegard von Klötze."

"A familiar name—"

"As she would tell you, if she spoke more English, she is a half-sister of Gertrude von Klötze."

"The nurse who accompanied me on my journey from Hanover. That explains why her eyes are likewise shockingly familiar to me," said Daniel. "Welcome to London, Fraülein," he said with a bow—a rather deeper and more formal bow than would normally be directed to a lady-in-waiting. "And welcome, all of you, to the Court of Technologickal Arts. If you would only be so good as to follow me."

"WHEN I WAS A GIRL in Constantinople," Eliza said, "I one day worked up the nerve to venture out from the *harim* of the Topkapi Palace and to explore certain reaches of that motley Pile that ought to have been forbidden to me. This I did by climbing up grape-vines, clambering over rooftops, and the like. And after a while I arrived at a place whence I could look down into a court-yard. This place was occupied by men of a mystickal sect called Darwayshes, who wore costumes, and observed rites, setting them apart from the rest of *al-Islam.* I lurked there for a few minutes, watching them, and then, having had my fill of strange sights, crept back to the *harim.*"

"The similitude is a good one," said Daniel Waterhouse. "Yes, now you are in another court full of Dervishes, as queer in their own way, yet as easy around their own kind, as those you spied in Constantinople." He and Eliza had paused in a relatively stagnant corner of the court. Above them, a beam had been thrown across a gap to make a lifting-point. Suspended from its middle was an elephant's tusk, an ivory crescent eight feet in diameter if it was an inch. Diverse clever baffles and charms had been fixed to its rope to prevent rodents from abseiling down for midnight picnics; the only creature allowed to gnaw at this treasure was a journeyman ivory-carver who was having at it with a fine-toothed saw. Nor was this the only oddity or wonder in the Court of Technologickal Arts. The yard was an irregular pentagon a hundred feet in breadth. It was closed in by an arcade of work-stalls, each little more than a lean-to sheltering some odd collection of tools. At a glance Eliza saw a glass-blower, a goldsmith, a watch-maker, and a lens-grinder, but there were many others who had their own collections of special-ized lathes, mills, hand-tools, and paraphernalia that were every bit as particular, especial, and jealously looked-after. Perhaps that old Jew with the stubby telescopes strapped to his face had once called himself a jeweler, and the obese German overflowing yon tiny stool had been a toy-maker, turning out music-boxes. Now whatever they did had been subsumed in a larger and more obscure purpose. Others simply could not be classified at all. There was a bloke who had a stall to himself, off in the corner—an exile even among Dervishes—where he had mounted a glass sphere on an axle. Spin-ning this around with the aid of a wan, jittery apprentice, he pro-duced unearthly crackling noises and summoned forth small lightning-bolts.

The open space of the court had mostly been claimed by one fac-tion or another and filled up with works both prodigal and practical. There were too many furnaces and forges to count at a glance, all of them quite small, and devoted to some sub-sub-specialty. These were fashioned of brick and mortar, each to a particular shape, reminding the visitors of so many shells cast up on some outlandish beach. There was a crane, moved by two men each trudging along in a great wooden wheel. This was situated in the back of the court where a gate led in from a warren of country cowpaths, none of which had yet been ennobled with a picturesque name. The court was further en-livened by diverse derricks, rigs, presses, frames, and Overhead Lift-ing Devices of unknown nature and purpose. There was even a barrow: a stony hummock that might have deserved the appellation of Ruin half a millennium ago, but had by now been mostly resorbed by the earth.

"Your budget for stationery must be generous," Eliza said. For another curious feature of the place was that scraps of paper were blowing round it like autumn leaves, and each had something scribbled on it. "I am put in mind of the 'Change." She snatched a scrap that had been dancing in a current of air in front of her, and stretched it out: it had been slashed, scribbled, and cross-hatched with furious pen-strokes. Once it might have been a fair rendition, in perspective, of something three-dimensional. But other hands had added, subtracted, modified, and annotated it so many times that half of the page was covered by ink. Perfected, it had been thrown away.

"We do spend a good bit on ink and paper," Daniel admitted, "but men such as these cannot think without them."

"I suppose I am meant to be impressed; but instead I confess myself bewildered," was the verdict of Johann von Hacklheber, who had never strayed more than arm's length from "Hildegard," but had never touched her, as they strolled round the court.

"The difficulty lies in the fact that there is little, so far, in the way of finished work," Daniel said, "and what has been finished has been shipped to Bridewell Palace." Then there was a respite as Johann attempted to explain the concept of Bridewell to the German girl, a project that did not seem to go very well.

"Allow me to demonstrate," Daniel said. He strode off across the court. Johann, "Hildegard," and Eliza followed, forming a queue that snaked and wended among forges, furnaces, and less namable constructs until it stopped at the foot of the barrow-mound.

This had been endowed with a set of wrought-iron gates, exceptionally massive, and closed with a lock the size of a Folio Bible, as might be seen on an Arsenal-Gate. Daniel had the key: a pound of brass wrought and carved into a lacy labyrinth. He blew on it, then inserted it into a hatch on the lock's front with the care of a surgeon lancing a King's boil. Snicking and clicking noises emanated from the penetralia of the device as it issued mechanical challenges, which were rebutted by the key; finally Daniel was given leave to spin a brass wheel that drew back several bolts. The gates came a-jar. Daniel excused himself and stepped through the opening. Peering round him the guests could just make out a sort of vestibule within: a small stone-paved landing at the top of a pit. Some torches were soaking in an oil-pot. Daniel drew one out, shook off lashings of excess oil, and handed it to Johann. "If you would be so kind," he said. Johann had no difficulty finding an open flame in this court, and handed it back, a-blaze, in a few moments. "I shall be back soon," Daniel announced. "If not, send down a search party in half an hour." With that, he stepped over the brink of the pit. "Hildegard" gasped, thinking that he was about to plummet straight down some old well-shaft. But it presently became obvious from the nature of Daniel's movements that he was in fact descending a stairway, hidden in shadow. Soon he was gone from view, and they were left to watch a quivering rectangle of fiery light, and to hear diverse scraping, squealing, and clanking noises. Then the light again became concentrated into a bobbing fire-brand, followed at a short interval, first by the face of Daniel Waterhouse, and then by a gleaming quadrilateral that he was carrying under one arm like a book.

"This was lent to me by a friend who suffered from an embarrassment of riches," Daniel explained after the torch had been extinguished and stowed, and the gate locked. They were examining a squarish plate of what appeared to be gold. It had been treated very disrespectfully and was scraped, battered out of plane, salt-caked, and tar-stained. But it was still obviously gold, hand-hammered to a thickness of perhaps an eighth of an inch. "As you have probably guessed, there are more of them stowed below; but we only withdraw as much as can be wrought in a single day."

For some minutes they followed Daniel around the court as he carried this treasure to several stations. A workman scrubbed it in a barrel of water to get rid of the salt. A goldsmith grasped it with tongs and thrust it into a furnace; for a few moments it was enveloped in fumes and colored flames as impurities were burnt off. Then it resolved to a pure glowing slab. He tugged it out, quenched it in water, and snipped off a corner for assay. Then Daniel took it to a weigher who tediously balanced it on a scale, and noted it in a book. Then it was across the yard to a mill consisting of two great brass rollers, one above the other like a mangle. A man fed the plate into the crevice between these as a boy whirled a crank on an elaborate gear-train. The rollers turned almost as slowly as minute-hands. What emerged from them was no longer a neat square: it had been mashed to an irregular oval blob, like pie-crust under a rolling-pin, thinner than a fingernail. It came out onto a kind of skid that had been fashioned from a whole ox-hide stretched over a frame the size of a dining-table. The plate lay on this like a lake of molten gold, almost smooth enough to bear reflections. Four men—one at each corner—now bore this across the court to a stall where a large shearing-machine had been established. The ox-hide pallet was mated to this, so that the golden sheet could be slid directly into the jaws of the shear. Two men now went to work slicing the lozenge of gold into a large number of strips, each about a hand-span in width. When this was finished they rotated the strips ninety degrees and fed them through a second time, cutting them into squares. Some of the cuttings, from near the edge, came out imperfectly shaped, and were pitched into a discard basket. The rest were piled into a neat stack. When they ran out of gold the shear-men twice counted and re-stacked the cards (for the gold squares resembled nothing so much as a deck of great playing-cards). All of the proceeds—including the basket of scraps—were given back to Daniel. He took them back to the weigher, who accounted for every iota of gold. Daniel then returned the scraps to the locked crypt.

The tour-group reconvened in the shop of the man called Saturn. The golden cards had been stacked and counted one more time, and loaded into a purpose-built, velvet-lined chest that was just the right size for them. They gathered round it instinctively.

"Well, Dr. Waterhouse, we now understand perhaps a tenth of the oddities housed in your court," said Eliza. "When shall we understand the remainder?"

"When we go to Bridewell!" Daniel returned, and picked up the chest as if he meant to leave.

"We are like jewels in a pirate's treasure-chest," said the Duchess of Arcachon-Qwghlm, trying to get her fellow-passengers to look on the bright side.

Daniel, Eliza, Johann, and "Hildegard" were sharing this booth-on-wheels, not only with a small chest of gold cards, but also with several bales of libels. To judge from their smell and their tendency to rub off on people's clothing, these had come off the press very recently. Everyone shied away from them save Daniel, who was dressed in clothes that were black to begin with.

According to some unwritten but universal rule of etiquette, people mashed together in a confined space tended not to look one another in the eye, or to converse. The fact that "Hildegard" was, in truth, obviously Princess Caroline of Hanover only exacerbated it. Thus Eliza's efforts to make cheery conversation.

After they had jolted some distance southwards along Saffron Hill, Daniel, mortified and bored, managed to work one of his arms free of the pile-up, and got a hand on the window-shutter, which he shot open. In London, actual sun-beams were too much to ask for; but he was rewarded with a nebulous in-flow of smoky gray light, which fell on the top-most sheet of a libel-bale.

LIBERTY
by *Dappa*

My Persecutor has been heard to say that my libels are used only to stop up chinks, and plug diverse other windy orifices, in the *garderobes* of Bankside gin-houses. Which if true raises the question of how *he* would know anything of such places; but let us pass over this mystery. For if Mr. Charles White's assertion *is* true, then you, reader, are enjoying but a few minutes' peaceful interlude in a House of Office somewhere in Southwark, and I had best get to the point before you have done with your business.

If you put your eye up to the chink that was vacated, when you pulled this document from its rightful place, you may be able to see a street—an eastward continuation of Bankside, tho' a bit further from the shore, running in front of Winchester Yard; that is called Clink Street, and forms a part of the boundary of the *Liberty of the Clink*. This parcel, 'tis said, long ago belonged to some abbots; but they granted it to the Bishop of Winchester, with the stipulation that that noble prelate would put it to work saving mens' souls, and gathering alms. Accordingly, a long line of Bishops ran brothels there for many hundreds of years. These were none of your latter-day whore-houses, infamous for disease and the degradation of women; nay, this was in the *Halcyon* days before the *French* Pox, and a certain great Patron and Regulator of Brothels, who dwelt not far off in St. James, issued a decree that no woman be forced to work in such a place against her will. So keenly were these Institutions inspected and ruled by the King and the Bishop that Labor, Management, and Customers all got along famously, and few disputes arose. But as in any human intercourse, trouble was foredoomed, and so a Prison was constructed here. It is from the Clink prison that I pen these words. Do not be concerned for my welfare. I am in a commodious flat, with a river-view; for this I have my patroness, and several of my readers, to thank. Below are several windowless chambers where some hundreds of my fellow-prisoners dwell, heavily ironed and lightly fed.

Why, you may ask, should the Clink be so crowded with wretches, when those Kings and Bishops had such care to make of this place an earthly Paradise? Why, because of certain degradations that have come with time. The Pox shut down the old Stews; the brothels moved from their proud stations on Bankside to a *Diaspora* of back-rooms, salted all over the Metropolis, where the Lords Spiritual and Temporal can scarcely find, much less rule, them. The Temples of Aphrodite were replaced by bull- and bear-baiting rings, which I should describe as Fields of Mars, if there were anything martial about them; but this is giving them more than they deserve. The Muses flourished here too, until Cromwell shut down the theatres. The merry god Dionysus once gamboled in the Liberty of the Clink, but alas, the good old drinks of ale and wine have been quite driven out by that infamous new-fangled poison, *Genebre*. Pox, poison, and pit-bulls rule this Clink now. It is a sad prospect, and enough to make a sapient prisoner reflect upon the nature of Liberties in general. For we all love to phant'sy that we live in some sort of Liberty—if not of the Clink, then of the City of London or some other Jurisdiction where men are proud to style themselves Free. But under close inspection, how often do we find those Freedoms to be Chimaeras, and our cherished Liberties to be little better than my private flat in the upper storey of the Clink? We may put it down, I suppose, to the nostalgia for Merry Olde England, whereby all things, be they never so *modern* or *outlandish,* are viewed through a perspective-glass of ancient design, which promises to deliver a true image, but in truth colors and distorts all that is seen through it. Merry Olde England did not have the modern Pox; and so brothels are no longer what they used to be. Bloody and vile baiting-pits it did not have either, at least, not in the numbers seen to-day, and not frequented nor managed by *respectable* men. And Merry Olde England did not have slavery: that queer institution whereby a man may own another, simply by saying that he does. But the true England of to-day has all of these things. So I do not much bemoan the fact that I am in the Clink while you, reader, are at Liberty; for the Liberties in which we dwell are but delusions. I would fainer dwell in a meaner Liberty with fewer delusions than roam about a great one while being used by the lies and deceptions of the Party in power.

"What do you think?" Eliza asked. She'd been watching Daniel read it.

"Oh, as an essay, 'tis well enough wrought. As a political tactic, I question whether 'tis well considered."

"When he writes 'reader, this' and 'reader, that' it is no empty figure," Eliza said. "He *does* have readers—though few of them would admit to it, in the current climate."

"There is the rub, my lady," Daniel said. He slammed the window to, for they were now rattling along the banks of Fleet Ditch, not all that far from the Royal Society's headquarters in Crane Court, and the ammoniacal stench had choked him and flooded his eyes with tears. "By publishing such things you are gambling that the Whigs shall win and the Tories shall lose."

Eliza seemed a bit put out by the criticism. But Caroline had been listening to their discourse, and was ready with an answer: "Ve are all gambling on zat, Doctor Vaterhouse. Including you."

IF JOHANN HAD NOT told Caroline that Bridewell was a whilom Royal Palace, she would have alighted from her carriage, swept her gaze over it, and dismissed it as a half-Gothick, half-Tudor ruin-cum-slum. But knowing what she knew, she was bound to stand a-mazed for some minutes, trying to reconstruct it in her mind's eye.

Visiting Dukes might once have passed an afternoon bowling in that court over yonder, which was now home to an immense Gordian tangle of worn-out cordage, fated to be worried into oakum by the chapped fingers of incarcerated whores. In that high window, where a twelve-year-old pick-pocket had just thrust his penis out between iron bars to urinate into plain air, a Princess might once have gazed out onto the Fleet, back when it had been a brook instead of a sewer. Knights might have stabled their chargers in that long building that was now a booming, dusty work-shop.

A young woman of a more romantic disposition might have been at hard labor, all day long, trying to make a presentable phant'sy out of this social and architectural midden. Caroline only sustained the effort until cat-calls from diverse barred and grilled windows reminded her that they were out of place, tarrying here in a court normally used to receive new prisoners.

"Pay them no mind," Daniel recommended, ushering them through a gateway to an inner court. "Persons of Quality come here frequently to gape at the prisoners, though 'tis said that Bedlam provides an infinitely more lurid spectacle. The inmates will all suppose that we are tourists."

It had become evident that the palace had at least two wings, albeit not very well matched. "We shan't go that way," Daniel said, nodding to the left, "it is all men: pick-pockets, procurers, and 'prentices who've broken their masters' noses. Please follow me to the women's side." He spoke deliberately, but moved in haste: a tactic intended to make them hurry along and to ignore the countless distractions strewn in their path. "I shall be preceding all of you through many doors—committing an unforgivable breach of etiquette each time—but as you have gathered by now, this palace is no Versailles. Do watch your step." This as he negotiated a series of pantries, stairs, and corridors that might once have been the province of some lower servants. Then he shouldered his way through a door that flushed them into a space that was startlingly broad and high-roofed: some sort of ancient Hall, where perhaps Earls had dined at long tables. But today it was populated mostly by women. There were two predominant types of furniture: blocks, and stocks. The blocks were nothing more than slices of great tree-trunks, rising to mid-thigh. Before each of these stood a woman. All of the women were young, for their task was too strenuous for girls or dowagers. Each of them wielded a huge mallet: a segment of hardwood tree-trunk a hand-span in diameter and a foot long, impaled on an axe-handle. Snaking along the tops of the blocks were punnies of retted hemp, which is to say, stalks of the hemp plant, a yard taller than a man, and a few inches in diameter, which some months ago had been shorn of their foliage and flung into stagnant ponds in the Lambeth Marshes and weighed down with stones. There, the water had infected and rotted the tissues of those stalks, attacking the interstitial glop that bound the fibers together, but sparing the fibers themselves. Dried in the sun, these had been barged across to Bridewell and piled up in a monstrous faggot at one end of the hall. Fresh punnies were continually being jerked out of this heap by younger girls, dragged down the pavement, and offered up as for sacrifice on vacant blocks. A punny had no sooner come to rest than a prowling man in an apron raised one hand in the air, brandishing a cane, and gazing hungrily at the sight of a woman's back, protected only by a thin layer of calicoe. If she did not raise her mallet and smash it down on the punny within a heart-beat, the cane would come down with no less violence on her back. Each punny had to be beaten over and over again, all up and down its length and round its circumference, to break loose the snot of rotted and desiccated pulp from the long dark fibers. The hammers boomed on the blocks in a never-ending fusillade, the debris fell to the floor like dirty snow, or shot up into the air in a roiling cloud. Caroline and Eliza immediately reached for their head-scarves and covered their coifs lest their hair be adulterated with coarse hemp-fibers. Soon enough both of the ladies had drawn the tails of those scarves across their mouths and noses too, for the air was saturated with a gas of tiny fiber-scraps that could not be seen but could most certainly be felt when they lodged in the throat or the eyes.

Besides blocks, the other furnishing in the hall was stocks. These had been erected around the walls at regular intervals. Each consisted of two planks mounted in a vertical frame so that they could be slid up and down, and pegged at various discrete altitudes by means of carved shear-pins. Matching half-moon-shaped notches, of diverse sizes and spacings, had been cut into the edges of these planks, so that wrists and necks of varying gauges could be fixed in whatever place and height was most inconvenient to the prisoner, and pleasing to the whims of the responsible official. Most of the stocks were vacant—signifying a well-run shop—but three were occupied by women with their hands stretched up high above their heads. The backs of their dresses were black with oozing and clotting blood.

"Now you know all that is known about the making of hemp and the reformation of morals," Daniel remarked, after they had darted out through a side exit and gotten into a stairway, where it was possible to hear and to breathe. There was a decent pause so that everyone could brush themselves off and blink debris from their eyes. "It astonishes me," Daniel reflected, "that men will see what we have just seen—and yet go out the next day to patronize a brothel. Personally I can imagine no scene less likely to stir amorous feelings in general, or an interest in prostitutes in particular—" but Johann harrumphed and Eliza glared. Caroline seemed to find the discourse interesting enough, but she'd been out-voted. "Very well, then, to the apartment of Miss Hannah Spates we go now. Do watch where you step," Daniel added, unnecessarily, as turds were plainly spread around all over the place.

BRIDEWELL PALACE WAS TYPICAL English in that, outside of whatever historical process had caused it to end up the way it was, it made no sense whatever. Like Botany, it could be Memorized but not Understood. The visitors had lost their bearings immediately, and by this point in the tour, none of them would have been surprised if Daniel had flung open a door to reveal a secret tunnel under the Thames, or a back entrance to the Inferno. But instead they found themselves on the uppermost storey of some wing, addition or out-building. Hannah Spates and her colleagues lived and worked here, in a large space under the heavy-burdened rafters of an ancient slate roof. It must have been as cold in the winter as it was stifling today; but it was dry, did not stink, had light from a few windows, and was not decorated with bleeding women. The rafters were steeply sloped, as if trying to shrug off their burden of stone flakes. This gave it the ambience of a Gothick church whose builders had succumbed to Black Death before they could kit it out with pews and pulpit.

It did at least have an organ—or so the visitors thought at first. The largest single object in the room was a box, the size of a Vagabond-shack but much more finely wrought, of oak planks cleverly joined together, and caulked at the corners with tar and oakum. To one side of it was a row of four large bellows, with a wooden rail mounted a few feet above them. Two women were gripping the rail. Each of them divided her weight between a pair of bellows, one under each foot; these had been rigged in such a way that as one foot descended, expelling air into the great wind-chest, the other inhaled and rose up. The women seemed to be scaling an endless stair. They were a matched set of great busty hippy frazzle-haired wenches with apple-red cheeks, getting riper and shinier by the moment, and they seemed to find this great fun. While gazing with open curiosity at the visitors, they kept an eye on a glass U-tube filled with mercury, which started one way whenever one of them took her weight off of a foot, and jerked back as she shifted it to the other. A level had been marked on one side of the tube by tying a red ribbon around it. None of the visitors needed to have it explained that the goal of the exercise was to make the mercury climb until it reached the height of that ribbon.

To the other side of the wind-chest was a console looking somewhat like the keyboard of a pipe-organ. But it had only thirty-two keys, with no sharps or flats, and a few of them were stuck down. The organist was a young woman with long cinnamon hair put up in a loose bun. Like every other woman in Bridewell she wore a dress that appeared to have been plucked by a blind man from a parish poor-box; but it was clean and she had obviously devoted many an hour to patching it and taking it in to respect the general shape of her body. As Daniel approached with his guests in train, she sat up straight, reached out, and pulled on an ivory knob. A sigh came from the works and the stuck keys all came unstuck at once.

"Your grace," Daniel said, turning to Eliza, "I present Miss Hannah Spates. Miss Spates, this is the lady I told you about."

Hannah Spates rose, and made a pass at a curtsey.

"I am pleased to make your acquaintance," said Eliza, having instantly donned a sincere but distant affect commonly seen among high-born philanthropists obliged to visit hospitals, orphanages, poor-houses, &c. "Pray, what is this instrument? Are we to hear a performance?"

Hannah was wrong-footed by the words "instrument" and "performance" but soon enough decrypted the question without any aid from Daniel. "It is the card-punching machine, your grace," she answered, "it cuts the bits out, as I'm to show you."

"We shall balance the books first," Daniel announced, and led his guests onwards to a back corner of the room, where a semblance of a *banca* had been established. There was a large desk, manned by a clerk. Standing behind him was a gentleman of about fifty, who now stepped forward to be introduced. "Mr. William Ham," Daniel identified him, "my nephew, and the money-goldsmith who tends to our affairs in the City."

Pleasantries were exchanged; Eliza allowed as how she had heard of Mr. Ham from friends of hers who were pleased to have done business with him, and William Ham made it known how honored he was by this. He seemed startled and pleased to have been recognized at all, as he was a quiet, well-dressed, but indifferent-looking sort, typical of the newish breed who had taken over the *banca* trade from the menagerie of chandelier-swinging adventurers, intoxicated poltroons, and pathological liars who'd launched it when Daniel had been a young man.

To business: Daniel handed the little box of gold cards to William Ham, who carried them over to a standing-desk by the window and weighed them on a scale. He called out numbers to the clerk, who repeated them aloud and pricked them down in a book. The cards were then placed in a strong-box that squatted on the floor-boards next to the *banca*. All, that is, save for one of them, which was handed to a third man: an aproned overseer, struck from the same mould as the ones down in the hemp-pounding shop, save that he was not brandishing a cane. With the care and pomp of a priest bearing the consecrated host across a chancel, he took this to the organ-like device, and set it down, for the nonce, on the music stand above the keyboard. Then he gripped a pair of heavy black wrought-iron handles that projected from the machine's front panel, just above the keyboard, and gave them a mighty jerk. A slab of iron emerged from the machine like a tongue being thrust out. It was flat and smooth as if it had been extruded from a rolling-mill, and for the most part it was devoid of markings or features of any kind. But at the back of it was a shallow square depression perforated by a dense grid of holes, so that it looked like a grille or screen. The overseer plucked the gold card from the music-stand and laid it into the depression, where it fit perfectly and covered up all of the holes with a margin to spare around the edges. Then he put the heels of his hands against the two iron handles and rammed the slab, along with its golden burden, back into the bowels of the machine. As it boomed into place, the discriminating listener could hear a metallic snap, as though some latches had engaged to hold it all in place.

He stepped back. Miss Spates now took up her perch on the bench before the keyboard, and smoothed out her patched skirt. Her first act was to bend forward and peer into a prism mounted on the top of the console. Evidently she did not like what she saw, and so she reached up with both hands and began to turn a pair of iron cranks this way and that, making some adjustment to the position of the pallet. When she was satisfied, she folded her hands demurely in her lap, and looked at Daniel's knees.

"Here is where I am suffered to play a small rôle," Daniel remarked, reaching into his breast-pocket and drawing out a card of stiff paper that had been the object of several hours' or days' attention from a fine quill-pen. Its edge was decorated with strings of digits and its interior mostly filled with writing in a cramped hand: blocks of text in LATIN and *English,* runes in the Real Character, and brief outbursts of digits. This he handed, with a suggestion of a bow, to Hannah, who rotated it and set it in place on the music-stand.

"She can read!?" Johann said incredulously.

"Actually, *she* can—thanks to her doting father—but this is unusual, and not strictly necessary," Daniel answered. "All they need to be able to do, is to distinguish between a one and a zero—as you may see for yourself by inspecting the card."

Johann, Eliza, and Caroline crowded in behind Miss Spates to peer over her shoulders at the specimen on the music-stand. It bore many styles of numbers and characters; but she had oriented it so that she could read a long string of digits printed along the edge. Every one of those digits was either a 1 or a 0. As the others had been talking, she had been sliding a finger along the keyboard, shoving down some keys but not others. Whenever a key was depressed, snicking and clunking noises would sound from some system of rods and levers back inside the mechanism, and the key would stay where she had put it. It was plain to see that the pattern she was making of those keys was the same as the pattern of ones and zeroes written on the edge of the card: wherever she saw a 1, she depressed the corresponding key, and wherever she saw a 0, she skipped over it.

The minute and exacting toil of Miss Spates was accompanied by loud, sweaty, vigorous labor from the bellows-pumping wenches, who had put on a crescendo, trying to stomp the mercury up to the red ribbon. "By your leave, sir," one of them gasped, "sometimes we sing a song, as sailors do when they heave on a hawser."

"Pray carry on!" Daniel returned, to the dismay of the overseer who had just opened his mouth to ban it.

> *Oh have you met Miss Sally Brown*
> *The country's fairest daughter,*
> *She works the handle up and down,*
> *To pump the farmer's water*
>
> *Pumpin' Sal, pumpin' Sal,*
> *No one does it like that little gal,*

Jump to the pump and work that rod,
And make your fellow a lucky sod!

Sally moved to London Town
And soon became misguided,
She pumped the men who came around,
And sent them home delighted.

Pumpin' Sal, pumpin' Sal, [etc.]

Sally lives in Bridewell now
Pumping is her chore 'gain.
She wears her legs out for to power
A Virtuoso's Organ.

Pumpin' Sal, pumpin' Sal, [etc.]

At the final beat, the quicksilver in the tube finally shot up to kiss the ribbon. Hannah Spates hauled back on an ivory knob that she had been gripping in sweaty expectation. The machine hissed, not from one place but from many, like fragments of a burst cannon raining into the sea.

Mounted to the top of the wind-box was a row of what had at first appeared to be organ-pipes. Each was several inches in diameter and a yard long. They were arranged in a segment of an arc whose center was a dense complex of rods and levers atop the console, and whose radius was a couple of yards. The pipes were joined to the console by brass levers that fanned out from the center like rays of the sun. Some of these, but not others, suddenly went into motion.

It now became obvious that pistons were concealed within those cylinders, and some of them were being pressed up by air from the wind-chest. As they moved they elevated the ends of the brass levers. Each lever pivoted around an oiled fulcrum that was far from the piston, and close to the central mechanism, giving it a large mechanical advantage at the latter end. The rapid upward thrust of each piston caused the opposite end of its lever to press downward slowly, but with great force; and each of those lever-ends bore down upon a slim vertical rod. The rods were thirty-two in number, arranged in a regular picket-line; each of them resisted movement for a few heart-beats and then gave way, as if some barrier had been breached. This sudden yielding enabled the piston at the opposite end to fly up until it tripped a lever affixed to a vertical pushrod on the outside of its pipe. The pushrod transmitted force down to some air-gate at the base of the pipe, which sprang open, allowing the piston to fall down to its starting-place. It was all over in a few moments. Miss Spates pulled the knob that caused all the keys to pop up to the zero position.

The *coda* to the performance was a faint skirling noise that emanated from the works for a few seconds. Then a little golden spume jetted from a cavity on the front of the console, and was caught by a porcelain bowl beneath. Daniel snatched this and showed it to the visitors. It contained several tiny disks of gold, like færy-coins, some of which were still spinning and buzzing round on their rims. "These bits," Daniel said, "are all of a common weight, which means that to *weigh* them is to *count* them; the count is then tallied."

"Tallied in what way?" Johann asked.

"The clerk examines the card," Daniel said, indicating the snarled document Miss Spates had been reading from, "and checks the sum of each number, to know how many bits ought to have been punched out; if this agrees not with the number of bits in the bowl, the card is in error, and is sent back to be re-melted. A rare occurrence, for *Miss Spates* does not make *Mis-takes*!"

Indeed Miss Spates had already reached up to grip a brass lever, and hauled back on it once; this had ratcheted the iron pallet a short distance deeper into the machine, as she verified by a glance into the prism. The bellows-wenches were singing again, and Miss Spates had found a new number on the card, and was registering it upon the keys. In a few moments came another climax of singing, hissing, and clunking; another convulsion of many levers and another rill of golden bits. After several more repetitions, Hannah Spates rose and got out of the way; the bellows-wenches climbed down and headed off in the direction of a beer-bucket; and the overseer stepped in to haul the iron pallet backwards out of the machine. He retrieved the golden card, which had been Swiss-cheesed by scores of neat round holes. Each of these was situated at an intersection of the Grid of Monsieur Descartes; but not all of the intersections had been punched. The result was a curious admixture of order and randomness, perhaps akin to what one would observe in a neatly printed message that was, however, written in some inscrutable cypher.

"My understanding of Clerkenwell Court has been much advanced," was Eliza's verdict, "and yet there remains much that is mysterious. I see, for example, why you have recruited organ-makers. But not the man who makes lightning."

"We bought a stock of parts from a Dutch organ-maker who was returning to his home country, and so this machine was fabricated using the tricks of that trade," Daniel allowed. "A toy-maker, a horologist, or *electrical* enthusiast might have reached the same destination, via a different route."

"But this is not, as I gather, the machine that does the thinking?"

"The Logic Mill will be a different machine entirely," Daniel said.

"*Will be?* And so it does not exist yet?"

"The punching of the cards will take a great deal of time, even if we build many more machines like this one, and put all of Bridewell to work," Daniel said. "Moreover, the Logic Mill cannot be designed, built, or tested, until we have some samples of cards to give it. And so in our work to date we have borne down very hard on the card-punching problem. As you have seen, that problem is solved. Additional machines like this one are now being made; but most of our efforts may now be devoted to the Logic Mill." Daniel cleared his throat delicately. "A significant infusion of Capital would be most welcome."

"I should say so!" Johann exclaimed. "Why are you making the cards out of *gold?*"

"It is ductile, hence easily made into cards of perfectly uniform thickness. Yet it is durable, for it is the only metal that does not rust or tarnish. But *that* is not why we need capital. Strange to relate, we already have enough gold locked away in our vault to transcribe all of the paper cards that I brought with me."

"Please say more on that—?" Eliza requested.

"Oh, when I came here from Boston I brought several boxes of these paper cards—enough to inform the logical kernel of a machine."

"Why did you?"

"Because, madame, the Massachusetts Bay Colony Institute of Technologickal Arts has been generously supported by men of some importance, and I thought they might like to see tangible evidence that I had actually been doing something. No, I did not anticipate any of this." He extended a hand toward the machine, and followed up with a judicious hooding of the eyelids, and a nod at Caroline.

"There are more cards still in Boston, then?"

"I left almost all of them behind in Massachusetts. But God willing they are at this very moment being loaded into the hold of a ship, *Minerva*, which I believe is known to you. She sailed from London in late April, and ought to have reached Boston Harbor last week."

"When *Minerva*, God willing, returns to London, then you shall have need of more gold for making into cards," Johann observed.

"By a happy coincidence," Daniel said with a dry smile, "more gold is expected to reach us, by sea, at the same time. And so when I speak of our need for capital, I am *not* referring to gold for card-making."

"As a sort of technologickal adventurer, Doctor, you are suffered, nay encouraged, to imbibe of a sort of optimism that in other disciplines—such as finance—would be reckoned incompetence," Eliza said. "*I* am being asked to act as a financier, and can afford myself no such luxury. I say that you are gambling too much on the likelihood that two ships—one freighted with cards, the other with gold—shall arrive in London safely and at the same time."

"The point is well taken," Daniel said, "and so let me simplify matters by letting you know that the cards and the gold *are on the same ship.*"

"*Minerva* carries both?"

"And I think you know what a fine ship she is. I would sooner trust gold to the bilge of *Minerva* than the vaults of many a *banca*. It is safe to predict that, round the beginning of August, she will drop anchor in the Pool, and we shall have all of the requisites to punch a large number of these cards. What is wanted, in the meantime, is financing to sustain the operations of Clerkenwell Court, so that we may build the Logic Mill."

"May I presume that you have already tried and failed to get additional support from your benefactor?"

"Roger Comstock is the one who proposed that I consult you, madame."

"I never thought one such as he could run out of money."

"Properly speaking, it is a question of *liquidity*. Much now hangs in the political balance, as you know. The perils that have forced Princess Caroline to seek refuge far from the gardens of Hanover, have not failed to press in, almost as hotly, on the Marquis of Ravenscar. He has extended his resources to the utmost, readying and arming himself for the coming struggle against Bolingbroke."

"And not without effect, if yesterday's news from Parliament be true," Johann put in.

"Yesterday was a victory for Comstock—but it was little more than a *skirmish*. Ahead lie *battles*."

"It is a wonder he has time or money for Logic Mills at all," Johann remarked.

"In truth, he does not, and has quite forgotten about us for now," Daniel said.

"So you require a sort of bridge loan," Eliza said.

"Indeed, madame."

"A bridge-builder cannot practice his trade, unless he knows the length of the span to be made—"

"The length is from now until a Hanover is crowned King or Queen of Great Britain."

"That could be never."

"And yet, as a wise woman once remarked, we are all gambling on it."

"It could be years, then."

"Queen Anne is as likely to live to the end of 1714 as I am to go to Naples and sell myself in the town square as a gigolo," Daniel averred.

"What is the amount you seek?"

"A stipend, delivered at regular intervals. Mr. Ham has drawn up some figures."

"That sounds boring," Eliza said, "and so I propose a parting of the ways. Johann, who has a head for numbers, can look at Mr. Ham's. Hildegard may wish to stay with him."

"And you, madame?"

"I have a head for relationships," Eliza said, "and so I shall join you in my carriage as you are delivered back to Clerkenwell Court, and I shall discourse to you of the relationship—or to be blunt, what precisely is to be my *security* for the proposed loan."

"It is a curious sort of Mint that you have created," Eliza remarked.

Daniel was startled out of a drowsy reverie. The Duchess of Arcachon-Qwghlm had been silent, staring out the window, as her carriage had taken them up the bank of Fleet Ditch and round the western approach of Holbourn Bridge. Now they were stuck in the absurdly mis-named Field Lane, a clogged chute of brick and horse-shit.

London had come awake reluctantly. The Mobility had devoted all of their energies, yesterday, to the Hanging-March; even those who had not actually pushed their way through the crowd to glimpse the awful Derrick raised above Tyburn Cross, had busied themselves picking the pockets, filling the bellies, or satisfying the urges of those who had. As for the Nobility, they had been as preoccupied with a violent and ghastly spectacle of a different character: down in Westminster, the Whigs had suddenly begun to ask pointed questions as to what had become of certain Asiento revenues. Persons of Quality had devoted yester evening and much of the night to liquidating their holdings in the South Sea Company, and gathering in Clubbs and coffee-houses to misinform one another.

But it was now mid-afternoon, and everyone, hanging-watchers and Parliamentarians alike, was finally awake. Except for Daniel Waterhouse, who had almost drifted off when pricked awake by this curious remark from Eliza. "I beg your pardon?" he mumbled, buying time to wake himself up.

"I am trying to hatch a similitude for what you are doing at Bridewell," Eliza returned. Then, sensing that this answer had been none too informative, she straightened her spine, like a cat, and turned her face toward Daniel. She was so beautiful that he flinched. "Gold is meant to be fungible—an ounce of it here is no different from an ounce in Amsterdam or Shahjahanabad."

I wish someone would explain that to Isaac, Daniel mused, then felt bad, as Isaac was a sick man just now—he'd collapsed in Westminster Palace a couple of weeks ago, and was still lying on a sick-bed at Roger Comstock's house.

"A financier, asked for a loan, carries out a diligent summing-up of the debtor's assets, to ensure that the loan shall be secured by something of worth," Eliza continued. "You have gold. This gold could be weighed, to find its worth. There could be no better security for a loan. But there is a complication. You are not using the gold *as gold.* You are using it as a medium for storage of information. Or I might say it thus: you are informing it. Once informed by the card-punching organ, it possesses value—to you, at least—that it did not have before. If it were to be melted down, it would lose that value. The only like procedure that I can call to mind, is that whereby blank disks of gold are informed by the blow of a die at the Mint, making 'em into guineas, and thereby imbuing 'em with additional worth—*seigneurage,* they name it. And so I say that your organ at Bridewell is like a little Mint, and your punched cards are the Coin of a new Realm."

"You have convinced me," Daniel said. "I only hope that Sir Isaac does not hear of it, and denominate me a rival."

"If the rumors as to Sir Isaac's condition are true," Eliza said, "you or *some* rival may soon be running the Mint at the Tower. But that is beside the point. Supposing you build the Logic Mill, and it works. Then the value—and I mean value not moral, æsthetic, or spiritual, but œconomic—of your Institute inheres in the ability to carry out logical and arithmetical work using the cards."

"Indeed, madame, that is all we can offer."

"If the cards were foreclosed upon by a creditor, and melted, the information would all be con-fused, the Logic Mill would not do work, and the value we just spoke of would be annihilated."

"True."

"It follows that the gold, once wrought into punched cards, be-comes a poor form of security indeed, as it cannot be spent, in a monetary sense, without destroying your enterprise."

"I agree without reservation that the gold cannot secure the loan."

"Moreover, if I understand the nature of the project, the cards and the machine are to be shipped to the Academy of Sciences in St. Petersburg when they are finished."

"That is true of the first set."

"But subsequent ones, supposing you build more, shall become the property of the Marquis of Ravenscar."

"As currently envisioned, yes."

"All that *I* would be left with would be some news that I might use to my advantage in certain markets. This is a sort of game I played to great advantage when I was young, and had nothing to lose, and no one who depended on me. But now I require tangible equity in exchange for my investments. I invest with my *head*, not my *heart*."

"And yet it is plain that you support Dappa, and I have heard that you contribute generously to hospitals for Veterans and Vagabonds."

"*As charities,* yes. But it is too late for you to remake your Institute as a charity."

"Then let me tell you something of the Logic Mill that not even Roger knows," Daniel sighed.

"You have my attention, Doctor."

"It will not work."

"The Logic Mill will not do logic?"

"Oh, yes, of course it will do that. Doing logic with a machine is not so very difficult. Leibniz took it up where Pascal dropped it, and I built upon Leibniz's work for fifteen years in Boston. Now I have turned it over to a cabal of ingenious fellows who in fifteen *weeks* have advanced further than I did."

"Then what do you mean, when you say it will not work?"

"When I returned from Hanover two days ago I devoted some time to reviewing the schemes that the *ingénieurs* have devised. I am most pleased with the results. But then I discovered a grave difficulty: we want power."

"Ah, you spoke to me of this in Hanover."

"Indeed, for then I had begun to *suspect* what I now *know*: that the Logic Mill shall require a source of Power, in the newfangled Mechanickal sense of that word, that is both *mighty* and *steady*. A very large water-wheel in a great river might serve; but much better would be—"

"The Engine for Raising Water by Fire!"

"If you were to invest in *that*, madame—and rest assured that it *does* want investors—you could obtain a controlling interest with little difficulty, thereby satisfying your requirement for Equity. With a new financial wind at his back, Mr. Newcomen could clear certain shoals on which the work has recently run aground, and drive on into open and beckoning seas. Meanwhile, here in London, the Logic Mill project shall arrive at an impasse, because of the dearth of Power. It shall happen soon—less than a year from now. You may then take the matter up with the Tsar, or with the Marquis of Ravenscar, or both; they will bargain with you then, madame, having no other choices."

Eliza gazed out the windows for some minutes. By now they had run the length of Saffron Hill, and the driver had made a detour to the edge of Clerkenwell Green and up Rag Street so as to spare himself, his horses, and his passengers a disagreeable and perilous transit of Hockley-in-the-Hole, where at this very moment outrages were being committed that would be punished six weeks hence at the next Hanging Day.

They had entered into the extension of Rag Street called Coppice Row, bringing them full circle. Daniel, gazing forward out his window, spied a carriage stopped before Clerkenwell Court. His heart forgot to beat when he recognized it. Matters were about to become more complicated than he'd have liked them to be. He thumped on the roof, and the driver reined in his team at the corner, a stone's throw short of the other carriage. "I will alight here," Daniel said, "as this is an easier place to get your lovely carriage turned round." Before Eliza could protest he opened the door, and one of her footmen jumped down to help him out.

"You have cast a new light on the matter," Eliza announced, giving him a prim smile that was the beginning of good-bye. "I am now willing to consider the proposal. But I cannot come to any conclusions until I have become well acquainted with the gentleman who founded the company."

"The Earl of Lostwithiel," said Daniel, raising his voice, as he was now out in the street, addressing Eliza through the open carriage-door. "For some weeks he has excused himself from the House of Lords. The illness of his third son forced him to withdraw to the west country. The poor child's demise extended his absence. I suspect that complications relating to the Engine have drawn it out even further. But even now, news is speeding westwards of yesterday's doings in Parliament. Lostwithiel must return now. He will be back in London anon. I shall see to it that he pays a call on your grace at Leicester House."

"THIRTY-SEVEN MINUTES AGO," said the big horologist named Saturn, "a strange old Tory appeared at our gates and begain baying for Doctor Waterhouse." He nodded at the carriage parked in front of his shop.

Daniel had already recognized it. "Where is Mr. Threader now?" he inquired.

"I have plied him with tea, and given him a brief look round the place—not letting him see any of the good bits—and then advanced from tea to brandy. He is drinking it three doors down, in that shop where the plasterers were finishing up yesterday."

"Thank you, Mr. Hoxton," Daniel said, putting a hand on the door to go out.

"You are welcome," Peter Hoxton said, in a guarded way, "but I must say, if I had known, when Fate brought us together, what sort of persons you associate with, I should never have pursued the acquaintance."

Daniel exited smiling. His expression changed over to one of surprise as a second carriage—a battered hackney, its wheel rims thumping from dents and clotted horse-turds—came up Coppice Row at reckless speed, and halted, in serial and ramshackle style, just ahead of Mr. Threader's. The door flew open. Out stepped a red-faced, white-haired, black-suited Nonconformist. Immediately behind him came a small man in breeches, waistcoat, &c., of a more conventional cut, though made of materials so florid as to be almost tribal. And behind him came a common-looking bloke who was even bigger than Saturn. He stayed behind to flick coins into the outstretched palm of the coachman.

"Brother Norman. Mr. Kikin. What a pleasure," Daniel said, moving to intercept them before they could reach the door of the clock-shop, and further damage Saturn's esteem for him. "I had not been notified that our Clubb was to meet to-day; but I welcome you to Clerkenwell Court, and I shall welcome our Treasurer too, when I have run him to ground."

"Mr. Threader is here?" said the astonished Mr. Kikin, and cast a comical look up and down Coppice Row. This was then mimicked by his bodyguard, who had taken up his usual station behind Mr. Kikin's shoulder.

"Why?" demanded Mr. Orney; but just then the door of a vacant storefront burst open, and out came Mr. Threader, already red in the ears from brandy.

"I haven't the vaguest notion of why *you* two are here," he proclaimed, "but since you are, I hereby call to order an emergency meeting of the Clubb for the Taking and Prosecution of the Party or Parties responsible for the Manufacture and Placement of the Infernal Engines lately Exploded at Crane Court, Orney's Ship-yard, *et cetera!*"

"First order of business: selecting a shorter name," Mr. Orney suggested.

"The first order of business, as ever, shall be the Collection of Dues—presuming as always that you are still solvent, Mr. Orney."

"If news from Westminster is true, it is not *my* solvency that bears examination— *Mr. Threader.*"

"It is of Parliament that I would discourse—which is why that is to be the *second* order of business—those Members who arrived *late* must wait their turn."

"How can we be *late* for a meeting that was called *after we arrived*!?"

"Gentlemen," Daniel said, "I fear we are disturbing our neighbors in Hockley-in-the-Hole. May we—please—take this inside?"

IT MIGHT ONE DAY serve as a pub or coffee-house, but for the nonce it was an empty room, freshly plastered, strewn with straw. The walls were white, darkling to overcast gray in the corners where still-damp plaster emitted palpable warmth and a nostril-stinging fragrance. The Clubb set up an impromptu Parliament there, using overturned buckets as chairs, and an upright barrel as lectern. These were improvised by Saturn and Mr. Kikin's bodyguard during the time that Mr. Threader raked in the Dues with all the weighing, biting, and microscopic examination of coins, and injurious commentary, that had become a Clubb custom. Then it was time for Mr. Threader to take command of the barrel. As he all too soon discovered, this was empty, and when struck with the fist emitted a tremendous boom, useful for rhetorical effect.

"When a Ship of Force appears before the breakwater, and lobs a mortar-shell *(boom)* into the town *(boom)*, you may be certain of two things: first *(boom)* that the enemy has been laying its plans for many months in advance; second *(boom)* that more *(boom)* mortar *(boom)* shells *(boom)* are shortly to follow *(boom boom boom)*."

"More brandy, Mr. Threader?" suggested Mr. Orney; but Threader ignored him.

"Yesterday," continued Mr. Threader, "the notorious leader of the Faction dropped *(boom)* a bomb *(boom)* in the House of Lords, discomposing the awful dignity, and shattering the traditional somnolence, of that August Body!"

"I have heard it said that if there were a way to invest in Apoplexy, one could have gotten rich in Westminster yesterday," said the Russian.

"As you are a Foreigner, sir, your amusement, like your person, are tolerated even if not welcomed. Those of us who live here must consider it *soberly*." He shot Orney a warning look to nip in the bud any plays on the word. "To revisit my similitude of the Ship and the Mortar-Shell, we must ask, how long has Ravenscar been planning this? And where will the next *(boom)* shell *(boom)* fall *(boom)*?"

"It'll fall on your head if you keep striking that barrel-head," Mr. Orney muttered.

"I have heard that yesterday was a lively one indeed for the South Sea Company, and doubtless for your enterprise, Mr. Threader," Daniel said. "In fact, such must be the demands upon your professional services, that I am astonished to find you here. Yes, Comstock has put Viscount Bolingbroke on the spot regarding that Asiento money. But what has that got to do with our Clubb?"

"It has been a strange fortnight for men whose business is to handle money," Mr. Threader said.

"Thank you for sharing that reflection with us, sir," returned Mr. Orney. "How does it bear on the very reasonable question just asked by Brother Daniel?"

"Men have been gathering up guineas, removing them from circulation, paying for them with French coins or other specie. It is all part of a subtile and covert investigation of the coinage, set afoot, 'tis said, by Bolingbroke."

"I move," said Daniel, "that we suspend Mr. Threader's remarks, and move him away from the Barrel, until such time as he professes a willingness to divulge, plainly and tersely, why the hell he is here; and in the meantime that either Brother Norman or Mr. Kikin take the Barrel and explain why *they* are here."

This motion passed by acclamation. Threader turned his back on all of them, a sullen gesture that elicited some hooting. Orney rose to speak; and in his Nonconformist get-up, standing before a barrel on a straw-covered floor, he looked for all the world like an itinerant preacher-man convening a barn-load of rustic believers.

"Though hangings might yesterday have been the talk of the Newgate-Tyburn axis, and the vanished Asiento money the sensation of Westminster and the City, the great happening of the day in Rotherhithe was the arrival—I shall employ dry understatement, and call it *startling*—of a Russian war-galley. She rowed here direct from St. Petersburg. To judge from the number of available places on her benches, she was driven with a speed fatal to several oarsmen; and the diverse large-caliber holes in her hull attest to at least one encounter with the Swedish Navy. At any rate, she got here, and now graces one of my docks, for she wants repairs. No sooner had she been made fast to my pier than several furry emissaries came down the gangplanks and fanned out into the city—"

"Rats?" guessed Mr. Threader.

"Russians," said Orney, "though of course there were some rats, too. One of the Russians brought a message to Mr. Kikin. Another brought one to me."

"No doubt the Tsar is running low on warships, and wants to know when you will be finished with those you are supposed to be building for him," said Mr. Threader.

"Oh I *am* building them, sir," Orney returned, "notwithstanding the best efforts of Infernal Engine-makers."

"I applaud you, Brother Norman," Daniel said, "for being the first man to say anything that is actually relevant to this Clubb's purpose."

"What shall your answer be, to the impatient Tsar?" Threader asked cruelly.

"Progress is being made," Orney said, "though I do confess it would be made *faster* if my fire-office would deign to make good on the losses for which they were supposedly insuring me."

"A-*ha!*" exclaimed Mr. Threader, satisfied.

"Why should your fire insurer not compensate you for what was plainly *a fire?*" Daniel asked.

"The policy that I bought from them contains an exemption for fires consequent to Acts of War. They have taken the position that the ship was set fire by *Swedish* incendiaries."

This was too much for Mr. Threader, who put both hands over his face to stifle a guffaw. Mr. Orney's deadly adversary he might be in nearly every regard; but in their hostility towards the insurance industry, the two men were as blood brothers. "Oh yes," he burst out, "a Londoner can scarce set foot out of his house nowadays without being set on fire by a roving Mobb of Swedish Incendiaries!"

"I think you have made your predicament clear, Brother Norman," said Daniel. "You require that the Clubb achieve its stated goal, so that you may claim the money you are due from your insurer; complete the ships; and escape the wrath of the Tsar." He turned now to the Muscovite. "Mr Kikin, are you at liberty to disclose the import of the message brought to you yesterday?"

"His Imperial Majesty made some references to Mr. Orney. To relate these now were redundant," said Kikin. "He takes the side of the insurance company in suspecting Swedish Incendiaries." A pause to clear his throat and inspect his nails as another juicy spate of laughter escaped from behind the hands of Mr. Threader. "His Imperial Majesty then wrote, or I should say, dictated to his scribe, a surpassingly bizarre discourse concerning some gold plates, which he desires ardently, notwithstanding the fact that they have been, in some sense, damaged; and he puts it all down to a fellow named Doctor Daniel Waterhouse—a name I never dreamed I should stumble across in an official communication from the Tsar of All the Russias."

"It's a long story," Daniel said, to end the long and profound silence that ensued—for Mr. Kikin's revelation had left even Mr. Threader dumbstruck.

"The Tsar has a long memory—and a long reach," Kikin reminded him.

"Very well, it's like this," Daniel said, and flipped open the latch on the little card-case he had been carrying around. At Bridewell he had dropped off the blank cards made this morning, and swopped them for ones that had been punched by Hannah Spates, and audited by the clerk. He displayed one to the Clubb, holding it up to a window so that light would shine through the holes. "As you can see, to describe it as *damaged* reflects an error in translation or transcription—what the Tsar meant was that it would have a lot of holes punched in it."

"It is hardly the first strange request that His Imperial Majesty has made," said Kikin. Indeed, the Russian was taking this much more matter-of-factly than Orney or Threader, who were so befuddled that they almost looked frightened.

Daniel said, "By the time that Brother Norman has this galley ship-shape, which will be—?"

"A week," said Orney. "God willing."

"By then I shall have damaged quite a few more, and they shall be ready to ship to St. Petersburg. If the Tsar is pleased by the results, the project in question may then move forward. But as this has nothing to do with the Clubb, let us set it aside for now." And he literally did, putting the card back in the chest and setting it aside.

"Well, if we're to speak no further of Brother Daniel's entanglements in Muscovy," said Mr. Orney, "perhaps Mr. Threader would now care to explain his presence."

"I would speak to the Clubb of an Opportunity," said Mr. Threader—who had finally composed himself and re-established his customary dry and dignified mien. He was gazing pensively out the window, and so did not witness the other members rolling their eyes and glancing at their watches. After a pause for effect, he made a half-turn and began looking them in the eye, each in turn. "Dr. Waterhouse has raised the possibility that the Infernal Device that nearly killed him and me in Crane Court, might not have been intended for either one of us—but rather for Sir Isaac Newton, who was known to frequent Crane Court late of a Sunday evening. This hypothesis was roundly hooted down at our previous meeting, and I shall be the first to confess that I was extremely skeptickal of it. But everything has changed. In the Clubbs and coffee-houses of the City, one name is now on every tongue: Jack the Coiner. At Westminster, in Lords, and in Star Chamber, who is the man they speak of? The

Duke of Marlborough? No. Prince Eugene? No. It is Jack the Coiner. At the Tower of London, rumors abound that Jack the Coiner goes in and out of the Mint at will. Why is my lord Bolingbroke investigating the fineness of Her Majesty's coinage? Why, because he fears it has been adulterated by Jack the Coiner. Why has Sir Isaac Newton suffered a nervous collapse? Because of the mischief committed against him by Jack the Coiner. Now, I ask you men of the Clubb: supposing, for the sake of argument, that we credit the extraordinary hypothesis of Dr. Waterhouse as to the intended victim of the first Infernal Device: what man would have a motive to assassinate him whose charge it is to prosecute all coiners, and send them to Tyburn to be torn apart? Why, a coiner! And among coiners, which would command the resources, which would have the cunning, to build and to place an Infernal Device?"

Kikin and Orney were silent, sullenly declining to participate in Threader's call-and-response.

"Jack the Coiner," said Daniel dutifully—since it was, after all, *his* hypothesis.

"Jack the Coiner. And therein lies the Opportunity I spoke of."

"An opportunity to have our throats slit from ear to ear?" Mr. Orney inquired.

"No! An opportunity to be of service to great men—men such as Her Britannic Majesty's Secretary of State Viscount Bolingbroke, Mr. Charles White, and Sir Isaac Newton!"

"Ah, yes, that *would* seem like an Opportunity for some," said Mr. Kikin, "but not for me, as I am already quite busy being of service to the Greatest Man in the World. Thank you anyway."

"As for myself," said Mr. Orney, "I am put in mind of Our Saviour, who made Himself of service to the poor by washing their feet with His own hands. Following His example as best a sinner may, I can have no larger ambition than to be of service to my common ordinary brethren, the salt of the earth. The Viscount Bolingbroke can look after himself."

Mr. Threader sighed. "I had phant'sied I might fire this Clubb with renewed lust for the pursuit."

Daniel said, "Mr. Kikin and Mr. Orney each has his own reason to join in that pursuit, as they have just explained to us—so why don't let's each pursue Jack for his own motives. If you wish to construe it as an Opportunity, it is of no account to me one way or the other."

"I have been making inquiries about this knave Jack," Mr. Threader said. "It is rumored that he is from time to time seen around the warehouses of Mr. Knockmealdown."

Orney scoffed. "That is like saying he has been spotted in England," he pointed out, "since the hideaways and bolt-holes of the East London Company spread across half of the Borough."

"Who is this person? What is this company?" Mr. Kikin wanted to know.

"Mr. Knockmealdown is the most notorious receiver of stolen goods in the metropolis," Daniel said.

"That is no mean distinction," Mr. Kikin said, "as this place has as many *fences* as *constables.*"

"To be sure, there are thousands of those," Daniel assured him, "but only a few dozen receivers of note."

Orney put in, "There is only one who has amassed capital sufficient to receive goods on a large scale—say, the whole contents of a pirated ship, as well as the ship itself. That is Mr. Knockmealdown."

"And this man has a *company*?!"

"Of course not," Orney said. "But he has an *organization,* which has ramified and spread from Rotherhithe—where I am sorry to say he got his start—up the bank to encompass a considerable part of the Bermondsey and Southwark waterfronts. Some wag once, drawing a facetious comparison to the British East India Company, dubbed it the Irish East London Company, and the name has stuck."

"So Mr. Threader has tracked our quarry as far as the south bank of the River Thames," Daniel said. "Meanwhile our missing member, Henry Arlanc, has, he assures me, been pursuing his investigations among the Vault-men of Fleet Ditch, so far to no practical effect. Has there been any progress in retaining a thief-taker?"

"I spent, or rather wasted, some time on it," said Mr. Kikin. "I posted a reward, and heard from several who feigned interest. But when I explained the nature of the work to them, they quickly lost interest."

"If the hypothesis of Brother Daniel and Mr. Threader is correct, this explains itself," said Mr. Orney. "Thief-takers, as I understand them, are petty scoundrels—poachers of small game. Such a varlet would not dare challenge Jack the Coiner."

"Perhaps, rather than posting a reward, it were better to find one thief-taker who is resolute, and treat with him directly," Mr. Threader suggested.

"It is most generous of the two of you to share these notions with me," said Mr. Kikin, "but I have anticipated you, and made efforts to reach Mr. Sean Partry."

"And that is—?" Orney asked.

"The most famous of all living thief-takers," Kikin announced.

"I have never heard of him," said Threader.

"Because you are a City man—why should you? Rest assured he

enjoys a high reputation in the *demimonde*—several of the petty thief-takers who came to me after I posted the reward, mentioned his name with great respect."

"Supposing that he is all that he's reputed to be—even so, can he challenge the likes of Jack the Coiner?" Daniel asked.

"More to the point, *will* he?" Threader added.

"He *will*," Kikin returned, "for 'tis said that his younger brother was slain by a member of Jack's gang. As to whether he *can*, this shall be discovered before we have to pay him very much money."

"Very well, provided we can settle on a clear definition of this troubling phrase *very much money*, I would be amenable to further contacts with Mr. Sean Partry," said Mr. Threader; and the others seemed to say, with little nods of their heads, that they did not disagree.

"We've not heard from you, Brother Daniel," said Orney. "Have you continued in your own investigation? How goes it?"

"It goes splendidly," Daniel returned, "but it is a slow strategy that I am pursuing, one that shall reward our patience. Notwithstanding which, results are beginning to develop: both the Marquis of Ravenscar and the Royal College of Physicians have been victims of burglary in the last month. I could not be more satisfied."

The other three exchanged looks, but none would be first to admit that he could not understand what Daniel was talking about. He was developing a reputation, it seemed, as a strange bloke who wandered about London in possession of perforated gold plates badly wanted by the Tsar; and the instincts of Mr. Orney, Mr. Threader, and Mr. Kikin were not to pry into the Pandora's Box that, it seemed, was the life of Dr. Waterhouse.

Westminster Palace
25 JUNE 1714

THE HOUSE BEING INFORMED, That the Secretary of the *South Sea* Company attended;

He was called in; and, at the Bar, presented to the House, a Book containing the Proceedings of the Directors of the *South Sea* Company, relating to the *Assiento* Trade; together with all Directions, Letters, and Informations, which the Directors, or any Committee of Directors, have received concerning the same.

And then he withdrew.

The Title of the said Book was read.

Ordered, That the said Book do lie upon the Table, to be perused by the Members of the House.

—*JOURNALS OF THE HOUSE OF COMMONS,*
VENERIS, 25° *DIE JULII;*
ANNO 13° ANNÆ REGINÆ, 1714

Dr. Daniel Waterhouse
c/o the Royal Society
Crane Court
London

Mr. Enoch Root
Thorn Bush Tavern
Boston
    25 June 1714
    Mr. Root,

Forgive the use of that barbarous convenience, the Pencil. For I write these words over a cup of Java in Waghorn's Coffee-house, which as you may know is a sort of annex to the lobby of the House of Lords.

From which you may infer that I am pressed in on all sides by that species of bipedal parasite known as the Lobbyer. Indeed, you may even be tugging fretfully at your red beard, wondering whether I have *become* a Lobbyer. The fact that I am writing a letter—instead of sidling up to well-dressed gentlemen and feigning interest in their children's welfare—is evidence to the contrary. My sojourn to Westminster today was occasioned by the need to speak to the Longitude Committee, and is being extended by my hope—vain, as it turns out—that Lords shall wind up their deliberations in a timely manner so that I may have a few words with one of their number. So perhaps in the end I *am* a Lobbyer.

I write to *you* because I wish to communicate with my *son*, Godfrey. This might seem a curiously indirect way of doing it. Indeed I often send the lad birthday-greetings and short paternal homilies, addressed to him care of my beloved wife. The little notes that come back to me months later, veering across the page in his deranged, expansive hand, and riddled with ink-bursts, are evidence that Faith is passing my correspondence on to him. Why, then, should I route this letter through the circuitous channel of Mr. Root's Table at the Thorn Bush Tavern? Because what I wish to convey to my son is not easily set down in phrases that a boy of his age has the wit to parse rightly.

It is known to everyone who has studied the life of my son's namesake, Gottfried Wilhelm von Leibniz, that when he was a boy, he was, for a time, locked out of the library of his dead father. A petty nobleman of Leipzig, learning of this atrocity, intervened on the boy's behalf, and saw to it that the library-door was unlocked, and little Gottfried was given the run of the place. What is less well known is that the mysterious nobleman was named Egon von Hacklheber—a contemporary of the mighty and orgulous banker, Lothar, who made the House of Hacklheber what it is, and is not, today. Rather than offering a physical description of Lother's little-known "stepbrother" Egon, I shall make this letter a good bit shorter by saying that he looked like you, Enoch. He vanished shortly after the conclusion of the Thirty Years' War and was presumed murdered by highwaymen.

Now in Boston lives a boy Godfrey William who may shortly find himself in the same plight that Gottfried Wilhelm faced in Leipzig sixty years ago. To wit, it is likely that his father shall turn up dead, and that the boy shall find himself in the care of a mother who is loving and well-intentioned but entirely too apt to be swayed by the counsels of neighbors, teachers, ministers, &c. I have spent enough time around Puritans in general, and Boston Puritans in particular, to know what these people will tell her: lock up the library! Or in other words—since I left only a paltry library behind—raise the boy to think of his father as a kindly but inept, fanciful but harmless character (rather like our neighbor, Mrs. Goose), who wandered off on a fool's errand, and met with a wholly predictable, and therefore rich-ly deserved, fate—a sort of fate that Godfrey may avoid, by steer-ing clear of his father's eccentricities and enthusiasms. In other words, Faith will let the boy partake of whatever nourishment he wants, provided it smacks not of Philosophy.

I charge you, Enoch, with saving the boy. A weighty burden I know; but much is afoot here. To assist you in this difficult task, I shall from time to time send you letters such as this one, that you may read in a few minutes what I have done in a few weeks. If these are shown to Godfrey when he is older, their contents may help to dispel any illusions as to my sanity and my seriousness that may have been planted in his mind by his fel-low colonists. Months may pass, however, during which I do not have leisure to write to you again, even hastily with a pen-cil, as now. The odds are high that during those months I shall have an encounter with a nicotine-smirched poniard, a Black-guard's bludgeon, a court-fop's epee, or Jack Ketch's rope. I may even—unlikely as it now seems—die of natural causes.

I have just been interrupted for some minutes by an acquaintance, one Mr. Threader. He is flitting and hopping about Waghorn's and the Lobby like a sparrow whose nest has just been blown down in a wind-storm. Most of his energies are directed towards what is going on in Lords, which has to do with some Asiento money that has gone missing (if you have not heard of this scandal, *vide* any of the newspapers on the ship that brought you this letter). But he has graciously spared a few minutes to feign some concern for Sir Isaac. Two weeks have passed since Newton came here to discourse of Longitude before Commons, was pulled aside to treat of Mint matters in Star Chamber, and suffered a nervous collapse. Countless rumors have circulated concerning the nature and gravity of his illness, and Mr. Threader has just recited *all* of them to me whilst studying my face. I cannot guess what my phizz told him, but my words let him know that the stories are all falsehoods. The truth of the matter is that Newton has been moved back to his house in St. Martin's, and is recovering satisfactorily. Today I addressed the Longitude Committee in his stead—not because he is really all that sick, but because no inducement will now prevail on him to come back to Westminster Palace, which he looks on as a thriving nest of vipers, hornets, Jesuits, &c., &c. If he ever sets foot in this place again—which will happen only if he is compelled to, by a Trial of the Pyx—he will not come naïve and unready, as he did a fortnight ago. He will come in the habit of a Grenadier, viz. as bedizened with Bombs as is the Apple Tree with Fruit.

You will be shocked to learn that *gambling* is the order of the hour, here in Waghorn's. The lobbyers have all lobbied one another to exhaustion, and still the Lords show grievously bad form by continuing to deliberate behind closed doors. Nothing is left to the lobbyers, as a way of passing the hours, than Vices. Having drunk up all the spiritous matter and smoked up all the air in Waghorn's, the only feasible vice left to them is the laying of wagers. Coins brought hither this morning for the honest purpose of bribing legislators, are being put to base uses.

When I began writing this letter, they were laying odds on whether Bolingbroke would achieve his paramount goal, which is to induce the Privy Council to call for a Trial of the Pyx. But the scraps of paper and snatches of gossip percolating out of Lords seem to say that things are not going Bolingbroke's way. His very survival may be at stake; the Pyx gambit, though excellent, may have to be set aside, for now, so that he may mass all his efforts on rebuttal of the Asiento allegations. Those who gambled on a Pyx trial an hour ago, have given up as lost whatever money they staked then, and are now trying to recoup their losses by betting that Her Britannic Majesty will prorogue Parliament simply to save her Secretary of State from going down—and perhaps taking the South Sea Company with him.

The doors to Lords have been opened. I shall close for now and continue when I can. A lot of money is changing hands. Lostwithiel is approaching.

I am writing this on my lap, sitting on the edge of the Thames embankment, legs adangle above the flow. I am, I should estimate, the ninety-fifth in a queue of a hundred, waiting for watermen at Westminster Stairs. The other ninety-nine regard me with scorn for my boyish posture; but as the eldest man in the queue I have certain perquisities, viz. I may sit down.

The reason I am so far back in the queue is that I stayed late at Waghorn's to chat with the Earl of Lostwithiel and with Mr. Threader, who irrupted upon us and would not be moved away. He noted, more than once, that by barging in upon us he was effecting a small re-union of three who were together in Devon in January. Indeed, it was there that I first drew Mr. Threader's notice by endorsing Lostwithiel's venture, the Proprietors of the Engine for Raising Water by Fire, and causing a small run on Mr. Threader's stock of capital, as several of his clients were (improbable as this must seem) moved by my discourse to invest. This was but the first disturbance I caused in Mr. Threader's well-regulated and steady life. Since then there have been explosions, arguments about politics, letters from the Tsar, and diverse other novelties: making me into a persistent and alarming presence in his life.

My relationship with the Silver Comstocks is ancient, and ambiguous in the extreme; but recent generations have seen fit to denominate me a friend of the family. So hereinafter I shall refer to my lord the Earl of Lostwithiel as Will Comstock. Will confirmed what was already implied by the settlement of diverse wagers all round us, namely, that the day had gone badly for Bolingbroke and the Tories. The Marquis of Ravenscar has—by dint of plots, maneuvers, and skirmishes too diverse and far-fetched for my tired brain to hold or my cramped hand to write down—literally called the Secretary of the South Sea Company on the carpet. The call went out (sensationally) a week ago. It was answered a few hours ago, when the said Secretary appeared before the bar in Commons, and presented a book—a compendium of all the Company's documents relating to the Asiento. The Tories regard this book as a lit granadoe, the Whigs as a golden apple, and it has moved back and forth between Commons and Lords this afternoon as the factions have exhausted all resources to put it where it can deal the most or the least damage. Important men have been reading from it aloud. It contains nothing to explain or excuse the disappearance of the slave-trade revenues. This shifts the burden of culpability to Bolingbroke, who was never viewed as an honest chap to begin with—even by his admirers.

Note that only yesterday Commons voted to post £100,000 as a reward to anyone who apprehends the Pretender should he dare to set foot on British soil. So the tide, which was running strongly in Bolingbroke's favor a fortnight ago, has quite reversed.

Thus news. I confess I did not attend closely to young Will during his narration, so fascinated was I by the phizz of Mr. Threader. As a rule there is nothing to see in his face; but today it was a fascinating study in warring passions, such as no van Dyck could have rendered. As a Tory, Mr. Threader is troubled to see the Tories back on their heels, and as a money-scrivener he is horrified by the public airing of the South Sea Company's soiled bedsheets. And yet, when Will told us that a Trial of the Pyx had been postponed indefinitely, it was impossible not to perceive relief, even elation, upon Mr. Threader's face. He has lately been coming by at all hours, or mailing me curious, hastily written notes, concerning the investigation of the coinage that has been set afoot by Bolingbroke. H.B.M.'s Sec'y of State pursues this (as everyone knows) to discredit the Whigs; yet it causes Mr. Threader the most intense anxiety. When Will let it be known that the Pyx would be unmolested for at least two months, Mr. Threader's face was suddenly illuminated from within, like a Jack-o'-lantern receiving its candle. He excused himself and lit out for the City.

Will and I both marked this. But Will is better bred than I, and does not like to gossip about others behind their backs. So he changed the subject, or rather deflected it, with a wry remark: "Mr. Threader's worries about the direction of the markets would be as nothing if the Duchess of Qwghlm got her hands round his neck." I inquired as to why Eliza would wish to strangle an old money-scrivener. Will replied that he and Eliza had met recently to discuss the Prop. of the Eng. for R.W. by F. Will had mentioned in passing that Engines were, in certain applications, an alternative to Slavery—and thereby triggered a spate of ranting from the Duchess as to the evils of that Institution, of the So. Sea Co., and all who like Mr. Threader credit its loathsome Equity. I had been chary of over-stressing this during my talks with Eliza, for fear that I would seem to manipulate her well-known passions on this subject, however it was clear from Will's account that she has been pondering it. The recent turning of the tide against the So. Sea Co. may give comfort to Eliza that to invest in the P.E.R.W.F. is not only Shrewd but Righteous. At any rate, Will seemed to say, by a well-timed wink, that such an investment is now in the works. He then changed subject again, inquiring as to the progress of the Logic Mill, and expressing polite curiosity about the same.

I let him know that, just as a printer sends proof-sheets to his client, we were making ready to ship a sample of our golden cards to our investor in the east. True to form, I did not fail to mention that we would benefit from certain financial expediencies. Will seemed to expect this; he allowed that he might be the bearer of some news concerning it, and handed me a sealed message from Eliza. Then he drained his coffee-cup and most courteously excused himself.

As I glance downriver I see a flotilla of watermen's boats approaching, drawn hither by the comely spectacle of a long queue of fuming Quality stamping their spurs in frustration. So I shall conclude directly. I opened Eliza's message. Out of it fell a smaller piece of paper. The message describes Will—grudgingly—as "a good Tory" and "worth knowing" and states that she and he have arrived at an agreement. This by itself would have been enough to *improve* my day considerably; but it was *perfected* by the smaller document, which was a goldsmith's note, drawn on the House of Hacklheber, and made out to your humble correspondent. There is enough here to support the operations of Clerkenwell Court for a week, and I flatter myself that she will see fit to provide another installment when it has been spent. We should have three card-punching organs installed at Bridewell within a fortnight; Hannah Spates is already training the women to make them work.

The queue is coming to life, like a torpid snake warmed by the sun; I close for now; an errand of a rather different nature awaits me.

Another damned coffee-house environs me—this time, it is in Warwick Court, behind the Old Bailey, and hard by the College of Physicians. I am surrounded half by barristers and half by Physicians, and cannot say which group I like less. Were I in legal trouble or sick or both I should of course change my tune.

When I reached the head of that queue I was complaining of, I took a water taxi to Black Friars Stairs, and thence a sedan chair up to the Old Bailey. It was even more crowded than the Houses of Parliament, for the Court of Sessions had been at work there for much of the day, and had just adjourned. I looked about until I saw a man who stood head and shoulders above the crowd. When I made my way over to him I discovered, as usual, Mr. Kikin, somewhere down about his midsection. He let it be known, by the look on his face, that I was late. After a curt exchange of greetings he turned his back on me and marched into the court-yard where the accused and their supporters and detractors mill about under the open sky, shelterless against rain and judicial wrath. In this he was working upstream against the flow of that Mobb who had come to mourn or to cheer the decisions of the magistrates. But he used his bodyguard to good effect, as a sort of human ram. Had he not been so precipitious I'd have counseled him to wait for the crowd to disperse, and the air to clear. By venturing in among them thus he was exposing himself to the gaol-fever, which is easily spread from the sheep-pen where the prisoners are kept, to the spectators, and thence out into the streets of London. But it was too late. I was on the horns of a dilemma: follow Kikin and risk the pestilence, or stay behind, alone, to be enveloped by a Mobb of persons no less dangerous than the convicted who were even now being herded off to their fates. I followed Kikin, not without some buffeting in that bottle-neck that leads into the court-yard from the street.

Once we had debouched into the yard, the crowding abated, and I breathed a little freer. Weather has been dry of late, so it was more dusty than muddy. The brazier in which the branding-irons are kept at the ready was still glowing, and spinning up a plume of sharply scented coal-smoke, which I phant'sied might cleanse the air of whatever miasma causes the gaol-fever. I stood near it, reading the red-hot letters of iron strewn about in the coals, viz. V for Vagabond, T for Thief, &c., and keeping an eye on Mr. Kikin to see where he would alight. The magistrates, clerks, &c., had already abandoned the high covered veranda from which justice is dispensed. Most of the spectators, as I have mentioned, had already departed. Those who remained had all gravitated to the wooden walls of the pens where the men and women prisoners are kept. They were reaching over the barriers to pass purses of coins, loaves of bread, apples, &c., to their friends, children, wives, and husbands on the other side, who raked in these prizes with fettered and scabrous hands. The bailiffs were of course herding all of the prisoners towards the Janus Gate. They made no move to interfere with the transactions I have just described, well knowing that most of the money being handed over in those shabby little purses would presently be in their own pockets. Of course, material goods were not all that passed over that barricade; there were kisses, hand-clasps, weeping, wailing, and declarations of love æternal, particularly in the cases of the ones who'd just been given tickets to

Tyburn. But I will elide these, on a pretext that they are not germane. In truth, it is too pathetic for words.

Standing at the northeast extremity of the yard, round the pillars of the Janus Gate, were several men who did not weep, wail, or proffer coin-purses. They only stood, backs to the gate, facing the flow of prisoners, and watched. It was a wonder to see them. From their postures you might identify them from a distance as mere idlers. But as I approached—following Mr. Kikin—I noted that these men wore curious expressions on their phizzes: each was as intent as a cat in the instant before it pounces upon an unsuspecting bird. These men were not idling, but *working,* practicing their profession with as full attention as the late Mr. Hooke when he would peer through his microscope at a swarm of animalcules. Some of the prisoners passing through the Janus Gate were oblivious; their faces were scanned and committed to memory. Others, wiser in the ways of the flash world, recognized these loiterers as thief-takers, and hid their faces behind their sleeves, or even walked backwards until they had passed safely through the gate. Some of the thief-takers stooped to childish but effective tricks, as calling out names: "John! Bob! Tom!" which made certain prisoners turn their way, the better for their faces to be inspected and their moles, scars, missing teeth, &c., to be memorized.

The only prisoners who are of no interest to the thief-takers are those who've just been condemned to Tyburn. The others stand a fair chance to get out of Newgate alive, and to return to their former ways and dwelling-places. Once a thief-taker has committed such a man's face to memory, he is liable to be re-arrested and prosecuted at any moment. It makes little difference whether he has in truth committed a crime; the Court wants a culprit, and the thief-taker wants reward-money.

Sean Partry was conspicuous, among thief-takers, by his age (I should estimate he is in his middle fifties) and by a bearing—I am tempted to call it dignity—wanting in the others. He has a good head of hair, only a bit thin on top, blond going gray, and sea-green eyes. He has an excellently carved set of teeth, but displays them rarely. He has a trim figure—unusual in a profession that consists largely of loitering round taverns—but any illusion that he is especially fit is dispelled when he begins to move, for he is a little bit halt and a little bit lame, stiff in the joints, and given to frequent sighs and grimaces that hint at pains internal.

Partry would on no account look us in the eye, or pay us any heed whatever, until the last of the prisoners had been herded through the gate. Then he began to interrogate us rather brusquely, wanting to know who we were, whom we represented, and why we desired to know so many things about Jack the Coiner. He was indifferent, and almost hostile, until we began to give substantive answers to his questions. Then he showed us more favor, and even consented to let Mr. Kikin buy him a drink at a public house down the way. He seemed well-informed as to politics, showing interest in my relation of the day's events at Westminster.

I told the story of the explosion in Crane Court, and listed the names of those who might have been its intended victim: Mr. Threader, Sir Isaac, Henry Arlanc, and your humble correspondent. Partry made some small remark about each, guessing rightly that Arlanc was a Huguenot name, and showing genuine curiosity about Newton. This is not so remarkable, as Newton has had many occasions to treat with thief-takers in catching and prosecuting coiners, and for all I know, might even have lined Partry's own pocket with some reward-money. He showed rather less interest in Mr. Kikin's account of the burning of the Russian ship at Rotherhithe. Partry is of the view that the latter event was a job that Jack was paid to do by Swedish or other foreign agents, and as such, offers little insight into Jack's motives. That Partry has bothered to consider this matter at all, and has already formed views on it, gave me a favorable character of the man. Kikin seemed to agree. We asked Partry whether he thought he might be of service to us, and he allowed as how he might; but not terribly soon. "My methods are my methods," he announced, by way of explaining that he would not be able to offer us any news until Friday, the 30th of July, or shortly before it. Kikin was dismayed. Partry reminded him that it would probably take that long anyway to negotiate a fee. Then he departed.

My conversation with Mr. Kikin now went into a few minutes' recess, as he does not like to stay in any one place for more than a few minutes. We paid our bill and wandered round a few corners to the coffee-house where I now sit writing these words. Kikin was nonplussed by the way Partry had moved from the *vague* assertion that it would take a long time, to the *specific* one that it would happen on the thirtieth of July. I treated it as a riddle, asking the addled Russian, could he not think of any event on that day that would explain Mr. Partry's confidence.

In the end Kikin resorted to pulling out the little waste-book where he writes down his social engagements. Flipping forward to 30 July, he found a page that was blank, save for one notation: HANGINGS. Meaning that the next Hanging-March to Tyburn was to be on that day, and so he had avoided making any appointments, knowing how difficult it would be to move through the Mobb-choked streets.

"Several men have lately been found guilty of coining," I explained. "On the thirtieth they shall be taken to Tyburn to be half-hanged, drawn, and quartered. Such men, being coiners, may have information about Jack. Being as they are afraid of Jack, they'll not let a word slip for the time being. But as the thirtieth of the month looms nearer, fear of Jack Ketch will grow to out-weigh fear of Jack Shaftoe. In those last few days, they may be persuaded, by one such as Sean Partry, to tell what they know concerning Jack, in exchange for lenient treatment at the Fatal Tree."

"You mean Partry can arrange a pardon!?" demanded Kikin, who was ready to be scandalized by our judicial laxity.

"No. But if we supply money to Partry, he may pass some of it on to Jack Ketch, who will then see to it that the prisoner in question receives a quick hanging—a neck-snapper instead of a slow strangler—so that he'll not be alive to know he is being disembowelled."

"This is a strange country," Kikin observed. I could say nothing.

Kikin is aghast that it will take so long to get answers. I believe he has made a mental calculation of how long it might take for the Russian galley, presently at Orney's Ship-yard in Rotherhithe, to get back to St. Petersburg, and then to return to London bringing some furious Russian count empowered to sack Mr. Kikin and bring him home in chains.

I let him know that I had a package of golden cards ready to ship out on that galley, which is supposed to depart very soon. This cheered him up, and he resolved to go to Clerkenwell Court that very instant to collect the plates. He is gone now, and I await here a trusted messenger who will bear the Duchess of Qwghlm's goldsmith's note to my banker in the City, William Ham. I am left, a strange man in a *strange country*, wondering how I got here, and what shall befall me next.

Your humble and obedient servant,
Daniel Waterhouse

Westminster Palace

9 JULY 1714

A Message from the Lords, by Mr. Holford *and Mr.* Lovibond:

Mr. Speaker,

We are commanded by the Lords to acquaint this House, That they, having this Day under their Examination Matters relating to the *South Sea* Company, which are of great Consequence to the Trade of this Kingdom, do desire that this House will give Leave to such Members of this House as are of the Committee of the *South Sea* Company for the *Assiento*; and *William Lowndes* Esquire; may have Leave to attend the House of Lords this Day.

And then the Messengers withdrew

Resolved, That this House doth give Leave to such Members . . . to go to the House of Lords, if they think fit.

And the Messengers were called in again, and Mr. Speaker acquainted them therewith.

Jovis, *8° die Julii;*

Anno 13° Annæ Reginæ, 1714

Ordered, That a Message be sent to the Lords, to desire, That they will direct the Painted Chamber, the Lobby, and the Passage to the House of Peers, to be cleared from any Crowd, when this House shall come up thither, by her Majesty's Command, to attend her Majesty.

Ordered, That Mr. Campion do carry the said Message.

Ordered, That the Serjeant at Arms attending this House do clear the Lobby of this House, and Passage leading to the Painted Chamber, from the Persons therein, for the better Passage of this House to the House of Peers . . .

A Message from her Majesty, by Sir William Oldes, Gentleman Usher of the Black Rod:

Mr. Speaker,

The Queen commands this honourable House to attend her Majesty in the House of Peers, immediately.

Accordingly, Mr. Speaker, with the House, went up to attend her Majesty, in the House of Peers: Where her Majesty was pleased to give the Royal Assent to several publick and private Bills:

After which her Majesty was pleased to make a most gracious Speech to both Houses of Parliament:

And afterwards the Lord High Chancellor of *Great Britain*, by her Majesty's Command, said

It is her Majesty's Royal Will and Pleasure, That this Parliament be prorogued to *Tuesday* the Tenth Day of *August* next: And this Parliament is accordingly prorogued to *Tuesday* the Tenth Day of *August* next.

Veneris, *9° die* Julii; *Anno 13° Annæ Reginæ, 1714*

A PAIR OF RAVENSCAR's strangely brawny aides had knocked Daniel up at Crane Court this morning, and bundled him into a sedan chair with such urgency that he could not discern whether he was being *summoned* or *abducted.* Encased in this box like a desiccated Specimen—a curious relic of the Cromwellian Epoch—he had been delivered up to Westminster's Old Palace Yard, and ejected in front of Waghorn's. A chap with a keen ear, if he'd sidled up close to Daniel about then, could have heard him muttering diverse outrageous calumnies and execrations against the Marquis of Ravenscar. For Daniel had been quite content at Crane Court with his pot of tea, one of Mrs. Arlanc's pastries, and a stack of vile newspapers. *This* place was dirty, crowded, and riotous. Not with the merry riotousness of Hockley-in-the-Hole on the eve of a Hanging-Day, but the snitty, bitchy sort practiced by men who were animated by the same base passions but who had too much to lose by giving them free rein. Everyone was in a hurry save Daniel. Most were in a hurry to get inside. They hustled along at cross-purposes to a small but troublesome moiety who were trying to move laterally between Commons and Lords, using the Old Palace Yard as a short-cut to circumvent the galleries and chambers within—which, it could be inferred, were too crowded to permit movement. There were scattered outbreaks of courtesy. But the third time Daniel saw some outraged second-rate hanger-on reach, in a theatrical manner, for his sword, he concluded that the place was not merely unpleasant but dangerous. He turned on his heel and began to walk away. Once he broke free of the crowd he could be at the Kit-Cat Clubb in half an hour . . . but then this lovely phant'sy was shivered by the words: "Dr. Waterhouse! I feared I should never reach you! If you'd care to follow me, we have saved a place for you at Waghorn's."

Daniel knew the voice. He had forgotten the name; but no matter, the chap's hairstyle was extremely memorable. He turned around expecting to see a young man coiffed as a Mohawk warrior. Alas, all he could make out were a lot of blokes in white periwigs. But one of them was staring right at him. If the wig were mentally subtracted, and the Mohawk added, the result was one of those young Whig gallants who were always prancing around on Roger-errands. Today's errand: rescue the doddering Doctor, frogmarch him into the Palace.

In Waghorn's, he sipped coffee and held a newspaper in front of his face, partly to read it, and partly as a barrier to conversation—for what he most dreaded was that the Mohawk had also been charged with keeping him company. Parliamentary babble surged and crashed about him like waves on rocks. They talked of everything save what was *really* going on. Mostly it was the Acts and Bills that had clogged their registers in recent weeks: Preventing the Growth of Schism (Bolingbroke's pet bill), Finding the Longitude (Roger's), the perennial issues of Woollen Manufacture, Quieting Corporations, endless Inclosures, and diverse Divorces, contested estates, and Insolvent Debtors; and what had come to be known as the Six R's: Raising the Militia, Running Brandy, Reducing Interest, Revenues of Scotch Bishops, Restraining the Growth of Popery, and (awkwardly) laws Relating to Vagrants. It was all hogwash. Either that, or they were speaking in a substitution code wherein every Act mentioned was a veiled reference to its sponsor.

The smoke and babble became too much for him at about the same time that his bladder—never his strongest organ—began to complain of all the coffee. He dropped the paper to discover that his Mohawk had vanished on some other errand—perhaps called away to a raiding-party on the upper Hudson River. So Daniel went out and found a place he could urinate (which actually was easier than finding a place he *couldn't*) and then took to strolling up and down the Painted Chamber and the Long Gallery. Consequently, he was swept up in the portentous series of room-clearings and gallery-evacuations ordered by Commons. Indeed, he was on the verge of being flushed clean off the Palace grounds when a different Mohawk found him, and escorted him, via circuitous back-passages, closets, and committee-rooms, into the House of Lords itself, and encouraged him to stand in Ravenscar's cheering-section, and to act as if he belonged there.

This gave Daniel over to grave forebodings. He had seen Charles I's head spurt and roll. He had attended Charles II almost to the moment of his death, fighting a bitter rear-guard action to keep the royal physicians at bay. He had watched, and been tempted to take part in, a tavern brawl that bloodied James II's nose, and more or less signalled the end of his reign. Quite prudently, he had absented himself from the country during the deaths of William and of Mary. But now he was back, and they were bringing the Queen to him. If she chose this time and place to give up the ghost, would every wigged head in the room turn and look at *him*? Would they tear him limb from limb on the spot, or ship him downriver for a proper beheading at the Tower? Would it come out that he had lately been riding round town in a carriage with a certain foreign Princess who was here *incognito* and uninvited?

These and other broodings so preoccupied him that he scarce noted a sudden silence, and the entry into the House of a rather gaudy sedan chair. He (and, admittedly, as many others as could be packed into the room) was in the Presence! 'Twas a Historick Moment! Or, at least, the sort of moment so apt to be writ down in History-Books. Yet despite this—or perhaps because of it—Daniel was afflicted by a maddening inability to *attend* to it. His own broodings were of greater interest—a sign of unforgivable arrogance?

Other men seemed to've been blessed with the ability to live in the moment, and to have experiences (Daniel imagined) in the raw vivid way that animals did. But not he. How would the ceremony, the pageantry of the Queen's visit to Parliament look, to one who could see them thus? Colorful, magnificent, mesmerizing, Daniel supposed. He'd never know. Daniel could only see this as a sick old lady paying a call on a room full of anxious blokes who hadn't bathed in a while.

The Kit-Cat Clubb
AN HOUR LATER

ISAAC NEWTON MUST THINK every room silent, for every room went silent when he walked into it. Even *this* one!

Daniel had recovered from the strange absence of mind that had troubled him during the Queen's address to Parliament. He was fully engaged in the moment. It must have had something to do with that here he could drink chocolate. Moreover, he could move about, talk to people, and attend to what *he* found interesting. Until Isaac hushed the place by walking in, this had been the spectacle of Roger—holding court at his favorite table—receiving the thanks, in the form of bad poetry, and the congratulations, in the form of expensive gifts, of Great Britain, one Briton at a time. Because this was the Kit-Cat Clubb, all of these encomia had to be delivered in verse: pithy epigrams if Roger were lucky, rambling trains of heroic couplets otherwise. One of the formal constraints observed in the Kit-Cat school of doggerel was that no one could be referred to by name. Classical allusions were *de rigueur*. Roger was almost always Vulcan.

Thus some viscount or other:

> *Vulcan* in his smoaky Forge† did smite*
> *of Gold bright Bolts‡ to fortify his Better§*
> *And, lest the Captives of the Gods take Flight,*
> *Titanic manacles and Olympian Fetters.*
> *Prometheus** who unwisely played with Fire*
> *Is bolted to a crag now all Alone*
> *When Juno†† did incite young Vulcan's ire*
> *His clever hand'work chained her to her Throne‡‡*

This particular Viscount, as everyone understood, could never have crafted such lines himself. He was accompanied by one of the young poets who loitered about the Clubb tossing off epigrams in exchange for pies and wine. Sir Isaac Newton broke in upon the touching exchange and began speaking to Roger. He had not gotten out of bed for a fortnight after his bludgeoning in Star Chamber, but he was

---

* Roger Comstock, Marquis of Ravenscar.

† The Kit-Cat Clubb.

‡ An allusion to the lightning-bolts forged by Vulcan; alternately, perhaps, golden guineas turned out by the Mint, which was no longer under Roger's direction since Oxford and Bolingbroke had overthrown the Whig Juncto, but still run by men associated with Roger, such as Newton.

§ Jupiter, to whom Vulcan supplied lightning-bolts; but possibly a cheeky allusion to George Louis of Hanover, for whom, it was hoped, the Mint would soon be turning out guineas.

** Bolingbroke.

†† Queen Anne.

‡‡ An allusion to a myth in which an angry Vulcan fashioned a trick throne containing hidden restraints, and gave it to his mother, Juno; when she sat on it, she was trapped, and only Vulcan could release her.

now walking about as spry as a twenty-year-old scholar gamboling on the banks of the Cam. He was completely unaware that he was jumping to the head of a snaking and redoubling queue of men who outranked him. Daniel had made slower head-way through the revelers because, unlike Isaac, he bothered to excuse himself as he went. So he could not hear Isaac's words at first. But he knew that Isaac must have been drawn hither by the news, and that he must be congratulating Roger on having *so* backed Bolingbroke into a corner that he had been forced to call for Mummy to come and rescue him. Substantial men, one after another, had been saying as much to Roger for hours now, and he had been receiving each plaudit with a nod so perfunctory it had dwindled to a vestigial tic. And yet when Isaac Newton said much the same sort of thing to him, Ravenscar took it with (if a play on words could be permitted) the utmost *gravity*. As if *other* men went about congratulating people almost at *random,* but *Newton* really *meant* it. Perhaps it helped that he was speaking in prose.

Daniel had thought that Roger seemed a bit distracted, even melancholy, as he'd sat there receiving the adulatory versifications of Whigdom. And Daniel thought he knew why. Roger loved the counter-attack. He'd spent the last month readying one, but now it was spent. He was in the position of a pistol-duellist who has discharged his weapon, and now stands defenseless, not knowing whether the foe is wounded mortally; merely dazed; or relishing the power to blow his brains out. He needed to be readying himself for Bolingbroke's *riposte;* instead he had to sit here and listen to bad poetry.

Roger took Isaac companionably by the arm and led him toward Daniel. By way of excusing himself he shouted: "Gentlemen—a moment, if you please—I have heard that the Queen to-day hath given the Royal Assent to the posting of a reward for him who finds out the Longitude!" He was feigning amazement at this turn of events. "And it is rumored that Sir Isaac knows something about it.

"If you would hope to find the Longitude,

"Find Newton first—and give him Food!"

Roger improvised, to light applause and heavy drinking. "Mr. Cat! If you would! Mutton-pies, please."

But by the time Daniel effected his rendezvous with Roger and Isaac, they had moved on to altogether different topics. "You are looking in the pink—splendid!—does this mean I shall get Catherine back? My household has gone to ruin since its Mistress went off to nurse her nuncle."

"Indeed, my lord, she has already gone back to resume her duties," Newton returned, bored, and a bit uneasy, with this subject.

"The house will be *glowing* in a few days, if she tends to it as well as she has to *you*."

"She has done well by her uncle," Newton allowed, "but in truth, the recent news from Westminster, and the prospect that Boling-broke would be baffled, and a Trial of the Pyx put off indefinitely, were the physic that cured me."

"Then do you and Dr. Waterhouse *carpe diem* and place your new-found vigor in service of some well-wrought plan of attack," Roger suggested, "for Parliament is only prorogued until the tenth of August, and that is more than enough time for such as Bolingbroke to dig a counter-counter-mine, and blow us all up to the sky."

"Dr. Waterhouse and I are accustomed to people attempting to blow us up," Newton returned. It was hard to make out whether this was a dry witticism or a clinical observation. Isaac startled Daniel, now, by looking him dead in the eye. "It is good that you are here. I wish to speak to you."

"Then with your indulgence I shall withdraw," Roger said, "that the two of you may speak. Please, speak of weighty matters, and keep your discourse to the matter at hand—for there is no more potent weapon for the Jacobites than to make the City, the Country, and the Mobb believe that the Whigs—and by extension the Hanovers—have secretly debased the coinage to make themselves rich!"

This was an awfully blunt thing to say to the Master of the Mint. Newton was shocked, which had probably been Roger's intention. Roger hovered just long enough to be certain that Newton was not going to collapse twitching on the floor. But instead Newton just glared at him. Daniel caught Roger's eye and threw him a wink. For Daniel had seen Isaac in this mood many times before, and it usually meant that he was going to work for forty-eight hours at a stretch un-til some problem or other was solved. Roger bowed and withdrew—depositing the whole burden on the shoulders of Daniel, who could already feel himself sagging.

"WE MUST HUNT DOWN JACK the Coiner, clap him in irons, and force him to testify that he adulterated a Pyx that, until he put his filthy hands into it, was filled with sound coins," said Sir Isaac Newton. He and Daniel had found a table in the corner. "What would be even better than his testimony, we might compel him to yield up any good guineas that he might have stolen from the Pyx, which would exon-erate me beyond even the powers of Jesuits."

"If that is your wish, Isaac, I am pleased to let you know that the pursuit of Jack has been underway for some months, and that it is being pressed forward by—"

"Your Clubb—yes, I know about your Clubb," Isaac said. "I shall require membership."

"The bylaws require a vote on such matters," Daniel said.

This was a jest. Isaac in this mood was not very receptive to it. "It should not be an obstacle. I propose, in effect, to merge the Mint's investigation of coiners with your Clubb's pursuit of those who wrought the Infernal Devices, since we have abundant reasons to believe that they are the same. The advantages to the Clubb are obvious."

"Then let us anticipate the Clubb's vote, and act as if you were already a member in good standing," Daniel said, placing both palms flat on the tabletop, and pressing himself up to his feet. Isaac rose, too. The mutton pies were coming toward them on a silver platter; Daniel redirected the waiter to an exit.

"The timing is felicitous," Daniel continued. "Haply, I have become aware of an important witness who wishes to have an interview with me."

Isaac was already in movement toward the exit. "I have hired a carriage for the day," he threw back over one shoulder. "Where shall I tell the driver we wish to go?"

"Tell him," Daniel returned, "that we are going to Bedlam."

The Carriage
MINUTES LATER

". . . AND SO WE HAVE MADE an arrangement with Mr. Partry—but not disbursed any money to him, of course—nor do we expect to, until the end of this month," Daniel said. He'd given Isaac an account of the Clubb's late doings, mercilessly abbreviated because of the aroma of the mutton pies, which were waiting on a platter in his lap. The platter was a twenty-pound slab of silver done up in full Barock style and engraved with miles of tangled script: a paean to the sexual powers of Newton's niece. Here she was referred to as Aphrodite, a code that Isaac was not likely to penetrate.

In an apt demonstration of the principle of Relativity, as propounded by Galileo, the bawdy platter, and the steaming morsels thereon, remained in the same position vis-à-vis Daniel, and hence were, in principle, just as edible, as if he had been seated before, and the pies had been resting upon, a table that was stationary with respect to the fixed stars. This was true despite the fact that the carriage containing Daniel, Isaac Newton, and the pies was banging around London. Daniel guessed that they were swinging round the northern limb of St. Paul's Churchyard, but he had no real way of telling; he had closed the window-shutters, for the reason that their journey to Bedlam would take them directly across the maw of Grub Street, and he did not want to read about today's adventure in all tomorrow's papers.

Isaac, though better equipped than Daniel or any other man alive to understand Relativity, shewed no interest in his pie—as if being in a state of movement with respect to the planet Earth rendered it somehow Not a Pie. But as far as Daniel was concerned, a pie in a moving frame of reference was no less a pie than one that was sitting still: position and velocity, to him, might be perfectly interesting physical properties, but they had no bearing on, no relationship to those properties that were *essential* to pie-ness. All that mattered to Daniel were relationships between his, Daniel's, physical state and that of the pie. If Daniel and Pie were close together both in position and velocity, then pie-eating became a practical, and tempting, possibility. If Pie were far asunder from Daniel or moving at a large relative velocity—e.g., being hurled at his face—then its pie-ness was somehow impaired, at least from the Daniel frame of reference. For the time being, however, these were purely Scholastic hypotheticals. Pie was on his lap and very much a pie, no matter what Isaac might think of it.

Mr. Cat had lent them silver table-settings, and Daniel, as he spoke, had tucked a napkin into his shirt-collar—a flag of surrender, and an unconditional capitulation to the attractions of Pie. Rather than laying down arms, he now picked them up—knife and fork. Isaac's question froze him just as he poised these above the flaky top-crust. "Is it the Clubb's intention to remain idle for the entire month of July?"

"Each member pursues whatever lines of inquiry strike him as most promising," Daniel returned. "As you and I are doing at this very moment." And he stabbed Pie.

"And the other members?"

"They have had little to report. Though at the most recent meeting, Mr. Threader mentioned that he had come by a scrap of information: Jack the Coiner is an associate of Mr. Knockmealdown, the infamous Receiver, and frequents the kens of the so-called East London Company in the Borough."

Now this, actually, shut Isaac up for long enough that Daniel was able to pitch a steaming load of mutton and gravy into his pie-hole. Isaac's eyes remained fixed in the direction of Daniel's face, but not focused on him—a good thing, since his phizz was in a state of gustatory rapture.

"You know my opinion of Mr. Threader," Isaac said.

Daniel nodded.

"He has had dealings with Jack—you may be certain of it," Isaac continued.

To Daniel this seemed about as likely as that his wife in Boston was secretly in league with Blackbeard. But his mouth was full of pie, he was contented, and he did not raise an objection—merely an eyebrow.

"Mr. Threader must be terrified that the recent investigation of the coinage, set afoot by Bolingbroke, will discover his sordid dealings with Jack. Men have been quartered at Tyburn Cross for less."

Here Isaac let it drop, in true mathematician's style, leaving the rest as an exercise for the reader. Daniel tried to communicate, with what he supposed were highly expressive shrugs, sighs, and brow-furrowings, that Isaac had quite lost him. But in the end the only thing for it was to swallow and say: "If Mr. Threader is *so* terrified of Jack's being apprehended, why should he *volunteer* information as to the man's habits?"

"It was a subtile message," Isaac said.

"To what effect?"

"To the effect that Mr. Threader is a willing turn-coat—for if there is little honor among thieves, there is even less among weighers and coiners—and would assist in catching Jack, in exchange for lenient treatment."

"Lenient treatment . . . from his own Clubb!?"

"From the Master of the Mint," Isaac said. "He wots perfectly well that you and I know each other."

"Thank you for making such a hypothesis known to me—unassisted, I never could have dreamed such a thing—so fanciful is it," Daniel said, a bit surly, and suspended further debate with more Pie.

LIKE A MELANCHOLICK in the corner of a crowded *salon*, Bedlam turned its broad back upon the City of London. It faced north across Moor Fields, the largest green space in the metropolis. Lunaticks with the good fortune to be lodged in north-facing cells en-

joyed a pleasant prospect across half a mile of open ground that separated the hospital from the next edifice of any size: Mr. Witanoont's Vinegar Yard on Worship Street at the foot of Holy-well
Mount. The broadest part of Moor Fields, directly before Bedlam,
had been outlined with a quadrilateral, and striped with a St.
George's Cross, of broad lanes bordered with regularly spaced trees.
The trees were all about forty years old, as they'd been planted by
the order of Hooke.

The lane forming the southern boundary of Moor Fields was
hemmed in between a picket-line of such trees on one side, and on
the other, an extremely formidable fence. A small iron-mine must
have been exhausted to supply those segments of this barrier that
consisted of wrist-thick pickets, and a quarry must have been eviscer-
ated to build up the parts consisting of stone blocks. As soon as this
awesome maniac-stopping technology appeared out the right-hand
window of the hackney-carriage, Daniel tossed down his flatware and
began cleaning himself up with his napkin, whilst scanning the little
poem that—by long-standing Kit-Cat tradition—had been carved
into the bottom crust:

> *Ye Product of* Pie *& ye Radius, Squared,*
> *Doth yield the Size of the Pan,*
> *An area vast enough to've been Shared,*
> *Not gobbled entire by One Man!*

Hooke had made the damned building something like seven hundred feet long—as wide as the whole Tower of London complex—a
luxury afforded only to architects working immediately after the
Fire. Though Daniel tried, he could not stop himself peering
through the iron bars to see if any inmates were out disporting themselves. All he saw were roaming claques of holiday-makers, and lone
prostitutes. No great loss; the really interesting madmen were not
given liberty to walk around out of doors.

Eventually the fence veered away from them on the right, and the
trees did likewise on the left, as they rattled into a broad oval forecourt spread below Bedlam's central cupola. This was lined with concentric rings of carriages and sedan chairs waiting for their owners
and renters to grow bored of the entertainments within. As he and
Isaac disembarked, Daniel paid the driver to take the silver back to
the Kit-Cat Clubb.

Despite being aged and distinguished Natural Philosophers,
they had to wait in the queue just like everyone else. The Gate
where every visitor had to pay his penny was commensurate with

the Fence. Vaulting over it was a stone cornice: a matched pair of gracefully curving ramps, rising up to almost kiss in the center. Each appeared to serve as a kind of chaise for a sculpted figure to lounge upon: on Daniel's left, like a straw-man that has been blown down from its armature, Melancholy reclined, gazing off dully into the space above Moor Fields. On his right, Mania perched, touching the cornice only with his elbows, hip-bone, and ankles, as every muscle in his body was chiseled taut. His fists were clenched as he strained against his fetters and his eyes rolled back as he gaped crazily up into the weather. Daniel knew these two stony fellows well, and even took a sort of godfatherly interest in them. He had visited Hooke in his atelier under Bedlam's cupola when Hooke had been sketching them, and had even dared to make suggestions, which Hooke had of course ignored. After they had been realized by sculptors, and hoisted into position, Daniel had walked beneath them many times, going to visit Hooke or to partake of the Royal Society's crack-pated madness-experiments. Never until today, though, had he felt such a *kinship* with them. For today Daniel, who on so many days was the personification of Melancholy, was standing in this queue to the left hand of Sir Isaac Newton: Mr. Mania himself. He looked back and forth a few times between sculpted Mania—or, as the Vulgar styled him, Raving Madness—and Isaac, hoping that the latter would note the similarity. For Daniel could not quite muster the nerve to voice his thoughts. Finally Isaac sighed, rolled his eyes, and said, "Yes, it is very droll."

In due course they ascended some broad steps to the gate and paid their pennies. This gave them liberty to ascend more steps to the entrance of the building, where they were given opportunities to pay supplementary bribes to the staff members loitering around the door. This was not strictly necessary, but would ensure that they'd be ushered straightaway to see the most entertaining madmen and -women in the whole establishment. Daniel merely scanned their faces and, not marking the one he sought, led Isaac into the building.

"I beg your pardon?" Isaac said, for he had heard Daniel muttering. "Did you say something?"

A deep voice behind them said, "Begging your pardon, Sir Isaac, but you need pay him no mind. Whenever Dr. Waterhouse crosses yonder threshold, it is his habit to say a prayer that he shall be permitted to leave."

Isaac made a point of ignoring this, supposing that the words had come from some inmate who was lurking by the door, hoping to receive a coin in payment for his waggish remarks. Which was a good guess, but wrong. Daniel turned about to face the man who had spoken. Finally Isaac did, too.

This was no lunatick, for his hair was long and lank. Inmates had their heads shaved. And his wrists and ankles were unfettered. Isaac stiffened, and drew back a step even as Daniel was approaching this fellow to shake his hand. For Isaac had recognized Saturn as a fellow with whom he had once had an encounter of an extremely dubious nature in a boozing-ken out back of Bridewell. But after a few moments' consideration—finding himself surrounded by shaven-headed, chain-dragging maniacs and melancholicks—Sir Isaac made up his mind that the company of Saturn was not so very distasteful after all.

At almost the same moment a fourth man, who'd been loitering near Saturn, presented himself for introduction. "Mr. Timothy Stubbs," said Saturn, "who as you can see from his red tresses does not live here. But as you may guess from his indigo suit, he does *work* here. Take your hand out of your pocket, Dr. Waterhouse; he has already been bribed."

"We have been attending to John Doe as you prescribed, Doctor," announced Timothy Stubbs after more formal introductions had been dragged out of Saturn. "He has been given every physic, every therapy known to modern medicine—but alas, he shows no sign of repenting from his delusions."

"Fancy that!" Daniel exclaimed. "I suppose you have had to keep him close, then."

"Indeed, Doctor, or he'd have knocked holes in *all* the walls by now. He is kept in a cell above."

"Where the most dangerous maniacs are pent up, on the upper storey," Saturn translated.

"Pray, where is Mr. Doe now?"

"He is in the Machine for Calming Violent Lunaticks, sir," said Stubbs, a bit startled by the question. "Just as you prescribed—four hours a day."

"Have the purges worked?"

"If you mean, do they purge him, sir, why, yes, they do, mightily. But if you mean, have they cured his madness, I am afraid not—so we have doubled them again."

"Excellent!" Daniel exclaimed. "Which way to the Machine?"

"It lies at the end of the men's wing—a bit of a walk, I'm afraid," said Stubbs, leading them carefully around a shaven-headed man who was lying on his stomach on the floor, darting his eyes from side to side and mumbling a stream of what sounded like military jargon, interrupted every few moments by spasmodic flinching as he reacted to imaginary shell-bursts.

"Not at all," Daniel returned cheerfully. "Bedlam is justly famed as the best Dry Walk in London."

"Small comfort on a sunny day I'm afraid," said Stubbs, skirting a group of three young men in Mohawk coiffures, who stood shoulder-to-shoulder critiquing the performance of a maniac who was playing a fiddle and dancing a jig at the same time:

"I'll give you a penny if you play another—and tuppence if you stop!"

"Why do we stand and watch *this* wretch, when there are *dishevelled madwomen* but a few paces away?"

"When you see what a dishevelled madwoman actually *looks* like, your question shall be answered."

They passed out of the central hall and entered a gallery that stretched away for some hundred yards. On the right it was lined with windows admitting light from the sky over Moor Fields. On the left was a succession of closely spaced doors, each sporting a small barred window at head-height. Except for the very noblest and the most destitute, the full range of Londoners—men, women, gentry, commoners, adults and children, small gangs of rowdy apprentices, flocks of well-dressed young women, solitary females even better-dressed (these were whores), doughty gaffers and crones taking their constitutionals, dashing squadrons of boys, strutting Mohawks, preening dandies, and perpetually amused Cockneys—strolled from door to door, peering in at each window to behold whatever spectacle lay within. Costermongers fed and beered the visitors from their push-carts. From place to place a knot of indigo-suited attendants ganged up on some inmate who had gotten out of hand. But for the most part the prisoners mixed freely with the visitors, or as freely as men could when ankle was fettered to ankle, and wrist to wrist, with generous lengths of heavy chain. Some of them—melancholicks—sat huddled on the floor, or shuffled to and fro, ignoring even those visitors who poked them in the ribs with walking-sticks. Others—maniacs—carried on furious disputes with entities not visibly present, or raved about whatever phant'sy was most on their minds; the most animated drew small crowds, which laughed at those rantings of a sexual or political nature, and goaded them to further outbursts. A maniac was trying to tell the world that Louis XIV was controlling London from a secret ærie atop the dome of St. Paul's, employing an army of Jesuits who could, through sorcery, metamorphose into gray doves. A young man told him that a whole flock of such doves had been sighted entering the cupola of Bedlam through a broken window. This news drove the maniac into transports of horror and sent him back to his cell as fast as he could waddle. The violent jangling of his chains mixed with the laughter and applause of the onlookers, making the gallery too noisy for conversation.

After it had died down, Stubbs announced "We've had to swop out the straw in John Doe's cell five times a day," in case Daniel still had lingering doubts as to the efficacy of those purges. "The other inmates have learnt to stand clear of him—except for the coprophiliacs, of course, who must be beaten back with sticks." He nodded to a door a short distance ahead. Coincidentally or not, an umber bullet flew out of its window and impacted on the wig of a passing fop, sending up a pretty burst of white powder. "*He* should have paid for a guide," Stubbs remarked, leading Daniel, Isaac, and Saturn on a long arc to keep them out of turd-range. "I do wonder whether Mr. Doe might respond well to beatings," Stubbs continued wistfully. "I know you have forbidden it, Doctor, but if you would allow me to have a go at him with the cane—"

"No," Daniel said. "Your message to me yesterday stated that he had requested an interview—"

"Indeed, guv'nor. Begged for it, more like."

"Let us withhold the cane, then, and see what the interview yields."

By this time they had come near enough to the end of the gallery to hear a persistent low hollow grinding and booming noise. Stubbs threw open a door at the end and led them into a spacious room—for they had entered into a sort of bastion anchoring the western end of the hospital, like the fist at the end of an arm—where that noise was a good deal louder. This salon was as cluttered with peculiar exhibits as the Court of Technologickal Arts at Clerkenwell, and as crowded with obstreperous madmen as a meeting of Her Majesty's Privy Council. But the biggest object in the room—and the source of the noise—was an immense wooden drum, mounted above the floor like a wheel. Its axle spanned the interval between a pair of massive upright timbers, each of which rose to slightly above Daniel's head. The drum was shaped like a fat coin, perhaps a yard thick. Its rim nearly grazed both floor and ceiling, which would make its diameter rather more than twelve feet. The circular faces of it—the heads and tails of the coin, as it were—had been fabricated in the same way as primitive cart-wheels, viz. of broad deals fastened side-by-side with long iron straps. The rim consisted of more planks pegged crosswise between these two disks.

Projecting from one end of the axle was an enormous crank with a handle as long as an oar. A stout little stairway led up to a platform, large enough for two or three men to stand abreast and bend their backs to the operation of that crank. One crew was doing so now, and another stood by, quaffing beer to replace the moisture they'd sweated into their clothes.

As the great wheel ground away on its axle of greased iron, muffled thumps and booms sounded from within: sometimes a steady tattoo, as of running feet, always culminating in a series of thuds like a man falling down stairs.

"The therapy is compleat!" Stubbs announced. The laborers gladly let go and stood up straight to stretch their tired backs, whilst keeping wary vigil on the crank-handle, which continued to rotate—its *vis inertiae* might break the jaw of an unwary man. After the drum had slowed to a low idling speed they seized the crank again and nudged it around a quarter-turn or so. It was now possible to see that the near face of the drum was fitted with a long narrow hatch nearly spanning the interval between hub and rim. The crank-men made sure that this was down and vertical, like an hour-hand at the stroke of six. Then they tromped down the stairs in quest of refreshment.

Stubbs leaned into the space between axle-support and drum-side and unlatched the door. It flew open all the way and banged against the outside of the Machine, revealing that its inner surface was entirely covered by a quilted canvas bag, so filthy that it gleamed with a hard shine, stuffed with straw or horse-hair. The open hatchway was mostly empty; but down low, something reminiscent of a human figure could be seen draining lumpily onto the floor, like a half-melted wax statue being poured out of a saucepan.

"You see?" Stubbs announced. "The Machine works!"

The man who had emerged from the Machine seemed to want in the worst way to get clear of it. But he knew better than to stand, or even sit. He straightened himself out on the floor, supporting himself on his forearms and his forehead, and began to creep along like an inchworm, pausing every few inches for an episode of dry heaves. In a minute or so he reached a waiting chamber-pot, dashed its lid off with a blind arm-swing, hugged it, and used it to pull himself up off the floor. With some further exertions, and the aid of a man in indigo, he got himself seated upon this vessel and immediately began to generate sounds of a hydraulic and pneumatic character.

"Has he assaulted any more walls?" Daniel asked.

"Only the one, Doctor. It is a part of his mania that he phant'sies he knows just where the treasure is hidden."

"What treasure do you refer to?" Isaac asked.

"Why, the same one all the lunaticks are searching for, sir," said Stubbs, "the Gold of King Solomon."

JOHN DOE WAS in no condition for an interview just yet. While the attendants busied themselves putting Doe's chains back on his wrists and ankles, and returning him to his cell, Daniel, Isaac, and Peter Hoxton ascended to the storey above and walked back to the center of Bedlam along a gantlet of cells similar to those below. Fewer visitors came up here. The ones who did tended to be gangs of bloody-minded 'prentices, or the most distasteful sort of fops, or solitary men who looked as if they might themselves benefit from a few hours in the Machine. The prisoners here remained locked in their cells, and for the best reasons. Daniel prudently walked as close to the windows, and as far from the doors, as was practical, and tried not to hear the mutterings of the faces framed in some of those little door-hatches. He led the others on, and they gladly followed, at a brisk pace. Presently they exeunted from the men's wing and entered the central part of the edifice, above the main entrance, and below the cupola. Here they ascended another stair into a vaulted space: technically an attic, but a carefully finished one, airy and well-lit.

Seen from Mr. Witanoont's Vinegar-Yard, Bedlam's center looked as if a squarish funnel had been turned upside-down and clapped on top of it. The broad part of the funnel was a high mansard roof enclosing the ample space in which Daniel, Isaac, and Saturn were now standing. The narrow nozzle was the cupola, which pierced the ceiling, admitting sky-light and (as its windows were ajar) exhausting the fouled air of the asylum. "This was Hooke's favorite part of the building, his ærie and his *atelier*," Daniel said, "though it then looked much different." He approached a railing and gazed down into the central well that vented cupola-light into the entrance hall. "This had planks thrown across it, making it into one great floor, uninterrupted."

"I only paid one visit, and that was for your going-away party," said Isaac.

This was of interest to Saturn, who had been distracted, leaning over the rail and beckoning to some blokes loitering on the ground floor, two storeys below them. Now those fellows were ascending the stair in a gang. A man in indigo was moving to intercept them on the landing. Saturn, whilst keeping an eye on their progress, attended to Daniel. "Was that before you went off to Massachusetts?" he inquired.

"*Long* before. I departed for Massachusetts, at long last, in 1695. The party to which Sir Isaac refers was in 1689."

"That makes no sense," Saturn pointed out. Then he leaned over the railing, turning his attention to what was happening on the landing below: the man in indigo had barred the path of the blokes—four in all—who had answered Saturn's call. They were big, rough-looking lads who could have mowed this man down in an instant, but they had piled to a stop anyway, and were looking up to Saturn for their cue.

"'S al'right, sir," Saturn called, "they're with us."

"And who the hell are you?"

Daniel silenced Saturn with a hand on his shoulder, and gave the answer: "Sir Isaac Newton, the Master of Her Majesty's Mint, investigates an act of High Treason. You are impeding his deputies. Pray stand aside."

Isaac was as startled to hear this, as was the indigo-suited maniac-wrangler, and stepped up to the railing. He did this not for effect, but simply to see what in heaven's name was going on. But the apparition of the ancient white-haired sorcerer-knight struck the attendant, and moved him aside, like a blast of wind blowing a door open. "I do beg your pardon, guv'nor," he said, in a much more moderate tone, after Saturn's ruffians had filed past him. "Is there any way I can be of service?"

"Prevent sight-seers from coming up here, thank you," Daniel returned, then wheeled round and began to scan the walls. This upper storey was not as prized by the Governors of Bedlam as it had been by Hooke; rather than situating their best offices here, they had sprinkled tables and trunks about the place, making it into a dovecote for clerks, and a dump for little-used documents.

"When we were here for my party it looked much as it does now," Daniel said to Isaac, "which is to say that these inward-sloping walls—which are, of course, the inner surface of the roof's structure—had been plastered over."

"Yes."

"But I often visited Hooke here much earlier—back in the seventies. This part of Bedlam went up first—as you'll recall, the wings took years to complete."

"Yes."

"I am trying to recollect what it looked like, before lath and plaster were put up. I phant'sy that behind these surfaces are large cavities—particularly—if memory serves—*here*, between where the chimney is hidden as it pierces the roof, and the corner. There are four chimneys—hence, four such cavities." Daniel had been dragging a hand along the plaster as he spoke, occasionally thumping with his knuckles. He'd stopped at a place, near the corner, where it answered with an especially resonant boom. Without allowing his hand to move, he turned round now to scan the other three corners.

His gaze lit on one that was stained with fresh plaster. Then—fortuitously—he noticed that Timothy Stubbs had finally caught up with them.

Pleasantly baffled might have described Stubbs's state of mind when he'd reached the head of the stairs; *horrified* was nearer the mark now. Daniel favored him with a thin smile. "Does my discourse have a familiar ring to you, Mr. Stubbs?"

"Indeed, Doctor, it is very like what John Doe was saying to his confederates, after I followed them hither that night."

"You showed commendable nerve, Mr. Stubbs, in sneaking up on a gang of madmen."

The praise caused Stubbs to relax a bit. "Wish I'd been so cool as to've tackled *all* of 'em, guv."

"You did just the proper thing by capturing their leader. Is that the place, over yonder, where they attacked the wall?" Daniel asked, pointing to the fresh plaster.

"Indeed, sir."

"Mad as hatters—or so 'twould seem," Daniel mused. "On the other hand, suppose there really is treasure, or something, hidden in one of these corners. Then John Doe is no madman, but a burglar or worse; and all of the treatments I have prescribed for him are to no purpose. They might even be detrimental! He should in that event be at Newgate awaiting justice, not at Bedlam seeking a cure. The only way to be certain is to look. I take it that Doe found nothing, when he broke through the wall?"

"Wasps' nests and bat droppings only," Stubbs returned, speaking slowly, as he was a bit lost.

"That is not surprising. Mr. Hooke would have placed his cache in the corner most sheltered from the prevailing winds—*there*," Daniel said, and pointed along the wall to the next corner. Saturn looked at him, and Daniel nodded. Saturn turned his back to the others and sauntered to the corner indicated. He gave his right arm a little twitch as he went, and a loggerhead of black iron dropped out of his sleeve, fat end first. His fingers closed round the narrow end just in time to keep it from dropping to the floor. Then with a sudden movement he brought it diagonally up and across his body, and with a ponderous swing of his whole trunk delivered a massive back-hand blow to the wall. The loggerhead burst through the plaster and the underlying lath like a musket-ball piercing a melon. Saturn drew it out, transferred the loggerhead to the other hand, and shoved half of his arm through the hole.

Mr. Timothy Stubbs was not in the least pleased by any of this, and looked as though the only thing preventing him from adding Saturn to Bedlam's roster was the implicit threat of the four lads Saturn had summoned up. But Peter Hoxton quickly settled the issue by declaring: "The verdict is in. John Doe is no lunatick, but a common burglar." And he drew his arm out of the hole, and held up, as proof, a rolled sheaf of dusty papers. "Or perhaps an *uncommon* one."

" 'Twould appear you had warned Mr. Stubbs to be on alert for madmen who would wish to knock holes in the walls," Isaac said, "but how could you have anticipated this?"

He and Daniel had retreated to the opposite corner of the upper storey to get away from the dust and noise created by the assault on the wall. Saturn's lads, who had come with diverse crowbars, stevedore's hooks, &c., secreted on their persons, had demolished a few square yards of plaster and lath, exposing a prism of dark space in which two or three bodies might have been concealed, if Hooke had been that sort of chap. Instead, he had packed in two wooden trunks, and a few leather wallets, then caulked the interstices with wadded or rolled papers. The dust was now settling to the point where Daniel and Isaac were tempted to approach. But first Isaac wanted an explanation.

"The story is not wholly known to me," Daniel said. "Several of Hooke's buildings, including the Royal College of Physicians and my lord Ravenscar's house, have recently been invaded."

"Catherine told me about the attack on *her* domicile," Isaac said. "A queer lot of burglars they were—knocking holes in my lord Ravenscar's walls to discover naught, while ignoring treasures that were sitting out in plain view."

"Simple extrapolation told me that Bedlam might be next. I paid Mr. Stubbs to show especial vigilance. John Doe was captured a week ago. He has done his utmost, I am told, to keep up the façade of a raving lunatick. Now that he knows what treatment lunaticks may expect in Bedlam, he may confess to simple burglary." Daniel caught Stubbs's eye—which was not easily done, as Stubbs was paralyzed with astonishment to see what was being dragged out of the walls. "Pray go to John Doe's cell. Tell him nothing about what has *really* occurred. Rather, tell him that Dr. Waterhouse has knocked holes in all four corners, and found *nothing*—proof that Doe is a madman indeed, who may, therefore, look forward to a stay here of indefinite duration."

Peter Hoxton had been carrying out a rough sort of the booty from the wall. Which was to say, he had raked out all that was of Saturnine interest and put the discards in another, larger pile. He had already culled out enough to keep him rapt for weeks: for the trunks were packed with small wooden chests, and the chests with fine instruments wrought of brass, and even of gold. Many of these were obviously clock-work. Saturn, wary of the dust, peered quickly at these, then closed them up and stacked them out of harm's way, covering them with a large drawing which he pressed into service as a tarpaulin. But the drawing itself—a phantastickal rendering of the skeleton of a bird—had now cozened him into rigid fascination. Isaac too was drawn to it. "I thought it were a rendering of a bird, at first," Saturn said, "until I spied this cull—" and he pointed to a snarl of lines that Hooke had, over the course of a few seconds' lazy yet furious drawing, scrawled and slashed onto the page. These by some miracle added up to a perfectly intelligible rendering of a man in breeches, waistcoat, and periwig, standing with arms raised above his head to support one joint of the wing. If this was supposed to be a bird, it would have a wingspan several times that of the largest albatross. But where a bird would have muscles to pull, this skeleton had pistons and cylinders to push, the great bones of the wings. It was inside-out and backwards, exoskeletal.

Daniel's gaze fell on a great leather wallet, gnawed at the corners by rodents, but still intact. He unwound the ribbon that held it closed, and spread it out on the lid of a trunk. It was a stack of foolscap sheets rising to the thickness of three fingers, creased and compressed from long immurement, but still perfectly legible. It contained notes, written in Hooke's hand, and illustrated with more admirable diagrams, on divers subjects:

Dr. Dee's Book of Spirits expos'd
Animadversions upon Dr. Vossius's Hypothesis of Gravitation
Acerbity in Fruits
Plagiarism in the *Parisian* Academy
Cryptography of Trithemius
Sheathing ships with lead, as practic'd by the *Chinese*
Telescopick Sights for Instruments Vindicated
Inconceivable Distance of the Fixt Stars
Parisian philosophers evade Proof from Observations,
    when they are unwilling to allow Consequences
272 Vibrations of a String in a Second, make the sound
    of G Sol re ut
Python explain'd
Of the Rowing of Ancient Gallies
Structure of Muscles explain'd

Iron and Sp. Salis take fire with explosion
Unguent for Burns, a *Receipt*
Ideas are corporeal, with their Explication, and the possible number
    that may be formed in a Man's Life
Monkeys wherein different from Men
How Light is produced in putrifying Bodies
Micrometer of a new contrivance
A Cause hinted of the Libration of the Moon
Flints: of their formation and former fluidity
French Academy have published some Matters first discovered here
Why freezing expands water
Effects of Earthquakes on the Constitution of Air
Hills generated by Earthquakes
Hob's Hypothesis of Gravity defective
Flying Fish, and of Flying in general
Center of the Earth not the Center of Gravity
Decay in human bodies observed
Anthelme's Opinion of Light refuted
The Genuine Receipt for making Orvietano
Why heat is not sensible in the Moon's Rays
Gravity and Light the two great Laws of Nature, are but different
    Effects of the same Cause
Hodometrickal Method for finding the Longitude
Effects on one Experimenter of the Plant, call'd Bangue by the
    Portugals, & Gange by the Moors
Mechanical Way of drawing Conical Figures
Burning-glasses of the Ancients

Implicit was that Hooke had concealed these in the walls of Bedlam because he would not entrust the Royal Society—specifically, Newton—with his legacy. And so Daniel began to read these titles aloud as a sort of rebuke to Isaac. But having started in on such a Litany, he found it difficult to stop. This was a sort of concentrated essence of that quicksilver spirit that had animated Daniel's, and the Royal Society's, halcyon days. To handle these pages was to drink deep from the Fountain of Youth.

What eventually stopped him was a page written, not in English like most of the others, and not in Latin like some of them, but in a wholly different alphabet. The characters on this page bore no relationship to any from the Roman, Greek, or Hebrew script; they were not Cyrillic, not Arabic, and yet bore no connection to any of the writing-systems of Asia. It was an admirably simple, clean, and lucid way of writing—if only one could understand it. And Daniel almost could. The sight of it stopped him cold for a minute. He was just beginning to decipher the glyphs of the title when Saturn put in: "I have already come across several of those, Doc—what tongue is that?"

Isaac, gazing at the leaf in Daniel's hand from three yards away, answered the question: "It is the Real Character," he said, "a language invented by the late John Wilkins, on *philosophical* principles, in hopes that it would drive out Latin. Hooke and Wren adopted it for a time. Can you still read it, Daniel?"

"Can you, Isaac?" Daniel asked; for it might be important for him to know this.

"Not without revising Wilkins's book."

"It is a receipt," Daniel said, elevating the page slightly, "for a restorative medicine, made from gold."

"Then pray do not waste time translating it," Isaac said, "for we all know of the late Mr. Hooke's susceptibility to quackery."

"This is not *Hooke's* receipt," Daniel said. "He wrote it out, but did not invent it. He gives credit to the same fellow who shewed the Royal Society how to make Phosphorus." To Saturn and diverse other cavesdroppers this signified nothing, but to Isaac it was as good as saying *Enoch the Red*. As such it drew Isaac's full and disconcertingly sharp attention. "Pray go on, Daniel."

"It begins with a sort of narration. An account of something Hooke witnessed somewhere . . ." A long pause now for difficult translation, then sudden knowledge: "No, here! Just here, where we are standing. The date given is . . . if my arithmetick is to be credited . . . *anno domini* 1689."

"The same year, and place, as your *strangely premature* going-away party," Saturn reflected.

This tripped Daniel up for a moment, being an acute observation on Saturn's part, and one that Daniel had entirely missed. But Isaac urged him to go on, and so he did, haltingly: "It began with a medical—no, a *surgical* procedure on a subject—human—male— aged two score and three."

"Ah, a contemporary of you two gentlemen!" Saturn put in. "Perhaps you knew him."

"He was quite ill because of a stone. A stone in his bladder. Hooke performed a lithotomy."

"What, *here*!?" Saturn exclaimed, looking about.

"I have seen them done in the *street*," Daniel said.

"It would not be the strangest thing Hooke did here," Isaac assured Saturn.

"That becomes the clearer, the more we go through his leavings," Saturn mused.

"Pray continue, Daniel!"

"The procedure went normally. However, the patient . . . the patient died," Daniel translated. He had begun to feel unaccountably woozy, and took a moment now to sit down atop a dusty trunk, lest he lose consciousness and topple over the balustrade into Bedlam's Well of Souls. "I beg your pardon . . . the patient died, as often happens, of shock. No pulse was evident. Whereupon the learned fellow I spoke of earlier emerged from a place of concealment, from which he had been observing the procedure."

"How convenient!" Saturn scoffed. "What, are we to believe this Alchemist lurks in Bedlam's shadows just waiting for someone to give up the ghost during an impromptu tabletop lithotomy?"

"The truth is not so fanciful. He had been present, earlier in the evening, for a social gathering. He overstayed to keep an eye on the procedure," Daniel said. This much was not written down on the page—it came from Daniel's memory.

"A social gathering—the oft-mentioned premature going-away party, perhaps!" Saturn said. He meant it as a jest. But neither Daniel nor Isaac laughed.

Daniel continued with the translation: "Hooke had in this room a Reverberatory Furnace, which was already hot for another experiment. The Alchemist went to work in some haste, using some chymicals from Hooke's own cupboard—which I can testify was well-stocked. For example, he used something that is rendered, on this page, as a bone-cube-cup . . ."

"Hooke must have meant a cupel."

"Ah, well done, Isaac. A cupel, and certain materials that he carried on his person in a small wooden chest. The receipt is not easy to translate—I too shall have to revise Wilkins." He skipped a page, then another. "The result: a small quantity of a light-bearing compound. Placed in the mouth of the dead patient, it caused his heart to resume beating, and cured him of his shock. Several minutes after, he came awake, and professed to have no memory of what had transpired. The Alchemist had by then departed, taking all the residues of the receipt with him. Hooke set it down as best he could from his recollections."

"This explains much," said Sir Isaac Newton, eyeing Daniel very oddly indeed. Daniel hardly cared; he had leaned back flaccid against the wall, and was gazing mindlessly at the oculus of silver light in the cupola. He felt no more alive than stone Melancholy.

"Yes, it does!" Saturn returned, "we now know what John Doe was looking for!" Then he shut up and swallowed hard, noting the odd, wordless tension joining Daniel to Isaac. "Or were you referring to something else?"

IN BOSTON DANIEL had known many Barbadian slaves, bred in the Caribbean from stock imported, a generation earlier, by the Duke of York's Royal Africa Company. They were the most superstition-ridden people he had ever met. It seemed that the most flimsy and volatile elements of African culture had survived the Middle Passage, even as the ballast of history and wisdom had been chucked over-board. Exported to northerly outposts, these slaves stepped off the gangplanks bedizened with *voudoun* fetishes and spouting the most bizarre words and phrases—'twas as if they lived in a perpetual hallu-cination. When such persons were placed in the households of literal-minded Puritans inclined to see devils and imps everywhere, the result was poisonous—as several Salemites had learned.

One phrase that Daniel had heard, more than once, from some such slaves, was *dead man walking.* It came out of a belief, endemic to the Caribbean, that corpses could be re-animated through sorcery, and made into sleep-walking Myrmidons who would do the sor-cerer's bidding.

It was impossible for Daniel to bar such thoughts from his mind for a little while. He was as helpless, as susceptible, as a man being tumbled in the Machine for Calming Violent Lunaticks. He was, if not a Dead Man Walking, then a Dead Man Sitting on his Arse for at least a quarter of an hour, as Saturn and his lads began to pack up the Hooke treasure and make it ready for shipment.

Gradually, that part of his mind where Enlightenment virtues were enshrined got the better of that part where grotesque supersi-tions waited for opportunities to jump out of the shadows and shout, "Boo!"

Precisely what Enoch Root *was,* was not known to Daniel. But Root most certainly was not a *voudoun* sorcerer. If he had ministered, in some wise, to Daniel following his lithotomy, he had not done so by necromancy. More likely, Daniel had not actually died, but gone into a coma, and Root had brewed up a stimulant to bring him back. It might have been as simple as smelling salts. Seeing which, Hooke—who *was* gullible about quack medicines—had let his imagi-nation carry him off.

It was amusing, though, that Daniel had written Root a letter, just the other day, stating his opinion that he, Daniel, was not likely to survive the next few weeks.

Isaac's repetition of the phrase "Crane Court" broke in on

Daniel's reverie. While Daniel had drifted away, Isaac had stepped in and begun issuing writs. He was telling them to take all of Hooke's treasures away to the headquarters of the Royal Society—precisely what Hooke had *not* wanted.

"Speaking as one who *lives* in the attic of the Royal Society," Daniel said, "I can witness that there is no room there. None."

"We can always make room," Isaac pointed out, "by rubbishing some beetles."

"But we do not wish to in this case," Daniel insisted.

"Where do you propose to take it, then?" Isaac asked, and sharp was his gaze on the document in Daniel's hands.

Before he forgot about this, Daniel folded it up the middle and slipped it into his breast pocket. "I propose it be stored at my lord Ravenscar's house," he said. "I go there frequently on Longitude and other business, so I can always get to it there. And as your niece is mistress of the household, you too may visit whenever you please."

"Then it were no different from keeping it at Crane Court."

"Pray walk with me, Isaac, to pay a call on Mr. John Doe, and I shall explain it as we go." Daniel rose to his feet, and found that he was as alive as he'd ever been. A live man walking.

"THE PIECE OF INFORMATION you are lacking," Daniel explained as they strolled down the gallery, "is that I suspect Henry Arlanc of involvement with the Infernal Devices."

"What, the porter?"

"Yes."

"But he is a member of the Clubb, is he not?"

"Indeed. I saw to it that he was made a member, on the pretext that he was nearly killed by the first Infernal Device, and so was as much a victim as any of us. But really I did so because I suspected him."

"On what grounds?"

"First: shortly after I arrived in London, some months ago, I began to make inquiries about the location of Hooke's papers and instruments. Henry Arlanc was the first man I asked. Not long after, I learned that word of my interest had spread through the *demimonde* with incredible rapidity, which made me suspect that Henry had talked to someone. Second: supposing that you, Isaac, were the intended victim of the first Infernal Device—that this was an attempt by Jack the Coiner to assassinate you, his most formidable foe—how would Jack have known that it was your habit to work late Sunday evenings at Crane Court? For you went to some pains to prevent this from being widely known, specifically so that you would not be disturbed by favor-seekers. Only Arlanc and a few others knew of this.

"Then I should say you have evidence enough, already, to prosecute Arlanc."

"But I would rather use Arlanc, somehow, to draw Jack out," Daniel returned. "We ought to do nothing that would make Arlanc phant'sy he is under suspicion. But it were obvious folly to place the items found today in the house where Arlanc dwells!"

"Very well. To the Temple of Vulcan they shall go, and I shall send a note to Catherine directing her to place them under lock and key. There is a vault in the cellar—"

"Can't think of a better place," Daniel said.

"I hope it is now plain to you that Threader is a villain," Isaac said. "Whatever evidence you may have to implicate Arlanc, is as nothing beside the fact that the Device was secreted on Threader's baggage-wain."

"Then do you add my name to the roster of those under suspicion," Daniel said, "as it was placed in *my* trunk. But in all seriousness, Isaac, I'll agree to this much: the Device could not have been placed where it was without the connivance—perhaps unwitting, or unwilling—of a servant in Threader's retinue."

"And it is certain that such Black-guards *are* numbered among his entourage. For Jack is a shrewd fellow, and would be at pains to plant spies in the households of his confederates."

They had paused before the door to John Doe's cell. Daniel said, "His confederates, yes—as well as his enemies. For as strange as it seems, he appears to have done just that in placing Arlanc at the Royal Society."

Isaac listened to this gravely, and then devoted a few seconds to a sort of clinical examination of Daniel's face: perhaps looking for symptoms of resurrection. "I suppose it *does* seem strange," he allowed. "On any other day, Daniel, I should be quite amazed."

The Launch Prudence
MONDAY, 12 JULY 1714

MR. ORNEY HAD SAID only that *Prudence* was a Simple and a Virtuous Vessel. No further warning was needed by the other members of the Clubb. They had come down to the stairs this morning laden with cushions, oilskins, umbrellas, spare clothes, food, drink, tobacco, and anti-emeticks. All of them were soon put to use as *Prudence* wallowed across the Pool of London and made a slow pass upstream before the waterfront of the Borough, struggling against the rain-swollen flow of the Thames towards London Bridge, which taunted them cruelly with visions of pubs and chocolate-houses.

Orney might be oblivious to rain, but, anticipating that the others would whinge about it, he had pitched a tarpaulin over *Prudence*'s midships. This was waterproof except along the seams; wherever any-one touched it; where it had been patched; round any of its constel-lations of moth-holes; and wherever else it happened to leak.

Prudence was, in essence, a fat cargo hold partitioned off from the rest of the universe by a carapace of bent planks, with a nod, here and there, to requirements of propulsion: diverse oar-locks, and a stubby mast with elementary rigging. There was no wind to-day—the rain was a steady soaker, not a lashing howler—and so he had hired four Rotherhithe lads to kneel on the deck and stir up the Thames with oars. The oarsmen were situated out-board, along the gunwales, shel-tered by naught but big-brimmed hats of waxy canvas. They looked as wretched as any Mediterranean galley-slaves. Daniel, Orney, Kikin, and Threader were in the hold, where Orney had improvised a bench by throwing a plank between two clapped-out sawbucks. When this was augmented by cushions, it rose just high enough that the four Clubb members could sit on it, all in a line like worshippers on a pew, and gaze out through a narrow horizontal slit between the fraying and weeping tarp-hem above, and the bashed and tar-slopped gun-wale below. This would make them perfectly invisible to any who might spy on them from the shore or the Bridge, as Orney had pointed out several times already, and would persist in doing until a plurality of the Clubb agreed with him, or told him to shut up. Orney used *Prudence* to make runs up and down and across the river for supplies, e.g., oakum, brown stuff, tar, and pitch, all of which the hold smelled like. There were other vessels like it scooting about the Pool.

"The point is granted," Mr. Threader said finally. "As a means to reconnoiter the demesne of the infamous Mr. Knockmealdown, it is better than packing a water-taxi with gentlemen in periwigs and sending them forth on a sunny day with parasols and spyglasses."

"There!" cried Daniel, who was tilting a hand-drawn map toward the feeble light lapping in through the slit, and menacing it with a Royal Society burning-glass the size of a dessert plate. This artifact, which was encrusted with a Rokoko frame and handle, had been a gift to Natural Philosophy from some member of the House of Tuscany. Beneath its splendour, the map looked very mean. The map had been cobbled together, as Daniel had explained, from rumors, recollections, and suppositions given to him by John Doe, Sean Partry, Peter Hoxton, Hannah Spates's father, and any of their drinking-companions who'd been in earshot when Daniel had interviewed them. "Mark yon brick warehouse," Daniel continued, indicating Bermondsey.

"There's been naught *but* brick warehouses for two hours," Threader pointed out, in a deprecating tone that moved Mr. Orney to muse:

"A man of the City, who lives off Byzantine manipulations of the Commerce of the Realm—like a fly, influencing the movements of a noble draught-horse by chewing on its arse—cannot perceive the beauty of this prospect. He will prefer the waterfront of Southwark: Bankside, and the Clink. For these were fashioned during indolent times, for the pleasure of idle wretches narcotized by Popery: being a succession of theatres, whorehouses, and baiting-pits strung together by a *corniche* well-made for preening strollers, beaux, fops, pimps, nancy-boys, *et cetera*. A lovely prospect doth it make—*to a certain type of observer*. But below the bridge, most of what meets the eye has been built in recent times—an age of industry and commerce. The same fellow who adores the Vanity Fair of Southwark will complain that Bermondsey and Rotherhithe are a monotonous succession of warehouses, all built to the same plan. But an industrious chap who lives by simple and honest labour will see a new Wonder of the World, not without a sort of beauty."

"The only wonder of the world I have seen to-day is a man who can speak for ten minutes about his own virtuousness, without stopping to draw breath," returned Mr. Threader.

"Gentlemen!" Daniel almost shouted, "I draw your notice to the Church of St. Olave, near the southern terminus of the Bridge."

"Does Mr. Knockmealdown also control *that*?" asked Mr. Kikin.

"No, though he is not above posting look-outs in the belfry," Daniel said. "But I point it out only as a land-mark. Directly below it, as seen from here, along the riverfront, may be seen a pair of wharves, of equal width, separated by a warehouse. The one on the right is Chamberlain's Wharf. The other is the Bridge Yard. Each communicates with streets in the hinter-land by a labyrinth of crazed alley-ways, whose tortuous wrigglings are only hinted at by this map. The warehouse between 'em, likewise, though it presents to us a straight and narrow front, rambles and ramifies as it grows back into the Borough—like—"

"A tumor spreading into a healthy organ?" suggested Mr. Kikin.

"A hidden fire, spreading invisibly from house to house, sensible from the street only by a smoak-pall of pick-pockets, outraged women, and abandoned property?" tried Threader.

"The abcesses of the Small-Pox, which present themselves first as a diaspora of tiny blisters, but soon increase until they have merged with one another to flay the patient alive?" said Mr. Orney.

For Daniel had employed all of these similitudes and more while drawing their attention to other East London Company facilities.

The oarsmen were giving them curious looks.

"I was going to liken it to a tree-stump in a garden," Daniel said forbearingly, "which to outward appearances stands alone, and may be easily plucked out; but a few minutes' work with a mattock suffice to prove it has a vast hidden root-system."

"Is it in any sense different from any of the *other* such places you've pointed to?" Threader asked.

"Without a doubt. Being so near the Bridge, it is convenient to the City, and so it is where Mr. Knockmealdown conducts a certain type of commerce: trade in objects small enough to be carried across the Bridge by hand, yet valuable enough to be worth the trouble. Whereas *bulk* contraband, as we've seen, is handled downriver."

"It certainly enjoys a fair prospect of the Bridge," observed Mr. Kikin, who had half-risen to a beetle-like squatting posture so that he could swivel his head back and forth.

"As does the Bridge of it," Daniel said. "The place is called the Tatler-Lock, which means, the Watch-Fence. We shall learn more of it in coming days!"

"Is that the end of the reconaissance?" Mr. Orney asked. "For we are getting into the turbulence of the Bridge, which on this rainy day, threatens to upset our boat."

"Or at least our stomachs," said Threader.

"Can we make it to Chapel Pier?" Daniel asked, pointing north across the flow to a mole that had been built upon the largest of the Bridge's twenty starlings, midway along the span. "For I have something to shew the Clubb, not far from it, that shall be of great interest."

"I vote we make the attempt," said Mr. Threader, "on the condition that Dr. Waterhouse desist from any more such foreboding, vague, oracular adumbrations, and simply come out and tell us directly what he means."

"Hear, hear!" said Orney, and after collecting a nod from Kikin, directed the oarsmen to turn north and cut across the river, allowing the current to sweep them away from the Bridge. Following which they were to turn *Prudence*'s blunt bow into the flow and work up to Chapel Pier. They executed their first turn directly in front of the Tatler-Lock, which Daniel gazed at raptly, as if he had a whole poke full of nicked watches he longed to fence there.

"Next order of business," said Mr. Threader, "to extract from Dr. Waterhouse an explanation of *why* we are here; which ought to include some intelligence as to why our Clubb's treasury, so prudently and jealously husbanded these months, is of a sudden brought to such a desperate pass."

"Our newest member—though he could not join us to-day, and forwards his regrets—will presently help make it whole," Daniel assured him.

"That is fortunate—*if true*—for our *other* absent member is in arrears."

"Mr. Arlanc has provided us with a wealth of *information* instead," Daniel returned.

"Then why is he not here, *further* to enrich us?"

"He does not *know* how useful he has been. I mean to keep him ill-informed."

"And the rest of us, too, 'twould seem," returned Mr. Orney, earning him a rare nod from Mr. Threader. As for Mr. Kikin, he had gone into the mode of the Long-Suffering Russian, smoking his pipe and saying naught.

"John Doe confessed he was no madman," Daniel said—for during lulls he had already narrated to his fellow passengers the first part of the tale of his and Isaac's raid on Bedlam. "But he said there was nothing we could do to him, to induce him to tell what he knew."

"A familiar predicament," mumbled Kikin around his pipe-stem. "He is more scared of Jack than of you. I know some tortures—"

"Sir!" huffed Mr. Threader, "this is England!"

"We bribe people here," Daniel said. "The negotiations were lengthy, the tale tedious. Suffice it to say that according to the parish records John Doe is dead, and a grave is being dug for him in Bethlem Burying Ground."

"How did you kill him?" Kikin inquired politely.

"The hole will be plugged with a cadaver from the cellars of the Royal Society, where it will never be missed. A man having marked similarities to John Doe, but a different name, is en route to Bristol. He will ship out to Carolina next week, to work for some years as an indentured servant. And as reward for having seen to all of these arrangements—which were complicated and *expensive*—we have had from him a full account of why he was knocking holes in the plaster-work of Bedlam."

"And may *we* hear it? Or will you, too, insist on being made a farm-hand in Carolina?" Threader said.

"That will not be necessary, thank you," Daniel returned politely. "John Doe let us know that he was only one of several Hoisters, Dubbers, and Mill-Layers—these are different specialties under the broad heading of House-Breakers—who took it upon themselves to respond to an Opportunity bruited about the Tatler-Lock and other such kens by a personage whose identity was not announced but who was suspected to be Jack the Coiner. This personage let it be known he was interested in certain buildings—specifically for what might be concealed in the walls of those buildings. Anyone who entered a building on the list, and extracted aught from its walls, was to take it to the Tatler-Lock and give the personage an opportunity to buy it. He is only interested in certain items, not others—so each must be carefully appraised before 'twill be paid for."

"Jack must desire these things—whatever they are—quite ardently, if he is truly willing to expose himself thus," said Orney.

"Perhaps this gives us a means to entrap him!" said Threader.

"Alas, it is not quite so simple," Daniel said. "For the goods were to be fenced through an *Arabian* auction."

Mr. Kikin was amused by the blank expressions on the faces of Orney and Kikin. "Shall I explain it?" he offered to Daniel. "For it is how Russians trade with Turks, even when we are at war with them."

"Prithee."

"When the Arab wishes to trade in dangerous circumstances—for example, across the Sahara with the Negro—he drives his caravan south to some oasis, and goes out some distance into the open waste, and piles up on the sand those goods he offers for trade. Then he withdraws to some remove beyond spear-range, yet still nigh enough that he is able to keep watch over his goods. The Negro now feels safe in venturing to the same place, where he piles up nearby those goods he offers in exchange. He withdraws and the Arab ventures out again, inspects the Negro's offerings, and adds to or takes from his pile. And so it goes, back and forth, until one is satisfied, which he betokens by packing up and hauling away the counterpart's offerings. The other waits until he has withdrawn, then goes out a last time to take possession of what remains."

"Provided one is willing to do without the exotic accoutrements of dunes, camels, *et cetera,* the same can be done in any empty room of the Tatler-Lock," Daniel said. "The Hoister and the Client need never see each other. They need only trust Mr. Knockmealdown— which, be it prudent or no, they do."

"I have a foreboding of what it is that you intend," Mr. Threader said, "since you are, as of three days ago, in possession of loot from the walls of Bedlam. But do you not think that a Fellow of the Royal Society, if he participates in this Arabian auction, shall be noticed by the sort of man who frequents the kens of Mr. Knockmealdown, and that word of the anomaly shall soon reach the ears of Jack?"

"The plan was proposed by none other than Sir Isaac himself," Daniel said. "He likened it to the hunter's stratagem whereby a goat or other expendable beast is tethered to a stake out in a clearing in the woods, to draw predatory animals to a place where they may be easily shot. We know not what Jack seeks, but very likely it is included among the goods we have found in Bedlam—therefore we have what is needed to establish a *Stake-out* of our own. Mr. Threader avers that this will never work if one of us attempts it. Sir Isaac has foreseen this objection. He suggests that we adopt his practice of going into the ken disguised as members of the criminal element."

This notion produced frigid silence among the Clubb. Before the others could recover their wits and throw Daniel overboard, he continued: "Fortunately we have already an understanding with Mr. Partry, who is as comfortable in such kens as Mr. Orney is in church. He has agreed to act as our representative in the auction."

"That is even *worse!*" Kikin cried. "Partry hunts and prosecutes thieves *for a living!*"

"No, no, no. You still don't understand," said Mr. Threader, finding Kikin's slowness just a bit distasteful. "*The whole point* of thief-takers is that *they are themselves criminals*—else, how could they get anything accomplished?"

"So you are going to give some valuables to a thief, entrusting him to take them to the most colossal thieves' market in Christendom, where he will sell them at auction to another thief—?"

"He is a very reputable thief," returned Mr. Threader. "I really do not understand you, sir—*you* are the one who recruited him."

At this Kikin could only roll his eyes, in the universal manner of foreigners in collision with Anglo-Saxon logic. He sighed and withdrew to his end of the plank.

"The Stake-out commences to-day," Daniel announced, patting a wooden chest on his lap. "We are going to make rendezvous with Partry at our head-quarters on London Bridge."

"That's *another* thing—I see that you have arrogated to yourself the authority to lease real estate on behalf of the Clubb!" Threader said.

It was Daniel's turn to roll his eyes. "Mr. Partry and Mr. Hoxton have, on our behalf, evicted a whore and twenty million bedbugs from a room above a tavern. If *that* is *leasing real estate,* then *Prudence* is the Spanish Armada."

"For the amount you have spent, we could have *gotten* the Spanish Armada," Orney returned, "but I supposed good old *Prudence* were less apt to draw fire from the Tower."

THE MEN WHO WERE PASSING the time of day under umbrellas and shed-roofs on and around Chapel Pier were oblivious to the charms and virtues of *Prudence,* and some even ventured out into the rain and tried to wave her off. Most of them were watermen who envisioned that the bulky launch would block half the Pier and create an Impediment to Commerce for some indefinite number of hours. They had ample opportunity to say so, by words and gestures, as Mr. Orney's stolid oarsmen fought up-current, closing on the Pier's butt at slower than walking speed. But after a little while the inhospitable watermen were joined by a man bigger than the rest, who ambled to and fro along the brink of the Pier, striking up a chat with each waterman he found. These exchanges tended to be brief, and always ended in the same manner: the obstreperous waterman turned away and withdrew to the shelter of the Bridge. By the time *Prudence* worked close enough for Orney to cast a line onto the Pier, this bulky cove was the only man left. He intercepted the lead with a flailing arm, passed it thrice around a bitt, and leaned back on it, inexorably ratcheting *Prudence* forward until she bumped against pier-side.

"Mind the Gap," Saturn suggested. The passengers did, and crossed it without any fatalities. Orney sent *Prudence* back to Rotherhithe. Saturn led them over the stony lid of the Pier to an uneven stair, perhaps under desultory repairs, perhaps ne'er finished. They ascended it in the hunched, splay-armed gait of drunks on ice. This got them to the upper world of the Bridge: an ordinary London shop-street that just happened to be thrust up into the air on stone stilts. To their left it was vaulted over, which is to say, the Bridge itself was bridged, by an ancient Chapel. To their right spread the open fire-break called The Square. Following Saturn's lead, they turned their backs on this and on London, and proceeded southwards, as if they were going off to the Borough to inspect the Tatler-Lock from the street. But far short of this—only a few score paces beyond the Chapel—Saturn side-stepped into a medieval doorway too narrow to admit him square-shouldered. Bracketed to the front of the building above this was a contraption consisting of a wooden platform, about the size of a cutting-board, impaled on a vertical spar, all cobwebbed with lank strands and net-works of hempen cord: a copy in miniature of ship's rigging, rotted by weather and deranged by nest-building birds. Standing on the platform was a miniature figure of a man, raising a grog-ration; and painted below upon the wall, for the entertainment of literate customers, was the name of the establishment: Ye Main-Topp.

Pursuing Saturn through this door, the Clubb found themselves in a public house, whose floor had been strewn with fresh hop-vines in a plucky but hopeless bid to freshen the air. Some half a dozen patrons were scattered against the walls as if they'd been blown into their current positions by the explosion of a shell in the center of the room. They were not mere seamen, for they had shoes; but neither were they Captains, for they wanted wigs. It could be inferred that the Main-Topp catered to the low middle class of Bridge people: ships' mates, watermen, hackney-drivers, &c. Several conversations were put in recess so that drinkers could devote all their powers of concentration to the newcomers. The barkeep, barricaded in his corner fortress, gave them all a nod. The Clubb nodded back and muttered diffident greetings, having no idea what sort of story Saturn had told the proprietor about the strange guests who'd soon be arriving. A door in the back of the room led to a steep and lightless staircase, which had no need of a banister, as a normal man could arrest his fall simply by squaring his shoulders against both sides and inhaling. In some way Saturn squirted to the top of it and through another elf-door into a room.

Though in truth 'twas not the Room they saw first, but what lay beyond its windows, which faced to the east: the Pool of London, so crowded with vessels of all sizes and descriptions that it struck the eye not so much as a body of liquid water as a morass, congested and nearly rafted over by floating wood. Aboard *Prudence* they had been maneuvering through it—which was to say, they'd been part of it—for a few hours, and so one might not expect the scene to've drawn their notice as strongly as it did. But viewed from above, and framed thusly in the lattice-work of the windows, it gave an entirely different impression; the hundreds of ships, variously bobbing, rocking, steaming, smoking, loading, unloading, undergoing diverse mendings, splicings, paintings, caulkings, and swabbings, shrugging off the rain from above while holding back and riding upon Thames-pressure from below, seemed as if they had been arrayed thus solely to be viewed by the Clubb from these windows. As if some tyrant prince had conceived an enthusiasm for seascape-painting and commanded that all the Realm's trees be cut and all its men pressed into service to create a striking Scene below his easel.

The room's floor was simply the obverse of the tavern's ceiling. It was fashioned of planks, generously spaced, so that stripes of light and fumaroles of tobacco-smoke leaked up through the fissures.

Over them was the roof of the building. It was thatched—a quaint touch never seen any more in parts of the city that had been reached by the Fire. This drew undue notice, for some moments, from the Clubb, who stood gaping up at it as if to say, *Ah yes, I have heard that once we made shelters out of grass.*

Buildings on London Bridge tended to be made by trial and error. Starting with a scheme that was more or less sane, in the broad sense that it had not fallen down yet, proprietors would enlarge their holdings by reaching out over the water with cantilevered add-ons, buttressed with diagonal braces. This was the *trial* phase. In the next, or *error* phase, the additions would topple into the Thames and wash up days later in Flanders, sometimes with furniture and dead people in them. Those that did not fall into the river were occupied, and eventually used to support further enhancements. Countless such iterations, spread thick over centuries, had made the Bridge as built-up as the laws of God and the ingenuity of Man would allow.

Daniel, venturing across springy floor-planks to this room's eastern extremity, found himself embraced by windows—for this had originally been a sort of experimental balcony that had been encased in glass after it had failed to collapse for several consecutive years. Like a curd held up out of the whey by a strainer, he was being kept out of the Thames by perhaps a finger's thickness of gappy planking. Between the boards he could see a gut of the river clashing and foaming along the edge of a starling. Vertigo—Hooke's nemesis— claimed his attention for a few moments. Then he got the better of it and turned to gaze southeast at the Borough. A few moments sufficed to identify the Tatler-Lock, whose façade of blackened bricks rose up from the bank no more than two hundred yards away. For the better viewing of which, a perspective-glass lay on the windowsill. Above it, a single diamond-shaped pane had been punched out to allow for clear viewing. Hidden as it was beneath the furry, dribbling brow of the thatched eave, this would never be noted from the Tatler-Lock.

"Enjoy a good look, then," said a new voice. "The glass is as good as any at your Society."

Daniel turned to spy Sean Partry sitting crosslegged in a back corner, surrounded by ironmongery, tamping tobacco into a pipe.

Daniel picked up the glass, telescoped it to full length, and set its wide end into the vee of the missing diamond, which had thoughtfully been lined with a rag. This held it perfectly steady, while allowing him to swivel the narrow end to and fro. Putting his eye to it, and making some small adjustments, he was rewarded with a magnified view of some windows on the upper storey of the Tatler-Lock. Several were boarded over, or else veiled with remnants of sails. One was but a vacant window-frame. Through this could be seen the floor-boards of an empty room, starry with bird-shit.

"There is little to see," Partry admitted. "Mr. Knockmealdown has a violent aversion to eavesdroppers."

"It is very good," was Daniel's verdict. "The hunter who stakes out bait, must establish a nearby blind, from which to observe his quarry. But not too close, lest the beast nose him, and be put on his guard. This room shall do. And you are correct, Mr. Partry, about the glass. The opticks were ground by a master."

A concentration of dust-bunnies and feather-shards marked the location of the previous tenant's Bed and Engine of Revenue. This had been cast into the river and supplanted by more furniture of the plank-and-cask school, on which Threader and Kikin had already claimed seats. Orney moved towards the windows to mark *Prudence*'s progress downriver but pulled up short as he felt the balcony losing altitude under his weight.

"What have you told the proprietor about who we are, and what we are doing?" Mr. Threader was asking Saturn.

"That you are Royal Society men making observations of the daily currency of the river."

"He's not going to believe *that*, is he?"

"You didn't ask me what he *believes*. You asked me what I *told* him. What he *believes*, is that you are City men investigating a case of insurance fraud by spying on a certain ship anchored out in the Pool."

"Fine—our true purpose shall not be suspected as long as he is telling people *that*."

"Oh no, he's not *telling* people that. He's *telling* them that you are a Sect of Dissenters forced to meet in secret because of the recent passage of Bolingbroke's Schism Act."

"Let the blokes in the tap-room think we are Dissenters then, is all I'm trying to say."

"That's not what they think. They think that you are Sodomites," Partry said. This silenced Threader for a while.

"No wonder we are paying such exorbitant rent," reflected Mr. Kikin, "considering the vast scope of activities going on in this one room."

Partry had spread a trapezoid of sail-cloth over the planks in the corner of the room and was sitting on it. He'd have looked like a tailor, except that he was working with the tools of the thief-taker's trade: an array of manacles, fetters, neck-rings, chains, bolts, and padlocks, which he was sorting, inspecting, and oiling. Probably this had done nothing to improve their reputation among the regulars drinking porter six feet below.

"What is it we are to put up for auction to-day?" Partry inquired.

Daniel stepped away from the window, handing the glass to Mr. Orney, and retrieved a small wooden chest he had earlier set down on a barrel-head. "Since you are a connoisseur of Opticks, Mr. Partry, you'll find this of interest. It is a collection of lenses, some no larger than mouse's eyes, but ground to perfection."

Partry narrowed his eyes. "You think Jack the Coiner has gone to so much trouble to get a box of lenses?"

"I think he desires Hooke-stuff. I know not what, or why. By proffering these, we show him our *bona fides*. That is, we prove that we have Hooke-stuff to sell, for only Hooke made lenses like these. Whether Jack buys them or not, we'll have his attention after to-day."

"To-day, or tomorrow, or a week hence," Partry corrected him. "There is no telling how long this will sit in the Tatler-Lock before Jack, or his deputy, comes round to appraise it." With that Partry accepted the box from Daniel, and tucked it under a sort of pea-coat he had put on as protection from the rain. He descended the stairs. Saturn followed after, and through the floor the Clubb could hear him asking the proprietor to send up four mugs of flip.

And so the Stake-out commenced. Daniel dragged an empty crate over to the balcony and sat down where he could keep an eye on the Tatler-Lock. It was unlikely there'd be anything to see, but he felt he ought to do this for the sake of form. Four mugs of steaming flip arrived on the shoulder of a fascinated bar-maid. It was, as a rule, a winter beverage, but suited them in to-day's weather. Orney produced an octavo Bible from his pocket and began memorizing it, oblivious to displays of withering scorn being directed his way by Mr. Threader. Kikin put on glasses and began to read an impressive document in Cyrillic letters. Threader grubbed a pencil out of his pocket and began to dash off notes using a barrel-head as desk. Daniel had not thought to bring anything to pass the time. Partry's hobby of fetters and chains held no allure. But Peter Hoxton, who was avidly literate, had already strewn reading materials about the place, viz. an English translation of Spinoza. This was too weighty for Daniel's mood. He picked up a libel instead.

A Diplomatick OVERTURE from the Queen of *Bonny*, to Her Britannic Majesty translated from the *Africk* by DAPPA, Ambassador to the *Liberty of the Clink*.

APOLOGY

Owing to a spell of confusion that hath gripped the mind of *Mr. Charles White*, and induced him to believe that he owns me, I have lately suspended my former habit, viz. of wandering about the Terraqueous Globe, for a life of dignified repose in the Clink where I am detained 'pon suspicion of having stolen myself. 'Tis a charge difficult to refute; for the Magistrate hath shrewdly asked me whether it was not true, that I was in possession of myself, and I, having always prided myself on being a self-possessed fellow, did answer in the *affirmative*. Whereupon the magistrate did bang his gavel and order me clapp'd in irons and dragged away to the Clink for the crime of receiving stolen goods.

My *stationary* habit has not been without benefit to the *stationers* of this and other Realms. For many of my old friends and relations, who had given up in despair of hitting such a restless target with a well-aim'd letter, have reached me here. Not a day goes by that I do not receive a weather-beaten and worm-eaten note from a far-off land. To-day I have got one that came in a ship lately active in the *Assiento* trade. This vessel came to London direct from the Slave Coast, bearing a chest laden with Spanish pieces of eight—part of the bounty due H.B.M.'s government, under the late Treaty of Peace, for the commerce between Africa [a great producer of Negroes] and the Caribbean [a ravenous gobbler-up of same]. The treasure-chest was removed by Mr. White, who carried it ashore in the company of several fellows, all of them bedizen'd with curious silver-greyhound badges. Later the same company was spied across town in Golden-Square, paying a call upon the Viscount *Bolingbroke*, who keeps a fine house there; but alas, somewhere along the way, the chest had *sprung a leak*, and those pieces of eight had dribbled out into the streets of London. Upon Mr. White's arrival at the Viscount's house, the chest was observed to be nearly empty. In haste his Messengers re-traced their path through the city, hoping to pick up what had spilt, but alas, the coins had already been plucked up by ordinary Londoners. As most common Englishmen have never laid eyes upon a coin of *silver*—pounds sterling being as rare in England as plainspoken Tories—no one recognized them for what they were. But seeing that each one was stamp'd with a face bearing the features of a *Bourbon*, these patriotic Englishmen took offence and flung the despicable medallions into Fleet Ditch, where they sank presently to the bottom. So the *Assiento* revenue is gone; though 'tis rumored among the Vault-men that on moonless nights a man resembling the Viscount Bolingbroke may be observed standing on the brink of that noisome *arroyo*, holding a cloak, and a fine suit of clothes, all embroider'd with *Greyhounds*, while a naked man splashes about in the *flume* below, like a pearl-diver in a Tropick lagoon, breaking the surface from time to time with a shiny new Bourbon piece of eight in his teeth. For which the man on the brink presently rewards him by tossing him an ear, much as a hunter doth take all the meat of the game while throwing the bones, gristle, &c. to his dogs, who are so foolish as to believe that they are being shown great favor.

Thus the latest shipment of *Assiento* money. But I am pleased to relate that a satchel of *mail*, brought to London on the same ship, escaped such a fate. For it was brought ashore by honest men who saw to it that the letters were delivered to their proper destinations—even such humble ones as the Clink.

Thus have I come into possession of a letter from Her Africk Majesty, the Queen of Bonny. It is addressed to Her Britannick Majesty. But since neither Queen Anne nor any of her Ministers is conversant with the tongue spoken by so many of her Caribbean subjects, H.A.M. has sent the letter to me, that I may have the honour of translating it to English. Which I have now done; but efforts to post it onwards to H.B.M. have failed. As many times as I send it, it comes back with a note to the effect that the recipient declined to pay. I see that the late disappearance of revenues, which hath led to such controversy at Westminster, hath been felt at St. James's. So as a favor to H.B.M. I have decided to publish the English text of the letter from H.A.M. in the form of this Libel or Broadside, in hopes that a gust of wind may loft it into St. James's, effecting, at no cost to H.B.M.'s Government, a delivery that otherwise were fiscally burdensome.

The letter begins thus:
Mon Cousine,

Such is the Radiance of your Enlightenment that the People of my Country, who formerly were as pale as Orphans in an Irish Work-House, have now been Tann'd quite Black . . .

[Translator's note: I here elide much more in the way of such lofty Apologies, Compliments, &c., and move directly to the substantive part of H.A.M.'s letter.]

Word hath reached me of late, that certain monies, sent to your Majesty as due profits of the Slave Trade, have not reached your coffers, and an assiduous search hath failed to turn them up. Which news, if true, is most remarkable, for Lapses of a similar nature have been observ'd at the other two Vertices of the Triangular Trade. Viz. to the Caribbean are supposed to be deliver'd a certain number of my subjects. At diverse slave-forts along the Guinea coast, these are packed aboard ship by captains who count 'em with exacting care, and prick 'em down in strict Inventories. Yet the same ships arriving some weeks later at the slave-marts of Jamaica, Barbados, &c., are found to be half-empty; and the few living slaves that are discharg'd from their stinking Hulls so wretched that many must be abandoned 'pon the Strand, as no planter is willing to buy 'em. Meanwhile, a failure of a like nature is easily to be observed from where I sit, in my royal palace of Bonny. For it was given us to understand that the Triangle Trade would deliver to our shores Civilization, Christianity, Enlightenment, and other vertues. Instead of Civilization, we are receiving daily ship-loads of white Sauvages who pillage our shore like so many Vikings having their way in a Nunnery. Instead of Christianity, we are the recipients of a Pagan mentality which holds Slavery to be good, because 'twas practiced by the Romans. And instead of Enlightenment, we are Benighted by the fell effects of the sins and outrages I have mentioned.

In consideration of the fact, which I have now prov'd beyond question, that no part of the Triangular Trade works as

489

it is supposed to—viz. Civilization not reaching Africa, Slaves not reaching America, and *Assiento* money not reaching Your Britannick Majesty's coffers—I propose we denominate it a fail'd Adventure, and bring it to an End immediately.

> *I have the honour to be,*
> *Your Britannick Majesty's Humble Servant,*
> *though not [yet anyway] her obedient Slave,*
> BONNY

Daniel looked up with a bright expression on his face, and was about to begin reading the libel aloud, when he was frozen by a cobra-like glare from Mr. Threader. "Tomorrow I shall supply this room with a copy of the King James Version," Threader announced, "so that Dr. Waterhouse may follow the fine example set by his co-religionist" (flicking his eyes at Orney) "and advance from Libels, to Bibles."

Daniel set the leaf down and gazed out the window for a time. After several minutes had gone by, his eyes were drawn to a tiny movement in the front of the Tatler-Lock. Something had changed in one of the upper windows. He rose slowly to his feet, not daring to take his eyes off of it; for so vast and various was the prospect of London, the Pool, and the Borough from these windows, that this iota was as easy to lose as a single bubble on a stormy sea. To get the perspective-glass extended, aimed, and focused took entirely too long. Nevertheless he was able to get a clear view of a window, mostly veiled behind canvas, but with a human arm, seemingly disembodied, projecting across the front of it and gathering it out of the way (he supposed) so that some light might spill into the room behind. The arm was attached, in the customary manner, to a man, who was standing in the room with his back to the curtain and had hooked his elbow round the edge of the canvas to pull it aside. Presently that man let his hand drop. His arm vanished as the curtain tumbled back to block the whole aperture of the window. At this moment, many a chap would have glanced away to say something to the others, and thereby lost track of which window he'd been gazing at; but Daniel, out of a mental discipline earned fifty years ago, remained still until he had memorized certain peculiarities of the Window in Question: the way a seam in the canvas angled across the upper right corner, and a pair of bricks in the sill that were not as dark as the rest. Only then did he begin to swing the telescope laterally, causing the image to sweep at greatly amplified speed. He counted the windows to the edge of the building—three—then reversed the movement and made sure he could find the Window in Question again. Only then did he withdraw his eye from the lens and announce to the others that he had seen something.

Partry was back half an hour later, and Saturn came in ten minutes after that. It had been their policy for Partry to go alone, and for Saturn to amble along some distance behind him to see if Partry was being followed—which was much more likely to happen on the return leg of the expedition. So Saturn had found a gin-house across the way from the Tatler-Lock and had tarried there until some minutes after Partry had quit the place. Partry, he reported, had indeed been followed up the Bridge by a pair of young culls; but it was Saturn's professional opinion that these were not spies of Jack's or Mr. Knockmealdown's, but merely a couple of enterprising young file-clys who, having consummated one transaction at the Tatler-Lock, were sizing up Sean Partry as a prospective next victim. Saturn knew the lads, and was known by them, because of certain past professional entanglements on which he was not keen to elaborate before the Clubb. Approaching them as if by happenstance on the Bridge, Saturn had remarked on the fact that none other than Sean Partry, the infamous thief-taker, had just gone into the Main-Topp, wearing thus-and-such. This had sent the boys off in quest of less dangerous prey.

Partry then told the tale—which was brief, as little had happened—of his visit to the Tatler-Lock. There was a sort of lobby, where refreshments could be got, and where (he speculated) loitering visitors were spied on through holes in the paneling. After having stated his business, and having waited for some time, he had been summoned by one "Roger Rodgers," a minion of Mr. Knockmealdown's, who had explained that the master of the establishment was downriver at one of his other factories, but that he had left standing orders as to how situations like this one were to be handled—orders that Rodgers had been at pains to carry out. But something in the way he did so gave Partry the idea that this was the first time any house-breaker had ever come in to the Tatler-Lock claiming to have the sort of goods called for in the general summons posted, so many weeks ago, by Jack. There was mounting confusion, leading to low comedy, as Rodgers led Partry from room to room trying to find a suitable place in which to conduct the Arabian auction. Here they stumbled upon a Pharaohanic hoard of stolen watches, there upon a whore dividing her attentions among three eleven-year-old pick-pockets, all addled with gin. Partry had begun to think aloud: a room with some light would enable the buyer better to appraise the proffered swag. A place in the back—towards the river-front—would afford more privacy. Something above street level were less tempting to the depredations of running-smoblers. By offering up such reflections just at those moments when Rodgers seemed most confused,

Partry had insensibly driven and steered him to an upper room above the river, and even induced Rodgers to draw back the canvas hanging in front of its window—which he'd hoped would be noticed by one of the Clubb from their blind in the Main-Topp, as it had been.

So the first bid in the Arabian auction had been placed, and all had gone by plan. The Clubb's deliberations now became radically tedious. This was a favorable omen, as this was the sort of tedium that men like Threader and Waterhouse excelled at, and profited from. The Stake-out ought to be maintained around the clock henceforth. Saturn volunteered to sleep here every night; this made the deliberations briefer than they might have been, and freed Saturn to bid them all good-bye and duck out. A schedule was drawn up whereby Orney, Kikin, Threader, and Waterhouse would take turns keeping an eye on the Tatler-Lock during the hours Saturn was not there. Some gaps remained in the schedule; it was hoped these might be plugged by Newton or even Arlanc. Partry was to stop by the Tatler-Lock once or twice a day to see if the buyer had placed a bid yet, then, after dodging round a bit to make sure he was not followed, come to the Main-Topp to report to whomever was on watch there. That person would make an entry in a log-book so that other members of the Clubb would know what had been going on.

THE PROGRESS OF THE STAKE-OUT, though it extended across never so many hours and days, could thenceforth be known by a few moments' study of the Log. The first entry was dated 12 July, and merely recounted what had just happened. It was written out by Daniel, who took the first watch, between the time that the rest of the Clubb departed and the time that Saturn returned, shoving a bed-roll up the stairs before him.

13 JULY A.M.

Passed a pleasanter than expected night. Amused self by lashing Mr. Partry's perspective-glass into a fix'd attitude, so that 'twill ever be pointed at the Window in Question. Not so much as a glimmer of candle-light rewarded my steadfast Attentions. Let us all pray that the "Stake-out" winds up before winter, as the room is cool at night even in this season—further explanation, as if any were wanted, for the previous Tenant's habit of remaining in bed night *and* day. At dusk, bats emerge from covert places between thatch and ridge-beam, and fly out between the floor-boards. But these should not trouble you of Diurnal habits.

Peter Hoxton, Esq.

13 JULY MIDDAY

Nothing.

Kikin

13 JULY P.M.

Mr. Partry called at four of the clock, having just come from the place of the auction. He reported finding a single copper token, of the lightest weight, laid down as proffer for the lenses. Sent word to Dr. Waterhouse. The next move is ours. Gentlemen?

Threader

13/14 JULY—NOCTURNAL RUMINATIONS

He might as well have offered us *nothing*. But he offered us *something*. It is difficult to make out the true signification of this humble disk of copper. But after a long night counting bats, here is what I believe: Jack [or his proxy] does not want the lenses. So he offers payment that is insultingly low. But he does wish to continue the Arabian auction. Our next move ought to be to make some adjustment to the contents of our Pile.

Peter Hoxton, Esq.

14 JULY MIDDAY

I agree with Saturn's hypothesis [*vide supra*]. Have brought the diagram of the flying-machine discovered in the wall of Bedlam. Will whoever next sees Mr. Partry please ask him to convey it to the Tatler-Lock and bring back the box of lenses.

Dr. Waterhouse

14 JULY P.M.

A most peculiar heathenish Negotiation. Have understood the instructions set forth above by Brother Daniel and read them aloud to the illiterate Mr. Partry. He has departed bearing the diagrams. God willing, he shall return the lenses. N.B. evening watch is vexatious owing to the singing and smoking of Main-Topp regulars below. Am willing to trade my evening watch scheduled for 17th, for a morning watch any day save tomorrow.

Orney

15 JULY A.M.

Lenses were returned by our Mercury[*] last night in good condition. Round midnight I detected light emanating from the Window in Question. A look through the perspective-glass revealed the enlarged and dis-

---

*Partry.

torted shadow of a man cast on the canvas window-covering by [one guesses] a candle or lantern within. Regret that I am unable to offer a useful description of him who cast the shadow. After some minutes the light waned and vanished.

At 2 A.M. a man knocked on the door hoping to find a Sodomite. I sent him away gravely disappointed.

Peter Hoxton, Esq.

15 JULY MIDDAY
No singing, no Sodomites, no Mercury.

Kikin

15 JULY P.M.
I renew my plea for some Respite from the damnable Vices practiced so freely Below. Will exchange evening for morning hours at favorable rates.

Partry reports a silver penny in fair condition has been offered for the diagrams. Sent word to Brother Daniel.

Orney

16 JULY A.M.
Yester eve the loneliness to which I'd grown accustomed was relieved by the unlooked-for, but welcome arrival of Dr. Waterhouse at five minutes past nine of the clock. He had received the note sent by Mr. Orney. He looks on today's news as supporting the view that Jack or his proxy is more interested in Hooke's *writings* than in his *artifacts*. He brought a wallet containing some of the *chymical* Notes, Receipts, &c., found in Bedlam's walls, and proposes that they be left in place of the Flying Machine Diagram. The response should then tell us whether we are [to borrow a figure from a children's game] getting Warmer or Colder.

Peter Hoxton, Esq.

16 JULY P.M.
I propose to Mr. Orney that in exchange for my taking his four hours scheduled tomorrow eve., he take my 18th A.M. and 19th midday watches.

Threader

P.S. Nothing happened.
P.P.S. I find the singing, etc. perfectly innocuous and even join in the choruses.

17 JULY WEE HOURS
Round seven of the clock, Mr. Orney, Mr. Partry, and I fortuitously overlapped. Mr. Partry collected the *chymical* Notes and departed for

the Tatler-Lock at 7:04, saying he should be back shortly. But when the bells of St. Olave and of St. Magnus Martyr next resumed their hourly dispute as to what time it was, he still had not returned. Keeping watch, I noted that the curtain had been drawn back entirely from the Window in Question, so as to flood the room of the Auction with what remained of the evening's light. Peering through the glass I saw a stout red-headed fellow, whom I believe to have been Mr. Knockmealdown, pacing about the room. Sitting at the table was a man dressed in a dark suit of clothes, going through the contents of the wallet in a methodical way—which told me, at least, that Mr. Partry had reached the Tatler-Lock and made his delivery. Moved partly by concern for the welfare of our thief-taker and partly by hope that I might contrive to get a better look at this dark-clad fellow [for the seeing through the window was poor], I departed the Main-Topp at 8:10, leaving Mr. Orney to man the post, and hurried south on London Bridge, reaching what I shall denominate the main entrance of the Tatler-Lock at 8:13. This door leads into the so-called *lobby*. Chary of exposing myself to the many prying eyes of that place, I did not go inside, but ambled about the surrounding streets for some little while—an exercise I do not recommend to any of the Clubb, as Mr. Knockmealdown's factories are as be-swarmed with footpads, &c., as a knacker's yard with flies—until at 8:24 my notice was drawn to a carriage [hackney, unmarked, unremarkable] emerging from an alleyway that is surrounded on three sides by out-buildings and other excrescences of the Tatler-Lock. I followed this on foot as far as the Great Stone Gate which it cleared at 8:26:30. Thence I watched it all the way across the Bridge. It passed St. Magnus Martyr, which is to say, it vanished into London, at 8:29:55: rather good time, as traffic on the Bridge was light. Be it noted that the City of London and the head-quarters of Mr. Knockmealdown are separated by a mere two hundred seconds—material for a Sermon should one of you homilists care to write it up. Returning towards the Tatler-Lock I encountered Mr. Partry in Tooly Street, carrying the Flying Machine Diagram under his arm. As is our practice, we pretended not to know each other. I swerved round several corners and followed him, at a distance, up the Bridge to the Main-Topp.

Mr. Partry explained that this auction is akin to a wheel that rubs and balks the first few times it is turned, but presently warms, and runs smoother. Previously the buyer did not come to inspect our proffers for a day or more. But today, as Mr. Partry was swopping the *chymical* Notes for the Flying Machine Diagram, he encountered Mr. Knockmealdown himself, who bruited that if Partry were to make himself comfortable and partake of some refreshment, he might afterwards nip back up to the Auction-room and find an answer waiting. So Partry did

just that—not in the "lobby" but in a more congenial and private tap-
room reserved for personal guests of the mismanagement—and at 8:23
[for I had taught him to tell time, and kitted him out with a watch, running in synchrony with mine], receiving the high sign from one of Mr.
Knockmealdown's minions, returned to the auction-room to find evidence that the wallet had been perused, and a gold coin—a *louis
d'or*—left as counter-proffer. Partry let it lie, which was a way of saying
to the buyer that he might have more to add to our pile in a day or two.

Mr. Orney departed to convey this news in person to Dr. Waterhouse. Before he departed, he took up a difficult matter with me, as follows. Mr. Orney is of the view that Mr. Threader's offer of a
two-for-one swop is beneath contempt, and unworthy of a civil response. He was at a loss as to how this information might be conveyed
to Mr. Threader. I told him that as I am a thoroughly uncivil person,
no one was better qualified than me to distribute this information. Consider it done.

Peter Hoxton, Esq.

18 JULY A.M.
Will members of the Clubb hereby desist from misusing the Log as a
bazaar for haggling over hours. The schedule is now all wrong anyway,
consequent to last night's events. I have conferred with Sir Isaac. He has
a notion of what it is that the buyer desires, and I agree with him. But we
are loath to sell the original to this buyer, whoever he is, and so we are
presently hard at work crafting a forg'd copy, with certain details altered,
so that it shall not be of any use [the document in question is a chymical
receipt, inscribed in a sort of philosophickal language that might as well
be a cypher; I know enough of the language, and Sir Isaac knows enough
of Alchemy, to produce a convincing fake]. Meanwhile Mr. Hoxton has
been directed to spend his days, and if need be his nights, at Clerkenwell
Court fabricating two wooden chests that look the same.

Other Clubb members, please confer amongst yourselves as to who
shall accept which watch, and do not involve this log-book.

Dr. Waterhouse

18 JULY P.M.
Spent nearly twenty-four hours here, alone. It is not the most disagreeable thing I have done, or would do, in service of the Tsar.

Kikin

18 JULY MIDNIGHT
Extemporaneous Jottings are best confin'd to Waste-books, not to be
perus'd by others. It is my Policy to write out several Draughts of any

Document that is important enough to pass under the eyes of Strangers
or Colleagues. But the Circumstances that have brought the Clubb into
being, and lately conferred upon me the Honour of Membership, are
most extraordinary, and may permit me to set down in this Log some
rude and hastily improvis'd Lines.

Dr. Waterhouse [who, as I write this, is sleeping on the Floor
nearby] and I did profit from the lengthy Vigil of Mr. Kikin thusly: we
have produced a Manuscript of several Leaves, similar in all observ-
ables to one that was written in 1689 by the late Mr. Hooke, viz. written
on the same sort of Paper, with similar Ink, in a similar Hand, expressed in the stately but obscure Cadences of the Philosophick Language, and written in the stark runes of the Real Character. Like Mr.
Hooke's *original*, whence 'twas in large part Cribbed, it claims to be a
Receipt for a restorative Elixir of such Potency as to bring back the
Dead, couched as a Narration of a strange Evening under Bedlam's
Cupola. In truth, the Receipt is of no practical utility, for the two reasons set forth below.

First, that, like Mr. Hooke's Original, it requires, as one of its Constituents, a mysterious Substance; and as the nature of this Ingredient
is not made clear, there is no way for Mr. Hooke's result to be dupli-
cated by any other Student of Chymical Arts [not the first time such a
Gravamen could be leveled at that Author's work—and perhaps sufficient Explanation of why he plaistered it up in a Wall].

Second, that certain of its Instructions were deliberately altered, at
my direction, to ensure that any effort to follow them would lead to
production of a formless and stinking Pot of what is denominated, by
Alchemists, *fæces.*

During our *chymical* Lucubrations in the Temple of Vulcan, Mr.
Hoxton and several Apprentices were as busy in the Court of Technologickal Arts [as it is styl'd by my somonolent Colleague] fabricating
two handsome Chests of Ebony-wood and Ivory. These were made to be
indistinguishable from each other by the simple expedient of making
two of each Part and assembling them side-by-side on the same Bench.
Each has a hing'd Lid closed by a Hasp that is not, however, presently
hinder'd by a Lock. Any Document, placed within such a Receptacle, is
imbued by it with seemingly greater importance and higher value—or
so may it seem to an impressionable Mind.

One of the twinned Chests bides at Clerkenwell where Mr. Hoxton
is committing further Improvements. The other has received the forg'd
Receipt and been convey'd to the Main-Topp by me and Dr. Waterhouse. We relieved the steadfast Mr. Kikin and waited for the arrival of
Mr. Partry.

As Partry is not able to read what is set down in ink on these pages, I

shall permit myself greater Liberties, in discoursing upon his Character, than I should if I suspected he might one day acquaint himself with
what I write down here. I beg the forbearance of the Clubb as I proffer
Advice for which they never asked. For though its members be worldly
and season'd Gentlemen all, yet the Clubb itself is of an age such that,
were it an Infant, it should not yet have the ability to crawl, or even to
roll over in its Cradle. Though I am its newest Member, it cannot be
disputed that I have been engag'd in Pursuit of Coiners for nigh on a
score of Years now; which giveth me Reason to suppose that some of my
thoughts and opinions, carefully considered, & judiciously set down,
might be of sufficient Interest to the Clubb as to be worth the few minutes it shall take to read them.

I would not have hired Partry. This gambit of hiring a thief-taker to
venture into the vile and perilous Haunts that are the natural Habitat
of Coiners, is easily understood; for to habituate such places is naturally repugnant, as well as dangerous, to a Gentleman. But *Dias* would
never have found the Cape of Good Hope, save by braving the journey,
and putting his own person in harm's way; and many are the tales in the
annals of the Royal Society of Natural Philosophers who expos'd themselves to disgusting and dangerous Circumstances, even to the point of
sacrificing Limb or Life, because no other means could be found to
their desir'd Ends. In consideration of which, it has long been my Habit
to alter my appearance, viz. by applying Latex of *Brasil* to my face to
give me a *pox-mark'd* Visage, &c., &c., and, thus disguised, to go out *incognito* into Gaols, Boozing-Kens, Taverns, &c., to see and hear with my
own Organs of Sense what I will not trust any villainous Thief-taker to
perceive clearly nor recount coherently.

Partry was already on the Clubb's pay-roll when I was given the
honour of membership, and I do not presume to suggest that he be
removed now. To fire Partry at the current stage of the Auction
would in any event only incite the gravest Unease in the mind of the
Buyer. In perusing this Log, however, I cannot but note that all of
the Clubb's impressions of the *Tatler-Lock,* save a few fleeting and
poorly resolved glimpses through the Window, have been supplied by
Mr. Partry. To be certain that he has not been, like Hamlet's uncle,
pouring Poison into your Ears while you sleep, I resolved to accompany Mr. Partry to the Tatler-Lock on his visit this evening. Dr.
Waterhouse, because he is concerned for my welfare, advised me not
to go, and, because he knows me well, surrendered before his warnings became tedious. To this plan Partry expressed a violent opposition, which at first excited my suspicions; but after the first flush of
astonishment had subsided he gave his assent. He did so grudgingly

at first, but upon seeing how my appearance was transfigured by a few moments' work with Latex and Spirit-Gum, a change of clothing, and adoption of a different posture and gait, he made peace with the idea, and offered no further complaints. We set out for the Tatler-Lock ten minutes apart. I went first, on the pretext of being a seller of watches, fallen upon hard times, who wished to replenish his inventory at prices not within reach of honest men. Only after I had ensconced myself in the *Lobby* did Mr. Partry enter the building, carrying the chest, wrapped up in a black cloth. Contained within it was the first page of the Receipt prepared by me and Dr. Waterhouse.

To relate further details were idle, since all that I observed there was more or less as Mr. Partry has led you to believe. My Suspicions, at least in so far as concern the Tatler-Lock and the operations of the Auction, are proven to be unfounded. The chest is in the Auction-room, awaiting the attention of the Buyer. Partry has gone away to wherever he spends his nights. During our absence Dr. Waterhouse fell asleep in the middle of his Watch: in the Army, a flogging offence, in the Clubb, I know not what. I shall take the first part of the night-watch myself and awaken him at the stroke of two.

Sir Isaac Newton

19 JULY A.M.

Sir Isaac did not fail to awaken me at the time mentioned. I have obsvd. naught since. But I should not be perfectly honest if I stated that my eyes were open for the whole duration of my watch.

Dr. Waterhouse

19 JULY MIDDAY

If Brother Daniel had found the Discipline to keep his eyes open, he might have seen candle-light in the Tatler-Lock during the wee hours. For Mr. Partry called at ten of the clock, bringing the News that a five-guinea piece [*sic*] has been laid down in the Auction-room. Someone has perused the first page of the Receipt, and liked what he has seen; I'd wager five guineas of my own that he'll offer us another such Coin for another Page.

Orney

19 JULY EVENING

Sent Partry to the Tatler-Lock with Page 2; but I do not like the Direction we are taking. What is to prevent the buyer from simply copying out the Receipt and then paying us nothing?

Threader

20 JULY VERY EARLY A.M.

Lights have been burning behind the rude Veil of the Window in Question for better than an hour, which would seem to confirm Mr. Threader's fears. I can allay these with a few particulars as to the Chest. As shall be obvious to anyone who gives it more than a few moments' inspection, it has a false bottom. There is a locked compartment beneath. This can only be opened with a key, which we have not offered yet. If the buyer reads all the way to the end of Page 4 he shall reach a Notation to the effect that an Ingredient, essential to the Receipt, is concealed in the bottom of the Chest. Merely to copy out all four pages shall avail him nothing, save writer's cramp. He must have the Chest and Key, and these he shall not get until he pays for them.

I also remind Mr. Threader that the purpose of the exercise is not to get paid, but to ensnare the Buyer.

Peter Hoxton, Esq.

20 JULY MIDDAY

Nothing.

Orney

20 JULY EVENING

Mr. Orney would have won his wager had anyone been foolhardy enough to accept it, for Partry reports a second five-guinea piece has been laid on top of the first. I have taken the liberty of sending down Page 3.

Kikin

21 JULY EARLY A.M.

Further Lucubrations obsvd. I suspect the Buyer is copying or translating the Receipt.

Peter Hoxton, Esq.

21 JULY MIDDAY

The point is conceded, that our Undertaking is a *snare* and not a legitimate commercial Transaction. But as this pile of five-guinea pieces ascends toward the sky I find myself sorely tempted to enter into the business of selling *philosophical* Arcana. Partry reports that the price offered is now fifteen [*sic*] guineas. I sent him back with the fourth and final Page.

Threader

21 JULY MIDNIGHT

Curtain was open in early eve. and I glimpsed our dark Philosopher at work once again. He goes hooded—this explains why I have not been able to see his face. Perhaps he is pox-marked, or burned in an Alchemical mishap. A gray goose-quill bobbed in the gloom next to his shoulder as he stain'd page after page of a Waste-book with ink. Later the curtain was dropp'd again, and my view replaced with dim flickerings that lasted until 11:12:30.

Peter Hoxton, Esq.

22 JULY MIDDAY

Disaster. Partry reports the five-guinea pieces are all gone, replaced by a silver penny.

Orney

22 JULY EVENING

I beg to differ with Brother Norman. This is not a disaster, but a clear sign from the Buyer that he has correctly decyphered the Receipt and understands that it is not useful to him without the Ingredient that is supposed to be contained in the bottom of the chest. I have sent Partry back to the Tatler-Lock with the key. Henceforth I shall remain here at the Main-Topp until the culmination of the Stake-out.

Dr. Waterhouse

23 JULY MIDDAY

Mr. Partry has been at the Tatler-Lock since day-break. He has persuaded Mr. Knockmealdown to allow him to sit vigil in a store-room directly beneath the place of the Auction. Such are the floor-boords of that edifice that not even a cat could stalk from the door to the table without producing a *fusillade* of cracks and booms. As soon as Mr. Partry hears anything of that nature he is to—

"Your pint, sirrah."

"That is very kind of you, Saturn," said Daniel, setting the quill into its pot, and glancing once more at the distant window where Partry was puffing on his pipe. "How did you guess I was in the mood for a pint?"

"*I* am in the mood for one," Saturn said.

"Then why didn't you bring up two?"

"You forget that I am a Paragon of Sobriety. I shall derive my pleasure from watching you drink yours."

"I am happy to oblige," Daniel said, and took a swallow. "There has been no signal from Mr. Partry," he said, for Saturn's dark eyes had strayed to the page of the Log, still dewy with unblotted ink. "I was merely refreshing the account."

"I must ask, why you do not write it in the Real Character," Saturn teased him, "if it is as excellent as all that."

"It *is* excellent. A much better way of setting down knowledge than Latin or English. Which is why I have devoted some years to making it more excellent yet, by transliterating it into numbers."

"Ah," said Saturn, "are you saying, then, that the cypher in which the women of Bridewell punch the cards, is a descendant of the Real Character?" By now he had changed places with Daniel, and taken up that position on the balcony of which they had all grown so weary in the last eleven days.

Daniel moved the Log over to its customary station on a crate-top, and busied himself blotting the latest entry with sand. "Not so much a *descendant* as a *sibling*," he said. "The father of both is the Philosophic Language, which is a system of classification of ideas. Once an idea has been enrolled or registered in the tables of the Philosophic Language, it may be addressed with a number, or a set of numbers—"

"Cartesian coordinates," Saturn mused, "for plotting the wand'rings of our thoughts, like."

"The similarity only holds to a point," Daniel cautioned him. "To avoid ambiguity, the Philosophic Language—Leibniz's version of it, anyway—employs only prime numbers. In this, it is quite different from the number-lines of Descartes. In any case, the Language, as it consists of ideas and numbers, may be writ down using any scheme one may care to choose. The binary cypher of our Logic Mill is one such. But when I was a young man, John Wilkins devised another— the Real Character—which for a time was all the rage in the Royal Society. Hooke and Wren used it fluently."

"Who uses it now?"

"No one."

"Then how is the Dark Philosopher able to read it?"

"The same question has been bedeviling me."

"This Wilkins cove must have published a dictionary or key—"

"Yes. I helped write it, during the Plague. The page-proofs were burnt up in the Fire. But it *was* published, and can be found in any number of libraries. But in order for our mysterious Buyer to go to such a library, and consult the book, he must first *recognize* the out-landish glyphs on the page as belonging to something called the Real Character. Think—if I shewed you, Peter, a page writ in the script of Malabar, would you know to consult a Malabar-Dictionary?"

"No—for these eyes, though they've seen much, have never seen Malabar-letters, and would not know 'em from Japanese or Æthiopian."

"Just so. Yet our buyer seems to have known the Real Character on sight."

"But is that really so extraordinary, when one considers that the same buyer knew that Hooke-stuff was to be found hidden in the walls of Bedlam? From which it's evident he knows much of your Society."

"I believe that the knowledge of where to look for the stuff came to the buyer through Henry Arlanc: the Royal Society's porter."

"I know who he is."

"Oh really? How do you know him?"

"He worked for a Huguenot watch-maker, with whom I had professional contacts before I turned to drink, and fell on black days. Several Fellows of the Royal Society patronized this horologist—that is how they got to know Henry Arlanc, and that is how Arlanc got the position at Crane Court."

"Until recently," Daniel said, "I had supposed that Arlanc was passing intelligence to Jack the Coiner, or someone in his organization, who was, at bottom, ignorant of Natural Philosophy."

"There's a hole in that hypothesis, Doc. Why'd such a cull want to rake through the mouse-eaten leavings of a dead Vertuoso?"

"Ignorant men have fanciful notions of what may be found in such residue. Alchemists frequently work with gold. Perhaps—"

"Still, the hypothesis does not hold up well under close examination."

"I agree!" said Daniel, exasperated. "I no longer believe in it."

"Well, *now* is a fine time to say so," said Saturn. "What's the *new* hypothesis?"

"That the buyer is a Fellow of the Royal Society, or else has made a close study of the Society's early years. He knows a great deal about Hooke and about the Real Character, and . . ." Daniel paused.

"And?"

"And about poison," Daniel said. "An attempt was recently made on the life of Princess Caroline. The weapon was a poniard smeared with nicotine, excellently prepared."

"Bloody peculiar," reflected Peter Hoxton, "when this benighted world doth so abound in simpler means of killing."

"During the 'sixties—Hooke's heyday, and the æra of the Real Character—several Fellows of the Royal Society took an interest in nicotine."

"It's obvious then, isn't it?" Saturn said.

"What is obvious?"

"The villain must be Sir Christopher Wren!"

Saturn clearly meant this as a preposterous jest, and so he was appalled to see Daniel considering it seriously. "Because he is one of the very few still living from that æra, you mean," Daniel finally said. "It is a good thought. But no. This is not being done by Wren, or Halley, or Roger Comstock, or any of the others who were in the Royal Society in those days. Supposing *I* wanted to kill someone—would I brew up nicotine? No. No, Peter, this is being done by some-one of a more recent generation. He has conceived a diseased Fascination with the Royal Society of the 1660s. He has poured an unhealthy amount of time into studying what we did, and reading our annals."

"Why?"

"Why? When a young man falls under the spell of a particular young woman, and will not leave her alone, though her father and brothers menace him with daggers drawn, ask you why?"

"But this is different."

"Perhaps."

"Trust me, 'tis different. The buyer desires something. I believe you know what the something is. Will you please let me in on the se-cret?"

"I have held it back, not because I wish to keep secrets from you," Daniel sighed, "but because I find the entire subject painfully embar-rassing. The buyer seeks the Philosopher's Stone."

Saturn slapped his forehead theatrically. "Why'd I even take the trouble to ask?"

"He has heard at least part of the story about the man who died in Bedlam when Hooke cut him for the stone, and who was (some would say) resurrected by the elixir of Enoch Root."

"Ah, that is the name of—?"

"Of the Alchemist in that story, yes. If you are the sort of chap who believes in Alchemy, then it is implicit, in that story, that the elixir must have been made using something akin to the Philosopher's Stone. Now, according to the lore of the Alchemists, that Stone is made by combining the Philosophic Mercury with the Philosophic Sulphur. Where, might you ask, does a bloke get his hands on such ingredients? The answers are many and various, depending on which Alchemist you talk to. But many believe that King Solomon was an Al-chemist, who knew how to get, or to make, the Philosophic Mercury, and who used it to turn lead into gold."

"Ah, that would explain why he was so rich!"

"Just so. Now, the story goes that if you could find some of King Solomon's gold and put it in a crucible, you could extract from it minute traces of the Philosophic Mercury. I believe that our buyer somehow got wind of this yarn about the Alchemical Resurrection in

Bedlam twenty-five years ago, and reckoned that the shortest and quickest way for him to get his hands on a sample of the Philosophic Mercury was—"

"To ransack London for Hooke's old notes and knick-knacks."

"Yes. Now, consider that, when I got back to London at the end of January, the first thing I did was to begin searching for Hooke's old notes and equipment. Arlanc was the first man I questioned. He must have mentioned this to his contact in Jack's organization. Shortly, word must have got round to our buyer."

"Who was already disposed to believe that this thing of infinite value had been hidden away, somewhere, by Hooke."

"Yes. Imagine the effect the news must have had upon him!"

"He must have been frantic," Saturn said, "believing that you were in quest of the same goods, and would get to them first."

"Indeed. As we now know, this led to the series of burglaries. I had only a dim and fragmentary understanding of these matters until a fortnight ago, when we found that document in the wall at Bedlam. Then all became clear. But, too, it was clear that the buyer's search was doomed to failure, for Hooke's receipt *mentions* a certain ingredient without offering any explanation of *how to obtain* it. For that reason, the document was useless as bait for the Stake-out."

"Which is why you and Sir Isaac had to produce the fake."

"The fake, and the box that it came in," Daniel said. "The buyer believes that a small amount of the Solomonic Gold is locked in the compartment in the bottom of that chest."

"Not for long," Saturn remarked. He was gazing fixedly out the window.

"Why do you say so?"

"Because Sean Partry is waving his arms at me from below the Window in Question."

Daniel's arm jerked and spilt his ink-bottle. It slicked the page of the log-book with a black parabola that streamed over the edge and spattered to the floor.

Saturn was on his feet. He waved back, but did not take his eye off the Tatler-Lock.

"Which direction is Partry indicating?" Daniel asked backing carefully away from the mess. The ink had already found a crevice between floor-planks. Sounds of havoc and dismay were coming up from the tap-room.

"He points toward the Bridge," said Saturn, and finally glanced away from Partry so that he could give his watch a study.

"Then the buyer ought to be coming our way—"

"In no more than two minutes," Saturn agreed. "But traffic is heavier now than when I clocked him before. I shall loop along the Bridge a-foot, and may out-pace him. Do you try to summon a hackney, or a sedan." And he preceded Daniel out the door, and down stairs. Which was fortunate for Daniel, as several ink-spattered Main-Topp patrons had by now formed up at the base of the stairs, in a retaliatory mood. Their ardor cooled when Saturn sallied forth, and through the little Mobb broke a path that Daniel was not slow to follow. "Our work above is concluded," Saturn announced, over his shoulder, as he went out, "and all losses shall be compensated anon—but not now." And with that he burst out the front door of the Main-Topp and into the streaming crowd of the Bridge.

Saturn glanced left—towards Southwark and the Tatler-Lock—but turned right, anticipating that the buyer's carriage would overtake him presently. By the time Daniel made it out the door, Saturn had already advanced several long strides in the direction of London. Daniel followed his example and glanced left—but it availed him nothing. He lacked both Peter Hoxton's *height,* which would have enabled him to see over the crowd as far as the Great Stone Gate, and his *youth,* which made eyes quicker to adjust to the sudden brightness of the unroofed street.

All he had was a vague instruction to hire a coach or a sedan. No hackney of sound mind would await customers in front of the Main-Topp. Daniel guessed there might be chairs or coaches for hire in the Square, a short distance to the north. So he turned right, and began to thread his way through the jostling crowd.

Like the captain of a brittle ship hemmed in on all sides by massive ice-floes, Daniel could not make his own path, but had to move along with the general flow, and avail himself of any leads that snaked open before him before they drew shut and crushed his ribs. He made feeble progress compared to Saturn. Before he had progressed so far as the vault of the Chapel, he had lost sight of Saturn's black head.

The artificial isles that supported the Bridge were called Starlings; the chutes between the Starlings, through which the divided River coursed, were denominated Locks. Daniel, unable to see much but heads and shoulders, estimated, by a kind of dead reckoning, that he must be passing over Long Entry Lock, which was the narrowest, hence most dangerous of them all, as the Chapel Pier to its north side had grown so fat over the centuries as to nearly pinch it shut. Then, looking up, he saw a stone vault overhead, and knew he was passing under the Chapel. Next (counting the Locks and Starlings in his head, like a Papist going through the Rosary) would be Chapel Lock—also quite narrow—but then St. Mary's Lock, one of the widest on the whole bridge, hence, popular among watermen. Directly over St. Mary's was the open fire-break called The Square. And it was there, Daniel reasoned, that hackney-drivers and sedan-porters would flock in hopes of swopping passengers with the watermen below.

Such was his plan. But as commonly happened to clever Natural Philosophers who have hatched elaborate schemes, he was overtaken by simple events. The crowd, hemmed in under the vault of the Chapel, suddenly pressed him from all sides. It was like being an atom of a gas in Boyle's Rarefying Engine when the piston was slammed down by a terrific weight. A carriage was trying to force its way through—and succeeding. The crowd, sensing danger not so much from the carriage itself as from its bow-wave of panic, surged out from the dangerous confines of the vault, and Daniel, like a wine-cork tossed into Long Entry Lock, was spewed forth.

He was in the open now, tottering, looking about warily lest some eddy of the Mobb-rush take him unawares and crush him against a store-front. So he saw the carriage that had caused the trouble as it emerged from the vault, pressing on toward London.

He did not doubt that this was the one. Its window-curtains had all been drawn and its driver had evidently been paid to force his way to the other end of the Bridge with no concern for life, limb, or liability.

They were over Chapel Lock. The Square was only ten yards farther along—but this hackney had already passed Daniel by, and at its mad pace would soon overtake Saturn as well. Daniel still nursed some hope that he might be able to summon a carriage or a chair in the Square—but it would not be easy to persuade a strange driver to light out in hot pursuit of a hackney being driven as recklessly as this one. They needed to keep the buyer in sight as long as they possibly could; for there was no way of telling how long he would wait to put the key he had just paid for into the key-hole in the bottom of the chest, and turn it.

Daniel had, by default, staggered into the sudden open space left in the wake of the hackney. He was so close that he almost could have reached out and climbed aboard, if he'd been that spry. So he could hear—or so he phant'sied—a muffled pop from within, like a musket misfiring. Then flickering light shone through the curtains, and he heard from within a man shouting *"Sacré bleu!"*

Without being aware of how fast he was moving—for if anyone had asked, he'd have insisted he was too old to run—Daniel had followed the hackney right into the Square. The way widened slightly here. He saw Saturn standing to one side. He'd been conversing with a sedan-porter, but had broken off to stare at the buyer's hackney.

Indeed *many* were now staring at it, for it was *smoking*. And it was making booms as the passenger flailed against the roof, signalling the driver to stop. The door on the right side flew open and disgorged a cloud of brown-gray smoke. So dense and voluminous was this, that a long and careful inspection was needed to see that there was a man in the middle of it. He was staggering away from the carriage, headed for the parapet that surrounded the Square to limit the number of pedestrians who toppled into St. Mary's Lock. The passenger looked like a figure from Ovid: a Cloud metamorphosing into a Man. For the smoke had saturated the long hooded cloak that he wore, and was still billowing out of it. Gagging, he shuffled toward the parapet. The hackney-driver scrambled round to the open door, probed into the smoke with his whip-handle, and after a bit of scratching about, dragged out a blackened carapace: a burnt box, still sputtering and jetting a sturdy plume of thick yellowish smoke. Its lid was open to reveal a sheaf of pages, still legible though they'd been burnt to gray leaves of ash; these tumbled onto the pavement and Daniel, only a fathom away, saw the angular glyphs of the Real Character. But then he turned his attention back to the buyer, who had finally cast off his raiment of smoke, and stood at the parapet, feet spread wide, hands planted to support him as he retched into St. Mary's Lock. Like a monk or wizard out of medieval times he looked in that robe. Then he was joined by a larger man who stepped in from the left and clapped his right hand on the other's left shoulder.

The response of the hooded man was immediate—too quick for Daniel, who had a foreboding of what was about to happen, to shout a warning. The hooded man spun toward Saturn, pivoting around the shoulder that Saturn had gripped. Much was hidden by the robe and by smoke; but the movements of his shoulders told that he was driving his right hand toward Saturn's belly.

But Peter Hoxton, by luck or by foresight, was ready for this. There had been something in the man's stance at the parapet that had looked posed, and poised: perhaps it had roused in Saturn's mind the same suspicions as in Daniel's. Saturn got his left arm well inside of the other's attack, and shouldered it aside. But then he jumped back. For as was now plain to everyone in the Square, the robed man was holding a small dagger in his hand. And as was clear to Daniel and to Saturn, the blade had been smeared with something.

In this brief melee the hood had fallen from the buyer's head to reveal his face. It was not burnt or pox-marked. On the contrary, it was a well-formed head of noble bearing. He had black hair going silver, and a goatee. That much was obvious as he surveyed the crowd on the Square, which had formed a ring around him and Saturn, well beyond dagger-range. Daniel recognized him (though it took a few moments) as Édouard de Gex.

De Gex made a move toward the parapet. Saturn, not very prudently, reached out and grabbed him. That stopped de Gex in his tracks. Or so it seemed for an instant until Daniel stepped forward through a shoal of smoke and perceived that de Gex had gone over the edge into St. Mary's Lock, leaving Saturn standing there alone, holding an empty robe.

Royal Society, Crane Court
24 JULY 1714

"WHEN I WAS A BOY, traveling the roads of France with my father— may God have mercy on his soul—and my brother Calvin, we would from time to time overtake a traveling knife-grinder, sweating with the labor of shoving his rig, which was very heavy because of the massive round grindstone. My father, God rest him, was a trader. A merchant. Everything he needed to conduct his business he carried in his head, or in his purse. This Calvin and I considered to be the normal state of affairs. How strange it was, therefore, to see these knife-sharpeners, who could not earn their bread without a great heavy stone! One day Father heard me and Calvin make some mocking comments after we had passed one of these poor hard-working men. He chided us for our arrogance, and gave us a lesson: the grindstone was set in motion by a shove, and kept turning by occasional slaps of the grinder's hand. If it lacked weight, it would run down so quickly as to be useless. But because of its tremendous mass, it continued to turn with the greatest impetuosity once set in motion. The stone acted, my father said, as a sort of *banca,* storing up the work that the grinder did sporadically with hand-slaps, and releasing it steadily. This faculty was so essential to the knife-grinder's work that he willingly pushed that heavy stone up and down hills every day of his life, like Sisyphus.

"When Jack Shaftoe came back to London, he had in his pocket some money given him by the King of France to finance certain schemes and intrigues that Jack was supposed to set afoot here. And, too, there was the promise that more money would be sent to Jack from time to time if *Le Roi* was pleased with his work. The gold he had in his pocket was like the first great shove that sets the grindstone in motion, and the sums promised later would be like the hand-slaps that keep it from losing its speed. But Jack had the wit to understand that he needed a *banca,* a store-house of wealth and power in London, so that his operations would run smooth and steady, even when the subsidies were balky and sporadic. It was not possible for him to rely upon proper *bancas,* and so he had to create one of his own, tailored to his designs. Making the acquaintance of a Mr. Knockmealdown—who in those days was a modestly successful fence, running a Lock in Limehouse, buying goods that had been rifled from ships by mudlarks—he offered up the following Proposition: that he, Jack Shaftoe, would use his 'French gold and English wits' to make Mr. Knockmealdown into a Colossus among receivers, vastly expanding his holdings, and building up his inventory. Mr. Knockmealdown would become a rich man, and his Irish East London Company, as 'twas waggishly called, would become, for Jack, the grindstone that would store up the produce of his labours.

"For the first several years that Jack was back in London, he applied himself to little else. And his wisdom in doing so was demonstrated presently, when the War of the Spanish Succession began to go badly for France, what with all the great blows struck at the armies of *Le Roi* by Marlborough and Prince Eugene. You may be sure that Louis sent Jack very little gold in those grim years. Jack should have been reduced to the estate of a Vagabond, and been rendered useless to *Le Roi,* had he not been able to sustain himself from the profits of the East London Company. As it was, Jack prospered even as Louis declined, and by the time that Marlborough crushed the French at Ramillies, and stood poised to drive into the heart of France (or so it seemed), Jack had built Mr. Knockmealdown up into the most powerful Receiver in Christendom: a sort of Pirate-King, able to absorb into his warehouses the entire contents of a stolen ship as a dog swallows a fly, and, on the same tide, to load the same ship to the gunwales with swag. The East London Company thereby became the Foundation upon which Jack could build his dark Edifice. Only in recent years has he built it high enough for men such as you to note it; but you may be certain it was a-building for many a year before then."

Here Henry Arlanc paused to sweep his gaze around the table. He gave each Clubb member a searching look in the eye, until he came to Sean Partry, who sat closest to him. Then he dropped his eyelids and bowed his head slightly, showing the thief-taker more respect than any other man in the room—even Sir Isaac. Perhaps this was for the simple reason that Partry had on his ring the keys to the manacles that now encircled Arlanc's wrists, and the fetters around his ankles. Arlanc raised his hands up out of his lap, which required some exertion as they were linked by twenty pounds of chain, and closed them round a mug of chocolate that his wife had brought to him.

Mrs. Arlanc had been *horrified* but not the least bit *surprised* when, at the beginning of the Clubb's meeting, as the first item of New Business, Sean Partry had stormed into the room and clapped her husband in irons. The prisoner, by contrast, had been astonished; but once this had faded he had shown no strong emotion, seeming to accept his personal ruin with true Huguenot fatalism. If anything, he seemed relieved.

"Explain to the Clubb how you became a minion of Jack Shaftoe," Sir Isaac demanded, "and do you speak slowly and clearly, that every word may be pricked down." For in lieu of Arlanc—who had, until minutes ago, been the Clubb's Secretary—they had brought in a Clerk from the Temple, who was scratching away with a quill as fast as he could, writing in shorthand.

"Very well. You will already have heard many tales of the horrors visited upon the French Calvinists after the Edict of Nantes in 1685, and so I shall spare you another, save to say that my father was caught up in a *dragonnade* and made a galley-slave—but not before he had contrived to smuggle me and Calvin across the Manche to England, packed in barrels, like herring. Later the galley on which my father served was destroyed in a battle against a Dutch fleet in the Mediterranean."

"But that must have occurred several years after the Edict," said Mr. Kikin, ever the student of history.

"Indeed, sir," said Arlanc, "for the War began, by most reckonings, in 1688, when Louis took the Palatinate and William took England."

"We prefer to say that England took William," Orney corrected him.

"Be that as it may, sir, the engagement that destroyed the galley of my father was a part of the said war, and it took place in the summer of 1690, off Crete."

"He was lost at sea, then, as I take it?" asked Mr. Threader, in a touchingly genteel and delicate way.

"On the contrary, sir—he was rescued by a pirate-galley commanded by none other than Jack Shaftoe."

At this claim, Kikin rolled his eyes, and Orney let out a "Poh!"

Isaac took no note of them, but sharpened his gaze, which remained locked on Arlanc's face. "It is consistent," he announced. "Jack Shaftoe turned Turk in the late 1680s. His Corsairs are known to have raided Bonanza during the summer of 1690. Thence they fled through the Gates of Hercules into the Mediterranean. By late summer they had reached Cairo, as all the world now knows. Mr. Arlanc's account is plausible."

"Thank you, sir," said Henry Arlanc. "Jack and his band of corsairs rescued my father, and other *galériens,* from the wrack of that galley. This much Calvin and I knew from letters we received in Limerick. But beyond that—"

"Hold. How did you and your brother get to Limerick?" asked Orney.

"I was getting to that, sir. When we were let out of our barrels in England, a pair of young lads, not yet fully grown, we could, I'm ashamed to say, muster very little interest in following our father's example and becoming merchants. We lusted after revenge— preferably violent, and if possible, glorious. We joined one of the Huguenot cavalry regiments forming in the Dutch Republic. By the time that William and Mary had come to England, we had risen in the ranks a bit—Calvin had become an assistant Chaplain and I was a non-commissioned officer. Our regiment was one of those that were despatched to Ireland during the early years of the war, to drive out the Pretender. We participated in the Siege of Limerick during the winter of '90 and '91, and that is where we received the miraculous tidings that our father—whom we had given up for dead—had been pulled out of the sea by the King of the Vagabonds."

"Did you receive any further communication from him?" asked Isaac.

"Not for several years, sir, as we were all so much on the move."

"If your father remained in the service of Jack Shaftoe, he would have called at such places as Mocha and Bandar-Congo during 1691 and followed the monsoon to Surat the year after," Newton said. "Beyond that it is difficult to reconstruct Jack's movements for several years. It is well known that he participated in a battle somewhere between Surat and Shahjahanabad in late 1693, and that in 1695 he had begun to organize a ship-building project."

"In February of 1698 our father posted us a letter from Batavia, where that ship had called to take on spices," Arlanc said. "We did not receive it until late in the year. By that time the war was over."

Orney snorted.

"Or so everyone believed at the time," Arlanc hastened to add. "In retrospect, of course, this was nothing more than a brief respite in a war that extended over twenty-five years. But few foresaw this, and so our regiment, like so many others, was disbanded the following year, when the Treaty of Partition was signed by William and Louis.

"It was difficult to find work in London with so many discharged veterans about, and dangerous to be there for the same reason. Calvin and I were more fortunate than some, for enough time had passed since the Edict of Nantes that the Huguenots had established themselves in England, and begun to prosper. Calvin secured a position as a pastor in a Huguenot church just outside of the city, and has been there ever since. I took jobs here and there as a servant to Huguenot businessmen.

"The last letter we received from our father was posted from Manila in August of the year of our Lord 1700, and it stated—"

"That Jack's ship was about to attempt the crossing of the Pacific," said Sir Isaac, "and he would be aboard it."

"Just so, sir. It is uncanny how much you know of Jack's movements about the world. Father said he would write to us again from Acapulco. But he died of scurvy en route, may God have mercy on his soul."

At this little prayer everyone in the room observed a respectful silence. Even Partry seemed moved. The first to speak was Sir Isaac. "And *how*, precisely, were you delivered this unhappy news?"

"Jack told me," said Arlanc.

This information silenced Isaac for a bit longer. Mrs. Arlanc could be heard indistinctly, sobbing into the shoulder of a scullery maid in the Royal Society's kitchen. But presently Isaac stirred again and said, "This would have occurred after his return to London in the last months of 1702."

"Again you are correct, sir."

"Do you phant'sy that Jack Shaftoe arranged this interview with you *solely* to deliver word of your father's passing?"

Here Henry Arlanc looked discomfited for the first time—odd, considering he was heavily ironed, and on his way to Newgate. He cast an uncertain glance at Sean Partry, and another at Sir Isaac. Then he answered: "Of course not, sir. However, I must tell you something you ought to know about Jack Shaftoe, which is that he is not utterly black-hearted. Did he have a selfish motive for paying a call on me? Of course, and I shall address that next. But his affection for my father was unfeigned, and when he told the tale of my father's passing, and his burial at sea, almost within sight of California, he shed tears. And I believe that the affection may even have been mutual, for by Jack's account, my father's dying words included certain warnings for Jack—warnings he'd have been well-advised to have heeded."

"How touching," Isaac said, very much as if he wanted to skip over this part as quickly as possible. But curiosity had already got the better of Daniel, who asked: "What did these warnings concern?"

This earned him a glare from Isaac, and so Daniel went on: "Forgive me, but it is clear that my father and yours had much in common with each other, Mr. Arlanc, and I cannot guess what sort of warnings a man like my father would have issued to a man like Jack, unless it was that his immortal soul was doomed to the Lake of Fire!"

Orney slapped the table and chuckled silently.

"My father implored Jack to beware of a certain passenger whom they'd plucked out of the Pacific following the wrack of the Manila Galleon. A Jesuit priest he was—an agent of the Inquisition, named Father Édouard de Gex."

Isaac, who had barely been able to hold back a sneer moments ago, was distinctly taken a-back. After a moment to compose himself he asked Partry to take the prisoner out of the room (which he did, a bit roughly) and out of earshot (which was seen to by Mrs. Arlanc, who rushed forth to embrace her husband and wail).

"He knows nothing of what happened yesterday on the Bridge," Daniel insisted.

"It is too soon for accounts to have appeared in newspapers," observed Mr. Kikin, an astute reader of all that spewed forth from Grub Street.

"Could Partry have mentioned anything to him? A slip of the tongue, perhaps?"

"Impossible," said Orney. "Partry and I spent all afternoon, and evening, scouring the banks of the Thames for evidence of de Gex."

"And I came here with Saturn, specifically to keep an eye on Arlanc," Daniel said. "He received no visitors."

"This is a singular piece of news, if it is to be credited," Isaac said. "For years it has been assumed, by many at Court, that de Gex—who spends much time in London—was an agent of the King of France. And many rumors have reached my ears that he was entangled, somehow, with Jack the Coiner. I had assumed that de Gex and Shaftoe operated hand-in-glove." He nodded at the place where Arlanc had just been sitting. "But this talk of a warning that went unheeded hints at a conflict of fourteen years' standing between the two of them."

"It hints at something else, too," Orney said. "If it is true that this de Gex survived the destruction of a ship on the open ocean, and stayed afloat long enough to be rescued, it implies that he knows how to swim—which means we cannot simply assume that he drowned in the Thames yesterday."

"Let us continue the interview," Isaac said.

"When Jack first returned to London, the war had resumed under its new name of the War of the Spanish Succession. But the armies had not yet been fully mobilized, and so many unemployed soldiers and sailors were still about, making the city infamously perilous. Jack had the wit to see that these men would presently be called back into service, and so he recruited as many as he could during his first months back. His interview with me was partly with an eye towards getting me to work for him."

"In what capacity? And did he succeed?" asked Isaac.

"Anyone who has paid the least notice to the newspapers, and to the discourse of Parliament, during the last decade, will know that war breeds corruption as flesh breeds maggots. The vast movements of men and matériel entailed by the maneuvers of the Allied Powers afforded Jack opportunities for profit that were almost inconceivably vast. For every case of peculation that was talked about openly in London, you may be certain there were a hundred others that went unremarked upon—and of those, Jack was probably involved, somehow, in fifty. His method was simple: he recruited soldiers and sailors before the Crown did, and he treated them better."

"You have answered my first question," Isaac said, "namely, in what capacity did Jack wish to hire you. But you have not touched on the second."

"Only because the answer is obvious," Arlanc said, and held up his manacles. "Oh, I did not do terrible things. But I am ashamed to say that I did look the other way when my regiment's deliveries of gunpowder, and other commodities, came up a bit short. This I did less out of a desire for profit than fear of a certain suttler who I'm sure would not have hesitated to cut my throat, or arrange for me to be shot in the back, had I raised any objection. God in his mercy took me out of this peril, for in ought-five I suffered a wound that forced me to retire from Her Majesty's service. I came back to London and, after I recovered, went to work as a porter for Monsieur Nevers, the horologist—"

"Which led in due course to your knowing several Fellows of the Royal Society, who hired Monsieur Nevers to make instruments," said Daniel.

"Yes, sir, and that is how I ended up working here."

"But you were also working for Jack," Isaac pointed out.

"Yes, sir, after a fashion," Arlanc admitted. "Though it hardly seemed like work. From time to time—perhaps once or twice a year—I was invited to go and meet a certain gentleman at a certain pub, and have a chat with him."

"If the work was all that trivial, why did you *bother*?" Isaac asked.

"Jack had power over me, as a result of our previous dealings," said Arlanc. "With a word he could destroy my marriage or blacken the reputation of my brother Calvin. What he asked of me seemed harmless—so I did it."

"What did you and this man talk about when you met in the pub?" asked Orney.

"He was an educated Frenchman. He professed to be a sort of Enthusiast, an *amateur* of Natural Philosophy. He simply wanted to know what the Royal Society was like. He asked all sorts of questions about what happened during the meetings, and what the Fellows were like—Sir Christopher Wren, Edmund Halley, and especially Sir Isaac Newton."

"Did you ever mention to this *amateur* that Sir Isaac made a practice of coming to Crane Court on Sunday evenings, and working late?" asked Daniel.

"I don't remember for certain, sir, but it is quite possible—that is the sort of thing this fellow loved to hear about, sir." Arlanc then paused, for everyone in the room had exhaled, and some who'd been studying his phizz for the last several minutes were now looking at their fingernails or gazing out the window. "Did I do wrong, sir?" asked Henry Arlanc. He was addressing the question to Daniel. "Foolish question! I know perfectly well I did wrong. But was it a crime? A crime for which a man can be charged, and brought before a magistrate?"

Daniel, moved by sympathy, looked him in the eye and got ready to say, *Of course not!* but Isaac was quicker: "You are guilty of Conspiracy, and to prove as much before a judge shall be simple enough. Mr. Partry, you may take this man away to Newgate Prison."

With no more ceremony than that, Partry loomed over Arlanc's shoulder and gathered up a fistful of lapel at the nape of the Huguenot's neck, by which he hauled him to his feet. Partry kicked Arlanc's chair aside and began to drag him backwards out of the room, leg-chains raking across the floor-boards. Approaching the exit the pair halted for a moment so that Partry could open the door with his free hand. Arlanc took this opportunity to say: "Beg pardon, sirs, but if I could add a word or two, concerning the man you seek—?"

"You may," answered Isaac, with a confirmatory nod at Partry. Partry remained in the doorway, watching over Arlanc's shoulder, while keeping a loose grip on the scruff of the other's neck. It seemed then to Daniel that this pair looked like a ventriloquist at a country fair, and his marionette. Arlanc began to speak. "I've been a student, you might say, of Jack for some years now—as Mr. Halley watches the movements of comets, and understands their nature without being able to alter their courses, why, so it is with me and Jack Shaftoe. And I say that if you think Jack is a slave of *Le Roi*, and dreams only of doing the bidding of Louis, why, you are underestimating the man. That hypothesis—if I may borrow a Royal Society word—does not do the man sufficient credit, and does not explain his actions."

"And what is *your* hypothesis, Mr. Arlanc?" asked Daniel.

"He's gone around the world, Jack has. He's had a pile of gold, lost it, got it back, and lost it again. He's been a Vagabond, a King, and everything in between. He has more swag now than a man could ever need. You must ask yourselves: what could *move* such a man? When Jack gets up in the morning, what does he think of? What does he desire?"

"You have been given leave to supply us with answers—not to ply us with questions," Sir Isaac pointed out.

"Very well then, sir, I'll tell you the answer. It is love that Jack seeks. The love of a woman. A certain particular woman, whom he loved once, and has never forgotten." Arlanc was looking Daniel in the eye. "She is known to some of you. Her name is—"

"I know her name," Daniel said, to cut off Arlanc's maudlin discourse before he could sully the name of some blameless lady or other; but he needn't have bothered, for Partry at the same instant had jerked back on Arlanc's shoulder so violently as to throttle his wind-pipe and draw him back through the door.

"Thank you, Mr. Partry," Isaac called out as Arlanc was removed with a fantastic cacophony: scraping and clanking of chains, gagging and coughing of the prisoner, curses from Partry, and above all the wailing and sobbing *redux* of Mrs. Arlanc. Doors up and down the hall were being hauled open, and diverse savants and vertuosos were thrusting their heads out to see what was the meaning of this. Kikin did the Clubb the favor of closing the door on that scene. This muffled the sound to the point where it was mere noises off: distracting but ignorable. There was a pause for the Clubb to regain its composure. Then Mr. Orney, who was running the meeting, said: "Right. Are there any other items of new business?"

"I have one," said Mr. Kikin, "which is that we all lie down and take a damned nap."

IF THE OTHERS WENT to sleep, Isaac did not, and neither did Daniel, for Isaac wanted to have words with him. They met in a study off the Library, where Isaac was wont to hold forth as President of the Royal Society.

"You will have seen the deficiency in Arlanc's account," was how Isaac opened the conversation.

"What, that nonsense about a woman?"

Isaac got that queasy look signifying that Daniel was being unforgivably slow. "For the Infernal Device to have been placed where it was, it was not sufficient simply for Jack to know that I work late here on Sunday evenings. He must have known, futhermore, that *you* were coming, in company of Mr. Threader, and that you should arrive on a Sunday evening."

"I sent more than one letter ahead, which Arlanc would have seen, to inform the Royal Society of my intentions . . ."

"Your intentions *in general*, yes. But the *specific* information that you should arrive on a Sunday evening—the fact that the Device was placed in your trunk on Mr. Threader's wagon—all this points to Threader's involvement."

"We have been over this before. That Jack has a spy in Threader's retinue I am willing to believe. But to say Mr. Threader himself is a *hashishin* is absurd!"

"Did you mark how quiet he was just now?"

"You call it *quiet*. I call it *asleep*. We have all been awake thirty-six hours!"

"You have learned from Arlanc how Jack builds power: he wheedles a small favor from someone, then comes back again asking for a larger one, and so on, until that person is ensnared, and has lost the power to refuse. Is it so difficult to believe that such a thing could have happened to an inveterate Weigher such as Mr. Threader?"

"I will consider it," Daniel said, "on the condition that you will entertain another, just as repugnant possibility: that the Royal Society harbors another, of infinitely higher rank than Henry Arlanc, who is working in league with Jack the Coiner."

Clerkenwell Court
27 JULY 1714

"I CAME AS SOON AS I COULD."

Daniel thought this very like Isaac: to open the conversation by defending himself against imagined allegations of tardiness. Since Daniel was the only man in the room (Saturn's clock-shop along Coppice Row), some might see it as an excess of caution; but when you were him you could never be too sure.

"Stunning alacrity is the phrase I should have used to describe your response to my message," Daniel assured him. "I did not expect you for another hour, and do not expect the rest of the Clubb to show up at all."

In case Daniel's reassurances were not in good faith, Isaac went on to bolster his rebuttal. "Some kind of storm has broken over the Court of St. James today. The Quality are all out in the streets—it is as if, at some moment in the middle of the day, every courtier and politician in London suddenly decided he was in the wrong place."

"That is not a bad description of what happened."

"I was at the Royal Society, going over some documents relating to Leibniz, and when I received your note, I found it nearly impossible to get out onto Fleet Street. At first I feared the Queen must have died; but the bells do not toll for her."

"I know a few things about what happened at *St. James's* today," Daniel said, "but as you came hither, instead of going thither, I presume you are more concerned with happenings at *Newgate*."

"When did he escape?" Isaac asked.

"Sometime during the night. Mr. Partry is there now, interviewing the gaolers."

"As we could not trust Mr. Partry to keep Mr. Arlanc in the gaol, I see no reason to entrust him with further responsibilities."

"It was not his task to *keep* Arlanc at Newgate but to *deliver* him there—which he did. There, the chains that Partry had put on him were removed, and replaced by much heavier ones, as is the usual practice of the gaolers."

"It is also their usual practice to accept money to replace those heavy chains with lighter ones."

"Indeed. After Arlanc had spent a night heavily ironed in the Condemned Hold, he got a new set of chains, which were so light as to be mere tokens, and he was moved—"

"To the Press-yard and Castle!?" Isaac shook his head, and turned his gaze to the traffic moving down Coppice Row. "Someone—obviously Jack, or one of his agents—came in and spread some money round the gaolers, then. They gave him a pleasant flat for a night and then looked the other way as he slid down a drainpipe. I should have anticipated it."

"Perhaps the reason you did *not,* was that it does not really *matter.*"

"I serve under a solemn Indenture, Daniel. To me, the administration of Justice *always* matters."

"Let me say it otherwise, then. All that was left in Arlanc's future was punishment. We should not have gotten any more information from him. This much was obvious. So the tedious business of looking after his incarceration and trial moved to the back of your mind. As it did to mine."

Both men now saw through the window Peter Hoxton and Sean Partry. They had been coming up Coppice Row from the general direction of Newgate. Saturn was walking in the lead, breaking a trail through the traffic, almost all of which was moving the opposite way.

This was Tuesday. Friday was a Hanging-Day at Tyburn. The streets would be impassable then, and on Thursday. Meat that was brought into the city on the hoof today or tomorrow would fetch a good price later in the week; accordingly, every few minutes a drover would come by, moving a small herd of doomed cattle down towards Smithfield. So the usual traffic of hay-wains, manure-carts, and holiday-makers coming back down from the open swales to the north of town, had to be crammed into the intervals between these herds. Northbound pedestrians, such as Saturn and Sean Partry, had a bad time of it. They entered the shop in a choleric mood, smelling of all the cow-shit they'd been forced to step in. But compared to Newgate this smelled like the gardens of Shalimar.

"There is not a man at Newgate but will aver that the disappearance of Henry Arlanc is a bottomless mystery," Partry announced, with no preliminaries. "From which you may assume—as you likely have done already—that it was arranged by that infamous Blackguard Jack Shaftoe."

"It was not worth your going to Newgate to collect that intelligence," said Newton, who might have been getting ready to accuse Partry of padding his bill.

But Partry was too quick for him. "In attending so keenly to Arlanc, Jack has forgotten about another inmate, scheduled to be drawn and quartered on Friday, whose testimony might be more useful to the Clubb, and more damaging to Jack, than that of Arlanc."

"Ah, you are speaking of that man who was convicted of coining some weeks ago, and whom you were planning to approach this week. I had quite forgotten about him," said Daniel.

"Do not punish yourself, Doc, for Jack has forgotten about him, too, and therein lies our opportunity."

"I have never *heard* of him," Isaac protested.

"You'd know his name, if I spoke it," Partry assured him, "he was caught up in one of your coining investigations some time ago, and duly convicted. But he made me swear I'd not reveal his name, and so you'll not know who he is until Thursday evening, at the Black Dogg, in the cellar of Newgate Prison."

"And then he shall be willing to talk to us of Jack?"

"Yes, sir—provided you come with guineas to put in his pockets."

"A gratuity for Jack Ketch so that this coiner shall die a swift merciful death the next day at Tyburn. It shall not be the first time I have enriched Mr. Ketch thus, to further my pursuit of bigger game," Isaac said, in a tone of exhausted resignation.

At this Partry nodded, and seemed satisfied—but only for an instant, because Daniel pulled him up short with a warning look, and a shake of the head. "Hold," he said, "the transaction as you have set it forth won't do."

"What do you mean it won't do?" asked Partry.

"Pray make yourself comfortable here, Mr. Partry," said Daniel, moving toward the back door, and staring at Isaac until Isaac noticed, and began staring back. "Or down the street at the pub, if you please. I must go for a stroll with Sir Isaac, and discuss with him certain complications."

Partry chewed his tongue for a few beats, and answered: "I shall husband my energies for yet another journey to Newgate and back. I wish you a pleasant stroll and a non-fatal."

"I'll see to the latter," offered Saturn, and followed Daniel and Isaac out the back into the Court of Technologickal Arts.

"What is it you wish to shew me here?"

It was necessary for Isaac to ask this, for as always the Court was a riot of invention. One of Mr. Newcomen's acolytes had come out from Devon with parts of an Engine, which had lately been put together in the middle of the yard to form a great smoking and steaming, sucking and thrashing terror, thronged with grimy admirers. In another corner, Mr. Hauksbee was trying out a new and yet more dangerous spark-maker, which had drawn in those few who were not fascinated by the Engine.

Daniel had hoped that Isaac would be enthralled. But he was not. And the tone in which he spoke, his rigid posture, his flared nostrils, all seemed calculated to let Daniel know that he did not especially like what he saw. It was perhaps a small act of mercy that Isaac did not ask any questions more grueling than *What is it you wish to shew me here?* For as Daniel surveyed the Court, he noted that very little progress was being made on the Logic Mill. If he were more responsible-minded, he should have been alarmed by that. Had he styled himself a leader of men, he should have taken measures to bring these aimless *ingénieurs* back to order. But he did not feel so moved. He had brought these men together here and given them what they most longed for: freedom to make things, and to work on whatever they found most interesting. For several months, the most interesting thing had been the Logic Mill, and all of them had glady worked together on it, without having to be told to. Of late they had become interested in new adventures. For a little while Daniel had been annoyed by their fickleness. Then he had reflected that the world, as of July 1714, was of a sudden crowded with interesting projects for men such as these: enough to keep them all busy for hundreds of years. If they let their attention drift from the Logic Mill, who was Daniel to command them not to be interested in sparks, or steam? And if Isaac was bored by the Engine for Raising Water by Fire, what power or right had Daniel to forbid it? It was nothing more than the Boyle/Hooke Rarefying Engine, built larger, and that was from fifty years ago.

"Nothing," Daniel finally answered. "It is merely a convenient way to get out of doors without being overrun by cattle." He led Isaac toward a side-exit of the Court, and Saturn—who'd fallen behind, as he'd gone to roust a pair of young culls who'd been playing at dice on a barrel-head—rushed up to grip its heavy bolt and toss it out of the way. The two dice-players fell in behind Daniel and Isaac, each stepping along smartly with a massive walking-stick in his hand, though neither of them seemed to have any trouble with rheumatism.

Preceded by Saturn and followed by the two bludgeon-men, Daniel and Isaac now embarked on a mockery of a country stroll. They were moving through a ragged net-work of paths and alleys chalking out small plots of dirt on the fringe of the metropolis— some still grazing sheep or growing turnips, others active construction sites. One day these would be streets, but now they were too

narrow, soft, and wandersome to support any traffic other than a pair
of elderly strollers and their van- and rear-guards. "From here we may
ramble north without too much unpleasantness."

"What is north of *here* that is worth a walk?" Isaac wanted to know.
Daniel ignored the question, and Isaac, after a moment's hesitation,
fell in step alongside.

"The arrangement proposed by Mr. Partry won't do," Daniel insisted. "We must have answers tomorrow—even tonight, if the prisoner can be induced to talk."

"Does this have something to do with whatever it was that happened at St. James's today?" Isaac asked. "For I have not heard such
urgency from you before now."

"Events have overtaken us; we must catch up," Daniel said. "Bolingbroke has a plan. I know not what it is. It may be a perfectly stupid
plan, or brilliant. Strangely, that does not matter. What matters is that
he has a plan, *he* moves, *he* acts, and all others are forced to observe
him and to respond. He is the center of all attention, which, I begin
to suspect, is more important to him than to achieve any particular
goal. Who does *not* have a plan is my lord Oxford, until recently the
Lord Treasurer—"

"What do you mean, *until recently*? Am I to understand that this
Realm has a new Lord Treasurer today?"

"I didn't say that—only that Oxford is gone. He surrendered the
White Staff to the Queen today in Council."

"Of his own volition or—"

"She demanded it of him. Strange to think of anyone so frail demanding anything; but that is what they say."

"And she still holds it?"

"She has not bestowed it on anyone else just yet, according to my
sources."

"Who *are* your sources, Daniel? They seem to be better than
mine—certainly *quicker*."

"That is another conversation. The point is that Oxford—and
with him all the moderate Tories—are out. Thus has the Queen let all
the world know, today, that she favors Bolingbroke and the Jacobites.
She has set in motion events that shall lead to the overturning of the
Settlement Act, the rejection of the Hanovers, and a Catholic King."

"In her dreams," Isaac corrected him. "In truth, Britain will
sooner have a second Civil War than a Popish King."

"Of course. Now, consider Bolingbroke's position. He has captured the Queen, and in the same instant, gained unquestioned
dominance of the Tories, and hence of Parliament. His next move
will be to parley with the Whigs: his only remaining opposition."

"Why should he bother?" Isaac asked. "I should think he is in a position to dictate terms."

"Behold Sir John Oldcastle's," was Daniel's answer. For they had come out into an open place where they could look across a hay-mow to an estate, on the other side of the main road, consisting of a few stately old buildings at the southern end, and a small wooded game-park extending to the north for perhaps two hundred yards, where it covered the slopes of a knobby little hill. Daniel drew Isaac's attention to the hill, which would have gone unnoticed and unnamed in most parts of England. Here on the boggy floodplain of the Fleet it was really something. One could see for hundreds of yards from its top! And indeed, three men were standing atop it right now, enjoying the prospect. "What do you make of them, Isaac? They put me in mind of observers posted on a height-of-land above a battlefield."

"That is a very romantick notion, I'm sure," Isaac said, "but in truth they are likely friends or kin of the Oldcastles, enjoying an afternoon ramble through the coppice."

"What? Through all of those tents, you mean!" Daniel answered, and pointed into the little wood. The growth at this time of year was too dense to allow a clear look, but a careful, keen-eyed observer—Sir Isaac Newton, for instance—could glimpse, through gaps between branches, taut canvas, and the occasional hemmed edge, tent-pole, or staked rope.

"Why, there is a little encampment there," Isaac said, "probably Vagabonds come to watch the hangings."

"Do you really think the lord of the manor would permit Vagabonds?"

"What is your explanation, if you do not favor mine?"

"That is a military encampment. But it is not one of the Queen's battalions. Ergo, a militia."

"Whig, or Tory?"

"Remember that Sir John Oldcastle was an early Protestant. The Oldcastles of today are not so fiery as he, but they still lean that way."

"Very well. It is a Whig Association company, then," Isaac said. "I have heard about them. But I admit that to see them out in force on the edge of London is a different matter."

"Let us stroll up a bit farther, and see what goes on up yonder, round Merlin's Cave," Daniel proposed, pointing north across fields to another up-cropping of buildings and trees, a quarter of a mile away. This was a good bit smaller, newer, and meaner than the Oldcastle estate, being a Spaw lately thrown up round a natural cave at the foot of the rise that led up eventually to Islington.

Presently it was hosting several who had ridden out from town on horseback. Though it was difficult to resolve much at this distance, it was obvious from the way these men handled their mounts that they were young, and skilled horsemen all, inclined to gallant and reckless displays. It was almost as if they were showing off in front of some ladies; but even at a quarter-mile it could be seen that no women were present. They were showing off for one another. As Daniel and Isaac drew nearer, which only took a minute or two, it became clear that all of these men affected the Mohawk. They, or rather their servants, were piling up branches to make a bonfire later.

"You have seen their like before. Whig gentlemen's sons," said Daniel, and stopped. "If we rambled deeper into the countryside we should see more like them, scattered about here and there, in parks and hamlets, or on high places where signal-fires may be kindled." He turned his back on the Mohawk camp before Merlin's Cave, and began walking back towards Clerkenwell. Isaac, after a pause for a last look, followed him.

Daniel continued, "Those we have seen are the spear-head. On a signal from my lord Ravenscar they should be the first to march down Saffron Hill and in through Newgate to take London. If we went to different suburbs, we should observe, on certain large estates, similar formations of Tory militia, who've already sworn allegiance to the Pretender."

Isaac was silent most of the way back.

Then he said, "What is going to happen tomorrow?"

"A dinner party," Daniel answered, "in Golden Square."

"I beg your pardon?"

"Bolingbroke has sent word round to Roger and the other Whigs, inviting them to join him tomorrow at his house on Golden Square. All of these great men who have been playing the game for so many years, and with such enormous stakes, must finally lay their cards on the table tomorrow evening. Bolingbroke has chosen the time and place of it, and he has done so most cunningly. The Queen is faring poorly indeed. After the meeting of the Council today she collapsed from the strain—strain placed upon her by Bolingbroke, perhaps with malice in his heart, or perhaps because he is oblivious to the damage he leaves in his own wake. Whatever the case may be, she is not expected to live long. And so Bolingbroke has this one moment—perhaps a day, perhaps as much as a week—when everything is perfect for him. Parliament is prorogued, and so he need not concern himself, for the moment, about the Asiento money. Oh, *he has the money*, mind you, or the influence he has bought with it, but has not yet begun to suffer the consequences of having stolen it. The Tories are united behind him; he has the Queen's favor; she is too weak to oppose him, but not weak enough to die; he has thrown all of us Dissidents and Nonconformists back on our heels with his Schism Act; and he has the Pyx. These are the cards he shall lay on the table tomorrow evening. What has Ravenscar in his hand? A few strong cards, to be sure."

"But we may strengthen his hand immeasurably," Isaac said, "and at the same instant weaken Bolingbroke's, by capturing Jack the Coiner, and exonerating the Pyx. It is very clear to me now. Thank you for the walk, Daniel."

"IT WILL NOT BE an easy negotiation," Sean Partry said, after giving the matter thorough consideration. "For it matters nothing, to this condemned wretch in Newgate, how high the political stakes may be. A civil war? Why should he care, when his boiled and tarred head shall watch the battle from the top of the Treble Tree?"

"Has he any family?" asked Daniel.

"Dead of the smallpox. Only one thing in all the world matters to this cull, and that is, how much pain shall he suffer on Friday?"

"Then it is a simple affair of bribing Jack Ketch," Daniel said. "I fail to see—"

"It is a not-so-very-simple affair," said Partry, "of bribing him *most* and *last,* even as Jack's men—who, as we've seen, infest Newgate Prison—are disputing the issue with us. This is why I was keen to do it on Thursday night. 'Twould afford Jack less time to offer a counter-bribe. But to do it on Tuesday evening—" He shook his head.

"Let us forget about today, then, and have a go at it on Wednesday," Daniel suggested.

"That will help—a little."

"But it must be in the afternoon—we cannot wait until the evening."

Partry mooted it, and finally gave up a shrug. "Anything is worth a try," he said. "But you had better show up with pounds sterling in your purse, and be ready to buy your information a word at a time."

"If it is simply a matter of showing up with pounds sterling," Isaac said, "then I know where I can get some."

Golden Square

"How much harm could a stiff drink possibly do you, at this stage of the game?" asked Roger Comstock, the Marquis of Ravenscar. "You and I are already off the charts of the Royal Society's annuity tables—living affronts to the Actuarial Profession."

"Hadn't you better go in there *sober*?" Daniel asked. He was facing, and Roger was showing his arse to, the best house on the Square. It put Daniel in mind of the stage of a theatre: not the new opera-house style, in which the actors were pent up behind a proscenium arch, but the W. Shakespeare wooden O, consisting of a flat patch of dirt (here the Square) walled in by galleries crowded with well-heeled voyeurs (the houses all round) and dominated by one magnificent edifice thrust out and over all (Bolingbroke's place) and cunningly shot through with passages, chutes, ladders, and stairs interconnecting diverse balconies, cupolas, windows, &c., where, at any moment, important personages might pop up for a conversation, tryst, complot, or sword-fight that would in some way move the drama along. An Arsenal of Possibilities it was. The groundlings salted about the Square could not take their eyes off of it. Except for Roger. But then, Roger was *not* a groundling. He was no mere spectator, but a leading man—a Capulet or a Montague, take your pick—who was using the Square as a sort of Green Room. He was making ready to enter stage left, and begin his performance; but his lines had not been written yet.

No wonder he was drinking. "*You've* been hoisting tankards in the Black Dogg. Fair is fair."

The mere idea of putting his lips against any of the available receptacles in the Black Dogg sent exquisite shudders up and down the length of Daniel's alimentary tract. "I would not even *sit down* there, much less *drink*."

"We're not sitting down *here*," Roger pointed out, "and that's not stopping *me*." One of his less dangerous-looking servants had drawn nigh, bearing a tray, desolate save for two amber thimbles. Roger pinched one off and projected its contents into his ivory-decked maw. Daniel snatched the other, only to prevent Roger from having a double.

"Your unwillingness to come right out and say how the negotiations are going is a kind of torture to me," Roger explained. Then, to the servant: "Another round, please, to dull the pain inflicted on me by my reticent chum."

"Stay," Daniel said, "we have not spoken to the prisoner yet."

Roger went into an orgasm of coughing.

"It is good news!" Daniel assured him. Which was so brazenly false that it silenced Roger, and straightened him up.

"You toy with me, sirrah."

"Not at all. Why should our prisoner be *so* apprehensive that he'll not even consent to show his face in the Black Dogg?"

"Because he's a bloody coward?"

"Even a *coward* should have naught to fear from Jack—unless he possessed information that was dangerous to Jack in the extreme."

"I have a question for you, Daniel."

"Pray ask it then, Roger."

"Have you ever participated in a negotiation in your entire life? For a quality oft found in persons who have, is an ability to look past some of the more fanciful assertions made by the adversary."

"Roger—"

"Like Cloudesley Shovell, seeing the Rocks of Scilly emerging from the murk, only after 'twas too late to turn his Fleet aside from its fatal Course, I now, on the very threshold of Bolingbroke's den, perceive my error in despatching you and that other Natural Philosopher to parley with this wily Black-guard."

"It is not quite as dismal as all that, Roger."

"Tell me something, then, that is not perfectly and utterly abominably bad news."

"We got an early start this afternoon, and have worked through all of the preliminary rounds of the Negotiation, using Sean Partry as our go-between. All of the posturing, bluffing, and nonsense is behind us. Now we are down to the final exchange. The prisoner holds out. We are taking a little recess, now, so that he may cool his heels and contemplate the terrors that await him on Friday. Meanwhile I come to you, wanting to know: what is the most we could offer this man, supposing he could bring us information, today, that should enable us to catch Jack—or at least prove that Jack tampered with the Pyx?"

"If it came down to that—Daniel, look me in the eye," Roger said.

"You must not offer this save as a last, desperate measure, and then only if it is sure to bring about our victory."

"I understand."

"If this chap can help me bring down Bolingbroke, I'll break him out of Newgate Prison and set him up with a farm in Carolina."

"Splendid, Roger."

"Not a *manor*, mind you, but a patch of dirt, a pointed stick, and a chicken."

"It is more than he deserves, and more than I'd hoped for."

"Now get thee gone to the Black Dogg. I can only draw out the evening's game for so long." Roger finally permitted himself a glance toward Bolingbroke's house. At least three Viscounts were looking back at him, from different windows. This reminded Daniel of something.

"We are to re-convene in an hour," said Daniel, checking his watch.

"An *hour*!?"

"Then all should go quickly. And I shall use that hour to our advantage. Enjoy your dinner, Roger, and don't drink too much."

"All I need do is drink less than my opponent. Easy."

"But I would that you were sober enough to enjoy your victory."

"I would that you were drunk enough to act a little less deliberately."

But Daniel was already scurrying up the portable steps of the phaethon that Roger had lent him. "Leicester Fields," he said to the driver.

Leicester House
HALF AN HOUR LATER

"In this country, as you may know, there is a tacit rule, observed by all the Nobility and Quality, Tory and Whig alike, forbidding the use of the Mobb in politics."

"I had no idea," said Princess Caroline, "but then I suppose that is what makes a thing tacit." Her English had gotten rather better during her weeks in London.

"No doubt when your royal highness shall reign over a peaceful and contented Britain, the rule shall be observed without fail," Daniel continued, "as it has been now for at least a quarter of a century."

"Except for during Parliamentary elections, of course," put in the Duchess of Arcachon-Qwghlm.

"Naturally," Daniel said, "and the odd church-burning or assassination. But I cannot be certain that it shall be obeyed *tonight.* On both sides of the Whig-Tory division I have lately seen a worrisome want of discretion. Bolingbroke's position, just now, is at once formidable, and fatally precarious. He is like a man who has scaled most of a stone wall with his fingernails and reached the point where he can just peek over the top, and see a safe place to stand—even as the danger of losing his grip and falling to the rocks below has never been greater. Now he will flail about and grasp at anything that might enable him to heave himself to safety. Why should he stick at violating this rule concerning the Mobb, just this once?"

They were in a chamber in Leicester House that had probably been styled a *Grand Salon* on the architect's drawings, æons ago. By the time the plaster had dried and the Stuarts had moved in, it had probably been called a salon; nowadays it would be a *salle,* or a walk-in closet. None of your froth of Rokoko plasterwork here. It was lined with wooden panels that never stopped popping. They were a shade of brown that was darker than black. Its several windows looked out over Leicester Fields, but these had been annihilated by clever shutters that could not be distinguished from wall-panels without assiduous knuckle-rapping. It was small, dark, and mean, but Eliza seemed to like it, and Daniel had to admit that on an evening such as this one there was something comforting about the place.

"This Mobb is oft spoken of, but never seen," said the Princess.

Daniel Waterhouse and Johann von Hacklheber, at the same instant, filled their lungs and opened their mouths to explain to her that she was wrong. But each hesitated, thinking to let the other speak first, and so the next voice heard was Caroline's. "You are about to curdle my blood with Mobb-tales, I know," she said. "But to me the notion is philosophically offensive. Doctor Leibniz has given much deep thought to the question of collective entities, such as a herd of sheep, and concluded that these must be regarded as aggregations of monads. What is true of a herd of sheep is more true of a Mobb of Londoners. They are all individual souls. This Mobb is a fabrication of minds too lazy to treat them as such."

"Yet I have seen the Mobb," said Daniel. "Some would say, I have *been* it."

"And yet you are as intelligent a man as ever God made," Caroline said. "This proves that the Mobb is an incoherent concept."

"I got a taste of the Mobb, the day Dappa was chased down Threadneedle Street with a bounty on his head," said Johann von Hacklheber. "Though made up of individual souls, it did have a sort of collective will about it."

"Pfui!"

"This is idle," said Eliza, "you can take it up with the Doctor in Hanover. We must tend to matters at hand. Johann, on the day that Dappa was taken, the Mobb had been incited by hand-bills printed and distributed by Charles White. How do you suppose Bolingbroke might animate the Mobb in the present crisis?"

"Understand, your grace, that ninety out of a hundred in the Mobb are simply criminals who want only the lamest of pretexts to run riot," Daniel said. "They are like the charge of coarse powder in a musket's barrel. It is detonated by a pinch of fine powder in the weapon's pan. Which is to say that one *provocateur,* moved by Party Malice, might incite ten or a hundred of the rabble to run amok. Bolingbroke will have such *provocateurs* posted in squares and streets where they can sway as many as possible. In order to inspire *them*—to put fire to the pan-powder—he needs only some small scandal or incident. Among other things, he might expose the presence of Hanoverian spies in London."

"I see," said the Princess. "It was foolish for me to have come, then."

"No, for it may have spared your royal highness's life from the assassins of de Gex," said Daniel.

"It *would* have been foolish," said Johann, "to have come here without having been prepared for this night." He locked eyes with his mother as he said this. Eliza stood up.

"Mother and son have been cleverly at work," Caroline guessed, "while the silly Princess has been delighting in her naughty adventure."

" 'Twas ever thus, and ever shall be, as long as we have Royals," said Eliza. "You may repay our labours by doing deeds that are beyond our scope."

"Easily said," said the Princess. "At this moment, what can I—"

"You can fly, and fly well," Eliza said. "Royal flight is a grand tradition. Elizabeth, Charles II, Louis XIV, the Winter Queen, all had to fly at some point in their lives, and all carried it off well."

"James II did it poorly," Daniel reflected. Then, not to be a party-pooper, recovered with: "But you are made of better stuff."

"And unlike him, the Princess has friends, and a plan," said Johann, "though she doesn't know it. I can set this plan in motion with a word. Is that what you recommend, Dr. Waterhouse?"

Now this was a rather weighty matter to have placed on Daniel's shoulders. As a younger man he'd have been paralyzed by the responsibility. But all decisions had come to him easier, somehow, since he had learnt that he was supposed to be dead anyway. "Oh, by all means," he said. "You must fly. But I would have a word with her grace, if the plan permits it."

Eliza smiled. "The plan calls for Johann and Caroline to change clothes first of all," she said, and excused the two of them with a smile, and a flicker of the eyelids. Johann turned away, blindly thrusting a hand behind him, and Caroline's hand dove into it like a falcon stooping on game, and thus they made for the door, he striding, bent forward, and she floating, erect as a Princess was supposed to be. As they gained the anteroom, Johann began to distribute commands, in German, to various persons who had quietly convened there during the quarter of an hour since Daniel had arrived. One of these thrust his head and arm into the room, favored Eliza with a deferential nod, and Daniel with a flash of the whites of his eyes, and pulled the door to so sharply that every panel in the room gave a sympathetic pop.

"You are alone with me," Eliza observed. "A *scenario* oft sung of by the poets of the Kit-Cat Clubb."

Daniel smiled. "If they sing of this, I shall be likened to Tithonus, who was granted æternal life, and turned into a cricket."

"As a ploy," Eliza said, "your modesty serves. I see how it must work on those who are young, vain, and do not know you well. To me who know you better, it is grating. Please speak plainly, without flattering me or deprecating yourself; we do not have time."

Daniel inhaled deeply, like a man who has just been doused with icy water. Then he said: "I bring you news concerning Jack Shaftoe."

It was Eliza's turn to gasp. She turned her back on him so quickly that the hem of her skirt sawed at his ankles. She retreated several steps, then arranged herself on a bench between two of the shuttered windows. Daniel stood sideways to her, so as not to dwell on the pinkness of her face.

"I was led to believe you were *pursuing* him. How can—"

"I am doing so, and I will catch him," Daniel said, "but this has not prevented him, clever chap that he is, from contriving a way to place in my ear certain words that were plainly intended for you."

"And what are those words, sir?"

"That everything he has been doing lately, he has been doing out of love for you."

"That is a very strange way of showing *love*," she returned. "Making counterfeit money for the King of France, and blowing people up."

"He has not actually blown anyone up," Daniel reminded her, "and as for the King of France, some would point out that he is also the liege-lord of Arcachon."

"Thank you for pointing it out," she said. "Is that the entire message?"

"That he loves you? Yes, I believe that is it."

"Well, when you catch him, you may give him my answer," she said, rising to her feet, "which is that the decision he made at the wharf in Amsterdam was the sort that cannot be unmade; and as proof, one need only behold what Jack has become in the thirty years since—all of which might have been predicted from the choice he made on that day."

"I have an inkling that Jack is now striving to become something rather different," Daniel said, "which you may *not* have predicted."

"That is what *young* Jack—who, I must admit, was a dreamy lad—would have done," Eliza said. "The wretch that he is now is not capable of it."

"Never was a mailed and spiked gauntlet more harshly thrown down. I am off to the Black Dogg now," Daniel said, excusing himself with a careful bow, "and I shall deliver that fell challenge to Jack, if fortune leads me to him."

Newgate Prison
HALF AN HOUR LATER

WHATEVER THE PLAN WAS that Johann von Hacklheber had laid for the extraction of Princess Caroline from the snares of London, it evidently did not rely on stealth. Such was the crowd and the commotion that Daniel half feared that the much-discussed Mobb had already conquered the stables of Leicester House. But not to worry, they were loyal servants and retainers all. Daniel found his phaethon and commanded the driver to take it round Leicester Fields and collect Sir Isaac Newton. This was achieved shortly and in absurdly conspicuous style. The diverse spies planted in and around Leicester Fields by political factions, foreign governments, nervous speculators, and Grub Street newspapers, would all report to their masters that a cricket-like geezer had scurried out of the London home of the Duchess of Arcachon-Qwghlm, hopped into an inappropriately seductive and libidinous Mode of Transport, swung round to snatch the World's Greatest Natural Philosopher, and thundered off in the direction of—Newgate Prison. What the recipients would make of this information was anyone's guess. Daniel was past caring.

THEY ENCOUNTERED PARTRY in the Gigger, which was a pit just off Newgate Street, under the actual Gate, where free men could swop words with prisoners through a grate. Partry was using it in lieu of an anteroom to the Black Dogg. "What news from Ravenscar?" came his voice through the grille.

"First, shall we have the privilege of meeting the other party to the negotiation?" Daniel asked. "It is difficult to parley with a phantom."

"As *you* are but a phantom to *him*, he would likely agree."

"Then let us get together in the same room at least!"

"It is arranged," Partry said. "I have rented the Black Dogg for the evening. We shall meet him there—the privacy of an empty tavern should loosen his tongue. But you must be prepared to loosen your purse-strings."

"That has been arranged as well," Daniel assured him. "If need be, we may offer the prisoner liberty, and a farm in Carolina. But only if need be."

"Now *that* is excessive!" Isaac said. "The promise of a quicker than usual hanging should be more than sufficient."

"As perhaps it shall be," Daniel said, "but if it does not suffice, why, we shall have room to bargain."

"Very well," said Partry, "to the Black Dogg! Mind your step as you descend the stairs, for they are quite slippery with crushed lice."

"More so than usual?" Daniel asked.

"Indeed," said Partry, "for as I just told you, I have cleared out the Dogg, and many have passed this way, only a few minutes ago, who had not stirred from their bar-stools and corners in a long while; there is no guessing what may have scattered from out of their rags."

"Aye, all of London is astir to-night!" Daniel remarked.

"All, save what is on the treads of these stairs," Partry insisted. "Pray, let me go ahead of you, and light your way with my lantern."

Following Partry, and preceding Isaac, down toward the Black Dogg, Daniel said: "How curious that to me it seemeth like any other stone stair-way in the world."

"Why is that so curious?" Isaac wanted to know.

"We speak of Newgate as a dread place," Daniel said, "but emptied of its prisoners, 'tis but another building—a bit stinkier than most, perhaps."

"The same might be remarked of its Pub," said Partry, heaving wide an iron-bound dungeon-door to release a surprising flood of candle-light, and an even worse than expected front of midden-stench.

"So it is really the *people* of Newgate who inspire us with dread, you are saying," said Isaac.

"Has the Black Dogg ever been so lit up in its whole sorry history?" asked Daniel as he passed through the door. For the place was as littered with candles as the steps had been with lice. And they were proper wax tapers, not rush-lights. Even the dining-room of Viscount Bolingbroke was not so finely illumined to-night. The Black Dogg was not the sort of tavern that contained a great deal of furniture— patrons either stood, or lay on the floor. There was a bar, of course, in the literal sense of a bulwark erected between the prisoners and the gin. This was now a palisade of burning tapers. Sean Partry led them over to it. Daniel followed half-way, but stopped in the center of the room to have a look round. His eyes were yet adjusting to the brightness, but he could see plainly enough that no one else was here.

"Where is the—" he began.

"How much in God's name has been spent on candles!?" Isaac demanded. "A fortune! Have you gone mad?"

"My going mad days are done," said Partry, turning his back on the bar, so that he became a shade halving the beam of fire. "Do not concern yourselves about it. I have paid for the candles with my own money. When we are finished I'll give 'em away to prisoners who cannot afford to buy even the mean grease-lights that are peddled by the gaolers, and whose eyes have forgotten light."

"You presume much," Isaac said. He and Daniel were shoulder-to-shoulder now, facing Partry, the heat of the candles on their faces like summer sun. "Nothing shall be paid you until we have achieved our goal. Where is the prisoner?"

"There is no prisoner," said Partry, "and never has been. I've been lying to you the entire time. Any information you are given to-night, concerning the whereabouts of Jack Shaftoe, shall come, not from some supposititious prisoner, but from me."

"Why have you lied to us?" Isaac asked.

"Lying to you enabled me to set up a meeting on neutral ground," answered Partry, and stomped his foot on the pavement. "Here, I feel safe in divulging my information."

"And what is that information, at long last?" Isaac demanded.

"That I am Jack Shaftoe," answered Jack Shaftoe, "*alias* Jack the Coiner, *alias* Quicksilver, and many other nick-names and titles besides; and that I am willing to wind up my career to-night, provided the right terms can be struck."

Golden Square
THE SAME TIME

IF THE POINT OF A dinner-party was to bring interesting people together and lay excellent food and wine in front of them, then the Viscount Bolingbroke's *soirée* was the event of the year. Some would complain that the guest-list was weighted too heavily to Whigs; but then, as of yesterday, Bolingbroke *was* Torydom, and as such needed no coterie. On the other hand, if the point of a dinner-party was to start fascinating conversations, then this was the grossest failure, to date, of the Age of Enlightenment; why, Robert Walpole was actually *humming* to fill in the silences. A dozen men were at the table; only two of them—Bolingbroke and Ravenscar—had authority to parley; and yet these two seemed perfectly content with plate and bottle, and with the dreadful silence of the room. From time to time one of the younger Whigs would try to launch a Topic of Conversation, and like a spark struck into moss it would sputter and smoke along for a few moments, until Bolingbroke or Ravenscar would dump a bucket of water on it by saying, "Pass the salt." The meal sprinted from one course to the next, as the guests had nothing to pass the time save chewing and swallowing. It was not until pudding that Bolingbroke could be troubled to make a Gambit. "My lord," he said to Roger, "it has been *ages* since I could free myself to attend a meeting of the good old R.S. Oh, are there any other Fellows present?" He looked round the table. His eyes were too close together, his nose was high-bridged and long: features more suited to a carnivorous beast than a human. So he was far from good-looking; yet his ugliness was of that sort that suggests caution, rather than mockery, to the onlooker. His mouth was tiny and pursed. But then, the muzzle of a gun was not so very large either. Bolingbroke's one adventure in the realm of fashion had been to wear a radically small and simple periwig one day, when he went to pay a call on the Queen. She had rewarded him by asking if, next time around, he intended to show up wearing a nightcap. Tonight he had donned the full wig: white curls tumbling down beyond his shoulders, over his lapels, to somewhere between the latitude of his nipples and of his waist. His cravat was white, and wrapped many times round his neck, like a bandage. It and the wig framed his face like an ostrich-egg swaddled in a shipping-crate. This was the face that scanned down the left, then up the right side of the table, until it fell upon the Marquis of Ravenscar, who was seated at his right hand.

"No, my lord," said Ravenscar, "there are only we two."

"The study of Natural Philosophy has not captivated the Whigs of the new generation," Bolingbroke concluded.

"The *Royal Society* has not captivated them," Ravenscar corrected him. "What they study besides *politics* and *wenches*, I know not."

At this, cautious laughter, less of amusement than of relief that a conversation seemed to be getting underway.

"My lord Ravenscar tries to stir up the old rumor that I know as much of wenches as Sir Isaac knows of gravity."

"Indeed, like gravity, the fair sex doth exert a continual pull on us all."

"But you change the subject—granted, to a more fascinating topic," Bolingbroke said. "Is not the Royal Society the world's foremost *salon* for the discussion of Natural Philosophy? How can a man claim to be an *amateur* of learning, and yet not aspire to become a Fellow? Or has it gone into decline? I've no way of knowing. Haven't been to a meeting in ages. A shame really."

"We have reached that part of dinner when we shove our chairs back, throw our napkins down, and pat our bellies," Ravenscar observed. "Does that signify that your party has gone into decline?"

"I understand," said Bolingbroke, after allowing those close-set blue eyes to wander round the ceiling for a few moments, as if deep in thought. "You mean to say that the Royal Society gorged itself on learning in the early decades, and now takes a respite, to digest all that it took in."

"Something like that."

"Too, is it not necessary, when one has *acquired* much, to *defend* it?"

"That sounds as if it might have a double meaning, my lord."

"Oh, don't be tedious. It has a single meaning, to do with Sir Isaac, and the fraudulent claims of the infamous *Hanoverian* plagiarist, Baron von what's-his-name—"

"All the Hanoverians *I* have met are sterling characters," said Ravenscar stolidly.

"Obviously you've not made the acquaintance of George Louis's wife!"

"No one can make her acquaintance as long as he keeps her locked up in that Schloß, my lord."

"Ah yes. Tell me, is it the *same* Schloß in which Princess Caroline is said to have taken refuge, when she took it into her mind that *hashishin* were stalking her through the gardens?"

"I haven't heard that story, my lord—or if I have, I have not *listened* to it."

"I have heard and listened—but I do not believe. *I* suspect that the Princess is somewhere *else.*"

"I have no idea where she is, my lord. But to get back to the Royal Society—"

"Yes. Let us do get back to it. Who can blame Sir Isaac, really?"

"Blame him for what, my lord?"

"For setting aside the pursuit of Natural Philosophy to defend his legacy from the aggression of the German."

"You place me in an impossible situation, my lord—I almost feel as if we are in the House of Lords again, disputing an Act. But I shall answer a question you have *not* asked, and say that if fewer young men are coming to the Royal Society of late, it is perhaps because listening to Sir Isaac rant about Leibniz; perusing the latest incriminating documents about Leibniz; and sitting on committees, tribunals, and Star Chambers intended to prosecute Leibniz in absentia, simply does not happen to be their notion of a Good Time."

"Von Leibniz. Thank you for reminding me of the man's name. How shall we keep all of these dreadful German names straight if not for the Whigs, who know them so intimately?"

"It is difficult to acquire the *German* tongue, when *French* ones are perpetually thrust into one's ears," Ravenscar answered; a jest that was greeted with awed and terrified silence round the table.

Bolingbroke reddened, then had a good chuckle. "My lord," he sputtered, "look at our fellow-revelers. Have you ever observed a more wooden bunch?"

"Only on a chessboard, my lord."

"It all comes of the fact that we have drifted off into prating of Natural Philosophy—the surest way to kill a conversation."

"On the contrary, my lord, you and I are having an excellent conversation."

"Indeed—but *they* are not. Which is why we have Withdrawing Rooms, you know, and the like—so that enthusiasts may cabal in the corners and not bore the company to death!"

"If this is all some sort of a ploy to get us to drink port wine, it is needlessly elaborate," observed Ravenscar.

"But *where* shall we drink it?" Bolingbroke asked.

"I dare not say, my lord, for 'tis *your* house."

"So it is. And I say that *these* chaps, who plainly do not give a fig for Natural Philosophy, may drink it in the comfort of my Withdrawing Room; but you and I, inveterate enthusiasts that we are, shall repair to the observatory, three storeys above—far enough away that the other guests shall not suffer our philosophical prattle."

"The Lord of the Manor has spoken; all must obey," announced Roger Comstock, Marquis of Ravenscar, and shoved his chair back; and that was how he and Bolingbroke ended up on the roof of the house, ogling the latter's Newtonian reflector. But as it was still twilight, and the stars were not out yet, her Majesty's Secretary of State had to content himself with aiming it at *terrestrial* targets. The facility with which he did so gave Roger the idea that this was not the first time he had used the instrument to spy upon neighbors, near and far.

"The seeing is excellent this evening," Bolingbroke sighed, "as the day was warm, and few have bothered to light fires."

"This port is of the best," Roger said, for they had brought a bottle up with them: the closest thing to manual labor that Bolingbroke's servants would suffer the master to perform.

"Spoils of political conquest, Roger. We all lust after such spoils, do we not?"

"The profession of politics would be altogether too disagreeable," Roger allowed, "without compensations above and beyond what is strictly appropriate."

"Well said." Bolingbroke was hunched over the eyepiece, twiddling the tube of the telescope this way and that, homing in on a target to the east. Roger phant'sied he might be pointing it at the dome of St. Paul's, two miles away; but no, his host had trained it downwards, as at some target nearer to hand. By far the biggest and closest structure along that general bearing was Leiceister House, seen from here as a great rambling L-shaped manor. It stood in its own compound, which was nearly as extensive as the green square of Leicester Fields to the south of it.

"Presently night shall fall and Venus shall shine forth—we shall admire her beauty then. But while we await the Goddess of Love, we may content ourselves peering at some of her earthly *worshippers*."

"I shouldn't think *you* of all people would need a *telescope* for that," Roger said, "other than the one God gave you."

Leicester House presented to the Fields a public façade with a small forecourt below, where callers could dismount from carriages, &c. This was all that most people could see of it. Looking down on it from the excellent vantage-point of Bolingbroke's roof, half a mile away, Roger was reminded that the house had quite a bit of property in back, hemmed in by newer buildings, so that most Londoners had no inkling it was there. Of this, about two-thirds, on the side nearer to Bolingbroke's, was a formal garden. The rest was an enclosed stable-yard. Separating them was a long thin wing extending from the main house—really little more than a gallery.

"Pity. They are not out this evening," Bolingbroke remarked.

"Who or what are not out, Henry?"

"The young lovers. A chap, strapping, blond, well-heeled, and a young woman, long chestnut hair, and an uncommonly erect—some would say noble, or royal—bearing. They tryst in yonder garden most every evening."

"Touching."

"Tell me, Roger. You, who know so much of these Germans who design to take over our country—have you met Princess Caroline?"

"I have had that honor once, on a visit to Hanover."

"They say she has the most lovely fall of chestnut hair—is it true?"

"It is a fair description."

"Ah! There she is now!"

"There *who* is, my lord?"

"The young lady I spoke of just now."

"*Which* young lady, my lord?"

"Come, have a look, and tell me."

Roger stepped forward with some reluctance.

"Oh, come and look!" Bolingbroke urged him. "It's harmless. Half the Tories in London have peered through this eyepiece, and seen her."

"That hardly constitutes a recommendation, but I shall humor you," Roger said, and bent to the task.

Through the tiny lens of the eyepiece shone a bubble of green light, which swelled in his sight as he moved towards it; then it was his whole world. A moment's work with the knob brought it to focus.

The gallery dividing the garden (foreground) from the stable-yard (background) was pierced in the center by a high vaulted pass-through: a gate, which was presently open. So Roger's view to the stable-yard was blocked by the gallery, except for in that one place, where it was possible to peer through the open arch-way and see a narrow swath of yellow gravel in the yard beyond. That was enough to make it obvious that the stables were busy this evening: hooves, booted feet, and carriage wheels were passing back and forth, all foreshortened, by the telescope's optics, into a flat impression, a living back-drop. Against which a solitary woman was visible, crouching in the center of that arch-way, in a sort of traveling-dress. She was changing out of her shoes, and into a pair of boots. The shoes discarded on the pavement beside her were mere slippers, only fit for wearing indoors. An open portmanteau rested nearby, overflowing with clothes. Suddenly a servant burst into the frame carrying a dress over her arm, and shoved it into the bag, then began hammering the contents down with the heel of her hand.

"I should call it a hasty departure," Bolingbroke said in his ear. "More Mercury than Venus."

Roger ignored him and sharpened the focus, trying to get a clear look at the young woman changing into her traveling-boots. She undoubtedly had a long fall of chestnut hair, which swept down over one shoulder and grazed the ground.

No, it was *on* the ground. In a heap. Roger blinked.

"What did you see!?" his host demanded. "Did you recognize her?"

"Stay, I'm not certain."

The hair had most definitely fallen to the ground. The woman calmly finished tying her boot-laces and then picked it up. She had light blonde hair, going a bit silvery, all pinned up close to her skull. She held the chestnut wig out at arm's length and gave it a shake, to make the tresses fall straight. Then she lifted it up and set it back in place atop her blonde head. The servant, who had somehow managed to get the bag closed, came round behind her to tug it into place and secure it with a long hair-pin.

"I'll be damned," Roger said. "The hair gives it away. If that young lady isn't Princess Caroline of Brandenburg-Ansbach, then I am not a Whig."

"Let me see! What is she doing now?" said Bolingbroke, and so Roger got out of his way. After a moment to adjust the focus and get his bearings, Bolingbroke said, "I can only see her from the back— her beau is nowhere to be seen—she is climbing into a carriage, I do believe."

"Then I believe it too, my lord."

The Black Dogg, Newgate Prison
THE SAME TIME

It happened sometimes in the practice of physics that the student, having wrestled for hours with a recalcitrant equation, would suddenly find a way to wreak some drastic simplification upon it. Of a sudden, two terms, which he had copied out time and again, and which had become as familiar to him as his own signature, would, through some insight, or the providence of some new scrap of information, turn out to be equal to each other, and vanish from the equation altogether, leaving a wholly new mathematical sentence to be pondered. The student's first reaction was exhiliration: pride at his own cleverness, mingled with a sense that at last he was getting somewhere. But soon sobriety took over, as he pondered the remade equation and became aware that he was really just starting on a new problem. Thus Daniel in the Black Dogg, trying to re-think all. For example: Jack Shaftoe was wearing a sword. When he had been Sean Partry, Daniel had scarce noted this, for many men went armed. But for Jack to be armed, here and now, was no mere affectation. He had set it all up so that he could kill Daniel and Isaac, if it came to that. And the king's ransom in fine bright candles: from Sean Partry this had been simply bizarre, but from Jack it was a way to get a good look at his interlocutors' faces whilst keeping his own phizz cloaked in the dazzle. And these were just the simple and superficial matters. Daniel would be puzzling over the deep bits for weeks.

"Newton is gobsmacked; Waterhouse nods as if he suspected this all along. Perhaps Waterhouse is cleverer than they give him credit for," said Jack.

"I knew *something* was going on; else I could not make sense of recent happenings," said Daniel. "But I did not expect *this.*"

"Can you make sense of it now?"

"No," Daniel said, and glanced over at Isaac, who for once was lagging pitiably behind; his bulging eyes strayed to the hilt of

Shaftoe's sword, lingered for a moment, then began to sweep the walls for exits.

"The entire month's work: Bedlam, the Main-Topp, and the Stake-out: why? What was the point?" Daniel asked.

"Ask de Gex," Jack said. "I had less than you might suppose to do with that tedious poppet-show. Through the most of it I was an amused spectator only. And an enraged, when I spied him swimming away, and knew he had survived."

"So it is true that you and he are at odds."

"Have *ever* been," Jack corrected him, "though he did not wot it, I think, until your nice bit of jugglery went off in his coach, and set him on fire. Now he seems at last to've got it through his head that I am not his friend."

"Because you engineered a double-cross," Daniel said.

"The whole time it has been my misfortune to know the man, he has turned minutes into hours, and hours into days, with his jabbering about Alchemy. The last few months—since he learned that *you* had been summoned home from Boston—it has been worse than ever. As he has made me suffer so much with it, I reckoned it mere justice to use it to kill him."

The mention of Alchemy had brought Isaac composure, and somehow made him willing to take part in the conversation. (This struck Daniel as an extremely familiar pattern; for when had Isaac ever been sociable, save when the company was Alchemists, and the topic Alchemy? Not for nothing did they call it the Esoteric Brotherhood. It was the only way he had ever made new acquaintances, with the sole exception of Daniel; it was his entire system for getting along with people, and that was its true magic.) "If ever was a moment, and a place, to ask a grossly indelicate question, 'twere now, and here," Isaac began.

"Let her rip, Ike," said Jack.

"If de Gex has been your hated foe for so long, why did you not kill him long ago? For unless I am mistaken this would not be difficult for one such as you to arrange."

"*You* who have slaughtered so many at Tyburn may suppose it is an easy thing to do, and may phant'sy that I have killed as many as Tamerlane," Jack returned, "but killing a wretch through the machinery of the Law is easy, compared with how it must be accomplished in my world, when the victim-to-be is Father Confessor to the Queen of France."

"So in de Gex's obsession with Alchemy you perceived a way to get rid of him *indirectly*," Daniel said.

Jack sighed. "It almost worked," he said. "And may work yet, through some convolution or other. But now is a perilous time, which is why we need to set matters straight, and get it done smartly."

"I cannot fathom your arrogance in supposing that, after all you have done, matters may simply be *set straight*!" Isaac exclaimed.

"Maybe you had better square that, guv, with the Marquis of Ravenscar," Jack returned. "If he's willing to give freedom and a farm in Carolina to a varlet who'll merely give information leading to my capture, why, what would he offer *me*, if he were in this room? What would *you* give me to have the former contents of the Pyx delivered to your house in St. Martin's this evening?"

Daniel's fear of being locked in a dungeon of Newgate with London's most infamous criminal had suddenly been shoved out of his mind by fear of what Roger would have to say when he learned just how utterly Daniel had bungled the negotiation.

In his distraction he was overtaken by Isaac, who, after a slow start, had now got up to full speed. "Supposing that there is anything to that offer," Isaac said, "how can you reconcile it with your duties as a paid agent of the King of France?"

"Ah, good, very important," Jack said. "Leroy is a far-sighted chap. Deserves all that's been said of him. Developed a scheme, in the respite between the wars, to win the next one by destroying the money of England. Excellent idea. Needed someone to do it for him. Haply I came along. I knew London. Knew of metals and coining. Had managerial experience, viz. Bonanza, Cairo, and other exploits. Was lacking in gentlemanly polish, though, and was of extremely dubious loyalty. How then to make good these deficits, that my salutary qualities might be put to work? De Gex. He knew me already. Is as noble as they come. Working in concert with me in London, he could get invited to *salons*—never my strong suit. He'd seen me make a fool of myself, more than once, over one Eliza—yes, Dr. Waterhouse, I spoke her name aloud—and knew she was the ticket to securing my loyalty. For by certain twists wrought on her by that perverted bitch Fortune, Eliza had married the young Duke of Arcachon, bore his children, and habitually spent half her time in France among the nobility of that land, who are prolific murderers of their own siblings, parents, *et cetera*. To poison her, or worse, should be as easy, for de Gex, as yanking out a troublesome nose-hair. Thus was the deal struck: Jack would to London to carry out the destruction of the vaunted Pound Sterling under the supervision of his tiresome overseer, de Gex, and in exchange, Eliza would be left alone.

"What a difference twelve years makes! The war is over, my friends, and France won. Oh, England wrung some scraps from them, but make no mistake, that is a Bourbon on Spain's throne.

Leroy would still see Jamie the Rover on the throne of Great Britain, but that is not as important to him, now, as was securing the Spanish Empire in 1701! This undertaking I have toiled at, of undermining the currency, has taken on a new cast. Before, the objective was to bring about a crash in this country's foreign trade—its only means of paying for war. Now, it is a petty matter: to create a scandal, and get the rich men of the City up in arms against the Whigs. Don't look so indignant, Ike, you know perfectly well this is what I've been up to. I am in a position to accomplish this now, or as soon as Bolingbroke can arrange a Trial of the Pyx. Shall I? Shall I betray my country to France? Perhaps! For there is much to hate about this place. Do I feel strongly moved? No longer. For Eliza's a widow. Her French children are grown up, dividing their time 'tween Paris and Arcachon. Her German boy is with her all the time. It has been two years since she graced the soil of *La France*. In sum it is a much more difficult matter, now, for de Gex to bring about her death—and it shall become more difficult yet, if *I* bring about *his*."

"Is this going to conclude with you asking for something?" Daniel asked.

"All I seek is a dignified retirement from the brawls of the World," Jack said, "though, since you mentioned the farm in Carolina, I think I should like to give that to my sons. They'll only get into scrapes if they stay in London."

"Oh yes," Daniel said, "it is quite unthinkable that anyone should get into trouble in America."

"*Different* trouble is all I seek for my lads," Jack said. "*Wholesome* trouble out in the fresh air."

Monmouth Street

THE SAME TIME

The Mob are outragious every where when they
think themselves provok'd.
> — *The Mischiefs That Ought Justly to Be*
> *Apprehended from a Whig-Government,*
> ANONYMOUS, ATTRIBUTED TO BERNARD
> MANDEVILLE, 1714

FROM THE STABLES of Leicester House, Johann and Caroline had
borrowed a pair of gray geldings: good but indifferent-looking
riding-horses in simple tack. They rode side-by-side up Monmouth
Street. Caroline was straddling her mount like a man, which was
made easier by wearing a man's pair of breeches. Her hair was
stuffed up under a man's white periwig and she even had a small-
sword joggling from her left hip. Johann was dressed similarly,
though he was armed with the big old rapier he had been carrying
around ever since mysterious persons had begun making attempts
on the lives of people who were close to him. They were supposed to
look like a pair of young gentlemen out for a ride in the town.

Caroline frequently turned round to look back towards Leicester
Fields. Johann had suggested that she not; but it was difficult for a
royal to accept such mundane suggestions. She was quite certain that
they were being followed by a fellow riding on a black horse. But
Monmouth Street curved steadily round to the left as it went, so she
lost sight of that rider from time to time. For the same reason they
could only see ahead for a certain distance, and every pace brought
new complications into view.

"When I made the plan, I had no way of knowing on what day it
might be set into motion," Johann said, "and so I did not take Hangings into account."

"Hanging-Day is not until Friday, is it not so?" asked Caroline. It
was Wednesday evening.

"Indeed. Tomorrow evening I should expect a crowd gathering along the route," said Johann. "I did not expect one *this* evening—but—" He trailed off as they rounded the final deflection. A stone's throw ahead, Monmouth Street joined together with two others, like tributaries of a river, to form a short but very wide thoroughfare that exhausted directly into a place called Broad St. Giles's. Their view into that district was blocked by a wide but shallow building erected square across their path, like a sandbar at the mouth of a river. It was brick below and timber above, with a pocked tile roof, and was so generally mean in its appearance that from this distance it might have been taken for a stable. But it had a few too many chimneys for that, all of them tottering into the weather like elderly pallbearers leaning into a gale. On the side facing Johann and Caroline it had a little front court running its whole width, supervised by a veranda. Several white-haired, gray-faced chaps were strewn upon some benches there. This was the St. Giles's alms-house, where parishioners who had outlived their means, their families, or their welcomes could be parked until they were ready for permanent berths in the nearby church-yard. For whatever reason, it had been built in the middle of the intersection so that Monmouth Street traffic must divert around it.

Now ordinarily, not being able to see into Broad St. Giles's would have been accounted some small act of Grace. It was not precisely a street, and not a square, but a kind of drain-trap plumbing High Holbourn (which ran off to the right, toward the City) to Oxford Street (left to Tyburn Cross). As a district of Greater London it no doubt had a history and a perfectly legitimate reason for existence; but as a conduit for traffic between Tyburn and London it was a lamentable improvisation. A few kegs of gunpowder detonated in the slum to the north side of it would create a direct through line uniting the two thoroughfares, and relegate Broad St. Giles's to a stagnant ox-bow lake, alienated from the main stream; but such improvements still lay in the future as Johann and Caroline rode toward it.

Tonight, however, not being able to get a clear view of what lay ahead was perilous. The district seemed more than normally crowded tonight. People—mostly roving tribes of young men—formed a slack eddy around the foundations of the alms-house. They did not appear to be bound for anywhere, unless Trouble could be considered a Destination; and some were already staring at Johann and Caroline, and pointing.

"Why so many people—the hanging?"

"Too soon, too soon—oh, if we *asked* one why he was here, he might claim it was for the Hanging-March—"

"But to believe it would be naïve," Caroline said. "You think then that it is as Dr. Waterhouse warned us."

"Yes—the Whigs and Tories have used the Hanging as a pretext to move their sympathizers—whatever you care to call them—"

"Militia?"

"Perhaps a little less than militia and a little better than the Mobb. I don't know. At any rate they are here, getting ready to light bonfires—"

"Look, they have done it already," Caroline said.

They had reached the place where the way broadened out, just before the front court of the alms-house. Off to their right, a bonfire had been kindled. It must have been carefully laid, and lit only a moment ago, for it suddenly flared very high, lofting a storm of incandescent twigs and leaves into its smoke-tower. It stood in the center of Broad St. Giles's, which was a good hundred feet wide there.

"That is meant to be a gathering-beacon for some faction or other, I'll wager," said Johann, rising up in his stirrups and looking about. Indeed, many had altered course, and set their faces toward the flame: some *reporting* to it smartly, others merely falling in, drawn by the curious instinct of the herd. "It is good for us. Look, the crowd dwindles over yonder, to the right side of the way—we shall slip through and be on High Holbourn presently. Then straight on to the city. Let's go!" and he drew back on his mount's right rein, demanding a sharp turn. Caroline did likewise; but she could not resist a look back down Monmouth. There was the fellow on the black horse, now so close behind that she could have called out to him. He was making no effort to hide himself, but waving his hat back and forth above his head as if trying to catch someone's eye. Succeeding in that, he then pointed deliberately at Johann and Caroline, and held up two fingers; then he joined those two fingers together to form a little blade, and drew it across his throat.

Caroline snapped her head round so sharply that her wig—an unfamiliar article—went askew on her head. She clapped a hand on it to hold it in place while she looked up and across the square, tracing the gaze of the man on the black horse. Immediately she saw a man standing on the roof of the alms-house, perched on the ridge, and keeping one hand on a chimney for balance. This fellow scrambled round as quickly as he could without falling, turning his back on Monmouth Street to gaze north across Broad St. Giles's and east to one of the street-ends that spilled into that side of it.

"Charles! Come, come!" Johann was calling. Caroline's name would be Charles for as long as she was wearing breeches. He had ridden about two lengths ahead. "Charles" could not answer without revealing her sex to anyone in earshot. She waited for a queue of boys to thread past, then rode up toward Johann. She was hoping to draw abreast of him so that she could talk, but he spurred his mount on as she drew within a length, and began to lead her through the crowd in the direction of London.

Caroline was beginning to perceive drawbacks to the plan. It had sounded too simple to go wrong. Eliza, wearing an outfit that made her look, from a distance, like Caroline, had boarded the finest carriage available at Leicester House and driven south, parading round the perimeter of Leicester Fields in full view of all the spies who had been loitering there. She was to have gone out near Sir Isaac Newton's house and then to have worked her way west in the direction of St. James's, as if trying to reach the Duke of Marlborough's house, which was not far from there. This was the sort of thing a conspiracy-minded Tory would expect Princess Caroline to do, had she been flushed out into the open; Marlborough was not back in the country yet, but had been conspicuously remodeling the house as a signal that his advent was drawing nigh. He had long-standing connexions with the Hanovers, and Caroline could seek refuge in his house in full confidence that no Mobb, Militia, or Faction would dare to molest her there.

Meanwhile Johann and Caroline had set out in the opposite direction, planning a ride of three miles or so straight through the heart of London to Billingsgate Stairs, immediately downstream of the Bridge, where a longboat would take them out to a Hanoverian sloop. A few days later they would be at Antwerp, and a few days after that, back at Hanover. So much for the plan; but Caroline had not considered until now that *if* the disguise worked, and caused their enemies to believe that she was not Caroline the princess, but Charles the nobody—why, what would it matter if such a nobody were found in Fleet Ditch with his throat cut and his purse missing?

An open space had appeared next to Johann, on his left side. She dug her heels into the horse's sides twice and goaded it until it was alongside him. "What lies over that way?" she asked, and gestured in the same direction (left, or north across Broad St. Giles's) that the man on the roof of the alms-house was looking.

Johann considered it. Several street-ends were visible on that side. From one of them a bobbling stream of manes, periwigs, and horse-tails issued: four, maybe as many as half a dozen riders. Their faces were indistinct at this range—but they caught the light of the bonfire clearly, as all of them were gazing up and across toward the alms-house. Caroline looked back that way; her view of the spy on the roof was now mostly blocked by the chimney, but she could see an arm gesticulating, waving the riders on a course to close with Johann and Caroline.

"The one where the riders are coming out is Dyot Street—it leads up to Great Russell, and—"

"Ravenscar's house?"

"Yes."

"Then I think we have confused our enemies, in a way that could be dangerous to us," Caroline said. "I think they believe that we are messengers, sent out from Eliza with an important note for the Marquis of Ravenscar, or whatever Whig commanders may be gathered at his house—those riders, I fear—"

"Were posted along Dyot to intercept any such communications," said Johann, "and now they are after us. Let us ride a little faster—but not gallop, we must not show fear—and turn to the right, on Drury Lane. That will lead us away from Ravenscar's and throw doubt on this idea that we are messengers."

"I have heard things about this Drury Lane—"

"We shall look like a pair of young gentlemen out questing for whores," Johann agreed. "Do not be concerned. Drury Lane is the *frontier* of a chancy district. Many of those who live there have strayed up to Broad St. Giles's this evening. Riding the border is not so terribly dangerous. Going through it would be a bad idea—but we shan't do that. Straight down Drury it is, all the way to the Strand." And with that Johann guided his mount round a right turn onto Drury Lane. Caroline's horse lurched forward in an effort to keep pace, and she almost lost her wig again. From here Drury Lane looked infinitely long, and hellishly disordered even by the standards of London: it narrowed and widened, narrowed and widened as if no surveyor had ever stretched out a line here, and buildings leaned away from it, or slumped over it, like a bench of drunks in a gin-house. She did not see any bonfires, which she counted as a sort of good news; perhaps Drury Lane would be left to the whores, procurers, and pickpockets tonight, even as other streets and intersections were employed as squares on the Whig/Tory chessboard.

"I saw something," she said, "a gesture. I fear that violence is going to be used against us." She could not help glancing at Johann's Italian rapier, wagging from his left flank.

Johann tried to deflect this with humor. "Then it is good that my right arm is free," he said, waving it in the air, "and on our vulnerable flank," indicating the benighted neighborhood on their right. "And good as well that you have a sword."

"A *small* one."

"Indeed, that is what they call it: a small-sword. No one carries the rapier and dagger any more. *I* am kitted out like an old man."

"I am glad of it," said Caroline, for Johann's weapon looked a fell relic of bygone times, much more formidable than the jeweled toothpick on her hip.

She could not help, now, turning round once more to look back. Drury Lane sported very few men on horseback at this hour and so it took but a moment to see two riders who had just entered from Broad St. Giles's. They let their mounts dawdle for a moment, as they took in the sordid prospect, and got their bearings; then, catching sight of Johann and Caroline, they spurred them forward at a trot.

Caroline did not care to argue the matter with Johann and so she kicked her mount up to a trot, which obliged him to do the same.

"As you can see the right side of the Lane is perforated by countless alleys," Johann said, loudly, in the manner of a jaded man about town explaining the lay of the land to his country cousin, "but there is a very broad street a short distance ahead that leads direct to Covent Garden Market, where are many wenches we euphemistically call flower-sellers and orange-girls. From there, several broad avenues lead to the Strand."

Caroline wanted to ask *Why are you telling me this* but she dared not speak aloud, for she sensed a pedestrian close by on her left hand. Then she was distracted by some commotion off to the right, not in Drury Lane but back in what she assumed to be a maze of alleys behind. Shod hooves were sparking on pavement back there, and a voice commanding, "Make way, damn you!" She knew enough English by now to know that this was the voice of someone well-bred, someone with the right to bear arms. She looked behind again to see that the two men following had made up half the distance separating them; then, turning back to give this news to Johann, she observed that he was gone, with no good-bye other than a tattoo of hoofbeats down an alley, and murmur of prostitutes in his wake.

What had he told her? Do not ride into the alleys; look for a broad avenue on the right. She did so, and almost did not see it, for it was much closer than she had supposed. A rider was just emerging from it, on a bothered and winded horse that he was forcing to walk. She hoped it might be Johann, but the horse was the wrong color (chestnut) and the rider was the wrong chap altogether. He was staring her in the face, and could easily have made her out to be a woman in disguise had the sun been shining.

This man, she reckoned, must have split off from the squadron that had ridden out of Dyot a minute ago, and galloped round through the alleys behind Drury Lane to cut them off here. But Johann, hearing the commotion that this fellow had made, had surmised what was going on, and had broken away to outflank the flanker.

The man on the chestnut horse showed the palm of his hand to the two riders who were trotting along after Caroline, seeming to ward them off. She could hear their mounts drop to a walk, then stop altogether. With his other hand he reached up to tip his hat to Caroline as she approached. Lacking a hat, she returned the greeting with a swirl of the hand and a nod. Whether she did it convincingly or not, she'd never know, for he did not bother to watch; he had already turned his gaze elsewhere, wondering what had become of Caroline's companion.

He was attending to his two friends behind Caroline. She looked back. They were pointing into the alley Johann had ridden into, and shouting. Caroline was forgotten; she was free to go; Johann's gambit was working.

Or did work, anyway, until someone stole her sword.

She felt a sharp tug and heard a hissing sound as the small-sword was plucked from its scabbard. This sound quite naturally got the attention of the man on the chestnut stallion; gentlemen who ignored the sound of a sword being drawn were not likely to live through their twenties. Caroline looked down belatedly, to see a boy of perhaps sixteen, missing his two front teeth, leering back at her with a fanged smile. He had brought the small-sword around so that it pointed at her. This was plainly a threat, but Caroline did not know what to make of it until the partner of the tail-drawer (as sword-thieves were known) came after the even more valuable scabbard. This hung at her hip from a rig called a baldric, which was just a broad leather strap that ran diagonally across her body and over her right shoulder. The second thief was smaller and nimbler—perhaps a younger brother—and his method of stealing it was straightforward: he grabbed it with both hands and yanked on it so hard that he lifted himself clean off the ground, while giving Caroline the following choice: fall sideways off the horse, or be decapitated by the strap. Long years of tedious riding-lessons had trained her to stay on the horse no matter what; she squeezed it hard between her legs, caught the saddle's rim with her right hand, and held on for dear life even while listing drastically to the left. The thief had planted a foot on the horse's flank and was leaning back almost horizontally, supporting his weight solely by the baldric. Caroline had no choice but to lean toward him even farther and cock her head over so that the baldric was stripped off over her head. It nearly sheared off her right ear as it went. She reached up to check if the ear was still attached to her head. It was; but the hair around it was her own. Not a wig. The wig was lying like a dead animal in the middle of Drury Lane. Or was, anyway, until a wig-thief darted in and snatched it. The tail-drawer let out a curse and lit out in pursuit of the wig-snatcher, menacing him with the weapon; the scabbard-stealer, who'd fallen hard on his arse, staggered to his feet and hobbled along behind.

Someone nearby was shouting: "It is the Princess! It is the Princess!" Caroline turned to see that it was the man on the chestnut stallion.

Another rider was galloping up behind him on a gray horse; this chap had his feet out of the stirrups and his boots up in the air, which looked like bad form indeed. Sharply the boots came down. The gray trotted riderless across Drury Lane. The chestnut was buckling as its hindquarters now supported the weight of a second man. It reared. The man in back threw his arms around the rider in the saddle, to keep from falling off backwards; one of his hands had something silver in it. A hand was beneath the rider's chin, pulling his head back; the silver object traveled sideways beneath it, not with a quick slash, but working its way through the neck one tube and ligament at a time. The rider fell over sideways, broadcasting a fan of blood that hissed down the wall of a nearby tavern. The man behind kicked the other's feet out of the stirrups and toppled him over into the street. Then Johann von Hacklheber took over the saddle. He scabbarded his bloody dagger, found the reins with that hand, then drew out his rapier with the other. He spurred the chestnut horse out into Drury Lane, nearly managing a head-on collision with Caroline's gray. As he went past he brought the flat of his sword down sharply on the croup of her mount, which responded by taking off with a lurch that nearly somersaulted her back out of the saddle. Lacking instructions from its rider, the horse headed for open space: the wide avenue that led to Covent Garden.

She was almost there by the time she got rightly arranged in the saddle again, and fished up the reins. Then she reflected that she was going west—the wrong direction—and did not really wish to appear in such a manner, viz. galloping across a large open square with her hair flowing behind her like a Hanoverian flag.

She ought to go back and help Johann. But whatever had happened in Drury Lane must be over and done with already; and if she showed up in the middle of it, he would be distracted and probably get killed. What, then, was the best way to help Johann? To follow his directions, so that he would know where to look for her. He had mentioned that from the vicinity of Covent Garden several streets led down to the Strand, which (even she knew) could take her east at least as far as St. Paul's. So she pulled back hard on the reins, bringing her mount to a skidding stop just short of the open space of the Garden, and insisted on a left turn down a promisingly broad street. This, inevitably, took her only a short distance to a tee with a smaller street. Guessing at a direction, she came to another, smaller tee; and so it went, as if the street-plan of the place were a diabolical snare made for one purpose only, which was to get people lost. By the third turn, she'd lost all sense of which direction she was going. By the fifth, she had a small crowd of boys after her. By the sixth, the boys had been joined by a couple of rough-looking men. The seventh turn led to a way that was very narrow indeed. Moreover, it was a cul-de-sac.

Yet, when she cast a glance back over her shoulder, she was astonished to see that all of her followers had disappeared.

Down at the end of the street were a few sedan chairs, waiting. Their porters stood about smoking and talking; though one by one they fell silent as Caroline rode up. There was a door at the very end of the street, lit with lanterns, and adorned with a sort of inn-sign in which was depicted a cat playing a fiddle. Beyond it, she could hear a lot of men chattering and laughing. A man was standing framed in that doorway, wearing porter's livery: a bit more nicely turned out than the ones who carried sedan chairs through gutters and puddles. He stirred as she rode closer, and removed the stem of his pipe from his mouth, and addressed Princess Caroline in a way no man had ever done before: "Well 'ello, missy, ain't you a smart lass in your britches, and all got up like a man! I can see one of our honourable members is planning a special evening indeed. You did bring your riding crop?"

It took her a moment to remember this word, for *crop* had diverse meanings, but then it came to her: it was *Reitgerte*, the little whip. One was dangling from her wrist. She groped it into her hand, and raised it up uncertainly.

The porter grinned and nodded. "I'll wager you're here for the Bishop of—"

"What is this place?" she asked.

"Oh, you've come to the right place, never fear," he answered, reaching for the door-handle.

"But what is it called?"

"Don't be a silly girl, this is the Kit-Cat Clubb!"

"Aha!" Caroline exclaimed, "is Doctor Waterhouse here? He is the one I would see!"

Leicester Fields

THE SAME TIME

ELIZA HAD RUN diverse errands fair and foul, and embraced many sacrifices, on behalf of these Hanover women, but this was in some ways the most disagreeable of all: going for a carriage-ride, here and now. For a carriage, be it never so finely decorated, and perforated with doors and windows, was unavoidably a box, and to shut herself up in a box at such a pass went against everything in her nature.

She had never quite got out of her mind a day when she and several other harem-girls, all in their *burqas,* had been herded into a tunnel beneath Vienna to be put to the sword. To *hear* the screams of the women, and *smell* their blood, and *know* what was going on while only being able to *see* a tiny patch of light, and being unable to use her hands, save by gripping things through the slippery fabric: this was for her the worst moment of her life, the thing she'd spent all her time since trying to put behind her.

Her view out the window of this carriage was no better than that from a *burqa,* and her ability to reach out and grab things even less. True, it was mounted on wheels, and pulled by a team of horses. But her usual retinue of dogs and armed footmen were absent, as they would have destroyed the illusion that this carriage contained Princess Caroline in disguise. The driver was trustworthy, but all someone had to do was aim a pistol at him, or knock him out of his perch and seize the reins; then she'd be even more helpless than she had been on that horrible day in Vienna.

Still and all, she rated the chances as good that the carriage would speed her to Marlborough House without let. The distance was less than half a mile as the crow flew, and once they worked clear of a few narrow streets south of Leicester Fields they would be speeding down such broad open avenues as Hay Market and Pall Mall. Whether it came to a good or a bad end, the ride would be over quickly, the revulsion she felt at being shut up in a wooden *burqa* she'd only have to tolerate for a few minutes.

It began well enough: an uneventful half-circuit of Leicester Fields, traversing the east side of the square, then swinging round to head west along its southern edge. This ought to have been a straight shot to Hay Market; but the driver called for a turn too soon, and she felt the box revolving leftwards onto St. Martin's. Out one window she could see a narrow *burqa*-view of Sir Isaac Newton's house; out the opposite, a flare of light where none ought to be. Someone had lit a bonfire in the southwestern corner of Leicester Fields, blocking the outlet to Hay Market. And they'd done it in the last minute or so, for Eliza had scanned the square carefully before suffering herself to be boxed, and seen nothing.

No matter; St. Martin's Street offered two different outlets that would lead them west. They reached the first of these in only a few moments, and slowed so that the driver could gaze down the side-street to see if it was clear. Eliza did the same. No more than fifty yards away, what looked like a squadron of cavalry was cantering into position to block them. They did not have banners, drums, or bugles, and did not wear uniforms, unless you considered Mode to be a kind of uniform. But they moved with a shared purpose, and Eliza sensed that they were looking to one man, in particular, for orders: a chap in a long cloak, on a black horse.

Before Eliza could take in much more, or say anything, the driver had made up his mind to try the second and last side-street. His whip skirled and cracked, touching off a barrage of noise: sixteen iron-shod hooves and four iron-rimmed wheels accelerating over cobble-stones as the box creaked, bobbled, and thudded in its suspension. To communicate with the driver was now next to impossible; she could pound and kick on the roof all she pleased, and scream through the grate until she was hoarse, and he likely would not hear a thing.

It was not clear what she *should* say to him. To maintain the illusion was all. To reach Marlborough House would be good, insofar as it enhanced the illusion. But it was not essential, and certainly not worth anyone's getting killed. To rattle around aimlessly for a while would serve as well, and perhaps better.

At the end of the street, where it turned to the right, there was enough room for the team and carriage to make a rapid sweeping turn. This the driver did—so swiftly that the carriage lost traction and slewed sideways for a yard or two, until its wheel-rims caught hard on a scarp in the road. Then its skid was arrested so sharply that the whole box lifted up and slanted as two wheels left the pavement for an instant. Presently the slack went out of the rig and jerked it forward again on its new, west-going course. The carriage crashed back down on four wheels again and Eliza was hurled to the right, then back as the team accelerated. She was left with the troubling memory of a momentary sound that, because it had been so sharp, had reached her ears even through all of the noise of this maneuver: the crack of the whip perhaps, or even a pistol-shot. But it had seemed to come from just outside the left window. She phant'sied it had had a splintering quality. Perhaps a wheel-spoke giving way as the lateral skid of the carriage had been arrested. Perhaps the driver should be directed to avoid violent right turns. Or had he heard the sound, too, and wanted no advice?

Her hatred of the box and passion to know what was going on urged her to shove her head out the window and look forward. Simple prudence said otherwise. The horses were *galloping* now. In a few yards they'd reach a tee, and be obliged to turn left or right on Hedge Lane; she braced her feet against the opposite bench, and her hands against the sides, and prayed they would go left. For she was convinced now that the heartbeat-like *thumpa-thumpa-thumpa* she heard on the left, and felt through the bones of the carriage, was a bad spoke or two.

This tactic—ramming-speed in the streets of London—seemed insane from within the box. But it was not really so, for (as she was recollecting) the carriage had a long pole—not unlike a ram on a galley—that extended all the way forward, between each pair of horses in the team, and to which all the harnesses were connected. People got killed by these things all the time: some by impalement and others by having their brains dashed out. Even supposing there *were* a squadron of Jacobite cavalry trying to bar their escape onto Hedge Lane—and that had to have been a phantasm, hadn't it?—all of them would get well clear of that deadly pole, once they perceived that it had built up too much speed to stop. What they might do *then*, when they'd regrouped and got their blood up, was another matter—but no point in fretting about that now.

It seemed to have worked, anyway, for the carriage's speed slackened even as she was tensed for a crash, and it began to manage a turn—a left turn, thank God, and not so fast—onto Hedge Lane. And really not so much a full turn as a quick leftward jog into the next west-going street, Little Suffolk, which would run straight to Hay Market, and dump them out directly across from the triple-arched façade of the Italian Opera House that Vanbrugh and the Whigs had built there.

She heard horses all round during this maneuver, and voices shouting; but could not make out words until they had got well established on Little Suffolk, and built up to a steady canter that would bring them to the Opera House in considerably less than one minute. There seemed no point in letting those seconds go to waste. Eliza could hear the riders all around shouting absurd things such as "Halt!" and "I demand that you stop this carriage." She wanted no such thing to occur; but neither did she want the driver to press forward if someone was about to shoot him. The important thing was the illusion.

She shot open the window on the carriage's left side and got a *burqa*-impression of several riders, all of whom abruptly went silent; which was so gratifying that she slid over to the right and shot *that* window open as well. She risked a peek out and forward, and saw a row of building-fronts ahead. This might have been any of London's newer streets. But her eye was arrested by one building-front twice or thrice as broad as its neighbors.

Like them it was made of brick, but so much of its façade was spoken for by arched windows and doorways, and by the massive grooved voussoirs that framed them, and the stacks of deeply rusticated blocks that ascended from its corner-stones, and the broad friezes and cornices that spanned its width between storeys, that it really seemed to have been fabricated out of massive clods of pale stone, with brick and mortar spackled into the narrow traces between. It was meant to look as dramatic as what went on inside of it: for this was the Italian Opera, and it stood in the Hay Market. Though Eliza loved and, like a good Whig, subscribed to it, it was of no utility whatever tonight, save as a landmark. Narrow streets such as Little Suffolk might be barricaded by a few men and a bonfire, but the Hay Market was nearly a hundred feet in breadth. It would take a company to stop them there.

"Ignore these men!" she said, "straight on, and stop for no one!" Which was only an indifferent snatch of libretto, as it went; but what made all the difference was that *she uttered it in German*. Eliza had been in many a *salon,* in Versailles and Amsterdam and elsewhere, and spoken many a clever or shocking *mot,* and created many a *frisson*—but all were as nothing compared to the effect that these words had on the riders around her. "It is she! It is the Princess!" one of them shouted, and spurred his horse to a gallop, riding forward to the intersection with Hay Market, now perhaps fifty yards away. Eliza was so pleased by this that she feared she might be recognized as an impostor, and spoil the effect; so before any of the riders on the right side could get too long a look at her, she withdrew and skidded back to the left side to have a look out *that* window.

But there enjoyment ended. Ahead, she saw meteors of flame

bobbing and swirling on the end of torch-handles. One of these stooped to the pavement and vanished in an orb of dull fire-glow, which broke open into a rush of brilliant yellow flame. Someone had put a torch to the base of a well-laid bonfire. The carriage faltered as the horses saw it. The driver cracked his whip over and over, and permitted the team to divert to the right as much as they could in the confines of Little Suffolk. Hope that they could skirt the fire, and fear of the whip and of the shouting riders, drove the horses into an undisciplined rush forward. Just as they burst through into Hay Market, someone tossed a handful of firecrackers into the flames. They went off in a barrage so close and hot that Eliza felt bursts of heat reaching in through the window to slap at her face. She tried to move to the right. But the team had gotten a worse scare than she, and moved away from it with all the power of several tons of muscle. The carriage veered right, and went up on its left wheels. Eliza would have dropped straight into the left door had she not lashed out to grip the sill of the window on the right. For a moment she was suspended, gazing up through the *burqa*-slot to see nothing but chimney-tops, storks' nests, and stars in the sky.

Then the left wheel collapsed. The entire carriage dropped an arm's length or so, and landed with its full weight on the end of the left axle. Or so she collected from the sounds and the movements. Her right hand was jarred loose from the windowsill, so she dropped like a sack of barley into the left door. Its latch gave way and it fell open; but it could only open so far, as it was nearly skidding along the pavement. The only thing holding it above the cobbles of Hay Market was that axle, which projected beyond the side of the vehicle for a short distance. And so Eliza, lying on her back on the broken door with the wind knocked out of her, was able to turn her head and see pavement rushing away only a few inches from her nose, taking her chestnut-colored wig with it.

But presently the pavement slowed and stopped. The horses—who must be driverless now—had decided that the place they had reached—the front court of the Opera, by the looks of it—was safer than any other place in view, and resolved to stop here. Eliza began trying to squirm out of the half-open door; she phant'sied there was enough space between the ground and the flank of the carriage to admit her body. This very soon turned out to have been overly optimistic, for the door was not open quite wide enough to let her out. She got her head, a shoulder, and an arm free, but the remainder of Eliza would not come unless the door were removed. It was held in place by hinges of ox-hide. Eliza's left arm was still imprisoned, but she could move it around, and find one of the hinges by groping.

She had a little Turkish watered-steel dagger in the waistband of her dress: a nasty old habit. She found it with her left hand, and drew it out. A few moments later she was sawing away at one of the leather hinges.

And she was thus busily engaged when a pair of polished black riding-boots presented themselves before her face. The hem of a long dark cloak roiled about them like a cloud. A chestnut wig fell to the pavement. "You are not the woman I was looking for," said a voice in French.

Eliza looked far, far up to see the face of Father Édouard de Gex staring down at her. He was perspiring freely. "But you will do, madame, you will do." In his gloved hands he was twirling a dagger that gave off an oily sheen in the light of the bonfires that were springing up all around.

The Black Dogg, Newgate Prison
A FEW MINUTES EARLIER

"I HAVE THE HEAVY GOLD. You know this," Jack said.

"The Solomonic Gold?" Isaac corrected him.

"Funny, that is what Father Ed calls it, too. Whatever you call it, I have it, and I know where I can get more. Now, suppose Bolingbroke demands a Trial of the Pyx. The refiner's furnace shall be set up in Star Chamber. A jury of London money-men shall open up the Pyx and take out a sample of coins—"

"Coins that *you* put in," Isaac said.

"That you can't prove—but in any case, *you* are personally responsible for every one of those coins," Jack reminded him. "They shall be counted and weighed first. And it may astonish you, Ike, to hear that the coins I put in there shall pass this first test. I made the blanks a bit thicker, you see—not enough so as you would notice, holding one between your fingers, but enough to make them of legal weight, even though they are allayed with base metal."

"But when they are assayed—?" Daniel said.

"When those same coins are melted in the cupel, and the quantity of gold in them is measured, they'll be found wanting. And this is where I may be of service to you, Ike, and to that Marquis who got you your post at the Mint."

"You can supply me with heavy gold, as you call it."

"Indeed. Which, slipped into the cupel by a bit of prestidigitation—easily arranged, have no fear—will give the assay greater weight, and make all the numbers come out as they should."

Isaac Newton, who had been strangely unmoved by all that infiltrated his nostrils and stuck to the soles of his shoes here in Newgate, was nauseated by this. Jack Shaftoe was quick to note it and to know why. "I disgust you, Ike, for the same reason I disgust Father Ed, which is that to me the heavy gold is only that. And when I offer it to you as a part of our present transaction, I offer it, not as a mystical essence for use in your divine sorcery, but as a bit o' spare weight to save your nuts during the Trial of the Pyx that is soon to come. Our conversation here would seem a good deal nobler, wouldn't it, if it were about *that* rather than *this;* if it were about *that,* why, you could phant'sy yourself living out a sort of latter-day sequel to the Bible, and Newgate, foul as it is, would be like those leper-towns where Jesus walked: not so foul, because part of a fair story. But because it is about *this,* namely, Ike Newton not getting his balls and his hand chopped off, why, you look about yourself and say, 'Eeeyuh, I am in the Black Dogg of Newgate Prison and it stinketh!' I see this clearly only because I have seen it so oft on the face of Father Ed, for whom all of London might as well be Newgate Prison when it is compared to Versailles. But I shall solace you with the same words I have spoke to Father Ed when he turns thus green about the gills."

"I am astonished that you have any words *left,*" said Isaac. "But as I have heard so many, a few more can do no harm."

"It is simply that when all of this has played out, and you are left holding a bit of that Solomonic Gold, why, you may believe, concerning it, whatever you choose, and do with it what you will."

"A question," Daniel said. "Since you know that Sir Isaac desires it, and you know he is aware that you have got some, why this elaborate scheme concerning the Pyx? Why did you not simply treat directly with Sir Isaac long ago?"

"Because there were other parties to be accounted for. On my side, there was de Gex, who had a say in the matter until I began trying to kill him a couple of weeks ago. On your side, Ravenscar, who does not believe in Alchemy any more than I do. To extract anything from *him* I needed something a bit more substantial than a spate of malarkey about King Solomon."

"Since you hold my views on the matter in such contempt, this conversation cannot be any more pleasant for you than it is for me. Let us bring it to a head directly," Isaac suggested. "You have offered a way to get me out of difficulty in the event that Bolingbroke demands a Trial of the Pyx. But this is of no utility to me if he *doesn't.* For as all the world knows, he has been gathering in guineas of late, preparing to assay those coins that have been circulating in her majesty's currency. Many counterfeits shall be encompassed in any such sample. At any time of Bolingbroke's choosing he may change his tune, and say, 'Behold, the Pyx was tampered with by Jack the Coiner, its contents are no reliable sample of the Mint's produce, we must instead assay the coins in circulation.' Such an assay shall prove deficient, both in the weight of the coins, and the fineness of the metal, because it shall include so many counterfeit guineas."

By way of an answer, Jack reached into the pocket of his breeches and drew out a little packet, which he tossed across the Black Dogg. Isaac got his hands up quickly enough, bobbled it, and trapped it against his breast. Daniel did not have to look to know what it was. "One of the Sinthias you stole from the Pyx in April."

"I have the rest stored away nice and safe," Jack said, "and can produce them when and where needed, to prove that you put only good coins into the Pyx, Ike. So, you see, whether Bolingbroke orders a Trial of the Pyx or no, I can save you: if he does, by supplying heavy gold, and if he doesn't, by supplying the rest of those." Jack nodded at the packet, which Isaac was now fondling near a candle-flame.

"In exchange for which, I suppose you require that you not be prosecuted, and that your sons get the farm in Carolina."

"My sons, and Tomba," Jack said. "That is an African who has been with me since we met him racing horses on the beach near Acapulco. Fine lad."

"I remind you that there is a reason why we insisted that this conversation happen *this evening*," Daniel said.

"Bolingbroke has Ravenscar backed up against the wall," Jack returned, "and Ravenscar needs something."

"Yes."

"Show Bolingbroke that, then." Jack nodded at the Sinthia. "It'll hit him like a bolt between the eyes; for he has pestered me without letup these many months, wanting them from me."

This silenced Daniel and Isaac for some moments. They had to look at each other for a while, before they looked at Jack. "Henry St. John, Viscount Bolingbroke, her majesty's Secretary of State, has been pestering *you?*"

"Call him by as many names as you like, the answer is yes."

"Let us go and see your *good friend* Bolingbroke, then," Daniel suggested, with a not very subtle look at his watch.

"He is not my friend, but a damned nuisance," Jack returned, "and I'd not go in to his house again even if he invited me. But you may have that packet, as proof of my *bona fides,* and I shall ride with you to Golden Square, and go for a constitutional round the green, as you go in to strike your bargain with him. When you have done, come out and tell me the results. I'm keen to know whether the next English King is going to be German or French."

"The only defect in your plan is a terribly mundane one," Daniel said. "We came in a phaethon."

"What a rake you are, Dr. Waterhouse! Do stay away from my sons!"

"Two may fit inside, only with a lot of stuffing and bending."

"Then do you stuff and bend yourselves into it," said Jack, walking over to the door. He hauled it open and extended a hand to say, *after you.* "I shall ride on the running-board, like a footman, as befits my station in life, and if any footpads or Jacobite fops get after us, why, I'll run 'em through."

The phaethon had been waiting in the Press-Yard next to the gaol. This opened onto Newgate Street *intra muros.* Driving west, they passed immediately beneath the vault of the city gate: a Gothick castle housing wealthy prisoners. Thence they could have got directly to Holbourn and taken a northerly route toward Golden Square, but Daniel knew it was an infernal gantlet of bonfires to-night: the bright line where Whig and Tory orders of battle were being drawn up. So he requested the southerly approach. The Old Bailey connected to the street *extra muros* and took them south to Ludgate Hill which, going west, became the last bridge over the Fleet Ditch, which became Fleet Street, which became the Strand.

The scheme of placing Jack on the running-board worked well, for the phaethon was equipped with a grate, situated next to where a footman's face was likely to be, so that master and servant could miscommunicate as freely and grievously on the road as they did at home. Daniel left it open. Jack was able to chat with the passengers almost as easily as if he were sharing the compartment with them. He was in a cheery mood—more so than Isaac, certainly—and offered up wry comments upon the Old Bailey, the odor of the Fleet, the Royal Society's headquarters, Drury Lane, the Kit-Cat Clubb, and other exhibits as they rattled past. Daniel took most of these in good humor, but Isaac, who suspected that Jack was baiting him, fumed quietly, like a beaker just tonged from a furnace. There were bonfires, fist-fights, and dogs fucking each other in Charing Cross, and

Jack was silent for a while, because alert. But Roger's driver—who was of the best—negotiated this adroitly and got them on the short street called Cockspur that would soon fork into Pall Mall and Hay Market just before the Opera House.

"There must be an opera tonight," Jack remarked through the grate.

" 'Tis not possible," Daniel returned. "It is out of season. I do believe they are erecting sets, and rehearsing, for a revival of *The Alchemist* by Ben Jonson."

"I saw that a hundred times as a boy," Jack said, "why ever are they reviving it now?"

"Because Herr Handel has written new music for it."

"What? It is a *play*, not an *opera*."

"Styles change," Daniel said. "Mr. Vanbrugh's theatre, there, is nothing like the theatres of your boyhood: it is all indoors, and ornate beyond description, and the actors are imprisoned on a stage, behind a proscenium."

"Stay, I have been to a few such," said Jack. "I could not hear a damned word. My ears are ruined; too much early horseplay with firearms."

"Your ears are fine. *No one* can hear what the actors are saying, in a place like that. And this one in Hay Market is worse than most."

"When Vanbrugh designed it," said Newton, suddenly thawing, "it was styled the Theatre Royal. When it opened, nine years ago, and the audience thought they were witnessing a mum-show, then they had to change the name of it to the Opera, which empowered the performers to make themselves heard, by bellowing at the tops of their lungs in the style that is customary in that Art."

"It chagrins me to hear that the good old *Alchymist* is being subjected to such perversion," said Jack. "I've a mind to pop Mr. Handel in the gob."

"It might not be so bad," Daniel said. "When yonder Opera got into financial straits—which did not take long—my lord Ravenscar stepped into the breach, and remodeled the inside—made it smaller, lowered the ceiling, *et cetera*."

"Ah, and that fixed the problem?"

"Of course not. So he had to rip it out and redo it again—anyway, he defrayed the expense by selling subscriptions for half a guinea."

"Only half! I'd have bought one, had I known."

"I shall ask my lord Ravenscar to throw one in as a *soupçon*," said Daniel.

"While you are at it, let him know his Opera is invested by the Mobb," said Jack. "For what I at first took to be the fireworks to celebrate an Opening Night, now takes on the appearance of a small Riot. There are several blokes on horseback, and I do believe I see a formation of infantry flanking them from behind the Opera House."

"Infantry!?"

"Some would call it more Mobb, but to my eye their movements are altogether too orderly and platoonishly clumped. They are some militia. Ah, and there is something else, just before the entrance: I think it is an overturned carriage."

Just then they swung round a curve onto Hay Market, and the Italian Opera House became visible out the left side of the phaethon. It was all as Jack had described it, save that Daniel did not see any of the phantom infantry spoken of by Jack. But he knew there was an open lot behind the building that was a perpetual construction camp as the theatre was gutted and remodeled by Ravenscar in his never-ending quest to make his performers audible, and where sets were erected for the operas. That was a very likely place for some Whig Association militia to have bivouacked. If it was really true that Jack had seen infantry, he'd have seen them there.

The phaethon bounded up on its suspension, as if they had driven over a sudden rise. Jack had jumped off. Looking back through the grate, Daniel saw him receding. He was standing in the middle of Hay Market, squarely in front of the Italian Opera. "I have just recognized that overturned carriage," he called. "I have deeds to do here."

"Our transaction is not finished!" Newton shouted back.

"It cannot be helped. I shall try to meet you in Golden Square later."

"If you do not, you may consider that the deal is null and void," Newton returned, his voice faltering, as he was no longer so sure that anyone was listening. Jack had dissolved into the Mobb.

> The Fabrick's Finish'd, and the Builder's part
> Has shown the Reformation of his Art.
> Bless'd with Success, thus have their first Essays
> Reform'd their Buildings, not Reform'd their Plays . . .
> Never was Charity so Ill Employ'd,
> Vice so Discourag'd, Vertue so Destroy'd;
> Never Foundation so abruptly laid,
> So Much Subscrib'd and yet so little Paid.
>
> —FROM DANIEL DEFOE'S ATTACK ON THE
> OPERA HOUSE IN HAY MARKET, *THE REVIEW*,
> NO. 26, 3 MAY 1705

The Kit-Cat Club is now grown *Famous* and *Notorious,*
all over the *Kingdom.* And they have Built a *Temple* for
their *Dagon,* the new *Play-house,* in the *Hay-Market.*
The *Foundation* was laid with great *Solemnity,* by a Noble Babe of *Grace.* And over or under the *Foundation
Stone* is a Plate of *Silver,* on which is Graven *Kit-Cat* on
the one side, and *Little Whigg** on the other. This is
in *Futuram re Memoriam,* that after *Ages* may know by
what *Worthy Hands,* and for what good *Ends* this
stately *Fabrick* was Erected.
        —JACOBITE JOURNALIST CHARLES LESLIE, *THE
    REHEARSAL OF OBSERVATOR,* NO. 41 (5/12 MAY
                                    1705)

BROAD AS IT WAS COMPARED to the town-houses hemming it in on left
and right, the part of the Opera House fronting on the Hay Market
could not contain a whole theatre. As anyone would discover who entered into one of its triad of massive arched doorways, this was only a
lobby. The auditorium proper, and the set-shops and backstage
spaces, were all under a mountainous roof that loomed in the interior of the block like a mountain-range over an Alpine town, and
threatened to bury the adjoining houses under an avalanche of roof-
tiles someday. Tonight the roof was hidden by darkness, occasionally
blushing a lambent red as a bonfire flared on the street below, and
betraying the presence of silent watchers posted on its roof. It over-
shadowed a stretch of Hay Market running some two hundred feet
from Bell Inn on the north (rumored to contain a secret subscribers'
entrance, used by the Kit-Catocracy) to the even narrower and
darker alley of Unicorn Court on the south (which, for those brave
enough to follow it all the way to its dead end, gave access to the
backstage). Overall this was neither the grandest nor meanest fabrique in London and one could easily go past it without a second
glance; but it happened to be the place where a lot of Jacobite Tories
had lit bonfires tonight. The squadrons of un-uniformed Tory cavalry
that had roved through the district to intercept messages between
Marlborough House and the Kit-Cat Clubb, or Marlborough House
and Leicester House, had converged hither, and turned their attention inward, toward the fires they had lit and the carriage they had
brought to bay, which was rumored to contain the Electoral Princess
of Hanover, here in London to spy and to cabal with Whigs *incognito.*

---

*In honor of Lady Anne Sunderland, the daughter of the Duke of Marlborough.

Not a one of them noted the sentries on the high dark roof of the Opera, who, for the last several minutes, had been busy with signal-flags. Those faced not towards the imbroglio in the Hay Market but west toward certain parks and undeveloped parcels of land, not far away, which in recent days had turned into strangely well-ordered Vagabond-camps.

"Money, and all that comes with it, disgusts me," said Father Édouard de Gex, speaking apparently to his own boots. For he had planted one to either side of the head of the Duchess of Arcachon-Qwghlm, and clamped her head between his ankle-bones, forcing her to look up into his face. "Within living memory, men and women of noble birth did not even have to *think* about it. Oh, there were rich nobles and poor, just as there were tall and short, beautiful and ugly. But it would never have entered the mind of even a *peasant* to phant'sy that a penniless Duke was any less a Duke, or that a *rich whore* ought to be made a Duchess. Nobles did not handle money, or speak of it; if they were guilty of *caring* about it, they took pains to hide it, as with any other vice. Men of the cloth did not need money, or use it, except for a few whose distasteful duty it was to take in the tithes from the poor-box. And ordinary honest peasants lived a life blessedly free of money. To nobles, clerics, and peasants—the only people needed or wanted in a decent Christian Realm—coins were as alien, eldritch, inexplicable as communion wafers to a Hindoo. They are, I believe, an artifact of the pagan necromancers of the Romans, talismans of the subterranean Cult of Mithras, which St. Constantine, after his conversion to the True Faith, somehow forgot to eradicate, even as the temples of the idolaters were being pulled down or made over into churches. The makers, users, and hoarders of money were a cult, a cabal, a parasitical infestation, enduring through many ages, no more Christian than the Jews—indeed, many *were* Jews. They convened in a few places like Venice, Genoa, Antwerp, and Seville, and spun round the globe a web or net-work of links along which money flowed, in feeble and fitful pulses. This was repugnant but endurable. But what has happened of late is monstrous. The money-cult has spread faster across what used to be Christendom than the faith of Mahomet did across Araby. I did not grasp the enormity of it until *you* came to Versailles as an infamous Dutch whore, a plaything of diseased bankers, and shortly were ennobled—made into a Countess, complete with a fabricated pedigree—and why? Because you had noble qualities? No. Only because you were Good with Money—a high sorceress of the coin-cult—and so were adored by the same sort of degraded Versailles court-fops who would gather in abandoned churches at midnight to recite the Black Mass.

"It was then that I formed my resolve to burn you at the stake, Eliza. It is to me what the Holy Grail was to Sir Galahad: an ambition that has sustained me through many trials and journeys. Oh, *by itself,* to see you slowly consumed by fire would be only an idle pleasure. Do not imagine I am so self-indulgent. Burning you, Eliza, was to be the climax, the catharsis of a great Work of purification. England was to fall to the armies of the Most Christian King, and the Dutch Republic was to fall next. Not just *you* but *many* were to have been consumed in *autos da fé* that would have illuminated the face of Europe as these bonfires do the Hay Market to-night. It was to have been the end of heresy—the heresy of the so-called Protestants, of the Jews, and, most of all, of the money-cult. Great canvases and frescoes would have been painted of the event, by the Michelangelos of a new age, who would work not for money but for the glory of God. These paintings would have been vast tableaux of countless figures; but in the center of all, taking pride of place, would have been you, Eliza, bound to a stake in Charing Cross, burning. During my voyage round the world, when I was sick or cold or exhausted, and my faith began to fail, I would think on this, and find new strength. The love of it beckoned me ever onward, even as fear of it drove Jack like the crack of a whip at an ox's ear."

All during this curious discourse, Eliza was trying to saw away, with her dagger, at the ox-hide strap that served as the hinge of the carriage door. This was difficult to achieve without a continual movement of the shoulder that must have been obvious to de Gex, and so she was trying to go about it subtly. Which meant slowly. He was evidently in no hurry to get on with her *auto da fé;* but she feared he was now drawing to some conclusion, and about to set fire to her carriage, or something. So she asked him a question. "It is just the opposite of what one would think, given your passion for Alchemy—who would've phant'sied you'd such an antipathy for money?"

De Gex shook his head sadly, and took his eyes away from Eliza's for the first time in a long while. The light of a bonfire glittered in the oily blade of his dagger, and caught his eye; he gazed into it, and twiddled it idly as he went on: "Of course some Alchemists are charlatans, seeking wealth; they are a mockery of people like *you,* sharing your avarice, wanting your artifice. But can you not see that Alchemy is the avenging angel to destroy your heresy? For what value shall your money have, if gold may be made as easily as straw?"

"So that is the end you seek," Eliza said, "to overturn and scatter the new System that has been built up, during your lifetime, by the ineffable workings of Money."

"Indeed! What right do Britain, and the Dutch Republic, have to exist? God did not mean for men to live in such places, or if He did,

He did not mean for them to *prosper* here. Look—look at this opera house! Built on the edge of the world by frostbitten shepherds—yet in its size, its glory, truly a monster, an abomination, only possible because of the unnatural distortions that Money has wreaked on the world. The same is true of all London! It should all burn. And you should be the spark to kindle it."

"Should be, or shall be?" Eliza asked. The ox-hide hinge was nearly sawn through; one good slash ought to drop the carriage-door to the pavement, and give her hips room to slither out. But this did her no good when her head was clamped between de Gex's feet. She arched her neck, pointing her chin up at de Gex's face, and thereby gained an upside-down view of a bonfire just a few paces away. If she could tempt him to go over and root around for a firebrand, she might be out from under the carriage by the time he got back.

"Grand beautiful schemes," said de Gex, with a regretful smile, "such as the one I have just laid out, oft arise more from *pride* than *piety*. To create an *auto da fé* here in the Hay Market to-night would gratify my pride. But it were too grand and gaudy a scheme, under present circumstances. I must show humility, instead, by doing the work quickly, with nicotine. You may take it as a moral lesson: though you have lived expensively, and in grand style, you shall die a simple and humble death in the gutter of Hay Market."

"Ain't it a shame," said an English voice, somehow familiar to Eliza, "when a noble holy man, who despises money, has to cut corners, and kill meanly, all because he and Leroy don't have two *louis d'or* to rub together."

At the first sound of this voice, de Gex stepped back half a pace, and broadened his stance. This freed Eliza's head. She turned it toward the speaker—who was framed in the center arch of the Italian Opera, as if just emerging from a play. Since there was no performance to-night, it seemed more likely that this was a chap who knew his way around the nearby alleyways. Unable to break through the cordon of Jacobite riders and flaming barricades, and the Mobb attracted thereby, he must have entered the Opera House covertly through the side entrance at Bell Inn, and worked his way through the building to burst in on their discourse from a direction unexpected and unwatched. So much so, in fact, that most of de Gex's riders, who were still out patrolling the fringe of the fire-light, did not even know yet that an interloper had penetrated to the core of their position.

Eliza, because startled, had let several seconds go to waste when she might have been cutting herself free. She went back to work now with the dagger.

De Gex took a step towards the interloper. "This is stupid even for you," he said. "You are sure to be dead within a few moments—behold, you are surrounded."

"You're a-mazed, Father Ed, because I've been such a shrewd and calculating sort the whole time you've known me. But in my youth I used to do stupid things, and even profit from them, all the time. All the cleverness I've shown since I got back to London has been to one end, namely, that I might get into position, as it were, to do something foolish for my Eliza. Here I am; now's the time."

"As you like it!" said de Gex. "It shall be my very great pleasure to punish you for your impulsiveness, Jack."

When this name reached Eliza's ears, her arm jerked, and the hinge slashed through. The carriage-door fell to the pavement under her weight, and made a crack. De Gex—who had taken a step toward Jack—hesitated, and looked back. Eliza did not have time to wriggle free. She flung the dagger at de Gex. It caught him in the back of the thigh, but was too light to penetrate more than a quarter of an inch. Still, it stung like a hornet, and he reached back to paw it out. "Bitch whore!" he cried, rounding on her and bringing his own dagger up to strike.

Jack flew down the steps of the Opera House, lunging toward de Gex and thrusting one hand forward. He looked less like a duellist than a wizard casting a spell, for no blade was in his hand, and the distance between them was too great for him to land a punch. But he had been cradling a small object in his palm, which flew outwards, spinning so fast that it made a buzzing hum, like the wings of a small bird. It shot past de Gex's upraised dagger-hand, but then, impossibly, reversed its direction and whipped around his wrist, going into a spiral orbit whose velocity waxed as its radius waned, finally becoming a whizzing blur that collided with his hand, and stuck there: for the thing that Jack had thrown was studded with glinting blades.

Jack drew back the hand that had thrown it, and de Gex's jerked toward him at the same instant, for the two were now joined by a silken cord that had been spooled about this curious throwing-weapon. Jack's other hand now came down. It was swinging a sword with a curved blade. The tip of it slashed the dagger out of de Gex's hand, and severed the cord. The dagger skittered away and was lost in darkness.

De Gex showed, now, that he had studied the art of defencing at some point in his life, for he spun away from Jack even as Jack wheeled into position to guard Eliza. His left, or dagger-, hand had been mangled by Jack's sword-stroke, but his right was still hale. With it he drew out a small-sword. He faced Jack, who had a watered-steel blade of Turkish design in his right, and nothing in his left. This would have created a reasonably even match, were it not for the fact that they were surrounded by armed men on horseback.

"Greetings Eliza," said Jack, "supposing that is you. I am back in your life, for better or worse, and I forgive you for harpooning me. Once you prophesied I should never look on your face again. To this point, it holds true, for I must keep a sharp eye on this de Gex until he and I have finished our duel. But after that—"

Eliza, busy squirming free, did not answer.

"A duel would be lovely, Jack," de Gex was saying, "but a commander on a field of battle must not so indulge himself." He was holding up his bloodied left hand, beckoning to someone out of Jack's field of view. His slashed glove flapped like a black flag, dripping blood onto the pavement. Hooves could be heard approaching; one of the gentleman riders trotted in from the perimeter, and stopped, framed in the arch of light through which Jack had just passed. Their route of escape had just been cut off. Eliza got to her feet finally. Jack, whilst keeping his eyes fixed on the face of de Gex, had maneuvered round between the latter and Eliza, and stood now with his back to her, guarding her.

"Captain Shelby," de Gex said to the horseman, "have you a pistol?"

"Indeed, my lord."

"Is it loaded?"

"Naturally, my lord."

"Do you fancy you can hit that bloke, there, him with the Turkish sword?"

"It should pose no great difficulty, my lord."

"Then pray do so. Good-bye, Jack; and please know that Eliza shall very soon be joining you on the shores of the Lake of Fire."

The next sound was the report of a firearm; but it came from the roof of an adjoining town-house, not from Captain Shelby. The only sound that came from Captain Shelby was a distasteful spattering, as his brains showered the forecourt of the Opera, followed by a thud as his body, all but decapitated, tumbled out of the saddle.

"That was one English musket-ball," said a voice, oddly similar to Jack's, from the parapet of the Opera above. "We have more."

"Identify yourselves!" demanded de Gex, raising his bloody hand to shield his eyes from the glare of the building's entrance.

"You are in no position to give orders. But it suits my purposes to let you know that you have been surrounded by the First Company of the First Regiment of Dragoons of the Whig Association Militia, once known, and soon to be known again, as the King's Own Black Torrent Guards. We have been bivouacked not far away to defend Marl-borough House should the need arise, and were drawn here by all of your disorderly conduct."

"Then do you return to your post, Captain," said de Gex.

"I am a lowly Sergeant, alas."

"Then get thee to Marlborough House, Sergeant," said de Gex, "for I daresay it shall require some defending, before the night is through. What goes on here is no concern of yours; you are away from your post without leave."

"It is, if truth be told, of direct concern to me, sir," said the Sergeant, "being a sort of family matter. For unless my eyes are telling me lies, my brother, who has ever been a disgrace to the family name, is down there attempting to redeem himself, and repent, and redress his sins, and so on and so forth, by the ancient and honorable trial of single combat—for the honour of a fair lady, no less! I have sworn, many times in the past, that I'd slay my brother myself if given a chance. And perhaps I will someday. But I'll not abandon him to be slain when he is about to do something honourable for once in his life. So have at it; but if any of your Horse try to intervene, they'll be as dead as Captain Shelby. We are Dragoons, and to make short work of foppish cavalry is our bread and butter."

So spoke Bob Shaftoe. The mounted Jacobites below all heard him, and heeded him; but Father Édouard de Gex missed the last bit, for he had darted inside the Opera House. Jack had lit out after him. After only a moment's pause, Eliza called out, "Thank you, Bob . . ."

"No time for it. You hesitate on the threshold," Bob said, "one part of you saying go with Jack, another saying you've no need of such a Vagabond wretch in your life. *My* voice bids you go in, Eliza, if a Sergeant may command a Duchess. The rabble beyond the fires, there, does not have the discipline or the discretion of these Jacobite riders. In a moment we may have open war here. Get inside! Stay near an exit. If you smell smoke, drop to your hands and knees, crawl out of the building, and run in any direction as fast as you can."

Bolingbroke's House, Golden Square
THE SAME TIME

"WE POLITICIANS," quoth Henry St. John, Viscount Bolingbroke, re-filling his goblet with port for the eleventh time, "are like men who live in frosty climes. It is the habit of such men that whenever they have nothing else to take up their time, they hie to the chopping-block, take up the axe, and set to work splitting and stacking cord-wood. They do it even in the heat of August, for they are ever driven by the memory of having been cold once. You and I have each had our days of bitter cold, Roger, and so whenever we are not otherwise busy, we go to work stacking up our *political* cord-wood. Each of us has a mountain of it. Other men, seeing the size of the woodpile, would call it enough, and leave off chopping. But you and I know 'tis meant to be burned, and shall burn quickly once lit. This whole Realm that we call the United Kingdom is one great pile of cord-wood now, or rather two piles, one called Whig and one called Tory. They are so near to each other that one cannot be lit without setting fire to the other. All that is wanted is tinder, and a spark. London is packed with tinder to-night, which is your doing, and mine: the militias, and the Mobb. They have been gathering round their bonfires in Hay Market, Holbourn, Smithfield, and Charing Cross, as we have stood here and watched them."

As Bolingbroke said this he drew Roger's attention to the districts named, sweeping his arm from one great intersection to another. He spoke truly, for once. Overhead, the stars had come out. One minute they weren't visible, the next they were. But they did not flare out all of a sudden, but asserted themselves quietly, as shoals rose from the sea while the tide ebbed. London this evening had become a constellation of bonfires in like fashion; they had not been lit at any one instant, yet every time Roger turned around and looked, there were more of them. Entire districts were dark, but between and among them was laced a flickering and pulsing net-work of fire, strewn, stretched, and rent like an old cobweb. Roger knew that like an old cobweb it was rooted, sticky, tenacious, no easy thing to sweep away. Really it had been present all the time, but invisible, like the strands of spider-silk one walks into in the dark. Fire only lit it up, and made glorious its immensity.

He gazed far downriver, past the dome of St. Paul's and the Monument to an old citadel by the side of the river, with a high, four-turreted keep in the middle: the Tower of London. It was dim and quiet tonight, for the Mint was idle. Tower Hill, the belt of open ground surrounding the moat, was speckled with bonfires. Roger lifted his gaze from that distraction and found the dark bulk of Legge Mount, thrust out toward the troublous City like a fist. Thence he indexed round the Tower walls anti-clockwise until he found Bloody Tower and Wakefield Tower, which were joined together side-by-side like misshapen conjoined twins, looking out over the Pool of London from the center of the southern wall. On the roof of each, a signal-fire had been kindled. Two fires, small sparks, easily resolved from this distance. One might have been just a fire. But two were a signal, sent by one who had an excellent view of goings-on in the Pool.

"I don't much care for your firewood similitude, Henry," Roger said, "for it is too obviously meant to affright me. And moreover, I know what you are about to say next: that your pile of firewood is greater than mine. You cannot deter me now with such loose hob-goblin-talk about civil war. For as bad as that would be, what you propose in its place is worse: you would take us all the way back to the days of Bloody Mary."

"Not so, Roger, not so! His Royal Highness is a Catholic, true, but—"

"As to the other thing, I am not yet overawed by your forces and your powers. Princess Caroline, whatever you might phant'sy about her, is not in London."

Bolingbroke laughed. "But, Roger, you told me, only an hour ago, that you had seen her through my telescope!"

"But, Henry, I was lying." It was Roger's turn to take up the decanter and replenish his glass. As he did, he turned his gaze south toward Hay Market. A contagion of bonfires had lately been spreading up and down its length, threatening to link up with a larger nexus in Charing Cross. They were particularly hot around the Italian Opera, which troubled Roger, for he'd put a lot of money into it, and did not want it burned down by a Mobb. His old eyes could not resolve individual figures from here, but he could see patterns: round and among the fires, dark currents swelled, ebbed, swirled, and splashed: the Mobb, yet wanting any clear purpose. But currents of order and purpose moved through the chaos, like rivers in the sea: disciplined groups, probably militia. The sight of it, so near to his beloved Opera, threw him into a woozy fit, and reminded him how much easier it would be to surrender to Bolingbroke.

But then his eyes picked out a black corpuscle, moving up Hay Market with implacable purpose, gleaming like a bead of lacquer as it slalomed round bonfires. At the great cross with Piccadilly it made the turn that would angle it up Shug Lane toward Golden Square. He knew then that this was *his* phaethon, hurtling across London like a black panther through a forest fire. He could not know what message it conveyed; but something in its desperate speed gave him hope it might be good news.

"We shall soon enough see whether you were lying *then* or *now*," said Bolingbroke—who had taken a moment to regain his hauteur. "But I would speak to you of the other matter—of the Prince."

"George Louis of Hanover? Splendid chap."

"No, Roger. His royal highness James Stuart, who by right, even if not by law, is our next King." He held up a hand. "The Queen has made up her mind, Roger. She cannot, will not abandon her own flesh and blood. She will make him her heir."

"Then let him have the china, the silver, the furniture for all I care. But not Great Britain. We are past this, Henry."

"We are never past *what is right*."

"Sometimes I phant'sy I am speaking to a medieval relic, when I talk to a Tory," Roger said. "What magical quintessence do you suppose it is that imbues a Stuart with the right to reign over a country *that hates him* and *that espouses a different religion*!?"

"The question is, shall we be ruled by Money, and the Mobb—which are one and the same to me, as neither serves any fixed principle—or by one who serves a higher good? That is the *point* of Royalty, Roger."

Roger paused. "'Tis an attractive prospect," he said. "And I do understand, Henry. We are at a fork in the road just now. One way takes us to a wholly new way of managing human affairs. It is a system I have helped, in my small way, to develop: the Royal Society, the Bank of England, Recoinage, the Whigs, and the Hanoverian Succession are all elements of it. The other way leads us to Versailles, and the rather different scheme that the King of France has got going there. I am not blind to the glories of the Sun King. I know Versailles is better than anything we have here, in many ways that count. But for every respect in which we are inferior to France, some compensation is to be found in the new System a-building here."

"It is a bankrupt System already," said Bolingbroke. "Come, it grows chilly up here, I have certain matters to attend to in my study."

He insisted that Roger precede him through the door and down the attic stairway. Presently they came to a small study on the second floor of the house, which had a view over Golden Square that must be pleasant in the daytime. Now, Golden Square had a view of *them,* for Bolingbroke had left the curtains open, and many lights burning. On the rooftop observatory they'd had privacy; it had been like the backstage of a theatre, where actors banter, out of character, before they go on.

But now they were on. Their audience was everyone in Golden Square. This included some late arrivals, who'd just drawn up in a phaethon. Roger could hear an argument beginning to catch fire between one who had just emerged from the carriage, and a servant of Bolingbroke's who had gone out to meet them. Clasping his hands behind his back Roger ambled over to a window and looked down to see Sir Isaac Newton saying something peremptory to Bolingbroke's butler, who was nodding and shrugging a lot—but not budging. Daniel Waterhouse paced slowly back and forth behind Newton, seeming at once agitated and bored.

Meanwhile Bolingbroke had gone straight to a standing desk— which had been situated directly in front of another window—where a gloriously ingrossed document was laid out, complete in every particular save that it wanted a signature.

"Gentlemen do not speak of money, as a rule . . ."

"Beg pardon, Henry?"

"I was remarking a minute ago that your System is already bankrupt. I did not wish you to think me uncouth."

"Furthest thing from my mind. But I do say, it is a bit stuffy with all these lights burning—mind if I open a window?"

"Please make yourself comfortable *here,* Roger. It will soon be very warm for you everywhere *else.* I have here a warrant, to be issued by the Privy Council to-morrow, calling for a Trial of the Pyx."

Roger was standing sideways to Bolingbroke, sliding up the window-sash. It shuddered as it rose, and caught the attention of Daniel Waterhouse outside. Daniel glanced away for an instant, then snapped back to stare at Roger.

"It pains me to stoop to this, Roger. But the bankruptcy of the Whigs is *financial* as well as *moral* and *intellectual;* and the insolvency of their accounts and the debasement of their money is a menace to the Realm. It must out."

Roger scarcely heard this. It was more speech than conversation, and besides, he knew what Bolingbroke was going to say before he said it. Roger was trying to work out a way to exchange a few words, at least, with good old Daniel, who was but a dozen feet below and twenty distant. Daniel had a preoccupied look, and was moving about curiously on the street, apparently trying to work clear of some shrubs and tree-branches that reached between him and Roger's window.

"I am placing my signature upon the warrant now," said Bolingbroke above scratching noises. "You may be my witness."

Roger turned his head to watch Bolingbroke marring the parchment, making the quill hop and skip across the page, like a dancer *en pointe,* as he dotted the *i*'s and crossed the *t*'s.

Then something whacked Roger on the side of the face. It thudded to the floor.

"What did you say, Roger?"

Roger blinked haze out of the impacted eye, and squatted down to pluck the missile off the floor. He knew it immediately. Hefting it in the palm of his hand, he strolled over to the desk, where Bolingbroke was blotting ink.

"Henry, since you have such a fascination with coins and coining, I thought you might like to have this as a souvenir of this evening. You might like to take it off to exile in France."

"Exile in France? What on earth are you talking about?"

"Your future, Henry, and mine." Roger clapped the object—still warm from Daniel's pocket—down atop the gaudy Warrant. It was a leathern bundle, sewn shut, written on in ink, and heavy as only gold could be.

"A Sinthia from the Pyx," Roger announced. "There are more, many more, where this came from. Jack the Coiner is ours. He has yielded all, and told all."

The Italian Opera
THE SAME TIME

SERGEANT BOB HAD given her good counsel, which was to seek refuge in the Opera, and not be swayed one way or the other by the knowledge that Jack was in the place. She moved quickly through the lobby, trying not to spy herself in any of the mirrors. The pins that had held her hair up underneath the Caroline-wig had either been torn out, or had gotten skewed around so that they dug at her scalp and tugged at her hair. She drew them out as she ran and let them tinkle to the floor, then gathered up her loose hair and whipped it around into a loose overhand knot behind her neck. Music beckoned: a strange sound on a night such as this. It meant Order and Beauty, two items that were in short supply in London generally, tonight particularly. She moved toward it, skidding on a thin spoor of blood that, she guessed, had dribbled from de Gex's wounded hand. It led away through a little door in the corner of the lobby. This blood-trail had already been smudged, here and there, by footprints: Jack pursuing de Gex. So, if her desire was to watch those two men fight with swords, she knew which way to go. But more appealing was the music of violins and violincellos: the modern instruments that could fill a whole opera-house with sound, be the acoustics never so wretched. She passed through a grand gilded door and into a dim foyer, redolent of Mr. Allcroft's Royal Essence for the Hair of the Head and Perriwigs. From there she entered into the back of the auditorium.

The house was sixty feet wide, and fifty from where Eliza came in to the front of the orchestra pit, where a man in a wig was standing with his back to her, moving a staff up and down in time with the music. The floor was scored into semicircular tracks by low walls that sprang in concentric arcs from one side-wall to the other, all focused inwards on center front stage. It recalled a Greek amphitheatre, without the weather and without the Greeks. An aisle ran down the middle in a straight line connecting Eliza to the man with the staff. She began to walk down that aisle. Bob had recommended she stay near an exit, in case the theatre should be torched by the Mobb; but the musicians did not suspect they were in any peril, and she ought to warn them. It would have been reasonable to shout out an alarum from the back of the house. But theatre-etiquette had somehow taken over from street-instincts, and she was disinclined to make a fuss. By the time she reached the place where she could rest her arms on the top of the little parapet that enclosed the orchestra pit, the music seemed to be drawing to some sort of coda; the up-and-down movement of the conductor's staff became more pronounced, and when he feared that matters were getting out of hand, he allowed it to slip down in his grip, so that it produced an audible thump on the floor with every beat.

The music stopped.

"Herr Handel," Eliza said, for she had recognized the conductor, "pardon me, but—"

She was interrupted by a voice from the stage, incredibly loud. It was Sir Epicure Mammon in the latest fashions, prancing across a London square with his dodgy sidekick, Surly.

> *Come on, sir. Now, you set your foot on shore*
> *In* novo orbe*; here's the rich* Peru*;*
> *And there within sir,*
> *[gesturing at the front of a noble town-house fronting on the square]*
> *are the golden mines, Great Solomon's Ophir!*

Eliza cowered for a moment—those theatre-going habits again. Then she returned to the pit wall to discover Georg Friedrich Handel looking at her, a bit slack-jawed. Having confirmed that this really was the Duchess of Arcachon-Qwghlm, albeit in a state of *déshabille* only dreamed of by most gentlemen, he executed a perfect court-bow, deploying his conducting-staff as counterbalance.

"I am sorry, I did not understand that this was a full rehearsal!" she exclaimed.

Behind Epicure Mammon and Surly, a carpenter was kneeling down to tack a bit of stage-dressing in place, and to one side, a painter was daubing away at a *trompe l'œil* sky. Mammon scowled at her. She raised a hand to her mouth in apology.

"My lady," exclaimed Handel, reverting, in his astonishment, to German, "what has brought you here?"

"This night," insisted Mammon, "I'll change all that is metal in thy house, to gold. And early in the morning, will I send to all the plumbers, and the pewterers, and buy their tin, and lead up; and to Lothbury, for all the copper."

"What, and turn that, too?" asked Surly, expertly feigning amazement, but at the same time, somehow managing to favor Eliza with a wink; Mammon might scorn her, but Surly knew a beautiful woman when he saw one.

"Yes," said Sir Epicure Mammon, "and I'll purchase Devonshire, and Cornwall, and make them perfect Indies! You admire now?"

"No, faith," said Surly. But he muttered the line distractedly. Having Eliza below was bad enough; but, too, it was impossible to ignore the uncouth noises off from stage right: blurted exclamations, grunts, and ring of steel on steel. Even the musicians, who had been transfixed, for a few moments, by the apparition of a Duchess, had begun turning their heads to look.

The stage of the Italian Opera was uncommonly deep, making it famous among those who loved magnificent sets, and infamous among those who wanted to hear the words. A vast canvas had been stretched across the back of it, and painted to look like an idealized vision of Golden Square, stretching off into a hazy distance; before it, model town-houses had been erected, to perfect the illusion. It tricked the eye very well until a bloody, slashed-up man vaulted over the parapets and rolled to the ground in the deep upstage; he looked like a giant, thirty feet tall, fe-fi-fo-fumming around Golden Square and bleeding on the bowling-green. Which was most inexplicable, until a moment later the very fabric of the Universe was rent open; for a blade of watered steel had been shoved through the taut canvas upstage, and slashed across it in a great arc, tearing the heavens asunder. Through the gap leapt Jack Shaftoe; and then giants duelled in Golden Square.

Jack had a blade that would slash through limbs as if they were melons, but it was heavy and slow. With his tiny small-sword, de Gex could not slash, but he could poke a man through in five places before the victim could say "ouch." Jack kept humming his scimitar through the space separating him from de Gex, to keep the other from advancing in range for a fatal lunge. De Gex maneuvered round those terrifying cuts, though diverse slashes on his arms suggested he had only just avoided some. He was studying Jack, awaiting the one mistake that would give him an opening to lunge through.

Epicure Mammon and Surly had conceded center stage to the duellists, and now stood at the edges of the proscenium—bit players, forgotten. The painter and the carpenter were on their feet, each torn between fear of the blades, and lust to avenge the damage wreaked on their work by Jack and de Gex respectively. It presently became clear that each of the duellists had a strategy as well as tactics. De Gex was waiting for Jack to become exhausted, which must happen soon. Jack was backing de Gex towards the brink of the stage; this would put him in a position to be hacked to pieces, unless he wanted to chance a jump down into the pit. Understanding this well enough, the musicians had already gone into motion: the violins and woodwinds were crowding into the corner farthest from de Gex and filing out through a door, not far from Eliza, that gave access to the floor of the house. The cellists and bassists were trying to decide between saving themselves, and saving their instruments. Handel was absolutely disgusted. "Get back in your chairs, all of you! You are being paid for five acts, not two!" But de Gex's boots were already at the edge of the stage, his blood was dripping onto the kettledrums, with faint sounds like reports of distant cannons, and the pit was depopulated. Handel tried to collar a fleeing cellist, and wound up holding a cello. Eliza passed its owner on his way out as she was going in. For she feared Handel did not reck the danger. She rushed across the pit and divested him of the cello and set it down on its tail-pin, cradling its narrow neck in her hand. "Let us find a way out," she said. She reached to place her hand on his epaulet but grasped only air, for the composer was storming toward the kettledrums. "Let us leave these very dangerous men to—"

But all was now overturned in an instant. Jack had got de Gex where he wanted him, and was winding up for a death-blow, when the painter ducked in, and flung a whole bucket of white paint into Jack's face.

There was a moment of stillness. Then de Gex began hopping round into a new position: he'd been ready for a leap into the percussion section, and now needed to make a lunge for Jack's heart. He had nearly gotten ready when Handel, standing below him in the pit, tossed his staff straight up, caught the end of it in both hands, and swung it round in a mighty hay-maker, catching one of de Gex's shins with such violence that the blood-slick foot was knocked back and off the edge of the stage. The rest of de Gex shortly followed. He made a flailing backwards fall into a kettledrum. One leg and an arm—his sword-arm—ruptured the drumhead and ended up beneath him in the immense copper kettle. The other limbs sprawled over its rim like claws of a lobster that does not wish to be cooked.

Handel had been left off-balance by his mighty swing. De Gex lashed out with his free hand and caught the composer's lace cravat in a bloody grip. He jerked hard, desperately trying to pull himself out. Eliza reacted before she could think. Her free hand dropped to the bridge of the cello. She raised it on high as her other hand levered the neck down toward the floor, and she launched it across the pit in a high arc. It rotated as it hurtled through apogee, and came down like a javelin, its whole weight concentrated behind the tail-pin. When it stopped, it was sitting on de Gex's chest. It lodged there at an angle, emitting a spectral chord as the life sighed out of de Gex. He let go of Handel's cravat.

The composer picked up his staff from the floor and righted his periwig. "Fifth page, second bar!" he called out. But the musicians were slow to return.

Eliza looked up and found a burst of paint where Jack had been, and a trail of white footprints leading out to backstage and Unicorn Court.

She was thinking about the prophecy Jack had alluded to. *Jack* styled it a prophecy, anyway; in her mind, it had been more in the nature of a blunt promise. She had spoken it to Jack twelve years ago, in the *Petit Salon* of the Hôtel Arcachon in Paris, with Louis XIV as witness. Most inconveniently, she had forgot the exact wording of it. It had been something along the lines of that Jack would never see her face nor hear her voice until the day he died. Eliza being something of a stickler for promises and commitments, she now reviewed the last few minutes' events in her mind, and satisfied herself that this one had not yet been broken. At no time had Jack gotten a look at her, for his gaze had been fixed on de Gex the whole time, or at least until he'd gotten a bucket of paint in the face. And she had not spoken any words he was likely to have heard.

And now he was gone, and could neither hear nor see her.

She turned around to face the house. Musicians and Actors had withdrawn to the farthest corners, and were looking to her, as if for a cue.

"It is safe now," she announced. "Jack Shaftoe has left the building."

Golden Square
THE SAME TIME

"YOU TOLD HIM *WHAT*!?" said Daniel.

"You heard me," said Roger; then, when he had grown weary of Daniel's gape and stare, "*Really.*"

"*Really?* What does *that* mean?"

"You are so tediously parson-like sometimes. I think it must be the lingering influence of Drake."

"I am being *pragmatic*. What if Bolingbroke demands *proof* that we have Jack? I haven't the faintest idea where the man *is*."

"Daniel, look about you."

Daniel did. He and Roger were at a corner of Golden Square, down the way a bit from Bolingbroke's house, in a sort of caravan-camp of pricey coaches and good horses: the field headquarters of Whigdom. Isaac had already gone home in the phaethon. Mohawks were galloping hither and cantering thither proclaiming news, and shaking encyphered writs. The house of Bolingbroke was desolate: the curtains and shutters had been drawn, most lights had been snuffed, and it was not really known whether Bolingbroke himself was still in the place. Rumor had it he'd gone to his club.

"Behold," Roger said, "we have won."

"How do you know that!?"

"I can just tell."

"How?"

"I saw it in his face."

Roger excused himself, not by word, or by gesture, but by some-how changing, for a moment, the way his eyes looked at Daniel. He strolled over to a little war party of Mohawks who were standing near their horses, and addressed them: "We have won. Let the word go forth; light the beacons." He then turned round and began making his way toward some cluster of notables. The Mohawks behind him began hip-hip-hooraying, and pretty soon everyone in Golden Square was doing it.

Daniel was slow to take up the cheer. But when he did, he meant it. This was politics. It was ugly, it was irrational, but it was preferable to war. Roger was being cheered because he had won. What did it mean to win? It meant being cheered. So Daniel huzzahed, as lustily as his dry pipes and creaky ribs would permit, and was astounded to see the way people came a-running: not only the Quality from their town-houses, but hooligans and Vagabonds from bonfire-strewn fields to the north, to throng around Roger and cheer him. Not be-cause they agreed with his positions, or even knew who he was, but because he was plainly enough the man of the hour.

Billingsgate Dock

A BIT LATER

"It is a wonder," exclaimed Johann von Hacklheber, wrapping an arm tight round Caroline's waist, and lifting her off the brink of the wharf, "how many people will do favors for one who is expected to be the next Queen of England." He was ankle-deep in Thames-water on Billingsgate Stair; severed fish-heads nuzzled his boot and ogled Car-oline's bum as he toddled round and got in position to set her into the waiting longboat. She had her arm round his neck very tight, as if meaning to shut him up by stuffing one of her breasts into his mouth.

He did not complain, but only gripped her buttock that much tighter through her breeches. All of these mutual gropings could be excused on grounds that the Princess must not be allowed to fall into the cold stew of fish-innards that was Billingsgate Dock. It was a chancy maneuver; the night was dark and the steps slick. Johann thought he was being decorous enough. But the thirty or so men who had brought Caroline here, in a royal progress of coaches, sedan-chairs, and out-riders, were having none of it. They were all drunk as lords. As a matter of fact, to judge by the escutcheons gilded onto their carriage-doors, most of them *were* lords. There was no aspect of the scene on the stairs that was not suggestive, to them, of *something*.

"I smell fish!" one of them shouted. And there were a hundred other remarks, most of them a good deal more direct and to the point.

"Gentlemen!" Johann shouted, once Caroline was in the long-boat, and her tit was out of his gob. "We are at Billingsgate, it is true; but this does not mean you must try to out-do the fishwives in exe-cration. They are not here now. Return in the day-time and woo them then."

"I say, who *are* these fishwives?" exclaimed someone, so intoxi-cated that his tongue was swishing around in his mouth like a mop in a bucket. "He makes them sound like very merry wenches indeed." He snorted a great draught of that bracing fish-market atmosphere into his nostrils. "And I *do* fancy their perfume."

Johann was getting it from both directions now. "You are too cyni-cal, love," said Caroline from the longboat, "and now you see I am pouting like a great big fish. They are *gallant,* nothing more. They do not even believe I am a Princess! They think I am a whore who came for Dr. Waterhouse."

"They know perfectly well who you are," said Johann. He offered a bow, sarcastically obsequious, to the men of the Kit-Cat Clubb, who stood above them at the top of the stairs, all spread out in a tableau, but difficult to make out in the dark—like a group portrait of them-selves gone almost black from tobacco-smoke.

The bow was returned many-fold, but Johann saw none of it, as he had turned to vault over the gunwale into the longboat. Caroline was waving to them—somehow even *that* made them think of indecent things and spew libidinous ravings up and down the dock.

"We truly are safe from exposure now," Johann muttered. "For those men, when they are sober, shall be ashamed to relate this story, and no one would believe it if they did."

The longboat was unnecessarily large for its present mission, viz. to ferry a Baron and a Princess to a ship in the Pool. It had five oars on a side, and ten stout sailors to swing them. As such it could quickly out-distance a waterman's boat, or most other craft that might try to pursue them. Johann and Caroline sat up in the bow to stay clear of the rowers.

"I am glad you had the wit to come here directly," Johann said.

"Not so directly, for I was made to be the object of several toasts in the Kit-Cat Clubb," she said.

Indeed, the toasting was not over yet. Enough time had elapsed, since it had become evident that she was going to depart by water, for the following to have been improvised by one of the crowd of domesticated poets who went round with Kit-Cats.

> *Off the sea came Aphrodite,*
> *To the Greeks whose lust was mighty.*
> *Soft of wit and firm of P—,*
> *Romans worshipped foam-borne Venus.*
> *'Pon the River dark as wine,*
> *Rides Britons' love-queen, Caroline.*

"That is lovely," Johann said. "It appears that Dr. Waterhouse shall have some explaining to do, at his Clubb."

"As shall I," Caroline said, "to my husband."

From Billingsgate a lone wag was chanting

> *May her Womb*
> *Be Popery's Tomb*
> *But pray the German*
> *Keeps his sperm in.*

He was immediately shouted down by indignant, even scandalized Kit-Cats. *Really! Some* chaps knew no bounds! Someone drew a sword halfway, and made a great show of having to be restrained, all the while glancing river-wards to be sure his gallantry was being noted by Caroline. But the longboat had been swallowed by shadow, from their point of view. The sword-fight fizzled. The Kit-Cat Caravan began to mount up: and so the last they saw of the Clubb were scintillations of cut-crystal stirrup-cups and of the silver trays on which they were brought around, faint as gleaming of fish-scales on the black waters that lapped at Billingsgate Stairs.

"I pray that *we* are vanishing from *their* ken as much as they from ours," Johann said. "We are going downriver some miles to make rendezvous with a sloop that rides at anchor before Greenwich. If we board the sloop quickly and get underway without delay, perhaps no one shall know that your royal highness is aboard."

"It is all a great farce," was Princess Caroline's verdict. In the darkness she could not see Johann collapsing, but she could see the air coming out of him. "I am sorry," she said.

"On the contrary. *La belle dame sans merci* is a role that becomes you—'twill serve you well when you are Queen, and Greenwich is one of your country houses."

"I am being without mercy to *myself*," Caroline said, "not just to you. It was stupid for me to have come to England."

"On the contrary—you were not safe, in Hanover, from that assassin."

"That assassin, who followed me to London without the least difficulty," Caroline said, "and might be preying on Eliza at this very moment."

"She is my mother, you do not need to remind me," Johann said. "But she knew you as a little child. When has she ever held back from letting you know her mind? If she felt, or if I did, that your being in London was unwise, we would have said so."

"But I am entitled to form my own views. I say that I stayed too long."

"Naturally it will seem so, when we are departing in such haste—it would be better if you had left a week ago, in leisurely fashion. But we could not have anticipated any of this then."

"How long has it been since Sophie's funeral? Six weeks. By the time we are back in Hanover, make it seven or eight weeks."

"That is not such a terribly long time for a grief-stricken Princess to be absent from Court."

"From Court and from Husband."

"Husband has other ways of sating himself."

"I wonder about that," said. "After what happened that night, can he have kept Henrietta Braithwaite as *maîtresse-en-titre*? Or will he have sent her packing, and acquired a new one? Or—?"

"Or what?"

"Or will he be looking forward to the return of his long-absent wife? His letters, lately, have been more interesting."

"More interesting than *what*? Or than *who*? Stay, you need not answer, we have gone into a place where angels fear to tread."

"It is a place where you went, knowingly and willingly, when you wooed a married Princess."

Johann was silent.

"There, you see? Now again I am *la belle dame sans merci*. I hope you fancy her."

"That I do," Johann said, "stupid plodding knight-errant that I am."

"Brave magnificent shining knight," Caroline said, "who needs to keep his visor closed, when he is whingeing."

That was the end of conversation for a while. The row down the Thames was long. Caroline struggled against drowsiness, and fought the urge to nestle up against Johann. Some of the time, negotiating the crowded Pool was a bit like running through a forest in the dark. At other times, watchmen on anchored ships mistook them for mudlarks, and shone lanterns at them, and aimed threats and blunderbusses their way. But as they rounded the bend before Rotherhithe and swept down along the Isle of Dogs, the ships became fewer and larger. Though the oarsmen were tired, the boat picked up speed, as it could now run down the current on a straighter course. Now that they had broken free from the noise and clutter of the city, they perceived small matters that before would have been lost among other impressions: bonfires being kindled upon hilltops, and riders galloping down the streets that flanked the river to right and left. It was impossible not to phant'sy that the fires and the riders alike bore strange information out of the city, into the country and down the river to the sea. Signal-fires on Channel cliffs might even speed news to the Continent this night. But what the news consisted of, and whether it be true or false, could not be known to the refugees on the longboat.

The transfer to the sloop went quickly, as Johann had hoped. The anchor was taken up and sails raised to catch what feeble breeze there was. Thus began a strange night-journey down the river, which to Caroline was a continuation of the longboat-passage, with everything spread out on a larger field: for queues of bonfires continued to grow across the countryside, radiating outwards from the city, and not a minute went by that her ears did not collect the faint report of galloping hooves on the post-road. In the end she only lulled herself to sleep by telling herself that this sloop, gliding silently down the dark river bearing a mysterious passenger, must be as sinister and disturbing to the riders on those horses, and the watchers on the hilltops, as *they* were to *her;* and perhaps with good reason, since (as she still had to remind herself) she intended to rule the country some day.

Sophia, *Mouth of the Thames*
MORNING OF THURSDAY, 29 JULY 1714

HANOVER WAS LANDLOCKED. Its greatest body of water was a three-mile-wide puddle. The rich might invest in, the rash might sail on, proper ships; but they had to travel abroad to Bremerhaven first. For most Hanoverians, the preferred way of getting to the other side of a body of water was to wait for it to freeze, then sprint across. *Sophia,* the sloop that Caroline and Johann had boarded in the dead of night off the Isle of Dogs, was technically a Hanoverian vessel, in that she carried impressive-looking documents asserting that she was. But the crew consisted mostly of boys from Friesland, the skipper was an Antwerp Protestant named Ursel, and the lads who had muscled the oars of the longboat last night had been hired, along with the boat, from a Danish whaler that was having her hull scraped in Rother-hithe. Those Danes were now waking up with sore backs in East London. Much water, some fresh and some brackish, had passed beneath *Sophia*'s keel in the meantime.

Left to form her own opinions, Caroline might have judged that they were now out in the sea, and well on their way to Antwerp. The fog made it impossible to see more than a stone's throw in any direction, but *Sophia* was being shouldered from one brawny roller to the next like a child being passed around by a crowd at a hanging. The temperature had dropped (which, as the Natural Philosopher in her knew, must account for the fog), and the air smelled different. But that this was pure landlubberly foolishness could be known by watching Ursel, who was no happier, here and now, than a Hanoverian, half-way across the Steinhuder Meer, when the ice he is treading on begins to crack and tilt. "*This* is why no one does this," he said to Johann, in a pidgin halfway between Dutch and German.

The second *this,* taken in the context of all that had happened in the last several hours, probably meant "to sneak out of the Pool in the middle of the night so that the Customs officials at Gravesend shall not board the vessel, inspect her cargo, and receive their customary gratuity, and then to run down the Hope, navigating by sounding-lead, in hopes of squirting past the fort at Sheerness before dawn so as not to be blown out of the water by the coastal artillery situated there for that purpose or overhauled by naval vessels sent out to run down smugglers." All of which looked to have been accomplished, to landlubberly eyes. A huge bell had bonged nine times, not long ago, and one of the mates, who knew the Thames, had identified it as the Cathedral in Canterbury. To Caroline, who had studied maps, this suggested they were well clear of the river's channel.

It was less clear what Ursel had meant by the first *this*. It was something so bad as to render self-evident the folly of having attempted the second *this*. Caroline looked at Johann. He was even more exhausted than she (for Caroline had slept and he had not), and more sea-sick to boot. It was clear from the look on his face that he did not know anything more than she did about the nature of the first *this*. And so Caroline stopped looking to him for answers, and watched the Frieslanders. They were very busy with sounding-leads, on port *and* starboard; one would think, to watch them, that *Sophia* was under assault by swimming pirates with daggers clenched in their teeth, and her only weapons were these slugs of lead on the ends of ropes. She had seen this procedure done before. Usually it took a good deal longer, as the lead took some time to strike bottom, and the rope had to be drawn back up one double arm-length, or fathom, at a time. *These* chaps were tossing their leads several times a minute, and calling out fathom-soundings without even bothering to draw in the lines. The numbers sounded funny in the dialect of Friesland; but they were small numbers.

She worked her way round the poop-deck rail toward Johann. "They all began to get terribly excited when the cock crowed."

"I heard no cock crow," answered Johann.

"Because you were crowing at the same moment."

"I beg your pardon?"

"Vomiting," she explained. "But a cock did crow, distinctly, over there." She waved vaguely to starboard.

Johann managed a confident smile. "Do not worry. Sounds carry strangely in fog. It could have been miles away. Or perhaps it was aboard another ship."

A cow mooed.

"The cock-crow could have a second meaning as well," Caroline pointed out, "no less troubling than the first: namely, that the fog is lifting." She had to raise her voice and lean closer to Johann, because Ursel had begun screaming. Like expert flautists, who could use the trick of circular breathing to play long continuous notes, Ursel had the ability, oft seen among sergeants, schoolteachers, wives, and other leaders of men, to scream for several minutes without letting up to replenish his lungs. "He has had an epiphany," Caroline said. "For quite a while, we wandered lost in the fog. Now, suddenly, he knows where we are."

"Yes," said Johann, "the wrong place." Which was so obvious that it was bad form for him to have mentioned it. For the issue of all Ursel's shouting, and the exertions of the sailors, was that *Sophia* came about, and, after a pause to carve her initials in the mushy bottom-sand with her keel, began to make head-way along a new course. In a few minutes' time, the soundings began to aspire past five, nay, even six fathoms. Of livestock the calls became less distinct, and the smell was replaced by that of creatures with fins and shells. The sky brightened from gray, to silver, to gold, and Caroline began to sense its warmth, faintly, on her lips, as she sensed Johann's body heat on cold nights in her bedchamber. Finally they emerged from the fog altogether. A shadowy blot off their port beam resolved itself into a Royal Navy brig paralleling them, and going about the task of opening up her gunports.

"At other moments during the execution of the present Plan I have had occasion to question whether it had been well-wrought; and yet troubles resolved, and we got *this* far," Johann said. "I shall pray to God and trust in Providence that this is not as bad as it would plainly seem on its face." *His* face was red: in some circumstances, adorable, here not a good sign.

"Poor Jean-Jacques. As out of place here as a rooster."

"If we could have *galloped* to Hanover, I would have so arranged it," he admitted. "But it is not for *you* to show concern for *me* in this pass."

"If we are overhauled, I shall put on the black sash that says I am in this country *incognito*," Caroline said. "*Somewhere* on yonder brig must be an officer, a man of breeding, who shall know what it means."

"The *incognito* worked for Sophie when she would go to visit Liselotte in the halcyon days of Versailles," Johann brooded, "but to expect Tories and Whigs to observe such a quaint conceit, in present circumstances, is like asking two gamecocks to toast the Queen's health before they commence slashing. No, I think I shall have to take responsibility, if it comes to that."

"What does *that* mean? You shall claim that you kidnapped me and brought me to London against my will?"

"Something like that."

"It is foolish. I will simply deny that I am who I am."

The discussion went on thus, tediously, circularly, and without result, even as the skipper Ursel was carrying on a parallel exchange with the captain of the Royal Navy brig. By signal-flags, the brig ordered *Sophia* to allow herself to be overhauled. *Sophia* affected not to see, then, not to understand, the message; the brig stiffened it with a cannon-shot across *Sophia*'s bow. *Sophia*, which by now had maneuvered into broader and deeper waters off Foulness Sand, raised sail, and began to make run for it by sailing closer to the wind than the square-rigged brig was capable of. This got them several miles nearer the open sea, for the wind was generally out of the east, which was the direction they wanted to go. They zigzagged, sometimes sailing a few points north, sometimes a few points south, of due east. The brig did likewise, but had to take wider and more pronounced zigzags, which ought to have made it slower. So it looked favorable for *Sophia*, at least by this simple account. But as the morning wore on, it became evident to Caroline (who was observing closely, as she looked forward to inheriting a Navy) that this was very much a devil-in-the-details sort of matter. The brig was capable of moving through the water faster than *Sophia*, so the difference in net speed was not quite as great as all that. And the brig had a proper pilot aboard, who knew where the shifting sands at the mouth of the river were *today*. Whereas Ursel had to work from a chart that had been printed ten years ago and was now a palimpsest of confusing hand-drawn cross-hatchings, and angry and emphatic notes in diverse Northern European languages. On account of which *Sophia*'s actual course, far from being the stately zigzag she would have traced across deep blue water, was a jangled fibrillation about due east, careering to one side or another whenever Ursel phant'sied they were approaching some peril rumored on the chart, or when the trend of the soundings was inauspicious, or the color of the water or the texture of its surface did not please him. Much time was spent, and much of *Sophia*'s forward momentum pissed away, in frequent course-changes, even as the brig loped easily back and forth across the estuary, plotting each tack to pierce invisible gaps between the Middle, the Warp, the Mouse, the Spile, the Spaniard, the Shivering Sand, and other Hazards to Navigation too small or too ephemeral to waste names on. It was altogether tense, chancy, and perilous, and so ought to have been thrilling. Yet it stretched out over half the day, and as much as an hour would sometimes go by without anything in particular happening. It was a bit like sitting by the bedside of a loved one with a grave illness: momentous, all-consuming, yet boring, hence exhausting.

In the end exhaustion caught up with Ursel. Or perhaps he had simply been outmaneuvered by the brig, which late in the morning began to draw within firing range of *Sophia,* and seemed as if she might be trying to get into position to fire a broadside. Forced suddenly to choose between cannon-fire and shallow water, Ursel chose the latter, and promptly ran *Sophia* aground on a ridge of ooze that in retrospect was implied by a squiggle on the chart. They were between Foreness and Foulness, in a place where the way was above twenty miles wide, and a river only in name; the entire eastern half of the horizon consisted of ocean, a full one hundred and eighty degrees of mockery to the poor skipper. When Caroline asked Ursel what they ought to do next, Ursel informed her that he was not competent to offer an opinion, for he was a skipper of ships, and *Sophia* was no longer that, but a wrack, owned not by Hanover but by whomever first happened along to salvage it. Then he retreated to his cabin to drink gin.

"Well, I know nothing of Admiralty law," said Caroline, "but this looks more ocean than river to me. I say we are on the high seas, minding our own business."

"We are *aground,*" Johann insisted.

"Then we *were* on the high seas minding our own business," Caroline said, "when along came that nasty brig and forced us to run aground. It is an act of piracy."

Johann rolled his eyes.

"We were on a pleasure cruise out of Antwerp when it happened," Caroline went on.

"What, and just happened to cross the North Sea by accident?"

"Blown off course in the night by that unusual easterly wind. Happens all the time. Come, don't be difficult! Last night in London you said I must do deeds beyond your scope. Re-writing history is a royal prerogative, is it not?"

"So 'twould seem, if you read much history."

"Who do you phant'sy is the more inventive writer: Queen Anne, or the woman before you?"

"*That* laurel goes to *you,* my love."

"Very well. In a trunk belowdecks is a Hanoverian flag. Run it up the mast. Let us show our colors, that all ships passing by may plainly see what rank piracy is committed this day by the Royal Navy!" And she struck a royal enough pose in the bows, gesturing with an arm to the waters spread out before them, which were flecked with sails of great ships.

"If it pleases your royal highness," Johann said.

"It does. Hop to it."

In response to *Sophia*'s having run aground, the brig had to conduct certain maneuvers that occupied close to half an hour: viz.

breaking off her tack, coming about, reducing sail, and making slow head-way to a point in deeper water some half a mile distant where she could tarry long enough to deploy a longboat without having to worry that wind, current, or tide would drive her aground. By the time all of these things had been achieved, *Sophia* had run a large set of Hanoverian colors to the top of her otherwise bare mast. And this seemed to give the brig's skipper second thoughts. For the arms of the House of Hanover were so close to those of the royal family of Great Britain as to be indistinguishable from this distance. The brig might be menacing *Sophia* with open gunports and run-out cannons; but Princess Caroline had just pressed a loaded pistol to the fore-head of the brig's skipper.

Last night, perhaps, some messenger, despatched from London by Bolingbroke, had galloped into the fort at Sheerness and presented this captain with an order to scour the estuary for such-and-such a sloop, and to capture the foreign spies aboard it. Which might have sounded straightforward enough at the time. Bolingbroke's seal dan-gling from the document, the exhausted post-horse blowing outside, the spattered and red-eyed messenger, the urgent missive in the dead of night: just the sort of thing ambitious naval officers prayed for. He had done his duty well this morning. But now something had gone awry: he had been presented with an opportunity to think. The royal arms rippling from the mast-head of the grounded sloop gave him much to think *about,* and much incentive to think carefully.

The brig's longboat was lowered, but not manned. Then it was supplied with oarsmen; but there seemed to be a debate in progress on the poop deck as to which officers should venture out. Was this a boarding-party? A rescue mission? A diplomatic envoy? Were the pas-sengers on the sloop foreign spies, fleeing smugglers, or the future owners and admirals of the Royal Navy? It was not the sort of situa-tion that lent itself to speedy resolves.

And it only grew more complicated. For immediately after *Sophia* had shown her true colors, one of the great ships passing from the ocean into the Thames had altered her course, and had been grow-ing ever since: a tiered battlement of white canvas spreading wider and looming higher by the minute. This thing was to the brig as a bear to a bulldog. She had three masts to the brig's two, and more courses on each mast, and more deck to carry cargo or guns—but mostly guns, for she was (as rapidly became obvious) an East India-man, hence not really distinguishable from a warship. She had at least thrice the brig's displacement. Farther up the Thames, her size would have put her at a disadvantage, but there was adequate room to maneuver here, at least, provided one had accurate charts and knew how to use them. This East Indiaman seemed every bit as confident as the brig in steering around unseen shallows. This despite the fact that she was not an English ship at all, nor a Dutch, but—as became clear, when she finally ran out *her* colors—

"*Mirabile dictu,*" said Johann, who had two-fistedly jammed a prospective-glass into his eye-socket. "What are the odds that two Hanoverian ships should meet?"

"What are the odds that *there would exist* two Hanoverian ships?" Caroline returned. She wrested the glass from Johann, and spent a minute admiring the Indiaman's figurehead: a bare-breasted Pallas, poised to bash her way through seas with her snaky-headed Ægis.

"My mother invested in a ship once," Johann said, "or rather Sophie did, and Mother handled the numbers."

"Let me try to guess the name of that ship. *Athena? Pallas? Minerva?*"

"That was it. *Minerva.* I thought she was in Boston, though."

"Maybe she was," said Caroline. "But now she's here."

Orney's Ship-yard, Rotherhithe
31 JULY 1714

"SHE IS A FAIR ENOUGH young lady, composed, civil, even when being man-handled off a sandbar by a boat-load of Filipino and Laskar swabbies. But, I was greatly relieved to get her off of my ship."

Otto van Hoek had the skin and the disposition of a hundred-year-old man, and the vigor of one closer to thirty. He had a steel hook in place of his right hand, and when he was distracted or nervous he would paw at things with it. Taverns, chambers, and cabins habituated by van Hoek sported sheaves of scratches on tabletops and walls, as if a giant cat had been there sharpening its claws. Now he was scoring the lid of a packing-crate lately off-loaded from *Minerva.* It rested on the wharf of Mr. Orney's Ship-yard in Rotherhithe. The address read

✠

Dr. Dan'l WATERHOUSE
Court of Technologickal Arts
Clerkenwell
London

✠

The planks of the lid were already scored half through, for van Hoek kept his hook sharp, and it had been a long and anxious morning for him. *Minerva* was in the dry-dock: a ditch slotted out of the bank of the river and walled off from it by doors wrought of whole tree-trunks. These, though they creaked alarmingly, and leaked copiously, held back the River. *Minerva* was propped up on many timbers rammed into the dry-dock's mucky and puddle-pocked floor. Her hull put Daniel in mind of a potato that has been left too long in the cellar and sprouted many tendrils, for one could phant'sy that the ship had thrust out a hundred bony legs below the water-line and crawled up out of the river. He had supposed that putting a ship as large as *Minerva* in dry-dock must be a stupendous operation extending over weeks, and had hoped that he'd arrive in time to see its opening phases. But it had been over and done with when he'd walked into the yard at eleven o'clock in the morning, and the only record of the adventure was a hundred parallel hook-scratches in the lid of this crate.

"I know that there is a—"

Daniel had been about to say *superstition*. "—a tradition that it is unlucky to have a woman aboard ship."

Van Hoek considered it. Van Hoek considered *everything*, which made it difficult to engage him in idle chitchat. "The first woman who spent any amount of time aboard this ship was Elizabeth de Obregon, whom we salvaged from the wrack of the Manila Galleon at the same time as him who burned it, one Édouard de Gex."

"He's dead, by the way."

"Again? I am glad to hear it. After that voyage, we did come in to some bad luck, to be sure; but I would have to be some sort of imbecile to blame it on the lady de Obregon, when the cause was obviously the malice and cunning of de Gex."

"That is just," Daniel said. "So you are not a believer that women are bad luck on a ship?"

"Such a belief would be difficult to reconcile with the well-established record of success of the Malabar pirate-queen."

"And yet it made you uneasy to have Princess Caroline aboard.

But I suppose there were *other* reasons for that. From the sounds of it, the Navy was after her."

"We had been tarrying in certain coves and inlets of Essex, frequented by smugglers—"

"I know those coves well," said Daniel with a smile, "it is where my father made his fortune."

"On the night of the 28th we received word that it was safe for us to enter the Thames—for the information that the Whigs were gaining the upper hand had been transmitted from London, at great speed, by signal-fires. I felt confident of this, or I should never have approached the Nore in the first place. When I spied that Navy brig harrying that sloop, I guessed that her skipper simply had not received word of the changes that were afoot in London. And indeed, as we made our way upriver with the Princess, we presently saw more than one Navy ship flying an ensign bearing the arms of Lord Berkeley—a Whig."

"And yet *still* you were glad to get her off your ship."

"Certain cargo is more trouble than it can possibly be worth," said van Hoek, and turned away from Daniel to regard *Minerva*. Cranes and windlasses were at work hoisting stout boxes of round river-rocks and cannonballs out of her bilge.

"You are not speaking only of Princesses, I detect," Daniel said.

"It was only meant to act as a sort of buffer, to see us through lean times," van Hoek said. "As a merchant keeps silver plate in his home, which may be melted down and coined when liquidity is wanted, so we have had those gold plates in our bilge. Not a single Customs inspector has ever suspected they were there. Most of our seamen do not even know. From time to time we would coin a little. I had no inkling we were in such peril."

"The only reason it *was* dangerous was that the Master of our Mint has an especial interest in this type of gold. As long as you did not coin it, you were safe. But to strike even one guinea and place it into circulation was like firing a pistol into the air in a church."

"Before he was arrested, Dappa said you had devised some scheme whereby we could extract the value of this gold without coining it," van Hoek said, "but beyond that, his discourse became murky. I thought I should hear the story from him during the passage to Boston; but of course we were forced to flee without him."

"Briefly, we have a buyer in Muscovy who will buy the gold from us, once we have altered its form in a particular way."

"You are going to make something out of it?"

"Yes, and then he will buy that something, and pay for it in *ordinary* gold. Or such was the plan, on the day Dappa was kidnapped, and you sailed for Boston."

"Do you mean to say there is a *new* plan now?" asked van Hoek, and made a deep gouge in the crate-lid.

"There *might* be," Daniel said. "Your erstwhile partner—"

"Jack?"

"Jack. Jack seems to have struck a deal with the Master of the Mint. Perhaps the danger I spoke of has passed. It might not be necessary to ship this gold—" and Daniel nodded at *Minerva* "—to Muscovy after all."

"It is of no account to me whether the Tsar or the Master buys it from me, provided we get the cursed stuff off our ship," van Hoek said, "but you had best make up your mind quickly." He had turned his gaze toward the river. Daniel turned around to espy a many-oared vessel crawling across the water, bearing directly for Orney's wharf.

"That is a very odd thing to see on the Thames," Daniel remarked. "What flag does she fly?" For van Hoek had unlimbered his prospective-glass.

"The double eagle. She is a war-galley of the Russian Navy," van Hoek said. Then, after a moment's pause, he laughed at the absurdity of such a thing.

"Come to collect the three warships that Mr. Orney has been building," Daniel surmised. "A great day for Mr. Orney!"

"And for Dr. Waterhouse?"

"It is all good. This is as I have expected."

"You do not say that with as much sincerity as I would like."

"I am not insincere, but distracted. Much has happened in recent days. The matter is far more complex than I have let on."

"Stab me! They do grow them big in Russia."

"What do you mean?"

"That man on the poop deck! If the others around him are of normal stature, then that is the biggest man I have ever seen. How he towers over that poor man who is getting the noogies!"

"You have me at a disadvantage. May I—?"

With some reluctance van Hoek handed over the perspective glass. Daniel found a place where he could brace it against the side of a piling, and arranged it so that he could get a view of the on-coming galley. She was still a bow-shot away from Orney's wharf; the oars continued to pulse, but more and more slowly as she lined up for the last few strokes. Daniel found the poop deck, which was exceptionally high, as was common with military galleys. Right away he saw the man van Hoek had been talking about. To judge his height rightly was made difficult by the presence of several dwarves around him. But there were some who seemed to be of normal stature: one pacing along the rail wearing an admiral's hat, after the French style. An old man with a long gray beard and a bald head protected under a dome of black felt. And a third about whose neck the tall man had wrapped one arm. Only the top of his bald pate was visible, as the giant had him bent forward in a headlock, and was rubbing the knuckles of his other hand over the poor fellow's skull. The broad grin on the giant's face, and the glee on the dwarves' faces, suggested it was all in good fun; the way that the victim hopped from toe to toe, and flailed his hands around, suggested he took a different view. Finally the big fellow released him, for the galley was now manuvering to the wharf, and passing between a pair of brand-new frigates riding at anchor before Orney's, which he seemed to find interesting. The victim scurried over and snatched up his periwig, then straightened his posture (slowly and judiciously, for he was an old man) and placed the adornment on his head. Not until he had patted it into place was Daniel able to focus distinctly on his face.

Daniel sighed.

"What is it?" van Hoek asked.

"Everything has suddenly become very complicated."

"I thought you said it was complicated *before*."

"Yes, I rather thought it was—before His Imperial Majesty Peter the Great showed up with Baron von Leibniz."

"That is the Tsar?"

"So I am guessing."

"What's he doing here?"

"I know not. But he is attired as a mere gentleman, with a black sash, hence *incognito*."

"Perhaps he has been routed by the Swedes, and fled here to exile."

"It does not have that air about it. A vanquished refugee does not show up attended by Dwarves and Philosophers."

"Why's he here, then?"

"I hope it is a whim."

"Why?"

"Because if it is not a whim, then it probably has something to do with *me*."

"I REGRET THAT I missed the funeral of Sophie," said Baron Gottfried Wilhelm von Leibniz. He had been on English soil for about an hour. Leibniz had never been precisely *handsome,* and never would be. But in the years since Daniel had last seen him, he had developed creases in his face, and shadows that went with his dark eyes, and (once he had put his wig on, and covered up the Tsar's knuckle-prints) at least made him look serious and formidable.

Peter was inspecting one of his new warships, accompanied by most of his entourage and by the startled but game Mr. Orney.

"Those who know and love you anyway, assumed your absence was for good reason," Daniel said. "Those courtiers who hold other opinions of you, had those opinions bolstered—if they noticed you were missing at all."

Leibniz nodded. "In May I had been summoned to St. Petersburg to work on the establishment of the Russian Academy of Sciences," he explained.

"Funny that *I* never get summoned on such errands."

"It is not all as delightful as you suppose. The place is literally and figuratively a swamp. Peter wants to do everything personally." Leibniz nodded at one of the new ships, which was still on the ways, ready to be launched; Peter was clambering up the rat-lines like a three-hundred-pound fly in a monstrous web, leaving his entourage on the deck below, helpless to do anything but cringe or applaud. "When he is out of town fighting the Swedes," Leibniz continued, "which is most of the time, then nothing happens at all. Then, when he returns, he is outraged that his projects have stagnated, and wants everything done immediately. The result, anyhow, is that I could not work out a way to leave." Here Leibniz trailed off and turned to look in the direction of the Tsar. His attention had been drawn thither, not by some sudden noise, but by its sudden absence. Peter Romanov had reached the mizzen-top and struck a pose there, peering through a perspective-glass as if he were commanding a naval engagement in the Baltic. As a matter of fact (as Leibniz had already mentioned to Daniel) he had been doing exactly that only a few days earlier, and his galley had the cannonball-holes and bloodstained decks to prove it.

But now Peter's glass was aimed, not at the distant sails of some Swedish fleet, but at the two aged Natural Philosophers conversing in Orney's yard below.

"Uh-oh," said Leibniz.

"His Tsarish Majesty has commanded that the plates be brought forth," confided Mr. Kikin to Daniel. For Kikin had dashed out from London as soon as he had got word that a Russian galley was approaching Rotherhithe and, to his credit, had only been struck catatonic for thirty seconds or so after he had walked into the ship-yard to be confronted with the spectacle of the Tsar of All the Russias debating the fine points of hull design with Mr. Orney. Now, he was acting as English interpreter.

"Which plates would those be?" Daniel asked.

"The very same ones we shipped to him, late in June," Kikin said.

Up and out of the war-galley's hold now came a solemn, and yet gaudy procession. First to emerge was the wig, the head, and then the body of a young gentleman, presumably of Peter's household. But he seemed to have been pressed into service as a sedan-carrier, for his arms were straight down to his sides, and in each hand was the end of a pole, carven of an immense tusk, and capped at the end with gold. Close behind him emerged the burden supported by those ivory poles: not a sedan-chair after all, but a box. To call it a box was like calling Versailles a hunting-blind, for this object was wrought mostly of amber, and what was not amber was ivory or gold. At a glance, from a distance, Daniel guessed that the finest jewelers in Christendom had devoted years to carving it. Not that his old eyes could resolve the details from here; he could just tell that it must be so, for this seemed to be how Peter went about things. Succeeding the amber chest, and supporting the aft ends of the tusks, was an outlandish-looking chap whom Daniel pegged as a Cossack. And bringing up the rear was the elderly man with the long gray beard and the black skullcap whom Daniel had noted earlier standing next to Peter on the poop deck. He was a Jew. What made Daniel realize as much was his juxtaposition against this phantastickal box-on-poles, which looked like nothing so much as the Ark of the Covenant, re-interpreted by Russians, and re-wrought in Nordic media and French styles. It was borne through a hushed entourage and set down upon a crate.

Leibniz cleared his throat and spoke in a voice meant to be heard by all. "The plates for the Logic Mill, which you were so good as to send us some weeks ago, arrived at the Academy in St. Petersburg on the tenth of July (reckoning it in English dates). Your humble servant, and His Tsarish Majesty's other representatives" (here he seemed to be looking at the old Jew) "have examined them thoroughly and reported to his majesty that they are in order." Kikin was trying to relate all of this in Russian, but Peter seemed to know more or less what was being said, and went over to the amber box. He lifted its lid and made as if to toss it aside; the Cossack intercepted it before it struck the ground, bowed, and backed away. Peter reached into the chest's velvet-lined interior and drew out several of the plates. The gold flashed in the midday light. Mr. Orney cringed and lifted his gaze to the public road that ran along the inland side of his shipyard. A sizable picket-line of mudlarks, freelance longshoremen, thief-takers, Black-guards, Vagabonds, bridle-culls, baggage-men, foot-scamperers, and runagates had already formed up there, like flies on the rim of a cider-glass.

Daniel was struck by a change in the appearance of the plates: while generally they seemed to have been well-treated, each of them was missing a piece. Someone had systematically sheared a fingernail-sized piece off the corner of each plate.

The Tsar noticed that Daniel had noticed. "I commanded Monsieur Kohan to assay the plates," he explained via Kikin, and nodded at the aged Jew.

"Solomon Kohan at your service," said the Jew in English. Beyond that, he had to resort to Latin to make himself understood. "Since none of the plates had holes punched in the *corners,* I reasoned that these corners were of no importance to the workings of your Logic Mill. And so I cornered, or quoined, each one of them, to try the fineness of your gold, as commanded by Cæsar."

All of which made sense to Daniel except for the reference to Cæsar. Then he recollected that "Tsar," or "Czar," was simply a rendering into Russian of that ancient Latin title.

"And what did you report concerning the quality of the gold to Cæsar?"

"The truth, of course."

"Of course. But different men have different views as to what truth is, and I would fain know yours, sir."

"No. The entire point of the assay is that it is not subject to opinion, taste, or debate. It is what it is."

"You invoke the Tetragrammaton. And yet men may dispute the meaning even of *that.* What were your findings?"

"The same as yours, I'm sure."

"That gold is gold?"

Peter broke in now, and there was a pause as Kikin translated: "The Tsar has decreed that, since the finest gold on earth was used to make the *first* batch of plates, with which he is well pleased, the *remainder* of the plates are to be made using the same stuff. What the hell do you suppose he means by that?"

Leibniz rolled his eyes. "Some have put it into his head that there exists a superior form of gold." He regarded Solomon Kohan none too benignly.

Meanwhile Peter had been unburdening himself further. Kikin translated: "Every plate sent to St. Petersburg henceforth shall, before it is accepted, be quoined in the same manner by Solomon Kohan."

"For your sake, and for your friend's," said Solomon to Daniel, with a glance toward Leibniz, "I hope you have an adequate supply of this type of gold."

"Perfectly adequate, thank you," said Daniel, and nodded at *Min-*

erva. He let a few moments elapse for Kikin to translate. By the time Daniel was ready to resume speaking, all the others had followed his gaze, and marked certain members of *Minerva*'s crew bringing up out of her hold flat packets of something heavy, wrapped in sack-cloth.

"Is that a Vroom?" asked Peter in Dutch. "She is a beauty."

"Indeed!" broke in van Hoek, who had been loitering on the edge of the crowd, "she is the last ship that the great Vroom ever designed, and if his Tsarish Majesty would care to—"

"I would," said Peter, and then he and van Hoek went off ranting in Dutch ship-jargon for some minutes. A lot of throat-clearing and eyebrow-wiggling on Daniel's part finally penetrated the awareness of van Hoek, who with reluctance brought the Tsar's attention back round to Daniel.

"Months ago," Daniel announced, "we set in motion work that has culminated, within the last few days, in the arrival of that Vroom that his Tsarish Majesty is admiring. She brought the gold that is to be used for the completion of the Logic Mill. It is being down-loaded at this very moment . . ." here Daniel trailed off, for Peter was already bounding across the muck of the yard to intercept one of those burlap bundles. Kikin ran after him, translating as he went, and the rest of the group hustled along behind. Daniel found himself bring-ing up the rear, alongside Solomon Kohan.

"It is curious," said Daniel, "that you take so keen an interest in this matter."

"It is curious," returned Solomon, "that *you* incorporate such gold into your device and expect that it shall go unnoticed by the Wise."

Solomon stared at Daniel with eyes that rarely blinked and that were such a pale gray as to be nearly colorless, though they were rimmed and flecked with black. His features were generally Semitic. This gave Daniel the idea that Monsieur Kohan had been born with dark eyes, befitting his race, but that they had become washed out and faded over time, like garments that have seen too many washings and too much sun. Immersed in that gaze, Daniel felt like a lump of sugar plunged into a stream of warm water. He was at a loss to answer, and so trudged across the churned muck of the yard in silence until he and Solomon had re-joined the group. All were gathered round a bundle that Peter had wrested from a barefoot seaman, thrown down on a barrel-head, and slashed open. The package was perhaps a foot and a half wide, four long, and an inch thick. Peeled bare, it was re-vealed as a metal plate, scratched and speckled, but unquestionably gold. Solomon muttered something in Hebrew. Peter regarded it with mild curiosity. "He says it looks like any other gold," Kikin explained.

"As how could it not," Leibniz said, "as there is no difference—" but here he was cut off by a sudden commotion. Mr. Orney, who as a rule was not the sort of chap one looked to to disrupt any proceedings with spontaneous outbursts, had thrust his way into the middle of the group, gathered up the dangling shreds of burlap, and begun trying to cover up the exposed gold as if it were no less shocking to him than a naked woman. Peter watched the frantic efforts of the Nonconformist with the same hungry curiosity as he applied to everything else, and asked Kikin a question. Kikin explained, gesturing to the scores of fascinated loiterers watching from along the road, from the branches of nearby trees, and from the roofs of houses. Suddenly Peter understood, and looked back at Orney, seeing him in a new light, and comprehending the reason for his pronounced nervousness. The Tsar looked over toward a formation of some two dozen Cossacks who had been prowling around the perimeter of the yard, and shouted some command at them.

"*Nyet!*" Kikin exclaimed; but the Cossacks were already fanning out towards the road, drawing sabers.

"What did he say?"

" 'Kill them all,' " Kikin said, and then began trying to explain to the Tsar something complicated that the Tsar was not in any sort of mood to learn about. Anyway, half of his words were drowned out by noises off. Cossacks were at large, and the game was afoot, in Rotherhithe, and the amount of shouting and screaming was prodigious. Peter plainly enough told Kikin to shut up. Kikin looked around pleadingly. Daniel spoke, catching Peter's eye briefly, afterwards staring at his belt-buckle. "So lax is the treatment of criminals here, and so disorderly is this country as a result, that even if his Tsarish Majesty had brought a whole *regiment* of Cossacks, and put everyone within a mile radius to the sword, the security of Mr. Orney's establishment could not be vouchsafed once the sun set, if the gold were known to be here. It must be transported to safekeeping in London. We could summon wagons; or—" and he nodded at the Russian galley.

"The Doctor's proposal is accepted," announced Kikin in due course. "Aboard the galley is yet more gold: some to pay Mr. Orney for the ships, provided they pass a thorough inspection, and some to pay the Institute of Technologickal Arts for the next phase of the Logic Mill. All of it must be conveyed safely to various places in London. His Tsarish Majesty has therefore decreed that the special gold from *Minerva* be transferred into the galley immediately. We shall then set out for London, all of us."

Van Hoek relayed all of this to his crew. Meanwhile Orney said:

"As much as part of me is pleased to see the blood of the *Mobile* running in the gutters of Rotherhithe, I would respectfully beseech Brother Peter to summon the furry chaps with the sabers back to the confines of my property."

"It shall be done," said Kikin after the usual pause; though Daniel thought Peter looked just a bit wounded. But then the Tsar's face screwed itself around as the result of some sort of neurological cock-up, and the moment passed.

Billingsgate Dock
LATER THAT DAY

PETER SPIED A queue of massive coal-wagons before the steelyard of Billingsgate, and decided that these were a better way to convey tons of gold around London than the frail coaches and sedan chairs scurrying like cockroaches up and down the river's banks. And so all commerce in fish and coal was suspended for an hour as the galley forced its way into Billingsgate Dock. It was most inadvisable for anyone but a visiting Tsar. Anyone the least bit English-looking would have been torn limb from limb by the fishwives the moment he stepped onto the wharf. Daniel—who *did* happen to be English-looking—was paralyzed by anxiety throughout this maneuver. But within thirty seconds of the Tsar's leaping from the gunwale of the galley to the scaly lid of Billingsgate Wharf, he was in the driver's seat, and holding the reins, of an empty coal-wagon. Its owner, seeing Peter stride toward him, had simply flung the reins at the Tsar's head and jumped out. Later he tossed the whip up in case Peter had need of it. The fishwives, too, were strangely compliant; they abandoned their stalls and lined up along wharf's edge to enjoy the spectacle. *That,* Daniel realized, was what enabled Peter to get away with it: not that he was the Tsar (for no one knew this), but the pageant of his coming. It did not matter how much business these people were losing; any money they made to-day would be spent to-morrow, but this event was one they'd tell tales of for as long as they lived. Moreover, the place was after all a Market, not a Palace, Parliament, College, or

Church. Markets drew a particular sort of person, just as those other places drew different sorts. And the sorts who found a market a congenial and rewarding place to be, were those who thought quickly on their feet, and adapted to unlooked-for happenings with facility; they were, in a word, mercurial. The driver of that coal-cart had perhaps ten seconds in which to make up his mind what he ought to do. Yet *he had decided.* And probably rightly. Daniel noted at least one purse being tossed at him by an aide of the Tsar.

They drove through the streets of London in this wagon, made to carry chalders of coal, now creaking under as great a mass of gold, Cossacks, and Natural Philosophers. The load was lightened somewhat on Threadneedle Street, where the gold that was to pay for the ships was deposited into the vaults of the Bank of England, and credited to an account controlled by Mr. Kikin. After that Daniel was made to sit in the driver's seat next to Peter, so that he could supply directions to Clerkenwell Court.

Kikin had been relegated somehow to the back of the coal-cart, where he was conversing in Russian with Solomon Kohan and a nobleman who seemed to have some say over affairs financial. Peter and Daniel, lacking an interpreter, batted sentence-fragments back and forth in diverse tongues until they settled on French. The Tsar spoke it passably, once he had set his mind to it; but to discourse in a second language demanded more patience than Peter generally had. Sensing as much, Daniel limited his remarks to the likes of "turn left at the next corner" and "to run over pedestrians is frowned on," &c. But after a while his curiosity got the better of him. Partly it was that they were passing along the back of Bedlam, and Daniel was terrified that Peter would take an interest in it, and go inside to learn all about lunaticks. *"Alors,"* Daniel said, "that Solomon Kohan is an interesting chap. Where on earth did you find him?"

"The Sack of Azov," Peter replied. "He had wandered there for some reason, and was dwelling in the Palace as a guest of the Pasha, when we laid siege to the place. Why do you ask?"

"Er . . . I don't know, really. Call it a commoner's curiosity as to how an Emperor goes about assembling his staff."

"There is no secret. Find the best people and don't let them go."

"How did you know that Monsieur Kohan was one of the best people?"

"The sheer quantity of gold we found on his person," Peter said, "served as his credentials."

They exited London at Cripplegate and thereby passed within a block of Grub Street. Yet they were not noticed, which confirmed in Daniel's mind a doubt that had been nagging him about newspapermen, and their choices as to what to be interested in, which struck him as bizarrely random. Though, as they worked their way to the west, he began to understand how it was that a gigantic Tsar could drive a coal-wagon full of gold and Don Cossacks through the city without attracting all that much notice. They were drawing nigh to Smithfield, with its connotations of cattle-drives, meat-markets, burnings at the stake, and seekers after violence. Many of the bonfires that had been lit on Wednesday evening were still burning now, on Saturday; for die-hard Tory Mobbs had persisted in clashing with their Whig counterparts all day Thursday, even as Ravenscar had been pressing his advantage on the loftier fronts of Whitehall and Westminster. Those disturbances had insensibly blended into the usual riotous panoply of the Hanging-March yesterday. So Smithfield, and all to its west, were now one vast smoking reeking aftermath. Peter had spoken of the Sack of Azov; Daniel wondered if it had looked anything like what they were now driving through. Shopkeepers and residents were beginning to place doors back on hinges, shovel human turds out of their forecourts, &c., but the place was still infested with feckless young men. Daniel mentally sorted these into such categories as armed irregulars, phanatiques, Vagabonds, and hanging-watchers—hasty judgments all, built on slight evidence. Any commerce-minded person passing through here must find it impossible to believe that any œconomically productive activity ever happened in England at all. And yet England prospered, and Peter knew it; how could he reconcile it with the evidence before his eyes?

"This place used to lie beyond the edge of the city," Daniel explained, "and bloody-minded young men would come here to practice at sword-play, or even to fight. This was more than a hundred years ago, when it was the fashion to have a wee shield on the left hand—a buckler. The sound of rapiers swashing against bucklers could be heard from far away, when they fought. Young men of that mentality came to be known, in the vernacular, as—"

"Bucklerswashers! Yes, I have heard of this," said Peter. "Which way do I go here?"

"Take the left fork, if you please, your Tsarish Majesty," Daniel said, "and then straight on to Clerkenwell."

> As for sense supernatural, which consisteth in revelation or inspiration, there have not been any universal laws so given, because God speaketh not in that manner but to particular persons, and to divers men divers things.
>
> —HOBBES, *Leviathan*

Upon arrival in Clerkenwell Court, Daniel discovered that Roger Comstock, or someone claiming to speak for him, had quartered two squadrons of Whig Association cavalry in the Court of Technologickal Arts: one Mohawk, the other normally coiffed. He was past caring, and no longer capable of being surprised by anything. It was fortuitous. The Templar-tomb made an impressive vault, with its new set of ironbound doors. The presence of the cavalry only made it seem that much better suited for storing a pile of gold, in Peter's eyes.

Daniel had been steeling himself, on the drive over, for a long day or two of explaining all of the marvels and oddities on view in the Court of Technologickal Arts—for really it was the worst kind of Peter-the-Great-bait. But most of the *ingénieurs* and projectors who frequented the place had locked their stuff up, or taken it away, when they had moved out to make room for the cavalry. So there was relatively little on view. Peter did venture underground for a cursory inspection of the Templar-tomb. But the ceiling was too low for him, and he seemed as bored as any other royal on any other ceremonial inspection, which gave Daniel the idea that hidden vaults of bizarre ancient military-religious sects must be altogether common and unremarkable in Russia. Solomon Kohan showed more interest in it than his boss. And so while Baron von Leibniz and Saturn (who had recovered admirably after having been rousted from bed at saber-point) showed the Tsar some of the machinery pertaining to the Logick Mill, Solomon and Daniel sat round a slate sarcophagus down below, and oversaw the transfer of the gold plates from *Minerva* into the Tomb of the Templars. This was a matter of weighing all that was brought down, and pricking down the weights in ledgers, and getting all of the numbers and the sums to agree: not especially demanding labor for two men such as these. During lulls they engaged in Solomon Kohan's idea of small talk:

"This is an interesting place."

"I am pleased you find it interesting."

"It puts me in mind of an operation I used to have in Jerusalem a long time ago."

"Now that you mention it, the full name of the Templars was the Knights of the Temple of Solomon. So if you are *that* Solomon—"

"Do not play word games with me. I refer, not to this hole in the ground, which is but an indifferent crypt for long-forgotten knights, but to what lies over."

"The Court of Technologickal Arts?"

"If that is what you call it."

"What would *you* call it?"

"A temple."

"Oh? Of what religion?"

"A religion that presupposes that we may draw closer to God by better understanding the World that He made."

"That being the only evidence available to us, you mean, as to what He was thinking."

"Available to *most* of us," Solomon allowed.

"Oh? Is there a *rest* of us who have *other* ways of knowing God?"

"In truth, yes," Solomon said, "but it is dangerous to say so, for almost all who claim to belong to this *rest* are charlatans."

"How gratifying, then, that you judge me fit to partake of this secret. Does this mean you have found me worthy to distinguish between the majority of charlatans and the minority of—"

"The Wise? Yes."

"Does that mean I am Wise?"

"No. You are not Wise but erudite. You are a member of the *Societas Eruditorum.*"

"Leibniz has spoken of it, but I did not know I was a member."

"It is not like these guys," Solomon said, rapping a knuckle on a Templar-sarcophagus, "with bylaws and initiation-rites and such."

"Are you a member?"

"No."

"Are you Wise?"

"Yes."

"Which means you have ways of knowing things that we erudite fellows don't. *We* have to be satisfied with practicing our religion."

"You make it sound unsatisfactory. Change your mind about this. It is better to know why you know things than simply to have things revealed to you."

"Enoch Root—is he Wise?"

"Yes."

"Leibniz?"

"Erudite."

"Newton?"

"Hard to say."

"It seems as though Newton just knows things. Finished knowledge appears in his head—no one else can make out how he did it; and no one else has a chance in hell of doing what he did."

"Yes."

"Is it a black-and-white distinction, Wise versus Erudite, or shades of gray? If I get lucky on some days, and a good idea pops into my head, am I being Wise?"

"You are partaking of the quality of Wiseness, or Wizardry, or whatever it is called in English."

"How many Wizards are there just now? You, Enoch, that's two. Possibly Isaac."

"I have no idea." But here Solomon was distracted by a faint noise from the direction of the stairs. He and Daniel looked that way, expecting to see a Cossack bearing more gold; but instead it was Saturn. He stepped toward them quietly. Daniel had no idea how long Saturn had been in the room with them, how much he might have heard. "Are you two quite finished with your sums?" he asked weakly.

"They are not all that difficult," Daniel returned. "Why do you ask? Is there some need of us?"

"Monsieur Romanov is anxious to go."

"Oh, really? Where does he wish to go all of a sudden?"

"During a lull in the conversation," said Peter Hoxton, "we heard the sounds of a crowd assembling in Hockley-in-the-Hole. He inquired. I made the mistake of telling him that it was most likely a bull-baiting. Now he ardently wishes to go and see it."

"Then who are we to keep him waiting?"

A Tavern, Hockley-in-the-Hole
LATER

"Two savants and a Jew walk into a bar . . ." Saturn began.

"I beg your pardon?"

"Never mind."

"Most people would call me a mere Natural Philosopher, not a savant," Daniel corrected him. He nodded across and down the table at Leibniz. "Now *he* is a savant."

"Yes," Saturn agreed, "and so is *he*." And he nodded toward the entrance of the tavern.

Daniel looked up just in time to see Sir Isaac Newton come through the door.

When the bull-baiting had concluded (the bull had lost), Peter the Great had insisted on buying a round of drinks, and turned to Saturn for a recommendation as to taverns. They had paraded into this place.

It had been Daniel's observation that all Public Houses fell into two categories, viz. ones that were much smaller than they looked from the outside, and ones that were much larger. This was one of the latter type, which was a good thing for several reasons. Item, that even when it had been shorn of Cossacks, dwarves, and other impedimenta, Peter's entourage still numbered a dozen. Item, that two of them (Peter and Saturn) were very large blokes. And item, that when Isaac suddenly walked into the place, Daniel at least had a few moments to compose himself as he made his way to the back.

Daniel and Saturn were sitting next to each other, facing the windows and the front door. Leibniz and the Tsar were on the opposite side of the table.

"Why would *he* suddenly show up here?" Daniel wondered.

"When we were at Clerkenwell Court," Saturn said, "the Tsar sent out a message. It seems that when he visited London some years ago, Sir Isaac gave him a tour of the Mint, which made a lively impression on him. Today when he saw the equipment we have made for handling the gold, he remembered this, and took it into his head that he wished to renew his acquaintance with that curious chap who once showed him around the Mint."

Peter stood up and turned around, which obliged everyone else to stand up, too. The exact moment of the meeting between Sir Isaac Newton and Baron Gottfried Wilhelm von Leibniz went unobserved by Daniel, who had become so upset that the blood stopped flowing to his brain for a little while; he remained standing, though, and his eyes stayed open, but it was as if his consciousness had gone into a total eclipse for half a minute or so.

When he was next aware of his surroundings, Saturn was tugging gently at his sleeve. Daniel looked round to discover that he was the only one still on his feet. The Tsar had moved around to Daniel's side of the table to make room for Isaac. Daniel wedged his skinny pelvis into the slot between the two Peters, Hoxton and The Great, the largest men in the room. Facing them across the table, Newton and Leibniz sat side-by-side in the most awkward arrangement imaginable. They were silhouettes against the window-light, and perhaps it was some small act of mercy that Daniel could see nothing of their facial expressions, only the shapes of their periwigs.

Through Kikin, Peter the Great said to Newton: "I thought of you today."

"I am honored, your Tsarish Majesty. May I ask in what connexion?" Newton's head-silhouette angled slightly toward Leibniz. He was guessing it had something to do with the calculus. And so imagine his surprise at Peter's response:

"Gold! I have never forgotten the day you showed me the Mint, and explained how gold flows to the Tower of London from every corner of the world to be made into guineas there. Today I have taken part in that currency. I have brought *ordinary* gold from Russia to your Bank, and *heavy* gold from the ship *Minerva* to Dr. Waterhouse's vault around the corner."

Lengthy was the silence of Newton. Daniel sensed, though he could not see, Isaac's gaze on him. His face was warm, as if feeling the heat of Isaac's wrath, and he wondered if his skin was still capable of turning pink.

Damn it anyway. This matter of the Solomonic Gold (he reminded himself) was not Daniel's affair. He could not care less about it. As a favor to Leibniz, whose name was being dragged through the mud every day by Newton, and as a way to further his own work on the Logick Mill, Daniel had brokered a one-for-one swop of normal for "Solomonic" gold that had finally and improbably been consummated within the last few hours. *Minerva* was at last free of her cursed burthen. Jack Shaftoe was well on his way to being free of the threat of prosecution and punishment for his past work in coining that gold. The stuff was sitting in the Templar-tomb now, legally under Ravenscar's control, but effectively Daniel's to do with as he pleased. Daniel had been working toward this moment for some months now, and ought to have been hoisting a glass or two in carefree celebration. There was this one complication, having to do with Isaac's notions about Alchemy; but Daniel had gotten better, with age, at accepting and ignoring the quirks and difficult peculiarities of his friends, perhaps even unto the point of self-induced blindness, and so he had not considered this very much until now.

What had ruined it all was the appearance of Monsieur Kohan. Most likely he was a lunatick; but indisputably he knew about the so-called Solomonic Gold, and looked forward to the day when every last ounce of it would be delivered to his custody in St. Petersburg. Whether or not Alchemy was claptrap, *some* believed in it, and some of them happened to be important, even dangerous. It might have been foolish for Daniel to have swallowed the phantastickal conceit that the heavy gold was infused with divine quintessence. But it would have suggested safer actions, which, had they been taken, would have led to simpler ends.

"That is a very remarkable thing, your Tsarish Majesty," said Isaac, "and explains much that until this moment has been obscured from me."

The front door of the tavern was kicked open. A huge man was standing there.

All went black, which Daniel, given his age, and his level of anxiety, was inclined to put down as resulting from the sort of devastating neurological event that was normally followed in a few minutes or hours by massive swelling of the brain and death.

On second thought, he was perfectly fine. Saturn had gripped the edge of the table and flung it up in the air whilst rising to his feet. The table—twelve feet long, and a hundred pounds of thick fir deals—had flipped up to create a barrier between all those sitting on that side of it, and the tavern's entrance. But only for an instant; then, as Newton might have predicted, gravity had its way, and the table fell edge-first to the floor. The number of toes broken on impact would be difficult to estimate, for it came down in between the two rows of men who had been sitting across from each other. Daniel looked down to see a quivering shaft, eight feet long if it was an inch, embedded in the tabletop. It had struck the table with such violence that its honed steel tip (for it seemed to be some sort of spear, or harpoon) had penetrated the entire thickness of the wood, and burst out the other side for an inch or two, creating a little wigwam of splinters lit from within by the gleam of the metal. Standing up (for everyone was getting to his feet) and bending forward a bit to see the other side, Daniel got a moment's horrifying glimpse of a human head impaled and spiked to the table. Then he understood it was nothing more than Leibniz's periwig. For the harpoon (it was clearly a harpoon) had passed through a narrow space between the two greatest brains in the world, albeit closer to Leibniz's, so that it had snagged the outer bulwarks of his out-moded, double-wide wig, and stripped it clean off his pate. The missile would have hurtled over the table and straight into the Tsar's chest if Saturn had not had the presence of mind to flip the table up.

So now there was a second awkward silence. The harpooneer was still standing in the doorway, in a deflated posture. His beard was almost as long as that of Solomon Kohan. One of his arms had been truncated near the elbow and enhanced with a prosthesis, which looked heavy.

"It is him," cried Mr. Kikin, "Yevgeny the Raskolnik! Where is my bodyguard when finally I need him!?"

"You do not need him, sir," said Saturn, stepping over the table, and reaching down to grip the shaft of the harpoon, "for as a long-time resident of Hockley-in-the-Hole, I take it as a personal affront that such incivility has been shown to our guest." He jerked the harpoon-shaft free from its steel head, which was going to remain embedded in the table for a long time. "I do view it as a personal obligation to now stave in the head of this Yevgeny." Saturn took a step towards the door, and Yevgeny took a step back, to get out in the clear and gain some melee-room; but Saturn's attack was arrested when a hand even larger than his closed over the harpoon-staff, and took it from him. "Your willingness is duly noted by his Tsarish Majesty," Kikin explained in a hurry, "but the conflict is strictly a Russians-versus-Russians sort of affair, most difficult to explain, and honor dictates that it be settled without embroiling our gracious hosts. Pray be seated and talk amongst yourselves." And he rushed out the door in pursuit of the Tsar.

Further developments were obscured by the crowd that gathered instantly around any conflict in this district, be it bulls vs. terriers or Tsars vs. Raskolniks. Out the window they could see only a lot of blokes' backs. Owing to the exceptional height of the combatants, they were from time to time able to glimpse a whirling quarter-stave, a hurtling flail, or a spray of blood silhouetted against the sky. But for the most part the progress of the duel had to be guessed at from watching the spectators, who moved in curious sympathy with the combatants. In much the same way as a man playing at lawn-bowls will twist and lean his body this way and that, as if he could thereby influence the course of a ball that has already left his hand, so those fight-watchers, almost in unison, juked and jived their shoulders and pelvises this way and that as they saw an opportunity to strike a blow, or cringed, smarted, and groaned when one was struck.

Saturn had been quite let down when Peter had disarmed him and gone forth into the fray. He did not recover for a minute or so; then, bewitched by the eldritch sympathy that conjoined all of the spectators, he squared his shoulders and headed for the exit, saying: "It has been great fun having the Tsar here *incognito,* but I suppose it was inevitable that word would get out and that this sort of thing would start to happen."

Of the group who'd been sitting round the table, the only ones now left were Daniel, Isaac, Leibniz, and (in the corner, a bit removed from the others) Solomon Kohan. The table itself, of course, was still resting on one edge.

"Had I not heard it direct from the Tsar," said Isaac to Daniel, "I could never have credited such a conceit: that, after all that has passed between us—"

"All that has passed between me and you, Isaac, is as nothing compared against the doings and machinations and skullduggery attending the damned gold. As to myself, I no longer give a fig where it goes. I would have been happy to give it all to you, until a few hours ago, for I phant'sied you were the only man on earth who knew of it, or cared."

"And what has changed so much in the last few hours?" Isaac asked, quite shocked.

"There is now, in the Ointment, not merely a Fly, but a Praying Mantis," said Daniel, nodding in the direction of the Peter-melee, "and one equipped with a mind that is excellent, not only by the standards of Mantises, but of men. He has claimed the Solomonic Gold. I am sorry."

Daniel now gave a few moments' thought to whether he should try to introduce Solomon, and how; but Isaac had got to his feet and stalked away. As Isaac went out the tavern-door he brushed past a chap who was coming in. Though this was not the most noble person who had ever set foot in the establishment (an honor that would have to go to Peter, or—who knows?—Solomon), he was unquestionably the best-dressed, and identifiable, from a thousand yards, as a courtier. Daniel, pent up behind the table, waved one arm in the air until he got the attention of the newcomer, who approached, looking befuddled. "Was that—?"

"Sir Isaac Newton? Yes. Daniel Waterhouse at your service."

"Frightfully sorry to intrude," said the courtier, "but word has reached the Household that an Important Man has come to London *incognito.*"

"It is true."

"From Muscovy, 'tis said."

"Also true."

"The Lady of said Household is deathly ill. On her behalf, I have come to greet the said Gentleman, and to observe the requisite formalities."

Daniel nodded out the window toward the melee. "As we say in Boston: get in line."

"Look for the chap in the sable hat," said Leibniz in French, "that is the chamberlain, you may take it up with him."

The courtier bowed and left.

"As may be obvious," Leibniz said, "my coming to London was brought about by *force majeure,* and was not part of any coherent plan. But as long as I am here, I thought I might stay on a bit, and try to patch matters up with Newton."

"Then I am sorry to tell you," Daniel said, "that your timing could not have been worse, for this matter of the gold will make it all much more complicated than you appreciate."

He was afraid he would now have to enter into discussion of Alchemy; but Leibniz nodded and said, "I knew a gentleman in Leipzig, also very interested in this gold."

"The heavy gold is of great political importance here, in that it could mean the difference between Newton's surviving a Trial of the Pyx, or not." And here he was forced to explain a great deal concerning Jack the Coiner, Bolingbroke, and the Clubb.

On balance, Leibniz seemed to take it as good news: "It sounds as if this difficulty can be cleared up, then. If this deal that you negotiated with Jack goes through as planned, Newton shall get what he requires to survive the Trial of the Pyx; and if not, why, how difficult can it possibly be to track down this gang of coiners when Newton, Waterhouse, and Leibniz are numbered among the thief-takers, and when two of the master-criminals—Édouard de Gex and Yevgeny the Thief-taker—have recently been slain in brawls?" For it was plain that the melee outside was over, and if the Tsar had lost, they probably would have heard about it by now.

"I find it difficult to believe, Gottfried, that, at this point in your career, what you really want to do is hang around the worst parts of London pursuing a band of criminals."

"All right, I admit it's only a pretext."

"What then is your *real* reason?"

"I would attempt, one last time, to attain some reconciliation with Newton, and to settle the calculus dispute in some way that is not squalid."

"A much sounder and nobler motive," Daniel said. "Now, let me explain to you why it shall not work, and why you should simply go home." And then he did, against his better judgment, discourse of Alchemy for a little while, explaining that Newton's desire to control the Solomonic Gold arose not simply out of a practical need to survive the Trial of the Pyx but out of a quest to obtain the Philosophick Mercury and the Philosopher's Stone.

But it was to no avail. It only confirmed Leibniz's desire to remain in London. "If what you are saying is true, Daniel, it means that the root of the problem is a philosophical confusion on Newton's part. And as I need not explain to you, it is the same confusion that underlies our disputes in the realm of Natural Philosophy."

"On the contrary, Gottfried, I think that the question of who invented the calculus first is very much one of the who-did-what-to-whom type; a what-did-you-know-and-when-did-you-know-it sort of affair."

"Daniel, it is true, is it not, that Newton kept his calculus work secret for decades?"

Daniel assented, very grudgingly. He was perfectly aware that to admit to any premise in a conversation with Leibniz would lead to a Socratic bear-trap banging shut on his leg a few minutes later.

"Who started the *Acta Eruditorum,* Daniel?"

"You, and that other chap. Listen, I stipulate that Newton tends to hide his work while you are very forward in publishing yours."

"And hiding one's results—restricting them to dissemination among a tiny fraternity—is a characteristic of what group?"

"The Esoteric Brotherhood."

"Otherwise known as—?"

"Alchemists," Daniel snapped.

"So the priority dispute would never have arisen if Sir Isaac Newton were not thoroughly infected with the the mentality of Alchemy."

"Granted," Daniel sighed.

"So it *is* a philosophical dispute. Daniel, I am an old man. I've not been in London since 1677. What are the chances I shall ever return? And Newton—who has never set foot outside of England—will not come to *me*. I shall not have another opportunity to meet with him. I will remain in London *incognito*—no one need never know I was here—and find some way to engage Newton in Philosophick discourse and help him out of the labyrinth in which he has wandered for so many years. It is a labyrinth without a roof, affording a clear view of the stars and the moon, which he understands better than any man; but behold, when Newton lowers his gaze to what is near to hand, he finds himself trapped and a-mazed in dark serpentine ways."

Daniel gave up. "Then consider yourself a member of our Clubb," he said. "You have my vote. Neither Kikin nor Orney shall dare withold his support from a savant whose pate still glows with the knuckle-prints of Peter the Great. Newton would doubtless vote against you. But he came to a separate peace with the Clubb's quarry a few evenings since, and no longer has any reason to attend our meetings."

YEVGENY THE RASKOLNIK had fallen like a tree in the dust of Hockley-in-the-Hole. From the looks of things he had given a fine account of himself. In this posture, viz. lying on his back, his face to the sky and framed in the iron-gray burst of his hair, it was obvious that he must be close to sixty years old. Had he been closer to Peter's age (the Tsar was forty-two) and in possession of both of his arms, the fight might have gone differently. As it was, Daniel could only interpret this as a spectacular form of suicide. He could not help but wonder whether Yevgeny knew about today's transfer of the gold from *Minerva,* and had somehow taken the notion into his head that, as a result, his time in the world was finished.

"This was an odd bloke, who was loyal to Jack for many years, but went his own way in recent years, and tried to burn the Tsar's new ships in Rotherhithe even as he was conniving with Jack to invade the Tower and sully the Pyx," Daniel explained to Leibniz. "He was a great villain. But it is a shame to see him, or anyone, lying thus unattended." At that moment, though, he spied Saturn approaching, with a few lads behind him and an empty wagon.

Daniel, Leibniz, and Solomon caught up with Peter and his entourage at Clerkenwell Court, just as they were mounting up to travel
back to Rotherhithe. Daniel sent with them a note to Mr. Orney, giving him the news that the incendiary who had attacked his shipyard
was dead. Leibniz took his leave of the Tsar, and Solomon promised
to rejoin the party later at Orney's. For it would take a few days to inspect and take delivery of the new ships, and to man them; then they
would sail directly into combat against the Swedes in the Baltic. Then
the Tsar and his company departed.

Daniel did not know why, but he now felt more energetic than at
any time in the last few weeks. Perhaps that was what made a Tsar a
Tsar: the ability to move those around him to great exertions. Perhaps the sight of the dead Yevgeny had reminded Daniel, as if he
needed it, that he should not live forever. Or perhaps it was a simple
desire to get the Solomonic Gold moving, to get it out of his possession as fast as he could. Others who toiled in the Court of Technologickal Arts seemed to feel likewise, for suddenly—after having
avoided the place for nearly a week, because of Whig/Tory strife and
Hanging-shenanigans—they began to show up and pry the planks off
the fronts of their little workshops around the Court and heave the
dust-cloths off their machines. Saturn came home, having seen to the
transfer of Yevgeny's body to a Russian church somewhere, and by
sundown the Court was in full production. They rolled, cut, and
weighed the largest batch of plates they had ever made in a single
day. Then Daniel pressed half a dozen idle but relatively sober Mohawks into service as escorts, and they took the plates down the
banks of the Fleet to Bridewell.

The very first cargo unloaded from *Minerva* upon her arrival on
Thursday had been the paper cards on which Daniel had, over the
course of a dozen years' toil at the Massachusetts Bay Colony Institute of Technologickal Arts, written out the tables of the Logick Mill.
These had already been forwarded to the card-punching workshop
in Bridewell, which now sported half a dozen organs.

"It's all right," insisted Hannah Spates, upon being rousted from
bed, "all the girls are accustomed to working nights anyway." And so
presently the shop was alight, and alive, with Hannah and five other
nimble-fingered girls working the keys of the organs, and several
pairs of big strumpets spelling each other on the bellows, fueled by
beer from a barrel that Saturn fetched from a brewery across the
ditch in Black Fryars. Some of the cards were punched even before
he returned with this enhancement, and a good many more after—
though Daniel insisted that the six women at the keys must remain
dry. The entire batch was finished before three in the morning, and

the banker William Ham, who'd been abducted by a Mohawk raiding-party from his bed in the city, did the sums, and weighed the cards and the bits that had been punched out of them, to the evident satisfaction of Solomon Kohan. The Jew had watched all with the keenest interest, but occasionally scowled at those aspects of the operation that looked as if they might be vulnerable to theft or embezzlement.

Daniel now presented him with a tiny purse sewn of the finest kid. It was no larger than a walnut, but plumped heavily in the palm of the hand, like a globule of quicksilver. "These are the tiny disks punched from the cards by the organs," Daniel explained. Solomon nodded; he had already observed how these motes of gold were harvested from the machines and weighed by Mr. Ham. "As a rule we take these back and melt them down to make more card-stock. To-night I make an exception and give them to you, Monsieur Kohan, as a memento of your visit to London, and a token of my esteem." Solomon clapped the wee purse between his hands and accepted the gift with a bow.

"Now," Daniel continued, "if you do not mind staying awake a little longer, you may see our provisions for keeping the finished plates safe until they are ready to be shipped to St. Petersburg."

Solomon said he didn't mind, so they loaded the chest of new plates into an open wagon and drove it through the streets of London, which were deserted save for the circulation of Vault-wagons to and from the brink of Fleet Ditch. Through Ludgate in the shadow of St. Paul's they entered into the city, and Daniel told the story of riding past Old St. Paul's, before the Fire, at the height of the Plague, when the City had been as empty and quiet as it was tonight, and the doomed church surrounded by a rampart of half-buried corpses. Presently they came out of the churchyard onto Cheapside and trundled east to the threshold of the money-district where the way forked into several streets: Threadneedle, Cornhill, and Lombard. They chose Threadneedle, and went up but a short distance to the fabrique of the Bank of England.

After a brief conversation with William Ham, the night porter suffered them to enter, and even offered to relieve Saturn of the burden in his arms: a strangely heavy locked chest. Saturn politely declined. William Ham dismissed the porter and sent him back to his bed. Lanthorns were distributed. Monsieurs Kohan, Waterhouse, Hoxton, and Ham moved through the Bank in their own pool of light, quickly leaving behind the parts of the establishment that looked like a bank (finished rooms with windows and furniture) and descending into its cellar.

By no stretch of the imagination could this be understood as a proper and rational basement. The ground under the Bank was a foam of cavities, some recent, some ancient, but mostly ancient. Most were connected to at least one other. This made it possible to navigate through the foam without resorting to shovels and blasting-powder, provided only that one understood the graph of their connexions. This was a job for a banker if ever there was one. Mr. Ham changed direction incessantly, but gave them all some reassurance by only rarely stopping to think, and only once backtracking. Anyone who had even a layman's knowledge of structures could see at a glance that, over the ages, more than one building had been erected on this site, and many a builder had stayed up late at night worrying about whether the foam could support it. The diverse vaults, arches, timbers, pilings, footings, and rubble-walls that threw back the light of their lanthorns, and forced William Ham into catastrophic reversals, were what those builders had effected when they had gotten worried enough. The timbered tunnels, linteled doorways, and arched passageways through which William conducted them were evidence that other builders had gambled that the interlocking foundation-works were strong enough, and would not give way if judiciously undermined.

"It is just the sort of hidden mare's nest about which one has bad dreams when putting one's money in a Bank," Saturn reflected, at a moment when he and Daniel were several convolutions behind Mr. Ham and Monsieur Kohan. But a moment later they caught up to find William Ham looking a bit huffy. He was directing their attention to a Gothik arch sealed off by a new portcullis of iron bars. Pyramidal beams of lanthorn-light, shining through the interstices, careered around the space on the other side. Slivers of gold and silver winked between the planks of crates. "The inherited complexities of the property," said Mr. Ham, "are, as you can see, giving way to a steady programme of rationalization. Where weaknesses are found, they are made strong. Several entire chambers have been infilled. Where sound vaults are discovered, they are fortified, as here." Mr. Ham then took them on a lengthy detour intended to bolster these and other assertions with evidence visual and anecdotal. By this point Daniel could no more have made his way out to the street than he could have balanced the Bank's accounts on his fingers. But he did feel that they were on average descending, for the air got damper and colder as they went, and the architecture changed. There was less wood, and what there was of it was rotten, and being replaced by masonry. They passed through a Gothik stratum into a Romanesque, or perhaps Roman—boundaries were ambiguous, as the site might have gone unchanged for half a millennium after the Romans had pulled out. Evidence of dampness was all round, though actual standing water was rare. It looked, in other words, as though they had found a way to channel groundwater and drain it out of the place—probably to Walbrook, a local creek that was famous because, at some point after the Fall of Rome, it had gone missing.

They came at some length to a chamber, sealed by a massive iron-bound door, which William unlocked with a key big enough to double as a bludgeon should the Bank come under attack. It was large for a subterranean vault, small for a parish church. Like a church, it had an aisle up the center, which had been made useful as a gutter. A trickle of groundwater two fingers wide meandered through crevices between close-set paving-stones. To either side of the aisle was a raised platform, also paved. Crates, lock-boxes, and money-bags had been piled up on these. William Ham led them up to the far end of the room, where the platforms gave way to a clear open space, and the trickle of aisle-water disappeared into a hole in the floor. He identified an open space at the end of a platform, and by a gesture indicated that Saturn should set the chest down there. Saturn did; but Solomon did not witness it, as he was inspecting the room.

Solomon shoved a sack of money aside to make a clear space on the platform, into which he spat, and then rubbed the saliva with a thumb until he had smeared away the patina of dust and congealed slime to reveal, in the light of Daniel's lanthorn, a few chips of colored stone set into the surface. A glimpse of a Mosaic.

"Roman?" Daniel guessed. Solomon nodded.

"As I think I have now demonstrated, the plates will be perfectly safe in this sealed vault until the time has come to ship them to St. Petersburg," William said to Solomon, as the ancient Jew came up to join them at the head of the chamber. But Solomon was staring at the floor. "Pray lend me your key," he said, holding out a hand.

William Ham did not like this proposition at all. But he could come up with no reason to refuse. He placed it in Solomon's hand. Solomon squatted down, felt the floor with his fingertips for some moments, then inserted the key's handle—which looked a bit like a very ornate trowel—into the drain-hole. A bit of exploratory wiggling and prying led to the sudden appearance of a large crescent-moon-shaped crevice. Saturn stepped forward. "Careful!" Solomon continued, "it will be a well."

"How do you know?"

"This is a Temple of Mithras, constructed by Roman soldiers," Solomon said, "and every such temple contained a well."

Saturn got his fingers into the crevice and pulled. A disk perhaps two feet in diameter came up out of the floor. It had been fashioned recently out of heavy planks. A lanthorn, let down into the cavity, revealed a well-shaft, lined with stones all the way down to the level of the water, which was perhaps three fathoms below.

"Your workmen found the well, and covered it," said Solomon. "But more for their own safety, than the Bank's security. I would wager the contents of this Bank that I could now leave the premises and meet you out in the street in half an hour's time without passing out through the building's front door."

"That is a bet I could not accept, even if the money were mine to wager," said William Ham, "for I can smell and feel the current of air rising up from the shaft as well as you."

"Indeed, the well has a side-channel!" exclaimed Saturn, who was on his stomach with head and shoulders thrust down into the shaft. "About halfway down. I have a mind to fetch one of the workmen's ladders and investigate!"

This was daft. But once Saturn had proposed, none could resist, it. Ladders were all over the place. They stabbed one down the well and planted it on the floor of the side-channel that Saturn had noticed. He went down first, and reported that the masons of the Temple of Mithras had carried out their duties well.

"As how could they not," Solomon returned, "for Mithras was the god of contracts."

"The *god of contracts*!?" exclaimed William Ham.

"Indeed," said Solomon, "and so it is a good thing for you that you have founded your Bank on his Temple."

"This Mithras does not appear in any Pantheon I have ever heard of."

"He was not a god of Olympus but one that the Greeks borrowed from the Persians, who had in their turn borrowed him from Hindoostan. From the Greeks his cult spread to the Romans, and became popular around the hundredth year of what you call *Anno Domini.* Or, as I would put it, some years after the destruction of the Temple of Solomon. Especially among soldiers, such as garrisoned Londinium, along the banks of the Walbrook."

Solomon had been clambering onto the ladder as he spoke.

"You aren't going down there?"

"Mr. Ham, I was sent here by the Tsar to investigate the Bank's security," said Solomon, "and inspect it I shall!"

Daniel followed Solomon down the ladder. Three of them now squatted together in a vaulted tunnel that ran off into the earth, sloping gently down toward the well so that it, too, acted as a drain. William Ham was left to sit sentry in the Temple of Mithras, and to run for help if they never emerged. But after a very brief shuffle down the tunnel they sensed space above their heads, and found stone steps, which turned to the right and led them down to the level of the groundwater. A creek, perhaps eight feet in breadth, ran sluggishly off into the dark, wending round pilings, moles, and foundations one could only assume supported buildings up on the street. In rainy weather they might have had to stop and turn back. But it was the first day of August and the level did not rise above their ankles as long as they stayed along the side of the channel. So they ventured downstream, shining their lights on walls and foundations as they went, and speculating as to which belonged to which building.

"During the Plague," Daniel said, "my uncle Thomas Ham—William's father—enlarged the cellar of his goldsmith's shop, which cannot be more than a stone's throw from us. He discovered a Roman mosaic, and diverse pagan coins and artifacts. My wife in Boston is wearing one of them in her hair."

"What did the mosaic depict?" Solomon asked.

"Some figures that called to mind Mercury. Mr. Ham styled it a Temple of Mercury and made of it a good omen. But it contained other images that would call his opinion into question—"

"Ravens?"

"Yes! How did you know?"

"*Corax,* the raven, was, to Persians, a messenger of the Gods—"

"As Mercury was to the Romans."

"Indeed. The worshippers of Mithras believed that as the soul descended from the sphere of the fixed stars to be incarnated on Earth, it passed through all of the planetary spheres along the way, and was influenced by each in turn. In passing through the sphere of Venus the soul became amorous, and so on. The innermost sphere, and the last to wreak its influence on the soul, was that of Mercury or Corax. The practitioners of this cult believed that as the soul prepared for death, and a return to the sphere of the fixed stars, it must reverse that transmigration, shedding first the trappings of Mercury-Corax, then those of Venus, *et cetera,* and finally—"

"Saturn?" guessed Saturn.

"Indeed."

"I am honored to be closest to the fixed stars, and least worldly of vices."

"Accordingly, there were seven ranks. For each rank was a chamber—always subterranean. Your uncle's cellar was that of Mercury-Corax, where new initiates were taken in. Later they would move through a gate or passage to the next chamber, which would have been decorated with images of Venus, and so on."

"What was the big chamber under the Bank?"

"You shall be pleased to know it was the chamber of Saturn, for the highest-ranking members," Solomon said.

"I did feel wondrously at home in the place!"

"If it is true that we are passing the foundations of the Ham gold-smith shop," said Solomon, "then we are traversing the hierarchy in reverse order, following the same course as souls coming down from the Cœlestial Sphere to be incarnated in the World."

"Funny that," Daniel said, "for I have just recognized the name of an old friend of mine, who'd be pleased to know where his work stood in the hierarchy."

They had stopped before a pile of relatively new stone-work, where heavy blocks had been laid to repair some ancient foundation, and to make it ready to support a new building. For the most part it was an uninterrupted bulwark of massive stones; but in one place a long slab had been laid like a lintel across a gap between two others, creating a low squarish opening through which the cellar on the other side could drain if need be. Carved on that lintel in spidery Roman letters was:

CHRISTOPHER WREN A.D. 1672

"This is the Church of St. Stephen Walbrook," said Daniel.

"No better place for souls to enter the world," Saturn mused.

They crawled up the drain—a tight fit—and emerged in the church's tombs. The bell was tolling above. "A grim birth," Daniel said. It took him a few moments to get his bearings, but then he led Saturn and Solomon up a stair to a room at the back of the church. They were surprised to see daylight coming in through windows—but not half so surprised as the vicar's wife was to see *them.* Her eyes were swollen half-shut from weeping, her cries of terror were relatively subdued, and her efforts to chase the muddy interlopers out of the building were desultory. No service was in progress, yet, strangely, many of the pews were occupied by persons who had come to do nothing but sit and pray in silence. Daniel, Saturn and Solomon stumbled out into the half light of early morning. A man was shuffling down Walbrook Street, headed for the Thames, bonging a hand-bell and shouting: "The Queen is dead, long live the King!"

BOOK 8

The System of the World

It remains that, from the same principles, I now demonstrate the frame of the System of the World.
—NEWTON, *Principia Mathematica*

Marlborough House

MORNING OF WEDNESDAY, 4 AUGUST 1714

'Tis a notion in the pamphlet shops that Whiggish libels sell best, so industrious are they to propagate scandal and falsehood.

—FROM A LETTER TO ROBERT HARLEY, 1ST EARL
OF OXFORD, QUOTED IN SIR WINSTON
CHURCHILL, *Marlborough: His Life and Times,*
VOL. VI

THE *LEVÉE,* OR RITUALIZED, semi-public getting-out-of-bed-in-the-morning, was an invention of Louis XIV, and like many of the Sun King's works was frowned upon by all right-minded Englishmen, who knew of it only from lurid yarns told of Versailles court-fops' prostituting their daughters to wangle an invitation to hold a candlestick or carry a shirt at a *levée* of the Sun King. This was all Daniel knew of the subject as of nine of the clock on the morning of August 4th, when a messenger knocked him up at Crane Court to inform him that he, Daniel, was one of half a dozen who had been summoned to take part in the Duke of Marlborough's first *levée* in London, which was going to commence in an hour's time.

"But my own *levée* is not yet finished," Daniel might have answered, wiping porridge from an unshaven chin. Instead he told the messenger to wait downstairs and that he would be along presently.

Marlborough House was invested by a crowd of several hundred Englishmen, the giddy-tired residue of an ecstatic Mobb that had sung the Duke through the streets of London yesterday: a Roman triumph thrown together on the spur of the moment by disorderly plebeians.

The Duke and his Duchess had reached Dover late on the 2nd. Yesterday had been devoted to an all-but-Royal progress through Rochester and other burgs lining the road to Londinium. So many of the Whig Quality had turned out to ride in the procession, and so many commoners had lined Watling Street, as to rouse suspicions in Daniel's mind that the rumors spread for so long by the Tories were true: Marlborough was the second coming of Cromwell. Now, to his very first *levée,* he had invited Daniel, who could still remember sitting on Cromwell's knee when he was a little boy.

Next to St. James's Palace, which was getting to look like a heap of architectural elements flung into a bin, Marlborough House shaped up as a proper building. The fence around its forecourt was a giant iron strainer, stopping everyone except for Daniel. The excluded had formed drifts of flesh on the other side, and watched eagerly, faces wedged between bars. As Daniel was helped down out of the carriage, and walked to the front door, he wondered how many of the crowd knew who he was, and of his ancient connexion to the terrible Puritan warlord. *Some* of them had to be Tory spies, who would mark Daniel, and note the connexion instantly. Daniel guessed that he had been summoned here to send a message of a vaguely threatening nature to all Torydom.

Vanbrugh had been remodeling the place in the expectation that the Duke would settle in for a long stay. Much of this work was still in its most brute stages and so Daniel had to be conducted under scaffolding and between piles of bricks and of timbers by a member of Marlborough's household. But as they got deeper into the building, it became more finished. The Duke's bedchamber had been done first, and the renovations propagated outwards from there. Before the Grinling Gibbons custom-carved double doors, a maid handed Daniel a large silver bowl full of steaming water, swathed in towels so it would not burn his hands. "Set it down beside my lord," he was instructed, and the doors were pulled open.

Like a beetle on a glacier the Duke of Marlborough sat in a chair in the white immensity of his bedchamber. Next to him was a table. The stubble on his scalp was dense: obviously it was Shaving-Day, and high time for it; as everyone had now heard, the Duke and Duchess had been held back in Ostend by contrary winds for a whole fortnight. Daniel, knowing no more of *levées* than any other Englishman, feared for a moment that he was about to be asked to lather the Duke's skull and scrape off two weeks' growth. But then he noted a valet standing by, stropping a razor, and understood, with immeasurable relief, that the blade-work would be left to a trained artisan.

Of the half-dozen who had been summoned to the *levée,* Daniel was the last to arrive—this much he could see even though his eyes were dazzled by August sunshine glancing off many tons of new plasterwork. So lofty was the ceiling that a Natural Philosopher could be forgiven for thinking that the festoons and friezes up along the ceiling had been carved from natural accumulations of snow and ice.

The Duke was in a dressing-gown of something that gleamed and whispered, and his neck had been swaddled in miles of linen in preparation for the shaving. It was as far from Puritan severity as one could possibly imagine. If there were any Tories without, on Pall Mall, who phant'sied that Daniel had come to pass the torch to the next Cromwell, a moment's glimpse into this room would have extinguished their fears. If Marlborough had come back in triumph to take over the country, he'd do so not as a military dictator but as a Sun King.

Marlborough half rose from his chair and bowed to Daniel—who nearly dropped the bowl. The other five participants in the *levée*—candle-holders, shirt-bearers, wig-powderers, mostly Earls or better—bowed even deeper. Daniel could still see little, but he could hear snickers as he staggered the last few yards.

"Dr. Waterhouse does not yet know about what was found in Baron von Bothmar's lock-box to-day," the Duke hazarded.

"I confess utter ignorance, my lord," Daniel said.

"The Hanoverian ambassador, Bothmar, brought with him a lock-box that was to be opened upon the death of Queen Anne. It contained orders from his majesty as to how the Realm was to be administered until such time as his majesty could come here to receive the crown, orb, and sceptre," explained the Duke. "This morning it was opened in the presence of the Council, and read out. The King has named twenty-five Regents to act in his stead until he arrives. You, Dr. Waterhouse, are one of the twenty-five."

"Bollocks!"

"Oh, it is quite true. And so when we bow to you, my lord, it is to acknowledge your authority as a Regent. You, and your two dozen colleagues, are the closest we have, just now, to a Sovereign."

Daniel had never been addressed before as "my lord," and certainly had never guessed that the first person ever to do so would be the Duke of Marlborough. It required some presence of mind not to spill the bowl. But he brought it home, with the help of a guiding hand from the valet, and stepped back, his formal duties completed. The valet rolled a sponge into the bowl, wrung it out, and placed it on the Duke's head like a soppy crown. The Duke blinked a rivulet out of his eye, elevated his chin, and commenced going through some papers that were on his lap—for apparently one of the attractions of the *levée* was watching the great man read his mail.

"Grub Street must be ten miles long now," the Duke remarked, tossing aside one newspaper after another.

"You may soon wish it were a good deal shorter."

"As may you, Dr. Waterhouse—your new prominence shall make you a Butt for innumerable Shafts." Marlborough had now cocked his head back so that soap would not run into his eyes, which placed him in the odd position of not being able to see into his own lap. He was groping through the papers there, golden cuff-tassels flailing, occasionally holding something up at arm's length. "Ah," he announced, finding today's *Lens,* "I give you this, Dr. Waterhouse. Just now, I was reading it aloud to these gentlemen, as we waited for the late arrival—*you* may read it yourself."

"Thank you, my lord, I am sure 'twas vastly more amusing than having me here on time."

"On the contrary, my lord, it is *we* who ought to amuse *you,*" said the Duke, and jerked in his chair as the razor planed off a ridge of scar-tissue. His noggin had acquired more than its share of high and low relief as he had overseen the deaths of several hundred thousand English, French, and other soldiers in the wars against Louis XIV. They now lurked below a fortnight's stubble like shoals under a murky tide, unseen Hazards to the blade's Navigation.

"What is it I am to read, my lord?" Daniel inquired, reaching out to accept the proffered newspaper.

Marlborough's eyes—which were uncommonly large and expressive—strayed for a moment to Daniel's hand. People did not, as a rule, bother to look at Daniel's hands—nay, neither the left nor the right. They had the full complement of fingers, they had not been branded in the Old Bailey, and they were unadorned—as a rule. But today Daniel wore, on his right hand, a simple ring of gold. Never having worn jewelry before, he was astonished at how this object caught people's attention.

"*A Meditation upon Power,*" Marlborough answered, "second page."

"It sounds meet, if I am as powerful as you say. Pray, who wrote it?"

"That's the thing," said Marlborough, "the extraordinary thing. There is a chap who goes by the *nom de plume* of Peer—"

"*He* wrote it!?"

"No, but he has discovered in the Clink a Blackamoor, a most remarkable specimen. He is not, of course, a sentient being—but he possesses the singular gift of being able to write and speak exactly as if he *were* one."

"I have met him," Daniel said. His eyes had finally adjusted to where he could make out the byline DAPPA. He glanced up at the Duke, then glanced away, as a thick bead of blood was coming out in front of his right ear and coursing along his jaw-line to stain the linen beneath his chin. The Duke jerked again. "Have a care, sirrah, I did not come hither to perish of lockjaw."

Daniel scanned the other five attendees, who favored him with excruciating smiles of a sort he'd not seen directed his way since he had been semi-important in the court of James II.

The Duke was bald again. Two valets were hovering behind him with rags, occasionally darting in to stanch gore. The Duke found a hand-mirror, held it up for a moment, and grimaced. "My word," he said, "is this a *shaving* or a *trepanning?*" He set the mirror down hastily, as if a life-time of musket- and sword-battles had hardly prepared him for this. There was a lot of mail in his lap—more than Daniel received per decade—and it was taking him some time to find what he was looking for. Daniel studied the Duke curiously. John Churchill had been the most beautiful young man in England, perhaps even in Christendom. The divine unfairness endured even now unto the Duke's sixty-fifth year. He was old, doughy, bald, and bleeding, but he actually did have a noble countenance—far from being true of all nobles—and his eyes were as large and beautiful as ever, unmarred by the sagging flesh and writhen brows that so oft made old Englishmen fearsome to behold.

"Here it is!" he announced, and whacked a letter against his knee a few times, as if this were necessary to get its words stacked up in the correct order. "From your fellow Regent!"

"My lord Ravenscar was also on Bothmar's list?" Daniel asked, for he had already spotted the handwriting and the seal.

"Oh my word, yes," said Marlborough, "odds-on favorite to be the next Lord Treasurer, you know. For who knows more about the workings of Bank, Mint, 'Chequer, and 'Change than Ravenscar?" He scanned the letter from Roger. "I shall not read it all," he assured them. "Greetings, congratulations, *et cetera*—and he invites me and Mrs. Churchill to attend a *soirée* at his house on the first of September." He lifted his eyes from the page and gazed at Daniel, a trace befuddled. "Do you think it is *decent* to have a party so soon after the Queen's death, my lord?"

"A month of mourning shall have elapsed, as of September the first, my lord," Daniel tried, "and I've no doubt it shall be a tasteful affair, duly restrained—"

"He promises right here to make his volcano erupt!" This elicited titters from the hitherto silent Five.

"Whilst mourning our late Queen, we must not omit to celebrate our new King, my lord."

"Oh, well, since you put it that way, I do believe I will attend," said the Duke. "I've never seen the famous Volcano, you know."

"It is said to be worth the trip, my lord."

"I've no doubt of that. I shall post an answer presently to the Temple of Vulcan. But if you should happen to see my lord Ravenscar, perhaps at one of the meetings of your Regency Council, you will tell him, won't you?"

"It would be my pleasure."

"Splendid! Now, may I arise, or shall it be necessary to cauterize my wounds?"

With the head-shaving, Daniel's direct relevance to the *levée* had ended. The Duke shifted his attention to others, whose roles it was to present him with shirt, wig, sword, &c. Each of these phases led to some chit-chat that was of essentially no interest to Daniel. Indeed, much of it was incomprehensible, because it was about people whom Daniel didn't know, or whose identities he could only guess at, as the Duke was referring to them by their Christian names, or in even more oblique ways. Nevertheless, Daniel had the clear sense it would be bad form to excuse himself. He was offered a chair on account of his age, and accepted it. Time passed. His eye drifted to the newspaper.

A MEDITATION UPON POWER
by Dappa

The Liberty of the Clink is as one with all of GREAT BRITAIN in lamenting the passage of our beloved Queen; the Prisoners have swopped their light, gay summer restraints for heavy mourning-fetters, and changed their gray rags for black, and all night long I am kept awake by moans and wails from the dungeons beneath, which proves that the inhabitants of the place are as sensible of the Tragedy, as my lord B—.

A week ago, that man was at the summit of the great mound of corpses that is Politics, and was accounted by many the most powerful in all the land. Since the Queen's demise, we hear nothing from him, or of him. What has become of B—?

It is an idle question, for no one cares what has become of that man. When people ask it, what they really mean is: what has become of B—'s Power? For a week ago he was agreed to have a great amount of it. To-day it seems he has none. Where has it got to? Many would fain know, for more men desire power than desire gold.

From Herr Leibniz we have heard that there is a Property of bodies called *vis viva*, and another called the *quantité d'avancement*, both of which are conserved through all collisions and transformations of a system. The first is equal to the product of the mass and the square of the velocity, and the second is simply the product of the mass and the velocity. At the beginning of time the Universe was endowed with a certain fund of both, which neither waxes nor wanes with time, but is merely exchanged among bodies, like silver pennies in a market-place. Which leads one to ask: is Power like the *vis viva*, and the *quantité d'avancement*, i.e., is it conserved by the Universe? Or is it like shares of a stock, which may have great value one day, and be worthless the next?

If Power is like stock-shares, then it follows that the immense sum thereof, lately lost by B—, has vanished like shadows in sunlight. For no matter how much wealth is lost in stock-crashes, it never seems to turn up. But if Power is conserved, then B—'s must have gone somewhere. Where is it? Some say 'twas scooped up by my lord R—, who hid it under a rock, lest my lord M— come from across the sea and snatch it away. My friends among the *Whigs* say that any Power lost by a Tory, is infallibly and insensibly distributed among all the People; but no matter how assiduously I search the lower rooms of the Clink for B—'s lost Power, I cannot seem to find any there, which explodes that argument, for there are assuredly very many People in those dark *salons*.

I propose a novel Theory of Power, which is inspired by the lucubrations of Mr. Newcomen, the Earl of Lostwithiel, and Dr. Waterhouse on the Engine for Raising Water by Fire. As a Mill makes Flour, a Loom makes Cloth, and a Forge makes Steel, so, we are assured, this Engine shall make Power. If the Backers of this Device speak truly—and I've no reason to deprecate their honesty—it proves that Power is *not* a Conserved Quantity, for of such Quantities it is never possible to make more. The amount of Power in the world, it follows, is ever-increasing, and the *rate* of increase grows ever faster as more of these Engines are built. A Man who hoards Power is therefore like a miser who sits on a heap of Coins, in a Realm where the Currency is being continually debased by production of more coins than the market can bear; so that what was a great Fortune when first he raked it together, insensibly becomes a slag-heap, and is found to be devoid of value, when at last he takes it to the market-place to be spent. Thus my lord B— and his vaunted Power-hoard. What is true of *him* is likely to be true of his lackeys, particularly his most base and slavish followers, such as MR. CHARLES WHITE. This varlet has asserted that he owns me. He phant'sies that to own a Man, is to have Power; yet he has got nothing by claiming to own me, while

I, who was supposed to be rendered Powerless, am now writing for a Grub Street newspaper that is being perused by you, esteemed reader.

As the Duke of Marlborough got dressed and accessorized, he told various of the courtiers to shove off, which they did, with deep bows, and almost tearful gratitude for having been invited; and before the hour of noon, Daniel found himself alone in the bedchamber with the Duke, suddenly formidable in full snow-white periwig, and understated yet shockingly fashionable suit of clothes, and small-sword. They went for a stroll in a rose-garden outside the Duke's bedchamber, which led to more conversation concerning roses than Daniel was really game for. Not that he didn't like roses as much as the next chap; but to talk about them was to miss the point.

"I have accepted Ravenscar's kind invitation," the Duke finally said, "and moreover I have done so in the presence of those other five, who are among the worst gossips in London—so much so that Roger has probably got wind of it already. But there is a *proviso* to my acceptance, which I did not mention to them. Neither shall I write it in the very courteous note I'll presently send to the Temple of Vulcan. I tell it privily to you, and rely upon you to convey it to him."

"I am ready, my lord," said Daniel, trying not to let his voice betray a certain *here we go again* weariness.

"Let me remind you of the agreement on which you and I shook hands, on the night of the Glorious Revolution, as we stood together on the causeway of the Tower."

"I recollect it clearly, my lord, but there's no harm in reviewing it."

"I said I would be your friend if you would help me to understand, or at least to keep track of, the machinations of the Alchemists."

"Indeed."

"I flatter myself that I have been of service to you, as occasions warranted, in the twenty-five years since then," said John Churchill. For now it seemed they were speaking not as Duke and Regent but as John and Daniel.

"Now that you mention it, it is a bit odd that my name turned up on Bothmar's list."

"I had many occasions, during and after the War, to sing the praises of certain Englishmen to the Electoral Prince," John said, "and the high esteem in which you are held by Princess Caroline cannot have hurt your chances, either."

"You have done the son of Drake unexpected honor, then," Daniel said.

"Now, Daniel, since we made our compact, much has changed—

Roger's Juncto re-shaped the country. He placed the world's leading Alchemist in charge of the Mint. That Alchemist is still there, and shows no sign of faltering. By some accounts he is diligent beyond compare. But reports have reached me concerning the Pyx, and such arcane and eldritch matters as the Solomonic Gold and the Philosophic Mercury and other such semi-occult doings as have no place in this the Eighteenth Century. Now that Anne is gone—may God rest her—and George is coming, I bear upon my shoulders the greatest imaginable responsibilities to help our new King—nay, our new Dynasty—understand what is going on in his Kingdom. I will ensure that the Mint is in the hands of officials *sane* and *competent,* and that the coinage is sound. Can Newton be trusted to run the Mint, Daniel? Will he run it as a mill for turning out disks of metal, or as a laboratory for Chiliastic researches? Is he a bloody sorcerer, Daniel? And if so, is he any good at it?"

The Temple of Vulcan
AN HOUR LATER

"WHAT DID YOU TELL HIM?" asked Roger, slightly more fascinated than aghast. He and Daniel were strolling in *Roger's* rose-garden, which was ten times the size of Marlborough's, though not so well located—Roger's gardeners couldn't nip over the fence and borrow a spade from the King of England's.

"I fear I was a bit too evasive for the Duke's taste," Daniel answered, after pondering it for some moments. "I assured him that whatever Newton does, he does very, very well, hence *if* he is a sorcerer, he must be a right clever one."

"Oh my lord," Roger exclaimed, "this cannot have improved the Duke's mood."

"I don't know. I believe I convinced him that Isaac is not a lunatick. That is no bad start."

"But it is *only* a start. Hmm."

"The *point* of the conversation, Roger, was not to condemn or exonerate Isaac. It was to send you a sort of warning."

"I am ready."

"Marlborough has accepted your invitation."

"Yes, I had the news hours ago."

"Consequently *all* the Quality will attend, whether you invite them or no."

"I have already laid in supplementary help, to cope with party-crashers. Is *that* the warning? That lots of people will come to my party?" Roger's attention had begun to wander, and his eyes lit on Daniel's gold ring. His brow furrowed, his lips parted. Daniel interrupted before he could change the subject to jewelry.

"No. Marlborough is profoundly unhappy about all of the mysteries and controversies surrounding the Mint. He is going to call for a Trial of the Pyx around the time of the Coronation—a couple of months from now, probably—to get all of those coins out of the Pyx, and ensure that all of those minted under George shall be free from any taint. In the meantime, he wishes to see progress made toward the resolution of these Mint troubles. He wishes to feel confident about Newton. If the situation has not begun to improve as of September the first, he'll not show up for your Party."

"Oh, horrors!"

"The humiliation shall be exquisite, and conspicuous. All London shall know that you are in disgrace, and shall never be made Lord Treasurer, or even Lord Dogcatcher. The first of September shall, in other words, mark the first day of your retirement."

After a suitably awe-full pause, and perhaps a few moments' silent prayer, Roger boomed: "Then let us ready the Volcano!" He revolved about his walking-stick, turning his back on Daniel, and marched through the garden to the main house. It was a fine show of bravado; but Daniel got the sense that Roger did not want Daniel, or anyone else, to see his face for some moments. And so Daniel did not inspect Roger's phizz too closely, but instead pretended to look at the plumbing of the Volcano.

And of its Maker; for MacDougall had removed one of the curved plates that made up the Volcano's slopes, and set it aside, and shoved his head deep into the apparatus.

"Your arse-crack is showing, Mr. MacDougall," Ravenscar shouted, "which I ever take as a sign of hard productive labor, in a man of your profession."

The arse in question began to shimmy as MacDougall attempted to disengage. There were two thuds and a curse. Then a head, crowned with a torch-flame of embarrassingly red hair, appeared. MacDougall's hair and cheeks were so red that everything near him looked dusky.

"MacDougall," Daniel said.

"It is a pleasure to see you, Dr. Waterhouse."

"Have you obtained the phosphorus yet?" Daniel asked.

"It's as I told you the other day, sir—I don't purchase it direct from the maker, but through a sort of go-between."

"And have you placed your order with this go-between yet?" Roger demanded.

"Oh, yes, my lord. Did it yesterday."

"Then go back to him and double it!" Roger commanded.

"Oh, I'm not certain they can make so much so fast, my lord!"

"Double it anyway, and if the Eruption of September the first is not the grandest ever, then the fault shall lie with our deficient phosphorus industry, and no man shall be able to claim that the Marquis of Ravenscar stinted or scrimped!"

"My lord, let's see if they don't rise to the challenge! I've a feeling they just might do it!"

"That is splendid, MacDougall," Daniel said, "will you please join me at my Clubb to deliver your report in person?"

"Oh, Dr. Waterhouse! I should be honored!"

"Then do you gather your tools together and meet me and my lord in the front of the house when you are ready."

Roger and Daniel departed the ballroom and circumvented the plashing fountain of Vulcan coming on Minerva's thigh. "Where is the lovely pair to-day?" Daniel inquired, unable to get his eyes off the goddess.

"I beg your pardon?" asked Roger—a bit distracted himself.

"Catherine Barton, and her Body."

"Ah. They are out shopping—the Body requires a new dress for the party."

"Magnificent."

"Say," Roger said, "you have quite foxed me. Why are you taking MacDougall to your Clubb?"

"I know MacDougall well. He has proved most invaluable at the Court of Technologickal Arts. Most ingenious."

"Very well, but *what has he to do with your Clubb?*"

They left the fountain behind and entered the part of the house that Daniel had designed: the original Temple of Vulcan, as it had been before the improvements of Hooke and Vanbrugh.

"The Infernal Devices used phosphorus," Daniel said. "Ergo, the chaps who built them must have had dealings with local suppliers. MacDougall is now dealing with them too, thanks to you. This provides the Clubb with a new line of investigation. Mr. Kikin and Mr. Orney are very keen to pursue it."

637

"But I thought you had struck a deal with Jack Shaftoe that would obviate the Clubb's purpose."

"We have not heard from Jack since he jumped off the back of your phaethon in the Hay Market a week ago, and, according to rumor, became embroiled at the Opera House—"

"Distasteful, that. Impaling Jesuits with 'cellos—not the done thing—I shall have to give him a sharp reprimand if he ever turns up."

"Well, that is the question, isn't it? Will Jack turn up? Isaac has already suggested that by jumping off the carriage before the transaction could be consummated, Jack forfeited anything he might have gained in the Black Dogg."

"Newton has already spoken to me concerning the Black Dogg," Roger confided. "He now maintains that everything said there, was said under duress—Jack had a sword, you didn't—and may be considered null and void."

"What think you, Roger?"

"I think that the Black Dogg deal was perfectly reasonable—if a bit over-generous to Jack—and so I find it disquieting that your Clubb is continuing to pursue him."

"Because it might queer the deal, and lead to the Duke not showing up for your party, you mean."

"Yes." They had reached the anteroom of the Temple, and now stood where they could enjoy the breeze coming in the house's open front door. They gazed down the steps like two priests of Vulcan taking a break from their sulphuric devotions.

"I cannot control Orney or Kikin," Daniel pointed out, "and of course to manage Isaac is impossible. You might have to fire him."

"I beg your pardon?"

"Marlborough is right, Roger. A sorcerer has no place at the Mint. It pains me to say for this, for Isaac is an old friend, and he makes good guineas. But he ought to be replaced with some chap who just wants to make coins."

"That is all well and good, but I do not have the power to fire him."

"Oh, really? You're a Regent, aren't you?"

"As are you, Daniel. Why don't *you* fire him?"

"It may come to that."

MacDougall emerged from the penetralia of the Temple, listing to starboard, as he carried a clanking tool-satchel in that hand. Sensing that the two Regents were embroiled in a State matter, he cringed and scurried out the door and did not check himself until he had dived into Daniel's hackney out on Great Russell Street and pulled the door shut after him.

"How *much* does Churchill hate Alchemists?" Roger asked. "Can he *ever* trust Newton?"

"Here is what I told the Duke of Marlborough concerning Alchemy," Daniel said, which brought Roger to attention. "It has been my view for some years that a new System of the World is being created around us. I used to suppose that it would drive out and annihilate any older Systems. But things I have seen recently, in the subterranean places beneath the Bank, have convinced me that new Systems never replace old ones, but only surround and encapsulate them, even as, under a microscope, we may see that living within our bodies are animalcules, smaller and simpler than us, and yet thriving even as we thrive. When we have stronger microscopes I should not be surprised to discover yet smaller and simpler organisms within those animalcules. And so I say that Alchemy shall not vanish, as I always hoped. Rather, it shall be encapsulated within the new System of the World, and become a familiar and even comforting presence there, though its name may change and its practitioners speak no more about the Philosopher's Stone. It shall be gone from view but it shall continue to run along beneath, as the lost river Walbrook streams beneath the Bank of England."

"Nice," said Roger, "but did the Duke buy it?"

"Unknown," said Daniel. "But I believe there is no harm in hedging our bets by continuing to investigate Jack, as we wait for the volcano to erupt."

The Kit-Cat Clubb
AN HOUR LATER

"Splendid bauble," said Mr. Threader, elevating his nose so that he could peer through his half-glasses at Daniel's hand. "I say, you're not turning into a Fopp, are you?"

"If I'd known all the fuss it would create I would never have put it on. May I have my hand back, please?"

"Who's the German?"

"Our newest member."

"I must remind you, Dr. Waterhouse, that this Clubb is bound by rules. Admission of new members is governed by several pages of the Bylaws, which you would do well to familiarize yourself with before showing up with—"

"The Baron is a court philosopher of Hanover, very influential there—"

"Right. He's in! What's his name?"

"He is here *incognito.* Just pretend you know who he is."

In an apt demonstration of the principle just expounded by Daniel, of systems encapsulated within systems, this claque of frustrated prosecutors had been swallowed up by the Kit-Cat Clubb. It was all because Newton had joined, and thereby endowed it with Mystery and Prestige. They met in a private room in the back, so that blokes like Saturn and MacDougall could take part. There was now a waiting list twenty names deep of men who wanted to join—none of whom had more than a vague idea of the Clubb's purpose. The fact that a Baron from the court of Hanover had secretly jumped this queue, on the very same day that a different member had been named a Regent, was going to make them all frantic. The Clubb would have to begin meeting in the Temple of Mithras just to get some privacy.

"Being a Regent has changed you!" Leibniz remarked, eyeing the ring.

"This damned thing is a present from that Solomon Kohan," Daniel confided.

"He does not strike me as the gift-giving type."

"After our visit to Bridewell, I presented him with a small purse containing bits of gold punched out of the cards. A few days later this ring was delivered to me by a Jew who has a goldsmith's shop along Lombard. With it was a note from Monsieur Kohan. He had the bits melted down and poured into a ring-mold. This is the result."

"It *seems* very courteous of him," Leibniz said.

"I agree."

But before they could enter into speculation as to Monsieur Kohan's *real* motives, that Silence fell over the room that heralded the arrival of Sir Isaac Newton. It was a different room, and a different meeting suddenly. Isaac made his way around shaking the hands of the Members and Guests: Mr. Kikin, Mr. Orney, Mr. Threader, Saturn, MacDougall, Leibniz, and finally Daniel. There was something markedly chilly in the way he looked at and spoke to Daniel. His greeting of Leibniz was warm by comparison. It was almost as if by some sorcery Isaac had listened in on the things Daniel had been saying about him earlier in the day.

"I must have a private word with my lord Regent," Isaac announced to the Clubb.

Shortly he and Daniel were facing off across a small table in the main room of the Kit-Cat. The intensity with which Isaac stared at Daniel held at bay any glad-handing Kit-Catters who might have wanted to come over and congratulate the new Regent.

"It is but a week since we spoke to Jack the Coiner in the Black Dogg," Isaac reminded him. "What are your intentions?"

"The Duke of Marlborough wants a Trial of the Pyx at the time of the Coronation," Daniel said, and paused for a moment in case Isaac was going to have a stroke. Isaac flinched and colored but went on living. "In the absence of any communications from Mr. Shaftoe— have you heard from him?"

"No."

"Neither have I. We must continue as before. If he wishes to resume negotiations, we may then deal from a position of greater strength."

Isaac was not even looking at him.

"What is your position?" Daniel asked.

"I desire what I have always desired," Isaac said. "Your machinations with Baron von Leibniz have made it harder to get—for much of it is now locked up in a tomb in Clerkenwell, and promised to the Tsar. But Jack might yet have some. Ergo, I must redouble my pursuit of Jack."

"What if a situation were to arise, Isaac, in which you were presented with a choice: on the one hand, striking a deal with Jack that would end the peril he poses to the currency and to the King, but leave you wanting what you seek. On the other, pursuing Jack to the bitter end in the hopes of getting his gold, but at the risk of failing the Trial of the Pyx?

"You ask questions like a Regent," Isaac said.

"Like it or not, I *am* one, and *must* ask such questions. And the question boils down to this: Do you respect the authority of the King, or of Regents appointed to act in his stead, and do you place the Mint and the Currency above other, more personal interests? Or does the Philosoper's Stone come first?"

"I find it astonishing that the son of Drake would even be capable of forming such a question in his mind, let alone asking it. Did you learn *nothing* from him?"

"You mistake me. I do not care a fig for the King. In this I am one with Drake. But Drake also taught me the value of money. I may not love money as much as some, but I do respect it. Do you?"

"Do you, Daniel, really believe that I left the Lucasian Chair of Mathematics at the College of the Holy and Undivided Trinity, and came to the Mint, solely out of an interest in *numismatics*?"

"Well answered," Daniel said. "Since we agree it is in our interests to continue the pursuit of Jack, let us rejoin the others in back."

YET ANOTHER NEW GUEST HAD come in through the alley-door, and joined the group in the back room, while Daniel and Isaac had been talking. He was a humble humble man, so hunched, so cringing in his posture that one might think Fellows of the Royal Society had waylaid him in the alley and surgically removed his collar-bones. He was kneading his hat to keep his hands from trembling. He smelled bad, and unlike many who do, he well knew it. Yet Mr. Threader was clapping him on the shoulder as if he were a favorite nephew being sworn in to the Bar. "I present Mr. Marsh!" Threader proclaimed. "Mr. Marsh has been the subject of the Clubb's deliberations before."

"I have forgotten those deliberations," Daniel confessed, "and some of us have never heard them in the first place."

"Infernal Devices require phosphorus," Threader said, "and we have already heard from Mr. MacDougall about the large order he has recently placed for same. It shall lead, in coming weeks, to the boiling-down of a stupendous volume of urine."

"We covered this in our meeting two days ago," Daniel reminded him, "but who is Mr. Marsh?"

"The last time the Clubb attempted to trace the flow of urine from Town to Country, we deputized Monsieur Arlanc, the now infamous, to canvass the Vault-men of Fleet Ditch. He directed our attention to the sad tale of a particular Vault-man who, for reasons unexplained, had driven his load out into Surrey. There he ran afoul of some young blades who were so offended by the fragrance of the vehicle that they drew their swords, and slew his horse, on the spot, depriving the poor owner of his livelihood. Henry Arlanc claimed he had made inquiries, up and down the lower Fleet, as to where the unfortunate fellow might be found, and had been assured that he had gone off to dwell with his family far away."

"Now I remember it," Daniel said. "We threw up our hands and no more pursued this thread of the investigation."

"Arlanc lied," Mr. Threader proclaimed. "After he was led away in chains, I asked myself, could we credit the representations he had made to us concerning the Vault-man? Since then I have made inquiries of my own. Very little effort was required to learn the truth: the Vault-man had *not* fled the city after losing his horse, but had gone to work for another chap in the same line of work, and could be found on the brink of the Fleet any night of the week. Last night, I found him. I present to you Mr. Marsh."

This actually produced a light round of applause—from the looks of it, not a familiar sound to the ears of Mr. Marsh.

"Long have I looked forward to asking you one question, Mr. Marsh," said Orney. "On the night your horse was slain, what on earth had induced you to drive your load into Surrey?"

"I was to be paid, guv'nor," said Mr. Marsh.

"Paid by whom?"

"By certain blokes in those parts who pay money for piss from time to time."

"Who are they, and where do they live?"

"No one knows, guv'nor."

"But if you bring them urine, and they pay you money, how can you not know?"

"You takes your wagon to a certain crossroads at midnight, and you blindfolds yourself. When they see you're blindfolded, they come out of hiding, and get into the driver's seat beside you without saying a word. Round and round and up and down and to and fro they drive, for an hour or more, so you've no notion of where you are. Finally you comes to a place where the wagon is emptied. Then they drive you back by the same mazy way you came. Off comes the blindfold. You're back where you started. A purse of money is on the seat beside you."

There was a silence as Mr. Marsh's singular narration was considered. Then Newton spoke: "Your horse is slain. But what became of your wagon?"

"It is still in Surrey, guv'nor."

"Then let us go and fetch it, and bring it to the Court of Technologickal Arts—assuming that Dr. Waterhouse gives his consent—for some repairs, and some alterations," Isaac said. "I have an idea."

Orney's Ship-yard, Rotherhithe
MORNING OF 13 AUGUST 1714

DANIEL ARRIVED EARLIER THAN most, and sat on a bale of Bridewell oakum. It was not a bad place to await the other members of the Clubb. The day was perfect. Later he would be hot, but for the nonce his suit was perfectly matched to the warmth of the sun and the temperate breeze off the river. Before him, three great greased skids declined into the Thames. They had exhausted their burdens—the Tsar's warships—and lay open to new projects. One of Orney's shipwrights stood at the head of the middle way. When he did not move for some minutes, Daniel guessed that something must be wrong. But then the man shifted his weight, cocked his head minutely, froze for a few seconds, then hunched his shoulders and let his chin drop almost to his breast-bone. Daniel perceived, then, that the man was thinking. And it was no aimless woolgathering, but a sort of work. As some built ships in bottles, this man was building one inside of his skull; and if Daniel had the fortitude to remain on this perch for some weeks or months, why, he would see the vision in the shipwright's mind take material form. A year hence, men would be sailing around on it! This Daniel found wondrous. He envied the shipwright. Not simply because he was a younger man but because he was being left alone in a quiet place to create something new, and, in sum, seemed, by grace or by craft, to have ensconced himself in a simpler and sweeter Story than the one Daniel was doomed to act out.

So much did he enjoy this interlude on the oakum, that he had to master a distinct flash of annoyance when the *tick, tick, tick* of a certain approaching wagon obtruded. The shipwright—lucky man—was free to ignore it. Daniel must attend.

The wagon was a great rank barrel mounted in a shallow wheeled box. Hunched on a plank bench at the front was a man, manipulating the reins of a single listless nag. He drove the rig down in to the middle of Orney's yard, then leaned back and let his head loll. Members of the Clubb were converging from diverse places round the Establishment where they had been smoking pipes, bowling, chatting, or tending to their very important correspondence.

When Mr. Marsh—for it was he—recovered from his exhaustion sufficiently to open his eyes and have a look round, he found himself surrounded by most of the would-be Prosecutors he had met nine days earlier at the Kit-Cat Clubb. The only one missing was Kikin. But Kikin's bodyguard was there, and so was Saturn. These two squatted down beneath the wagon and went to work with prybars. Another man in his position might have raised objections to having his wagon dismantled while was still sitting on it, but Mr. Marsh seemed past caring. Planks were removed from the vehicle's flat underbelly; Saturn stood and tossed them into the bed of the wagon while the big Russian carefully extracted a smuggled burden from a hidden cavity. This looked, for a moment, like a bale of clothing; but presently it sprouted extremities, and began to stretch, writhe, and complain. The bodyguard stood it upright next to the wagon. The head of Mr. Kikin could now be seen, wigless, hatless, hairless, red-eyed, blinking, and emitting swear-words that would make Cossacks clap their hands over their ears and run home to their mothers. A wig was produced and jammed over Kikin's pate. He was disgorging all manner of stuff from his pockets: paper scraps, pencil stubs, a compass, a watch.

"I ween we shall now hear a long disquisition from Mr. Kikin," said Mr. Threader. "Once, that is, he has remembered his manners. Let us hear first, and briefly, the report of Mr. Marsh."

"Oh, from that I am here, and alive, you must know that it came off as planned, sirs," said Mr. Marsh.

"You met the mysterious personage in the night-time? You were blindfolded and conveyed to the place where the urine is collected? You emptied your load, and were returned to the lonely crossroads, and were paid, and were sent on your way?" Threader inquired. Marsh answered with a stately procession of nods.

"Very well, then," said Daniel Waterhouse, "as we agreed, the horse is yours, and you are free to go forth and ply your trade. We ask only that you speak of this to no one."

"Right, guv'nor," answered Marsh, with a slight roll of the eyes: his way of pointing out that it would be suicidal for him to relate the story anywhere in Christendom. Then, exhausted though he was, he drove out of Orney's Ship-yard and began putting distance between him and the mad Clubb as fast as his new cart-horse could manage.

Mr. Orney had spread out a large-scale map of Surrey on an open-air table normally used for unfurling ship-plans. Kikin, moving in a stiff tottering gait, brought his paper-scraps and began to arrange them according to some inscrutable scheme while quaffing beer from a sort of earthenware tureen. Breezes discomposed the scraps; rocks were procured. Kikin placed his pocket-compass on the map. The three Natural Philosophers all noted that Orney—as always, a master of detail—had so oriented the map that its north-arrow was aligned with the compass's needle.

When Mr. Kikin felt himself capable of human speech, he announced, with no greetings, complaints, or other preliminaries: "We commenced from *here.*" And he deposited a pebble on a Surrey cross-roads not far off the high road from London Bridge. "To the south-east we proceeded, on a good road—"

"You were able to perceive the compass in the dark, then?" Orney asked.

"The phosphorus paint compounded by Freiherr von Leibniz, and daubed upon its card by Mr. Hoxton, performed as expected. It was right in my face, as bright as a full moon. I say we were going southeast on a good road—almost certainly *this* one," insisted Kikin, streaking his finger across the map. "I counted, er . . ." and here he consulted his notes. "Seventy-eight revolutions of the wheel." For Newton had proposed, and Saturn had constructed, a little device that produced a click every time the wheel went round.

"One thousand and thirty feet, then," said Newton, having worked out the product in his head. For all of them knew by heart the circumference of the wheel in question.

But here Orney had anticipated, and prepared: he produced a ribbon of paper, marked with regularly spaced pen-lines, each neatly indexed with a number: 50, 100, 200, and so on. It was a scale that he had drawn up, demarcated not in feet, furlongs, or miles, but in revolutions of the wheel of Mr. Marsh's vault-wagon. By snaking it down the road drawn on the map (for the road was not perfectly straight) he was able to show that, at a place near the eighty mark, there was an intersection with a smaller road. "That must be it," Kikin said, and reviewed a spate of Cyrillic notations. "Yes, west-southwest for fifty ticks—then an elbow in the road, bringing us round to almost due south—three hundred and thirty ticks later we went up and over a stone bridge."

This led to some back-tracking and head-scratching, for it was not clear which of several possible roads the wagon might have taken; but presently Leibniz noticed a bridge whose position was found to be consistent with all of Kikin's *data,* and so they went on reckoning from there.

All in all, Kikin had marked down a couple of dozen changes in direction, three bridges, diverse segments of noticeably good or bad road, and the odd hill, village, obstreperous canine, or swampy bit. It became obvious, as they plotted his trajectory as a line of pebbles on the map, that the route was circuitous by design. But eventually it had come to an end in some place described by Kikin as reeking of *sal ammoniac.* There the wagon had been emptied. A different winding and looping course had then been traced to bring Mr. Marsh (and his hidden stowaway) back to the starting-place. Getting the outbound and the inbound *data* to agree with each other, so that they started and ended in the same places, while not blatantly contradicting the map's assertions as to the locations of bridges, hills, &c., took twice as long as had been required for the wagon to actually cover the ground, and devolved into a lengthy progress of disputes about applied Euclidean geometry and the nature of absolute space: arguments that Newton and Leibniz were perhaps a bit too eager to engage in, so that Daniel had to intervene from time to time and ban Metaphysics. The accuracy of Mr. Kikin's observations was called into question; he defended himself with less and less vehemence as the morning wore on, and in early afternoon could be seen dozing on a piled cargo-net. Factions developed, fissures opened within factions, alliances were forged and betrayed, outrage was manifested against the turncoats, who professed dedication only to higher principles of Truth.

But at some point it all fell into place and they came up with an answer—Daniel's gold ring, set down at a particular location on the map—that was obviously right, and made them wonder why they had not seen it right away. Mr. Kikin, who only minutes earlier had been characterized as an innumerate poltroon, under suspicion of having fallen asleep between observations, was now hailed as the best chap ever; toasted; and likened to Vasco da Gama.

It was Daniel who ruined the celebratory mood by asking the question: "Now what?"

"If the map is to be trusted," said Newton, "Jack's urine-boiling operation is situated on a large estate, high in the North Downs."

"As it would have to be," Orney put in, "or the neighbors would complain of the stink."

"Taking into consideration the size of the estate, the openness of the countryside, and the notorious and vicious character of Jack's gang, I say 'twere foolhardy to approach the place without a company or more of armed men."

"Then it is fortunate that *you* are a member of the Clubb, Sir Isaac," Saturn said, "for I have seen you summon up just such a force when you were in need." He was referring to the raid on the boozing-ken in St. Bride's.

"The men you saw—and escaped from—on that occasion were Queen's Messengers," Newton said, "though of course they are called King's Messengers as of two weeks ago. They are under the command of Mr. Charles White, who is a loyal minion of Bolingbroke. He aided me *then*, only as part of leading me into a trap. I do not phant'sy Mr. White will be disposed to aid us *now*."

"But the power of Bolingbroke is destroyed," said Kikin, "or so people are saying."

"Not destroyed, sir," Newton corrected him, "as long as his man guards the Mint, and the Pyx."

"Is the Queen's—pardon me, the *King's* Own Black Torrent Guard not garrisoned at the Tower, and charged with guarding the coinage?" Orney inquired.

"Yes, but they are *also* under the command of Charles White," said Newton.

"After Jack compromised the Pyx in April," Daniel explained in an aside to Leibniz, "Bolingbroke made hay of it in Parliament, and said that this shewed the Whigs could not be trusted with the Mint. Thus did he gain authority over such matters."

"Which he then delegated to White?"

"Indeed. Now, he is bound to be stripped of that authority when the Hanovers come in and the Whigs take power; but for now he commands both the King's Messengers and the Black Torrent Guards; and he controls the Mint, and the Pyx."

All faces had turned their way. Daniel's sidebar with Leibniz had become the center of attention. Newton, in particular, was gazing into Daniel's eyes, and had an expectant look about him.

"Since the events of a fortnight ago," Daniel volunteered, "tensions between Whig and Tory, Hanover and Jacobite, have ebbed, but not altogether vanished. The troops of the Whig Association are still bivouacked all round the capital, ready to be called out in the event Bolingbroke attempts to seize power. Perhaps a company of such troops could be detailed to assist us in this matter. I shall make inquiries among men who have a say in such matters."

The meeting went on for some little while after that, but in truth Daniel's utterance had been the end of it. Isaac soon thought up a pretext for leaving. Kikin was gone a few minutes after that, and he took Leibniz with him so that they could transact unspecified Tsar-business en route. Threader and Orney were left to bait each other, as was their practice; though neither of them would dream of admitting to it, they had developed a kind of friendship.

Daniel and Saturn shared a water-taxi. Long before it reached

London, Saturn had cause to regret this, for Daniel—who had been so content at the beginning of the day, sitting on his bale and watching the river flow by—had now become gloomy and brooding even by Saturnine standards. "Isaac will bring this to a head," Daniel predicted. "Not for him the dodge, the accommodation, the quiet understanding. The armistice we made with Jack in the Black Dogg is forgotten. He must slay the *bête noire*. Ha! I wonder what he has in mind for *me*."

Saturn had been squinting at some inconsequential thing on the river's bank, hoping that his fellow-passenger would shut up if ignored long enough. This last remark, however, caused him to turn his head and fix his gaze on Daniel. "Why should he have anything in mind for you?"

"I am all that stands between him and the Solomonic Gold, or so he imagines."

"Is it true?"

"The Tsar, and various of his minions, such as Monsieurs Kohan and Kikin, would have something to say about it, if Isaac confiscated the stuff," Daniel allowed, "but they are far away, and not really part of Newton's world. He will not take such persons into consideration. *Me* he will hate for having done the wrong thing."

"What are the practical consequences of being so hated?" Saturn wondered.

Daniel thought of Hooke, and how Hooke's legacy had disappeared. But if that happened after one was dead, did it really matter?

Saturn went on, "He is civil to you when the Clubb is together—"

"And I had wondered *why*, until today," Daniel said. "Isaac no longer has the King's Messengers and the Black Torrent Guard at his disposal. Bolingbroke has stripped him of the temporal power he had, or phant'sied he had, a few months ago. To act against Jack the Coiner, Isaac requires that sort of power—and I have got such power, at least indirectly, through Roger."

"But why on earth," asked Saturn, "should you consent to any such thing, if you hold it to be the case that Sir Isaac counts you as a foe, and would sweep you out of his way?"

"A perfectly sensible question," said Daniel. "I think it is simple for him, complicated for me, snared as I am in a mare's nest of compromises and accommodations, which to him would seem like one of those hair-balls we used to pull from cows' bellies—a nasty mess that ought to be swept away. He'll not be satisfied with anything less than the destruction of Bolingbroke, Charles White, Jack Shaftoe, Leibniz, and—if I've been so foolish as to get tangled up with 'em—me.

Peter, I cannot summon anything like the fury of Newton, hot as a refiner's fire. Perhaps I and the others really are nothing more than schlock to be raked off the top of his crucible and dumped on the ground to harden and blacken."

Surrey

BEFORE DAWN, 15 AUGUST 1714

And armes shal stand on his parte, and thei shal pollute the Sanctuarie of strength, & shal take away the dailie *sacrifice,* & they shal set up the abominable desolation.

—DANIEL 11:31

When ye therefore shal se the abomination of desolation spoken of by Daniel the Prophet, standing in the holie place (let him that readeth consider it). Then let them which be in Iudea, flee into the mountaines. Let him who is on the house top, not come downe to fetch anie thing out of his house. And he that is in the field, let not him returne back to fetch his clothes.

—MATTHEW 24:15–18

HE HATED TO BE LEADING troops across English soil. Ireland, Belgium, Holland, and France were the natural *champs de Mars;* armies roamed across and fed off them like sheep on English downs. But to lead a company of armed troopers across an English field made him reconsider his choice of profession.

That was, as he knew, confused and stupid thinking, for armies were no more natural and no more welcome in Belgium than they were here; but anyway it was how he felt. As always, he would be keeping those feelings to himself.

They had crossed over to Lambeth on the horse ferry two hours after midnight and marched, or rather walked, south on the

Clapham road. The beating tromp of a proper march would be heard for miles across this drowsy landscape, and they did not want alarms to race across the countryside. So they had broken stride, separated into platoons, and made their way southwards, dividing and merging around the odd settlement. Watchmen, insomniacs, and busybodies who came out on to the road to pose troublesome questions, were told to mind their own business, and then asked for directions to Epsom. The strategy was to march faster than Rumor, but if some eager messenger were to get out ahead of them on horseback, they hoped he would spread the lie that they were going generally southwest. Which was just what they did, for some hours; but then, having gathered together in a dell off to the side of the way to eat their rations of biscuit, they executed a sharp change in direction, double-timed four miles eastwards along a road, then took to the fields. Scouts led them up and down gentle slopes that they could feel but not yet see. He thought there was rather more of up, than of down, but then it always felt thus to a tired infantryman. His ears were bad, and so he could not hear the rustling of leaves, but he sensed the presence of trees by their auras of stillness and of scent. These developed into copses that had to be circumvented, lest in walking through them the soldiers disperse, rustle leaves, and pop branches.

The light sifted down out of the sky like motes and flakes of ash from a burning city. At some point there was suddenly enough of it that he could make sense of the blobs and vestiges that, for the last hour or so, had marred the darkness. He stopped to look round. He had imagined, until now, that they had been marching across open ground, diverting around the occasional wood. But it was not like that. Trees grew more or less densely everywhere, and made it impossible to see more than a stone's throw in any direction, except where a hill rolled up in the distance. Through the mottled shadow of the wood meandered a pale river: a way paved with grass that was becoming prickly and tinder-like in the summer heat. This chalky soil was as powerless to retain moisture as the fingers of a skeleton to hold money. It set off a hue and cry in his mind: he had marched a company into a high place where ponds and streams would not exist! In a few hours they would be out of water! He silenced these alarms by means of elaborate thinking and exhausting mental effort; ten paces later they started back up again, and reigned over his mind for an age. The thoughts became dry and worn-out, like straw that has been slept on too many times, and finally disintegrated in the first clear light of the morning.

Like boys who have waded along a creek-bed to the place where it loses itself in river, the troops had come to a broad swale that rolled up from undulating farm-country below—generally to their left—and, to their right, fetched up against the limey buttresses of a chalk hill—a down, as they named it in this part of the country. There this convenient highway of dry fescue and sporadic trees was barred by a furry tonsure of beeches that gripped the rougher parts of the down, indeed seemed to cover it all the way to the top—until he peered through spare places in the wood and saw pale, sere meadows on the high side.

The order of battle would have been clear to him at that point, even if he'd been a private soldier with no hand in its planning: there was an estate on the top of this down, hedged on this approach by the beech-belt. Proper visitors would approach it by (he guessed) some sort of carriageway that would come up the gentler slope on its yonder side; he and his company, however, were going to assault it from its (he hoped) unguarded and unwatched rear by toiling up the wooded chalk-bluff until they could break out of the trees and into the open ground above and beyond.

As he was collecting all of this together in his head, the wee hairs on the back of his neck stirred. He turned and drew this new breeze into his nostrils. It was damp and smelled of the river. It was going to precede them up through the trees.

He spoke now for the first time in hours, and gave the word to begin at once, each platoon holding hands, to use a figure of speech, with those to either side of it, so that they'd not lose one another in the fog, and fragment the line. "What fog, Sergeant?" someone asked, for the air was as clear as snow-melt. But Sergeant Bob only turned his back on this fellow and began stalking up-hill. One measure of soldierly experience, he had found, was how long it took for a man to wot that an engagement had commenced. For Bob Shaftoe, it had commenced the moment this moist breeze had begun its journey up from the Thames, and the battle was now more than half over. For this chap who had just asked him "What fog?" the onset of the battle still lay at some indefinite point in the future. Taken to its extreme, this particular form of military incompetence led to men being surrounded and slaughtered while sleeping, or eating. In less extreme forms it caused excessive casualties. Bob knew of no remedy for it other than to act, which would shock and embarrass laggardly sergeants and corporals to follow him. By the time he reached the verge of the beech-wood, he could feel the moisture clammy on his arms. By the time he led his company out on to the high pasture-land on the lid of the down, it was hushed under a new fog. He had not gone ten paces into this hilltop estate when a dog began to bark. The company had been moving with admirable quiet; but the breeze was at their backs, their scent had preceded them, indeed was now a mile in their van, and the dog knew they were coming.

They were now seven-eighths of the way through this engagement that, in the minds of most of his men, still lay in the future. Bob was not the only one who heard the dog barking: voices up ahead were calling it by name, telling it to shut up. If Bob was lucky, they'd still be lying in their beds cursing the dog at the moment he kicked the door down. But that would have been very lucky indeed. A squall of whinnies and hoofbeats erupted from far ahead, off to their right: Whig Association cavalry, which had converged on this place from another quarter. Even Bob's wrecked ears could make out that much, and one of the younger soldiers insisted that he could hear a carriage moving somewhere off to their right. It was too soon for the inhabitants of this farm, estate, or whatever it was, to have gotten a carriage of their own out on to the road, and so Bob supposed this must be some officers or gentlemen come to observe, remark, criticize, countermand, or otherwise improve upon Bob's conduct of the operation.

"Permission is given to be audible," he said, loudly, and loudness spread like panic down the line to his left and to his right. Though because of the fog it was not so much a line as a chopped-up scribble. The drummers began to beat an advance, and sergeants began to scream in outrage as they understood, from that, just how badly spattered over the field they had become. One platoon was far to the rear, and confused, and (what was much worse) unwilling to accept just how badly they'd got it wrong; Bob crossed them off his mental Order of Battle as *hors de combat*. Other platoons seemed to be moving perpendicular to the line of march. And so Bob finally screamed an order that all should simply march toward the barking dog. This worked better than anything else he had tried. It forced them to go up-slope. Word propagated up the line that a wall had been encountered on the right, and Bob ordered them to hold there. Presently the middle, and finally the left, found that wall, and stopped, forming (Bob supposed) an arc a few hundred yards long, curved inwards to face in the general direction of the dog. Its barking had been joined by the blowing of a post horn; shouting; colliding blades; and pistol-shots. The wall was a linear rock-pile, snarled and teeming with hedge-life. Bob vacillated there, for a few moments, until he heard cavalry behind him, and noted that the fog was beginning to dissolve into the light of day. Then he gave the order to clamber over the wall and proceed double-time toward the melee. They would serve better as beaters than as hunters. The horsemen coming round across their rear could round up anyone who dashed through their line.

THE STREETS OF LONDON, EACH so particular and unique to the terrified, benighted pedestrian, were, to a coach-passenger, as anonymous and same as waves on the sea. As Waterhouse, Newton, and Leibniz had sailed through them during the early hours of the morning, Daniel had teased himself with the phant'sy that they would settle the Calculus Dispute *now*, perhaps with Christian reconciliation or perhaps with a roadside duel in the dead of night. But Sir Isaac had made it plain that he had no intention of talking about *anything*, and had pretended to sleep, and shifted and glared when Leibniz and Waterhouse disturbed his repose with candle-light and chit-chat. This made perfect sense. Isaac held the upper hand in the dispute, and was going to triumph; why talk to Leibniz at all? Leibniz would have to make Newton *want* to talk.

Daniel neither slept, nor pretended to. As soon as there was light, he dropped the carriage's window-shutters, giving them a pleasant enough view of a tree-lined Surrey carriageway. But this lasted only for a quarter of an hour or so before it dissolved in fog. Leibniz, then Newton, stirred from feigned or genuine sleep. "Do you suppose we are riding to the Clubb's final meeting, then?" Daniel asked, now desperate to get them talking about *something*.

"If by that what you are really asking is, 'are we about to catch Jack?' then I should say no," Isaac answered. "This does not seem his sort of place. It looks like the country house of some lord."

"You seem disquieted by that," Leibniz said, "but has it not been obvious from the beginning that Jack must be conniving with men of high rank?"

"Of course," said Isaac, "but I had not expected to drive right through the gate of some Duke's country-house! Where are we?"

"Be at ease," said Daniel, who sat facing forward, and had a view ahead. "We are being hailed by one of Roger's pseudo-Mohawks. He is bidding the driver turn left."

"And what is to the left?"

"A lesser road—not so impressively tree-lined as this. Perhaps it leads away to some humble down-top farm-stead."

But having turned on to that road they immediately drove through a stone gate: clearly not the formal main entrance, but a side door, of some substantial demesne. It seemed to Daniel, as they trundled along the rutted road, that they must be following in the steps of the Whig Association Foot, who must all have paused along this stretch to void their bladders. But then he got it. And for once in his life, he got it slightly quicker than Newton or Leibniz. The last few minutes' travel—the roads, the turns, and the odor—tallied with the penultimate leg of Mr. Kikin's journey. They were there— almost. "Driver!" Daniel exclaimed, "tell me—do you see, up ahead, a place where one might turn to the right, and go up-hill a short distance on an old track that is paved in patches with flat stones?"

"No, guv'nor," said the driver. But then they rounded a bend and he saw just what Daniel had described. As did Newton and Leibniz, who by this point had their heads thrust out of windows. "Go that way!" they all began to shout, for all of them recognized this from Mr. Kikin's narration. The driver complied. They were now ascending a knoll.

At its top was a cluster of old Norman-looking farm-buildings, very down at heels. A dog was barking. Hooves sounded behind; it was their minder from the cavalry. "Turn about! You are going the wrong way!" he called.

"We are going the right way!" insisted Newton, Leibniz, and Waterhouse in unison; which set them all to laughing, and sent the dog into a frenzy.

"Who goes there?" came a call from far away down the hill, and something in the tone of voice gave Daniel the idea that this was not some resident of the place, challenging an intruder, but a fellow intruder, trying to make out what was going on. Which was quite striking, and (an instant later) a wee bit disturbing. Until now, he'd been supposing that they were going over ground that had already been traversed, and laid claim to, by friendlies, operating according to some coherent plan. But now he could hear a simply ludicrous amount of effort being expended by several units and individuals, all within earshot of one another, and all on the same side, for the simple purpose of trying to make out who the other blokes were, what direction they were headed, *et cetera*. So for all he knew, he and Newton and Leibniz might be *in front of* the rest of the force. And finally—as a sort of crowning ornament to this edifice of startling realizations that had been set a-building by the shouted "Who goes there?"—he understood that all military operations were this way, that no one here, other than Daniel, was surprised by any of it, and that (as in so many other situations in life) no remedy was possible and no apologies would be forthcoming.

It kept his mind occupied, anyway, until they crested the knoll and found themselves lost in and surrounded by the Odor: a stench of *sal ammoniac* so bad that it panicked the horses and forced the driver to use every bit of his wit, will, and whip-skill to rein them in, wheel them about, and drive them up-wind, out of the bad air. This confused and wild U through the hilltop lasted for all of ten seconds, and left a farrago of weird impressions in Daniel's mind: the hysterical dog at the end of its tether, the gutted buildings, stained ground. The phrase "abomination of desolation" hung in his head; he could hear the voice of Drake intoning the words out of the Geneva Bible. The ancient half-timbered buildings of the farmstead—which had probably been in ruins even before Jack and his gang had gotten to them—had been attacked, as beetles scavenge a fallen carcass, and holed, torn, gutted, stripped, and remade into some monstrous novelty. The sides that faced out into the surrounding countryside had not been changed much, but the middle of the compound had been turned into something that was part giant machine, part Alchemist's laboratory. Vast boilers, stained black with smoke, narrowed to serpentine tubes of hammered copper, frosted with dripping beads of solder and fuzzy with fertile encrustations of chymical crystals. Patches of soil lay burned and dead where they'd been plashed with murderous tinctures.

It finally occurred to him to look at Isaac to see how the arch-Alchemist reacted to this glimpse of the Art writ large. Daniel saw in Isaac's face neither fascination nor disgust but a kind of pensive bewilderment: the look he got when he was drawing connexions in his mind that were beyond Daniel's powers. But he looked suddenly at Daniel and remarked, "Clarke's house."

Which was a reference to a thing he had taken Daniel to see fifty years earlier, on a visit to Grantham, Lincolnshire: an apothecary's house where Isaac had boarded as a schoolboy. Clarke had dabbled in Alchemy and had filled a side yard of the house with wreckage of his experiments. It was much smaller than what they had just seen, but to young Isaac must have seemed as large, and as glamourous with hazards, and as seething with mystery. In the half-century since, all things Alchemical had become familiar to Isaac; but what he had just seen must have jolted him with the same emotions he had known as a boy making illicit forays into Mr. Clarke's laboratory.

For Daniel's part, he wanted to loathe what Jack had made of this good old farm, and to be outraged, and to hate Jack all the more for it. But none of these feelings came to him. They would never come, because Daniel had already seen in Devon the works of Mr. Thomas Newcomen, which were like a harbinger of this thing. Or perhaps the Engine for Raising Water by Fire, and Jack's phosphorus-mill, were both harbingers of something else, which he could scarce picture in his mind—and scarcely wished to. He had once said to Mr. Threader, in a very self-righteous way, that England did not need

Slaves, if she could learn to make Engines, and that Engines, being clever, were a more English sort of thing than toiling Negroes; but now he was beginning to think that he ought to be more careful of what he wished for. The *first* phosphorus laboratory ever made—that of the Alchemist Heinrich Brand—had been *so* clever that it had inspired Leibniz to write a poem about it. But Daniel could see from the look on Leibniz's face that he'd be writing no poems about *this* place, unless it was a supplementary Canto of Dante's *Inferno.*

They debarked from the carriage, for the horses would on no account draw any nearer to the noisome Works. They knew that the dog was tethered, for they had nearly run over it, and they knew that no humans would be about, because who could or would sleep atop such a hell-mouth? So Newton, Leibniz, and Waterhouse strode rather than crept toward the Factory, and when they heard hoofbeats coming up behind, none of them paid it much mind, knowing that it was the young Mohawk who had been detailed to keep an eye out for them.

The last breaths of the fog had at last blown off from this hilltop, though the low places among the downs were still gloomed under fat gray rivers. One could see ten miles from this place—and anyone save a Natural Philosopher would turn his back to the ugly scene in the center to enjoy the prospect. But these men, who thought nothing of dissecting a beautiful corpse to examine a necrotic ulcer, had eyes only for the phosphorus-works.

The compound was ringed by an old hedgerow that had been viciously trimmed back by its new tenants, and cut down to the height of a man's mid-section. Newton, Leibniz, and Waterhouse passed through a gap where it was pierced by a little side-track, and the Mohawk, who was angling in from another direction, jumped it easily on his mount, wheeled round, and trotted toward them. Waterhouse, well knowing his place, assumed the tedious duty of talking to the rider so that the great ones' observations would not be disturbed. "Never mind what orders you have been given," said Daniel, "this place is the objective of the day—it is why we have all come here."

"Shall I go and summon others?"

"I do not think it necessary—they'll find us anon."

"I meant, sir, in case we should meet with resistance."

"There will be none," said Daniel, "except for *that!*" And he pointed toward the dog, who was sprinting for them.

It turned out that this animal's tether was very long indeed, so that it could range over the entire hilltop, provided it did not commit the classic error of getting the rope wound around anything—and it was one of those dogs who was clever enough to avoid that. Having (or so it imagined) chased off the carriage of Newton, Leibniz, et al., it had found employment on the opposite side of the compound, barking at some untoward noises. But now it was coming for them, angling in on their larboard quarter. It faltered as it perceived a choice between going for Newton and Leibniz—who were several paces ahead—or Daniel and the mounted Mohawk. Wisely, it chose the former. Newton and Leibniz, so different in matters of high philosophy, were absolutely the same when it came to being chased across a farm-yard by a huge ravening mastiff. They cheated to the right, and got up against the hedgerow, prepared to clamber over it if they had to—but this was a last resort, at their age. Then they hustled forward, hoping to get out of the tether's fatal radius. But that tether simply kept uncoiling—just when it looked as if it were about to jerk taut, fresh miles of it would appear, as if by some conjuror's trick. Newton almost tripped over something, and Leibniz bent down and picked it up: it was a long wooden paddle, chymically gnawed and stained, its handle snapped off at one end, but still a fathom long. For they had drawn nigh the boiler where such implements were used to stir and test the thickening coction. Leibniz waved this find around, sending a message that the dog collected instantly; it broke off the frontal assault and shifted fluidly into a feinting-and-lunging style of flank-attack. Daniel caught up with the others about now, and, passing behind Leibniz's defense, went to haul Isaac Newton up off the ground. Meanwhile the Mohawk had ridden up behind the dog and was shouting to draw its attack: a plan his mount well understood and little favored, so that this rider must devote all his powers to managing the mental states of the dog on one hand and the horse on the other.

Isaac was down, not because he had tripped, but because he had gotten interested in something. He held out his hand. A reddish nodule lay in the middle of his palm. "Behold," he announced, "Jack has learnt the art of making *red* phosphorus. It is scattered all about."

"That would be the source of ignition for the Infernal Devices, then," said Leibniz over his shoulder. He was still *en garde* with the paddle, protecting the other two, who were crouched behind him at the base of the hedgerow. But this was less and less necessary, as the Mohawk now had the dog's undivided attention. The horse kept rearing so that it might bring down its hooves on the mastiff's head.

The rider had his pistol out.

"Hold your fire, sir," said Daniel, who long ago had grown sick of seeing dogs killed in the name of Natural Philosophy. He stood up, and pulled Newton to his feet. Something in that word *fire* was troubling him.

"*Hold your fire!*" cried Leibniz, who had glanced down to see red phosphorus all over the ground. But the Mohawk heard them not. The dog's tether had come round to touch the horse's hind legs, and made it panic. The cavalryman leveled his gun at the dog. Leibniz whirled about, turning his back on what was about to happen. Seeing the others a few paces away, side by side, he spun the paddle round to make it horizontal, and held it before him at chest height. Then he hurled himself forward. The implement caught Daniel just below the collar-bone and forced him back until the stiff old vegetation of the murdered hedgerow chopped him just below the buttocks. His last clear impression was of a bolt of fire jerking out of the muzzle of the pistol. Then the sky spun round him—a Ptolemaic illusion, of course, as in truth he was executing a backward somersault over the hedgerow. He—and Newton beside him—tumbled all the way over on the other side, and ended up sprawled face down in the lee of the hedge. The backs of his calves were being broiled by a sea of white flame that had reached over the wall like sunrise.

BOB HAD LOST THE FACULTY of hearing sounds of a high sharp timbre, but had grown very keen to thuds, bumps, and rumbles, which he heard not with his ears but with his feet and his ribs. What he listened for, with said organs, was hoofbeats, door-slams, gunfire, &c. Of guns he had heard only a little thus far. Hooves were spattering the earth to their rear: the Whig Association cavalry, dashing across the back of the line. Bob was leading his company across a pasture toward a hedgerow that bordered its up-hill side. Like all the other hedgerows on this estate, it had been trimmed short, which Bob looked on as a military preparation; the height was good for men to kneel behind and shoot over.

Three such hedgerows, dividing perhaps a quarter mile of more or less open ground, stood between Bob's line and a hilltop farm that seemed to be the source of the barking. Bob glimpsed a carriage careering to and fro up among its buildings but could make no sense of this, and so forced himself to ignore it. His line had instinctively wheeled so that it was parallel to the next hedgerow. When they were just reaching it, and slinging arms and breaking stride to clamber over, Bob felt something in his feet, and shouted, "Cavalry! Less than a squadron—much less. Hold the line. They are coming from beyond those trees." Which was merely a reasonable guess, based on the fact that he could not see them yet. His men's heads all turned— they were hearing something he couldn't. Following their eye-line, Bob locked his gaze upon the edge of the little copse ahead of them—it was growing in a little pocket of the landscape—and saw horses' legs, lit by the orange-amber sun of early morning, scissoring against tree-trunks.

A moment later three riders tore around the corner of the wood and made straight for them. They'd been apt in their timing—waiting for the moment when the approaching foot broke stride to address the hedge-climbing project. "About face—backs against the hedge!" Bob commanded, and they did it.

The three riders had formed a diagonal spread as a result of wheeling round the corner of the wood—the one who'd taken the outside track now trailed. The one in the middle was—his eyes had to be deceiving him—black. Had he been burned? A weapon burst in his face? No time to ponder it now. Bob drew out his sword in case he needed to parry a saber-cut from above. But none of the riders had drawn. The foremost jumped the hedgerow very near Bob, and Bob was almost felled, not by any physical contact but by dizzy awe at the magnificence of the horse and the power of its movement. The black man made the jump just behind Bob. At the same moment a flash lit up the top of the hill, and a moment later came a roaring whoosh and a clatter of booms. The third rider was just fixing to jump the hedgerow when all of this occurred; his mount faltered, clipped the top of the hedge, landed awry, and broke a leg.

The rider tumbled free and rolled to his feet only a little hurt. But two platoons of Foot were crouching with their backs to the hedgerow, all aiming their muskets at him from such short range that his riddled corpse would be scorched by powder-burns if Bob gave the order to fire.

"Take that bloody thing out of my face and shoot my horse," said this fellow to the nearest.

The other two riders—first the black man, then the white—wheeled about in the middle of the pasture, a stone's throw away. In the distance Bob saw several Whig cavalry rounding to intercept them. "Jimmy! Tomba!" shouted the dismounted man. "Go! You can get through 'em! It's a few fops on some nags, and they don't know the territory, and they won't fight!"

All of which, Bob suspected, was true. If "Jimmy" and "Tomba" had kept on at a gallop they could, with a bit of luck, have survived a volley from Bob's musketeers and probably shot through the Whig line. But they showed no gust for it. They exchanged a look, then turned back, and began riding toward their comrade. Bob came out from the shade of the hedgerow, glancing back one time—unnecessarily—to verify that all three of the men had muskets trained on them. A word from Bob and they were dead. They knew this. But they took no notice of Bob or anyone else. As the white rider approached, he said, "Don't be such a tosser, Danny. We are not a devil-take-the-hindmost sort of family, are we?"

Bob now recognized these two—Jimmy and Danny—as his nephews, whom he had not seen in about twenty years.

"Oh, Jesus Christ!" he said.

It was an expression of disgust and chagrin—hardly of surprise. He had been running into too many Shaftoes lately to be surprised by anything. Hearing the oath, they turned to look his way, and knew him in turn. "Aagh! Shit!" exclaimed Danny.

"I knew 'twould come to this sooner or later, uncle," said Jimmy, with a sad, wise shake of the head, "if you kept trafficking with the *legitimate authorities.*"

"You know this man!?" said the black fellow, his mop-like hairdo all a-swing.

"He's our friggin' uncle," said Danny. "Hope you're *satisfied,* Bob."

Bob's heart was thudding. His feet were, too; that because of the cavalry, who were charging across the pasture, having perceived, in all of this, an opportunity to lop some heads, or at least limbs—the sort of entertainment Horse-men lived for. This clear and present danger unfroze Bob's tongue, and his legs. He stumbled out into the path of the cavalry, and held up a hand to stay them; their captain had the good sense to call off the attack. They dropped to a canter and came on in a line to seal off any possible escape.

"You boys have been Absent Without Leave from the King's, and then the Queen's, and then the King's Own Black Torrent Guard for twenty years," said Bob.

"Don't be such a prick!" was Danny's response; but Jimmy—dismounting—said: "*You* don't be such a friggin' *idiot,* brother of mine. Our Uncle Bob phant'sies he's doing us a *boon* by bringing us under *military* justice, so's we'll be hanged *fast* instead of drawn and quartered at Tyburn Cross."

Danny was impressed. "Good one, uncle! Sorry I called you a prick. But just as Jimmy and Tomba would not abandon *me,* so me and Jimmy won't leave Tomba behind to be gutted by Jack Ketch all by his lonesome, will we, Jimmy? Jimmy? Jimmy? *Seamus Shaftoe,* I be talking to ye, shite-for-brains!"

"I suppose not," said Jimmy at last, "but it does put a friggin' strain on me like this, having to do the decent thing *twice* in, what, two friggin' minutes."

"You've had twenty years to do the wrong things," said Bob. "These two minutes won't kill you."

"What about the two minutes at Tyburn?" was Danny's answer—which left Bob so tongue-tied that Tomba laughed out loud at him.

DANIEL HAD NEVER HEARD ISAAC admit to feeling pain, until he and Leibniz each took one of his hands and pulled him to his feet. Then Isaac got an astonished look, as though he'd never hurt before in his life, and let out an "Ooh-oh! Ah! Ah!" He clenched his eyes shut, grimaced, and steepled his brow, then froze just long enough to convince Daniel that he was suffering a cardiac event that would terminate his life. But finally the pain appeared to leak away in slow increments, and his conscious mind assumed control over the nerves that led to the muscles of the face. He could now wear the expression he wished to: one of forced unconcern. "It is," he said, and stopped to sip air, "nothing. The muscles . . . about the ribs . . . were not ready . . . for Baron von Leibniz's . . . *intervention.*"

"Might you have broken a rib?" Daniel asked.

"I do not believe so," said Newton in one long down-hill gout of breath. Then he regretted having said so much at a go, as this obliged him to breathe deeply once. The grimace came back.

"Let us fetch the carriage, so you do not have to walk," suggested Leibniz. "Daniel, you might remain with Sir Isaac?"

Daniel stood by Newton while Leibniz—who because of gout moved in an awkward shrugging-and-rolling gait even on a good day—went off to find their carriage. Its team must have fled screaming when the top of the hill had gone off. The place had not precisely exploded—though embedded in the event had been many small explosions. It had, rather, caught fire and burned to cinders very rapidly, as if a fire that ought to have extended over some hours had been compressed into as many seconds. The place had been a kind of slum, growing and running without plan—senseless. But unlike a normal slum, which about itself created middens of bones, gristle, shit, and ash, this one had become filthy with chymical wastes and by-products, many of them highly inflammable. The fire kindled by the Mohawk's pistol-shot had hopped and rushed across the phosphorus-pocked soil until it had struck a vein: a rivulet of waste trickling from one of the boilers. It had raced up this fuse and ignited, then exploded, one or more of the giant copper retorts, and this blast, like the firing of powder in a musket's pan, had ignited the main conflagration: some large store of red phosphorus in what had been a barn. The barn had been erased. Not even wreckage remained. The boilers were strewn scraps of copper, some of which was still molten. The dog, horse, and rider were steaming, intertangled bone-piles; they'd been incinerated by the roasting heat of the burning barn—a sort of action at a distance whereby heat was transmitted across space like gravity. It traveled, like light, in straight lines. This explained why Leibniz, Newton, and Waterhouse still lived, for in tumbling over the hedgerow they had fallen into its shadow, and so intercepted none of the fire's radiance. The side of the hedgerow facing the barn was now a sterile stone spine with a few stalagmites of charcoal reaching out of it. The opposite side, a few inches away, was unchanged.

These and other impressions fully occupied their Natural-Philosophick faculties for some minutes. Then Daniel's attention began to wander about. He had never taken a proper look round the area. First fog, then flames had baffled careful observations. He had no idea where they were, save that it was in Surrey, on some elevated stretch of the North Downs. Casting an eye down the hill, he saw undulating country spread out for many miles, church-steeples poking up here and there. Turning about, he saw a sort of cottage a few hundred yards down the road. But before he could gather many impressions of that, his eye was drawn to a much larger building spreading its wings across the breadth of a rise in the distance, and embracing one end of a system of formal gardens. "By god, that is a Great House!" he exclaimed. A stupid remark, but one that had to be gotten out of the way. His eyes were now able to find the tree-lined carriageway from which they had turned off some minutes before. It led around to the opposite face of that house and came up, he supposed, to its front door. "Whose is it?"

Newton had not noticed it before. But when he did, he looked bemused rather than surprised. "If you were a Tory, you would know it by heart. That is a place that my lord Bolingbroke bought, some years ago, from my lord—" and Isaac mentioned the name of a Whig lord who had famously gone bankrupt during an especially festive run on the Bank of England.

"I did not know Bolingbroke had a house in these parts," Daniel confessed.

"That is because he has not occupied it yet," said Isaac, "only subjected it to an endless series of remodeling-projects." Then he paused to sift his own words. "Remodeling means that diverse tradesmen are forever passing in and out of the place with wagon-loads of stuff. The local people grow accustomed to such traffic . . ."

"You are saying that a criminal enterprise, headquartered on some of the out-buildings of the manor, could conceal its presence and its activities by blending in with such traffic," said Daniel. He did not want to oblige Isaac to speak any more than was necessary, as it was quite obviously painful. "It is remarkable. We have suspected some link between Bolingbroke and Jack. But who would have imagined that the Secretary of State would suffer such goings-on in his own property?"

"Perhaps not *so* remarkable," said Isaac. "He does not actually *live* here. We have lately seen that Bolingbroke was weaker, and more desperate, than we had supposed when he was at the zenith of his power and we in terror of him. He may have been beholden to Jack in ways we can only guess at. So for Jack to make use of some outbuildings on a piece of surplus property owned by Bolingbroke, and probably paid for by the King of France . . ." Newton shrugged to indicate it was not all that surprising, but then he wished he hadn't, as the movement seemed to ignite racking pains in his ribs.

"I see another carriage headed this way," said Daniel, "probably that of Monsieurs Kikin, Orney, and Threader." He waved to it and the driver waved back. "Let us sit down and await it."

"I prefer to stand," said Isaac, "so that I shall not have to get up again."

"Whither shall we ask the driver to convey us?" asked Daniel, hoping Isaac would say, *the nearest physician.*

"To yonder cottage," Isaac said. "Let us discover what Jack has got going in *there.* Though I think I know already."

"IT IS AS I THOUGHT," he was saying twenty minutes later. He was seated at a work table in the cottage. Daniel, Leibniz, Orney, Threader, and Kikin were gathered about, standing on shards of glass that had been blown out of the frames during the recent entertainments. The carriage in which Daniel, Newton, and Leibniz had come out from London had been hunted down and driven back here, and a certain box of instruments fetched from it. From this Newton had selected an excellent convex lens mounted in a loupe, which he was using to inspect some pieces of evidence they had found lying out in plain sight on this table.

On the upper storey of this cottage, in a bedchamber, under a bed, the "Mohawks" had found three men who spoke no English. One was middle-aged and the other two might have been apprentices, sons, or both. They had been herded down stairs, and Leibniz had figured out that they were Saxons. They were relieved he could speak German but terrified that he was a Baron. He had been conversing with them, and Kikin (who knew German) had listened in, while Newton had inspected the exhibits on the work table. Left with nothing to do, Orney and Threader stood by, and Daniel was struck by the difference in their faces: Orney as ebullient as he was ever likely to get, Threader curiously distracted and rigid.

"Before I relate my findings," said Newton, "have you learned anything from these men, Baron von Leibniz?"

"This will hardly surprise anyone, given the nature of these tools and workpieces," said Leibniz, "but these men are engravers. They came from Dresden."

"And the elder is quite obviously a master," said Newton. "Please tell him who I am, and give him my highest compliments."

Leibniz did so. The mention of Newton's name nearly struck the Saxons dead with terror, but the compliment that followed close on its heels caused the oldest of the three to go all pink. He bowed very low—then, perhaps fearing that this was not obsequious enough, he got down on both knees. The younger men followed suit. Daniel had rarely seen humans so abject. "Isaac," he said, "they are probably wondering whether you intend to kill them."

"What they have been doing here would be High Treason, were they Englishmen," Isaac allowed. "Whether Saxons can be accused of treason against the United Kingdom is a question for scholars of the law."

"They have told me," said Leibniz, "that they were induced to come here on false pretenses. Having arrived, they were made prisoners in this cottage, and told that they would neither be paid nor allowed to depart until they had accomplished a certain work, which is now nearly finished."

"That it is!" said Newton. From the table before him he picked up a dun-colored wafer that earlier had come in for prolonged inspection under his glass. "This is a wax impression of a die for a one-guinea piece. I invite you all to inspect it." He handed it to Daniel. It was quite familiar, and at the same time very strange.

"This bears an image of George Louis of Hanover!" he exclaimed.

"A fortnight ago, I directed the engravers at the Tower Mint to begin work on a die for the new King George guineas," Newton said. "Since then—as many can testify—I have not once set foot in the Liberty of the Tower. I have never seen the dies from which that wax impression was struck. And yet here in this cottage in Surrey—the property of my lord Bolingbroke—we find the impression, and—" he picked up a cylinder of metal, bearing on one end an engraved mirror-image of the relief on the wax "—an essentially perfect copy of the die, which may be put to use in coining counterfeit guineas! This evidence, and the testimony of the Saxons, have delivered our enemies into our hands. Those charged with guarding the Mint—under the command of Charles White—have quite obviously colluded in making the wax impression, and delivering it here, where we have found coining-equipment, and caught the two sons of Jack Shaftoe red-handed. And since I have taken care not to enter the

Mint, Bolingbroke cannot accuse me of having had a hand in any of this. I'll see them all at Tyburn—and as for these Saxons, they shall be free to go home after they have assisted us with our inquiries."

Norman Orney—a heavy-built man, but strong and even spry from working in his ship-yard—was able to catch the smaller and frailer Mr. Threader before he struck the floor.

Assisted by one of the younger Saxons, he carried Threader up-stairs and heaved him on to a bed. Hankies were waved, hands rubbed, feet propped up, &c., and presently blood seeped back in to the old money-scrivener's face and he woke up. But, plainly enough, he wished he hadn't.

"Oh, Sir Isaac," he said, and began flailing for a handhold. "Help me to rise," he said to no one.

"I think you should stay down," said Daniel.

"That moment has arrived I prayed would never come," said Threader. "I must get down on my knees and pray to Sir Isaac New-ton for my life—or, barring that, an honorable death—or if that is not feasible, an expeditious."

"Then you admit collusion with coiners?" said Isaac, quite as bored as the others were astonished.

"You figured it out ages ago, didn't you, Sir Isaac? Yes. Collusion with coiners. With *the* coiner. Now, mind you, in the beginning—"

"It seemed like nothing," said Isaac, and waved his hand as if shooing off a wasp. "Forgive me, but I detect the onset of a long and well-rehearsed narration, for which I have no sufferance. The longer you make the story, the more gradual, insensible, and innocent seems your descent into . . . *High Treason*."

Threader jumped, if such a thing was possible for a man lying flat on his back.

"But no matter how you stretch it, the *beginning* and the *end* are the same, are they not?" Isaac continued. "At the *beginning* you fall into the seemingly harmless practice of weighing guineas, and culling out those that are infinitesimally heavier. At the *end* you have been thoroughly compromised by Jack the Coiner. He has placed his agents in your company—he *owns* you so completely that he can even place an Infernal Device in your luggage-wagon, in the hope of assas-sinating the Master of the Mint at the Royal Society."

"Oh, Sir Isaac, I did not know about that!"

"*That* much I believe. Jack would have had no reason to warn you—on the contrary. Yet even if the matter of the Infernal Device is left out of the accompt, you too are guilty of High Treason!"

"Oh, but what if I testify? Put me before a magistrate, Sir Isaac! No counter-tenor at the Italian Opera ever sang as I shall!"

"I do not need to hear you sing," said Isaac. "Your offer has come too late. With no assistance from you, I have obtained all I wished for."

"What if I could give you Jack the Coiner?" said Mr. Threader. Which struck Daniel and the others as frightfully dramatic; but Newton smiled thinly, like a chess-master who always knew that his foe would bring his Queen out eventually.

"Then there is an opportunity for negotiation," said Newton. "Give me what you have."

"Every Sunday evening, it is my lord Bolingbroke's habit to go to a certain Clubb frequented by Tories. There is a back room, a private salon with a servants' door leading back into the kitchens. At a certain signal Bolingbroke withdraws to that room on some pretext or other. Meanwhile Jack has entered the same Clubb through the back, in the guise of a knife-grinder who has come to whet the cooks' cutlery. He comes into that salon through the servants' door and doffs his disguise, and there the two villains hatch their plots and co-ordinate their schemes. It should happen again, just as I've said, in only a few hours, this being Sunday."

"Perhaps Jack will have heard about what has happened this morning, and will know better than to attend the meeting," said Isaac.

"Who shall bring him intelligence of it? The estate has been sealed off."

"Everyone in the county saw the top of the hill explode."

"Perhaps news of it shall reach Jack, perhaps not," said Mr. Threader. "He must still meet with Bolingbroke from time to time. If this fails, why, I know other things about Jack, and can suggest other stratagems."

"Then let us go to London so that the snare may be laid," said Newton; and with that, the Clubb's most eventful meeting (to date anyway) was adjourned, and its Treasurer manacled.

Library of Leicester House
MORNING OF 18 AUGUST 1714

For the sovereign is the public soul, giving life and motion to the commonwealth; which expiring, the members are governed by it no more, than the carcase of a man, by his departed, though immortal, soul.

— HOBBES, *Leviathan*

THE PLACE HAD NOT been fixed up in more than a hundred years, and was irredeemably Tudor: one could easily imagine Gloriana calling Sir Walter Raleigh on the carpet in here. No books by living authors were in evidence. The coastlines on the globe were hopelessly out of fashion.

Sir Isaac Newton did not have leisure to peruse this convex Artifact, however. He had been escorted to the library by young Johann von Hacklheber—a Leipziger baron. And so he was not extremely surprised to recognize a second North German baron—Gottfried Wilhelm von Leibniz—rising from a chair to bid him welcome. Newton's face showed that he was annoyed to have been ensnared into yet another extraordinary and irregular meeting with his Nemesis, but that he would stiffen his upper lip and get through it. He glanced for only a moment at the young woman seated in an armchair near the globe. His eyes then snapped back to Leibniz. "I was led to believe I should be paying a call on the Duchess of Arcachon-Qwghlm," he began. But his protest trailed off as his eyes wandered back to behold the young woman. It was not just that she was good looking, though she more or less was. It was rather that she was turned out in clothing and jewels— especially, jewels—the likes of which Newton had not feasted his protruberant eyes on since the last time he had been summoned into the presence of Royalty. The woman was, in fact, wearing an actual tiara, and something in her bearing told Newton that it was no affectation, and that the sparkly bits were no rhinestones.

Johann von Hacklheber had already ducked out. Leibniz had the floor. "Your royal highness," he said to the young woman, "this is Sir Isaac Newton. Sir Isaac, it is my honor to present Her Royal Highness Caroline, Princess of Wales, Electoral Princess of Hanover, *et cetera, et cetera.*"

"Stay! Do not move, Sir Isaac," said Caroline, causing the savant to freeze in the opening of what promised to be a deep and lengthy formal bow. "We have heard already the story of how you were injured in our service—an inadvertent consequence of Baron von Leibniz's heroics. You are in no condition for courtly bowing. Pray sit down."

"You need not narrow your eyes thus at Freiherr von Leibniz," said another voice, from the corner. Newton looked over to see Daniel Waterhouse, who had been delving into a brown and crusty Tome. "It is *I*, not the Baron, who related the story to her royal highness, and I who ought to be blamed for any misapprehensions I may have planted in her mind. True, it's not every day that a German Baron has a go at Sir Isaac Newton with a great stick. *Some* might be tempted to make something out of it; but I suffered the same, and have forgiven him, and thanked him."

"As do I," said Newton easily, and then sat down—with conspicuous stiffness—in the side chair indicated by Caroline. Now it was Caroline in the big throne-like armchair next the globe, symmetrically flanked by Newton and Leibniz. Waterhouse prowled about the dim periphery, like a furtive librarian or, as it were, a philosophick Butler.

Caroline broke the ice—which was passing thick and cold—with small talk of the last days' events in London. Were the rumors true?

This was *just* the gambit to use on Sir Isaac, who desired more than anything to set the new Dynasty's mind at ease about the coinage of their Realm.

"Jack Shaftoe is ours!" he proclaimed. "The Coiner shall coin no more in *this* world."

"If our understanding of the thing is correct," said Caroline, "then this is momentous news indeed, and I am surprised I have not heard more of it."

"Ah, but your royal highness, I did not know you were in London until I stepped over the threshold of this room—otherwise your royal highness should have been notified within the hour of Mr. Shaftoe's arrest."

"That is not what I meant. I refer to the fact that we have not heard anything of it from Grub Street."

"He was taken in the back room of a certain Clubb, only a few minutes' walk from here, frequented by Tories—many of whom, you may be sure, are sorely embarrassed. Certain Whigs would make political hay of it—and presently *shall.* I bear most of the men of this Clubb no ill-will and did not wish to expose them to obloquy. The true villain of the piece is a certain Tory Lord who was the first man in England for a time—"

"I know who you mean."

"*He* may deserve exposure and shame, but this is not to be achieved without grave embarrassment to the entire Realm. The matter is delicate—" and here Isaac looked, uncharacteristically, to one who would know more about it: Daniel Waterhouse, Lord Regent.

Daniel responded by raising his voice in the direction of a side door of the library, which stood ajar. "Bring it in," he commanded.

The door was drawn open by some unseen servant. Another servant, a butler, came in gripping a tray mostly covered by a blue velvet cushion. Bedded in that were two ingots of metal, deeply wrought with intricate circular depressions, made so that they could be clapped together like a huge locket. These were borne over to the Princess so that she could inspect them; Newton and Leibniz stole sidelong glances. "It is my honor," said Daniel, "to present to your royal highness the Seals that are used by His Majesty's Secretary of State on his official correspondence. Until yesterday these were, of course, in the possession of my lord Bolingbroke. But as your royal highness may have heard, Bolingbroke has decided to spend more time with his family."

"Yes—*in France,*" said Caroline drily.

"He was last seen southbound at a speed normally seen only among men who have been projected from high cliffs," Daniel allowed. "Of course, being a man of honor, he first gave the Seals of his former office to one of His Majesty's Regents. I had the privilege of catching them when they slipped from his sweaty and trembling hands, and now present them to your royal highness. They are your family property. You may take them back to Hanover or—"

"They shall be ever so much more useful here," said Caroline. "You and the other Regents will look after them, won't you?"

"We shall consider it our honor and our privilege, highness."

"Very well. Then since Bolingbroke appears to have departed the stage, I would that these be set aside, and I would hear more of Jack Shaftoe. Did he fight?"

The butler backed away and set the Seals on a library table near Daniel, then backed out of the room bowing. This gave Newton some moments to frame a response. Isaac, who until now had been at pains to respond instantly to the Princess's every word and gesture, bated for a moment before answering. Daniel searched his face and thought he perceived a quiver of triumph—a rare self-indulgence for a Puritan. He was sitting at the right hand of the Princess of Wales telling the tale of how he'd caught the arch-villain Jack the Coiner, and, as a soupçon, the Seals of his most terrible persecutor had been brought in as a sort of trophy. Only Bolingbroke's scalp on a stick would have given satisfaction more complete.

"Fight? No. Rather, he feigned a sort of boredom, or so I am told by the bailiffs who arrested him."

"Boredom?"

"Yes, highness, as if he had known all along that he was walking into a trap."

"Is he in the Tower of London, then?"

Isaac could not prevent a patronizing smile from spreading across his face. "As Mr. Shaftoe is a traitor and an important one, your royal highness anticipates, correctly, that he shall be held in the Tower. In this case, however, there are extenuating circumstances that have dictated a less conventional accommodation. Jack the Coiner and his gang seized the Tower complex in an elaborate *coup de main* some months ago. It was hushed up, explained away. But the fact is that he did it; from which we may conclude that he had, and has, many confederates among the people who dwell there, and that he knows its secrets all too intimately. Effective control of the Tower is still vested in Charles White, captain of the King's Messengers, and he is an old crony of Bolingbroke."

"I should have thought the Regents might have found another man for such a position," said Caroline, shifting her attention to Daniel.

"In England such changes are not made lightly or swiftly," said Daniel, "and rarely without cause. We have no firm evidence against Mr. White—though this might change—"

"If Jack talks to us, and tells us what he knows," Newton concluded.

"I see," said Caroline, "which is yet another reason to keep him out of the Tower, and out of the Power, of Charles White. Where then is he?"

"He is in Newgate Prison," said Newton, "and others of his gang are in Fleet Prison. We deemed it wisest not to put all of them together in one building."

"Indeed," said Caroline, looking a little dismayed. "But is Newgate not a very common pit? Can he be kept close in such a place?"

"Newgate is several prisons lumped into one," said Daniel. "The most notorious part of it is indeed an execrable dungeon. But connected with it is the Press-Yard and Castle, where Persons of Quality are held, if they can afford it."

"We are paying the Gaolers of Newgate to keep him in an apartment there, heavily ironed," Newton announced.

"Can Jack not pay them even more?"

"Perhaps. But if they collude in his escape, the gaolers lay themselves open to charges of High Treason. And, working as they do at Newgate, and discoursing with Jack Ketch every day, they know better than most what is the penalty for *that* crime."

"I thank you, Sir Isaac, and Dr. Waterhouse, for acquainting me with these things," said Caroline, in a tone of voice, and with a shift of posture, that made it plain that this part of the conversation was at an end. "Now I would hear of matters far more important." She settled back in her chair, letting its padded arms support her elbows, and as she talked, her right hand strayed over to rest upon the antique globe and nudge it this way and that in its felt-lined cradle. Her pose recalled that of a Monarch with one hand on an Orb, though the other hand seemed to be missing its Sceptre. "As you may know, Sir Isaac, I have known Baron von Leibniz for many years, and learned from him much of what I know of Mathematicks, Metaphysicks, and the younger discipline of Natural Philosophy. Concerning the first of these, reports have reached me of an unpleasant dispute concerning the origin of the Calculus. The particulars are tedious. Lesser minds, confronted with such complexities, have seized on simple explanations. One such is that you stole the calculus from Freiherr von Leibniz; another is that he stole it from you. I find both of these hypotheses unconvincing."

During Caroline's remarks Daniel had observed a change in the weather pass across Isaac's face. If he had expected lavish thanks and praise, he had been disappointed; Caroline had found the news of Jack and Bolingbroke interesting but, in the end, not all that remarkable. 'Twas as if the exhausted and bloodied Knight had dragged a pair of freshly slain dragons into the forecourt of the Princess's castle, and after a look-see and a polite question or two, she had gone back to filing her nails. Isaac had been irked for a moment, then resigned himself to it. 'Twas ever thus, for Isaac. Everything he had done had been under-appreciated and over-criticized. The pink flush of victory, which earlier had been so plain on his face, had vanished, to be replaced by the visage he was used to wearing: gray and stiff as the figurehead on a worn-out ship.

"Your royal highness knows Leibniz better than I," said Newton. "As you have confided your view in me, highness, I shall accept it, and say nothing against it, either here, or in public. Of course, I have no power to compel other philosophers to adopt that, or any other, view."

"Then let us wash our hands of the Calculus Dispute and move on to Metaphysicks and Natural Philosophy. For I have long suspected—and Dr. Waterhouse will support me on this—that the Calculus Dispute was really an epiphenomenon of a far more profound, interesting, and momentous debate. Baron von Leibniz has served my House well as court philosopher; Sir Isaac, I trust, is desirous of doing likewise."

"It is chief among my aspirations, highness," Newton responded. This elicited a slight eye-roll from Leibniz, who glanced toward Daniel for support, but Daniel affected not to notice, and remained grave of aspect.

"I wonder if any royal House in the history of this world has enjoyed the distinction of being served, at the same time, by two such eminent philosophers! It is a rare thing, and I mean to make the most of it. You are both Christians, believers in a living and active God. You both hold that humans are made in God's image, possessing free will. In Mathematicks and Natural Philosophy, your interests run on very similar lines. And yet there is between you a schism as deep as that between Scylla and Charybdis—a fundamental divergence of views that makes it impossible for you to collaborate with each other. Which were not such a bad thing, perhaps, if I were still Princess of Ansbach or some other tiny place, and you, sir, a Librarian and you, sir, a Vicar. But I am Princess of Wales. The House you both now serve is a great one—some would say, second only to the House of Bourbon. If the philosophy of that House is confused, why, it shall have dreadful consequences, dificult to foretell. A year ago, I asked Dr. Waterhouse to journey hither from Boston, that we might go to work healing this breach. That you, Sir Isaac, and you, Baron von Leibniz, are here together in this room now, is all his doing; but he did it at my command. His part in the thing is done and he has my gratitude forever. *Your* parts, gentlemen, begin now."

"Highness," said Newton, "I am grateful to you for having stated with such clarity the *truth* of my views on God, the human spirit, and free will. For Baron von Leibniz, I am sorry to report, has disseminated the slander that I am some sort of Atheist. While it is true that I reject the doctrine of the Trinity, please know that I do so only out of a belief that the Homoousian doctrine promulgated at the Council of Nicaea was an error, a straying from what Christians had believed until then, and ought to believe now—"

"Any person who seeks *slander* need not look so far afield, nor delve so deep!" Leibniz exclaimed, rising to his feet so forcefully that he had to take half a step toward Newton to steady himself. "I saved this man's life three days ago, and gossip has already reached my ears that I am guilty of *assaulting* him! These willful distortions, sir, do nothing to bring us nigher true Philosophy!"

"I cannot imagine any slander more base than that I am an Atheist!" returned Newton. Because of his ribs, it was much more difficult for him to rise from his chair, but now he got his walking-stick under his folded hands as if he were about to give it a go.

"An Atheist? No. Never would I spread such a calumny—on my honor! But *spreading doctrines that incline others toward Atheistical views* is another matter. Of that you are, I regret to say, culpable."

"Can one believe the incoherence of the man?!" Newton burst out, and regretted it, for it hurt to speak so vehemently. As long as his ribs were complaining anyway, he rose to his feet, then continued the outburst in a voice distorted by pain. "I am not an Atheist, he claims to admit—then he turns around and accuses me of spreading Atheism! It is typical of his slippery discourse, his slippery metaphysics!"

They were interrupted, but only for a moment, by a thud emanating from the floor between them. For Princess Caroline, disgruntled and bored, had used the palm of her hand to roll the globe up out of its cradle and over the rim of the felt-padded Great Circle that held it captive. It had tumbled to the rug between Newton and Leibniz. She put a foot up on it—a most undignified posture, for a Princess—and began to roll it back and forth idly as the argument went on.

"I do not think it is the least bit slippery," said Leibniz. "You may be the most sincere Christian in the world, sir, but if you publish doctrines that are obscure, incoherent, contradictory, and impossible for readers to follow, why, they may go a-stray in their thinking and tend towards doctrines you would never espouse."

"This is how you make amends for a false accusation of Atheism—by saying my life's work is incoherent and contradictory? Pray do not make any more such apologies, sirrah, or *I* shall have to make amends to *you* by challenging you to a duel!"

Princess Caroline gave the globe a hard shove, and it rolled for a few yards across the carpet and scored a goal, as it were, in a large fireplace that accounted for most of one wall of the room. The hearth was slightly lower than the floor of the room, so the globe lodged there, and came to a stop between two andirons. "That globe will never do, for a modern Monarch," she announced. "When the Prince of Wales and I move to this house, it shall have to be replaced by a new one, with more of geography and fewer of monsters and mermaids. One that shall be ready to receive Lines of Longitude whensoever that Roger Comstock finds someone to award his Prize to." She rose now to her feet, and Newton and Leibniz, finally remembering their manners, turned to track her as she walked toward the fireplace. First, though, she wrenched a burning taper from a chair-side candelabrum. "As a rule I am averse to burning things found in Libraries, but this must be reckoned no loss at all, compared to the damage that the two of you are inflicting on Philosophy by your bickering." She bent her knees and executed a graceful descent until she was sitting on the floor beside the hearth, skirts arranged around her. "I see things sometimes, in dreams or in daydreams—some of them I quite fancy, for they seem to carry meaning. Those I remember, and think back on. There is one such vision that has got stuck in my head, quite as melodies often do, and I can't seem to get rid of it. I shall try to do justice to it thusly." And she reached out with the candle and let its flame lave the underside of the globe. The globe was of wood, and too heavy to catch fire readily; but paper gores printed with images of continents had been pasted over it. The paper caught fire, and a ragged flame-ring began to spread, consuming the cartographer's work and leaving behind it a blackened and featureless sphere. "Sophie kept trying to tell me, before she died, that a new System of the World was being made. Oh, it is not a terribly novel thing to say. I know, and Sophie knew, that the third volume of your *Principia Mathematica* bears that name, Sir Isaac. Since she died, I have become quite convinced that she was correct—and moreover that the System is to be born, not at Versailles, but here—that this shall be its Prime Meridian, and all else shall be reckoned, and ruled, from here. It is a pleasing notion that there is to be such a System, and that I might play some small part in being its midwife. I think of the globe, with its neat parallels and meridians, as the Emblem of this System—what the Cross is to Christianity. But I am troubled by the vision of such a Globe in flames. What you are looking at here is a poor rendition of it; in my nightmares, it is ever so much more lovely and dreadful."

"What do you suppose that vision signifies, highness?" asked Daniel Waterhouse.

"That this System, if it is set up wrong, might be doomed from the start," said Caroline. "Oh, it shall be a wonder to behold at first, and all shall marvel at its regularity, its œconomy, and the ingenuity of them who framed it. Perhaps it shall work as planned for a decade, or a century, or more. And yet if it has been made wrong at the beginning, it shall burn, in the end, and my vision shall be realized in a manner infinitely more destructive than *this*." She gave the smoking globe a nudge. It had been wholly scoured by the flames and become a trackless black orb.

Daniel now stepped over and gave her a hand up. "I do not concern myself so much," said Caroline, turning toward Leibniz and

Newton, "with bankers, merchants, clock-makers, or Longitude-finders, and their rôles in the creation of this System. Or even with Astronomers and Alchemists. But I am terribly concerned with my Philosophers, for if *they* get it wrong, then the System *is* flawed, and *shall* burn, in the end. Stop your bickering and get to work."

"As it pleases your highness," said Sir Isaac. "What would you have us work on?"

"Baron von Leibniz may be on to something," said Caroline, "which is that, though you, and most other Fellows of the Royal Society, are true Christians, and believers in Free Will, the very doctrines and methods that the Royal Society has promulgated have caused many to question the existence of God, the divinity of Christ, the authority of the Church, the premise that we have souls endowed with Free Will. Why, Dr. Waterhouse himself has lately given me the lamentable news that he has quite abandoned all such doctrines."

This earned Daniel perturbed and puzzled looks from Newton and Leibniz. All he could do, in the face of such disapproval from such minds, was make a frail smile and shrug. Caroline continued, "As so much of civilization is rooted in those beliefs, this strikes me as one way in which our System of the World might be set up wrongly and thus self-doomed. Neither you, Sir Isaac, nor you, Baron von Leibniz, sees the slightest contradiction between your Faith and the true and fearless pursuit of Natural Philosophy. But you differ radically in how you reconcile the one with the other. If you two cannot manage it, no one can; and so I would like for you to work on *that*, if you please."

"Your royal highness's discourse concerning the System of the World, and the threat of its running awry at some future time, puts me in mind of a thing I do not understand in the philosophy of Sir Isaac Newton," Leibniz began. "Sir Isaac describes that System by which the heavenly bodies are kept in their gyres, and made to orbit round and round forever. Fine. But he seems to say that God, who created this system and set it in motion, must from time to time reach in and tinker with it, as a horologist adjusts the workings of his clock. As if God lacked the foresight, or the power, to make it a perpetual motion."

"You are over-reacting to a passage from my *Opticks* that is really not all that important," Isaac began.

"On the contrary, sir, it is very important indeed, *if it is wrong*, and puts wrong ideas in people's heads!"

"Then as you are at such pains to correct my errors, Herr Leibniz, let me return the favor in kind. This similitude, likening the universe to a clock, and God to a horologist, is faulty. A horologist is presented with certain laws or facts of nature, viz. that weights descend towards the center of the earth and springs push back when deflected. Taking these as givens, he hacks away at his bench to produce some mechanism that exploits these properties in a more or less ingenious way. Ones who are more ingenious, make clocks that require adjustment less often, and one who was perfect would, I suppose, make one that would never need it at all. But God does not merely compose the objects and forces that were given to Him, but is Himself the Author of those objects and forces. Author, and preserver. Nothing happens in this world without His government and His inspection. Think of Him not as a watch-maker but as a King. Suppose there were a Kingdom where all things ran forever in an orderly and regular way without the King ever having to attend, make judgments, or exercise his powers. If it were, in sum, so ordered that the King could be removed from it without any diminution, then he would be a King only in name, and not deserving of the respect and loyalty of his subjects."

"Like the God of Spinoza," said Caroline, "if I am following your similitude correctly."

"Indeed, highness. And so if Baron von Leibniz is of the view that the world can go on forever without the continual inspection and governance of God, why, then, I say that it is *his* philosophy that shall incline men towards Atheism."

"That is *not* my view, as I think you know," said Leibniz equably. "I believe that God takes part in the world's workings at every moment—but *not* in the sense of mending it when it has gone awry. To say otherwise is to say God makes mistakes, and changes His mind. Instead of which I believe in a pre-established harmony, reflecting that God has foreseen all, and provided for it."

To which Sir Isaac was about to make some rejoinder when he was interrupted by Daniel. "This, I believe, is the least interesting topic that the two of you could debate. It is really an argument about the signification of certain words, and the applicability of certain metaphors: the clock-maker, the King, *et cetera.*"

Both Leibniz and Newton were pressing their lips together to keep all of their objections and rejoinders from bursting forth in a Pandoran onslaught. Rather than see the rest of the day devoted to the aftermath, Daniel turned to Princess Caroline and continued, without letup: "Or to put it another way: your royal highness, are you willing to stipulate that Sir Isaac and Baron von Leibniz both believe in a God who is aware of and active in the Universe? And that this God, in framing the Universe, was not chargeable of any errors?"

"Indeed, Dr. Waterhouse, it is plain to see that both of them believe as much—though I wish *you* would believe it, too."

"I am not really a participant, highness, so let us leave my views out of the reckoning."

"On the contrary, Dr. Waterhouse," said the Princess, "every philosophical dialogue I have ever read, requires one interlocutor who is of a Skeptickal habit of mind—"

"Or of a Stupid," Daniel put in.

"Be he Skeptickal, Stupid, or both, the others try to win him over to their view of things." Caroline had suddenly gone all flushed and girlish, and looked to Newton and Leibniz for their support in the venture. Phant'sying she saw what she wanted, she turned back to the bemused Daniel, who was saying: "Am I to understand that the purpose of the discussion is now to subject me to a *religious conversion?*"

"*You* are the one who complained, a moment ago, of feeling Stupid," said Caroline, a bit miffed. "So listen, and be enlightened."

"I am yours to command, highness, and ready for Enlightenment. But I'd have you know that my Stupidity and my Skepticism are two sides of the same coin, and are of a very particular kind, which is carefully thought out. John Locke was of the same mind, and set it down in words better than I ever could. To go into it here would be half an hour's digression; suffice it to say, that as a result of being near men like Newton and Leibniz, men like Locke and I are all too keenly aware of the limits of our own intellects, and the dullness of our own senses. And not only of ours but of most other people's, too. And as a result of studying Natural Philosophy we have got glimmerings of the immensity and complexity of the Universe that were not available to anyone until of late, and are known only to a few now. The imbalance between the grand mysteries of the Universe as opposed to our own feeble faculties, leads us to set very modest expectations as to what we shall and shan't be able to understand—and makes us passing suspicious of anyone who propounds dogma or seems to phant'sy he has got it all figured out. Having said which I must concede that if *anyone* can figure it all out, it would be these two; and so I'll listen, provided they confine their discussion to topics that are *interesting.*"

"And what would you denominate interesting, Doctor Waterhouse?" asked the Princess.

"The two labyrinths."

Caroline and Leibniz both smiled; Newton looked stormy. "I do not know what this is meant to signify."

"Doctor Leibniz mentioned to me long ago that there are two sorts of intellectual labyrinths into which all thinking people are sooner or later drawn," said Caroline. "One is the composition of the continuum, which is to say, what is matter made of, what's the nature of space, *et cetera.* The other is the problem of free will: Do we have a choice in what we do? Which is like saying, do we have souls?"

"I'll agree with Baron von Leibniz at least to this point: these are interesting questions, and so many spend so much time thinking on them that the similitude of a labyrinth is well taken."

Daniel reminded them, "The Princess has requested that this discussion be productive of a better System of the World. I put it to you that the latter question—free will, and the spirit—is, as far as that goes, the more important. Myself, I am comfortable with the notion that we are Machines made of Meat, that there's no more free will in us than there is in a cuckoo-clock, and that the spirit, soul, or whatever you want to call it, is a færy-tale. Many who study Natural Philosophy will arrive at the same conclusion, unless the two of you find a way of convincing them otherwise. Her royal highness seems to be of the view that such beliefs, if they should be imbued into the new System that her House is erecting, shall lead to the realization of her nightmare. So, if I am to be Simplicio in this dialogue, pray explain how it is that there may be such a thing as free will, and a spirit that may do as it pleases, unbound by the *Mathematick* laws of our Mechanical Philosophy."

"Well, if you put it that way, it's an old problem," said Leibniz. "Descartes saw straight away that Mechanical Philosophy might spell trouble for free will, in that it led to a new sort of predestinationism—*not* rooted in theology, like that of the Calvinists, but rather growing out of the simple fact that matter obeys predictable laws."

"Yes," said Daniel, "and then he got it all wrong, by putting the soul in the pineal gland."

"I'd rather say he got it wrong *before* then, by dividing the universe into matter, and cogitation," Leibniz said.

"And I'd say he got it wrong even before then, by supposing that there was a problem," said Newton. "There's nothing wrong in recognizing that part of the universe is a passive mechanism, and part of it is active and thinking. But Monsieur Descartes, seeing what was done to Galileo by the Papists, was in such terror of the Inquisition that his resolve failed."

"Very well, in any case we agree that Descartes perceived a problem, and came up with a wrong answer," said Daniel. "Does either of you have a better one to offer up? Sir Isaac, it sounds as if you deny the very *existence* of any such problem."

"You may read *Principia Mathematica* without finding discourse of souls, spirits, cogitation, or what-have-you," said Isaac. "It is about planets, forces, gravity, and geometry. I do not address, and certainly do not pretend to solve, the riddles that so confounded Monsieur Descartes. Why should we attempt to frame hypotheses about such matters?"

"Because if *you* do not, Sir Isaac, others, of less brilliance, will; and they will frame the wrong ones," Caroline said.

Newton bristled. "My work on gravity and opticks has brought me a kind of fame, which is a thing I never sought, nor wanted. It has done me nothing good, and much bad—as now, when I am expected to utter profundities on topics far afield from what I have chosen to study."

"So says the public Sir Isaac Newton," said Daniel, "Author of *Principia Mathematica,* and Master of the Mint. But this is a private gathering, which might benefit from the participation of the *private* Sir Isaac: the author of the *Praxis.*"

"*Praxis* has not been published," Isaac pointed out, "and not because I have deemed it somehow *private* but because 'tis yet unfinished, and so not fit to talk of."

"What is *Praxis?*" Caroline inquired.

"What *Principia Mathematica* was to Mechanical Philosophy, *Praxis* would be to Alchemy," said Isaac.

"A laconic answer! May we hear more?"

"If I may say so, highness," said Daniel, "Sir Isaac learned early that anything he openly professed was liable to come under attack, to his great aggravation and embarrassment, and so became chary of professing anything until he had got it perfect, and made it impervious. *Praxis* is not ready yet."

"Then it seems I shall not have any satisfaction whatsoever!" said Caroline, a bit poutingly.

"Which is entirely my fault, for having mentioned *Praxis,*" Daniel hastened to say. "But I had a reason for doing it, which was to say that, though *the public* Sir Isaac might profess not to see the problem that so captured the attention of Descartes, I believe that *the private* Sir Isaac has been working on just that problem."

"As I state quite plainly in *Principia Mathematica,*" said Isaac, in a bit of a high clarion self-righteous tone, "it is not my intention, in that work, to consider the causes and seats of Force. That gravity exists, and acts at a distance, is taken as a given. Why and how it does so are not considered. I would not be human if I did not have some curiosity as to what gravity was, and how it works; and even if 'twere otherwise, Baron von Leibniz and his Continental supporters would never allow me a moment's peace on the matter. So, yes! I would understand Force. I have toiled at it. The ignorant have styled my toils Alchemy."

At this Daniel threw him an irritated look, which Isaac, to his credit, did not fail to notice. *"C'est juste!"* Isaac said. "It's not *wrong* to call this work Alchemy, but that word, so laden with the baggage of centuries, doesn't do justice to it."

"May I ask a question about your research in this area—however you choose to denote it?" Leibniz asked.

"Provided it contains no hidden barbs or spryngs," Isaac allowed.

Leibniz now achieved the difficult feat of rolling his eyes, heaving a great sigh of exasperation, and voicing his question all at the same time. "If I understand what 'force' means, in your metaphysicks—"

"Which is the only coherent definition of 'force' that I know of!" Newton slipped in, glancing at the Princess.

Leibniz, with some visible straining, affected a saintly mien during this. "It appears to mean some invisible influence, acting across what you think of as the vacuum of space at infinite speed, which causes objects to accelerate—even though nothing seems to be touching them."

"Setting aside your strangely hedged and qualified way of talking about 'vacuum' and 'space,' that is a reasonable description of gravitational force," Newton allowed.

"Now in your metaphysicks—which I concede happens to be that used by just about everyone—there is this thing called space, which is mostly empty, but has lumpy bits here and there, called bodies; some big heavy spherical ones which we call planets, but also any amount of clutter, such as this poker, yonder candelabrum, the rug, and these bipedal animated bodies answering to the names Daniel Waterhouse, Princess Wilhelmina Caroline of Brandenburg-Ansbach, *et cetera?*"

"That much is so obvious that some of us are amazed to hear a learned man waste breath pointing it out," said Newton.

"Some of those bodies answer only to the deterministic laws of the mechanical philosophy," said Leibniz, "such as the globe, which rolled into the fireplace because her royal highness gave it a shove. But the bodies denominated Daniel Waterhouse, *et cetera*, are somehow different. True, they are subject to the same forces as the globe—our friend Daniel plainly feels Gravity's pull, or else he would float away! But such bodies act in complicated ways not explainable by the laws set forth in your *Principia Mathematica*. When Dr. Waterhouse sits down to write an essay, let us say about the *Latitudinarian* philosophy espoused by him and the late Mr. Locke, we may observe his quill maneuvering all over the page in the most complicated paths imaginable. Here are none of the conic sections of the *Principia*! No equation can predict the trajectory of Daniel's nib over the

page, for it results from innumerable and unfathomable minute con-
tractions of the small muscles of his fingers and his hand. If we dis-
sect a man's hand, we find that these muscles are governed by nerves,
which may easily enough be traced back to the brain, as rivers come
from springs in the mountains. Remove the brain, or sever its connexions to the hand, and lo, that limb becomes as simple as yonder
globe; that is, we may predict its future movements from the *Principia,* and plot them in Conics. And so it is evident that, to the Force
of Gravity—which acts on everything—are superadded other forces,
observable only in animals,* and productive of infinitely more complicated and interesting movements."

"I am with you so far," said Newton, "if all you are saying is that
forces other than Gravity act on Dr. Waterhouse's pen when he is
writing something, and that such forces do not appear to motivate
rocks or comets."

"Hooke was fascinated by muscles," Daniel put in, "and looked at
them under his microscope, and labored at making artificial ones, so
that he could fly. *Those,* I predict, could have been described by Mechanical Philosophy; after all, they were naught more than practical
applications of the Rarefying Engine, and as such, subject to Boyle's
Law. With more time and better microscopes, Hooke might have
found, within muscles, tiny mechanisms, likewise describable by
mathematical laws, and thereby put to rest any supposed mysteries—"

But he stopped as both Newton and Leibniz were making the
same sort of hand-waving gestures employed to bat away farts. "You
miss the point!" said Leibniz. "I have no interest in the physics of
muscles! Think, sir, if Hooke had made his flying-machine, driven, in
a deterministic fashion, by Rarefying Engines, what more then would
he have had to add to this device, to make it flutter to a safe perch
atop the cupola of Bedlam, and balance there as 'twas buffeted by
divers wind-gusts, and take flight again without o'ersetting and tumbling to the ground like a shot squab? I am trying to draw our attention to what it is that comes down those nerves from the brain: the
decisions, or rather, the physical manifestations thereof—the characters, as it were, in which they are writ—and transmitted to the muscles, that they may *inform* what would otherwise be without form and
void."

"I understand that," said Daniel, "and I say it is all pistons and
cylinders, weights and springs, to the very top. And that's all I need to

---

*As everyone in the room knew, Leibniz was using the word *animal* in an ancient and
somewhat technical sense of something animated, i.e., possessing, or possessed by,
an anima, or spirit.

explain how I inform ink on a page, and how a bird informs the air with its wings."

"And I agree with you!" said Leibniz.

This produced a dumbfounded pause. "Have I converted you to the doctrine of Materialism so easily, then?" Daniel inquired.

"By no means," said Leibniz. "I say only that, though the machine of the body obeys deterministic laws, *it does so in accordance with the desires and dictates of the soul,* because of the pre-established harmony."

"Of that, we must needs hear more, for it is very difficult to understand," said the Princess.

"Chiefly because it is *wrong*!" said Sir Isaac.

Caroline now had to literally step between the two philosophers. "Then we are all in agreement that further discourse concerning the pre-established harmony is wanted from Baron von Leibniz," she said. "But first, I would fain hear Sir Isaac address the phænomena of which Drs. Waterhouse and Leibniz have just been discoursing. Sir Isaac, we have heard from both of these gentlemen that they are wholly satisfied it is all mechanism to the very top. What of you? Do you require something more?"

Newton said, "If we allow, not only the muscles, but the nerves, and even the brain itself, to be 'pistons and cylinders, weights and springs' as you put it, whose machinations might be observed and described by some future Hooke, then we must still explain how those mechanisms are informed by the soul, spirit, or whatever we are going to call it—the thing that has free will, that is not subject to deterministic laws, and that accounts for our being human. This is ultimately the same problem as we discoursed of earlier—the problem *you* find boring, Daniel—of God's relationship to the Universe. For the relationship that our souls bear to our bodies, is akin to the relationship that God bears to the entire Universe. If God is to be something more than an Absentee Landlord—something more than the perfect watch-maker, who sets His clock a-run, and walks away from it—then we must account for how He influences the movements of things in the world. This gets us round to that mysterious phænomenon called Force. And when we discourse of animal motion we must in the end address a like problem, namely of how the soul that inhabits a body may influence the operation of what is in the end just a big soggy clock."

"I could not disagree more, by the way," said Leibniz. "The soul and body influence each other not at all."

"Then how does my soul know that yonder candle is flickering?" asked Princess Caroline. "For I can only know such a thing through my eyes, which are parts of my body."

"Because God has put into your soul a principle representative of the candle-flame and everything else in the Universe," said Leibniz. "But that is most certainly *not* how *God* perceives things! *He* perceives all things, because He continually produces them. And so I reject any such analogies likening God's relationship to the Universe and ours to our bodies."

"I do not understand Baron von Leibniz's hypothesis at all," Isaac confessed.

"What is *your* hypothesis, Sir Isaac?"

"That most of the animal body is a determined machine, I'll grant. That it is controlled from the brain, has been proved, by Willis and others. It follows, simply, that, by laws of God's choosing, the soul has the power to operate upon the brain, and thereby to influence animal movements."

"This is just Descartes and the pineal gland all over again!" Leibniz scoffed.

"He was wrong about the pineal gland," Newton said, "but I'll grant a certain formal resemblance between his way of thinking about it, and mine."

"In each case," Daniel translated, "there is some sense in which a free, non-corporeal, non-mechanical spirit can effect physical changes in the workings of the machinery of the brain."

"I think that much is obvious; as is the fact that God—Who is likewise a non-corporeal Spirit—has power to effect physical changes—that is, to exert Force—upon any thing whatsoever in this Universe."

"And is it the case that when you study the causes and seats of Force in your *Praxis* work, you seek to understand Forces of that type as well?"

"I do not think that any account of Force that failed to address this topic could be deemed complete."

"When Sir Isaac was working on the *Principia*," said Daniel, "I paid him a visit up at Trinity. He had requested what seemed to me to be an odd lot of information: tables of the tides, *data* on a certain comet, astronomical observations of Jupiter and Saturn. Well, it was a long ride, and by the time I had reached Cambridge I'd managed to work out that there was a common thread running through all of these: gravity. Gravity causes the tides and determines the orbits of comets and planets alike. To us it is obvious now; but back *then* it was by no means agreed that a comet, let us say, might be bound by the same force that kept the Earth in its gyre. Isaac's triumph was to perceive that all of these phænomena were attributable to the same cause, working everywhere in the same way. Now, I have long been nonplussed by Isaac's Alchemical research, but as years have gone by I have perceived that he would achieve a similar triumph by finding a single common underlying explanation for phænomena that we think of as diverse, and unrelated: free will, God's presence in the Universe, miracles, and the transmutation of chymical elements. Couched in the willfully obscure jargon of the Alchemists, this cause, or principle, or whatever one wants to call it, is known as the Philosopher's Stone, or other terms such as the Philosophic Mercury, the Vital Agent, the Latent or Subtile Spirit, the Secret Fire, the Material Soul of Matter, the Invisible Inhabitant, the Body of Light, the Seed, the Seminal Virtue."

"You are confusing a number of different ideas," said Isaac, "but this does at least prove that you *perused* my notes before *burning* them."

At this Caroline was taken aback for a moment; then curiosity got the better of her. "What is this Agent or Spirit? Have you seen it, Sir Isaac?"

"I see it now, in the emotions and thoughts flickering across your face, highness. I see its *effect* everywhere," was the somewhat evasive response of Newton. "In Nature I perceive two categories of actions: *mechanical* and *vegetable*. By *mechanical* I mean, of course, just the sort of thing that Drs. Waterhouse and Leibniz discoursed of earlier: in a word, clock-work. By *vegetable* I do not mean turnips. That is a new and vulgar meaning of the word. I use it in its ancient sense of something animate, living, growing. It describes generative and creative processes. Clocks, even good ones, run down and wear out. The mechanical world decays. Counterpoised against this tendency to decline must be some creative principle: the active seed—the Subtile Spirit. An unimaginably tiny quantity of this, acting upon a vastly larger bulk of insipid, dead, inactive matter, wreaks immense, even miraculous transformations, to which I give the general name *vegetation*. Just as the general principle of Gravity manifests itself in diverse specific ways, such as tides, the orbits of comets, and the trajectories of bullets, so the vegetative principle may be perceived, by those who know how to look for it, in diverse places. Just to mention one example, which we discoursed of earlier: a flying-machine, constructed of artificial muscles, would be a mechanical device, whose fate, I believe, would be to crash to the ground, like the corpse of a bird that has died on the wing. If that machine were to take flight—which would mean sensing every fluctuation of the air, and responding in the correct way—I should ascribe that, ultimately, to the workings of some sort of vegetative principle. But Daniel is correct in thinking that it is also related to such matters as souls, miracles, and certain of the more profound and astonishing chymical transformations."

"But do you think that there is ultimately some physical substance at work—something you could touch and observe?"

"Yes, I do, and have been searching for it. And I think I know where to find some," Isaac said, and turned to glower at Daniel. But the Princess missed this, as she was turning to Leibniz. "Baron von Leibniz," said she, "can your view be reconciled with Sir Isaac's?"

Leibniz sighed. "It is . . . awkward," he said. "To my ears, all of this sounds like a rear-guard action fought by a good Christian retreating before the onslaught of Mechanical Philosophy."

"That could not be more wrong!" snapped Newton. "There is Mechanical, and there is Vegetable. I study both."

"But you have already ceded half the battlefield to Mechanical!"

"There is no *ceding*, sir. Have you not read my *Principia*? The Mechanical world exists, the Mechanical philosophy describes it."

"Dr. Waterhouse would say that Mechanism describes not just *half*, but *all* of it," Leibniz said. "I take the opposite view, which is that Vegetable is all, and what we think of as mechanical is only the superficies of underlying processes that are not mechanical at all."

"We await a coherent explanation," said Isaac.

"Philosophers of a Mechanick frame of mind break all things down into atoms, to which they ascribe properties that, to them, seem reasonable—which means Mechanical properties. Mass, extension, and the ability to collide with and stick to one another. Then from this they try to explain Gravity and Souls and Miracles. It leads them into difficulties. Instead, I break all things down into *monads*, to which I ascribe what some would call soul-like properties: they can perceive, thnk about their perceptions, decide, and act. From this it is no great difficulty to explain those things that are so troublesome, in a mechanical-minded Atomic philosophy—everything that you put under the rubric of Vegetation, including our own ability to think, decide, and act. However, it is difficult to explain the things that are, in an Atomic philosophy, idiotically simple and obvious. Such as space and time."

"Space and Time! Two minor omissions that no one is likely to notice," grumbled Newton.

"If I may say so, your own conception of Space is by no means as straightforward as it seems at first," Leibniz said, very much in the style of one who was firing the opening salvo of another long argument. But before this could get going, the door of the room opened, and Johann von Hacklheber could be seen standing there, holding, in a very significant way, a Letter. Behind him Eliza was pacing back and forth with a fist balled up in front of her lips.

Princess Caroline stared into Johann's eyes, and cocked her head. She did not say aloud *I told you not to bother me,* but it came through so distinctly that all heads turned back toward Johann, expecting from him an immediate apology. Instead he raised his eyebrows and stood his ground.

Caroline closed her eyes and sighed. Newton, Leibniz, and Waterhouse stepped back to clear her path out of the room. For they had all understood at the same moment that there was only one person who had this authority: Caroline's father-in-law, the as-yet-uncrowned King of England.

"Dr. Waterhouse, pray accept the rôle of my knight-errant, and put this thing to rest," she said, and swept out.

"Well! That's a bit of a tall order," Daniel reflected, after the door had been closed behind her.

"Not so," said Newton, "if you'll only release the Solomonic Gold."

"That Jew who works for the Tsar," said Daniel—not wishing to utter the name Solomon, for fear it would send Isaac into chiliastic transports—"has detected that the trial batch of plates were made of heavier-than-normal gold, and the decree has gone forth from the Academy of Sciences in St. Petersburg that *all* succeeding plates be made of the same stuff. If we disobey, punishment will ensue, in the *Russian* style. Were it not for this, I'd swop the gold without hesitation. For I believe it has no special properties whatsoever."

"Then how do you explain your personal resurrection, at the hands of Enoch Root, in 1689?"

"Say *what!*?" asked Leibniz.

"Or," said Isaac, "is that the one thing Hooke wrote, in all his life, that you'll not believe?"

"Hooke's account states that Enoch gave me some medicine, which helped."

"*Helped!?* You have a marvelous gift for understatement, Daniel."

"It could have been anything . . . or *nothing.* It has been known to occur that seemingly dead men will revive after a few minutes."

"I hated Hooke," Isaac admitted, "but even I will admit that he was the most acute observer who ever lived. Do you really expect me to believe that he, of all people, could not distinguish between a living patient and a dead?"

"I see that your mind is quite made up. What point is there in debating it?"

Both Newton and Leibniz laughed out loud.

"What is funny?" Daniel demanded.

"You have made *us* debate for hours!" Leibniz exclaimed. "Now that you are challenged on a troublesome question, you claim to see no point in it."

"I need only a small sample, Daniel," said Newton. "Do not forget that for many years I have sought evanescent traces of this in samples of gold that had been infinitely diluted and debased. My techniques are now highly developed. I do not need a brick of the stuff. Just an ounce, or less—a scrap."

"I tell you that Peter's assayer weighed every ounce of it. There are no ounces to spare. I could *ask* him for permission to take a small sample, but . . ."

"No," said Isaac, "I do not think it would be wise for you to tip your hand."

At this remark Daniel was suddenly conscious of the ring on his finger: the one that Solomon had given him, made of con-fused bits punched from the plates at Bridewell. A tingle ran up his arm to his scalp; but he froze there, and said nothing, and hoped that Isaac would not take note of his horripilation.

"Isaac," said a voice. Daniel had to look up to verify that it was that of Leibniz: a bit shocking, only in that the German had addressed Newton by his Christian name, without the "Sir."

"Gottfried," said Newton, not to be gainsaid.

"Thirty-seven years ago I came *incognito* to these shores to propose an alliance between myself and you. It was about two years after I'd developed the calculus, only to realize I was only following in your footsteps. It had occurred to me that we might share other interests as well, and that by joining forces we might achieve more, sooner. Daniel had encouraged me in this."

"I well remember the match, and the matchmaker," said Isaac, "and his weakness for playing with matches."

This witticism, because it was such a rare thing from Isaac, cut all the more deeply. Daniel's right arm had begun to feel terribly heavy, as if the ring were weighing it down—or as if the strain of the day had caused him to suffer a stroke. He put the heavy hand in the pocket of his breeches, and hung his head.

"Then you remember as well as I that the match flared, only to fail," said Gottfried. "Now I am back, certainly for the last time. Will you not reconsider, Isaac? Will you not obey your Princess—*my* Princess—and work with me, and lay a strong foundation beneath the System of the World?"

"I *am* and *have been* working on just that," said Isaac. "Should I not ask *you*, Gottfried, if *you* would work with *me*? It might entail giving up on monads, by the way. Ah, I see by your look that you have no thought of doing so."

"The answer then is no."

"The answer is *yes*. But it is a question of *timing*, sir. It is not for you, or me, or our Princess, to dictate how long it shall take, and when it shall be accomplished! *She* would have it settled *now*—today! *You* are likewise in a great hurry. For you are an old man—we are all old men—and fearful of running out of time. But this is neither here nor there. Nature will reveal her secrets at times of her own choosing, and has no thought of our convenience. *Principia Mathematica* might never have come about had Nature not sent a spate of comets our way in the 1680s, and so arranged their trajectories that we could make telling observations. It might be ten years, a hundred, or a thousand before she sends us the clew that will enable us to solve the riddles we have been speaking of today. Though the Gold of Solomon might be might be just that clew—I don't know until I can inspect some of it."

Daniel smiled. "You are infinitely patient, it seems, save where the Solomonic Gold is concerned. It is amusing. Of the three of us, I'm the only one who is convinced he is really going to die soon—both of you, Isaac and Gottfried, are believers in life æternal. Why don't you have the courage of your convictions, and agree to re-convenc the discussion a few centuries from now, or whenever there are sufficient *data* to resolve these issues philosophically?"

Which was a little bit of a cheap trick—forcing their hands thus, by challenging the sincerity of their religious convictions. But Daniel was exhausted, and could see that the thing was doomed, and wanted only to wind it up.

"I accept!" said Leibniz. "It is a sort of duel—a *philosophick* duel, to be settled, not with weapons, but with ideas, at a time and on a field yet to be chosen. I accept." And he held out his hand toward Isaac.

"Then I'll look for you on that field, sir," said Newton. "Though our philosophies are so different that I do not really expect *both* of us can possibly be there; for *one* of us must be wrong." He shook Leibniz's hand.

"Every duellist needs a second," said Leibniz. "Perhaps Daniel shall act in that capacity for both of us."

Daniel snorted. "*Isaac* may believe I was resurrected, but I did not think *you* would hold with such beliefs, Gottfried. No, if you require seconds, it now seems that there are any number of immortal personages who shall be willing to show up on the appointed date, and hold your coats: for you, Gottfried, there is Enoch Root, and for you,

Isaac, that ancient Jew who works for the Tsar and calls himself Solomon." And so he did not take his right hand from his pocket to shake hands with them, for the ring felt terribly heavy and obvious, and he had a sort of lurid phant'sy that Gottfried and Isaac would suddenly recognize it for what it was, and fall to scuffling over it.

"Brr, my father-in-law is frightfully cross with me," Caroline announced, "at least, if I have made sense of his letter correctly." She had read through it three times as Johann and Eliza watched. Leicester House resounded with booming and dragging noises: the sound of Royal baggage being packed and positioned.

"So much time has passed, and so many things have occurred, since I claimed I was going away to that Schloß to recover from June's traumas, that I had quite forgotten that his majesty was expecting me back. But now he seems to have figured out where I am."

"Probably some intelligence reached him after our little adventure on the Thames," Johann suggested. His discourse had been clipped and gloomy, and he'd been supporting his head on his fingertips—or perhaps that was self-administered massage. To Caroline, being bawled out by the King of England and Elector of Hanover might have been a trivial family dust-up, but for him it was a different matter.

"Very well," said Caroline, "it's back to Hanover I go, then."

"Right!" said Johann, and got up and strode out. If anyone had had the temerity to stop him and ask him *why*, he'd have said he was off to do something ever so practical and important. But as both Caroline and Eliza understood perfectly well, the fact of the matter was that he had become so agitated that he'd go mad if he spent any more time sitting and talking.

"Off to Hanover," Caroline repeated, "only to return in a few weeks! It says here that his majesty intends to reach England late in September. Supposing that the Prince of Wales and I are to accompany him, that means that as soon as I reach Hanover I shall have to turn round and come right back."

"Geographically, yes, you shall return to the same latitude and longitude," said Eliza, after thinking about this one for a moment. "But you will no longer be *incognito*. And so *socially* you shall be coming to a city you have never before visited, and to a different life altogether."

"I suppose that shall be quite true, as long as we dwell in places like St. James's Palace, with all the courtiers and the ambassadors, and the Duke of Marlborough right next door," said Caroline. "But if there's one thing I learned from Sophie, it's that there are very practical reasons for a Princess to have more than one Palace. For her, the Leine Schloß served as St. James's shall for me and George Augustus. But at every chance she got, she removed herself to Herrenhausen, where she could live as she pleased, and walk in the garden. That's why I have been so keen on *this* place. It's going to be my Herrenhausen," Caroline announced, "and *you* are going to be its doyenne."

"Thank God," said Eliza, "I was afraid you were about to say, 'dowager.'"

"Lady of the Bedchamber or Mistress of the Stole or something," Caroline said, a bit absently. "We shall have to choose the right English title for you. Whatever you're called, the point is that I'd like you to live here, at least part of the time, and walk in the garden with me, and talk to me."

"That doesn't sound too onerous," said Eliza with a smile. "But know that any place where I live is liable to have a flux of odd persons running through it, connected with the work that I pursue on the abolition of Slavery, and so on."

"So much the better! It'll remind me that much more of the Charlottenburg back when Sophie Charlotte was still alive."

"Some of my lot may be odder and rougher yet . . ."

"You have a faraway look in your eye when you say that . . . are you thinking of your long-lost beau?"

At this Eliza sighed and threw Caroline a mean look.

"I have not forgotten our fascinating chat in Hanover," Caroline said.

"Let's speak of a different fascinating chat!" said Eliza. "What tidings from the Library?"

"When I left, they were still having at each other. They are both very proud men. Newton, especially, is not of a mind to back down. The court is coming *here*, and leaving poor Leibniz behind in Hanover. Advantage Newton. Newton has won the calculus dispute, or so it is believed by the savants of the Royal Society. And the recent controversies surrounding the Mint have cleared up, or so it would seem."

"Is that what he told you? Now *that* would be some kind of a miracle, if true," Eliza said.

"Why do you say so?"

"Is it not the case that the Pyx is still under the control of Charles White? And is Newton not still answerable to a Trial of the Pyx?"

"That is what they tell me," said Caroline, "but Newton seems to believe he has now got the upper hand where that is concerned, by arresting the arch-villain known as Jack the Coiner. The fiend is now utterly in Sir Isaac's power, and doomed to be half-hanged, drawn, and quartered at Tyburn Cross . . . Johann? *Johann!* Bring the smelling salts, the Duchess has got the vapors!"

Johann banged into the room only a few moments later, but by then his mother had got her color back, and prevented a slide to the floor by getting a white-knuckled grip on the arms of her chair. "It is nothing," she said, swiveling her eyes at her first-born. "Carry on, please, as you were."

Johann departed, seething and quizzical.

"It is just a sort of catalepsis that comes over me sometimes, when suddenly I have got rather a lot to think about all at once. Shortly it passes. I am fine. Thank you for your expression of concern, highness. Moving on—"

"We shall *not* move on!" announced the Princess of Wales. "We shall stick right here, on this, the most fascinating topic of conversation in the history of the world! *You* are in love with the most infamous Black-guard ever!"

"Stop that! It's not like that at all," said Eliza. "*He* happens to be in love with *me,* that is all."

"Oh, well, that's different altogether."

"There is no call for sarcasm."

"How did you meet? I love to hear stories of how true lovers met."

"We are *not* true lovers," said Eliza, "and as to how we met—well—it's none of your business."

Another door whacked open and in came Leibniz. He bowed to the ladies, looking very solemn. "I take it that a departure for Hanover is planned, and soon," he said. "If your royal highness will have me, I will accompany you." He turned toward Eliza. "My lady. The friendship that began in Leipzig thirty years ago, when our paths crossed at the Fair, and I shared a little adventure with you and your Vagabond beau—"

"Aha!" shouted Caroline.

"Draws now to a close. The Princess's noble and splendid attempt to effect a philosophical reconciliation—so ably and patiently assisted by Dr. Waterhouse—has, I am sorry to say—"

"Failed?" said Caroline.

"Adjourned," Leibniz said.

"For how long?"

"Hundreds, perhaps thousands of years."

"Hmm," said Caroline, "that will be of little practical utility to the House of Hanover, when it comes time to select a new Privy Council."

"I am sorry," said Leibniz, "but there is no rushing certain things.

While *other* matters, such as my departure from London, happen entirely too soon."

"Where are Sir Isaac, and Dr. Waterhouse?" the Princess inquired.

"Sir Isaac has taken his leave, and forwards apologies for not having said good-bye in person," said Leibniz, "but one gets the idea he had terribly important things to do. Dr. Waterhouse said he would await you in the garden, just in case you might be of a mind to behead him for failing in his mission."

"By no means! I shall go and thank him for his good offices—and I'll see you on the boat tomorrow!" said Caroline, and swept out of the place.

"Eliza," said the savant.

"Gottfried," said the Duchess.

London Bridge
THE NEXT DAY

"IT WAS NOT HALF so blubbery as it might have been," said Leibniz, "when one considers how long the Duchess and I have known each other, and all we have been through, and whatnot. We shall keep in touch, of course, through letters."

He was describing his leave-taking from Eliza at Leicester House the day before; but he might as well have been talking of the one that was happening now, on London Bridge, between him and Daniel.

"Forty-one years," Daniel said.

"I was thinking the same thing!" Leibniz said, practically before Daniel had got the words out. "It was forty-one years ago when you and I first met, right here, on this very what-do-you-call-it."

"Starling," Daniel said. They were standing on the one beneath the Square, near the mid-point of the Bridge, and not awfully far from the Main-Topp where the Clubb had of late conducted its Stake-out. But Daniel's memory of that, though only a few weeks old, was already quite washed-out and indistinct compared to what Leibniz was speaking of: the day in 1673 when a young Leibniz (no Baron in those days) with an Arithmetickal Engine tucked under his arm had disembarked from a ship that had brought him over from Calais, and been conveyed to this starling—to this very *spot*—by a lighter, and first made the acquaintance of young Daniel Waterhouse of the Royal Society.

Leibniz's memory was no less distinct. "I believe it was—here!" (tapping a flat rock at starling's edge with his toe) "where I first touched down."

"That is how I remember it."

"Of course we are both wrong, if Absolute Space is correct," Leibniz went on. "For during those forty-one years the Earth has rotated, and revolved about the Sun, and the Sun, for all we know, has careered for some vast distance. So I did not really touch down *here* but in some *other* place that is now far out in the interstellar vacuum."

Daniel did not rise to this bait. He was fearful that Leibniz was about to burst out into some bitter declamation against Newton and Newton's philosophy. But Leibniz drew back from that brink, even as he was drawing back from the stony rim of the starling. A longboat was working up towards them. It was the lighter that would take Leibniz out to the Hanoverian sloop *Sophia,* where Princess Caroline had already settled into her cabin.

"What do I remember of that day? We were espied, and glared at, by Hooke, who was over yonder surveying a wharf," said Leibniz, pointing at the London bank. "We went to pay a call on poor old Wilkins, who lay some great responsibility on your shoulders—"

"He wanted me to 'make it all happen,' " said Daniel.

Leibniz laughed. "What do you suppose the rascal meant by that?"

"I have thought about it a million times," said Daniel. "Religious toleration? The Royal Society? Pansophism? The Arithmetickal Engine? I cannot be sure. But all of those things were linked together in Wilkins's mind."

"He had a prefiguring of what Caroline calls the System of the World."

"Perhaps. At any rate, I have tried to preserve in my mind, since then, that linkage—the notion that all of those things must move together, somewhat like prisoners on a common chain—"

"A cheerful image!" Leibniz remarked.

"And if there has been any plan whatever to my life in those forty-one years, it's been that I have tried to keep an eye out for whichever of them was lagging farthest behind, and chivvy it along. For two decades, the laggard has been Arithmetickal Engines and Logic Mills, *et cetera.*"

"And so you have toiled on that," said Leibniz, "for which you have my æternal gratitude. But who knows? With the support of the Tsar, and the motive Power of the Engine for Raising Water by Fire, perhaps it shall be laggardly no more."

"Perhaps," said Daniel. "It grieves me, now—especially since yesterday—that I went off into seclusion, and did not involve myself in the Metaphysickal rift until it was too late."

"But if you *had,* you'd be now berating yourself over having neglected some *other* matter—good Puritan that you are."

Daniel snorted.

"Remember that in those days Newton was known chiefly as a very clever telescope-maker," Leibniz went on. "Wilkins could not have foreseen the rift you spoke of—and so could not have charged you with healing it. You are clear of any such burthen."

"But the grand project of Pansophism was a thing he saw very clearly, and, I'm sure, wanted me to support in whatever way I could," Daniel said. "I wonder now if I did the best possible job of it."

"And I should say the answer is yes," said Leibniz, "for that we live in the best of all possible worlds."

"I hope that is not true," said Daniel, "as it seems to me now that my journey here from Boston, which I confess I undertook with a certain kind of foolish and thrilling hope in my heart, has concluded in tragedy—and not even *grand* tragedy but something much more futile and ignominious."

"After we visited Wilkins on his death-bed," said Leibniz, "we went to a coffee-house, did we not, and talked. We spoke of Mr. Hooke's observations of snowflakes—their remarkable property, which is that each of the six arms grows outwards from a common center, and each grows independently, of its own internal rules. One arm cannot affect the others. And yet the arms are all alike. To me this is an embodiment of the pre-established harmony. Now, Daniel, in like manner, there grows out of the core of Natural Philosophy more than one system for understanding the Universe. They grow according to their own internal principles, and one does not affect another—as Newton and I demonstrated yesterday by utterly failing to agree on anything! But if it's true—as I believe—that they are rooted in a common seed, then in the fullness of time they must adopt a like form, and become reflections of one another, as a snowflake's arms."

"I hope the poor snowflake does not melt before it reaches that perfection," said Daniel, "in the heat of those fires that Caroline dreams of."

"That is beyond our ability to predict or prevent. We can only do all in our power to move the work forward," said Leibniz.

"Speaking of which," said Daniel, "here is something for you."

During Leibniz's remarks he had from time to time glanced up at the traffic coming out of London on the Bridge. Now he raised a hand and waved to someone up in the Square. Leibniz followed his eyeline up to behold William Ham, the banker, waving back from atop a cart that had just drawn to a halt at the head of the stairs. It was populated by a conspicuously large number of beefier-than-average porters, some of whom remained where they were, engaging all and sundry passersby in stare-downs. Others hopped off and went to work carrying several small crates down the stairs and piling them at Leibniz's feet. At about the same time, the lighter from *Sophia* drew close enough to pelt them with rope-ends, and several watermen who loitered on the starling caught them out of the air and made the boat fast. A Hanoverian servant vaulted over the gunwale and bent to take and move the first of the crates; but Leibniz asked him in German if he would terribly mind waiting for a moment. "If these are what I think they are—" he said to Daniel.

"Indeed."

"Then later they shall be counted by men who are ever so sharp when it comes to weights and measures; and I would that all of the numbers add up!"

So the crates accumulated until the wagon up above was empty. Each had been sealed with a medallion of wax bearing the imprint of the Bank of England—for that is where they had been stored until a few minutes ago, and one could still smell the damp of the Bank's cellars escaping from the pores in the wood. William Ham came down with a great wallet of musty paperwork, on which was traced the provenance of what was in the crates, beginning with Solomon Kohan's accompt of the gold taken from *Minerva,* and passing through all of the intermediate stages of rolling and cutting at the Court of Technologickal Arts and punching at Bridewell. Leibniz examined it all, and finally counted the crates (7) and counted them again (7) and asked Daniel to verify the count (7). Finally he signed the papers GOTTFRIED FREIHERR VON LEIBNIZ in diverse places, and Daniel counter-signed as Witness. At last Leibniz gave leave for the crates to be moved aboard the lighter; but he counted them as they were moved (7).

"It is a start," Daniel said. "There are many more yet to come, as you know. But as long as you were making a journey to Hanover anyway, I thought I might as well give you all that we have managed to bang out so far."

"It adds a most pleasing *coda* to what might otherwise be a melancholy parting," said Leibniz, and squared off before Daniel, forcing his features into a simulacrum of a smile. "And it really ought to put to rest any mistaken thoughts that might have been troubling your sleep as to whether you have done right by Wilkins. You have, sir, done him proud."

Daniel was now helpless to say anything and so he stepped forward and embraced Leibniz hard. Leibniz returned the embrace, giving as good as he got, then broke away and turned his back on Daniel before Daniel could see his face and vaulted into the boat almost in the same motion. He counted the crates, or pretended to, one last time as lines were cast off and the boat fell away and yawed in the turbulent gulf of the lock.

"Seven?" Daniel shouted.

"Seven exactly!" came the answer. "I shall see you, Daniel, on Parnassus, or wherever it is that Philosophers end up!"

"I think they end up in old books," said Daniel, "and so I shall look for you, sir, in a Library."

"That is what I am building," said Leibniz, "and that is where you shall find me. Good-bye, Daniel!"

"Good-bye, Gottfried!" Daniel shouted, and then stood and watched for some time as the boat became indistinct, and quite lost itself, in the welter of shipping in the Pool of London, there below the charred battlements of the Tower. It was almost a mirror image of the way Leibniz had appeared, out of nowhere, forty-one years earlier, except that the mirror was a misty and a streaky one. For much had changed in those years and Daniel could not watch with the clear eyes of a young man.

Greenwich

Let other Princes, surrounded with couching Slaves, glory in the unlimited Obedience of stupid Wretches that have no sense of Liberty, and little else to brag of, than that like so many Stocks or Stones, they can bear being kick'd and trod upon, whilst a King of *Great Britain,* almost alone in all the Universe, may boast himself to be a Monarch over Rational Creatures.

— *The Mischiefs That Ought Justly to Be Apprehended from a Whig-Government,* ANONYMOUS, ATTRIBUTED TO BERNARD MANDEVILLE, 1714

"NOW *THERE* IS SOMETHING you don't see every day!" exclaimed Roger Comstock, Marquis of Ravenscar. It was the first thing he had said in a quarter of an hour—a long time, for him—and it prodded Daniel out of a sort of walking coma into which he had sunk during this, the third hour he and Roger had spent standing in this queue.

Daniel started awake and looked round.

Philosophers came to Greenwich all the time, and some even lived here, for the Observatory was up on the hill. Kings and Queens came here rarely, even though the place belonged to them. Architects came here frequently, and almost always wished they hadn't. For building-projects at Greenwich always had money trouble, and things seemed to decay faster than they could be erected. Inigo Jones had been adroit enough to scamper in and out of this Slough of Despond and actually get a thing built and roofed before it got bogged down: this was the Queen's House, and the secret to its success was that it was small. The bloody thing seemed to be a mile from the river. Or so it felt to Daniel and the others in the queue, whose head was lodged somewhere in Mr. Jones's Opus and whose tail wandered all the way to bankside. Some stone steps descended to the river there. A gaudy barge had been made fast. Beyond, anchored in a deeper part of the Thames, was the Navy ship that had fetched George, King, over from the Eurasian landmass. Daniel was only able to see these things because he and Roger had, at long last, reached the foot of, and (half an hour later) trudged to the top of, one of the curving stairways that led up to the terrace of the Queen's House. From there a few minutes' shuffling and doddering had got them as far as the front door. They were on the threshold. Daniel had his back to the entrance and was enjoying the view—such as it was—down to the river. Roger, with his stoat-like instinct for dark, seething, infested places, faced opposite. The open doors expired a miasma of rose-water and armpits, cut with the tang of new paint, a-throb with a sort of Beowulfian mélange of German and English. Daniel couldn't bear to turn round and see whatever Roger found so interesting, and so he and Roger passed over the threshold in this Janus-like configuration. Daniel was convinced he had caught a glimpse of Sir Christopher Wren, about an hour behind them in the queue, and had been trying to work out some way of getting Wren's attention, and of inducing him, by furtive gesticulations, to jump the line. But it was perfectly hopeless; this was the worst place in the world for it. Twenty-some years ago, Wren had been brought in to impose some order on this place, as only Wren could. It had been his place ever since. He was working for free—the idea was to build a hospital for Naval pensioners. Queen Mary had started flogging the plan after the battle at La Hougue in '92, but she had expired in '94. There was no telling when a driblet of cash might spill forth from the Royal coffers. Whenever this occurred, Wren would blow it immediately on great blocks of stone and slam them down at the corners, and later along the perimeters, of the things he proposed to build here. For he could see perfectly well that he'd be dead before it went up. Later, and lesser, architects might botch the details, but none would be able to place the actual buildings other than where Wren had flung these plinths into the earth. His deputy Nick Hawksmoor, perceiving the genius of this strategy, and very much getting into the spirit, had lately bought a great bloody block of sculpture-grade marble at some scandalously low price and arranged for it to be vomited up on to the riverbank; when they could get enough money to hire someone to beat on it with a chisel, they'd make it into a brilliant statue of whomever happened to be King or Queen then. And so the general picture that Daniel was seeing from the terrace—and that owned Wren's attention—was one of colossal foundations, laid by giants: a tiered echelon of rectangles—a Pythagorean dream. In that it was all foundations and no actual buildings, it seemed to confirm all that the Princess of Wales had said, a month ago, about the System, and the importance of putting it on a sound philosophical base. But what Newton and Leibniz had come up with—or failed to—seemed rickety compared to the works of Wren: further evidence that Wren had chosen wisely by turning away from pure philosophy and applying his genius to architecture.

Daniel gave up all hope of catching Wren's eye and turned round to see what Roger was on about.

"All right," he had to admit, after a few moments' taking it in, "you don't see it every day."

Two jowls, stapled together by a grimace, and supervised by a stare: the face of George. Lots of clothing to hide his body—nothing unusual *there,* though, beyond that the clothes were nicer than those of the people massed around him: his Court. Most of these Daniel recognized from his visit to Hanover. He pointed out a few of them to Roger, who had heard of all of them—knew more about them, as it turned out, than Daniel did—but needed a sort of key by which rumors, slanders, calumnies, and salacious anecdotes could be mapped to faces. Pretty soon they were all shooting chilly looks Daniel's way, even though he was only about the dozenth person in the queue. Perhaps it was because they had caught him pointing and muttering to Roger. More likely, though, it was because the last time they'd seen him, in Hanover, round the time of Sophie's death, he had been pretending to be senile and useless. Then he had been named a Regent. No proof of *compos mentis,* that, but they'd read into it that he had pull over *someone. Certainly* not George. By process of elimination, then, he'd been influencing Princess Caroline.

Caroline did not even seem to be in the room. No, on second thought, there she was in the corner with her husband. They'd already drawn their own little shadow Court of mostly young, witty Londoners, all talking too much, laughing, and drawing evil looks from the old and not so witty, who tended to keep their faces turned toward the new King. It was weirdly obvious and bold: if you thought you'd live long enough to march in George I's funeral procession, why then you would gravitate toward the future George II. Most had the decency and good form to hew to this general principle, but Daniel Waterhouse was fouling it up by being an old man in the young people's camp. And here he was on the arm of the Marquis of Ravenscar!

"I'd best stop pointing and staring now, as we seem to've been noticed," he said to Roger, trying to look as if he were making a remark about yesterday's weather, "but in closing I'll just add that you can see plainly enough the fat one and the skinny one."

As *tout le monde* knew, these were George's mistresses; his actual wife, of course, was still locked up in a dank Schloß somewhere beyond the Weser.

"I had already marked them, sir," said Roger drily. "And *they* seem to have marked *me*—for death!"

"I think you altogether misinterpret their glaring," Daniel said, after verifying that the fat one and the skinny one were, in fact, attempting to set fire to Roger's eyebrows with the heat of their scrutiny. "A she-wolf in the Thüringerwald stares thus at her prey, before pouncing. But it is not out of *hate* that the feral bitch of the north does so, but rather a cool understanding that it's from the hapless rabbit, sheep, or what-have-you, that she is to derive her sustenance."

"Oh, is *that* all they want? Money?"

"In a word, yes."

"I'd supposed that they wanted me to draw out my sword and plunge it into my own vitals, or something, from the way they were looking at me."

"No," Daniel confirmed, "they want your money."

"It is good to know this."

"Why? Are you going to give them some of your money now?"

"That would be impolite," said Roger, blushing at the very thought. "But I see no obstacle to giving them someone else's."

Finally they had drawn near enough that it was no longer the done thing for them to acknowledge anyone other than their (as yet uncrowned) King. For once Daniel got precedence over Roger, because of being a Regent; and his majesty even recognized him. "Dr. Vaterhouse of der Royal Society," he rattled off, as he allowed Daniel to kiss his hand—the very last occasion, or so Daniel hoped, that Daniel would ever give his Puritan ancestors occasion to roll over in their graves. Daniel was so consumed by the horror of what he was doing, and by wondering whether he was going to catch anything from that hand, which had already been kissed, today, by half of the syphilitics in England, that he failed to attend to what the King was saying. The problem was that his majesty had jumped over to some other language—some language, that is, that he actually spoke—and Daniel had not kept up—had not re-tuned his ear to follow it. With his unkissed left hand, George was gesturing toward the windows in the back, or south wall of the house, which provided a pleasant enough view over a rising green lawn, crossed here and there by paths, and tufted with carefully managed outbreaks of trees. Jutting from the biggest and most elevated of these, off to the right, was the queer edifice known as the Royal Observatory: two bookends imprisoning one book. But other than that, few buildings were visible, as the whole point was for it to be a park.

Daniel, belatedly coming alive to the fact that he was being personally addressed in an as-yet-unidentified language by the King, got only a single word: *Rüben*. What did it mean? To rub something? Perhaps the King was remarking that the custodians of the Queen's House had rubbed the windows very clean? Daniel was just beginning to nod when the King helpfully said *"navet."* Daniel realized in some horror that he'd switched to French to make himself better understood—but Daniel still didn't understand! Was he talking about the Navy? That would be reasonable in a way, since the activities of the Royal Observatory were of great importance to the Navy. Daniel kept nodding. Finally Bothmar intervened—Baron von Bothmar, who'd been the Hanoverian ambassador to the Court of St. James back in the days when Hanover and England had been different countries. "His majesty hates to see good land go to waste," Bothmar translated, "and has been eyeing yonder open space all morning, wondering how it might be put to some practical use; the difficulty being that it inclines toward the north and does not, in consequence, receive good sunlight. Knowing that you, Dr. Waterhouse, are a man of great Natural-philosophick acumen, his majesty asks you whether you are in agreement with him in thinking that, in the springtime, one might, with some hope of success, plant on that ground *Rüben—navets*—turnips."

"Tell his majesty that if I had a shovel I'd go plant some right now," Daniel said hopelessly.

The King, having been made aware of this, blinked and nodded. He had got a distant look now in his eyes, which reflected the green light of the future turnip-patch. Daniel could almost see the man's jowls fill up with saliva as he envisioned a grand turnip-feast in a year's time.

Ravenscar was chuckling. "How your shovel-work would discomfit those prancing, Frenchified Tory courtiers," he remarked, "who, seeing such an excellent plot of land as that, have not the wit to imagine any use for it save to parade about on their gaudy *chevals*."

"The Marquis of Ravenscar," von Bothmar explained, and Daniel now had to avert his gaze from the not especially appetizing spectacle of Roger planting a smooch on George's hand.

When Daniel felt it was safe to look back, the King seemed to have been put in mind of something. He was casting about for an eye-line to the Duke of Marlborough, and presently got one—Marlborough was one of the few actual English people suffered to stand anywhere near the King of England. Much as iron filings stand up and get organized in the presence of a magnet, certain facts and memories that had been scattered round the King's periwig came into alignment when his visual cortex was stimulated by the face of Marlborough. He harrumphed and began to burp out some phrases having to do with a *soirée* and a *Vulkan* that were translated into prose, and into English, by Bothmar. "His majesty has heard from my lord Marlborough that the Duke very much enjoyed your recent party, at which the famous Volcano was made to erupt. His majesty would fain witness this amusement. Not now. Later. But my lord Marlborough spoke well of how the Royal Mint has been looked after, and of the quality of the coinage. His majesty will require good men to look after the Treasury. Good *men*—not a good man. For such is the importance of this task that he has decided to change the tradition of appointing a Lord Treasurer, and place that office in commission. His majesty is pleased to nominate my lord Ravenscar First Lord of the Treasury. And he is also pleased to nominate Daniel Waterhouse a member of that same Commission."

All of which came as news to Daniel—though Roger had been winking at and elbowing him even more than usual in recent days, which ought to have given him a clew.

Rather a lot of bowing and scraping occurred round now, as tremendous gratitude had to be expressed, *et cetera*. Daniel happened to glance Marlborough's way, and caught the Duke glaring at Roger. Roger, who had peripheral vision subtending a full three hundred and sixty degrees, was well aware of it; it was some sort of arranged cue. "What will be my lord's first act as First Lord of the Treasury?" inquired Bothmar, who, too, had taken part in these silent, fevered exchanges.

"Why, to make a clean start of his majesty's coinage!" Roger answered. "Not that there was anything wrong with that of Queen Anne—this is well established. It is more of a procedural matter—some would call it superficial pomp, but we English have a weakness for that sort of thing—there is this special box, called the Pyx, which we keep in the Tower, all locked up, and put samples of the new coins into it as they are produced. And from time to time his majesty's council will say, 'Let's have a look at the old Pyx, shall we,' just as a routine precaution, as gunners try their powder before a battle. And so out comes the Pyx, and it is carried in a sort of solemn procession to the Star Chamber at Westminster where a furnace has been set up for the occasion, and the Pyx is unlocked in the presence of his majesty's Lords of the Council and the coins are taken out and assayed by goldsmiths from the City and compared against a trial plate, which is, as a rule, kept locked up in a crypt below Westminster

Abbey along with a lot of old saints' bones and whatnot." Here the new King's attention began to drift very noticeably and Roger seemed to come aware that he might as well be a witch-doctor dancing about in a fright wig and a carven mask. "Never mind, it is *quite the rite,* and it gives the City men a warm feeling. And when they have such a feeling it is rather a good thing for your majesty's commerce."

Bothmar had taken to raising his eyebrows at Roger so violently that it seemed they might fly off and stick to the ceiling. "*Anyway,*" Roger concluded, "time to clean out the Pyx! It is half full of most excellent coins bearing the stamp of the late Queen Anne, R.I.P. One Charles White has been looking after it—you may inquire among others as to the man's character. In fact, you'll probably meet him today!"

"In about ten minutes," said Bothmar, and glanced over toward the door. "That is, if you'll *finish.*" Daniel couldn't help following Bothmar's gaze, and had his day ruined by the sight of Mr. White, just inside the threshold, staring at him interestedly.

Roger polished it off thus: "To put to rest any possible confusion, I say, before we begin throwing new King George guineas into the Pyx, and mixing them up with Anne's, why, let's have a Trial of the Pyx, empty the thing out, kill the rumors, and start off your majesty's reign with a lot of sparkling new coins."

"For a while the schedule is terribly busy—"

"Not to worry," Roger assured him, "the Mint would not go into production anyway until after the coronation, which I'm told is scheduled for the twentieth of October. Give us, then, say, a week for the festivities to subside . . ."

"Sir Isaac Newton suggests Friday, the twenty-ninth."

"Worst *possible* day, I am afraid. That is a Hanging-Day at Tyburn. Impossible to move."

"Sir Isaac is aware of the fact," said Bothmar, "but says it is good, because on that day the Coiner shall be executed."

"I see. Yes. Yes. On one day—practically at the same moment—the Pyx shall be put to the trial, Sir Isaac shall be vindicated, and the most notorious of all coiners shall be put to death before an audience of, oh, half a million. Practicalities aside, Sir Isaac's proposal is, come to think of it, very clever."

"Well," Bothmar pointed out, "he *is* a genius."

"That he is!"

"And," Bothmar added, "his majesty thinks highly of Sir Isaac's philosophickal prowess."

"Did Sir Isaac have an opinion about the turnips?" Daniel inquired, but Roger stepped on his foot and Bothmar politely omitted to translate it.

"So," said Bothmar, "unless you object—"

"Not in the least! Friday, October the twenty-ninth, it is! Get the Privy Council to wave a quill over it, and we shall make ready for a Trial of the Pyx!"

ROGER AND DANIEL were permitted to stay and mingle. But Daniel hated mingling worse than anything. He launched a desperate escape attempt via the terrace in the back, but could not work out how to get round to the Thames side and flag down a passing Ship without making a spectacle of himself. He stared across the Lawn and pretended to philosophize about the turnip farm. When he felt this pretense might be wearing a bit thin, he stared up the hill at the Observatory and wondered if Flamsteed was awake yet, and whether he'd raise objections if Daniel went up there to tinker with the equipment. This too was wearing thin when haply he came across that old last resort of introverts at cocktail parties: a document that he could pretend to be utterly absorbed in. It was a broadside, lying face down on the stone pavement of the terrace with gentlemen's boot-prints all over it. Daniel raked it up over his toe with the tip of his walking-stick and from there was able to coax it up into a hand, and flip it over.

At the top of the sheet were two portraits of equal size, arrayed next to each other. One looked like an ink-blot. It was a miserable rendering of a black-haired black man in a black suit with two white eyes poking out. Beneath was a caption: *Dappa as rendered in April 1714 by the renown'd portraitist, Charles White.* The other was a rather good engraving of an African gentleman with silvery dreadlocks and a beard, dusky, of course, but with a range of skin tones suggested by the hatchures and other tricks of the engraver's art. It was captioned *DAPPA as rendered in September 1714 by* —, and here was given the name of a highly regarded artist. Looking more closely Daniel saw, in the background of the picture, a barred window, through which could be espied the skyline of London rising above the Thames. It was the view from the Liberty of the Clink.

The title was ADDITIONAL REMARKS on FAME by DAPPA. Daniel began to read it. It took the form of a sugary and, Daniel suspected, sarcastic encomium to the Duke of Marlborough.

"That was inadvertent," remarked a man who had been standing nearby, smoking a pipe. From the corner of his eye, Daniel had already marked this chap as a military man, for he was wearing an officer's uniform. Reckoning him to be a fellow non-Mingler, he had had the simple decency to ignore him. Now this general or colonel or whatever he was had shown the poor form to irrupt in on Daniel while he was pretending to read something so as not to have to talk to anyone. Daniel looked up and saw, first, that the facings, piping, cuffs, &c. of the uniform were those of the King's Own Black Torrent Guard. Second, that this was Marlborough.

"What was inadvertent, my lord?"

"When you came to call on me at my *levée,* just after I returned to this city, a month and a half ago, I had been reading some of this chap's work," said Marlborough. "Must have made some remark. Those other chaps must have gone forth and spread the rumor that I was a devotee of Mr. Dappa's work. It seems he has only become more popular since. People have sent him money—he lives now in the finest apartment that the Clink has to offer, and strolls on a private balcony there, and is called on by fops and whatnot. He says in the document you are holding in your hand there, that he has all but become a white man as a result, and presents these portraits as evidence. He still wears chains; but those are less restrictive than the chains of the mind that bind some to out-moded ideas such as Slavery. So he deems himself a Gentleman now, and has begun to place donations in escrow, in the hopes that he may purchase Charles White as soon as the price drops low enough."

"My word! You practically have the thing memorized!" Daniel exclaimed.

"I have had to spend many hours of late waiting for his majesty to wax talkative. Dappa writes well."

"You have command of your old regiment again, I gather?"

"Yes. The details are quite unfathomable. Others are toiling away at them. Colonel Barnes has been located, and put in charge of rounding up certain elements who were scattered during the amusements of the summer. I am glad I was not here. It all would have vexed me to no end. I understand congratulations are in order for you."

"Thank you," said Daniel. "I have no idea what are the duties of a member of the Treasury Commission—"

"Keep an eye on my lord Ravenscar. See to it that the Trial of the Pyx goes rather well."

"That, my lord, hangs on what is in the Pyx."

"Yes. I was meaning to ask you. Does *anyone* really know what's in the bloody thing?"

"Perhaps *he* does," said Daniel, and inclined his head toward a nearby window. A red-wigged gentleman was in there, mingling with Germans, but glancing frequently at them.

"Charles White," said Marlborough, "is, it's true, still in command of the King's Messengers, who pretend to guard the Pyx. I am pleased to let you know that they are now surrounded, and carefully observed, by the King's Own Black Torrent Guard. So Mr. White cannot make any more mischief with the Pyx. And Colonel Barnes has related to me that White was downriver with you and Sir Isaac Newton at the moment that the Pyx was molested in April."

"Very well," said Daniel, since, plainly enough, Marlborough had figured this all out on his own: "The only one who really knows what is in the Pyx is Jack Shaftoe."

"Hmm. If that is the case, then I am astonished that there is not a queue before Newgate Prison quite as long as that yonder."

"Perhaps there is," Daniel said.

White came out on the terrace and bowed. "My lord," he said to Marlborough. "Doctor Waterhouse."

"Mr. White," they both said. Then they all took turns saying, "God save the King."

"I trust you'll be *even more busy* than usual," White said to Daniel, "now that you've two Mints to look after."

"Two Mints? I do not understand, Mr. White. There is only one Mint that I know of."

"Oh, perhaps I was misinformed," said White, mock-confused. "People are saying there is another."

"Do you mean Jack Shaftoe's coining house in Surrey? The *Tory* Mint?" Daniel asked, and let the handbill snap in the breeze, hoping that White would notice it. He did.

"You really ought to have better sources of information. Don't read that rubbish. Listen to what Persons of Quality are saying."

Marlborough turned his back, which was a rude thing to do; but the way this was going, it would soon become a duelling matter unless the Duke pretended he wasn't hearing it.

"And what are Persons of Quality saying, Mr. White?"

"That Ravenscar is coining, too."

"People are accusing the Marquis of Ravenscar of committing High Treason? Seems audacious."

"Everyone knows he raised a private army. 'Tis a small step from that, to a private Mint."

"Bored toffs in drawing-rooms may believe any phant'sies they please! Such accusations require at least some evidence."

"They say that evidence may be found in abundance," said White, "at Clerkenwell Court, and at Bridewell, and in the cellars of the Bank of England. Good day." And he left. Which was fortunate for Daniel. A few seconds ago he had been amused at the sheer idiocy of the notion that Roger had been coining. Now he had become too flustered to speak.

"What was that about?" Marlborough very much wanted to know.

"It is a philosophical project I have been undertaking with Leibniz," said Daniel, "that, to make a long story—" and he gave a sketchy account of the thing to the Duke, explaining the movement of the gold from Clerkenwell to Bridewell to the Bank to Hanover. "Someone seems to have gathered rather a lot of information about it," Daniel concluded, "and spreads now a twisted version according to which it is a *coining* operation."

"We know who is *spreading* it—we have just been conversing with him," said Marlborough. "It matters not where the rumor originated." To this Daniel said nothing, for a sickening awareness had come over him that this might all have originated with Isaac.

"What *does* matter—very much—is that two members of the new Treasury Commission are mixed up in it," said Marlborough.

"Mixed up in *what*? A science experiment?"

"In something that looks a bit dodgy."

"I can't help it if it looks dodgy *to an ignoramus*!"

"But you *can* help that you are mixed up in it."

"What do you mean, my lord?"

"I mean that your experiment is at an end, sir. It must stop. And the moment it has stopped, responsible persons, trusted by the King and the City alike, must go to this Clerkenwell Court, and to Bridewell, and into the vaults of the Bank, and inspect them, and find *nothing* of what Mr. White has been talking of."

"It could be *stopped* at any time," Daniel said, "but to wind it up properly and cast away the residue is impossible in a day, or a week."

"How long will it take then?"

"October twenty-ninth," said Daniel, "is the date that has just been set for the Trial of the Pyx, the execution of Jack the Coiner, and the elimination of all doubt as to the soundness of his majesty's coinage. No later than that date, my lord, you'll be able to visit the places mentioned with as many inspectors as you might care to bring along with you—including even Sir Isaac himself—and you shall find nothing save Templar-tombs at Clerkenwell, hemp-pounders at Bridewell, and Coin of the Realm at the Bank."

"Done," said the Duke of Marlborough, and strode away, pausing to bow to a young lady crossing the terrace alone: the Princess of Wales.

"Dr. Waterhouse," Caroline said, "I need something from you."

Roger Comstock's House

3:30 A.M., FOUR DAYS LATER (22 SEPTEMBER 1714)

DANIEL HAD BARELY GOT in the front door when the most exquisite body in Britain was pressed up against him, hard. He wondered, not for the first time, how the world might have been different had said body been united in one person with her uncle's mind. Not much was separating him from Catherine Barton; having been rousted by a most urgent message, he'd come over in his nightshirt. *She* was wearing something diaphanous that he only glimpsed in the fraction of a second before she impacted on him. She smelled good: not an easy thing to accomplish in 1714. Daniel began to get his first erection since—since—well, since the *last* time he'd seen Catherine Barton. It was most inappropriate, as she was distraught. She was most certainly the sort of girl who would notice—but not the sort who would take it the wrong way.

She took him by the hand and led him back through the courtyard, round the fountain, and into the Ballroom, which smelled of oil, and was eerily lit up by the white-green glow of *kaltes feuer:* Phosphorus. A new thing had been added to the place. Seen from the entrance it looked like the rounded prow of a ship that happened to be made of silver, wreathed and festooned with garlands smitten of gold. Some manner of bas-relief Classical frieze had been molded into it. A sort of ram projected up and out of the thing, explicitly Priapic; Daniel recoiled and edged round this, for its tip was like to have caught him in the face. Iron rings, straps, &c., dangled from it. Coming now round the side of the object he discovered that it sat between a pair of wheels, made of wood but covered in gold leaf. This solved the mystery of how so heavy an object could have been moved into the ballroom. It was nothing less than a chariot—a huge one, eight feet wide. It was, he realized, a Chariot of the Gods. Coming finally around the open back of it, which faced towards the Volcano only a few yards away, he saw that the whole floor of the vehicle was a tongue-shaped expanse of Bed: as wide as the Chariot and ten feet long, upholstered in crimson silk and bestrewn with furs, and silk- and velvet-covered pillows in diverse glandular shapes. Sprawled in the middle of it was Roger Comstock, the Marquis of Ravenscar. A laurel wreath was awry on his bald head. Mercifully, his purple toga had not been altogether torn off, but the middle of it was poked up, producing a Turkish tent effect that echoed the shape of the nearby Volcano. But the Volcano, mechanism that it was, still pumped away faithfully, its hidden Screw sending spurt after spurt of Oil of Phosphorus down its slopes. Whereas Roger was, or had been, animated by what Newton would call a Vegetative Spirit, which had quite fled his body. The toga-lifter was rigor mortis. He'd have to be buried in a special coffin.

"He was sworn in today as First Lord of the Treasury," said Miss Barton—who, bless her, had the presence of mind to know that *some* explanation was wanting. "And so we celebrated the Rites of Vulcan."

"Of course you did," said Daniel, who was crawling on all fours up the treacherous (because silky as well as oily) slope of the stupendous Bed, glancing up from time to time to navigate by the landmark of the Pole Star.

"It is a thing Roger liked to do, to celebrate a great triumph. The *last* time was after he crushed Bolingbroke. The Rites are lengthy and elaborate—"

"I had already inferred that," Daniel said. He had finally got to the place where he could behold Roger's face in softly pulsing phosphorus-light.

"Just at the moment of the—Eruption—he suffered an attack—"

"Stroke, probably."

"He said, 'Get Daniel! No Bleeders—I don't want to go out like King Chuck.' I ran out to send you the message. When I returned, he was—like he is now."

"You mean, dead?" said Daniel. For he had completed the rite of checking for a pulse. It was superfluous—no man had ever looked more dead than Roger. But his engorged Member had raised doubts.

DANIEL REMAINED STRANGELY CALM UNTIL servants sledded Roger's corpse down to the Chariot's threshold, transferred him to a litter, and took him away. Even when he was dead, it seemed, Roger's presence had some chymical power to reassure Daniel, to make him feel sure everything would come out all right. But something in the way Roger's limbs tumbled as he was being moved, cruelly struck Daniel as proof that Roger's adroitness, his intelligence, his force were all flown. By the time the ballroom doors had slammed behind the retreating litter, Daniel had already begun to dissolve.

The Chariot, as it turned out, had a cover: a sort of brocaded tarpaulin that could be drawn over its open top and rear, probably to catch dust and bird-shit when it was languishing in Roger's stables awaiting a Triumph. This had been reefed and tied about the vehicle's rim with many tasseled golden ropes. The Priestess of Vulcan went round undoing these, and presently unfurled the cover, and drew it down to envelop the whole bed. Daniel was sitting up in the middle of it, elbows on knees, hands clamped over his phizz, tears leaking out.

"I do not wish to live in a world that does not have Roger in it," he heard himself saying; and then he thanked God that Roger was not alive to hear him talking this way. "He was my Complement—my protector—my partner—my patron—it's almost as if he were my wife or something."

"Or you his," said Miss Barton. Having finished with this project of enclosing Daniel in the womb-like interior of the Chariot of Vulcan, she hitched up her skirts and knee-walked up the slope of the bed until she reached Daniel's side, then put a comforting hand on his shoulder.

"God! I really am on the wrong Planet henceforth!" Daniel exclaimed. "What am I going to do?"

"Roger has made out the most exacting Will. He showed it to me. There is money for the Royal Society. For a Museum he wishes to have made here. For the Kit-Cat Clubb, the Italian Opera, and the Massachusetts Bay Colony of Technologickal Arts."

Daniel did not say what he was thinking, which was that for every asset Roger could claim, there would be equal or greater liabilities. He had held his creditors at bay by amazing them, threatening them, distracting them, and drinking them under the table. But now, like ants swarming a defenseless carcass, they would come.

Daniel pulled his hands from his face and made himself leave off blubbering. "No. It is not that sort of thing I am thinking of. I have much to do before the twenty-ninth of October. Much to do! It seemed nearly impossible even when Roger was about to do most of it *for* me. The others on the Treasury Commission are mountebanks and time-servers. So it is *I* who must organize the Trial of the Pyx. What do I know of it? Nothing! Clerkenwell Court and Bridewell must be shut down, liquidated. The Institute of Technologickal Arts has got to be considered dead—I'll send word to Enoch to sell the cabin. What else!? Oh, yes. The Princess of Wales wants me to help a dear friend of hers sort out her love life—which happens to be more fraught with dangers and complexities than, let us say, the foreign policy of the Venetian Republic."

711

"I am sorry to laugh, on such a sad occasion," said the Priestess of Vulcan, "but *that* strikes me as most absurd!"

Which Daniel might have taken in a resentful spirit, had she not begun to knead the tight muscles at the base of his neck and between his scapulae.

"In some things you are a very clever chap, or so Roger always used to say. But what would a man such as you know of affairs of the heart? Why, your muscles tie themselves up in knots at the very mention of these things! Roll over on your belly, sir, or else the oil will run down your back."

"Oil? What oil!?"

"*This* oil . . ."

"Oh, my word!"

"*That's* better. Now I can straddle you—your buttocks can take most of my weight—thus—and it becomes easier for me to reach those parts of you that are most in need of lubrication and a good stiff massage."

"Is *this* how Roger did it?" Daniel said wonderingly, a long time later.

"No, Roger liked to get up on all fours like a—"

"No, no, no, Miss Barton. I meant something different. Is this how Roger managed to—to keep so many balls in the air—as it were—and not go mad?"

"Now you ask me to speculate on matters quite beyond my scope, Dr. Waterhouse. Roll over on your back!"

"I was just reflecting that those affairs that so troubled my mind only a little while ago, seem to have quite fled my mind—oh, my goodness, Miss Barton!"

"It sounded as if your troubles were beginning to sneak back into your awareness," she explained, "and so I rather phant'sied some drastic action was called for."

"What . . . what . . . what troubles, Miss . . . Miss . . . Miss Barton?"

"My point exactly. Tilt your pelvis t'other way, if you please, sir . . . there! Much better, you'll admit. Now, leave the rest to me, sir—the balance of this chariot can be a bit . . . *tricky* . . . the ride . . . a bit rough."

Indeed, the axle-bearings of the Chariot of Vulcan presently began to creak as it got to rocking forward and back, forward and back, on its wheels. Daniel was old, and the ride was correspondingly long. But the *primum mobile*—the Body of Miss Barton—was young and, as everyone in London agreed, in the most superb condition, and more than equal to the work. Daniel felt a-drift in Absolute Space, and phant'sied that the Chariot had worked its way out the ballroom doors, off the property, down Tottenham Court Road, and was gliding across the dewy turf of Lambs Conduit Fields . . . on and on . . . until suddenly it toppled down a well. He opened his eyes. It was over. She executed a back-somersault off of him, and rolled to her feet, poking up the tarpaulin with her head, and artfully stuffed a fistful of Roman priestess vestments up between her thighs.

"Perhaps your uncle knows something after all," Daniel said. "It seems so obvious, when one contrasts a dead Roger with a live Daniel, that there is something one lacks and the other has!"

"You have a bit less of it now," Miss Barton said playfully. Then she turned her head to one side, attending to some subtle noise without, that Daniel had not heard. "Who is there?" she called, and gathered up an arm-load of tarp, ready to give it a heave. "Don't!" Daniel called, for he was most indecent.

"The servants have seen ever so much worse!" she returned with a roll of the eyes, and heaved. The curtain flew back and ended up creased over Daniel's head like a little roof. He gazed out upon the face of Sir Isaac Newton, who was standing there with his back to the volcano, beaming lanthorn-light at him.

"I came as soon as I heard the dreadful news," he announced crisply, at some point during the approximately half an hour during which Daniel was rendered speechless. Isaac had not evinced the slightest surprise at seeing Daniel here, in this pose. This raised interesting questions. Had he been eavesdropping the entire time, and therefore had ample time to master his rage and astonishment? Or was his opinion of Daniel's character now so abyssal that he simply felt nothing at all?

"It seems, however," Isaac went on, "that matters are well in hand here."

"That they are, uncle," said Miss Barton, and glided down off the bed of the chariot to give her kinsman a chaste peck on the cheek.

"Is there any way that I might be of assistance?" Isaac was desirous of knowing.

Daniel could not think of anything to say. He would have ample time to re-live the moment later, to savor and amplify his embarrassment. What struck him now, as he sat there in a half-ripped-off nightshirt, gazing upon fully dressed Isaac, was that word of Roger's death must be out; and all over the metropolis at this instant, people were awake, and out-maneuvering Daniel in ways that he probably would never even know about.

The Castle, Newgate Prison

29 SEPTEMBER 1714

A TURRETED CASTLE BESTRODE Holborn. On the side where the gentleman and his host were taking tea, the building sported a noble façade, to make a great impression on riders entering into London from the west. The ground floor was mostly accounted for by the vaulted arch of the gateway. The floor above that contained the machinery for raising and lowering the siege-grade portcullis; this was hidden behind a row of niches in which Liberty, Justice, and other noble ladies took shelter from the rains. This had not prevented their turning a mottled black from coal-smoke. So they glared down like Furies at all who passed beneath. But the next floor up was adorned by a triple Gothick window centered above the highway, rather like the hatch at the top of a German clock, whence the cuckoo popped out on the hour. Behind those windows lay Jack's new abode. He would not be popping out, however, as they were heavily barred. Indeed, the first resident of this flat must have been a blacksmith, who must've lived there for a month, forging those gridirons and setting them into the stone frames. But they were excellent windows, taller than Jack and wider than the span of his arms, and despite the massive bars they admitted a fortune in light.

The Castle, as this part of Newgate Prison was called, was meant for Prisoners of Quality. So it lacked certain facilities that were present in abundance in other parts of the gaol, e.g., iron wall-rings to which difficult prisoners could be fettered. The gaolers had been forced to improvise. A hundred pounds of chain had been looped round some of the window-bars and dragged along the floor to Jack and locked to his ankle-fetters. The chain was long enough that he could hobble to any part of the apartment, save the exit. For the nonce, he was seated at his table, sipping tea.

Standing before his great window and gazing through the gridwork, the visitor enjoyed a view along the road up Snow Hill to the place where it bridged the Fleet Ditch some quarter of a mile away.

Beyond that it swelled to twice or thrice the width, and rambled off among posh squares and courts that had been cow-pastures when Jack was a lad. Much nearer to hand, no more than a bow-shot away, to the right, lay the Church of St. Sepulchre. It was an ancient English church of that school of architecture known to scholars as A Big Pile of Rocks. There, Jack and his fellow Tyburn commuters would be subjected to a tedious rite in one month's time. So Jack preferred not to let his gaze rest on that Church and especially not its Yard, which had swallowed more dead than it could cleanly digest.

"All of the best apartments in London, it seems, are in bloody Prisons," said the visitor, "and all of them are occupied by men who are troublesome to me, in one way or another."

Against those windows he made a perfect Fopp-silhouette, like something snipped out of black paper by an ingenious miniaturist on the Pont-Neuf. From the high-styled ringlets of his periwig down to the bows on his shoes, back up the curves of his well-muscled calves and the perfectly cut skirts of his coat, traveled the eyes of Jack. He wore a scabbard and a small-sword, and Jack thought of flattening him with a swing of the mighty chain, and snatching the weapon. But this would boot him nothing and so to think of it was idle. Jack snapped out of this hyper-violent reverie, and tried to make conversation.

"What, are you speaking of that bloke in the Clink? The famous Dappa?"

"You know that I am," said Charles White, and turned his back to the view. He reached out absent-mindedly and stroked Jack's chain where it was looped about the window-bars. "Before this country became so disorderly, *all* of those who were troublesome to their betters were pent up in places such as this. I am pleased that there are still remaining *some* vestiges of civilization."

"But isn't that Dappa *more* trouble for you in the Clink?"

"I have plans for Dappa," said White, "and I have plans for you. And *that* is why facilities such as the Clink and Newgate are so useful; they hold men like you in one place long enough for men like me to make plans."

"All right," said Jack, "I knew we'd get round to this, and I am ready for it. You are a tedious and obvious bloke, Mr. White. So I need only ask myself, what's the most tedious and obvious plan that a man could devise? Why, to have me done away with. Not much of a threat, as one month from to-day I've an appointment with Mr. Jack Ketch at Tyburn Cross; and there is no way you could murder me *here* that could be worse than how he'll carry it off *there*. So you are powerless to issue threats. You must, therefore, offer inducements."

"You rush ahead so!" White exclaimed. "It were proper, first, to speak of what it is that you must do."

"There's nothing in the world I *must* do," Jack reminded him. "In that sense I'm the freest man in the world. What is it that you are trying to *get* me to do?"

"You are charged with High Treason in the form of coining. Sir Isaac Newton has enough to prove it; there's little point in offering up a defense. You'll be asked to plead, guilty or not guilty. It is a necessary formality. If you refuse to enter a plea, you'll be subject to the *peine forte et dur*—pressing under weights—until you die, or change your mind."

"I have been coming to Newgate since I was a wee lad, and well know the Standard Procedures," said Jack. "What is your point?"

"If you agree to make a statement, I'll see to it that several men are present—not just Sir Isaac. In the presence of those men, you will say that Sir Isaac Newton debased the coinage, and took the gold that he skimmed from Her Majesty's coffers, and—"

"Pocketed it?"

"No."

"Gave it to prostitutes?"

"No."

"Drank it up?"

"No. Used it to perform Alchemical research in the Tower."

"Oh! Of course. Stupid me," said Jack, and slapped himself in the forehead so briskly that his ankle-chains jingled. "That were a far more credible accusation."

"My lord Bolingbroke got wind of it," White went on, in a peculiar singsong cadence meant to remind Jack that this was the made-up Romance that he was supposed to be memorizing, "and quite properly began to make preparations for a Trial of the Pyx. Hearing of this, the guilty Newton flew into a panic, and reached you, Jack, and induced you and your gang—"

"Gang. Gang. Why is it ever 'Gang?' Don't call them that. It sounds so—I don't know—*criminal.* They are my family and friends."

"Induced you and your *associates* to break in to the Tower, open the Pyx, remove the debased guineas that would prove Newton's guilt, and replace them with sound ones. To make this possible Newton led me and others on a wild goose chase to Shive Tor. You achieved your mission; but it went awry in some small way—here you can make up something plausible—and people found out about it, and now Newton is trying to commit judicial murder on you and your . . . *associates,* to cover his traces."

" 'Twould make for a lively half-hour, relating such a yarn in the presence of my persecutor, and a panel of a-mazed Big-wigs," Jack admitted. "As if 'twere a Statue set up in the middle of my Apartment, I shall, in weeks to come, circle round your Proposition and view it from diverse angles and in different lights, and peruse it for Defects."

"Did you say, *weeks?*" asked the amused/perplexed White. "Because—"

"There is ample time for me to consider it," Jack said authoritatively. "And I shall consider it far more seriously if you can let me know what I might get out of it, other than a few minutes' entertainment."

"Escape," said Charles White. "Escape to America for you and your . . . associates in the Fleet Prison."

Now at this Jack felt moved, at last, to bestir himself, and shuffled across the floor, dragging the chain behind him until he stood at the window, next to Charles White. It had been the tendency of White to gaze down the street and off to the right, which was his not especially subtle way of trying to draw Jack's attention to the Church of St. Sepulchre, and other grisly land-marks and way-stations along the route of the Hanging-March. But Jack looked rather to the left. Several buildings of note happened to be arranged in a straight line marching off to the southwest. Nearest to hand, just within musketry range, and therefore almost as convenient to the Old Bailey as Newgate, was the Fleet Prison. It was a great thick wall of Building, fuzzy with myriad chimney-pipes, spreading along the banks of the mighty shit-ditch after which it was named. Beyond that, on the opposite side of said ditch, and down a bit, sprawled Bridewell, infested with Females in Trouble. Then there was the Thames, and finally, miles off, he could see the odd spire belonging, he thought, to the Hall or the Abbey at Westminster. All of these were packed firmly in a matrix of unremarkable London buildings, post-Fire, therefore made of coal-blackened brick, and built wall to wall with nothing green, except for the odd fleck where some nest-building bird had stolen a bit of moss or turf from somewhere and been forced to drop it to evade assault by ravens, Nature's footpads. The only reason that the Fleet Prison could be identified as a separate Institution was that its buildings rose up from the middle of an open plaza; it had grounds, and a perimeter.

"You'd have me believe, then," said Jack, "that you can spring three blokes out of *there,* as well as *me* out of *here,* on the same night? For you'll have to do both at the same time. To me it would seem a most difficult thing to put into execution—even if the Whigs *hadn't* beaten the stuffing out of your party and sent half of 'em packing to *La France.*"

"I must say that I am disappointed to hear such timid and doubtful words from the conqueror of the Tower," White said.

"*I* had *resources*. You—"

"You underestimate the tenacity and the wealth of my Party. Do not be misled by the temporary departure of Bolingbroke. Rebellion is brewing, Jack. It might take a year or two, but mark my words: Jacobite armies will soon be on the march in this country and shall sweep away the Spawn of the Usurper."

"That would be the King of England you're referring to, there?"

"As some style him. To arrange a simple jail-break, or two of them on the same evening, is really a trivial matter, Jack. Particularly from Newgate Prison, which has a history of escapes, by prominent prisoners, almost as illustrious as that of the Tower."

"As to that I shall have to accept your word," said Jack, "since none of the blokes I knew here as a lad, ever escaped save via the Treble Tree."

"Then only ponder the immense value, to my Party, of discrediting Sir Isaac Newton, the coinage of this Realm, and the Whigs, all at a stroke; set aside which, the cost of arranging two jail-breaks is derisory."

"Sir, you may consider your proposal On the Table," said Jack, "and after I have waited a decent interval for competing proposals to join it, I shall weigh them all, and arrive at some judicious decision, provided that my old mate, the Imp of the Perverse, does not get the better of me."

The Black Dogg of Newgate
4 OCTOBER 1714

NEWGATE WAS THE MOST versatile building in town. It was the Middlesex county gaol, not only for malefactors, but for debtors of both the honest and the dishonest type, and for fines as well. But this was also the City of London's prison for criminals. It was in that capacity that it now played host to Jack Shaftoe, and hundreds of others who only *wished* they were Jack Shaftoe. But grades and distinctions could be found even within that class. Not all London criminals were footpads, horsepads, shoplifters, file-clys, night-gamesters, running-smoblers, or till-divers. There were also the Unfortunate Gentlemen, guilty of Treason, Murder, Highway Robbery, Rape, Scandal, Debt, Duelling, Bankruptcy, or Coining. Of all of these except for Rape and Debt, Jack Shaftoe was guilty as charged.

To create a distinct Ward or Hold for each of these classes were a task to which only Noah were equal. But to mix them all in one room were unnatural, or, at least, un-English. Accordingly, Newgate possessed three great divisions. Below the aristocratic confines of the Press-Yard and Castle, where Toffs in Trouble paid their debts to society playing cards in ventilated apartments, but above the loathsome flesh-pits of the Common-Side, was the Master-Side of Newgate. One part of this was for Felons, the other for mere Debtors, but in practice they were all commingled, especially in that part of the prison called the Black Dogg.

Inhabitants of the Press-Yard and Castle looked indistinguishable from any other Persons of Quality, save that they were fettered. Common-Side prisoners tended to be flagrantly, almost gloriously wretched, and even without the heavy chains that they were obliged to wear, could never have been mistaken for anything other than prisoners. Occupants of the Master-Side, however, bore to free Londoners the same relationship as a dried and salted cod, hanging on a rack, did to a live one swimming in the sea: which was to say that most of the same bits were there, and with some squinting, head-cocking, and generous dollops of imagination, you could make in your mind's eye a picture of what they'd once been. Family and friends would show up from time to time bearing clothing, food, candles, and toiletries, and so most of these were able to keep up some vestiges of whatever looks they'd had before they'd been clapped into irons.

The Visitor looked like one of those. The patches that held his clothing together might have been taken as stigmata of poverty up on Newgate Street, but down here in the Black Dogg, people were apt to look on them as badges or decorations proving that someone out there still knew his name. His black periwig, so ratty and bedraggled, would have earned him mockery had he worn it in Charing Cross, but in the Black Dogg it proved—well, it proved he still had a periwig. More remarks in the same vein could be made concerning his shoes, his stockings, and the three-cornered hat pulled down low over his face. Even his insistent, raspy cough was very typical of Newgate prisoners, as was his low murmuring way of speaking. All in all, anyone familiar with Newgate would have marked him, without a moment's thought, as a long-term Master-Side Debtor. But then, upon a second look, they would have noted two oddities about the man: one, that there were no irons round his ankles. He was free to leave. Two, that the ankle-chained bloke he was conversing with was a clean and well-dressed Press-Yard and Castle prisoner, only slumming for a short interval here in the Black Dogg. Divers cudgel-wielding Gaolers and Bailiffs had crowded into the place to keep an eye on this inmate while he passed the time of day with his visitor. But soon enough it had become evident that this old, coughing, out-of-breath, patched, raggedy, down-at-heels gager could not possibly be here as part of any scheme to break Jack Shaftoe out of prison. Or if he were, he could be stopped simply by throwing him an elbow. So the guards had relaxed, and shooed prisoners off benches and away from tables, and taken seats, bought drink from the prisoner-barman, and bided their time, each keeping an eye on Jack from across the room.

"Thank you for coming round," Jack said to his visitor. "I'd have nipped round to see you, but I'm chained to a great bloody window-grille most days."

The Visitor twitched and coughed.

"Thought you might like to know," Jack continued, "that I have been receiving offers from other quarters that are right tempting. More attractive, by a long chalk, than aught that I've heard from *you.*"

The Visitor murmured some hot words, and, when words failed him, made flat slicing gestures.

"Oh, I've no illusions as to *that,*" Jack assured him. "All has changed since we met here on the 28th of July. There is abundant evidence—as people never tire of telling me—to send me and the boys to Tyburn. So, I am not about to ask you for what we spoke of before: the farm in Carolina. *That* is a pipe-dream. But for Christ's sake! A man of your intelligence must know that *this* is no kind of tempting offer! A merciful hanging, that is to say, a long drop, a short stop, and a decent burial for me and the boys. You cannot seriously expect me to assist you in exchange for such floor-sweepings. Bloody hell, if I want to die fast, I can make it so in the privacy of my own apartment!"

The Visitor spoke for some little while now, but was cut off, at the end, by a coughing fit; which seemed to bring him such discomfort that he shifted about and writhed on his chair.

"Sore ribs," was the diagnosis of Doctor Jack Shaftoe. "Oh, I've had what you've got, sir, a time or two. Bloody torture, ain't it? An arm or a leg heals in a trice, but ribs take forever." This seemed to be a sort of patter while he waited for the Visitor's fit to subside. When the other had finally stifled himself with a handkerchief to the lips, Jack went on: "It is easy enough for me to stand up before anyone you like, put my hand on a Bible, and testify that the coins I took out of the Pyx—*your* coins—were sound, and the ones I put into it—*my* fakes—were debased. But you quite correctly ask, who the hell is going to take *my* word for it? No one in his right mind. So. Yes. Indeed. You, sir, require *hard* evidence, in the form of the *hard* currency that I stole. Where is it, you'd like to know? Well, I already told you before that I gave all of that swag to the late Marquis of Ravenscar. I hoped that'd satisfy you. But as you have been so tiresome on this topic, I have, since the Marquis's death, made certain inquiries among those of my friends you've not yet murdered, thrown into prison, or chased out of the country. And they tell me, sir, that those Sinthias from the Pyx were taken out of Ravenscar's house after he died by that friend of his, that Daniel Waterhouse, and that this Waterhouse cove placed 'em for safekeeping in a vault or something below the ground out in Clerkenwell—I see by your face that you know the place I mean!" For the greasy wig had begun to bob up and down as the Visitor nodded.

The Visitor pointed something out, and then it was Jack's turn to nod. "You'll never come out and say what you mean, but I can translate it well enough into plain talk: without the King's Messengers to act as your bully boys, you must go through channels now. You can no longer just raid a place like Clerkenwell Court on your personal say-so. You must secure the Authority first. If you would like me to testify before a magistrate that the Pyx coins are secured in that vault, why, I'll do that, sir, I will. But in exchange I must have freedom for Jimmy and Danny and Tomba. And for myself I want life, is all. Keep me locked up forever, if that is your will; but I'll not be subjected to all of that rudeness out at Tyburn, and my parts pickled in Jack Ketch his Kitchen."

The Visitor mumbled something, and clawed at the tabletop until he'd dragged himself to his feet. "See you in a week, then!" Jack said. The Visitor said nothing in return, but turned round, keeping his face to the wall, and tottered out of the Black Dogg.

Now some of the Gaolers were of a mind to jump up and fetch Jack straightaway back to his parlor up in the Castle. But others had not yet finished their pints. Jack himself had ordered a round for the house only a minute earlier, and had not even begun to quaff from the fresh mug that had just been set before him. It seemed indecent to drag him out just now. So Jack sat, and shook hands and exchanged pleasantries with several prisoners who had the temerity to approach his table, and even kissed a Common-Side wench—almost certainly a Felon, by the looks of her—on the cheek. But after a few minutes there was movement from an adjacent table. Two free men had been sitting there all through Jack's interview with his visitor: one, younger and quite bulky, the other, of indeterminate age (because of a wig and a turned-up collar) but with the bony physique of one of those fortunate chaps who has found the knack of spiting age. The big one stayed in his chair, only shifting position so as to bring Jack's table into the corner of his eye. The slight one got up, went into the corner, and helped himself to a seat. He was gripping a mug—courtesy of Jack! He had not, however, brought it to his lips. Rather, he kept it clenched between his hands so that they would not shake so much. They wanted to shake with rage. No, they wanted to close round the throat of Jack Shaftoe.

Jack enjoyed watching his new visitor for a few minutes. For it took that long for the old man to contain his fury enough to speak.

"How long," he finally said, "how long have you been whispering those—those abominable lies into the ear of Sir Isaac Newton?"

"For as long as I have been *privy* to his eager ears," said Jack, "going on two months now. It is something I never looked for. Great men in this town will do backflips to get Ike's attention for even a moment. Who'd have thought he would listen so avidly to a Vagabond? And yet since he clapped me in irons, I've had better entrée to him than the bloody King of England himself. I snap my fingers—there he is, ready to listen for hours."

"Since the Marquis of Ravenscar went to his long home," said Daniel, "Isaac Newton is my oldest friend. Or *was*; for your lies have made him into a bitter and dangerous enemy."

Jack snorted. "I could see what excellent *friends* you were when you came here to parley with me on the evening of July the 28th. The suspicion on old Ike's face was quite obvious. Oh, not suspicion *of you only* but of *everyone*. I knew then that a few words from me would set him off. And so now you are enemies. Which is of as much significance to me, as that flies are, at this moment, swarming on camels' arses in Cairo. Your old friend, enemy, or whatever he is, wishes to tear me limb from limb. Now. This bloke, who would do this terrible thing to me, is, it seems, a sorcerer or alchemist of some stripe, straight out of a bleeding færy-tale! Just like elves and trolls, his sort are fading away, and soon to vanish from this world. A state of affairs that is as plain to *them*, as it is to you and me! But where you and I look on this as a dying-off—and good riddance!—Ike and his chums mistake it for an Apocalypse that will be their great and final triumph. Ones such as he used to come and pester us in Vagabond-camps, and we would sport with them, lacking other diversions. Just as the proprietor of a gin-house uses his customers' lust for booze to get money to feed his family, why, I am using Ike's lust for the Solomonic Gold to get what I require for myself and the boys. Which I'll go on doing until I have achieved satisfaction. If the result is a raid upon the Whig Mint hidden at Clerkenwell Court, and if in consequence you and your learned associates are brought hither in chains, it is nothing to me."

"Fine. It is all clear. What is it then that you want?"

"Jimmy, Danny, Tomba, and I, free men, on a ship bound for America."

"It is so noted," said the other. "However, there is a complication of which I am obliged to make you aware."

"My glass is only half empty, Dr. Waterhouse, and you have not even touched yours; so it seems there is ample time, if you will abandon this guarded cryptic way of speaking and only come out and say what you mean."

"*You* may—supposing some escape were to be possible—board ship and go to America. But *she* will not."

Jack almost shot back some waggish riposte, but then a serious look spread over his phizz, and he settled back, and waited. "You cannot possibly be talking about what I *think* you're talking about!" he said finally.

"I know it is difficult to believe," said Daniel.

"Even supposing—well—supposing any number of things I'm unwilling to suppose—why would she employ *you* as a go-between?"

"It is an eminently reasonable question," said Daniel. "The answer is that she is not. I am doing this at the bidding of another—a friend of the lady in question."

"Then I do not think much of this person's friendship," said Jack, "for a true friend would not dream of trying to mend what was broken so long ago. Some friend! Ha!"

"None the less," Daniel said, "I have been asked, by the friend in question, to make inquiries. The friend is young, and she has fanciful notions concerning the power of true love, *et cetera, et cetera*."

"Yes, as depicted in plays," Jack said. "And by that I do not mean the vile, merry plays of the Restoration but older ones such as I attended as a lad."

"Of a simpler æra."

"Indeed. Yes. Though I am by no means fatuous enough to believe in such mawkish phant'sies, sir, I know how it is that young ladies, perhaps over-fond of the Theatre and the Italian Opera, can fall under its influence for a time, until Age and Experience slap them back to their senses. And so I'll allow that this young lady who sent you may be merely *daft*, and not the least bit malicious."

"She will be ever so gratified," said Daniel, "to know that the King of the Vagabonds thinks so."

"No need to jab at me, there, Doctor. 'Tis a sufficiently trying conversation, even without your biting asides. I am getting round to telling you something of great moment, which you must relay to this meddlesome lass, and that is as follows: the woman in question said to me, a long time ago, that I'd never again see her nor hear her voice until the day I died. And she's not the sort to renege."

"Well, then, it follows that if you escape death, and board ship for America, you won't get to see her or speak to her," Daniel pointed out.

"That were a very sad fate indeed," said Jack, "but it is the fate to which I have been doomed for twelve years; and another few years of it wouldn't kill me; whereas hanging around London *would*."

Fleet Prison
AFTERNOON OF 5 OCTOBER 1714

'TWAS NATURAL TO ASSUME of a prison that, like the *Inferno* of Dante, it would only get worse as one worked one's way in through the gate and pierced its concentric wards. Daniel had been circumventing the Fleet—a largely autonomous city of about a thousand souls— since he'd been tiny. The prison building proper (burned down in 1666, rebuilt in 1670) was a bit shy of two hundred fifty feet in length from the Poor Side common-room on the south end, to the Chapel on the north; forty feet deep; and forty high (sufficient for five storeys of low-ceilinged apartments, if one counted its half-buried cellar). But this structure, big as it was, could no more be confused with the Prison as a whole, than, say, the White Tower could be mistaken for the Tower of London complex. The Fleet Prison, as Daniel had always known it, was a squarish town about five hundred feet on a side—so, on paper, six acres or so. But seen up close it was like one of those writhing horrors that Hooke used to view under his microscope, which was to say it felt a thousand times larger than it was, because so complex and seething. Its outer boundary was understood to run, on the western side, right up the bank of the Fleet Ditch. On the north, all of Fleet Lane lay within it, but the buildings on the north side of the street lay without; so a prisoner could walk down the lane, trailing a hand along the fronts of the buildings, but if he or she stepped thro' a doorway it would be deemed an Escape, and set in motion a train of financial consequences for the Warden. Similarly on the street called the Great Old Bailey (which coincided with the eastern boundary) and Ludgate Hill (southern), though along the latter it was more complicated because the prison had thrust out three narrow tendrils along as many small Courts that depended from the south side of Ludgate. Thus the squarish, six-acre *rules* (as it was, for some reason, called) within which certain prisoners could roam about unchained and unguarded, provided that they had taken out a *Warrant of Attorney to confess a judgment to the amount of the debt with which the prisoner stands charged, with a defeazance on the back declaring it is to be void in case no escape should take place.* This and other such securities, by very long-standing tradition, made it at least theoretically possible for those who'd been put in prison for debt—which meant most of the Fleet's population—to move, and in some cases set up domiciles, outside of the Prison proper but within the *rules,* which was nearly indistinguishable from other seedy neighborhoods of London. The only way you'd really know you were in a prison was that certain chaps had odd habits of locomotion—in the interior of the six acres they'd move about like anyone else, but as they approached the boundary streets they'd become tentative, as if they could sense an invisible barrier, and would sidle along cautiously, lest a misstep or traffic accident push them over the border and make them guilty of Escape.

All of this was an accommodation that like other institutions in this country had grown up insensibly during the half-dozen centuries since the Norman Conquest. When those actual Normans had burst in on the place, they'd found a patch nearer to one acre in extent, shaped like the hoof-print of a horse, its flat side defined by the bank of the Fleet River (in those days, one phant'sied, a babbling rural freshet) and the rest of it bulging out to the east. In any case it had somehow picked up a privileged legal status: the Bishop of London had authority over all the land around it, but not this one-acre hoofprint. Which anomaly could presumably be traced back to some more or less interesting yarn involving mailed Angles whaling on each other with gory battle-axes, but none of that mattered now—what mattered was that this oddity had somehow been leveraged, over the better part of a millennium, into the hoofprint's current status as the Prison for the Courts of Common Pleas, Chancery, Exchequer, and Curia Regis. It had served in like capacity for the Court of Star Chamber until that had been abolished, and so Drake had once been chained up here, before Daniel had been born. In those days, for that reason, it had been a more interesting place, and more profitable to the Warden. But now it was thought of almost entirely as a debtors' prison. There were a few exceptions to that rule, which had lately become very important to Daniel. But in order for him to come to grips with the *exceptions* he had first to know and understand the *norms*.

This had entailed a negligible amount of preliminary research. Negligible because small, but also because he simply could not believe what he'd been reading about how the place was run. Like a general planning a campaign, he'd sought to draw up an Order of Battle: a list of the opposing forces, an inventory of their battalions. Yet no matter how many documents he perused, or debtors he bought gin for in the sad taverns that competed against cut-rate slaughterhouses and brothels for real estate in the *rules,* he could only turn up references to the following officials:

✠ A Warden, who had bought the title as a sort of Investment— possibly the most complicated financial security in the history of the world—and who was never there.

✠ A Deputy Warden, who had entered into some manner of indenture with the Warden, so as to shield the Warden from the liability he ought to have incurred whenever a prisoner was found to have escaped—the details made Daniel's head spin, and were not important—suffice it to say that the arrangement only made sense if the Deputy Warden were essentially no better than an imprisoned debtor himself, so that when any liability fell on *him* as a result of an escape, he could simply shrug off the now inconvenient title, plead insolvency, and dissolve back into the Fleet's general population.

✠ A few Tipstaffs, who were officials charged with escorting prisoners to and from the several Courts; these were not resident in the Prison and had no weapons [other than painted staves] and no power to help or hinder Daniel.

✠ A Scavenger, who as far as could be made out was a parasitical species of janitor.

✠ A Crier.

✠ A Chaplain.

✠ Three Turnkeys.

No matter how many times he went over the list, Daniel could not fathom how order could be maintained over a one-acre prison housing, every night, upwards of a thousand men, women, and children, by a staff whose executive arm, as it were, numbered three turnkeys.

He would have to go and see it. Anyone could do so; they did not charge a fee for admission, as at Bedlam. Daniel blended in as long as he wore old clothes and did not go around announcing that he was a Lord Regent.

The Fleet presented itself along the bank of the Ditch as a sheer wall, ventilated by a few stoutly gridironed windows where the *poor debtors* would sit all day long rattling tin cups that they thrust out between the bars. Passers-by could chuck coins into these; but since to be a passer-by meant to stroll along the brink of the Sceptered Isle's *Cloaca Maxima,* these were not superabundant. Hooke had wanted to bridge the whole Ditch over, i.e., to bury it. This would have perked up the cup-rattling business no end; but it had not been done.

Next to the poor debtors' begging-grate was a massive archway tunneling, for an intimidating distance of some forty feet, through this wall of Prison buildings that rose above the Ditch-brink. The tunnel was lined on both sides by stone benches occupied, most of the time, by Disagreeable Persons. In entering this tunnel one crossed over the ancient boundary and so departed, albeit temporarily, from the see of the Bishop of London. Wretched ministers sat here all day long, hoping to earn a shilling or two by performing quick no-questions-asked weddings. The same rite, celebrated a few yards away, would be illegal and illegitimate, but here the Bishop had no power to ban it. There were too many such men of the cloth to fit on the finite bench space under the arch; the more enterprising were all parading up and down the bank of the Fleet hoping to draw in business.

The other people on the bench tended to be male and female prostitutes, or their customers, hoping to conduct business, which was to be negotiated here, and consummated within the Prison.

At a certain point the arched passage was severed by a stone wall no more than about eight feet high, with a row of iron spikes protruding cheerfully from its top. Set into the middle of this was a grated doorway. Anyone could pass in, but only some could pass out. Daniel slowed as he approached this. Peter Hoxton had been acting as a sort of rear-guard, and almost piled into him. "You are permitted to go on," Saturn pointed out, looking this way and that at the Bench-people. For these had noted Daniel and begun to tender diverse proposals. Daniel ignored him, and them. He was staring at his feet. He flipped his walking-stick around and rapped its massive head against the paving-stones, moved to the side a couple of feet, and did it again. Finally he resolved to go in. But he got into a nasty collision, just before the door, with a young man. It was not nasty in the sense of being violent, nor in the sense of being acrimonious, for the young man tried to avoid it, and proffered a sort of apology after. He had been walking along behind Daniel and Saturn in traffic, and when they'd bated before the door, he had sought to go around them. The nastiness came from that he was a butcher's boy, employed probably by one of the many shambles out in the *rules* along Fleet Lane, and so his clothes were soggy with blood and other body fluids of dead animals, and clotted with fæces and brains and feathers and hair. Some of it ended up on Daniel. The boy was aghast, particularly when he got it in his head that Saturn might retaliate; but Daniel smiled benignly and said, "After you, young man," and held out a hand. The boy pushed through the door, smearing it anew—for it looked as if many of his colleagues had preceded him—and civilly held it open for Daniel. Daniel and Saturn went in, passing by a whore (tertiary syphilis) and client (primary) waiting to go out, walked through the scrutiny of a turnkey, and emerged from the tunnel into one side of a stripe of open ground that lay athwart their path. The Prison building was directly ahead of them, an immense barrier stretching more than a hundred feet to the left as well as to the right, and looming high above. In half a dozen strides they could have ascended a few steps and gone right into it. But Daniel drew up short, and stopped again. His attention had been seized by a peculiar triptych of figures who were standing just within the gate, and who had no thought of getting out of Daniel's, or anyone's, way. One was a scruffy and beaten-down-looking chap, who kept turning to the left and right, as if mounted on a vertical spit. Next to him, looking on, was a fellow, slightly better dressed, leaning on a staff daubed all over with paint. A few paces distant stood a grim, heavy man who was staring at the first fellow in a way that normally would have provoked a row. The staring went on for an uncannily long time, and Daniel began to collect that it was some sort of rite. He noticed that the turnkey who was stationed by the gate was *also* staring, when he was not busy scrutinizing the faces of departing visitors; and this detail solved the puzzle for him, just as Saturn—who had been amusing himself watching Daniel try to make sense of it—gave the explanation: "New prisoner. These turnkeys have a faculty in common with thief-takers: they never forget a face, once they've given it a keen study."

Daniel now felt a strong disinclination to be studied, or even glimpsed, by men with such gifts, and so he moved forward, and stopped in a place a bit nearer the Prison and away from the eldritch scrutiny of the turnkeys. He rapped on the pavement again, and looked both ways. They were in a sort of choke-point; the prison grounds were narrowest here, broader to the right (south) and more so to the north. That was because the bit to the north was separated from the Ditch outside, not by a thick row of buildings, as here, but only by a stone curtain-wall, twenty-five feet high, with rotating spikes at the top. To spruce things up it had been painted, down low, with scenery. But Daniel only glimpsed a few vertical splints of this because the place was crowded with smokers, strollers, and conversationalists. The day was a bit nippy, but the walls and the Prison's bulk kept out all wind, and so the prisoners and the guests were making the most of it. Which gave him an insight. Seeing self-described *poor debtors* begging outside, he'd always assumed they were committing a tautology. But now that he was on the inside, he could see debtors who were *affluent,* and so he understood that the cup-rattlers without called themselves *poor* to distinguish themselves from these.

Daniel turned his back on the Painted Ground, as the yard to the north was called, and, at a prudent distance, followed the butcher's boy who had collided with him a moment earlier. The gruesome lad moved purposefully but was obliged to meander somewhat over the course of a sixty-pace journey, channeled between the Prison on his left and the backs of the Fleet Ditch–facing buildings on his right. He was headed for a row of small buildings put up against the base of the Prison wall, directly ahead of him, which was to say along the southern verge. Even from a distance Daniel could tell plainly enough that this was a Convenience, a Necessary House, a Shite-Hole. The boy went in to use it, and Daniel said a silent prayer for whomever would have to use it next. Presently the boy emerged, retraced his steps, walked past the turnkey (who studied him shrewdly, but did not move or speak), merged with the incoming and outgoing traffic of visitors, whores, &c., and went out.

Daniel Waterhouse and Peter Hoxton meanwhile had paused about halfway between the gate and the privy, for two reasons.

(1) The Prison building consisted almost entirely of apartments, no better and no worse than any other London slum-apartments, to which prisoners had their own keys. Nevertheless, it did have a few strong-rooms, or, less politely, dungeons in which people could be placed *without* the privilege of having a door-key! Daniel was especially curious about these. There was a row of them in the Ditch-facing buildings whose back doors and windows were on Daniel's right hand as he looked south toward the privies. But to inspect these closely would have been indiscreet.

However, haply

(2) Another strange rite was getting underway to the left side of the gate-privy axis. They had approached the Poor Side of the prison:

a couple of very large rooms at the extremity of the south wing, where prisoners who could not afford apartments slept and lived all crowded together. Against the exterior wall of one of those teeming halls was a cistern, fed by a pump. This was sunk into the earth less than a hundred feet away from Fleet Ditch itself and so Daniel had to will himself not to imagine what sort of water came out of it. A dozen or so persons were approaching it: a tight cluster of four, surrounded by a ragged entourage. They spread out around the cistern and Daniel perceived that one of them had his elbows pinioned behind his back with a shaggy hank of twine. He was uncovered, and being frogmarched by others who were every bit as down-at-heels as he was but had managed to round up artifacts recognizable as hats and wigs. Heads turned toward the oldest of these, and he went into a peroration that sounded, for all the world, like a legal judgment: certainly it went on that long, and was that hard to follow. It was as pompous as these men were shabby, but when the leprous verbiage was scraped away to expose its grammatical bones, what it said was that these fellows (except for the one who was tied up) were something called the Court of Inspectors and that he, the one who was talking, was the Steward thereof, and that in some proceeding just concluded they had found the bare-headed one guilty of having entered so-and-so's apartment yesterday and stealing a clay bottle containing gin from out of a hole in the wall where its rightful owner was generally known to park it, when not pressing it against his lips; and that the sentence for said crime was to be carried out forthwith. Whereupon the gin-nicker was spun around so that his back was to the cistern, and its rim behind his knees, and then shoved back so that his feet went out and up, and his head pierced the glaze of scum that covered the reservoir, and went under. Maintaining a fierce grip on the man's shoulders, his captors maneuvered him so that his face was directly beneath the spout of the pump, and a third officer of the "Court of Inspectors" set to work jacking the pump-handle as vigorously as he could. It was difficult to monitor the results because a crowd of prisoners had gathered round to be edified by it. Daniel glimpsed the prisoner's feet dancing an air tarantella. Debtors had gathered in all of the Prison's windows to learn from the booze-hound's errors. Saturn had a fair view, being tall. Daniel sidled around behind him and stood with his back pressed against Saturn's and looked the other way, at what he took to be the strong-rooms.

These certainly looked the part, having heavy doors with redundant bars and locks, and little to nothing in the way of windows. He'd heard that some of the strong-rooms were near the Ditch, the Privies, and the prison's dung-midden, and that was true of these, though the stench was not so bad as all this implied because it was a crisp day. But Daniel did not see any of the precautions he'd have expected if members of the Shaftoe gang had been locked up here. Moreover, at their other side, these rooms faced the Ditch-brink, and might have windows or grates communicating with the outside, which made them a less fitting place for locking up really infamous criminals.

The gin-thief having been fully reformed, the pumping ended, and its beneficiary was dragged out half-dead and left on the ground next to the cistern. The crowd dispersed. Some of them went south round the nearer end of the great building, squeezing through a narrow and loathsome pass between it and the privies and the midden; here the surrounding wall was forty feet high, because it came so close to the upper-storey windows of the building that it put anyone who looked at it in mind of rope-based strategies. But once Daniel and Saturn had rounded the corner and turned north again, now on the east side of the building, the space between it and the wall broadened decisively into a close a hundred feet or more across, which Daniel identified from his preliminary readings as the Racket Ground. This adjoined the north or Master's Side of the prison, where more affluent debtors dwelled in apartments that were more or less crowded depending on how much money they had—this being one of the Warden's primary Engines of Revenue. Despite the chill in the air there were too many games of rackets, bowls, skittles, &c. underway here for Daniel to sort out. Around the edges were a few scabrous tables where it looked like card-games might be prosecuted during summer. Daniel took a seat at one of these to rest his legs. His back was to the prison wall and he could survey the entire Racket Ground and the Master's Side opposite. Some distance off to his right, the prison's northeastern lobe was described by the curve of the wall. Nestled in its lee were a few separate buildings: a kitchen, which had its own pump and cistern. To one side of it, another midden, threatening to engulf another privy—all of this disconcertingly close to the prison chapel. To the other side, a building in the crook of the wall that Daniel would have been hard pressed to identify— that is, if not for the fact that two armed soldiers were standing in front of it. Two tents, standard military issue, and a cook-fire encroached on the Racket Ground nearby.

Daniel had been carrying a map-case slung over one shoulder. He unlimbered it now and unbuckled its lid. When he overturned it, the first thing that emerged was a wee avalanche of dust and of plaster-crumbs still bound together in clusters by horse-hair. But with a bit of shaking he was able to produce a roll of documents.

Saturn had last seen these when he'd rooted them out of a shattered wall in the cupola of Bedlam. "When you were abusing the pavement with your stick, some of the prisoners espied you, and speculated you were mad," he said. "Now I do begin to wonder—"

"It suits me very well for them to suppose I am mad!" Daniel exclaimed, pleased to hear about it. "You may explain to them that I am not only daft but senile, and convinced that treasure was buried here long ago by a counterfeiter—"

"Counterfeiter! Here?"

"Yes, from time to time coiners and smugglers have been committed to this place by the Court of Exchequer or Curia Regis. So the story makes sense to that point, as all madman-stories must, in their beginnings. I've got it into my head that I can find this treasure. You are a manservant, charged, by my exasperated family, with following me around, keeping me out of trouble, and tending to my needs."

"In that capacity," said Peter Hoxton, "I'll just nip down to the Tap-Room, if it's all the same to you, and get chocolate for myself and—?"

"Coffee for me, thank you," said Daniel, and began to wrestle the drawings out on the pitted tabletop, weighing them down at the edges with shattered bowling-pins. Saturn ambled across the Racket Ground, dodging airborne or rolling balls as need be, and giving the cold shoulder to an acquaintance who'd recognized him. He worked his way north round the aperture between kitchen and chapel so that he could go in at the northern extremity of the building—the Tap-Room and coffeehouse were there, hard by the chapel.

As he had been doing on and off for fifty years, Daniel communed with the mind of Robert Hooke through Hooke's curious notes and jottings, and his exquisite pictures.

Anno Domini 1335 ye Warden of ye Fleet hired laborers to dig a Moat around ye Prop'ty (ye Court & ye Building withal). Width of ye Excav'n was 10 Feet. Of Necessity (or else how could it have been Filled with Water) we say that this communicated with ye Fleet at two places, forming an ox-bow lying to ye East side of that River, & that its Pos'n agrees approx. with ye present Wall . . . a later Record complains that Sewers & Tannery-drains & as many as 1 doz. Latrines have been made to discharge into said Moat from adjoining Prop'ties, making of it an open Sewer that must needs have been no less Offensive then, than is the Fleet Ditch to-day . . . ye Moat no longer exists, & yet ye Rec'ds want any sugg'n of its having been Filled. Whence I venture to Conclude, 'twas never Filled, but rather Roofed, to shield ye Environs from its noisome damps, & yet discharges into ye Fleet, most probably at A and B, & doth account for much of what is loathsome about that Ditch . . . and here Hooke went on to develop his argument that the same treatment ought to be given to the Ditch itself.

A and B referred to two locations on the east bank of Fleet Ditch, near the prison's northwest and southwest corners. These were marked on a survey plat, done by Hooke after the Fire. Comparing this against what he could see from his present vantage point, Daniel had now the satisfying experience of its all coming together coherently in his mind. Few human monuments were as permanent, as unmoveable, as a stone shithouse—especially one that by long-standing tradition was used by everyone in a crowded neighborhood. If Fleet Lane butcher's boys were taking a shite at the southern end of the place in 1714, it probably meant they'd been doing so in 1614, 1514, 1414, &c. That row of privies must be among the dozen or so that had been erected over the moat. And the privy that Daniel was now looking at, next to the kitchen, must be over the moat, too—but on the opposite prong of the ox-bow. The back of that edifice was the Prison wall. Just on its other side would be a row of buildings that fronted on Fleet Lane. Some of these were slaughterhouses that, long ago, must have gathered along the north brink of that moat like flies, and employed it to carry away their offal. Likewise the prison kitchen, just there next to that privy.

And the next building along was the one that was being guarded by the soldiers.

Daniel had read legal filings made by prisoners who had been incarcerated in a certain strong-room on the Master's Side of the Fleet, and who had hired lawyers to get them out of it at all costs. For such prisoners tended not to be debtors. They had been put there by Curia Regis or Star Chamber, and were dangerous and wealthy. The place was described, in these documents, as being situated on the south side of a ditch, which made no sense unless it was taken as a reference to the vanished moat. The dungeon was described as "infested with toads and vermin" and "surcharged with loathsome vapors" and "impervious to the least ray of light." Prisoners there were chained to floor-staples and condemned to lie in sewage—their own (for there was not even a bucket) as well as what seeped in through the walls.

These happy ruminations were interrupted by Saturn, who had come back with a serving-woman in tow. She set out the drinks. Saturn had borrowed some newspapers from the Tap-Room (which was said to be as well-stocked with current reading material as any Clubb in the metropolis) and sat down to peruse these over his chocolate.

Daniel scrutinized the woman—though perhaps not as rudely as a turnkey—and guessed she was no whore, but perhaps the wife of a debtor, obliged to live here for a long time (perhaps forever) and trying to make some pin-money by helping out in the Tap-Room (another Engine of Revenue for the Warden). She gave as good as she got in the way of scrutiny, from which Daniel knew that Saturn had already told her the daft treasure-hunter story.

"My good woman," Daniel said, rooting his coin-purse from his pocket so that she would not wander off, "are you connected with the Management?"

"Y'mean, the Court of Inspectors, like?"

Daniel smiled. "I had in mind the Warden—"

The woman was taken aback that the Warden should be brought into the conversation, even by a senile madman; Daniel might as well have asked her if she took tea with the Pope of Rome.

"The Court of Inspectors, then, if *they* are the responsible parties."

"They are *responsible* for a lot of *parties,* know-what-I-mean!" She exchanged a twinkly look with Saturn: having a bit of harmless fun baiting the gager.

"Those men with the muskets would not allow me to investigate yonder dungeon!" Daniel complained, pointing to the soldiers. "I had been led to believe that the Fleet was open to all, but—"

"You're in luck, then," the woman announced.

"How so, madame?"

"Well, it's like this: if you wanted near *aught* else, it'd be a cold day in Hell 'fore the Steward would give you the least bit of satisfaction,'less you paid him, of course. But on the matter of them soldiers, the Steward is *exercised,* he is, and been making all manner of tedious speeches at the Wine-Clubb and the Beer-Clubb, and filing briefs against the Powers that Be! Your complaints shan't fall on deaf ears, sir, if you go to the Steward direct—'specially if you make a contribution, like, know-what-I-mean."

During this Daniel had been extracting coins from his purse and sorting them on the tabletop, which had not gone unnoticed. He placed the tip of an index finger on one of modest value and slid it across the table so that the woman could take it—which she did. Her gaze was now rapt on Daniel's index finger, which continued to hover above the array of coins.

"Am I correct in gathering, then, that the garrisoning of armed soldiers in the Fleet is an *unusual* procedure?"

It took her a moment to decode this. "Armed soldiers here unusual, why yes! I should say so!"

"They've not been here long, then?"

"Since August, I'd say. Guarding them new prisoners—or so 'tis claimed. The Steward scoffs—calls it a ruse—a press-what-do-you-call-it—"

"A precedent."

"Yeah."

"That must not be allowed to stand, lest the Fleet insensibly begin to lose its ancient privileges," Daniel guessed, exchanging a look with Saturn. Which might have sounded incredibly pretentious and high-flown; but Saturn had insisted that the debtors of the Fleet spent a third of their lives sleeping, a third drinking, gambling, smoking, &c., and a third pursuing abstract legal disputes with the Warden.

"The Steward is the chief of the Court of Inspectors?" Daniel asked.

"Yes, sir."

"Elected, or—"

"It's complicated, like. Most often he is the eldest debtor."

"The senior debtors run the place through this made-up Court, then."

The woman's eyes widened. "Course!" Then they narrowed. "But ain't *all* Courts made-up?"

Daniel liked this so much that he paid her more than it was probably worth. "Now, you say that there is a Wine-Clubb?"

"Yes, sir, Monday nights. And Beer-Clubb Thursdays. Leastwise, men gather and drink, and call it a Clubb."

"Prisoners or visitors or—"

"Both."

"So it is finished at ten of the clock?"

The woman had no idea what Daniel was on about, so he had to explain: "At that hour, the turnkeys call 'strangers all out,' do they not?"

"What matters it, if they do? The Clubbs roar until one or two in the morning, sir, and then they disperse to apartments, and carry on through sunrise."

Daniel slid her another coin, feeling stupid in retrospect. For everyone said this was the greatest brothel in London, and how could such a thing be, if everyone really was shooed away at ten?

"Of the Wine-Clubb and the Beer-Clubb, which is the loudest?"

"Loudest? Wine-Clubb, loud early, quiet late. Beer-Clubb, other way round, know-what-I-mean."

"Do the soldiers ever partake?" asked Daniel, nodding at the tents.

"Ooh, every so often a pair of 'em'll nip round for a pint," she said, "but it's been dicey, 'tween us 'n' them, know-what-I-mean—"

"Because of the Steward's legal proceedings."

"Yeah. Yeah. That's it."

"How can they sleep, in those tents, with all of the noise from the tap-room nearby?"

"They can't. But sleep's always a problem in the Fleet," she said, "for them as have ambitions of sleepin', know-what-I-mean."

"I know precisely what you mean, madame," said Daniel, sliding a final coin. "Do take this and buy some cotton to stuff in your ears."

"Thank you ever so kindly, sir," she said, backing away. "Hope to see you on Monday or Thursday evening, as you prefer."

"IF THIS GETS ANY EASIER," said Daniel to Saturn, "I shall feel a bit let down."

"It doesn't look easy to me! Have you seen the locks on that dungeon?"

"It shall be as easy as throwing a party," Daniel returned. "Now, come—let's go out—supposing that the turnkeys will let us!—and look for real estate on Fleet Lane."

Saturn looked gloomier than usual.

"What, the idea doesn't please you?"

"It is no more displeasing than any of your other recent notions," said Peter Hoxton, Esq.

"Is that your idea of diplomacy?"

"It is the best I can muster just now. You should not have looked in Hockley-in-the-Hole, if you sought a diplomat."

"Then as long as we are being blunt," said Daniel, "this is as good a time as any for me to inform you that I know you made the Infernal Devices for Jack."

"Was wondering," said Peter Hoxton, motionless and red.

"I had suspected, but it became more than obvious in July, when you crafted that excellent snare that caught de Gex."

Peter Hoxton commenced inhaling now, and, over the next quarter-minute or so, drew into his lungs a few hogsheads of air, and grew and grew until it seemed his ribcage was going to press up against the building to one side and the wall to the other, and begin cracking the masonry. But finally he reached his limit, and let all of the air out in a whistling hurricanoe.

"Was wondering," he repeated, as if he'd only been trying the phrase on for size, the first time he'd said it. "Have been on tenterhooks, a bit."

"I know you have."

"I am gratified" said Saturn, cherishing this word, "gratified that you did not simply *prosecute* me."

"No one was killed," Daniel pointed out. "The explosions did not continue."

"One of the reasons I sought you out in the first place, you know, was that . . ."

"You wanted to keep an eye on me, and my investigation."

"Oh, to be sure, but also because . . ."

"You felt bad that you'd had a hand in Blowing me Up."

"Yes—exactly! It's as if you read my mind."

"I read your face, your manner, which is what a Father Confessor is *supposed* to do. What do you know concerning the Pyx?"

"I opened it. Jack took some things out, placed others in."

"What did Jack put in? Was it fine gold? Or allayed with base metal?"

Saturn shrugged. "I sometimes purchase gold to make watches," he said, "but that is all I know of gold."

After this Daniel was silent for such a long time that Saturn progressed through diverse stages of irritability, nervousness, and melancholy. He looked up and regarded the Fleet Prison. "Would you like me to go yonder and pick out a cell, then, or—"

"Wrong place for Infernal Device makers. You would find the company of debtors tedious. You would fall to drinking." Daniel pushed himself to his feet and drained his coffee, which had been tepid when served and was cold now. "Now, about that real estate," said Daniel. "My life began getting really complicated round the time the King of England blew up my house, and killed my dad; now I may have to blow up another house to make things simple again; if so, I'll need a man of your skills."

Saturn finally stood up. "That, at least, is more interesting than what we have been doing, and so I shall join you."

NOTICE

of a PUBLICK AUCTION
to be conducted in the LIBERTY *of the* CLINK
ONE WEEK FROM TODAY
[*that is, on the* 20th *October A.D.* 1714]
Item for sale: MR. CHARLES WHITE, ESQ.

'Tis well enough known, alike to the Nobility and the Mobility, that when the Earl of O— [known in some Clubbs by the sobriquet, Last of the Tories] was presented to the King of England at Greenwich, and crept up to kiss the King his hand, his majesty only glared at the poor Supplicant, then turned the royal Backside without suffering a Word to spill from his lips. Whereupon the blushing Earl fled in almost as profound Disgrace as his fellow Tory, my lord B—, who was last seen on the packet to Calais practicing his genuflections to any French gentleman who strolled near enough.

From these and diverse other Auspices we may see that Torydom is bank-rupt. It is an ancient Tradition that when the final

Scion of a noble House breathes his last, an Executor—by tradition, a respected Gentleman of the town—disposes of the surviving Effects, viz. livestock, wine-bottles, furnishings, carriages, &c.—by the expedient of a publick Auction. And indeed 'tis a very beneficial and *ennobling* practice; for many a Viscount, &c., of recent Coinage, whose grandpère was a cobbler or a smuggler, would otherwise be unable to stuff his town-house with family heirlooms dating back to the Norman Conquest.

So dismal and thorough-going has been the Tories' fall, that there is little left to sell off to the triumphant Whigs, and to my knowledge no good man has yet stepped forward to proffer his service as Executor [many would gladly nominate themselves for the rôle of Executioner; but that position is spoken for by one Jack Ketch, and he is said to be passing jealous of it, and a dangerous man to get on the wrong side of, as he has slain many].

Having as I do much time on my hands [for I can only spend so many hours *per diem* counting my readers' generous Contributions] and enjoying to no small degree the respect of the Duke of M— and other august figures [as how else could it be explained that the Whigs now print my scribblings in their Paper], I have lately stepped forward to appoint myself Executor of the wretched leavings that answer to the name of the Tories' Estate. I approached this responsibility with aweful Trepidation, supposing I should have to toil for years at selling off the Tories' abandoned Assets: mountains of debas'd paper Currency, acres of country-house-lawns, a warehouse of ill will, and diverse odds and ends such as French-English phrasebooks and Papist regalia. To my considerable relief, however, I have found that even these feeble assets are gone, dissolved, liquidated, and so my task is infinitely simpler than I had supposed. For the Tories have only one thing remaining, and that is Mr. Charles White, who professes to be my owner. Mr. White's vocal and oft-repeated support for Slavery [a primitive and savage custom whereby one soul may own another] has simplified what would otherwise have been a most awkward matter. For thanks to the generosity of my readers I am sanguine that I have coin sufficient to purchase Mr. White at auction, which will be conducted immediately following the new King's coronation on the 20th instant. Owning Mr. White, who asserts a claim to ownership of *me* shall mean, infallibly, that I shall then be the owner of myself again; which is all that I really seek. I shall then eliminate the middle-man, as 'twere, by confiscating all of Mr. White's assets, including myself. Mr. White I shall set free, naked as the day he was born, so that he can hie to France and mug some Fopp for his clothes; though I may prevail on him first to shine my boots—which, being such a notorious Black-guard, he is well capable of doing.

Signed,

DAPPA *of the* LIBERTY OF THE CLINK
13 October A.D. 1714

The Tap-Room, Fleet Prison
BEER-CLUBB NIGHT (THURSDAY, 14 OCTOBER 1714)

DAPPA HAD ONLY WRITTEN THE bloody thing yesterday and the Tap-Room was already plastered with them—as was every other coffee-house and Clubb in the metropolis. Or so Daniel assumed, as he sat in the corner, pretending to have a beer, and reading it. He had not actually set foot in the Kit-Cat or any other such place since his memorable encounter with Jack Shaftoe in the Black Dogg ten days earlier. Rather, this Tap-Room had become his new College, and the debtors—especially the elders of the Court of Inspectors—his new fellows. They were no more tedious than most of the Kit-Cat's membership, and Daniel often found them easier to get along with, as they had no purpose in life other than to go on existing as merrily as possible. Daniel could make them a good deal merrier by purchasing the occasional round for the house.

And also by discoursing of buried treasure. For that yarn, which Daniel had made up on the spur of the moment, had spread through the Fleet's population as quick as pink-eye. Not one in ten believed a word of it, of course; but that still left a few dozen who were ready to assault with spades and prybars any snatch of ground, floor, or wall whereon Daniel fixed his gaze for more than a few moments. Daniel had never meant to draw so much attention to himself, and was now worried that, if he did break the Shaftoes out of prison somehow, he'd be identified and prosecuted. But it was too late. All he could do now was fling out red herrings that might slow the investigations of future prosecutors. He wore a large brown wig, and gave out that his family name was Partry, and encouraged the prisoners of the Fleet to call him "Old Partry."

This, he now understood, was how men like Bolingbroke got into big trouble—not by doing anything identifiably stupid, but through an insensible narrowing of choices that compelled them, in the end, to take some risk or other.

Of those credulous souls who believed in the buried-gold story, not a single one belonged to the Court of Inspectors. This led to some tension between the two factions whenever Daniel took up his seat in the Tap. For the Steward and his Court desired proximity to "Old Partry" so that they might get free drinks, and the gold-diggers wanted to hear about his latest researches. Daniel played them off against each other shamelessly—not a prudent long- (or even medium-) term strategy, but just barely sustainable for ten days. He began to drop hints that he had narrowed the gold's location down to the prison's northeast corner—that being the one where Jimmy and Danny Shaftoe and Tomba were locked in the strong-room. It did not take more than an hour for the gold-digging faction to arrive at the furious conclusion that the soldiers lately garrisoned in that corner were really there to provide cover for a treasure extraction project being conducted, illicitly of course, by High Officialdom, probably Tories under the control of the sinister Charles White! The Court of Inspectors did not credit a word of it, but saw merit in the legend anyway, in that it gave them yet another pretext to file writs against the Warden, and so they began disingenuously to spread and to foster the story, and even to improve upon it. This was all so absurd that Daniel's orderly mind could never have predicted it; never would he have advanced any such thing as a strategy. But once underway, it could not be stopped.

Two days had sufficed for him to learn everything worth knowing concerning the Fleet and how it worked. He had then pissed away nearly a week learning something he ought to have known already: in London, real estate, be it never so smelly and disreputable, was valuable, and jealously looked after. The shambles along Fleet Lane might have seemed unutterably disgusting and mean, but to them who labored in their back rooms and dwelled, or operated brothels, on their upper storeys, they were little kingdoms, and every square foot was looked after as carefully as a statue or flower-patch in Versailles. Daniel *knew*, as well as he knew that the shortest distance between two points was a straight line, that in the backs of these buildings' cellars must be drains—the most execrable hair-raising drains conceivable—that communicated with the Fleet Prison's long-buried ox-bow moat—the same moat whose contents were seeping, through porous walls, into the cellar where the Shaftoes were locked up. But in several days' hard trying, and phantastickal lying, he was not able even to get past the front rooms of these establishments, much less down into their backs. Those drains were *valuable*, because they would carry away the objectionable byproducts of certain types of profit-making activities, e.g., butchery and soap-making. Men made livings and supported families on those drains. They found it senseless that an elderly stranger ought to be let in to see these miracles, simply because he voiced curiosity about them. He could have offered money in exchange for a look-see, but this would only have drawn even more attention.

Points A and B on Hooke's drawing—the places in the sheer bank of Fleet Ditch where it connected to the moat—were clearly identifiable, but they had been sealed by a pastiche of iron grille-work and masonry with gaps between bricks to let stuff flow through. Saturn with a skiff and a powder-keg could have made short work of these, but it would have been rather noticeable, there in the midst of the city, all of a quarter-mile from St. Paul's Churchyard.

In the end the only way to gain access to that scaled-off moat was via Fleet Prison itself, by capitalizing on its very peculiarities, and on the unlooked-for currency of the buried gold story. "Old Partry," well into his cups during the Beer-Clubb of Thursday, 7 October, had let slip a notion that the soldiers might be circumvented, and the treasure reached, by tunneling in from the moat. The following morning, it was found that the privy adjacent to the kitchen, along the north wall of the Prison, had been vandalized. This was a two-holer: a wooden bench having a pair of orifices that communicated (as was obvious enough, after it had been vandalized) with a common shaft that descended into an inscrutable and noxious blackness. Half the bench was still in good working order, but the other had been gone at with a hatchet, and the hole made a good deal broader and ruder.

Now this was a grave matter to the general population of the Fleet, because the buildings were famously in decay, and the Warden infamously reluctant to dent his cash flow by effecting repairs. The Court of Inspectors would have to prosecute lawsuits for an hundred years before the Privy got fixed. The Steward came round and had words with "Old Partry." The aged, daft visitor and his huge manservant were welcome to pass the time of day in the Tap-Room or the Racket Ground, but all buried-treasure talk must cease forthwith. Some of the less acute inmates were getting ideas, and beginning to tear the place up. The privy-basher, if found, would be Pumped.

Another thing that Daniel had been learning was that even if real estate was expensive, people were cheap. Which ought to have been obvious to him from that, in exchange for tiny bits of silver, people were forever shinnying up chimneys, climbing into bed with syphilitics, or taking musket-balls in Belgium. But like most who did not do such things, he went out of his way not to dwell on it, and had quite put it out of his mind until it was brought to his notice forcefully by Peter Hoxton. In exchange for what he wanted people to do for him, Daniel offered a lot of silver, relatively speaking; and even as Saturn had forewarned him, word got round, and they had to turn people away and deflect their efforts to under-bid those who'd already been hired.

The work consisted of going into Fleet Prison ostensibly to take a shit; entering the vandalized privy when no one was paying especially keen attention; and jumping down the hole. The first boy who did it got paid extra, because there was no telling what he would find, or what would find him; but he climbed back up the (provided) rope a few minutes later with the sensational intelligence that he had found himself in a long, gently curving tunnel with a firm floor beneath several inches of slimy muck, and, flowing sluggishly over that, sewage that came up to mid-thigh.

The young men that Daniel hired went down that hole with bags on their backs (nothing bulky enough to draw the notice of the turnkeys) and came up empty-handed. They constructed a wooden ladder down below so that they might re-ascend to the privy without having to use climbing-ropes (as the pioneers had done). They went down with measuring-ropes and came up with numbers in their heads, which were mapped by Saturn: eight feet to the east of the privy-orifice, on the north side of the tunnel, was a drain-opening two hand-spans in breadth, which from time to time vomited cattle-guts. Eleven feet beyond that was the output shaft of a House of Office that must be in the back room of some other edifice. Two fathoms beyond that, on the right, a drain that must belong to the prison's kitchen. Thirty sloshing paces beyond that, around a bend, a tiny in-flow of fresh water: the overflow drain of a pump and cistern that stood between the Prison kitchen and the dungeon. Up and down the tunnel these explorations spread, a picture filled in, one scrap at a time, by the accounts of the eager, reeking lads who emerged from the privy at all hours. Within a day they had found a stretch of rotten masonry wall, ninety to a hundred feet east of the privy, that could not be anything other than the outside wall of the dungeon itself. By listening with ears pressed against this, they convinced themselves that they heard chains rattling: the massive irons that the Warden of the Fleet had borrowed from Newgate Prison to bind the Shaftoe Gang. Now they went down with iron bars, chisels, and muffled hammers to peck and scrape away the crazed mortar that held that wall together. After two days of this, a chap on the other side—black, and so presumably Tomba—pulled a brick out of the way to make a fist-sized hole, and said that the miners must on no account remove any more material, lest their gaolers notice changes in the wall. So after that they moved on to other sorts of preparations. Several privy-shafts were ascended by boys recruited from London's surplus of chimney-sweeps, hence, very much at home in filthy and cramped verticals. A particularly accommodating one was identified, and mapped to a house of prostitution in a corner of Bell Savage Inn: one of several culs-de-sac that lay just outside the prison wall, in the smoky labyrinth of boozing-kens and spunging-houses between it and the Great Old Bailey.

For a few days in the second week of October, Daniel felt as though Thursday Night Beer-Clubb would never roll around. For the traffic in and out of the damaged privy had begun to attract notice—not so much the comings and goings of the boys themselves (for they employed a system of lookouts, so that their entries to and exits from the shaft would not be be seen by ordinary privy-users), but the trail of nostril-singeing moisture that they tended to leave on their way out. This admittedly was not as obvious in a dark, wet, stinking London prison shit-house as it might have been in some other settings, but some had noted it and begun to talk, which made Daniel very ill at ease. Not that there was any want of other things to feel ill at ease about! The more time he spent in the Tap-Room, the worse he felt; but during the final days, he could not tear himself away from the place for more than a few hours at a time. During the afternoon of the fourteenth, he read Dappa's auction piece half a dozen times, between re-reading that day's newspapers, and yesterday's. But finally the sky got dark and the place began to fill up with Beer-seekers, and Saturn ambled through and gave him a wink, and then, of course, it was all coming too fast! Happening too soon! He wasn't ready! It was a little bit like a year ago, when *Minerva* had been stalled off the coast of Massachusetts for week after tedious week by contrary winds, and Daniel, irreligious though he was, had prayed for a shift in the wind—only to be assaulted by Blackbeard's pirate-fleet when that day finally arrived. Another change was in the air now, and another adventure in the offing. He was alarmed. But he reasoned with himself thus: men like Jack Shaftoe had adventures all their lives. Even his maths tutor at Cambridge, Isaac Barrow, had once duelled Corsairs in the Mediterranean. Everything since Enoch had come to his door a year and two days ago, had been an adventure, albeit with lulls. So why not let's get on with it!

Daniel summoned one of the Tap-Room's crack staff, and ordered that a certain keg of beer be tapped, and paid for it in gold. This was received, by the Debtors, with no less awe than a Biblical miracle. They responded with a miracle of their own: they transmogrified a full keg into an empty one. Daniel bought another, for word had gone out into the *rules* and beyond that Old Partry was buying a round for London, and people were thronging the place—coming in through the gate, Daniel was informed, in such a solid stream that no one could get out. To Daniel it only seemed like a more crowded than usual Beer-Clubb (and a more appreciative!), but when finally he was hoisted up onto the shoulders of several debtors, and huzzahed a good many times, and made the object of divers toasts, he was able from that vantage point to see over the heads of the Clubb and out the open door and windows into the Racket Ground, where he saw: fog. Not the usual London sea-fog, but the condensed breath of hundreds of persons who had backed up outside the doors because the Tap-Room was full. It might have been alarming, had these been Red Indians or Turks. But they were Englishmen. Daniel recognized here only the normal traits of Englishmen, viz. a wont to convene, drink, and be sociable, especially on chilly dark nights. He deemed this an apt moment to trigger another English predilection: joining together in mad projects.

"I have spent all of my gold," he announced, when a speech had been called for, and the Clubb had got as quiet as it was ever likely to. "I have spent it all," he repeated, "and my family, who look a-skance at my researches, would opine that I am now likely to become your fellow-inmate here in the Fleet; which they would be ashamed of, but I would deem a higher honor than to be made a Knight of the Garter." Now, a pause for toasting and huzzahing. "But this is not to happen. I have only spent my gold thus in the Tap-Room, because I am so sure of finding more anon, out yonder. For lately I have uncovered new documents that shall enable me positively to fix the location of the cache of coins buried in these precincts one hundred and forty years ago by coiners locked up on orders of Sir Thomas Gresham!"

This utterance had begun promisingly, but then degenerated (in the opinion of most) into a windy and recondite history-lesson, and so the applause was not as vigorous as it might have been, had he simply ordered another keg tapped. But that suited his purposes well enough. The true believers in the buried-gold story had suspected, all evening long, that some new ferment was at work in Old Partry's mind, and they now surged toward him, waving shovels and pointed sticks. The Court of Inspectors were extremely dismayed, and of a mind to have Daniel Pumped; but they were helpless as long as engulfed in a Mobb of visitors whose bellies were full of beer paid for by Old Partry.

"Now if you would be so accommodating as to bear me round to the Poor Side," Daniel said, "I shall find the treasure, and we shall extract it, and divide it up! I make only one demand of you, which is that you remain well clear of the soldiers, and in no way menace or molest them. They are armed, after all; and if we are so rash as to hand them a pretext, why, they might just seize what's rightfully ours!"

This, he thought, percolated to the edge of the crowd reasonably well. As well, it gave the Court of Inspectors an excuse to exercise their authority. He saw the Steward and three of his high council making for the dungeon straightaway, presumably to explain to the soldiers what was going on.

"To the Poor-Side Cistern!" Daniel commanded, and in a few moments was borne there, followed by a thrilled company of shovelmen. This was the place where Daniel had seen a prisoner Pumped on his first visit. He drew out a document. It was written in the Real Character: perfectly impenetrable to even the litcrate among the debtors, which was a good thing, since it was actually a description of a clock-work mechanism written a long time ago by Hooke. "The inscription says, proceed from here along a line parallel to the Ditch for fifty paces, until a certain Tree is reached," he announced, and let it be known that he wished to dismount. His bearers let him down, and he backed up to the edge of the cistern, faced north, and began to pace: "One, two, three . . ."

By the time he had reached ten, they had begun to count along with him. Fifty found them all goose-stepping and chanting in perfect unison in the Painted Ground.

"No tree," Daniel observed in the silence that ensued. "Of course, it was burned in the Fire. We must proceed anyway, keeping in mind that there is likely to be some error." He scrutinized the document, turning it this way and that, until many had grown restive, and some had even begun to dig holes. "'Turn to the right and go another hundred,' it says, which foxed me for a bit," said Daniel, gazing up at the wall of the Prison, which barred all rightward movement. "Until one considers that the prison that stood in those days was *smaller*. We must measure a distance of one hundred paces *that way*." And he thrust his hand at the Prison.

Now, everyone in the whole party had a different notion of how this was to be achieved, and so for ten minutes the Fleet seemed to have swopped inmates with Bedlam, as all over the place people were clambering through windows, stretching bits of twine across other inmates' cells, pacing along exterior walls, and dragging sticks through dirt. But after a while, two-thirds of them reconvened on the near edge of the Racket Ground. Smaller clusters of dissident pacers and measurers staked out more or less far-flung positions which they insisted were the correct ones.

"There is supposed to be another tree here, but it's gone," said Daniel. He spent a while reading, and squinting up at the dome of St. Paul's. "Of course the turret of old St. Paul's was in a slightly different place," he reminded them, "but fortunately I am old enough to remember it." He paced toward that remembered landmark all the way across the Racket Ground, parallelled by the several dissident groups, who counted his paces jealously. He stopped just short of the Prison wall, then sidestepped five paces to the left, until he was standing on the rim of a shallow stone gutter that ran for some distance along the wall's base. He looked both ways, pretending to check for landmarks; but really he was performing reconaissance on the soldiers. All dozen of them had been rousted from their tents by their sergeant, and now stood in a picket-line across the front of the dungeon-building, facing outwards, with fixed bayonets. The sergeant stood in front of the line. In front of him were several worthies of the Court of Inspectors, who seemed to want to create a buffer between the soldiers and the shovelers. All of these had been watching Daniel alertly, as he had drawn to within half a dozen yards of the nearest soldiers. But that was as close as he came. "Here is where the instructions tell us to dig," he announced, and stamped the ground. And then he danced out of the way, lest his foot be taken off by the blade of a shovel. He glanced up to see the soldiers looking somewhat relieved. In the dimness behind them, a large man sprinted at the privy as though his bowels were about to give way. Old Partry had been quite forgotten, and was shouldered to the edge of the crowd, and his wig knocked off (actually, he abetted this by shaking his head at the right moment). In the shadow of the Prison wall he shrugged off his cloak, and then stepped out into the clear, uncovered, and dressed in shabby attire that blended well with what most people wore around here. He walked south, all the way around the poor wing, and doubled back along the western side of the prison and walked north past the cistern and the main gate (thronged, now, with Beer-Clubbers wishing to go home, so that all three turnkeys were kept busy inspecting their faces). Up across the Painted Ground he strolled, and then around the north end of the prison building. The vandalized privy was directly ahead of him. He had made almost a complete circuit of the Fleet to reach it; but in this way he had been able to approach it without parading in front of the soldiers. He entered, sat on the bench, took a deep breath, raised his knees, and spun around on his arse until his feet were poised above the hole. As soon as he dipped them in, strong hands grabbed his ankles and pulled down. Faster than he'd have liked, the rest of him followed. Only his head and shoulders were still showing when he was blinded by sudden lanthorn-glare. Someone was coming in the door of the privy! There was a gasp. Daniel was yanked downwards, barking his chin on the edge of the hole. A scream sounded from the world above, and a crash as the visitor dropped the lanthorn. The ragged oval of light above was snuffed out.

"Do you s'pose she got a good look at your face?" Saturn grunted in his ear. But Daniel was unable to respond. A kind of paralyzing dismay had come over him, as precursor to horror and, in all likelihood, sickness. He was finally now understanding what it really meant to be in a London sewer—and he wasn't even really down in it yet, for Saturn was bearing him over one shoulder, sloshing down the tunnel toward a source of illumination hidden round the curve of the ox-bow.

Daniel would have fled, if not for the shameful knowledge that he'd been paying other people to do this for a week.

He suffered. Time passed. They were in a different part of the tunnel, with more light and more people. A great hole had been knocked through the wall. Men were working in a low-ceilinged vault. On its far wall was a massive door; wedges had been driven into the crack between it and its jamb, so that even if the soldiers heard something above the din of the Mobb and came down to investigate they would not be able to get it open. Three of the worst-looking wretches Daniel had ever seen were reclining on the floor, as if taking their leisure; but of course they were sick, and weak, and fettered by hundred-pound irons from Newgate. A bloke with a hammer and a punch was striking the irons off of them, one wrist or ankle at a time. By the time Daniel reached them, one was free, and sitting up to rub his wrists. "We been complainin' for weeks they didn't give us a latrine," he observed, "and now we're going to go *down* one."

"*Up* one is more like," said Saturn. "I hope you are in condition to climb a ladder, Danny."

"I hope that gager slung over your shoulder is," Danny returned.

"He has hidden reserves," Saturn said.

"He'd better stop hiding them," said the black man—though it was not easy to discern skin tones under these circumstances.

Moved, finally, by this and more such mockery, Daniel wriggled, and insisted that he be set upright in the tunnel. The stuff came up to his knees. He got through it by reminding himself that he would, in some sense, survive. "If some of us are ready to go, then let us go," he suggested.

"We'll stay together, thank'ee kindly," said Danny. Tomba had been struck free, but the hammer-man was only beginning to work on Jimmy. "But feel free to lead the way—supposin' there *is* one."

"Oh, there is," Saturn assured him, "Only the final inch needs to be cleared." And he hefted a thick iron bar.

THE FINAL INCH CONSISTED OF planks. It was a floor built over a relatively wide shaft that led down into the sewer. It was all that separated that cloacal world from the House of Office in the back of the brothel in Bell Savage Inn.

Saturn was, in general, not one to throw his weight around, and make much of his bigness; he was a big man of the understated type. Which made it all the more impressive when he decided to make the most of his endowments. Nothing could have prepared the ladies of the establishment for the sight of him erupting from the floor of their toilet in a volcano of shards and splinters. They made no pretense of trying to puzzle it out, but only ran for the exits, abandoning customers in various states of *déshabille* and divers levels of excitement. The brothel had two bouncers: these were naturally posted at the front door, and so some minutes passed before they were made to believe that their services were needed in the House of Office. Eventually they came, swinging coshes, and found themselves outnumbered, out-muscled, and out-weaponed by seven filthy men who had, by that time, emerged from the hole inaugurated by Saturn.

"If you have come to eject us," Daniel said to them, "you might like to know that our only desire is to leave. Pray, where is the exit?"

OUT IN THE CLOSE of Bell Savage Inn a large flat-bed cart was biding its time behind a four-horse team. Upright in the back of it was a barrel of fresh water, and a lad with a bucket, who cheerfully doused them as they were clambering aboard. This did not even come close to making them clean, but it knocked away what was more solid, and diluted what was more wet, and made them feel better. Best of all, it did not take very long. They threw the empty barrel out on to the ground. Of those who'd taken part in this project, half had escaped via the broken privy and would be going out via the prison gate, and two others had come up via the brothel. These two now walked away. Jimmy, Danny, Tomba, Saturn, and Daniel lay side-by-side in the bed of the wagon. The lad flung a tarp over them. They kicked off fouled boots and breeches as the wagon negotiated the labyrinthine ways of the *rules*. Anyone who tried to track them would find an obvious trail of discarded clothing across Prujeon Close, Black and White Court, and other such attractions. But then they would come out into The Great Old Bailey, a broad and busy London thoroughfare, and not know which way to turn. For once the cart had gone beyond that point, they took care to throw no more clews out of it.

Southward, The Great Old Bailey ran to Ludgate. Thence, under the name of Water Street, it went to Black Fryars Stairs along the river.

Northwards, a stone's throw away, the Court of Sessions lay on the opposite side of the street, and just up from that was Newgate Prison. A pursuer might be forgiven for supposing that the escapees would have turned south toward the river and freedom, not north toward judgment and the worst prison in the city. But north was where they went, and in a very short time the wagon had stopped. Saturn stood up, shouldering the tarpaulin aside, and fetched a lanthorn from the driver. Jimmy, Danny, and Tomba sat up and looked about, bewildered. They were at a crossing of The Great Old Bailey with another street, even broader. That street was bridged, only a few yards away, by a mighty turreted Gothick castle that brooded over the square, and barred the great way with a portcullis.

"Newgate Prison," Jimmy said.

"Do not attend too much to the low dark places," said Saturn, opening the lanthorn's shutters, "but elevate your gaze, and regard the great treble window, there, above those statues." He looked up to demonstrate. The windows in question were thirty feet above the level of the pavement. A single candle was gleaming between the iron bars. It leapt up, briefly illuminating a face—but only long enough for the flame to be blown out. And yet in that instant the face had been recognized.

"Da—" cried Jimmy, but the final consonant was muffled by the hand of Tomba, which had clamped down over his mouth.

From that alone, Jack Shaftoe might have guessed who was in that wagon; but Saturn now removed all doubt by playing the lanthorn-beam over the faces of Jimmy, Danny, and Tomba in turn. Then, finally, he illuminated Daniel. For that they'd escaped was only part of what had to be communicated to Jack; who was responsible for it was as important.

"You must all fly like birds," Jack said. He was not shouting, but somehow projecting his voice right at them. "Fly, and stop for nothing until you've reached America."

"You mean, 'we'! Don't you, Dad!? It's we all who must fly together!" Jimmy called.

"If wanting, alone, could tear down prisons, all men would be free," Jack returned. "No. I am here. You are there. Tomorrrow I'll be here still, and you had better be far away!"

"Dad, we can't just *leave* you up there," Danny said.

"Shut up! You must go now. Now! Listen. I have been saying for thirty years that I must provide for my boys. It was all bollocks until this moment. But now I've done it, finally! That is what you must remember me by—none of the other shite. Go! Go to America, find wives, have children, tell them what Grandfather did for his sons—and tell them they're expected to do no less. Good-bye!"

His voice broke as he got to the end of this, and he swam dimly into view once more as he sagged against the bars. Saturn gestured to the driver, who popped his whip and got the wagon turned west out of town, making a cacophony that drowned out the farewell cries of the three escaped prisoners. Their dim and distant view of Jack Shaftoe was killed by the descent of the tarpaulin. The wagon rattled away. The square was left empty. High above it, five human forms could be made out: Jack slumped against the window, and below him, in their niches, the statues of Liberty, Justice, Mercy, and Truth. These all seemed to have turned their backs on Jack, and they pointedly ignored the muffled sobbing noises that continued to escape from the window for some minutes after.

THEY STAYED ON HIGH HOLBOURN only as far as Chancery Lane. There they doubled back south toward the river, and passed down through the middle of the Temple to the stairs, where a boat waited, manned by several oarsmen who had been well paid to be deaf, dumb, and blind for one night. All five of them boarded this, and it sprang away from Temple Stairs and angled across the river and upstream, headed for a row of timber wharves along the Lambeth bank.

"There's no telling when your escape will be noted," Daniel said, once he felt that they'd recovered sufficiently from that brutal leave-taking that they might hear and mark his words. The escapees had been stuffing their faces with bread and cheese and boiled eggs waiting for them in the boat, and their eyes turned toward him as he spoke. He got the idea, from this, that they were used to listening with care, and heeding instructions.

"First thing they'll do is send word downriver to look for men matching your descriptions trying to get out via Gravesend. So, you don't go that way. Swift horses and clean clothes await you on yonder shore. There is a man there who shall guide you to a place in Surrey, where you'll change over to fresh horses—and so on all the way to Portsmouth. With luck you can ship out there tomorrow, on a vessel bound for Carolina—you'll be in the guise of indentured servants, going in company of many such to labor on Mr. Ickham's plantation there. But if word of your escape should reach Portsmouth before the ship sails, you may have to pay some smuggler or other to take you over to France."

"Dad said he wants us in Carolina, though," Danny said, "and so Carolina's where we'll go."

"I don't doubt it," Daniel said. "America will suit you, I think."

"We know," said Jimmy, "we've already friggin' been there."

So ACCUSTOMED WERE THE MEN of the Shaftoe organization to dashing night-time escapades that they had galloped off into the darkness of Lambeth before Daniel had even climbed out of the boat to bid them farewell. There was nothing to do but sit down and let himself be rowed, along with Saturn, back over to the London side.

"I never knew how bloody complicated it was, to be a criminal master-mind," Daniel complained. He had been excited until a few minutes ago but was now feeling more exhausted than he had in years.

"Most people work their way up to it gradual-like, beginning with simpler jobs, such as snatching watches," Saturn said. "It is very unusual to go straight to the top. Only a distinguished Fellow of the Royal Society could have managed it. My hat would be off to you, sir, if I had one."

"I wonder if my inexperience will be looked on as a mitigating circumstance when I am put on trial for all of this."

"*If*, not *when*. Though it would behoove you to think about going back to America."

"Fine. I shall think about it," Daniel said. "First, though, we have got more sewer-work to do."

"Oh, I'll never again look on Walbrook as a sewer—not after to-night," said Saturn. "It is more like a wee brook that has been walled up, and made privy to us and a few other in-the-know blokes."

CRANE COURT WAS LESS THAN a quarter of a mile away. Daniel hired a sedan chair and reached it in a few minutes' time. Isaac Newton, as it turned out, had been working here late. But someone had found him, and got word to him. A carriage had been sent round to fetch him, and it all but blocked the narrow court. Daniel bade the sedan chair's porters to move off to one side of the street and make way.

Isaac emerged, white in the shine of the street lights, drawn, coughing. He settled himself in the carriage and immediately opened all the windows to get more air.

"To Newgate," he commanded. "I'll sit up all night watching Jack

Shaftoe, if that is what I have to do; and tomorrow I'll have him before a magistrate. We'll see how much trouble he can cause when he is pinned under a ton of stones." This was what he was saying as the carriage rattled past Daniel's sedan chair, only an arm's length away, and it seemed he was addressing some important person or other who was facing him. But as Isaac spoke, he stared out the window full into Daniel's face. Daniel was hid behind a dense black screen, and knew he must be perfectly invisible; but he caught his breath anyway, and for the next few moments found himself a little short of wind, like a prisoner being pressed.

Under a Pile of Lead Weights, the Press-Room, Newgate Prison
20 OCTOBER 1714

> Then said Apollyon, "I am sure of thee now," and
> with that he had almost pressed him to death, so that
> Christian began to despair of life.
> —JOHN BUNYAN, *The Pilgrim's Progress*

MERCURY DID NOT KNOW the way to Newgate. Strange that the Messenger of the Gods should absent himself from a great Gate astride a high Road leading into what Jack Shaftoe was pleased to denominate the greatest metropolis in the world. Yet Mercury had never been spied here. Nor (for that matter, and to be perfectly honest) was he wont to visit most of the other locales where Jack had spent his life. For that swift prancing God, accustomed to the swept marble floors of Olympus, would never wish to get shit on his dove-white ankle-wings. Indeed, considering the places he had frequented, Jack might have lived his life in a perfect informational void—and been a happier man for it—were it not for the fact that fastidious Mercury had three cupbearers or, in plain language, butt-boys, viz. Light, Sound, and Stink. These swarmed and ranged round him somewhat as Panic and Terror were said to do around

Mars, and conveyed news into and out of places where the Boss feared to tread.

Light was rarely seen around Newgate. For that matter 'twas not oft spied in London generally. There was a yard at one end of the prison, so narrow that a young man could stand with his back against the building and piss against the enclosing wall. On days when the sun appeared above London, it shone into that yard for some minutes about noon. But for that very reason, the apartments (as they were styled, despite a lot of stout ironmongery about the windows) that looked out on that yard were reserved for prisoners who had a lot of money.

Jack had a lot of money—much of which he had, indeed, manufactured himself—but he was not in one of those apartments on this day, for reasons having to do with certain auncient hallowed canons of the English judiciary. He was, rather, in the Common Felons' side, where Light was a stranger, unless a shred of it be arrested, and sentenced to a brief term of imprisonment in a lanthorn.

By and large, *Sound,* that lusty runagate, had a much easier time of it here than his ethereal brother Light. The inmates of Newgate loved Sound, and never let off making as much of it as they could. Partly it was the want of Light, which made Sound their only medium for the exchange of intelligence, or, as the case might be, stupidity. And partly it was that everyone in the place—rich, poor, felon, debtor, male, female, adult, child—had the means of making noise with every movement, in that they all wore iron fetters from the moment they were admitted to when they were discharged. Rich could afford light chains, poor must make do with heavy, but chains they all had, and they loved to make them clink and rattle. As if sheer volume of noise might shake the stench from the air, and scare away the lice.

Jack lay in the Press-Room in the center of the prison, on the second floor. Next door was the Women Felons' hold, which contained about a hundred females packed head to foot like chocolate soldiers in a box. Their sole source of diversion was to scream the most foul things they could think of out a grate set into the stone wall at one end of the room, communicating with the street. And as it turned out there were plenty of free Londoners who had nothing better to do than to stand out there and listen to them. As this practice had been continuously practiced and maintained on this spot for something like one thousand years, with only occasional lapses attributable to plague, fire, gaol-fever, or wholesale tear-downs and re-builds of the prison fabrique itself, it had been developed to a high art. To blaspheming, these women were what the Duke of Marlborough was to generalship. Fortunately for Jack, who liked a bit of quiet so that he might lapse into unconsciousness from time to time, the Press-Room walls were thick, and muffled those execrations into a vague clamor.

But if Jack heard more than he saw, he smelt a thousand times as much as he heard. For, of all of Mercury's aides-de-camp, that base, insinuating wretch, *Stink,* was most at home in Newgate. Mostly what Jack smelt was himself, and what had lately been squeezed out of him. But from time to time he got a whiff of fire being kindled, and then he nosed hot oil, pitch, and tar. For the Press-Room lay near Jack Ketch his Kitchen, where that high official took the heads and limbs of his clients to boil them in the substances mentioned, so that they should endure longer when put up on spikes round city gates.

He had been put into this place on the eighteenth of October. After he had been here for a long time, the door had opened, and a gaoler had come in and stuffed a heel of black bread into his mouth. Then another long time had elapsed. Then the door had opened again, and another gaoler had come in with a ladle that he had dragged through a puddle on the floor a few moments earlier. He had poured the proceeds into Jack's mouth to spit out or swallow as he saw fit. Jack, impetuous fellow, had swallowed. Now, he knew that a prisoner on bread and water (e.g., himself) was served once a day, the bread alternating with the water. He'd had two servings; ergo, it must be nigh on the twentieth of October. On that date the new King was to be crowned at Westminster Abbey, a mile and a half from here.

What a shame that he could not attend the Coronation! Oh, he had not been invited. But then, he had made a long career of venturing into places where he'd not been welcome, and so this need not have stopped him.

The diverse parades, processions, and rites of the Coronation were attended by respectable men and women: bishops, doctors, yeomen, and earls. Every single one of them hoped and trusted that major portions of Jack Shaftoe would end up in Jack Ketch his Kitchen soon. For that to happen, though, he should have to be convicted. Specifically, he'd have to be convicted of High Treason. Mere robbers, murderers, &c. were only hanged. And a hanged body, entire, was a grocery too gross to maneuver up the stairs to yonder Kitchen. The penalty for High Treason, on the other hand, was to be hanged until half dead (whatever that meant), then cut down, drawn, and separated—with the aid of four teams of horses galloping in opposite directions—into at least four pieces, of a convenient size for the oil, pitch, and tar spa operated just a few steps away from here by Jack Ketch. Shaftoe had been booked for a lengthy and painful round trip via Tyburn, and only one formality prevented it: in order for Jack to be convicted, there'd have to be a proper trial; and according to the rules of such things, the trial could not progress beyond a certain point until Jack pleaded one way or the other.

Accordingly the bailiff, two days ago, had rousted him from his clean, well-lighted apartment in the Castle, and chivvied him down a long narrow alley, a sort of sheep-chute that ran direct to the holding-pen of the Old Bailey. Thence into a Yard where a magistrate (or so it could be presumed from his mien and his Wig) had peered down at him from a balcony (for it had been learnt long ago that magistrates who swapped air with Newgate prisoners soon died of gaol fever). Jack had declined to plead, and so the usual procedure had been effected: back up that alley to Newgate. But to the Press-Room instead of his lovely apartment. There Jack had been stripped to his drawers and very very strongly encouraged to lie down flat on his back on the stone floor. The four corners of the Press-Room were adorned with iron staples set into the floor. These had been connected to his wrists and ankles by chains. Then, in an uncanny prefigurement of the penalty for High Treason, the chains had been drawn tight, so that he was spread-eagled.

A stout wooden box, open on the top—therefore reminiscent of a manger—was suspended from the ceiling in the middle of the room by some tackle. This had been let down until it had dangled a few inches above Jack's breast-bone. The gaolers had gone to work ferrying lead cylinders from a strangely tidy display against the wall, and piling them into the manger with unnerving hollow booms. They had kept at it for rather a long time, and like lawyers they had cited precedents the whole way—now we are above the hundredweight mark, which is for elderly ladies and tubercular children—now we are at two hundred pounds, which was enough to induce Lord so-and-so to plead after a mere three hours—but we have more respect for you than him, Jack—so now we are up nearing three hundred pounds, which killed Bob the Stabber but which Jephthah Big withstood for three days.

And now, Jack, we are ready for you. As you're plainly ready for us.

They'd let the box of weights down onto him then, the pulley overhead supplying all of the squeals and screams that Jack would've, if he could've. The weight had not hit him all at once, but had grown and grown, like the tide. He'd understood right away why so many of the people alluded to by the gaolers had broken, or simply died: it was not the weight, and not the pain, though both were extraordinary, but rather the sheer gloom of it. This Jack was able to master, though just barely, by reminding himself that this was not the worst spot he'd ever been in. Not by a long chalk. And this kept him settled until that thread was broken that connected him to the here and now, and his mind, unleashed, began to dream of the old days.

Through many old stories his mind rambled then, and like a translucent ghost he haunted vivid scenes of Port-Royal in Jamaica, the Siege of Vienna, Barbary, Bonanza, Cairo, Malabar, Mexico, and other places, seeing faces he well remembered, loving most of them, hating a few. To some of those persons he called out. He called out so loud that the gaolers of Newgate heard him, and came in to the Press-Room to see whether he had given up, and was ready to plead. But they found only that he was a-mazed in his own memories, and not conscious of his true surroundings. And he was in a kind of anguish, not because of the weights—for he'd ceased to be aware of them—but because those memories were fixed, and would in no way respond to his outcries. He might as well have been in a Chapel calling out to the frescoes on the ceiling: gorgeous, but dead, and deaf. One time he saw Mr. Foote, in a flowered tunic, hoisting a colorful drink on a Queenah-Kootah beach, as if drinking Jack's health; but this was the nearest anyone came to taking notice of him.

Strangely, the only one who would speak to him was the one he hated the most: Father Édouard de Gex.

"Of all the people! I can't imagine anything more offensive!" Jack raged.

"Yes, but you have to admit I am just the sort who would turn up in a time and place such as this." De Gex had dropped that annoying French accent.

"Well, yes . . . you have me there," Jack said weakly.

Jesuit that he was, de Gex was ready with a glib explanation: "The others who haunt your memories, Jack, are still alive, or else gone on to their destinies, and are too far removed from this world to hear you. It is only I who haunts this world thus."

"You didn't go to Hell? I had you prick'd down as a straight-to-Hell man."

"As I once told you in a moment of weakness, my status was, and is, ambiguous."

"Ah, yes—your devious *cousine* muddied those waters, did she not—I had forgotten."

"Not even St. Peter can sort the matter out," said the ghost of de Gex, "so I must wander the earth until Judgment Day."

"What do you do to pass the time, then, Father Ed?"

Father Ed shrugged. "I seek to redeem myself, by giving good advice, and steering others, who still have some prospect of reaching Heaven, into the path of righteousness."

"Haw! *You* of all people?"

De Gex shrugged. "Since you're chained to the floor, you have no choice but to *listen to,* but it is your choice whether you shall *heed,* my advice."

"And what is your advice? Speak up, you are fading."

"I do not fade," de Gex explained. "The gaolers have heard you shouting at me, and opened the door of your cell; voilà, it's morning, the windows of Newgate Prison have been opened to admit fresh air, light floods in to the place. I remain here with you. Ignore the gaolers; they are confused, they see me not, they suppose you to be not in your right mind."

"Ha! Fancy that! Me, not in my right mind!"

"You have accepted the proposal that was tendered by Daniel Waterhouse . . . why?"

"Oh, I adjudged him the most capable of bringing it off. Charles White is a powerful man, but in a precarious spot, liable to be chased out of the country at any moment. I dared not gamble all on *him.* Newton I simply could not fathom. Waterhouse, though . . . he's dependable, he is, and was in touch with Saturn, and had every incentive to see the matter through. He has already sprung the boys out of the Fleet—that explains why Sir Isaac was so furious yester evening . . ."

"That was *three* evenings ago, Jack," said de Gex, "and they put you under these weights two days ago, on the eighteenth."

"Stab me, that's a hell of a long time, I had quite lost track."

"You have held out longer than anyone; word has leaked out, through the windows of Newgate, into the streets, and the Mobb have begun to sing songs about you:

> *"Put another Weight on the Stack*
> *Said the Vagabond Half-cocked Jack*
> *For the night is still young*
> *I've got air in me lungs*
> *And I don't think I'm ready to crack."*

"Is *that* what they were caterwauling? I had wondered. It is not so bad, I suppose, for a snatch of Mobb doggerel. And very touching. But I trust that the Mobb can improve on it. Perhaps take up a collection and hire a proper Poet, with some taste. I'd fancy something in heroic couplets, iambic hexameter perhaps, and capable of being set to music . . ."

"Jack! Has it occurred to you to wonder why you can hear me, a departed spirit, while none of the gaolers knows I am in here?"

"No, but it has occurred to me to wonder why you leave me alone here for two whole bloody days—*then* show up to trouble my repose with ghastly Advice."

"The answer is the same in both cases. You are standing before the threshold of the portal that joins your world to the next."

"Is that a poetickal way of saying I'm about to croak?"

"Yes."

"Well, I shall see you in a minute or two, then, I can feel myself going . . . I can hear the bells of Heaven ringing . . ."

"Actually, those are the bells of Westminster Abbey, carrying down the river on the morning breeze."

"Why? Someone died?"

"No, it is the tradition to toll the great Bell of the Abbey as the carriage of the new Sovereign draws up before the west door. That Bell is calling all England to the Church, Jack, to celebrate the Coronation of George."

"Did they reserve a seat for me?"

"Try and concentrate, Jack, or the ringing of that bell will be the last thing you ever hear."

"I would like to remind you that the *alternative* is for me to plead. No matter how I plead, I'm bound for Tyburn, where I'll die a much worse death than *this*. Hell, this is practically painless!"

"Are you not forgetting an important part of the plan?"

"What? The plan of Daniel Waterhouse?"

"Yes."

"Oh, no. I know where you are leading me now, Father Ed, and it's not a place to which I will be led. You did this once before: forged a letter from *her,* to draw me in to a snare!"

"You are spread-eagled to the floor of Newgate Prison with three hundred pounds of weight on your chest and you have sixty seconds to live. It strikes me as *funny* that you are so wary, at such a moment, of being drawn in to a *trap!*"

"I just don't wish to be made a fool of again, is all. That's all I ask for, is a bit of pride."

"*Pride* is not what you are wanting. You've plenty. Has it got you what you desired? No. You don't want *pride*. You want *Faith*."

"Oh, Jesus Friggin' Christ!"

"All right. Barring that, wouldn't you like to stay on another nine days, just to see how it all comes out in the end?"

"If dying means that I end up on the same plane of existence with you, and must suffer more of your prating, then nine days here begins to sound pretty good."

"So—?"

"Oh, all right. What the hell. I'll plead."

"Say it louder!" de Gex implored him. "They can't hear you! They are hearkening to the fanfare of distant trumpets!"

"Funny, so am I—I phant'sied I'd died, and that was angels blowing golden horns for me!"

"It is the trumpeter of the Household Royal announcing the entry of George Louis to Westminster Abbey. And those are the drums of his solemn procession!"

"I'll friggin' plead!" Jack shouted, "now take this shit off of me, already, and eject yonder Ghost."

Westminster Abbey

20 OCTOBER 1714

LATER, THE QUALITY who had witnessed it (as well as many who only wanted people to *think* they had) would swear that the villain's lips had parted, baring his teeth, and that a hungry and feral look had come over his face. For Charles White had been a great man in the land, and it was no small matter to bring him down. He had to be made over, first, in people's minds, into a kind of beast.

It happened before the west front of Westminster Abbey. All of the great persons of Britain, as well as Ambassadors and other guests from other realms, were standing about, a little bit dumbfounded from several hours of Church. For the Coronation of George was nothing more or less than an uncommonly tedious church-service, spiced up, here and there, with trotting-out of the gaudiest Regalia this side of Shahjahanabad. Through diverse Processionals and Recessionals they had sat, or stood, and every time the King had shooed away a fly it had been answered by a fifteen-minute Fanfare and a solemn Incantation. The Archbishop, the Lord Chancellor, the Chamberlain, and everyone on down to the Bluemantle Pursuivant had all checked in with one another to verify that George Louis of Hanover was the correct chap, and then they had double- and triple-checked, and run it by various phalanxes and bleacher-loads of Bishops, Peers, Nobles, *et cetera,* who could never affirm anything with a quick nod or thumbs-up but must bellow out pompous circumlocutions in triplicate, bating whenever the trumpet-section, organist, or choir got a whim to break out in half an hour of joyful polyphony. A busy traffic in Bibles, Faldstools, Chalices, Patens, Ampoules, Spoons, Copes, Spurs, Swords, Robes, Orbs, Sceptres, Rings, Coronets, Medals, Crowns, and Rods had cluttered the aisle, as if the world's poshest pawn-shop were being sacked by a Mobb of under-employed Clerics and Peers, and not a jot or tittle of this swag could ever be moved from Point A to Point B without several prayers and hymns pointing out what a splendid and yet frightfully solemn event it was. Paeans flew thick and fast. Prayers were a penny a pound. The name of Our Lord was just about worn through. Christ's ears burned. Everything was pretty resounding. Spit-slicks sprawled between trumpeters' feet. Bellows-pumpers were sent down with busted guts. The boys' choir grew beards.

When finally the new King had lumbered down the aisle in his purple robe and left the building, the congregants had scarce believed their eyes—as when the world's most tedious and tenacious dinner-guest finally exits at four in the morning. There had followed a supplemental half-hour of programmed recessionals as the various guests had retreated, and gone outside to stand, blink, mingle, and chat. All the church-bells in London were pealing. The King, and the Prince and Princess of Wales, had long since gone their separate ways.

It was then that the person of Mr. Charles White had been violated by a hand that had clapped him on the shoulder. As Captain of the King's Messengers, he was dressed for the occasion in a glorious and out-moded get-up. But even through his tasseled epaulet, he felt the hand on his shoulder, and knew its meaning. It was then—some said—that the hungry look came over him, and his lips parted.

He rounded on the fellow who had dared touch him. But then he was dismayed, and stopped. He had been looking for an ear to bite. But the man who stood before him—middle-aged, solid, well-dressed, in a yellow wig—did not have an ear on the right side of his head, just a lumpy orifice. And this so flummoxed Charles White that he quite lost the moment. He looked around to notice that he had been discreetly surrounded by several gentles and nobles, notorious Whigs all, and that they were ready to draw their swords.

"Charles White, I arrest you in the name of the King," said the man in the yellow wig. And it was then that White knew him: this was Andrew Ellis. White had bitten his ear off twenty years ago, in a coffee-house, as Roger Comstock, Daniel Waterhouse, and a roomful of Whigs had looked on. Ellis was a Viscount or something now, and in and out of Parliament.

"I do not recognize the usurper King," White announced—a rather impolite thing to say, under the circumstances—"but I *do* recognize the threat of those weapons you are so eager to draw, and so I shall go, under duress, as a man being kidnapped by Black-guards."

"You may name it kidnapping or any thing else," said Ellis, "but make no mistake, it is an arrest, upon the authority of the Lord Chancellor."

"And am I allowed to know the charge?"

"That at the behest of the King of France, you did conspire with one Jack Shaftoe and Édouard de Gex to trespass upon the Liberty of the Tower and adulterate the Pyx."

"So Jack Shaftoe has broken," White muttered, as he was being walked, in the midst of this knot of armed Whigs, across the Old Palace Yard, toward the Stairs where a boat waited to take him down to the Tower.

"He has *denounced you*," Ellis returned. "No one knows whether he is *broken*, or pursuing his own ends."

"His own," said White, "or someone else's."

But the men who were arresting or abducting him were merely amused by that, and so to any passer-by who had stood on the bank of the Thames to watch them bundling their catch into a waiting river-barge, they'd have seemed a merry band of Englishmen, pleased to have a new King and to have survived his Coronation.

The Court of the Old Bailey
20 OCTOBER 1714

"GUILTY!" SAID THE MAGISTRATE.

"That's what I said," said Jack Shaftoe. He worried that the magistrate had not heard his plea. His voice was enfeebled, as his breathing-musculature was fashed from having worked against three hundred pounds of resistance for days. And the other people sharing this patch of dirt with him were making a lot more noise than he was capable of.

"This court finds you, Jack Shaftoe, Guilty of High Treason!" the magistrate said, in case it had been missed in the uproar.

"This court doesn't *have* to find me Guilty, as that is how I pleaded!" Jack protested, but it was useless.

He was a bit giddy from the removal of the weights, and from the light and food and water that had been lavished upon him when he had cried uncle, and owned up to invading the Tower of London, and blamed the whole thing on Charles White, and agreed to come down here and plead. So he saw things in an odd way, like a traveler from China to whom everything is impossibly strange. Some sort of judicial proceeding had been underway here, involving him. But he had paid no attention to it at all. He just could not bring himself to attend to the wigged chap up on the balcony. Of much more interest was the scene down here.

Court was a good English word meaning a yard. A slab of earth. A patch of dirt. Some courts, such as those on the Isle of Dogs when Jack had been a boy, were surrounded by scraps of wood, and full of pigs and of pig-shit. Other courts were surrounded by stone walls with arrow-slits in the top; people on the insides of such courts tended to have a better time of it than those who shared their courts with swine. The Queen had a court. No, scratch that, the Queen was dead. Long live the King! The King had a court. It was infested with courtiers. The theatres of Southwark were a particular type of court. There were countless other specialized types, e.g., tennis courts, fore-courts, and the Court of Directors of the East India Company. One entire category of Courts was devoted to inflicting punishment on bad men. This, the Old Bailey, was one such.

Jack had familial ties to the Irish nation and knew that *Baile Atha Cliath* was their name for the city of Dublin. Bailey, it seemed, was just another word for Court. The bailiff brought you to the bailey and put you in the bail-dock, and you dasn't stray from his bailiwick until you posted bail.

During this mental divagation of Jack's, on the subject of Courts and Baileys, the magistrate up on the balcony had been washing the place down with a spate of legal mumbo-jumbo, as well as a homily about the error of Jack's ways, and the error of his mother's ways, and his father's, and their mothers' and fathers', all the way back to the progenitor of their race, presumed to be one Cain. Little of this reached Jack's ears, because of the uproar, and none of it penetrated his head, because he was not paying attention. He knew what the magistrate was saying: that Jack was a bad man—beyond bad, if truth be told—so surpassingly and transcendently bad that it was necessary for him to be put to death by the most gruesome and, hence, enter-taining means that the English mind could conceive of.

The Old Bailey employed a man called a crier, whose chief qualification was that he could engrave his own words on a pane of glass, simply by shouting at it. He was deployed, from time to time, to quell the uproar. For the groundlings in this court cared naught for the words of the Justices. But the crier they respected for his loudness. He put it to work now: "Oyez! Oyez! Oyez! My Lords, the King's Justices, strictly charge and command *all manner* of persons to keep silence while Sentence of Death is passing on the prisoner at the bar, on pain of imprisonment." By the time he was finished, the crowd had actually heeded his words. No one was talking except for a few daft and/or deaf stragglers tucked away in the corners, who were quickly shushed by the others. Silence was a rare thing around Newgate, and fragile; but this was a different kind of silence altogether, it was contagious as smallpox.

The magistrate was on his feet, treading heavily up to the railing of his balcony. Clearly he was in a foul temper. He'd rather be at the Coronation festivities, drinking the health of the fresh-minted King. Really, the whole country ought to count this a holiday. It was extraordinary that a Judicial Proceeding was underway here on such a day! What could account for it? Certain Powers must have reached into a courtly revel with a long shepherd's crook and fetched this magistrate out by the neck.

"The law is," he bellowed, "that thou shalt return from hence, to the Place whence thou camest, and from thence to Tyburn Cross, where thou shalt hang by the neck, but not unto Death; that thou shalt thereafter be drawn and quartered, till the body be Dead! Dead! Dead! And the Lord have Mercy upon thy Soul."

Those milling shades in the dimness behind the magistrate's balcony must be those selfsame Powers, practically hopping from foot to foot in their eagerness to run back to Westminster and proclaim the news: Jack Shaftoe was broken by the *peine forte et dure,* he came to the court, he pleaded, and even now lies in chains in the Condemned Hold! That was the preordained Moral of the Morality Play being enacted in this place, which looked more like a theatre the longer Jack stood here. There were even extras, or, in Theatrical cant, spear-carriers. For the Justice's kind final words, *and the Lord have Mercy upon thy Soul,* were nearly drowned out by the humble-bumble of many boots on the stairs within the building, and before the audience could even consider launching a riot, they found themselves surrounded by a company of Guards brandishing half-pikes.

Some might welcome the new King with toasts, medals, statues, or concubines. But there were men in London who could not think of any better party favor to present to their new Sovereign than Jack Shaftoe's head on a platter. At an earlier stage of his life he'd have strained his eyes to resolve the faces lurking back there in the shadows behind the balcony, perhaps shouted something of a defiant nature. But he really could not care less about them now. Truth be told, he hadn't heard a word the magistrate had uttered (aside, that is, from the terrible Sentence) in the last quarter of an hour. It was all because of the noise of the people who were down here in the dirt—the Court—the Old Bailey—with him. His people.

Something got crushed down atop his head. His knees buckled in alarm for a moment. But he was not being assaulted from behind. Someone had bestowed a hat on him. By the time he turned round, that someone had been chased back into the chanting rabble by a furious corporal of the Guard. But the rabble were very pleased by what they saw. A chant formed of the roar: "God save the King! God save the King! God save the King!"

The magistrate had stood up to make himself heard, his face was red, he was bellowing with such force that his wig was shuddering, but nothing reached the court. A bailiff snatched the thing from Jack's head and flung it down. Before his boots crushed and treaded it down into the mud of the Bailey, Jack saw what it was: a makeshift crown, sporting a letter V in the middle. Not that Jack knew much about letters; but he recognized that one, because the same symbol was burnt into the brawn of his right thumb, and had been there for most of his life. For Jack had first been branded Vagabond when he'd been a young man.

It was a common designation. King of the Vagabonds, however, was a high title indeed, and one that had not been attached to his name until he had, through inconceivable exertions, earned it.

The Tower of London
LATE AFTERNOON, 20 OCTOBER 1714

"So-near-and-yet-so-far. That what you've been thinking all this time?" said Charles White. He spoke with remarkable aplomb for a man whose elbows were bound together behind his back with rope. He was displaying those elbows to the whole room, almost as if it was the latest fashion from Paris. For he had turned his back on Newton, and on the Beefeaters who were now guarding him, so that he could gaze out a window that overlooked Mint Street.

As Master of the Mint, Newton could have claimed whatever space he'd taken a whim to. But he'd always been a most practical Master, keen to better the productivity of the place, and so he had situated his personal atelier so as not to impede the coiners' work. It was about forty feet on a side, divided into several closets, a wee chamber that communicated with the interior of Brick Tower and thence to the Inner Ward, and a single great laboratory-cum-office that commanded a view up, and down, and across this leg of Mint Street. Scarlet late-afternoon sun was angling in through rents in northwestern clouds, setting White's left cheek and shoulder aglow, but only because they were elevated above the ground here; below them, Mint Street had already fallen into twilight, being over-shadowed by the glum row of casemates that lined the near surface of the outer wall. The casemate situated across from Newton's laboratory and a bit off to the right was at once the best and the worst of these. Its sole practical function, lately, had been to enclose the Vault that housed the Pyx. As such it had been guarded round the clock by men identifying themselves as Queen's, and more recently King's, Messengers. Which amounted to that they wore silver-greyhound badges and had bits of paper bearing the signature and the seal of Charles White.

This view of the house—which was to say, Sir Isaac Newton's view—was one that Charles White had never had the opportunity to enjoy until a few moments ago, when the Yeomen had frogmarched him in to the laboratory. He was making it clear now that he was well pleased with the picture his hand-picked Messengers made, standing there as a finely dressed and heavily-armed barrier between Newton and his magic box. When the Messengers spied White up in the window, lit up by the sun, they took to hip-hip-huzzahing him, perhaps not realizing that he was under arrest, and on a serious charge indeed—

"High Treason," Newton was saying. He was seated at a vast table, which had turned black from hard employment. He was still wearing the crimson robes he had donned, this morning, for the Coronation. "I cannot think of any other word to describe what you stand accused of doing."

"Accused!?" White asked merrily, and now, at last, tore himself from the window, and turned in to the room to face Newton. The sunset-light filled the laboratory like a refulgent gas, making all dull-colored things, such as the table and the faded beams of the low ceiling, even dimmer than they were. But anything that had an iota of

shine or of color gleamed out of the dark like colored stars: Newton's robes, the ribbons trapped between pages of his fat, ragged, ancient books, the brass and gold of his many scales and balances, samples of gold and silver piled here and there. "Who has accused me?"

"Jack Shaftoe."

"Don't suppose that has anything to do with your putting three hundred pounds of lead on his chest?"

"I do not suppose so," said Newton, "for I suppose that you are quite guilty. But I do admit that an adroit barrister could build a case that Jack Shaftoe is an unreliable witness to begin with, made more so by the torment of the *peine forte et dure.*"

White now, for the first time, seemed taken aback. He had not expected Isaac Newton, of all people, to lend him a hand in erecting his legal defense. "You care not what happens to Jack—whether he is believed, or no!" White tried.

"I care not whether he was your puppet, or you his, or both of you de Gex's."

"But you need to establish that the Pyx was adulterated *by someone,* so that you'll not be held responsible for what is found there. And Jack's testimony, perhaps, is not deemed reliable enough to prove that beyond doubt. You need *my* word on it."

"You shall have adequate time to develop that and other theories in your new lodgings," said Newton, who stood up abruptly, and nodded to the Beefeaters. He had heard some sort of commotion down below, and wanted to go have a look. As did White; but, obeying gestures from Newton, the Yeomen laid hands on the prisoner and dragged him back before he could get near Newton, or the window. White became agitated for the first time, and cursed and made unrealistic demands, then fanciful threats as the Beefeaters dragged him back to the inner chamber, and thence into Brick Tower; from there, it would be a short march across the Parade to one of the Yeomen's houses where White would be an involuntary guest from now on.

A Letter

Charles White, Esq.
The Tower
Dappa
The Clink
Mr. Dappa,

It has been brought to my notice that in the press have appeared diverse libels, broadsides, essays, &c., supposed to have been written by you, in which my name is dishonoured. I demand satisfaction of a kind that may only be achieved if you and I come together in the same place for a short time: preferably an open field, removed from crowds and habitations. You will, I am certain, take my meaning.

I am unable to set foot beyond the Liberty of the Tower without in so doing sacrificing my honour as a Gentleman; consequently, I must beg your indulgence in a small favour, viz. that you might pay a call on me here, that we may settle the thing in these precincts.

This cannot be achieved while you remain imprisoned on charges of thievery. As you will remember, I preferred these charges against you some months ago, but the prosecution has been delayed and stretched out by the machinations of the diverse lawyers retained on your behalf by your notorious Benefactress. Know then that I shall tomorrow (21 October) inform the Magistrate that no further efforts shall be made to advance your Prosecution and that you should be released forthwith. Accordingly, I shall look for you at the Tower of London at dawn of the 22nd instant.

It is a tradition that when one gentleman challenges another in this wise, the challengee shall have the privilege of choosing the weapons to be used. As you are no gentleman, you might not have been aware of this; and one must rate it as unlikely that you shall possess the mastery of the art of Defensing that would be required in order to contend with one such as me. It is my expectation, therefore, that you shall elect to try the matter with firearms, at such-and-such number of paces. If your estate as a recently freed prisoner, your blackness, or your poverty render it infeasible for you to lay hands on two suitable weapons, pray inform me and I shall see to it that they are provided.

> *I am, until daybreak of the 22nd,*
> *Your Humble & Obedient Svt.,*
> *Charles White, Esq.*

Mint Street, the Tower of London

DUSK, 20 OCTOBER 1714

SO NEAR AND YET SO FAR, White had said; but emerging from the sally-port stairs into the purple shades of Mint Street, Isaac Newton was nearer yet, and yet more far than he had been half a minute ago. A lot of men had arrived at once, and they had come in two distinct blocs: the first, which he had spied from his window, was a posse of half a dozen noblemen, generally young, and all of them mounted: at a glance, most likely cavalry officers, still in their Coronation plumage. These had ridden up to, and surrounded, the knot of King's Messengers who guarded the door of the Warden's House. The latter were at a prohibitive disadvantage, being on foot. But they all possessed a little of their master's bluster, and were making a terrific show of thrusting their chests in the air and nudging their swords out of their scabbards, and letting it be known, in an oratorio of sonorous vowels and a rush of trilled R's, just what a grievous and unsconscionable and actionable affront this all was.

But this hubbub was dying away at the moment Newton emerged from the sally-port and came out into the Street—where, for the first time in a while, no one paid him any note. All eyes had collected on one of the mounted nobles: a young man, well- but not extravagantly dressed, who had remained silent through all of the insults and the bluff of Charles White's Messengers. In the moment before the man moved or spoke, there was a cæsura; and during it, one could hear the muffled *tromp* of massed boots coming up Mint Street. The second, larger bloc of men was marching this way.

The leader of the riders peeled back his cloak to reveal a prodigious Document sealed by a swingeing ruby of wax.

"The German's been busy with his dictionary," cracked one of the Messengers.

A nearby rider commanded, "Silence, and pay due respect when speaking of our King."

"Long live the King," said the leader of the riders, and all of his companions echoed it. The Messengers could summon up no more than an incoherent murmur. The rider now broke the seal, unrolled the page, and read it: "Know all men by these presents that I, George, by the Grace of God King of the United Kingdom of Great Britain, *et cetera*, do hereby relieve Mr. Charles White, Esq., of the post of Captain of the King's Messengers, and appoint in his place William, the Earl of Lostwithiel." He lifted his gaze from the document and began to roll it up. "I am the Earl of Lostwithiel," he let them know, almost shyly, "and as Captain of the King's Messengers I hereby relieve you all of your positions—" sweeping his eyes across the faces of the men on foot "—and bid you stand down. The men you see around you are the new King's Messengers, and have assumed all of your duties and responsibilities."

During all of this the *tromp, tromp, tromp* of the soldiers' boots had been growing louder; it echoed from the fronts of the casemates down around Mint Street's northern elbow, where the Moneyers lived, and had been dining in their halls. But they had all put their faces in the windows to see what was going on. A white charger came into view, followed, at half a length, by a gray one, both ridden by men wearing uniforms of officers in the King's Own Black Torrent Guard; behind them marched a column of regulars. Even if the Old Messengers had been of a mind to cross swords with the New and be massacred there in the middle of Mint Street, this might have given them second thoughts. One, then another, then all of them punched their swords back in to their scabbards, peeled off their silver-greyhound badges, and flung them on the cobbles, turned their backs, and walked away in the direction of Brass Mount, dividing to pass round Isaac Newton who was coming the other way.

"My lord," said Newton.

"Sir Isaac," said Lostwithiel, and doffed his hat.

"I am pleased that his majesty has been so quick to rid the Mint of those men. I welcome you to the Tower. It is a great day."

"Here's thanks for that," said Lostwithiel, and doffed his hat again.

"Those men, you must know, have stood between me and his majesty's Pyx ever since that day in June when I was made aware that it might have been compromised."

Even as Newton was speaking these words he was edging nearer the door of the Warden's House, watched interestedly by all of the new Messengers.

The column of soldiers stomped to a halt just at the elbow in the street below Bowyer Tower. The second officer—a Colonel, it could now be seen, with a peg-leg—gave some inaudible command to some subordinates in his wake, touching off a long train of ramifications that ended with sergeants bellowing incomprehensible things to the troops. The outcome was that the troops marched away towards their barracks-houses all around the Liberty of the Tower.

Meanwhile the officer on the white charger—a General—rode forward to join the King's Messengers, and presently drew up alongside the Earl of Lostwithiel. This was the Duke of Marlborough, and so a bit of time was devoted, now, to everyone's showing him various degrees of respect. His peg-legged colonel was bringing up the rear; and behind him was a platoon that had not yet been given leave to go back to its quarters. But this kept a respectful distance, and so Newton was left the sole unmounted man on the street, a smudge of red, and a head of white steam, in a gloomy crevasse.

"My lord," Marlborough announced to Lostwithiel, "in yonder House is a Vault. Within that Vault is a lock-box belonging to his majesty, denominated the Pyx. The Pyx has a unique status in this Realm. It is a repository of Evidence. From time to time that box is opened and the evidence subjected to a judicious examination by a jury of men who have been chosen by the Sovereign. The object of that Trial is to find out whether or not the Master of his majesty's Mint—" and here Marlborough permitted himself a cock of the head toward Newton "—has been fulfilling the terms of the solemn Indenture that bears his name. You will appreciate that the Trial of the Pyx is a matter of utmost gravity; and yet it is only meaningful insofar as the evidence being weighed—which is to say, the Pyx—has been kept sacrosanct. No one who has an interest in the outcome of that Trial, which shall occur in nine days, must be suffered to approach the Pyx. This is the will of the King."

"My will, your grace, is to please his majesty."

"Very good, then," said Marlborough. "Colonel Barnes, you will assist my lord Lostwithiel in keeping an eye on the place, won't you?"

"With pleasure, your grace," said the peg-legged colonel, and then made a head-jerking move that sent the platoon of Black Torrent Guards in to motion. They took up positions flanking the house's doors, and a moment later they were joined by the new Messengers, who had begun to dismount. The Duke of Marlborough turned his charger around and rode away. Newton turned around and went back to his laboratory.

A Letter
21 OCTOBER 1714

Dappa
The Clink
White
The Tower
Mr. White:

Am in receipt of yours of yester evening.

Gentlemen do not fight duels with slaves, nor do they honourably quit claim on property that by rights belongs to them, and so I, along with all London, shall interpret this as a renunciation of the doctrine of Slavery. To rid the world of that repugnant Institution shall require many more such renunciations, as well as legal precedents hard fought and slowly won, but by your letter you have done so much to further this cause that I shall politely overlook the fact that it is really nothing more than a way for you to commit suicide, homicide, or both, before Jack Ketch can lay a glove on you.

I look forward to despatching you on Tower Hill tomorrow at daybreak. In supposing that I would prefer firearms to swords, you have guessed correctly; but once again you have under-rated me by supposing that I'd not be able to supply the requisite hard-ware. On the contrary, I have made arrangements for a matched set to be on hand, and, in accordance with the traditions that govern such things, I shall give you the choice as to which weapon you shall prefer.

The gaolers are coming to take my chains off.

See you tomorrow.

Dappa

The Condemned Hold, Newgate Prison

21 OCTOBER 1714

Newgate is the Horse of Troy, in whose Womb are
shut up all the Mad Greeks that were Men of Action.
— *Memoirs of the Right Villanous John Hall*,
1708

THERE WAS AN OLD JOKE that Newgate must be like Heaven, for the
way to it was straight and narrow. It must have originated with a waggish prisoner, not with any free man. For a free man would approach
Newgate through ways (from the west, Holborn, from the east, Newgate Street) that were broad and crooked. For the convenience of
Newgate's exclusive membership, however, there was a short-cut, a
chute or gutter running *straight and narrow* for about an hundred
paces from the holding-pens of the Court to the southeastern corner
of the Prison. It was one of those sacred and inviolable English rights-
of-way, hemmed in by high walls to either side. For the owners of the
properties to the left and to the right sides of it did not love to see
long necklaces of chained prisoners marching to and fro across their
back yards.

In particular, the property to the right, as one went from the Bailey to the Prison, had notably fastidious and particular tenants. For
that parcel, a good acre and a half, was the demesne of the College of
Physicians. Your common Newgate felon knew it only as a mystery
and a terror. A mystery because no part of it could be seen, owing to
the high featureless wall that lined the chute. A terror because the
bodies of poor men, cut down from the Treble Tree, were sold to that
College by the enterprising Jack Ketch. And there, instead of being
given a Christian burial, they were cut up into pieces, ensuring that
the unquiet spirit that once animated those dismembered parts must
roam the earth until Judgment Day.

To Jack Shaftoe it was no terror because when Ketch had done
with him there'd be little left of him to cut up. And neither was it a

mystery. For he had made a bit of a study of the place. Just on the other side of that wall, he knew, was a garden, where Physicians could stroll about and stretch their legs, or relax on benches, after a long night of cutting up dead criminals. The remainder of the ground was claimed by a great building that had been thrown up, after the Fire, by one Robert Hooke. It was famous because its turret was decorated with a large golden Pill. But it faced the other way, toward Warwick Lane, turning its back upon Newgate. Dead prisoners were brought in through the back way: a cul-de-sac, running from Prison to College, called Phoenix Court.

In the Old Bailey yesterday, a certificate had been bestowed upon him, a sort of diploma. A considerate bailiff had toted that rare document back up the straight and narrow way to Newgate, following Jack and Jack's entourage of cudgel-toting gaolers, and presented it to the officialdom there. The import of this paper was that Jack had graduated from the Press-Room, and might now be admitted to the Condemned Hold.

According to the ways of the place, this meant that he exchanged the Press-Room's lead weights for fetters of iron.

These now sprawled around him on the oaken planking. For the Condemned Hold was furnished with wooden shelves that kept some of its occupants up above the floor, and at the moment Jack had the whole place to himself. Jack did not feel the weight of his chains unless he attempted to move.

The discomforts that the chains inflicted upon his body, though, troubled him less than the unmistakable whiff of Mockery present in these arrangements. What ink was to a writer, fine metals—mercury, silver, gold, and watered steel—had always been to Jack.

That metals consisted partly of water was obvious from the fact that, when you heated them up, they became fluids. But some other substance must be combined with water in order to create a metal. The missing ingredient was supplied by invisible rays from the planets, which penetrated the ground and combined with the water that was there in the earth. The rays from that dimmest and most sluggish of planets, Saturn, created the basest of all metals, lead. Jupiter was responsible for tin and Mars for iron. Venus did copper, the moon silver, Mercury, obviously, accounted for mercury, and the Sun made gold. This was why the gold-hungry Spaniards, in their explorations and conquests, had never strayed far from the Equator, for that was where the Sun beat down most directly, and produced the richest deposits of its precious Element.

As even the most ignorant miner understood, base metals were continually being transmuted into nobler ones by a kind of dark vegetation within the earth. A deposit of lead, left to ripen in the ground for some centuries, would become silver, and silver would in time become gold.

For many years Jack had derived pride and fame from a supposed affinity between himself and Quicksilver, that shimmering fluid spirit. According to a learned man Jack knew, by the name of Enoch, Mercury (the planet) ran closer to the Sun than any other body, and whipped round it at terrific speed, without being consumed. Jack had flattered himself by seeing, in that, a token of his relationship with the Sun King. For as the Alchemists loved to jabber, "What is above is as that which is below, and what is below is as that which is above." Jack might have sprung from the basest imaginable stock, the commonest folk in the whole world, but he had been transmuted over time into a man linked in the common mind with quicksilver and with gold.

Which made it all the more offensive that, since he had been brought to Newgate, he'd been been immobilized by the basest of metals, substances that did not in any way partake of the spirit of quicksilver. The best face he could put on it was that he had moved from lead (in the Press-Room) to iron (in the Condemned Hold)—a small but indisputable step up the ladder.

These Alchemical ruminations were now most rudely broken in upon by a persistent choking and gagging noise. Some one else had entered the Condemned Hold; and, from the sounds of it, he had swallowed his own tongue. This was most irregular. It was a common enough thing for free men to pay a gaoler to let them go in to the Condemned Hold for a few minutes' time and gape at the soon-to-be-dead men, much as people would go to Bedlam to see the Raving Mad; but the practice had been suspended for as long as Jack Shaftoe was in the place, for Ike Newton was leery of escape-plots. So this choking wretch, whoever he was, must have some special dispensation. Jack rotated his head—carefully, for the iron neck-collar had a few nasty burrs on it—and saw naught save a wee hand gripping a rope. Rotating his head a bit more, and sacrificing some neck-skin, he at last got sight of a boy, standing on tiptoe, and hanging himself. That is, he had a noose round his neck and was holding the free end of the rope up above him, acting as his own gallows. Seeing that he had at last got Jack's attention, he now went in to a phantastickal parody of a hanged man, rolling his eyes, pawing at the noose with his free hand, and dancing about the Condemned Hold on tippy-toe when he wasn't spasmodically twitching.

"It is not bad," was Jack's verdict after a particularly affecting round of convulsions, "but I have seen better. In fact, I have *done* better. I once followed your trade, boy."

"What trade is that, Jack Shaftoe, King of the Vagabonds?" asked the boy, letting the rope drop.

"That of hanging from condemned men's legs to make 'em die faster, and thereby undercutting Jack Ketch, who demands far too much silver for a quick death."

"Then you know why I'm here," said the boy.

"Knew it the moment I spied the noose. What's the going rate nowadays?"

"A guinea."

"Oh, you're a sly one. Don't you know I can't afford guineas?"

"Everyone knows. Don't hurt to ask, though."

"Very shrewd. I commend you. But tell me this: does the Mobb mock me now, for having had so much, and lost it?"

"No," said the boy, "they love you for it."

"Never!"

"When you were Jack the Coiner, and flyin' above London in yer Sky-Chariot, in a golden waistcoat, with that Papist henchman, they din't care for none of that," said the boy. "But now you've been brought low, and lost all, and are Jack the Vagabond again, why, the people are sayin', he's all right, he is! One of us, like."

"And that is why they came to the Court of Sessions to crown me even as the King was being crowned at Westminster," Jack said. "So 'twasn't mockery at all."

"Blokes are raising pints and saying 'God save the King,' and they don't mean George the German."

"You know, I got a homily the other day, when I was being Pressed, from the ghost of that Papist henchman, as you called him, and he had some things to say concerning Pride. And my mind went back to Amsterdam, 1685, when I had to choose between two Opportunities. One, to go out into the world and become a man of affairs and make a lot of money, all to impress a certain Lady and make her think I was the right man for her. Two, to write off that venture, lose all, remain in Amsterdam, and go on being the feckless Vagabond I'd always been, and to rely upon the said Female for food, shelter, *et cetera.*"

"Which did you choose?" asked the boy.

"Don't blame you for not being able to guess," said Jack, "for as all London knows, I have been a money-man, Jack the Coiner, and I have been a Vagabond, too, in the estate you see me here. The answer is, I chose to seek my fortune. Failed. Lost all. Then got a fortune I had not ever looked for. Lost it though. Got it back. Lost it. Got another—the story is somewhat repetitious."

"Yes, I was noticing."

"Anyway, point is, now I'm back where I started again, and have been presented, I am beginning to realize, with the same choice as before—yet now all is changed! If I'd stayed in Amsterdam, would she've loved me—or found me tiresome company? Would I've loved her? Or found her too bossy and tight-laced?"

These and other rhetorical questions and imponderable Mysteries of Creation spilled from Jack's lips, until he became aware that he had thereby driven the boy away, or put him to sleep. He was alone again in the Condemned Hold, and would be for some time yet. It was a bargaining ploy on the part of the gaolers, no less effective for being crude and obvious. In time they would come and offer to lighten his chains in trade for some silver, or move him to an apartment along the Press-Yard, in exchange for gold. Obviously they might expect to fetch a higher price if they let him suffer for a while first. The Condemned Hold was not as dark as the Press-Room was, for there was a window high in the wall that admitted some light from Newgate Street. But in due time the sun set and that window went dark. Jack, who had not even a copper to buy himself a candle, was left with naught to entertain him but remembered images.

He was thinking back to that straight and narrow passage. At its far end there was a sort of wicket, called by some the Gate of Janus, where prisoners entering the Bailey from the prison went to the left if they were females, and to the right if they were males, so that each sex was conducted into a different holding-pen. This was done strictly for appearances. *Within* Newgate, men and women mixed freely. But visitors to the Old Bailey saw strict segregation in the pens, and (Jack supposed) heaved great sighs of relief to see that the place was run in a virtuous manner. As the sessions proceeded, the prisoners were let out of the pens one by one, and each returned a few minutes later. The lucky ones were literally smoking from freshly applied brands, the unlucky came back whole and unmarked, as they were destined for Tyburn, or for America. But at the end of the session, all of them—male and female, branded and condemned—were bottlenecked together through the Gate of Janus where they began their return up the chute to Newgate Prison. And just there, in the Old Bailey, near that gate, was a place where a free person might stand and gaze directly into the face of every prisoner who passed by.

Most of the men who collected in that place were thief-takers. Plenty such had been there yesterday, after Jack had been sentenced. But Jack, reviewing the scene in his mind, phant'sied that there had been a woman there, too, a woman veiled in black scrim so that he could not see her face. But *she* wanted to see *his,* evidently. He was just drifting in to a delightful reverie, concerning this, when he was molested by sudden lanthorn-light, and then by a hand shaking his shoulder. He opened his eyes a crack, then grumbled and closed them. The light waned as it was directed elsewhere. Jack opened his eyes full, and gazed up into the face of Sir Isaac Newton.

The Gallows, Tower Hill
DAWN, 22 OCTOBER 1714

WHEN IT GREW LIGHT enough for them to move around without having to tote flaming objects, four men converged on the scaffold that stood in the middle of Tower Hill. Two came from the sea: a black man, and a short red-head with a hook in place of a hand. Two issued from the outlying fortification of the Tower known as the Bulwark; both of them gentlemen, but afoot, and surrounded by several Yeomen of the Guard, and followed, at a respectful distance, by half a dozen mounted dragoons.

The gallows would not be put to use today, save as a landmark by which the two gentlemen from the Tower, and the two seafarers, could find each other. For Tower Hill was a considerable expanse, mostly open parade-ground, but complicated here and there by earth-works where the Tower's garrison might conduct rehearsals for Continental siege-wars. It would not be suitable for the duellists to blunder about trying to find each other until daylight had washed broad over the land, and so they had agreed to meet at the scaffold where sometimes the Tower's lordly inmates were put to death. The Yeomen who had conducted the two gentlemen out the Bulwark's gates peeled away as soon as the timbers of the scaffold came in view, and kept their distance. The legalities were interesting. There was nothing unusual about a noble prisoner strolling about the Liberty of the Tower, of which Tower Hill was a part. Nor for such a prisoner to be shadowed, on his perambulations, by Yeomen of the Guard, to make sure he would not escape or engage in treasonable discourse with free men. But duelling, though a frequent enough practice, was illegal. And so it could be inferred that Charles White had arrived, in advance, with some understanding with the Lieutenant of the Tower. He would go for an early-morning stroll on Tower Hill. At some point the Yeomen might lose him, for a few minutes, in the fog. A pistol-shot or two might be heard. White would be found dead or alive. If dead, he'd be buried. If alive, he'd go back to his lodging in the Tower. Either way the incident would be explained: the strollers had run afoul of footpads; there'd been a struggle; White had wrested a pistol from one of the attackers; *et cetera*. It was threadbare, but no more so than any of the other fictions that were routinely put forth to explain duels. Accordingly the Yeomen kept their distance, so as to sustain the lies that they would have to tell in an hour's time; but the dragoons spread out to surround the area, lest White try to flee into the streets of London, only a hundred running paces distant.

"Where are the pistols?" White demanded.

If his opponent, and his opponent's second, had been gentlemen, he might have greeted them first. But these were Vagabonds of the sea and so that was how he said hello.

"Pistols? What pistols?" asked Dappa.

"You stated in your letter that you would supply a matched set of pistols," White said, suspecting tomfoolery.

"Firearms are what I said I would supply," said Dappa, "and I said I'd let you choose. If you will now follow me and Captain van Hoek, please, I'll show you the first of 'em." And Dappa strode into the fog. Van Hoek stepped out of the way to let White and his second—a young gent name of Woodruff—follow. They were leery of being followed by van Hoek and so after an awkward few seconds' feinting and after-youing, they all fell into step abreast of one another and out of mutual stabbing-range.

"Where is it?" Charles White demanded.

"Less than a hundred paces from here," Dappa returned.

The ground reared up under their feet. They had come to the base of a brief but stiff rise in the Hill, which traditionally was employed as a natural viewing-stand for Londoners eager to see Lords being hanged. Rather than attempting to scale this slope, Dappa deflected to the right and walked along its base, following fresh wheel-ruts that scarred the ground.

He led them to an artillery-piece, mounted on a two-wheeled carriage, and turned round so that the earth rose up behind it. Directions were not easy to keep track of in this dim light, but it seemed to be aimed generally toward the bank of the river. Resting on the ground beside the piece were a powder-keg, a pyramidal stack of five balls, and relevant tools, viz. scoop, ramrod, &c.

Before White could fully take this in, Dappa had made an about-face and begun goose-stepping toward the Thames, counting paces: "One, two, three . . ."

They were approaching the base of another rise in the ground: this one part of the earthen rampart that surrounded the Bulwark. The sky had brightened, and the fog dissolved, to the point where they could see that he was leading them toward another field-piece, arrayed in the same manner as, and aimed back towards, the first; which loomed down on them from its shelf halfway up Tower Hill.

The hundred paces had given White time to grow accustomed to the idea—even to see humor in it. "Where did you get these guns?" he wanted to know.

"It is a passably entertaining story," Dappa answered, "but if you are about to die, there's no point in relating it to you. And if *I* am, then one of the ways I mean to spite you is by leaving you in the dark. Technically, by the way, they are called Hobbits, or Haubitzes," said Dappa. "Not guns. A *gun* has a longer barrel, and is much heavier; it throws heavy balls at great speed, to batter down walls. A Haubitz is like a horizontal mortar: it uses a smaller powder-charge. I judged it a more suitable weapon, for a duel. Cannon-shot would carry in to the city, if we mis-aimed. Haubitz-balls, being lighter, will fall to the ground nearby."

"How can they be lighter if they are made of the same stuff?" asked Woodruff, who had apparently been studying his Natural Philosophy.

"They are hollow, you see," said Dappa, picking one of them up with only modest effort, even though it was a good six inches in diameter. He spun it over between his hands to reveal a drilled orifice, and a spray of gray strings, radiating outwards, like meridians, to cover one hemisphere of its surface. "Hollow, so that they may be packed with powder. Otherwise, we'd be here all day trying to hit each other with a lucky shot. These shells will burst and kill anything within a few yards."

"I see. It is quite practical," said Woodruff, though he seemed a bit preoccupied by the implications of that for *him*. Van Hoek was eyeing him with amusement.

"Please take as much time as you will to inspect these bombs, the Haubitzes, and anything else you please; I assure you they are quite identical."

"No need," said White, "and little time. Quite obviously the most advantageous position is the one on high." He nodded up toward the first Haubitz. "For that reason, you'd look to me to choose it, and if one of the Haubitzes were deficient, that's where you'd place it. And so I choose *this;* you may have the high ground."

"Very well," said Dappa, "shall we to the midway-point then?"

They stood back-to-back on the field, each staring in to the muzzle of the gun he'd soon be loading. Their seconds stood off to the side, watching to be sure that all of the rules and formalities were observed.

"It is perfect," White reflected. "Over yonder I have had victory over Newton, and the Whigs; for make no mistake, he will fail the Trial of the Pyx a week hence. Here I shall have victory over *you*, or else die; either way I could hardly have expected better."

"One," said Dappa, and took a pace away from him—as much to shut the man up as anything else.

"Very well. One," said White, and took a pace. Thence they counted, and paced, in unison; and round about the time they reached forty (for they were taking very long paces) they dropped all pretense of dignity and fell to work upon the Haubitzes.

White was aided, in this, by his second. Dappa wasn't. Van Hoek stood with his back to the Haubitz, as if he were an early-morning perambulator pausing to take in the view of Tower Hill's lower reaches and the Pool. When Dappa gave him a dirty look, van Hoek licked his hook and held it up in the air as if to test the wind.

Dappa cuffed him on the back. "Stop it!"

"Look at them scurrying around down there," said van Hoek. "They have no idea what they are doing."

"That's what concerns me."

"In Cairo you were much cooler," van Hoek reminded him, "and it was I who looked on irritably."

"In Cairo I had nothing to lose!" Dappa reminded him. He had rolled the powder-keg to a safer distance from the Haubitz, and was prying the bung out with a dagger. "Did White and Woodruff move their keg?"

"Ah, you see? *Now* you ask for the knowledge that I have been collecting."

"You could have collected it, and done something else useful, at the same time."

"Oh, very well," said van Hoek, and ambled round to the butt of the Haubitz. He sighted down the barrel, then changed focus to the target. "Yes. They moved their keg. But not as far as they ought to've." He picked up a stone and used it as a mallet to whack the quoin under the weapon's butt, depressing its muzzle slightly. "Do you think we need to allow for the rotation of the Earth?"

Dappa studiously ignored this baiting. He had filled a long-handled scoop with powder, and now introduced it to the muzzle. The scoop's diameter was markedly smaller than the weapon's bore.

"This is the part they are likely to get wrong," Dappa reflected, as he prodded away, trying to get the scoop into a narrower chamber concealed in the butt. "I hope they'll charge it full bore, and blow themselves up!"

"That would not be sporting," van Hoek chided him, and used his hook to scrape away some chymical encrustation surrounding the touch-hole. Because of his disability, he could not very easily pick up a shell, and so this duty fell to Dappa, who stuffed in a ball, then set to beating it down the barrel with a ramrod, while gazing attentively down-hill.

"This is what you get for your slowness!" he pointed out. For both he and van Hoek had noticed that White, with a grin, was putting fire to the touch-hole of a fully loaded and ready-to-go Haubitz.

A cloud of flame the size of a parish church appeared between them and their opponents, then winked out and was smoke.

"And that is what they get for their lubberly haste," said van Hoek.

As both van Hoek and Dappa understood, White and Woodruff had over-charged the weapon. The force of the fire had crushed the shell inside the barrel, causing it to vomit forth a cloud of gunpowder, most of which (fortunately for them) had burned in the open air.

There was nothing to do until the smoke-cloud drifted over them and gave them a clear view of White and Woodruff, who looked woozy and badly sunburned. Then van Hoek put fire to the touch-hole. The Haubitz discharged correctly and, as they were standing nearly behind it, they got to glimpse the shell in flight for a fraction of a second. It spattered against the stone wall of the Bulwark, above and behind and a bit to the left of the opposition, and failed to ignite altogether. Instead it sprayed shell-shards and powder-corns all over White and Woodruff, who scarcely noticed, as they had shaken off their shock and turned their attention back to the Haubitz.

"Now's when they'll blow themselves up," Dappa offered, thrusting a swab into a bucket.

"On the contrary, they found the water you so considerately left out for them, and are swabbing out their Haubitz just as you are. But we have the advantage—we got information about how to adjust our aim, and they did not." Van Hoek belabored the quoin some more, then kicked at one of the gun-carriage's wheels to adjust its azimuth. Dappa meanwhile re-loaded. After which he was very keen on firing; but van Hoek kept presenting himself at the weapon's muzzle with sticks, handfuls of dry grass, leaves, and other such debris, which he stuffed in to the bore until it was full, and even over-full; it ended up looking like a bronze vase sporting a dead bouquet. Dappa grew most peevish and took to waving the torch over the touch-hole, and feinting toward it. Van Hoek was oblivious, and did not even turn around when White's second shot screamed past his shoulder and buried itself in the embankment behind them. But he saw it strike, and pointed it out to Dappa, who spat on his fingers and reached into the cave it had made, then yanked out a fizzing net-work of fuze. He flung it on the ground and cursed. Van Hoek finally left his blocking-position before the Haubitz's barrel and used his hook to catch the bail of their water-bucket; he went over to the fizzing and writhing fuze, and doused it. While he was thus occupied Dappa put fire to their Haubitz and got off their second shot; it struck the ground just at the base of the embankment behind White and Woodruff, and a couple of yards to the right of them. Instead of burying itself in the earth, this one caromed straight up in the air and disappeared. Several seconds later, having apparently risen to an apogee and begun to drop, it exploded perhaps ten yards above the ground, and not terribly far from White and Woodruff. But they had marked its ascent and descent, with avid finger-pointing, and scampered clear of it and flung themselves to the ground. They were not injured.

Van Hoek was disgusted. "I've a mind to walk down there and put one through White's skull," he said.

"Why? It is my duel, not yours," said Dappa, busy again.

Van Hoek began to rake up such sticks and dry grass as had escaped his first sweep. "As your second, it is my job to have a go at your opponent if he tries to run away. White ran away."

"It is a gray area," Dappa averred. "It is expected of a ship-captain in battle that he'll not flinch when broadsides come at him; on the other hand, if a fizzing shell lands nearby, he is not expected to stand there and watch it burst."

"Hmmph," said van Hoek, repeating his performance of barrel-stuffing; and this time, as if to add emphasis, he ripped off his auburn periwig and jammed it down the throat of the gun to tamp down all of the loose vegetation he'd emptied into it. A shell flew past him. This time, White and Woodruff had used less powder yet, and so it had already caromed once off the ground by the time it reached them. It went by knee-high and executed a loop-the-loop off the hillside, landing directly in front of Dappa: a black, smoking sphere with a burning fuze projecting from one side. It was rolling down-hill, but too slowly for their purposes, and so Dappa bolted toward it and kicked out wildly; missed; drew his leg back, and gave it a hard shove. In almost the same motion he spun round and flung himself full-length on the ground. Van Hoek meanwhile had turned his back on the thing and embraced the powder-keg, spreading out his coat around him to make it a curtain against sparks. The shell rolled and toddled down-hill for one, two, three heartbeats and then blew up.

It was answered a moment later by a second boom, for it seemed that a spark had flown close enough to their Haubitz to ignite the powder in the touch-hole, and fired the weapon prematurely. Dappa and van Hoek were both several moments getting to their feet, as each had suffered survivable wounds from shell-fragments or pebbles, and both were a bit stunned. They saw their shell explode over the Thames.

The blast of White's shell had knocked their Haubitz askew. A trail of smouldering sticks and grass was, however, spread down the hillside like a road of fire, and Woodruff could be seen kicking furiously at something that emitted dense smoke, and kept adhering to his foot in a way that made him very cross: the wig. White meanwhile was making preparations to re-load.

It was then that they ceased to exist. Dappa's and van Hoek's view of the Bulwark was eliminated, replaced by a sphere of flame with ugly dark bits spiraling out of it. Once again they threw themselves to the ground. Burning debris began to shower their position. They jumped up and ran, putting distance between themselves and their stock-piles of explodables. They made rendezvous at the scaffold, which was gaily decorated by the prostrate forms of several Beefeaters who had all sought cover there. About then a ripping *BABABA* sounded from below as all of White's shells detonated. This was the signal for Dappa and van Hoek to depart at a sprightly pace for the waterfront. If any of the Yeomen of the Guard lifted his head to watch, he saw them simply disappear into a storm-front of powder-smoke that now obnubilated the lower reaches of the Hill.

Within that immense pall, however, it was possible to see for short distances. And so Dappa and van Hoek paused, or at least slowed down, as they passed by the erstwhile position of White and Woodruff. They did not see anything identifiable as a body; though Dappa was fairly certain he had tripped over someone's spine.

"Here's a marvel," van Hoek said reflectively. He was staring at something down on the scorched earth, using his hook in lieu of an index finger to count several small objects, over and over again. "One, two, three, four, *five*! One, two, three, four, *five*!"

"What is it?"

"There are too many ears!" van Hoek exclaimed.

Dappa went over and touched heads with him. There were, indeed, five ears: four all together, all wizened, and, off to one side, a fifth, which looked fresh, as it had blood on it.

"This is explainable, actually," said Dappa, kicking some dirt over the four dry ones, "but not now. Let's back to my ship, if you please. The Yeomen, the Watch, the Dragoons: they'll be all over us!"

"They'll all be scared shitless."

"The point is granted; but I really am eager to see my ship again."

Dappa and van Hoek still could not see far, but they both stumbled down-hill: an infallible trick for locating oceans. "I hope this means you have finally put an end to this writing foolishness. It has grown most tiresome."

"I have discharged my cannonball. I shan't be quick to re-load. As a writer, however, I am ever a devoted slave to the Muse, whose privilege it is to command me . . ."

"Then let's *do* get to the ship," said van Hoek, quickening his pace, "and prepare to sail out on to the high seas where the bitch won't be able to reach you with any such directions."

The Press-Yard and Castle, Newgate Prison
23 OCTOBER 1714

STRANGE WHAT A DIFFERENCE was made by moving twenty feet. For that was the distance separating Jack's four-posted feather-bed in the Castle from the middle of the Press-Room, which happened to be situated just on the other side of the apartment's back wall. A few days earlier, he'd lain naked on a stone floor with a box of weights on his chest; now, clad in a clean linen nightshirt, he reclined on goose-down.

A month or two ago, Jack could have bought his way into this apartment without difficulty. But since then most of his assets had been spent. And what hadn't been spent had been seized, or otherwise put out of his reach, by his febrile Persecutor, Sir Isaac Newton.

There was no fixed rent for the apartments of the Press-Yard and Castle. Rather, the Keeper applied a sliding scale, depending upon the Degree of the personage imprisoned. A Duke—let us say, a rebel

Scottish lord—would be expected to pay a premium of five hundred guineas upon admission to the gaol, simply to escape from the Common-Side and Master-Side. Having got over that hurdle he would, each week, then have to pay the gaoler about a mark, or thirteen shillings and change, for the privilege of staying in a room such as this one.

Now Jack was going to be dead in a week, and so the rent would not add up to much—not even a pound. But the *premium* was a different matter. A commoner with means, having no other distinctions to his name, would be charged at a much lower rate than a Duke— say twenty pounds. What, then, would be the rate for a Jack Shaftoe? Some would say he was less than a commoner, and ought to pay fewer than twenty pounds sterling. But others—probably to include the Gaoler of Newgate—would insist he was greater, in his way, than a Duke, and ought to pay a king's ransom.

In sum, he could not possibly have been sprung from the Condemned Hold for less than several hundred pounds. He did not have such money, not any more. Neither did any of his surviving friends. Where had it come from?

This was *not* part of the deal he'd struck the other night with Sir Ike in the Condemned Hold. Newton had asked for Jack to dictate an affidavit, stating that evidence of a Whig coining-ring was to be found in a subterranean vault in one of the late Roger Comstock's real estate developments in Clerkenwell. Newton had tediously rehearsed the statement with him all night long, it seemed, and Jack had prattled it back to a Stenographer and a line-up of dumbfounded worthies the next morning. But Newton had not offered to put Jack back into his Castle apartment, and Jack hadn't asked, because he sensed that Newton was running low on money. The *quid pro quo*, rather, was that Jack's punishment might be reduced: at the very least, to a conventional (and speedy) hanging, perhaps even to a fine he'd never be able to pay, so that he'd spend the rest of his life on the Master Debtor's side of Newgate.

No, someone else—someone with lots of money—had caused Jack to be moved here. It was a further step on the road to Faith that de Gex had prated about: Jack had nothing, but he was somehow being cared for and looked after. It hurt his pride, yes, but not as much as some things he could mention.

It seemed unlikely that his benefactress (for Jack liked to indulge himself in the phant'sy that it was a female) had done so only to make Jack more comfortable during this, his final week on Earth. Jack preferred to suppose that this had been meant as some way of sending him a message. To decypher that message was now the only thought in his mind; but he soon stopped making any progress on the riddle, and postponed further work on it, pending arrival of fresh clews.

Instead he divided his time between thinking about Eliza and cursing himself for being so fatuous as to think of her. On the other hand, he had to admit, there was no great harm in it. It could no longer lead him astray, as it had done in years past. He was now as astray as it was possible for anyone to be in this world. He was at a pole. Van Hoek had explained to him once that if you went to the South Pole, then east and west and south would cease to exist, and any direction you went would be north. Thus Jack's current status in the world.

Clerkenwell Court
MORNING OF 23 OCTOBER 1714

ROGER WOULD SOMEHOW HAVE got advance intelligence of this raid. Roger would have confronted them—no, strike that, he would have had coffee and hot cross buns waiting, and he would have served them up to Isaac Newton, the Earl of Lostwithiel, and the King's Messengers, so that by the time they invaded the Court, the whole affair would have been re-conjured into a guided tour, invitation-only.

But Daniel was not Roger, and so, by the time he arrived, the raid had already been in progress for two hours. It would have been over and done with, had it been better managed. But more than one apparatus of His Majesty's Government had become interested, and so it had waxed cumbersome, and been both over- and under-planned. There had been meetings; that much was obvious. Bright young things had attended them, shaped the agendas, had their say, been noted down in the minutes. Someone had anticipated a need to remove the doors of the Vault by main force. Petards, winches, ox-teams had been concatenated to the Bill of Necessaries. Delays and misunderstandings had propagated. No one had showed up at exactly the right time. Important men had missed opportunities to see the humorous side. Obstinacy and indignation were the order of the day. The foot-soldiers cooled their heels, awaiting orders, and shook their heads incredulously.

This, in sum, was what Daniel walked in to at about nine of the clock. Walked because the raid and its unintended consequences had blocked traffic on Coppice Row and forced him to abandon his sedan chair a quarter of a mile short of the destination. This was for the better. The sedan chair would have dumped him into the midst of the broil; he'd have been noticed, and men who'd been to those meetings would have been keen to exchange words with him. As it was, he approached the thing gradually and quietly.

With one exception: halfway there, he passed the carriage of the Duchess of Arcachon-Qwghlm, stuck in traffic.

"Coming to look in on your investment, my lady?" he inquired, as if talking to himself, as he walked past the helpless vehicle.

There was a rustle within; he guessed she was at her correspondence.

"Good morning, Dr. Waterhouse. May I call on you there, in a few minutes' time?"

"I invite you to let yourself in to the vacant apartment on the first floor, above the clock-shop," Daniel called back over his shoulder. "Think of it as a private box from which you may view the Comedy of Errors."

A minute later, he was there. He went in through a side-wicket and got in to the middle of the thing before anyone had recognized him; then they all wanted to know how long he'd been there. "Dr. Waterhouse!" exclaimed the Earl of Lostwithiel, "how long have you been here?"

"Long enough," said Daniel, trying to be oracular.

"It's a bit of a shame," said the Earl. Which Daniel found most irritating, until he recollected that the Earl was a man of breeding, and tended to understate things to the point where they were nearly subliminal. He was trying to let Daniel know that he was very sorry. Daniel tried to respond in kind. "It must have been awkward for you."

"Not at all," said the Earl, meaning *it has been a living hell.*

"The thing became complicated, didn't it," Daniel went on. "Your responsibilities as Captain of the King's Messengers, of course, supersede all other considerations. I see you have discharged them well."

"God save the King," said the Earl, which, Daniel guessed, was a way of saying *you have got it right and thank you for not being cross with me.*

". . . save the King" said Daniel, meaning *you're welcome.*

"Sir Isaac is . . . below," said the Earl, looking down toward the gates of the Templar-tomb, which stood open and, as far as Daniel could make out, unwrecked.

"How did you get them open?" Daniel asked.

"We stood about them, discussing the use of force, until finally a great big chap showed up and undid the lock for us."

Daniel took his leave and walked towards the gates, ignoring two different Persons of Quality who spotted him and demanded to know how long he had been there.

"HOW LONG HAVE YOU been here?" asked Sir Isaac Newton.

The Templar-tomb was a bubble of warm, oily smoke, for many candles and lanthorns had been brought down. The steam pulsing from the nostrils of half a dozen shovel-and-rake-wielding workmen, and the moist vapors rising from all of those lights, condensed on the chilly stone and brass of the sarcophagi and streaked them with rivulets.

"Long enough," Daniel snapped. There was much here for him to be peevish about, but the worst of it was that Isaac, who was capable of being so interesting, had, by involving himself in these worldly doings, made himself so dull.

But it was all for the most ethereal of reasons. Daniel must keep reminding himself of that.

"This cannon-duel that was fought on Tower Hill the other day: it's all about that, isn't it?" Daniel tried.

"That, and the escape of the Shaftoes," Isaac admitted. "My witnesses have a way of disappearing when they are most needed. Only Jack now remains."

"You are not going to find anything by digging up these poor Templars," Daniel said. "It must be obvious to you that what was here, has been moved."

"Of course it is," Isaac said, "but other Powers have involved themselves in the thing, as you can see, and they are not as quick to notice what is *obvious,* as you and I."

This sounded almost like a compliment: Isaac reaching down to pull Daniel up to his plane for a moment. Daniel was pleased, then wary.

"It is all White's fault," Isaac went on. "I do think that he meant to die—to put himself beyond the grasp of Justice. But the *manner* of his death he could not have foreseen—and it has wrought in my favor."

"By throwing the new government into a sort of panic, you mean."

By way of an answer, Isaac spread his hands, and looked about at all of the perfervid diggers. "When they have grown as bored as I am with the ransacking of this place, they'll move on to Bridewell, and if nothing is found there, they'll follow the trail to the Bank of England."

Daniel knew that there was an appendix to this sentence, which need hardly be spoken aloud: *unless you help me by giving me some of what I need.* And for a moment Daniel was ready to nip down to the Bank and fetch out a bit of Solomonic Gold for good old Isaac. Why not? Solomon Kohan would notice that it had gone missing, and Peter the Great would wax wroth, but there would probably be a way to patch it up.

Then Isaac spoke: "They say that to hide the escape of the Shaftoes from the strong-room of the Fleet, an old gager got the Mobb drunk, and told them tall tales of buried gold."

This curdled the whole thing. Daniel remembered, now, why he had good reason to hold on to every grain of the gold: because people wanted it, and so having it gave Daniel power he might need. And, too, he was reminded of the farcical nature of the whole Alchemical world-view. So he said nothing more of substance, but excused himself, and went up above ground, and a minute later had joined the Duchess of Arcachon-Qwghlm in that vacant apartment above what had been the Court of Technologickal Arts.

"You should never have left me alone here," she said to him.

Somehow Daniel did not get the idea that she was complaining of a social *faux pas.* "Your grace?"

She was standing at a window that looked out over the Court, and talking over her shoulder at him. He approached, and drew up next to her, but well off to the side, so that the scurrying big-wigs below would not see them together in the window.

"Something has been troubling me about this investment ever since I agreed to it," she continued.

These words, had they been spoken in anger, might have made Daniel spin on his heel and run all the way to Massachusetts. But she was bemused and a little distracted, with the makings of a smile on her lips.

She explained, "It came clear to me when I looked out this window. The last time I saw your Court of Technologickal Arts, it was a bazaar of the mind—all those clever men, each in his own wee shop, pursuing his peculiar interests, but exchanging ideas with the others when he went to fetch a cup of coffee or to use the House of Office. That seemed to work very well, didn't it? And because I am curious about the same things, I was cozened by it—I admit that I was! And yet as enchanted as I was, a little voice kept whispering to me that it was not, *au fond,* a sound investment. *Today* I came here and found it all gone. All the clever fellows have packed up their tools and absconded. Only the land and the building remain. For those, your investors have overpaid. This place is destined to be just another suburban shop-block, of no greater value than the ones to the left and to the right."

"As to the value of the property, I agree," Daniel said. "Does that mean it was not a sound investment for you and for Roger Comstock?"

"Yes," she said, again with a smile, "that is what it means!"

"In an accompt-book, maybe that is true—"

"Oh, believe me. It is."

"But Roger never set much store by strict accompts, did he? He pursued more than strictly financial gain."

"That is perfectly all right," Eliza said. "You misunderstand me. I too have many goals that cannot be assessed or rendered in an accompt-book. But it has been my practice to keep those separate, in my head, from the sorts of projects that would make sense to *any* investor. In the case of the Court of Technologickal Arts, I made the error of confusing one with the other. That is all. I do not think one can ever *own* the quicksilver spirit that circulates among the minds of philosophers and *ingénieurs*. It is like trying to catch in a bucket the electrickal fluid of Mr. Hauksbee."

"So it is hopeless, then?"

"Is *what* hopeless, Dr. Waterhouse?"

"Trying to support, to invest in such projects?"

"Oh, no. Not hopeless. I think it could be done. I got it wrong the first time. That's all."

"Is there to be a second time?"

Silence. Daniel tried again. "What is to be the final accounting, then? Even if I did not have any interest in the thing, I should need to know, for I am involved in the settling of Roger's estate."

"Oh. You need to know what this is all worth," Eliza said.

"Yes. Your grace. Thank you."

"It is worth whatever the building next to it is worth. You could, then, pursue claims on the value of the discoveries that were made here. Conceivably. For example, if six months from now a horologist who was once a tenant here builds a clock that wins the Longitude Prize, then Roger's estate could lay claim to some part of the money. But it would be a fool's errand. It would only enrich lawyers."

"Very well. We shall write it off. But what of the Logic Mill—?"

"I heard that the card-punching organs had been torn out of Bridewell, and cast into the river."

"Oh, yes. I made sure of that. Everything is gone from Bridewell."

"The cards themselves—?"

"Are to be shipped to Hanover, and thence to the Tsar's Academy in St. Petersburg."

"So they neither add to nor subtract from the balance-sheet. What is it, then, that you are asking me about?"

Daniel was appalled, in some sense, by the pitiless brutality of this financial discourse. But he was also fascinated. It was a bit like vivisection: savage, but just interesting enough to keep him from slinking out of the room and going straight to the nearest boozing-ken. "I suppose I am asking you about the whole structure of ideas that gives the cards of the Logic Mill their value," he said.

"Value?"

"Power, then. Power to effect computations."

"You are asking, what are those ideas worth?"

"Yes."

"That depends on how soon a true Logic Mill can be made. You have not made one, have you?"

"No," Daniel admitted. "We learned much from making the card-punching organs—"

"*We* meaning—" and Eliza cocked her head out the window, reminding him of the vacant stalls being pillaged by soldiers and Messengers.

"All right," Daniel admitted, "the *we* no longer exists. *We* have been scattered. It shall be most difficult to re-assemble the *we*."

"And the organs are on the bottom of the river."

"Yes."

"You have drawings? Plans?"

"Mostly in our heads."

"Here's what I would say, then," Eliza began, "if I were rendering this accompt. The ideas are very good ones. The quality of the work, excellent. However, they are Leibniz's ideas, and they stand or fall with the Doctor and his reputation. His repute is very low with his House, the House of Hanover, which is now the sovereign power in this Realm. Caroline loves the Doctor, and has tried to effect a reconciliation between him and Sir Isaac, but this came to naught. Even when she is Queen she will have little power to change this—so irreconcilable are Leibniz's ideas with Newton's. It would be different if Leibniz's ideas were useful, but they are not—not yet, not compared to Newton's. It might be a long time before a Logic Mill can be constructed—a hundred years or more. And so the answer is that it is all devoid of *monetary* value at this time."

"Hmm. My life's work, devoid of value. That's hard to hear."

"I am only saying that you'll never find anyone who'll give you money for it. But you have a great Prince in the East who is happy to support the work. Ship it all to him. The golden cards, your notes and drawings, all that Enoch Root shipped over from Boston—send it all into the East, where someone values it."

"Very well. I have been arranging to do just that."

Eliza had turned away from the window and made Daniel Waterhouse the object of her scrutiny. She had, in fact, quite backed him into a corner. Something had occurred to her just now: a wild idea she did not like very much. "You phant'sy that's all there is, don't you? When you, Daniel, speak of your life's work, the only thing you include in that is what you have done on the Logic Mill."

Daniel showed empty hands to her. "What else is there?"

"At the very least, there is your son Godfrey, whom you ought to go home and look in on! One child in Boston today is a million descendants at some time in the future."

"Yes, but in what estate, in what sort of country?"

"That is for you to determine. And setting aside Godfrey—consider all you have done in the year since you received the letter from Princess Caroline!"

"I feel it's all been a muddle."

"You have done much for this country. For the Engine for Raising Water by Fire. For the abolition of Slavery. For Newton and Leibniz both, though neither of them might appreciate it."

"As I said before,'tis all a muddle to me. But I am a great brooder, and you have given me something to brood on for the rest of my days."

"Don't only brood on it, if you please. Work it out. See what you have done."

"In your rendering of the accompt," said Daniel, "do you find anything at all in the way of assets?"

"Oh, yes," Eliza said. "The Engine for Raising Water by Fire shall more than pay for all of the losses that I have complained of."

"I didn't feel that you were *complaining* so much as facing facts," Daniel said.

"I lose money all the time," she assured him. "I have spent rather a lot on this Slavery project, and it is only beginning—it'll take at least as long to do away with Slavery as it will to construct a proper Logic Mill, of that I'm sure."

"Ah, so I'm no worse than you—very kind of you to say so. What is to be your next project, if I may inquire?"

"As far as this investment is concerned? To cut the losses, liquidate what is to no purpose, and redouble investment in what is actually working: the Engine."

"It seems very reasonable when you put it that way," said Daniel, for some reason feeling quite relieved. "If the Engine succeeds, by the way, it will help your Cause, by reducing the demand for slave labor—"

"And yours," she said, "by supplying motive Power for a Logic Mill. Now you are beginning to understand."

"As Roger liked to say,'tis a good thing to be educable."

"Very well!" she said, and clapped her hands. "But there are details for us to attend to, aren't there, before we become distracted by these grand schemes?"

"We have a way to keep the cards safe from men of that type," said Daniel, gesturing with his head in the direction of the authorities sacking the Court.

"I had guessed as much. I was thinking of Friday."

"Two things are happening on Friday: the Trial of the Pyx, and the Hanging-March," Daniel reminded her. "Which of them do you mean?"

Eliza got that rueful half-smile again. "Both," she said simply, "for they are one thing now."

"Then you and I have arrived at the same conclusion," Daniel said. "It is between Isaac and Jack. For Jack almost certainly placed base metal in the Pyx. If he testifies to that effect, Newton is absolved, and the currency is upheld."

"Would there be any way to save Newton, and the Currency, *without* such testimony from Jack?"

"Wouldn't it be easier to persuade Jack to testify? That would have the added benefit of saving Jack from execution, supposing a deal could be struck—"

"A very questionable supposition, that," she pointed out, "and at any rate, I don't want him to make any such deal. I want him to be executed on Friday."

Daniel was so dumbfounded by this bald utterance that he kept on talking, like a man who has been shot through the head but keeps walking a stride or two before he crumples. "Er—well—even if that is what you want—why not strike a deal that would give him a quick merciful hanging, at least?"

"The original sentence," she insisted, "is what I want to be carried out against Jack Shaftoe on Friday."

"So—" Daniel blinked and shook his head, unable to fathom her placid cruelty. "So you are asking me, is there a way for Newton to triumph, in a Trial of the Pyx, even without testimony from Jack?"

"That is what I am asking you, as a Natural Philosopher."

"You are asking me, then, if the Trial of the Pyx can be *rigged!*"

"Good day, Dr. Waterhouse; both of us have many things to tend to before Friday," said Eliza, and walked out of the room.

The Chapel, Newgate Prison
24 OCTOBER 1714

I beseech you, Brethren, by the Mercies of God, that you present your Bodies a Living Sacrifice, Holy, Acceptable unto God; which is your Reasonable Service.

—ROMANS 12:1

ENGLAND'S POWERS TEMPORAL WERE NOT precisely *finished* with Jack Shaftoe. But they'd done everything to him that was within their scope, found him guilty of the worst of all crimes, thrown him in the worst of all places, sentenced him to the worst of all punishments. They were spent. Their Avenging Sword needed a good working-over with a whetstone, and their terrible quiver was empty. And so they had turned him over to the Powers Spiritual of the Realm, viz. the Church of England. This was the first time—and quite obviously the last—in Jack's life that he had attracted the notice of that organization. He did not know how to behave under its strange gaze.

The Vagabond-camps of his youth had been more than amply supplied with lunaticks. Indeed Newgate was the only place he had ever been since that contained a higher proportion of madmen.

He and Bob had learnt very early that the Nation of the Insane comprised diverse classes, sects, and parties, each of which must be treated with in a different way. A matched pair of starving ragamuffins, roving around a camp in the middle of some ducal game-park, exerted a powerful draw on maniacs of many types. But for those boys to survive, they had to learn to distinguish between, say, the religious Phanatiques and the pædophiles. For the consequences of being caught by them were wholly different. A Phanatique might even take it upon himself to defend a couple of boys from the sort of mad Vagabond who was bent on buggery. For this service he might exact a price, namely, to make them hear a sermon. It was in his nature to give sermons, just as it was to lambaste sodomites. As these two behaviors expressed the same nature, they could not be teased apart. The boys had to accept one with the other. From such sermons had the Shaftoe boys learned everything there was to know about the Anglican Church.

Later in his life, Jack was to recollect those open-air sermons with the skepticism of a world-weary adult. The sermonizers were religious maniacs who'd liefer rove the countryside in the company of pestilential Vagabonds than submit to the authority of Anglicans; and so how could such be expected to give a fair and impartial account of what went on in the Church of England? Of the slanders and calumnies that they flung against that Church's shiny red door, most were probably hallucinations; the remainder might have a germ of truth, but must still consist mostly of perfervid phant'sies. It was not that Jack had any affinity for the Church, any need to hold up their end of the argument. It was rather that he got sick of preachers early on. If he were to give credit to their ravings about the Anglican Church, he must give equal credit to their assertions, so tediously repeated, that he was bound for Hell. He preferred to take a dim view of everything they said, rather than picking and choosing.

This chapel he was sitting in now made him think that everything those Phanatiques told him might have been literally true.

The Phanatiques said that Anglican churches—unlike the open-air conventicles and simple barnlike meeting-houses of the Nonconformists—were divided up into boxes called pews. And lest this sound too attractive to a lot of bored Vagabonds who were standing in the mud or, at best, sitting on logs, they likened those pews to livestock pens, in which the churchgoers were pent up like so many sheep waiting to be fleeced, or slaughtered.

Now, here Jack sat, in his first ever Anglican service, and what did he observe but that the floor of the chapel—which was situated on the uppermost storey of Newgate Prison—was indeed divided into boxes. These were pens, and then some. Pens were open to the sky; but these pews (as they were styled by the management) had stout lids on them, to prevent Malefactors from vaulting over the top, or Dissident holy men from ascending directly into Heaven without the intermediation of a deputized representative of the Church of England.

The Phanatiques said that in Anglican churches, Persons of Quality got the best seats; the classes could not mingle freely, as they did in a Gathered church. Sure enough, the pews of Newgate chapel were strictly segregated according to degree. Prisoners from the Common Side were penned on one side of the aisle, to the left hand of the Ordinary as he stood in his corner pulpit. Those from the Master Side went to the right. Debtors were boxed separately from Felons, Males walled off from Females. But the very best seats in the house, directly below the pulpit, were reserved for the aristocracy: persons lately condemned to die at Tyburn. These were granted the luxury of an open pew, though they were chained to it, like galley-slaves to their bench.

The Phanatiques said that the Anglican Church was a place of death, a portal to Hell. Which sounded like lunacy; but this place was hung in black, swathed in funeral-shrouds. Directly before the Condemned pew, between it and the pulpit, was a stout altar; but what rested upon the Lord's Table was not a breakfast of bread and wine, but a coffin. And lest they fail to apprehend the message, the lid of that coffin had been removed, to make it plain that it was vacant, and wanted a lodger. It yawned at them through the service, and the Ordinary wasted no chance to direct their attention thither.

The Phanatiques said that people went to Anglican churches, not to hear and heed the Word of God, but to see and be seen. That it was a Show, nothing better than a play in a theatre, and probably worse, in that plays made no bones about being vile and bawdy, while Anglican services arrogated to themselves a sort of holiness. It was a claim difficult to make about the front of this chapel, which was full of smelly persons in boxes, peering out through grates. But when Jack tired of staring at the open coffin on the altar, and let his attention wander up the aisle, he noted that the back half of the church was supplied with several rows of open pews, and that they were packed full of churchgoers. Not "parishioners," mind you, for that would mean people who lived in or near Newgate, but "churchgoers," meaning, in this case, free Londoners who had got out of bed this morning, put on their Sunday best, and made a positive decision to travel here—a place so miasmic, that passersby had been known to drop dead in the street from breathing what wafted out of its gratings—and sit in a place draped all in black and listen to a gaol-house preacher rant about Death for a couple of hours.

Never one to affect false modesty, or any sort of modesty at all for that matter, Jack knew perfectly well that they had come to stare at the Condemned, and particularly at him. He stared right back. The Ordinary had been explicating a paltry few lines from Paul's Epistle to the Romans for more than an hour. No one was paying attention. Jack screwed himself around, looked back, and met the eye of each churchgoer in turn, challenging him or her to a stare-down, and he won every one, knocking them down one pew at a time like archery targets pinned to a fencerail. Except, that is, for one whose gaze he could not meet, because her face was hidden behind a veil. It was the same woman who had gone to the Gate of Janus the other day, just to get a look at him. On that occasion, she had flashed by so quickly that he hadn't fixed her clearly in his memory. This Sunday morning, he had a good hour to stare at her. Her face might be hidden, but he could see plainly enough she was rich; there was a lacy *fontange* perched atop her head, adding six inches to her height, and serving as a sort of mainmast from which the veil was deployed. Her dress was far from gaudy, being almost as dark and dour as mourning weeds, but he could see the sheen on the silk from here; the fabric alone probably cost as much as the whole contents of an average Londoner's wardrobe. And she'd brought a bloke, a young man, bit of a bruiser, blond and blue-eyed. Not a husband and not a beau, but a bodyguard. Jack lost the stare-down with him, but only because he, Jack, was distracted. Something was afoot.

Halfway Along Cheapside
DAWN, MONDAY, 25 OCTOBER 1714

"Did Roger come to you in a dream, or something?"

"I beg your pardon!?"

Saturn opened his eyes for the first time since he had upended his body into the carriage, back at Clerkenwell Court, a quarter of an hour ago. Since then he had only made himself more comfy with every bump and swerve. Confronted now with evidence that his companion had been conscious, and cogitating, the entire time, Daniel was mildly indignant.

Saturn pushed himself up a notch. "It is so unlike you to know of something before it happens. I wondered if you had had a spectral Visitation from the Shade of the late Marquis of Ravenscar."

"My intelligence came from another source."

"The Earl of Lostwithiel?"

"Shut up!"

"I thought so. Mortification was writ all over his lordship's face the other day, at the Sack of Clerkenwell."

"It'll be worse if word gets round that he has been talking to me, and so please curtail this!"

"Hmph. I do not think that Ravenscar got people to be discreet by *shushing* them. I think rather he was an *ingénieur* of a sort, who balanced interests."

"What is your point, other than that I am no substitute for Roger?"

"Clerkenwell Court was to me what a Gathered Church was to your dad's lot. Now what you Gathered has been Scattered by the Powers that Be. Just as certain of your co-religionists, in such a pickle, would abscond to Massachusetts to erect a City on a Hill or something, I phant'sy that I shall get out of this bloody town and go to what, for a Mechanick, will be what Plymouth Rock was for Puritans."

"And where, pray tell, is that?"

"Another place called Plymouth, but older, and easier to get to."

The carriage, following Daniel's instructions, had managed a right turn; Daniel had lost track of where they were, and was disoriented for a moment, until he saw the Church of St. Stephen Walbrook go by to their left. A light or two was already burning in a window there; good.

Saturn seemed a little provoked that Daniel had not risen to this most excellent bait. "Plymouth is where Mr. Newcomen is building his Engine, is it not?"

"Close enough," Daniel said. "I shall buy you a map of the west country as a going-away present, and on the journey you can master the fine distinctions between Plymouth, Dartmouth, Teignmouth, *et cetera.*"

"'Sblood, the place has as many Mouths as Parliament," Saturn muttered, and watched Daniel carefully—warily, even. Perhaps he had been worried as to how Daniel would react.

Daniel said, "I shall give Mr. Newcomen an excellent character of you."

"Thank you."

"I'll not say a word about Infernal Devices, or bursting out of whores' toilets in the dead of night."

"I would be indebted."

"Please don't think of it in that light . . . look on it rather as a selfish deed on my part," Daniel said. "Newcomen needs fewer smiths, and more men like you."

"I heard he was banging out great bloody monstrosities."

"That he is. But where he wants help is in the fabricating of the small clever bits—the valves, and so on. Just the job for a Horologist Gone Bad."

"Right! Let's sort this, then!" said a radically more energetic Peter Hoxton, rolling out the carriage door even though it had not yet come to a full stop. Daniel smelled River, and felt it condensing on his brow; they'd pulled round on the Three Cranes, a wharf not far from where the lost river of Walbrook buried itself in the Thames. A row of warehouses fronted on it, running parallel to the riverbank and a stone's throw back from the water. Separating two of these buildings was a narrow chink that anyone might have overlooked in the dark and the fog. Daniel was only able to pick it out because a light was burning some distance along this alley-way, on its right side. As Saturn shambled toward this, his head or shoulders would occult it from time to time. After a minute this stopped happening. Daniel heard a door opening, and eroded stumps of a few words, and then the door closing again.

The alley would broaden, after some distance, into the spacious back-court of the Vintners' Hall. Many of the establishments around it, including the one Saturn had gone into, were cooperages.

"Back to the Church of St. Stephen Walbrook," Daniel said to the coachman.

WILLIAM HAM WAS WAITING FOR them there, out front of the church where he'd been baptized. He climbed through the carriage door and settled into Saturn's former perch with a grunt. "Never has a church been put to such uses," he remarked.

"I've explained to the vicar—and will gladly explain again if need be—that it is all in pursuit of a righteous and Christian undertaking."

"Pray don't speak of *undertaking,* uncle. Not today."

That got them as far as the front entrance of the Bank of England, all of seven hundred feet away.

"I would like you to know something," Daniel said, as William was fumbling with his keys. For Daniel had the sense that William's slowness, his clumsiness, were not due to cold fingers alone.

"What is that, uncle?"

"I've never spoken of this to you before, as I know it is delicate. But after your father passed away, and his Vault was opened—forcibly—by order of the Lord Chancellor, I was among the party that went down into it, and found that it was empty."

"It is a very odd time for you to bring that up," William said, right snappishly, and smacked the Bank's door open. His irritation had at least got the blood running through his fingers, and perhaps to his brain. There was now a short interlude in the foyer while he soothed the porter's nerves, and urged him to get back in bed. Then he began to lead Daniel down into the labyrinthine basements and sub-basements of the Bank. While they walked, Daniel talked.

"Your choler is up, William. And no wonder! King Charles took from your father the plate, specie, and bullion that had been entrusted to the House of Ham by its depositors. The House was ruined. Your father died of shame. Others in the goldsmith trade had suffered likewise—though not as much—and understood that your father had been given no choice. The King had taken the gold by invoking his divine right to it. That's why you've never wanted for a position in the banking trade—because the story is proverbial among money-goldsmiths, and you are a living link to it.

"Anyway," Daniel continued, "after we found your father's vault empty we went up on the roof of your house—"

"We?"

"Your uncles Raleigh and Sterling and I, and Sir Richard Apthorp. And do you know what happened up there on the roof?"

"Can't imagine."

"Sir Richard founded the Bank of England."

"What do you mean!? This was not founded until twenty years later! And in any case, how can one man found a bank on the roof of a goldsmith's shop that is being burned down by the Mobb?"

"I mean he saw it all together in his head. He saw that banks would never work right if the King could sack their vaults whenever he ran low on revenue. This was a revolutionary thought. Probably would not have entered his mind had he not been thrown together with the sons of Drake the King-killer, the enemy of Divine Right, the champion of Enterprise. But when Sir Richard put those elements together in his mind, he created—all this."

"Bully for him," said William. "Wish I'd been the one to do that. You know. Redeem the family honour and whatnot." He had stopped before the door to the vault where the Logic Mill cards had been accumulating, as they had been brought in from Bridewell. There would be more messing about with keys now. Daniel relieved his nephew of the lanthorn and stood there Diogenes-like, shining light on his hands while he worked.

"As you know perfectly well, you were too young to found a Bank," Daniel reminded him. "Instead, you are redeeming the family honour now. At this moment."

"How do you reckon?" William said, gingerly pushing a gaudy key into one of the door-locks.

"The King—or some limb or other of his government—is coming, in a little while, to steal what I have deposited here. Oh, it is not my property. But is it the King's?! He has no bloody right to it. If you were to hang your head and let him steal it, the family curse would be confirmed—it would be indelible, then."

William Ham hauled open the Vault door. Stale air drained out of it. Daniel caught a whiff of sewer—nothing like the Fleet, but enough to stir the memory. "After you, uncle," said William, sounding rather more serene than he had some minutes earlier.

"No, William, after you! You have precedence. This is *your* deed. A small one, but a great one. People around the City shall hear of it, and the stock of the Bank shall rise, because of the stand you have made. But more important: your father, if he can see this, is saying to the other departed spirits, this is my son, in whom I am well pleased."

"Good of you to say so—since I know you don't believe in any of that!" said William, a bit huskily. Daniel had averted his gaze from the sight of tears filling the pouches under his nephew's eyes, and so was startled, and almost dropped the lanthorn, when William socked him on the shoulder. "But I *do* believe in such things, and I say that if my dad's looking on, why, *yours* is right there next to him, and couldn't be happier to see you poking your brand-new King in the eye with a sharp stick!"

A MINUTE LATER DANIEL was alone in the Temple of Mithras, and William Ham was on the other side of the Vault door, locking him in there.

In William's hip-pocket was a document, freshly signed, in which Daniel took possession of his deposits, and relieved the Bank of all responsibility for them. If nothing else, it would slow the King's men down for as long as it took them to read it.

Those deposits, of course, were all here and accounted for, stacked on the floor in front of Daniel. The golden cards of the Logick Mill had been sent over from Bridewell in frequent small shipments. After Daniel had visited this place with Solomon Kohan, and become aware of the well-shaft in its floor, he had instituted changes in how the cards were packaged for shipment. He had struck a deal with a cooper near the Vintner's Yard, and this cooper, Mr. Anderton, had fabricated a run of purpose-built boxes of peculiar design. Most anyone who looked on one of these would guess it was either a snare-drum or a hat-box, about a foot in diameter and half that in height. They were lightweight and not especially rugged, made from splits of soft wood no more than an eighth of an inch thick, steam-bent into hoops, sewed together with rawhide, and sealed with pitch. Each arrived at Bridewell with wood-shavings (a resource produced in superabundance by Mr. Anderton's arsenal of block-planes and draw-knives). Each had a close-fitting lid. These had been stockpiled at one end of the card-punching shop, handy to the desk where Mr. Ham weighed and accounted for all of the gold. Whenever a batch of cards was complete, and the paperwork all made out, one of these hat-boxes would be pulled off the stack and the lid set aside. Into the bed of wood-shavings would be pressed the stack of cards, all wrapped in paper, and next to it would go a wee purse containing the holes that had been punched out of them. The papers for this batch would be set atop, and finally the lid would be put on, laced down with more rawhide, and sealed all around its rim with tar. Then it was ready for dispatch to the Bank of England.

These containers were nothing like true barrels for strength, water-tightness, or cost. But they would fit down the well-shaft, and they would float, at least for a little while. Which was all that Daniel wanted. As soon as William Ham locked him in to the Vault, Daniel went over and pulled up the plank disk that covered the well-shaft. He was dizzy with a kind of terror that something would have gone wrong, and no one would be there. For a minute his fears were borne out. But then he began to hear voices, and a minute later he observed shreds of light skating and veering around, and finally a candle-flame, directly below. "Ready," came a voice.

Daniel dropped a hat-box down the shaft. No crashing or splintering noises were returned: only a firm *splunk* as it was caught by two out-stretched hands, followed by some conversation, and a brief surge of laughter. Then: "Ready!" and Daniel dropped another. It was uneven the first dozen times, with too much conversation and apologizing. Then it seemed as though the men down below had got a bucket-brigade organized, and Daniel ended up being the bottle-neck, as he could not seem to ferry the boxes to the hole rapidly enough. In the end Peter Hoxton had to climb up into the vault and assist him. After that, the place emptied out in a very short time.

But by the time the last of the Solomonic Gold went down the hole, voices—angry ones—could already be heard on the other side of the door, and hasty men were rattling the locks and picking curiously at the hasps and the hinges. William had promised to delay as long as he could by being indolent, then argumentative, and finally by pretending he couldn't find the key; but clearly enough these pretenses were all wearing thin. Worse, Daniel was growingly certain that Isaac was on the other side of that door, and Isaac could pick any lock ever made. After a last look round to make sure no box had been forgotten, Daniel inserted himself into the shaft, and began to seek the ladder's rungs with his toes. Saturn was not far behind, but he paused at the top of the ladder to fiddle with a bit of rope, and then to set the plank-disk lid into place above his head—closing the door behind him, as it were. That rope still dangled through a small hole bit from the rim of the lid. It led, as Daniel knew, to the underside of a large, ancient-looking crate that rested on the floor of the Vault next to the well-shaft. When Saturn was sure that Daniel had reached the base of the ladder and gotten well out of harm's way by retreating into the side-shaft, he wrapped that rope around his hands and trusted his whole weight to it. He plunged straight down for about an arm's length, then was caught short, and had to kick for a rung. The crate had shifted over and, or so they hoped, covered the lid. This might or might not buy them a few minutes of extra time, depending on how closely the Vault was searched.

Saturn pulled the ladder down and carried it with him as he followed Daniel to the bank of Walbrook. The stream's course was now marked out, spottily, by a series of candles. One or two men could be heard sloshing downriver. Saturn here discarded the ladder and then followed Daniel down the current, snuffing out candles as he went, and both of them keeping an eye peeled for hat-boxes that had gone astray.

A few minutes' wading brought them to the orifice that served as cellar-drain for St. Stephen Walbrook. Daniel went through first, crawling up it on his belly until rough hands grasped his, and drew him out in one long heave. He could not see very well for a minute, because there was suddenly too much light coming into his eyes. But he could smell the mineral tang of fresh mortar, and he knew from the calluses on those hands that they must have belonged to masons. There was a minute of bother trying to get Saturn up through the drain, which turned to hilarity when he popped loose; then he jumped to his feet and shushed them all furiously, saying that he had heard voices echoing down Walbrook from the Bank, and he thought one of them might be an angry Sir Isaac.

Daniel could see now. There was quite a crowd there in the crypt under the church: a mason and two younger assistants, two coopers from Mr. Anderton's company, Daniel, Saturn, and a pair of mudlarks who had been part of the bucket brigade. As well as a very old and bent-over chap, in good clothes and good humor, seemingly fascinated by the hole in the floor whence so many novelties had just emerged.

"I had quite forgotten about it!" exclaimed Sir Christopher Wren.

"I am indebted to you, Daniel. It is in the nature of building-projects, you know, that one gets a thing ninety-nine percent finished, then drifts away. Quite right of you to call this to my attention."

By the time he had reached the end of this sentence, the drain had ceased to exist. The masons had brought with them a length of wrist-thick lead pipe, which they thrust down the tunnel, then buried in a wheelbarrow-avalanche of mixed mortar and rubble. The head of the pipe was stomped down until it was flush with the floor, and then the eldest of the masons set about finish-work, arranging a few small flat paving-stones around the orifice to cover up the rubble fill beneath.

At the other end of the room, Anderton's men were stacking the hat-boxes into barrels. These were unfinished; the staves at the top were splayed apart, restrained by temporary hoops. A groove had been carved around their inner surfaces, near the ends, to accept the end-pieces. Each barrel was tall enough to accommodate a stack of half a dozen hat-boxes; more wood-shavings were dumped in around these, so they would not rattle around, and then the end-pieces were set in loose. In this state the barrels were dragged up stairs and out into the court behind the church, which communicated with a bigger court out back of Salters' Hall: a place where no sight was more unremarkable than a huddle of barrels ready to be finished.

By day's end, all of the barrels had been conveyed to the work-shop of Mr. Anderton, and his coopers had bent the staves inward to imprison the end-pieces, and put on the permanent hoops.

Daniel was tired, and wanted to call it a day, but he could not bring himself to leave the cooperage until the last of the hat-boxes had been sealed up within the last of the barrels. He made himself at home in a corner of Anderton's shop, stimulating himself as needed with coffee or tobacco, until the job was done. The barrels were then rolled down to Three Cranes and entrusted to a shipping-company; the destination marked on each one of them was LEIBNIZ-HAUS HANOVER. After all the care and bother that the Solomonic Gold had occasioned during its eventful passage from the Solomon Islands to the Palace of the Viceroy in Mexico, to its theft before Bonanza, to Cairo and Malabar and its many travels on or in the hull of *Minerva,* it felt very strange to turn one's back on it and walk away, leaving it stacked out in the open on a wharf. But now, disguised as salt cod and placed in the care of a reputable shipping-agent, it was probably safer than it had ever been.

Poop Deck of Minerva, the Pool of London

DANIEL HAD FEARED going back to Cranc Court yesterday evening for the reason that Isaac would probably find him there and belabor him, and lambaste him, and browbeat him, and altogether make him feel bad. So he had fetched on the notion of requesting permission to come aboard *Minerva*, which was more convenient to the Three Cranes, and more hospitable. For weeks the management of that fair ship had been urging him to pay them a call, and for weeks he had been finding excuses not to. They were delighted when Daniel's water-taxi hove up alongside shortly before midnight, and gave him too much to drink and then bedded him down in his old cabin.

When he woke up, he knew in his bones that he had slept for a very, very long time—probably owing to his inexpressible relief at having rid himself of the Solomonic Gold.

But he also knew that he could have slept much longer if not for all of the crashing and cursing.

He pulled on—with some reluctance—the crusty duds he had worn the day before. It felt like *they* were wearing *him* now. A strange man flung his cabin-door open without thinking to knock. Daniel was just in the act of buckling his shoe. He and the intruder studied each other, mutually shocked. The other was young, well-dressed, and properly brought up—mortified, therefore, that he had disturbed an old man at his *levée*. Why, then, was he here? The answer was suggested by the silver-greyhound badge.

"Sir! I do beg your pardon. But, er . . ."

"By the King's command, you must search this cabin?" Daniel guessed.

"Yes, sir. That's right."

"For . . . what, if I may ask? Sleepy old men? Here's one."

"No, sir, beg pardon . . ."

"If you will only tell me what you have been ordered to search for, then perhaps I can assist you."

"It's gold, sir. Contraband gold."

"Ah," Daniel said, "I'm afraid the only gold in this chamber is this ring on my finger." Daniel slipped it off and held it up. "Will you be confiscating it, then?"

Now the King's Messenger was downright embarrassed. "Oh, no, sir, of course not, that is not the sort of thing we are looking for at all. And I really am *terribly* sorry to be disturbing you. But if you could only . . . well . . ."

"Get out of the way, so that you could give this cabin a thorough search? My good man, I was just on my way out!" Daniel said, and after slipping the ring back on to his finger he raised his eyebrows at the Messenger, pushed himself to his feet, and got out.

He found Dappa above, on the poop deck, sighting through a prospective-glass toward the Tower of London. Last night Daniel had reached *Minerva* without getting a clear notion of where she was situated in the Pool. Now that the sun was up, he was struck by how near she was to the Tower: practically within shouting-distance.

He knew better than to startle Dappa by speaking: this was bad etiquette, when the other chap's attention was fixed on something far away. And he did not bother inquiring after van Hoek. The Captain's whereabouts were obvious, for he never let off cursing in Dutch, Sabir, and all other tongues at his command, as he followed the King's Messengers about his ship.

"It could have been worse," Dappa said, after an especially bracing out-burst of van Hoekian execration burgeoned from an open hatch. "We are light-laden just now, and there is little difficulty in making a thorough search. A fortnight from now we'd have been laden to the scuppers and it would have been awkward." He withdrew the glass from his eye and squinted at Daniel. "They are scratching our guns."

"I beg your pardon?"

"Someone important has fallen under the spell of a phant'sy that this magic gold might have been cast into the form of a gun, and painted black, as a way of smuggling it out, and so they have scratched each and every one of our guns with an awl, to be sure they are made of brass."

"Incredible."

"There are those among our crew who look on you, now, as bad luck."

"Ah. I see. Because the first time I came aboard, it led to being assaulted by Blackbeard. And now this."

"Yes, Doc."

"Since they are so superstitious," Daniel said, "perhaps they have heard the saying, 'Third time's a charm.'"

"What do you have in mind?" Dappa asked, and then could not help smiling.

"I gather from what you said that a voyage is in the offing?"

"We'll take on some cargo here. Then to Plymouth."

"Really!"

"When we set you ashore there, ten months ago, we chanced to embark on a little venture that is still playing out. At any rate, we must needs put in there. Then south to Oporto. Then a crossing of the Atlantic Ocean is contemplated, in balmier latitudes than these."

"And then back to London in the spring-time?"

"We have had quite enough of London, thank you! No," Dappa said, and laughed. "We go the other way round. Enoch Root has been pestering us to take him to the Islands of Solomon . . ."

"But those are halfway around the world from Boston!"

"We know where they are," said Dappa. "They are on our way, though."

"On your way to *where*?!"

"Queena-Kootah, where we'd visit old friends, or their grave-sites as the case might be, and then Malabar, where we have an Investrix who, it is safe to say, is now waxing a bit *obstreperous*. She'll not accept her Dividend in the form of a Bill of Exchange. We must sail there and stack bullion on the shore."

"Awkward."

"When we make profits in London, yes, I should say it is awkward. We'll go there and stack gold on her beach and I shall make love to her and in time she'll forgive us."

"Then?"

"I've no idea."

"Your Solomon Islands passenger has been working as my proxy in Boston," Daniel said, "winding up the Massachusetts Bay Colony Institute of Technologickal Arts, liquidating the assets, assuaging the creditors, and paying the bar tabs. Before he absconds to the Antipodes I really ought to sit down with him and settle accounts."

"Then you'll need to go *there*, and do it *soon*, for I can assure you he is not coming *this* way."

"You said you were going first to Plymouth—?"

"That I did."

"I, too, have business in the west country," said Daniel. "Perhaps I could make rendezvous with you there, and obtain passage back home?"

"Perhaps," Dappa said. Then, startled by his own rudeness, he made haste to add, "Oh,'tis all good where I am concerned. But after *this* van Hoek'll have questions. He'll want to know just where *is* this troublous gold. I shall give you a Hint: a satisfactory answer would be *far, far away.*"

"I've an even better answer," said Daniel, "which is: *I don't know.*" He held up his hands as if to indicate all thousand ships in the Pool, and it turned into a shrug.

"It is in transit," Dappa understood. "You have shipped it."

"It has been solved," Daniel said, "con-fused in the currency of the Thames, and it will make its way to Hanover, mysteriously but reliably, even as Pieces of Eight converge, as if they had minds of their own, on Shahjahanabad."

The more poetic Daniel waxed, the more Dappa's interest waned, and by the end of this sentence he had plugged the glass back into his eye-socket and trained it again on the Tower.

"What is it you are looking at up there?" Daniel asked. The wind was strong, and cold, and out of the north, and Daniel had no wig or hat. As he had ascended to the poop deck a minute ago, he had looked once toward the Tower, to get his bearings, but since then he had stood with his back to it and the collar of his coat turned up to shield his neck and the base of his skull. Dappa faced resolutely into the breeze, fighting it off with a fixed grimace. He said, "It is easier for you to turn around and see for yourself than for me to explain all."

"But you have a prospective-glass, and I don't."

"It is hardly needed at this range!"

"Why are you you using it, then?"

"Trying to resolve certain details. I am watching a group of men on the top of Lanthorn Tower," Dappa said, "who are obviously enough responsible for this outrage."

"Meaning, the ransack of your ship?"

"Yes. These Messengers, you may've noticed, keep looking to them for instructions. They have been communicating with semaphores. I think that one of them is Sir Isaac Newton."

This was altogether predictable, and yet it was enough to make Daniel turn around and brave the wind. In a few moments he had picked out the group that Dappa had described. "Where is he?" Daniel asked.

"In the middle, peering right back at us with a spyglass."

"Oh, bloody hell, he'll probably recognize me!" Daniel burst out. He ought to have whirled right back around. But like a field-mouse caught in a raptor's gaze, he found himself curiously unable to move.

"It's all right, he is lowering the glass—no, I'm wrong, he *dropped* the bloody thing!"

"Isaac dropped it!?" Daniel could not conceive of Isaac Newton dropping a telescope.

"He's a-gawp. Looking our way. Can't make out his face really . . . his posture calls to mind such undignified words as gobsmacked, stamagast. Stricken. Oh! Oh! Oh, my god!"

"What! What is it?" Daniel demanded, and mastered the urge to snatch the glass. For all he could see with his naked eye was that the crowd on the top of the tower was puckering inwards toward the center, where Isaac stood—or *had* stood a moment earlier.

"He's gone down! Straight down. Lucky that bloke on his right caught him."

"*Caught* him!?"

"He just toppled over," said Dappa, "dropped the glass and like to have landed right on top of it. Look, someone is running for help . . . they are calling to the soldiers down below them, waving their hats . . . Jesus Christ, they're all in a bloody panic!" Dappa finally took the glass from his eye, and looked at Daniel. His brow furrowed above the bridge of his nose, as finally he made sense of what he had just seen. Then it hit Daniel, too, and he had to reach out one hand and steady himself on a railing.

"He's not dead, or they would not be in such a hurry," Dappa reasoned. "Sir Isaac Newton has had a stroke. That's what I'd say."

"Perhaps he only fainted. He has been ailing of late."

"A stroke fits better with what I saw. It hit him on his right side— that's why he dropped the glass, that's why his right leg gave way. Whether it was a swoon, or a stroke, I do believe it was occasioned—" But here he bit his tongue, and winced.

"By his recognizing my face, when I turned around," Daniel said, "thereby proving all his darkest and strangest fears. Which fears have been tormenting him ever since I returned to London and got entangled in the weird saga of the Solomonic Gold. Shit! I killed my friend."

"He is neither dead, nor your friend," Dappa corrected him.

"If you would be so good as to summon me a water-taxi," said Daniel, "I must make haste to his niece's house—which is probably where they'll take him—and defend him from the physicians."

The Temple of Vulcan
WEDNESDAY, 27 OCTOBER 1714

THE OPTIMISTIC SIDE OF DANIEL's nature put in a rare appearance on the evening of Tuesday and convinced Daniel that Isaac's collapse had been neither swoon nor stroke, but only another of those mad panics that would come over him from time to time and later subside. Daniel was so sure of this that he paid a call on Isaac's house in St. Martin's that evening, expecting that Isaac would be there. But he was not. He was in the care of Catherine Barton at the house of the late Roger Comstock.

Daniel went there on Wednesday, then, and found Miss Barton distraught. In retrospect he now saw it as a marvel that Isaac hadn't died a long time ago. His troubles had begun in August when Leibniz had knocked him and Daniel over a wall. This had saved them from being roasted by phosphorus-fire, but had done damage to Isaac's ribs, with the result that he'd breathed but shallowly for weeks afterwards. He'd picked up a catarrh that ought to have been minor, but had been unable to cough effectively because of the pain in his ribs, and so had not been clearing his lungs. This catarrh had entrenched itself and become a pneumonia.

The event yesterday probably had been a stroke, but not as grave as it might have been; according to Catherine, Isaac had suffered weakness on his right side for a time, but seemed to have regained some of his strength since then. That did not concern her so much as his rapidly mounting fever.

"Fever!?" Daniel exclaimed, and insisted on going in to see the patient. Isaac had left strict orders to keep all physicians out of his room, and Catherine had obeyed them; but Daniel Waterhouse was no physician.

Isaac was spread-eagled on a four-poster bed, dressed in a flimsy nightshirt. He had kicked the bedclothes off onto the floor and he or someone else had opened a window to let in cold air. Daniel had to stuff his hands into his pockets to keep them from freezing. "Isaac?" he said.

The patient's head stirred, triggering a shift of his flowing white hair, and beneath half-closed lids his eyes focuscd. But the eyes were not looking Daniel's way. Daniel came over to the bedside. Isaac was breathing rapidly and shallowly. Daniel bent down and pressed an ear to Isaac's ribcage, wincing at the heat that came out of his body— like a loaf fresh out of the oven. In the bases of Isaac's lungs, it sounded as though bacon was being fried. His heart was beating weakly but quickly, albeit with alarming skips and pauses.

During this examination, Daniel could not help but notice a rash on those parts of Isaac's chest not covered by the nightshirt. He sat on the edge of the bed and unbuttoned the garment. Isaac's eyes, then his head moved slightly as Daniel did so; the movement had caught his eye. He watched Daniel's hands work their way down his heaving sternum, one button at a time, and when Daniel spread the nightshirt apart, Isaac's eyes tracked his right hand. Daniel recognized it: Natural-Philosophic curiosity.

Isaac's torso was covered with the rash. It was most obvious around the left armpit.

"When was the last time you were in Newgate Prison?" Daniel asked. For he had the sense that Isaac was entering in to a lucid phase.

"Ah!" Isaac said, and then had to cough for a minute, in a frothy way, to clear the pipes for action. "You and I agree on the diagnosis of gaol-fever, then. That is a comfort. We agree on so little else." Long pauses held these phrases apart.

"When was the last time . . ." Daniel reiterated patiently.

Isaac cut him off with the answer: "A week ago. I went and spoke to Jack in the Condemned Hold."

"Normally the incubation period for gaol-fever would be—"

"Longer, a bit. Yes. I know. But I am old. And weakened by other maladies. You are being tedious. I have little time. I stipulate that I have gaol-fever. It will get worse before it gets better. If it gets better at all. Now I am getting chilly. Will you please button me back up. My right hand has lost some of its dexterity."

Daniel could hardly deny such a request, and so he began to re-button the shirt—even though he was sure that this was a ploy by Isaac to bring Daniel's hands into view again so that he could observe the ring. Daniel ignored this, and worked the buttons as fast as he could, and cursed his own stupidity for not having simply pocketed the thing before entering the room.

"It looks heavy," Isaac remarked. "You know of what I speak. Does it weigh heavy on your finger?"

"Sometimes."

"Who gave it you? Not a woman, surely."

Daniel finished with the buttons, and thrust his hands back in his pockets.

"I should like to give you something as well," Isaac remarked. His gaze had tracked the bauble all the way to Daniel's pocket and now flicked up to settle on Daniel's eyes.

"And what might that be, Isaac?"

"Not so much give it you, as draw it to your notice," Isaac corrected himself. "That stuff of Hooke's. Found at Bedlam. Reposited here. For me it was neither the most . . . nor the least . . . convenient place to look at it. Since the death . . . of Roger . . . I have come here more often. For I could not attend to my work . . . when he was hovering . . . you know . . . and asking all manner of questions. I have made a study of that document. The one that figured in the Stake-out . . . of last summer. You know the one I mean. Hooke's account of a patient . . . who died after a lithotomy . . . and was resurrected . . . there is no other word for it . . . by a certain receipt. A remarkable document."

"You forged a fake version of it as bait for de Gex," Daniel said, "but—"

"But I have returned to it. In recent weeks. As my health was failing. And I took many notes. And interpreted what was cryptic. And set down clearly what Hooke—who was no Alchemist—did not understand. I know you think it is all rubbish. But if you would look after it . . . and see that it finds its way into the right . . . *hands* . . . it would be a comfort to me."

"Of course. Where is it?"

"Roger's library. Table before the window. Top drawer on the right."

"I'll fetch it now," Daniel said, "and take it to your house straightaway."

"That is good," Isaac said. "Take it to my laboratory. Put it with the rest."

"The rest of what?" Daniel asked. But he could see plainly he'd not be getting an answer. Isaac drew in his limbs, curled up on his side, and began to shiver like a dog fresh out of the water that cannot fight the urge to shake. Daniel called for Catherine, and together they sorted out the bedclothes and drew them over Isaac's body.

"He has asked me to tend to some things," Daniel announced to justify leaving. "I shall send word to the Council that Isaac is unwell, and cannot attend the Trial of the Pyx, day after tomorrow."

"No! You must do no such thing!" Miss Barton said, and laid a hand on Daniel's wrist. For she knew well enough that her words would penetrate a man's brain as effectively as a musket-ball, if she touched him while she spoke.

"Miss Barton," Daniel said, "look at the poor man! He can't possibly—"

"Uncle Isaac told me that he must be present at the Trial of the Pyx no matter what. Even if he's dead."

"Pardon me, but did you really mean that?"

" 'Even if I am dead,' he told me, 'you stuff my corpse in a sedan chair and carry me to Star Chamber on Friday morning.' And that, Doctor Waterhouse, is just what I mean to do."

"Well, God willing, he'll still be alive," Daniel said, and gently disengaged himself from Miss Barton's smooth grasp, and headed for Roger's library.

Newgate Prison
28 OCTOBER 1714

> . . . the Bell-man, who is the Prelude to the Hang-man, like a Flourish before a damn'd Melancholy Tune, comes next to Torture them with his Inhu-mane Stanza's, as if Men in their Condition cou'd have any Stomach to Unseasonable Poetry; for the Night before Execution, placing himself under their Window, he harangues them with the following Sere-nade, set to the Tune of the Bar Bell at the Black Dog.
>
> — *Memoirs of the Right Villanous*
> *John Hall,* 1708

SINCE SENTENCE OF DEATH had been pronounced upon him, the gaol-keepers had kept Jack's apartment-door locked, and posted armed men outside to ensure it stayed that way. They'd never once let him go down to the good old Dogg. Jack's only way of com-

muning with the Dogg's merry company had been to hear the ringing of its bell every night, at curfew. At that moment it had been his
custom to lift a glass of Oporto, chosen from the rather large collection of bottles that had been sent up to his room, during the last
week, by admirers.

This evening, however, his libation was rudely interrupted by the
clanging of a hand-bell down below, in the vaulted passage-way that
tunneled below his Castle and passed by the grated vent-hole of the
Condemned Hold. Jack was not the only man slated to die at Tyburn
tomorrow. Six more were going there with him, all Common-Side
Malefactors who lacked means, or mysterious friends, to buy their
way out of the said Hold. This nocturnal Bell-Man was plying his
trade to a captive audience down there, spewing noxious poetry
through the grating:

> *All you that in the Condemn'd Hold do lye,*
> *Prepare you, for to Morrow you must die.*
> *Think well upon your Sins, in Time repent,*
> *Lest you are Headlong into Satan sent.*
> *Watch then, and Pray, that so you may be fit*
> *T'Appear so soon before the Judgment-Seat:*
> *And when St. Pulcher's Bell to Morrow Tolls,*
> *The Lord above have Mercy on your Souls.*

Having discharged his obligations there, the Bell-Man removed
himself from the stink of the vault. He retreated through the
portcullis and out into the middle of Holborn. He planted himself in
the middle of the road directly beneath Jack Shaftoe's triple window,
like a swain getting ready to serenade his lady love. Which maneuvers
would normally be both dark (as the sun had set quite some time
ago) and dangerous (as men who stood in the middle of a highway
leading into a gate of the City of London normally did not long survive). But the Bell-Man's progress was well-lighted by a crowd of Londoners with torches, who had thronged the highway from one side to
the other, throwing up a barrier of flame that would dazzle and ter-
rify any horses whose drivers were foolish enough to bring them this
way. Newgate was closed for the evening. The Bell-Man stood in a
fiery semicircle, blinking in surprise, as normally he must carry out
his duties alone and unheralded.

Jack had been playing the recluse since he had been condemned.
In the first days, crowds had gathered in Holborn from time to time,
apparently drawn by rumors that Jack Shaftoe was going to get out of
bed and stand in his window to be viewed, like a King taking the air

in St. James's. All of them had been driven away, disappointed, by constables. But tonight was a special occasion, for how many times in his life would Jack be half-hanged, drawn, and quartered? Jack busied himself for a minute or two, lighting tapers. For sources of illumination were another luxury that was famously in short supply at Newgate, and those sycophants who lacked the Yellow Boys (that is to say, Guineas) to buy Jack bottles of Oporto might at least scratch together thrums (that is to say, three pence) to buy him a taper, so that he might take good aim at his chamber-pot later. He had not been burning many of these, but at this point there was little reason to hoard them, and so he went round and set every one of them alight. The room immediately filled with lambent smoke, and the fragrance of rancid tallow, which took him right back to his boyhood on the Isle of Dogs. There was a small ironbound hatch in one of his windows, which might be opened to admit air. He did so now, to spill out the smoke, and was spotted by the crowd down in Holborn, who phant'sied that Jack Shaftoe had nothing better to do on this, his last night, than to banter with them. That damned bell started up, quieting a surge of excitement from the crowd, and the Bell-Man roared out his stanza.

Jack was ready for him. He put his face to the open grate and shouted back,

> *O tedious Man, who with thy Bell*
> *Dost ring me down the road to Hell,*
> *Tomorrow eve, at half past seven,*
> *I'll hock a spit on you from Heaven.*
> *For if, as preachers say, the afterlife*
> *Smells sweet, sounds pleasant, is free of strife,*
> *And is, in sum, a Kingdom of Felicity,*
> *It must be any place that does not harbor Thee.*

The performance was extremely well-received by all hearers save the Bell-Man himself, who slinked away in the direction of St. Sepulchre, stepping a bit lively as turds and expired vegetables began to pelt him in the back.

Now that he'd been sent away in disgrace, the only people remaining were members in good standing of the Mobility, a.k.a. the Mobb, a class of people divided by their tendency to rape, murder, and steal from one another, but united in their admiration for Jack. They were expecting something from him, without a doubt. A few groups were trying to sing songs to him, in different keys and meters, but no one tune had taken hold yet. Jack—who must be nothing more, to them, than a silhouette against a smoky candle-lit chamber, half-obscured by the reticule of massive iron bars—waved his arms a bit to quiet them down, then put his face to the grate again, and shouted:

"The curfew-bell has sounded, and the gentleman from St. Sepulchre has given me his stanzas, and I am retiring! As should you all! For we have a long and busy day ahead of us tomorrow! I have an appointment at Tyburn in the morning, to which you are all invited! And then another at the College of Physicians in the afternoon. For even though my *body* is to be quartered, my *head* is expected to come through the ceremony more or less intact, and those Natural Philosophers around the corner there—straight up Newgate Street, take a right on Warwick Lane just across from Grey Fryars, there, then down to the first entry on your right, the large building with the golden pill on the top—they're going to cut open my skull tomorrow and peer inside, to see if they can ascertain why I am such a bad fellow."

He was answered by a general scream of rage, so disturbing to the peace and quiet of his gentlemanly abode, that he shut the hatch immediately. And a good thing, too, for moments later, a hailstorm struck. The noise of small objects assaulting the windowpanes grew until it was louder than the screaming was. Jack approached the window again, out of curiosity, and saw that farthings and pennies, and even a few shillings, were piling up on the stone windowsill outside, so thick that they were forming up into drifts. The people were throwing money at him, money to pay for a Christian burial, to keep him out of the hands of the College of Physicians. And the ones who couldn't afford to fling coins, were charging up Newgate Street in a torchlight stampede, looking for that first right turn that Jack just told them about. It promised to be a long and eventful night at the College of Physicians; but at least Jack Shaftoe would get some privacy, and some sleep.

Sir Isaac Newton's House in St. Martin's
EVENING, THURSDAY, 28 OCTOBER 1714

"MR. THREADER," the butler announced.

Daniel looked up, and turned around.

Mr. Threader stood in the laboratory doorway, hat in hand, decidedly cringing, looking about the room as if expecting Sir Isaac Newton to spring out from behind a glowing furnace and turn him into a newt.

"He is not here," Daniel said gently. "He is at his niece's house."

"Recuperating—or so 'tis rumored—from an *attaque* of some sort—?" Mr. Threader, emboldened, stepped over the threshold. The butler closed the door behind him and walked away.

"We shall help him recuperate, you and I. Please, please, come in!" Daniel beckoned with one, then both hands. Mr. Threader obeyed with extreme reluctance. He was not accustomed to Alchemical laboratories. The glowing furnaces, the smells, the open flames, the jars and retorts with their cryptic labels, were all vaguely threatening to him. Seeing as much, Daniel felt, for a moment, what a second-rate Alchemist must feel when a gullible person ventures into his shop: a smug self-satisfaction in the bamboozlement and bewilderment of one's fellow-man, and a perverse urge to milk the wretch for all he is worth.

But alas, he had other errands, and must needs put Mr. Threader at ease.

"It must all seem quite foreign to you. I was fortunate: I was chumming with Isaac during the years that he turned our domicile into one great smoking Lab. So, all the stuff you see around you here was moved in to our house one bit at a time, and I could ask Isaac what it was, and how to use it." Daniel laughed. "I am more at home here than I should care to admit!"

Mr. Threader permitted himself a dry chuckle. "I must say that you *look* quite at home here, which is quite amusing after all of the unkind remarks you have made about Alchemy."

Daniel wondered what Mr. Threader would make of it if Daniel were to let him know that tomorrow he, Daniel, might be the most eminent Alchemist since King Solomon went in to the East. But he shook it off as being too uncanny to speak of just now.

"Is Sir Isaac expected to be in any condition to attend the Trial?"

"He would not miss it for anything."

"It is good to know his condition improves."

Daniel said nothing. Isaac's condition was not improving; he suspected that the gaol-fever was creating a lesion on Isaac's heart. As a boy Isaac had tried to make perpetual motion machines, seeing in them a model of the heart. But Isaac's heart, Daniel suspected, was about to give out. Men had not been able to fashion perpetual motion machines because men were mechanics who only knew how to work with inert matter. Hearts pumped longer than any machine could, because the matter of which they were made—or so Alchemists supposed—was suffused with the vegetative spirit.

"Let's make some money!" Daniel said. "Did you bring the molds?"

What Daniel had mentioned was so perilous that Mr. Threader, by way of an answer, could only flinch. "Do you have a bit of gold?" he returned.

Daniel flourished his right hand, then pulled off the gold ring and tossed it without ceremony into a small crucible. Picking this up with a pair of tongs, he made to thrust it into a small, keening, and radiating furnace. "Is it fine gold?" Mr. Threader wanted to know.

"It is finer than fine," Daniel said, and maneuvered the crucible into the glowing heart of the furnace. "It is heavier than pure gold."

Mr. Threader blinked. "I'm afraid that is quite impossible."

"You may verify it in a minute or two."

"How can such a thing be?"

"A divine quintessence fills its pores, which, in ordinary gold, are vacant cavities."

Mr. Threader stared at him, to see if Daniel was having him on; but Daniel himself was not certain. In the end Mr. Threader believed it, not because of weighing the gold or because he found Alchemy convincing, but because of the political, the human logic of the thing. "I say! I say! You want me to—to—you are *up* to something! Aren't you!"

"We are *all* up to something," Daniel said, and gave Mr. Threader what was meant to be a chilly look. He was afraid that the other was about to launch into some self-righteous peroration. But Mr. Threader had the decency to stifle himself.

"You have been chosen by the Jury of the Citizens to serve in the rôle of Pesour tomorrow, have you not?"

"Dr. Waterhouse, you are strangely well-informed about what is supposed to have been a secret, and so I shall not make a fool of myself denying it."

"You are, therefore, the adversary—the challenger—of the Master of the Mint."

"That is how the avarice of the Mint-men has been kept in check since ancient days," Mr. Threader said agreeably. "It is the gold-smiths' duty and their honour."

"It poses a curious conflict of interests," Daniel remarked, "when one considers that Sir Isaac had it in his power, a few weeks ago, to send you to Tyburn along with Jack Shaftoe, but elected not to."

Mr. Threader only made a seething noise at that, which was nearly lost in like noises emitted by the furnace. In August he had been pitiable, abject, almost a little disgusting. But now he'd got used to the whole affair's having been swept under the rug, and considered it very bad manners indeed for Daniel to have revisited it. Daniel was distracted now, for a moment, by the curious sight of the ring beginning to melt: most of it was yet unchanged, but where it touched the walls of the crucible it was sagging and ponding.

"The only ones who can testify against me are Jack and his boys," Mr. Threader reminded him. "Jack has not implicated me, and will be dead in a few hours. The boys have escaped—"

"I know," Daniel said, "I broke them out of prison. I know where they are. Got affidavits from them, before they left the country. Witnessed and sealed affidavits stating that you took part in coining. Speaking of which, I do believe we are just about ready for that mold."

Mr. Threader reached into his coat-pocket. "To own this thing is a death-warrant," he said, "but you already have mine in your hip pocket, it seems, and so this is redundant." And he took out a cylinder of clay, a bit larger in diameter than a guinea coin, and as long as a finger. In the middle it had been broken or chopped into two halves that had been rejoined with slip and fired to make the thing whole. He lay this on its side on the workbench and then rolled it until a tapered hole, like a tiny funnel, came round to the top. Then he chocked it between a pair of fire-bricks. "Be my guest," he offered, "but this is hardly the way to forge a proper guinea!"

"It need not be all that convincing," Daniel said, "as we are going to chop it up anyway."

Mr. Threader was startled, then baffled by this remark; then he understood, and nodded. Meanwhile Daniel had taken up the tongs again, and reached in to the furnace. The crucible came out a-glow. Daniel swung it round over the bench-top and let the tongs rest on one of the fire-bricks, to steady himself. Then he twisted his wrists. Liquid fire spilled out of the crucible. A bead or two went astray, but most of it went down the hole in the clay cylinder.

"There," said Mr. Threader, "we are in the same boat now—you have just committed High Treason!"

"It is an old failing of my family," Daniel admitted. He tapped the last drips of gold from the crucible; they beaded on the table and instantly congealed. He set the tongs and crucible aside, and closed the furnace door. With a pair of tweezers he picked up every bead of gold that had gone astray and dropped them into a little cup. Then he took up the clay mold, which was warm, and snapped it in half. A guinea fell out of it and spun on the table. As Mr. Threader had warned him, it was not a very good guinea: the gold had not evenly filled the mold, so parts of it were indistinct. The edging was no good at all, and it had a bubble trapped in it. A prong stuck out of its rim where the filling-hole had been. Daniel flicked it into a bowl of water to cool it down, then plucked it out with his bare fingers and attacked it with a pair of heavy shears. His hands almost were not equal to this task, and he thought for a moment that he might have to send for Saturn. But Mr. Threader, warming to the task, wrapped his hands around Daniel's and they squeezed together, grunting like swine, and finally there was a *snap* and two halves of the guinea went flying opposite directions. Daniel had so arranged things that one of these halves included the prong and most of the other gross imperfections. This he placed in the bowl with the other surplus. But the other half was more presentable. Daniel fetched this off the floor and brought it back, and they halved it again, and again—a little bit like cutting a Piece of Eight into *reales*, except they made the bits smaller and quite irregular—reducing the false half-guinea into a rubble of mangled shards. When Mr. Threader deemed that they had a suitable range of shapes and sizes, they raked it all into a scale-pan and weighed it—both men jotting down the number.

And then both agreed, without having to say it, that they were finished. Daniel saw the visitor out; Mr. Threader had taken a sedan chair so that no one might see the Pesour paying a call on the Master of the Mint, something that would have seemed very fishy indeed.

"Did you—somehow—*influence* the Jury to choose *me?*" Mr. Threader wanted to know.

"I used what influence I could muster."

"Because of my guilty conscience."

"No, in truth, *any* member of the Jury probably could have been swayed, one way or another," Daniel said. "I thought of you because of your skill at prestidigitation. And I hope you can do tricks with coin-snips as well as with whole guineas."

"Most of it is a matter of misdirecting the audience's attention— less dexterity is involved than is commonly supposed. But I shall practice with these tonight."

"Then I shall practice making a distracting spectacle of myself," Daniel promised him.

"Then you shall be up all night long, for it does not come naturally to you."

"I'll be up all night *anyway*," Daniel said, "doing all kinds of unnatural things."

FRIDAY
29 October 1714

✠

Westminster Abbey

MORNING

HE GETS THERE much too early because he overestimated the Hanging-Traffic. *So* many people want to see Jack Shaftoe drawn and quartered that *everyone* has gone early to line the route. Daniel need only walk out of Sir Isaac Newton's town-house, turn his back on the dim roar that resounds against the vault of heaven to the north—a sort of Aurora Borealis of Crowd-clamour—and stroll for a few minutes on quiet streets, and there he is in the Broad Sanctuary: a sweep of open ground splayed out north and west of the Abbey.

He must be a very old and strange man indeed to be approaching a stained Pile such as this one *on official business*. So peculiar is his errand that he falters, knowing not which entrance to use, which presbyter to accost. But the place is all out of kilter anyway because laborers are still taking down the galleries and bleachers put up for the Coronation. Cockney and Irish demolition-men are strutting out the doors with great rough-sawn planks on their shoulders. There is nary a churchman in sight. Daniel elects to go in the west entrance, which seems a bit less congested than the north with bulky blokes and baulks of wood. Moments later he is struck to find himself walking over the stone where Tompion was planted eleven months ago. It being a great peculiarity of this æra that a horologist should be given a resting-place that one or two generations before would have been reserved for a knight or a general.

He puts Tompion's bones behind him, ducks beneath a moving plank, and gets out in to the cloisters. This is a square courtyard framed in a quadrilateral of roofed stone galleries, but otherwise open to the elements. Those elements today consist of raw bright autumn sun and cold turbulent air. Daniel shoves hands in pockets, hunches, and stiff-legs it to the next corner, turns right, follows the East Cloister to its end. There on the left wall is an unmarked medieval fortress-door, massive planks hinged, strapped, gridded, and pierced with black iron. Diverse ancient hand-crafted padlocks depend from its hasp-system like medals on the breast of a troll-general. Daniel has a key to only one of them, and no one else is here. He is freezing. *Men half your age and double your weight have been slain on these wastes by Extremity of Cold.* The cloister blocks the eastern sun but does nothing to shelter him from the breeze, which is coming out of the northwest, striking down into the Cloisters and nearly pinning him to this door. So he back-tracks a few paces and passes through a doorway that does happen to be open. This gets him into a corridor that is out of the wind, but cold and dark. Light beckons at its other end, and he can sense warmth on his face, so he goes that way for several paces, and is rewarded, and astonished, to find himself all alone in the most beautiful room in Britain.

Any other Brit would have known in advance that this was the Chapter House. But because of his Revolutionary up-bringing, this was the least likely place on the Isle for Daniel ever to have set foot—until this day. It is a great octagon whose walls seem to consist entirely of stained glass—a structural impossibility given that the vault overhead consists of numberless tons of stone. It is all held up, he reasons, by pillars at the eight vertices, and a ninth one in the center of the room, so tall and slender it seems doomed to buckle. But it has stayed up for something like four hundred years, and only the most bitter and skeptickal Empiricist would inspect it with such a jaded eye. The place is not going to collapse on him. Those windows are harvesting the sunlight and warming the place. Daniel falls into an orbit around the central pillar. Some of his lessons are coming back to him, and he recalls that this was where the King's Council, and later Parliament, convened until the monks got sick of their hollering and kicked them out and across the street to Westminster Palace. From the way one old man's footfalls and breathing echo around the place, Daniel can't imagine how raucous it must have been when it was filled with politicians.

The brilliant windows capture his attention during the first few orbits, but later his eyes are drawn to the wooden panels below them, at head level. These are painted with scenes that Daniel recognizes, almost without even having to look at them, as the Revelation of that scary lunatick St. John the Divine. The Four Horsemen on their color-coded steeds, the Great Beast spitting terrified Saints, misguided humans queueing up to receive the Mark of the Beast. The Whore drunk on the Blood of the butchered Saints, and later being burned for it. Christ leading the armies of Heaven on a white horse. Much of this is so faded that it can only be made out by one such as Daniel who had to memorize it when he was a boy, so that, like an actor standing backstage awaiting his scene, he'd be able to follow the script, and know his cue, when it happened for real. In the more di-lapidated Mobb-scenes, only the eyes stand out among the faded and peeling pigmentation: some sleepy, some upraised, some darting about for Earthly advantage, others attending to the faraway deeds of Angels, still others lost in contemplation of what it all means. He can not help seeing this all as a final message from Drake. A reminder that, in spite of all Isaac's lucubrations, Isaac still does not know the date and time of the Last Trumpet, and that in spite of all Drake's methodical preparations, Daniel has yet to step out of the wings and play his assigned role.

Footsteps and jolly hallooing come his way: sounds more terrible to his ears than the hoofbeats of the Four Horsemen, for they signify that he shall have to be civil to chaps he barely knows. He turns toward the entrance. In comes the First Lord of the Treasury his Clarke, Writer of the Tallies, and Auditor of the Receipt of the King's Exchequer (one man) in his finest clothes. On his arm is the almost-as-well-turned-out Chamberlain's Deputy of the Receipt of the King's Exchequer. These men, of course, have names and lives, but Daniel has forgot the for-mer, and has no interest in the latter. This is one of those occasions in England when names do not matter, only titles. "Good morning, Dr. Waterhouse!" exclaims the first, "have you your Key?"

It is an inane question, as there'd be no point in Daniel's being here if he didn't have the bloody key; but the man who asks it does so with a twinkle in his eye. It is nothing more than a rhetorical and facetious chat-starter, and perhaps a way of taking Daniel's measure.

"Have you yours, sir?" Daniel returns, and the oppressively cheer-ful Writer of the Tallies (&c.) whips it out of his pocket. Not to be outdone, the Chamberlain's Deputy (&c.) pats his breast; a key hangs on a ribbon there.

Daniel's key is in his left coat-pocket and his hand is clenched around it. In the right pocket, his other hand cradles a small wooden box, like a jewelry-chest, that he nicked from a storage-closet at Isaac's a couple of hours ago. He is struck by a little spell of dizziness for a mo-ment, and spreads his feet wider, as a precaution against toppling and splitting his head on the old floor-tiles. The Key and the Chest, the rite of the Six Padlocks—why, it's as if he's been dropped in to some hid-den, never-published Chapter of the Revelation—perhaps even a whole separate book, an apocryphal sequel to the Bible.

Other voices can be heard out in the cloisters, and Daniel reckons they must be nearing a quorum. Noting Daniel's interest, the Writer of the Tallies steps aside and settles into an after-you posture—whether because of age, rank, or general obsequiousness, Daniel can't tell. Daniel's here as one of the Treasury delegation. He leads the Writer of the Tallies and the Chamberlain's Deputy back out to the gusty Cloister. Men have gathered before the door of the Pyx Chamber, some sitting on the huge mottled stone benches, others standing on stones bearing the names of middling-famous dead people. But when they spy Daniel and the others approaching, all rise and turn—as if he's in charge! Which—given what he's got in his pockets—he has every right to be. "Good morning, gentlemen," he says, and waits for the answering murmur to die down. "Are we all present, then?" He sees a gaudy cleric, but not a bishop (no mitre), and pegs him as the Dean of Westminster. Two other gentlemen step up fondling great keys. Some very junior Church-men stand by with lanthorns at the ready, and there is a contingent of befuddled/suspicious Hanoverian nobles, escorted by a personable English Duke who's been despatched to explain matters to them, and Johann von Hacklheber, serving as interpreter.

"His Majesty's Privy Council have demanded a Trial of the Pyx," Daniel reminds them, "and so provided there are no objections I say that we should give them satisfaction by fetching the necessary bits and conveying them to Star Chamber with no further ado."

There are no objections and so Daniel turns significantly toward the locked door. The First Lord of the Treasury his Clarke, Writer of the Tallies, and Auditor of the Receipt of the King's Exchequer moves into position on one side of him, and another Key-holder on the other. They make a second echelon behind another group of three Key-holders who form up directly in front of the door: the Dean of Westminster, the Chamberlain's Deputy of the Receipt of the King's Exchequer, and a representative of the Company of Goldsmiths. The Dean steps up, pulling off a key that has been dangling on his breast-bone on a golden rope, and sets to work on one of the three padlocks visible on this, the outer door. When he is finished, the other two Key-holders play their parts. The padlocks are carried away in pomp and laid out on the stone bench where important men make it their business to keep an eye on them. The great hasp is dismantled by a brawny Acolyte and the door is pulled open.

Two steps lead down into a small anteroom. The way is barred by a second door, no less formidable than the first. Daniel steps forward and down in to this space, takes out his key, and after a few moments' trial and error, works out which lock it is meant to open. That achieved, he ascends back to cloister level, for there is only room there for one Key-holder and one lanthorn-man. Presently all three inner-door locks have been removed, and brought out into the light, and the hasp is undone. Eyes turn to Daniel again. He goes down in there and puts his shoulder to the door and shoves. It swings halfway open and stops resolutely, as he knew it would. The vault beyond is twice as ancient as the Chapter House. It was rifled during some 13th-Century disturbance—for this is where the Abbey stores its plate and other treasures—and so they installed a stone kerb on the floor so that the door could not be swung fully a-gape, and any future looters would have to ferry the goods out one bauble at a time, as opposed to by the chest-load.

It is Daniel's privilege now to go in, so he takes possession of a lanthorn and side-steps into the Pyx chamber—then quells a misanthropic urge to slam it behind him and bar it, and live here for a thousand years on the Philosopher's Stone. The place is bigger than he'd expected: thirty feet square, with a single squat pillar in the center holding up the four low-slung vaults that converge there and give the place such a hunched, dwarvish feel. After all of this fuss, Daniel's bemused to find that it is just a dusty old storage-cellar with black lock-boxes strewn about according to no especial plan.

Others follow him in. Some seem to know their way around the place. They converge on certain of the treasure-chests, and there is much more finagling with keys. The last group to sack the place were Cromwell's men, who shot the locks off the chests and helped themselves to the Coronation regalia. But Cromwell had needed a sound coinage as badly as any King of old, and so he'd had to mend the chests and replace the locks. Daniel is tempted to point this out as he watches hereditary nobles fumbling with the Puritan hard-ware, but he stifles himself.

Three important objects come out from their respective lock-boxes:

(item) A leather case containing Terrible Documents: the counterpanes of the indentures signed by Isaac and other Mint officials. The First Lord of the Treasury his Clarke takes possession of these.

(item) A boxy wooden chest containing standard weights.

(item) A broader and flatter chest containing standard plates: sheets of precious metal of known fineness, produced in the furnaces of the Company of Goldsmiths. It is against these that Isaac's coins are to be compared.

These three treasures are borne up into the Cloister as if they were royal triplets being trotted out for some fresh air. Long and loud is the clicking of keys and clanging of hasps in their wake. This rite must have been a lot more efficient, Daniel reflects, back in the days when Parliament and the Council both held their deliberations a few paces away in the Chapter House. When the monks booted them out, there must have been some discussion along the lines of "Oh yes, and one of these days we must fetch the Pyx stuff out of the

Abbey and store it where it is actually used." But that was one of those errands that, if not achieved in the first twelve hours, would remain undone centuries later. And, as all of this was shewing, the fetching-out of these three items had long since ossified into a ceremony.

A procession forms up and marches back along the Cloister, into the Transept of the Abbey, and across the Quire. The demolition-crews taking down the galleries in the North Transept seem to sense that something very grave is underway, and shush one another, and clear a path for them; some take their hats off, others stand at attention, holding their crowbars at parade rest. As soon as the last of the parade has gone out the north door, they descend back into joyous mayhem.

The procession right-faces as it clears the door, entering in to a pass between the Abbey and St. Margaret's Church. Their path toward the River is squarely barred by the gloomy, encrusted hulk of Westminster Hall. To the left or north end of it lie those encrustations belonging to the Exchequer, including the Star Chamber. This is where Sir Isaac Newton's travail began, back in June. It is where the final settling of accounts is going to take place now, or as soon as Daniel and the others cross the street.

Chapel of Newgate Prison

IT IS A WHOLE new look for the chapel: the black window treatments have been pulled down, and sentenced to a period of confinement, not to exceed one-eighth of a year, in a wooden box where moths will feed upon them. Light is cautiously admitted through the window-grates. The tourists in the back pews are absent. On the altar before the Condemned pew, the coffin has been replaced with a platter of bread and wine. The wine looks as if it's to be metered out in thimbles, which is an offense to Jack. For if the Church believes, as it plainly does, that a little bit of communion wine is a good thing, then why should not a bucket of it be excellent?

But there'll be plenty of opportunities to get drunk on the way to Tyburn, and so this is a mere passing flicker of annoyance. He is here

to be Churchified. It is the next in the steadily building rite of morti-
fications and tortures that began with the Bell-Man last night and will
culminate, in a few hours, with quartering.

Jack Shaftoe is brought in separately, after the wretches who spent
the night in the Condemned Hold have already been frogmarched
up the aisle and chained to the awful Pew. He feels like a bride, the
last one into the church, the one all heads turn to look at. As well
they might! For Jack got up two hours ago, not wanting to waste a
single minute of this most special of all days, and has spent the intervening time getting dressed up in his Hanging-Suit.

He does not know whence the Hanging-Suit came. It arrived at
dawn, delivered, the turnkey insisted, by a blond man who roared up
in an immense black carriage, and did not speak a word.

Several boxes were needed to contain the entire Hanging-Suit. By
the time Jack first saw it, they'd all been gone through by the gaolers,
to make sure that no shivs, pistols, saws, or Infernal Devices were
wrapped up in the finery. So all was in disarray, all blotched with
grimy hand-prints. And yet the inherent majesty of the Hanging-Suit
was in no way diminished.

The innermost of the Hanging-Suit's three layers—the part that
touches Jack—comprises white drawers of Egyptian cotton, white
hose of Turkish silk, and a shirt made from enough fine white Irish
linen to keep a company of Foot in tourniquets and bandages
through a brief foreign war. And it must be understood that the ad-
jective "white" here means a true, blinding salt-white, and not the
dirty beige that passes for white in poorly illuminated textile markets.

The next layer comprises a pair of breeches, a long-skirted waistcoat, and a coat. All of these are in metallic hues. As a matter of fact,
Jack's pretty sure that they are literally made out of metal. The waistcoat seems to be cloth-of-gold. The breeches and coat are silver. All
of the buttons are golden, which Jack takes to mean that, like counterfeit guineas, they are lumps of solder, cleverly jacketed in whispers
of gold. But when he bites one, it bites back. Only faint impressions
are left by his [false] teeth, and he can see no trace of gray in them—
no evidence of base metal underlying the gold. These buttons were
made by pouring molten metal into a mold, so each one bears the
same imprint: a figure too tiny and involved for Jack's eyes to make it
out in the dimness of his Castle apartment.

The third layer—what comes into contact with the dirt of the
world—consists of black leather shoes with silver buckles; a cape,
purple on the outside, lined with fur, and hemmed and piped and
bebuttoned with additional silver and gold; and a white periwig.

The Hanging-Suit is replete with pockets, several of which came pre-loaded with coins, placing Jack in a position to dispense Civility Money to the sundry turnkeys, gaolers, blacksmiths, drivers, and executioners who'll be handling him during the course of the day. It is extraordinary that those coins were not pilfered and the buttons not ripped off by the gaolers when they inspected the Hanging-Suit; Jack concludes that the Mysterious Personage who brought it to him must have employed not only bribery, but threats of Prosecution and of Physical Violence as well.

On his way up stairs to the chapel here, he has advanced the turnkey a shilling for the following favor:

Upon entering the Chapel, every denizen of Newgate stops in his tracks for a few moments because staggered by a blast of light, a sort of optical fanfare. To be honest, the chapel is just sufficiently illuminated for the Ordinary to read from his hundred-pound Bible. But compared to the rest of Newgate, it's brilliant.

The Lord's House gets the best part of the prison, viz. the southeastern corner of the top floor. This means a few windows face the morning sun, and several more take the sun during the day—assuming there is any sun. Today the sky is cloudless. The favor that Jack has requested of the turnkey is simply that he would like to have a few moments to bask in the sun that streams into one of those east-facing windows, at the back of the chapel, before he is led up to the doleful Pew.

The transaction comes off as agreed. Into the southeast corner Jack goes, and stands in a prism of sunlight for a few moments. His eyes are seared by the radiance of his own clothing. He is forced to gaze out the window for a few moments, to give his stiff creaky old pupils time to shrink down to the size of fleas. He is therefore gazing roughly eastwards, down the length of Phoenix Court. Just below him, Phoenix Court makes a sort of intersection with the Straight and Narrow Way that connects Newgate with the Court of Sessions in the Old Bailey. Moving away from the prison, then, it forms the northern boundary of the garden that spreads behind the College of Physicians.

Gazing over the wall from this privileged vantage-point, Jack is just a bit let down to see that the College of Physicians is still standing. Oh, there are columns of smoke rising from its property. But this is not because the Mobb burned it down last night. The smoke issues rather from cook-fires. The garden in the back has been turned into a bivouac for (counting the tents) a company of soldiers. No, strike that, they are (examining the colours) grenadiers. Of soldiers, these are the biggest (in that they are obliged to march around with large numbers of iron bombs strapped to their bodies), stupidest (obviously), and the most dangerous to the Mobility (considering the effect of a grenade lobbed into a crowd). Just the lot you'd want to have camped out in your garden if you were Noble, and expecting a nocturnal visit from the Mobile.

As long as he's here, Jack takes a moment to fondle one of his golden buttons, and to twist it round for a good look. He notes, first of all, that it's not attached very firmly: just a few threads hold it in place. But he already knew that from fumbling with it in the dark, back in his apartment. What he really wants is to examine the emblem that is molded into every one of those buttons. Now that he has light, he recognizes it instantly: this is the symbol written by Alchemists to denote quicksilver.

These preliminaries, small as they might seem, put all into a new light—and not just literally—for Jack. He allows himself to be escorted up the aisle, very much like a radiant bride, and very much to the dazzlement of his pew-mates and the dismay of the Ordinary.

The only thing lacking is the bridegroom, one Jack Ketch, who is down in his kitchen putting on his black formal attire and getting ready for the big day. But that part of the ceremony will be conducted later, *al fresco,* before, give or take a multitude, the entire population of Southeastern England.

The service follows the usual pattern, complete with Old and New Testament readings chosen to fit the occasion. The Ordinary has pre-positioned bookmarks. The Old Testament one is a length of black grosgrain ribbon that takes him into the type of passage whose sole purpose, in a Christian service, is to demonstrate just how much trouble we would all be in, if we were still Jews. Finishing this, the Ordinary grips three inches' and fifty pounds' worth of pages and heaves them over, bypassing a lot of zany Prophets and tedious Psalms, and dropping smack dab into the New Testament. A small adjustment then takes him to a page that has been marked with the gaudiest, most whorish bookmark Jack's ever seen, a fat swath of yellow silk with a gold medallion dangling from the end. The Ordinary pulls this exhibit all the way out of the Book, gripping the golden disk in his hand, and letting the yellow silk dangle before them, and rather deliberately folds it up and *slips it into his pocket,* all the while keeping a curious eye on Jack.

It occurs to Jack that he is being Sent a Message.

The Ordinary reads. It is not a single continuous selection but a whole series of snippets, for worshippers with short attention spans, and short life expectancies.

"Now about eight days after these sayings he took with him Peter and John and James, and went up on the mountain to pray. And as he was praying, the appearance of his countenance was altered, and his raiment became dazzling white. Luke 9:28–29.

"As they were going along the road, a man said to him, 'I will follow you wherever you go.' And Jesus said to him, 'Foxes have holes, and birds of the air have nests; but the Son of man has nowhere to lay his head.' Luke 9:57–58.

"A man was going down from Jerusalem to Jericho, and he fell among robbers, who stripped him and beat him, and departed, leaving him *half dead*. Now by chance a priest was going down that road; and when he saw him he passed by on the other side. So likewise a Levite, when he came to the place and saw him, passed by on the other side. But a Samaritan, as he journeyed, came to where he was; and when he saw him, he had compassion, and went to him and bound up his wounds, pouring on oil and wine; then he set him on his own beast and brought him to an inn, and took care of him. Luke 10:30–34.

"There was a rich man, who was clothed in purple and fine linen and who feasted sumptuously every day. And at his gate lay a poor man named Lazarus, full of sores, who desired to be fed with what fell from the rich man's table; moreover the dogs came and licked his sores. The poor man died and was carried by the angels to Abraham's bosom. The rich man also died and was buried; and in Hades, being in torment, he lifted up his eyes, and saw Abraham far off and Lazarus in his bosom. Luke 16:19–23."

"I'll be damned, that Luke was a hell of a scribbler," says Jack.

The Ordinary pauses and stares at Jack over his half-glasses.

Bribing the Ordinary is nothing new, of course, it is nearly as ancient and hallowed a ritual as celebrating the Eucharist. But the yellow silk, the gold—this is a kind of signature, a way of letting Jack know just *who* did the bribing.

"Your Reverence, could I trouble you to read the Old Testament passage one more time?"

"I beg your pardon?"

"Read it again. Consider it, sir, to be part of those Duties for which you have been already Compensated."

With great rakings and shovelings of pages, the Ordinary returns to the very beginning of the Tome. The other condemned prisoners shift and mutter; some even rattle their chains. To be hanged by the neck until dead is one thing; but to be forced to listen to a reading from the Old Testament *twice*, why, that is not only Unusual but Cruel.

"Cain knew his wife," the Ordinary intones, "and she conceived and bore Enoch; and he built a City, and called the name of the city after the name of his son, Enoch . . ." There now follows a quarter of an hour of men knowing their wives, and becoming the fathers of other men and living for hundreds and hundreds of years. This was the bit where Jack lost his concentration on the first read-through. And to be perfectly honest he loses it again now, somewhere around the time when Kenan becomes the father of Mahalalel. But he snaps to attention later when the name of Enoch comes up again. "When Enoch had lived sixty-five years, he became the father of Methuselah. Enoch walked with God after the birth of Methuselah three hundred years, and had other sons and daughters. Thus all the days of Enoch were three hundred and sixty-five years. Enoch walked with God; and he was not, for God took him. The Book of Genesis, Chapter 5." And the Ordinary heaves an immense sigh, for he has been reading for a long time, and lo, he thirsteth mightily for the wine on the Lord's Table, for his throat is as dry as a place in the wilderness without water, amen.

"What the hell does that mean? 'Enoch walked with God, and he was not, for God took him'?"

"Enoch was translated," the Ordinary says.

"Even an unlettered mudlark like me knows that the Bible was translated from another tongue, your Reverence, but—"

"No, no, no, I don't mean translated that way. It is a term of *theology*," the Ordinary says, "it means that Enoch did not die."

"Pardon?"

"At the point of death, he was taken away bodily into the afterlife."

"Bodily?"

"His body, rather than dying, was translated away," says the Ordinary. "Is it all right with you if we continue now with the service as planned?"

"Carry on, sir," Jack says. "Carry on."

New Palace Yard, Westminster

EVEN AS DANIEL'S PROCESSION has been assembling in the Cloisters of Westminster Abbey, in other buildings, palaces, and compounds around London other groups have been coalescing in more or less ancient and awesome buildings and converged on Westminster by boat, foot, or gilded carriage, and are now stacked outside of Star Chamber like so many battalions waiting to be summoned onto the Fields of Mars. It is no mean similitude. The Trial of the Pyx is so pompous precisely because it is such a dire and vicious clash. In its rudiments, this is a four-way knife-fight among the Sovereign (here represented by the Lords of the Council and the King's Remembrancer), the Exchequer (which is playing host to the Trial), the Mint (today, synonymous with Sir Isaac Newton), and a medieval guild called the Company of Goldsmiths. In effect, what they are all here to do is to construct an airtight legal case against Sir Isaac, and find him guilty beyond doubt of Treason, in the form of embezzling from the Royal Mint, so that he may be punished straightaway and with no thought of any appeal. The penalties might range from æternal shame and obloquy on up to loss of the right hand (the traditional fate of fraudulent coiners) or even to the same treatment that Jack Shaftoe is about to receive at Tyburn. The challengers are the Goldsmiths, here represented by a jury of chaps in suitably medieval-looking garb, flashy with cloth-of-gold. They are Prosecutors, Mercenaries, and Inquisitors all rolled in to one. The choice is cunningly made, for the Goldsmiths have a natural and long-standing suspicion of the Mint and its produce, which from time to time flares up to out-and-out hostility. Hostility has been the rule during Sir Isaac's tenure. Isaac has found ways to reduce the profit that the Goldsmiths reap when they deliver bullion to the Mint to be coined, and they have retaliated by crafting new trial plates of such fineness that Isaac has been hard pressed to mint guineas pure enough. For the Goldsmiths, as well as others in the money trade, such as Mr. Threader, the rewards of bringing down Isaac shall be immense.

The Serjeant at Arms Attending the Great Seal comes out in to the yard and summons Daniel's contingent. They troop into the Palace and enter presently into Star Chamber. Last time Daniel was in this place, he was tied to a chair and being tortured for sport by Jeffreys. Today the scene's a bit different. The furniture has been removed or pushed to the walls. In the middle of the chamber, planks have been laid down to protect the floor, and bricks piled atop them to make a platform at about the height of a man's midsection. Resting atop this is a small furnace, similar to the one in which Daniel melted his ring last night. Someone must have been up tending it since the wee hours, for it's already heated through, cherry red, and ready to go.

They pass out into a side chamber. Marlborough's here, seated at the high end of a table along with the Lord Chancellor, the Chancellor of the Exchequer, the new First Lord of the Treasury—Roger's replacement—and other Lords of the Council. Seated in the middle of the table, facing the door, and flanked by clerks and aides, is a chap in a white judicial wig, a three-cornered baron's hat, and black robes. This, Daniel reckons, would be the King's Remembrancer: one of the most ancient positions in the Realm. He is the keeper of the Seal that is the *sine qua non* of the power of the Chancellor of the Exchequer, and in the King's name he rides herd on the Exchequer in diverse ways—including presiding over Trials of the Pyx.

Such a Trial cannot even get underway without the necessaries that it has been Daniel's honor to fetch from the Abbey vault. And so what occurs next, encrusted as it might be with protocol and ceremony, is ever so straightforward: Daniel and the other five Keyholders are summoned to the table. The King's Remembrancer asks for the Indentures, the Weights, and the Plates. These are handed over, but not before Daniel and the others have sworn on stacks of Bibles that they are the genuine articles. One of the King's Remembrancer's Clarkes opens up the chest containing the trial plates. There are two of these, one of silver and one of gold: slabs of metal inscribed with great hairballs of cursive asserting just how fine and just how authentic they are, and pocked here and there with goldsmiths' seals. The Clarke reads these aloud. Another contingent of blokes is summoned and sworn: these have come from his majesty the King's Treasury at Westminster, whence they've fetched out a little chest, sealed shut with a lump of wax. The seal is that of the Lord Mayor. The Lord Mayor himself is hauled in, at the head of a jury of twelve Citizens, Mr. Threader among them. The Lord Mayor verifies the seal on the chest. It is opened and a die is removed from a velvet bed. The die is compared, by the Mayor and the Citizens, to the stamps on the trial plates, and all agree that the match is perfect. These are indeed the true plates made by the Goldsmiths as a challenge to Sir Isaac Newton; the Trial may proceed.

Similar rites attend the box of weights. This is lined in green velvet, with neat depressions to contain the individual weights: the largest, a full pint or so of brass, marked *500 shillings* and much smaller ones for *1 shilling* and *4 pence* and *one pence,* &c., &c., and finally a set of ivory-handled tweezers for manipulating the tiniest of them.

"Summon the Goldsmiths," intones the King's Remembrancer. To Daniel and his coterie, he says, "You may stand over there," and waves at an open space in the corner. Daniel leads the group over, and turns around to find the eyes of the Duke of Marlborough on him: a reminder—as if Daniel needed any—that this is it. The new System is facing its first test, and it's doing so under the most adverse possible circumstances: a sick and possibly demented Alchemist is in charge of the Mint and a Vagabond has tampered with the Pyx and is now going to meet his Maker without having coughed up the evidence they want. And Roger's no longer around to make it all better.

The Stone Anvil, the High Hall, Newgate Prison

"I HAVE FOUND GOD!" Jack Shaftoe announces.

"What, *here*!?" says his interlocutor, a heavy-set chap in a black leather hood.

They are standing in a queue in the High Hall. Or rather Jack Shaftoe is, and the hooded man has come up to him, the better to inspect Jack's Hanging-Suit.

The High Hall might be a bit of a grand name for it. It is simply the biggest room in the gaol, outside of the Chapel, and so it is where fitness-conscious felons come to toddle around, in an endless ragged procession. The center of their orbit is a block of stone set in the middle of the floor, and equipped with a few basic smithy-tools. Normally they are a wordy bunch, the Hall a hurricanoe of profanity, a Vortex of Execration. Today they are gagged by their own amazement. All stare inwards toward the two most famous Jacks in London: Shaftoe and Ketch, exchanging civilities like Addison and Steele. There is no sound except for the scraping of their chains on the floor, and the organized chants of the Mobb outside.

Then an ear-splitting clang sounds from the stone anvil. Another prisoner has just had his ankle-fetters struck off. The only restraint upon him now is a length of cord with which Ketch has lately bound his elbows together behind his back.

"The communion-bread, you know, is in the shape of coins," Shaftoe remarks.

Then he thinks better of it, for Ketch thinks it's funny, and forgets himself, and exposes his empty tooth-sockets, as well as a few that are soon to be empty. For the hood unfortunately stops at the level of his nose. Somewhere, Ketch must have a whole foot-locker filled with false teeth, as no man in London is in a better position to collect them; but he has not worn any today.

"But how richer a treasure are those coins of bread, than ones of gold!" Shaftoe exclaims. "For gold and silver may buy admission to a Clubb, or other place of debauchery. But coins of bread have bought me admission to the Kingdom of Heaven. Assuming I can manage a few things in the next couple of hours."

Ketch has utterly lost interest. How many times has he heard this identical speech from a client? He excuses himself very civilly, jumps to the head of the queue, and devotes a few moments to pinioning the next prisoner's elbows with another length of cord.

When Ketch comes back, it is evident he has been thinking about Jack's Hanging-Suit. "After this," he remarks, "it will not be possible for you to change clothes."

"Oh, you are a subtile one, Jack Ketch!" Shaftoe remarks.

"It is just that—according to some who style themselves in the know—you are destitute."

"You think I *borrowed* this suit!? Fie on all such gossip-mongers, Mr. Ketch, you know better than to pay heed to them. This suit is every bit as much my own property, as that handsome hood is yours."

Another clang. Ketch excuses himself again and binds up the bloke who's directly in front of Jack. While he is doing so, he sniffles once or twice, juicily, as if the air in the High Hall does not agree with him. But of all men in London, Ketch must be the least sensitive to miasmas, damps, and vapours.

When Ketch turns back round, Shaftoe's startled, and even a bit alarmed, to see, below the fringe of the hood, a teardrop trickling down his cheek. Ketch steps close to Shaftoe, close enough that Shaftoe, craning his neck (for Ketch is a head taller) can resolve individual cavities in Ketch's last remaining incisor. "You can't imagine what this means to me, Mr. Shaftoe."

"No, I cannot, Mr. Ketch. What does it mean to you?"

"I'm in debt, Mr. Shaftoe, deep in debt."

"You don't say!"

"My Betty—the missus—can't stop having little ones. Every year for the last eight."

"You have eight little Ketches? How remarkable, that a man in your line of work should be such a fount of new life."

"After the last hanging, one of my creditors tried to arrest me in the street! I've never been so ashamed."

"Indeed! For a man in such a respectable profession, to be accosted in a public place, and accused of indebtedness, that is a grave humiliation!"

"What would my boys think of me if I wound up *here*, in Newgate?"

"You *have* wound up here in Newgate, Mr. Ketch. But never mind, I take your meaning."

"They'd have to come and live with me. Here."

"It is not the best environment for raising small children," Shaftoe allowed.

"That's why—excuse me—" Ketch steps behind Shaftoe, draws out another length of cord, and strings it between the latter's elbows. Ketch makes a sliding knot, and begins to draw it tighter, bringing Shaftoe's elbows closer together—but only a bit.

"It would be a shame to wrinkle the Hanging-Suit," Shaftoe remarks.

"A great shame, Mr. Shaftoe, but more important to me is your comfort."

Shaftoe smiles in spite of himself at this polite evasion. And with that smile on his face, he steps forward, raises a knee, and places one immaculate polished shoe on the stone anvil. "Do have a care with that hammer, my good man," he says to the smith—a pox-ravaged prisoner who looks like he has been in Newgate since the Fire. "These clothes mean nothing to me, but they will soon be *inherited* by my good friend Mr. Ketch here. For he is not only my friend, and my sole heir, but the *executor* of my will. By the immemorial traditions of this Realm, all that I wear upon my person, and the contents of its pockets, are *his* at the moment of my expiration. In those pockets reside several coins of diverse denominations. If you go about your work soberly, and leave my shoes unmarked, Mr. Ketch may choose to reach into one of my pockets and fish out a rather large coin for your Civility Money; but if you ruin them, Mr. Ketch may have to recoup his losses by giving you *nothing*."

In consequence of this, the smith spends more time getting Jack's chains off than all the other condemnees put together. But get them off he does, and for his pains receives a handsome shilling from Shaftoe's pocket and Ketch's hand.

The Trial of the Pyx

No two Trials of the Pyx are the same. Details vary depending on whose ox is being gored at the time, and who's goring it. Anciently the Mayor and Citizens of London would stand by and witness the whole rite, which was the most reasonable thing in the world given that the City men had a greater stake in the soundness of the coinage than anyone else. It made for some crowded and riotous Trials, and so at some point a jury of twelve respected City men came to stand in for the whole Citizenry. They would take a hand in those parts of the Trial that did not require any special Guild expertise, and observe the Jury of Goldsmiths carrying out those that did, and when the assayers had rendered their verdict, they would go out into London and relate the good or bad news to their fellow-Citizens.

In recent centuries the presence of the City men has slowly dwindled, to the point where Sir Isaac Newton has felt moved to complain that Trials of the Pyx have become a shadowy rite conducted by a cabal or conspiracy of Goldsmiths, unobserved and unaccountable. It is safe to say the Goldsmiths are no more pleased by these remarks than by anything else Isaac has done during his tenure at the Mint. Still and all, the entire point of the exercise is to prove Isaac a traitorous fraud, and, if at all possible, to see his hand chopped off in New Palace Yard. All of which is less likely to come to pass if Isaac can make a credible case that the Trial is rigged by a shadowy Guild. So for today's Trial the pendulum has swung back as far as it can without inviting the whole City. It is a full-dress, dual-Jury affair. The City's represented not only by the Lord Mayor but also by a full jury of twelve Citizens, separate from and independent of the jury of Goldsmiths. And they'll not just watch but—mostly through their chosen delegate, Mr. Threader—participate. Only after these dozen Citizens have been recognized and sworn and shunted off to their own corner is it time for the Principals to be brought in and the Trial to begin in earnest.

The King's Remembrancer asks for the Pyx. Out goes the Serjeant at Arms. A minute later he's back with the Earl of Lostwithiel in tow, and behind Lostwithiel are four more King's Messengers carrying a palanquin on which rests the Pyx. This is set down before the table, and Lostwithiel avers that it really is the Pyx and that he fetched it in good order straight from the Tower, and no monkey business along the way.

The King's Remembrancer then asks the Serjeant to summon the second Jury: that of the Goldsmiths. A minute later, the Twelve troop in, all a-gleam, and line up before him. They cannot take their eyes off the Pyx, at least not until the King's Remembrancer speaks, as follows: "Do you swear that you shall well and truly, after your knowledge and discretion, make the assays of the monies of gold and silver that have been reposited in the Pyx, and truly report if the said monies be in weight and fineness according to the King's standards of his Treasury, and also if the same monies be sufficient in allay, *et cetera*, according to the Covenant comprised in the Indenture thereof made between the King's grace and the Master of his Mint, so help you God?"

"We do," say the Jury of Goldsmiths.

Satisfied of that, the King's Remembrancer asks for the Master of the Mint: the man, and the moment, everyone has been waiting for. All bodies and heads and eyes turn to follow the Serjeant out of the room, then remain motionless as his boot-steps recede through Star Chamber and the gallery beyond.

They wait, and wait, and wait, until every man jack in the room is quite certain that it really is taking longer than it ought to—*much* longer—*something* must be out of joint. A member of the City jury can be heard mumbling some kind of witticism. One of the goldsmiths says clearly, "Perhaps he's at the hanging!" and another responds, "Perhaps he's run off to France!" whereupon he is furiously shushed by no less than the Duke of Marlborough.

When all of that noise and bother die down, it is finally possible to hear people approaching Star Chamber—rather more people than the King's Remembrancer asked for. The entourage, if that's what it is, bates outside. The Serjeant comes in. On his arm is a young woman. They cross the floor of Star Chamber; her head turns to gaze curiously at the assayer's furnace, whose red light shines on her, so that Daniel recognizes her as Catherine Barton.

She comes in to the chamber and is heralded by the Serjeant. Great is her fame, of course, and so the amount of ogling that now takes place is beyond all boundaries of dignity. It almost would have been better if she had showed up stark naked. "My lords," she says, for with so many dignitaries in the room she daren't speculate as to who is in charge, "Sir Isaac Newton is ill. I have sat by his bed this last week and I beseeched him not to answer your summons. He would not heed me, but gave orders that he was to be brought here this morning no matter what. He is very weak, and so, if it please my lords, I have arranged to bring him here in his sedan chair. With your permission, I'll have him brought in thusly."

"As his nurse, Miss Barton, is it your opinion that he is fit to understand what is going on around him, and to be tried?" asks the King's Remembrancer.

"Oh, yes. He knows," Miss Barton insists, "however, because he is so very weak, he requests that Dr. Daniel Waterhouse act as his spokesman." And, having now fixed on the King's Remembrancer as the boss, she steps forward and hands him a letter, presumably written in Isaac's hand, saying as much.

Generally not one to seize the moment, Daniel acts all out of character now by striding in to the middle of the room while most eyes are still trying to pick him out in the crowd. "If Sir Isaac's proposal is acceptable to my lords, then I shall be honoured to serve as his hand and voice."

There is a certain amount of looking back and forth now, but this does not alter what is inside the Pyx, or what is written on the indenture, and so in the end it does not really matter. Suddenly, important heads are nodding all around the room. "It is so ordered," says the King's Remembrancer, not before reading the letter through twice. "You have the gratitude of the Council, Dr. Waterhouse. Er, shall we have Sir Isaac's chair brought in, then?"

"There is no precedent for this, and so pray allow me to suggest one," Daniel says. "We are soon to move in to the Star Chamber for the Assay, are we not? Then rather than move Sir Isaac twice, I suggest we make him comfortable straightaway in Star Chamber. He can hear the indenture being read from there."

"So ordered!"

Miss Barton curtseys her way out and flits across Star Chamber, calling to Daniel with her eyes. Daniel excuses himself and backs out. Heads lean in and faces turn to line the doorway. Daniel is confronted by the black obelisk of Isaac's sedan chair, suspended between two astonished-looking porters. Miss Barton is hissing directions: "In the corner! The corner! No, that one!" There is some almost comical turning about, but finally they understand what she wants: for the sedan's door to face toward a corner of Star Chamber so that when the door is open Isaac, in his pitiful state, won't be visible to the entire Chamber. Finally they get it set down the way she wants it. Daniel side-steps through a narrow gap between pole and wall, and backs in to the corner. He glances up one time to see all of those faces in the next room peering through the doorway at him. Then he undoes the latch on the sedan chair's door and opens it. The first thing he sees is a hand, pale and still, gripping an ornate key. He opens the door farther, letting light shine in so that he can see Isaac sprawled against the wall of his black box, eyes open and mouth a-gape, perfectly still. Daniel need not check his pulse to be certain that what he is looking at, here, is the recently deceased corpse of Sir Isaac Newton, dead at age seventy-one of Newgate gaol-fever.

The Press-Yard, Newgate Prison

TEN MINUTES LATER they are down in the Press-Yard, just off Phoenix Court. It is called a Yard but is really nothing more than a fortified alley. A short caravan is drawn up there, waiting to convey them all to Tyburn: a wagon containing various tools of Mr. Ketch's trade; a spacious open cart, already loaded with empty coffins; and, drawing up the rear, a sledge. The cart is for most of the condemnees, for Ketch, and for the Ordinary. The sledge is reserved for Shaftoe, it being the tradition that a traitor be dragged to his death facing backwards. Mere hanging is too good for such a vile person, wheels are too nice.

As the condemnees progress from each stage to the next, their entourage grows. Here in the Press-Yard there must be two score men, mostly gaolers with cudgels, but a few constables as well. Jack's beginning to see blunderbusses. A sort of corridor is formed, tending to funnel them straight to the big cart. The other prisoners clamber up and sit down, using coffin-lids as benches. Jack is directed to his wheelless land-barge, which has a plank to sit on, but no coffin; by the end of the day, a coffin, or indeed any other container, will be quite wasted on him.

Mr. Ketch, who is nothing if not organized, opens one of the several lockers on his supply-wagon, and pulls out several lengths of rope. Each of them has a hangman's noose in one end. He tosses all but one of them into the big cart, then circles around to the rear where he addresses Jack.

"It's a fine one, eh?" he exclaims, holding up the noose.

"If you were not wearing a black hood you'd be glowing with pride, Mr. Ketch. But I do not know why."

"This rope I got from a pirate-captain I hanged last year."

"He supplied his own rope?"

"Indeed. A hawser, he called it. Look at the thickness of it."

"He wanted to be sure the rope would not break? That seems very odd to me."

"No, no, I'll show you!" And Ketch steps round to Shaftoe's left side and fits the noose over the latter's head. The rope is so thick and stiff, the noose so tight, that it can barely close around Shaftoe's throat. But the knot lodges under his left ear like a great bony fist. "Feel that leverage—now you'll take my meaning, sir!" Ketch says, pulling up once or twice on the loose end of the rope. Each time he does, the knot, bearing on the heel of Shaftoe's skull, crowbars his entire head forward and to one side. "And look at the length of it!" Shaftoe turns to see that Ketch has retreated to a distance of some two fathoms, but still has not run out of rope. "With this I can give you a drop such as few men are afforded, Mr. Shaftoe, very few. By the time you get to the end of this rope you'll be moving as fast as a cannonball. You'll be smoking a pipe in Heaven long before I chop off your testicles and shovel your guts out; and the quartering will mean as little to you, as coffin-worms to a dead bishop."

"You are a princely fellow, Mr. Ketch, and Betty is fortunate to have you."

"Mr. Shaftoe," says Jack Ketch in a lower voice, stepping up very close to him now, and absent-mindedly wrapping the loose rope into a neat coil, "I shan't have leisure to exchange words with you again, until we are standing beneath the Tree. For I've other prisoners to tend to, as you can see, and the journey to Tyburn promises to be, er . . ."

"Festive?"

"I was going to say 'eventful,' not wanting to show disrespect. I'll be in the cart. We shall not be able to hear each other. Since you're facing backwards, we shall not be able to *see* each other. Even when we are face to face beneath the Tree, the noise will be such that we'll not be able to exchange a word, though we scream in each other's ears. So I say to you now, sir, thank you! Thank you! And know that you shall feel less pain today than a man who bangs his head on a door-frame in a dark room."

"In the way of pain, I ask for nothing more nor less than what I deserve," says Shaftoe, "and I shall entrust you, Mr. Ketch, with that determination."

"And I shall prove worthy of that trust sir! Farewell!" says Jack Ketch.

He turns his back on Shaftoe as if he's afraid he might cry again. He straightens his back, works on his composure, smooths down his hood, and steps up into the cart, where he has other clients waiting.

Star Chamber

THE NEXT TIME Daniel has his wits about him, the King's Remembrancer is reading some document aloud, declaiming in the hoarse lope of one who has been reading for quite a long while. Daniel looks through the doorway to see the King's Remembrancer peering through half-glasses at a generously sized parchment with a zigzag edge: one of the counterpanes of an indenture. This would be the contract that Isaac signed when he became Master of the Mint. It is one of the treasures that Daniel fetched out of the Abbey vault. What it says is that Isaac accepts sole personal responsibility for whatever is about to be found in the Pyx. It probably seemed like a lot of dry legal gibberish when Isaac signed it, but as the words resound through Star Chamber in the hearing of all the most important men in the Realm, it strikes him as so very grave and formidable as to make Isaac almost lucky to be dead. Daniel notes that he is the object of curious scrutiny by several of those men, and so he fixes his gaze on Isaac's dead face, smiles, nods, and makes a *sotto voce* remark as if chatting with the sick man.

The Indenture draws to a thunderous end with invocations of God and of the Sovereign, and then the King's Remembrancer looks up and demands the three keys of the Pyx.

In taking Isaac's key out of his hand, Daniel notes that *rigor mortis* has not set in yet. He can't have been dead for long.

The other Key-holders of the Pyx have already undone their respective locks by the time Daniel gets in there. Only one lock remains: a beauty, made to look like the front of the Temple of Solomon. Daniel gets it open and flips the hasp out of the way. Two members of the City jury step up and raise the lid of the Pyx. The cervical vertebrae of the Great and the Good pop and creak all round as they vie to see what's in it: a pile of wee leather packets, called Sinthias, each labeled with a month and a year.

"Very well," says the King's Remembrancer, "the Jurors may withdraw to Star Chamber to conduct the Assay."

While the Jurors are still mumbling and shuffling, Daniel strides out, key in hand, and makes for the sedan chair. Miss Barton has taken up a position in front of it, facing into the room, as if to block any well-wishers—or ill-wishers, for that matter—from trying to get close to her uncle. She's a bit red around the eyes, but when Daniel comes up to place a steadying hand on her shoulder, she feels solid and strong beneath the sleeve of her frock, and after a moment she shrugs him off and directs him toward the corner with a flick of her eyes. Many a London man-about-town has dreamed of receiving a come-hither look from those lovely Orbs, but Daniel will have to settle for what he's just been given: a go-thither look. "He said," she says, "that you would know what to do."

So he goes into the corner, opens the door again, and verifies that Isaac's still dead (which might seem a safe enough thing to assume; but with Isaac, you never know). He leans his head and shoulders into the box now, and checks under Isaac's armpit: still tepid. Looking up, he has a full view of the back of Catherine Barton's bodice and all of Star Chamber beyond. The black screen darkens everything somewhat, but his eyes soon enough adjust. No one, of course, can see him or Isaac.

On a large table next to the furnace, the City jurors dump out the contents of the Pyx. Sinthias gush out and mound up. A few roll to the floor and are chased down and snatched back. The Pyx is set upright, open, and empty, on the floor. The twenty-four Jurors—Goldsmiths and Citizens working all together, for the nonce—go through the heap, reading the label on each Sinthia, and divide them into two piles: one containing silver coins—shillings, sixpence, and various other penny denominations—and the other gold: guineas, and the odd five-guinea piece. Daniel notes that Mr. Theader has established a commanding position at the end of the table where the gold coins are being piled. Before him is a great two-pan scale. He is wielding a jack-knife, making quick work of the Sinthias, cutting the Yellow Boys out of their leathern straitjackets and stacking them on the table. From time to time he will cup one in his hand and toss it: as always, Daniel cannot make out whether this is a mere nervous tic, or a studied effort to judge its weight.

As the Trial of the Pyx seems well in hand, Daniel turns his attention to matters inside the sedan chair.

He said you would know what to do. Well, yes and no.

Daniel has studied a document, written in Hooke's hand, asserting that a patient (who happened to be one Daniel Waterhouse, but that is neither here nor there) died, and was brought back to life by a coction brewed up by an Alchemist. Hooke set down the receipt as best as he could from memory. Later Isaac went through and studied this, as only Isaac could study a thing, and made any number of annotations to it, all in the mythology-ridden argot and the queer symbology of the Esoteric Brotherhood. Daniel knows more than he'd like to of such things, from having spent so much of his young life around such people, and he's had a few days to go over Hooke's receipt and Newton's commentary and puzzle out what they mean. Isaac has made several attempts in recent weeks to carry out all of the steps in the procedure save the last, and so all of the necessary crucibles, retorts, &c. were lying out in plain sight on his laboratory-table when Daniel began work a couple of days ago, and all of the ingredients were there, too. All, that is, except for the last and most crucial.

Out of his pocket Daniel now takes the small wooden chest. He sets it on Isaac's lap and opens it. The contents are a stoppered glass flask containing a red liquid, and a paper packet, like a wee Sinthia no bigger than Daniel's fingernail. Daniel unfolds this with great care to expose a small quantity of gold dust. This is what remains of the ring that Solomon Kohan gave him, which Daniel melted last night to make a counterfeit guinea. Half of that guinea was snipped up into tiny shards that ought to be up Mr. Threader's sleeve just now. The rest of it Daniel tediously rubbed against a file until it was all gone, and collected the dust of it into this paper packet. The particles are so fine that one needs a microscope to view them; this ought to mean that their superficies are enormous, and easily penetrable by any surrounding menstruum. Right now that happens to be air, and not much seems to be happening. But it is time to carry out the last step, which is to place them in a very different menstruum, altogether more reactive. Daniel picks up the phial of scarlet fluid and thumbs the cork out of it, then, practically in the same motion, pours the dust of the Solomonic Gold into the fluid. He replaces the cork and, holding the flask between his palms, clamps the stopper in place with both thumbs and gives it a shake.

A red-orange glow suffuses the interior of the sedan chair. Daniel perceives that it is light shining through the flesh of his hands. But there is no warmth: this is like *kaltes feuer*, the cold fire of Phosphorus.

He stuffs the phial under the flap of Isaac's coat so that the unearthly light won't shine through the window of the sedan chair, then risks taking the cork off. It is like staring into the swirling and lambent clouds of a thunderstorm. A scent reaches his nostrils, which he cannot identify, but he knows he's smelled it before, and it brings a powerful urge to lift this draught to his lips and drink it down. He masters this, and considers how to get it into Isaac. It is to be administered orally, he knows that. But how does one get a dead man to drink? Hooke's notes said something about a spatula. Tilting the vial, Daniel observes that the magma is thick, like porridge—it is congealing. If he waits much longer, he fears, it will be solid and unusable. Daniel grabs the only spatulate object near to hand: the key to Isaac's padlock. Using this as a spoon, he digs out a gob of the bright stuff as big as the last joint of his little finger, and introduces it to Isaac's mouth, flips it upside-down, and wipes it off on Isaac's tongue.

He looks out the window, fearful that someone will have noticed the light. But all eyes are on a grave rite being conducted by Mr. Threader: a pile of guineas has been placed on one pan of his great Barock scale, and on the opposite pan, one of the standard weights from the Abbey vault.

He spoons out another gob. Half of the stuff is now gone from the phial. It continues to congeal, but it is still manageable. It has the useful property of adhering to itself more than to anything else, somewhat like mercury; it leaves no wetness, no residue on the inside of the phial or on the key. The final spoonful seems to take with it every last trace of the stuff, and the key emerges from Isaac's mouth clean. Daniel notes that the glow has vanished, and now for the first time risks bringing his trembling hand to Isaac's mouth and pulling his jaw down so that he can inspect the inside of the mouth. He is shocked to find that all of the stuff is gone, as if it had never existed. It has diffused into Isaac's flesh: the vegetative spirit, if that's what it really is, pervading the inert matter of the corpse.

"I find that these coins are satisfactory for weight," Mr. Threader announces, "and so I propose that we now prevail upon our good friends, the Company of Goldsmiths, to assay the metal for fineness." As Mr. Threader says this, he glances toward Daniel.

"The Company of Goldsmiths stands ready to conduct the assay," announces the eldest of that jury. "We have nominated Mr. William Ham as Fusour."

William steps forward and addresses Mr. Threader. "I shall require a fair sample of the metal having an aggregate weight of twelve grains, if you please, sir."

"It is my honour to have been nominated Pesour by the Jury of Citizens," says Mr. Threader agreeably. "I propose to give you your twelve grains by cutting small amounts from several coins, as is the established practice."

"The Company of Goldsmiths assents," says the Fusour.

"Then let the guineas from the Sinthias be mixed that a fair sample may be drawn," says the Pesour.

With that, all the stacks of guineas piled on the table are swept off, in a clashing golden avalanche, into the Pyx. Watched intently by twenty-three other jurors—and now by Daniel, who has withdrawn from the sedan chair, and come over to observe—one of the Citizens stirs through the guineas with his hand, mixing them thoroughly. When that has gone on for long enough, he averts his gaze, displays an empty hand to the room, thrusts it into the middle of the Pyx, and pulls out a single guinea, which he places on the table before the Pesour.

Each of the other eleven City men does the same. A dozen guineas, chosen at random, are now lined up on the table before Mr. Threader.

Church of St. Sepulchre

All good people, pray heartily unto God for these poor Sinners, who are now going to their Death, for whom this great Bell doth toll. You that are con-demned to die, repent with lamentable Tears; ask Mercy of the Lord for the Salvation of your souls through the Merits, Death, and Passion of Jesus Christ, who now sits on the right Hand of God, to make intercession for as many of you as penitently return unto Him. Lord have Mercy upon you! Christ have Mercy upon you!
—THE BELL-MAN OF ST. SEPULCHRE'S

WHEN THEY DRAG HIM OUT of the Press-Yard he's startled to see that they've actually dropped the portcullis, severing Newgate Street *intra muros* from Holborn *extra*. He can hear a seething Mobb on the other side of it, but not see them, as a squadron of mounted soldiers is drawn up on the near side of the mighty Grate, forming up as if to mount a sally.

Presently, his private ceremonial sledge slews itself round in the street so that he is facing abaft, which means gazing down Newgate toward the heart of old London Town. This ought to provide him a more or less straight view down Newgate and Cheapside all the way to the 'Change, miles away; but instead all he sees is more soldiers. Squadrons are issuing from Phoenix Court on the right, and the grounds of Christ's Hospital on the left, and forming up in the wide part of the street behind him. This is unusual.

The air feels heavy, pushing in queerly on his skull. Because of the crowd-noise it is difficult to discern why, at first; then he recollects that every bell in London is ringing, muffled, to announce the Hanging-March.

The first leg of the three-mile journey encompasses somewhat less than a hundred yards, that being the distance from the portcullis of Newgate to the Church-Yard of St. Sepulchre's. It only takes them about twenty minutes, which makes Jack phant'sy this isn't going to be so very difficult as popular legend would have one believe. He remembers these things as being a good deal bigger and rowdier. But then he hasn't attended one since before the Plague, and everything seemed larger through a child's eyes.

Still and all, he has plenty of time to rid himself of the cord that Jack Ketch used to link his elbows. Being loose to begin with, it scrapes off easily on the rough planks of the sledge. He's about to toss it away into the crowd when he gets to looking at it, and thinks it might have other uses. Jack—who's lived on ships, and knows his knotwork—has a bowline in the end of it before the Mobb can chant "Jack Shaftoe!" and slips this over the toe of his shoe. It catches on the heel, and makes a kind of stirrup. With a few undignified gestures he is able to thread it up his leg, beneath his breeches. Then, reaching down his front, he pulls it up under his shirt so that it emerges from his collar, just at the base of his throat. And now his seamanship once again comes into play as he whips that cord round the noose a few times, and makes it fast.

Though he can't see forward, he knows they are before St. Sepulchre's, because its muffled bell has become very loud, and is now reinforced by a familiar but unwelcome clang. The Bell-Man once again has added his monotonous note. He is reinforced by the Vicar of that church and diverse acolytes and hangers-on. Most of these, Jack peevishly suspects, only agreed to this duty so that they could get excellent front-row seats to the Hanging-March.

Some sort of ritual—completely inaudible to Jack, who is half-deaf in the best of circumstances—plays out on the steps of the church. It is for his benefit, he knows. He is ready to give the Bell-Man another round of abuse. But he bates. Tiresome though these people are, they have his best interests at heart, and some of the lesser criminals up on the cart might derive comfort from this.

The general idea, here, is that back in the old days, when St. Sepulchre's sat outside the City Gate on the Edge of Nowhere, this was the last church that any Tyburn-bound prisoner would ever see, and hence marked his absolutely final opportunity to repent. This being the London of today, they'll pass any number of Wren-churches between here and the Fatal Tree. But tradition is tradition. And so the Church of England gets a few points for sheer persistence.

The rite, whatever it is, doesn't last long, and then the church-folk come out with little nosegays for the prisoners, and cups of wine. Jack accepts both with good grace, reaching deep into his pockets for Civility Money. This gesture is noted by the crowd and garners a roar of approval, which comes to Jack's ears as a great sea tearing into a pebbly beach a mile away. And so Jack beckons the Bell-Man over and gives him a whole guinea for his pains—though not before biting down on it. This jest elicits laughs even from the soldiers. Finally, since this is going over so well, he gets the Vicar to descend the steps, and hands over another guinea—his last—for the poor-box, and shakes his hand. And nearly jerks the poor fellow's arm out of its socket, as the sledge has started up again. This thanks to Ketch, who has not failed to notice Shaftoe's guineas—which is to say, *Ketch's* guineas—disappearing into the undeserving hands of Church-men! Ketch gets the caravan moving double-time, as if they were being menaced from the rear by a Horde of Mongols. Not until they are well clear of the danger, and moving along at a good steady clip, does Ketch turn his attention back to Shaftoe. His mouth is half-open. His rotting jaw is slack. *What on earth were you thinking!?* he seems to say, *I could have fed my family for a year on what you just gave away!*

Thus is Jack jerked away from St. Sepulchre's behind without even having had time to think about repentance—which was supposed to have been the entire point of stopping there. Either he has already repented, back in Newgate Chapel this morning, or else he never will.

But, in all seriousness, he thinks he might have repented. Something happened there, in truth. A sort of portcullis clanged down, severing the long, bad part of his life from a shorter and better part of it. It is all bound up, somehow, with that procedure of eating the coin of bread. But there is a powerful point to that rite, and he reckons it has something to do with a joining together, a sharing with everyone else who's ever accepted payment in that coinage, God's Legal Tender. In sum, Jack feels strangely one with all of Christendom this morning—which is not by any means a familiar way for him to feel—and Christendom seems to reciprocate those tender feelings, for all of it has turned out to see him off.

Now at last he begins to comprehend the immensity and power of the Mobb. Until this point he has seen it at a remove, like a man watching a play. Now there is a reversal. Jack is the poor player having his hour on the stage, and the audience is all of London. Or since so many appear to have come in from out of town, let's just call it all of the Universe. They react to his merest gesture. They even react to things he hasn't actually done. Seams of laughter rip through the crowd in response to jests he is rumored to have uttered. Not one person in an hundred even knows of his own knowledge that Jack is here, because most of them (as Jack recollects from having been a part of such Mobbs) can only see others' backs. They have been drawn here by the legend that Jack Shaftoe will be drawn to Tyburn on a sledge, and having come, and being unable to see him, they get by on the suspicion that he is out there somewhere. Jack Ketch—still stung and dismayed by the loss of those two guineas—is without a doubt the foremost member of the audience, viewing Jack's performance from, as it were, his own private box-on-wheels.

Jack guesses that every constable, beadle, bailiff, watchman, and gaoler in London is included in the entourage. Even for a normal Hanging-Day this does not suffice to hold back the crowd, and so there are always soldiers with half-pikes. But today there are these mounted squadrons as well. Jack had supposed at first that they were cavalry, but quickly knew from their colors that they were actually the King's Own Black Torrent Guards—no less than the terrible Dragoons who keep the Tower. Awfully nice of them to come out for his execution considering all of the trouble he has put them to in recent months. 'Tis a splendid gesture, and probably a calculated one. Of all His Majesty's regiments, none would be more avid to witness his death, none less likely to allow him to slip away. And so all that Jack sees of the Mobb, he sees by peering, through his low, sledge-back vantage-point, between the scissoring legs of the Dragoons' mounts. But he sees plenty.

The King's Own Black Torrent Guards have blundered into a sort of pincer now, and allowed themselves to be enveloped. For to the north of St. Sepulchre's is Smithfield, a largish open space, site of the cattle market, and used for occasional burnings at the stake.* The two great streets that curve down from Smithfield are Gilt-Spur, which they've already passed, and Cow-Lane, which is ahead. Smithfield, it is now obvious, has served as an immense gathering-place and holding-pen for hanging-watchers; for at least the past day, and

---

*Females who are found guilty of High Treason are punished thus, rather than being subjected to the indecency of what is about to happen to Jack.

probably longer, revelers have congregated there to hurl spent gin-bottles into howling bonfires. The ringing of the church-bells has served as their signal, and now they are flooding down Gilt-Spur Street and Cow-Lane. This puts a million of them in front of the procession and a million behind.

Cow-Lane joins Holborn near the eastern end of the bridge that Hooke threw over Fleet Ditch some years ago. This is therefore a strategic intersection. If the procession were somehow blocked there by the Mobb, it would have no way of getting across the streaming shit-flume of the Fleet, it would be bottled up, unable to reach the killing-ground. Jack can't see it, but he knows they're headed that way, because the earth is tilting beneath the sledge, causing him to recline ever so gently. They are descending Snow Hill. The whole parade should grind to a halt at any moment. But to his surprise they make the turn at the base of the hill without delay, and cross onto the pavers of the bridge. They are halfway across the Fleet Ditch before Jack perceives why: a company of artillery has established a bridgehead there, and set up several cannons, presumably loaded with grapeshot and chains, pointed up Cow-Lane towards Smithfield. A few yards farther along is another battery aimed south along the stony brink of the Ditch, holding back a hundred thousand or so who have formed up there. The Mobb is thus obliged to watch his passage from a remove. Jack stands up in his sledge and waves an arm. Ten thousand people surge to glimpse the great event. It is difficult to guess how many are crushed; but at least a hundred of them are projected over the kerb into the Ditch. Jack sits down, not wishing to be responsible for any more such mayhem. Another score of spectators tumble into the Fleet.

Star Chamber

TWELVE GRAINS IS A FORTIETH of an ounce; and gold being the densest thing in the world, a fortieth of an ounce is smaller than a pea. Yet such is the precision of the Goldsmiths' techniques that they can conduct a reliable assay with so tiny a sample. To take the twelve grains from a single coin would defeat the purpose of the whole undertaking, for such a test might be queered by a freak of chance: a meaningless surplus or deficit of gold in one particular coin. Hence the mixing and sampling that has led to Mr. Threader's having a dozen guineas set out on the cloth before him. He has come armed with a pair of mighty long-handled snips. He stands up for better leverage, and in short order has cut each of the dozen guineas into halves. He then works his way down the row of twenty-four half-guineas, snipping off their sharp corners. There ought to be forty-eight of these. They are so tiny that they appear to Daniel as points of fire on Threader's black velvet cloth, echoing the stars painted on the ceiling of this chamber. Like a mad demiurge, Mr. Threader creates a little cosmos crowded with half-moons and strewn stars. He then begins to impose Order on his own Chaos, picking up the halved guineas and setting them to one side, while herding the stars into a globular cluster in the middle. It seems that his old fingers have difficulty picking up the wee bits, for he raises his hand to his mouth once or twice and licks his fingertips, like a scholar who is having difficulty getting traction on a page. Everyone is watching this closely, though Daniel's mind is a bit distracted still because of that business with Isaac. He turns his head thataway, and notes that the Lord Privy Seal has ventured out of the side chamber where he and all of the great big-wigs are supposed to be awaiting the verdict of the Jury. His lordship has got it into his head that he is going to say hello to Sir Isaac, and turns that way purposefully. But Catherine has read his mind, has tracked his doddering progress, giving him the evil eye the whole way. He's too blind or careless to notice. She steps into his path. Daniel averts his gaze, not wishing to see the Catastrophe of Manners that's in the offing.

"Pray, my lord, do *not*, I beg you," cries Catherine Barton from the corner of the room. All heads turn that way except for that of Daniel, who is just turning round the other way.

Mr. Threader glances up over his half-glasses, reaches down, and puts the tip of his long finger on a star. When he withdraws his hand, it's gone—the star has been snuffed out. But another one tumbles to the cloth in its place. This he seizes between thumb and index finger, picks up, and drops upon the little mound that he's making in the middle. He brings his fingertips to his mouth again to lick them, and Daniel sees a fleck of gold come away on the tip of his tongue and disappear, he supposes, right down Mr. Threader's epiglottis. Then Mr. Threader rubs his hands together as if they're chilly—which they probably are. He favors Daniel with a wink.

The crisis in the corner has been sorted out somehow; heads are turning back toward the Pesour. He stands there motionless, hands at his sides, as if he has not moved a muscle during this little *con-tretemps*. "Sir Isaac is grown so reclusive of late, one can't but wonder what it is he's trying to hide from us!" Mr. Threader remarks, in a clearly audible aside to one of the Goldsmiths. "I daresay all his se-crets shall be discovered in a few minutes' time; he can hide from Lord Privy Seal but not from *this*." Nodding at the furnace.

Daniel is by and large a great stifler of urges and hider of feelings; but he knows that this is a cue. "You *dog*!" he exclaims, and takes half a step forward, reaching around himself, groping for the ridiculous sword he's hung on himself for the occasion, and half yanking it from its scabbard. In that moment every face in the room turns to-ward him. Mr. Threader snuffs out another star, lets another one fall from between his fingers, and reloads.

"Dr. Waterhouse," he says, mumbling a bit, probably because he is in the act of swallowing a bit of a guinea, "my old friend! Are you feel-ing quite all right?"

"I am no friend of *yours*, sir!" Daniel cries, and makes to draw the sword all the way out; but then younger and stronger hands are on his arm, and someone has moved to block his path to Mr. Threader. "I am a true friend of Sir Isaac Newton—a man so dedicated, so loyal to his King and to his craft that he has come here to-day in spite of being laid low with illness!" Daniel shoves the sword back in to its sheath, spins, and takes a few paces back into the open space between the Jurors and Miss Barton. All eyes track him except for those of Mr. Threader, who is up to more conjuring. "You would do well to remember, sir, that it is your solemn duty to conduct this assay justly and truly, and in spite of the enmity that your profession bears toward Sir Isaac. The Lords of the Council—" and here Daniel turns to gesture with one hand toward the door of the side chamber. The unfamiliar scabbard swings around and whacks him on the ankle, which gives him an idea—he hooks a toe over it, flails his arms, and tumbles to the floor.

It's all the Jurors can do not to laugh out loud. But soon enough they are struck dumb by two very different, yet equally mesmerizing sights: first of all Catherine Barton rushing forward and bending down to assist Daniel, so that everyone's able to stare down her bodice. Second, the Duke of Marlborough striding in from the next room in high dudgeon.

"What in the name of—" he begins, then stops, lost in contempla-tion of Miss Barton's cleavage.

" 'Tis nothing, my lord, if you please, a momentary flaring of warm feelings, as when a log bursts on a hearth, and sparks fly," says Mr. Threader. "The only sparks that matter to us are these." He ges-tures with both hands at the pile of golden bits he has made on the cloth. "If, as I hope, Dr. Waterhouse's exertions have left him quite uninjured, then I shall weigh out twelve grains of these."

"I am . . . fine," Daniel announces. "Thank you, Miss Barton," he says, for she's just hauled him to his feet, and is spanking the dust from him. "I am sorry," he concludes. "Pray continue, Mr. Threader."

Working now with a pair of tweezers, Mr. Threader moves granules of gold one by one from the pile of snips to one of the pans of his great Scale. On the opposite pan he places a twelve-grain weight from the set that was stored in the Abbey. After a minute the scale-pans begin to move. The Pesour goes into a protracted and tedious work of swapping larger bits for smaller ones, or sometimes snipping a bit in half to make change, as it were.

Finally Mr. Threader steps back from the table, hands upraised like a priest's. "I say," he intones, "that on the pan of yonder scale is a sample of metal fairly chosen from the coins in the Pyx, weighing twelve grains exactly; and I invite the Fusour to assay it."

William Ham steps up.

William has not worked as a goldsmith since he was a boy. But like his father before him he's a member in good standing of the Company. Daniel reckons that they tapped him as Fusour for a reason: he defied Sir Isaac and the King's Messengers in the Bank of England a few days ago, asserting that they had no right to enter the vault and seize a deposit. They honor him for it now. This steadfast Goldsmith protected the sanctity of England's commerce by his actions in the bank, and now he'll perform a like service by challenging the produce of the Mint.

He has been at work preparing some necessaries over by the furnace. He approaches the Scale now carrying a wooden tray between his hands. On the tray are a sheet of lead, hammered out to a thin irregular disk, like a miniature pie-crust; a bullet-mold; pliers; and a cube of gray-white material rather less than an inch on a side, with a round depression in its upper surface. William Ham sets this down before the scale and tilts the scale-pan so that the twelve grains of gold-bits slide off and shower down into the center of the leaden sheet. He then folds the sheet together to imprison the gold, and wraps it up into a lumpy wad about the size of a hazelnut. He places this into one half of the bullet-mold, settles the other half over it, and squeezes the mold together with the pliers. When the packet comes out it has been rendered almost perfectly spherical: a wee globe, less like the Earth than the pitted gray Moon. He sets this into the depression in the top of the cupel—for that is the name of the cube of burnt bone ash. The sample fits into this neatly, recalling diagrams Daniel once studied in Geometry of spheres inscribed within cubes. William carries the tray over and sets it beside the furnace. A pair of tongs awaits. He uses these to pick up the cupel and thrust it into the heart of the furnace. It is dark and gray at first, but in a few moments it begins to absorb and then to give back some of the radiance in which it's immersed. The lead softens and sags. William Ham consults his watch. A dome of surface tension forms in the cupel as its contents become liquid. The gray ash darkens as the molten metals saturate it.

Written right on the gold trial plate is the following: *This standard composed of 22 carracts of fine gold, 2 carracts of alloy in the pound troy of Great Britain made the 13th day of April 1709.* The late Sir Isaac Newton begged to differ—he suspected that the true numbers were more like 23 and 1, and that the goldsmiths had fixed the plate to make it more likely he'd fail the Trial—but in any case, the point is that Sir Isaac's guineas are supposed to be made almost entirely of gold, with small amounts of base metals permitted. That is to say that out of the twelve grains of guinea-shards that made up the sample, eleven grains (if the inscription on the trial plate is taken at face value) or more (if the Goldsmiths fudged it) must be pure gold. The way to verify this is chymically to separate the gold from the not-gold, then weigh the former. The Company of Goldsmiths learned, ages ago, that when an assay is made in a cupel according to this receipt, the base metals in the sample will dissolve into the lead and be drawn, along with it, into the bone ash, like water into a sponge. But the pure gold will remain aloof, and form an ingot in the depression in the cupel's top. And that is what happens now, before the eyes of Daniel and all the Jurors. Though it is an everyday procedure, it seems nearly as magical, to Daniel, as what occurred a few moments ago in the sedan chair. The release of the body of pure radiant gold from the dissolving globe of lead reminds him of the dream-vision of which Princess Caroline spoke.

If the assay is left in the furnace for too long, the gold will evaporate and lose weight, which is not fair to the Master of the Mint. If it is not left in long enough, some base metal will remain allayed with the ingot of gold, which is not fair to the King. Knowing how long to leave it in there is a black art of the Goldsmiths, and Daniel gets the sense that William is silently polling the other eleven members of his Jury for their opinions. When a consensus seems to have been reached, he picks up the tongs again and withdraws the cupel and sets it on a brick to cool down. The lead jacket has vanished and the cupel has turned charcoal-gray. Remaining in the top of the cupel is the ingot: a tiny round lake of gold. The stars and moons that decorated Mr. Threader's black firmament have been changed by alchemy into this little sun. They need only wait for its heat to subside before they take the weight of it.

Holbourn

HOLBOURN OUGHT TO BE the Valley of the Shadow of Death for Jack. Perhaps he'd see it that way if he were facing forwards, watching Tyburn creep toward him. But they've faced him the other way, towards the London he's leaving. There is intended to be a message in this: he is supposed to be looking back ruefully on his traitorous doings. But it is not working out thus. Jack is a spark dragged through a trench full of gunpowder. Far from being the Valley of the Shadow of Death, it is a roaring flume of vibrant riotous life, perfectly arrayed for viewing by Jack, and as such, a great distraction for one who really ought to be attending to his sins.

He does not recognize any one person in particular, but London, as an entire thing, is as familiar to him as the faces in a parish church, on Sunday morn, would be to an aged vicar. Groups are recognizable too. There's a battalion of fishwives, of approximately regimental size, who have outflanked the artillery batteries at the Bridge and, by a covert march along Chick Lane, worked their way round to the west bank of the Fleet. There they seem to have divided into companies and squads, and mustered themselves within striking-distance in such places as Saffron Hill, the Dyers' Court, the Plough-Yard, and Bleeding Heart Court. These are tributaries that empty into Holbourn along the hill that climbs up from the Fleet crossing, where the Hanging-March is doomed to move slowly. Triggered by the westward-propagating Mobb-roar, the fishwives mount vicious sallies from their nests and burst into the road, shouldering between the pikemen and the dragoons, pulling fistfuls of black coins from their aprons and flinging them at Jack's head. They pock the sledge like grapeshot, they ricochet and ring in the air like færy-bells. Jack rips a button from his coat and underhands it to a fishwife who has actually penetrated to within a few yards of the sledge. She's too astonished to do anything but clap it out of the air. A knot of fish-guts strikes him square on the bridge of the nose. He returns fire with another golden button.

Having beaten back the assault of the Fishwives' Regiment with only light casualties, they crest the hill and enter into the widest part of Holbourn, which runs for a mile to St. Giles's, passing between diverse expensive squares, all converted from cow-pastures during Jack's lifetime. A Puritan in a black frock stands up on the street-island at Holbourn Bar, holding a Bible over his head, open to some passage he guesses Jack should know about. Another breaks through the cordon and climbs into the sledge with Jack and gets ready to baptize him with a bucket of water he's brought along; but the Ordinary of Newgate, who's been riding in the cart, isn't having any of that. He's down on the pavement in a trice, hustling along beside the sledge, and makes a grab for the handle of the Baptismal pail. This leads to a tug-of-war, and creates enough of a diversion that a short procession of Catholics—or so he assumes, from the monks' robes they're all wearing—is able to slip in, and make itself part of the parade. One is a priest, the others are burly monks, which makes perfect sense as a lone Papist wouldn't survive for ten seconds in this crowd. The priest strides along behind the sledge, looks Jack in the eye, and begins to declaim rapidly in what Jack assumes is Latin. Jack is being given last rites! A very considerate gesture on someone's part. This tiny and intrepid Popish strike force was probably despatched by Louis XIV from a secret chapel-headquarters in a vault beneath Versailles.

The procession bumps to a stop for some reason Jack can't see. Getting into the Christian spirit, he takes this opportunity to whip off his purple cape and toss it to the priest. He then indicates that the priest is to give it to a poor old woman, over yonder, who has somehow fought her way to the front of the crowd.

The rich people are having their say now. The procession has passed Chancery Lane and travels now among the homes of the high and the mighty: Red Lyon Square, Waterhouse Square, Bloomsbury. All to the north side. To the south, Drury Lane plugs in, running up from Covent Garden and Long Acre. Which is to say that Dukes and Merchant Princes control one side of the parade route, whores and actresses the other. Captains of Commerce, worth millions of pounds sterling, practically topple from balconies and rooftops in their eagerness to shake their fists at him. The ladies on the other side are much more forgiving. Jack, on an impulse, stands up, shrugs off his coat, and throws it into a phalanx of prostitutes. It's shredded in a heartbeat. He's down to his cloth-of-gold vest now, already missing a few buttons. He turns around to make sure that Jack Ketch is getting a load of this. And indeed he is. The executioner was dismayed by Jack's alms-giving at St. Sepulchre, but after a while he seemed to put it out of his mind, reckoning it was an aberration, a moment of weakness, on Shaftoe's part. Which must have made it all the more painful for him when Shaftoe began to disrobe and hurl his priceless raiments into the Mobb.

At St. Giles's, there's another ritual: the procession stops so that bowls of ale may be brought out and given to the prisoners. Jack drinks several, paying for each with a golden button. By the time they start moving again, and round the Tottenham Court bend into Oxford Road, his vest is hanging loose on his shoulders, not a single button remaining.

A carriage is stopped in the intersection, like a boat run aground in the middle of a torrent. Standing atop it is a fat Duke who has positioned himself so that Jack will get a good long look at him as he is dragged away to the west. He screams something that must be very unpleasant, and, realizing that Jack cannot quite make out what he's saying over the general noise, turns red in the face and begins to bellow and gesticulate with such fury that his wig shudders askew. But the meaner sort of people, leaving aside the occasional angry fishwife, are much more forgiving. At the crossing of Marybone Lane, where the countryside finally opens up to the north side of the road, a common-looking fellow comes trotting alongside with a pint of wine for Jack, and Jack pays him by handing him the golden vest.

They have reached Tyburn Cross. It is a desert the size of the Pacific Ocean, paved with human faces. A few tall objects protrude above the flood, here and there: a stranded carriage, a tree that's about to collapse from the weight of the people who've climbed it, occasional men on horseback, and the Triple Tree itself. Which Jack does not see until he's underneath it. It is an alienated frame-work of six mighty timbers—three vertical pilings and three cross-bars forming a triangle high above—beautiful in a strange way. The feeling is of entering a house without a roof, a home whose ceiling is Heaven.

A space about a stone's throw in width has been cleared round the base of the Deadly Nevergreen. The crowd's held at bay by pikemen, now reinforced by the King's Own Black Torrent Guards. Some bestride their war-horses facing outwards with sabers drawn and pistols cocked; others have dismounted and fixed bayonets.

The preliminary hangings seem to take forever. Jack enlivens the proceedings by stripping off his breeches, whipping them around his head a few times, showering coins in all directions, and flinging them off into the crowd. Somewhere along the line he's lost his periwig, too. So now he's stripped down to white undergarments, shoes, and a noose. Going to his destiny a pauper, like that Lazarus the Ordinary read about in chapel this morning.

The others are all dead, decorating two of the Three-Legged Mare's cross-bars. The third is reserved exclusively for Jack. He climbs up onto the cart, and the driver maneuvers it beneath the clear space. Jack's eyes are tired from seeing so much, and so he tilts his head back for a moment so that all he can see is the sky, divided in half by the rope-worn timber above.

Gunfire sounds from nearby. He swings his chin down again. This is the first time he's seen the crowd from a high vantage-point. Yet still he cannot find the edge of it. Gunpowder-smoke is drifting up from a black phalanx of Quakers or Barkers or some such. No one knows why.

Below, preparations are being made.

Flies explode from Jack Ketch's man-rated butcher block as Ketch heaves a rolled bundle onto it. He loosens a couple of ties and shakes out the contents: a complete suite of disembowelling-tools. The table is a scab the size of a bed. Ketch distributes his tools around it, occasionally testing an edge with a thumb. He takes particular care with some rusty shackles. This is a way of letting Shaftoe know that he can expect to be alive and conscious during the later phases of the operation.

When they pulled out of the Press-Yard some hours ago, Ketch had every expectation of being a rich man at the end of the day. All of those golden buttons, all of those rich clothes, the coins in the pockets, all were for him. He was going to get out of debt and buy shoes for his children.

Now Ketch is going to get nothing. Shaftoe has avoided meeting Ketch's eye until now, not knowing, and not caring, whether Ketch was responding to the relentless destruction of his fortune with curses, tears, or shocked disbelief. But they do look at each other now, Shaftoe up on his cart, and Ketch down at his abattoir, and Shaftoe sees that Ketch is perfectly calm. There's no trace of the warm emotion he showed earlier, in the Press-Yard. It's as if that never occurred. Even if Ketch removed his hood, the face beneath would be no more expressive than is the black leather mask. He has gone into a cool professional mode. In a way, revenge is easy for Ketch, because he need only carry out the Court's sentence to the letter, and put him to death *in terrorem*.

Jack now wonders whether this strategy was a good idea. A younger man would be scared. But it's normal to have second thoughts at this stage. It's the sign of a good plan.

He is expected to say a few words now.

"I, Jack Shaftoe, also known as *L'Emmerdeur*, the King of the Vagabonds, Ali Zaybak, Quicksilver, Lord of Divine Fire, Jack the Coiner, do hereby repent of all my sins and commend my soul to God," he says, "and ask only that I receive a decent Christian burial, with all of my quarters, if they can be rounded up, to be put together in the same box. And my head, too. For it is well known that the College of Physicians is gathered, as I speak, round their dissection-table on Warwick Lane, sharpening their scalpels, and getting ready to cut my head open so that they may rummage through my brains looking for the house where the Imp of the Perverse has dwelt lo these many years. I would prefer that this not happen. Having said that, Mr. Ketch, I turn myself over to your care. And I ask only that you check your knotwork twice over, for last night when Betty came to service me and these other fellows in the Condemned Hold, she was saying that you had quite lost your enthusiasm for the job, and were looking for a position as a maid-of-all-work. Step to it, man, the Physicians are waiting—"

And that is all he can get out, for during this last bit, Ketch has slung the loose end of the rope over the timber above, and pulled it taut. Very taut. Earlier, he'd promised to put a lot of slack in it and give Shaftoe a nice long drop, so that it would be over quickly; but that was before Shaftoe breached a certain implied contract. Ketch pulls the rope so taut that Jack is only appearing to stand on the cart; in truth, the tips of his toes are barely grazing the floor-boards now. "I shall tend to you in a few minutes' time, Jack," he mumbles into Shaftoe's ear.

Jack's head is forced down by the knot behind his ear; he can't help but notice that the cart is no longer beneath him. He remembers the cord that he earlier strung from his shoe to the noose beneath his drawers, and pushes off against it with one leg. This relieves some of the pressure. Behind him on the cart, the Ordinary and the Catholic priest are striving to out-pray each other.

Four teams of horses stand at the ready in the clear space below, facing different ways like the cardinal points on a compass-card, ready for the final and most spectacular part of the operation. A few people, presumably connected in one way or another with aspects of the drawing-and-quartering, are standing around down there, watching him.

One of these is a solitary man, dressed in a monk's robe. Come to think of it, he's one of the monks who was escorting the Catholic priest up Holbourn. He takes up a position in the open, next to the giant butcher block. The man's hood is drawn nearly closed, so that he looks out at the world down a tunnel of black homespun. He turns to face Jack, cleverly arranging it so that a tube of sunlight will shine onto his face. Jack's expecting Enoch Root or, barring that, some wild holy man.

Instead he recognizes the face of his brother Bob.

And that explains how a lone monk is able to be here at all, because Bob, of course, knows his way around the King's Own Black Torrent Guard.

For one glorious moment of stupidity, Jack supposes that some kind of rescue is about to happen.

Then there's a moment of terror as he wonders if Bob is going to run up and hang from his legs to kill him fast. Or barring that, perhaps he'll pull a pistol and put Jack out of his misery directly.

The cord snaps! Jack drops a couple of inches, the noose clubs him in the back of the head, the rope draws tighter.

Jack keeps watching his brother. Now, as in the early years of his life, there is no one else in the world.

Bob until now has kept his hands together in front of him, tucked into the capacious sleeves of his garment. Now, seeing Jack's distress, he draws them apart, and holds them up in the air like a saint. The sleeves churn. Two larks fly out of the right one, and a blackbird from the left. They flutter aimlessly about the gallows for a few moments, then identify it as Not a Real Tree, and ascend into the light.

Jack feels the pressure of the world being relieved.

He has no trouble taking the birds' meaning: *they have escaped.* All three of them. They are headed for America.

There is a roaring. He cannot know if it is the blood in his ears, or the Mobb, or, perhaps, a legion of demons and a choir of angels fighting for possession of his soul. Jack rolls his eyes high up in their sockets, trying to keep those birds in view. The sky, which was blue a moment ago, has turned uniformly gray, and its compass is narrowing. It shrinks to a lead coin with two white birds and a black one minted on its face.

Star Chamber

IN DUE TIME MR. THREADER seizes the cupel with tongs and upends it over the freshly polished scale-pan of the balance. The ingot—an oblate bead—falls out, and spins and buzzes on the pan. Some flecks of burnt bone fall around it; Mr. Threader blows these away and then gives the ingot an exploratory nudge or two with his tweezers, to satisfy himself that no other impurities have stuck to it. When he is certain that there's nothing on that pan except for pure gold, he places a ten-grain standard weight on the opposite pan. This is not nearly enough to balance the ingot—which is good, as far as it goes—and so, now wielding the ivory-handled tweezers, he adds a one-grain weight. Then a half-grain. The scale has gone into motion but still inclines toward the ingot of gold. Mr. Threader is working now with standard weights so small that Daniel can hardly see them: they are evanescent squares of gold foil stamped with fractions. He makes a messy pile of them and then stops, stumped. He removes a lot of small ones and replaces them with a larger one, and hems and haws. Finally he removes every single one of the standard weights, sets them back in their niches in the case, and puts on the single twelve-grain weight that he used earlier to weigh the sample of guinea fragments.

The pans oscillate for a long time, the needle making equal excursions to either side of dead center. After a while, friction prevails, and it stops. It is so close to being perfectly centered that in order to read it Mr. Threader must place his hand over his nose and mouth, so that his breathing won't startle it, and practically polish the thing with his eyelashes.

Then he draws back: the only man in the room who is moving so much as a muscle. For everyone has marked the delay, and noticed the twelve-grain weight on the other pan: very odd.

"The ingot weighs twelve grains," Mr. Threader proclaims.

"There must be some error," says a flummoxed senior Goldsmith. "Such a thing is impossible unless all the guineas contain no base metals whatsoever!"

"Or," says Mr. Threader under his breath to Daniel, "the base metals were converted to gold in the cupel!"

"There must have been some error in the assay," the senior Goldsmith continues, beginning now to look to his Guild-fellows, to erect a consensus.

But William Ham is having none of it. "That is a difficult accusation to sustain, without evidence," he points out.

"The evidence is right there before our eyes!" complains the elder, gesturing at the balance.

"*That* is evidence only that Sir Isaac makes good guineas, and that the British coin is the soundest currency of the whole world," William says doggedly. "Every member of this Jury watched—nay, *participated in*—the Assay. Did we not? None of us saw anything amiss. By our silence we have already consented to it, and vouchsafed its result. To reverse ourselves *now*, and say 'twas all done wrong, is to go before *that* man and say, 'My lord, we do not know how to do an assay!'"

William gestures toward the end of Star Chamber, where the Duke of Marlborough's absorbed in conversation with some other dignitary.

William's a banker, not a practicing Goldsmith. In the councils of that Company he is of low rank and little account. But outside their Clubb-house, in the City of London, he has earned a *gravitas* that makes heads turn his way when he speaks. This is why they nominated him as Fusour. Perhaps it is why the senior Goldsmith is calling the Assay into question; he's spooked by William's influence. Such political currents are too subtle for Daniel to follow; all he needs to know is that the Goldsmiths and the City men alike are swayed by William's words. If they trouble to look at the senior Goldsmith at all, it is in glances over their shoulders, as if looking back curiously at one who has fallen behind.

To his credit, the elder sees clearly enough the way it's going. He cringes once at what he's being forced to do, then his face slackens. "Very well," he says, "let us give Sir Isaac his due, then. He has exasperated us more than any other Master of the Mint; but no one has ever claimed he did not know his way around a furnace." He turns toward Marlborough, as do the other Goldsmiths, and they all bow. Marlborough notes it and nods to the chap he's been talking to, who turns around to see it. Daniel recognizes the fellow as Isaac Newton, and feels a kind of pride that his friend is being honored in this way, and that he seems at last to have earned the trust of Marlborough. A moment passes before Daniel remembers that Isaac is dead.

This courtly scene is disturbed by trouble in the gallery leading in from New Palace Yard: some uncivil person is trying to crash the party, and the Serjeant is dutifully trying to stop him. Their dispute and their footsteps draw nearer.

"What business—"

"The King's business, sir!"

"Whom would you—"

"My captain, sir! The Duke of Marlborough! Perhaps you will have heard of him!" The speaker stomps right into Star Chamber, moving in an uneven gait: a uniformed Colonel with a peg-leg of carven ebony. Then he stops, realizing he's just burst in upon a solemn moment, and doesn't know what to say. It promptly gets worse: recent evolutions have given the Lords waiting in the side chamber the idea that they have been missing out on something. Most of them choose this moment to debouche into the Star Chamber wearing expressions that say, "Explain, or be hanged!"

Daniel by now has recognized the peg-legged colonel: this is Barnes of the Black Torrent Guard. Barnes was already of a mind to dig his own grave and jump into it even before the King's Remembrancer, the Chancellor of the Exchequer, First Lord of the Treasury, Lord Privy Seal, and Lord Chancellor filed into the room, followed by enough Hanoverian Dukes and Princes to conquer Saxony. Barnes is now not only peg-legged but peg-tongued and peg-brained. The only man who dares make a sound is Marlborough.

"My lords," he says, when the side-chamber has emptied out, "we have news from the Jurors. And unless I have mistaken the signs, we have got news from Tyburn Cross as well."

Daniel glances at Barnes, who is going through a chrestomathy of head-shaking, throat-slitting, eye-bulging, and hand-waving. But Marlborough is oblivious; he's got eyes only for the Lords of the Council, and the Hanoverians. He goes on, "Would the Juries care to make a preliminary report?"

The Pesour and the Fusour make after-you gestures at each other. Finally William Ham steps forward, and bows. "We shall of course draw up the document presently, and give it to the King's Remembrancer," he says, "but it is my great pleasure to inform my lords that the assay has been performed, and it has proved beyond doubt that His Majesty's currency is sounder than it has ever been in all the history of this Realm, and that the highest accolades are owed to the Master of his majesty's Mint, Sir Isaac Newton!"

Isaac is diffident, but the Fusour's announcement starts up a round of hip-hip-huzzahs that only bates when he steps forward and bows to the room. Which he does gracefully and with perfect balance; he has not looked so spry in years. Daniel searches the room for Miss Barton, and only finds her when she appears at his side, seizes him by the right arm, and plants a kiss on his cheek.

"It is my very great honor," says Isaac, "to do what I can for my country. Some distinguish themselves in battle" (a nod at Marlborough), "others in sage advice" (a nod—astonishingly—at Daniel), "still others in grace and beauty" (Miss Barton). "I make coins, and strive to make them sound, as a foundation on which the Commerce of this Realm may be builded by her thrifty and industrious Citizens." A nod to the Jurors.

"There is another thing that you do very well, besides making coins, is there not, Sir Isaac?"

This Marlborough enunciates very clearly, for the benefit of the Hanoverians, and he waits for Johann von Hacklheber to effect a translation before he goes on: "I refer, of course, to your duty of prosecuting those who make *bad* coins."

"That, too, is the charge of the Master of the Mint," Isaac admits.

Barnes has gone back into frantic pantomiming, but he can't

seem to get the eye of Marlborough, who is rapt on the Germans. Marlborough goes on, "Sir Isaac's triumph here, in the Trial of the Pyx, has, as I understand it, been matched—some would even say, surpassed—by a simultaneous triumph at Tyburn! Colonel Barnes?" And all eyes turn to Barnes. But he has dropped the gesticulations and now stands there the very picture of martial dignity.

"Indeed, my lord," he announces. "Jack Shaftoe, *L'Emmerdeur,* the King of the Vagabonds, a.k.a. Jack the Coiner, has been hanged."

"Hanged, drawn, and quartered, according to the sentence pronounced against him?" Marlborough says, so fiercely that it is more assertion than query.

"Hanged, my lord," Barnes says. It dangles there for a terrible long time, like a kicking wretch on a gallows, and he feels a need to make improvements: "Hanged by the neck until dead."

"*Half* dead, I should say, and then cut down, drawn, and quartered?"

"Mr. Ketch was balked from carrying out the, er, supplemental eviscerations and dismemberments and whatnot, upon the *hanged* and *dead, corpse* of *the late* villain Shaftoe."

"Prevented by *what,* pray tell? Squeamishness? Did Mr. Ketch forget to bring his cutlery?"

"Prevented by the Mobb. By the violence and the menace of the greatest and surliest Mobb that has ever assembled upon this Island."

A murky side-conversation now starts up in the Hanover contingent, as Johann von Hacklheber tries to translate "Mobb" into High German.

"I ordered the King's Own Black Torrent Guard to defend the gallows, precisely because I expected a larger than usual Mobb," says Marlborough distractedly, in a sort of quiet prodrome to raging anger. Recognizing it as such, Barnes says: "And that is precisely what we accomplished, my lord, and the hangings were all carried out in good order, and Jack Ketch and the bailiffs and gaolers conveyed out of there safe and sound. The gallows will, alas, have to be rebuilt, but that's a job for carpenters, not soldiers."

"I see. But you deemed it prudent to retreat before the drawing and quartering could be performed."

"Yes my lord, 'twas at that moment when the Mobb became most frenzickal, and rushed the Gallows to cut him down—"

"*Him,* or *his corpse?*" Isaac Newton asks.

"Colonel Barnes," says Marlborough, "*did they cut him down,* or did they merely *rush the gallows to cut him down?* There is a difference, you see."

"If you want to know whose hand wielded the knife that severed the rope, I cannot give you his name," Barnes says. "Just then, I was preoccupied with the larger task of *leading my troops.*"

"How did you lead them? What orders did you give?"

"To form a cordon with fixed bayonets around Jack Ketch and those other participants *who were still alive.*"

"Did you give an order to fire?"

"No," says Barnes, "as I judged it would be suicidal; and though I am ever ready to die in the line of duty, I was of the view that for us to commit suicide would have impeded us in the conduct of our mission."

"I have often thought that the Vicar and the Warrior in you were struggling to achieve dominance, Colonel Barnes. Now I see that the Warrior has at last prevailed. For the Vicar would have opened fire and trusted to God. It is only the Warrior who would have chosen the difficult path of an orderly retreat."

Barnes—who has been expecting anything but praise—salutes, and goes red in the face.

"They wish to know why the soldiers did not fire on the Mobb to restore order!" says Johann von Hacklheber, speaking on behalf of a formation of very disgruntled-looking Hanoverians.

"Because this is England and we don't massacre people in England!" Marlborough announces. "Or rather, we *do* but we are striving to turn over a new leaf. Pray translate that into more diplomatic language, Freiherr von Hacklheber, and see to it that the new King quite gets the message, so that we don't have to send the Barkers after him." Marlborough winks at Daniel.

Isaac has paid little heed to these last few exchanges. "In truth it is just as well for my purposes that Jack Shaftoe's corpse was left intact, for I have been looking forward to conducting an autopsy on the wretch at the College of Physicians, to find out what on earth made him the way he was."

"I know," says Barnes. "All London knows, for Jack announced as much—somewhat more colorfully—from the gallows. It was this very thing that so infuriated the Mobb."

"So be it," says Isaac, with a shrug. "Have your men take the corpse to the College of Physicians."

"We don't know where it is," says Colonel Barnes.

"On Warwick Lane, off Newgate."

"No. I meant, we don't know where *the corpse* is."

"I beg your pardon?" says Isaac, and looks to Marlborough. But the Duke is in a frank Cultural Exchange with his Hanoverian counterparts and has no time for Isaac. It has taken the Germans some time to fully comprehend the impertinence of Marlborough's quip about the Barkers, and to believe that the Duke actually said something that rude; now they are waxing wroth, getting a bit foamy even. Johann von Hacklheber, seeing he's caught in a perilous crossfire, is edging away, trying to make himself party to the safer and more interesting conversation re: Jack Shaftoe's carcass.

"After the dead body was cut down," Barnes continues, "some of the Mobb raised it up. I sent soldiers to wrest it from them. The Mobb scampered away and gave it a right good heave."

"On to the ground?"

"No, it was caught and raised up on high again by *others* of the Mobb; and when they spied my soldiers coming for them, they gave it another heave, so that others, farther from the gallows, took up the burthen. And from there it developed into a sort of, well, *orderly* procedure, and I had to climb up on to the scaffold to see where it went. He sort of *glided*. Like a leaf, floating on a turbulent and swirling stream, dodging and spinning in unseen Mobb-currents, but ever moving in same general direction: away from *me*."

Isaac sighs, and begins to look his age again. "Spare me any further poetick description and just say forthrightly, please, where did you last see the body of Jack Shaftoe?"

"Sort of dissolving into the western horizon."

Isaac stares at him.

"The Mobb was of tremendous size," Barnes explains.

"You are quite certain he was dead at the time he was cut down?"

"If I may, sir, that's easily answered!" says Johann von Hacklheber. "Anyone who was at Newgate this morning can tell you he was wearing a king's ransom in cloth-of-gold, and that his pockets bulged with coins. All of which, of course, was payment for Jack Ketch—"

"To hang him fast—break his neck in an instant," Isaac says. "Very well! Let the Mobb have him then. Let him end up in a potter's field somewhere."

"Yes," says Daniel Waterhouse, "it is a most fitting end for such a villainous man. And this—the new King, the strong Bank, the sound coinage, and all the works of Natural Philosophers and *ingénieurs*— are a fine beginning for a new System of the World."

At this, Johann von Hacklheber looks askance at Marlborough, who is close to getting into a sword-fight with some Duke of Germany.

"Never you mind *that*," Daniel reassures him, "for it is all part of the System."

Epilogs

For Time, though in Eternitie, appli'd
To motion, measures all things durable
By present, past, and future
    —MILTON, *Paradise Lost*

Leibniz-Haus, Hanover
NOVEMBER 1714

MOST MEN, standing knee-deep in gold, would talk about that. But not these two eccentric Barons.

"Then he stepped out of his sedan chair and looked perfectly all right," says Johann von Hacklheber.

He sits down upon an empty barrel. Leibniz, cringing and mincing from the gout, has been seated for some while. They are beneath Leibniz's great house, in a cellar made to store victuals. But the bottles of wine, the kegs of beer, the turnips, potatoes, and belching buckets of sauerkraut have been hauled out and given to the poor. The place has been filled up with barrels of a different sort. Leibniz, unwilling now to trust anyone in Hanover, left them sealed until Johann arrived. Johann's been dismantling them, removing the gold plates, and placing them in orderly stacks.

"It sounds as though he was re-animated by the *Elixir Vitae*," Leibniz admits.

"I thought you didn't believe in such things," says Johann, and gestures at the gold plates all around.

"I don't think about such matters the way *he* does," says Leibniz, "but I can't rule out the possibility that monads, ordered in the right way, might do things that would seem like miracles to us."

"Well, you have got all the magic gold you could ever desire, if you want to cure that gout, or—"

"Live forever?"

Johann looks abashed, and instead of answering, picks up his prybar, and goes to work on another barrel.

"I suspect that there are some of us who *have been* living forever," Leibniz says, "such as your supposed great-uncle, and my benefactor, Egon von Hacklheber. Or Enoch Root, as others know him. Let us suppose that Enoch knows how to manipulate the Subtile Spirit in such a way as to heal diseases and extend life. What of it, then? What has he accomplished? How has it changed anything?"

"Hardly at all," says Johann.

"Hardly at all," agrees Leibniz, "save that from time to time he may grant a few years' undeserved life to someone who would otherwise have perished. Enoch must have been asking himself, these last couple of millennia, what is the point of it all. It is obvious that he took a lively interest in Natural Philosophy, and did what he could to foster it. Why?"

"Because Alchemy was not bringing him satisfaction."

"Evidently not. Now, Johann, it would seem that Sir Isaac has been granted a few more years by Alchemy, and yet clearly it has not brought him any happiness or enlightenment that he did not possess before. Which gives us another hint as to why it does not satisfy Enoch. You point out that I, likewise, could use the Solomonic Gold in this cellar to extend my life. Let us suppose that it's true. But obviously this is not the goal toward which I have been directed by Enoch, or by Solomon Kohan. On the contrary! Those two have sought to sequester the gold and keep it out of the hands of the one man who knows how to wield it: Isaac Newton. For me to take up Alchemy at my age, and melt those plates down to make an elixir—why, it'd be Doctor Faustus all over again! And with the same dismal result in the last act."

"I can't bear to see Newton triumph, while you sicken and dwindle here in Hanover."

"I've got all of the Solomonic Gold. He doesn't. That is a triumph. It does not make me glad. No, triumph will not be mine if I only ape what he did. That is surrender. If I am to outlive Newton, it will not be by extending the span of my life with unnatural coctions. We must do all in our power to see that the Logic Mill is built."

"In St. Petersburg?"

"Or wherever, and whenever, some great prince sees fit to build it."

"I'll make arrangements to have some stout crates built," says Johann, "and delivered here. I'll take them into this cellar myself and pack the golden cards into them with my own two hands, and nail them shut so that no one will have cause to think that they contain anything more valuable than musty old letters. Once that is done, you may ship them to St. Petersburg, if that is the right place for them, with a stroke of a quill. But if what I hear from Russia has any color of truth, the Tsar is distracted, and may not see the thing through."

Leibniz smiles. "That's why I was careful to say *whenever some great prince sees fit to build it.* If not the Tsar, then someone else who will come along after my death."

"Or after mine, or my son's or my grandson's," Johann says. "Human nature being what it is, I fear that this will only happen when the things that the Logic Mill is good at become important to a war. And that is a difficult thing to imagine."

"Then pray bring up your son and your grandson, if you have any, to be imaginative. Then impress on them the importance of looking after those dusty old crates in the Leibniz-Archiv. Speaking of which—"

"The Princess of Wales," says Johann, holding up a hand, "has become most imperious since she got her new lands and titles, and has ordered me to find a woman I have some actual prospect of marrying. My dear mother has weighed in, too. I beg *you* not to start."

"Very well," says Leibniz, and lets a respectful silence fall. "That must have been a difficult conversation. I am sorry."

"It was a difficult conversation that I had been expecting," says Johann, "and I find it's easier to have it *behind* me than *in front of* me. I am here now. I'll go to London from time to time, and dance with her at a ball, and take tea with my mother, and remember. Then I shall return to Hanover and live my life."

"What about them? What do you hear from those two great ladies?"

"They are on this Continent," says Johann, "mending fences with their cousins, now that the war is finally over."

Gardens of Trianon, Royal Château of Versailles

A CRACK SOUNDS across still water. Wild geese squawk and take to the air on tired wings. A second crack, and a single bird drops to the bank. A water-dog swims after it, marring the pond's surface with a vee-shaped wake that could almost be a reflection of the goose-formations high above. A window shatters, a lady whoops in surprise. The laughter of two men can be heard.

A panel of chopped and lashed-down foliage moves suddenly aside, like a door, to reveal a small barge: a floating blind. It is just large enough for two hunters, but rich enough for two kings. For once the panel of sticks and dead leaves is out of the way, it is all gold leaf and bas-reliefs of Diana and Orion. Two men sit in gilded campaign-chairs. Each cradles a fowling-piece of ridiculous length. They are helpless with mirth, for a while, at the breaking of the window.

One of them is very old, pink, bloated, half buried in furs and blankets that settle toward the deck as he jiggles them with his laughter. He slaps an ermine pelt to keep it from sliding into the pond. *"Mon cousin,"* he says, "you have bagged two birds with one shot: a goose, and a chambermaid!"

The other is in his middle fifties, active, but not spry, for it seems that a life of adventures has left him carrying a vast inventory of aches, pains, cramps, cricks, clicks, pops, and charley-horses. He shuffles across the deck of the barge and heaves open another camouflage-panel to let in the morning sun and release stale air. This gives him time to compose a sentence in bad French: "If she was hurt bad we'd hear more screaming. She was only scared."

"I believe you scored a hit on the Trianon-sous-Bois: the residence of my sister-in-law, Liselotte."

"She sounds ever so high and mighty," says the younger man. "I dare not talk to one such. Maybe you could let her know how sorry I am."

"Oh? How sorry *are* you?" asks the older.

"Ah, you are a sly one there, Leroy. Tell me, does this Liselotte know the Duchess of Arcachon-Qwghlm?"

"But yes, they are old partners in mischief, those two! Probably having breakfast together as we speak."

"Then maybe Eliza can be my apologist. She speaks better French than you anyway."

"Ho-ho-ho!" chortles the King. "You only think so because you are so besotted with her. I can see it."

There's sudden thrashing in the brush beside the water. *"Merde!"* says the King, "we are found out! Close the blind! Hurry!"

The other turns and reaches for the panel, then stops short, grimaces, and cocks his head. "Bloody hell."

"The neck again?"

"Worst bleeding crick in the neck I've ever had." He reaches up to rub a raw place, then flinches, and settles for re-composing his silk neckerchief.

"You should try to avoid being hanged."

"I did try to avoid it, but the thing was complicated."

She appears on the bank, holding up one hand with thumb and index finger pressed together.

"Morning, Jack."

"Bonjour, Madame la Duchesse." The one named Jack executes a courtly bow, so exaggerated as to border on open mockery. Each and every one of his vertebrae has something to say about it.

"I've something here that you lost!" she announces.

"My heart?"

She hurls the bird-pellet at him. The men on the barge avert their eyes as it impacts on a chair-arm and ricochets around. "*La Palatine* wants you two to know that she is too old to be the target of musket-fire."

"Fortunately Pepe is bringing you a peace-offering," says the King, and indicates the curly-haired dog, who's up on the bank now, wagging his tail at Eliza. He trots up and drops the dead bird at her feet.

"I've little taste for such things," she says, "but Liselotte was a great huntress in her day and so it might placate her." She bends down, pinches the bird's neck, and walks away from them holding it out at arm's length. The men watch in awe. Leroy gives Jack a dig in the ribs.

"*Magnifique*, eh?"

"Old goat."

"Ah, she is a great woman," says the King, "and you, *mon cousin*, are a fortunate man."

"To meet her in the first place was fortunate, I'll give you that. To lose her was stupid. Now, I don't know the word to describe what I am, besides tired."

"You will have ample time to rest from your travails, and lovely places in which to do it," says Leroy.

Jack, suddenly alert, pulls one of the blind doors to, and crouches behind it. A trio of French courtiers, drawn by the sound of the fowling-pieces, are approaching. "Lovely places indeed," says Jack, "as long as I stay out of sight, and out of gossip."

"Ah, but in such places as La Zeur and St.-Malo, this is not so terribly difficult, eh?"

"That is where I shall live out my retirement," Jack allows, "as long as she'll have me."

The King looks mock-astonished. "And if she throws you out?"

"Back to England, and back to work," says Jack.

"As a coiner?"

"As a gardener."

"I do not believe such a thing!"

"Believe it, Leroy, for 'tis a notorious weakness of Englishmen who are too old to do anything useful. My brother has found a position on a rich man's estate. If Eliza ever grows weary of supporting a broken-down old Vagabond, I may go thither and live out my days killing the Duke's weeds and poaching his game."

Blenheim Palace

"Fine! So be it, then! I'll get along unshod!" bellows a man of similar age and proportions to Jack. He seizes one of his knees with both hands and yanks up. A bare foot emerges from a boot, which is sunk almost to its top in the mud. He plants the foot, grabs the other knee, and repeats. Bob Shaftoe now stands, a free man, in mud almost up to his knees. His boots are stranded nearby, rapidly filling with rain. He salutes them. "Good riddance!"

"Hear, hear!" calls a voice from a tent, pitched nearby on slightly higher and firmer ground. A man rises from a table and turns toward him. The table is lit by several candles even though it is two o'clock in the afternoon.

Bob's wearing a broad-brimmed felt hat, which supports approximately a gallon of rainwater, distributed among several discrete pools. He cocks his head in a most deliberate and calculating manner, and the pools slide, merge, slalom round the hat's contours, and spring off its back brim, splatting into the mud behind him. This enables him to get a clear sight-line into the tent.

The man who has just spoken stands in its entrance, gazing down on him; at the table, a peg-legged fellow sits on a folding chair and graciously accepts a cup of chocolate from a woman who has been at work over a little cook-fire in the rear. "Bob," calls the standing gentleman, "you are now barefoot in the rain, which calls to mind how I first saw you nigh on fifty years ago, and I say it becomes you, and may you leave those boots there to rot, and never again wear such odious contraptions. Now, do come back to us before you catch your death. Abigail has made chocolate."

Bob wrenches a foot clear of the mud, plants it on a rock, and uses this as a foundation on which to pull the opposite one free. He risks a glance back at the abandoned boots. "Do the bloody *plans* call for a pair o'boots there?"

"They call for a shrubbery!" announces the peg-leg, peering at Bob through a transit, and consulting a garden-plan spread out on the table. "But never you mind, those boots will be eaten by vermin long before planting-season."

"What would the Vicar of Blenheim know about planting-season?"

"As much as I know about being a vicar."

"And that is as much as *I* know about being a country gentleman," says the Duke of Marlborough, gazing fretfully across a half-mile of mud and stumps at the still-building pile of Blenheim. "But we must all adapt—we must all learn. Except for Abigail, who is already perfect." Abigail gives him a skeptical look and a cup of chocolate. Bob squelches another step closer. The gaze of (formerly) Colonel, (and now) the Reverend Barnes strays back to the great map, which looks ever so fanciful when contrasted against the gloomy reality outside. His eye wanders across the orderly geometry of the plan until it fixes upon a wee Chapel and a nearby Vicarage.

Marlborough says, "We shall mount a last Campaign from this tent, and pick off the vermin who are drawn hither by the intoxicating fragrance of Bob's boots. Bob shall study how to look after plants, Barnes shall learn how to look after souls, I shall learn how to be idle, and Abigail shall look after all of us."

"It sounds as if it ought to work," says Bob, "so long as my brother does not show up."

"He is dead," Marlborough avers. "But if he shows up, we'll shoot him. And if he recovers, we'll pack him off to Carolina, where he may work alongside his offspring. For I am told that you are not the only Shaftoe, Bob, to have turned over a new leaf, and become a tiller of the soil."

Bob has finally reached the tent's threshold. "It is a strange fate indeed," he mutters, "but only fitting."

"Why fitting?"

"Jack, Jimmy, and Danny ought by rights to become tillers of the soil," says Bob, "because they have made so much trouble in the past, as soilers of the till."

"If you are going to make such jests," says Barnes, "you are welcome to stay out in the rain."

Carolina

"I SPIED 'EM AGAIN this morning, Tomba! The weather cleared, just after sunup, and I looked to the West and saw 'em, all lit up by the red sun shining in off the sea. A line of hills, or mountains if you please. Laid out, waiting for us, like baked apples in a pan."

Tomba is lying face down on the sack of desiccated pine-branches that answers to the name of bed here, in the indentured servants' quarters of Mr. Ickham's Plantation. Not for the first time in his life, his back is striped with long whip-cuts. Jimmy Shaftoe hauls a sopping mass of rags out of a bucket, wrings it out, and lays it on Tomba's raw flesh. Tomba opens his mouth to scream, but makes no sound. Danny keeps talking, trying to get Tomba to think about something else. "A week's hard traveling," he says, "less than that if we steal some horses. We can manage without food for that long. When we make it to those hills, there'll be game a-plenty."

"Game," says Tomba, "and Indians."

"Tomba, look at the state you're in, and tell me Indians are worse than the Overseer."

"Nothing's worse than him," Tomba admits. "But I'm in no condition to run cross-country for seven days."

"Then we wait until those stripes are healed. Then we do it—"

"Boys, you do not understand. There will *always* be something. The Overseer *knows* how to keep men downtrodden. Especially black men. I didn't understand that, when I came here. It's different, the way he treats me. Look at my back, and tell me it isn't so."

Lines of fire run in parallel courses across the walls of the shack where the sun glares between unchinked wall-planks. A pig roots outside, undermining the corner of their dwelling, but they can't shoo it away or eat it because it is the Overseer's pride and joy. They can hear him now, bellowing in the distance. "Jimmy? Danny! Jimmy? Danny! Where the hell have you got to?"

"Lookin' after our mate you just beat half to death, you bastard," mutters Jimmy.

"I want to see red necks on the lot of you," says Tomba, repeating the Overseer's favorite aphorism. "Tomorrow, red necks all around, save for this Blackamoor—there's only one way to give *him* a red neck and that's with the lash." Tomba gets his hands underneath him, and pushes himself up on to all fours, then hangs his head low and lets his dreadlocks sweep the floor, he's so woozy.

"Jimmy? Danny! Jimmy? Danny! Are you feedin' your pet Black-amoor?" By process of elimination, the Overseer has figured out where they are, and is drawing nigh.

"You're right," says Tomba, "he means to kill me today. It is time to *unpack*."

"Then *unpack* we shall," says Danny.

He bends down and seizes the hay-bag that served him for a bed, and rips it open from one end to the other. Out tumbles an elongated bundle. Jimmy snatches it and tears away several rope ties. The two Shaftoes work together to unroll the bundle, Danny holding his arms out like a pair of shelf-brackets while Jimmy unwinds the bolt of canvas. Tomba paws one hand up the shack's wall until he finds a hand-hold on one of the hewn logs that make up its frame, and pulls himself to his feet. "They're not in here, Master!" he calls, "no one in here but poor Tomba!"

"You're a damned liar!" bellows the Overseer, and hammers the door open with the butt of his whip-handle. He stops, framed in the entrance, unable to see into the darkness of the shed. He can hear, though, the unexpected sounds of two gently curved blades—a longer one and a shorter one—being whisked from their scabbards. Perhaps he even glimpses the unaccustomed sight of Carolina sunlight gleaming from watered steel.

"Don't tell us," says Danny, "you want to see some red necks around this place. Is that what you were about to say?"

"What—get back to work, you lazy bastards! Or I'll give you more of what Tomba got!" The Overseer steps into the shed, and raises his whip; but before he can bring it down, steel skirls past his ear, and the amputated lash drops to the dirt floor at his feet. Tomba staggers outside and closes the shed door behind himself. He squints about at several acres of mud, which he knows to be red in color, though it looks gray to him because his vision has gone black and white. A big white house stands at one end. Indentured servants toil with mattocks and shovels. Behind him, the Overseer has become uncharacteristically silent. Perhaps his eyes have adjusted to the point where he can see he's locked in a confined space with a pair of enraged Samurai.

"There's more'n one way to make a red neck," Danny points out, "and here's how they do it in Nagasaki!" There follows a rapid sequence of noises that Tomba has not heard in quite a while, though he recognizes them well enough. Blood rushes out from under the shed wall and puddles in the wallow rooted out by the Overseer's pig. Drawn by its fragrance, the pig waddles over, snuffles, then begins to lap it up.

Jimmy and Danny burst out of the shed. Danny wipes his blade on his pant-leg and re-sheathes it. Jimmy hollers to the other indentured servants: "You all can take the rest of the day off! And when Mr. Ickham comes back from Charleston, and wants to know what happened, why, you just tell him that it was done by the Red-Neck Ronin, and that we went that-away!" And he thrusts his *wakizashi* into the untamed West. Then he sheaths it and turns to his companions.

"Let's head for the hills, boys."

Cornwall

WILL COMSTOCK, the Earl of Lostwithiel, has been worrying that they'll become trapped in one of the sudden mists that wander about the moors like ghosts through a haunted house, and lose their way. And indeed such mists wash up round them on two occasions. He insists, then, that they stop right where they are, and bide their time until the air clears. Daniel frets that *Minerva* shall lose patience, and sail without him. But around midday the mists blow off on a stiff north wind that presses and pursues them down-valley toward the sea, now visible far off, pea-green, and pied with cloud-shadows and sun-shafts.

The land is chopped by stone walls into parcels so irregular it's almost as if this country had to be pieced together from shreds of other worlds. In the high open country that tumbles down from the moors, the walls are lacy and irregular. Later, as the company of travelers traverse down into the valley, they pass through forests of stunted oaks, no taller than Daniel's head, that cling to the slopes like wool to a sheep's back and refuse to give up their leaves even at this time of year. There the walls run straight and solid, drenched with moss and saturated with life.

From such a wood, the company emerges into a smoky bottomland, where shaggy anthracite-colored cattle engage in desultory shoving-matches. They fall in along the course of a rushing river that has vaulted down off the moor. Not far below them, it slows, flattens, and broadens to an estuary. There is the longboat waiting to take Daniel out to *Minerva*, which is anchored somewhere hereabouts, making ready for the run to Oporto and thence, eventually, to Boston.

But the travelers from London have not followed the Earl of Lost-withiel and Thomas Newcomen all this way to look at cows or boats. As they come out from under the dripping eaves of the last little oak-coppice, Daniel Waterhouse, Norman Orney, and Peter Hoxton begin to note certain oddments and novelties round the foot of the valley. Above the high tide mark, the ground runs gently up-hill for no more than a bow-shot before leaping up to make a rocky bluff that looms over the estuary. It's obvious enough, even to visitors who are not aficionadoes of the Technologickal Arts, that men have been digging coal out of the roots of that bluff for many generations. The flat ground along the shore is strewn with dunnage and gouged with marks where they have trundled and dragged the coal down to meet the boats. To that point, it is typical of a certain type of small mine that might prosper until the miners delved to the waterline, and then be abandoned.

There is a flattish out-cropping not far above the foot of the bluff. On it stands a thing that might have been cobbled together from pieces of drawbridges and siege engines. Two free-standing stone walls are held apart by an unroofed void perhaps four yards in breadth. That void has been congested with a dark web of timbers that reminds Daniel of a gallows. This supports some arrangement of platforms, stairs, ladders, and Machinery that is quite difficult to sort out, even as they draw closer to it. From its complexities emerges a sucking and hissing and booming, like the beating of a giant's heart, one might think, in the last moments before it dies. This does not die, however, but keeps going in a steady cadence. With each beat comes a sudden rushing noise, which their ears can follow as it me-anders down a crooked wooden aqueduct and finally leaps out and spatters on the tidal flat below, where it has carved a little water-course—a man-made streambed—down into the surf.

"Ground-water, pumped from the depths of the mine, by Mr. New-comen's Engine," announces Lostwithiel. This is unnecessary, since the three visitors have come all the way out from London expressly to see it. And yet it's important for Lostwithiel to come out and say it, as when the pastor at a wedding intones, *I now pronounce you man and wife.*

Orney and Saturn are keen to clamber down into the bowels of the Engine and know the particulars. Daniel goes with them as far as a plank platform from which he can get a good prospect of the valley. There he stops for a look round. It is the closest thing to solitude he'll have until he reaches Massachusetts. He can now see *Minerva* anchored beyond the bar, some miles down where the estuary joins the sea. The crew of the longboat have already marked him through their prospective-glasses and are rowing directly for him, building speed to ground their keel in the soft sand where the Engine spits out the mine-water.

Slowly shaking its fist above Daniel's head is an arm made of giant, knot-ridden timbers joined by iron hasps that must have been sledge-hammered out in a forge somewhere nearby. Depending from its end is a gargantuan chain, its links about the size of a grown man's femur, joined together by hand-forged cotter pins as big as bears' claws. In Newcomen's mind, Daniel knows, these links are meant to be of uniform size. In practice each is a little different, the differences averaging out as the chain disappears over the horizon of the curving arch-head that terminates the great arm. From it depends the piston, which fills a vertical cylinder the size of a mine-shaft. Packed round the piston's edge to form a seal is a matted O of old rope yarn, called junk, clamped down by a junk ring, secured with rustic nuts. Plenty of steam leaks out around it, but most stays where it belongs. The opposite end of the arm is linked to a pump rod consisting of several tree-trunks squared off and bound together with iron bands, plunging into the earth and pulling on giant sucking and splurging equipment too deep down for Daniel to see. Compared to all of this, the brains of the thing are tiny, and easy to miss: a man, on a platform a storey or two below where Daniel is standing, surrounded by pushrods, bell-cranks, and levers and supplying information to the machine when needed, which is not very frequently. At the moment, he is supplying information to Orney and Saturn, who have joined him down there.

This platform is dripping wet, and yet it's warm, for the used steam exhaled by the Engine drifts round it and condenses on the planks. Daniel lets the Engine breathe down his neck while he surveys the other works of the Proprietors of the Engine for Raising Water by Fire. He means to dash off a note to Eliza, letting her know just what has been done here with the capital that she and the other investors have entrusted to Lostwithiel and Newcomen. Mr. Orney will then take the letter back to London and see that she receives it. Orney will have a lot more to say, of course. Being a man of commerce, he'll mark things to which Daniel would be blind, and he'll know, without having to think about it, just which details Eliza shall and shan't find interesting. For Orney himself has put a bit of money in this thing now, and if he likes what he sees here, he'll go back to London and talk it up among his brethren.

So there's no need for Daniel to make some foolish pretense of seeing this venture through the shrewd eyes of a businessman. He tries, rather, to see it as what he is: a Natural Philosopher. As such it is the experimental aspects of it—its failures—that draw his notice. The level ground below the Engine is pocked, all around, with wreckage of Newcomen's boilers. The natural and correct form for such a thing is a sphere. Knowing as much, Newcomen has been learning how to fabricate large spherical shells out of iron. And just as a schoolboy's waste-book is littered, page after page, with smeared and scratched-out failures, so the deep soil of the river-bottom is strewn with ineradicable records of every idea that Newcomen has ever had on the subject, and striking visual proof of why and how certain of those ideas were bad. He can't possibly beat out a single billet of iron into a vast seamless bubble and so he has to piece the things together of many smaller curved plates, lapped and riveted.

Fifty years ago Hooke had caught sparks struck off of a steel, and put them under the microscope, and shown Daniel what they really were: pocked spheres of shiny metal, like iron planets. Daniel had supposed they were solid, until he saw some that had been blown open by internal pressure. For the sparks weren't globules, but hollow bubbles, of molten steel that flailed, then froze, when they burst, leaving wild out-flung extremities that looked a little bit like clawing hands and a little bit like ancient tree-roots cast up on a beach. Some of Mr. Newcomen's failed boilers look like those exploded sparks. Others have failed in ways not so obvious, and lie half-embedded in the earth, like meteors fallen out of the sky.

Some miners come up out of the ground talking in a language he's never heard before: half a dozen Cornish men in black, sodden clothes. Daniel can see just from their stumbling gait that their feet are half frozen, and from the way they carry themselves that they've been working hard for a long time. They fetch hampers and gather round the one boiler in the vale that actually works: the one below Daniel, which is driving the Engine. This rests in a massive collar of masonry with holes in the bottom to admit air and coal. The miners pull off their boots and their dripping socks and stretch their feet out in the fire-glow and take great loaf-sized pasties out of the hamper and begin to tear out mouthfuls. Their faces are all black from coal, much blacker than Dappa's. Their eyes are white as stars. A pair of eyes leaps up and marks Daniel on the platform, and then all the others follow suit. There's a moment, then, when Daniel's looking down at them and they are all looking up trying to decide what to make of this strange visitor. How must he seem to them? He's in a long woolen coat and his head is swaddled in a knit sailor's cap. He's growing a beard. He looms above them wreathed in whorls of exhausted steam. He wonders if these Cornish men have the faintest idea that they are sitting around an explosive device. He concludes that they are probably as intelligent as anyone else, and know it perfectly well, but have made peace with the idea, and have decided that they can accommodate it in their day-to-day lives in exchange for what passes, around here, for prosperity. It's no different from what a sailor does when he takes ship knowing that he might drown. Daniel supposes that the wizards of the Technologickal Arts will be proffering many more such choices to people in years to come.

This journey began with a wizard walking into his door. Now it ends with a new kind of wizard standing on an Engine. Gazing down on this boiler from above, the wizard has the sense of being an angel or demon regarding Earth from Polaris. For, chastened by his failures, Mr. Newcomen has become most regular in his practices, and in this, his master-work, the seams and rivet-lines joining one curved plate to the next radiate from top center just like meridians of Longitude spreading from the North Pole. Below is a raging fire, and within is steam at a pressure that would blow Daniel to Kingdom Come (just like Drake) if a rivet were to give way. But that does not come to pass. The steam is piped off to raise water, and the wasted heat of the fire affords a measure of comfort to the miners, and for the time being it all works as it is supposed to. At some point the whole System will fail, because of the flaws that have been wrought into it in spite of the best efforts of Caroline and Daniel. Perhaps new sorts of Wizards will be required then. But— and perhaps this is only because of his age, and that there's a long-boat waiting to take him away—he has to admit that having some kind of a System, even a flawed and doomed one, is better than to live forever in the poisonous storm-tide of quicksilver that gave birth to all of this.

He has done his job.

"I'm going home now," he says.

Here Ends *The BAROQUE CYCLE*

This I have now published; not for the public good [which I do not think my poor abilities can promote], but to gratify my brother the Stationer. The benefits of that trade do chiefly consist in the printing of copies; and the vanity of this age is more taken with matters of curiosity, than those of solid benefit. Such a pamphlet as this, may be salable, when a more substantial and useful discourse is neglected.

—*John Wilkins*

Acknowledgments

THE BAROQUE CYCLE would have been unthinkable—in the most literal sense of that word—had it not been for the efforts of scholars, scientists, explorers, poets, preachers, pamphleteers, raconteurs, artists, translators, and cartographers dating back to the era of Wilkins and Comenius, and extending into the present day. A few of them are listed below. Some lived three hundred years ago, but others are still alive. I am a little hesitant to publish the names of the latter because it is much easier than it used to be to look people up, and so I am afraid that it will lead to these people being pestered. Nearly all of the people who bother to read three-thousand-page novels *and their acknowledgments pages* wouldn't dream of disturbing the privacy of the acknowledged, but there are always a few exceptions; if you are one of those, please leave these people alone!

The project would not have happened at all had it not been for serendipitous conversations seven years ago with George Dyson and Steven Horst. A crucial midcourse correction, equally unlooked-for, was supplied by Piers Bursill-Hall after he sat through an infamously long lecture delivered by yours truly in Cambridge in 2002.

The following scholars (in alphabetical order) have done work that was essential to the completion of this project. While eager to give them due credit, I am aware that those who are still among us, and who actually bother to read my work, may be chagrined by my tendency to whip out my artistic license and make stuff up whenever it's convenient: Frank Dawson Adams, E. J. Aiton, Maurice Ashley, Julian Barbour, J. M. Beattie, Olivier Bernier, Peter L. Bernstein, Bryan Bevan, Roger Lee Brown, Florian Cajori, Gale E. Christianson, Sir Archibald Geikie, David M. Gitlitz, A. Rupert Hall, John E. N. Hearsey, David Kahn, Henry Kamen, John Maynard Keynes, Mark Kishlansky, Meir Kohn, Maria Kroll, Andrew Lossky, Robert K. Massie, Nicholas Mayhew, John Read, H. Stanley Redgrove, Bertrand Russell, Hans Georg Schulte-Albert, Barbara J. Shapiro, J. G. Simms,

Lee Smolin, William Spencer, Hugh Thomas, David Underdown, Henri and Barbara van der Zee, Maureen Waller, Richard Westfall, D. T. Whiteside. Though her biography of Hooke came out too late to influence this project, Lisa Jardine should also be mentioned, simply out of the hope that readers who would like to learn more about this period will read her work. Likewise Carl Zimmer and his recent biography of Thomas Willis, and Vladimir I. Arnol'd for *Huygens and Barrow, Newton and Hooke.*

In general there is not room to mention specific titles here, but I'll make exceptions for Fernand Braudel's Civilization and Capitalism series; Sir Winston Spencer Churchill's six-volume biography of Marlborough; Giovanni Franceso Gemelli Careri's incredible *Voyage Round the World;* and every ribald, scabrous, mordant, teeming libel Ned Ward ever wrote. I am thankful Ned was around to describe Baroque England, and even more thankful that he died before he could get around to describing me.

Period writers were indispensable: John Bunyan, Richard F. Burton (who was not really of this period but who wrote much that was useful), Daniel Defoe, John Evelyn, George Farquhar, Henry Fielding, (the Right Villainous) John Hall, Liselotte, John Milton, Samuel Pepys, the Duc de Saint-Simon, Jean-Baptiste Tavernier, Jean de Thevenot, Joseph de la Vega, John Wilkins, Lt.-Gen. Adam Williamson of the Tower of London, and the translators of the Geneva Bible. And of course, Hooke, Newton, and Leibniz. But an author of my limitations would be unable to make heads or tails of Leibniz's body of work without the help of scholars, translators, and editors such as Robert Merrihew Adams, H. G. Alexander, Roger Ariew, Richard Francks, Daniel Garber, and R. S. Woolhouse. Likewise Subrahmanyan Chandrasekhar for his *Newton's Principia for the Common Reader.*

A certain kind of debt, which might make sense only to novelists, ought to be acknowledged to the late Dorothy Dunnett and to Alexandre Dumas.

People who fund and staff museums—especially wee, peculiar museums—ought to be acknowledged. I don't have any of those people's names, but here are some interesting museums: Newton's Room at Babson College in Wellesley, Massachusetts; Newton's house at Woolsthorpe; Musée Carnavalet in Paris; the Bank of England Museum; the Hague Historical Museum; the Upper Harz Mining Museum and the Bergapothek in Clausthal-Zellerfeld; and the Bergbaumuseum Röhrigschacht in Wettelrode.

Thanks to Béla and Gabriella Bollobás; Doug Carlston and Tomi

Pierce; and Barry Kemp of Connell Cars for providing me with access to places I could not have seen (Bollobás), worked in (Carlston/ Pierce), or found (Kemp) otherwise. George Jewsbury and Catherine and Hugo Durandin provided timely assistance. Charles McAleese had a thing or two to say about Irish history. Likewise the balance of the HBC on all other topics under the sun. Greg Bear lent me two books and did not object when the loan stretched out to a length that a lesser man might have denominated theft (the books have now been returned in front of many witnesses).

Many others have, knowingly or not, contributed to a milieu in which it was possible for me to consider writing something like this without seeming completely mad. And here I am tempted to list the names of a lot of mathematicians and physicists. But out of a concern for their privacy and a desire not to seem like I'm clinging to their ankles, I'll draw a veil over those conversations. Suffice it to say that the Royal Society crowd written about in these books has many descendants and heirs today, who are capable of talking learnedly about monads, cellular automata, the calculus dispute, absolute time and space, &c. at the drop of a hat, and that it's been my privilege to know a few of them. They seem pleasantly surprised to learn that someone actually wants to write a novel about such topics, and I in turn have been pleasantly surprised to find that they are actually willing to spend time talking to me, and out of this, quite a few good conversations have arisen over the years.

Helping in many ways to make this possible on the publishing end, and exhibiting superhuman patience over its seven-year span, were Jennifer Hershey, Liz Darhansoff, Jennifer Brehl, and Ravi Mirchandani.

Jeremy Bornstein, Alvy Ray Smith, and Lisa Gold read the penultimate drafts and supplied useful commentary. The latter two, along with the cartographer Nick Springer, participated in creation of maps, diagrams, and family trees.

The dialect spoken by Lord Gy in the third volume is a good faith effort by the author to approach eighteenth-century Scottish with all due respect and to get it as right as possible. If I've botched it; and if you know enough Scottish to know that I have; and if you're thinking of giving me a piece of your mind, know that I am one-quarter MacPhail. The uncanny vibrations you have been feeling in the soles of your feet the last couple of years are seismic disturbances created by my ancestors turning over in their graves at Preston Pans and other locations. Worse, the clan's last chieftain—no admirer of the Hanovers, apparently—was transported to Virginia in 1715 but died en route. He probably haunts the sea-lanes even now, and, for all I know, may have a bone to pick with me. Which is a roundabout way of saying that even before the ink has dried on the manuscript page, novelists' families—nuclear and extended—have had to put up with a lot from us. The greatest share of my gratitude, always, goes to them.

Neal Stephenson
May 2004